Ethel M. Dell, best novels

In this book:
The Lamp in the Desert
The Keeper of the Door
The Way of an Eagle

Ethel M. Dell (1881 -- 1939) was a British writer of over 30 popular romance novels and several short stories from 1911 to 1939. Ethel Dell worked on a novel for several years, but it was rejected by eight publishers. Finally the publisher T. Fisher Unwin bought the book for their First Novel Library, a series which introduced a writer's first book. This book, entitled *The Way of an Eagle*, was published in 1911 and by 1915 it had gone through thirty printings. Her debut novel is very characteristic of Ethel M. Dell's novels. There is a very feminine woman, an alpha male, a setting in India, passion galore liberally mixed with some surprisingly shocking violence and religious sentiments sprinkled throughout. While readers adored Ethel M. Dell's novels, critics hated them with a passion; but she did not care what the critics thought. She considered herself a good storyteller – nothing more and nothing less. Ethel M. Dell continued to write novels for a number of years. She made quite a lot of money, from £20,000 to £30,000 a year, but remained quiet and almost pathologically shy.

In this book:
The Lamp in the Desert..................Pag. 3
The Keeper of the Door.................Pag. 173
The Way of an Eagle....................Pag. 421

The Lamp in the Desert

PART I
CHAPTER I
BEGGAR'S CHOICE

A great roar of British voices pierced the jewelled curtain of the Indian night. A toast with musical honours was being drunk in the sweltering dining-room of the officers' mess. The enthusiastic hubbub spread far, for every door and window was flung wide. Though the season was yet in its infancy, the heat was intense. Markestan had the reputation in the Indian Army for being one of the hottest corners in the Empire in more senses than one, and Kurrumpore, the military centre, had not been chosen for any especial advantages of climate. So few indeed did it possess in the eyes of Europeans that none ever went there save those whom an inexorable fate compelled. The rickety, wooden bungalows scattered about the cantonment were temporary lodgings, not abiding-places. The women of the community, like migratory birds, dwelt in them for barely four months in the year, flitting with the coming of the pitiless heat to Bhulwana, their little paradise in the Hills. But that was a twenty-four hours' journey away, and the men had to be content with an occasional week's leave from the depths of their inferno, unless, as Tommy Denvers put it, they were lucky enough to go sick, in which case their sojourn in paradise was prolonged, much to the delight of the angels.

But on that hot night the annual flitting of the angels had not yet come to pass, and notwithstanding the heat the last dance of the season was to take place at the Club House. The occasion was an exceptional one, as the jovial sounds that issued from the officers' mess-house testified. Round after round of cheers followed the noisy toast, filling the night with the merry uproar that echoed far and wide. A confusion of voices succeeded these; and then by degrees the babel died down, and a single voice made itself heard. It spoke with easy fluency to the evident appreciation of its listeners, and when it ceased there came another hearty cheer. Then with jokes and careless laughter the little company of British officers began to disperse. They came forth in lounging groups on to the steps of the mess-house, the foremost of them—Tommy Denvers—holding the arm of his captain, who suffered the familiarity as he suffered most things, with the utmost indifference. None but Tommy ever attempted to get on familiar terms with Everard Monck. He was essentially a man who stood alone. But the slim, fair-haired young subaltern worshipped him openly and with reason. For Monck it was who, grimly resolute, had pulled him through the worst illness he had ever known, accomplishing by sheer force of will what Ralston, the doctor, had failed to accomplish by any other means. And in consequence and for all time the youngest subaltern in the mess had become Monck's devoted adherent.

They stood together for a moment at the top of the steps while Monck, his dark, lean face wholly unresponsive and inscrutable, took out a cigar. The night was a wonderland of deep spaces and glittering stars. Somewhere far away a native *tom-tom* throbbed like the beating of a fevered pulse, quickening spasmodically at intervals and then dying away again into mere monotony. The air was scentless, still, and heavy.

"It's going to be deuced warm," said Tommy.

"Have a smoke?" said Monck, proffering his case.

The boy smiled with swift gratification. "Oh, thanks awfully! But it's a shame to hurry over a good cigar, and I promised Stella to go straight back."

"A promise is a promise," said Monck. "Have it later!" He added rather curtly, "I'm going your way myself."

"Good!" said Tommy heartily. "But aren't you going to show at the Club House? Aren't you going to dance?"

Monck tossed down his lighted match and set his heel on it. "I'm keeping my dancing for to-morrow," he said. "The best man always has more than enough of that."

Tommy made a gloomy sound that was like a groan and began to descend the steps by his side. They walked several paces along the dim road in silence; then quite suddenly he burst into impulsive speech.

"I'll tell you what it is, Monck!"

"I shouldn't," said Monck.

Tommy checked abruptly, looking at him oddly, uncertainly. "How do you know what I was going to say?" he demanded.

"I don't," said Monck.

"I believe you do," said Tommy, unconvinced.

Monck blew forth a cloud of smoke and laughed in his brief, rather grudging way. "You're getting quite clever for a child of your age," he observed. "But don't overdo it, my son! Don't get precocious!"

Tommy's hand grasped his arm confidentially. "Monck, if I don't speak out to someone, I shall bust! Surely you don't mind my speaking out to you!"

"Not if there's anything to be gained by it," said Monck.

He ignored the friendly, persuasive hand on his arm, but yet in some fashion Tommy knew that it was not unwelcome. He kept it there as he made reply.

"There isn't. Only, you know, old chap, it does a fellow good to unburden himself. And I'm bothered to death about this business."

"A bit late in the day, isn't it?" suggested Monck.

"Oh yes, I know; too late to do anything. But," Tommy spoke with force, "the nearer it gets, the worse I feel. I'm downright sick about it, and that's the truth. How would you feel, I wonder, if you knew your one and only sister was going to marry a rotter? Would you be satisfied to let things drift?"

Monck was silent for a space. They walked on over the dusty road with the free swing of the conquering race. One or two 'rickshaws met them as they went, and a woman's voice called a greeting; but though they both responded, it scarcely served as a diversion. The silence between them remained.

Monck spoke at last, briefly, with grim restraint. "That's rather a sweeping assertion of yours. I shouldn't repeat it if I were you."

"It's true all the same," maintained Tommy. "You know it's true."

"I know nothing," said Monck. "I've nothing whatever against Dacre."

"You've nothing in favour of him anyway," growled Tommy.

"Nothing particular; but I presume your sister has." There was just a hint of irony in the quiet rejoinder.

Tommy winced. "Stella! Great Scott, no! She doesn't care the toss of a halfpenny for him. I know that now. She only accepted him because she found herself in such a beastly anomalous position, with all the spiteful cats of the regiment arrayed against her, treating her like a pariah."

"Did she tell you so?" There was no irony in Monck's tone this time. It fell short and stern.

Again Tommy glanced at him as one uncertain. "Not likely," he said.

"Then why do you make the assertion? What grounds have you for making the assertion?" Monck spoke with insistence as one who meant to have an answer.

And the boy answered him, albeit shamefacedly. "I really can't say, Monck. I'm the sort of fool that sees things without being able to explain how. But that Stella has the faintest spark of real love for that fellow Dacre,—well, I'd take my dying oath that she hasn't."

"Some women don't go in for that sort of thing," commented Monck dryly.

"Stella isn't that sort of woman." Hotly came Tommy's defence. "You don't know her. She's a lot deeper than I am."

Monck laughed a little. "Oh, you're deep enough, Tommy. But you're transparent as well. Now your sister on the other hand is quite inscrutable. But it is not for us to interfere. She probably knows what she is doing—very well indeed."

"That's just it. Does she know? Isn't she taking a most awful leap in the dark?" Keen anxiety sounded in Tommy's voice. "It's been such horribly quick work, you know. Why, she hasn't been out here six weeks. It's a shame for any girl to marry on such short notice as that. I said so to her, and she—she laughed and said, 'Oh, that's beggar's choice! Do you think I could enjoy life with your angels in paradise in unmarried bliss? I'd sooner stay down in hell with you.' And she'd have done it too, Monck. And it would probably have killed her. That's partly how I came to know."

"Haven't the women been decent to her?" Monck's question fell curtly, as if the subject were one which he was reluctant to discuss.

Tommy looked at him through the starlight. "You know what they are," he said bluntly. "They'd hunt anybody if once Lady Harriet gave tongue. She chose to eye Stella askance from the very outset, and of course all the rest followed suit. Mrs. Ralston is the only one in the whole crowd who has ever treated her decently, but of course she's nobody. Everyone sits on her. As if," he spoke with heat, "Stella weren't as good as the best of 'em—and better! What right have they to treat her like a social outcast just because she came out here to me on her own? It's hateful! It's iniquitous! What else could she have done?"

"It seems reasonable—from a man's point of view," said Monck.

"It was reasonable. It was the only thing possible. And just for that they chose to turn the cold shoulder on her,—to ostracize her practically. What had she done to them? What right had they to treat her like that?" Fierce resentment sounded in Tommy's voice.

"I'll tell you if you want to know," said Monck abruptly. "It's the law of the pack to rend an outsider. And your sister will always be that—married or otherwise. They may fawn upon her later, Dacre being one to hold his own with women. But they will always hate her in their hearts. You see, she is beautiful."

"Is she?" said Tommy in surprise. "Do you know, I never thought of that!"

Monck laughed—a cold, sardonic laugh. "Quite so! You wouldn't! But Dacre has—and a few more of us."

"Oh, confound Dacre!" Tommy's irritation returned with a rush. "I detest the man! He behaves as if he were conferring a favour. When he was making that speech to-night, I wanted to fling my glass at him."

"Ah, but you mustn't do those things." Monck spoke reprovingly. "You may be young, but you're past the schoolboy stage. Dacre is more of a woman's favourite than a man's, you must remember. If your sister is not in love with him, she is about the only woman in the station who isn't."

"That's the disgusting part of it," fumed Tommy. "He makes love to every woman he meets."

They had reached a shadowy compound that bordered the dusty road for a few yards. A little eddying wind made a mysterious whisper among its thirsty shrubs. The bungalow it surrounded showed dimly in the starlight, a wooden structure with a raised verandah and a flight of steps leading up to it. A light thrown by a red-shaded lamp shone out from one of the rooms, casting a shaft of ruddy brilliance into the night as though it defied the splendour without. It shone upon Tommy's face as he paused, showing it troubled and anxious.

"You may as well come in," he said. "She is sure to be ready. Come in and have a drink!"

Monck stood still. His dark face was in shadow. He seemed to be debating some point with himself.

Finally, "All right. Just for a minute," he said. "But, look here, Tommy! Don't you let your sister suspect that you've been making a confidant of me! I don't fancy it would please her. Put on a grin, man! Don't look bowed down with family cares! She is probably quite capable of looking after herself—like the rest of 'em."

He clapped a careless hand on the lad's shoulder as they turned up the path together towards the streaming red light.

"You're a bit of a woman-hater, aren't you?" said Tommy.

And Monck laughed again his short, rather bitter laugh; but he said no word in answer.

5

CHAPTER II
THE PRISONER AT THE BAR

In the room with the crimson-shaded lamp Stella Denvers sat waiting. The red glow compassed her warmly, striking wonderful copper gleams in the burnished coils of her hair. Her face was bent over the long white gloves that she was pulling over her wrists, a pale face that yet was extraordinarily vivid, with features that were delicate and proud, and lips that had the exquisite softness and purity of a flower.

She raised her eyes from her task at sound of the steps below the window, and their starry brightness under her straight black brows gave her an infinite allurement. Certainly a beautiful woman, as Monck had said, and possessing the brilliance and the wonder of youth to an almost dazzling degree! Perhaps it was not altogether surprising that the ladies of the regiment had not been too enthusiastic in their welcome of this sister of Tommy's who had come so suddenly into their midst, defying convention. Her advent had been utterly unexpected—a total surprise even to Tommy, who, returning one day from the polo-ground, had found her awaiting him in the bachelor quarters which he had shared with three other subalterns. And her arrival had set the whole station buzzing.

Led by the Colonel's wife, Lady Harriet Mansfield, the women of the regiment had—with the single exception of Mrs. Ralston whose opinion was of no account—risen and condemned the splendid stranger who had come amongst them with such supreme audacity and eclipsed the fairest of them. Stella's own simple explanation that she had, upon attaining her majority and fifty pounds a year, decided to quit the home of some distant relatives who did not want her and join Tommy who was the only near relation she had, had satisfied no one. She was an interloper, and as such they united to treat her. As Lady Harriet said, no nice girl would have dreamed of taking such an extraordinary step, and she had not the smallest intention of offering her the chaperonage that she so conspicuously lacked. If Mrs. Ralston chose to do so, that was her own affair. Such action on the part of the surgeon's very ordinary wife would make no difference to any one. She was glad to think that all the other ladies were too well-bred to accept without reservation so unconventional a type.

The fact that she was Tommy's sister was the only consideration in her favour. Tommy was quite a nice boy, and they could not for his sake entirely exclude her from the regimental society, but to no intimate gathering was she ever invited, nor from the female portion of the community was there any welcome for her at the Club.

The attitude of the officers of the regiment was of a totally different nature. They had accepted her with enthusiasm, possibly all the more marked on account of the aloofness of their women folk, and in a very short time they were paying her homage as one man. The subalterns who had shared their quarters with Tommy turned out to make room for her, treating her like a queen suddenly come into her own, and like a queen she entered into possession, accepting all courtesy just as she ignored all slights with a delicate self-possession that yet knew how to be gracious when occasion demanded.

Mrs. Ralston would have offered her harbourage had she desired it, but there was pride in Stella—a pride that surged and rebelled very far below her serenity. She received favours from none.

And so, unshackled and unchaperoned, she had gone her way among her critics, and no one—not even Tommy—suspected how deep was the wound that their barely-veiled hostility had inflicted. In bitterness of soul she hid it from all the world, and only her brother and her brother's grim and somewhat unapproachable captain were even vaguely aware of its existence.

Everard Monck was one of the very few men who had not laid themselves down before her dainty feet, and she had gradually come to believe that this man shared the silent, side-long disapproval manifested by the women. Very strangely that belief hurt her even more deeply, in a subtle, incomprehensible fashion, than any slights inflicted by her own sex. Possibly Tommy's warm enthusiasm for the man had made her more sensitive regarding his good opinion. And possibly she was over ready to read condemnation in his grave eyes.

But—whatever the reason—she would have given much to have had him on her side. Somehow it mattered to her, and mattered vitally.

But Monck had never joined her retinue of courtiers. He was never other than courteous to her, but he did not seek her out. Perhaps he had better things to do. Aloof, impenetrable, cold, he passed her by, and she would have been even more amazed than Tommy had she heard him describe her as beautiful, so convinced was she that he saw in her no charm.

It had been a disheartening struggle, this hewing for herself a way along the rocky paths of prejudice, and many had been the thorns under her feet. Though she kept a brave heart and never faltered, she had tired inevitably of the perpetual effort it entailed. Three weeks after her arrival, when the annual exodus of the ladies of the regiment to the Hills was drawing near, she became engaged to Ralph Dacre, the handsomest and most irresponsible man in the mess.

With him at least her power to attract was paramount. He was blindly, almost fulsomely, in love. Her beauty went to his head from the outset; it fired his blood. He worshipped her hotly, and pursued her untiringly, caring little whether she returned his devotion so long as he ultimately took possession. And when finally, half-disdainfully, she yielded to his insistence, his one all-mastering thought became to clinch the bargain before she could repent of it. It was a mad and headlong passion that drove him—not for the first time in his life; and the subtle pride of her and the soft reserve made her all the more desirable in his eyes.

He had won her; he did not stop to ask himself how. The women said that the luck was all on her side. The men forebore to express an opinion. Dacre had attained his captaincy, but he was not regarded with great respect by any one. His fellow-officers shrugged their shoulders over him, and the commanding officer, Colonel Mansfield, had been heard to call him "the craziest madman it had ever been his fate to meet." No one, except Tommy, actively disliked him, and he had no grounds for so doing, as Monck had pointed out. Monck, who till then had occupied the same bungalow, declared he had nothing against him, and he was surely in a position to form a very shrewd opinion. For Monck was neither fool nor madman, and there was very little that escaped his silent observation.

He was acting as best man at the morrow's ceremony, the function having been almost thrust upon him by Dacre who, oddly enough, shared something of Tommy's veneration for his very reticent brother-officer. There was scant friendship between them. Each had been accustomed to go his own way wholly independent of the other. They were no more than casual acquaintances, and they were content to remain such. But undoubtedly Dacre entertained a certain respect for Monck and observed a wariness of behaviour in his presence that he never troubled to assume for any other man. He was careful in his dealings with him, being at all times not wholly certain of his ground.

Other men felt the same uncertainty in connection with Monck. None—save Tommy—was sure what manner of man he was. Tommy alone took him for granted with whole-hearted admiration, and at his earnest wish it had been arranged between them that Monck should take up his abode with him when the forthcoming marriage had deprived each of a companion. Tommy was delighted with the idea, and he had a gratifying suspicion that Monck himself was inclined to be pleased with it also.

The Green Bungalow had become considerably more homelike since Stella's arrival, and Tommy meant to keep it so. He was sure that Monck and he would have the same tastes.

And so on that eve of his sister's wedding, the thought of their coming companionship was the sole redeeming feature of the whole affair, and he turned in his impulsive fashion to say so just as they reached the verandah steps.

But the words did not leave his lips, for the red glow flung from the lamp had found Monck's upturned face, and something—something about it—checked all speech for the moment. He was looking straight up at the lighted window and the face of a beautiful woman who gazed forth into the night. And his eyes were no longer cold and unresponsive, but burning, ardent, intensely alive. Tommy forgot what he was going to say and only stared.

The moment passed; it was scarcely so much as a moment. And Monck moved on in his calm, unfaltering way.

"Your sister is ready and waiting," he said.

They ascended the steps together, and the girl who sat by the open window rose with a stately movement and stepped forward to meet them.

"Hullo, Stella!" was Tommy's greeting. "Hope I'm not awfully late. They wasted such a confounded time over toasts at mess to-night. Yours was one of 'em, and I had to reply. I hadn't a notion what to say. Captain Monck thinks I made an awful hash of it though he is too considerate to say so."

"On the contrary I said 'Hear, hear!' to every stutter," said Monck, bowing slightly as he took the hand she offered.

She was wearing a black lace dress with a glittering spangled scarf of Indian gauze floating about her. Her neck and shoulders gleamed in the soft red glow. She was superb that night.

She smiled at Monck, and her smile was as a shining cloak hiding her soul. "So you have started upon your official duties already!" she said. "It is the best man's business to encourage and console everyone concerned, isn't it?"

The faint cynicism of her speech was like her smile. It held back all intrusive curiosity. And the man's answering smile had something of the same quality. Reserve met reserve.

"I hope I shall not find it very arduous in that respect," he said. "I did not come here in that capacity."

"I am glad of that," she said. "Won't you come in and sit down?"

She motioned him within with a queenly gesture, but her invitation was wholly lacking in warmth. It was Tommy who pressed forward with eager hospitality.

"Yes, and have a drink! It's a thirsty right. It's getting infernally hot. Stella, you're lucky to be going out of it."

"Oh, I am very lucky," Stella said.

They entered the lighted room, and Tommy went in search of refreshment.

"Won't you sit down?" said Stella.

Her voice was deep and pure, and the music in it made him wonder if she sang. He sat facing her while she returned with apparent absorption to the fastening of her gloves. She spoke again after a moment without raising her eyes. "Are you proposing to take up your abode here to-morrow?"

"That's the idea," said Monck.

"I hope you and Tommy will be quite comfortable," she said. "No doubt he will be a good deal happier with you than he has been for the past few weeks with me."

"I don't know why he should be," said Monck.

"No?" She was frowning slightly over her glove. "You see, my sojourn here has not been—a great success. I think poor Tommy has felt it rather badly. He likes a genial atmosphere."

"He won't get much of that in my company," observed Monck.

She smiled momentarily. "Perhaps not. But I think he will not be sorry to be relieved of family cares. They have weighed rather heavily upon him."

"He will be sorry to lose you," said Monck.

"Oh, of course, in a way. But he will soon get over that." She looked up at him suddenly. "You will all be rather thankful when I am safely married, Captain Monck," she said.

There was a second or two of silence. Monck's eyes looked straight back into hers while it lasted, but they held no warmth, scarcely even interest.

"I really don't know why you should say that, Miss Denvers," he said stiffly at length.

Stella's gloved hands clasped each other. She was breathing somewhat hard, yet her bearing was wholly regal, even disdainful.

"Only because I realize that I have been a great anxiety to all the respectable portion of the community," she made careless reply. "I think I am right in classing you under that heading, am I not?"

8

He heard the challenge in her tone, delicately though she presented it, and something in him that was fierce and unrestrained sprang up to meet it. But he forced it back. His expression remained wholly inscrutable.

"I don't think I can claim to be anything else," he said. "But that fact scarcely makes me in any sense one of a community. I think I prefer to stand alone."

Her blue eyes sparkled a little. "Strangely, I have the same preference," she said. "It has never appealed to me to be one of a crowd. I like independence—whatever the crowd may say. But I am quite aware that in a woman that is considered a dangerous taste. A woman should always conform to rule."

"I have never studied the subject," said Monck.

He spoke briefly. Tommy's confidences had stirred within him that which could not be expressed. The whole soul of him shrank with an almost angry repugnance from discussing the matter with her. No discussion could make any difference at this stage.

Again for a second he saw her slight frown. Then she leaned back in her chair, stretching up her arms as if weary of the matter. "In fact you avoid all things feminine," she said. "How discreet of you!"

A large white moth floated suddenly in and began to beat itself against the lamp-shade. Monck's eyes watched it with a grim concentration. Stella's were half-closed. She seemed to have dismissed him from her mind as an unimportant detail. The silence widened between them.

Suddenly there was a movement. The fluttering creature had found the flame and fallen dazed upon the table. Almost in the same second Monck stooped forward swiftly and silently, and crushed the thing with his closed fist.

Stella drew a quick breath. Her eyes were wide open again. She sat up.

"Why did you do that?"

He looked at her again, a smouldering gleam in his eyes. "It was on its way to destruction," he said.

"And so you helped it!"

He nodded. "Yes. Long-drawn-out agonies don't attract me."

Stella laughed softly, yet with a touch of mockery. "Oh, it was an act of mercy, was it? You didn't look particularly merciful. In fact, that is about the last quality I should have attributed to you."

"I don't think," Monck said very quietly, "that you are in a position to judge me." She leaned forward. He saw that her bosom was heaving. "That is your prerogative, isn't it?" she said. "I—I am just the prisoner at the bar, and—like the moth—I have been condemned—without mercy."

He raised his brows sharply. For a second he had the look of a man who has been stabbed in the back. Then with a swift effort he pulled himself together.

In the same moment Stella rose. She was smiling, and there was a red flush in her cheeks. She took her fan from the table.

"And now," she said, "I am going to dance—all night long. Every officer in the mess—save one—has asked me for a dance."

He was on his feet in an instant. He had checked one impulse, but even to his endurance there were limits. He spoke as one goaded.

"Will you give me one?"

She looked him squarely in the eyes. "No, Captain Monck."

His dark face looked suddenly stubborn. "I don't often dance," he said. "I wasn't going to dance to-night. But—I will have one—I must have one—with you."

"Why?" Her question fell with a crystal clearness. There was something of crystal hardness in her eyes.

But the man was undaunted. "Because you have wronged me, and you owe me reparation."

"I—have wronged—you!" She spoke the words slowly, still looking him in the eyes.

9

He made an abrupt gesture as of holding back some inner force that strongly urged him. "I am not one of your persecutors," he said. "I have never in my life presumed to judge you—far less condemn you."

His voice vibrated as though some emotion fought fiercely for the mastery. They stood facing each other in what might have been open antagonism but for that deep quiver in the man's voice.

Stella spoke after the lapse of seconds. She had begun to tremble.

"Then why—why did you let me think so? Why did you always stand aloof?"

There was a tremor in her voice also, but her eyes were shining with the light half-eager, half-anxious, of one who seeks for buried treasure.

Monck's answer was pitched very low. It was as if the soul of him gave utterance to the words. "It is my nature to stand aloof. I was waiting."

"Waiting?" Her two hands gripped suddenly hard upon her fan, but still her shining eyes did not flinch from his. Still with a quivering heart she searched.

Almost in a whisper came his reply. "I was waiting—till my turn should come."

"Ah!" The fan snapped between her hands; she cast it from her with a movement that was almost violent.

Monck drew back sharply. With a smile that was grimly cynical he veiled his soul. "I was a fool, of course, and I am quite aware that my foolishness is nothing to you. But at least you know now how little cause you have to hate me."

She had turned from him and gone to the open window. She stood there bending slightly forward, as one who strains for a last glimpse of something that has passed from sight.

Monck remained motionless, watching her. From another room near by there came the sound of Tommy's humming and the cheery pop of a withdrawn cork.

Stella spoke at last, in a whisper, and as she spoke the strain went out of her attitude and she drooped against the wood-work of the window as if spent. "Yes; but I know—too late."

The words reached him though he scarcely felt that they were intended to do so. He suffered them to go into silence; the time for speech was past.

The seconds throbbed away between them. Stella did not move or speak again, and at last Monck turned from her. He picked up the broken fan, and with a curious reverence he laid it out of sight among some books on the table.

Then he stood immovable as granite and waited.

There came the sound of Tommy's footsteps, and in a moment the door was flung open. Tommy advanced with all a host's solicitude.

"Oh, I say, I'm awfully sorry to have kept you waiting so long. That silly ass of a *khit* had cleared off and left us nothing to drink. Stella, we shall miss all the fun if we don't hurry up. Come on, Monck, old chap, say when!"

He stopped at the table, and Stella turned from the window and moved forward. Her face was pale, but she was smiling.

"Captain Monck is coming with us, Tommy," she said.

"What?" Tommy looked up sharply. "Really? I say, Monck, I'm pleased. It'll do you good."

Monck was smiling also, faintly, grimly. "Don't mix any strong waters for me, Tommy!" he said. "And you had better not be too generous to yourself! Remember, you will have to dance with Lady Harriet!"

Tommy grimaced above the glasses. "All right. Have some lime-juice! You will have to dance with her too. That's some consolation!"

"I?" said Monck. He took the glass and handed it to Stella, then as she shook her head he put it to his own lips and drank as a man drinks to a memory. "No," he said then. "I am dancing only one dance to-night, and that will not be with Lady Harriet Mansfield."

"Who then?" questioned Tommy.

It was Stella who answered him, in her voice a note that sounded half-reckless, half-defiant. "It isn't given to every woman to dance at her own funeral," she said: "Captain Monck has kindly consented to assist at the orgy of mine."

10

"Stella!" protested Tommy, flushing. "I hate to hear you talking like that!"

Stella laughed a little, softly, as though at the vagaries of a child. "Poor Tommy!" she said. "What it is to be so young!"

"I'd sooner be a babe in arms than a cynic," said Tommy bluntly.

CHAPTER III
THE TRIUMPH

Lady Harriet's lorgnettes were brought piercingly to bear upon the bride-elect that night, and her thin, refined features never relaxed during the operation. She was looking upon such youth and loveliness as seldom came her way; but the sight gave her no pleasure. She deemed it extremely unsuitable that Stella should dance at all on the eve of her wedding, and when she realized that nearly every man in the room was having his turn, her disapproval by no means diminished. She wondered audibly to one after another of her followers what Captain Dacre was about to permit such a thing. And when Monck— Everard Monck of all people who usually avoided all gatherings at the Club and had never been known to dance if he could find any legitimate means of excusing himself—waltzed Stella through the throng, her indignation amounted almost to anger. The mess had yielded to the last man.

"I call it almost brazen," she said to Mrs. Burton, the Major's wife. "She flaunts her unconventionality in our faces."

"A grave mistake," agreed Mrs. Burton. "It will not make us think any the more highly of her when she is married."

"I am in two minds about calling on her," declared Lady Harriet. "I am very doubtful as to the advisability of inviting any one so obviously unsuitable into our inner circle. Of course Mrs. Ralston," she raised her long pointed chin upon the name, "will please herself in the matter. She will probably be the first to try and draw her in, but what Mrs. Ralston does and what I do are two very different things. She is not particular as to the society she keeps, and the result is that her opinion is very justly regarded as worthless."

"Oh, quite," agreed Mrs. Burton, sending an obviously false smile in the direction of the lady last named who was approaching them in the company of Mrs. Ermsted, the Adjutant's wife, a little smart woman whom Tommy had long since surnamed "The Lizard."

Mrs. Ralston, the surgeon's wife, had once been a pretty girl, and there were occasions still on which her prettiness lingered like the gleams of a fading sunset. She had a diffident manner in society, but yet she was the only woman in the station who refused to follow Lady Harriet's lead. As Tommy had said, she was a nobody. Her influence was of no account, but yet with unobtrusive insistence she took her own way, and none could turn her therefrom.

Mrs. Ermsted held her up to ridicule openly, and yet very strangely she did not seem to dislike the Adjutant's sharp-tongued little wife. She had been very good to her on more than one occasion, and the most appreciative remark that Mrs. Ermsted had ever found to make regarding her was that the poor thing was so fond of drudging for somebody that it was a real kindness to let her. Mrs. Ermsted was quite willing to be kind to any one in that respect.

They approached now, and Lady Harriet gave to each her distinctive smile of royal condescension.

"I expected to see you dancing, Mrs. Ermsted," she said.

"Oh, it's too hot," declared Mrs. Ermsted. "You want the temperament of a salamander to dance on a night like this."

She cast a barbed glance towards Stella as she spoke as Monck guided her to the least crowded corner of the ball-room. Stella's delicate face was flushed, but it was the exquisite flush of a blush-rose. Her eyes were of a starry brightness; she had the radiant look of one who has achieved her heart's desire.

"What a vision of triumph!" commented Mrs. Ermsted. "It's soothing anyway to know that that wild-rose complexion won't survive the summer. Captain Monck looks curiously out of his element. No doubt he prefers the bazaars."

"But Stella Denvers is enchanting to-night," murmured Mrs. Ralston.

Lady Harriet overheard the murmur, and her aquiline nose was instantly elevated a little higher. "So many people never see beyond the outer husk," she said.

Mrs. Burton smiled out of her slitty eyes. "I should scarcely imagine Captain Monck to be one of them," she said. "He is obviously here as a matter of form to-night. The best man must be civil to the bride—whatever his feelings."

Lady Harriet's face cleared a little, although her estimate of Mrs. Burton's opinion was not a very high one. "That may account for Captain Dacre's extremely complacent attitude," she said. "He regards the attentions paid to his *fiancée* as a tribute to himself."

"He may change his point of view when he is married," laughed Mrs. Ermsted. "It will be interesting to watch developments. We all know what Captain Dacre is. I have never yet seen him satisfied to take a back seat."

Mrs. Burton laughed with her. "Nor content to occupy even a front one at the same show for long," she observed. "I marvel to see him caught in the noose so easily."

"None but an adventuress could have done it," declared Mrs. Ermsted. "She has practised the art of slinging the lasso before now."

"My dear," said Mrs. Ralston, "forgive me, but that is unworthy of you."

Mrs. Ermsted flicked an eyelid in Mrs. Burton's direction with an *insouciance* that somehow robbed the act of any serious sting. "Poor Mrs. Ralston holds such a high opinion of everybody," she said, "that she must meet with a hundred disappointments in a day."

Lady Harriet's down-turned lips said nothing, but they were none the less eloquent on that account.

Mrs. Ralston's eyes of faded blue watched Stella with a distressed look. She was not hurt on her own account, but she hated to hear the girl criticized in so unfriendly a spirit. Stella was more brilliantly beautiful that night than she had ever before seen her, and she longed to hear a word of appreciation from that hostile group of women. But she knew very well that the longing was vain, and it was with relief that she saw Captain Dacre himself saunter up to claim Mrs. Ermsted for a partner.

Smiling, debonair, complacent, the morrow's bridegroom had a careless quip for all and sundry on that last night. It was evident that his *fiancée's* defection was a matter of no moment to him. Stella was to have her fling, and he, it seemed, meant to have his. He and Mrs. Ermsted had had many a flirtation in the days that were past and it was well known that Captain Ermsted heartily detested him in consequence. Some even hinted that matters had at one time approached very near to a climax, but Ralph Dacre knew how to handle difficult situations, and with considerable tact had managed to avoid it. Little Mrs. Ermsted, though still willing to flirt, treated him with just a tinge of disdain, now-a-days; no one knew wherefore. Perhaps it was more for Stella's edification than her own that she condescended to dance with him on that sweltering evening of Indian spring.

But Stella was evidently too engrossed with her own affairs to pay much attention to the doings of her *fiancé*. His love-making was not of a nature to be carried on in public. That would come later when they walked home through the glittering night and parted in the shadowy verandah while Tommy tramped restlessly about within the bungalow. He would claim that as a right she knew, and once or twice remembering the methods of his courtship a little shudder went through her as she danced. Very willingly would she have left early and foregone all intercourse with her lover that night. But there was no escape for her. She was pledged to the last dance, and for the sake of the pride that she carried so high she would not shrink under the malicious eyes that watched her so unsparingly. Her dance with Monck was quickly over, and he left her with the briefest word of thanks. Afterwards she saw him no more.

The rest of the evening passed in a whirl of gaiety that meant very little to her. Perhaps, on the whole, it was easier to bear than an evening spent in solitude would have been. She knew that she would be too utterly weary to lie awake when bedtime came at last. And the night would be so short—ah, so short! And so she danced and laughed with the gayest of the merrymakers, and when it was over at last even the severest of her critics had to admit that her triumph was complete. She had borne herself like a queen at a banquet of rejoicing, and like a queen she finally quitted the festive scene in a 'rickshaw drawn by a team of giddy subalterns, scattering her careless favours upon all who cared to compete for them.

As she had foreseen, Dacre accompanied the procession. He had no mind to be cheated of his rights, and it was he who finally dispersed the irresponsible throng at the steps of the verandah, handing her up them with a royal air and drawing her away from the laughter and cheering that followed her.

With her hand pressed lightly against his side, he led her away to the darkest corner, and there he pushed back the soft wrap from her shoulders and gathered her into his arms.

She stood almost stiffly in his embrace, neither yielding nor attempting to avoid. But at the touch of his lips upon her neck she shivered. There was something sensual in that touch that revolted her—in spite of herself.

"Ralph," she said, and her voice quivered a little, "I think you must say good-bye to me. I am tired to-night. If I don't rest, I shall never be ready for to-morrow."

He made an inarticulate sound that in some fashion expressed what the drawing of his lips had made her feel. "Sweetheart—to-morrow!" he said, and kissed her again with a lingering persistence that to her overwrought nerves had in it something that was almost unendurable. It made her think of an epicurean tasting some favourite dish and smacking his lips over it.

A hint of irritation sounded in her voice as she said, drawing slightly away from him, "Yes, I want to rest for the few hours that are left. Please say good night now, Ralph! Really I am tired."

He laughed softly, his cheek laid to hers. "Ah, Stella!" he said. "What a queen you have been to-night! I have been watching you with the rest of the world, and I shouldn't mind laying pretty heavy odds that there isn't a single man among 'em that doesn't envy me."

Stella drew a deep breath as if she laboured against some oppression. "It's nice to be envied, isn't it?" she said.

He kissed her again. "Ah! You're a prize!" he said. "It was just a question of first in, and I never was one to let the grass grow. I plucked the fruit while all the rest were just looking at it. Stella—mine! Stella—mine!"

His lips pressed hers between the words closely, possessively, and again involuntarily she shivered. She could not return his caresses that night.

His hold relaxed at last. "How cold you are, my Star of the North!" he said. "What is it? Surely you are not nervous at the thought of to-morrow after your triumph to-night! You will carry all before you, never fear!"

She answered him in a voice so flat and emotionless that it sounded foreign even to herself. "Oh, no, I am not nervous. I'm too tired to feel anything to-night."

He took her face between his hands. "Ah, well, you will be all mine this time to-morrow. One kiss and I will let you go. You witch—you enchantress! I never thought you would draw old Monck too into your toils."

Again she drew that deep breath as of one borne down by some heavy weight. "Nor I," she said, and gave him wearily the kiss for which he bargained.

He did not stay much longer, possibly realizing his inability to awake any genuine response in her that night. Her remoteness must have chilled any man less ardent. But he went from her too encompassed with blissful anticipation to attach any importance to the obvious lack of corresponding delight on her part. She was already in his estimation his own property, and the thought of her happiness was one which scarcely entered into his consideration. She had accepted him, and no doubt she realized that she was doing very well for herself. He had no misgivings on that point. Stella was a young woman who knew her own mind very thoroughly. She had secured the finest catch within reach, and she was not likely to repent of her bargain at this stage.

So, unconcernedly, he went his way, throwing a couple of *annas* with careless generosity to a beggar who followed him along the road whining for alms, well-satisfied with himself and with all the world on that wonderful night that had witnessed the final triumph of the woman whom he had chosen for his bride, asking nought of the gods save that which they had deigned to bestow—Fortune's favourite whom every man must envy.

CHAPTER IV
THE BRIDE

It was remarked by Tommy's brother-officers on the following day that it was he rather than the bride who displayed all the shyness that befitted the occasion.

As he walked up the aisle with his sister's hand on his arm, his face was crimson and reluctant, and he stared straight before him as if unwilling to meet all the watching eyes that followed their progress. But the bride walked proudly and firmly, her head held high with even the suspicion of an upward, disdainful curve to her beautiful mouth, the ghost of a defiant smile. To all who saw her she was a splendid spectacle of bridal content.

"Unparalleled effrontery!" whispered Lady Harriet, surveying the proud young face through her lorgnettes.

"Ah, but she is exquisite," murmured Mrs. Ralston with a wistful mist in her faded eyes.

"'Faultily faultless, icily regular, splendidly null,'" scoffed little Mrs. Ermsted upon whose cheeks there bloomed a faint fixed glow.

Yes, she was splendid. Even the most hostile had to admit it. On that, the day of her final victory, she surpassed herself. She shone as a queen with majestic self-assurance, wholly at her ease, sublimely indifferent to all criticism.

At the chancel-steps she bestowed a brief smile of greeting upon her waiting bridegroom, and for a single moment her steady eyes rested, though without any gleam of recognition, upon the dark face of the best man.

Then the service began, and with the utmost calmness of demeanour she took her part.

When the service was over, Tommy extended his hesitating invitation to Lady Harriet and his commanding officer to follow the newly wedded pair to the vestry. They went. Colonel Mansfield with a species of jocose pomposity specially assumed for the occasion, his wife, upright, thin-lipped, forbidding, instinct with wordless disapproval.

The bride,—the veil thrown back from her beautiful face,—stood laughing with her husband. There was no fixity in the soft flush of those delicately rounded cheeks. Even Lady Harriet realized that, though she had never seen so much colour in the girl's face before. She advanced stiffly, and Ralph Dacre with smiling grace took his wife's arm and drew her forward.

"This is good of you, Lady Harriet," he declared. "I was hoping for your support. Allow me to introduce—my wife!"

His words had a pride of possession that rang clarion-like in every syllable, and in response Lady Harriet was moved to offer a cold cheek in salutation to the bride. Stella bent instantly and kissed it with a quick graciousness that would have melted any one less austere, but in Lady Harriet's opinion the act was marred by its very impulsiveness. She did not like impulsive people. So, with chill repression, she accepted the only overture from Stella that she was ever to receive.

But if she were proof against the girl's ready charm, with her husband it was quite otherwise. Stella broke through his pomposity without effort, giving him both her hands with a simplicity that went straight to his heart. He held them in a tight, paternal grasp.

"God bless you, my dear!" he said. "I wish you both every happiness from the bottom of my soul."

She turned from him a few seconds later with a faintly tremulous laugh to give her hand to the best man, but it did not linger in his, and to his curtly proffered felicitations she made no verbal response whatever.

Ten minutes later, as she left the vestry with her husband, Mrs. Ralston pressed forward unexpectedly, and openly checked her progress in full view of the whole assembly.

"My dear," she murmured humbly, "my dear, you'll allow me I know. I wanted just to tell you how beautiful you look, and how earnestly I pray for your happiness."

It was a daring move, and it had not been accomplished without courage. Lady Harriet in the background stiffened with displeasure, nearer to actual anger than she had ever before permitted herself to be with any one so contemptible as the surgeon's wife. Even

Major Ralston himself, most phlegmatic of men, looked momentarily disconcerted by his wife's action.

But Stella—Stella stopped dead with a new light in her eyes, and in a moment dropped her husband's arm to fling both her own about the gentle, faded woman who had dared thus openly to range herself on her side.

"Dear Mrs. Ralston," she said, not very steadily, "how more than kind of you to tell me that!"

The tears were actually in her eyes as she kissed the surgeon's wife. That spontaneous act of sympathy had pierced straight through her armour of reserve and found its way to her heart. Her face, as she passed on down the aisle by her husband's side, was wonderfully softened, and even Mrs. Ermsted found no gibe to fling after her. The smile that quivered on Stella's lips was full of an unconscious pathos that disarmed all criticism.

The sunshine outside the church was blinding. It smote through the awning with pitiless intensity. Around the carriage a curious crowd had gathered to see the bridal procession. To Stella's dazzled eyes it seemed a surging sea of unfamiliar faces. But one face stood out from the rest—the calm countenance of Ralph Dacre's magnificent Sikh servant clad in snowy linen, who stood at the carriage door and gravely bowed himself before her, stretching an arm to protect her dress from the wheel.

"This is Peter the Great," said Dacre's careless voice, "a highly honourable person, Stella, and a most efficient bodyguard."

"How do you do?" said Stella, and held out her hand.

She acted with the utmost simplicity. During her four weeks' sojourn in India she had not learned to treat the native servant with contempt, and the majestic presence of this man made her feel almost as if she were dealing with a prince.

He straightened himself swiftly at her action, and she saw a sudden, gleaming smile flash across his grave face. Then he took the proffered hand, bending low over it till his turbaned forehead for a moment touched her fingers.

"May the sun always shine on you, my *mem-sahib!*" he said.

Stella realized afterwards that in action and in words there lay a tacit acceptance of her as mistress which was to become the allegiance of a lifelong service.

She stepped into the carriage with a feeling of warmth at her heart which was very different from the icy constriction that had bound it when she had arrived at the church a brief half-hour before with Tommy.

Her husband's arm was about her as they drove away. He pressed her to his side. "Oh, Star of my heart, how superb you are!" he said. "I feel as if I had married a queen. And you weren't even nervous."

She bent her head, not looking at him. "Poor Tommy was," she said.

He smiled tolerantly. "Tommy's such a youngster."

She smiled also. "Exactly one year younger than I am."

He drew her nearer, his eyes devouring her. "You, Stella!" he said. "You are as ageless as the stars."

She laughed faintly, not yielding herself to the closer pressure though not actually resisting it. "That is merely a form of telling me that I am much older than I seem," she said. "And you are quite right. I am."

His arm compelled her. "You are you," he said. "And you are so divinely young and beautiful that there is no measuring you by ordinary standards. They all know it. That is why you weren't received into the community with open arms. You are utterly above and beyond them all."

She flinched slightly at the allusion. "I hope I am not so extraordinary as all that," she said.

His arm became insistent. "You are unique," he said. "You are superb."

There was passion barely suppressed in his hold and a sudden swift shiver went through her. "Oh, Ralph," she said, "don't—- don't worship me too much!"

Her voice quivered in its appeal, but somehow its pathos passed him by. He saw only her beauty, and it thrilled every pulse in his body. Fiercely almost, he strained her to him.

And he did not so much as notice that her lips trembled too piteously to return his kiss, or that her submission to his embrace was eloquent of mute endurance rather than glad surrender. He stood as a conqueror on the threshold of a newly acquired kingdom and exulted over the splendour of its treasures because it was all his own.

It did not even occur to him to doubt that her happiness fully equalled his. Stella was a woman and reserved; but she was happy enough, oh, she was happy enough. With complacence he reflected that if every man in the mess envied him, probably every woman in the station would have gladly changed places with her. Was he not Fortune's favourite? What happier fate could any woman desire than to be his bride?

CHAPTER V
THE DREAM

It was a fortnight after the wedding, on an evening of intense heat, that Everard Monck, now established with Tommy at The Green Bungalow, came in from polo to find the mail awaiting him. He sauntered in through the verandah in search of a drink which he expected to find in the room which Stella during her brief sojourn had made more dainty and artistic than the rest, albeit it had never been dignified by the name of drawing-room. There was light green matting on the floor and there were also light green cushions in each of the long wicker chairs. Curtains of green gauze hung before the windows, and the fierce sunlight filtering through gave the room a strangely translucent effect. It was like a chamber under the sea.

It had been Monck's intention to have his drink and pass straight on to his own quarters for a bath, but the letters on the table caught his eye and he stopped. Standing in the green dimness with a tumbler in one hand, he sorted them out. There were two for himself and two for Tommy, the latter obviously bills, and under these one more, also for Tommy in a woman's clear round writing. It came from Srinagar, and Monck stood for a second or two holding it in his hand and staring straight out before him with eyes that saw not. Just for those seconds a mocking vision danced gnomelike through his brain. Just at this moment probably most of the other men were opening letters from their wives in the Hills. And he saw the chance he had not taken like a flash of far, elusive sunlight on the sky-line of a troubled sea.

The vision passed. He laid down the letter and took up his own correspondence. One of the letters was from England. He poured out his drink and flung himself down to read it.

It came from the only relation he possessed in the world—his brother. Bernard Monck was the elder by fifteen years—a man of brilliant capabilities, who had long since relinquished all idea of worldly advancement in the all-absorbing interest of a prison chaplaincy. They had not met for over five years, but they maintained a regular correspondence, and every month brought to Everard Monck the thin envelope directed in the square, purposeful handwriting of the man who had been during the whole of his life his nearest and best friend. Lying back in the wicker-chair, relaxed and weary, he opened the letter and began to read.

Ten minutes later, Tommy Denvers, racing in, also in polo-kit, stopped short upon the threshold and stared in shocked amazement as if some sudden horror had caught him by the throat.

"Great heavens above, Monck! What's the matter?" he ejaculated.

Perhaps it was in part due to the green twilight of the room, but it seemed to him in that first startled moment that Monck's face had the look of a man who had received a deadly wound. The impression passed almost immediately, but the memory of it was registered in his brain for all time.

Monck raised the tumbler to his lips and drank before replying, and as he did so his customary grave composure became apparent, making Tommy wonder if his senses had tricked him. He looked at the lad with sombre eyes as he set down the glass. His brother's letter was still gripped in his hand.

"Hullo, Tommy!" he said, a shadowy smile about his mouth. "What are you in such a deuce of a hurry about?"

Tommy glanced down at the letters on the table and pounced upon the one that lay uppermost. "A letter from Stella! And about time, too! She isn't much of a correspondent now-a-days. Where are they now? Oh, Srinagar. Lucky beggar—Dacre! Wish he'd taken me along as well as Stella! What am I in such a hurry about? Well, my dear chap, look at the time! You'll be late for mess yourself if you don't buck up."

Tommy's treatment of his captain was ever of the airiest when they were alone. He had never stood in awe of Monck since the days of his illness; but even in his most familiar moments his manner was not without a certain deference. His respect for him was unbounded, and his pride in their intimacy was boyishly whole-hearted. There was no sacrifice great or small that he would not willingly have offered at Monck's behest.

And Monck knew it, realized the lad's devotion as pure gold, and valued it accordingly. But, that fact notwithstanding, his faith in Tommy's discretion did not move him to bestow his unreserved confidence upon him. Probably to no man in the world could he have opened his secret soul. He was not of an expansive nature. But Tommy occupied an inner place in his regard, and there were some things that he veiled from all beside which he no longer attempted to hide from this faithful follower of his. Thus far was Tommy privileged.

He got to his feet in response to the boy's last remark. "Yes, you're right. We ought to be going. I shall be interested to hear what your sister thinks of Kashmir. I went up there on a shooting expedition two years after I came out. It's a fine country."

"Is there anywhere that you haven't been?" said Tommy. "I believe you'll write a book one of these days."

Monck looked ironical. "Not till I'm on the shelf, Tommy," he said, "where there's nothing better to do."

"You'll never be on the shelf," said Tommy quickly. "You'll be much too valuable."

Monck shrugged his shoulders slightly and turned to go. "I doubt if that consideration would occur to any one but you, my boy," he said.

They walked to the mess-house together a little later through the airless dark, and there was nothing in Monck's manner either then or during the evening to confirm the doubt in Tommy's mind. Spirits were not very high at the mess just then. Nearly all the women had left for the Hills, and the increasing heat was beginning to make life a burden. The younger officers did their best to be cheerful, and one of them, Bertie Oakes, a merry, brainless youngster, even proposed an impromptu dance to enliven the proceedings. But he did not find many supporters. Men were tired after the polo. Colonel Mansfield and Major Burton were deeply engrossed with some news that had been brought by Barnes of the Police, and no one mustered energy for more than talk.

Tommy soon decided to leave early and return to his letters. Before departing, he looked round for Monck as was his custom, but finding that he and Captain Ermsted had also been drawn into the discussion with the Colonel, he left the mess alone.

Back in The Green Bungalow he flung off his coat and threw himself down in his shirt-sleeves on the verandah to read his sister's letter. The light from the red-shaded lamp streamed across the pages. Stella had written very fully of their wanderings, but her companion she scarcely mentioned.

It was like a gorgeous dream, she said. Each day seemed to bring greater beauties. They had spent the first two at Agra to see the wonderful Taj which of course was wholly beyond description. Thence they had made their way to Rawal Pindi where Ralph had several military friends to be introduced to his bride. It was evident that he was anxious to display his new possession, and Tommy frowned a little over that episode, realizing fully why Stella touched so lightly upon it. For some reason his dislike of Dacre was increasing rapidly, and he read the letter very critically. It was the first with any detail that she had written. From Rawal Pindi they had journeyed on to exquisite Murree set in the midst of the pines where only to breathe was the keenest pleasure. Stella spoke almost wistfully of this place; she would have loved to linger there.

"I could be happy there in perfect solitude," she wrote, "with just Peter the Great to take care of me." She mentioned the Sikh bearer more than once and each time with growing affection. "He is like an immense and kindly watch-dog," she said in one place. "Every material comfort that I could possibly wish for he manages somehow to procure, and he is always on guard, always there when wanted, yet never in the way."

Their time being limited and Ralph anxious to use it to the utmost, they had left Murree after a very brief stay and pressed on into Kashmir, travelling in a *tonga* through the most glorious scenery that Stella had ever beheld.

"I only wished you could have been there to enjoy it with me," she wrote, and passed on to a glowing description of the Hills amidst which they had travelled, all grandly beautiful and many capped with the eternal snows. She told of the River Jhelum, swift and splendid, that flowed beside the way, of the flowers that bloomed in dazzling profusion on every side—wild roses such as she had never dreamed of, purple acacias, jessamine yellow and white, maiden-hair ferns that hung in sprays of living green over the rushing waterfalls, and the vivid, scarlet pomegranate blossom that grew like a spreading fire.

And the air that blew through the mountains was as the very breath of life. Physically, she declared, she had never felt so well; but she did not speak of happiness, and again Tommy's brow contracted as he read.

For all its enthusiasm, there was to him something wanting in that letter—a lack that hurt him subtly. Why did she say so little of her companion in the wilderness? No casual reader would have dreamed that the narrative had been written by a bride upon her honeymoon.

He read on, read of their journey up the river to Srinagar, punted by native boatmen, and again, as she spoke of their sad, droning chant, she compared it all to a dream. "I wonder if I am really asleep, Tommy," she wrote, "if I shall wake up in the middle of a dark night and find that I have never left England after all. That is what I feel like sometimes—almost as if life had been suspended for awhile. This strange existence cannot be real. I am sure that at the heart of me I must be asleep."

At Srinagar, a native *fête* had been in progress, and the howling of men and din of *tom-toms* had somewhat marred the harmony of their arrival. But it was all interesting, like an absorbing fairy-tale, she said, but quite unreal. She felt sure it couldn't be true. Ralph had been disgusted with the hubbub and confusion. He compared the place to an asylum of filthy lunatics, and they had left it without delay. And so at last they had come to their present abiding-place in the heart of the wilderness with coolies, pack-horses, and tents, and were camped beside a rushing stream that filled the air with its crystal music day and night. "And this is Heaven," wrote Stella; "but it is the Heaven of the Orient, and I am not sure that I have any part or lot in it. I believe I shall feel myself an interloper for all time. I dread to turn each corner lest I should meet the Angel with the Flaming Sword and be driven forth into the desert. If only you were here, Tommy, it would be more real to me. But Ralph is just a part of the dream. He is almost like an Eastern potentate himself with his endless cigarettes and his wonderful capacity for doing nothing all day long without being bored. Of course, I am not bored, but then no one ever feels bored in a dream. The lazy well-being of it all has the effect of a narcotic so far as I am concerned. I cannot imagine ever feeling active in this lulling atmosphere. Perhaps there is too much champagne in the air and I am never wholly sober. Perhaps it is only in the desert that any one ever lives to the utmost. The endless singing of the stream is hushing me into a sweet drowsiness even as I write. By the way, I wonder if I have written sense. If not, forgive me! But I am much too lazy to read it through. I think I must have eaten of the lotus. Good-bye, Tommy dear! Write when you can and tell me that all is well with you, as I think it must be—though I cannot tell—with your always loving, though for the moment strangely bewitched, sister, Stella."

Tommy put down the letter and lay still, peering forth under frowning brows. He could hear Monck's footsteps coming through the gate of the compound, but he was not paying any attention to Monck for once. His troubled mind scarcely even registered the coming of his friend.

Only when the latter mounted the steps on to the verandah and began to move along it, did he turn his head and realize his presence. Monck came to a stand beside him.

"Well, Tommy," he said, "isn't it time to turn in?"

Tommy sat up. "Oh, I suppose so. Infernally hot, isn't it? I've been reading Stella's letter."

Monck lodged his shoulder against the window-frame. "I hope she is all right," he said formally.

His voice sounded pre-occupied. It did not convey to Tommy the idea that he was greatly interested in his reply.

He answered with something of an effort. "I believe she is. She doesn't really say. I wish they had been content to stay at Bhulwana. I could have got leave to go over and see her there."

"Where exactly are they now?" asked Monck.

Tommy explained to the best of his ability. "Srinagar seems their nearest point of civilization. They are camping in the wilderness, but they will have to move before long. Dacre's leave will be up, and they must allow time to get back. Stella talks as if they are fixed there for ever and ever."

"She is enjoying it then?" Monck's voice still sounded as if he were thinking of something else.

Tommy made grudging reply. "I suppose she is, after a fashion. I'm pretty sure of one thing." He spoke with abrupt force. "She'd enjoy it a deal more if I were with her instead of Dacre."

Monck laughed, a curt, dry laugh. "Jealous, eh?"

"No, I'm not such a fool." The boy spoke recklessly. "But I know—I can't help knowing—that she doesn't care twopence about the man. What woman with any brains could?"

"There's no accounting for women's tastes or actions at any time," said Monck. "She liked him well enough to marry him."

Tommy made an indignant sound. "She was in a mood to marry any one. She'd probably have married you if you'd asked her."

Monck made an abrupt movement as if he had lost his balance, but he returned to his former position immediately. "Think so?" he said in a voice that sounded very ironical. "Then possibly she has had a lucky escape. I might have been moved to ask her if she had remained free much longer."

"I wish to Heaven you had!" said Tommy bluntly.

And again Monck uttered his short, sardonic laugh. "Thank you, Tommy," he said.

There fell a silence between them, and a hot draught eddied up through the parched compound and rattled the scorched twigs of the creeping rose on the verandah with a desolate sound, as if skeleton hands were feeling along the trellis-work. Tommy suppressed a shudder and got to his feet.

In the same moment Monck spoke again, deliberately, emotionlessly, with a hint of grimness. "By the way, Tommy, I've a piece of news for you. That letter I had from my brother this, evening contained news of an urgent business matter which only I can deal with. It has come at a rather unfortunate moment as Barnes, the policeman, brought some disturbing information this evening from Khanmulla and the Chief wanted to make use of me in that quarter. They are sending a Mission to make investigations and they wanted me to go in charge of it."

"Oh, man!" Tommy's eyes suddenly shone with enthusiasm. "What a chance!"

"A chance I'm not going to take," rejoined Monck dryly. "I applied for leave instead. In any case it is due to me, but Dacre had his turn first. The Chief didn't want to grant it, but he gave way in the end. You boys will have to work a little harder than usual, that's all."

Tommy was staring at him in amazement. "But, I say, Monck!" he protested. "That Mission business! It's the very thing you'd most enjoy. Surely you can't be going to let such an opportunity slip!"

"My own business is more pressing," Monck returned briefly.

Then Tommy remembered the stricken look that he had surprised on his friend's face that evening, and swift concern swallowed his astonishment. "You had bad news from Home! I say, I'm awfully sorry. Is your brother ill, or what?"

"No. It's not that. I can't discuss it with you, Tommy. But I've got to go. The Chief has granted me eight weeks and I am off at dawn." Monck made as if he would turn inwards with the words.

"You're going Home?" ejaculated Tommy. "By Jove, old fellow, it'll be quick work." Then, his sympathy coming uppermost again, "I say, I'm confoundedly sorry. You'll take care of yourself?"

"Oh, every care." Monck paused to lay an unexpected hand upon the lad's shoulder. "And you must take care of yourself, Tommy," he said. "Don't get up to any tomfoolery while I am away! And if you get thirsty, stick to lime-juice!"

"I'll be as good as gold," Tommy promised, touched alike by action and admonition. "But it will be pretty beastly without you. I hate a lonely life, and Stella will be stuck at Bhulwana for the rest of the hot weather when they get back."

"Well, I shan't stay away for ever," Monck patted his shoulder and turned away. "I'm not going for a pleasure trip, and the sooner it's over, the better I shall be pleased."

He passed into the room with the words, that room in which Stella had sat on her wedding-eve, gazing forth into the night. And there came to Tommy, all-unbidden, a curious, wandering memory of his friend's face on that same night, with eyes alight and ardent, looking upwards as though they saw a vision. Perplexed and vaguely troubled, he thrust her letter away into his pocket and went to his own room.

CHAPTER VI
THE GARDEN

The Heaven of the Orient! It was a week since Stella had penned those words, and still the charm held her, the wonder grew. Never in her life had she dreamed of a land so perfect, so subtly alluring, so overwhelmingly full of enchantment. Day after day slipped by in what seemed an endless succession. Night followed magic night, and the spell wound closer and ever closer about her. She sometimes felt as if her very individuality were being absorbed into the marvellous beauty about her, as if she had been crystallized by it and must soon cease to be in any sense a being apart from it.

The siren-music of the torrent that dashed below their camping-ground filled her brain day and night. It seemed to make active thought impossible, to dull all her senses save the one luxurious sense of enjoyment. That was always present, slumbrous, almost cloying in its unfailing sweetness, the fruit of the lotus which assuredly she was eating day by day. All her nerves seemed dormant, all her energies lulled. Sometimes she wondered if the sound of running water had this stultifying effect upon her, for wherever they went it followed them. The snow-fed streams ran everywhere, and since leaving Srinagar she could not remember a single occasion on which they had been out of earshot of their perpetual music. It haunted her like a ceaseless refrain, but yet she never wearied of it. There was no thought of weariness in this mazed, dream-world of hers.

At the beginning of her married life, so far behind her now that she scarcely remembered it, she had gone through pangs of suffering and fierce regret. Her whole nature had revolted, and it had taken all her strength to quell it. But that was long, long past. She had ceased to feel anything now, but a dumb and even placid acquiescence in this lethargic existence, and Ralph Dacre was amply satisfied therewith. He had always been abundantly confident of his power to secure her happiness, and he was blissfully unconscious of the wild impulse to rebellion which she had barely stifled. He had no desire to sound the deeps of her. He was quite content with life as he found it, content to share with her the dreamy pleasures that lay in this fruitful wilderness, and to look not beyond.

He troubled himself but little about the future, though when he thought of it that was with pleasure too. He liked, now and then, to look forward to the days that were coming when Stella would shine as a queen—his queen—among an envious crowd. Her position assured as his wife, even Lady Harriet herself would have to lower her flag. And how little Netta Ermsted would grit her teeth! He laughed to himself whenever he thought of that. Netta had become too uppish of late. It would be amusing to see how she took her lesson.

And as for his brother-officers, even the taciturn Monck had already shown that he was not proof against Stella's charms. He wondered what Stella thought of the man, well knowing that few women liked him, and one evening, as they sat together in the scented darkness with the roar of their mountain-stream filling the silences, he turned their fitful conversation in Monck's direction to satisfy his lazy curiosity in this respect.

"I suppose I ought to write to the fellow," he said, "but if you've written to Tommy it's almost the same thing. Besides, I don't suppose he would be in the smallest degree interested. He would only be bored."

There was a pause before Stella answered; but she was often slow of speech in those days. "I thought you were friends," she said.

"What? Oh, so we are." Ralph Dacre laughed, his easy, complacent laugh. "But he's a dark horse, you know. I never know quite how to take him. Your brother Tommy is a deal more intimate with him than I am, though I have stabled with him for over four years. He's a very clever fellow, there's no doubt of that—altogether too brainy for my taste. Clever fellows always bore me. Now I wonder how he strikes you."

Again there was that slight pause before Stella spoke, but there was nothing very vital about it. She seemed to be slow in bringing her mind to bear upon the subject. "I agree with you," she said then. "He is clever. And he is kind too. He has been very good to Tommy."

"Tommy would lie down and let him walk over him," remarked Dacre. "Perhaps that is what he likes. But he's a cold-blooded sort of cuss. I don't believe he has a spark of real affection for anybody. He is too ambitious."

"Is he ambitious?" Stella's voice sounded rather weary, wholly void of interest.

Dacre inhaled a deep breath of cigar-smoke and puffed it slowly forth. His curiosity was warming. "Oh yes, ambitious as they're made. Those strong, silent chaps always are. And there's no doubt he will make his mark some day. He is a positive marvel at languages. And he dabbles in Secret Service matters too, disguises himself and goes among the natives in the bazaars as one of themselves. A fellow like that, you know, is simply priceless to the Government. And he is as tough as leather. The climate never touches him. He could sit on a grille and be happy. No doubt he will be a very big pot some day." He tipped the ash from his cigar. "You and I will be comfortably growing old in a villa at Cheltenham by that time," he ended.

A little shiver went through Stella. She said nothing and silence fell between them again. The moon was rising behind a rugged line of snow-hills across the valley, touching them here and there with a silvery radiance, casting mysterious shadows all about them, sending a magic twilight over the whole world so that they saw it dimly, as through a luminous veil. The scent of Dacre's cigar hung in the air, fragrant, aromatic, Eastern. He was sleepily watching his wife's pure profile as she gazed into her world of dreams. It was evident that she took small interest in Monck and his probable career. It was not surprising. Monck was not the sort of man to attract women; he cared so little about them—this silent watcher whose eyes were ever searching below the surface of Eastern life, who studied and read and knew so much more than any one else and yet who guarded knowledge and methods so closely that only those in contact with his daily life suspected what he hid.

"He will surprise us all some day," Dacre placidly reflected. "Those quiet, ambitious chaps always soar high. But I wouldn't change places with him even if he wins to the top of the tree. People who make a specialty of hard work never get any fun out of anything. By the time the fun comes along, they are too old to enjoy it."

And so he lay at ease in his chair, feasting his eyes upon his young wife's grave face, savouring life with the zest of the epicurean, placidly at peace with all the world on that night of dreams.

It was growing late, and the moon had topped the distant peaks sending a flood of light across the sleeping valley before he finally threw away the stump of his cigar and stretched forth a lazy arm to draw her to him.

"Why so silent, Star of my heart? Where are those wandering thoughts of yours?"

She submitted as usual to his touch, passively, without enthusiasm. "My thoughts are not worth expressing, Ralph," she said.

"Let us hear them all the same!" he said, laying his head against her shoulder.

She sat very still in his hold. "I was only watching the moonlight," she said. "Somehow it made me think—of a flaming sword."

"Turning all ways?" he suggested, indolently humorous. "Not driving us forth out of the garden of Eden, I hope? That would be a little hard on two such inoffensive mortals as we are, eh, sweetheart?"

"I don't know," she said seriously. "I doubt if the plea of inoffensiveness would open the gates of Heaven to any one."

He laughed. "I can't talk ethics at this time of night, Star of my heart. It's time we went to our lair. I believe you would sit here till sunrise if I would let you, you most ethereal of women. Do you ever think of your body at all, I wonder?"

He kissed her neck with the careless words, and a quick shiver went through her. She made a slight, scarcely perceptible movement to free herself.

But the next moment sharply, almost convulsively, she grasped his arm. "Ralph! What is that?"

She was gazing towards the shadow cast by a patch of flowering azalea in the moonlight about ten yards from where they sat. Dacre raised himself with leisurely self-assurance and peered in the same direction. It was not his nature to be easily disturbed.

But Stella's hand still clung to his arm, and there was agitation in her hold. "What is it?" she whispered. "What can it be? I have seen it move—twice. Ah, look! Is it—is it—a panther?"

"Good gracious, child, no!" Carelessly he made response, and with the words disengaged himself from her hand and stood up. "It's more probably some filthy old beggar who fondly thinks he is going to get *backsheesh* for disturbing us. You stay here while I go and investigate!"

But some nervous impulse goaded Stella. She also started up, holding him back. "Oh, don't go, Ralph! Don't go! Call one of the men! Call Peter!"

He laughed at her agitation. "My dear girl, don't be absurd! I don't want Peter to help me kick a beastly native. In fact he probably wouldn't lower himself to do such a thing."

But still she clung to him. "Ralph, don't go! Please don't go! I have a feeling—I am afraid—I—" She broke off panting, her fingers tightly clutching his sleeve. "Don't go!" she reiterated.

He put his arm round her. "My dear, what do you think a tatterdemalion gipsy is going to do to me? He may be a snake-charmer, and if so the sooner he is got rid of the better. There! What did I tell you? He is coming out of his corner. Now, don't be frightened! It doesn't do to show funk to these people."

He held her closely to him and waited. Beside the flowering azalea something was undoubtedly moving, and as they stood and watched, a strange figure slowly detached itself from the shadows and crept towards them. It was clad in native garments and shuffled along in a bent attitude as if deformed. Stella stiffened as she stood. There was something unspeakably repellent to her in its toadlike advance.

"Make one of the men send him away!" she whispered urgently. "Please do! It may be a snake-charmer as you say. He moves like a reptile himself. And I—abhor snakes."

But Dacre stood his ground. He felt none of her shrinking horror of the bowed, misshapen creature approaching them. In fact he was only curious to see how far a Kashmiri beggar's audacity would carry him.

Within half a dozen paces of them, in the full moonlight, the shambling figure halted and salaamed with clawlike hands extended. His deformity bent him almost double, but he was so muffled in rags that it was difficult to discern any tangible human shape at all. A tangled black beard hung wisplike from the dirty *chuddah* that draped his head, and above it two eyes, fevered and furtive, peered strangely forth.

The salaam completed, the intruder straightened himself as far as his infirmity would permit, and in a moment spoke in the weak accents of an old, old man. "Will his most gracious excellency be pleased to permit one who is as the dust beneath his feet to speak in his presence words which only he may hear?"

It was the whine of the Hindu beggar, halting, supplicatory, almost revoltingly servile. Stella shuddered with disgust. The whole episode was so utterly out of place in that moonlit paradise. But Dacre's curiosity was evidently aroused. To her urgent whisper to send the man away he paid no heed. Some spirit of perversity—or was it the hand of Fate upon him?—made him bestow his supercilious attention upon the cringing visitor.

"Speak away, you son of a centipede!" he made kindly rejoinder. "I am all ears—the *mem-sahib* also."

The man waved a skinny, protesting arm. "Only his most gracious excellency!" he insisted, seeming to utter the words through parched lips. "Will not his excellency deign to give his unworthy servant one precious moment that he may speak in the august one's ear alone?"

"This is highly mysterious," commented Dacre. "I think I shall have to find out what he wants, eh, Stella? His information may be valuable."

"Oh, do send him away!" Stella entreated. "I am not used to these natives. They frighten me."

"My dear child, what nonsense!" laughed Dacre. "What harm do you imagine a doddering old fool like this could do to any one? If I were Monck, I should invite him to join the party. Not being Monck, I propose to hear what he has to say and then kick him out. You run along to bed, dear! I'll soon settle him and follow you. Don't be uneasy! There is really no need."

He kissed her lightly with the words, flattered by her evident anxiety on his behalf though fully determined to ignore it.

Stella turned beside him in silence, aware that he could be immovably obstinate when once his mind was made up. But the feeling of dread remained upon her. In some fantastic fashion the beauty of the night had become marred, as though evil spirits were abroad. For the first time she wanted to keep her husband at her side.

But it was useless to protest. She was moreover half-ashamed herself at her uneasiness, and his treatment of it stung her into the determination to dismiss it. She parted with him before their tent with no further sign of reluctance.

He on his part kissed her in his usual voluptuous fashion. "Good-night, darling!" he said lightly. "Don't lie awake for me! When I have got rid of this old Arabian Nights sinner, I may have another smoke. But don't get impatient! I shan't be late."

She withdrew herself from him almost with coldness. Had she ever been impatient for his coming? She entered the tent proudly, her head high. But the moment she was alone, reaction came. She stood with her hands gripped together, fighting the old intolerable misgiving that even the lulling magic all around her had never succeeded in stilling. What was she doing in this garden of delights with a man she did not love? Had she not entered as it were by stealth? How long would it be before her presence was discovered and she thrust forth into the outermost darkness in shame and bitterness of soul?

Another thought was struggling at the back of her mind, but she held it firmly there. Never once had she suffered it to take full possession of her. It belonged to that other life which she had found too hard to endure. Vain regrets and futile longings—she would have none of them. She had chosen her lot, she would abide by the choice. Yes, and she would do her duty also, whatever it might entail. Ralph should never know, never dimly suspect. And that other—he would never know either. His had been but a passing fancy. He trod the way of ambition, and there was no room in his life for anything besides. If she had shown him her heart, it had been but a momentary glimpse; and he had forgotten already. She was sure he had forgotten. And she had desired that he should forget. He had penetrated her stronghold indeed, but it was only as it were the outer defences that had fallen. He had not reached the inner fort. No man would ever reach that now—certainly, most certainly, not the man to whom she had given herself. And to none other would the chance be offered.

No, she was secure; she was secure. She guarded her heart from all. And she could not suffer deeply—so she told herself—so long as she kept it close. Yet, as the wonder-music of the torrent lulled her to sleep, a face she knew, dark, strong, full of silent purpose, rose before her inner vision and would not be driven forth. What was he doing to-night? Was he wandering about the bazaars in some disguise, learning the secrets of that strange native India that had drawn him into her toils? She tried to picture that hidden life of his, but could not. The keen, steady eyes, set in that calm, emotionless face, held her persistently, defeating imagination. Of one thing only was she certain. He might baffle others, but by no amount of ingenuity could he ever deceive her. She would recognize him in a moment whatever his disguise. She was sure that she would know him. Those grave, unflinching eyes would surely give him away to any who really knew him. So ran her thoughts on that night of magic till at last sleep came, and the vision faded. The last thing she knew was a memory that awoke and mocked her—the sound of a low voice that in spite of herself she had to hear.

"I was waiting," said the voice, "till my turn should come."

With a sharp pang she cast the memory from her—and slept.

CHAPTER VII
THE SERPENT IN THE GARDEN

"Now, you old sinner! Let's hear your valuable piece of information!" Carelessly Ralph Dacre sauntered forth again into the moonlight and confronted the tatterdemalion figure of his visitor.

The contrast between them was almost fantastic so strongly did the arrogance of the one emphasize the deep abasement of the other. Dacre was of large build and inclined to stoutness. He had the ruddy complexion of the English country squire. He moved with the swagger of the conquering race.

The man who cringed before him, palsied, misshapen, a mere wreck of humanity, might have been a being from another sphere—some underworld of bizarre creatures that crawled purblind among shadows.

He salaamed again profoundly in response to Dacre's contemptuous words, nearly rubbing his forehead upon the ground. "His most noble excellency is pleased to be gracious," he murmured. "If he will deign to follow his miserably unworthy servant up the goat-path where none may overhear, he will speak his message and depart."

"Oh, it's a message, is it?" With a species of scornful tolerance Dacre turned towards the path indicated. "Well, lead on! I'm not coming far—no, not for untold wealth. Nor am I going to waste much time over you. I have better things to do."

The old man turned also with a cringing movement. "Only a little way, most noble!" he said in his thin, cracked voice. "Only a little way!"

Hobbling painfully, he began the ascent in front of the strolling Englishman. The path ran steeply up between close-growing shrubs, following the winding of the torrent far below. In places the hillside was precipitous and the roar of the stream rose louder as it dashed among its rocks. The heavy scent of the azalea flowers hung like incense everywhere, mingling aromatically with the smoke from Dacre's newly lighted cigar.

With his hands in his pockets he followed his guide with long, easy strides. The ascent was nothing to him, and the other's halting progress brought a smile of contemptuous pity to his lips. What did the old rascal expect to gain from the interview he wondered?

Up and up the narrow path they went, till at length a small natural platform in the shoulder of the hill was reached, and here the ragged creature in front of Dacre paused and turned.

The moonlight smote full upon him, revealing him in every repulsive detail. His eyes burned in their red-rimmed sockets as he lifted them. But he did not speak even after the careless saunter of the Englishman had ceased at his side. The dash of the stream far below rose up like the muffled roar of a train in a tunnel. The bed of it was very narrow at that point and the current swift.

For a moment or two Dacre stood waiting, the cigar still between his lips, his eyes upon the gleaming caps of the snow-hills far away. But very soon the spell of them fell from him. It was not his nature to remain silent for long.

With his easy, superior laugh he turned and looked his motionless companion up and down. "Well?" he said. "Have you brought me here to admire the view? Very fine no doubt; but I could have done it without your guidance."

There was no immediate reply to his carelessly flung query, and faint curiosity arose within him mingling with his strong contempt. He pulled a hand out of his pocket and displayed a few *annas* in his palm.

"Well?" he said again. "What may this valuable piece of information be worth?"

The other made an abrupt movement; it was almost as if he curbed some savage impulse to violence. He moved back a pace, and there in the moonlight before Dacre's insolent gaze—he changed.

With a deep breath he straightened himself to the height of a tall man. The bent contorted limbs became lithe and strong. The cringing humility slipped from him like a garment. He stood upright and faced Ralph Dacre—a man in the prime of life.

"That," he said, "is a matter of opinion. So far as I am concerned, it has cost a damned uncomfortable journey. But—it will probably cost you more than that."

"Great—Jupiter!" said Dacre.

He stood and stared and stared. The curt speech, the almost fiercely contemptuous bearing, the absolute, unwavering assurance of this man whom but a moment before he had so arrogantly trampled underfoot sent through him such a shock of amazement as nearly deprived him of the power to think. Perhaps for the first time in his life he was utterly and completely at a loss. Only as he gazed at the man before him, there came upon him, sudden as a blow, the memory of a certain hot day more than a year before when he and Everard Monck had wrestled together in the Club gymnasium for the benefit of a little crowd of subalterns who had eagerly betted upon the result. It had been sinew *versus* weight, and after a tough struggle sinew had prevailed. He remembered the unpleasant sensation of defeat even now though he had had the grit to take it like a man and get up laughing. It was one of the very few occasions he could remember upon which he had been worsted.

But now—to-night—he was face to face with something of an infinitely more serious nature. This man with the stern, accusing eyes and wholly merciless attitude—what had he come to say? An odd sensation stirred at Dacre's heart like an unsteady hand knocking for admittance. There was something wrong here— something wrong.

"You—madman!" he said at length, and with the words pulled himself together with a giant effort. "What in the name of wonder are you doing here?" He had bitten his cigar through in his astonishment, and he tossed it away as he spoke with a gesture of returning confidence. He silenced the uneasy foreboding within and met the hard eyes that confronted him without discomfiture. "What's your game?" he said. "You have come to tell me something, I suppose. But why on earth couldn't you write it?"

"The written word is not always effectual," the other man said.

He put up a hand abruptly and stripped the ragged hair from his face, pushing back the heavy folds of the *chuddah* that enveloped his head as he did so. His features gleamed in the moonlight, lean and brown, unmistakably British.

"Monck!" said Dacre, in the tone of one verifying a suspicion.

"Yes—Monck." Grimly the other repeated the name. "I've had considerable trouble in following you here. I shouldn't have taken it if I hadn't had a very urgent reason."

"Well, what the devil is it?" Dacre spoke with the exasperation of a man who knows himself to be at a disadvantage. "If you want to know my opinion, I regard such conduct as damned intrusive at such a time. But if you've any decent excuse let's hear it!"

He had never adopted that tone to Monck before, but he had been rudely jolted out of his usually complacent attitude, and he resented Monck's presence. Moreover, an unpleasant sense of inferiority had begun to make itself felt. There was something judicial about Monck—something inexorable and condemnatory—something that aroused in him every instinct of self-defence.

But Monck met his blustering demand with the utmost calm. It was as if he held him in a grip of iron intention from which no struggles, however desperate, could set him free.

He took an envelope from the folds of his ragged raiment. "I believe you have heard me speak of my brother Bernard," he said, "chaplain of Charthurst Prison."

Dacre nodded. "The fellow who writes to you every month. Well? What of him?"

Monck's steady fingers detached and unfolded a letter. "You had better read for yourself," he said, and held it out.

But curiously Dacre hung back as if unwilling to touch it.

"Can't you tell me what all the fuss is about?" he said irritably.

Monck's hand remained inflexibly extended. He spoke, a jarring note in his voice. "Oh yes, I can tell you. But you had better see for yourself too. It concerns you very nearly. It was written in Charthurst Prison nearly six weeks ago, where a woman who calls herself your wife is undergoing a term of imprisonment for forgery."

"Damnation!" Ralph Dacre actually staggered as if he had received a blow between the eyes. But almost in the next moment he recovered himself, and uttered a quivering laugh. "Man alive! You are not fool enough to believe such a cock-and-bull story as that!" he said. "And you have come all this way in this fancy get-up to tell me! You must be mad!"

Monck was still holding out the letter. "You had better see for yourself," he reiterated. "It is damnably circumstantial."

"I tell you it's an infernal lie!" flung back Dacre furiously. "There is no woman on this earth who has any claim on me—except Stella. Why should I read it? I tell you it's nothing but damned fabrication—a tissue of abominable falsehood!"

"You mean to deny that you have ever been through any form of marriage before?" said Monck slowly.

"Of course I do!" Dacre uttered another angry laugh. "You must be a positive fool to imagine such a thing. It's preposterous, unheard of! Of course I have never been married before. What are you thinking of?"

Monck remained unmoved. "She has been a music-hall actress," he said. "Her name is—or was—Madelina Belleville. Do you tell me that you have never had any dealings whatever with her?"

Dacre laughed again fiercely, scoffingly. "You don't imagine that I would marry a woman of that sort, do you?" he said.

"That is no answer to my question," Monck said firmly.

"Confound you!" Dacre blazed into open wrath. "Who the devil are you to enquire into my private affairs? Do you think I am going to put up with your damned impertinence? What?"

"I think you will have to." Monck spoke quietly, but there was deadly determination in his words. "It's a choice of evils, and if you are wise you will choose the least. Are you going to read the letter?"

Dacre stared at him for a moment or two with eyes of glowering resentment; but in the end he put forth a hand not wholly steady and took the sheet held out to him. Monck stood beside him in utter immobility, gazing out over the valley with a changeless vigilance that had about it something fateful.

Minutes passed. Dacre seemed unable to lift his eyes from the page. But it fluttered in his hold, though the night was still, as if a strong wind were blowing.

Suddenly he moved, as one who violently breaks free from some fettering spell. He uttered a bitter oath and tore the sheet of paper passionately to fragments. He flung them to the ground and trampled them underfoot.

"Ten million curses on her!" he raved. "She has been the bane of my life!"

Monck's eyes came out of the distance and surveyed him, coldly curious. "I thought so," he said, and in his voice was an odd inflection as of one who checks a laugh at an ill-timed jest.

Dacre stamped again like an infuriated bull. "If I had her here—I'd strangle her!" he swore. "That brother of yours is an artist. He has sketched her to the life—the she-devil!"

His voice cracked and broke. He was breathing like a man in torture. He swayed as he stood.

And still Monck remained passive, grim and cold and unyielding. "How long is it since you married her?" he questioned at last.

"I tell you I never married her!" Desperately Dacre sought to recover lost ground, but he had slipped too far.

"You told me that lie before," Monck observed in his even judicial tones. "Is it—worth while?"

Dacre glared at him, but his glare was that of the hunted animal trapped and helpless. He was conquered, and he knew it.

Calmly Monck continued. "There is not much doubt that she holds proof of the marriage, and she will probably try to establish it as soon as she is free."

"She will never get anything more out of me," said Dacre. His voice was low and sullen. There was that in the other man's attitude that stilled his fury, rendering it futile, even in a fashion ridiculous.

"I am not thinking of you." Monck's coldness had in it something brutal. "You are not the only person concerned. But the fact remains—this woman is your wife. You may as well tell the truth about it as not—since I know."

Dacre jerked his head like an angry bull, but he submitted. "Oh well, if you must have it, I suppose she was—once," he said. "She caught me when I was a kid of twenty-one. She was a bad 'un even then, and it didn't take me long to find it out. I could have divorced her several times over, only the marriage was a secret and I didn't want my people to know. The last I heard of her was that her name was among the drowned on a wrecked liner going to America. That was six years ago or more; and I was thankful to be rid of her. I regarded her death as one of the biggest slices of luck I'd ever had. And now—curse her!"—he ended savagely—"she has come to life again!"

He glanced at Monck with the words, almost as if seeking sympathy; but Monck's face was masklike in its unresponsiveness. He said nothing whatever.

In a moment Dacre took up the tale. "I've considered myself free ever since we separated, after only six weeks together. Any man would. It was nothing but a passing fancy. Heaven knows why I was fool enough to marry her, except that I had high-flown ideas of honour in those days, and I got drawn in. She never regarded it as binding, so why in thunder should I?" He spoke indignantly, as one who had the right of complaint.

"Your ideas of honour having altered somewhat," observed Monck, with bitter cynicism.

Dacre winced a little. "I don't profess to be anything extraordinary," he said. "But I maintain that marriage gives no woman the right to wreck a man's life. She has no more claim upon me now than the man in the moon. If she tries to assert it, she will soon find her mistake." He was beginning to recover his balance, and there was even a hint of his customary complacence audible in his voice as he made the declaration. "But there is no reason to believe she will," he added. "She knows very well that she has nothing whatever to gain by it. Your brother seems to have gathered but a vague idea of the affair. You had better write and tell him that the Dacre he means is dead. Your brother-officer belongs to another branch of the family. That ought to satisfy everybody and no great harm done, what?"

He uttered the last word with a tentative, disarming smile. He was not quite sure of his man, but it seemed to him that even Monck must see the utter futility of making a disturbance about the affair at this stage. Matters had gone so far that silence was the only course—silence on his part, a judicious lie or two on the part of Monck. He did not see how the latter could refuse to render him so small a service. As he himself had remarked but a few moments before, he, Dacre, was not the only person concerned.

But the absolute and uncompromising silence with which his easy suggestion was received was disquieting. He hastened to break it, divining that the longer it lasted the less was it likely to end in his favour.

"Come, I say!" he urged on a friendly note. "You can't refuse to do this much for a comrade in a tight corner! I'd do the same for you and more. And remember, it isn't my happiness alone that hangs in the balance! We've got to think of—Stella!"

Monck moved at that, moved sharply, almost with violence. Yet, when he spoke, his voice was still deliberate, cuttingly distinct. "Yes," he said. "And her honour is worth about as much to you, apparently, as your own! I am thinking of her—and of her only. And, so far as I can see, there is only one thing to be done."

"Oh, indeed!" Dacre's air of half-humorous persuasion dissolved into insolence. "And I am to do it, am I? Your humble servant to command!"

Monck stretched forth a sinewy arm and slowly closed his fist under the other man's eyes. "You will do it—yes," he said. "I hold you—like that."

Dacre flinched slightly in spite of himself. "What do you mean? You would never be such a—such a cur—as to give me away?"

Monck made a sound that was too full of bitterness to be termed a laugh. "You're such an infernal blackguard," he said, "that I don't care a damn whether you go to the devil or not. The only thing that concerns me is how to protect a woman's honour that you have dared to jeopardize, how to save her from open shame. It won't be an easy matter, but it can be done, and it shall be done. Now listen!" His voice rang suddenly hard, almost metallic. "If this thing is to be kept from her—as it must be—as it shall be—you must drop out—vanish. So far as she is concerned you must die to-night."

"I?" Dacre stared at him in startled incredulity. "Man, are you mad?"

"I am not." Keen as bared steel came the answer. Monck's impassivity was gone. His face was darkly passionate, his whole bearing that of a man relentlessly set upon obtaining the mastery. "But if you imagine her safety can be secured without a sacrifice, you are wrong. Do you think I am going to stand tamely by and see an innocent woman dragged down to your beastly level? What do you suppose her point of view would be? How would she treat the situation if she ever came to know? I believe she would kill herself."

"But she never need know! She never shall know!" There was a note of desperation in Dacre's rejoinder. "You have only got to hush it up, and it will die a natural death. That she-devil will never take the trouble to follow me out here. Why should she? She knows very well that she has no claim whatever upon me. Stella is the only woman who has any claim upon me now."

"You are right." Grimly Monck took him up. "And her claim is the claim of an honourable woman to honourable treatment. And so far as lies in your power and mine, she shall have it. That is why you will do this thing—disappear to-night, go out of her life for good, and let her think you dead. I will undertake then that the truth shall never reach her. She will be safe. But there can be no middle course. She shall not be exposed to the damnable risk of finding herself stranded."

He ceased to speak, and in the moonlight their eyes met as the eyes of men who grip together in a death-struggle.

The silence between them was more terrible than words. It held unutterable things.

Dacre spoke at last, his voice low and hoarse. "I can't do it. There is too much involved. Besides, it wouldn't really help. She would come to know inevitably."

"She will never know." Inexorably came the answer, spoken with pitiless insistence. "As to ways and means, I have provided for them. It won't be difficult in this wilderness to cover your tracks. When the news has gone forth that you are dead, no one will look for you."

A hard shiver went through Dacre. His hands clenched. He was as a man in the presence of his executioner. The paralysing spell was upon him again, constricting as a rope about his neck. But sacrifice was no part of his nature. With despair at his heart, he yet made a desperate bid for freedom.

"The whole business is outrageous!" he said. "It is out of the question. I refuse to do it. Matters have gone too far. To all intents and purposes, Stella is my wife, and I'm damned if any one shall come between us. You may do your worst! I refuse."

Defiance was his only weapon, and he hurled it with all his strength; but the moment he had done so, he realized the hopelessness of the venture. Monck made a single, swift movement, and in a moment the moonlight glinted upon the polished muzzle of a Service revolver. He spoke, briefly, with iron coldness.

"The choice is yours. Only—if you refuse to give her—the sanctuary of widowhood—I will! After all it would be the safest way for all concerned."

Dacre went back a pace. "Going to murder me, what?" he said.

Monck's teeth gleamed in a terrible smile. "You need not—refuse," he said.

"True!" Dacre was looking him full in the eyes with more of curiosity than apprehension. "And—as you have foreseen—I shall not refuse under those circumstances. It would have saved time if you had put it in that light before."

"It would. But I hoped you might have the decency to act without—persuasion." Monck was speaking between his teeth, but the revolver was concealed again in the folds of his garment. "You will leave to-night—at once—without seeing her again. That is understood."

It was the end of the conflict. Dacre attempted no further resistance. He was not the man to waste himself upon a cause that he realized to be hopeless. Moreover, there was about Monck at that moment a force that restrained him, compelled instinctive respect. Though he hated the man for his mastery, he could not despise him. For he knew that what he had done had been done through a rigid sense of honour and that chivalry which goes hand in hand with honour—the chivalry with which no woman would have credited him.

That Monck had nought but the most disinterested regard for any woman, he firmly believed, and probably that conviction gave added strength to his position. That he should fight thus for a mere principle, though incomprehensible in Dacre's opinion, was a circumstance that carried infinitely more weight than more personal championship. Monck was the one man of his acquaintance who had never displayed the smallest desire to compete for any woman's favour, who had never indeed shown himself to be drawn by any feminine attractions, and his sudden assumption of authority was therefore unassailable. In yielding to the greater power, Dacre yielded to a moral force rather than to human compulsion. And though driven sorely against his will, he respected the power that drove. His dumb gesture of acquiescence conveyed as much as he turned away relinquishing the struggle.

He had fought hard, and he had been defeated. It was bitter enough, but after all he had had his turn. The first hot rapture was already passing. Love in the wilderness could not last for ever. It had been fierce enough—too fierce to endure. And characteristically he reflected that Stella's cold beauty would not have held him for long. He preferred something more ardent, more living. Moreover, his nature demanded a certain meed of homage from the object of his desire, and undeniably this had been conspicuously lacking. Stella was evidently one to accept rather than to give, and there had been moments when this had slightly galled him. She seemed to him fundamentally incapable of any deep feeling, and though this had not begun to affect their relations at present, he had realized in a vague fashion that because of it she would not hold him for ever. So, after the first, he knew that he would find consolation. Certainly he would not break his heart for her or for any woman, nor did he flatter himself that she would break hers for him.

Meantime—he prepared to shrug his shoulders over the inevitable. Things might have been much worse. And perhaps on the whole it was safer to obey Monck's command and go. An open scandal would really be a good deal worse for him than for Stella, who had little to lose, and there was no knowing what might happen if he took the risk and remained. Emphatically he had no desire to face a personal reckoning at some future date with the she-devil who had been the bane of his existence. It was an unlikely contingency but undoubtedly it existed, and he hated unpleasantness of all kinds. So, philosophically, he resolved to adjust himself to this burden. There was something of the adventurer in his blood and he had a vast belief in his own ultimate good luck. Fortune might frown for awhile, but he knew that he was Fortune's favourite notwithstanding. And very soon she would smile again.

But for Monck he had only the bitter hate of the conquered. He cast a malevolent look upon him with eyes that were oddly narrowed—a measuring, speculative look that comprehended his strength and registered the infallibility thereof with loathing. "I wonder what happened to the serpent," he said, "when the man and woman were thrust out of the garden."

Monck had readjusted his disguise. He looked back with baffling, inscrutable eyes, his dark face masklike in its impenetrability. But he spoke no word in answer. He had said his say. Like a mantle he gathered his reserve about him again, as a man resuming a solitary journey through the desert which all his life he had travelled alone.

CHAPTER VIII
THE FORBIDDEN PARADISE

Looking back later upon that fateful night, it seemed to Stella that she must indeed have slept the sleep of the lotus-eater, for no misgivings pierced the numb unconsciousness that held her through the still hours. She lay as one in a trance, wholly insensible of the fact that she was alone, aware only of the perpetual rush and fall of the torrent below, which seemed to act like a narcotic upon her brain.

When she awoke at length broad daylight was all about her, and above the roar of the stream there was rising a hubbub of voices like the buzzing of a swarm of bees. She lay for awhile listening to it, lazily wondering why the coolies should bring their breakfast so much nearer to the tent than usually, and then, suddenly and terribly, there came a cry that seemed to transfix her, stabbing her heavy senses to full consciousness.

For a second or two she lay as if petrified, every limb struck powerless, every nerve strained to listen. Who had uttered that dreadful wail? What did it portend? Then, her strength returning, she started up, and knew that she was alone. The camp-bed by her side was empty. It had not been touched. Fear, nameless and chill, swept through her. She felt her very heart turn cold.

Shivering, she seized a wrap, and crept to the tent-entrance. The flap was unfastened, just as it had been left by her husband the night before. With shaking fingers she drew it aside and looked forth.

The hubbub of voices had died down to awed whisperings. A group of coolies huddled in the open space before her like an assembly of monkeys holding an important discussion.

Further away, with distorted limbs and grim, impassive countenance, crouched the black-bearded beggar whose importunity had lured Ralph from her side the previous evening. His red-rimmed, sunken eyes gazed like the eyes of a dead man straight into the sunrise. So motionless were they, so utterly void of expression, that she thought they must be blind. There was something fateful, something terrible in the aloofness of him. It was as if an invisible circle surrounded him within which none might intrude.

And close at hand—so close that she could have touched his turbaned head as she stood—the great Sikh bearer, Peter, sat huddled in a heap on the soft green earth and rocked himself to and fro like a child in trouble. She knew at the first glance that it was he who had uttered that anguished wail.

To him she turned, as to the only being she could trust in that strange scene.

"Peter," she said, "what has happened? What is wrong? Where—where is the captain *sahib*?"

He gave a great start at the sound of her voice above him, and instantly, with a rapid noiseless movement, arose and bent himself before her.

"The *mem-sahib* will pardon her servant," he said, and she saw that his dark face was twisted with emotion. "But there is bad news for her to-day. The captain *sahib* has gone."

"Gone!" Stella echoed the word uncomprehendingly, as one who speaks an unknown language.

Peter's look fell before the wide questioning of hers. He replied almost under his breath: "*Mem-sahib*, it was in the still hour of the night. The captain *sahib* slept on the mountain, and in his sleep he fell—and was taken away by the stream."

"Taken away!" Again, numbly, Stella repeated his words. She felt suddenly very weak and sick.

Peter stretched a hand towards the inscrutable stranger. "This man, *mem-sahib*," he said with reverence, "he is a holy man, and while praying upon the mountain top, he saw the *sahib*, sunk in a deep sleep, fall forward over the rock as if a hand had touched him. He came down and searched for him, *mem-sahib*; but he was gone. The snows are melting, and the water runs swift and deep."

"Ah!" It was a gasp rather than an exclamation. Stella was blindly tottering against the tent-rope, clutching vaguely for support.

The great Sikh caught her ere she fell, his own distress subdued in a flash before the urgency of her need. "Lean on me, *mem-sahib!*" he said, deference and devotion mingling in his voice.

She accepted his help instinctively, scarcely knowing what she did, and very gently, with a woman's tenderness, he led her back into the tent.

"My *mem-sahib* must rest," he said. "And I will find a woman to serve her."

She opened her eyes with a dizzy sense of wonder. Peter had never failed before to procure anything that she wanted, but even in her extremity she had a curiously irrelevant moment of conjecture as to where he would turn in the wilderness for the commodity he so confidently mentioned.

Then, the anguish returning, she checked his motion to depart. "No, no, Peter," she said, commanding her voice with difficulty. "There is no need for that. I am quite all right. But—but—tell me more! How did this happen? Why did he sleep on the mountain?"

"How should the *mem-sahib's* servant know?" questioned Peter, gently and deferentially, as one who reasoned with a child. "It may be that the opium of his cigar was stronger than usual. But how can I tell?"

"Opium! He never smoked opium!" Stella gazed upon him in fresh bewilderment. "Surely—surely not!" she said, as though seeking to convince herself.

"*Mem-sahib*, how should I know?" the Indian murmured soothingly.

She became suddenly aware that further inaction was unendurable. She must see for herself. She must know the whole, dreadful truth. Though trembling from head to foot, she spoke with decision. "Peter, go outside and wait for me! Keep that old beggar too! Don't let him go! As soon as I am dressed, we will go to—the place—and—look for him."

She stumbled over the last words, but she spoke them bravely. Peter straightened himself, recognizing the voice of authority. With a deep salaam, he turned and passed out, drawing the tent-flap decorously into place behind him.

And then with fevered energy, Stella dressed. Her hands moved with lightning speed though her body felt curiously weighted and unnatural. The fantastic thought crossed her brain that it was as though she prepared herself for her own funeral.

No sound reached her from without, save only the monotonous and endless dashing of the torrent among its boulders. She was beginning to feel that the sound in some fashion expressed a curse.

When she was ready at length, she stood for a second or two to gather her strength. She still felt ill and dizzy, as though the world she knew had suddenly fallen away from her and left her struggling in unimaginable space, like a swimmer in deep waters. But she conquered her weakness, and, drawing aside the tent-flap once more, she stepped forth.

The morning sun struck full upon her. It was as if the whole earth rushed to meet her in a riot of rejoicing; but she was in some fashion outside and beyond it all. The glow could not reach her.

With a sharp sense of revulsion, she saw the deformed man squatting close to her, his *chuddah*-draped head lodged upon his knees. He did not stir at her coming though she felt convinced that he was aware of her, aware probably of everything that passed within a considerable radius of his disreputable person. His dark face, lined and dirty, half-covered with ragged black hair that ended in a long thin wisp like a goat's beard on his shrunken chest, was still turned to the east as though challenging the sun that was smiting a swift course through the heavens as if with a flaming sword. The simile rushed through her mind unbidden. Where would she be—what would have happened to her—by the time that sword was sheathed?

She conquered her repulsion and approached the man. As she did so, Peter glided silently up like a faithful watch-dog and took his place at her right hand. It was typical of the position he was to occupy in the days that were coming.

Within a pace or two of the huddled figure, Stella stopped. He had not moved. It was evident that he was so rapt in meditation that her presence at that moment was no more to him than that of an insect crawling across his path. His eyes, red-rimmed, startlingly bright, still challenged the coming day. His whole expression was so grimly aloof, so sternly unsympathetic, that she hesitated to disturb him.

Humbly Peter came to her assistance. "May I be allowed to speak to him, *mem-sahib?*" he asked.

She turned to him thankfully. "Yes, tell him what I want!"

Peter placed himself in front of the stranger. "The noble lady desires your service," he said. "Her gracious excellency is waiting."

A quiver went through the crouching form. He seemed to awake, his mind returning as it were from a far distance. He turned his head, and Stella saw that he was not blind. For his eyes took her in, for the moment appraised her. Then with ungainly, tortoiselike movements, he arose.

"I am her excellency's servant," he said, in hollow, quavering accents. "I live or die at her most gracious command."

It was abjectly spoken, yet she shuddered at the sound of his voice. Her whole being revolted against holding any converse with the man. But she forced herself to persist. Only this monstrous, half-bestial creature could give her any detail of the awful thing that had happened in the night. If Ralph were indeed dead, this man was the last who had seen him in life.

With a strong effort she subdued her repugnance and addressed him. "I want," she said, "to be guided to the place from which you say he fell. I must see for myself."

He bent himself almost to the earth before her. "Let the gracious lady follow her servant!" he said, and forthwith straightened himself and hobbled away.

She followed him in utter silence, Peter walking at her right hand. Up the steep goat-path which Dacre had so arrogantly ascended in the wake of his halting guide they made their slow progress in dumb procession. Stella moved as one rapt in some terrible dream. Again that drugged feeling was upon her, that sense of being bound by a spell, and now she knew that the spell was evil. Once or twice her brain stirred a little when Peter offered his silent help, and she thanked him and accepted it while scarcely realizing what she did. But for the most part she remained in that state of awful quiescence, the inertia of one about whom the toils of a pitiless Fate were closely woven. There was no escape for her. She knew that there could be no escape. She had been caught trespassing in a forbidden paradise, and she was about to be thrust forth without mercy.

High up on a shelf of naked rock their guide stood and waited—a ragged, incongruous figure against the purity of the new day. The early sun had barely topped the highest mountains, but a great gap between two mighty peaks revealed it. As Stella pressed forward, she came suddenly into the splendour of the morning.

It affected her strangely. She felt as Moses must have felt when the Glory of God was revealed to him. The brightness was intolerable. It seemed to pierce her through and through. She was not able to look upon it.

"Excellency," the stranger said, "it was here."

She moved forward and stood beside him. Quiveringly, in a voice she hardly recognized as her own, she spoke. "You were with him. You brought him here."

He made a gesture as of one who repudiates responsibility. "I, excellency, I am the servant of the Holy Ones," he said. "I had a message for him. I knew that the Holy Ones were angry. It was written that the white *sahib* should not tread the sacred ground. I warned him, excellency, and then I left him. And now the Holy Ones have worked their will upon him, and lo, he is gone."

Stella gazed at the man with fascinated eyes. The confidence with which he spoke somehow left no room for question.

"He is mad," she murmured, half to herself and half to Peter. "Of course he is mad."

And then, as if a hand had touched her also, she moved forward to the edge of the precipice and looked down.

The rush of the torrent rose up like the tumult of many voices calling to her, calling to her. The depth beneath her feet widened to an abyss that yawned to engulf her. With a sick sense of horror she realized that ghastly, headlong fall—from warm, throbbing life on the enchanted height to instant and terrible destruction upon the green, slimy boulders over which the water dashed and roared continuously far below. Here he had sat, that arrogant lover of hers, and slipped from somnolent enjoyment into that dreadful gulf. At her feet—proof indisputable of the truth of the story she had been told—lay a charred fragment of the cigar that had doubtless been between his lips when he had sunk into that fatal sleep. The memory of Peter's words flashed through her brain. He had smoked opium. She wondered if Peter really knew. But of what avail now to conjecture? He was gone, and only this mad native vagabond had witnessed his going.

And at that, another thought pierced her keen as a dagger, rending its way through living tissues. The manner of the man's appearing, the horror with which he had inspired her, the mystery of him, all combined to drive it home to her heart. What if a hand had indeed touched him? What if a treacherous blow had hurled him over that terrible edge?

She turned to look again upon the stranger, but he had withdrawn himself. She saw only the Indian servant, standing close beside her, his dark eyes following her every action with wistful vigilance.

Meeting her desperate gaze, he pressed a little nearer, like a faithful dog, protective and devoted. "Come away, my *mem-sahib!*" he entreated very earnestly. "It is the Gate of Death."

That pierced her anew. Her desolation came upon her in an overwhelming wave. She turned with a great cry, and threw her arms wide to the risen sun, tottering blindly towards the emptiness that stretched beneath her feet. And as she went, she heard the roar of the torrent dashing down over its grim boulders to the great river up which they two had glided in their dream of enchantment aeons and aeons before....

She knew nothing of the sinewy arms that held her back from death though she fought them fiercely, desperately. She did not hear the piteous entreaties of poor harassed Peter as he forced her back, back, back, from those awful depths. She only knew a great turmoil that seemed to her unending—a fearful striving against ever-increasing odds—and at the last a swirling, unfathomable darkness descending like a wind-blown blanket upon her—enveloping her, annihilating her....

And British eyes, keen and grey and stern, looked on from afar, watching silently, as the Indian bore his senseless *mem-sahib* away.

PART II
CHAPTER I
THE MINISTERING ANGEL

"And what am I going to do?" demanded Mrs. Ermsted fretfully. She was lounging in the easiest chair in Mrs. Ralston's drawing-room with a cigarette between her fingers. A very decided frown was drawing her delicate brows. "I had no idea you could be so fickle," she said.

"My dear, I shall welcome you here just as heartily as I ever have," Mrs. Ralston assured her, without lifting her eyes from the muslin frock at which she was busily stitching.

Mrs. Ermsted pouted. "That may be. But I shan't come very often when she is here. I don't like widows. They are either so melancholy that they give you the hump or so self-important that you want to slap them. I never did fancy this girl, as you know. Much too haughty and superior."

"You never knew her, dear," said Mrs. Ralston.

Mrs. Ermsted's laugh had a touch of venom. "As I have tried more than once to make you realize," she said, "there are at least two points of view to everybody. You, dear Mrs. Ralston, always wear rose-coloured spectacles, with the unfortunate result that your opinion is so unvaryingly favourable that nobody values it."

Mrs. Ralston's faded face flushed faintly. She worked on in silence.

For a space Netta Ermsted smoked her cigarette with her eyes fixed upon space; then very suddenly she spoke again. "I wonder if Ralph Dacre committed suicide."

Mrs. Ralston started at the abrupt surmise. She looked up for the first time. "Really, my dear! What an extraordinary thing to say!"

Little Mrs. Ermsted jerked up her chin aggressively. "Why extraordinary, I wonder? Nothing could be more extraordinary than his death. Either he jumped over the precipice or she pushed him over when he wasn't looking. I wonder which."

But at that Mrs. Ralston gravely arose and rebuked her. She never suffered any nervous qualms when dealing with this volatile friend of hers. "It is more than foolish," she said with decision; "it is wicked, to talk like that. I will not sit and listen to you. You have a very mischievous brain, Netta. You ought to keep it under better control."

Mrs. Ermsted stretched out her dainty feet in front of her and made a grimace. "When you call me Netta, I always know it is getting serious," she remarked. "I withdraw it all, my dear angel, with the utmost liberality. You shall see how generous I can be to my supplanter. But do like a good soul finish those tiresome tucks before you begin to be really cross with me! Poor little Tessa really needs that frock, and *ayah* is such a shocking worker. I shan't be able to turn to you for anything when the estimable Mrs. Dacre is here. In fact I shall be driven to Mrs. Burton for companionship and counsel, and shall become more catty than ever."

"My dear, please"—Mrs. Ralston spoke very earnestly—"do not imagine for an instant that having that poor girl to care for will make the smallest difference to my friendship for you! I hope to see as much of you and little Tessa as I have ever seen. I feel that Stella would be fond of children. Your little one would be a comfort to any sore heart."

"She can be a positive little devil," observed Tessa's mother dispassionately. "But it's better than being a saint, isn't it? Look at that hateful child, Cedric Burton—detestable little ape! That Burton complacency gets on my nerves, especially in a child. But then look at the Burtons! How could they help having horrible little self-opinionated apes for children?"

"My dear, your tongue—your tongue!" protested Mrs. Ralston.

Mrs. Ermsted shot it out and in again with an impudent smile. "Well, what's the matter with it? It's quite a candid one—like your own. A little more pointed perhaps and something venomous upon occasion. But it has its good qualities also. At least it is never insincere."

"Of that I am sure." Mrs. Ralston spoke with ready kindliness. "But, oh, my dear, if it were only a little more charitable!"

Netta Ermsted smiled at her like a wayward child. "I like saying nasty things about people," she said. "It amuses me. Besides, they're nearly always true. Do tell me what you think of that latest hat erection of Lady Harriet's! I never saw her look more aristocratically hideous in my life than she looked at the Rajah's garden-party yesterday. I felt quite sorry for the Rajah, for he's a nice boy notwithstanding his forty wives, and he likes pretty things." She gave a little laugh, and stretched her white arms up, clasping her hands behind her head. "I have promised to ride with him in the early mornings now and then. Won't darling Dick be jealous when he knows?"

Mrs. Ralston uttered a sigh. There were times when all her attempts to reform this giddy little butterfly seemed unavailing. Nevertheless, being sound of principle and unfailingly conscientious, she made a gallant effort. "Do you think you ought to do that, dear? I always think that we ought to live more circumspectly here at Bhulwana than down at Kurrumpore. And—if I may be allowed to say so—your husband is such a good, kind man, so indulgent, it seems unfair to take advantage of it."

"Oh, is he?" laughed Netta. "How ill you know my doughty Richard! Why, it's half the fun in life to make him mad. He nearly turned me over his knee and spanked me the last time."

"My dear, I wish he had!" said Mrs. Ralston, with downright fervour. "It would do you good."

"Think so?" Netta flicked the ash from her cigarette with a disdainful gesture. "It all depends. I should either worship him or loath him afterwards. I wonder which. Poor old Richard! It's silly of him to stay in love with the same person always, isn't it? I couldn't be so monotonous if I tried."

"In fact if he cared less about you, you would think more of him," remarked Mrs. Ralston, with a quite unusual touch of severity.

Netta Ermsted laughed again, her light, heartless laugh. "How crushingly absolute! But it is the literal truth. I certainly should. He's cheap now, poor old boy. That's why I lead him such a dog's life. A man should never be cheap to his wife. Now look at your husband! Indifference personified! And you have never given him an hour's anxiety in his life."

Mrs. Ralston's pale blue eyes suddenly shone. She looked almost young again. "We understand each other," she said simply.

A mocking smile played about Mrs. Ermsted's lips, but she said nothing for the moment. In her own fashion she was fond of the surgeon's wife, and she would not openly deride her, dear good soul.

"When you've quite finished that," she remarked presently, "there's a tussore frock of my own I want to consult you about. There's one thing about Stella; she won't be wanting many clothes, so I shall be able to retain your undivided attention in that respect. I really don't know what Tessa and I would do without you. The tiresome little thing is always tearing her clothes to pieces."

Mrs. Ralston smiled, a soft mother-smile. "You're a lucky, lucky girl," she said, "though you don't realize it, and probably never will. When are you going to bring the little monkey to see me again?"

"She will probably come herself when the mood takes her," carelessly Mrs. Ermsted made reply. "I assure you, you stand very high on her visiting list. But I hardly ever take her anywhere. She is always so naughty with me." She chose another cigarette with the words. "She is sure to be a pretty frequent visitor while Tommy Denvers is here. She worships him."

"He is a nice boy," observed Mrs. Ralston. "I wish he could have got longer leave. It would have comforted Stella to have him."

"I suppose she can go down to him at Kurrumpore if she doesn't mind sacrificing that rose-leaf complexion," rejoined Mrs. Ermsted, shutting her matchbox with a spiteful click. "You stayed down last hot weather."

"Gerald was not well and couldn't leave his post," said Mrs. Ralston. "That was different. I felt he needed me."

"And so you nearly killed yourself to satisfy the need," commented Mrs. Ermsted. "I sometimes think you are rather a fine woman, notwithstanding appearances." She glanced at the watch on her wrist. "By Jove, how late it is! Your latest *protégée* will be here immediately. You must have been aching to tell me to go for the last half-hour. You silly saint! Why didn't you?"

"I have no wish for you to go, dear," responded Mrs. Ralston tranquilly. "All my visitors are an honour to my house."

Mrs. Ermsted sprang to her feet with a swift, elastic movement. "Mary, I love you!" she said. "You are a ministering angel, faithful friend, and priceless counsellor, all combined. I laugh at you for a frump behind your back, but when I am with you, I am spellbound with admiration. You are really superb."

"Thank you, dear," said Mrs. Ralston.

She returned the impulsive kiss bestowed upon her with a funny look in her blue eyes that might almost have been compassionate if it had not been so unmistakably humorous.

She did not attempt to make the embrace a lingering one, however, and Netta Ermsted took her impetuous departure with a piqued sense of uncertainty.

"I wonder if she really has got any brains after all," she said aloud, as she sped away in her "rickshaw." "She is a quaint creature anyhow. I rather wonder that I bother myself with her."

At which juncture she met the Rajah, resplendent in green *puggarree* and riding his favourite bay Arab, and forthwith dismissed Mrs. Ralston and all discreet counsels to the limbo of forgotten things. She had dubbed the Rajah her Arabian Knight. His name for her was of too intimate an order to be pronounced in public. She was the Lemon-scented Lily of his dreams.

CHAPTER II
THE RETURN

Stella's first impression of Bhulwana was the extremely European atmosphere that pervaded it. Bungalows and pine-woods seemed to be its main characteristics, and there was about it none of the languorous Eastern charm that had so haunted the forbidden paradise. Bhulwana was a cheerful place, and though perched fairly high among the hills of Markestan it was possible to get very hot there. For this reason perhaps all the energies of its visitors were directed towards the organizing of gaieties, and in the height of the summer it was very gay indeed.

The Rajah's summer palace, white and magnificent, occupied the brow of the hill, and the bungalows that clustered among the pines below it looked as if there had been some competition among them as to which could get the nearest.

The Ralstons' bungalow was considerably lower down the hill. It stood upon more open ground than most, and overlooked the race-course some distance below. It was an ugly little place, and the small compound surrounding it was a veritable wilderness. It had been named "The Grand Stand" owing to its position, but no one less racy than its present occupant could well have been found. Mrs. Ralston's wistful blue eyes seldom rested upon the race-course. They looked beyond to the mist-veiled plains.

The room she had prepared for Stella's reception looked in an easterly direction towards the winding, wooded road that led up to the Rajah's residence. Great care had been expended upon it. Her heart had yearned to the girl ever since she had heard of her sudden bereavement, and her delight at the thought of receiving her was only second to her sorrow upon Stella's account.

Higher up the hill stood the dainty bungalow which Ralph Dacre had taken for his bride. The thought of it tore Mrs. Ralston's tender heart. She had written an urgent epistle to Tommy imploring him not to let his sister go there in her desolation. And, swayed by Tommy's influence, and, it might be, touched by Mrs. Ralston's own earnest solicitude, Stella, not caring greatly whither she went, had agreed to take up her abode for a time at least with the surgeon's wife. There was no necessity to make any sudden decision. The whole of her life lay before her, a dreary waste of desert. It did not seem to matter at that stage where she spent those first forlorn months. She was tired to the soul of her, and only wanted to rest.

She hoped vaguely that Mrs. Ralston would have the tact to respect this wish of hers. Her impression of this the only woman who had shown her any kindness since her arrival in India was not of a very definite order. Mrs. Ralston with her faded prettiness and gentle, retiring ways did not possess a very arresting personality. No one seeing her two or three times could have given any very accurate description of her. Lady Harriet had more than once described her as a negligible quantity. But Lady Harriet systematically neglected everyone who had no pretensions to smartness. She detested all dowdy women.

But Stella still remembered with gratitude the warmth of affectionate admiration and sympathy that had melted her coldness on her wedding-day, and something within her, notwithstanding her utter weariness, longed to feel that warmth again. Though she scarcely realized it, she wanted the clasp of motherly arms, shielding her from the tempest of life.

Tommy, who had met her at Rawal Pindi on the dreadful return journey, had watched over her and cared for her comfort with the utmost tenderness; but Tommy, like Peter, was somehow outside her confidence. He was just a blundering male with the best intentions. She could not have opened her heart to him had she tried. She was unspeakably glad to have him with her, and later on she hoped to join him again at The Green Bungalow down at Kurrumpore where they had dwelt together during the weeks preceding her marriage. For Tommy was the only relative she had in the world who cared for her. And she was very fond of Tommy, but she was not really intimate with him. They were just good comrades.

As a married woman, she no longer feared the veiled shafts of malice that had pierced her before. Her position was assured. Not that she would have cared greatly in any case. Such trivial things belonged to the past, and she marvelled now at the thought that they had ever seriously affected her. She was changed, greatly changed. In one short month she had left her girlhood behind her. Her proud shyness had utterly departed. She had returned a grave, reserved woman, indifferent, almost apathetic, wholly self-contained. Her natural stateliness still clung about her, but she did not cloak herself therewith. She walked rather as one rapt in reverie, looking neither to the right nor to the left.

Mrs. Ralston nearly wept when she saw her, so shocked was she by the havoc that strange month had wrought. All the soft glow of youth had utterly passed away. White and cold as alabaster, a woman empty and alone, she returned from the forbidden paradise, and it seemed to Mrs. Ralston at first that the very heart of her had been shattered like a beautiful flower by the closing of the gates.

But later, when Stella had been with her for a few hours, she realized that life still throbbed deep down below the surface, though, perhaps in self-defence, it was buried deep, very far from the reach of all casual investigation. She could not speak of her tragedy, but she responded to the mute sympathy Mrs. Ralston poured out to her with a gratitude that was wholly unfeigned, and the latter understood clearly that she would not refuse her admittance though she barred out all the world beside.

She was deeply touched by the discovery, reflecting in her humility that Stella's need must indeed have been great to have drawn her to herself for comfort. It was true that nearly all her friends had been made in trouble which she had sought to alleviate, but Mary Ralston was too lowly to ascribe to herself any virtue on that account. She only thanked God for her opportunities.

On the night of their arrival, when Stella had gone to her room, Tommy spoke very seriously of his sister's state and begged Mrs. Ralston to do her utmost to combat the apathy which he had found himself wholly unable to pierce.

"I haven't seen her shed a single tear," he said. "People who didn't know would think her heartless. I can't bear to see that deadly coldness. It isn't Stella."

"We must be patient," Mrs. Ralston said.

There were tears in the boy's own eyes for which she liked him, but she did not encourage him to further confidence. It was not her way to discuss any friend with a third person, however intimate.

Tommy left the subject without realizing that she had turned him from it.

"I don't know in the least how she is left," he said restlessly. "Haven't an idea what sort of state Dacre's affairs were in. I ought to have asked him, but I never had the chance; and everything was done in such a mighty hurry. I don't suppose he had much to leave if anything. It was a fool marriage," he ended bitterly. "I always hated it. Monck knew that."

"Doesn't Captain Monck know anything?" asked Mrs. Ralston.

"Oh, goodness knows. Monck's away on urgent business, been away for ever so long now. I haven't seen him since Dacre's death. I daresay he doesn't even know of that yet. He had to go Home. I suppose he is on his way back again now; I hope so anyway. It's pretty beastly without him."

"Poor Tommy!" Mrs. Ralston's sympathy was uppermost again. "It's been a tragic business altogether. But let us be thankful we have dear Stella safely back! I am going to say good night to her now. Help yourself to anything you want!"

She went, and Tommy stretched himself out on a long chair with a sigh of discontent over things in general. He had had no word from Monck throughout his absence, and this was almost the greatest grievance of all.

Treading softly the passage that led to Stella's door, Mrs. Ralston nearly stumbled over a crouching, white-clad figure that rose up swiftly and noiselessly on the instant and resolved itself into the salaaming person of Peter the Sikh. He had slept across Stella's threshold ever since her bereavement.

"My *mem-sahib* is still awake," he told her with a touch of wistfulness. "She sleeps only when the night is nearly spent."

"And you sleep at her door?" queried Mrs. Ralston, slightly disconcerted.

The tall form bent again with dignified courtesy. "That is my privilege, *mem-sahib*," said Peter the Great.

He smiled mournfully, and made way for her to pass.

Mrs. Ralston knocked, and heard a low voice speak in answer. "What is it, Peter?"

Softly she opened the door. "It is I, my dear. Are you in bed? May I come and bid you good night?"

"Of course," Stella made instant reply. "How good you are! How kind!"

A shaded night-lamp was burning by her side. Her face upon the pillow was in deep shadow. Her hair spread all around her, wrapping her as it were in mystery.

As Mrs. Ralston drew near, she stretched out a welcoming hand. "I hope my watch-dog didn't startle you," she said. "The dear fellow is so upset that I don't want an *ayah*, he is doing his best to turn himself into one. I couldn't bear to send him away. You don't mind?"

"My dear, I mind nothing." Mrs. Ralston stooped in her warm way and kissed the pale, still face. "Are you comfortable? Have you everything you want?"

"Everything, thank you," Stella answered, drawing her hostess gently down to sit on the side of the bed. "I feel rested already. Somehow your presence is restful."

"Oh, my dear!" Mrs. Ralston flushed with pleasure. Not many were the compliments that came her way. "And you feel as if you will be able to sleep?"

Stella's eyes looked unutterably weary; yet she shook her head. "No. I never sleep much before morning. I think I slept too much when I was in Kashmir. The days and nights all seemed part of one long dream." A slight shudder assailed her; she repressed it with a shadowy smile. "Life here will be very different," she said. "Perhaps I shall be able to wake up now. I am not in the least a dreamy person as a rule."

The quick tears sprang to Mrs. Ralston's eyes; she stroked Stella's hand without speaking.

"I wanted to go back to Kurrumpore with Tommy," Stella went on, "but he won't hear of it, though he tells me that you stayed there through last summer. If you could stand it, so could I. I feel sure that physically I am much stronger."

"Oh no, dear, no. You couldn't do it." Mrs. Ralston looked down upon the beautiful face very tenderly. "I am tough, you know, dried up and wiry. And I had a very strong motive. But you are different. You would never stand a hot season at Kurrumpore. I can't tell you what it is like there. At its worst it is unspeakable. I am very glad that Tommy realizes the impossibility of it. No, no! Stay here with me till I go down! I am always the first. And it will give me so much pleasure to take care of you."

Stella relinquished the discussion with a short sigh. "It doesn't seem to matter much what I do," she said. "Tommy certainly doesn't need me. No one does. And I expect you will soon get very tired of me."

"Never, dear, never." Mrs. Ralston's hand clasped hers reassuringly. "Never think that for a moment! From the very first day I saw you I have wanted to have you to love and care for."

A gleam of surprise crossed Stella's face. "How very kind of you!" she said.

"Oh no, dear. It was your own doing. You are so beautiful," murmured the surgeon's wife. "And I knew that you were the same all through—beautiful to the very soul."

"Oh, don't say that!" Sharply Stella broke in upon her. "Don't think it! You don't know me in the least. You—you have far more beauty of soul than I have, or can ever hope to have now."

Mrs. Ralston shook her head.

"But it is so," Stella insisted. "I—What am I?" A tremor of passion crept unawares into her low voice. "I am a woman who has been denied everything. I have been cast out like Eve, but without Eve's compensations. If I had been given a child to love, I might have had hope. But now I have none—I have none. I am hard and bitter,—old before my time, and I shall never now be anything else."

"Oh, darling, no!" Very swiftly Mrs. Ralston checked her. "Indeed you are wrong. We can make of our lives what we will. Believe me, the barren woman can be a joyful mother of children if she will. There is always someone to love."

Stella's lips were quivering. She turned her face aside. "Life is very difficult," she said.

"It gets simpler as one goes on, dear," Mrs. Ralston assured her gently. "Not easy, oh no, not easy. We were never meant to make an easy-chair of circumstance however favourable. But if we only press on, it does get simpler, and the way opens out before us as we go. I have learnt that at least from life." She paused a moment, then bent suddenly down and spoke into Stella's ear. "May I tell you something about myself—something I have never before breathed to any one—except to God?"

Stella turned instantly. "Yes, tell me!" she murmured back, clasping closely the thin hand that had so tenderly stroked her own.

Mrs. Ralston hesitated a second as one who pauses before making a supreme effort. Then under her breath she spoke again. "Perhaps it will not interest you much. I don't know. It is only this. Like you, I wanted—I hoped for—a child. And—I married without loving—just for that. Stella, my sin was punished. The baby came—and went—and there can never be another. I thought my heart was broken at the time. Oh, it was bitter—bitter. Even now—sometimes—" She stopped herself. "But no, I needn't trouble you with that. I only want to tell you that very beautiful flowers bloom sometimes out of ashes. And it has been so with me. My rose of love was slow in growing, but it blossoms now, and I am training it over all the blank spaces. And it grew out of a barren soil, dear, out of a barren soil."

Stella's arms were close about her as she finished. "Oh, thank you," she whispered tremulously, "thank you for telling me that."

But though she was deeply stirred, no further confidence could she bring herself to utter. She had found a friend—a close, staunch friend who would never fail her; but not even to her could she show the blackness of the gulf into which she had been hurled. Even now there were times when she seemed to be still falling, falling, and always, waking or sleeping, the nightmare horror of it clung cold about her soul.

CHAPTER III
THE BARREN SOIL

No one could look askance at poor Ralph Dacre's young widow. Lady Harriet Mansfield graciously hinted as much when she paid her state call within a week of her arrival. Also, she desired to ascertain Stella's plans for the future, and when she heard that she intended to return to Kurrumpore with Mrs. Ralston she received the news with a species of condescending approval that seemed to indicate that Stella's days of probation were past. With the exercise of great care and circumspection she might even ultimately be admitted to the fortunate circle which sunned itself in the light of Lady Harriet's patronage.

Tommy elevated his nose irreverently when the august presence was withdrawn and hoped that Stella would not have her head turned by the royal favour. He prophesied that Mrs. Burton would be the next to come simpering round, and in this he was not mistaken; but Stella did not receive this visitor, for on the following day she was in bed with an attack of fever that prostrated her during the rest of his leave.

It was not a dangerous illness, and Mrs. Ralston nursed her through it with a devotion that went far towards cementing the friendship already begun between them. Tommy, though regretful, consoled himself by the ready means of the station's gaieties, played tennis with zest, inaugurated a gymkhana, and danced practically every night into the early morning. He was a delightful companion for little Tessa Ermsted who followed him everywhere and was never snubbed, an inquiring mind notwithstanding. Truly a nice boy was Tommy, as everyone agreed, and the regret was general when his leave began to draw to a close.

On the afternoon of his last day he made his appearance on the verandah of The Grand Stand for tea, with his faithful attendant at his heels, to find his sister reclining there for the first time on a *charpoy* well lined with cushions, while Mrs. Ralston presided at the tea-table beside her.

She looked the ghost of her former self, and for a moment though he had visited her in bed only that morning, Tommy was rudely startled.

"Great Jupiter!" he ejaculated. "How ill you look!"

She smiled at his exclamation, while his small, sharp-faced companion pricked up attentive ears. "Do people look like that when they're going to die?" she asked.

"Not in the least, dear," said Mrs. Ralston tranquilly. "Come and speak to Mrs. Dacre and tell us what you have been doing!"

But Tessa would only stand on one leg and stare, till Stella put forth a friendly hand and beckoned her to a corner of her *charpoy*.

She went then, still staring with wide round eyes of intensest blue that gazed out of a somewhat pinched little face of monkey-like intelligence.

"What have you and Tommy been doing?" Stella asked.

"Oh, just hobnobbing," said Tessa. "Same as Mother and the Rajah."

"Have some cake!" said Tommy. "And tell us all about the mongoose!"

"Oh, Scooter! He's such a darling! Shall I bring him to see you?" asked Tessa, lifting those wonderful unchildlike eyes of hers to Stella's. "You'd love him! I know you would. He talks—almost. Captain Monck gave him to me. I never liked him before, but I do now. I wish he'd come back, and so does Tommy. Don't you think he's a nice man?"

"I don't know him very well," said Stella.

"Oh, don't you? That's because he's so quiet. I used to think he was surly. But he isn't really. He's only shy. Is he, Aunt Mary?" The blue eyes whisked round to Mrs. Ralston and were met by a slightly reproving shake of the head. "No, but really," Tessa protested, "he is a nice man. Tommy says so. Mother doesn't like him, but that's nothing to go by. The people she likes are hardly ever nice. Daddy says so."

"Tessa," said Mrs. Ralston gently, "we don't want to hear about that. Tell us some more about Captain Monck's mongoose instead!"

Tessa frowned momentarily. Such nursery discipline was something of an insult to her eight years' dignity, but in a second she sent a dazzling smile to her hostess, accepting the rebuff. "All right, Aunt Mary, I'll bring him to see you to-morrow, shall I?" she said brightly. "Mrs. Dacre will like that too. It'll be something to amuse us when Tommy's gone."

Tommy looked across with a grin. "Yes, keep your spirits up!" he said. "It's dull work with the boys away, isn't it, Aunt Mary? And Scooter is a most sagacious animal—almost as intelligent as Peter the Great who coils himself on Stella's threshold every night as if he thought the bogeyman was coming to spirit her away. He's developing into a habit, isn't he Stella? You'd better be careful."

Stella smiled her faint, tired smile. "I like to have him there," she said. "I am not nervous, of course, but he is a friend."

"You'll never shake him off," predicted Tommy. "He comes of a romantic stock. Hullo! Here is his high mightiness with the mail! Look at the sparkle in Aunt Mary's eyes! Did you ever see the like? She expects to draw a prize evidently."

He stretched a leisurely arm and took the letter from the salver that the Indian extended. It was for Mrs. Ralston, and she received it blushing like an eager girl.

"Why does Aunt Mary look like that?" piped Tessa, ever observant. "It's only from the Major. Mother never looks like that when Daddy writes to her."

"Perhaps Daddy's letters are not so interesting," suggested Tommy.

Tessa chuckled. "Shall I tell you what? She'd ever so much rather have a letter from the Rajah. I know she would. She keeps his locked up, but she never bothers about Daddy's. I can't think what the Rajah finds to write about when they are always meeting. I think it's silly, don't you?"

"Very silly," said Tommy. "I hate writing letters myself. Beastly dull work."

"Perhaps you will excuse me while I read mine," said Mrs. Ralston.

Stella smiled at her. "Oh do! Perhaps there will be some interesting news of Kurrumpore in it."

"News of Monck perhaps," suggested Tommy. "There's a fellow who never writes a letter. I haven't the faintest idea where he is or what he is doing, except that he went to his brother somewhere in England. He is due back in about a fortnight, but I probably shan't hear a word of him until he's there."

"You have not written to him either?" questioned Stella.

"I couldn't. I didn't know where to write." Tommy's eyes met hers with slight hesitation. "I haven't been able to tell him anything of our affairs. It's quite possible though that he will have heard before he gets back to The Green Bungalow. He generally gets hold of things."

"It need not make any difference." Stella spoke slowly, her eyes fixed upon the green race-course that gleamed in the sun below them. "So far as I am concerned, he is quite welcome to remain at The Green Bungalow. I daresay we should not get in each other's way. That is," she looked at her brother, "if you prefer that arrangement."

"I say, that's jolly decent of you!" Tommy's face was flushed with pleasure. "Sure you mean it?"

"Quite sure." Stella spoke rather wearily. "It really doesn't matter to me—except that I don't want to come between you and your friend. Now that I have been married—" a tinge of bitterness sounded in her voice—"I suppose no one will take exception. But of course Captain Monck may see the matter in a different light. If so, pray let him do as he thinks fit!"

"You bet he will!" said Tommy. "He's about the most determined cuss that ever lived."

"He's a very nice man," put in Tessa jealously.

Tommy laughed. "He's one of the best," he agreed heartily. "And he's the sort that always comes out on top sooner or later. Just you remember that, Tessa! He's a winner, and he's straight—straight as a die." "Which is all that matters," said Mrs. Ralston, without lifting her eyes from her letter.

"Hear, hear!" said Tommy. "Why do you look like that, Stella? Mean to say he isn't straight?"

"I didn't say anything." Stella still spoke wearily, albeit she was faintly smiling. "I was only wondering."

"Wondering what?" Tommy's voice had a hint of sharpness; he looked momentarily aggressive.

"Just wondering how much you knew of him, that's all," she made answer.

"I know as much as any one," asserted Tommy quickly. "He's a man to be honoured. I'd stake my life on that. He is incapable of anything mean or underhand."

Stella was silent. The boy's faith was genuine, she knew, but, remembering what Ralph Dacre had told her on their last night together, she could not stifle the wonder as to whether Tommy had ever grasped the actual quality of his friend's character. It seemed to her that Tommy's worship was of too humble a species to afford him a very comprehensive view of the object thereof. She was sure that unlike herself—he would never presume to criticize, would never so much as question any action of Monck's. Her own conception of the man, she was aware, had altered somewhat since that night. She regarded him now with a wholly dispassionate interest. She had attracted him, but she much doubted if the attraction had survived her marriage. For herself, that chapter in her life was closed and could never, she now believed, be reopened. Monck had gone his way, she hers, and they had drifted apart. Only by the accident of circumstance would they meet again, and she was determined that when this meeting took place their relations should be of so impersonal a character that he should find it well-nigh impossible to recall the fact that any hint of romance had ever hovered even for a fleeting moment between them. He had his career before him. He followed the way of ambition, and he should continue to follow it, unhindered by any thought of her. She was dependent upon no man. She would pick up the threads of her own life and weave of it something that should be worth while. With the return of health this resolution was forming within her. Mrs. Ralston's influence was making itself felt. She believed that the way would open out before her as she went. She had made one great mistake. She would never make such another. She would be patient. It might be in time that to her, even as to her friend, a blossoming might come out of the barren soil in which her life was cast.

CHAPTER IV
THE SUMMONS

During those months spent at Bhulwana with the surgeon's wife a measure of peace did gradually return to Stella. She took no part in the gaieties of the station, but her widow's mourning made it easy for her to hold aloof. Undoubtedly she earned Lady Harriet's approval by so doing, but Mrs. Ermsted continued to look at her askance, notwithstanding the fact that her small daughter had developed a warm liking for the sister of her beloved Tommy.

"Wait till she gets back to Kurrumpore," said Mrs. Ermsted. "We shall see her in her true colours then."

She did not say this to Mrs. Ralston. She visited The Grand Stand less and less frequently. She was always full of engagements and seldom had a moment to spare for the society of this steady friend of hers. And Mrs. Ralston never sought her out. It was not her way. She was ready for all, but she intruded upon none.

Mrs. Ralston's affection for Stella had become very deep. There was between them a sympathy that was beyond words. They understood each other.

As the wet season drew on, their companionship became more and more intimate though their spoken confidences were few. Mrs. Ralston never asked for confidences though she probably received more than any other woman in the station.

It was on a day in September of drifting clouds and unbroken rain that Stella spoke at length of a resolution that had been gradually forming in her mind. She found no difficulty in speaking; in fact it seemed the natural thing to do. And she felt even as she gave utterance to the words that Mrs. Ralston already knew their import.

"Mary," she said, "after Christmas I am going back to England."

Mrs. Ralston betrayed no surprise. She was in the midst of an elaborate darn in the heel of a silk sock. She looked across at Stella gravely.

"And when you get there, my dear?" she said.

"I shall find some work to do." Stella spoke with the decision of one who gives utterance to the result of careful thought. "I think I shall go in for hospital training. It is hard work, I know; but I am strong. I think hard work is what I need."

Mrs. Ralston was silent.

Stella went on. "I see now that I made a mistake in ever coming out here. It wasn't as if Tommy really wanted me. He doesn't, you know. His friend Captain Monck is all-sufficing—and probably better for him. In any case—he doesn't need me."

"You may be right, dear," Mrs. Ralston said, "though I doubt if Tommy would view it in the same light. I am glad anyhow that you will spend Christmas out here. I shall not lose you so soon."

Stella smiled a little. "I don't want to hurt Tommy's feelings, and I know they would be hurt if I went sooner. Besides I would like to have one cold weather out here."

"And why not?" said Mrs. Ralston. She added after a moment, "What will you do with Peter?"

Stella hesitated. "That is one reason why I have not come to a decision sooner. I don't like leaving poor Peter. It occurred to me possibly that down at Kurrumpore he might find another master. Anyway, I shall tell him my plans when I get there, and he will have the opportunity"—she smiled rather sadly—"to transfer his devotion to someone else."

"He won't take it," said Mrs. Ralston with conviction. "The fidelity of these men is amazing. It puts us to shame."

"I hate the thought of parting with him," Stella said. "But what can I do?"

She broke off short as the subject of their discussion came softly into the room, salver in hand. He gave her a telegram and stood back decorously behind her chair while she opened it.

Mrs. Ralston's grave eyes watched her, and in a moment Stella looked up and met them. "From Kurrumpore," she said.

Her face was pale, but her hands and voice were steady.

"From Tommy?" questioned Mrs. Ralston.

"No. From Captain Monck. Tommy is ill—very ill. Malaria again. He thinks I had better go to him."

"Oh, my dear!" Mrs. Ralston's exclamation held dismay.

Stella met it by holding out to her the message. "Tommy down with malaria," it said. "Condition serious. Come if you are able. Monck."

Mrs. Ralston rose. She seemed to be more agitated than Stella. "I shall go too," she said.

"No, dear, no!" Stella stopped her. "There is no need for that. I shall be all right. I am perfectly strong now, stronger than you are. And they say malaria never attacks newcomers so badly. No. I will go alone. I won't be answerable to your husband for you. Really, dear, really, I am in earnest."

Her insistence prevailed, albeit Mrs. Ralston yielded very unwillingly. She was not very strong, and she knew well that her husband would be greatly averse to her taking such a step. But the thought of Stella going alone was even harder to face till her look suddenly fell upon Peter the Great standing motionless behind her chair.

"Ah well, you will have Peter," she said with relief.

And Stella, who was bending already over her reply telegram, replied instantly with one of her rare smiles. "Of course I shall have Peter!"

Peter's responding smile was good to see. "I will take care of my *mem-sahib*," he said.

Stella's reply was absolutely simple. "Starting at once," she wrote; and within half an hour her preparations were complete.

She knew Monck well enough to be certain that he would not have telegraphed that urgent message had not the need been great. He had nursed Tommy once before, and she knew that in Tommy's estimation at least he had been the means of saving his life. He was a man of steady nerve and level judgment. He would not have sent for her if his faith in his own powers had not begun to weaken. It meant that Tommy was very ill, that he might be dying. All that was great in Stella rose up impulsively at the call. Tommy had never really wanted her before.

To Mrs. Ralston who at the last stood over her with a glass of wine she was as a different woman. There was nothing headlong about her, but the quiet energy of her made her realize that she had been fashioned for better things than the social gaieties with which so many were content. Stella would go to the deep heart of life.

She yearned to accompany her upon her journey to the plains, but Stella's solemn promise to send for her if she were taken ill herself consoled her in a measure. Very regretfully did she take leave of her, and when the rattle of the wheels that bore Stella and the faithful Peter away had died at last in the distance she turned back into her empty bungalow with tears in her eyes. Stella had become dear to her as a sister.

It was an all-night journey, and only a part of it could be accomplished by train, the line ending at Khanmulla which was reached in the early hours of the morning. But for Peter's ministrations Stella would probably have fared ill, but he was an experienced traveller and surrounded her with every comfort that he could devise. The night was close and dank. They travelled through pitch darkness. Stella lay back and tried to sleep; but sleep would not come to her. She was tired, but repose eluded her. The beating of the unceasing rain upon the tin roof, and the perpetual rattle of the train made an endless tattoo in her brain from which there was no escape. She was haunted by the memory of the last journey that she had made along that line when leaving Kurrumpore in the spring, of Ralph and the ever-growing passion in his eyes, of the first wild revolt within her which she had so barely quelled. How far away seemed those days of an almost unbelievable torture! She could regard them now dispassionately, albeit with wonder. She marvelled now that she had ever given herself to such a man. By the light of experience she realized how tragic had been her blunder, and now that the awful sense of shock and desolation had passed she could be thankful that no heavier penalty had been exacted. The man had been taken swiftly, mercifully, as she believed. He had been spared much, and she—she had been delivered from a fate far worse. For she could never have come to love him. She was certain of that. Lifelong misery would have been her portion, school herself to submission though she might. She believed that the awakening from that dream of lethargy could not have been long deferred for either of them, and with it would have come a bitterness immeasurable. She did not think he had ever honestly believed that she loved him. But at least he had never guessed at the actual repulsion with which at times she had been filled. She was thankful to think that he could never know that now, thankful that now she had come into her womanhood it was all her own. She valued her freedom almost extravagantly since it had been given back to her. And she also valued the fact that in no worldly sense was she the richer for having been Ralph Dacre's wife. He had had no private means, and she was thankful that this was so. She could not have endured to reap any benefit from what she now regarded as a sin. She had borne her punishment, she had garnered her experience. And now she walked once more with unshackled feet; and though all her life she would carry the marks of the chain that had galled her she had travelled far enough to realize and be thankful for her liberty.

The train rattled on through the night. Anxiety came, wraith-like at first, drifting into her busy brain. She had hardly had time to be anxious in the rush of preparation and departure. But restlessness paved the way. She began to ask herself with growing uneasiness what could be awaiting her at the end of the journey. The summons had been so clear and imperative. Her first thought, her instinct, had been to obey. Till the enforced inaction of this train journey she had not had time to feel the gnawing torture of suspense. But now it came and racked her. The thought of Tommy and his need became paramount. Did he know that she was hastening to him, she wondered? Or had he—had he already passed beyond her reach? Men passed so quickly in this tropical wilderness. The solemn music of an anthem she had known and loved in the old far-off days of her girlhood rose and surged through her. She found herself repeating the words:

"Our life is but a shadow;So soon passeth it away,And we are gone,—So soon,—so soon."

The repetition of those last words rang like a knell. But Tommy! She could not think of Tommy's eager young life passing so. Those words were written for the old and weary. But for such as Tommy—a thousand times No! He was surely too ardent, too full of life, to pass so. She felt as if he were years younger than herself.

And then another thought came to her, a curious haunting thought. Was the Nemesis that had overtaken her in the forbidden paradise yet pursuing her with relentless persistence? Was the measure of her punishment not yet complete? Did some further vengeance still follow her in the wilderness of her desolation? She tried to fling the thought from her, but it clung like an evil dream. She could not wholly shake off the impression that it had made upon her.

Slowly the night wore away. The heat was intense. She felt as if she were sitting in a tank of steaming vapour. The oppression of the atmosphere was like a physical weight. And ever the rain beat down, rattling, incessant, upon the tin roof above her head. She thought of Nemesis again, Nemesis wielding an iron flail that never missed its mark. There was something terrible to her in this perpetual beating of rain. She had never imagined anything like it.

It was in the dark of the early morning that she began at last to near her destination. A ten-mile drive through the jungle awaited her, she knew. She wondered if Monck had made provision for this or if all arrangements would be left in Peter's capable hands. She had never felt more thankful for this trusty servant of hers than now with the loneliness and darkness of this unfamiliar world hedging her round. She felt almost as one in a hostile country, and even the thought of Tommy and his need could not dispel the impression.

The train rattled into the little iron-built station of Khanmulla. The rainfall seemed to increase as they stopped. It was like the beating of rods upon the station-roof. There came the usual hubbub of discordant cries, but in foreign voices and in a foreign tongue.

Stella gathered her property together in readiness for Peter. Then she turned, somewhat stiff after her long journey, and found the door already swinging open and a man's broad shoulders blocking the opening.

"How do you do?" said Monck.

She started at the sound of his voice. His face was in the shadow, but in a moment his features, dark and dominant, flashed to her memory. She bent to him swiftly, with outstretched hand.

"How good of you to meet me! How is Tommy?"

He held her hand for an instant, and she was aware of a sharp tingling throughout her being, as though by means of that strong grasp he had imparted strength. "He is about as bad as a man can be," he said. "Ralston has been with him all night. I've borrowed his two-seater to fetch you. Don't waste any time!"

Her heart gave a throb of dismay. The brief words were as flail-like as the rain. They demanded no answer, and she made none; only instant submission, and that she gave.

She had a glimpse of Peter's tall form standing behind Monck, and to him for a moment she turned as she descended.

"You will see to everything?" she said. "You will follow."

"Leave all to me, my *mem-sahib*!" he said, deeply bowing; and she took him at his word.

Monck had a military overcoat on his arm in which he wrapped her before they left the station-shelter. Ralston's little two-seater car shed dazzling beams of light through the dripping dark. She floundered blindly into a pool of water before she reached it, and was doubly startled by Monck lifting her bodily, without apology, out of the mire, and placing her on the seat. The beat of the rain upon the hood made her wonder if they could make any headway under it. And then, while she was still wondering, the engine began to throb like a living thing, and she was aware of Monck squeezing past her to his seat at the wheel.

He did not speak, but he wrapped the rug firmly about her, and almost before she had time to thank him, they were in motion.

That night-ride was one of the wildest experiences that she had ever known. Monck went like the wind. The road wound through the jungle, and in many places was little more than a rough track. The car bumped and jolted, and seemed to cry aloud for mercy. But Monck did not spare, and Stella crouched beside him, too full of wonder to be afraid.

They emerged from the jungle at length and ran along an open road between wide fields of rice or cotton. Their course became easier, and Stella realized that they were nearing the end of their journey. They were approaching the native portion of Kurrumpore.

She turned to the silent man beside her. "Is Tommy expecting me?" she asked.

He did not answer her immediately; then, "He was practically unconscious when I left," he said.

He put on speed with the words. They shot forward through the pelting rain at a terrific pace. She divined that his anxiety was such that he did not wish to talk.

They passed through the native quarter as if on wings. The rain fell in a deluge here. It was like some power of darkness striving to beat them back. She pictured Monck's face, grim, ruthless, forcing his way through the opposing element. The man himself she could barely see.

And then, almost before she realized it, they were in the European cantonment, and she heard the grinding of the brakes as they reached the gate of The Green Bungalow. Monck turned the little car into the compound, and a light shone down upon them from the verandah.

The car came to a standstill. "Do you mind getting out first?" said Monck.

She got out with a dazed sense of unreality. He followed her immediately; his hand, hard and muscular, grasped her arm. He led her up the wooden steps all shining and slippery in the rain.

In the shelter of the verandah he stopped. "Wait here a moment!" he said.

But Stella turned swiftly, detaining him. "No, no!" she said. "I am coming with you. I would rather know at once."

He shrugged his shoulders without remonstrance, and stood back for her to precede him. Later it seemed to her that it was the most merciful thing he could have done. At the time she did not pause to thank him, but went swiftly past, taking her way straight along the verandah to Tommy's room.

The window was open, and a bar of light stretched therefrom like a fiery sword into the streaming rain. Just for a second that gleaming shaft daunted her. Something within her shrank affrighted. Then, aware of Monck immediately behind her, she conquered her dread and entered. She saw that the bar of light came from a hooded lamp which was turned towards the window, leaving the bed in shadow. Over the latter a man was bending. He straightened himself sharply at her approach, and she recognized Major Ralston.

And then she had reached the bed, and all the love in her heart pulsed forth in yearning tenderness as she stooped. "Tommy!" she said. "My darling!"

He did not stir in answer. He lay like a figure carved in marble. Suddenly the rays of the lamp were turned upon him, and she saw that his face was livid. The eyes were closed and sunken. A terrible misgiving stabbed her. Almost involuntarily she drew back.

In the same moment she felt Monck's hands upon her. He was unbuttoning the overcoat in which she was wrapped. She stood motionless, feeling cold, powerless, strangely dependent upon him.

As he stripped the coat back from her shoulders, he spoke, his voice very measured and quiet, but kind also, even soothing.

"Don't give up!" he said. "We'll pull him through between us."

A queer little thrill went through her. Again she felt as if he had imparted strength. She turned back to the bed.

Major Ralston was on the other side. Across that silent form he spoke to her.

"See if you can get him to take this! I am afraid he's past it. But try!"

She saw that he was holding a spoon, and she commanded herself and took it from him. She wondered at the steadiness of her own hand as she put it to the white, unconscious lips. They were rigidly closed, and for a few moments she thought her task was hopeless. Then very slowly they parted. She slipped the spoon between.

The silence in the room was deathly, the heat intense, heavy, pall-like. Outside, the rain fell monotonously, and, mingling with its beating, she heard the croaking of innumerable frogs. Neither Ralston nor Monck stirred a finger. They were watching closely with bated breath.

Tommy's breathing was wholly imperceptible, but in that long, long pause she fancied she saw a slight tremor at his throat. Then the liquid that had been in the spoon began to trickle out at the corner of his mouth.

She stood up, turning instinctively to the man beside her. "Oh, it's no use," she said hopelessly.

He bent swiftly forward. "Let me try! Quick, Ralston! Have it ready! That's it. Now then, Tommy! Now, lad!"

He had taken her place almost before she knew it. She saw him stoop with absolute assurance and slip his arm under the boy's shoulders. Tommy's inert head fell back against him, but she saw his strong right hand come out and take the spoon that Ralston held out. His dark face was bent to his task, and it held no dismay, only unswerving determination.

"Tommy!" he said again, and in his voice was a certain grim tenderness that moved her oddly, sending the tears to her eyes before she could check them. "Tommy, wake up, man!

If you think you're going out now, you're damn well mistaken. Wake up, do you hear? Wake up and swallow this stuff! There! You've got it. Now swallow—do you hear?—swallow!"

He held the spoon between Tommy's lips till it was emptied of every drop; then thrust it back at Ralston.

"Here take it! Pour out some more! Now, Tommy lad, it's up to you! Swallow it like a dear fellow! Yes, you can if you try. Give your mind to it! Pull up, boy, pull up! play the damn game! Don't go back on me! Ah, you didn't know I was here, did you? Thought you'd slope while my back was turned. You weren't quick enough, my lad. You've got to come back."

There was a strange note of passion in his voice. It was obvious to Stella that he had utterly forgotten himself in the gigantic task before him. Body and soul were bent to its fulfillment. She could see the perspiration running down his face. She stood and watched, thrilled through and through with the wonder of what she saw.

For at the call of that curt, insistent voice Tommy moved and made response. It was like the return of a departing spirit. He came out of that deathly inertia. He opened his eyes upon Monck's face, staring up at him with an expression half-questioning and half-expectant.

"You haven't swallowed that stuff yet," Monck reminded him. "Get rid of that first! What a child you are, Tommy! Why can't you behave yourself?"

Tommy's throat worked spasmodically, he made a mighty effort and succeeded in swallowing. Then, through lips that twitched as if he were going to cry, weakly he spoke.

"Hullo—hullo—you old bounder!"

"Hullo!" said Monck in stern rejoinder. "A nice game this! Aren't you ashamed of yourself? You ought to be. I'm furious with you. Do you know that?"

"Don't care—a damn," said Tommy, and forced his quivering lips to a smile.

"You will presently, you—puppy!" said Monck witheringly. "You're more bother than you're worth. Come on, Ralston! Give him another dose! Tommy, you hang on, or I'll know the reason why! There, you little ass! What's the matter with you?"

For Tommy's smile had crumpled into an expression of woe in spite of him. He turned his face into Monck's shoulder, piteously striving to hide his weakness.

"Feel—so beastly—bad," he whispered.

"All right, old fellow, all right! I know." Monck's hand was on his head, soothing, caressing, comforting. "Stick to it like a Briton! We'll pull you round. Think I don't understand? What? But you've got to do your bit, you know. You've got to be game. And here's your sister waiting to lend a hand, come all the way to this filthy hole on purpose. You are not going to let her see you go under. Come, Tommy lad!"

The tears overflowed down Stella's cheeks. She dared not show herself. But, fortunately for her, Tommy did not desire it. Monck's words took effect upon him, and he made a trembling effort to pull himself together.

"Don't let her see me—like this!" he murmured. "I'll be better presently. You tell her, old chap, and—I say—look after her, won't you?"

"All right, you cuckoo," said Monck.

CHAPTER V
THE MORNING

Day broke upon a world of streaming rain. Stella sat before a meal spread in the dining-room and wanly watched it. Peter hovered near her; she had a suspicion that the meal was somehow of his contriving. But how he had arrived she had not the least idea and was too weary to ask.

Tommy had fallen into natural sleep, and Ralston had persuaded her to leave him in his care for a while, promising to send for her at once if occasion arose. She had left Monck there also, but she fancied Ralston did not mean to let him stay. Her thoughts dwelt oddly upon Monck. He had surprised her; more, in some fashion he had pierced straight through her armour of indifference. Wholly without intention he had imposed his personality upon her. He had made her recognize him as a force that counted. Though Major Ralston had been engaged upon the same task, she realized that it was his effort alone that had brought Tommy back. And—she saw it clearly—it was sheer love and nought else that had obtained the mastery. This man whom she had always regarded as a being apart, grimly self-contained, too ambitious to be capable of more than a passing fancy, had shown her something in his soul which she knew to be Divine. He was not, it seemed, so aloof as she had imagined him to be. The friendship between himself and Tommy was not the one-sided affair that she and a good many others had always believed it. He cared for Tommy, cared very deeply. Somehow that fact made a vast difference to her, such a difference as seemed to reach to the very centre of her being. She felt as if she had underrated something great.

The rush of the rain on the roof of the verandah seemed to make coherent thought impossible. She gazed at the meal before her and wondered if she could bring herself to partake of it. Peter had put everything ready to her hand, and in justice to him she felt as if she ought to make the attempt. But a leaden weariness was upon her. She felt more inclined to sink back in her chair and sleep.

There came a sound behind her, and she was aware of someone entering. She fancied it was Peter returned to mark her progress, and stretched her hand to the coffee-urn. But ere she touched it she knew that she was mistaken. She turned and saw Monck.

By the grey light of the morning his face startled her. She had never seen it look so haggard. But out of it the dark eyes shone, alert and indomitable, albeit she suspected that they had not slept for many hours.

He made her a brief bow. "May I join you?" he said.

His manner was formal, but she could not stand on her dignity with him at that moment. Impulsively, almost involuntarily it seemed to her later, she rose, offering him both her hands. "Captain Monck," she said, "you are—splendid!"

Words and action were alike wholly spontaneous. They were also wholly unexpected. She saw a strange look flash across his face. Just for a second he hesitated. Then he took her hands and held them fast.

"Ah—Stella!" he said.

With the name his eyes kindled. His weariness vanished as darkness vanishes before the glare of electricity. He drew her suddenly and swiftly to him.

For a few throbbing seconds Stella was so utterly amazed that she made no resistance. He astounded her at every turn, this man. And yet in some strange and vital fashion her moods responded to his. He was not beyond comprehension or even sympathy. But as she found his dark face close to hers and felt his eyes scorch her like a flame, expediency rather than dismay urged her to action. There was something so sublimely natural about him at that moment that she could not feel afraid.

She drew back from him gasping. "Oh please—please!" she said. "Captain Monck, let me go!"

He held her still, though he drew her no closer. "Must I?" he said. And in a lower voice, "Have you forgotten how once in this very room you told me—that I had come to you—too late? And—now!"

The last words seemed to vibrate through and through her. She quivered from head to foot. She could not meet the passion in his eyes, but desperately she strove to cope with it ere it mounted beyond her control.

"Ah no, I haven't forgotten," she said. "But I was a good deal younger then. I didn't know much of life. I have changed—I have changed enormously."

"You have changed—in that respect?" he asked her, and she heard in his voice that note of stubbornness which she had heard on that night that seemed so long ago—the night before her marriage.

She freed one hand from his hold and set it pleadingly against his breast. "That is a difficult question to answer," she said. "But do you think a slave would willingly go back into servitude when once he has felt the joy of freedom?"

"Is that what marriage means to you?" he said.

She bent her head. "Yes."

But still he did not let her go. "Stella," he said, "I haven't changed since that night."

She trembled again, but she spoke no word, nor did she raise her eyes.

He went on slowly, quietly, almost on a note of fatalism. "It is beyond the bounds of possibility that I should change. I loved you then, I love you now. I shall go on loving you as long as I live. I never thought it possible that you could care for me—until you told me so. But I shall not ask you to marry me so long as the thought of marriage means slavery to you. All I ask is that you will not hold yourself back from loving me—that you will not be afraid to be true to your own heart. Is that too much?"

His voice was steady again. She raised her eyes and met his look. The passion had gone out of it, but the dominance remained. She thrilled again to the mastery that had held Tommy back from death.

For a moment she could not speak. Then, as he waited, she gathered her strength to answer. "I mean to be true," she said rather breathlessly. "But I—I value my freedom too much ever to marry again. Please, I want you to understand that. You mustn't think of me in that way. You mustn't encourage hopes that can never be fulfilled."

A faint gleam crossed his face. "That is my affair," he said.

"Oh, but I mean it." Quickly she broke in upon him. "I am in earnest. I am in earnest. It wouldn't be right of me to let you imagine—to let you think—" she faltered suddenly, for something obstructed her utterance. The next moment swiftly she covered her face. "My dear!" he said.

He led her back to the table and made her sit down. He knelt beside her, his arms comfortingly around her.

"I've made you cry," he said. "You're worn out. Forgive me! I'm a brute to worry you like this. You've had a rotten time of it, I know, I know. No, don't be afraid of me! I won't say another word. Just lean on me, that's all. I won't let you down, I swear."

She took him at his word for a space and leaned upon him; for she had no alternative. She was weary to the soul of her; her strength was gone.

But gradually his strength helped her to recover. She looked up at length with a quivering smile. "There! I am going to be sensible. You must be worn out too. I can see you are. Sit down, won't you, and let us forget this?"

He met her look steadily. "No, I can't forget," he said. "But I shan't pester you. I don't believe in pestering any one. I shouldn't have done it now, only—" he broke off faintly smiling—"it's all Tommy's fault, confound him!" he said, and rose, giving her shoulder a pat that was somehow more reassuring to her than any words.

She laughed rather tremulously. "Poor Tommy! Now please sit down and have a rational meal! You are looking positively gaunt. It will be Tommy's and my turn to nurse you next if you are not careful."

He pulled up a chair and seated himself. "What a pleasing suggestion! But I doubt if Tommy's assistance will be very valuable to any one for some little time to come. No milk in that coffee, please. I will have some brandy."

Looking back upon that early breakfast, Stella smiled to herself though not without misgiving. For somehow, in spite of what had preceded it, it was a very light-hearted affair. She had never seen Monck in so genial a mood. She had not believed him capable of it. For though he looked wretchedly ill, his spirits were those of a conqueror.

Doubtless he regarded the turn in Tommy's illness as a distinct and personal victory. But was that his only cause for triumph? She wished she knew.

CHAPTER VI
THE NIGHT-WATCH

When Stella saw Tommy again, he greeted her with a smile of welcome that told her that for him the worst was over. He had returned. But his weakness was great, greater than he himself realized, and she very quickly comprehended the reason for Major Ralston's evident anxiety. Sickness was rife everywhere, and now that the most imminent danger was past he was able to spare but little time for Tommy's needs. He placed him in Stella's care with many repeated injunctions that she did her utmost to fulfil.

For the first two days Monck helped her. His management of Tommy was supremely arbitrary, and Tommy submitted himself with a meekness that sometimes struck Stella as excessive. But it was so evident that the boy loved to have his friend near him, whatever his mood, that she made no comments since Monck was not arbitrary with her. She saw but little of him after their early morning meal together, for when he could spare the time to be with Tommy, she took his advice and went to her room for the rest she so sorely needed.

She hoped that Monck rested too during the hours that she was on duty in the sick-room. She concluded that he did so, though his appearance gave small testimony to the truth of her supposition. Once or twice coming upon him suddenly she was positively startled by the haggardness of his look. But upon this also she made no comment. It seemed advisable to avoid all personal matters in her dealings with him. She was aware that he suffered no interference from Major Ralston whose time was in fact so fully occupied at the hospital and elsewhere that he was little likely to wish to add him to his sick list.

Tommy's recovery, however, was fairly rapid, and on the third night after her arrival she was able to lie down in his room and rest between her ministrations. Ralston professed himself well satisfied with his progress in the morning, and she looked forward to imparting this favourable report to Monck. But Monck did not make an appearance. She watched for him almost unconsciously all through the day, but he did not come. Tommy also watched for him, and finally concluded somewhat discontentedly that he had gone on some mission regarding which he had not deemed it advisable to inform them.

"He is like that," he told Stella, and for the first time he spoke almost disparagingly of his hero. "So beastly discreet. He never thinks any one can keep a secret besides himself."

"Ah well, never mind," Stella said. "We can do without him."

But Tommy had reached the stage when the smallest disappointment was a serious matter. He fretted and grew feverish over his friend's absence.

When Major Ralston saw him that evening he rated him soundly, and even, Stella thought, seemed inclined to blame her also for the set-back in his patient's condition.

"He must be kept quiet," he insisted. "It is absolutely essential, or we shall have the whole trouble over again. I shall have to give him a sedative and leave him to you. I can't possibly look in again to-night, so it will be useless to send for me. You will have to manage as best you can."

He departed, and Stella arranged to divide the night-watches with Peter the Great. She did not privately believe that there was much ground for alarm, but in view of the doctor's very emphatic words she decided to spend the first hours by Tommy's side. Peter would relieve her an hour after midnight, when at his earnest request she promised to go to her room and rest.

The sedative very speedily took effect upon Tommy and he slept calmly while she sat beside him with the light from the lamp turned upon her book. But though her eyes were upon the open page her attention was far from it. Her thoughts had wandered to Monck and dwelt persistently upon him. The memory of that last conversation she had had with Ralph Dacre would not be excluded from her brain. What was the meaning of this mysterious absence? What was he doing? She felt uneasy, even troubled. There was something about this Secret Service employment which made her shrink, though she felt that had their mutual relations been of the totally indifferent and casual order she would not have cared. It seemed to her well-nigh impossible to place any real confidence in a man who deliberately concealed so great a part of his existence. Her instinct was to trust him, but her reason forbade. She was beginning to ask herself if it would not be advisable to leave India just as soon as Tommy could spare her. It seemed madness to remain on if she desired to avoid any increase of intimacy with this man who had already so far overstepped the bounds of convention in his dealing with her.

And yet—in common honesty she had to admit it—she did not want to go. The attraction that held her was as yet too intangible to be definitely analyzed, but she could not deny its existence. She did not love the man—oh, surely she did not love him—for she did not want to marry him. She brought her feelings to that touchstone and it seemed that they were able to withstand the test. But neither did she want to cut herself finally adrift from all chance of contact with him. It would hurt her to go. Probably—almost certainly—she would wish herself back again. But, the question remained unanswered, ought she to stay? For the first time her treasured independence arose and mocked her. She had it in her heart to wish that the decision did not rest with herself.

It was at this point, while she was yet deep in her meditations, that a slight sound at the window made her look up. It was almost an instinctive movement on her part. She could not have said that she actually heard anything besides the falling rain which had died down to a soft patter among the trees in the compound. But something induced her took up, and so doing, she caught a glimpse of a figure on the verandah without that sent all the blood in her body racing to her heart. It was but a momentary glimpse. The next instant it was gone, gone like a shadow, so that she found herself asking breathlessly if it had ever been, or if by any means her imagination had tricked her. For in that fleeting second it seemed to her that the past had opened its gates to reveal to her a figure which of late had drifted into the back alleys of memory—the figure of the dreadful old native who, in some vague fashion, she had come to regard as the cause of her husband's death.

She had never seen him again since that awful morning when oblivion had caught her as it were on the very edge of the world, but for long after he had haunted her dreams so that the very thought of sleep had been abhorrent to her. But now—like the grim ghost of that strange life that she had so resolutely thrust behind her—the whole revolting personality of the man rushed vividly back upon her.

She sat as one petrified. Surely—surely—she had seen him in the flesh! It could not have been a dream. She was certain that she had not slept. And yet—how had that horrible old Kashmiri beggar come all these hundreds of miles from his native haunts? It was not likely. It was barely possible. And yet she had always been convinced that in some way he had known her husband beforehand. Had he come then of set intention to seek her out, perhaps to attempt to extract money from her?

She could not answer the question, and her whole being shrank from the thought of going out into the darkness to investigate. She could not bring herself to it. Actually she dared not.

Minutes passed. She sat still gazing and gazing at the blank darkness of the window. Nothing moved there. The wild beating of her heart died gradually down. Surely it had been a mistake after all! Surely she had fallen into a doze in the midst of her reverie and dreamed this hateful apparition with the gleaming eyes and famished face!

She exerted her self-command and turned at last to look at Tommy. He was sleeping peacefully with his head on his arm. He would sleep all night if undisturbed. She laid aside her book and softly rose.

Her first intention was to go to the door and see if Peter were in the passage. But the very fact of moving seemed to give her courage. The man's rest would be short enough; it seemed unkind to disturb him.

Resolutely she turned to the window, stifling all qualms. She would not be a wretched coward. She would see for herself.

The night was steaming hot, and there was a smell of mildew in the air. A swarm of mosquitoes buzzed in the glare thrown by the lamp with a shrill, attenuated sound like the skirl of far-away bagpipes. A creature with bat-like wings flapped with a monstrous ungainliness between the outer posts of the verandah. From across the compound an owl called on a weird note of defiance. And in the dim waste of distance beyond she heard the piercing cry of a jackal. But close at hand, so far as the rays of the lamp penetrated, she could discern nothing.

Stay! What was that? A bar of light from another lamp lay across the verandah, stretching out into the darkness. It came from the room next to the one in which she stood. Her heart gave a sudden hard throb. It came from Monck's room.

That meant—that meant—what did it mean? That Monck had returned at that unusual hour? Or that there really was a native intruder who had found the window unfastened and entered?

Again the impulse to retreat and call Peter to deal with the situation came upon her, but almost angrily she shook it off. She would see for herself first. If it were only Monck, then her fancy had indeed played her false and no one should know it. If it were any one else, it would be time enough then to return and raise the alarm.

So, reasoning with herself, seeking to reassure herself, crying shame on her fear, she stepped noiselessly forth into the verandah and slipped, silent as that shadow had been, through the intervening space of darkness to the open window of Monck's room.

She reached it, was blinded for a moment by the light that poured through it, then, recovering, peered in.

A man, dressed in pyjamas, stood facing her, so close to her that he seemed to be in the act of stepping forth. She recognized him in a second. It was Monck,—but Monck as she never before had seen him, Monck with eyes alight with fever and lips drawn back like the lips of a snarling animal. In his right hand he gripped a revolver.

He saw her as suddenly as she saw him, and a rapid change crossed his face. He reached out and caught her by the shoulder.

"Come in! Come in!" he said, his words rushing over each other in a confused jumble utterly unlike his usual incisive speech. "You're safe in here. I'll shoot the brute if he dares to come near you again."

She saw that he was not himself. The awful fire in his eyes alone would have told her that. But words and action so bewildered her that she yielded to the compelling grip. In a moment she was in the room, and he was closing and shuttering the window with fevered haste.

She stood and watched him, a cold sensation beginning to creep about her heart. When he turned round to her, she saw that he was smiling, a fierce, triumphant smile.

He threw down the revolver, and as he did so, she found her voice. "Captain Monck, what does that man want? What—what is he doing?"

He stood looking at her with that dreadful smile about his lips and the red fire leaping, leaping in his eyes. "Can't you guess what he wants?" he said. "He wants—you."

"Me?" She gazed back at him astounded. "But why—why? Does he want to get money out of me? Where has he gone?"

Monck laughed, a low, terrible laugh. "Never mind where he has gone! I've frightened him off, and I'll shoot him—I'll shoot him—if he comes back! You're mine now—not his. You were right to come to me, quite right. I was just coming to you. But this is better. No one can come between us now. I know how to protect my wife."

He reached out his hands to her as he ended. His eyes shocked her inexpressibly. They held a glare that was inhuman, almost devilish.

She drew back from him in open horror. "Captain Monck! I am not your wife! What can you be thinking of? You—you are not yourself."

She turned with the words, seeking the door that led into the passage. He made no attempt to check her. Instinct told her, even before she laid her hand upon it, that it was locked.

She turned back, facing him with all her courage. "Captain Monck, I command you to let me go!"

Clear and imperious her voice fell, but it had no more visible effect upon him than the drip of the rain outside. He came towards her swiftly, with the step of a conqueror, ignoring her words as though they had never been uttered.

"I know how to protect my wife," he reiterated. "I will shoot any man who tries to take you from me."

He reached her with the words, and for the first time she flinched, so terrible was his look. She shrank away from him till she stood against the closed door. Through lips that felt stiff and cold she forced her protest.

"Indeed—indeed—you don't know what you are doing. Open the door and—let me—go!"

Her voice sounded futile even to herself. Before she ceased to speak, his arms were holding her, his lips, fiercely passionate, were seeking hers.

She struggled to avoid them, but her strength was as a child's. He quelled her resistance with merciless force. He choked the cry she tried to utter with the fiery insistence of his kisses. He held her crushed against his heart, so overwhelming her with the volcanic fires of his passion that in the end she lay in his hold helpless and gasping, too shattered to oppose him further.

She scarcely knew when the fearful tempest began to abate. All sense of time and almost of place had left her. She was dizzy, quivering, on fire, wholly incapable of coherent thought, when at last it came to her that the storm was arrested.

She heard a voice above her, a strangely broken voice. "My God!" it said. "What—have I done?"

It sounded like the question of a man suddenly awaking from a wild dream. She felt the arms that held her relax their grip. She knew that he was looking at her with eyes that held once more the light of reason. And, oddly, that fact affected her rather with dismay than relief. Burning from head to foot, she turned her own away.

She felt his hand pass over her shamed and quivering face as though to assure himself that she was actually there in the flesh. And then abruptly—so abruptly that she tottered and almost fell—he set her free.

He turned from her. "God help me! I am mad!" he said.

She stood with throbbing pulses, gasping for breath, feeling as one who had passed through raging fires into a desert of smouldering ashes. She seemed to be seared from head to foot. The fiery torment of his kisses had left her tingling in every nerve.

He moved away to the table on which he had flung his revolver, and stood there with his back to her. He was swaying a little on his feet.

Without looking at her, he spoke, his voice shaky, wholly unfamiliar. "You had better go. I—I am not safe. This damned fever has got into my brain."

She leaned against the door in silence. Her physical strength was coming back to her, but yet she could not move, and she had no words to speak. He seemed to have reft from her every faculty of thought and feeling save a burning sense of shame. By his violence he had broken down all her defences. She seemed to have lost both the power and the will to resist. She remained speechless while the dreadful seconds crept away.

He turned round upon her at length suddenly, almost with a movement of exasperation. And then something that he saw checked him. He stood silent, as if not knowing how to proceed.

Across the room their eyes met and held for the passage of many throbbing seconds. Then slowly a change came over Monck. He turned back to the table and deliberately picked up the revolver that lay there.

She watched him fascinated. Over his shoulder he spoke. "You will think me mad. Perhaps it is the most charitable conclusion you could come to. But I fully realize that when a thing is beyond an apology, it is an insult to offer one. The key of the door is under the pillow on the bed. Perhaps you will not mind finding it for yourself."

He sat down with the words in a heavy, dogged fashion, holding the revolver dangling between his knees. There was grim despair in his attitude; his look was that of a man utterly spent. It came to Stella at that moment that the command of the situation had devolved upon her, and with it a heavier responsibility than she had ever before been called upon to bear.

She put her own weakness from her with a resolution born of expediency, for the need for strength was great. She crossed the room to the bed, felt for and found the key, returned to the door and inserted it in the lock. Then she paused.

He had not moved. He was not watching her. He sat as one sunk deep in dejection, bowed beneath a burden that crushed him to the earth. But there was even in his abasement a certain terrible patience that sent an icy misgiving to her heart. She did not dare to leave him so.

It needed all the strength she could muster to approach him, but she compelled herself at last. She came to him. She stood before him.

"Captain Monck!" she said.

Her voice sounded small and frightened even in her own ears. She clenched her hands with the effort to be strong.

He scarcely stirred. His eyes remained downcast. He spoke no word.

She bent a little. "Captain Monck, if you have fever, you had better go to bed."

He moved slightly, influenced possibly by the increasing steadiness of her voice. But still he did not look at her or speak.

She saw that his hold upon the revolver had tightened to a grip, and, prompted by an inner warning that she could not pause to question, she bent lower and laid her hand upon his arm. "Please give that to me!" she said.

He started at her touch; he almost recoiled. "Why?" he said.

His voice was harsh and strained, even savage. But the needed strength had come to Stella, and she did not flinch.

"You have no use for it just now," she said. "Please be sensible and let me have it!"

"Sensible!" he said.

His eyes sought hers suddenly, involuntarily, and she had a sense of shock which she was quick to control; for they held in their depths the torment of hell.

"You are wrong," he said, and the deadly intention of his voice made her quiver afresh. "I have a use for it. At least I shall have—presently. There are one or two things to be attended to first."

It was then that a strange and new authority came upon Stella, as if an unknown force had suddenly inspired her. She read his meaning beyond all doubting, and without an instant's hesitation she acted.

"Captain Monck," she said, "you have made a mistake. You have done nothing that is past forgiveness. You must take my word for that, for just now you are ill and not in a fit state to judge for yourself. Now please give me that thing, and let me do what I can to help you!"

Practical and matter-of-fact were her words. She marvelled at herself even as she stooped and laid a steady hand upon the weapon he held. Her action was purposeful, and he relinquished it. The misery in his eyes gave place to a dumb curiosity.

"Now," Stella said, "get to bed, and I will bring you some of Tommy's quinine."

She turned from him, revolver in hand, but paused and in a moment turned back.

"Captain Monck, you heard what I said, didn't you? You will go straight to bed?"

Her voice held a hint of pleading, despite its insistence. He straightened himself in his chair. He was still looking at her with an odd wonder in his eyes—wonder that was mixed with a very unusual touch of reverence.

"I will do—whatever you wish," he said.

"Thank you," said Stella. "Then please let me find you in bed when I come back!"

She turned once more to go, went to the door and opened it. From the threshold she glanced back.

He was on his feet, gazing after her with the eyes of a man in a trance.

She lifted her hand. "Now remember!" she said, and with that passed quietly out, closing the door behind her.

Her brain was in a seething turmoil and her heart was leaping within her like a wild thing suddenly caged. But, very strangely, all fear had departed from her.

Only a brief interval before, she had found herself wishing that the decision of her life's destiny had not rested entirely with herself. It seemed to her that a great revelation had been vouchsafed between the amazing present and those past moments of troubled meditation. And she knew now that it did not.

CHAPTER VII
SERVICE RENDERED

The news that Monck was down with the fever brought both the Colonel and Major Ralston early to the bungalow on the following morning.

They found Stella and the ever-faithful Peter in charge of both patients. Tommy was better though weak. Monck was in a high fever and delirious.

Stella was in the latter's room, for he would not suffer her out of his sight. She alone seemed to have any power to control him, and Ralston noted the fact with astonishment.

"There's some magic about you," he observed in his blunt fashion. "Are you going to take on this job? It's no light one but you'll probably do it better than any one else."

It was a tacit invitation, and Stella knowing how widespread was the sickness that infected the station, accepted it without demur.

"It rather looks as if it were my job, doesn't it?" she said. "I am willing, anyway to do my best."

Ralston looked at her with a gleam of approval, but the Colonel drew her aside to remonstrate.

"It's not fit for you. You'll be ill yourself. If Ralston weren't nearly at his wit's end he'd never dream of allowing it."

But Stella heard the protest with a smile. "Believe me, I am only too glad to be able to do something useful for a change," she assured him. "As to being ill myself, I will promise not to behave so badly as that."

"You're a brick, my dear," said Colonel Mansfield. "I wish there were more like you. Mind you take plenty of quinine!" With which piece of fatherly advice he left her with the determination to keep an eye on her and see that Ralston did not work her too hard.

Stella, however, had no fears on her own account. She went to her task resolute and undismayed, feeling herself actually indispensable for almost the first time in her life. Her influence upon Monck was beyond dispute. She alone possessed the power to calm him in his wildest moments, and he never failed to recognize her or to control himself to a certain extent in her presence.

The attack was a sharp one, and for a while Ralston was more uneasy than he cared to admit. But Monck's constitution was a good one, and after three days of acute illness the fever began to subside. Tommy was by that time making good progress, and Stella, who till then had snatched her rest when and how she could, gave her charge into Peter's keeping and went to bed for the first time since her arrival at Kurrumpore.

Till she actually lay down she did not realize how utterly worn out she was, or how little the odd hours of sleep that she had been able to secure had sufficed her. But as she laid her head upon the pillow, slumber swept upon her on soundless wings. She slept almost before she had time to appreciate the exquisite comfort of complete repose.

That slumber of hers lasted for many hours. She had given Peter express injunctions to awake her in good time in the morning, and she rested secure in the confidence that he would obey her orders. But it was the light of advancing evening that filled the room when at last she opened her eyes.

There had come a break in the rain, and a bar of misty sunshine had penetrated a chink in the green blinds and lay golden across the Indian matting on the floor. She lay and gazed at it with a bewildered sense of uncertainty as to her whereabouts. She felt as if she had returned from a long journey, and for a time her mind dwelt hazily upon the Himalayan paradise from which she had been so summarily cast forth. Vague figures flitted to and fro through her brain till finally one in particular occupied the forefront of her thoughts. She found herself recalling every unpleasant detail of the old Kashmiri beggar who had lured Ralph Dacre from her side on that last fateful night. The old question arose within her and would not be stifled. Had the man murdered and robbed him ere flinging him down to the torrent that had swept his body away? The wonder tormented her as of old, but with renewed intensity. She had awaked with the conviction strong upon her that the man was not far away, that she had seen him recently, and that Everard Monck had seen him also.

That brought her thoughts very swiftly to the present, to Monck's illness and dependence upon her, and in a flash to the realization that she had spent nearly the whole day as well as the night in sleep. In keen dismay she started from her bed and began a rapid toilet.

A quarter of an hour later she heard Peter's low, discreet knock at the door, and bade him enter. He came in with a tea-tray, smiling upon her with such tender solicitude that she had it not in her heart to express any active annoyance with him.

"Oh, Peter, you should have called me hours ago!" was all she found to say.

He set down the tray with a deep salaam. "But the captain *sahib* would not permit me," he said.

"He is better?" Stella asked quickly.

"He is much better, my *mem-sahib*. The doctor *sahib* smiled upon him only this afternoon and told him he was a damn' fraud. So my *mem-sahib* may set her mind at rest."

Obviously the term constituted a high compliment in Peter's estimation and the evident satisfaction that it afforded to Stella seemed to confirm the impression. He retired looking as well pleased as Stella had ever seen him.

She finished dressing as speedily as possible, ate a hasty meal, and hastened to Tommy's room. To her surprise she found it empty, but as she turned on the threshold the sound of her brother's laugh came to her through the passage. Evidently Tommy was visiting his fellow sufferer.

With a touch of anxiety as to Monck's fitness to receive a visitor, she turned in the direction of the laugh. But at Monck's door she paused, constrained by something that checked her almost like a hand laid upon her. The blood ran up to her temples and beat through her brain. She found she could not enter.

As she stood there hesitating, Monck's voice came to her, quiet and rational. She could not hear what he said, but Tommy's more impetuous tones cutting in were clearly audible.

"Oh, rats, my dear fellow! Don't be so damn' modest! You're worth a score of Dacres and you bet she knows it."

Stella tingled from head to foot. In another moment she would have passed swiftly on, but even as the impulse came to her it was frustrated. The door in front of her suddenly opened, and she was face to face with Monck himself.

He stood leaning slightly on the handle of the door. He was draped in a long dressing-gown of Oriental silk that hung upon him dejectedly as if it yearned for a stouter tenant. In it he looked leaner and taller than he had ever seemed to her before. He had a cigarette between his lips, but this he removed with a flicker of humour as he observed her glance.

"Caught in the act," he remarked. "Please come in!"

Something that was very far from humour impelled Stella to say quickly, "I hope you don't imagine I was eavesdropping."

He looked sardonic for an instant. "No, I do not so far flatter myself," he said. "I was referring to my cigarette."

She entered, striving for dignity. Then as his attitude caught her attention she forgot herself and turned upon him in genuine dismay. "What are you doing out of bed? You know you are not fit for it. Oh, how wrong of you! Take my arm!"

He transferred his hand from the door to her shoulder, and she felt it tremble though his hold was strong.

"May I not sit up to tea with you, nurse *sahib*?" he suggested, as she piloted him firmly to the bedside.

"Of course not," she made answer. The consciousness of his weakness had fully restored her confidence and her authority. "Besides, I have had mine. Tommy, you too! It is too bad, I shall never dare to close my eyes again."

At this point Monck laughed so suddenly and boyishly that she found it utterly impossible to continue her reproaches. He humbly apologized as he subsided upon the bed, and turning to Tommy who, fully dressed, was reclining at his ease in a deck-chair by its side said with a smile, "You get back to your own compartment, my son. It isn't good for me to have two people in the room with me at the same time. And your sister wants to take my pulse undisturbed."

"Or listen to your heart?" suggested Tommy irreverently as he rose.

"Turn him out!" said Monck, leaning luxuriously upon the pillows that Stella arranged for him.

Tommy laughed as he sauntered away, pulling the door carelessly after him but recalled by Monck to shut it.

A sudden silence followed his departure. Stella was at the window, looping back the curtains. The vague sunlight still smote across the dripping compound; the whole plain was smoking like a mighty cauldron. Stella finished her task and stood still.

Across the silence came Monck's voice. "Aren't you going to give me my medicine?"

She turned slowly round. "I think you are nearly equal to doctoring yourself now," she said.

He was lying raised on his elbow, his eyes, intent and searching, fixed upon her. Abruptly, in a different tone, he spoke. "In other words, quit fooling and play the game!" he said. "All right, I will—to the best of my ability. First of all, may I tell you something that Ralston said to me this morning?"

"Certainly." Stella's voice sounded constrained and formal. She remained with her back to the window; for some reason she did not want him to see her face too clearly.

"It was only this," said Monck. "He said that I had you to thank for pulling me through this business, that but for you I should probably have gone under. Ralston isn't given to saying that sort of thing. So—if you will allow me—I should like to thank you for the trouble you have taken and for the service rendered."

"Please don't!" Stella said. "After all, it was no more than you did for Tommy, nor so much." She spoke nervously, avoiding his look.

The shadow of a smile crossed Monck's face. "I chance to be rather fond of Tommy," he said, "so my motive was more or less a selfish one. But you had not that incentive, so I should be all the more grateful. I am afraid I have given you a lot of trouble. Have you found me very difficult to manage?"

He put the question suddenly, almost imperiously. Stella was conscious of a momentary surprise. There was something in the tone rather than the words that puzzled her. She hesitated over her reply.

"You have?" said Monck. "That means I have been very unruly. Do you mind telling me what happened on the night I was taken ill?"

She felt a burning blush rush up to her face and neck before she could check it. It was impossible to attempt to hide her distress from him. She forced herself to speak before it overwhelmed her. "I would rather not discuss it or think of it. You were not yourself, and I—and I—"

"And you?" said Monck, his voice suddenly sunk very low.

She commanded herself with a supreme effort. "I wish to forget it," she said with firmness.

He was silent for a moment or two. She began to wonder if it would be possible to make her escape before he could pursue the subject further. And then he spoke, and she knew that she must remain.

"You are very generous," he said, "more generous than I deserve. Will it help matters at all if I tell you that I would give all I have to be able to forget it too, or to believe that the thing I remember was just one of the wild delusions of my brain?"

His voice was deep and sincere. In spite of herself she was moved by it. She came forward to his side. "The past is past," she said, and gave him her hand.

He took it and held it, looking at her in his straight, inscrutable way. "True, most gracious!" he said. "But I haven't quite done with it yet. Will you hear me a moment longer? You have of your goodness pardoned my outrageous behaviour, so I make no further allusion to that, except to tell you that I had been tempted to try a native drug which in its effects was worse than the fever pure and simple. But there is one point which only you can make clear. How was it you came to seek me out that night?"

His grasp upon her hand was reassuring though she felt the quiver of physical weakness in its hold. It was the grasp of a friend, and her embarrassment began to fall away from her.

"I came," she said, "because I had been startled. I had no idea you were anywhere near. I was really investigating the verandah because of—of something I had seen, when the light from this window attracted me. I thought possibly someone had broken in."

"Will you tell me what startled you?" Monck said.

She looked at him. "It was a man—an old native beggar. I only saw him for a moment. I was in Tommy's room, and he came and looked in at me. You—you must have seen him too. You were talking very excitedly about him. You threatened to shoot him."

"Was that how you came to deprive me of my revolver?" questioned Monck.

She coloured again vividly. "No, I thought you were going to shoot yourself. I will give it back to you presently."

"When you consider that I can be safely trusted with it?" he suggested, with his brief smile. "But tell me some more about this mysterious old beggar of yours! What was he like?"

She hesitated momentarily. "I only had a very fleeting glimpse of him. I can't tell you what he was really like. But—he reminded me of someone I never want to think of or suffer myself to think of again if I can help it."

"Who?" said Monck.

His voice was quiet, but it held insistence. She felt as if his eyes pierced her, compelling her reply.

"A horrible old native—a positive nightmare of a man—whom I shall always regard as in some way the cause of my husband's death."

In the pause that followed her words, Monck's hand left hers. He lay still looking at her, but with that steely intentness that told her nothing. She could not have said whether he were vitally interested in the matter or not when he spoke again.

"You think that he was murdered then?"

A sharp shudder went through her. "I am very nearly convinced of it," she said. "But I shall never know for certain now."

"And you imagine that the murderer can have followed you here?" he pursued.

"No! Oh no!" Hastily she made answer. "It is ridiculous of course. He would never be such a fool as to do that. It was only my imagination. I saw the figure at the window and was reminded of him."

"Are you sure the figure at the window was not imagination too?" said Monck. "Forgive my asking! Such things have happened."

"Oh, I know," Stella said. "It is a question I have been asking myself ever since. But, you know—" she smiled faintly—"I had no fever that night. Besides, I fancy you saw him too."

His smile met hers. "I saw many things that night as they were not. And you also were overwrought and very tired. Perhaps you had had an exciting supper!"

She saw that he meant to turn the subject away from her husband's death, and a little thrill of gratitude went through her. He had seen how reluctant she was to speak of it. She followed his lead with relief.

"Perhaps—perhaps," she said. "We will say so anyhow. And now, do you know, I think you had better have your tea and rest. You have done a lot of talking, and you will be getting feverish again if I let you go on. I will send Peter in with it."

He raised one eyebrow with a wry expression. "Must it be Peter?" he said.

She relented. "I will bring it myself if you will promise not to talk."

"Ah!" he said. "And if I promise that—will you promise me one thing too?"

She paused. "What is that?"

His eyes met hers, direct but baffling. "Not. to run away from me," he said.

The quick blood mounted again in her face. She stood silent.

He lifted an urgent hand. "Stella, in heaven's name, don't be afraid of me!"

She laid her hand again in his. She could not do otherwise. She wanted to beg him to say nothing further, to let her go in peace. But no words would come. She stood before him mute.

And—perhaps he knew what was in her mind—Monck was silent also after that single earnest appeal of his. He held her hand for a few seconds, and then very quietly let it go. She knew by his action that he would respect her wish for the time at least and say no more.

CHAPTER VIII
THE TRUCE

Tommy was in a bad temper with everyone—a most unusual state of affairs. The weather was improving every day; the rains were nearly over. He was practically well again, too well to be sent to Bhulwana on sick leave, as Ralston brutally told him; but it was not this fact that had upset his internal equilibrium. He did not want sick leave, and bluntly said so.

"Then what the devil do you want?" said Ralston, equally blunt and ready to resent irritation from one who in his opinion was too highly favoured of the gods to have any reasonable grounds for complaint.

Tommy growled an inarticulate reply. It was not his intention to confide in Ralston whatever his grievance. But Ralston, not to be frustrated, carried the matter to Monck, then on the high road to recovery.

"What in thunder is the matter with the young ass?" he demanded. "He gets more lantern-jawed and obstreperous every day."

"Leave him to me!" said Monck. "Discharge him as cured! I'll manage him."

"But that's just what he isn't," grumbled Ralston. "He ought to be well. So far as I can make out, he is well. But he goes about looking like a sick fly and stinging before you touch him."

"Leave him to me!" Monck said again.

That afternoon as he and Tommy lounged together on the verandah after the lazy fashion of convalescents, he turned to the boy in his abrupt fashion.

"Look here, Tommy!" he said. "What are you making yourself so conspicuously unpleasant for? It's time you pulled up."

Tommy turned crimson. "I?" he stammered. "Who says so? Stella?"

There was the suspicion of a smile about Monck's grim mouth as he made reply. "No; not Stella, though she well might. I've heard you being beastly rude to her more than once. What's the matter with you? Want a kicking, eh?"

Tommy hunched himself in his wicker chair with his chin on his chest. "No, want to kick," he said in a savage undertone.

Monck laughed briefly. He was standing against a pillar of the verandah. He turned and sat down unexpectedly on the arm of Tommy's chair. "Who do you want to kick?" he said.

Tommy glanced at him and was silent.

"Significant!" commented Monck. He put his hand with very unwonted kindness upon the lad's shoulder. "What do you want to kick me for, Tommy?" he asked.

Tommy shrugged the shoulder under his hand. "If you don't know, I can't tell you," he said gruffly.

Monck's fingers closed with quiet persistence. "Yes, you can. Out with it!" he said.

But Tommy remained doggedly silent.

Several seconds passed. Then very suddenly Monck raised his hand and smote him hard on the back.

"Damn!" said Tommy, straightening involuntarily.

"That's better," said Monck. "That'll do you good. Don't curl up again! You're getting disgracefully round-shouldered. Like to have a bout with the gloves?"

There was not a shade of ill-feeling in his voice. Tommy turned round upon him with a smile as involuntary as his exclamation had been.

"What a brute you are, Monck! You have such a beastly trick of putting a fellow in the wrong."

"You are in the wrong," asserted Monck. "I want to get you out of it if I can. What's the grievance? What have I done?"

Tommy hesitated for a moment, then finally reached up and gripped the hand upon his shoulder. "Monck! I say, Monck!" he said boyishly. "I feel such a cur to say it. But—but—" he broke off abruptly. "I'm damned if I can say it!" he decided dejectedly.

Monck's fingers suddenly twisted and closed upon his. "What a funny little ass you are, Tommy!" he said.

Tommy brightened a little. "It's infernally difficult—taking you to task," he explained blushing a still fiercer red. "You'll never speak to me again after this."

Monck laughed. "Yes, I shall. I shall respect you for it. Get on with it, man! What's the trouble?"

With immense effort Tommy made reply. "Well, it's pretty beastly to have to ask any fellow what his intentions are with regard to his sister, but you pretty nearly told me yours."

"Then what more do you want?" questioned Monck.

Tommy made a gesture of helplessness. "Damn it, man! Don't you know she is making plans to go Home?"

"Well?" said Monck.

Tommy faced round. "I say, like a good chap,—you've practically forced this, you know—you're not going to—to let her go?"

Monck's eyes looked back straight and hard. He did not speak for a moment; then, "You want to know my intentions, Tommy," he said. "You shall. Your sister and I are observing a truce for the present, but it won't last for ever. I am making plans for a move myself. I am going to live at the Club."

"Is that going to help?" demanded Tommy bluntly.

Monck looked sardonic. "We mustn't offend the angels, you know, Tommy," he said.

Tommy made a sound expressive of gross irreverence. "Oh, that's it, is it? Now we know where we are. I've been feeling pretty rotten about it, I can tell you."

"You always were an ass, weren't you?" said Monck, getting up.

Tommy got up too, giving himself an impatient shake. He pushed an apologetic hand through Monck's arm. "I can't expect ever to get even with a swell like you," he said humbly,

Monck looked at him. Something in the boy's devotion seemed to move him, for his eyes were very kindly though his laugh was ironic. "You'll have an almighty awakening one of these days, my son," he said. "By the way, if we are going to be brothers, you had better call me by my Christian name."

"By Jove, I will," said Tommy eagerly. "And if there is anything I can do, old chap—anything under the sun—"

"I'll let you know," said Monck.

So, like the lifting of a thunder cloud, Tommy's very unwonted fit of temper merged into a mood of great benignity and Ralston complained no more.

Monck took up his abode at the Club before the brief winter season brought the angels flitting back from Bhulwana to combine pleasure with duty at Kurrumpore.

Stella accepted his departure without comment, missing him when gone after a fashion which she would have admitted to none. She did not wholly understand his attitude, but Tommy's serenity of demeanour made her somewhat suspicious; for Tommy was transparent as the day.

Mrs. Ralston's return made her life considerably easier. They took up their friendship exactly where they had left it and found it wholly satisfactory. When Lady Harriet Mansfield made her stately appearance, Stella's position was assured. No one looked askance at her any longer. Even Mrs. Burton's criticism was limited to a strictly secret smile.

Netta Ermsted was the last to leave Bhulwana. She returned nervous and fretful, accompanied by Tessa whose joy over rejoining her friends was as patent as her mother's discontent. Tessa had a great deal to say in disparagement of the Rajah of Markestan, and said it so often and with such emphasis that at last Captain Ermsted's patience gave way and he forbade all mention of the man under penalty of a severe slapping. When Tessa had ignored the threat for the third time he carried it out with such thoroughness that even Netta was startled into remonstrance.

"You are quite right to keep the child in order," she said. "But you needn't treat her like that. I call it brutal."

"You can call it what you like," said Ermsted. "I did it quite as much for your benefit as for hers."

Netta tossed her head. "I'm not a sentimental mother," she observed. "You won't punish me in that way. I object to a commotion, that's all."

He took her by the shoulder. "Do you?" he said. "Then I advise you to be mighty careful, for, I warn you, my blood is up."

She made a face at him, albeit there was a quality of menace in his hold. "Are you going to treat me as you have just treated Tessa?"

His teeth were clenched upon his lower lip. "Don't be a little devil, Netta!" he said.

She snapped her fingers. "Then don't you be a big fool, most noble Richard! It doesn't pay to bully a woman. She can always get her own back one way or another. Remember that!"

He gripped her suddenly by both arms. "By Heaven!" he said passionately. "I'll do worse than beat you if you dare to trifle with me!"

She tried to laugh, but his look frightened her. She turned as white as the muslin wrap she wore. "Richard—Dick—don't," she gasped helplessly.

He held her locked to him. "You've gone too far," he said.

"I haven't, Dick! I haven't!" she protested. "Dick, I swear to you—I have never—I have never—"

He stopped the words upon her lips with his own, but his kiss was terrible. She shrank from it trembling, appalled.

In a moment he let her go, and she sank upon her couch, hiding her quivering face with convulsive weeping.

"You are cruel! You are cruel!" she sobbed.

He remained beside her, looking down at her till some of the sternness passed from his face.

He bent at last and touched her. "I'm not cruel," he said. "I'm just in earnest, that's all. You be careful for the future! There's a bit of the devil in me too when I'm goaded."

She drew herself away from him, half-frightened still and half petulant. "You used to be—ever so much nicer than you are now," she said, keeping her face averted.

He answered her sombrely as he turned away, "I used to have a wife that I honoured before all creation."

She sprang to her feet. "Dick! How can you be so horrid?"

He shrugged his shoulders as he walked to the door. "I was—a big fool," he said very bitterly.

The door closed upon him. Netta stood staring at it, tragic and tear-stained.

Suddenly she stamped her foot and whirled round in a rage. "I won't be treated like a naughty child! I won't—I won't! I'll write to my Arabian Knight—I'll write now—and tell him how wretched I am! If Dick objects to our friendship I'll just leave him, that's all. I was a donkey ever to marry him. I always knew we shouldn't get on."

She paused, listening, half-fearing, half-hoping, that she had heard him returning. Then she heard his voice in the next room. He was talking to Tessa.

She set her lips and went to her writing-table. "Oh yes, he can make it up with his child when he knows he has been brutal; but never a single kind word to his wife—not one word!"

She took up a pen with fingers that trembled with indignation, and began to write.

CHAPTER IX
THE OASIS

For two months Tommy possessed his impulsive soul in patience. For two months he watched Monck go his impassive and inscrutable way, asking no further question. The gaieties of the station were in full swing. Christmas was close at hand.

Stella was making definite plans for departure in the New Year. She could not satisfy herself with an idle life, though Tommy vehemently opposed the idea of her going. Monck never opposed it. He listened silently when she spoke of it, sometimes faintly smiling. She often saw him. He came to the Green Bungalow in Tommy's company at all hours of the day. She met him constantly at the Club, and he never failed to come to her side there and by some means known only to himself to banish the crowd of subalterns who were wont to gather round her. He asserted no claim, but the claim existed and was mutely recognized. He never spoke to her intimately. He never attempted to pass the bounds of ordinary friendship. Only very rarely did he make her aware that her company was a pleasure to him. But the fact remained that she was the only woman that he ever sought, and the tongues of all the rest were busy in consequence.

As for Stella, she still told herself that she would escape with her freedom. He would speak, she was convinced, before she left. She even sometimes told herself that after what had passed between them, it was almost incumbent upon him to speak. But she believed that he would accept her refusal philosophically, possibly even with relief. She restrained herself forcibly from dwelling upon the thought of him. Again and again she reminded herself that he trod the way of ambition. His heart was given to his work, and a man may not serve two masters. He cared for her, probably, but in a calm, judicial fashion that could never satisfy her. If she married him she would come second—and a very poor second—to his profession. And so she did not mean to marry him. And so she checked the fevered memory of passionate kisses that had burned her to the soul, of arms that had clasped and held her by a force colossal. That had been only the primitive man in him, escaped for the moment beyond his control—the primitive man which he had well-nigh succeeded in stifling with the bonds of his servitude. Had he not told her that he would have given all he had to forget that single wild lapse into savagery? She was sure that he despised himself for it. He would never for an instant suffer such an impulse again. He did not really love her. It was not in him to love any woman. He would make her a formal offer of marriage, and when she had refused him he would dismiss the matter from his mind and return to his work undisturbed.

So she schooled herself to make her plans, leaving him out of the reckoning, telling herself ever that her newly restored freedom was too dear ever to be sacrificed again. In Mrs. Ralston's company she attended some of the social gatherings of the station, but she took no keen pleasure in them. She disliked Lady Harriet, she distrusted Mrs. Burton, and more often than not she remained away. The coming Christmas festivities did not attract her. She held aloof till Tommy who was in the thick of everything suddenly and vehemently demanded her presence.

"It's ridiculous to be so stand-offish," he maintained. "Don't let 'em think you're afraid of 'em! Come anyway to the moonlight picnic at Khanmulla on Christmas Eve! It's going to be no end of a game."

Stella smiled a little. "Do you know, Tommy, I think I'd rather go to bed?"

"Absurd!" declared Tommy. "You used to be much more sporting."

"I wasn't a widow in those days," Stella said.

"What rot! What damn' rot!" cried Tommy wrathfully.

"There is no altering the fact," said Stella.

He left her, fuming.

That evening as she sat on the Club verandah with Mrs. Ralston, watching some tennis, Monck came up behind her and stood against the wall smoking a cigarette.

He did not speak for some time and after a word of greeting Stella turned back to the play. But presently Mrs. Ralston got up and went away, and after an interval Monck came silently forward and took the vacant seat.

Tommy was among the players. His play was always either surprisingly brilliant or amazingly bad, and on this particular evening he was winning all the honours.

Stella was joining in the general applause after a particularly fine stroke when suddenly Monck's voice spoke at her side.

"Why don't you take a hand sometimes instead of always looking on?"

The question surprised her. She glanced at him in momentary embarrassment, met his straight look, and smiled.

"Perhaps I am lazy."

"That isn't the reason," he said. "Why do you lead a hermit's life? Do you follow your own inclination in so doing? Or are you merely proving yourself a slave to an unwritten law?"

His voice was curt; it held mastery. But yet she could not resent it, for behind it was a masked kindness which deprived it of offence.

She decided to treat the question lightly. "Perhaps a little of both," she said. "Besides, it seems scarcely worth while to try to get into the swim now when I am leaving so soon."

He made an abrupt movement which seemed to denote suppressed impatience. "You are too young to say that," he said.

She laughed a little. "I don't feel young. I think life moves faster in tropical countries. I have lived years since I have been here, and I am glad of a rest."

He was silent for a space; then again abruptly he returned to the charge. "You're not going to waste all the best of your life over a memory, are you? The finest man in the world isn't worth that."

She felt the colour rise in her face as she made reply. "I hope I am not going to waste my life at all. Is it a waste not to spend it in a feverish round of social pleasures? If so, I do not think you are in a position to condemn me."

She saw his brief smile for an instant. "My life is occupied with other things," he said. "But I don't lead a hermit's existence. I am going to the officers' picnic at Khanmulla on the twenty-fourth for instance."

"Being a case of 'Needs must'," suggested Stella.

"By no means." Monck leaned forward to light another cigarette. "I am going for a particular purpose. If that purpose is not fulfilled—" he paused a moment and she felt his eyes upon her again—"I shall come straight back," he ended with a certain doggedness of determination that did not escape her.

Stella's gaze was fixed upon the court below her and she kept it there, but she saw nothing of the game. Her heart was beating oddly in leaps and jerks. She felt curiously as if she were under the influence of an electric battery; every nerve and every vein seemed to be tingling.

He had not asked a question, yet she felt that in some fashion he had made it incumbent upon her to speak in answer. In the silence that followed his words she was aware of an insistence that would not be denied. She tried to put it from her, but could not. In the end, more than half against her will, she yielded.

"I suppose I shall have to go," she said, "if only to pacify Tommy."

"A very good and sufficient reason," commented Monck enigmatically.

He lingered on beside her for a while, but nothing further of an intimate nature passed between them. She felt that he had gained his objective and would say no more. The truce between them was to be observed until the psychological moment arrived to break it, and that moment would occur some time on Christmas Eve in the moonlit solitudes of Khanmulla.

Later she reflected that perhaps it was as well to go and get it over. She could not deny him his opportunity, and it would not take long—she was sure it would not take long to convince him that they were better as they were.

Had he been younger, less wedded to his work, less the slave of his ambition, things might have been different. Had she never been married to Ralph Dacre, never known the bondage of those few strange weeks, she might have been more ready to join her life to his.

But Fate had intervened between them, and their paths now lay apart. He realized it as well as she did. He would not press her. Their eyes were open, and if the oasis in the desert had seemed desirable to either for a space, yet each knew that it was no abiding-place.

Their appointed ways lay in the waste beyond, diverging ever more and more, till presently even the greenness of that oasis in which they had met together would be no more to either than a half-forgotten dream.

CHAPTER X
THE SURRENDER

The moon was full on Christmas Eve. It shone in such splendour that the whole world was transformed into a fairyland of black and silver. Stella stood on the verandah of the Green Bungalow looking forth into the dazzling night with a tremor at her heart. The glory of it was in a sense overwhelming. It made her feel oddly impotent, almost afraid, as if some great power menaced her. She had never felt the ruthlessness of the East more strongly than she felt it that night. But the drugged feeling that had so possessed her in the mountains was wholly absent from her now. She felt vividly alive, almost painfully conscious of the quick blood pulsing through her veins. She was aware of an intense longing to escape even while the magic of the night yet drew her irresistibly. Deep in her heart there lurked an uncertainty which she could not face. Up to that moment she had been barely aware of its existence, but now she felt it stirring, and strangely she was afraid. Was it the call of the East, the wonder of the moonlight? Or was it some greater thing yet, such as had never before entered into her life? She could not say; but her face was still firmly set towards the goal of liberty. Whatever was in store for her, she meant to extricate herself. She meant to cling to her freedom at all costs. When next she stood upon that verandah, the ordeal she had begun to dread so needlessly, so unreasonably, would be over, and she would have emerged triumphant.

So she told herself, even while the shiver of apprehension which she could not control went through her, causing her to draw her wrap more closely about her though there was nought but a pleasant coolness in the soft air that blew across the plain.

She and Tommy were to drive with the Ralstons to the ruined palace in the jungle of Khanmulla where the picnic was to take place. She had never seen it, but had heard it described as the most romantic spot in Markestan. It had been the site of a fierce battle in some bye-gone age, and its glories had departed. For centuries it had lain deserted and crumbling. Yet some of its ancient beauty remained. Its marble floors and walls of carved stone were not utterly obliterated though only owls and flying-foxes made it their dwelling-place. Natives regarded it with superstitious awe and seldom approached it. But Europeans all looked upon it as the most beautiful corner within reach, and had it been nearer to Kurrumpore, it would have been a far more frequented playground than it was.

The hoot of a motor-horn broke suddenly upon the silence, and Stella started. It was the horn of Major Ralston's little two-seater; she knew it well. But they had not proposed using it that night. She and Tommy were to accompany them in a waggonette. The crunching of wheels and throb of the engine at the gate told her it was stopping. Then the Ralstons had altered their plans, unless—Something suddenly leapt up within her. She was conscious of a curious constriction at the throat, a sense of suffocation. The fuss and worry of the engine died down into silence, and in a moment there came the sound of a man's feet entering the compound. Standing motionless, with hands clenched against her sides, she gazed forth. A tall, straight figure was coming towards her between the whispering tamarisks. It was not Major Ralston. He walked with a slouch, and this man's gait was firm and purposeful. He came up to the verandah-steps with unfaltering determination. He was looking full at her, and she knew that she stood revealed in the marvellous Indian moonlight. He mounted the steps with the same absolute self-assurance that yet held nought of arrogance. His face remained in shadow, but she did not need to see it. The reason of his coming was proclaimed in every line, in every calm, unwavering movement.

He came to her, and she waited there in the merciless moonlight; for she had no choice.

"I have come for you," he said.

The words were brief, but they thrilled her strangely. Her eyes fluttered and refused to meet his look.

"The Ralstons are taking us," she said.

Her tone was cold, her bearing aloof. She was striving for self-control. He could not have known of the tumult within her. Yet he smiled. "They are taking Tommy," he said.

She heard the stubborn note in his voice and suddenly and completely the power to resist went from her.

She held out her hand to him with a curious gesture of appeal, "Captain Monck, if I come with you—"

His fingers closed about her own. "If?" he said.

She made a rather piteous attempt to laugh. "Really I don't want to," she said.

"Really?" said Monck. He drew a little nearer to her, still holding her hand. His grasp was firm and strong. "Really?" he said again.

She stood in silence, for she could not give him any answer.

He waited for a moment or two; then, "Stella," he said, "are you afraid of me?"

She shook her head. Her lips had begun to tremble inexplicably. "No—no," she said.

"What then?" He spoke with a gentleness that she had never heard from him before. "Of yourself?"

She turned her face away from him. "I am afraid—of life," she told him brokenly. "It is like a great Wheel—a vast machinery. I have been caught in it once—caught and crushed. Oh can't you understand?"

"Yes," he said.

Again for a space he was silent, his hand yet holding hers. There was subtle comfort in his grasp. It held protection.

"And so you want to run away from it?" he said at length. "Do you think that's going to help you?"

She choked back a sob. "I don't know. I have no judgment. I don't trust myself."

"You believe in sincerity?" he said. "In being true to yourself?" Then, as she winced, "No, I don't want to go over old ground. We are talking of present things. I'm not going to pester you, not going to ask you to marry me even—" again she was aware of his smile though his speech sounded grim—"until you have honestly answered the question that you are trying to shirk. Perhaps you won't thank me for reminding you a second time of a conversation that you and I once had on this very spot, but I must. I told you that I had been waiting for my turn. And you told me that I had come—too late."

He paused, but she did not speak. She was trembling from head to foot.

He leaned towards her. "Stella, I'm not such a fool as to make the same mistake twice over. I'm not going to miss my turn a second time. I loved you then—though I had never flattered myself that I had a chance. And my love isn't the kind that burns and goes out." His voice suddenly quivered. "I don't know whether you have any use for it. You have been too discreet and cautious to betray yourself. Your heart has been a closed book to me. But to-night—I am going to open that book. I have the right, and you can't deny it to me. If you were queen of the whole earth I should still have the right, because I love you, to ask you—as I ask you now—have you any love for me? There! I have done it. If you can tell me honestly that I am nothing to you, that is the end. But if not—if not—" again she heard a deep vibration in his voice—"then don't be afraid—in the name of Heaven! Marriage with me would not mean slavery."

He stopped abruptly and turned from her. From the room behind them there came a cheery hail. Tommy came tramping through.

"Hullo, old chap! You, is it? Has Stella been attending to your comfort? Have you had a drink?"

Monck's answer had a sardonic note, "Your sister has been kindness itself—as she always is. No drinks for me, thanks. I am just off in Ralston's car to Khanmulla." He turned deliberately back again to Stella. "Will you come with me? Or will you go with Tommy—and the Ralstons?"

There was neither anxiety nor persuasion in his voice. Tommy frowned over its utter lack of emotion. He did not think his friend was playing his cards well.

But to Stella that coolness had a different meaning. It stirred her to an impulse more headlong than at the moment she realized.

"I will come with you," she said.

"Good!" said Monck simply, and stood back for her to pass.

She went by him without a glance. She felt as if the wild throbbing of her heart would choke her. He had spoken in such a fashion as she had dreamed that he could ever speak.

He had spoken and she had not sent him away. That was the thought that most disturbed her. Till that moment it had seemed a comparatively easy thing to do. Her course had been clear. But he had appealed to that within her which could not be ignored. He had appealed to the inner truth of her nature, and she could not close her ears to that. He asked her only to be true to herself. He had taken his stand on higher ground than that on which she stood. He had not urged any plea on his own behalf. He had only urged her to be honest. And in so doing he had laid bare that ancient mistake of hers that had devastated her life. He did not desire her upon the same terms as those upon which she had bestowed herself upon Ralph Dacre. He made that abundantly clear. He did not ask her to subordinate her happiness to his. He only asked for straight dealing from her, and she knew that he asked it as much for her sake as for his own. He would not seek to hold her if she did not love him. That was the great touchstone to which he had brought her, and she knew that she must face the test. The mastery of his love compelled her. As he had freely asserted, he had the right—just because he was an honourable man and he loved her honourably.

But how far would that love of his carry him? She longed to know. It was not the growth of a brief hour's passion. That at least she knew. It would not burn and go out. It would endure; somehow she realized that now past disputing. But was it first and greatest with him? Were his cherished career, his ambition, of small account beside it? Was he willing to do sacrifice to it? And if so, how great a sacrifice was he prepared to offer?

She yearned to ask him as he sped her in silence through the chequered moonlight of the Khanmulla jungle. But some inner force restrained her. She feared to break the spell.

The road was deserted, just as it had been on that dripping night when she had answered his summons to Tommy's sick bed. She recalled that wild rush through the darkness, his grim strength, his determination. The iron of his will had seemed to compass her then. Was it the same to-night? Had her freedom already been wrested from her? Was there to be no means of escape?

Through the jungle solitudes there came the call of an owl, weird and desolate and lonely. Something in it pierced her with a curious pain. Was freedom then everything? Did she truly love the silence above all?

She drew her cloak closer about her. Was there something of a chill in the atmosphere? Or was it the chill of the desert beyond the oasis that awaited her?

They emerged from the thickest part of the jungle into a space of tangled shrubs that seemed fighting with each other for possession of the way. The road was rough, and Monck slackened speed.

"We shall have to leave the car," he said. "There is a track here that leads to the ruined palace. It is only a hundred yards or so. We shall have to do it on foot."

They descended. The moonlight poured in a flood all about them. They were alone.

Stella turned up the narrow path he indicated, but in a moment he overtook her. "Let me go first!" he said.

He passed her with the words and walked ahead, holding the creepers back from her as she followed.

She suffered him silently, with a strange sense of awe, almost as though she trod holy ground. But the old feeling of trespass was wholly absent. She had no fear of being cast forth from this place that she was about to enter.

The path began to widen somewhat and to ascend. In a few moments they came upon a crumbling stonewall crossing it at right angles.

Monck paused. "One way leads to the palace, the other to the temple," he said. "Which shall we take?"

Stella faced him in the moonlight. She thought he looked stern. "Is not the picnic to be at the palace?" she said.

"Yes." He answered her without hesitation. "You will find Lady Harriet and Co. there. The temple on the other hand is probably deserted."

"Ah!" His meaning flashed upon her. She stood a second in indecision. Then "Is it far?" she said.

She saw his faint smile for an instant. "A very long way—for you," he said.

"I can come back?" she said.

"I shall not prevent you." She heard the smile in his voice, and something within her thrilled in answer.

"Let us go then!" she said.

He turned without further words and led the way.

They entered the shadow of the jungle once more. For a space the path ran beside the crumbling wall, then it diverged from it, winding darkly into the very heart of the jungle. Monck walked without hesitation. He evidently knew the place well.

They came at length upon a second clearing, smaller than the first, and here in the centre of a moonlit space there stood the ruined walls of a little native temple or mausoleum.

A flight of worn, marble steps led to the dark arch of the doorway. Monck stretched a hand to his companion, and they ascended side by side. A bubbling murmur of water came from within. It seemed to fill the place with gurgling, gnomelike laughter. They entered and Monck stood still.

For a space of many seconds he neither moved nor spoke. It was almost as if he were waiting for some signal. They looked forth into the moonlight they had left through the cave-like opening. The air around them was chill and dank. Somewhere in the darkness behind them a frog croaked, and tiny feet scuttled and scrambled for a few moments and then were still.

Again Stella shivered, drawing her cloak more closely round her. "Why did you bring me to this eerie place?" she said, speaking under her breath involuntarily.

He stirred as if her words aroused him from a reverie. "Are you afraid?" he said.

"I should be—— by myself," she made answer. "I don't think I like India at too close quarters. She is so mysterious and so horribly ruthless."

He passed over the last two sentences as though they had not been uttered. "But you are not afraid with me?" he said.

She quivered at something in his question. "I am not sure," she said. "I sometimes think that you are rather ruthless too."

"Do you know me well enough to say that?" he said.

She tried to answer him lightly. "I ought to by this time. I have had ample opportunity."

"Yes," he said rather bitterly. "But you are prejudiced. You cling to a preconceived idea. If you love me—it is in spite of yourself."

Something in his voice hurt her like the cry of a wounded thing. She made a quick, impulsive movement towards him. "Oh, but that is not so!" she said. "You don't understand. Please don't think anything so—so hard of me!"

"Are you sure it is not so?" he said. "Stella! Stella! Are you sure?"

The words pierced her afresh. She suddenly felt that she could bear no more. "Oh, please!" she said. "Oh, please!" and laid a quivering hand upon his arm. "You are making it very difficult for me. Don't you realize how much better it would be for your own sake not to press me any further?"

"No!" he said; just the one word, spoken doggedly, almost harshly. His hands were clenched and rigid at his sides.

Almost instinctively she began to plead with him as one who pleads for freedom. "Ah, but listen a moment! You have your life to live. Your career means very much to you. Marriage means hindrance to a man like you. Marriage means loitering by the way. And there is no time to loiter. You have taken up a big thing, and you must carry it through. You must put every ounce of yourself into it. You must work like a galley slave. If you don't you will be—a failure."

"Who told you that?" he demanded.

She met the fierceness of his eyes unflinchingly. "I know it. Everyone knows it. You have given yourself heart and soul to India, to the Empire. Nothing else counts—or ever can count now—in the same way. It is quite right that it should be so. You are a builder, and you must follow your profession. You will follow it to the end. And you will do great things,—immortal things." Her voice shook a little. "But you must keep free from all hampering burdens, all private cares. Above all, you must not think of marriage with a woman whose chief desire is to escape from India and all that India means, whose sympathies are utterly alien from her, and whose youth has died a violent death at her hands. Oh, don't you see the madness of it? Surely you must see!"

A quiver of deep feeling ran through her words. She had not meant to go so far, but she was driven, driven by a force that would not be denied. She wanted him to see the matter with her eyes. Somehow that seemed essential now. Things had gone so far between them. It was intolerable now that he should misunderstand.

But as she ceased to speak, she abruptly realized that the effect of her words was other than she intended. He had listened to her with a rigid patience, but as her words went into silence it seemed as if the iron will by which till then he had held himself in check had suddenly snapped.

He stood for a second or two longer with an odd smile on his face and that in his eyes which startled her into a momentary feeling that was almost panic; then with a single, swift movement he bent and caught her to him.

"And you think that counts!" he said. "You think that anything on earth counts—but this!"

His lips were upon hers as he ended, stopping all protest, all utterance. He kissed her hotly, fiercely, holding her so pressed that above the wild throbbing of her own heart she felt the deep, strong beat of his. His action was passionate and overwhelming. She would have withstood him, but she could not; and there was that within her that rejoiced, that exulted, because she could not. Yet as at last his lips left hers, she turned her face aside, hiding it from him that he might not see how completely he had triumphed.

He laughed a little above her bent head; he did not need to see. "Stella, you and I have got to sink or swim together. If you won't have success with me, then I will share your failure."

She quivered at his words; she was clinging to him almost without knowing it. "Oh, no! Oh, no!" she said.

His hand came gently upwards and lay upon her head. "My dear, that rests with you. I have sworn that marriage to me shall not mean bondage. If India is any obstacle between us, India will go."

"Oh, no!" she said again. "No, Everard! No!"

He bent his face to hers. His lips were on her hair. "You love me, Stella," he said.

She was silent, her breathing short, spasmodic, difficult.

His cheek pressed her forehead. "Why not own it?" he said softly. "Is it—so hard?"

She lifted her face swiftly; her arms clasped his neck. "And if—if I do,—will you let me go?" she asked him tremulously.

The smile still hovered about his lips. "No," he said.

"It is madness," she pleaded desperately.

"It is—Kismet," he made answer, and took her face between his hands looking deeply, steadily, into her eyes. "Your life is bound up with mine. You know it. Stella, you know it."

She uttered a sob that yet was half laughter. "I have done my best," she said. "Why are you so—so merciless?"

"You surrender?" he said.

She gave herself to the drawing of his hands. "Have I any choice?"

"Not if you are honest," he said.

"Ah!" She coloured rather painfully. "I have at least been honest in trying to keep you from this—this big mistake. I know you will repent it. When this—fever is past, you will regret—oh, so bitterly."

He set his jaw and all the grim strength of the man was suddenly apparent. "Shall I tell you the secret of success?" he said abruptly. "It is just never to look back. It is the secret of happiness also, if people only realized it. If you want to make the best of life, you've got to look ahead. I'm going to make you do that, Stella. You've been sitting mourning by the wayside long enough."

She smiled almost in spite of herself, for the note of mastery in his voice was inexplicably sweet. "I've thought that myself," she said. "But I'm not going to let you patch up my life with yours. If this must be—and you are sure—you are sure that it must?"

"I have spoken," he said.

She faced him resolutely. "Then India shall have us both. Now I have spoken too."

His face changed. The grimness became eagerness. "Stella, do you mean that?" he said. "It's a big sacrifice—too big for you."

Her eyes were shining as stars shine through a mist. She was drawing his head downwards that her lips might reach his. "Oh, my darling," she said, and the thrill of love triumphant was in her words, "nothing would be—too big. It simply ceases to be a sacrifice—if it is done—for your dear sake."

Her lips met his upon the words, and in that kiss she gave him all she had. It was the rich bestowal of a woman's full treasury, than which it may be there is nought greater on earth.

PART III
CHAPTER I
BLUEBEARD'S CHAMBER

Bhulwana in early spring! Bhulwana of the singing birds and darting squirrels! Bhulwana of the pines!

Stella stood in the green compound of the bungalow known as The Grand Stand, gazing down upon the green racecourse with eyes that dreamed.

The evening was drawing near. They had arrived but a few minutes before in Major Ralston's car, and the journey had taken the whole day. Her mind went back to that early hour almost in the dawning when she and Everard Monck had knelt together before the altar of the little English Church at Kurrumpore and been pronounced man and wife. Mrs. Ralston and Tommy alone had attended the wedding. The hour had been kept a strict secret from all besides. And they had gone straight forth into the early sunlight of the new day and sped away into the morning, rejoicing. A blue jay had laughed after them at starting, and a blue jay was laughing now in the budding acacia by the gate. There seemed a mocking note in its laughter, but it held gaiety as well. Listening to it, she forgot all the weary miles of desert through which they had travelled. The world was fair, very fair, here at Bhulwana. And they were alone.

There fell a step on the grass behind her; she thrilled and turned. He came and put his arm around her.

"Do you think you can stand seven days of it?" he said.

She leaned her head against him. "I want to catch every moment of them and hold it fast. How shall we make the time pass slowly?"

He smiled at the question. "Do you know, I was afraid this place wouldn't appeal to you?"

Her hand sought and closed upon his. "Ah, why not?" she said.

He did not answer her. Only, with his face bent down to hers, he said, "The past is past then?"

"For ever," she made swift reply. "But I have always loved Bhulwana—even in my sad times. Ah, listen! That is a *koïl*!"

They listened to the bird's flutelike piping, standing closely linked in the shadow of a little group of pines. In the bungalow behind them Peter the Great was decking the table for their wedding-feast. The scent of white roses was in the air, languorous, exquisite.

The blue jay laughed again in the acacia by the gate, laughed and flew away. "Good riddance!" said Monck.

"Don't you like him?" said Stella.

"I'm not particularly keen on being jeered at," he answered.

She laughed at him in her turn. "I never thought you cared a single *anna* what any one thought of you."

He smiled. "Perhaps I have got more sensitive since I knew you."

She lifted her lips to his with a sudden movement. "I am like that too, Everard. I care—terribly now."

He kissed her, and his kiss was passionate. "No one shall ever think anything but good of you, my Stella," he said.

She clung to him. "Ah, but the outside world doesn't matter," she said. "It is only we ourselves, and our secret, innermost hearts that count. Everard, let us be more than true to each other! Let us be quite, quite open—always!"

He held her fast, but he made no answer to her appeal.

Her eyes sought his. "That is possible, isn't it?" she pleaded. "My heart is open to you. There is not a single corner of it that you may not enter."

His arms clasped her closer. "I know," he said. "I know. But you mustn't be hurt or sorry if I cannot say the same. My life is a more complex affair than yours, remember."

"Ah! That is India!" she said. "But let me share that part too! Let me be a partner in all! I can be as secret as the wiliest Oriental of them all. I would so love to be trusted. It would make me so proud!"

He kissed her again. "You might be very much the reverse sometimes," he said, "if you knew some of the secrets I had to keep. India is India, and she can be very lurid upon occasion. There is only one way of treating her then; but I am not going to let you into any unpleasant secrets. That is Bluebeard's Chamber, and you have got to stay outside."

She made a small but vehement gesture in his arms. "I hate India!" she said. "She dominates you like—like—"

"Like what?" he said.

She hid her face from him. "Like a horrible mistress," she whispered.

"Stella!" he said.

She throbbed in his hold. "I had to say it. Are you angry with me?"

"No," he said.

"But you don't like me for it all the same." Her voice came muffled from his shoulder. "You don't realize—very likely you never will—how near the truth it is."

He was silent, but in the silence his hold tightened upon her till it was almost a grip.

She turned her face up again at last. "I told you it was madness to marry me," she said tremulously. "I told you you would repent."

He looked at her with a strange smile. "And I told you it was—Kismet," he said. "You did it because it was written that you should. For better for worse—" his voice vibrated—"you and I are bound by the same Fate. It was inevitable, and there can be no repentance, just as there can be no turning back. But you needn't hate India on that account. I have told you that I will give her up for your sake, and that stands. But I will not give you up for India—or for any other power on earth. Now are you satisfied?"

Her face quivered at the question. "It is—more than I deserve," she said. "You shall give up nothing for me."

He put his hand upon her forehead. "Stella, will you give her a trial? Give her a year! Possibly by that time I may tell you more than I am able to tell you now. I don't know if you would welcome it, but there are always a chosen few to whom success comes. I may be one of the few. I have a strong belief in my own particular star. Again I may fail. If I fail, I swear I will give her up. I will start again at some new job. But will you be patient for a year? Will you, my darling, let me prove myself? I only ask—one year."

Her eyes were full of tears. "Everard! You make me feel—ashamed," she said. "I won't—won't—be a drag on you, spoil your career! You must forgive me for being jealous. It is because I love you so. But I know it is a selfish form of love, and I won't give way to it. I will never separate you from the career you have chosen. I only wish I could be a help to you."

"You can only help me by being patient—just at present," he said.

"And not asking tiresome questions!" She smiled at him though her tears had overflowed. "But oh, you won't take risks, will you? Not unnecessary risks? It is so terrible to think of you in danger—to think—to think of that horrible deformed creature who sent—

Ralph—" She broke off shuddering and clinging to him. It was the first time she had ever spoken of her first husband by name to him.

He dried the tears upon her cheeks. "My own girl, you needn't be afraid," he said, and though his words were kind she wondered at the grimness of his voice. "I am not the sort of person to be disposed of in that way. Shall we talk of something less agitating? I can't have you crying on our wedding-night."

His tone was repressive. She was conscious of a chill. Yet it was a relief to turn from the subject, for she recognized that there was small satisfaction to be derived therefrom. The sun was setting moreover, and it was growing cold. She let him lead her back into the bungalow, and they presently sat down at the table that Peter had prepared with so much solicitude.

Later they lingered for awhile on the verandah, watching the blazing stars, till it came to Monck that his bride was nearly dropping with weariness and then he would not suffer her to remain any longer.

When she had gone within, he lit a pipe and wandered out alone into the starlight, following the deserted road that led to the Rajah's summer palace.

He paced along slowly with bent head, deep in thought. At the great marble gateway that led into the palace-garden he paused and stood for a space in frowning contemplation. A small wind had sprung up and moaned among the cypress-trees that overlooked the high wall. He seemed to be listening to it. Or was it to the hoot of an owl that came up from the valley?

Finally he drew near and deliberately tapped the ashes from his half-smoked pipe upon the shining marble. The embers smouldered and went out. A black stain remained upon the dazzling white surface of the stone column. He looked at it for a moment or two, then turned and retraced his steps with grim precision.

When he reached the bungalow, he turned into the room in which they had dined; and sat down to write.

Time passed, but he took no note of it. It was past midnight ere he thrust his papers together at length and rose to go.

The main passage of the bungalow was bright with moonlight as he traversed it. A crouching figure rose up from a shadowed doorway at his approach. Peter the Great looked at him with reproach in his eyes.

Monck stopped short. He accosted the man in his own language, but Peter made answer in the careful English that was his pride.

"Even so, *sahib*, I watch over my *mem-sahib* until you come to her. I keep her safe by night as well as by day. I am her servant."

He stood back with dignity that Monck might pass, but Monck stood still. He looked at Peter with a level scrutiny for a few moments. Then: "It is enough," he said, with brief decision. "When I am not with your *mem-sahib*, I look to you to guard her."

Peter made his stately *salaam*. Without further words, he conveyed the fact that without his permission no man might enter the room behind him and live.

Very softly Monck turned the handle of the door and passed within, leaving him alone in the moonlight.

CHAPTER II
EVIL TIDINGS

They walked on the following morning over the pine-clad hill and down into the valley beyond, a place of running streams and fresh spring verdure. Stella revelled in its sweetness. It made her think of Home.

"You haven't told me anything about your brother," she said, as they sat together on a grey boulder and basked in the sunshine.

"Haven't I?" Monck spoke meditatively. "I've got a photograph of him somewhere. You must see it. You'll like my brother," he added, with a smile. "He isn't a bit like me."

She laughed. "That's a recommendation certainly. But tell me what he is like! I want to know."

Monck considered. "He is a short, thick-set chap, stout and red, rather like a comedian in face. I think he appreciates a joke more than any one I know."

"He sounds a dear!" said Stella; and added with a gay side-glance, "and certainly not in the least like you. Have you written yet to break the news of your very rash marriage?"

"Yes, I wrote two days ago. He will probably cable his blessing. That is the sort of chap he is."

"It will be rather a shock for him," Stella observed. "You had no idea of changing your state when you saw him last summer."

There fell a somewhat abrupt silence. Monck was filling his pipe and the process seemed to engross all his thoughts. Finally, rather suddenly, he spoke. "As a matter of fact, I didn't see him last summer."

"You didn't see him!" Stella opened her eyes wide. "Not when you went Home?"

"I didn't go Home." Monck's eyes were still fixed upon his pipe. "No one knows that but you," he said, "and one other. That is the first secret out of Bluebeard's chamber that I have confided in you. Keep it close!"

Stella sat and gazed; but he would not meet her eyes. "Tell me," she said at last, "who is the other? The Colonel?"

He shook his head. "No, not the Colonel, You mustn't ask questions, Stella, if I ever expand at all. If you do, I shall shut up like a clam, and you may get pinched in the process."

She slipped her hand through his arm. "I will remember," she said. "Thank you—ever so much—for telling me. I will bury it very deep. No one shall ever suspect it through me."

"Thanks," he said. He pressed her hand, but he kept his eyes lowered. "I know I can trust you. You won't try to find out the things I keep back."

"Oh, never!" she said. "Never! I shall never try to pry into affairs of State."

He smiled rather cynically. "That is a very wise resolution," he said. "I shall tell Bernard that I have married the most discreet woman in the Empire—as well as the most beautiful."

"Did you marry her for her beauty or for her discretion?" asked Stella.

"Neither," he said.

"Are you sure?" She leaned her cheek against his shoulder. "It's no good pretending with me you know, I can see through anything, detect any disguise, so far as you are concerned."

"Think so?" said Monck.

"Answer my question!" she said.

"I didn't know you asked one." His voice was brusque; he pushed his pipe into his mouth without looking at her.

She reached up and daringly removed it. "I asked what you married me for," she said. "And you suck your horrid pipe and won't even look at me."

His arm went round her. He looked down into her eyes and she saw the fiery worship in his own. For a moment its intensity almost frightened her. It was like the red fire of a volcano rushing forth upon her—a fierce, unshackled force. For a space he held her so, gazing at her; then suddenly he crushed her to him, he kissed her burningly till she felt as if caught and consumed by the flame.

"My God!" he said passionately. "Can I put—that—into words?"

She clung to him, but she was trembling. There was that about him at the moment that startled her. She was in the presence of something terrible, something she could not fathom. There was more than rapture in his passion. It was poignant with a fierce defiance that challenged all the world.

She lay against his breast in silence while the storm that she had so unwittingly raised spent itself. Then at last as his hold began to slacken she took courage.

She laid her cheek against his hand. "Ah, don't love me too much at first, darling," she said. "Give me the love that lasts!"

"And you think my love will not last?" he said, his voice low and very deep.

She softly kissed the hand she held. "No, I didn't say—or mean—that. I believe it is the greatest thing that I shall ever possess. But—shall I tell you a secret? There is something in it that frightens me—even though I glory in it."

"My dear!" he said.

She raised her lips again to his. "Yes, I know. That is foolish. But I don't know you yet, remember. I have never yet seen you angry with me."

"You never will," he said.

"Yes, I shall." Her eyes were gazing into his, but they saw beyond. "There will come a day when something will come between us. It may be only a small thing, but it will not seem small to you. And you will be angry because I do not see with your eyes. And I think the very greatness of your love will make it harder for us both. You mustn't worship me, Everard. I am only human. And you will be so bitterly disappointed afterwards when you discover my limitations."

"I will risk that," he said.

"No. I don't want you to take any risks. If you set up an idol, and it falls, you may be—I think you are—the kind of man to be ruined by it."

She spoke very earnestly, but his faint smile told her that her words had failed to convince.

"Are you really afraid of all that?" he asked curiously.

She caught her breath. "Yes, I am afraid. I don't think you know yourself, your strength, or your weakness. You haven't the least idea what you would say or do—or even feel—if you thought me unkind or unjust to you."

"I should probably sulk," he said.

She shook her head. "Oh, no! You would explode—sooner or later. And it would be a very violent explosion. I wonder if you have ever been really furious with any one you cared about—with Tommy for instance."

"I have," said Monck. "But I don't fancy you will get him to relate his experiences. He survived it anyway."

"You tell me!" she said.

He hesitated. "It's rather a shame to give the boy away. But there is nothing very extraordinary in it. When Tommy first came out, he felt the heat—like lots of others. He was thirsty, and he drank. He doesn't do it now. I don't mind wagering that he never will again. I stopped him."

"Everard, how?" Stella was looking at him with the keenest interest.

"Do you really want to know how?" he still spoke with slight hesitation.

"Of course I do. I suppose you were very angry with him?"

"I was—very angry. I had reason to be. He fell foul of me one night at the Club. It doesn't matter how he did it. He wasn't responsible in any case. But I had to act to keep him out of hot water. I took him back to my quarters. Dacre was away that night and I had him to myself. I kept my temper with him at first—till he showed fight and tried to kick me. Then I let him have it. I gave him a licking—such a licking as he never got at school. It sobered him quite effectually, poor little beggar." An odd note of tenderness crept through the grimness of Monck's speech. "But I didn't stop then. He had to have his lesson and he had it. When I had done with him, there was no kick left in him. He was as limp as a wet rag. But he was quite sober. And to the best of my belief he has never been anything else from that day to this. Of course it was all highly irregular, but it saved a worse row in the end." Monck's faint smile appeared. "He realized that. In fact he was game enough to thank me for it in the morning, and apologized like a gentleman for giving so much trouble."

"Oh, I'm glad he did that!" Stella said, with shining eyes. "And that was the beginning of your friendship?"

"Well, I had always liked him," Monck admitted. "But he didn't like me for a long time after. That thrashing stuck in his mind. It was a pretty stiff one certainly. He was always very polite to me, but he avoided me like the plague. I think he was ashamed. I left him alone till one day he got ill, and then I went round to see if I could do anything. He was pretty bad, and I stayed with him. We got friendly afterwards."

"After you had saved his life," Stella said.

Monck laughed. "That sort of thing doesn't count in India. If it comes to that, you saved mine. No, we came to an understanding, and we've managed to hit it ever since."

Stella got to her feet. "Were you very brutal to him, Everard?"

He reached a brown hand to her as she stood. "Of course I was. He deserved it too. If a man makes a beast of himself he need never look for mercy from me."

She looked at him dubiously. "And if a woman makes you angry—" she said.

He got to his feet and put his arm about her shoulders. "But I don't treat women like that," he said, "not even—my wife. I have quite another sort of treatment for her. It's curious that you should credit me with such a vindictive temperament. I don't know what I have done to deserve it."

She leaned her head against him. "My darling, forgive me! It is just my horrid, suspicious nature."

He pressed her to him. "You certainly don't know me very well yet," he said.

They went back to the bungalow in the late afternoon, walking hand in hand as children, supremely content.

The blue jay laughed at the gate as they entered, and Monck looked up, "Jeer away, you son of a satyr!" he said. "I was going to shoot you, but I've changed my mind. We're all friends in this compartment."

Stella squeezed his hand hard. "Everard, I love you for that!" she said simply. "Do you think we could make friends with the monkeys too?"

"And the jackals and the scorpions and the dear little *karaits*," said Monck. "No doubt we could if we lived long enough."

"Don't laugh at me!" she protested. "I am quite in earnest. There are plenty of things to love in India."

"There's India herself," said Monck.

She looked at him with resolution shining in her eyes. "You must teach me," she said.

He shook his head. "No, my dear. If you don't feel the lure of her, then you are not one of her chosen and I can never make you so. She is either a goddess in her own right or the most treacherous old she-devil who ever sat in a heathen temple. She can be both. To love her, you must be prepared to take her either way."

They went up into the bungalow. Peter the Great glided forward like a magnificent genie and presented a scrap of paper on a salver to Monck.

He took it, opened it, frowned over it.

"The messenger arrived three hours ago, *sahib*. He could not wait," murmured Peter.

Monck's frown deepened. He turned to Stella. "Go and have tea, dear, and then rest! Don't wait for me! I must go round to the Club and get on the telephone at once."

The grimness of his face startled her. "To Kurrumpore?" she asked quickly. "Is there something wrong?"

"Not yet," he said curtly. "Don't you worry! I shall be back as soon as possible."

"Let me come too!" she said.

He shook his head. "No. Go and rest!"

He was gone with the words, striding swiftly down the path. As he passed out on to the road, he broke into a run. She stood and listened to his receding footsteps with foreboding in her heart.

"Tea is ready, my *mem-sahib*" said Peter softly behind her.

She thanked him with a smile and went in.

He followed her and waited upon her with all a woman's solicitude.

For a while she suffered him in silence, then suddenly, "Peter," she said, "what was the messenger like?"

Peter hesitated momentarily. Then, "He was old, *mem-sahib*," he said, "old and ragged, not worthy of your august consideration."

She turned in her chair. "Was he—was he anything like—that—that holy man—Peter, you know who I mean?" Her face was deathly as she uttered the question.

"Let my *mem-sahib* be comforted!" said Peter soothingly. "It was not the holy man—the bearer of evil tidings."

"Ah!" The words sank down through her heart like a stone dropped into a well. "But I think the tidings were evil all the same. Did he say what it was? But—" as a sudden memory shot across her, "I ought not to ask. I wish—I wish the captain—*sahib* would come back."

"Let my *mem-sahib* have patience!" said Peter gently. "He will soon come now."

The blue jay laughed at the gate gleefully, uproariously, derisively. Stella shivered.

"He is coming!" said Peter.

She started up. Monck was returning. He came up the compound like a man who has been beaten in a race. His face was grey, his eyes terrible.

Stella went swiftly to the verandah-steps to meet him. "Everard! What is it? Oh, what is it?" she said.

He took her arm, turning her back. "Have you had tea?" he said.

His voice was low, but absolutely steady. Its deadly quietness made her tremble.

"I haven't finished," she said. "I have been waiting for you."

"You needn't have done that," he said. "I won't have any, Peter," he turned on the waiting servant, "get me some brandy!"

He sat down, setting her free. But she remained beside him, and after a moment laid her hand lightly upon his shoulder, without words.

He reached up instantly, caught and held it in a grip that almost made her wince. "Stella," he said, "it's been a very short honeymoon, but I'm afraid it's over. I've got to get back at once."

"I am coming with you," she said quickly.

He looked up at her with eyes that burned with a strange intensity but he did not speak in answer.

An awful dread clutched her. She knelt swiftly down beside him. "Everard, listen! I don't care what has happened or what is likely to happen. My place is by your side—and nowhere else. I am coming with you. Nothing on earth shall prevent me."

Her words were quick and vehement, her whole being pulsated. She challenged his look with eyes of shining resolution.

His arms were round her in a moment; he held her fast. "My Stella! My wife!" he said.

She clung closely to him. "By your side, I will face anything. You know it, darling. I am not afraid."

"I know, I know," he said. "I won't leave you behind. I couldn't now. But a time will come when we shall have to separate. We've got to face that."

"Wait till it comes!" she whispered. "It isn't—yet."

He kissed her on the lips. "No, not yet, thank heaven. You want to know what has happened. I will tell you. Ermsted—you know Ermsted—was shot in the jungle near Khanmulla this afternoon, about half an hour ago."

"Oh, Everard!" She started back in horror and was struck afresh by the awful intentness of his eyes.

"Yes," he said. "And if I had been here to receive that message, I could have prevented it."

"Oh, Everard!" she said again.

He went on doggedly. "I ought to have been here. My agent knew I was in the place. I ought to have stayed within reach. These warnings might arrive at any time. I was a damned lunatic, and Ermsted has paid the price." He stopped, and his look changed. "Poor girl! It's been a shock to you," he said, "a beastly awakening for us both."

Stella was very pale. "I feel," she said slowly, "as if I were pursued by a remorseless fate."

"You?" he questioned. "This had nothing to do with you."

She leaned against him. "Wherever I go, trouble follows. Haven't you noticed it? It seems as if—as if—whichever way I turn—a flaming sword is stretched out, barring the way." Her voice suddenly quivered. "I know why,—oh, yes, I know why. It is because once—like the man without a wedding-garment, I found my way into a forbidden paradise. They hurled me out, Everard. I was flung into a desert of ashes. And now—now that I have dared to approach by another way—the sentence has gone forth that wherever I pass, something shall die. That dreadful man—told me on the day that Ralph was taken away from me—that the Holy Ones were angry. And—my dear—he was right. I shall never be pardoned until I have—somehow—expiated my sin."

"Stella! Stella!" He broke in upon her sharply. "You are talking wildly. Your sin, as you call it, was at the most no more than a bad mistake. Can't you put it from you?—get above it? Have you no faith? I thought all women had that."

She looked at him strangely. "I wasn't brought up to believe in God," she said. "At least not personally, not intimately. Were you?"

"Yes," he said.

"Ah!" Her eyes widened a little. "And you still believe in Him—still believe He really cares—even when things go hopelessly wrong?"

"Yes," he said again. "I can't talk about Him. But I know He's there."

She still regarded him with wonder. "Oh, my dear," she said finally, "are you behind me, or a very, very long way in front?"

He smiled faintly, grimly. "Probably a thousand miles behind," he said. "But I have been given long sight, that's all."

She rose to her feet with a sigh. "And I," she said very sadly, "am blind."

Down by the gate the blue jay laughed again, laughed and flew away.

CHAPTER III
THE BEAST OF PREY

In a darkened room Netta Ermsted lay, trembling and unnerved. As usual in cases of adversity, Mrs. Ralston had taken charge of her; but there was very little that she could do. It was more a matter for her husband's skill than for hers, and he could only prescribe absolute quiet. For Netta was utterly broken. Since the fatal moment when she had returned from a call in her 'rickshaw to find Major Burton awaiting her with the news that Ermsted had been shot on the jungle-road while riding home from Khanmulla, she had been as one distraught. They had restrained her almost forcibly from rushing forth to fling herself upon his dead body, and now that it was all over, now that the man who had loved her and whom she had never loved was in his grave, she lay prostrate, refusing all comfort.

Tessa, wide-eyed and speculative, was in the care of Mrs. Burton, alternately quarrelling vigorously with little Cedric Burton whose intellectual leanings provoked her most ardent contempt, and teasing the luckless Scooter out of sheer boredom till all the animal's ideas in life centred in a desperate desire to escape.

It was Tessa to whom Stella's pitying attention was first drawn on the day after her return to The Green Bungalow. Tommy, finding her raging in the road like a little tiger-cat over some small *contretemps* with Mrs. Burton, had lifted her on to his shoulders and brought her back with him.

"Be good to the poor imp!" he muttered to his sister. "Nobody wants her."

Certainly Mrs, Burton did not. She passed her on to Stella with her two-edged smile, and Tessa and Scooter forthwith cheerfully took up their abode at The Green Bungalow with whole-hearted satisfaction.

Stella experienced little difficulty in dealing with the child. She found herself the object of the most passionate admiration which went far towards simplifying the problem of managing her. Tessa adored her and followed her like her shadow whenever she was not similarly engrossed with her beloved Tommy. Of Monck she stood in considerable awe. He did not take much notice of her. It seemed to Stella that he had retired very deeply into his shell of reserve during those days. Even with herself he was reticent, monosyllabic, obviously absorbed in matters of which she had no knowledge.

But for her small worshipper she would have been both lonely and anxious. For he was often absent, sometimes for hours at a stretch wholly without warning, giving no explanation upon his return. She asked no questions. She schooled herself to patience. She

76

tried to be content with the close holding of his arms when they were together and the certainty that all the desire of his heart was for her alone. But she could not wholly, drive away the conviction that at the very gates of her paradise the sword she dreaded had been turned against her. They were back in the desert again, and the way to the tree of life was barred.

Perhaps it was natural that she should turn to Tessa for consolation and distraction. The child was original in all her ways. Her ideas of death were wholly devoid of tragedy, and she was too accustomed to her father's absence to feel any actual sense of loss.

"Do you think Daddy likes Heaven?" she said to Stella one day. "I hope Mother will be quick and go there too. It would be better for her than staying behind with the Rajah. I always call him 'the slithy tove.' He is so narrow and wriggly. He wanted me to kiss him once, but I wouldn't. He looked so—so mischievous." Tessa tossed her golden-brown head. "Besides, I only kiss white men."

"Hear, hear!" said Tommy, who was cleaning his pipe on the verandah. "You stick to that, my child!"

"Mother said I was very silly," said Tessa. "She was quite cross. But the Rajah only laughed in that nasty, slippy way he has and took her cigarette away and smoked it himself. I hated him for that," ended Tessa with a little gleam of the tiger-cat in her blue eyes. "It—it was a liberty."

Tommy's guffaw sounded from the verandah. It went into a greeting of Monck who came up unexpectedly at the moment and sat down on a wicker-chair to examine a handful of papers. Stella, working within the room, looked up swiftly at his coming, but if he had so much as glanced in her direction he was fully engrossed with the matter in hand ere she had time to observe it. He had been out since early morning and she had not seen him for several hours.

Tessa, who possessed at times an almost uncanny shrewdness, left her and went to stand on one leg in the doorway. "Most people," she observed, "say 'Hullo!' to their wives when they come in."

"Very intelligent of 'em," said Tommy. "Do you think the Rajah does?"

"I don't know," said Tessa seriously. "I went to the palace at Bhulwana once to see them. But the Rajah wasn't there. They were very kind," she added dispassionately, "but rather silly. I don't wonder the Rajah likes white men's wives best."

"Oh, quite natural," agreed Tommy.

"He gave Mother a beautiful ring with a diamond in it," went on Tessa, delighted to have secured his attention and watching furtively for some sign of interest from Monck also. "It was worth hundreds and hundreds of pounds. That was the last thing Daddy was cross about. He was cross."

"Why?" asked Tommy.

"'Cos he was jealous, I expect," said Tessa wisely. "I thought he was going to give her a whipping. And I hid in his dressing-room to see. Mother was awful frightened. She went down on her knees to him. And he was just going to do it. I know he was. And then he came into the dressing-room and found me. And so he whipped me instead." Tessa ended on a note of resentment.

"Served you jolly well right," said Tommy.

"No, it didn't," said Tessa. "He only did it 'cos Mother had made him angry. It wasn't a child's whipping at all. It was a grown-up's whipping. And he used a switch. And it hurt—worse than anything ever hurt before. That's why I didn't mind when he went to Heaven the other day. I hope I shan't go there for a long time yet. It isn't nice to be whipped like that. And I wasn't going to say I was sorry either. I knew that would make him crosser than anything."

"Poor chap!" said Tommy suddenly.

Tessa came a step nearer to him. "*Ayah* says the man who did it will be hanged if they catch him," she said. "If it is the Rajah, will you manage so as I can go and see? I should like to."

"Tessa!" exclaimed Stella.

Tessa turned flushed cheeks and shining eyes upon her. "I would!" she declared stoutly. "I would! There's nothing wrong in that. He's a horrid man. It isn't wrong, is it, Captain Monck? But if he shot my Daddy?" She went swiftly to Monck with the words and leaned ingratiatingly against him. "You'd kill a man yourself that did a thing like that, wouldn't you?"

"Very likely," said Monck.

She gazed at him admiringly. "I expect you've killed lots and lots of men, haven't you?" she said.

He smiled with a touch of grimness. "Do you think I'm going to tell a scaramouch like you?" he said.

"Everard!" Stella rose and came to the window. "Do—please—make her understand that people don't murder each other just whenever they feel like it—even in India!"

He raised his eyes to hers, and an odd sense of shock went through her. It was as if in some fashion he had deliberately made her aware of that secret chamber which she might not enter. "I think you would probably be more convincing on that point than I should," he said.

She gave a little shudder; she could not restrain it. That look in his eyes reminded her of something, something dreadful. What was it? Ah yes, she remembered now. He had had that look on that night of terror when he had first called her his wife, when he had barred the window behind her and sworn to slay any man who should come between them.

She turned aside and went in without another word. India again! India the savage, the implacable, the ruthless! She felt as a prisoner who battered fruitlessly against an iron door.

Tessa's inquisitive eyes followed her. "She's going to cry," she said to Monck.

Tommy turned sharply upon his friend with accusation in his glance, but the next instant he summoned Tessa as if she had been a terrier and walked off into the compound with the child capering at his side.

Monck sat for a moment or two looking straight before him; then he packed together the papers in his hand and stepped through the open window into the room behind. It was empty.

He went through it without a pause, and turned along the passage to the door of his wife's room. It stood half-open. He pushed it wider and entered.

She was standing by her dressing-table, but she turned at his coming, turned and faced him.

He came straight to her and took her by the shoulders. "What is the matter?" he said.

She met his direct look, but there was shrinking in her eyes. "Everard," she said, "there are times when you make me afraid."

"Why?" he said.

She could not put it into words. She made a piteous gesture with her clasped hands.

His expression changed, subtly softening. "I can't always wear kid gloves, my Stella," he said. "When there is rough work to be done, we have to strip to the waist sometimes to get to it. It's the only way to get a sane grip on things."

Her lips were quivering. "But you—you like it!" she said.

He smiled a little. "I plead guilty to a sporting instinct," he said.

"You hunt down murderers—and call it—sport!" she said slowly.

"No, I call it justice." He still spoke gently though his face had hardened again. "That child has a sense of justice, quite elementary, but a true one. If I could get hold of the man who killed Ermsted, I would cheerfully kill him with my own hand—unless I could be sure that he would get his deserts from the Government who are apt to be somewhat slack in such matters."

Stella shivered again. "Do you know, Everard, I can't bear to hear you talk like that? It is the untamed, savage part of you."

He drew her to him. "Yes, the soldier part. I know. I know quite well. But my dear, do me the justice at least to believe that I am on the side of right! I can't do other than talk generalities to you. You simply wouldn't understand. But there are some criminals who can only be beaten with their own weapons, remember that. Nicholson knew that—and applied it. I follow—or try to follow—in Nicholson's steps."

She clung to him suddenly and closely. "Oh, don't—don't! This is another age. We have advanced since then."

"Have we?" he said sombrely. "And do you think the India of to-day can be governed by weakness any more successfully than the India of Nicholson's time? You have no idea what you say when you talk like that. Ermsted is not the first Englishman to be killed in this State. The Rajah of Markestan is too wily a beast to go for the large game at the outset, though—probably—the large game is the only stuff he cares about. He knows too well that there are eyes that watch perpetually, and he won't expose himself—if he can help it. The trouble is he doesn't always know where to look for the eyes that watch."

A certain exultation sounded in his voice, but the next instant he bent and kissed her.

"Why do you dwell on these things? They only trouble you. But I think you might remember that since they exist, someone has to deal with them."

"You don't trust Ahmed Khan?" she said. "You think he is treacherous?"

He hesitated; then: "Ahmed Khan is either a tiger or—merely a jackal," he said. "I don't know which at present. I am taking his measure."

She still held him closely. "Everard," her voice came low and breathless, "you think he was responsible for Captain Ermsted's death. May he not have been also for—for—"

He checked her sharply before Ralph Dacre's name could leave her lips. "No. Put that out of your mind for good! You have no reason to suspect foul play where he was concerned."

He spoke with such decision that she looked at him in surprise. "I often have suspected it," she said.

"I know. But you have no reason for doing so. I should try to forget it if I were you. Let the past be past!"

It was evident that he would not discuss the matter, and, wondering somewhat, she let it pass. The bare mention of Dacre seemed to be unendurable to him. But the suspicion which his words had started remained in her mind, for it was beyond her power to dismiss it. The conviction that he had met his death by foul means was steadily gaining ground within her, winding serpent-like ever more closely about her shrinking heart.

Monck went his way, whether deeply disappointed or not she knew not. But she realized that he would not reopen the subject. He had made his explanation, but—and for this she honoured him—he would not seek to convince her against her will. It was even possible that he preferred her to keep her own judgment in the matter.

They dined at the Mansfields' bungalow that night, a festivity for which she felt small relish, more especially as she knew that Mrs. Ralston would not be present. To be received with icy ceremony by Lady Harriet and sent in to dinner with Major Burton was a state of affairs that must have dashed the highest spirits. She tried to make the best of it, but it was impossible to be entirely unaffected by the depressing chill of the atmosphere. Conversation turned upon Mrs. Ermsted, regarding whom the report had gone forth that she was very seriously ill. Lady Harriet sought to probe Stella upon the subject and was plainly offended when she pleaded ignorance. She also tried to extract Monck's opinion of poor Captain Ermsted's murder. Had it been committed by a mere *budmash* for the sake of robbery, or did he consider that any political significance was attached to it? Monck drily expressed the opinion that something might be said for either theory. But when Lady Harriet threw discretion to the winds and desired to know if it were generally believed in official circles that the Rajah was implicated, he raised his brows in stern surprise and replied that so far as his information went the Rajah was a loyal servant of the Crown.

Lady Harriet was snubbed, and she felt the effects of it for the rest of the evening. Walking home with her husband through the starlight later, Stella laughed a little over the episode; but Monck was not responsive. He seemed engrossed in thought.

He went with her to her room, and there bade her good-night, observing that he had work to do and might be late.

"It is already late," she said. "Don't be long! I shall only lie awake till you come."

He frowned at her. "I shall be very angry if you do."

"I can't help that," she said. "I can't sleep properly till you come."

He looked her in the eyes. "You're not nervous? You've got Peter."

"Oh, I am not in the least nervous on my own account," she told him.

"You needn't be on mine," he said.

She laughed, but her lips were piteous. "Well, don't be long anyway!" she pleaded. "Don't forget I am waiting for you!"

"Forget!" he said. For an instant his hold upon her was passionate. He kissed her fiercely, blindly, even violently; then with a muttered word of inarticulate apology he let her go.

She heard him stride away down the passage, and in a few moments Peter came and very softly closed the door. She knew that he was there on guard until his master should return.

She sat down with a beating heart and leaned back with closed eyes. A heavy sense of foreboding oppressed her. She was very tired, but yet she knew that sleep was far away. Just as once she had felt a dread that was physical on behalf of Ralph Dacre, so now she felt weighed down by suspense and loneliness. Only now it was a thousand times magnified, for this man was her world. She tried to picture to herself what it would have meant to her had that shot in the jungle slain him instead of Captain Ermsted. But the bare thought was beyond endurance. Once she could have borne it, but not now—not now! Once she could have denied her love and fared forth alone into the desert. But he had captured her, and now she was irrevocably his. Her spirit pined almost unconsciously whenever he was absent from her. Her body knew no rest without him. From the moment of his leaving her, she was ever secretly on fire for his return.

Had they been in England she knew that it would have been otherwise. In a calm and temperate atmosphere she could have attained a serene, unruffled happiness. But India, fevered and pitiless, held her in scorching grip. She dwelt as it were on the edge of a roaring furnace that consumed some victims every day. Her life was strung up to a pitch that frightened her. The very intensity of the love that Everard Monck had practically forced into being within her was almost more than she could bear. It hurt her like the searing of a flame, and yet in the hurt there was rapture. For the icy blast of the desert could never reach her now. Unless—unless—ah, was there not a flaming sword still threatening her wherever she pitched her camp? Surround herself as she would with the magic essences of love, did not the vengeance await her—even now—even now? Could she ever count herself safe so long as she remained in this land of treachery and terrible vengeance? Could there ever be any peace so near to the burning fiery furnace?

Slowly the night wore on. The air blew in cool and pure with a soft whispering of spring and the brief splendour of the rose-time. The howl of a prowling jackal came now and then to her ears, making her shiver with the memory of Monck's words. Away in the jungle the owls were calling upon notes that sounded like weird cries for help.

Once or twice she heard a shuffling movement outside the door and knew that Peter was still on guard. She wondered if he ever slept. She wondered if Tommy had returned. He often dropped into the Club on his way back, and sometimes stayed late. Then, realizing how late it was, she came to the conclusion that she must have dozed in her chair.

She got up with a sense of being weighted in every limb, and began to undress. Everard would be vexed if he returned and found her still up. Not that she expected him to return for a long time. His absence lasted sometimes till the night was nearly over.

She never questioned him regarding it, and he never told her anything. Dacre's revelation on that night so long ago had never left her memory. He was engaged upon secret affairs. Possibly he was down in the native quarter, disguised as a native, carrying his life in his hand. He had a friend in the bazaar, she knew; a man she had never seen, but whose shop he had once pointed out to her though he would not suffer her—and indeed she had no desire—to enter. This man—Rustam Karin—was a dealer in native charms and trinkets. The business was mainly conducted by a youth of obsequious and insincere demeanour called Hafiz. The latter she knew and instinctively disliked, but her feeling for the unknown master was one of more active aversion. In the depths of that dark native stall she pictured him, a watcher, furtive and avaricious, a man who lent himself and his shrewd and covetous brain to a Government he probably despised as alien.

Tommy had once described the man to her and her conception of him was a perfectly clear one. He was black-bearded and an opium-smoker, and she hated to think of Everard as in any sense allied with him. Dark, treacherous, and terrible, he loomed in her imagination. He represented India and all her subtleties. He was a serpent underfoot, a knife in the dark, an evil dream.

She could not have said why the personality of a man she did not know so affected her, save that she believed that all Monck's secret expeditions were conceived in the gloom of that stall she had never entered in the heart of the native bazaar. The man was in Monck's confidence. Perhaps, being a woman, that hurt her also. For though she recognized—as in the case of that native lair down in the bazaar—that it were better never to set foot in that secret chamber, yet she resented the thought that any other should have free access to it. She was beginning to regard that part of Monck's life with a dread that verged upon horror—a feeling which her very love for the man but served to intensify. She was as one clinging desperately to a treasure which might at any moment be wrested from her.

Stiffly and wearily she undressed. Tommy must surely have returned ages ago, though probably late, or he would have come to bid her good-night. Why did not Everard return?

At the last she extinguished her light and went to the window to gaze wistfully out across the verandah. That secret whispering—the stirring of a thousand unseen things—was abroad in the night. The air was soft and scented with a fragrance intangible but wholly sweet. India, stretched out beneath the glittering stars, stirred with half-opened eyes, and smiled. Stella thought she heard the flutter of her robe.

Then again the mystery of the night was rent by the cry of some beast of prey, and in a second the magic was gone. The shadows were full of evil. She drew back with swift, involuntary shrinking; and as she did so, she heard the dreadful answering cry of the prey that had been seized.

India again! India the ruthless! India the bloodthirsty! India the vampire!

For a few palpitating moments she leaned against the wall feeling physically sick. And as she leaned, there passed before her inner vision the memory of that figure which she had seen upon the verandah on that terrible night when Everard had been stricken with fever. The look in her husband's eyes that day had brought it back to her, and now like a flashlight it leapt from point to point of her brain, revealing, illuminating.

That figure on the verandah and the unknown man of the bazaar were one. It was Rustam Karin whom she had seen that night—Rustam Karin, Everard's trusted friend and ally—the Rajah's tool also though Everard would never have it so—and (she was certain of it now with that certainty which is somehow all the greater because without proof) this was the man who had followed Ralph Dacre to Kashmir and lured him to his death. This was the beast of prey who when the time was ripe would destroy Everard Monck also.

CHAPTER IV
THE FLAMING SWORD

The conviction which came upon Stella on that night of chequered starlight was one which no amount of sane reasoning could shake. She made no attempt to reopen the subject with Everard, recognizing fully the futility of such a course; for she had no shadow of proof to support it. But it hung upon her like a heavy chain. She took it with her wherever she went.

More than once she contemplated taking Tommy into her confidence. But again that lack of proof deterred her. She was certain that Tommy would give no credence to her theory. And his faith in Monck—his wariness, his discretion—was unbounded.

She did question Peter with regard to Rustam Karin, but she elicited scant satisfaction from him. Peter went but little to the native bazaar, and like herself had never seen the man. He appeared so seldom and then only by night. There was a rumour that he was leprous. This was all that Peter knew.

And so it seemed useless to pursue the matter. She could only wait and watch. Some day the man might emerge from his lair, and she would be able to identify him beyond all dispute. Peter could help her then. But till then there was nothing that she could do. She was quite helpless.

So, with that shrinking still strongly upon her that made all mention of Ralph Dacre's death so difficult, she buried the matter deep in her own heart, determined only that she also would watch with a vigilance that never slackened until the proof for which she waited should be hers.

The weeks had begun to slip by with incredible swiftness. The tragedy of Ermsted's death had ceased to be the talk of the station. Tessa had gone back to her mother who still remained a semi-invalid in the Ralstons' hospitable care. Netta's plans seemed to be of the vaguest; but Home leave was due to Major Ralston the following year, and it seemed likely that she would drift on till then and return in their company.

Stella did not see very much of her friend in those days. Netta, exacting and peevish, monopolized much of the latter's time and kept her effectually at a distance. The days were growing hotter moreover, and her energies flagged, though all her strength was concentrated upon concealing the fact from Everard. For already the annual exodus to Bhulwana was being discussed, and only the possibility that the battalion might be moved to a healthier spot for the summer had deferred it for so long.

Stella clung to this possibility with a hope that was passionate in its intensity. She had a morbid dread of separation, albeit the danger she feared seemed to have sunk into obscurity during the weeks that had intervened. If there yet remained unrest in the State, it was below the surface. The Rajah came and went in his usual romantic way, played polo with his British friends, danced and gracefully flattered their wives as of yore.

On one occasion only did he ask Stella for a dance, but she excused herself with a decision there was no mistaking. Something within her revolted at the bare idea. He went away smiling, but he never asked her again.

Definite orders for the move to Udalkhand arrived at length, and Stella's heart rejoiced. The place was situated on the edge of a river, a brown and turgid torrent in the rainy weather, but no more than a torpid, muddy stream before the monsoon. A native town and temple stood upon its banks, but a sandy road wound up to higher ground on which a few bungalows stood, overlooking the grim, parched desert below.

The jungle of Khanmulla was not more than five miles distant, and Kurrumpore itself barely ten. But yet Stella felt as if a load had been lifted from her. Surely the danger here would be more remote! And she would not need to leave her husband now. That thought set her very heart a-singing.

Monck said but little upon the subject. He was more non-committal than ever in those days. Everyone said that Udalkhand was healthier and cooler than Kurrumpore and he did not contradict the statement. But yet Stella came to perceive after a time something in his silence which she found unsatisfactory. She believed he watched her narrowly though he certainly had no appearance of doing so, and the suspicion made her nervous.

There were a few—Lady Harriet among the number—who condemned Udalkhand from the outset as impossible, and departed for Bhulwana without attempting to spend even the beginning of the hot season there. Netta Ermsted also decided against it though Mrs. Ralston declared her intention of going thither, and she and Tessa departed for that universal haven The Grand Stand before any one else.

This freed Mrs. Ralston, but Stella had grown a little apart from her friend during that period at Kurrumpore, and a measure of reserve hung between them though outwardly they were unchanged. A great languor had come upon Stella which seemed to press all the more heavily upon her because she only suffered herself to indulge it in Everard's absence. When he was present she was almost feverishly active, but it needed all her strength of will to achieve this, and she had no energy over for her friends.

Even after the move to Udalkhand had been accomplished, she scarcely felt the relief which she so urgently needed. Though the place was undoubtedly more airy than Kurrumpore, the air came from the desert, and sand-storms were not infrequent.

She made a brave show nevertheless, and with Peter's help turned their new abode into as dainty a dwelling-place as any could desire. Tommy also assisted with much readiness though the increasing heat was anathema to him also. He was more considerate for his sister just then than he had ever been before. Often in Monck's absence he would spend much of his time with her, till she grew to depend upon him to an extent she scarcely realized. He had taken up wood-carving in his leisure hours and very soon she was fully occupied with executing elaborate designs for his workmanship. They worked very happily together. Tommy declared it kept him out of mischief, for violent exercise never suited him in hot weather.

And it was hot. Every day seemed to bring the scorching reality of summer a little nearer. In spite of herself Stella flagged more and more. Tommy always kept a brave front. He was full of devices for ameliorating their discomfort. He kept the punkah-coolie perpetually at his task. He made the water-coolie spray the verandah a dozen times a day. He set traps for the flies and caught them in their swarms.

But he could not take the sun out of the sky which day by day shone from horizon to horizon as a brazen shield burnished to an intolerable brightness, while the earth—parched and cracked and barren—fainted beneath it. The nights had begun to be oppressive also. The wind from the desert was as the burning breath from a far-off forest-fire which hourly drew a little nearer. Stella sometimes felt as if a monster-hand were slowly closing upon her, crushing out her life.

But still with all her might she strove to hide from Monck the ravages of the cruel heat, even stooping to the bitter subterfuge of faintly colouring the deathly whiteness of her cheeks. For the wild-rose bloom had departed long since, as Netta Ermsted had predicted, though her beauty remained—the beauty of the pure white rose which is fairer than any other flower that grows.

There came a burning day at last, however, when she realized that the evening drive was almost beyond her powers. Tommy was on duty at the barracks. Everard had, she believed, gone down to Khanmulla to see Barnes of the Police. She decided in the absence of both to indulge in a rest, and sent Peter to countermand the carriage.

Then a great heaviness came upon her, and she yielded herself to it, lying inert upon the couch in the drawing-room dully listening to the creak of the punkah that stirred without cooling the late afternoon air.

Some time must have passed thus and she must have drifted into a species of vague dreaming that was not wholly sleep when suddenly there came a sound at the darkened window; the blind was lifted and Monck stood in the opening.

She sprang up with a startled sense of being caught off her guard, but the next moment a great dizziness came upon her and she reeled back, groping for support.

He dropped the blind and caught her. "Why, Stella!" he said.

She clung to him desperately. "I am all right—I am all right! Hold me a minute! I—I tripped against the matting." Gaspingly she uttered the words, hanging upon him, for she knew she could not stand alone.

He put her gently down upon the sofa. "Take it quietly, dear!" he said.

She leaned back upon the cushions with closed eyes, for her brain was swimming. "I am all right," she reiterated. "You startled me a little. I—didn't expect you back so soon."

"I met Barnes just after I started," he made answer. "He is coming to dine presently."

Her heart sank. "Is he?" she said faintly.

"No." Monck's tone suddenly held an odd note that was half-grim and half-protective. "On second thoughts, he can go to the Mess with Tommy. I don't think I want him any more than you do."

She opened her eyes and looked up at him. "Everard, of course he must dine here if you have asked him! Tell Peter!"

Her vision was still slightly blurred, but she saw that the set of his jaw was stubborn. He stooped after a moment and kissed her forehead. "You lie still!" he said. "And mind—you are not to dress for dinner."

He turned with that and left her.

83

She was not sorry to be alone, for her head was throbbing almost unbearably, but she would have given much to know what was in his mind.

She lay there passively till presently she heard Tommy dash in to dress for mess, and shortly after there came the sound of men's voices in the compound, and she knew that Monck and Barnes were walking to and fro together.

She got up then, summoning her energies, and stole to her own room. Monck had commanded her not to change her dress, but the haggardness of her face shocked her into taking refuge in the remedy which she secretly despised. She did it furtively, hoping that in the darkened drawing-room he had not noted the ghastly pallor which she thus sought to conceal.

Before she left her room she heard Tommy and Barnes departing, and when she entered the dining-room Monck came in alone at the window and joined her.

She met him somewhat nervously, for she thought his face was stern. But when he spoke, his voice held nought but kindness, and she was reassured. He did not look at her with any very close criticism, nor did he revert to what had passed an hour before.

They were served by Peter, swiftly and silently, Stella making a valiant effort to simulate an appetite which she was far from possessing. The windows were wide to the night, and from the river bank below there came the thrumming of some stringed instrument, which had a weird and strangely poignant throbbing, as if it voiced some hidden distress. There were a thousand sounds besides, some near, some distant, but it penetrated them all with the persistence of some small imprisoned creature working perpetually for freedom.

It began to wear upon Stella's nerves at last. It was so futile, yet so pathetic—the same soft minor tinkle, only a few stray notes played over and over, over and over, till her brain rang with the maddening little refrain. She was glad when the meal was over, and she could make the excuse to move to the drawing-room. There was a piano here, a rickety instrument long since hammered into tunelessness. But she sat down before it. Anything was better than to sit and listen to that single, plaintive little voice of India crying in the night.

She thought and hoped that Monck would smoke his cigarette and suffer himself to be lulled into somnolence by such melody as she was able to extract from the crazy old instrument; but he disappointed her.

He smoked indeed, lounging out in the verandah, while she sought with every allurement to draw him in and charm him to blissful, sleepy contentment. But it presently came to her that there was something dogged in his refusal to be so drawn, and when she realized that she brought her soft *nocturne* to a summary close and turned round to him with just a hint of resentment.

He was leaning in the doorway, the cigarette gone from his lips. His face was turned to the night. His attitude seemed to express that patience which attends upon iron resolution. He looked at her over his shoulder as she paused.

"Why don't you sing?" he said.

A little tremor of indignation went through her. He spoke with the gentle indulgence of one who humours a child. Only once had she ever sung to him, and then he had sat in such utter immobility and silence that she had questioned with herself afterwards if he had cared for it.

She rose with a wholly unconscious touch of majesty. "I have no voice to-night," she said.

"Then come here!" he said.

His voice was still absolutely gentle but it held an indefinable something that made her raise her brows.

She went to him nevertheless, and he put his hand through her arm and drew her close to his side. The night was heavy with a brooding heat-haze that blotted out the stars. The little twanging instrument down by the river was silent.

For a space Monck did not speak, and gradually the tension went out of Stella. She relaxed at length and laid her cheek against his shoulder.

His arm went round her in a moment; he held her against his heart. "Stella," he said, "do you ever think to yourself nowadays that I am a very formidable person to live with?"

"Never," she said.

His arm tightened about her. "You are not afraid of me any longer?"

She smiled a little. "What is this leading up to?"

He bent suddenly, his lips against her forehead. "Dear heart, if I am wrong—forgive me! But—why are you trying to deceive me?"

She had never heard such tenderness in his voice before; it thrilled her through and through, checking her first involuntary dismay. She hid her face upon his breast, clasping him close, trembling from head to foot.

He turned, still holding her, and led her to the sofa. They sat down together.

"Poor girl!" he said softly. "It hasn't been easy, has it?"

Then she realized that he knew all that she had so strenuously sought to hide. The struggle was over and she was beaten. A great wave of emotion went through her. Before she could check herself, she was shaken with sobs.

"No, no!" he said, and laid his hand upon her head. "You mustn't cry. It's all right, my darling. It's all right. What is there to cry about?"

She clung faster to him, and her hold was passionate. "Everard," she whispered, "Everard,—I—can't leave you!"

"Ah!" he said "We are up against it now."

"I can't!" she said again. "I can't."

His hand was softly stroking her hair. Such tenderness as she had never dreamed of was in his touch. "Leave off crying!" he said. "God knows I want to make things easier for you—not harder."

"I can bear anything," she told him brokenly, "anything in the world—if only I am with you. I can't leave you. You won't—you can't—force me to that."

"Stella! Stella!" he said.

His voice checked her. She knew that she had hurt him. She lifted her face quickly to his.

"Oh, darling, forgive me!" she said. "I know you would not."

He kissed the quivering lips she raised without words, and thereafter there fell a silence between them while the mystery of the night seemed to press closer upon them, and the veiled goddess turned in her sleep and subtly smiled.

Stella uttered a long, long sigh at last. "You are good to bear with me like this," she said rather piteously.

"Better now?" he questioned gently.

She closed her eyes from the grave scrutiny of his. "I am—quite all right, dear," she said. "And I am taking great care of myself. Please—please don't worry about me!"

His hand sought and found hers. "I have been worrying about you for a long time," he said.

She gave a start of surprise. "I never thought you noticed anything."

"Yes." With a characteristic touch of grimness he answered her. "I noticed when you first began to colour your cheeks for my benefit. I knew it was only for mine, or of course I should have been furious."

"Oh, Everard!" She hid her face against him again with a little shamed laugh.

He went on without mercy. "I am not an easy person to deceive, you know. You really might have saved yourself the trouble. I hoped you would give in sooner. That too would have saved trouble."

"But I haven't given in," she said.

His hand closed upon hers. "You would kill yourself first if I would let you," he said. "But—do you think I am going to do that?"

"It would kill me to leave you," she said.

"And what if it kills you to stay?" He spoke with sudden force. "No, listen a minute! I have something to tell you. I have been worried about you—as I said—for some time. To-day I was working in the orderly-room, and Ralston chanced to come in. He asked me how you were. I said, 'I am afraid the climate is against her. What do you think of her?' He replied, 'I'll tell you what I think of you, if you like. I think you're a damned fool.' That opened my eyes." Monck ended on the old grim note. "I thanked him for the information, and told him to come over here and see you on the earliest opportunity. He has promised to come round in the morning."

"Oh, but Everard!" Stella started up in swift protest. "I don't want him! I won't see him!"

He kept her hand in his. "I am sorry," he said. "But I am going to insist on that."

"You—insist!" She looked at him curiously, a quivering smile about her lips.

His eyes met hers uncompromisingly. "If necessary," he said.

She made a movement to free herself, but he frustrated her, gently but with indisputable mastery.

"Stella," he said, "things may be difficult. I know they are. But, my dear, don't make them impossible! Let us pull together in this as in everything else!"

She met his look steadily. "You know what will happen, don't you?" she said. "He will order me to Bhulwana."

Monck's hand tightened upon hers. "Better that," he said, under his breath, "than to lose you altogether!"

"And if it kills me to leave you?" she said. "What then?"

He made a gesture that was almost violent, but instantly restrained himself. "I think you are braver than that," he said.

Her lips quivered again piteously. "I am not brave at all," she said. "I left all my courage—all my faith—in the mountains one terrible morning—when God cursed me for marrying a man I did not love—and took—the man—- away."

"My darling!" Monck said. He drew her to him again, holding her passionately close, kissing the trembling lips till they clung to his in answer. "Can't you forget all that," he said, "put it right away from you, think only of what lies before."

Her arms were round his neck. She poured out her very soul to him in that close embrace. But she said no word in answer, and her silence was the silence of despair. It seemed to her that the flaming sword she dreaded had flashed again across her path, closing the way to happiness.

CHAPTER V
TESSA

The blue jay was still laughing on the pine-clad slopes of Bhulwana when Stella returned thither. It was glorious summer weather. There was life in the air—such life as never reached the Plains.

The bungalow up the hill, called "The Nest," which once Ralph Dacre had taken for his bride, was to be Stella's home for the period of her sojourn at Bhulwana. It was a pretty little place twined in roses, standing in a shady compound that Tessa called "the jungle." Tessa became at once her most constant visitor. She and Scooter were running wild as usual, but Netta was living in strict retirement. People said she looked very ill, but she seemed to resent all sympathy. There was an air of defiance about her which kept most people at a distance.

Stories were rife concerning her continued intimacy with the Rajah who was now in residence at his summer palace on the hill. They went for gallops together in the early morning, and in the evenings they sometimes flashed along the road in his car. But he was seldom observed to enter the bungalow she occupied, and even Tessa had no private information to add to the general gossip. Netta seldom went to race course or polo-ground, where the Rajah was most frequently to be found.

Stella, who had never liked Netta Ermsted, took but slight interest in her affairs. She always welcomed Tessa, however, and presently, since her leisure was ample and her health considerably improved, she began to give the child a few lessons which soon became the joy of Tessa's heart. She found her quick and full of enthusiasm. Her devotion to Stella made her tractable, and they became fast friends.

It was in June just before the rains, that Monck came up on a week's leave. He found Tessa practically established as Stella's companion. Her mother took no interest in her doings. The *ayah* was responsible for her safety, and even if Tessa elected to spend the night with her friend, Netta raised no objection. It had always been her way to leave the child to any who cared to look after her, since she frankly acknowledged that she was quite incapable of managing her herself. If Mrs. Monck liked to be bothered with her, it was obviously her affair, not Netta's.

And so Stella kept the little girl more and more in her own care, since Mrs. Ralston was still at Udalkhand, and no one else cared in the smallest degree for her welfare. She would not keep her for good, though, so far as her mother was concerned, she might easily have done so. But she did occasionally—as a great treat—have her to sleep with her, generally when Tessa's looks proclaimed her to be in urgent need of a long night. For she was almost always late to bed when at home, refusing to retire before her mother, though there was little of companionship between them at any time.

Stella investigated this resolution on one occasion, and finally extracted from Tessa the admission that she was afraid to go to bed early lest her mother should go out unexpectedly, in which event the *ayah* would certainly retire to the servants' quarters, and she would be alone in the bungalow. No amount of reasoning on Stella's part could shake this dread. Tessa's nerves were strung to a high pitch, and it was evident that she felt very strongly on the subject. So, out of sheer pity, Stella sometimes kept her at "The Nest," and Tessa's gratitude knew no bounds. She was growing fast, and ought to have been in England for the past year at least; but Netta's plans were still vague. She supposed she would have to go when the Ralstons did, but she saw no reason for hurry. Lady Harriet remonstrated with her on the subject, but obtained no satisfaction. Netta was her own mistress now, and meant to please herself.

Monck arrived late one evening on the day before that on which he was expected, and found Tessa and Peter playing with a ball in the compound. The two were fast friends and Stella often left Tessa in his charge while she rested.

She was resting now, lying in her own room with a book, when suddenly the sound of Tessa's voice raised in excited welcome reached her. She heard Monck's quiet voice make reply, and started up with every pulse quivering. She had not seen him for nearly six weeks.

She met him in the verandah with Tessa hanging on his arm. Since her great love for Stella had developed, she had adopted Stella's husband also as her own especial property, though it could scarcely be said that Monck gave her much encouragement. On this occasion she simply ceased to exist for him the moment he caught sight of Stella's face. And even Stella herself forgot the child in the first rapture of greeting.

But later Tessa asserted herself again with a determination that would not be ignored. She begged hard to be allowed to remain for the night; but this Stella refused to permit, though her heart smote her somewhat when she saw her finally take her departure with many wistful backward glances.

Monck was hard-hearted enough to smile. "Let the imp go! She has had more than her share already," he said. "I'm not going to divide you with any one under the sun."

Stella was lying on the sofa. She reached out and held his hand, leaning her cheek against his sleeve. "Except—" she murmured.

He bent to her, his lips upon her shining hair. "Ah, I have begun to do that already," he said, with a touch of sadness. "I wonder if you are as lonely up here as I am at Udalkhand."

She kissed his sleeve. "I miss you—unspeakably," she said.

His fingers closed upon hers. "Stella, can you keep a secret?"

She looked up swiftly. "Of course—of course. What is it? Have they made you Governor-General of the province?"

He smiled grimly. "Not yet. But Sir Reginald Bassett—you know old Sir Reggie?—came and inspected us the other day, and we had a talk. He is one of the keenest empire-builders that I ever met." An odd thrill sounded in Monck's voice. "He asked me if presently—when the vacancy occurred—I would be his secretary, his political adviser, as he put it. Stella, it would be a mighty big step up. It would lead—it might lead—to great things."

"Oh, my darling!" She was quivering all over. "Would it—would it mean that we should be together? No," she caught herself up sharply, "that is sheer selfishness. I shouldn't have asked that first."

His lips pressed hers. "Don't you know it is the one thing that comes first of all with me too?" he said. "Yes, it would mean far less of separation. It would probably mean Simla in the hot weather, and only short absences for me. It would mean an end of this beastly regimental life that you hate so badly. What? Did you think I didn't know that? But it would also mean leaving poor Tommy at the grindstone, which is hard."

"Dear Tommy! But he has lots of friends. You don't think he would get up to mischief?"

"No, I don't think so. He is more of a man than he was. And I could keep an eye on him—even from a distance. Still, it won't come yet,—not probably till the end of the year. You are fairly comfortable here—you and Peter?"

She smiled and sighed. "Oh yes, he keeps away the bogies, and Tessa chases off the blues. So I am well taken care of!"

"I hope you don't let that child wear you out," Monck said. "She is rather a handful. Why don't you leave her to her mother?"

"Because she is utterly unfit to have the care of her." Stella spoke with very unusual severity. "Since Captain Ermsted's death she seems to have drifted into a state of hopeless apathy. I can't bear to think of a susceptible child like Tessa brought up in such an atmosphere."

"Apathetic, is she? Do you often see her?" Monck spoke casually, as he rolled a cigarette.

"Very seldom. She goes out very little, and then only with the Rajah. They say she looks ill, but that is not surprising. She doesn't lead a wholesome life!"

"She keeps up her intimacy with His Excellency then?" Monck still spoke as if his thoughts were elsewhere.

Stella dismissed the subject with a touch of impatience. She had no desire to waste any precious moments over idle gossip. "I imagine so, but I really know very little. I don't encourage Tessa to talk. As you know, I never could bear the man."

Monck smiled a little. "I know you are discretion itself," he said. "But you are not to adopt Tessa, mind, whatever the state of her mother's morals!"

"Ah, but I must do what I can for the poor waif," Stella protested. "There isn't much that I can do when I am away from you,—not much, I mean, that is worth while."

"All right," Monck said with finality, "so long as you don't adopt her."

Stella saw that he did not mean to allow Tessa a very large share of her attention during his leave. She did not dispute the point, knowing that he could be as adamant when he had formed a resolution.

But she did not feel happy about the child. There was to her something tragic about Tessa, as if the evil fate that had overtaken the father brooded like a dark cloud over her also. Her mind was not at rest concerning her.

In the morning, however, Tessa arrived upon the scene, impudent and cheerful, and she felt reassured. Her next anxiety became to keep her from annoying Monck upon whom naturally Tessa's main attention was centered. Tessa, however, was in an unusually tiresome mood. She refused to be contented with the society of the ever-patient Peter, repudiated the bare idea of lesson books, and set herself with fiendish ingenuity to torment the new-comer into exasperation.

Stella could have wept over her intractability. She had never before found her difficult to manage. But Netta's perversity and Netta's devilry were uppermost in her that day, and when at last Monck curtly ordered her not to worry herself but to leave the child alone, she gave up her efforts in despair. Tessa was riding for a fall.

It came eventually, after two hours' provocation on her part and stern patience on Monck's. Stella, at work in the drawing-room, heard a sudden sharp exclamation from the verandah where Monck was seated before a table littered with Hindu literature, and looked up to see Tessa, with a monkey-like grin of mischief, smoking the cigarette which she had just snatched from between Monck's lips. She was dancing on one leg just out of reach, ready to take instant flight should the occasion require.

Stella was on the point of starting up to intervene, but Monck stopped her with a word. He was quieter than she had ever seen him, and that fact of itself warned her that he was angry at last.

"Come here!" he said to Tessa.

Tessa removed the cigarette to poke her tongue out at him, and continued her war-dance just out of reach. It was Netta to the life.

Monck glanced at the watch on his wrist. "I give you one minute," he said, and returned to his work."

"Why don't you chase me?" gibed Tessa.

He said nothing further, but to Stella his silence was ominous. She watched him with anxious eyes.

Tessa continued to smoke and dance, posturing like a *nautch-girl* in front of the wholly unresponsive and unappreciative Monck.

The minute passed, Stella counting the seconds with a throbbing heart. Monck did not raise his eyes or stir, but there was to her something dreadful in his utter stillness. She marvelled at Tessa's temerity.

Tessa continued to dance and jeer till suddenly, finding that she was making no headway, a demon of temper entered into her. She turned in a fury, sprang from the verandah to the compound, snatched up a handful of small stones and flung them full at the impassive Monck.

They fell around him in a shower. He looked up at last.

What ensued was almost too swift for Stella's vision to follow. She saw him leap the verandah-balustrade, and heard Tessa's shrill scream of fright. Then he had the offender in his grasp, and Stella saw the deadly determination of his face as he turned.

In spite of herself she sprang up, but again his voice checked her. "All right. This is my job. Bring me the strap off the bag in my room!"

"Everard!" she cried aghast.

Tessa was struggling madly for freedom. He mastered her as he would have mastered a refractory puppy, carrying her up the steps ignominiously under his arm.

"Do as I say!" he commanded.

And against her will Stella turned and obeyed. She fetched the strap, but she held it back when he stretched a hand for it.

"Everard, she is only a child. You won't—you won't——"

"Flay her with it?" he suggested, and she saw his brief, ironic smile. "Not at present. Hand it over!"

She gave it reluctantly. Tessa squealed a wild remonstrance. The merciless grip that held her had sent terror to her heart.

Monck, still deadly quiet, set her on her feet against one of the wooden posts that supported the roof of the verandah, passed the strap round her waist and buckled it firmly behind the post.

Then he stood up and looked again at the watch on his wrist. "Two hours!" he said briefly, and went back to his work at the other end of the verandah.

Stella went back to the drawing-room, half-relieved and half-dismayed. It was useless to interfere, she saw; but the punishment, though richly deserved, was a heavy one, and she wondered how Tessa, the ever-restless, wrought up to a high pitch of nervous excitement as she was, would stand it.

The thickness of the post to which she was fastened made it impossible for her to free herself. The strap was a very stout one, and the buckle such as only a man's fingers could loosen. It was an undignified position, and Tessa valued her dignity as a rule.

She cast it to the winds on this occasion, however, for she fought like a wild cat for freedom, and when at length her absolute helplessness was made quite clear even to her, she went into a paroxysm of fury, hurling every kind of invective that occurred to her at Monck who with the grimness of an executioner sat at his table in unbroken silence.

Having exhausted her vocabulary, both English and Hindustani, Tessa broke at last into tears and wept stormily for many minutes. Monck sat through the storm without raising his eyes.

From the drawing-room Stella watched him. She was no longer afraid of any unconsidered violence. He was completely master of himself, but she thought there was a hint of cruelty about him notwithstanding. There was ruthlessness in his utter immobility.

The hour for *tiffin* drew near. Peter came out on to the verandah to lay the cloth. Monck gathered up books and papers and rose.

The great Sikh looked at the child shaken with passionate sobbing in the corner of the verandah and from her to Monck with a touch of ferocity in his dark eyes. Monck met the look with a frown and turned away without a word. He passed down the verandah to his own room, and Peter with hands that shook slightly proceeded with his task.

Tessa's sobbing died down, and there fell a strained silence. Stella still sat in the drawing-room, but she was out of sight of the two on the verandah. She could only hear Peter's soft movements.

Suddenly she heard a tense whisper. "Peter! Peter! Quick!"

Like a shadow Peter crossed her line of vision. She heard a murmured, "Missy *baba*!" and rising, she bent forward and saw him in the act of severing Tessa's bond with the bread-knife. It was done in a few hard-breathing seconds. The child was free. Peter turned in triumph,—and found Monck standing at the other end of the verandah, looking at him.

Stella stepped out at the same moment and saw him also. She felt the blood rush to her heart. Only once had she seen Monck look as he looked now, and that on an occasion of which even yet she never willingly suffered herself to think.

Peter's triumph wilted. "Run, Missy *baba*!" he said, in a hurried whisper, and moved himself to meet the wrath of the gods.

Tessa did not run. Neither did she spring to Stella for protection. She stood for a second or two in indecision; then with an odd little strangled cry she darted in front of Peter, and went straight to Monck.

"It—it wasn't Peter's fault!" she declared breathlessly. "I told him to!"

Monck's eyes went over her head to the native beyond her. He spoke—a few, brief words in the man's own language—and Peter winced as though he had been struck with a whip, and bent himself in an attitude of the most profound humility.

Monck spoke again curtly, and as if at the sudden jerk of a string the man straightened himself and went away.

Then Tessa, weeping, threw herself upon Monck. "Do please not be angry with him! It was all my fault. You—you—you can whip me if you like! Only you mustn't be cross with Peter! It isn't—it isn't—fair!"

He stood stiffly for a few seconds, as if he would resist her; and Stella leaned against the window-frame, feeling physically sick as she watched him. Then abruptly his eyes came to hers, and she saw his face change. He put his hand on Tessa's shoulder.

"If you want forgiveness for yourself—and Peter," he said grimly, "go back to your corner and stay there!"

Tessa lifted her tear-stained face, looked at him closely for a moment, then turned submissively and went back.

Monck came down the verandah to his wife. He put his arm around her, and drew her within.

"Why are you trembling?" he said.

She leaned her head against him. "Everard, what did you say to Peter?"

"Never mind!" said Monck.

She braced herself. "You are not to be angry with him. He—is my servant. I will reprimand him—if necessary."

"It isn't," said Monck, with a brief smile. "You can tell him to finish laying the cloth."

He kissed her and let her go, leaving her with a strong impression that she had behaved foolishly. If it had not been for that which she had seen in his eyes for those few awful seconds, she would have despised herself for her utter imbecility. But the memory was one which she could not shake from her. She did not wonder that even Peter, proud Sikh as he was, had quailed before that look. Would Monck have accepted even Tessa's appeal if he had not found her watching? She wondered. She wondered.

She did not look forward to the meal on the verandah, but Monck realized this and had it laid in the dining-room instead. At his command Peter carried a plate out to Tessa, but it came back untouched, Peter explaining in a very low voice that 'Missy *baba* was not hungry.' The man's attitude was abject. He watched Monck furtively from behind Stella's chair, obeying his every behest with a promptitude that expressed the most complete submission.

Monck bestowed no attention upon him. He smiled a little when Stella expressed concern over Tessa's failure to eat anything. It was evident that he felt no anxiety on that score himself. "Leave the imp alone!" he said. "You are not to worry yourself about her any more. You have done more than enough in that line already."

There was insistence in his tone—an insistence which he maintained later when he made her lie down for her afternoon rest, steadily refusing to let her go near the delinquent until she had had it.

Greatly against her will she yielded the point, protesting that she could not sleep nevertheless. But when he had gone she realized that the happenings of the morning had wearied her more than she knew. She was very tired, and she fell into a deep sleep which lasted for nearly two hours.

Awakening from this, she got up with some compunction at having left the child so long, and went to her window to look for her. She found the corner of Tessa's punishment empty. A little further along the verandah Monck lounged in a deep cane chair, and, curled in his arms asleep with her head against his neck was Tessa.

Monck's eyes were fixed straight before him. He was evidently deep in thought. But the grim lines about his mouth were softened, and even as Stella looked he stirred a little very cautiously to ease the child's position. Something in the action sent the tears to her eyes. She went back into her room, asking herself how she had ever doubted for a moment the goodness of his heart.

Somewhere down the hill the blue jay was laughing hilariously, scoffingly, as one who marked, with cynical amusement the passing show of life; and a few seconds later the Rajah's car flashed past, carrying the Rajah and a woman wearing a cloudy veil that streamed far out behind her.

CHAPTER VI
THE ARRIVAL

Two months later, on a dripping evening in August, Monck stood alone on the verandah of his bungalow at Udalkhand with a letter from Stella in his hand. He had hurried back from duty on purpose to secure it, knowing that it would be awaiting him. She had become accustomed to the separation now, though she spoke yearningly of his next leave. Mrs. Ralston had joined her, and she wrote quite cheerfully. She was very well, and looking forward—oh, so much—to the winter. There was certainly no sadness to be detected between the lines, and Monck folded up the letter and looked across the dripping compound with a smile in his eyes.

When the winter came, he would probably have taken up his new appointment. Sir Reginald Bassett—a man of immense influence and energy—was actually in Udalkhand at that moment. He was ostensibly paying a friendly visit at the Colonel's bungalow, but Monck knew well what it was that had brought him to that steaming corner of Markestan in the very worst of the rainy season. He had come to make some definite arrangement with him. Probably before that very night was over, he would have begun to gather the fruit of his ambition. He had started already to climb the ladder, and he would raise Stella with him, Stella and that other being upon whom he sometimes suffered his thoughts to dwell with a semi-humorous contemplation as—his son. A fantastic fascination hung about the thought. He could not yet visualize himself as a father. It was easier far to picture Stella as a mother. But yet, like a magnet drawing him, the vision seemed to beckon. He walked the desert with a lighter step, and Tommy swore that he was growing younger.

There was an enclosure in Stella's letter from Tessa, who called him her darling Uncle Everard and begged him to come soon and see how good she was getting. He smiled a little over this also, but with a touch of wonder. The child's worship seemed extraordinary to him. His conquest of Tessa had been quite complete, but it was odd that in consequence of it she should love him as she loved no one else on earth. Yet that she did so was an indubitable fact. Her devotion exceeded even that of Tommy, which was saying much. She seemed to regard him as a sacred being, and her greatest pleasure in life was to do him service.

He put her letter away also, reflecting that he must manage somehow to make time to answer it. As he did so, he heard Tommy's voice hail him from the compound, and in a moment the boy raced into sight, taking the verandah steps at a hop, skip, and jump.

"Hullo, old chap! Admiring the view eh? What? Got some letters? Have you heard from your brother yet?"

"Not a word for weeks." Monck turned to meet him. "I can't think what has happened to him."

"Can't you though? I can!" Tommy seized him impetuously by the shoulders; he was rocking with laughter. "Oh, Everard, old boy, this beats everything! That brother of yours is coming along the road now. And he's travelled all the way from Khanmulla in a—in a bullock-cart!"

"What?" Monck stared in amazement. "Are you mad?" he inquired.

"No—no. It's true! Go and see for yourself, man! They're just getting here, slow and sure. He must be well stocked with patience. Come on! They're stopping at the gate now."

He dragged his brother-in-law to the steps. Monck went, half-suspicious of a hoax. But he had barely reached the path below when through the rain there came the sound of wheels and heavy jingling.

"Come on!" yelled Tommy. "It's too good to miss!"

But ere they arrived at the gate it was blocked by a massive figure in a streaming black mackintosh, carrying a huge umbrella. "I say," said a soft voice, "what a damn' jolly part of the world to live in!"

"Bernard!" Monck's voice sounded incredulous, yet he passed Tommy at a bound.

"Hullo, my boy, hullo!" Cheerily the newcomer made answer. "How do you open this beastly gate? Oh, I see! Swelled a bit from the rain. I must see to that for you presently. Hullo, Everard! I chanced to find myself in this direction so thought I would look up you and your wife. How are you, my boy?"

An immense hand came forth and grasped Monck's. A merry red face beamed at him from under the great umbrella. Twinkling eyes with red lashes shone with the utmost good-will.

Monck gripped the hand as if he would never let it go. But "My good man, you're mad to come here!" were the only words of welcome he found to utter.

"Think so?" A humorous chuckle accompanied the words. "Well, take me indoors and give me a drink! There are a few traps in the cart outside. Had we better collect 'em first?"

"I'll see to them," volunteered Tommy, whose sense of humour was still somewhat out of control. "Take him in out of the rain, Everard! Send the *khit* along!"

He was gone with the words, and Everard, with his brother's hand pulled through his arm, piloted him up to the bungalow.

In the shelter of the verandah they faced each other, the one brother square and powerful, so broad as to make his height appear insignificant; the other, brown, lean, muscular, a soldier in every line, his dark, resolute face a strange contrast to the ruddy open countenance of the man who was the only near relation he possessed in the world.

"Well,—boy! I believe you've grown." The elder brother, surveyed the younger with his shrewd, twinkling eyes. "By Jove, I'm sure you have! I used not to have to look up to you like this. Is it this devilish climate that does it? And what on earth do you live on? You look a positive skeleton."

"Oh, that's India, yes." Everard brushed aside all personal comment as superfluous. "Come along in and refresh! What particular star have you fallen from? And why in thunder didn't you say you were coming?"

The elder man laughed, slapping him on the shoulder with hearty force. His clean-shaven face was as free from care as a boy's. He looked as if life had dealt kindly with him.

"Ah, I know you," he said. "Wouldn't you have written off post-haste—if you hadn't cabled—and said, 'Wait till the rains are over?' But I had raised my anchor and I didn't mean to wait. So I dispensed with your brotherly counsel, and here I am! You won't find me in the way at all. I'm dashed good at effacing myself."

"My dear good chap," Everard said, "you're about the only man in the world who need never think of doing that."

Bernard's laugh was good to hear. "Who taught you to turn such a pretty compliment? Where is your wife? I want to see her."

"You don't suppose I keep her in this filthy place, do you?" Everard was pouring out a drink as he spoke. "No, no! She has been at Bhulwana in the Hills for the past three months. Now, St. Bernard, is this as you like it?"

The big man took the glass, looking at him with a smile of kindly criticism. "Well, you won't bore each other at that rate, anyhow," he remarked. "Here's to you both! I drink to the greatest thing in life!" He drank deeply and set down the glass. "Look here! You're just off to mess. Don't let me keep you! All I want is a cold bath. And then—if you've got a spare shakedown of any sort—going to bed is mere ritual with me. I can sleep on my head—anywhere."

"You'll sleep in a decent bed," declared Everard. "But you're coming along to mess with me first. Oh yes, you are. Of course you are! There's an hour before us yet though. Hullo, Tommy! Let me introduce you formally to my brother! St. Bernard,—my brother-in-law Tommy Denvers."

Tommy came in through the window and shook hands with much heartiness.

"The *khit* is seeing to everything. Pleased to meet you, sir! Beastly wet for you, I'm afraid, but there's worse things than rain in India. Hope you had a decent voyage."

Bernard laughed in his easy, good-humoured fashion. "Like the niggers, I can make myself comfortable most anywheres. We had rather a foul time after leaving Aden. Ratting in the hold was our main excitement when we weren't sweating at the pumps. Oh no, I didn't come over in one of your majestic liners. I have a sailor's soul."

A flicker of admiration shot through the merriment in Tommy's eyes. "Wish I had," he observed. "But the very thought of the sea turns mine upside down. If you're keen on ratting, there's plenty of sport of that kind to be had here. The brutes hold gymkhanas on the verandah every, night. I sit up with a gun sometimes when Everard is out of the way."

"Yes, he's a peaceful person to live with," remarked Everard. "Have something to eat, St. Bernard!"

"No, no, thanks! My appetite will keep. A cold bath is my most pressing need. Can I have that?"

"Sure!" said Tommy. "You're coming to mess with us of course? Old Reggie Bassett is honouring us with his presence to-night. It will be a historic occasion, eh, Everard?"

He smiled upon the elder brother with obvious pleasure at the prospect. Bernard Monck always met with a welcome wherever he went, and Tommy was prepared to like any one belonging to Everard. It was good too to see Everard with that eager light in his eyes. During the whole of their acquaintance he had never seen him look so young.

Bernard held a somewhat different opinion, however, and as he found himself alone again with his brother he took him by the shoulders, and held him for a closer survey.

"What has India been doing to you, dear fellow?" he said. "You look about as ancient as the Sphinx. Been working like a dray-horse all this time?"

"Perhaps." Everard's smile held something of restraint. "We can't all of us stand still, St. Bernard. Perpetual youth is given only to the favoured few."

93

"Ah!" The older man's eyes narrowed a little. For a moment there existed a curious, wholly indefinite, resemblance between them. "And you are happy?" he asked abruptly.

Everard's eyes held a certain hardness as he replied, "Provisionally, yes. I haven't got all I want yet—if that's what you mean. But I am on the way to getting it."

Bernard Monck looked at him a moment longer, and let him go. "Are you sure you're wanting the right thing?" he said.

It was not a question that demanded an answer, and Everard made none. He turned aside with a scarcely perceptible lift of the shoulders.

"You haven't told me yet how you come to be here," he said. "Have you given up the Charthurst chaplaincy?"

"It gave me up." Bernard spoke quietly, but there was deep regret in his voice. "A new governor came—a man of curiously rigid ideas. Anyway, I was not parson enough for him. We couldn't assimilate. I tried my hardest, but we couldn't get into touch anywhere. I preached the law of Divine liberty to the captives. And he—good man! preferred to keep them safely locked in the dungeon. I was forced to quit the position. I had no choice."

"What a fool!" observed Everard tersely.

Bernard's ready smile re-appeared. "Thanks, old chap!" he said. "That's just the point of view I wanted you to take. Now I have other schemes on hand. I'll tell you later what they are. I think I'd better have that cold bath next if you're really going to take me along to mess with you. By Jove, how it does rain! Does it ever leave off in these parts?"

"Not very often this time of the year. I'm not going to let you stay here for long." Everard spoke with his customary curt decision. "It's no place for fellows like you. You must go to Bhulwana and join my wife."

"Many thanks!" Bernard made a grotesque gesture of submission. "What sort of woman is your wife, my son? Do you think she will like me?"

Everard turned and smote him on the shoulder. "Of course she will! She will adore you. All women do."

"Oh, not quite!" protested Bernard modestly. "I'm not tall enough to please everyone of the feminine gender. But you think your wife will overlook that?"

"I know," said Everard, with conviction.

His brother laughed with cheery self-satisfaction. "In that case, of course I shall adore her," he said.

CHAPTER VII
FALSE PRETENCES

They were a merry party at mess that night. General Sir Reginald Bassett was a man of the bluff soldierly order who knew how to command respect from his inferiors while at the same time he set them at their ease. There was no pomp and circumstance about him, yet in the whole of the Indian Empire there was not an officer more highly honoured and few who possessed such wide influence as "old Sir Reggie," as irreverent subalterns fondly called him.

The new arrival, Bernard Monck, diffused a genial atmosphere quite unconsciously wherever he went, and he and the old Indian soldier gravitated towards each other almost instinctively. Colonel Mansfield declared later that they made it impossible for him to maintain order, so spontaneous and so infectious was the gaiety that ran round the board. Even Major Ralston's leaden sense of humour was stirred. As Tommy had declared, it promised to be a historic occasion.

When the time for toasts arrived and, after the usual routine, the Colonel proposed the health of their honoured guest of the evening, Sir Reginald interposed with a courteous request that that of their other guest might be coupled with his, and the dual toast was drunk with acclamations.

"I hope I shall have the pleasure of seeing more of you during your stay in India," the General remarked to his fellow-guest when he had returned thanks and quiet was restored. "You have come for the winter, I presume."

Bernard laughed. "Well, no, sir, though I shall hope to see it through. I am not globe-trotting, and times and seasons don't affect me much. My only reason for coming out at all was to see my brother here. You see, we haven't met for a good many years."

The statement was quite casually made, but Major Burton, who was seated next to him, made a sharp movement as if startled. He was a man who prided himself upon his astuteness in discovering discrepancies in even the most truthful stories.

"Didn't you meet last year when he went Home?" he said.

"Last year! No. He wasn't Home last year." Bernard looked full at his questioner, understanding neither his tone nor look.

A sudden silence had fallen near them; it spread like a widening ring upon disturbed waters.

Major Burton spoke, in his voice, a queer, scoffing inflection. "He was absent on Home leave anyway. We all understood—were given to understand—that you had sent him an urgent summons."

"I?" For an instant Bernard Monck stared in genuine bewilderment. Then abruptly he turned to his brother who was listening inscrutably on the other side of the table. "Some mistake here, Everard," he said. "You haven't been Home for seven years or more have you?"

There was dead silence in the room as he put the question—a silence, so full of expectancy as to be almost painful. Across the table the eyes of the two brothers met and held.

Then, "I have not," said Everard Monck with quiet finality.

There was no note of challenge in his voice, neither was there any dismay. But the effect of his words upon every man present was as if he had flung a bomb into their midst. The silence endured tensely for a couple of seconds, then there came a hard breath and a general movement as if by common consent the company desired to put an end to a situation, that had become unendurable.

Bertie Oakes dug Tommy in the ribs, but Tommy was as white as death and did not even feel it. Something had happened, something that made him feel giddy and very sick. That significant silence was to him nothing short of tragedy. He had seen his hero topple at a touch from the high pinnacle on which he had placed him, and he felt as if the very ground under his feet had become a quicksand.

As in a maze of shifting impressions he heard Sir Reginald valiantly covering the sudden breach, talking inconsequently in a language which Tommy could not even recognize as his own. And the Colonel was seconding his efforts, while Major Burton sat frowning at the end of his cigar as if he were trying to focus his sight upon something infinitesimal and elusive. No one looked at Monck, in fact everyone seemed studiously to avoid doing so. Even his brother seemed lost in meditation with his eyes fixed immovably upon a lamp that hung from the ceiling and swayed ponderously in the draught.

Then at last there came a definite move, and Bertie Oakes poked him again. "Are you moonstruck?" he said.

Tommy got up with the rest, still feeling sick and oddly unsure of himself. He pushed his brother-subaltern aside as if he had been an inanimate object, and somehow, groping, found his way to the door and out to the entrance for a breath of air.

It was raining heavily and the odour of a thousand intangible things hung in the atmosphere. For a space he leaned in the doorway undisturbed; then, heralded by the smell of a rank cigar, Ralston lounged up and joined him.

"Are you looking for a safe corner to catch fever in?" he inquired phlegmatically, after a pause.

Tommy made a restless movement, but spoke no word.

Ralston smoked for a space in silence. From behind them there came the rattle of billiard-balls and careless clatter of voices. Before them was a pall-like darkness and the endless patter of rain.

Suddenly Ralston spoke. "Make no mistake!" he said. "There's a reason for everything."

The words sounded irrelevant; they even had a sententious ring. Yet Tommy turned towards him with an impulsive gesture of gratitude.

"Of course!" he said.

Ralston relapsed into a ruminating silence. A full minute elapsed before he spoke again. Then: "You don't like taking advice I know," he said, in his stolid, somewhat gruff fashion. "But if you're wise, you'll swallow a stiff dose of quinine before you turn in. Good-night!"

He swung round on his heel and walked away. Tommy knew that he had gone for his nightly game of chess with Major Burton and would not exchange so much as another half-dozen words with any one during the rest of the evening.

He himself remained for a while where he was, recovering his balance; then at length donned his mackintosh, and tramped forth into the night. Ralston was right. Doubtless there was a reason. He would stake his life on Everard's honour whatever the odds.

In a quiet corner of the ante-room sat Everard Monck, deeply immersed in a paper. Near him a group of bridge-players played an almost silent game. Sir Reginald and his brother had followed the youngsters to the billiard-room, the Colonel had accompanied them, but after a decent interval he left the guests to themselves and returned to the ante-room.

He passed the bridge-players by and came to Monck. The latter glanced up at his approach.

"Are you looking for me, sir?"

"If you can spare me a moment, I shall be glad," the Colonel said formally.

Monck rose instantly. His dark face had a granite-like look as he followed his superior officer from the room. The bridge-players watched him with furtive attention, and resumed their game in silence.

The Colonel led the way back to the mess-room, now deserted. "I shall not keep you long," he said, as Monck shut the door and moved forward. "But I must ask of you an explanation of the fact which came to light this evening." He paused a moment, but Monck spoke no word, and he continued with growing coldness. "Rather more than a year ago you refused a Government mission, for which your services were urgently required, on the plea of pressing business at Home. You had Home leave—at a time when we were under-officered—to carry this business through. Now, Captain Monck, will you be good enough to tell me how and where you spent that leave? Whatever you say I shall treat as confidential."

He still spoke formally, but the usual rather pompous kindliness of his face had given place to a look of acute anxiety.

Monck stood at the table, gazing straight before him. "You have a perfect right to ask, sir," he said, after a moment. "But I am not in a position to answer."

"In other words, you refuse to answer?" The Colonel's voice had a rasp in it, but that also held more of anxiety than anger.

Monck turned and directly faced him. "I am compelled to refuse," he said.

There was a brief silence. Colonel Mansfield was looking at him as if he would read him through and through. But no stone mask could have been more impenetrable than Monck's face as he stood stiffly waiting.

When the Colonel spoke again it was wholly without emotion. His tones fell cold and measured. "You obtained that leave upon false pretences? You had no urgent business?"

Monck answered him with machine-like accuracy. "Yes, sir, I deceived you. But my business was urgent nevertheless. That is my only excuse."

"Was it in connection with some Secret Service requirement?" The Colonel's tone was strictly judicial now; he had banished all feeling from face and manner.

And again, like a machine, Monck made his curt reply. "No, sir."

"There was nothing official about it?"

"Nothing."

"I am to conclude then—" again the rasp was in the Colonel's voice, but it sounded harsher now—"that the business upon which you absented yourself was strictly private and personal?"

"It was, sir."

The commanding officer's brows contracted heavily. "Am I also to conclude that it was something of a dishonourable nature?" he asked.

Monck made a scarcely perceptible movement. It was as if the point had somehow pierced his armour. But he covered it instantly. "Your deductions are of your own making, sir," he said.

"I see." The Colonel's tone was openly harsh. "You are ashamed to tell me the truth. Well, Captain Monck, I cannot compel you to do so. But it would have been better for your own sake if you had taken up a less reticent attitude. Of course I realize that there are certain shameful occasions regarding which any man must keep silence, but I had not thought you capable of having a secret of that description to guard. I think it very doubtful if General Bassett will now require your services upon his staff."

He paused. Monck's hands were clenched and rigid, but he spoke no word, and gave no other sign of emotion.

"You have nothing to say to me?" the Colonel asked, and for a moment the official air was gone. He spoke as one man to another and almost with entreaty.

But, "Nothing, sir," said Monck firmly, and the moment passed.

The Colonel turned aside. "Very well," he said briefly.

Monck swung round and opened the door for him, standing as stiffly as a soldier on parade.

He went out without a backward glance.

CHAPTER VIII
THE WRATH OF THE GODS

It was nearly an hour later that Everard Monck and his brother left the mess together and walked back through the dripping darkness to the bungalow on the hill overlooking the river. The rush of the swollen stream became audible as they drew near. The sound of it was inexpressibly wild and desolate.

"It's an interesting country," remarked Bernard, breaking a silence. "I don't wonder she has got hold of you, my son. What does your wife think of it? Is she too caught in the toils?"

Not by word or look had he made the smallest reference to the episode at the mess-table. It was as if he alone of those present had wholly missed its significance.

Everard answered him quietly, without much emphasis. "I believe my wife hates it from beginning to end. Perhaps it is not surprising. She has been through a good deal since she came out. And I am afraid there is a good deal before her still."

Bernard's big hand closed upon his arm. "Poor old chap!" lie said. "You Indian fellows don't have any such time of it, or your women folk either. How long is she a fixture at Bhulwana?"

"The baby is expected in two months' time." Everard spoke without emotion, his voice sounded almost cold. "After that, I don't know what will happen. Nothing is settled. Tell me your plans now! No, wait! Let's get in out of this damned rain first!"

They entered the bungalow and sat down for another smoke in the drawing-room.

Down by the river a native instrument thrummed monotonously, like the whirring of a giant mosquito in the darkness. Everard turned with a slight gesture of impatience and closed the window.

He established his brother in a long chair with a drink at his elbow, and sat down himself without any pretence at taking his ease.

"You don't look particularly comfortable," Bernard observed.

"Don't mind me!" he made curt response. "I've got a touch of fever to-night. It's nothing. I shall be all right in the morning."

"Sure?" Bernard's eyes suddenly ceased to be quizzical; they looked at him straight and hard.

Everard met the look, faintly smiling. "I don't lie about—unimportant things," he remarked cynically. "Light up, man, and fire away!"

He struck a match for his brother's pipe and kindled his own cigarette thereat.

There fell a brief silence. Bernard did not look wholly satisfied. But after a few seconds he seemed to dismiss the matter and began to talk of himself.

"You want to know my plans, old chap. Well, as far as I know 'em myself, you are quite welcome. With your permission, I propose, for the present, to stay where I am."

"I shouldn't if I were you." Everard spoke with brief decision. "You'd be far better off at Bhulwana till the end of the rains."

Bernard puffed forth a great cloud of smoke and stared at the ceiling. "That is as may be, dear fellow," he said, after a moment. "But I think—if you'll put up with me—I'll stay here for the present all the same."

He spoke in that peculiarly gentle voice of his that yet held considerable resolution. Everard made no attempt to combat the decision. Perhaps he realized the uselessness of such a proceeding.

"Stay by all means!" he said, "but what's the idea?"

Bernard took his pipe from his mouth. "I have a big fight before me, Everard boy," he said, "a fight against the sort of prejudice that kicked me out of the Charthurst job. It's got to be fought with the pen—since I am no street corner ranter. I have the solid outlines of the campaign in my head, and I have come out here to get right away from things and work it out."

"Going to reform creation?" suggested Everard, with his grim smile.

Bernard shook his head, smiling in answer as though the cynicism had not reached him. "No, that's not my job. I am only a man under authority—like yourself. I don't see the result at all. I only see the work, and with God's help, that will be exactly what He intended it should be when He gave it to me to do."

"Lucky man!" said Everard briefly.

"Ah! I didn't think myself lucky when I had to give up the Charthurst chaplaincy." Bernard spoke through a haze of smoke. "I'm afraid I kicked a bit at first—which was a short-sighted thing to do, I admit. But I had got to look on it as my life-work, and I loved it. It held such opportunities." He broke off with a sharp sigh. "I shall be at it again if I go on. Can't you give me something pleasanter to think about? Haven't you got a photograph of your wife to show me?"

Everard got up. "Yes, I have. But it doesn't do her justice." He took a letter-case from his pocket and opened it. A moment he stood bent over the portrait he withdrew from it, then turned and handed it to his brother.

Bernard studied it in silence. It was an unmounted amateur photograph of Stella standing on the creeper-grown verandah of the Green Bungalow. She was smiling, but her eyes were faintly sad, as though shadowed by the memory of some past pain.

For many seconds Bernard gazed upon the pictured face. Finally he spoke.

"Your wife must be a very beautiful woman."

"Yes," said Everard quietly.

He spoke gravely. His brother's eyes travelled upwards swiftly. "That was not what you married her for, eh?"

Everard stooped and took the portrait from him. "Well, no—not entirely," he said.

Bernard smiled a little. "You haven't told me much about her, you know. How long have you been acquainted?"

"Nearly two years. I think I mentioned in my letter that she was the widow of a comrade?"

"Yes, I remember. But you were rather vague about it. What happened to him? Didn't he meet with a violent death?"

There was a pause. Everard was still standing with his eyes fixed upon the photograph. His face was stern.

"What was it?" questioned Bernard. "Didn't he fall over a precipice?"

"Yes," abruptly the younger man made answer. "It happened in Kashmir when they were on their honeymoon."

"Ah! Poor girl! She must have suffered. What was his name? Was he a pal of yours?"

"More or less." Everard's voice rang hard. "His name was Dacre."

"Oh, to be sure. The man I wrote to you about just before poor Madelina Belleville died in prison. Her husband's name was Dacre. He was in the Army too, and she thought he was in India. But it's not a very uncommon name." Bernard spoke thoughtfully. "You said he was no relation."

"I said to the best of my belief he was not." Everard turned suddenly and sat down. "People are not keen, you know, on owning to shady relations. He was no exception to the rule. But if the woman died, it's of no great consequence now to any one. When did she die?"

Bernard took a long pull at his pipe. His brows were slightly drawn. "She died suddenly, poor soul. Did I never tell you? It must have been immediately after I wrote that letter to you. It was. I remember now. It was the very day after.... She died on the twenty-first of March—the first day of spring. Poor girl! She had so longed for the spring. Her time would have been up in May."

Something in the silence that followed his words made him turn his head to look at his brother. Everard was sitting perfectly rigid in his chair staring at the ground between his feet as if he saw a serpent writhing there. But before another word could be spoken, he got up abruptly, with a gesture as of shaking off the loathsome thing, and went to the window. He flung it wide, and stood in the opening, breathing hard as a man half-suffocated.

"Anything wrong, old chap?" questioned Bernard.

He answered him without turning. "No; it's only my infernal head. I think I'll turn in directly. It's a fiendish night."

The rain was falling in torrents, and a long roll of thunder sounded from afar. The clatter of the great drops on the roof of the verandah filled the room, making all further conversation impossible. It was like a tattoo of devils.

"A damn' pleasant country this!" murmured the man in the chair.

The man at the window said no word. He was gasping a little, his face to the howling night.

For a space Bernard lay and watched him. Then at last, somewhat ponderously he arose.

Everard could not have heard his approach, but he was aware of it before he reached him. He turned swiftly round, pulling the window closed behind him.

They stood facing each other, and there was something tense in the atmosphere, something that was oddly suggestive of mental conflict. The devils' tattoo on the roof had sunk to a mere undersong, a fitting accompaniment as it were to the electricity in the room.

Bernard spoke at length, slowly, deliberately, but not unkindly. "Why should you take the trouble to—fence with me?" he said. "Is it worth it, do you think?"

Everard's face was set and grey like a stone mask. He did not speak for a moment; then curtly, noncommittally, "What do you mean?" he said.

"I mean," very steadily Bernard made reply, "that the scoundrel Dacre, who married Madelina Belleville and then deserted her, left her to go to the dogs, and your brother-officer who was killed in the mountains on his honeymoon, were one and the same man. And you knew it."

"Well?" The words seemed to come from closed lips. There was something terrible in the utter quietness of its utterance.

Bernard searched his face as a man might search the walls of an apparently impregnable fortress for some vulnerable spot. "Ah, I see," he said, after a moment. "You must have believed Madelina to be still alive when Dacre married. What was the date of his marriage?"

"The twenty-fifth of March." Again the grim lips spoke without seeming to move.

A gleam of relief crossed his brother's face. "In that case no one is any the worse. I'm sorry you've carried that bugbear about with you for so long. What an infernal hound the fellow was!"

"Yes," assented Everard.

He moved to the table and poured himself out a drink.

His brother still watched him. "One might almost say his death was providential," he observed. "Of course—your wife—never knew of this?"

"No." Everard lifted the glass to his lips with a perfectly steady hand and drank. "She never will know," he said, as he set it down.

"Certainly not. You can trust me never to tell her." Bernard moved to his side, and laid a kindly hand on his shoulder. "You know you can trust me, old fellow?"

Everard did not look at him. "Yes, I know," he said.

His brother's hand pressed upon him a little. "Since they are both gone," he said, "there is nothing more to be said on the subject. But, oh, man, stick to the truth, whatever else you let go of! You never lied to me before."

His tone was very earnest. It held urgent entreaty. Everard turned and met his eyes. His dark face was wholly emotionless. "I am sorry, St. Bernard," he said.

Bernard's kindly smile wrinkled his eyes. He grasped and held the younger man's hand. "All right, boy. I'm going to forget it," he said. "Now what about turning in?"

They parted for the night immediately after, the one to sleep as serenely as a child almost as soon as he lay down, the other to pace to and fro, to and fro, for hours, grappling—and grappling in vain—with the sternest adversary he had ever had to encounter.

For upon Everard Monck that night the wrath of the gods had descended, and against it, even his grim fortitude was powerless to make a stand. He was beaten before he could begin to defend himself, beaten and flung aside as contemptible. Only one thing remained to be fought for, and that one thing he swore to guard with the last ounce of his strength, even at the cost of life itself.

All through that night of bitter turmoil he came back again and again to that, the only solid foothold left him in the shifting desert-sand. So long as his heart should beat he would defend that one precious possession that yet remained,—the honour of the woman who loved him and whom he loved as only the few know how to love.

PART IV
CHAPTER I
DEVILS' DICE

"It's a pity," said Sir Reginald.

"It's a damnable pity, sir," Colonel Mansfield spoke with blunt emphasis. "I have trusted the fellow almost as I would have trusted myself. And he has let me down."

The two were old friends. The tie of India bound them both. Though their ways lay apart and they met but seldom, the same spirit was in them and they were as comrades. They sat together in the Colonel's office that looked over the streaming parade-ground. A gleam of morning sunshine had pierced the clouds, and the smoke of the Plains went up like a furnace.

"I shouldn't be too sure of that," said Sir Reginald, after a thoughtful moment. "Things are not always what they seem. One is apt to repent of a hasty judgment."

"I know." The Colonel spoke with his eyes upon the rising cloud of steam outside. "But this fellow has always had my confidence, and I can't get over what he himself admits to have been a piece of double-dealing. I suppose it was a sudden temptation, but he had always been so straight with me; at least I had always imagined him so. He has rendered some invaluable services too."

"That is partly why I say, don't be too hasty," said Sir Reginald. "We can't afford—India can't afford—to scrap a single really useful man."

"Neither can she afford to make use of rotters," rejoined the Colonel.

Sir Reginald smiled a little. "I am not so sure of that, Mansfield. Even the rotters have their uses. But I am quite convinced in my own mind that this man is very far from being one. I feel inclined to go slow for a time and give him a chance to retrieve himself. Perhaps it may sound soft to you, but I have never floored a man at his first slip. And this man has a clean record behind him. Let it stand him in good stead now!"

"It will take me some time to forget it," the Colonel said. "I can forgive almost anything except deception. And that I loathe."

"It isn't pleasant to be cheated, certainly," Sir Reginald agreed. "When did this happen? Was he married at the time?"

"No." The Colonel meditated for a few seconds "He only married last spring. This was considerably more than a year ago. It must have been the spring of the preceding year. Yes, by Jove, it was! It was just at the time of poor Dacre's marriage. Dacre, you know, married young Denvers' sister—the girl who is now Monck's wife. Dacre was killed on his honeymoon only a fortnight after the wedding. You remember that, Burton?" He turned abruptly to the Major who had entered while he was speaking.

Burton came to a stand at the table. His eyes were set very close together, and they glittered meanly as he made reply. "I remember it very well indeed. His death coincided with this mysterious leave of Monck's, and also with the unexpected absence of our man Rustam Karin just at a moment when Barnes particularly needed him."

"Who is Rustam Karin?" asked Sir Reginald.

"A police agent. A clever man. I may say, an invaluable man." Colonel Mansfield was looking hard at the Major's ferret-like face as he made reply. "No one likes the fellow. He is suspected of being a leper. But he is clever. He is undoubtedly clever. I remember his absence. It was at the time of that mission to Khanmulla, the mission I wanted Monck to take in hand."

"Exactly." Major Burton rapped out the word with a sound like the cracking of a nut. "We—or rather Barnes—tried to pump Hafiz about it, but he was a mass of ignorance and lies. I believe the old brute turned up again before Monck's return, but he wasn't visible till afterwards. He and Monck have always been thick as thieves—thick as thieves." He paused, looking at Sir Reginald. "A very fishy transaction, sir," he observed.

Sir Reginald's eyes met his. "Are you," he said calmly, "trying to establish any connection between the death of Dacre and the absence from Kurrumpore of this man Rustam Karin?"

"Not only Rustam Karin, sir," responded the Major sharply.

"Ah! Quite so. How did Dacre die?" Sir Reginald still spoke quietly, judicially. There was nothing encouraging in his aspect.

Burton hesitated momentarily, as if some inner warning prompted him to go warily.

"That was what no one knew for certain, sir. He disappeared one night. The story went that he fell over a precipice. Some old native beggar told the tale. No one knows who the man was."

"But you have your eye upon Rustam Karin?" suggested Sir Reginald.

Burton hesitated again. "One doesn't trust these fellows, sir," he said.

"True!" Sir Reginald's voice sounded very dry. "Perhaps it is a mistake to trust any one too far. This is all the evidence you can muster?"

"Yes, sir." Burton looked suddenly embarrassed. "Of course it is not evidence, strictly speaking," he said. "But when mysteries coincide, one is apt to link them together. And the death of Captain Dacre always seemed to me highly mysterious."

"The death of Captain Ermsted was no less so," put in the Colonel abruptly. "Have you any theories on that subject also?"

Burton smiled, showing his teeth. "I always have theories," he said.

Sir Reginald made a slight movement of impatience. "I think this is beside the point," he said. "Captain Ermsted's murderer will probably be traced one day."

"Probably, sir," agreed Major Burton, "since I hear unofficially that Captain Monck has the matter in hand. Ah!"

He broke off short as, with a brief knock at the door, Monck himself made an abrupt appearance.

He came forward as if he saw no one in the room but the Colonel. His face wore a curiously stony look, but his eyes burned with a fierce intensity. He spoke without apology or preliminary of any sort.

"I have just had a message, sir, from Bhulwana," he said. "I wish to apply for immediate leave."

The Colonel looked at him in surprise. "A message, Captain Monck?"

"From my wife," Monck said, and drew a hard breath between his teeth. His hands were clenched hard at his sides. "I've got to go!" he said. "I've got to go!"

There was a moment's silence. Then: "May I see the message?" said the Colonel.

Monck's eyelids flickered sharply, as if he had been struck across the face. He thrust out his right hand and flung a crumpled paper upon the table. "There, sir!" he said harshly.

There was violence in the action, but it did not hold insolence. Sir Reginald leaning forward, was watching him intently. As the Colonel, with a word of excuse to himself, took up and opened the paper, he rose quietly and went up to Monck. Thin, wiry, grizzled, he stopped beside him.

Major Burton retired behind the Colonel, realizing himself as unnecessary but too curious to withdraw altogether.

In the pause that followed, a tense silence reigned. Monck was swaying as he stood. His eyes had the strained and awful look of a man with his soul in torment. After that one hard breath, he had not breathed at all.

The Colonel looked up. "Go, certainly!" he said, and there was a touch of the old kindliness in his voice that he tried to restrain. "And as soon as possible! I hope you will find a more reassuring state of affairs when you get there."

He held out the telegram. Monck made a movement to take it, but as he did so the tension in which he gripped himself suddenly gave way. He blundered forward, his hands upon the table.

"She will die," he said, and there was utter despair in his tone. "She is probably dead already."

Sir Reginald took him by the arm. His face held nought but kindliness, which he made no attempt to hide. "Sit down a minute!" he said. "Here's a chair! Just a minute. Sit down and get your wind! What is this message? May I read it?"

He murmured something to Major Burton who turned sharply and went out. Monck sank heavily into the chair and leaned upon the table, his head in his hands. He was shaking all over, as if seized with an ague.

Sir Reginald read the message, standing beside him, a hand upon his shoulder. "Stella desperately ill. Come. Ralston," were the words it contained.

He laid the paper upon the table, and looked across at the Colonel. The latter nodded slightly, almost imperceptibly.

Monck spoke without moving. "She is dead," he said. "My God! She is dead!" And then, under his breath, "After all,—counting me out—it's best—it's best. I couldn't ask for anything better at this devils' game. Someone's got to die."

He checked himself abruptly, and again a terrible shivering seized him.

Sir Reginald bent over him. "Pull yourself together, man! You'll need all your strength. Please God, she'll be better when you get there!"

Monck raised himself with a slow, blind movement. "Did you ever dice with the devil?" he said. "Stake your honour—stake all you'd got—to save a woman from hell? And then lose—my God—lose all—even—even—the woman?" Again he checked himself. "I'm talking like a damned fool. Stop me, someone! I've come through hell-fire and it's scorched away my senses. I never thought I should blab like this."

"It's all right," Sir Reginald said, and in his voice was steady reassurance. "You're with friends. Get a hold on yourself! Don't say any more!"

"Ah!" Monck drew a deep breath and seemed to come to himself. He lifted a face of appalling whiteness and looked at Sir Reginald. "You're very good, sir," he said. "I was knocked out for the moment. I'm all right now."

He made as if he would rise, but Sir Reginald checked him. "Wait a moment longer! Major Burton will be back directly."

"Major Burton?" questioned Monck.

"I sent him for some brandy to steady your nerves," Sir Reginald said.

"You're very good," Monck said again. He leaned his head on his hand and sat silent.

Major Burton returned with Tommy hovering anxiously behind him. The boy hesitated a little upon entering, but the Colonel called him in.

102

"You had better see the message too," he said. "Your sister is ill. Captain Monck is going to her."

Tommy read the message with one eye upon Monck, who drank the brandy Burton brought and in a moment stood up.

"I am sorry to have made such a fool of myself, sir," he said to Sir Reginald, with a faint, grim smile. "I shall not forget your kindness, though I hope you will forget my idiocy."

Sir Reginald looked at him closely for a second. His grizzled face was stern. Yet he held out his hand.

"Good-bye, Captain Monck!" was all he said.

Monck stiffened. The smile passed from his face, leaving it inscrutable, granite-like in its composure. It was as the donning of a mask.

"Good-bye, sir!" he said briefly, as he shook hands.

Tommy moved to his side impulsively. He did not utter a word, but as they went out his hand was pushed through Monck's arm in the old confidential fashion, the old eager affection was shining in his eyes.

"He has one staunch friend, anyhow," Sir Reginald muttered to the Colonel.

"Yes," the Colonel answered gravely. "He has done a good deal for young Denvers. It's the boy's turn to make good now. There isn't much left him besides."

"Poor devil!" said Sir Reginald.

CHAPTER II
OUT OF THE DARKNESS

"You said Everard was coming. Why doesn't he come? It's very dark—it's very dark! Can he have missed the way?"

Feebly, haltingly, the words seemed to wander through the room, breaking a great silence as it were with immense effort. Mrs. Ralston bent over the bed and whispered hushingly that it was all right, all right, Everard would be there soon.

"But why does he take so long?" murmured Stella. "It's getting darker every minute. And it's so steep. I keep slipping—slipping. I know he would hold me up." And then after a moment, "Oh, Mary, am I dying? I believe I am. But—he—wouldn't let me die."

Mrs. Ralston's hand closed comfortingly upon hers. "You're quite safe, dearest," she said. "Don't be afraid!"

"But it's so dreadfully dark," Stella said restlessly. "I shouldn't mind if I could see the way. But I can't—I can't."

"Be patient, darling!" said Mrs. Ralston very tenderly. "It will be lighter presently."

It was growing very late. She herself was listening for every sound, hoping against hope to hear the firm quiet step of the man who alone could still her charge's growing distress.

"It would be so dreadful to miss him," moaned Stella. "I have waited so long. Mary, why don't they light a lamp?"

A shaded lamp was burning on the table by the bed. Mrs. Ralston turned and lifted the shade. But Stella shook her head with a weary discontent.

"That doesn't help. It's in the desert that I mean—so that he shan't miss me when he comes."

"He cannot miss you, darling," Mrs. Ralston assured her; but in her own heart she doubted. For the doctor had told her that he did not think she would live through the night.

Again she strained her ears to listen. She had certainly heard a sound outside the door; but it might be only Peter who, she knew, crouched there, alert for any service.

It was Peter; but it was not Peter only, for even as she listened, the handle of the door turned softly and someone entered. She looked up eagerly and saw the doctor.

He was a thin, grey man for whom she entertained privately a certain feeling of contempt. She was so sure her own husband would have somehow managed the case better. He came to the bedside, and looked at Stella, looked closely; then turned to her friend watching beside her.

"I wonder if it would disturb her to see her husband for a moment," he said.

Mrs. Ralston suppressed a start with difficulty. "Is he here?" she whispered.

"Just arrived," he murmured back, and turned again to look at Stella who lay motionless with closed eyes, scarcely seeming to breathe.

Mrs. Ralston's whisper smote the silence, and it was the doctor's turn to start. "Send him in at once!" she said.

So insistent was her command that he stood up as if he had been prodded into action. Mrs. Ralston was on her feet. She waved an urgent hand.

"Go and get him!" she ordered almost fiercely. "It's the only chance left. Go and fetch him!"

He looked at her doubtfully for a second, then, impelled by an authority that overrode every scruple, he turned in silence and tiptoed from the room.

Mrs. Ralston's eyes followed him with scorn. How was it some doctors managed—notwithstanding all their experience—to be such hopeless idiots?

The soft opening of the door again a few seconds later banished her irritation. She turned with shining welcome in her look, and met Monck with outstretched hands.

"You're in time," she said.

He gripped her hands hard, but he scarcely looked at her. In a moment he was bending over the bed.

"Stella girl! Stella!" he said.

"Everard!" The weak voice thrilled like a loosened harp-string, and the man's dark face flashed into sudden passionate tenderness.

He went down upon his knees beside the bed and gathered her to his breast. She clung to him feebly, her lips turned to his.

"My darling—oh, my darling—have you come at last?" she whispered. "Hold me—hold me!—Don't let me die!"

He held her closer and closer to his heart, so that its fierce throbbing beat against her own. "You shan't die," he said, "you can't die—with me here."

She laughed a little, sobbingly. "You saved Tommy—twice over. I knew you would save me—if you came in time. Oh, darling, how I have wanted you! It's been—so dark and terrible."

"But you held on!" Monck's voice was very low; it came with a manifest effort. He was holding her to his breast as if he could never let her go.

"Yes, I held on. I knew—I knew—how—how it would hurt you—to find me gone." Her trembling hands moved fondly about his head and finally clasped his neck. "It's all right now," she said, with a sigh of deep content.

Monck's lips pressed hers again and again, and Mrs. Ralston went away to the window to hide her tears. "Please, God, don't separate them now!" she whispered.

It was many minutes later that Stella spoke again, softly, into Monck's ear. "Everard—darling husband—the baby—our baby—don't you—wouldn't you like to see it?"

"The baby!" He spoke as if startled. Somehow he had concluded from the first that the baby would be dead, and the rapture of finding her still living had driven the thought of everything else from his mind.

"Don't move!" whispered Stella, clasping him closer. "Ask them to bring it!"

He spoke over his shoulder to Mrs. Ralston, his voice oddly cold, almost reluctant. "Would you be good enough to bring the baby in?"

She turned at once, smiling upon him shakily. But his dark face remained wholly inscrutable, wholly unresponsive. There was something about him that smote her with a curious chill, but she told herself that he was worn out with hard travel and anxiety as she went from the room to comply with his curt request.

Lying against his shoulder, Stella whispered a few halting sentences. "It—happened so suddenly. The Rajah drives so fiercely—like a man possessed. And the car skidded on the hill. Netta Ermsted was in it, and she screamed, and I—I was terrified because Tessa—Tessa—brave mite—sprang in front of me. I don't know what she thought she could do. I think partly she was angry, and lost her head. And she meant—to help—to protect me—somehow. After that, I fainted—and when I came round, they had brought me back here.

104

That was ever so long ago." She shuddered convulsively. "I've been through a lot since then."

Monck's teeth closed upon his lip. He had not suspected an accident.

Tremulously Stella went on. "It—was so much too soon. I was—dreadfully—afraid for the poor wee baby. But the doctor said—the doctor said—it was all right—only small. And oh, Everard—" her voice thrilled again with a quivering joy—"it is a boy. I so wanted—a son—for you."

"God bless you!" he said almost inarticulately, and kissed her white face again burningly, even with violence. She smiled at his intensity, though it made her gasp. "I know—I know—you will be great," she said. "And—your son—must carry on your greatness. He shall learn to love—the Empire—as you do. We will teach him together—you and I."

"Ah!" Monck said, and drew the hard breath of a man struggling in deep waters.

Mrs. Ralston returned softly with a white bundle in her arms, and Stella's hold relaxed. Her heavy lids brightened eagerly.

"My dear," Mrs. Ralston said, "the doctor has commanded me to turn your husband out immediately. He must just peep at the darling baby and go."

"Tell him to go himself—to blazes!" said Monck forcibly, and then reached up, still curiously grim to Mrs. Ralston's observing eyes, and, without rising from his knees, took his child into his arms.

He laid it against the mother's breast, and tenderly uncovered the tiny, sleeping face.

"Oh, Everard!" she said.

And Mrs. Ralston turned away with a little sob. She did not believe any longer that Stella would die. The sweet, thrilling happiness of her voice seemed somehow to drive out the very thought of death. She had never in her life seen any one so supremely happy. But yet—though she was reassured—there was something else in the atmosphere that disturbed her. She could not have said wherefore, but she was sorry for Monck—deeply, poignantly sorry. She was certain, with that inner conviction that needs no outer evidence, that it was more than weariness and the strain of anxiety that had drawn those deep lines about his eyes and mouth. He looked to her like a man who had been smitten down in the pride of his strength, and who knew his case to be hopeless.

As for Monck, he went through his ordeal unflinching, suffering as few men are called upon to suffer and hiding it away without a quiver. All through the hours of his journeying, he had been prepared to face—he had actually expected—- the worst. All through those hours he had battled to reach her indeed, straining every faculty, resisting with almost superhuman strength every obstacle that arose to bar his progress. But he had not thought to find her, and throughout the long-drawn-out effort he had carried in his locked heart the knowledge that if when he came at last to her bedside he found her—this woman whom he loved with all the force of his silent soul—white and cold in death, it would be the best fate that he could wish her, the best thing that could possibly happen, so far as mortal sight could judge, for either.

But so it had not been. At the very Gate of Death she had waited for his coming, and now he knew in his heart that she would return. The love between them was drawing her, and the man's heart in him battled fiercely to rejoice even while wrung with the anguish of that secret knowledge.

He hardly knew how he went through those moments which to her were such pure ecstasy. The blood was beating wildly in his brain, and he thought of that devils' tattoo on the roof at Udalkhand when first that dreadful knowledge had sprung upon him like an evil thing out of the night. But he held himself in an iron grip; he forced his mind to clearness. Even to himself he would not seem to be aware of the agony that tore him.

They whispered together for a while over the baby's head, but he never remembered afterwards what passed or how long he knelt there. Only at last there came a silence that drifted on and on and he knew that Stella was asleep.

Later Mrs. Ralston stooped over him and took the baby away, and he laid his head down upon the pillow by Stella's and wished with all his soul that the Gate before which her feet had halted would open to them both.

Someone came up behind them, and stood for a few seconds looking down upon them. He was aware of a presence, but he knelt on without stirring—as one kneeling entranced in a sacred place. Then two hands he knew grasped him firmly by the shoulders, raising him; he looked up half-dazed into his brother's face.

"Come along, old chap!" Bernard whispered. "You mustn't faint in here."

The words roused him. The old sardonic smile showed for a moment about his lips. He faint! But he had not slept for two nights. That would account for that curious top-heavy feeling that possessed him. He suffered Bernard to help him up,—good old Bernard who had watched over him like a mother refusing flatly to remain behind, waiting upon him hand and foot at every turn.

"You come into the next room!" he whispered. "You shall be called immediately if she wakes and wants you. But you'll crumple up if you don't rest."

There was truth in the words. Everard realized it as he went from the room, leaning blindly upon the stout, supporting arm. His weariness hung upon him like an overwhelming weight.

He submitted himself almost mechanically to his brother's ordering, feeling as if he moved in a dream. As in a dream also he saw Peter at the door move, noiseless as a shadow, to assist him on the other side. And he tried to laugh off his weakness, but the laugh stuck in his throat.

Then he found himself in a chair drinking a stiff mixture of brandy and water, again at Bernard's behest, while Bernard stood over him, watching with the utmost kindness in his blue eyes.

The spirit steadied him. He came to himself, sat up slowly, and motioned Peter from the room. He was his own master again. He turned to his brother with a smile.

"You're a friend in need, St. Bernard. That dose has done me good. Open the window, old fellow, will you? Let's have some air!"

Bernard flung the window wide, and the warm wet air blew in laden with the fragrance of the teeming earth. Everard turned his face to it, drawing in great breaths. The dawn was breaking.

"She is better?" Bernard questioned, after a few moments.

"Yes. I believe she has turned the corner." Everard spoke without turning. His eyes were fixed.

"Thank God!" said Bernard gently.

Everard's right hand made a curious movement. It was as if it closed upon a weapon. "You can do that part," he said, and he spoke with constraint. "But you'd do it in any case. It's a way you've got. See the light breaking over there? It's like a sword—turning all ways." He rose with an obvious effort and passed his hand across his eyes. "What of you, man?" he said. "Have they been looking after you?"

"Oh, never mind me!" Bernard rejoined. "Have something to eat and turn in! Yes, of course I'll join you with pleasure." He clapped an affectionate hand upon his brother's shoulder. "It's a boy, I'm told. Old fellow, I congratulate you—may he be a blessing to you all your lives! I'll drink his health if it isn't too early."

Everard broke into a brief, discordant laugh. "You'd better go to church, St. Bernard," he said, "and pray for us!"

He swung away abruptly with the words and crossed the room. The crystal-clear rays of the new day smote full upon him as he moved, and Bernard saw for the first time that his hair was streaked with grey.

CHAPTER III
PRINCESS BLUEBELL

To Bernard, sprawling at his ease with a pipe on the verandah some hours later, the appearance of a small girl with bare brown legs and a very abbreviated white muslin frock, hugging an unwilling mongoose to her breast, came as a surprise; for she entered as one who belonged to the establishment.

"Who are you, please?" she demanded imperiously, halting before him while she disentangled the unfortunate Scooter's rebellious legs from her hair.

Bernard sat up and removed his pipe. Meeting eyes of the darkest, intensest blue that he had ever seen, he gave her appropriate greeting,

"Good morning, Princess Bluebell! I am a humble, homeless beggar, at present living upon the charity of my brother, Captain Monck."

She came a step nearer. "Why do you call me that? You are not Captain Monck's brother really, are you?"

He spread out his hands with a deprecating gesture. "I never contradict royal ladies, Princess, but I have always been taught to believe so."

"Why do you call me Princess?" she asked, halting between suspicion and gratification.

"Because it is quite evident that you are one. There is a—bossiness about you that proclaims the fact aloud." Bernard smiled upon her—the smile of open goodfellowship. "Beggars always know princesses when they see them," he said.

She scrutinized him severely for a moment or two, then suddenly melted into a gleaming, responsive smile that illuminated her little pale face like a shaft of sunlight. She came close to him, and very graciously proffered Scooter for a caress. "You needn't be afraid of him. He doesn't bite," she said.

"I suppose he is a bewitched prince, is he?" asked Bernard, as he stroked the furry little animal.

The great blue eyes were still fixed upon him. "No," said Tessa, after a thoughtful moment or two. "He's only a mongoose. But I think you are a bewitched prince. You're so big. And they always pretend to be beggars too," she added.

"And the princesses always fall in love with them before they find out," said Bernard, looking quizzical.

Tessa frowned a little. "I don't think falling in love is a very nice game," she said. "I've seen a lot of it."

"Have you indeed?" Bernard's eyes screwed up for a moment, but were hastily restored to an expression of becoming gravity. "I don't know much about it myself," he said. "You see, I'm an old bachelor."

"Haven't you—ever—been in love?" asked Tessa incredulously.

He held out his hand to her. "Yes, I'm in love at the present moment—quite the worst sort too—love at first sight."

"You are rather old, aren't you?" said Tessa dispassionately, but she laid her hand in his notwithstanding.

"Quite old enough to be kissed," he assured her, drawing her gently to him. "Shall I tell you a secret? I'm rather fond of kissing little girls."

Tessa went into the circle of his arm with complete confidence. "I don't mind kissing white men," she said, and held up her red lips. "But I wouldn't kiss an Indian—not even Peter, and he's a darling."

"A very wise rule, Princess," said Bernard. "And I feel duly honoured."

"How is my darling Aunt Stella this morning?" demanded Tessa suddenly. "You made me forget. *Ayah* said she would be all right, but *Ayah* says just anything. Is she all right?"

"She is better," Bernard said. "But wait a minute!" He caught her arm as she made an impetuous movement to leave him. "I believe she's asleep just now. You don't want to wake her?"

Tessa turned upon him swiftly—wide horror in her eyes. "Is that your way of telling me she is dead?" she said in a whisper.

"No, no, child!" Bernard's reply came with instant reassurance. "But she has been—she still is—ill. She was upset, you know. Someone in a car startled her."

"I know I was there." Tessa came close to him again, speaking in a tense undertone; her eyes gleamed almost black. "It was the Rajah that frightened her so—the Rajah—and my mother. I'm never going to ask God to bless her again. I—hate her! And him too!"

107

There was such concentrated vindictiveness in her words that even Bernard, who had looked upon many bitter things, was momentarily startled.

"I think God would be rather sorry to hear you say that," he remarked, after a moment. "He likes little girls to pray for their mothers."

"I don't see why," said Tessa rebelliously, "not if He hasn't given them good ones. Mine isn't good. She's very, very bad."

"Then there's all the more reason to pray for her," said Bernard. "It's the least you can do. But I don't think you ought to say that of your mother, you know, even if you think it. It isn't loyal."

"What's loyal?" said Tessa.

"Loyalty is being true to any one—not telling tales about them. It's about the only thing I learnt at school worth knowing." Bernard smiled at her in his large way. "Never tell tales of anyone, Princess!" he said. "It isn't cricket. Now look here! I've an awfully interesting piece of news for you. Come quite close, and I'll whisper. Do you know—last night—when Aunt Stella was lying ill, something happened. An angel came to see her."

"An angel!" Tessa's eyes grew round with wonder, and bluer than the bluest bluebell. "What was he like?" she whispered breathlessly. "Did you see him?"

"No, I didn't. I think it was a she," Bernard whispered back. "And what do you think she brought? But you'll never guess."

"Oh, what?" gasped Tessa, trembling.

Bernard's arm slipped round her, and Scooter with a sudden violent effort freed himself, and was gone.

"Never mind! I can get him again," said Tessa. "Or Peter will. Tell me—quick!"

"She brought—" Bernard was speaking softly into her ear—"a little boy-baby. Think of that! A present straight from God!"

"Oh, how lovely!" Tessa gazed at him with shining eyes. "Is it here now? May I see it? Is the angel still here?"

"No, the angel has gone. But the baby is left. It is Stella's very own, and she is to take care of it."

"Oh, I hope she'll let me help her!" murmured Tessa in awe-struck accents. "Does Uncle Everard know yet?"

"Yes. He and I got here in the night two or three hours after the baby arrived. He was very tired, poor chap. He is resting."

"And the baby?" breathed Tessa.

"Mrs. Ralston is taking care of the baby. I expect it's asleep," said Bernard. "So we'll keep very quiet."

"But she'll let me see it, won't she?" said Tessa anxiously.

"No doubt she will, Princess. But I shouldn't disturb them yet. It's early you know."

"Mightn't I just go in and kiss Uncle Everard?" pleaded Tessa. "I love him so very much. I'm sure he wouldn't mind."

"Let him rest a bit longer!" advised Bernard. "He is worn out. Sit down here, on the arm of my chair, and tell me about yourself! Where have you come from?"

Tessa jerked her head sideways. "Down there. We live at The Grand Stand. We've been there a long time now, nearly ever since Daddy went away. He's in Heaven. A *budmash* shot him in the jungle. Mother made a great fuss about it at the time, but she doesn't care now she can go motoring with the Rajah. He is a nasty beast," said Tessa with emphasis. "I always did hate him. And he frightened my darling Aunt Stella at the gate yesterday. I—could have—killed him for it."

"What did he do?" asked Bernard.

"I don't know quite; but the car twisted round on the hill, and Aunt Stella thought it was going to upset. I tried to take care of her, but we were both nearly run over. He's a horrid man!" Tessa declared. "He caught hold of me the other day because I got between him and Mother when they were sitting smoking together. And I bit him." Vindictive satisfaction sounded in Tessa's voice. "I bit him hard. He soon let go again."

"Wasn't he angry?" asked Bernard.

"Oh, yes, very angry. So was Mother. She told him he might whip me if he liked. Fancy being whipped by a native!" High scorn thrilled in the words. "But he didn't. He laughed in his slithery way and showed his teeth like a jackal and said—and said—I was too pretty to be whipped." Tessa ground her teeth upon the memory. It was evidently even-more humiliating than the suggested punishment. "And then he kissed me—he kissed me—" she shuddered at the nauseating recollection—"and let me go."

Bernard was listening attentively. His eyes were less kindly than usual. They had a steely look. "I should keep out of his way, if I were you," he said.

"I will—I do!" declared Tessa. "But I do hate the way he goes on with Mother. He'd never have dared if Daddy had been here."

"He is evidently a bounder," said Bernard.

They sat for some time on the verandah, growing pleasantly intimate, till presently Peter came out with an early breakfast for Bernard. He invited Tessa to join him, which she consented to do with alacrity.

"We must find Scooter afterwards," she said, as she proudly poured out his coffee. "And then perhaps, if I keep good, Aunt Mary will let me see the baby."

"Wonder if you will manage to keep good till then," observed a voice behind them.

She turned with a squeak of delight and sprang to meet Everard.

He was looking haggard in the morning light, but he smiled upon her in a way she had never seen before, and he stooped and kissed her with a tenderness that amazed her.

"Stella tells me you were very brave yesterday," he said.

"Was I? When?" Tessa opened her blue eyes to their widest extent. "Oh, I was only—angry," she said then. "Darling Aunt Stella was frightened."

He patted her shoulder. "You meant to take care of her, so I'm grateful all the same," he said.

Tessa clung to his arm. "I'd like to come and take care of her always," she said, rather wistfully. "I can easily be spared, Uncle Everard. And I'm really not nearly so naughty as I used to be."

He smiled at the words, but did not respond. "Where's Scooter?" he said.

They spent some time hunting for him, but it was left to Peter finally to unearth him, for in the middle of the search Mrs. Ralston came softly out upon the verandah with the baby in her arms, and at once all Tessa's thoughts were centred upon the new arrival. She had never before seen anything so tiny, so red, or so utterly beautiful!

Bernard left his breakfast to join the circle of admirers, and when the doctor arrived a few minutes later he was in triumphant possession of the small bundle that held them all spellbound. He knew how to handle a baby, and was extremely proud of the accomplishment.

It was not till two days later, however, that he was admitted to see the mother. She had turned the corner, they said, but she was terribly weak. Yet, as soon as she heard of the presence of her brother-in-law, she insisted upon seeing him.

Everard brought him in to her, but for the first time in her life she dismissed him when the introduction was effected.

"We shall get on better alone," she said, with a smile. "You come back—afterwards."

So Everard withdrew, and Bernard sat down by her side, his big hand holding hers.

"That is nice," she said, her pale face turned to him. "I have been wanting to know you ever since Everard first told me of you."

He bent with a little smile and kissed the slender fingers he held. "Then the desire has been mutual," he said.

"Thank you." Stella's eyes were fixed upon his face. "I was afraid," she said, with slight hesitation, "that you might think—when you saw Everard—that marriage hadn't altogether agreed with him."

Bernard's kindly blue eyes met hers with absolute directness. "No, I shouldn't have thought that," he said. "But I see a change in him of course. He is growing old much too fast. What is it? Overwork?"

"I don't know." She still spoke with hesitation. "I think it is a good deal—anxiety."

"Ah!" Bernard's hand closed very strongly upon hers. "He is not the only person that suffers from that complaint, I think."

She smiled rather wanly. "I ought not to worry. It's wrong, isn't it?"

"It's unnecessary," he said. "And it's a handicap to progress. But it's difficult not to when things go wrong, I admit. We need to keep a very tight hold on faith. And even then—"

"Yes, even then—" Stella said, her lips quivering a little—"when the one beloved is in danger, who can be untroubled?"

"We are all in the same keeping," said Bernard gently. "I think that's worth remembering. If we can trust ourselves to God, we ought to be able to trust even the one beloved to His care."

Stella's eyes were full of tears. "I am afraid I don't know Him well enough to trust Him like that," she said.

Bernard leant towards her. "My dear," he said, "it is only by faith that you can ever come to knowledge. You have to trust without definitely knowing. Knowledge—that inner certainty—comes afterwards, always afterwards. You can't get it for yourself. You can only pray for it, and prepare the ground."

Her fingers pressed his feebly. "I wonder," she said, "if you have ever known what it was to walk in darkness."

Bernard smiled. "Yes, I have floundered pretty deep in my time," he said. "There's only one thing for it, you know; just to keep on till the light comes. You'll find, when the lamp shines across the desert at last, that you're not so far out of the track after all—if you're only keeping on. That's the main thing to remember."

"Ah!" Stella sighed. "I believe you could help me a lot."

"Delighted to try," said Bernard.

But she shook her head. "No, not now, not yet. I want you—to take care of Everard for me."

"Can't he take care of himself?" questioned Bernard. "I thought I had taught him to be fairly independent."

"Oh, it isn't that," she said. "It is—it is—India."

He leaned nearer to her, the smile gone from his eyes. "I thought so," he said. "You needn't be afraid to speak out to me. I am discretion itself, especially where he is concerned. What has India been doing to him?"

With a faint gesture she motioned him nearer still. Her face was very pale, but resolution was shining in her eyes. "Don't let us be disturbed!" she whispered. "And I—I will tell you—all I know."

CHAPTER IV
THE SERPENT IN THE DESERT

The battalion was ordered back to Kurrumpore for the winter months, ostensibly to go into a camp of exercise, though whispers of some deeper motive for the move were occasionally heard. Markestan, though outwardly calm and well-behaved, was not regarded with any great confidence by the Government, so it was said, though, officially, no one had the smallest suspicion of danger.

It was with mixed feelings that Stella returned at length to The Green Bungalow, nearly three months after her baby's birth. During that time she had seen a good deal of her brother-in-law, who, nothing daunted by the discomforts of the journey, went to and fro several times between Bhulwana and the Plains. They had become close friends, and Stella had grown to regard his presence as a safeguard and protection against the nameless evils that surrounded Everard, though she could not have said wherefore.

He it was who, with Peter's help, prepared the bungalow for her coming. It had been standing empty all through the hot weather and the rains. The compound was a mass of overgrown verdure, and the bungalow itself was in some places thick with fungus.

When Stella came to it, however, all the most noticeable traces of neglect had been removed. The place was scrubbed clean. The ragged roses had been trained along the verandah-trellis, and fresh Indian matting had been laid down everywhere.

The garden was still a wilderness, but Bernard declared that he would have it in order before many weeks had passed. It was curious how, with his very limited knowledge of natives and their ways, he managed to extract the most willing labour from them. Peter the Great smiled with gratified pride whenever he gave him an order, and all the other servants seemed to entertain a similar veneration for the big, blue-eyed *sahib* who was never heard to speak in anger or impatience, and yet whose word was one which somehow no one found it possible to disregard.

Tommy had become fond of him also. He was wont to say that Bernard was the most likable fellow he had ever met. An indefinable barrier had grown up between him and his brother-in-law, which, desperately though he had striven against it, had made the old easy intercourse impossible. Bernard was in a fashion the link between them. Strangely they were always more intimate in his presence than when alone, less conscious of unknown ground, of reserves that could not be broached.

Strive as he might, Tommy could not forget that evening at the mess—the historic occasion, as he had lightly named it—when like an evil magic at work he had witnessed the smirching of his hero's honour. He had sought to bury the matter deep, to thrust it out of all remembrance, but the evil wrought was too subtle and too potent. It reared itself against him and would not be trampled down.

Had any of his brother-officers dared to mention the affair to him, he would have been furious, would strenuously have defended that which apparently his friend did not deem it worth his while to defend. But no one ever spoke of it. It dwelt among them, a shameful thing, ignored yet ever present.

Everard came and went as before, only more reticent, more grim, more unapproachable than he had ever been in the old days. His utter indifference to the cold courtesy accorded him was beyond all scorn. He simply did not see when men avoided him. He was supremely unaware of the coldness that made Tommy writhe in impotent rebellion. He had never mixed very freely with his fellows. Upon Tommy alone had he bestowed his actual friendship, and to Tommy alone did he now display any definite change of front. His demeanour towards the boy was curiously gentle. He never treated him confidentially or spoke of intimate things. That invincible barrier which Tommy strove so hard to ignore, he seemed to take for granted. But he was invariably kind in all his dealings with him, as if he realized that Tommy had lost the one possession he prized above all others and were sorry for him.

Whatever Tommy's mood, and his moods varied considerably, he was never other than patient with him, bearing with him as he would never have borne in the byegone happier days of their good comradeship. He never rebuked him, never offered him advice, never attempted in any fashion to test the influence that yet remained to him. And his very forbearance hurt Tommy more poignantly than any open rupture or even tacit avoidance could have hurt him. There were times when he would have sacrificed all he had, even down to his own honour, to have forced an understanding with Monck, to have compelled him to yield up his secret. But whenever he braced himself to ask for an explanation, he found himself held back. There was a boundary he could not pass, a force relentless and irresistible, that checked him at the very outset. He lacked the strength to batter down the iron will that opposed him behind that unaccustomed gentleness. He could only bow miserably to the unspoken word of command that kept him at a distance.

He was too loyal ever to discuss the matter with Bernard, though he often wondered how the latter regarded his brother's attitude. At least there was no strain in their relationship though he was fairly convinced that Everard had not taken Bernard into his confidence. This fact held a subtle solace for him, for it meant that Bernard, who was as open as the day, was content to be in the dark, and satisfied that it held nothing of an evil nature. This unquestioning faith on Bernard's part was Tommy's one ray of light. He knew instinctively that Bernard was not a man to compromise with evil. He carried his banner that all might see. He was not ashamed to confess his Master before all men, and Tommy mutely admired him for it.

He marked with pleasure the intimacy that existed between this man and his sister. Like Stella, though in a different sense, he had grown imperceptibly to look upon him as a safeguard. He was a sure antidote to nervous forebodings. The advent of the baby also gave him keen delight. Tommy was a lover of all things youthful. He declared he had never felt so much at home in India before.

Peter also was almost as much in the baby's company as was its *ayah*. The administration of the bottle was Peter's proudest privilege, and he would walk soft-footed to and fro for any length of time carrying the infant in his arms. Stella was always content when the baby was in his charge. Her confidence in Peter's devotion was unbounded. The child was not very strong and needed great care. The care Peter lavished upon it was as tender as her own. There was something of a feud between him and the *ayah*, but no trace of this was ever apparent in her presence. As for the baby, he seemed to love Peter better than any one else, and was generally at his best when in his arms.

The Green Bungalow became a favourite meeting-place with the ladies of the station, somewhat, to Stella's dismay. Lady Harriet swept in at all hours to hold inspections of the infant's progress and give advice, and everyone who had ever had a baby seemed to have some fresh warning or word of instruction to bestow.

They were all very kind to her. She received many invitations to tea, and smiled over her sudden popularity. But—it dawned upon her when, she had been about three weeks in the station—no one but the Ralstons seemed to think of asking her and her husband to dine. She thought but little of the omission at first. Evening entertainments held but slight attraction for her, but as time went on and Christmas festivities drew near, she could not avoid noticing that practically every invitation she received was worded in so strictly personal a fashion that there could be no doubt that Everard was not included in it. Bernard was often asked separately, but he generally refused on the score of the evening being his best working time.

Also, after a while, she could not fail to notice that Tommy was no longer at his ease in Everard's presence. The old careless *camaraderie* between them was gone, and she missed it at first vaguely, later with an uneasiness that she could not stifle. There was something in Tommy's attitude towards his friend that hurt her. She knew by instinct that the boy was not happy. She wondered at first if there could be some quarrel between them, but decided in face of Everard's unvarying kindness to Tommy that this could not be.

Another thing struck her as time went on. Everard always checked all talk of his prospects. He was so repressive on the subject that she could not possibly pursue it, and she came at last to conclude that his hope of preferment had vanished like a mirage in the desert.

He was very good to her, but his absences continued in the old unaccountable way, and her dread of Rustam Karin, which Bernard's presence had in a measure allayed, revived again till at times it was almost more than she could bear.

She did not talk of it any further to Bernard. She had told him all her fears, and she knew he was on guard, knew instinctively that she could count upon him though he never reverted to the matter. Somehow she could not bring herself to speak to him of the strange avoidance of her husband that was being practised by the rest of the station either. She endured it dumbly, holding herself more and more aloof in consequence of it as the days went by. Ever since the days of her own ostracism she had placed a very light price upon social popularity. The love of such women as Mary Ralston—and the love of little Tessa—were of infinitely greater value in her eyes.

Tessa and her mother were once more guests in the Ralstons' bungalow. Netta had desired to stay at the new hotel which—as also at Udalkland—native enterprise had erected near the Club; but Mrs. Ralston had vetoed this plan with much firmness, and after a little petulant argument Netta had given in. She did not greatly care for staying with the Ralstons. Mary was a dear good soul of course, but inclined to be interfering, and now that the zest of life was returning to Netta, her desire for her own way was beginning to reassert itself. However, the Ralstons' bungalow also was in close proximity to the Club, and in consideration of this she consented to take up her abode there. Her days of seclusion were over. She had emerged from them with a fevered craving for excitement of any description mingled with that odd defiance that had characterized her almost ever since her husband's death. She had never kept any very great control upon her tongue, but now it was positively venomous. She seemed to bear a grudge against all the world.

Tessa, with her beloved Scooter, went her own way as of yore, and spent most of her time at The Green Bungalow where there was always someone to welcome her. She arrived there one day in a state of great indignation, Scooter as usual clinging to her hair and trying his utmost to escape.

Like a whirlwind she burst upon Stella, who was sitting with her baby in the French window of her room.

"Aunt Stella," she cried breathlessly, "Mother says she's sure you and Uncle Everard won't go to the officers' picnic at Khanmulla this year. It isn't true, is it, Aunt Stella? You will go, and you'll take me with you, won't you?"

The officers' picnic at Khanmulla! The words called up a flood of memory in Stella's heart. She looked at Tessa, the smile of welcome still upon her face; but she did not see her. She was standing once more in the moonlight, listening to the tread of a man's feet on the path below her, waiting—waiting with a throbbing heart—for the sound of a man's quiet voice.

Tessa came nearer to her, looking at her with an odd species of speculation. "Aunt Stella," she said, "that wasn't—all—Mother said. She made me very, very angry. Shall I tell you—would you like to know—why?"

Stella's eyes ceased to gaze into distance. She looked at the child. Some vague misgiving stirred within her. It was the instinct of self-defence that moved her to say, "I don't want to listen to any silly gossip, Tessa darling."

"It isn't silly!" declared Tessa. "It's much worse than that. And I'm going to tell you, cos I think I'd better. She said that everybody says that Uncle Everard won't go to the picnic on Christmas Eve cos he's ashamed to look people in the face. I said it wasn't true." Very stoutly Tessa brought out the assertion; then, a moment later, with a queer sidelong glance into Stella's face, "It isn't true, dear, is it?"

Ashamed! Everard ashamed! Stella's hands clasped each other unconsciously about the sleeping baby on her lap. Strangely her own voice came to her while she was not even aware of uttering the words. "Why should he be ashamed?"

Tessa's eyes were dark with mystery. She pressed against Stella with a small protective gesture. "Darling, she said horrid things, but they aren't true any of them. If Uncle Everard had been there, she wouldn't have dared. I told her so."

With an effort Stella unclasped her hands. She put her arm around the little girl. "Tell me what they are saying, Tessa," she said. "I think with you that I had better know."

Tessa suffered Scooter to escape in order to hug Stella close. "They are saying things about when he went on leave just after you married Captain Dacre, how he said he wanted to go to England and didn't go, and how—how—" Tessa checked herself abruptly. "It came out at mess one night," she ended.

A faint smile of relief shone, in Stella's eyes. "But I knew that, Tessa," she said. "He told me himself. Is that all?"

"You knew?" Tessa's eyes shone with sudden triumph. "Oh, then do tell them what he was doing and stop their horrid talking! It was Mrs. Burton began it. I always did hate her."

"I can't tell them what he was doing," Stella said, feeling her heart sink again.

"You can't? Oh!" Keen disappointment sounded in Tessa's voice. "But p'raps he would," she added reflectively, "if he knew what beasts they all are. Shall I ask him to, Aunt Stella?"

"Tell me first what they are saying!" Stella said, bracing herself to face the inevitable.

Tessa looked at her dubiously for a moment. Somehow she would have found it easier to tell this thing to Monck himself than to Stella. And yet she had a feeling that it must be told, that Stella ought to know. She clung a little closer to her.

"I always did hate Major Burton," she said sweepingly. "I know he started it in the first place. He said—and now she says—that—that it's very funny that the leave Uncle Everard had when he pretended to go to England should have come just at the time that Captain Dacre was killed in the mountains, and that a horrid old man Uncle Everard knows called Rustam Karin who lives in the bazaar was away at the same time. And they just wonder if p'raps he—the old man—had anything to do with Captain Dacre dying like he did, and if Uncle Everard knows—something—about it. That's how they put it, Aunt Stella. Mother only told me to tease me, but that's what they say."

She stopped, pressing Stella's hand very tightly to her little quivering bosom, and there followed a pause, a deep silence that seemed to have in it something of an almost suffocating quality.

Tessa moved at last because it became unbearable, moved and looked down into Stella's face as if half afraid. She could not have said what she expected to see there, but she was undoubtedly relieved when the beautiful face, white as death though it was, smiled back at her without a tremor.

Stella kissed her tenderly and let her go. "Thank you for telling me, darling," she said gently. "It is just as well that I should know what people say, even though it is nothing but idle gossip—idle gossip." She repeated the words with emphasis. "Run and find Scooter, sweetheart!" she said. "And put all this silly nonsense out of your dear little head for good! I must take baby to *ayah* now. By and by we will read a fairy-tale together and enjoy ourselves."

Tessa ran away comforted, yet also vaguely uneasy. Her tenderness notwithstanding, there was something not quite normal about Stella's dismissal of her. This kind friend of hers had never sent her away quite so summarily before. It was almost as if she were half afraid that Tessa might see—or guess—too much.

As for Stella, she carried her baby to the *ayah*, and then shut herself into her own room where she remained for a long time face to face with these new doubts.

He had loved her before her marriage; he had called their union Kismet. He wielded a strange, almost an uncanny power among natives. And there was Rustam Karin whom long ago she had secretly credited with Ralph Dacre's death—the serpent in the garden—the serpent in the desert also—whose evil coils, it seemed to her, were daily tightening round her heart.

CHAPTER V
THE WOMAN'S WAY

It was three days later that Tommy came striding in from the polo-ground in great excitement with the news that Captain Ermsted's murderer had been arrested.

"All honour to Everard!" he said, flinging himself into a chair by Stella's side. "The fellow was caught at Khanmulla. Barnes arrested him, but he gives the credit of the catch to Everard. The fellow will swing, of course. It will be a sensational trial, for rumour has it that the Rajah was pushing behind. He, of course, is smooth as oil. I saw him at the Club just now, hovering round Mrs. Ermsted as usual, and she encouraging him. That girl is positively infatuated. Shouldn't wonder if there's a rude awakening before her. I beg your pardon, sir. You spoke?" He turned abruptly to Bernard who was seated near.

"I was only wondering what Everard's share had been in tracking this charming person down," observed the elder Monck, who was smiling a little at Tommy's evident excitement.

"Oh, everyone knows that Everard is a regular sleuth-hound," said Tommy. "He is more native than the natives when there is anything of this kind in the wind. He is a born detective, and he and that old chap in the bazaar are such a strong combination that they are practically infallible and invincible."

"Do you mean Rustam Karin?" Stella spoke very quietly, not lifting her eyes from her work.

Tommy turned to her. "That's the chap. The old beggar fellow. At least they say he is. He never shows. Hafiz does all the show part. The old boy is the brain that works the wires. Everard has immense faith in him."

"I know," Stella said.

Her voice sounded strangled, and Bernard looked across at her; but she continued to work without looking up.

Tommy lingered for a while, expatiating upon Everard's astuteness, and finally went away to dress for mess still in a state of considerable excitement.

Stella and Bernard sat in silence after his departure. There seemed to be nothing to say. But when, after a time, he got up to go, she very suddenly raised her eyes.

"Bernard!"

"My dear!" he said very kindly.

She put out a hand to him, almost as if feeling her way in a dark place. "I want to ask you," she said, speaking hurriedly, "whether you know—whether you have ever heard—the things that are being said about—about Everard and this man—Rustam Karin."

She spoke with immense effort. It was evident that she was greatly agitated.

Bernard stopped beside her, holding her hand firmly in his. "Tell me what they are!" he said gently.

She made a hopeless gesture. "Then you do know! Everyone knows. Naturally I am the last. You knew I connected that dreadful man long ago with—with Ralph's death. I had good reason for doing so after—after I had actually seen him on the verandah here that awful night. But—but now it seems—because he and Everard have always been in partnership—because they were both absent at the time of Ralph's death, no one knew where—people are talking and saying—and saying—" She broke off with a sharp, agonized sound. "I can't tell you what they are saying!" she whispered.

"It is false!" said Bernard stoutly. "It's a foul lie of the devil's own concocting! How long have you known of this? Who was vile enough to tell you?"

"You knew?" she whispered.

"I never heard the thing put into words but I had my own suspicions of what was going about," he admitted. "But I never believed it. Nothing on this earth would induce me to believe it. You don't believe it, either, child. You know him better than that."

She hid her face from him with a smothered sob. "I thought I did—once."

"You did," he asserted staunchly. "You do! Don't tell me otherwise, for I shan't believe you if you do! What kind friend told you? I want to know."

"Oh, it was only little Tessa. You mustn't blame her. She was full of indignation, poor child. Her mother taunted her with it. You know—or perhaps you don't know—what Netta Ermsted is."

Bernard's face was very grim as he made reply. "I think I can guess. But you are not going to be poisoned by her venom. Why don't you tell Everard, have it out with him? Say you don't believe it, but it hurts you to hear a damnable slander like this and not be able to refute it! You are not afraid of him, Stella? Surely you are not afraid of him!"

But Stella only hid her face a little lower, and spoke no word.

He laid his hand upon her as she sat. "What does that mean?" he said. "Isn't your love equal to the strain?"

She shook her head dumbly. She could not meet his look.

"What?" he said. "Is my love greater than yours then? I would trust his honour even to the gallows, if need be. Can't you say as much?"

She answered him with her head bowed, her words barely audible. "It isn't a question of love. I—should always love him—whatever he did."

"Ah!" The flicker of a smile crossed Bernard's face. "That is the woman's way. There's a good deal to be said for it, I daresay."

"Yes—yes." Quiveringly she made answer. "But—if this thing were true—my love would have to be sacrificed, even—even though it would mean tearing out my very heart. I couldn't go on—with him. I couldn't—possibly."

Her words trembled into silence, and the light died out of Bernard's eyes. "I see," he said slowly. "But, my dear, I can't understand how you—loving him as you do—can allow for a moment, even in your most secret heart, that such a thing as this could be true. That is where you begin to go wrong. That is what does the harm."

She looked up at last, and the despair in her eyes went straight to his heart. "I have always felt there was—something," she said. "I can't tell you exactly how. But it has always been there. I tried hard not to love him—not to marry him. But it was no use. He mastered me with his love. But I always knew—I always knew—that there was something hidden which I might not see. I have caught sight of it a dozen times, but I have never really seen it." She suppressed a quick shudder. "I have been afraid of it, and—I have always looked the other way."

"A mistake," Bernard said. "You should always face your bogies. They have a trick of swelling out of all proportion to their actual size if you don't."

"Yes, I know. I know." Stella pressed his hand and withdrew her own. "You are very good," she said. "I couldn't have said this to any one but you. I can't speak to Everard. It isn't entirely my own weakness. He holds me off. He makes me feel that it would be a mistake to speak."

"Will you let me?" Bernard suggested, taking out his pipe and frowning over it.

She shook her head instantly. "No!—no! I am sure he wouldn't answer you, and—and it would hurt him to know that I had turned to any one else, even to you. It would only make things more difficult to bear." She stopped short with a nervous gesture. "He is coming now," she said.

There was a sound of horse's hoofs at the gate, and in a moment Everard Monck came into view, riding his tall Waler which was smothered with dust and foam.

He waved to his wife as he rode up the broad path. His dark face was alight with a grim triumph. A *saice* ran forward to take his animal, and he slid to the ground and stamped his feet as if stiff.

Then without haste he mounted the steps and came to them.

"I am not fit to come near you," he said, as he drew near. "I have been right across the desert to Udalkhand, and had to do some hard riding to get back in time." He pulled off his glove and just touched Stella's cheek in passing. "Hullo, Bernard! About time for a drink, isn't it?"

He looked momentarily surprised when Stella swiftly turned her head and kissed the hand that had so lightly caressed her. He stopped beside her and laid it on her shoulder.

"I am afraid you won't approve of me when I tell you what I have been doing," he said.

She looked up at him. "I know. Tommy came in and told us. You—seem to have done something rather great. I suppose we ought to congratulate you."

He smiled a little. "It is always satisfactory when a murderer gets his deserts," he said, "though I am afraid the man who does the job is not in all cases the prime malefactor."

"Ah!" Stella said. She folded up her work with hands that were not quite steady; her face was very pale.

Everard stood looking down at the burnished coils of her hair. "Are you going to the dance at the Club to-night?" he asked, after a moment.

She shook her head instantly. "No."

"Why not?" he questioned.

She leaned back in her chair, and looked up at him. "As you know, I never was particularly fond of the station society."

He frowned a little. "It's better than nothing. You are too given to shutting yourself up. Bernard thinks so too."

Stella glanced towards her brother-in-law with a slight lift of the eyebrows. "I don't think he does. But in any case, we are engaged to-night. It is Tessa's birthday, and she and Scooter are coming to dine."

"Coming to dine! What on earth for?" Everard looked his astonishment.

"My doing," said Bernard. "It's a surprise-party. Stella very kindly fell in with the plan, but it originated with me. You see, Princess Bluebell is ten years old to-day, and quite grown up. Mrs. Ralston had a children's party for her this afternoon which I was privileged to attend. I must say Tessa made a charming hostess, but she confided to me at parting that the desire of her life was to play Cinderella and go out to dinner in a 'rickshaw all by herself. So I undertook then and there that a 'rickshaw should be waiting for her at the gate at eight o'clock, and she should have a stodgy grown-up entertainment to follow. She was delighted with the idea, poor little soul. The Ralstons are going to the Club dance, and of course Mrs. Ermsted also, but Tommy is giving up the first half to come and amuse Cinderella. Mrs. Ralston thinks the child will be ill with so much excitement, but a tenth birthday is something of an occasion, as I pointed out. And she certainly behaved wonderfully well this afternoon, though she was about the only child who did. I nearly throttled the Burton youngster for kicking the *ayah*, little brute. He seemed to think it was a very ordinary thing to do." Bernard stopped himself with a laugh. "You'll be bored with all this, and I must go and make ready. There are to be Chinese lanterns to light the way and a strip of red cloth on the steps. Peter is helping as usual, Peter the invaluable. We shan't keep it up very late. Will you join us? Or are you also bound for the Club?"

"I will join you with pleasure," Everard said. "I haven't seen the imp for some days. There has been too much on hand. How is the boy, Stella? Shall we go and say good-night to him?"

Stella had risen. She put her hand through his arm. "Bernard and Tommy are to do all the entertaining, and you and I can amuse each other for once. We don't often have such a chance."

She smiled as she spoke, but her lips were quivering. Bernard sauntered away, and as he went, Everard stooped and kissed her upturned face.

He did not speak, and she clung to him for a moment passionately close. Wherefore she could not have said, but there was in her embrace something to restrain her tears. She forced them back with her utmost resolution as they went together to see their child.

CHAPTER VI
THE SURPRISE PARTY

Punctually at eight o'clock Tessa arrived, slightly awed but supremely happy, seated in a 'rickshaw, escorted by Bernard, and hugging the beloved Scooter to her eager little breast.

Her eyes were shining with mysterious expectation. As her cavalier handed her from her chariot up the red-carpeted steps she moved as one who treads enchanted ground. The little creature in her arms wore an air of deep suspicion. His pointed head turned to and fro with ferret-like movements. His sharp red eyes darted hither and thither almost apprehensively. He was like a toy on wires.

"He is going—p'raps—to turn into a fairy prince soon," explained Tessa. "I'm not sure that he quite likes the idea though. He would rather kill a dragon. P'raps he'll do both."

"P'raps," agreed Bernard.

He led the little girl along the vernadah under the bobbing lanterns. Tessa looked about her critically. "There aren't any other children, are there?" she said.

"Not one," said Bernard, "unless you count me. We are going to dine together, you and I, quite alone—if you can put up with me. And after that we will hold a reception for grown-ups only."

"I shall like that," said Tessa graciously. "Ah, here is Peter! Peter, will you please bring a box for Scooter while I have my dinner? He wants to go snake-hunting," she added to Bernard. "And if he does that, I shan't have him again for the rest of the evening."

"You don't get snakes this time of year, do you?" asked Bernard.

"Oh yes, sometimes. I saw one the other day when I was out with Major Ralston. He tried to kill it with his stick, but it got away. And Scooter wasn't there. They like to hide under bits of carpet like this," said Tessa in an instructive tone, pointing to the strip that had been laid in her honour. "Are you afraid of snakes, Uncle St. Bernard?"

"Yes," said Bernard with simplicity. "Aren't you?"

Tessa looked slightly surprised at the admission. "I don't know. I expect I am. Peter isn't. Peter's very brave."

"He has been more or less brought up with them," said Bernard. "Scorpions too. He smiled the other day when I fled from a scorpion in the garden. And I believe he has a positively fatherly feeling for rats."

Tessa shivered a little. "Scooter killed a rat the other day, and it squealed dreadfully. I don't think he ought to do things like that, but of course he doesn't know any better."

"He looks as if he knows a lot," said Bernard.

"Yes, I wish he would learn to talk. He's awful clever. Do you think we could ever teach him?" asked Tessa.

Bernard shook his head. "No. It would take a magician to do that. We are not clever enough, either of us. Peter now—"

"Oh, is Peter a magician?" said Tessa, with shining eyes. "Peter, dear Peter," turning to him ecstatically as he appeared with a box in which to imprison her darling, "do you think you could possibly teach my little Scooter to talk?"

Peter smiled all over his bronze countenance. "Missy *sahib*, only the Holy Ones can do that," he said.

Tessa's face fell. "That's as bad as telling you to pray for anything, isn't it?" she said to Bernard. "And my prayers never come true. Do yours?"

"They always get answered," said Bernard, "some time or other."

"Oh, do they?" Tessa regarded him with interest. "Does God come and talk to you then?" she said.

He smiled a little. "He speaks to all who wait to hear, my princess," he said.

"Only to grown-ups," said Tessa, looking incredulous.

Bernard put his arm round her. "No," he said. "It's the children who come first with Him. He may not give them just what they ask for, but it's generally something better."

Tessa stared at him, her eyes round and dark. "S'pose," she said suddenly, "a big snake was to come out of that corner, and I was to say, 'Don't let it bite me, Lord!' Do you think it would?"

"No," said Bernard very decidedly.

"Oh!" said Tessa. "Well, I wish one would then, for I'd love to see if it would or not."

Bernard pulled her to him and kissed her. "We won't talk any more about snakes or you'll be dreaming of them," he said. "Come along and dine with me! Rather sport having it all to ourselves, eh?"

"Where's Aunt Stella and Uncle Everard?" asked Tessa.

"Oh, they're preparing for the reception. Let me take your Highness's cloak! This is the banqueting-room."

He threw the cloak over a chair in the verandah, and led her into the drawing-room, where a small table lighted by candles with crimson shades awaited them.

"How pretty!" cried Tessa, clapping her hands.

Peter in snowy attire, benign and magnificent, attended to their wants, and the feast proceeded, vastly enjoyed by both. Tessa had never been so *fêted* in all her small life before.

When, at the end of the repast, to an accompaniment of nuts and sweetmeats, Bernard poured her a tiny ruby-coloured liqueur glass of wine, her delight knew no bounds.

"I've never enjoyed myself so much before," she declared. "What a ducky little glass! Now I'm going to drink your health!"

"No. I drink yours first." Bernard arose, holding his glass high. "I drink to the Princess Bluebell. May she grow fairer every day! And may her cup of blessing be always full!"

"Thank you," said Tessa. "And now, Uncle St. Bernard, I'm going to drink to you. May you always have lots to laugh at! And may your prayers always come true! That rhymes, doesn't it?" she added complacently. "Do I drink all my wine now, or only a sip?"

"Depends," said Bernard.

"How does it depend?"

"It depends on how much you love me," he explained. "If there's any one else you love better, you save a little for him."

She looked straight at him with a hint of embarrassment in her eyes. "I'm afraid I love Uncle Everard best," she said.

Bernard smiled upon her with reassuring kindliness. "Quite right, my child. So you ought. There's Tommy too and Aunt Stella. I am sure you want to drink to them."

118

Tessa slipped round the table to his side, clasping her glass tightly. As she came within the circle of his arm she whispered, "Yes, I love them ever such a lot. But I love you best of all, except Uncle Everard, and he doesn't want me when he's got Aunt Stella. I s'pose you never wanted a little girl for your very own did you?"

He looked down at her, his blue eyes full of tenderness. "I've often wanted you, Tessa," he said.

"Have you?" she beamed upon him, rubbing her flushed cheek against his shoulder. "I'm sure you can have me if you like," she said.

He pressed her to him. "I don't think your mother would agree to that, you know."

Tessa's red lips pouted disgust. "Oh, she wouldn't care! She never cares what I do. She likes it much best when I'm not there."

Bernard's brows were slightly drawn. His arm held the little slim body very closely to him.

"You and I would be so happy," insinuated Tessa, as he did not speak. "I'd do as you told me always. And I'd never, never be rude to you."

He bent and kissed her. "I know that, my darling."

"And when you got old, dear Uncle St. Bernard,—really old, I mean—I'd take such care of you," she proceeded. "I'd be—more—than a daughter to you."

"Ah!" he said. "I should like that, my princess of the bluebell eyes."

"You would?" she looked at him eagerly. "Then don't you think you might tell Mother you'll have me? I know she wouldn't mind."

He smiled at her impetuosity. "We must be patient, my princess," he said. "These things can't be done offhand, if at all."

She slid her arm round his neck and hugged him. "But there is the weeniest, teeniest chance, isn't there? 'Cos you do think you'd like to have me if I was good, and I'd—love—to belong to you. Is there just the wee-est little chance, Uncle St. Bernard? Would it be any good praying for it?"

He took her little hand into his warm kind grasp, for she was quivering all over with excitement.

"Yes, pray, little one!" he said. "You may not get exactly what you want. But there will be an answer if you keep on. Be sure of that!"

Tessa nodded comprehension. "All right. I will. And you will too, won't you? It'll be fun both praying for the same thing, won't it? Oh, my wine! I nearly spilt it."

"Better drink it and make it safe!" he said with a twinkle. "I'm going to drink mine, and then we'll go on to the verandah and wait for something to happen."

"Is something going to happen?" asked Tessa, with a shiver of delighted anticipation.

He laughed. "Perhaps,—if we live long enough."

Tessa drank her wine almost casually. "Come on!" she said. "Let's go!"

But ere they reached the French window that led on to the verandah, a sudden loud report followed by a succession of minor ones coming from the compound told them that the happenings had already begun. Tessa gave one great jump, and then literally danced with delight.

"Fireworks!" she cried. "Fireworks! That's Tommy! I know it is. Do let's go and look!" They went, and hung over the verandah-rail to watch a masked figure attired in an old pyjama suit of vivid green and white whirling a magnificent wheel of fire that scattered glowing sparks in all directions.

Tessa was wild with excitement. "How lovely!" she cried. "Oh, how lovely! Dear Uncle St. Bernard, mayn't I go down and help him?"

But Bernard decreed that she should remain upon the verandah, and, strangely, Tessa submitted without protest. She held his hand tightly, as if to prevent herself making any inadvertent dash for freedom, but she leapt to and fro like a dog on the leash, squeaking her ecstasy at every fresh display achieved by the bizarre masked figure below them.

Bernard watched her with compassionate sympathy in his kindly eyes. Little Tessa had won a very warm place in his heart. He marvelled at her mother's attitude of callous indifference.

Certainly Tessa had never enjoyed herself more thoroughly than on that evening of her tenth birthday. Time flew by on the wings of delight. Tommy's exhibition was appreciated with almost delirious enthusiasm on the verandah, and a little crowd of natives at the gate pushed and nudged each other with an admiration quite as heartfelt though carefully suppressed.

The display had been going on for some time when Stella came out alone and joined the two on the verandah. To Tessa's eager inquiry for Uncle Everard she made answer that he had been called out on business, and to Bernard she added that Hafiz had sent him a message by one of the servants, and she supposed he had gone to Rustam Karin's stall in the bazaar. She looked pale and dispirited, but she joined in Tessa's delighted appreciation of the entertainment which now was drawing to a close.

It was getting late, and as with a shower of coloured stars the magician in the compound accomplished a grand *finale*, Bernard put his arm around the narrow shoulders and said, with a kindly squeeze, "I am going to see my princess home again now. She mustn't lose all her beauty-sleep."

She lifted her face to kiss him. "It has been—lovely," she said. "I do wish I needn't go back to-night. Do you think Aunt Mary would mind if I stayed with you?"

He smiled at her whimsically. "Perhaps not, princess; but I am going to take you back to her all the same. Say good-night to Aunt Stella! She looks as if a good dose of bed would do her good."

Tommy, with his mask in his hand, came running up the verandah-steps, and Tessa sprang to meet him.

"Oh, Tommy—darling, I have enjoyed myself so!"

He kissed her lightly. "That's all right, scaramouch. So have I. I must get out of this toggery now double-quick. I suppose you are off in your 'rickshaw? I'll walk with you. It'll be on the way to the Club."

"Oh, how lovely! You on one side and Uncle St. Bernard on the other!" cried Tessa.

"The princess will travel in state," observed Bernard. "Ah! Here comes Peter with Scooter! Have your cloak on before you take him out!"

The cloak had fallen from the chair. Peter set down Scooter in his prison, and picked it up. By the light of the bobbing, coloured lanterns he placed it about her shoulders.

Tessa suddenly turned and sat down. "My shoe is undone," she said, extending her foot with a royal air. "Where is the prince?"

The words were hardly out of her mouth before another sound escaped her which she hastily caught back as though instinct had stifled it in her throat. "Look!" she gasped.

Peter was nearest to her. He had bent to release Scooter, but like a streak of light he straightened himself. He saw—before any one else had time to realize—- the hideous thing that writhed in momentary entanglement in the folds of Tessa's cloak, and then suddenly reared itself upon her lap as she sat frozen stiff with horror.

He stooped over the child, his hands outspread, waiting for the moment to swoop. "Missy *sahib*, not move—not move!" he said softly above her. "My missy *sahib* not going to be hurt. Peter taking care of Missy *sahib*."

And, with glassy eyes fixed and white lips rigid, Tessa's strained whisper came in answer. "O Lord, don't let it bite me!"

Tommy would have flung himself forward then, but Bernard caught and held him. He had seen the look in the Indian's eyes, and he knew beyond all doubting that Tessa was safe, if any human power could make her so.

Stella knew it also. In that moment Peter loomed gigantic to her. His gleaming eyes and strangely smiling face held her spellbound with a fascination greater even than that wicked, vibrating thing that coiled, black and evil, on the white of Tessa's frock could command. She knew that if none intervened, Peter would accomplish Tessa's deliverance.

But there was one factor which they had all forgotten. In those tense seconds Scooter the mongoose by some means invisible became aware of the presence of the enemy. The lid of his box had already been loosened by Peter. With a frantic effort he forced it up and leapt free.

In that moment Peter, realizing that another instant's delay might be fatal, pounced forward with a single swift swoop and seized the serpent-in his naked hands.

Tessa uttered the shriek which a few seconds before sheer horror had arrested, and fell back senseless in her chair.

Peter, grim and awful in the uncertain light, fought the thing he had gripped, while a small, red-eyed monster clawed its way up him, fiercely clambering to reach the horrible, writhing creature in the man's hold.

It was all over in a few hard-breathing seconds, over before either of the men in front of Peter or a shadowy figure behind him that had come up at Tessa's cry could give any help.

With a low laugh that was more terrible than any uttered curse, Peter flung the coiling horror over the verandah-rail into the bushes of the compound. Something else went with it, closely locked. They heard the thud of the fall, and there followed an awful, voiceless struggling in the darkness.

"Peter!" a voice said.

Peter was leaning against a post of the verandah. "Missy *sahib* is quite safe," he said, but his voice sounded odd, curiously lifeless.

The shadow that had approached behind him swept forward into the light. The lanterns shone upon a strange figure, bent, black-bearded, clothed in a long, dingy garment that seemed to envelop it from head to foot.

Peter gave a violent start and spoke a few rapid words in his own language.

The other made answer even more swiftly, and in a second there was the flash of a knife in the fitful glare. Bernard and Tommy both started forward, but Peter only thrust out one arm with a grunt. It was a gesture of submission, and it told its own tale.

"The poor devil's bitten!" gasped Tommy.

Bernard turned to Tessa and lifted the little limp body in his arms.

He thought that Stella would follow him as he bore the child into the room behind, but she did not.

The place was in semi-darkness, for they had turned down the lamps to see the fireworks. He laid her upon a sofa and turned them up again.

The light upon her face showed it pinched and deathly. Her breathing seemed to be suspended. He left her and went swiftly to the dining-room in search of brandy.

Returning with it, he knelt beside her, forcing a little between the rigid white lips. His own mouth was grimly compressed. The sight of his little playfellow lying like that cut him to the soul. She was uninjured, he knew, but he asked himself if the awful fright had killed her. He had never seen so death-like a swoon before.

He had no further thought for what was passing on the verandah outside. Tommy had said that Peter was bitten, but there were three people to look after him, whereas Tessa—poor brave mite—had only himself. He chafed her icy cheeks and hands with a desperate sense of impotence.

He was rewarded after what seemed to him an endless period of suspense. A tinge of colour came into the white lips, and the closed eyelids quivered and slowly opened. The bluebell eyes gazed questioningly into his.

"Where—where is Scooter?" whispered Tessa.

"Not far away, dear," he made answer soothingly. "We will go and find him presently. Drink another little drain of this first!"

She obeyed him almost mechanically. The shadow of a great horror still lingered in her eyes. He gathered her closely to him.

"Try and get a little sleep, darling! I'm here. I'll take care of you."

She snuggled against him. "Am I going to stay all night!" she asked.

"Perhaps, little one, perhaps!" He pressed her closer still. "Quite comfy?"

"Oh, very comfy; ever—so—comfy," murmured Tessa, closing her eyes again. "Dear—dear Uncle St. Bernard!"

She sank down in his hold, too spent to trouble herself any further, and in a very few seconds her quiet breathing told him that she was fast asleep.

He sat very still, holding her. The awful peril through which she had come had made her tenfold more precious in his eyes. He could not have loved her more tenderly if she had been indeed his own. He fell to dreaming with his cheek against her hair.

CHAPTER VII
RUSTAM KARIN

How long a time passed he never knew. It could not in actual fact have been more than a few minutes when a sudden sound from the verandah put an end to his reverie.

He laid the child back upon the sofa and got up. She was sleeping off the shock; it would be a pity to wake her. He moved noiselessly to the window.

As he did so, a voice he scarcely recognized—a woman's voice—spoke, tensely, hoarsely, close to him.

"Tommy, stop that man! Don't let him go! He is a murderer,—do you hear? He is the man who murdered my husband!"

Bernard stepped over the sill and closed the window after him. The lanterns were still swaying in the night-breeze. By their light he took in the group upon the verandah. Peter was sitting bent forward in the chair from which he had lifted Tessa. His snowy garments were deeply stained with blood. Beside him in a crouched and apelike attitude, apparently on the point of departure, was the shadowy native who had saved his life. Tommy, still fantastic and clown-like in his green and white pyjama-suit, was holding a glass for Peter to drink. And upright before them all, with accusing arm outstretched, her eyes shining like stars out of the shadows, stood Stella.

She turned to Bernard as he came forward. "Don't let him escape!" she said, her voice deep with an insistence he had never heard in it before. "He escaped last time. And there may not be another chance."

Tommy looked round sharply. "Leave the man alone!" he said. "You don't know what you're talking about, Stella. This affair has upset you. It's only old Rustam Karin."

"I know. I know. I have known for a long time that it was Rustam Karin who killed Ralph." Stella's voice vibrated on a strange note. "He may be Everard's chosen friend," she said. "But a day will come when he will turn upon him too. Bernard," she spoke with sudden appeal, "you know everything. I have told you of this man. Surely you will help me! I have made no mistake. Peter will corroborate what I say. Ask Peter!"

At sound of his name Peter lifted a ghastly face and tried to rise, but Tommy swiftly prevented him.

"Sit still, Peter, will you? You're much too shaky to walk. Finish this stuff first anyhow!"

Peter sank back, but there was entreaty in his gleaming eyes. They had bandaged his injured arm across his breast, but with his free hand he made a humble gesture of submission to his mistress.

"*Mem-sahib,*" he said, his voice low and urgent, "he is a good man—a holy man. Suffer him to go his way!"

The man in question had withdrawn into the shadows. He was in fact beating an unobtrusive retreat towards the corner of the bungalow, and would probably have effected his escape but for Bernard, who, moved by the anguished entreaty in Stella's eyes, suddenly strode forward and gripped him by his tattered garment.

"No harm in making inquiries anyway!" he said. "Don't you be in such a hurry, my friend. It won't do you any harm to come back and give an account of yourself—that is, if you are harmless."

He pulled the retreating native unceremoniously back into the light. The man made some resistance, but there was a mastery about Bernard that would not be denied. Hobbling, misshapen, muttering in his beard, he returned.

"*Mem-sahib!*" Again Peter's voice spoke, and there was a break in it as though he pleaded with Fate itself and knew it to be in vain. "He is a good man, but he is leprous. *Mem-sahib,* do not look upon him! Suffer him to go!"

Possibly the words might have had effect, for Stella's rigidity had turned to a violent shivering and it was evident that her strength was beginning to fail. But in that moment Bernard broke into an exclamation of most unwonted anger, and ruthlessly seized the ragged wisp of black beard that hung down over his victim's hollow chest.

"This is too bad!" he burst forth hotly. "By heaven it's too bad! Man, stop this tomfool mummery, and explain yourself!"

The beard came away in his indignant hand. The owner thereof straightened himself up with a contemptuous gesture till he reached the height of a tall man. The enveloping *chuddah* slipped back from his head.

"I am not the fool," he said briefly.

Stella's cry rang through the verandah, and it was Peter who, utterly forgetful of his own adversity, leapt up like a faithful hound to protect her in her hour of need.

The glass in Tommy's hand fell with a crash. Tommy himself staggered back as if he had been struck a blow between the eyes.

And across the few feet that divided them as if it had been a yawning gulf, Everard Monck faced the woman who had denounced him.

He did not utter a word. His eyes met hers unflinching. They were wholly without anger, emotionless, inscrutable. But there was something terrible behind his patience. It was as if he had bared his breast for her to strike.

And Stella—Stella looked upon him with a frozen, incredulous horror, just as Tessa had looked upon the snake upon her lap only a little while before.

In the dreadful silence that hung like a poisonous vapour upon them, there came a small rustling close to them, and a wicked little head with red, peering eyes showed through the balustrade of the verandah.

In a moment Scooter with an inexpressibly evil air of satisfaction slipped through and scuttled in a zigzag course over the matting in search of fresh prey.

It was then that Stella spoke, her voice no more than a throbbing whisper. "Rustam Karin!" she said.

Very grimly across the gulf, Everard made answer. "Rustam Karin was removed to a leper settlement before you set foot in India."

"By—Jupiter!" ejaculated Tommy.

No one else spoke till slowly, with the gesture of an old and stricken woman, Stella turned away. "I must think," she said, in the same curious vibrating whisper, as though she held converse with herself. "I must—think."

No one attempted to detain her. It was as though an invisible barrier cut her off from all but Peter. He followed her closely, forgetful of his wound, forgetful of everything but her pressing need. With dumb devotion he went after her, and they vanished beyond the flicker of the bobbing lanterns.

Of the three men left, none moved or spoke for several difficult seconds. Finally Bernard, with an abrupt gesture that seemed to express exasperation, turned sharply on his heel and without a word re-entered the room in which he had left Tessa asleep, and fastened the window behind him. He left the tangle of beard on the matting, and Scooter stopped and nosed it sensitively till Everard stooped and picked it up.

"That show being over," he remarked drily, "perhaps I may be allowed to attend to business without further interference."

Tommy gave a great start and crunched some splinters of the shattered glass under his heel. He looked at Everard with an odd, challenging light in his eyes.

"If you ask me," he said bluntly, "I should say your business here is more urgent than your business in the bazaar."

Everard raised his brows interrogatively, and as if he had asked a question Tommy made sternly resolute response.

"I've got to have a talk with you. Shall I come into your room?"

Just for a second the elder man paused; then: "Are you sure that is the wisest thing you can do?" he said.

"It's what I'm going to do," said Tommy firmly.

"All right." Everard stooped again, picked up the inquiring Scooter, and dropped him into the box in which he had spent the evening.

Then without more words, he turned along the verandah and led the way to his own room.

Tommy came close behind. He was trembling a little but his agitation only seemed to make him more determined.

He paused a moment as he entered the room behind Everard to shut the window; then valiantly tackled the hardest task that had ever come his way.

"Look here!" he said. "You must see that this thing can't be left where it is."

Everard threw off the garment that encumbered him and gravely faced his young brother-in-law.

"Yes, I do see that," he said. "I seem to have exhausted my credit all round. It's decent of you, Tommy, to have been as forbearing as you have. Now what is it you want to know?"

Tommy confronted him uncompromisingly. "I want to know the truth, that's all," he said. "Can't you stop this dust-throwing business and be straight with me?"

His tone was stubborn, his attitude almost hostile. Yet beneath it all there ran a vein of something that was very like entreaty. And Everard, steadily watching him, smiled—the faint grim smile of the fighter who sees a gap in his enemy's defences.

"I'm afraid not," he said. "I don't want to be brutal, but—you see, Tommy—it's not your business."

Tommy flinched a little, but he stood his ground. "I think you're forgetting," he said, "that Stella is my sister. It's up to me to protect her."

"From me?" Everard's words came swift and sharp as a sword-thrust.

Tommy turned suddenly white, but he straightened himself with a gesture that was not without dignity. "If necessary—yes," he said.

An abrupt silence followed his words. They stood facing each other, and the stillness between them was such that they could hear Scooter beyond the closed window scratching against his prison-walls for freedom.

It seemed endless to Tommy. He came through it unfaltering, but he felt physically sick, as if he had been struck in the back.

When Everard spoke at last, his hands clenched involuntarily. He half expected violence. But there was no hint of anger about the elder man. He had himself under iron control. His face was flint-like in its composure, his mouth implacably grim.

"Thanks for the warning!" he said briefly. "It's just as well to know how we stand. Is that all you wanted to say?"

The dismissal was as definite as if he had actually seized and thrown him out of the room. And yet there was not even suppressed wrath in his speech. It was indifferent, remote as a voice from the desert-distance. His eyes looked upon Tommy without interest or any sort of warmth, as though he had been a total stranger.

In that moment Tommy saw that sacred thing, their friendship, shattered and lying in the dust. It was not he who had flung it there, yet his soul cried out in bitter self-reproach. This was the man who had been closer to him than a brother, the man who had saved him from disaster physically and morally, watching over him with a grim tenderness that nothing had ever changed.

And now it was all done with. There was nothing left but to turn and go.

But could he? He stood irresolute, biting his lips, held there by a force that seemed outside himself. And it was Everard who made the first move, turning from him as if he had ceased to count and pulling out a note-book that he always carried to make some entry.

Tommy stood yet a moment longer as if, had it been possible, he would have broken through the barrier between them even then. But Everard did not so much as glance in his direction, and the moment passed.

In utter silence he turned and went out as he had entered. There was nothing more to be said.

CHAPTER VIII
PETER

Tessa went back to the Ralstons' bungalow that night borne in Bernard's arms. She knew very little about it, for she scarcely awoke, only dimly realizing that her friend was at hand. Tommy went with them, carrying Scooter. He said he must show himself at the Club, though Bernard suspected this to be merely an excuse for escaping for a time from The Green Bungalow. For it was evident that Tommy had had a shock.

He himself was merely angry at what appeared to him a wanton trick, too angry to trust himself in his brother's company just then. He regarded it as no part of his business to attempt to intervene between Everard and his wife, but his sympathies were all with the latter. That she in some fashion misconstrued the whole affair he could not doubt, but he was by no means sure that Everard had not deliberately schemed for some species of misunderstanding. He had, to serve his own ends, personated a man who was apparently known to be disreputable, and if he now received the credit for that man's misdeeds he had himself alone to thank. Obviously a mistake had been made, but it seemed to him that Everard had intended it to be made, had even worked to bring it about. What his object had been Bernard could not bring to conjecture. But his instinctive, inborn hatred of all underhand dealings made him resent his brother's behaviour with all the force at his command. He was too angry to attempt to unravel the mystery, and he did not broach the subject to Tommy who evidently desired to avoid it.

The whole business was beyond his comprehension and, he was convinced, beyond Stella's also. He did not think Everard would find it a very easy task to restore her confidence. Perhaps he would not attempt to do so. Perhaps he was too engrossed with the service of his goddess to care that he and his wife should drift asunder. And yet—the memory of the morning on which he had first seen those streaks of grey in his brother's hair came upon him, and an unwilling sensation of pity softened his severity. Perhaps he had been drawn in in spite of himself. Perhaps the poor beggar was a victim rather than a worshipper. Most certainly—whatever his faults—he cared deeply.

Would he be able to make Stella realize that? Bernard wondered, and shook his head in doubt.

The thought of Stella turning away with that look of frozen horror on her face pursued him through the night. Poor girl! She had looked as though the end of all things had come for her. Could he have helped her? Ought he to have left her so? He quickened his pace almost insensibly. No, he would not interfere of his own free will. But if she needed his support, if she counted upon him, he would not be found wanting. It might even be given to him eventually to help them both.

He had not seen her again. She had gone to her room with Peter in attendance, Peter who owed his life to the knife in Everard's girdle. He had had a strong feeling that Peter was the only friend she needed just then, and certainly Tessa had been his first responsibility. But the feeling that possibly she might need him was growing upon him. He wished he had satisfied himself before starting that this was not the case. But he comforted himself with the thought of Peter. He was sure that Peter would take care of her.

Yes, Peter would care for his beloved *mem-sahib*, whatever his physical disabilities. He would never fail in the execution of that his sacred duty while the power to do so was his. If all others failed her, yet would Peter remain faithful. Even then with his dog-like devotion was he crouched upon her threshold, his dark face wrapped in his garment, yet alert for every sound and mournfully aware that his mistress was not resting. Of his own wound he thought not at all. He had been very near the gate of death, and the only man in the world for whom he entertained the smallest feeling of fear had snatched him back. To his promptitude alone did Peter owe his life. He had cut out that deadly bite with a swiftness and a precision that had removed all danger of snake-poison, and in so doing he had exposed the secret which he had guarded so long and so carefully. The first moment of contact had betrayed him to Peter, but Peter was very loyal. Had he been the only one to recognize him, the secret would have been safe. He had done his best to guard it, but Fate had been against them. And the *mem-sahib*—the *mem-sahib* had turned and gone away as one heart-broken.

Peter yearned to comfort her, but the whole situation was beyond him. He could only mount guard in silence. Perhaps—presently—the great *sahib* himself would come, and make all things right again. The night was advancing. Surely he would come soon.

Barely had he begun to hope for this when the door he guarded was opened slightly from within. His *mem-sahib*, strangely white and still, looked forth.

"Peter!" she said gently.

He was up in a moment, bending before her, his black eyes glowing in the dim light.

She laid her slender hand upon his shoulder. She had ever treated him with the graciousness of a queen. "How is your wound?" she asked him in her soft, low voice. "Has it been properly bathed and dressed?"

He straightened himself, looking into her beautiful pale face with the loving reverence that he always accorded her. "All is well, my *mem-sahib*," he said. "Will you not be graciously pleased to rest?"

She shook her head, smiling faintly—a smile that somehow tore his heart. She opened her door and motioned him to enter. "I think I had better see for myself," she said. "Poor Peter! How you must have suffered, and how splendidly brave you are! Come in and let me see what I can do!"

He hung back protesting; but she would take no refusal, gently but firmly overruling all his scruples.

"Why was the doctor not sent for?" she said. "I ought to have thought of it myself."

She insisted upon washing and bandaging his wound anew. It was a deep one. Necessity had been stern, and Everard had not spared. It had bled freely, and there was no sign of any poisonous swelling. With tender hands Stella treated it, Peter standing dumbly submissive the while.

When she had finished, she arranged the injured arm in a sling, and looked him in the eyes.

"Peter, where is the captain *sahib*?"

"He went to his room, my *mem-sahib*," said Peter. "Bernard *sahib* carried the little missy *sahib* back, and Denvers *sahib* went with him. I did not see the captain *sahib* again."

He spoke wistfully, as one who longed to help but recognized his limitations.

Stella received his news in silence, her face still and white as the face of a marble statue. She felt no resentment against Peter. He had acted almost under compulsion. But she could not discuss the matter with him.

At length: "You may go, Peter," she said. "Please let no one come to my door to-night! I wish to be undisturbed."

Peter salaamed low and withdrew. The order was a very definite one, and she knew she could rely upon him to carry it out. As the door closed softly upon him, she turned towards her window. It opened upon the verandah. She moved across the room to shut it; but ere she reached it, Everard Monck came noiselessly through on slippered feet and bolted it behind him.

CHAPTER IX
THE CONSUMING FIRE

As he turned towards her, there came upon Stella, swift as a stab through the heart, the memory of that terrible night more than a year before when he had drawn her into his room and fastened the window behind her—against whom? His wild words rushed upon her. She had deemed them to be directed against the unknown intruder on the verandah. She knew now that the madness that had loosed his tongue had moved him to utter his fierce threat against a man who was dead—against the man whom he had—She stopped the thought as she would have checked the word half-spoken. She turned shivering away. The man on the verandah, that vision of the night-watches, she saw it all now—she saw it all. And he had loved her before her marriage. And he had known—and he had known—that, given opportunity, he could win her for his own.

Like a throbbing undersong—the fiendish accompaniment to the devils' chorus—the gossip of the station as detailed by Tessa ran with glib mockery through her brain. Ah, they only suspected. But she knew—she knew! The door of that secret chamber had opened wide to her at last, and perforce she had entered in.

He had moved forward, but he had not spoken. At least she fancied not, but all her senses were in an uproar. And above it all she seemed to hear that dreadful little thrumming instrument down by the river at Udalkhand—the tinkling, mystic call of the vampire goddess,—India the insatiable who had made him what he was.

He came to her, and every fibre of her being was aware of him and thrilled at his coming. Never had she loved him as she loved him then, but her love was a fiery torment that burned and consumed her soul. She seemed to feel it blistering, shrivelling, in the cruel heat.

Almost before she knew it, she had broken her silence, speaking as it were in spite of herself, scarcely knowing in her anguish what she said.

"Yes, I know. I know what you are going to say. You are going to tell me that I belong to you. And of course it is true,—I do. But if I stay with you, I shall be—a murderess. Nothing will alter that."

"Stella!" he said.

His voice was stern, so stern that she flinched. He laid his hand upon her, and she shrank as she would have shrunk from a hot iron searing her flesh. She had a wild thought that she would bear the brand of it for ever.

"Stella," he said again, and in both tone and action there was compulsion. "I have come to tell you that you are making a mistake. I am innocent of this thing you suspect me of."

She stood unresisting in his hold, but she was shaking all over. The floor seemed to be rising and falling under her feet. She knew that her lips moved several times before she could make them speak.

"But I don't suspect," she said. "The others suspect. I—know."

He received her words in silence. She saw his face as through a shifting vapour, very pale, very determined, with eyes of terrible intensity dominating her own.

Half mechanically she repeated herself. It was as if that devilish thrumming in her brain compelled her. "The others suspect. I—know."

"I see," he said at last. "And nothing I can say will make any difference?"

"Oh, no!" she made answer, and scarcely knew that she spoke, so cold and numb had she become. "How could it—now?"

He looked at her, and suddenly he saw that to which his own suffering had momentarily blinded him. He saw her utter weakness. With a swif passionate movement he caught her to him. For a second or two he held her so, strained against his heart, then almost fiercely he turned her face up to his own and kissed the stiff white lips.

"Be it so then!" he said, and in his voice was a deep note as though he challenged all the powers of evil. "You are mine—and mine you will remain."

She did not resist him though the touch of his lips was terrible to her. Only as they left her own, she turned her face aside. Very strangely that savage lapse of his had given her strength.

"Physically—perhaps—but only for a little while," she said gaspingly. "And in spirit, never—never again!"

"What do you mean?" he said, his arms tightening about her.

She kept her face averted. "I mean—that some forms of torture are worse than death. If it comes to that—if you compel me—I shall choose death."

"Stella!" He let her go so suddenly that she nearly fell. The utterance of her name was as a cry wrung from him by sheer agony. He turned from her with his hands over his face. "My God!" he said, and again almost inarticulately, "My—God!"

The low utterance pierced her, yet she stood motionless, her hands gripped hard together. He had forced the words from her, and they were past recall. Nor would she have recalled them, had she been able, for it seemed to her that her love had become an evil thing, and her whole being shrank from it in a species of horrified abhorrence, even though she could not cast it out.

He had turned towards the window, and she watched him, her heart beating in slow, hard strokes with a sound like a distant drum. Would he go? Would he remain? She almost prayed aloud that he would go.

But he did not. Very suddenly he turned and strode back to her. There was purpose in every line of him, but there was no longer any violence.

He halted before her. "Stella," he said, and his voice was perfectly steady and controlled, "do you think you are being altogether fair to me?"

She wrung her clasped hands. She could not answer him.

He took them into his own very quietly. "Just look me in the face for a minute!" he said.

She yearned to disobey, but she could not. Dumbly she raised her eyes to his.

He waited a moment, very still and composed. Then he spoke. "Stella, I swear to you—and I call God to witness—that I did not kill Ralph Dacre."

A dreadful shiver went through her at the bald brief words. She felt, as Tommy had felt a little earlier, physically sick. The beating of her heart was getting slower and slower. She wondered if presently it would stop.

"Do you believe me?" he said, still holding her eyes with his, still clasping her icy hands firmly between his own.

She forced herself to speak before that horrible sense of nausea overcame her. "Perhaps—David—said the same thing—about Uriah the Hittite."

His face changed a little, but it was a change she could not have defined. His eyes remained inscrutably fixed upon hers. They seemed to enchain her quivering soul.

"No," he said quietly. "Nor did I employ any one else to do it."

"But you were there!" The words seemed suddenly to burst from her without her own volition.

He drew back sharply, as if he had been struck. But he kept his eyes upon hers. "I can't explain anything," he said. "I am not here to explain. I only came to see if your love was great enough to make you believe in me—in spite of all there seems to be against me. Is it, Stella? Is it?"

His words seemed to go through her, tearing a way to her heart; the agony was more than she could bear. She uttered an anguished cry, and wrenched herself from him. "It isn't a question of love!" she said. "You know it isn't a question of love! I never wanted to love you. I never wholly trusted you. But you forced my love—though you couldn't compel my trust. And now that I know—now that I know—" her voice broke as if the torture were too great for her; she flung out her hands with a gesture of driving him from her—"oh, it is hell on earth—hell on earth!"

He drew back for a second before her, his face deathly white. And then suddenly an awful light leapt in his eyes. He gripped her outflung hands. The fire had kindled to a flame and the torture was too much for him also.

"Then you shall love me—even in hell!" he said, through his clenched teeth, and locked her in the iron circle of his arms.

She did not resist him. She was very near the end of her strength. Only, as he held her, her eyes met his, mutely imploring him....

It reached him even in his madness, that unspoken appeal. It checked him in the mid-furnace of his passion. His hold relaxed as if at a word of command. He put her into a chair and turned himself from her.

The next moment he was fumbling desperately at the window fastening. The night met him on the threshold. He heard her weeping, piteously, hopelessly, as he went away.

CHAPTER X
THE DESERT PLACE

A single light shone across the verandah when Bernard Monck returned late in the night. It drew his steps though it did not come from any of the sitting-rooms. With the light tread often characteristic of heavy men, he approached it, realizing only at the last moment that it came from the window of his brother's room.

Then for a second he hesitated. He was angry with Everard, more angry than he could remember that he had ever been before. He questioned with himself as to the wisdom of seeing him again that night. He doubted if he could be ordinarily civil to him at present, and a quarrel would help no one.

Still why was the fellow burning a light at that hour? An unacknowledged uneasiness took possession of him and drove him forward. People seemed to do all manner of extravagant things in this fantastic country that they would never have dreamed of doing in homely old England. There must be something electric in the atmosphere that penetrated the veins. Even he had been aware of it now and then, a strange and potent influence that drove a man to passionate deeds.

He reached the window without sound just as Stella had reached it on that night of rain long ago. With no consciousness of spying, driven by an urgent impulse he could not stop to question, he looked in.

The window was ajar, as if it had been pushed to negligently by someone entering, and in a flash Bernard had it wide. He went in as though he had been propelled.

A man—Everard—was standing half-dressed in the middle of the room. He was facing the window, and the light shone with ghastly distinctness upon his face. But he did not look up. He was gazing fixedly into a glass of water he held in his hand, apparently watching some minute substance melting there.

It was not the thing he held, but the look upon his face, that sent Bernard forward with a spring. "Man!" he burst forth. "What are you doing?"

Everard gave utterance to a fierce oath that was more like the cry of a savage animal than the articulate speech of a man. He stepped back sharply, and put the glass to his lips. But no drop that it contained did he swallow, for in the same instant Bernard flung it violently aside. The glass spun across the room, and they grappled together for the mastery. For a few seconds the battle was hot; then very suddenly the elder man threw up his hands.

"All right," he said, between short gasps for breath. "You can hammer me—if you want someone to hammer. Perhaps—it'll do you good."

He was free on the instant. Everard flung round and turned his back. He did not speak, but crossed the room and picked up the glass which lay unbroken on the floor.

Bernard followed him, still gasping for breath, "Give that to me!" he said.

His soft voice was oddly stern. Everard looked at him. His hand, shaking a little, was extended. After a very definite pause, he placed the glass within it. There was a little white sediment left with a drain of water at the bottom. With his blue eyes full upon his brother's face, Bernard lifted it to his own lips.

But the next instant it was dashed away, and the glass shivered to atoms against the wall. "You—fool!" Everard said.

A faint, faint smile that very strangely proclaimed a resemblance between them which was very seldom perceptible crossed Bernard's face. "I—thought so," he said. "Now look here, boy! Let's stop being melodramatic for a bit! Take a dose of quinine instead! It seems to be the panacea for all evils in this curious country."

His voice was perfectly kind, even persuasive, but it carried a hint of authority as well, and Everard gave him a keen look as if aware of it.

He was very pale but absolutely steady as he made reply. "I don't think quinine will meet the case on this occasion."

"You prefer another kind of medicine," Bernard suggested. And then with sudden feeling he held out his hand. "Everard, old chap, never do that while you've a single friend left in the world! Do you want to break my heart? I only ask to stand by you. I'll stand by you to the very gates of hell. Don't you know that?"

His voice trembled slightly. Everard turned and gripped the proffered hand hard in his own.

"I suppose I—might have known," he said. "But it's a bit rash of you all the same."

His own voice quivered though he forced a smile. He would have turned away, but Bernard restrained him.

"I don't care a tinker's damn what you've done," he said forcibly. "Remember that! We're brothers, and I'll stick to you. If there's anything in life that I can do to help, I'll do it. If there isn't, well, I won't worry you, but you know you can count on me just the same. You'll never stand alone while I live."

It was generously spoken. The words came straight from his soul. He put his hand on his brother's shoulder as he uttered them. His eyes were as tender as the eyes of a woman.

And suddenly, without warning, Everard's strength failed him. It was like the snapping of a stretched wire. "Oh, man!" he said, and covered his face.

Bernard's arm was round him in a moment, a staunch, upholding arm. "Everard—dear old chap—can't you tell me what it is?" he said. "God knows I'll die sooner than let you down."

Everard did not answer. His breathing was hard, spasmodic, intensely painful to hear. He had the look of a man stricken in his pride.

For a space Bernard stood dumbly supporting him. Then at length very quietly he moved and guided him to a chair.

"Take your time!" he said gently. "Sit down!"

Mutely Everard submitted. The agony of that night had stripped his manhood of its reserve. He sat crouched, his head bowed upon his clenched hands.

"Wait while I fetch you a drink!" Bernard said.

He was gone barely two minutes. Returning, he fastened the window and drew the curtain across. Then he bent again over the huddled figure in the chair.

"Take a mouthful of this, old fellow! It'll pull you together."

Everard groped outwards with a quivering hand. "Give me strength—to shoot myself," he muttered.

The words were only just audible, but Bernard caught them. "No,—give you strength to play the game," he said, and held the glass he had brought to his brother's lips.

Everard drank with closed eyes and sat forward again motionless. His face was bloodless. "I'm sorry, St. Bernard," he said, after a moment. "Forgive me for manhandling you—and all the rest, if you can!" He drew a long, hard breath. "Thanks for everything! Good-night!"

"But I'm not leaving you," said Bernard, gently. "Not like this."

"Like what?" Everard opened his eyes with an abrupt effort. "Oh, I'm all right. Don't you bother about me!" he said.

Their eyes met. For a second longer Bernard stood over him. Then he went down upon his knees by his side. "I swear I won't leave you," he said, "until you've told me this trouble of yours."

Everard shook his head instantly, but his hand went out and closed upon the arm that had upheld him. He was beginning to recover his habitual self-command. "It's no good, old chap. I can't," he said. And added almost involuntarily, "That's—the hell of it!"

"But you can," Bernard said. He still looked him straight in the eyes. "You can and you will. Call it a confession—I've heard a good many in my time—and tell me everything!"

"Confess to you!" A hint of surprise showed in Everard's heavy eyes. "You'd better not tempt me to do that," he said. "You might be sorry afterwards."

"I will risk it," Bernard said.

"Risk being made an accessory to—what you may regard as a crime?" Everard said. "Forgive me—you're a parson, I know,—but are you sure you can play the part?"

Bernard smiled a little at the question. "Yes, I can," he said. "A confession is sacred—whatever it is. And I swear to you—by God in Heaven—to treat it as such."

Everard was looking at him fixedly, but something of the strain went out of his look at the words. A gleam of relief crossed his face.

"All right. I will—confess to you," he said. "But I warn you beforehand, you'll be horribly shocked. And—you won't feel like absolving me afterwards."

130

"That's not my job, dear fellow," Bernard answered gently. "Go ahead! You're sure of my sympathy anyway."

"Am I? You're a good chap, St. Bernard. Look here, don't kneel there! It's not suitable for a father confessor," Everard's faint smile showed for a moment.

Bernard's hand closed upon his. "Go ahead!" he said again, "I'm all right."

Everard made an abrupt gesture that had in it something of surrender. "It's soon told," he said, "though I don't know why I should burden you with it. That fellow Ralph Dacre—I didn't murder him. I wish to Heaven I had. So far as I know—he is alive."

"Ah!" Bernard said

Jerkily, with obvious effort, Everard continued. "I'm a murderous brute no doubt. But if I had the chance to kill him now, I'd take it. You see what it means, don't you? It means that Stella—that Stella—" He broke off with a convulsive movement, and dropped back into a tortured silence.

"Yes. I see what it means," Bernard said.

After an interval Everard forced out a few more words. "About a fortnight after their marriage I got your letter telling me he had a wife living. I went straight after them in native disguise, and made him clear out. That's the whole story."

"I see," Bernard said again.

Again there fell a silence between them. Everard sat bowed, his head on his hand. The awful pallor was passing, but the stricken look remained.

Bernard spoke at last. "You have no idea what became of him?"

"Not the faintest. He went. That was all that concerned me." Grimly, without lifting his head, he made answer. "You know the rest—or you can guess. Then you came, and told me that the woman—Dacre's wife—died before his marriage to Stella. I've been in hell ever since."

"I wish to Heaven I'd stopped away!" Bernard exclaimed with sudden vehemence.

Everard shifted his position slightly to glance at him. "Don't wish that!" he said. "After all, it would probably have come out somehow."

"And—Stella?" Bernard spoke with hesitation, as if uncertain of his ground. "What does she think? How much does she know?"

"She thinks like the rest. She thinks I murdered the hound. And I'd rather she thought that," there was dogged suffering in Everard's voice, "than suspected the truth."

"You think—" Bernard still spoke with slight hesitation—"that will hurt her less?"

"Yes." There was stubborn conviction in the reply. Everard slowly straightened himself and faced his brother squarely. "There is—the child," he said.

Bernard shook his head slightly. "You're wrong, old fellow. You're making a mistake. You are choosing the hardest course for her as well as yourself."

Everard's jaw hardened. "I shall find a way out for myself," he said. "She shall be left in peace."

"What do you mean?" Bernard said. Then as he made no reply, he took him firmly by the shoulders. "No—no! You won't. You won't," he said. "That's not you, my boy—not when you've sanely thought it out."

Everard suffered his hold; but his face remained set in grim lines. "There is no other way," he said. "Honestly, I see no other way."

"There is another way." Very steadily, with the utmost confidence, Bernard made the assertion. "There always is. God sees to that. You'll find it presently."

Everard smiled very wearily at the words. "I've given up expecting any light from that quarter," he said. "It seems to me that He hasn't much use for the wanderers once they get off the beaten track."

"Oh, my dear chap!" Bernard's hands pressed upon him suddenly. "Do you really believe He has no care for that which is lost? Have you blundered along all this time and never yet seen the lamp in the desert? You will see it—like every other wanderer—sooner or later, if you only have the pluck to keep on."

"You seem mighty sure of that." Everard looked at him with a species of dull curiosity. "Are you sure?"

"Of course I am sure." Bernard spoke vigorously. "And so are you in your heart. You know very well that if you only push on you won't be left to die in the wilderness. Have you never thought to yourself after a particularly dark spell that there has always been a speck of light somewhere—never total darkness for any length of time? That's the lamp in the desert, old chap. And—whether you realize it or not—God put it there."

He ceased to speak, and rose quietly to his feet; then, as Everard stretched a hand to him, gave him a steady pull upwards. They stood face to face.

"And that," Bernard added, after a few moments, "is all I've got to say. You turn in now and get a rest! If you want me, well, you know where to find me—just any time."

"Thanks!" Everard said. His hand held his brother's hard. "But—before you go—there's one thing I want to say—no, two." A shadowy smile touched his grim lips and vanished. His eyes were still and wholly remote, sheltering his soul.

"Go ahead!" said Bernard gently.

Everard paused for a second. "You have asked no promise of me," he said then; "but—I'll make you one. And I want one from you in return."

Again he paused, as if he had some difficulty in finding words.

"You can rely on me," Bernard said.

"Yes, old fellow." For an instant his eyes smiled also. "I know it. It's by that fact alone that you've gained your point. And so I'll hang on somehow for the present—find another way—anyhow hang on, just because you are what you are—and because—" his voice sank a little—"you care."

"Don't you know I love you before any one else in the world?" Bernard said, giving him a mighty grip.

"Yes," Everard looked him straight in the face, "I do. And it means more to me than perhaps you think. In fact—it's everything to me just now. That's why I want you to promise me—whatever happens—whatever I decide to do—that you will stay within reach of—that you will take care of—my—my—of Stella." He ended abruptly, with a quick gesture that held entreaty.

And Bernard's reply came instantly, almost before he had ceased to speak. "Before God, old chap, I will."

"Thanks," Everard said again. He stood for a few moments as if debating something further, but in the end he freed himself and turned away. "She will be all right, with you," he said. "You're—safe anyhow."

"Quite safe," said Bernard steadily.

PART V

CHAPTER I
GREATER THAN DEATH

"If you ask me," said Bertie Oakes, propping himself up in an elegant attitude against a pillar of the Club verandah, "it's my belief that there's going to be—a bust-up."

"Nobody did ask you," observed Tommy rudely.

He generally was rude nowadays, and had been haled before a subalterns' court-martial only the previous evening for that very reason. The sentence passed had been of a somewhat drastic nature, and certainly had not improved his temper or his manners. To be stripped, bound scientifically, and "dipped" in the Club swimming-bath till, as Oakes put it, all the venom had been drenched out of him, was an experience for which only one utterly reckless would qualify twice.

Tommy had come through it with a dumb endurance which had somewhat spoilt the occasion for his tormentors, had gone back to The Green Bungalow as soon as his punishment was over, and for the first time had drunk heavily in the privacy of his room.

He sat now in a huddled position on the Club verandah, "looking like a sick chimpanzee" as Oakes assured him, "ready to bite—if he dared—at a moment's notice."

Mrs. Ralston was seated near. She had a motherly eye upon Tommy.

"Now what exactly do you mean by a 'bust-up,' Mr. Oakes?" she asked with her gentle smile.

Oakes blew a cloud of smoke upwards. He liked airing his opinions, especially when there were several ladies within earshot.

"What do I mean?" he said, with a pomposity carefully moulded upon the Colonel's mode of delivery on a guest-night. "I mean, my dear Mrs. Ralston, that which would have to be suppressed—a rising among the native element of the State."

"Ape!" growled Tommy under his breath.

Oakes caught the growl, and made a downward motion with his thumb which only Tommy understood.

Mrs. Burton's soft, false laugh filled the pause that followed his pronouncement. "Surely no one could openly object to the conviction of a native murderer!" she said. "I hear that the evidence is quite conclusive. Captain Monck has spared no pains in that direction."

"Captain Monck," observed Lady Harriet, elevating her long nose, "seems to be exceptionally well qualified for that kind of service."

"Set a thief to catch a thief, what?" suggested Oakes lightly. "Yes, he seems to be quite good at it. Just as well in a way, perhaps. Someone has got to do the dirty work, though it would be preferable for all of us if he were a policeman by profession."

It was too carelessly spoken to sound actively malevolent. But Tommy, with his arms gripped round his knees, raised eyes of bloodshot fury to the speaker's face.

"If any one could take a first class certificate for dirty work, it would be you," he said, speaking very distinctly between clenched teeth.

A sudden silence fell upon the assembly. Oakes looked down at Tommy, and Tommy glared up at Oakes.

Then abruptly Major Ralston, who had been standing in the background with a tall drink in his hand, slouched forward and let himself down ponderously on the edge of the verandah by Tommy's side.

"Go away, Bertie!" he said. "We've listened to your wind instrument long enough. Tommy, you shut up, or I'll give you the beastliest physic I know! What were we talking about? Mary, give us a lead!"

He appealed to his wife, who glanced towards Lady Harriet with a hint of embarrassment.

Major Ralston at once addressed himself to her. He was never embarrassed by any one, and never went out of his way to be pleasant without good reason.

"This murder trial is going to be sensational," he said, "I've just got back from giving evidence as to the cause of death and I have it on good authority that a certain august personage in Markestan is shaking in his shoes as to the result of the business."

"I have heard that too," said Lady Harriet.

It was a curious fact that though she was always ready, and would even go out of her way, to snub the surgeon's wife, she had never once been other than gracious to the surgeon.

"I don't suppose he will be actively implicated. He's too wily for that," went on Major Ralston. "But there's not much doubt according to Barnes, that he was in the know—very much so, I should imagine." He glanced about him. "Mrs. Ermsted isn't here, is she?"

"No dear. I left her resting," his wife said. "This affair is very trying for her—naturally." He assented somewhat grimly. "I wonder she stayed for it. Now Tessa on the other hand yearns for the murderer's head in a charger. That child is getting too Eastern in her ideas. It will be a good thing to get her Home."

Mrs. Burton intervened with a simper. "Yes, she really is a naughty little thing, and I cannot say I shall be sorry when she is gone. My small son is at such a very receptive age."

"Yes, he's old enough to go to school and be licked into shape," said Major Ralston brutally. "He flings stones at my car every time I pass. I shall stop and give him a licking myself some day when I have time."

"Really, Major Ralston, I hope you will not do anything so cruel," protested Mrs. Burton. "We never correct him in that way ourselves."

"Pity you don't," said Major Ralston. "An unlicked cub is an insult to creation. Give him to me for a little while! I'll undertake to improve him both morally and physically to such an extent that you won't know him."

Here Tommy uttered a brief, wholly involuntary guffaw.

"What's the matter with you?" said Ralston.

"Nothing." His gloom dropped upon him again like a mantle. "Have you been at Khanmulla all day?"

"Yes; a confounded waste of time it's been too." Ralston took a deep drink and set down his glass.

"You always think it's a waste of time if you can't be doctoring somebody," muttered Tommy.

"Don't be offensive!" said Ralston. "I know what's the matter with you, my son, but I should keep it to myself if I were you. As a matter of fact I did give medical advice to somebody this afternoon—which of course he won't take."

Tommy's face was suddenly scarlet. It was solely the maternal protective instinct that induced Mrs. Ralston to bend forward and speak.

"Do you mean Captain Monck, Gerald?" she asked.

Major Ralston cast a comprehensive glance around the little group assembled near him, finishing his survey upon Tommy's burning countenance. "Yes—Monck," he said. "He's staying with Barnes at Khanmulla to see this affair through. If I were Mrs. Monck I should be pretty anxious about him. He says it's insomnia."

"Is he ill?" It was Tommy who spoke, his voice quick and low, all the sullen embarrassment gone from his demeanour.

The doctor's eyes dwelt upon him for a moment longer before he answered. "I never saw such a change in any man in such a short time. He'll have a bad break-down if he doesn't watch out."

"He works too hard," said Mrs. Ralston sympathetically.

Her husband nodded. "If it weren't for that sickly baby of hers, I should advise his wife to go straight to him and look after him. But perhaps when this trial is over he will be able to take a rest. I shall order the whole family to Bhulwana if I get the chance." He got up with the words, and faced the company with a certain dogged aggressiveness that compelled attention. "It's hard," he said, "to see a fine chap like that knocked out. He's about the best man we've got, and we can't afford to lose him."

He waited for someone to take up the challenge, but no one showed any inclination to do so. Only after a moment Tommy also sprang up as if there was something in the situation that chafed him beyond endurance.

Ralston looked at him again, critically, not over-favourably. "Where are you off to in such a hurry?" he said.

Tommy hunched his shoulders, all defiance in a second. "Going for a ride," he growled. "Any objection?"

Ralston turned away. "None whatever, my young porcupine. Have mercy on your nag, that's all—and don't break your own neck!"

Tommy strode wrathfully away to the sound of Mrs. Burton's tittering laugh. With the exception of Mrs. Ralston, who really did not count, he hated every one of the party that he left behind on the Club verandah, and he did not attempt to disguise the fact.

But when an hour later he rolled off his horse in the compound of the policeman's bungalow at Khanmulla, his mood had undergone a complete change. There was nothing defiant or even assertive about him as he applied for admittance. He looked beaten, tried beyond his strength.

It was growing rapidly dark as he followed Barnes's *khansama* into the long bare room which he used as his private office. The man brought him a lamp and told him that the *sahibs* would be back soon. They had gone down to the Court House again, but they might return at any time.

He also brought him whisky and soda which Tommy did not touch, spending the interval of waiting that ensued in fevered tramping to and fro.

He had not seen Monck alone since the evening of Tessa's birthday-party nearly three weeks before. On the score of business connected with the approaching trial, Monck had come to Khanmulla immediately afterwards, and no one at Kurrumpore had had more than an occasional glimpse of him since. But he meant to see him alone now, and he had given very explicit instructions to that effect to the servant, accompanied by a substantial species of persuasion that could not fail to achieve its object.

When the sound of voices told him at last of the return of the two men, he drew back out of sight of the window while the obsequious *khansama* went forth upon his errand. Then a moment or two later he heard them separate, and one alone came in his direction. Everard entered with the gait of a tired man.

The lamp dazzled him for a second, and Tommy saw him first. He smothered an involuntary exclamation and stepped forward.

"Tommy!" said Monck, as if incredulous.

Tommy stood in front of him, his hands at his sides. "Yes, it's me. I had to come over—just to have a look at you. Ralston said—said—oh, damn it, it doesn't matter what he said. Only I had to—just come and see for myself. You see, I—I—" he faltered badly, but recovered himself under the straight gaze of Everard's eyes—"I can't get the thought of you out of my mind. I've been a damn' cur. You won't want to speak to me of course, but when Ralston started jawing about you this afternoon, I found—I found—" he choked suddenly—"I couldn't stand it any longer," he said in a strangled whisper.

Monck was looking full at him by the merciless glare of the lamp on the table, which revealed himself very fully also. All the grim lines in his face seemed to be accentuated. He looked years older. The hair above his temples gleamed silver where it caught the light.

He did not speak at once. Only as Tommy made a blind movement as if to go, he put forth a hand and took him by the arm.

"Tommy," he said, "what have you been doing?"

Out of deep hollows his eyes looked forth, indomitable, relentless as they had ever been, searching the boy's downcast face.

Tommy quivered a little under their piercing scrutiny, but he made no attempt to avoid it.

"Look at me!" Monck commanded.

He raised his eyes for a moment, and in spite of himself Monck was softened by the utter misery they held.

"You always were an ass," he commented. "But I thought you had more strength of mind than this."

Tommy made an impotent gesture. "I'm a beast—I'm a skunk!" he declared, with tremulous vehemence. "I'm not fit to speak to you!"

The shadow of a smile crossed Monck's face. "And you've come all this way to tell me so?" he said. "You've no business here either. You ought to be at the Mess."

"Damn the Mess!" said Tommy fiercely. "They'll tell me I ratted to-morrow. I don't care. Let 'em say what they like! It's you that matters. Man, how infernally ill you look!"

Monck checked the personal allusion. "I'm not ill. But what have you been up to? Are you in a row?"

Tommy essayed a laugh. "No, nothing serious. The blithering idiots ducked me yesterday for being disrespectful, that's all. I don't care. It's you I care about, Everard, old chap!"

His voice held sudden pleading, but his face was turned away. He had meant to say more, but could not. He stood biting his lips desperately in a mute struggle for self-control.

Everard waited a few seconds, giving him time; then abruptly he moved, slapped a hand on Tommy's shoulder and gave him a shake.

"Tommy, don't be so beastly cheap! I'm ashamed of you. What's the matter?"

Tommy yielded impulsively to the bracing grip, but he kept his face averted. "That's just it," he blurted out. "I feel cheap. Fact is, I came—I came to ask you to—forgive me. But now I'm here,—I'm damned if I have the cheek."

"What do you want my forgiveness for? I thought I was the transgressor." Everard's voice was a curious blend of humour and sadness.

Tommy turned to him with a sudden boyish gesture so spontaneous as to override all barriers. "Oh, I know all that. But it doesn't count. See? I don't know how I ever had the infernal presumption to think it did, or to ask you—you, of all men—to explain your actions. I don't want any explanation. I believe in you without, simply because I can't help it. I know—without any proof,—that you're sound. And—and—I beg your pardon for being such a cur as to doubt you. There! That's what I came to say. Now it's your turn."

The tears were in his eyes, but he made no further attempt to hide them. All that was great in his nature had come to the surface, and there was no room left for self-consciousness.

Monck realized it, and it affected him deeply, depriving him of the power to respond. He had not expected this from Tommy, had not believed him capable of it. But there was no doubting the boy's sincerity. Through those tears which Tommy had forgotten to hide, he saw the old loving trust shine out at him, the old whole-hearted admiration and honour offered again without reservation and without stint.

He opened his lips to speak, but something rose in his throat, preventing him. He held out his hand in silence, and in that wordless grip the love which is greater than death made itself felt between them—a bond imperishable which no earthly circumstance could ever again violate—the Power Omnipotent which conquers all things.

CHAPTER II
THE LAMP

The orange light of the morning was breaking over the jungle when two horsemen rode out upon the Kurrumpore road and halted between the rice fields.

"I say, come on a bit further!" Tommy urged. "There's plenty of time."

But the other shook his head. "No, I can't. I promised Barnes to be back early. Good-bye, Tommy my lad! Keep your end up!"

"I will," Tommy promised, and thrust out a hand. "And you'll hang on, won't you? Promise!"

"All right; for the present. My love to Bernard." Everard spoke with his usual brevity, but his handclasp was remembered by Tommy for a very long time after.

"And to Stella?" he said, pushing his horse a little nearer till it muzzled against its fellow.

Everard's eyes, grave and dark, looked out to the low horizon. "I think not," he said. "She has—no further use for it."

"She will have," said Tommy quickly.

But Everard passed the matter by in silence. "You must be getting on," he said, and relaxed his grip. "Good-bye, old chap! You've done me good, if that is any consolation to you."

"Oh, man!" said Tommy, and coloured like a girl. "Not—not really!"

Everard uttered his curt laugh, and switched Tommy's mount across the withers. "Be off with you, you—cuckoo!" he said.

And Tommy grinned and went.

Half-an-hour later he was sounding an impatient tatto upon his sister's door.

She came herself to admit him, but the look upon her face checked the greeting on his lips.

"What on earth's the matter?" he said instead.

She was shivering as if with cold, though the risen sun had filled the world with spring-like warmth. It occurred to him as he entered, that she was looking pinched and ill, and he put a comforting arm around her.

"What is it, Stella girl? Tell me!"

She relaxed against him with a sob. "I've been—horribly anxious about you," she said.

"Oh, is that all?" said Tommy. "What a waste of time! I was only over at Khanmulla. I spent the night at Barnes's bungalow because they wouldn't trust me in the jungle after dark."

"They?" she questioned.

"Barnes and Everard," Tommy said, and faced her squarely. "I went to see Everard."

"Ah!" She caught her breath. "Major Ralston has been here. He told me—he told me—" her voice failed; she laid her head down upon Tommy's shoulder.

He tightened his arm about her. "It's a shame of Ralston to frighten you. He isn't ill." Then a sudden thought striking him, "What was he doing here so early? Isn't the kid up to the mark?"

She shivered against him again. "He had a strange attack in the night, and Major Ralston said—said—oh, Tommy," she suddenly clung to him, "I am going to lose him. He—isn't—like other children."

"Ralston said that?" demanded Tommy.

"He didn't tell me. He told Bernard. I practically forced Bernard to tell me, but I think he thought I ought to know. He said—he said—it isn't to be desired that my baby should live."

"What?" said Tommy in dismay. "Oh, my darling girl, I am sorry! What's wrong with the poor little chap?"

With her face hidden against him she made whispered answer. "You know he—came too soon. They thought at first he was all right, but now—symptoms have begun to show themselves. We thought he was just delicate, but it isn't only that. Last night—in the night—" she shuddered suddenly and violently and paused to control herself—"I can't talk about it. It was terrible. Major Ralston says he doesn't suffer, but it looks like suffering. And, oh, Tommy,—he is all I have left."

Tommy held her comfortingly close. "I say, wouldn't you like Everard to come to you?" he said.

"Oh no! Oh no!" Her refusal was instant. "I can't see him. Tommy, why suggest such a thing? You know I can't."

"I know he's a good man," Tommy said steadily. "Just listen a minute, old girl! I know things look black enough against him, so black that it's probable he'll have to send in his papers. But I tell you he's all right. I didn't think so at first. I thought the same as you do. But somehow that suspicion has got worn out. It was pretty beastly while it lasted, but I came to my senses at last. And I've been to tell him so. He was jolly decent about it, though he didn't tell me a thing. I didn't want him to. Besides, he always is decent. How could he be otherwise? And now we're just as we were—friends."

There was no mistaking the satisfaction in Tommy's voice. He even spoke with pride, and hearing it, Stella withdrew herself slowly and wearily from his arms.

"It's rather different for you, Tommy," she said. "A man's standards are different, I know. There may be what you call extenuating circumstances—though I can't quite imagine it. I'm too tired to argue about it, Tommy dear, and you mustn't be vexed with me. I can't go into it with you, but I feel as if it is I—I myself—who have committed an awful sin. And it has got to be expiated, perhaps that is why my baby is to be taken from me. Bernard says it is not so. But then—Bernard is a man too." There was a sound of heartbreak in her voice as she ended. She put up her hands with a gesture as of trying to put away some monstrous thing that threatened to crush her—a gesture that went straight to Tommy's warm heart.

"Oh, poor old girl!" he said impulsively, and took the hands into his own. "I say, ought I to be in here? Aren't you supposed to be resting?"

She smiled at him wanly. "I believe I am. Major Ralston left a soothing draught, but I wouldn't take it, in case—" she broke off. "Peter is on guard as well as *Ayah*, and he has promised to call me if—if—" Again she stopped. "I don't think *Ayah* is much good," she resumed. "She was nearly frightened out of her senses last night. She seems to think there is something—supernatural about it. But Peter—Peter is a tower of strength. I trust him implicitly."

"Yes, he's a good chap," said Tommy. "I'm glad you've got him anyway. I wish I could be more of a help to you."

She leaned forward and kissed him. "You are very dear to me, Tommy. I don't know what I should do without you and Bernard."

"Where is the worthy padre?" asked Tommy.

"He may be working in his room. He is certainly not far away. He never is nowadays."

"I'll go and find him," said Tommy. "But look here, dear! Have that draught of Ralston's and lie down! Just to please me!"

She began to refuse, but Tommy could be very persuasive when he chose, and he chose on this occasion. Finally, with reluctance she yielded, since, as he pointed out, she needed all the strength she could muster.

He tucked her up with motherly care, feeling that he had accomplished something worth doing, and then, seeing that exhaustion would do the rest, he left her and went softly forth in search of Bernard.

The latter, however, was not in the bungalow, and since it was growing late Tommy had a hurried bath and dressed for parade. He was bolting a hasty *tiffin* in the dining-room when a quiet step on the verandah warned him of Bernard's approach, and in a moment or two the big man entered, a pipe in his mouth and a book under his arm.

"Hullo, Tommy!" he said with his genial smile. "So you haven't been murdered this time. I congratulate you."

"Thanks!" said Tommy.

"I congratulate myself also," said Bernard, patting his shoulder by way of greeting. "If it weren't against my principles, I should have been very worried about you, my lad. For I couldn't get away to look for you."

"Of course not," said Tommy. "And I was safe enough. I've been over to Khanmulla. Everard made me spend the night, and we rode back this morning."

"Everard! He isn't here?" Bernard looked round sharply.

"No," said Tommy bluntly. "But he ought to be. He went back again. He is wanted for that trial business. I say, things are pretty rotten here, aren't they? Is the little kid past hope?"

"I am afraid so." Bernard spoke very gravely. His kindly face was more sombre than Tommy had ever seen it.

"But can nothing be done?" the boy urged. "It'll break Stella's heart to lose him."

Bernard shook his head. "Nothing whatever I am afraid. Major Ralston has suspected trouble for some time, it seems. We might of course get a specialist's opinion at Calcutta, but the baby is utterly unfit for a journey of any kind, and it is doubtful if any doctor would come all this way—especially with things as they are."

"What do you mean?" said Tommy.

Bernard looked at him. "The place is a hotbed of discontent—if not anarchy. Surely you know that!"

Tommy shrugged his shoulders. "That's nothing new. It's what we're here for."

"Yes. And matters are getting worse. I hear that the result of this trial will probably mean the Rajah's enforced abdication. And if that happens there is practically bound to be a rising."

Tommy laughed. "That's been the situation as long as I've been out. We're giving him enough rope, and I hope he'll hang, though I'm afraid he won't. The rising will probably be a sort of Chinese cracker affair—a fizz, a few bangs, and a splutter-out. No honour and glory for any one!"

"I hope you are right," said Bernard.

"And I hope I'm wrong," said Tommy lightly. "I like a run for my money."

"You forget the women," said Bernard abruptly.

Tommy opened his eyes. "No, I don't. They'll be all right. They'll have to clear out to Bhulwana a little earlier than usual. They'll be safe enough there. You can go and look after 'em, sir. They'll like that."

"Thank you, Tommy." Bernard smiled in spite of himself. "It's kind of you to put it so tactfully. Now tell me what you think of Everard. Is he really ill?"

"No; worried to death, that's all. He's talking of sending in his papers. Did you know?"

"I suspected he would," Bernard spoke thoughtfully.

"He mustn't do it!" said Tommy with vehemence. "He's worth all the rest of the Mess put together. You mustn't let him."

Bernard lifted his brows. "I let him!" he said. "Do you think he is going to do what I tell him?"

"I know you have influence—considerable influence—with him," Tommy said. "You ought to use it, sir. You really ought. It's up to you and no one else."

He spoke insistently. Bernard looked at him attentively.

"You've changed your tune somewhat, haven't you, Tommy?" he said.

"Yes," said Tommy bluntly. "I have. I've been a damn' fool if you want to know—the biggest, damnedest fool on the face of creation. And I've been and told him so."

"For no particular reason?" Bernard's blue eyes grew keener in their regard. He looked at Tommy with more interest than he had ever before bestowed upon him.

Tommy's face was red, but he replied without embarrassment. "Certainly. I've come to my senses, that's all. I've come to realize—what I really knew all along—that he's a white man, white all through, however black he chooses to be painted. And I'm ashamed that I ever doubted him."

"He hasn't told you anything?" questioned Bernard, still closely surveying the flushed countenance.

"No!" said Tommy, and his voice rang on a note of indignant pride. "Why the devil should he tell me anything? I'm his friend. Thank the gods, I can trust him without."

Bernard held out his hand suddenly. The interest had turned to something warmer. He looked at the boy with genuine admiration. "I take off my hat to you, Tommy," he said. "Everard is a deuced lucky man."

"What?" said Tommy, and turned deep crimson. "Oh, rot, sir! That's rot!" He gripped the extended hand with warmth notwithstanding. "It's all the other way round. I can't tell you what he's been to me. Why, I—I'd die for him, if I had the chance."

"Yes," Bernard said with simplicity. "I'm sure you would, boy. And it's just that I like about you. You're just the sort of friend he needs—the sort of friend God sends along to hold up the lamp when the night is dark. There! You want to be off. I won't keep you. But you're a white man yourself, Tommy, and I shan't forget it."

"Oh, rats—rats—rats!" said Tommy rudely, and escaped through the window at headlong speed.

CHAPTER III
TESSA'S MOTHER

"It really isn't my fault," said Netta fretfully. "I don't see why you should lecture me about it, Mary. I can't help being attractive."

"My dear," said Mrs. Ralston patiently, "that was not my point. I am only urging you to show a little discretion. You do not want to be an object of scandal, I am sure. The finger of suspicion has been pointed at the Rajah a good many times lately, and I do think that for Tessa's sake, if not for your own, you ought to put a check upon your intimacy with him."

"Bother Tessa!" said Netta. "I don't see that I owe her anything."

Mrs. Ralston sighed a little, but she persevered. "The child is at an age when she needs the most careful training. Surely you want her to respect you!"

Netta laughed. "I really don't care a straw what she does. Tessa doesn't interest me. I wanted a boy, you know. I never had any use for girls. Besides, she gets on my nerves at every turn. We shall never be kindred spirits."

"Poor little Tessa!" said Mrs. Ralston gently. "She has such a loving heart."

"She doesn't love me," said Tessa's mother without regret. "I suppose you'll say that's my fault too. Everything always is, isn't it?"

"I think—in fact I am sure—that love begets love," said Mrs. Ralston. "Perhaps when you and she get to England together, you will become more to each other."

"Out of sheer *ennui*?" suggested Netta. "Oh, don't let's talk of England—I hate the thought of it. I'm sure I was created for the East. Hence the sympathy that exists between the Rajah and myself. You know, Mary, you really are absurdly prejudiced against him. Richard was the same. He never had any cause to be jealous. They simply didn't come into the same category."

Mrs. Ralston looked at her with wonder in her eyes. "You seem to forget," she said, "that Richard's murderer is being tried, and that this man is very strongly suspected of being an abettor if not the actual instigator of the crime."

Netta flicked the ash from her cigarette with a gesture of impatience. "I only wish you would let me forget these unpleasant things," she said. "Why don't you go and preach a sermon to the beautiful Stella Monck on the same text? Ralph Dacre's death was quite as much of a mystery. And the kindly gossips are every bit as busy with Captain Monck's reputation as with His Excellency's. But I suppose her devotion to that wretched little imbecile baby of hers renders her immune!"

She spoke with intentional malice, but she scarcely expected to strike home. Mary was not, in her estimation, over-endowed with brains, and she never seemed to mind a barbed thrust or two. But on this occasion Mrs. Ralston upset her calculations.

She arose in genuine wrath. "Netta!" she said. "I think you are the most heartless, callous woman I have ever met!"

And with that she went straight from the room, shutting the door firmly behind her.

"Good gracious!" commented Netta. "Mary in a tantrum! What an exciting spectacle!"

She stretched her slim body like a cat as she lay with the warm sunshine pouring over her, and presently she laughed.

"How funny! How very funny! Netta, my dear, they'll be calling you wicked next."

She pursed her lips over the adjective as if she rather enjoyed it, then stretched herself again luxuriously, with sensuous enjoyment. She had riden with the Rajah in the early morning, and was pleasantly tired.

The sudden approach of Tessa, scampering along the verandah in the wake of Scooter, sent a quick frown to her face, which deepened swiftly as Scooter, dodging nimbly, ran into the room and went to earth behind a bamboo screen.

Tessa sprang in after him, but pulled up sharply at sight of her mother. The frown upon Netta's face was instantly reflected upon her own. She stood expectant of rebuke.

"What a noisy child you are!" said Netta. "Are you never quiet, I wonder? And why did you let that horrid little beast come in here? You know I detest him."

"He isn't horrid!" said Tessa, instantly on the defensive. "And I couldn't help him coming in. I didn't know you were here, but it isn't your bungalow anyway, and Aunt Mary doesn't mind him."

"Oh, go away!" said Netta with irritation. "You get more insufferable every day. Take the little brute with you and shut him up—or drown him!"

Tessa came forward with an insolent shrug. There was more than a spice of defiance in her bearing.

"I don't suppose I can catch him," she said. "But I'll try."

The chase of the elusive Scooter that followed would have been an affair of pure pleasure to the child, had it not been for the presence of her mother and the growing exasperation with which she regarded it. It was all sheer fun to Scooter who wormed in and out of the furniture with mirth in his gleaming eyes, and darted past the window a dozen times without availing himself of that means of escape.

Netta's small stock of patience was very speedily exhausted. She sat up on the sofa and sternly commanded Tessa to desist.

"Go and tell the *khit* to catch him!" she said.

Tessa, however, by this time had also warmed to the game. She paid no more attention to her mother's order than she would have paid to the buzzing of a mosquito. And when

Scooter dived under the sofa on which Netta had been reclining, she burrowed after him with a squeal of merriment.

It was too much for Netta whose feelings had been decidedly ruffled before Tessa's entrance. As Scooter shot out on the other side of her, running his queer zigzag course, she snatched the first thing that came to hand, which chanced to be a heavy bronze weight from the writing-table at her elbow, and hurled it at him with all her strength.

Scooter collapsed on the floor like a broken mechanical toy. Tessa uttered a wild scream and flung herself upon him.

Netta gasped hysterically, horrified but still angry. "It serves him right—serves you both right! Now go away!" she said.

Tessa turned on her knees on the floor. Scooter was feebly kicking in her arms. The missile had struck him on the head and one eye was terribly injured. She gathered him up to her little narrow chest, and he ceased to kick and became quite still.

Over his lifeless body she looked at her mother with eyes of burning furious hatred. "You've killed him!" she said, her voice sunk very low. "And I hope—oh, I do hope—some day—someone—will kill you!"

There was that about her at the moment that actually frightened Netta, and it was with undoubted relief that she saw the door open and Major Ralston's loose-knit lounging figure block the entrance.

"What's all this noise about?" he began, and stopped short.

Behind him stood another figure, broad, powerful, not overtall. At sight of it, Tessa uttered a hard sob and scrambled to her feet. She still clasped poor Scooter's dead body to her breast, and his blood was on her face and on the white frock she wore.

"Uncle St. Bernard! Look! Look!" she said. "She's killed my Scooter!"

Netta also arose at this juncture. "Oh, do take that horrible thing away!" she said. "If it's dead, so much the better. It was no more than a weasel after all. I hate such pets."

Major Ralston found himself abruptly though not roughly pushed aside. Bernard Monck swooped down with the action of a practised footballer and took the furry thing out of Tessa's hold. His eyes were very bright and intensely alert, but he did not seem aware of Tessa's mother.

"Come with me, darling!" he said to the child. "P'raps I can help."

He trod upon the carved bronze that had slain Scooter as he turned, and he left the mark of his heel upon it—the deep impress of an angry giant.

The door closed with decision upon himself and the child, and Major Ralston was left alone with Netta.

She looked at him with a flushed face ready to defy remonstrance, but he stooped without speaking and picked up the thing that Bernard had tried to grind to powder, surveyed it with a lifted brow and set it back in its place.

Netta promptly collapsed upon the sofa. "Oh, it is too bad!" she sobbed. "It really is too bad! Now I suppose you too—are going to be brutal."

Major Ralston cleared his throat. There was certainly no sympathy in his aspect, but his manner was wholly lacking in brutality. He was never brutal to women, and Netta Ermsted was his guest as well as his patient.

After a moment he sat down beside her, and there was nothing in the action to mark it as heroic, or to betray the fact that he yearned to stamp out of the room after Bernard and leave her severely to her hysterics.

"No good in being upset now," he remarked. "The thing's done, and crying won't undo it."

"I don't want to undo it!" declared Netta. "I always did detest the horrible ferrety thing. Tessa couldn't have taken it Home with her either, so it's just as well it's gone." She dried her eyes with a vindictive gesture, and reached for the cigarettes. Hysterics were impossible in this man's presence. He was like a shower of cold water.

"I shouldn't if I were you," remarked Major Ralston with the air of a man performing a laborious duty. "You smoke too many of 'em."

Netta ignored the admonition. "They soothe my nerves," she said. "May I have a light?"

He searched his pockets, and apparently drew a blank.

Netta frowned in swift irritation. "How stupid! I thought all men carried matches."

Major Ralston accepted the reproof in silence. He was like a large dog, gravely presenting his shoulder to the nips of a toy terrier.

"Well?" said Netta aggressively.

He looked at her with composure. "Talking about going Home," he said, "at the risk of appearing inhospitable, I think it is my duty to advise you very strongly to go as soon as possible."

"Indeed!" She looked back with instant hostility. "And why?"

He did not immediately reply. Whether with reason or not, he had the reputation for being slow-witted, in spite of the fact that he was a brilliant chess-player.

She laughed—a short, unpleasant laugh. She was never quite at her ease with him, notwithstanding his slowness. "Why the devil should I, Major Ralston?"

He shrugged his shoulders with massive deliberation. "Because," he said slowly, "there's going to be the devil's own row if this man is hanged for your husband's murder. We have been warned to that effect."

She shrugged her shoulders also with infinite daintiness, "Oh, a native rumpus! That doesn't impress me in the least. I shan't go for that."

Major Ralston's eyes wandered round the room as if in search of inspiration. "Mary is going," he observed.

Netta laughed again, lightly, flippantly. "Good old Mary! Where is she going to?"

His eyes came down upon her suddenly like the flash of a knife. "She has consented to go to Bhulwana with the rest," he said. "But I beg you will not accompany her there. As Captain Ermsted's widow and—" he spoke as one hewing his way—"the chosen friend of the Rajah, your position in the State is one of considerable difficulty—possibly even of danger. And I do not propose to allow my wife to take unnecessary risks. For that reason I must ask you to go before matters come to a head. You have stayed too long already."

"Good gracious!" said Netta, opening her eyes wide. "But if Mary's sacred person is to be safely stowed at Bhulwana, what is to prevent my remaining here if I so choose?"

"Because I don't choose to let you, Mrs. Ermsted," said Major Ralston steadily.

She gazed at him. "You—don't—choose! You!"

His eyes did battle with hers. Since that slighting allusion to his wife, he had no consideration left for Netta. "That is so," he said, in his heavy fashion. "I have already pointed out that you would be well-advised on your own account to go—not to mention the child's safety."

"Oh, the child!" There was keenness about the exclamation which almost amounted to actual dislike. "I'm tired to death of having Tessa's welfare and Tessa's morals rammed down my throat. Why should I make a fetish of the child? What is good enough for me is surely good enough for her."

"I am afraid I don't agree with you," said Major Ralston.

"You wouldn't," she rejoined. "You and Mary are quite antediluvian in your idea. But that doesn't influence me. I am glad to say I am more up to date. If I can't stay here, I shall go to Udalkhand. There's a hotel there as well as here."

"Of sorts," said Major Ralston. "Also Udalkhand is nearer to the seat of disturbance."

"Well, I don't care." Netta spoke recklessly. "I'm not going to be dictated to. What a mighty scare you're all in! What can you think will happen even if a few natives do get out of hand?"

"Plenty of things might happen," he rejoined, getting up. "But that by the way. If you won't listen to reason I am wasting my time. But—" he spoke with abrupt emphasis—"you will not take Tessa to Udalkhand."

Netta's eyes gleamed. "I shall take her to Kamtchatka if I choose," she said.

For the first time a smile crossed Major Ralston's face. He turned to the door. "And if she chooses," he said, with malicious satisfaction.

The door closed upon him, and Netta was left alone.

She remained motionless for a few moments showing her teeth a little in an answering smile; then with a swift, lissom movement, that would have made Tommy compare her to a lizard, she rose.

With a white, determined face she bent over the writing-table and scribbled a hasty note. Her hand shook, but she controlled it resolutely.

Words flicked rapidly into being under her pen: "I shall be behind the tamarisks to-night."

CHAPTER IV
THE BROAD ROAD

Bernard Monck never forgot the day of Scooter's death. It was as indelibly fixed in his memory as in that of Tessa.

The child's wild agony of grief was of so utterly abandoned a nature as to be almost Oriental in its violence. The passionate force of her resentment against her mother also was not easy to cope with though he quelled it eventually. But when that was over, when she had wept herself exhausted in his arms at last, there followed a period of numbness that made him seriously uneasy.

Mrs. Ralston had gone out before the tragedy had occurred, but Major Ralston presently came to his relief. He stooped over Tessa with a few kindly words, but when he saw the child's face his own changed somewhat.

"This won't do," he said to Bernard, holding the slender wrist. "We must get her to bed. Where's her *ayah*?"

Tessa's little hand hung limply in his hold. She seemed to be half-asleep. Yet when Bernard moved to lift her, she roused herself to cling around his neck.

"Please keep me with you, dear Uncle St. Bernard! Oh, please don't go away!"

"I won't, sweetheart," he promised her.

The *ayah* was nowhere to be found, but it was doubtful if her presence would have made much difference, since Tessa would not stir from her friend's sheltering arms, and wept again weakly even at the doctor's touch.

So it was Bernard who carried her to her room, and eventually put her to bed under Major Ralston's directions. The latter's face was very grave over the whole proceeding and he presently fetched something in a medicine-glass and gave it to Bernard to administer.

Tessa tried to refuse it, but her opposition broke down before Bernard's very gentle insistence. She would do anything, she told him piteously, if only—if only—he would stay with her.

So Bernard stayed, sending a message to The Green Bungalow to explain his absence, which found Mrs. Ralston as well as Stella and brought the former back in haste.

Tessa was in a deep sleep by the time she arrived, but, hearing that Stella did not need him, Bernard still maintained his watch, only permitting Mrs. Ralston to relieve him while he partook of luncheon with her husband.

Netta did not appear for the meal to the unspoken satisfaction of them both. They ate almost in silence, Major Ralston being sunk in a species of moody abstraction which Bernard did not disturb until the meal was over.

Then at length, ere he rose to go, he deliberately broke into his host's gloomy reflections. "Will you tell me," he said courteously, "exactly what it is that you fear with regard to the child?"

Major Ralston continued to be abstracted for fully thirty seconds after the quiet question; then, as Bernard did not repeat it but merely waited, he replied to it.

"There are plenty of things to be feared for a child like that. It's a criminal shame to have kept her out here so long. What I actually believe to be the matter at the present moment, is heart trouble."

"Ah! I thought so." Bernard looked across at him with grave comprehension. "She had a bad shock the other day."

"Yes; a shock to the whole system. She lives on wires in any case. I am going to examine her presently, but I am pretty sure I am right. What she really wants—" Major

Ralston stopped himself abruptly, so abruptly that a twinkle of humour shone momentarily in Bernard's eyes.

"Don't jam on the brakes on my account!" he protested gently. "I am with you all the way. What does she really want?"

Major Ralston uttered a gruff laugh. It was practically impossible not to confide in Bernard Monck. "She wants to get right away from that vicious little termagant of a mother of hers. There's no love between them and never will be, so what's the use of pretending? She wants to get into a wholesome bracing, outdoor atmosphere with someone who knows how to love her. She'll probably go straight to the bad if she doesn't—that is, if she lives long enough."

The humour had died in Bernard's eyes. They shone with a very different light as he said, "I have thought the same thing myself." He paused a moment, then slowly, "Do you think her mother would be persuaded to hand her over to me?" he said.

Ralston's brows went up. "To you! For good and all do you mean?"

"Yes." In his steady unhurried fashion Bernard made answer. "I have been thinking of it for some time. As a matter of fact, it was to consult you about it that I came here to-day. I want it more than ever now."

Ralston was staring openly. "You'd have your hands full," he remarked.

Bernard smiled. "I daresay. But, you see, we're chums. To use your own expression I know how to love her. I could make her happy—possibly good as well."

Ralston never paid compliments, but after a considerable pause he said, "It would be the best thing that ever happened to the imp. So far as her mother's permission goes, I should say she is cheap enough to be had almost without asking. You won't need to use much persuasion in that direction."

"An infernal shame!" said Bernard, the hot light again in his eyes.

Ralston agreed with him. "All the same, Tessa can be a positive little demon when she likes. I've seen it, so I know. She has got a good deal of her mother's temperament only with a generous allowance of heart thrown in."

"Yes," Bernard said. "And it's the heart that counts. You can do practically anything with a child like that."

Ralston got up. "Well, I'm going to have another look at her, and then I'm due at The Green Bungalow. I can't say what is going to happen there. You ought to clear out, all of you; but a journey would probably be fatal to Mrs. Monck's infant just now. I can't advise it."

"Wherever Stella goes, I go," said Bernard firmly.

"Yes, that's understood." Ralston gave him a keen look. "You're in charge, aren't you? But those who can go, must go, that's certain. That scoundrel will be convicted in a day or two. And then—look out for squalls!"

Bernard's smile was scarcely the smile of the man of peace. "Oh yes, I shall look out," he said mildly. "And—incidentally—Tommy is teaching me how to shoot."

They returned to Tessa who was still sleeping, and Mrs. Ralston gave up her place beside her to Bernard, who settled down with a paper to spend the afternoon. Major Ralston departed for The Green Bungalow, and the silence of midday fell upon the place.

It was still early in the year, but the warmth was as that of a soft summer day in England. The lazy drone of bees hung on the air, and somewhere among the tamarisks a small, persistent bird, called and called perpetually, receiving no reply.

"A fine example of perseverance," Bernard murmured to himself.

He had plenty of things to think about—to worry about also, had it been his disposition to worry; but the utter peace that surrounded him made him drowsy. He nodded uncomfortably for a space, then finally—since he seldom did things by halves—laid aside his paper, leaned back in his chair, and serenely slept.

Twice during the afternoon Mrs. Ralston tiptoed along the verandah, peeped in upon them, and retired again smiling. On the second occasion she met her husband on the same errand and he drew her aside, his hand through her arm.

"Look here, Mary! I've talked to that little spitfire without much result. She talks in a random fashion of going to Udalkhand. What her actual intentions are I don't know. Possibly she doesn't know herself. But one thing is certain. She is not going to be attached to your train any longer, and I have told her so."

"Oh, Gerald!" She looked at him in dismay. "How—inhospitable of you!"

"Yes, isn't it?" His hand was holding her arm firmly. "You see, I chance to value your safety more than my reputation for kindness to outsiders. You are going to Bhulwana at the end of this week. Come! You promised."

"Yes, I know I did." She looked at him with distress in her eyes. "I've wished I hadn't ever since. There is my poor Stella in bad trouble for one thing. She says she will have to change her *ayah*. And there is—"

"She has got Peter—and her brother-in-law. She doesn't want you too," said her husband.

"And now there is little Tessa," proceeded Mrs. Ralston, growing more and more worried as she proceeded.

"Yes, there is Tessa," he agreed. "You can offer to take her to Bhulwana with you if you like. But not her mother as well. That is understood. It won't break her heart to part with her, I fancy. As for you, my dear," he gave her a whimsical look, "the sooner you are gone the better I shall be pleased. Lady Harriet and the Burton contingent left to-day."

"I hate going!" declared Mrs. Ralston almost tearfully. "I shouldn't have promised if I could have foreseen all that was going to happen."

He squeezed her arm. "All the same—you promised. So don't be silly!"

She turned suddenly and clung to him.

"Gerald! I want to stay with you. Let me stay! I can't bear the thought of you alone and in danger."

He stared for a moment in astonishment. Demonstrations of affection were almost unknown between them. Then, with a shamefaced gesture, he bent and kissed her.

"What a silly old woman!" he said.

That ended the discussion and she knew that her plea had been refused. But the fashion of its refusal brought the warm colour to her faded face, and she was even near to laughing in the midst of her woe. How dear of Gerald to put it like that! She did not feel that she had ever fully realized his love for her until that moment.

Seeing that her presence in her own bungalow was not needed just then, she betook herself once more to Stella, and again the afternoon silence fell like a spell of enchantment. That there could be any element of unrest anywhere within that charmed region seemed a thing impossible. The peace of Eden brooded everywhere.

The evening was drawing on ere Bernard slowly emerged from his serene slumber and looked at the child beside him. Some invisible influence—or perhaps some bond of sympathy between them—had awakened her at the same moment, for her eyes were fixed upon him. They shone intensely, mysteriously blue in the subdued light, wistful, searching eyes, wholly unlike the eyes of a child.

Her hand came out to his. "Have you been here all the time, dear?" she said.

She seemed to be still half-wrapped in the veil of sleep. He leaned to her, holding the little hand up against his cheek.

"Almost, my princess," he said.

She nestled to him snuggling her fair head into his shoulder. "I've been dreaming," she whispered.

"Have you, my darling?" He gathered her close with a compassionate tenderness for the frailty of the little throbbing body he held.

Tessa's arms crept round his neck. "I dreamt," she said, "that you and I, Uncle St. Bernard, were walking in a great big city, and there was a church with a golden spire. There were a lot of steps up to it—and Scooter—" a sob rose in her throat and was swiftly suppressed—"was sunning himself on the top. And I tried to run up the steps and catch him, but there were always more and more and more steps, and I couldn't get any nearer. And I cried at last, I was so tired and disappointed. And then—" the bony arms tightened—

"you came up behind me, and took my hand and said, 'Why don't you kneel down and pray? It's much the quickest way.' And so I did," said Tessa simply. "And all of a sudden the steps were gone, and you and I went in together. I tried to pick up Scooter, but he ran away, and I didn't mind 'cos I knew he was safe. I was so happy, so very happy. I didn't want to wake again." A doleful note crept into Tessa's voice; she swallowed another sob.

Bernard lifted her bodily from the bed to his arms. "Don't fret, little sweetheart! I'm here," he said.

She lifted her face to his, very wet and piteous. "Uncle St. Bernard, I've been praying and praying—ever such a lot since my birthday-party. You said I might, didn't you? But God hasn't taken any notice."

He held her close. "What have you been praying for, my darling?" he said.

"I do—so—want to be your little girl," answered Tessa with a break in her voice. "I never really prayed for anything before—only the things Aunt Mary made me say—and they weren't what I wanted. But I do want this. And I believe I'd get quite good if I was your little girl. I told God so, but I don't think He cared."

"Yes. He did care, darling." Very softly Bernard reassured her. "Don't you think that ever! He is going to answer that prayer of yours—pretty soon now."

"Oh, is He?" said Tessa, brightening. "How do you know? Is He going to say Yes?"

"I think so." Bernard's voice and touch were alike motherly. "But you must be patient a little longer, my princess of the bluebell. It isn't good for us to have things straight off when we want them."

"You do want me?" insinuated Tessa, squeezing his neck very hard.

"Yes. I want you very much," he said.

"I love you," said Tessa with passionate warmth, "better—yes, better now than even Uncle Everard. And I didn't think I ever could do that."

"God bless you, little one!" he said.

Later, when Major Ralston had seen her again, they had another conference. The doctor's suspicions were fully justified. Tessa would need the utmost care.

"She shall have it," Bernard said. "But—I can't leave Stella now. I shall see my way clearer presently."

"Quite so," Ralston agreed. "My wife shall look after the child at Bhulwana. It will keep her quiet." He gave Bernard a shrewd look. "Perhaps you—and Mrs. Monck also—will be on your way Home before the hot weather," he said. "In that case she could go with you."

Bernard was silent. It was impossible to look forward. One thing was certain. He could not desert Stella.

Ralston passed on. Being reticent himself he respected a man who could keep his own counsel.

"What about Mrs. Ermsted?" he said. "When will you see her?"

"To-night," said Bernard, setting his jaw.

Ralston smiled briefly. That look recalled his brother. "No time like the present," he said.

But the time for consultation with Netta Ermsted upon the future of her child was already past. When Bernard, very firm and purposeful, walked down again after dinner that night, Ralston met him with a wry expression and put a crumpled note into his hand.

"Mrs. Ermsted has apparently divined your benevolent intentions," he said.

Bernard read in silence, with meeting brows.

DEAR MARY:

This is to wish you and all kind friends good-bye. So that there may be no misunderstanding on the part of our charitable gossips, pray tell them at once that I have finally chosen the broad road as it really suits me best. As for Tessa—I bequeath her and her little morals to the first busybody who cares to apply for them. Perhaps the worthy Father Monck would like to acquire virtue in this fashion. I find the task only breeds vice in me. Many thanks for your laborious and, I fear, wholly futile attempts to keep me in the much too narrow way.

146

Yours,

NETTA.

Bernard looked up from the note with such fiery eyes that Ralston who was on the verge of a scathing remark himself had to stop out of sheer curiosity to see what he would say.

"A damnably cruel and heartless woman!" said Bernard with deliberation.

Ralston's smile expressed what for him was warm approval. "She's nothing but an animal," he said.

Bernard took him up short. "You wrong the animals," he said. "The very least of them love their young."

Ralston shrugged his shoulders. "All the better for Tessa anyhow."

Bernard's eyes softened very suddenly. He crumpled the note into a ball and tossed it from him. "Yes," he said quietly. "God helping me, it shall be all the better for her."

CHAPTER V
THE DARK NIGHT

An owl hooted across the compound, and a paraquet disturbed by the outcry uttered a shrill, indignant protest. An immense moon hung suspended as it were in mid-heaven, making all things intense with its radiance. It was the hour before the dawn.

Stella stood at her window, gazing forth and numbly marvelling at the splendour. As of old, it struck her like a weird fantasy—this Indian enchantment—poignant, passionate, holding more of anguish than of ecstasy, yet deeply magnetic, deeply alluring, as a magic potion which, once tasted, must enchain the senses for ever.

The extravagance of that world of dreadful black and dazzling silver, the stillness that was yet indescribably electric, the unreality that was allegorically real, she felt it all as a vague accompaniment to the heartache that never left her—the scornful mockery of the goddess she had refused to worship.

There were even times when the very atmosphere seemed to her charged with hostility—a terrible overwhelming antagonism that closed about her in a narrowing ring which serpent-wise constricted her ever more and more, from which she could never hope to escape. For—still the old idea haunted her—she was a trespasser upon forbidden ground. Once she had been cast forth. But she had dared to return, braving the flaming sword. And now—and now—it barred her in, cutting off her escape.

For she was as much a prisoner as if iron walls surrounded her. Sentence had gone forth against her. She would not be cast forth again until she had paid the uttermost farthing, endured the ultimate torture. Then only—childless and desolate and broken—would she be turned adrift in the desert, to return no more for ever.

The ghastly glamour of the night attracted and repelled her like the swing of a mighty pendulum. She was trying to pray—that much had Bernard taught her—but her prayer only ran blind and futile through her brain. The hour should have been sacred, but it was marred and desecrated by the stark glare of that nightmare moon. She was worn out with long and anxious watching, and she had almost ceased to look for comfort, so heavy were the clouds that menaced her.

The thought of Everard was ever with her, strive as she might to drive it out. At such moments as these she yearned for him with a sick and desperate longing—his strength, his tenderness, his understanding. He, and he alone, would have known how to comfort her now with her baby dying before her eyes. He would have held her up through her darkest hours. His arm would have borne her forward however terrible the path.

She had Bernard and she had Tommy, each keen and ready in her service. She sometimes thought that but for Bernard she would have been overwhelmed long since. But he could not fill the void within her. He could not even touch the aching longing that gnawed so perpetually at her heart. That was a pain she would have to endure in silence all the rest of her life. She did not think she would ever see Everard again. Though only a few miles lay between them at present he might have been already a world away. She was sure he would not come back to her unless she summoned him. The manner of his going, though he had taken no leave of her, had been somehow final. And she could not call him back even if she would. He had deceived her cruelly, of set intention, and she could never trust him again. The memory of Ralph Dacre tainted all her thoughts of him. He had sworn he had not killed him. Perhaps not—perhaps not! Yet was the conviction ever with her that he had sent him to his death, had intended him to die.

She had given up reasoning the matter. It was beyond her. She was too hopelessly plunged in darkness. Tommy with all his staunchness could not lift that overwhelming cloud. And Bernard? She did not know what Bernard thought save that he had once reminded her that a man should be regarded as innocent unless he could be proved guilty.

It was common talk now that Everard's Indian career was ended. It was only the trial at Khanmulla that had delayed the sending in of his papers. He was as much a broken man, however hotly Tommy contested the point, as if he had been condemned by a court-martial. Surely, had he been truly innocent he would have demanded a court-martial and vindicated himself. But he had suffered his honour to go down in silence. What more damning evidence could be supplied than this?

The dumb sympathy of Peter's eyes kept the torturing thought constantly before her. She felt sure that Peter believed him guilty of Dacre's murder though it was more than possible that in his heart he condoned the offence. Perhaps he even admired him for it, she reflected shudderingly. But his devotion to her, as always, was uppermost. His dog-like fidelity surrounded her with unfailing service. The *ayah* had gone, and he had slipped into her place as naturally as if he had always occupied it. Even now, while Stella stood at her window gazing forth into the garish moonlight, was he softly padding to and fro in the room adjoining hers, hushing the poor little wailing infant to sleep. She could trust him implicitly, she knew, even in moments of crisis. He would gladly work himself to death in her service. But with Mrs. Ralston gone to Bhulwana, she knew she must have further help. The strain was incessant, and Major Ralston insisted that she must have a woman with her.

All the ladies of the station, save herself, had gone. She knew vaguely that some sort of disturbance was expected at Khanmulla, and that it might spread to Kurrumpore. But her baby was too ill for travel; she had practically forced this truth from Major Ralston, and so she had no choice but to remain. She knew very well at the heart of her that it would not be for long.

No thought of personal danger troubled her. Sinister though the night might seem to her stretched nerves, yet no sense of individual peril penetrated the weary bewilderment of her brain. She was tired out in mind and body, and had yielded to Peter's persuasion to take a rest. But the weird cry of the night-bird had drawn her to the window and the glittering splendour of the night had held her there. She turned from it at last with a long, long sigh, and lay down just as she was. She always held herself ready for a call at any time. Those strange seizures came so suddenly and were becoming increasingly violent. It was many days since she had permitted herself to sleep soundly.

She lay for awhile wide-eyed, almost painfully conscious, listening to Peter's muffled movements in the other room. The baby had ceased to cry, but he was still prowling to and fro, tireless and patient, with an endurance that was almost superhuman.

She had done the same thing a little earlier till her limbs had given way beneath her. In the daytime Bernard helped her, but she and Peter shared the nights.

Her senses became at last a little blurred. The night seemed to have spread over half a lifetime—a practically endless vista of suffering. The soft footfall in the other room made her think of the Sentry at the Gate, that Sentry with the flaming sword who never slept. It beat with a pitiless thudding upon her brain....

Later, it grew intermittent, fitful, as if at each turn the Sentry paused. It always went on again, or so she thought. And she was sure she was not deeply sleeping, or that haunting cry of an owl had not penetrated her consciousness so frequently.

Once, oddly, there came to her—perhaps it was a dream—a sound as of voices whispering together. She turned in her sleep and tried to listen, but her senses were fogged, benumbed. She could not at the moment drag herself free from the stupor of weariness that held her. But she was sure of Peter, quite sure that he would call her if any emergency arose. And there was no one with whom he could be whispering. So she was sure it must be a dream. Imperceptibly she sank still deeper into slumber and forgot....

It was several hours later that Tommy, returned from early parade, flung himself impetuously down at the table opposite Bernard with a brief, "Now for it!"

Bernard was reading a letter, and Tommy's eyes fastened upon it as his were lifted.

"What's that? A letter from Everard?" he asked unceremoniously.

"Yes. He has written to tell me definitely that he has sent in his resignation—and it has been accepted." Bernard's reply was wholly courteous, the boy's bluntness notwithstanding. He had a respect for Tommy.

"Oh, damn!" said Tommy with fervor. "What is he going to do now?"

"He doesn't tell me that." Bernard folded the letter and put it in his pocket. "What's your news?" he inquired.

Tommy marked the action with somewhat jealous eyes. He had been aware of Everard's intention for some time. It had been more or less inevitable. But he wished he had written to him also. There were several things he would have liked to know.

He looked at Bernard rather blankly, ignoring his question. "What the devil is he going to do?" he said. "Dropout?"

Bernard's candid eyes met his. "Honestly I don't know," he said. "Perhaps he is just waiting for orders."

"Will he come back here?" questioned Tommy.

Bernard shook his head. "No. I'm pretty sure he won't. Now tell me your news!"

"Oh, it's nothing!" said Tommy impatiently. "Nothing, I mean, compared to his clearing out. The trial is over and the man is condemned. He is to be executed next week. It'll mean a shine of some sort—nothing very great, I am afraid."

"That all?" said Bernard, with a smile.

"No, not quite all. There was some secret information given which it is supposed was rather damaging to the Rajah, for he has taken to his heels. No one knows where he is, or at least no one admits he does. You know these Oriental chaps. They can cover the scent of a rotten herring. He'll probably never turn up again. The place is too hot to hold him. He can finish his rotting in another corner of the Empire; and I wish Netta Ermsted joy of her bargain!" ended Tommy with vindictive triumph.

"My good fellow!" protested Bernard.

Tommy uttered a reckless laugh. "You know it as well as I do. She was done for from the moment he taught her the opium habit. There's no escape from that, and the devil knew it. I say, what a mercy it will be when you can get Tessa away to England."

"And Stella too," said Bernard, turning to the subject with relief.

"You won't do that," said Tommy quickly.

"How do you know that?" Bernard's look had something of a piercing quality.

But Tommy eluded all search. "I do know. I can't tell you how. But I'm certain—dead certain—that Stella won't go back to England with you this spring."

"You're something of a prophet, Tommy," remarked Bernard, after an attentive pause.

"It's not my only accomplishment," rejoined Tommy modestly. "I'm several things besides that. I've got some brains too—just a few. Funny, isn't it? Ah, here is Stella! Come and break your fast, old girl! What's the latest?"

He went to meet her and drew her to the table. She smiled in her wan, rather abstracted way at Bernard whom she had seen before.

"Oh, don't get up!" she said. "I only came for a glimpse of you both. I had *tiffin* in my room. Peter saw to that. Baby is very weak this morning, and I thought perhaps, Tommy dear, when you go back you would see Major Ralston for me and ask him to come up soon." She sat down with an involuntary gesture of weariness.

"Have you slept at all?" Bernard asked her gently.

"Oh yes, thank you. I had three hours of undisturbed rest. Peter was splendid."

"You must have another *ayah*," Bernard said. "It isn't fit for you to go on in this way."

"No." She spoke with the docility of exhaustion. "Peter is seeing to it. He always sees to everything. He knows a woman in the bazaar who would do—an elderly woman—I think he said she is the grandmother of Hafiz who sells trinkets. You know Hafiz, I expect? I don't like him, but he is supposed to be respectable, and Peter is prepared to vouch for the woman's respectability. Only she has been terribly disfigured by an accident, burnt I think he said, and she wears a veil. I told him that didn't matter. Baby is too ill to notice, and he evidently wants me to have her. He says she has been used to English children, and is a good nurse. That is what matters chiefly, so I have told him to engage her."

"I am very glad to hear it," Bernard said.

"Yes, I think it will be a relief. Those screaming fits are so terrible." Stella checked a sharp shudder. "Peter would not recommend her if he did not personally know her to be trustworthy," she added quietly.

"No. Peter's safe enough," said Tommy. He was bolting his meal with great expedition. "Is the kiddie worse, Stella?"

She looked at him with that in her tired eyes that went straight to his heart. "He is a little worse every day," she said.

Tommy swore into his cup and asked no further.

A few moments later he got up, gave her a brief kiss, and departed.

Stella sat on with her chin in her hand, every line of her expressing the weariness of the hopeless watcher. She looked crushed, as if a burden she could hardly support had been laid upon her.

Bernard looked at her once or twice without speaking. Finally he too rose, went round to her, knelt beside her, put his arm about her.

Her face quivered a little. "I've got—to keep strong," she said, in the tone of one who had often said the same thing in solitude.

"I know," he said. "And so you will. There's special strength given for such times as these. It won't fail you now."

She put her hand into his. "Thank you," she said. And then, with an effort, "Do you know, Bernard, I tried—I really tried—to pray in the night before I lay down. But—there was something so wicked about it—I simply couldn't."

"One can't always," he said.

"Oh, have you found that too?" she asked.

He smiled at the question. "Of course I have. So has everybody. We're only children, Stella. God knows that. He doesn't expect of us more than we can manage. Prayer is only one of the means we have of reaching Him. It can't be used always. There are some people who haven't time for prayer even, and yet they may be very near to God. In times of stress like yours one is often much nearer than one realizes. You will find that out quite suddenly one of these days, find that through all your desert journeying, He has been guiding you, protecting you, surrounding you with the most loving care. And—because the night was dark—you never knew it."

"The night is certainly very dark," Stella said with a tremulous smile. "If it weren't for you I don't think I could ever get through."

"Oh, don't say that!" he said. "If it weren't me it would be someone else—or possibly a closer vision of Himself. There is always something—something to which later you will look back and say, 'That was His lamp in the desert, showing the way.' Don't fret if you can't pray! I can pray for you. You just keep on being brave and patient! He understands."

Stella's fingers pressed upon his. "You are good to me, Bernard," she said. "I shall think of what you say—the next time I am alone in the night."

His arm held her sustainingly. "And if you're very desolate, child, come and call me!" he said. "I'm always at hand, always glad to serve you."

She smiled—a difficult smile. "I shall need you more—afterwards," she said under her breath. And then, as if words had suddenly become impossible to her, she leaned against him and kissed him.

He gathered her up close, as if she had been a weary child. "God bless you, my dear!" he said.

CHAPTER VI
THE FIRST GLIMMER

It was from the Colonel himself that Stella heard of Everard's retirement.

He walked back from the Mess that night with Tommy and asked to see her for a few minutes alone. He was always kinder to her in his wife's absence.

She was busy installing the new *ayah* whom Peter with the air of a magician who has but to wave his wand had presented to her half an hour before. The woman was old and bent and closely veiled—so closely that Stella strongly suspected her disfigurement to be of a very ghastly nature, but her low voice and capable manner inspired her with instinctive confidence. She realized with relief from the very outset that her faithful Peter had not made a mistake. She was sure that the new-comer had nursed sickly English children before. She went to the Colonel, leaving the strange woman in charge of her baby and Peter hovering reassuringly in the background.

His first greeting of her had a touch of diffidence, but when he saw the weary suffering of her eyes this was swallowed up in pity. He took her hands and held them.

"My poor girl!" he said.

She smiled at him. Pity from an outsider did not penetrate to the depths of her. "Thank you for coming," she said.

He coughed and cleared his throat. "I hope it isn't an intrusion," he said.

"But of course not!" she made answer. "How could it be? Won't you sit down?"

He led her to a chair; but he did not sit down himself. He stood before her with something of the air of a man making a confession.

"Mrs. Monck," he said, "I think I ought to tell you that it was by my advice that your husband resigned his commission."

Her brows drew together a little as if at a momentary dart of pain. "Has he resigned it?" she said.

"Yes. Didn't he tell you?" He frowned. "Haven't you seen him? Don't you know where he is?"

She shook her head. "I can only think of my baby just now," she said.

He swung round abruptly upon his heel and paced the room. "Oh yes, of course. I know that. Ralston told me. I am very sorry for you, Mrs. Monck,—very, very sorry."

"Thank you," she said.

He continued to tramp to and fro. "You haven't much to thank me for. I had to think of the Regiment; but I considered the step very carefully before I took it. He had rendered invaluable service—especially over this Khanmulla trial. He would have been decorated for it if—" he pulled up with a jerk—"if things had been different. I know Sir Reginald Bassett thought very highly of him, was prepared to give him an appointment on his personal staff. And no doubt eventually he would have climbed to the top of the tree. But—this affair has destroyed him." He paused a moment, but he did not look at her. "He has had every chance," he said then. "I kept an open mind. I wouldn't condemn him unheard until—well until he refused flatly to speak on his own behalf. I went over to Khanmulla and talked to him—talked half the night. I couldn't move him. And if a man won't take the trouble to defend his own honour, it isn't worth—that!" He snapped his fingers with a bitter gesture; then abruptly wheeled and came back to her. "I didn't come here to distress you," he said, looking down at her again. "I know your cup is full already. And it's a thankless task to persuade any woman that her husband is unworthy of her, besides being an impertinence. But what I must say to you is this. There is nothing left to wait for, and it would be sheer madness to stay on any longer. The Rajah has been deeply incriminated and is in hiding. The Government will of course take over the direction of affairs, but there is certain—absolutely certain—to be a disturbance when Ermsted's murderer is executed. I hope an adequate force will soon be at our disposal to cope with it, but it has not yet been provided. Therefore I cannot possibly permit you to stay here any longer. As Monck's wife, it is more than likely that you might be made an object of vengeance. I can't risk it. You and the child must go. I will send an escort in the morning."

He stopped at last, partly for lack of breath, partly because from her unmoved expression he fancied that she was not taking in his warning words. She sat looking straight before her as one rapt in reverie. It was almost as though she had forgotten him, suffered some more absorbing matter to crowd him out of her thoughts.

"You do follow me?" he questioned at length as she did not speak.

She lifted her eyes to him again though he felt it was with a great effort. "Oh, yes," she said. "I quite understand you, Colonel Mansfield. And—I am quite grateful to you. But I am not staying here for my husband's sake at all. I—do not suppose we shall ever see each other any more. All that is over."

He started. "What! You have given him up?" he said, uttering the words almost involuntarily, so quiet was she in her despair.

She bent her head. "Yes, I have given him up. I do not know where he is—or anything about him. I am staying here now—I must stay here now—for my baby's sake. He is too ill to bear a journey."

She lifted her face again with the words, and in its pale resolution he saw that he would spend himself upon further argument in vain. Moreover, he was for the moment too staggered by the low-spoken information to concentrate his attention upon persuasion. Her utter quietness silenced him.

He stood for a moment or two looking down at her, then abruptly bent and took her hand. "You're a very brave woman," he said, a quick touch of feeling in his voice. "You've had a fiendish time of it out here from start to finish. It'll be a good thing for you when you can get out of it and go Home. You're young; you'll start again."

It was clumsy consolation, but his hand-grip was fatherly. She smiled again at him, and got up.

"Thank you very much, Colonel. You have always been kind. Please don't bother about me any more. I am really not a bit afraid. I have too much to think about. And really I don't think I am important enough to be in any real danger. You will excuse me now, won't you? I have just got a new *ayah*, and they always need superintending. Perhaps you will join my brother-in-law. I know he will be delighted."

She extricated herself with a gentle aloofness more difficult to combat than any open opposition, and he went away to express himself more strongly to Bernard Monck from whom he was sure at least of receiving sympathy if not support.

Stella returned to her baby with a stunned feeling of having been struck, and yet without consciousness of pain. Perhaps she had suffered so much that her faculties were getting numbed. She knew that the Colonel was surprised that his news concerning Everard had affected her so little. She was in a fashion surprised herself. Was she then so absorbed that she had no room for him in her thoughts? And yet only the previous night how she had yearned for him!

It was the end of everything for him—the end of his ambition, of his career, of all his cherished hopes. He was a broken man and he would drop out as other men had dropped out. His love for her had been his ruin. And yet her brain seemed incapable of grasping the meaning of the catastrophe. The bearing of her burden occupied the whole of her strength.

The rest of the Colonel's news scarcely touched her at all, save that the thought flashed upon her once that if the danger were indeed so great Everard would certainly come to her. That sent a strange glow through her that died as swiftly as it was born. She did not really believe in the danger, and Everard was probably far away already.

She went back to her baby and the *ayah*, Hanani, over whom Peter was mounting guard with a queer mixture of patronage and respect. For though he had procured the woman and obviously thought highly of her, he seemed to think that none but himself could be regarded as fully qualified to have the care of his *mem-sahib's* fondly cherished *baba*.

Stella heard him giving some low-toned directions as she entered, and she wondered if the new *ayah* would resent his lordly attitude. But the veiled head bent over the child expressed nothing but complete docility. She answered Peter in few words, but with the utmost meekness.

Her quietness was a great relief to Stella. There was a self-reliance about it that gave her confidence. And presently, tenderly urged by Peter, she went to the adjoining room to rest, on the understanding that she should be called immediately if occasion arose. And that was the first night of many that she passed in undisturbed repose.

In the early morning, entering, she found Peter in sole possession and very triumphant. They had divided the night, he said, and Hanani had gone to rest in her turn. All had gone well. He had slept on the threshold and knew. And now his *mem-sahib* would sleep through every night and have no fear.

She smiled at his solicitude though it touched her almost to tears, and gathered in silence to her breast the little frail body that every day now seemed to feel lighter and smaller. It would not be for very long—their planning and contriving. Very soon now she would be free—quite free—to sleep as long as she would. But her tired heart warmed to Peter and to that silent *ayah* whom he had enlisted in her service. Through the dark night of her grief the love of her friends shone with a radiance that penetrated even the deepest shadows. Was this the lamp in the desert of which Bernard had spoken so confidently—the Lamp that God had lighted to guide her halting feet? Was it by this that she would come at last into the Presence of God Himself, and realize that the wanderers in the wilderness are ever His especial care?

Certainly, as Peter had intimated, she knew her baby to be safe in their joint charge. As the days slipped by, it seemed to her that Peter had imbued the *ayah* with something of his own devotion, for, though it was proffered almost silently, she was aware of it at every turn. At any other time her sympathy for the woman would have fired her interest and led her to attempt to draw her confidence. But the slender thread of life they guarded, though it bound them with a tie that was almost friendship, seemed so to fill their minds that they never spoke of anything else. Stella knew that Hanani loved her and considered her in every way, but she gave Peter most of the credit for it, Peter and the little dying baby she rocked so constantly against her heart. She knew that many an *ayah* would lay down her life for her charge. Peter had chosen well.

Later—when this time of waiting and watching was over, when she was left childless and alone—she would try to find out something of the woman's history, help her if she could, reward her certainly. It was evident that she was growing old. She had the stoop and the deliberation of age. Probably, she would not have obtained an *ayah's* post under any other circumstances. But, notwithstanding these drawbacks, she had a wonderful endurance, and she was never startled or at a loss. Stella often told herself that she would not have exchanged her for another woman—even a white woman—out of the whole of India had the chance offered. Hanani, grave, silent, capable, met every need.

CHAPTER VII
THE FIRST VICTIM

An ominous calm prevailed at Khanmulla during the week that followed the conviction of Ermsted's murderer and the disappearance of the Rajah. All Markestan seemed to be waiting with bated breath. But, save for the departure of the women from Kurrumpore, no sign was given by the Government of any expectation of a disturbance. The law was to take its course, and no official note had been made of the absence of the Rajah. He had always been sudden in his movements.

Everything went as usual at Kurrumpore, and no one's nerves seemed to feel any strain. Even Tommy betrayed no hint of irritation. A new manliness had come upon Tommy of late. He was keeping himself in hand with a steadiness which even Bertie Oakes could not ruffle and which Major Ralston openly approved. He had always known that Tommy had the stuff for great things in him.

A species of bickering friendship had sprung up between them, founded upon their tacit belief in the honour of a man who had failed. They seldom mentioned his name, but the bond of sympathy remained, oddly tenacious and unassailable. Tommy strongly suspected, moreover, that Ralston knew Everard's whereabouts, and of this even Bernard was ignorant at that time. Ralston never boasted his knowledge, but the conviction had somehow taken hold of Tommy, and for this reason also he sought the surgeon's company as he had certainly never sought it before.

Ralston on his part was kind to the boy partly because he liked him and admired his staunchness, and partly because his wife's unwilling departure had left him lonely. He and Major Burton for some reason were not so friendly as of yore, and they no longer spent their evenings in strict seclusion with the chess-board. He took to walking back from the Mess with Tommy, and encouraged the latter to drop in at his bungalow for a smoke whenever he felt inclined. It was but a short distance from The Green Bungalow, and, as he was wont to remark, it was one degree more cheerful for which consideration Tommy was profoundly grateful. Notwithstanding Bernard's kind and wholesome presence, there were times when the atmosphere of The Green Bungalow was almost more than he could bear. He was powerless to help, and the long drawn-out misery weighed upon him unendurably. He infinitely preferred smoking a silent pipe in Ralston's company or messing about with him in his little surgery as he was sometimes permitted to do.

On the evening before the day fixed for the execution at Khanmulla, they were engaged in this fashion when the *khitmutgar* entered with the news that a *sahib* desired to speak to him.

"Oh, bother!" said Ralston crossly. "Who is it? Don't you know?"

The man hesitated, and it occurred to Tommy instantly that there was a hint of mystery in his manner. The *sahib* had ridden through the jungle from Khanmulla, he said. He gave no name.

"Confounded fool!" said Ralston. "No one but a born lunatic would do a thing like that. Go and see what he wants like a good chap, Tommy! I'm busy."

Tommy rose with alacrity. His curiosity was aroused. "Perhaps it's Monck," he said.

"More likely Barnes," said Ralston. "Only I shouldn't have thought he'd be such a fool. Keep your eyes skinned!" he added, as Tommy went to the door. "Don't get shot or stuck by anybody! If I'm really wanted, I'll come."

Tommy grinned at the caution and departed. He had ceased to anticipate any serious trouble in the State, and nothing really exciting ever came his way.

He went through the bungalow to the dining-room still half expecting to find his brother-in-law awaiting him. But the moment he entered, he had a shock. A man in a rough tweed coat was sitting at the table in an odd, hunched attitude, almost as if he had fallen into the chair that supported him.

He turned his head a little at Tommy's entrance, but not so that the light revealed his face. "Hullo!" he said. "That you, Ralston? I've got a bullet in my left shoulder. Do you mind getting it out?"

Tommy stopped dead. He felt as if his heart stopped also. He knew—surely he knew—that voice! But it was not that of Everard or Barnes, or of any one he had ever expected to meet again on earth.

"What—what—" he gasped feebly, and went backwards against the door-post. "Am I drunk?" he questioned with himself.

The man in the chair turned more fully. "Why, it's Tommy!" he said.

The light smote full upon him now throwing up every detail of a countenance which, though handsome, had begun to show unmistakable signs of coarse and intemperate habits. He laughed as he met the boy's shocked eyes, but the laugh caught in his throat and turned to a strangled oath. Then he began to cough.

"Oh—my God!" said Tommy.

He turned then, horror urging him, and tore back to Ralston, as one pursued by devils. He burst in upon him headlong.

"For heaven's sake, come! That fellow—it's—it's——"

"Who?" said Ralston sharply.

"I don't know!" panted back Tommy. "I'm mad, I think. But come—for goodness' sake—before he bleeds to death!"

Ralston came with a velocity which exceeded even Tommy's wild rush. Tommy marvelled at it later. He had not thought the phlegmatic and slow-moving Ralston had it in him. He himself was left well behind, and when he re-entered the dining-room Ralston was already bending over the huddled figure that sprawled across the table.

"Come and lend a hand!" he ordered. "We must get him on the floor. Poor devil! He's got it pretty straight."

He had not seen the stricken man's face. He was too concerned with the wound to worry about any minor details for the moment.

Tommy helped him to the best of his ability, but he was trembling so much that in a second Ralston swooped scathingly upon his weakness.

"Steady man! Pull yourself together! What on earth's the matter? Never seen a little blood before? If you faint, I'll—I'll kick you! There!"

Tommy pulled himself together forthwith. He had never before submitted to being bullied by Ralston; but he submitted then, for speech was beyond him. They lowered the big frame between them, and at Ralston's command he supported it while the doctor made a swift examination of the injury.

Then, while this was in progress, the wounded man recovered his senses and forced a few husky words. "Hullo,—Ralston! Have they done me in?"

Ralston's eyes went to his face for the first time, shot a momentary glance at Tommy, and returned to the matter in hand.

"Don't talk!" he said.

A few seconds later he got to his feet. "Keep him just as he is! I must go and fetch something. Don't let him speak!"

He was gone with the words, and Tommy, still feeling bewildered and rather sick, knelt in silence and waited for his return.

But almost immediately the husky voice spoke again. "Tommy—that you?"

Tommy felt himself begin to tremble again and put forth all his strength to keep himself in hand. "Don't talk!" he said gruffly.

"I've—got to talk." The words came, forced by angry obstinacy. "It's no—damnation—good. I'm done for—beaten on the straight. And that hell hound Monck—"

"Damn you! Be quiet!" said Tommy in a furious undertone.

"I won't be quiet. I'll have—my turn—such as it is. Where's Stella? Fetch Stella! I've a right to that anyway. She is—my lawful wife!"

"I can't fetch her," said Tommy.

"All right then. You can tell her—from me—that she's been duped—as I was. She's mine—not his. He came—with that cock-and-bull story about—the other woman. But she was dead—I've found out since. She was dead—and he knew it. He faked up the tale—to suit himself. He wanted her—the damn skunk—wanted her—and cheated—cheated—to get her."

He stopped, checked by a terrible gurgle in the throat. Tommy, white with passion, broke fiercely into his gasping silence.

"It's a damned lie! Monck is a white man! He never did—a thing like that!"

And then he too stopped in sheer horror at the devilish hatred that gleamed in the rolling, bloodshot eyes.

A few dreadful seconds passed. Then Ralph Dacre gathered his ebbing life in one last great effort of speech. "She is my wife. I hold the proof. If it hadn't been for this—I'd have taken her from him—to-night. He ruined me—and he robbed me. But I—I'll ruin him now. It's my turn. He is not—her husband, and she—she'll scorn him after this—if I know her. Consoled herself precious soon. Yes, women are like that. But they don't forgive so easily. And she—is not—the forgiving sort—anyway. She'll never forgive him for tricking her—the hound! She'll never forget that the child—her child—is a bastard. And—the Regiment—won't forget either. He's down—and out."

He ceased to speak. Tommy's hands were clenched. If the man had been on his feet, he would have struck him on the mouth. As it was, he could only kneel in impotence and listen to the amazing utterance that fell from the gasping lips.

He felt stunned into passivity. His anger had strangely sunk away, though he regarded the man he supported with such an intensity of loathing that he marvelled at himself for

155

continuing to endure the contact. The astounding revelation had struck him like a blow between the eyes. He felt numb, almost incapable of thought.

He heard Ralston returning and wondered what he could have been doing in that interminable interval. Then, reluctant but horribly fascinated, his look went back to the upturned, dreadful face. The malignancy had gone out of it. The eyes rolled no longer, but gazed with a great fixity at something that seemed to be infinitely far away. As Tommy looked, a terrible rattling breath went through the heavy, inert form. It seemed to rend body and soul asunder. There followed a brief palpitating shudder, and the head on his arm sank sideways. A great stillness fell....

Ralston knelt and freed him from his burden. "Get up!" he said.

Tommy obeyed though he felt more like collapsing. He leaned upon the table and stared while Ralston laid the big frame flat and straight upon the floor.

"Is he dead?" he asked in a whisper, as Ralston stood up.

"Yes," said Ralston.

"It wasn't my fault, was it?" said Tommy uneasily. "I couldn't stop him talking."

"He'd have died anyhow," said Ralston. "It's a wonder he ever got here if he was shot in the jungle as he must have been. That means—probably—that the brutes have started their games to-night. Odd if he should be the first victim!"

Tommy shuddered uncontrollably.

Ralston gripped his arm. "Don't be a fool now! Death is nothing extraordinary, after all. It's an experience we've all got to go through some time or other. It doesn't scare me. It won't you when you're a bit older. As for this fellow, it's about the best thing that could happen for everyone concerned. Just rememer that! Providence works pretty near the surface at times, and this is one of 'em. You won't believe me, I daresay, but I never really felt that Ralph Dacre was dead—until this moment."

He led Tommy from the room with the words. It was not his custom to express himself so freely, but he wanted to get that horror-stricken look out of the boy's eyes. He talked to give him time.

"And now look here!" he said. "You've got to keep your head—for you'll want it. I'll give you something to steady you, and after that you'll be on your own. You must cut back to The Green Bungalow and find Bernard Monck and tell him just what has happened—no one else mind, until you've seen him. He's discreet enough. I'm going round to the Colonel. For if what I think has happened, those devils are ahead of us by twenty-four hours, and we're not ready for 'em. They've probably cut the wires too. When you've done that, you report down at the barracks! Your sister will probably have to be taken there for safety. And there may be some tough work before morning."

These last words of his had a magical effect upon Tommy. His eyes suddenly shone. Ralston had accomplished his purpose. Nevertheless, he took him back to the surgery and made him swallow some *sal volatile* in spite of protest.

"And now you won't be a fool, will you?" he said at parting. "I should be sorry if you got shot to no purpose. Monck would be sorry too."

"Do you know where he is?" questioned Tommy point-blank.

"Yes." Blunt and uncompromising came Ralston's reply. "But I'm not going to tell you, so don't you worry yourself! You stick to business, Tommy, and for heaven's sake don't go round and make a mush of it!"

"Stick to business yourself!" said Tommy rudely, suddenly awaking to the fact that he was being dictated to; then pulled up, faintly grinning. "Sorry: I didn't mean that. You're a brick. Consider it unsaid! Good-bye!"

He held out his hand to Ralston who took it and thumped him on the back by way of acknowledgment.

"You're growing up," he remarked with approval, as Tommy went his way.

CHAPTER VIII
THE FIERY VORTEX

"There is nothing more to be done," said Peter with mournful eyes upon the baby in the *ayah's* arms. "Will not my *mem-sahib* take her rest?"

Stella's eyes also rested upon the tiny wizen face. She knew that Peter spoke truly. There was nothing more to be done. She might send yet again for Major Ralston. But of what avail? He had told her that he could do no more. The little life was slipping swiftly, swiftly, out of her reach. Very soon only the desert emptiness would be left.

"The *mem-sahib* may trust her *baba* to Hanani," murmured the *ayah* behind the enveloping veil. "Hanani loves the *baba* too."

"Oh, I know," Stella said.

Yet she hung over the *ayah's* shoulder, for to-night of all nights she somehow felt that she could not tear herself away.

There had been a change during the day—a change so gradual as to be almost imperceptible save to her yearning eyes. She was certain that the baby was weaker. He had cried less, had, she believed, suffered less; and now he lay quite passive in the *ayah's* arms. Only by the feeble, fluttering breath that came and went so fitfully could she have told that the tiny spark yet lingered in the poor little wasted frame.

Major Ralston had told her earlier in the evening that he might go on in this state for days, but she did not think it probable. She was sure that every hour now brought an infinitesimal difference. She felt that the end was drawing near.

And so a great reluctance to go possessed her, even though she would be within call all night. She had a hungry longing to stay and watch the little unconscious face which would soon be gone from her sight. She wanted to hold each minute of the few hours left.

Very softly Peter came to her side. "My *mem-sahib* will rest?" he said wistfully.

She looked at him. His faithful eyes besought her like the eyes of a dog. Their dumb adoration somehow made her want to cry.

"If I could only stay to-night, Peter!" she said.

"*Mem-sahib*," he urged very pleadingly, "the *baba* sleeps now. It may be he will want you to-morrow. And if my *mem-sahib* has not slept she will be too weary then."

Again she knew that he spoke the truth. There had been times of late when she had been made aware of the fact that her strength was nearing its limit. She knew it would be sheer madness to neglect the warning lest, as Peter suggested, her baby's need of her outlasted her endurance. She must husband all the strength she had.

With a sigh she bent and touched the tiny forehead with her lips. Hanani's hand, long and bony, gently stroked her arm as she did so.

"Old Hanani knows, *mem-sahib*," she whispered under her breath.

The tears she had barely checked a moment before sprang to Stella's eyes. She held the dark hand in silence and was subtly comforted thereby.

Passing through the door that Peter held open for her, she gave him her hand also. He bent very low over it, just as he had bent on that first wedding-day of hers so long—so long—ago, and touched it with his forehead. The memory flashed back upon her oddly. She heard again Ralph Dacre's voice speaking in her ear. "You, Stella,—you are as ageless as the stars!" The pride and the passion of his tones stabbed through her with a curious poignancy. Strange that the thought of him should come to her with such vividness to-night! She passed on to her room, as one moving in a painful trance.

For a space she lingered there, hardly knowing what she did; then she remembered that she had not bidden Bernard good-night, and mechanically her steps turned in his direction.

He was generally smoking and working on the verandah at that hour. She made her way to the dining-room as being the nearest approach.

But half-way across the room the sound of Tommy's voice, sharp and agitated, came to her: Involuntarily she paused. He was with Bernard on the verandah.

"The devils shot him in the jungle, but he came on, got as far as Ralston's bungalow, and collapsed there. He was dead in a few minutes—before anything could be done."

The words pierced through her trance, like a naked sword flashing with incredible swiftness, cutting asunder every bond, every fibre, that held her soul confined. She sprang for the open window with a great and terrible cry.

"Who is dead? Who? Who?"

The red glare of the lamp met her, dazzled her, seemed to enter her brain and cruelly to burn her; but she did not heed it. She stood with arms flung wide in frantic supplication.

"Everard!" she cried. "Oh God! My God! Not—Everard!"

Her wild words pierced the night, and all the voices of India seemed to answer her in a mad discordant jangle of unintelligible sound. An owl hooted, a jackal yelped, and a chorus of savage, yelling laughter broke hideously across the clamour, swallowing it as a greater wave swallows a lesser, overwhelming all that has gone before.

The red glare of the lamp vanished from Stella's brain, leaving an awful blankness, a sense as of something burnt out, a taste of ashes in the mouth. But yet the darkness was full of horrors; unseen monsters leaped past her as in a surging torrent, devils' hands clawed at her, devils' mouths cried unspeakable things.

She stood as it were on the edge of the vortex, untouched, unafraid, beyond it all since that awful devouring flame had flared and gone out. She even wondered if it had killed her, so terribly aloof was she, so totally distinct from the pandemonium that raged around her. It had the vividness and the curious lack of all physical feeling of a nightmare. And yet through all her numbness she knew that she was waiting for someone—someone who was dead like herself.

She had not seen either Bernard or Tommy in that blinding moment on the verandah. Doubtless they were fighting in that raging blackness in front of her. She fancied once that she heard her brother's voice laughing as she had sometimes heard him laugh on the polo-ground when he had executed a difficult stroke. Immediately before her, a Titanic struggle was going on. She could not see it, for the light in the room behind had been extinguished also, but the dreadful sound of it made her think for a fleeting second of a great bull-stag being pulled down by a score of leaping, wide-jawed hounds.

And then very suddenly she herself was caught—caught from behind, dragged backwards off her feet. She cried out in a wild horror, but in a second she was silenced. Some thick material that had a heavy native scent about it—such a scent as she remembered vaguely to hang about Hanani the *ayah*—was thrust over her face and head muffling all outcry. Muscular arms gripped her with a fierce and ruthless mastery, and as they lifted and bore her away the nightmare was blotted from her brain as if it had never been. She sank into oblivion....

CHAPTER IX
THE DESERT OF ASHES

Was it night? Was it morning? She could not tell. She opened her eyes to a weird and incomprehensible twilight, to the gurgling sound of water, the booming croak of a frog.

At first she thought that she was dreaming, that presently these vague impressions would fade from her consciousness, and she would awake to normal things, to the sunlight beating across the verandah, to the cheery call of Everard's *saice* in the compound, and the tramp of impatient hoofs. And Everard himself would rise up from her side, and stoop and kiss her before he went.

She began to wait for his kiss, first in genuine expectation, later with a semi-conscious tricking of the imagination. Never once had he left her without that kiss.

But she waited in vain, and as she waited the current of her thoughts grew gradually clearer. She began to remember the happenings of the night. It dawned upon her slowly and terribly that Everard was dead.

When that memory came to her, her brain seemed to stand still. There was no passing on from that. Everard had been shot in the jungle—just as she had always known he would be. He had ridden on in spite of it. She pictured his grim endurance with shrinking vividness. He had ridden on to Major Ralston's bungalow and had collapsed there,—collapsed and died before they could help him. Clearly before her inner vision rose the scene,—Everard sinking down, broken and inert, all the indomitable strength of him shattered at last, the steady courage quenched.

Yet what was it he had once said to her? It rushed across her now—words he had uttered long ago on the night he had taken her to the ruined temple at Khanmulla. "My love is not the kind that burns and goes out." She remembered the exact words, the quiver in the voice that had uttered them. Then, that being so, he was loving her still. Across the desert—her bitter desert of ashes—the lamp was shining even now. Love like his was immortal. Love such as that could never die.

That comforted her for a space, but soon the sense of desolation returned. She remembered their cruel estrangement. She remembered their child. And that last thought, entering like an electric force, gave her strength. Surely it was morning, and he would be needing her! Had not Peter said he would want her in the morning?

With a sharp effort she raised herself; she must go to him.

The next moment a sharp breath of amazement escaped her. Where was she? The strange twilight stretched up above her into infinite shadow. Before her was a broken archway through which vaguely she saw the heavy foliage of trees. Behind her she yet heard the splash and gurgle of water, the croaking of frogs. And near at hand some tiny creature scratched and scuffled among loose stones.

She sat staring about her, doubting the evidence of her senses, marvelling if it could all be a dream. For she recognized the place. It was the ruined temple of Khanmulla in which she sat. There were the crumbling steps on which she had stood with Everard on the night that he had mercilessly claimed her love, had taken her in his arms and said that it was Kismet.

It was then that like a dagger-thrust the realization of his loss went through her. It was then that she first tasted the hopeless anguish of loneliness that awaited her, saw the long, long desert track stretching out before her, leading she knew not whither. She bowed her head upon her arms and sat crushed, unconscious of all beside....

It must have been some time later that there fell a soft step beside her; a veiled figure, bent and slow of movement, stooped over her.

"*Mem-sahib*!" a low voice said.

She looked up, startled and wondering. "Hanani!" she said.

"Yes, it is Hanani." The woman's husky whisper came reassuringly in answer. "Have no fear, *mem-sahib!* You are safe here."

"What—happened?" questioned Stella, still half-doubting the evidence of her senses. "Where—where is my baby?"

Hanani knelt down by her side. "*Mem-sahib*," she said very gently, "the *baba* sleeps—in the keeping of God."

It was tenderly spoken, so tenderly that—it came to her afterwards—she received the news with no sense of shock. She even felt as if she must have somehow known it before. In the utter greyness of her desert—she had walked alone.

"He is dead?" she said.

"Not dead, *mem-sahib*," corrected the *ayah* gently. She paused a moment, then in the same hushed voice that was scarcely more than a whisper: "He—passed, *mem-sahib*, in these arms, so easily, so gently, I knew not when the last breath came. You had been gone but a little space. I sent Peter to call you, but your room was empty. He returned, and I went to seek you myself. I reached you only as the storm broke."

"Ah!" A sharp shudder caught Stella. "What—happened?" she asked again.

"It was but a band of *budmashes, mem-sahib*." A note of contempt sounded in the quiet rejoinder. "I think they were looking for Monck *sahib*—for the captain *sahib*. But they found him not."

"No," Stella said. "No. They had killed him already—in the jungle. At least, they had shot him. He died—afterwards." She spoke dully; she felt as if her heart had grown old within her, too old to feel poignantly any more. "Go on!" she said, after a moment. "What happened then? Did they kill Bernard *sahib* and Denvers *sahib*, too?"

"Neither, my *mem-sahib*." Hanani's reply was prompt and confident. "Bernard *sahib* was struck on the head and senseless when we dragged him in. Denvers *sahib* was not touched. It was he who put out the lamp and saved their lives. Afterwards, I know not how, he raised a great outcry so that they thought they were surrounded and fled. Truly, Denvers *sahib* is great. After that, he went for help. And I, *mem-sahib*, fearing they might return to visit their vengeance upon you—being the wife of the captain *sahib* whom they could not find—I wrapped a *saree* about your head and carried you away." Humble pride in the achievement sounded in Hanani's voice. "I knew that here you would be safe," she ended. "All evil-doers fear this place. It is said to be the abode of unquiet spirits."

Again Stella gazed around the place. Her eyes had become accustomed to the green-hued twilight. The crumbling, damp-stained walls stretched away into darkness behind her, but the place held no terrors for her. She was too tired to be afraid. She only wondered, though without much interest, how Hanani had managed to accomplish the journey.

"Where is Peter?" she asked at last.

"Peter remained with Bernard *sahib*," Hanani answered. "He will tell them where to seek for you."

Again Stella gazed about the place. It struck her as strange that Peter should have relinquished his guardianship of her, even in favour of Hanani. But the thought did not hold her for long. Evidently he had known that he could trust the woman as he trusted himself and her strength must be almost superhuman. She was glad that he had stayed behind with Bernard.

She leaned her chin upon her hands and sat silent for a space. But gradually, as she reviewed the situation, curiosity began to struggle through her lethargy. She looked at Hanani crouched humbly beside her, looked at her again and again, and at last her wonder found vent in speech.

"Hanani," she said, "I don't quite understand everything. How did you get me here?"

Hanani's veiled head was bent. She turned it towards her slowly, almost reluctantly it seemed to Stella.

"I carried you, *mem-sahib*," she said.

"You—carried—me!" Stella repeated the word incredulously. "But it is a long way—a very long way—from Kurrumpore."

Hanani was silent for a moment or two, as though irresolute. Then: "I brought you by a way unknown to you, *mem-sahib*," she said. "Hafiz—you know Hafiz?—he helped me."

"Hafiz!" Stella frowned a little. Yes, by sight she knew him well. Hafiz the crafty, was her private name for him.

"How did he help you?" she asked.

Again Hanani seemed to hesitate as one reluctant to give away a secret. "From the shop of Hafiz—that is the shop of Rustam Karin in the bazaar," she said at length, and Stella quivered at the name, "there is a passage that leads under the ground into the jungle. To those who know, the way is easy. It was thus, *mem-sahib*, that I brought you hither."

"But how did you get me to the bazaar?" questioned Stella, still hardly believing.

"It was very dark, *mem-sahib*; and the *budmashes* were scattered. They would not touch an old woman such as Hanani. And you, my *mem-sahib*, were wrapped in a *saree*. With old Hanani you were safe."

"Ah, why should you take all that trouble to save my life?" Stella said, a little quiver of passion in her voice. "Do you think life is so precious to me—now?"

Hanani made a protesting gesture with one arm. "Lo, it is yet night, *mem-sahib*," she said. "But is it not written in the sacred Book that with the dawn comes joy?"

"There can never be any joy for me again," Stella said.

Hanani leaned slowly forward. "Then will my *mem-sahib* have missed the meaning of life," she said. "Listen then—listen to old Hanani—who knows! It is true that the *baba* cannot return to the *mem-sahib*, but would she call him back to pain? Have I not read in her eyes night after night the silent prayer that he might go in peace? Now that the God of gods has answered that prayer—now that the *baba* is in peace—would my *mem-sahib* have it otherwise? Would she call that loved one back? Would she not rather thank the God of spirits for His great mercy—and so go her way rejoicing?"

Again the utterance was too full of tenderness to give her pain. It sank deep into Stella's heart, stilling for a space the anguish. She looked at the strange, draped figure beside her that spoke those husky words of comfort with a dawning sense of reverence. She had a curious feeling as of one being guided through a holy place.

"You—comfort me, Hanani," she said after a moment. "I don't think I am really grieving for the *baba* yet. That will come after. I know that—as you say—he is at peace, and I would not call him back. But—Hanani—that is not all. It is not even the half or the beginning of my trouble. The loss of my *baba* I can bear—I could bear—bravely. But the loss of—of—" Words failed her unexpectedly. She bowed her head again upon her arms and wept the bitter tears of despair.

Hanani the *ayah* sat very still by her side, her brown, bony hands tightly gripped about her knees, her veiled head bent slightly forward as though she watched for someone in the dimness of the broken archway.

At last very, very slowly she spoke.

"*Mem-sahib*, even in the desert the sun rises. There is always comfort for those who go forward—even though they mourn."

"Not for me," sobbed Stella. "Not for those—who part—in bitterness—and never—meet again!"

"Never, *mem-sahib*?" Hanani yet gazed straight before her. Suddenly she made a movement as if to rise, but checked herself as one reminded by exertion of physical infirmity. "The *mem-sahib* weeps for her lord," she said. "How shall Hanani comfort her? Yet never is a cruel word. May it not be that he will—even now—return?"

"He is dead," whispered Stella.

"Not so, *mem-sahib*." Very gently Hanani corrected her. "The captain *sahib* lives."

"He—lives?" Stella started upright with the words. In the gloom her eyes shone with a sudden feverish light; but it very swiftly died. "Ah, don't torture me, Hanani!" she said. "You mean well, but—it doesn't help."

"Hanani speaks the truth," protested the old *ayah*, and behind the enveloping veil came an answering gleam as if she smiled. "My lord the captain *sahib* spoke with Hafiz this very night. Hafiz will tell the *mem-sahib*."

But Stella shook her head in hopeless unbelief. "I don't trust Hafiz," she said wearily.

"Yet Hafiz would not lie to old Hanani," insisted the *ayah* in that soft, insinuating whisper of hers.

Stella reached out a trembling hand and laid it upon her shoulder. "Listen, Hanani!" she said. "I have never seen your face, yet I know you for a friend."

"Ask not to see it, *mem-sahib*," swiftly interposed the *ayah*, "lest you turn with loathing from one who loves you!"

Stella smiled, a quivering, piteous smile. "I should never do that, Hanani," she said. "But I do not need to see it. I know you love me. But do not—out of your love for me—tell me a lie! It is false comfort. It cannot help me."

"But I have not lied, *mem-sahib*." There was earnest assurance in Hanani's voice—such assurance as could not be disregarded. "I have told you the truth. The captain *sahib* is not dead. It was a false report."

"Hanani! Are you—sure?" Stella's hand gripped the *ayah's* shoulder with convulsive, strength. "Then who—who—was the *sahib* they shot in the jungle—the *sahib* who died at the bungalow of Ralston *sahib*? Did—Hafiz—tell you that?"

"That—" said Hanani, and paused as if considering how best to present the information,—"that was another *sahib*."

"Another *sahib*?" Stella was trembling violently. Her hold upon Hanani was the clutch of desperation, "Who—what was his name?"

She felt in the momentary pause that followed that the eyes behind the veil were looking at her strangely, speculatively. Then very softly Hanani answered her.

"His name, *mem-sahib*, was Dacre."

"Dacre!" Stella repeated the name blankly. It seemed to hold too great a meaning for her to grasp.

"So Hafiz told Hanani," said the *ayah*.

"But—Dacre!" Stella hung upon the name as if it held her by a fascination from which she could not shake free. "Is that—all you know?" she said at last.

"Not all, my *mem-sahib*," answered Hanani, in the soothing tone of one who instructs a child. "Hafiz knew the *sahib* in the days before Hanani came to Kurrumpore. Hafiz told a strange story of the *sahib*. He had married and had taken his wife to the mountains beyond Srinagar. And there an evil fate had overtaken him, and she—the *mem-sahib*—had returned alone."

Hanani paused dramatically.

"Go on!" gasped Stella almost inarticulately.

Hanani took up her tale again in a mysterious whisper that crept in eerie echoes about the ruined place in which they sat. "*Mem-sahib*, Hafiz said that there was doubtless a reason for which he feigned death. He said that Dacre *sahib* was a bad man, and my lord the captain *sahib* knew it. Wherefore he followed him to the mountains and commanded him to be gone, and thus—he went."

"But who—told—Hafiz?" questioned Stella, still struggling against unbelief.

"How should Hanani know?" murmured the *ayah* deprecatingly "Hafiz lives in the bazaar. He hears many things—some true—some false. But that Dacre *sahib* returned last night and that he now is dead is true, *mem-sahib*. And that my lord the captain *sahib* lives is also true. Hanani swears it by her grey hairs."

"Then where—where is the captain *sahib*?" whispered Stella.

The *ayah* shook her head. "It is not given to Hanani to know all things," she protested. "But—she can find out. Does the *mem-sahib* desire her to find out?"

"Yes," Stella breathed.

The fantastic tale was running like a mad tarantella through her brain. Her thoughts were in a whirl. But she clung to the thought of Everard as a shipwrecked mariner clings to a rock. He yet lived; he had not passed out of her reach. It might be he was even then at Khanmulla a few short miles away. All her doubt of him, all evil suspicions, vanished in a great and overwhelming longing for his presence. It suddenly came to her that she had wronged him, and before that unquestionable conviction the story of Ralph Dacre's return was dwarfed to utter insignificance. What was Ralph Dacre to her? She had travelled far— oh, very far—through the desert since the days of that strange dream in the Himalayas. Living or dead, surely he had no claim upon her now!

Impulsively she stooped towards Hanani. "Take me to him!" she said. "Take me to him! I am sure you know where he is."

Hanani drew back slightly. "*Mem-sahib*, it will take time to find him," she remonstrated. "Hanani is not a young woman. Moreover—" she stopped suddenly, and turned her head.

"What is it?" said Stella.

"I heard a sound, *mem-sahib*." Hanani rose slowly to her feet. It seemed to Stella that she was more bent, more deliberate of movement, than usual. Doubtless the wild adventure of the night had told upon her. She watched her with a tinge of compunction as she made her somewhat difficult way towards the archway at the top of the broken marble steps. A flying-fox flapped eerily past her as she went, dipping over the bent, veiled head with as little fear as if she were a recognized inhabitant of that wild place.

A sharp sense of unreality stabbed Stella. She felt as one coming out of an all-absorbing dream. Obeying an instinctive impulse, she rose up quickly to follow. But even as she did so, two things happened.

Hanani passed like a shadow from her sight, and a voice she knew—Tommy's voice, somewhat high-pitched and anxious—called her name.

Swiftly she moved to meet him. "I am here, Tommy! I am here!"

And then she tottered, feeling her strength begin to fail.

"Oh, Tommy!" she gasped. "Help me!"

He sprang up the steps and caught her in his arms. "You hang on to me!" he said. "I've got you."

She leaned upon him quivering, with closed eyes. "I am afraid I must," she said weakly. "Forgive me for being so stupid!"

"All right, darling. All right," he said. "You're not hurt?"

"No, oh no! Only giddy—stupid!" She fought desperately for self-command. "I shall be all right in a minute."

She heard the voices of men below her, but she could not open her eyes to look. Tommy supported her strongly, and in a few seconds she was aware of someone on her other side, of a steady capable hand grasping her wrist.

"Drink this!" said Ralston's voice. "It'll help you."

He was holding something to her lips, and she drank mechanically.

"That's better," he said. "You've had a rough time, I'm afraid, but it's over now. Think you can walk, or shall we carry you?"

The matter-of-fact tones seemed to calm the chaos of her brain. She looked up at him with a faint, brave smile.

"I will walk,—of course. There is nothing the matter with me. What has happened at Kurrumpore? Is all well?"

He met her eyes. "Yes," he said quietly.

Her look flinched momentarily from his, but the next instant she met it squarely. "I know about—my baby," she said.

He bent his head. "You could not wish it otherwise," he said, gently.

She answered him with firmness, "No."

The few words helped to restore her self-possession. With her hand upon Tommy's arm she descended the steps into the green gloom of the jungle. The morning sun was smiting through the leaves. It gleamed in her eyes like the flashing of a sword. But—though the simile held her mind for a space—she felt no shrinking. She had a curious conviction that the path lay open before her at last. The Angel with the Flaming Sword no longer barred the way.

A party of Indian soldiers awaited her. She did not see how many. Perhaps she was too tired to take any very vivid interest in her surroundings. A native litter stood a few yards from the foot of the steps. Tommy guided her to it, Major Ralston walking on her other side.

She turned to the latter as they reached it. "Where is Hanani?" she said.

He raised his brows for a moment. "She has probably gone back to her people," he answered.

"She was here with me, only a minute ago," Stella said.

He glanced round. "She knows her way no doubt. We had better not wait now. If you want her, I will find her for you later."

"Thank you," Stella said. But she still paused, looking from Ralston to Tommy and back again, as one uncertain.

"What is it, darling?" said Tommy gently.

She put her hand to her head with a weary gesture of bewilderment. "I am very stupid," she said. "I can't think properly. You are sure everything is all right?"

"Quite sure, dear," he said. "Don't try to think now. You are done up. You must rest."

Her face quivered suddenly like the face of a tired child. "I want—Everard," she said piteously. "Won't you—can't you—bring him to me? There is something—I want—to say to him."

There was an instant's pause. She felt Tommy's arm tighten protectively around her, but he did not speak.

It was Major Ralston who answered her. "Certainly he shall come to you. I will see that he does."

The confidence of his reply comforted her. She trusted Major Ralston instinctively. She entered the litter and sank down among the cushions with a sigh.

As they bore her away along the narrow, winding path which once she had trodden with Everard Monck so long, long ago, on the night of her surrender to the mastery of his love, utter exhaustion overcame her and the sleep, which for so long she had denied herself, came upon her like an overwhelming flood, sweeping her once more into the deeps of oblivion. She went without a backward thought.

CHAPTER X
THE ANGEL

It was many hours before she awoke and in all those hours she never dreamed. She only slept and slept and slept in total unconsciousness, wrapt about in the silence of her desert.

She awoke at length quite fully, quite suddenly, to a sense of appalling loneliness, to a desolation unutterable. She opened her eyes wide upon a darkness that could be felt, and almost cried aloud with the terror of it. For a few palpitating moments it seemed to her that the most dreadful thing that could possibly happen to her had come upon her unawares.

And then, even as she started up in a wild horror, a voice spoke to her, a hand touched her, and her fear was stayed.

"Stella!" the voice said, and steady fingers came up out of the darkness and closed upon her arm.

Her heart gave one great leap within her, and was still. She did not speak in answer, for she could not. She could only sit in the darkness and wait. If it were a dream, it would pass—ah, so swiftly! If it were reality, surely, surely he would speak again!

He spoke—softly through the silence. "I don't want to startle you. Are you startled? I've put out the lamp. You are not afraid?"

Her voice came back to her; her heart jerked on, beating strangely, spasmodically, like a maimed thing. "Am I awake?" she said. "Is it—really—you?"

"Yes," he said. "Can you listen to me a moment? You won't be afraid?"

She quivered at the repeated question. "Everard—no!"

He was silent then, as if he did not know how to continue. And she, finding her strength, leaned to him in the darkness, feeling for him, still hardly believing that it was not a dream.

He took her wandering hand and held it imprisoned. The firmness of his grasp reassured her, but it came to her that his hands were cold; and she wondered.

"I have something to say to you," he said.

She sat quite still in his hold, but it frightened her. "Where are you?" she whispered.

"I am just—kneeling by your side," he said. "Don't tremble—or be afraid! There is nothing to frighten you. Stella," his voice came almost in a whisper. "Hanani—the *ayah*—told you something in the ruined temple at Khanmulla. Can you remember what it was?"

"Ah!" she said. "Do you mean about—Ralph Dacre?"

"I do mean that," he said. "I don't know if you actually believed it. It may have sounded—fantastic. But—it was true."

"Ah!" she said again. And then she knew why he had turned out the lamp. It was that he might not see her face when he told her—or she his.

He went on; his hold upon her had tightened, but she knew that he was unconscious of it. It was as if he clung to her in anguish—though she heard no sign of suffering in his low voice. "I have done the utmost to keep the truth from you—but Fate has been against me all through. I sent him away from you in the first place because I heard—too late—that he had a wife in England. I married you because—" he paused momentarily—"ah well, that doesn't come into the story," he said. "I married you, believing you free. Then came Bernard, and told me that the wife—Dacre's wife—had died just before his marriage to you. That also came—too late."

He stopped again, and she knew that his head was bowed upon his arms though she could not free her hand to touch it.

"You know the rest," he said, and his voice came to her oddly broken and unfamiliar. "I kept it from you. I couldn't bear the thought of your facing—that,—especially after—after the birth of—the child. Even when you found out I had tricked you in that native rig-out, I couldn't endure the thought of your knowing. I nearly killed myself that night. It seemed the only way. But Bernard stopped me. I told him the truth. He said I was wrong not to tell you. But—somehow—I couldn't."

"Oh, I wish—I wish you had," she breathed.

"Do you? Well,—I couldn't. It's hard enough to tell you now. You were so wonderful, so beautiful, and they had flung mud at you from the beginning. I thought I had made you safe, dear, instead of—dragging you down."

"Everard!" Her voice was quick and passionate. She made a sudden effort and freed one hand; but he caught it again sharply.

"No, you mustn't, Stella! I haven't finished. Wait!"

His voice compelled her; she submitted hardly knowing that she did so.

"It is over now," he said. "The fellow is dead. But, Stella,—he had found out—what I had found out. And he was on his way to you. He meant to—claim you."

She shuddered—a hard, convulsive shudder—as if some loathsome thing had touched her. "But—I would never have gone back," she said.

"No," he answered grimly, "you wouldn't. I was here, and I should have shot him. They saved me that trouble."

"You were—here!" she said.

"Yes,—much nearer to you than you imagined." Almost curtly he answered. "Did you think I would leave you at the mercy of those devils? You!" He stopped himself sharply. "No I was here to protect you—and I would have done it—though I should have shot myself afterwards. Even Bernard would have seen the force of that. But it didn't come to pass that way. It wasn't intended that it should. Well, it is over. There are not many who know—only Bernard, Tommy, and Ralston. They are going—if possible—to keep it dark, to suppress his name. I told them they must." His voice rang suddenly harsh, but softened again immediately. "That's all, dear—or nearly all. I hope it hasn't shocked you unutterably. I think the secret is safe anyhow, so you won't have—that—to face. I'm going now. I'll send—Peter—to light the lamp and bring you something to eat. And you'll undress, won't you, and go to bed? It's late."

He made as if he would rise, but her hands turned swiftly in his, turned and held him fast.

"Everard—Everard, why should you go?" she whispered tensely into the darkness that hid his face.

He yielded in a measure to her hold, but he would not suffer himself to be drawn nearer.

"Why?" she said again insistently.

He hesitated. "I think," he said slowly "that you will find an answer to that question—possibly more than one—when you have had time to think it over."

"What do you mean?" she breathed.

"Must I put it into words?" he said.

She heard the pain in his voice, but for the first time she passed it by unheeded. "Yes, tell me!" she said. "I must know."

He was silent for a little, as if mustering his forces. Then, his hands tight upon hers, he spoke. "In the first place, you are Dacre's widow, and not—my wife."

She quivered in his hold. "And then?" she whispered.

"And then," he said, "our baby is dead, so you are free from all—obligations."

Her hands clenched hard upon his. "Is that all?"

"No." With sudden passion he answered her. "There are two more reasons why I should go. One is—that I have made your life a hell on earth. You have said it, and I know it to be true. Ah, you had better let me go—and go quickly. For your own sake—you had better!"

But she ignored the warning, holding him almost fiercely. "And the last reason?" she said.

165

He was silent for a few seconds, and in his silence there was something of an electric quality, something that pierced and scorched yet strangely drew her. "Someone else can tell you that," he said at length. "It isn't that I am a broken man. I know that wouldn't affect you one way or another. It is that I have done a thing that you would hate—yet that I would do again to-morrow if the need arose. You can ask Ralston what it is! Say I told you to! He knows."

"But I ask you," she said, and still her hands gripped his. "Everard, why don't you tell me? Are you—afraid to tell me?"

"No," he said.

"Then answer me!" she said, her breathing sharp and uneven. "Tell me the truth! Make me understand you—once and for all!"

"You have always understood me," he said.

"No—no!" she protested.

"Well, nearly always," he amended. "As long as you have known my love—you have known me. My love for you is myself—the immortal part. The rest—doesn't count."

"Ah!" she said, and suddenly the very soul of her rose up and spoke. "Then you needn't tell me any more, dear love—dear love. I don't need to hear it. It doesn't matter. It can't make any difference. Nothing ever can again, for, as you say, nothing else counts. Go if you must,—but if you do—I shall follow you—I shall follow you—to the world's end."

"Stella!" he said.

"I mean it," she told him, and her voice throbbed with a fiery force that was deeper than passion, stronger than aught human. "You are mine and I am yours. God knows, dear,—God knows that is all that matters now. I didn't understand before. I do now, I think—suffering has taught me—many things. Perhaps it is—His Angel."

"The Angel with the Flaming Sword," he said, under his breath.

"But the Sword is turned away," she said. "The way is open."

He got to his feet abruptly. "Wait!" he said. "Before you say that—wait!"

He freed himself from her hold gently but very decidedly. She knew that for a second he stood close above her with arms outflung before he turned away. Then there came the rasp of a match, a sudden flare in the darkness. She looked to see his face—and uttered a cry.

It was Hanani, the veiled *ayah*, who stooped to kindle the lamp....

CHAPTER XI
THE DAWN

"This country is like an infernal machine," said Bernard. "You never know when it's going to explode. There's only one reliable thing in it, and that's Peter."

He turned his bandaged head in the latter's direction, and received a tender, indulgent smile in answer. Peter loved the big blue-eyed *sahib* with the same love which he had for the children of the *sahib-log*.

"Whatever happens," Bernard continued, "there's always Peter. He keeps the whole show going, and is never absent when wanted. In fact, I begin to think that India wouldn't be India without him."

"A very handsome compliment," said Sir Reginald.

"It is, isn't it?" smiled Bernard. "I have a vast respect for him—a quite unbounded respect. He is the greatest greaser of wheels I have ever met. Help yourself, sir, won't you? I am sorry I can't join you, but Major Ralston insists that I must walk circumspectly, being on his sick list. I really don't know why my skull was not cracked. He declares it ought to have been and even seems inclined to be rather disgusted with me because it wasn't."

"You had a very lucky escape," said Sir Reginald. "Allow me to congratulate you!"

"And a very enjoyable scrap," said Bernard, with kindling eyes. "Thanks! I wouldn't have missed it for the world,—the damn' dirty blackguards!"

"Was Mrs. Monck much upset?" asked Sir Reginald. "I have never yet had the pleasure of meeting her."

"She was more upset on my brother's account than her own," Bernard said, giving his visitor a shrewd look. "She thought he had come to harm."

"Ah!" said Sir Reginald, and held his glass up to the light. "And that was not so?"

"No," said Bernard, and closed his lips.

There was a distinct pause before Sir Reginald's eyes left his glass and came down to him. They held a faint whimsical smile.

"We owe your brother a good deal," he said.

"Do we?" said Bernard.

Sir Reginald's smile became more pronounced. "I have been told that it is entirely owing to him—his forethought, secrecy, and intimate knowledge obtained at considerable personal risk—that this business was not of a far more serious nature. I was of course in constant communication with Colonel Mansfield. We knew exactly where the danger lay, and we were prepared for all emergencies."

"Except the one which actually rose," suggested Bernard.

"That?" said Sir Reginald. "That was a mere flash in the pan. But we were prepared even for that. My men were all in Markestan by daybreak, thanks to the promptitude of young Denvers."

"If all our throats had been slit the previous night, that wouldn't have helped us much," Bernard pointed out.

Sir Reginald broke into a laugh. "Well, dash it, man! We did our best. And anyway they weren't, so you haven't much cause for complaint."

"You see, I was one of the casualties," explained Bernard. "That accounts for my being a bit critical. So you expected something worse than this?"

"I did." Sir Reginald spoke soberly again. "If we hadn't been prepared, the whole of Markestan would have been ablaze by now from end to end."

"Instead of which, you have only permitted us a fizz, a few bangs, and a splutter-out, as Tommy describes it," remarked Bernard. "And you haven't even caught the Rajah."

"I wasn't out to catch him," said Sir Reginald. "But I will tell you who I am out to catch, though I am afraid I am applying in the wrong quarter."

Bernard's eyes gleamed with a hint of malicious amusement. "I thought my health was not primarily responsible for the honour of your visit, sir," he said.

"No," said Sir Reginald, with simplicity. "I really came because I want to take you into my confidence, and to ask for your confidence in return."

"I thought so," said Bernard, and slowly shook his head. "I'm afraid it's no go. I am sealed."

"Ah! And that even though I give you my word it would be to your brother's interest to break the seal?" questioned Sir Reginald.

Bernard's eyes suddenly drooped under their red brows. "And betray my trust?" he said lazily.

"I beg your pardon," said Sir Reginald.

He finished his drink with a speed that suggested embarrassment, but the next moment he smiled. "You had me there, padre. I withdraw the suggestion. I should not have made it if I could see the man himself. But he has disappeared, and even Barnes, who knows everything, can't tell us where to look for him."

"Neither can I," said Bernard. "I am not in his confidence to that extent."

"Why don't you ask his wife?" a low voice said.

Both men started. Sir Reginald sprang to his feet. "Mrs. Monck!"

"Yes," Stella said. She stood a moment framed in the French window, looking at him. Then she stepped forward with outstretched hand. The morning sunshine caught her as she moved. She was very pale and her eyes were deeply shadowed, but she was exceedingly beautiful.

167

"I heard your voices," she said, looking at Sir Reginald, while her hand lay in his. "I didn't mean to listen at first. But I was tempted, because you were talking of—my husband, and—" she smiled at him faintly, "I fell."

"I think you were justified," Sir Reginald said.

"Thank you," she answered gently. She turned from him to Bernard, and bending kissed him. "Are you better? Peter told me it wasn't serious. I would have come to you sooner, but I was asleep for a very long time, and afterwards—Everard wanted me."

"Everard!" he said sharply. "Is he here?"

"Sit down!" murmured Sir Reginald, drawing forward his chair.

But Stella remained standing, her hand upon Bernard's shoulder. "Thank you. But I haven't come to stay. Only to tell you—just to tell you—all the things that Bernard couldn't, without betraying his trust."

"My dear, dear child!" Bernard broke in quickly, but Sir Reginald intervened in the same moment.

"No, no! Pardon me! Let her speak! She wishes to do so, and I—wish to listen."

Stella's hand pressed a little upon Bernard's shoulder, as though she supported herself thereby.

"It is right that you should know, Sir Reginald," she said. "It is only for my sake that it has been kept from you. But I—have travelled the desert too long to mind an extra stone or two by the way. First, with regard to the suspicion which drove him out of the Army. You thought—everyone thought—that he had killed Ralph Dacre up in the mountains. Even I thought so." Her voice trembled a little. "And I had less excuse than any one else, for he swore to me that he was innocent—though he would not—could not—tell me the truth of the matter. The truth was simply this. Ralph Dacre was not dead."

"Ah!" Sir Reginald said softly.

Bernard reached up and strongly grasped the hand that rested upon him. But he spoke no word.

Stella went on with greater steadiness, her eyes resolutely meeting the shrewd old eyes that watched her. "He—Everard—came between us because only a fortnight after our marriage he received the news that Ralph had a wife living in England. Perhaps I ought to tell you—though this in no way influenced him—that my marriage to Ralph was a mistake. I married him because I was unhappy, not because I loved him. I sinned, and I have been punished."

"Poor girl!" said Sir Reginald very gently.

Her eyelids quivered, but she would not suffer them to fall. "Everard sent him away from me, made him vanish completely, and then came himself to me—he was in native disguise—and told me he was dead. I suppose it was wrong of him. If so, he too has been punished. But he wanted to save my pride. I had plenty of pride in those days. It is all gone now. At least, all I have left is for him—that his honour may be vindicated. I am afraid I am telling the story very badly. Forgive me for taking so long!"

"There is no hurry," Sir Reginald answered in the same gentle voice. "And you are telling it very well."

She smiled again—her faint, sad smile. "You are very kind. It makes it much easier. You know how clever he is in native disguise. I never recognized him. I came back, as I thought, a widow. And then—it was nearly a year after—I married Everard, because I loved him. It was just before Captain Ermsted's murder. We had to come back here in a hurry because of it. Then when the summer came we had to separate. I went to Bhulwana for the birth of my baby. And while I was there, he heard that Ralph Dacre's wife had died in England only a few days before his marriage to me. That meant of course that I was not Everard's legal wife, that the baby was illegitimate. But—I was very ill at the time—he kept it from me."

"Of course he did," said Sir Reginald.

"Of course he did," said Bernard.

"Yes," she assented. "He couldn't help himself then. But he ought to have told me afterwards—when—when I began to have that horrible suspicion that everyone else had, that he had murdered Ralph Dacre."

"A difficult point," said Sir Reginald.

"I told him he was making a mistake," said Bernard.

Stella glanced down at him. "It was a mistake," she said. "But he made it out of love for me, because he thought—he thought—that my pride was dearer to me than my love. I don't wonder he thought so. I gave him every reason. For I wouldn't listen to him, wouldn't believe him. I sent him away." Her breath caught suddenly, and she put a quick hand to her throat. "That is what hurts me most," she said after a moment,—"just to remember that,—to remember what I made him suffer—how I failed him—when Tommy, even Tommy, believed in him—went after him to tell him so."

"But we all make mistakes," said Sir Reginald gently, "or we shouldn't be human."

She controlled herself with an effort. "Yes. He said that, and told me to forget it. I don't know if I can, but I shall try. I shall try to make up to him for it for as long as I live. And I thank God—for giving me the chance."

Her deep voice quivered, and Bernard's hand tightened upon hers. "Yes," he said, looking at Sir Reginald. "Ralph Dacre is dead. He was the unknown man who was shot in the jungle two nights ago."

"Indeed!" said Sir Reginald sharply.

"Yes," Stella said. "He too had found out—about the death of his first wife. And he was on his way to me. But—" she suddenly covered her eyes—"I couldn't have borne it. I would have killed myself first."

Bernard reached up and thrust his arm about her, without speaking.

She leaned against him for a few seconds as if the story had taxed her strength too far. Then Sir Reginald came to her and with a fatherly gesture drew her hand away from her face.

"My dear," he said very kindly, "thank you a thousand times for telling me this. I know it's been infernally hard. I admire you for it more than I can say. It hasn't been too much for you I hope?"

She smiled at him through tears. "No—no! You are both—so kind."

He stooped with a very courtly gesture and carried her hand to his lips. "Everard Monck is a very lucky man," he said, "but I think he is almost worthy of his luck. And now—I want you to tell me one thing more. Where can I find him?"

Her hand trembled a little in his. "I—am not sure he would wish me to tell you that."

Sir Reginald's grey moustache twitched whimsically. "If his desire for privacy is so great, it shall be respected. Will you take him a message from me?"

"Of course," she said.

Sir Reginald patted her hand and released it. "Then please tell him," he said, "that the Indian Empire cannot afford to lose the services of so valuable a servant as he has proved himself to be, and if he will accept a secretaryship with me I think there is small doubt that it will eventually lead to much greater things."

Stella gave a great start. "Oh, do you mean that?" she said.

Sir Reginald smiled openly. "I really do, Mrs. Monck, and I shall think myself very fortunate to secure him. You will use your influence, I hope, to induce him to accept?"

"But of course," she said.

"Poor Stella!" said Bernard. "And she hates India!"

She turned upon him almost in anger. "How dare you pity me? I love anywhere that I can be with him."

"So like a woman!" commented Bernard. "Or is it something in the air? I'll never bring Tessa out here when she's grown up, or she'll marry and be stuck here for the rest of her life."

"You can do as you like with Tessa," said Stella, and turned again to Sir Reginald. "Is that all you want of me now?"

"One thing more," he answered gently. "I hope I may say it without giving offence."

169

With a gesture all-unconsciously regal she gave him both her hands. "You may say—anything," she said impulsively.

He bent again courteously. "Mrs. Monck, will you invite me to witness the ratification of the bond already existing between my friend Everard Monck, and the lady who is honouring him by becoming his lawful wife?"

She flushed deeply but not painfully. "I will," she said. "Bernard, you will see to that, I know."

"Yes; leave it to me, dear!" said Bernard.

"Thank you," she said; and to Sir Reginald: "Good-bye! I am going to my husband now."

"Good-bye, Mrs. Monck!" he said. "And many thanks for your graciousness to a stranger."

"Oh no!" she answered quickly. "You are a friend—of us both."

"I am proud to be called so," he said.

As she passed back into the bungalow her heart fluttered within her like the wings of a bird mounting upwards in the dawning. The sun had risen upon the desert.

CHAPTER XII
THE BLUE JAY

"Tommy says his name is Sprinter; but Uncle St. Bernard calls him Whisky. I wonder which is the prettiest," said Tessa.

"I should call him Whisky out of compliment to Uncle St. Bernard," said Mrs. Ralston.

"He certainly does whisk," said Tessa. "But then—Tommy gave him to me." She spoke with tender eyes upon a young mongoose that gambolled at her feet. "Isn't he a love?" she said. "But he isn't nearly so pretty as darling Scooter," she added loyally. "Is he, Aunt Mary?"

"Not yet, dear," said Mrs. Ralston with a smile.

"I wish Uncle St. Bernard and Tommy would come," said Tessa restlessly.

"I hope you are going to be very good," said Mrs. Ralston.

"Oh yes," said Tessa rather wearily. "But I wish I hadn't begun quite so soon. Do you think Uncle St. Bernard will spoil me, Aunt Mary?"

"I hope not, dear," said Mrs. Ralston.

Tessa sighed a little. "I wonder if I shall be sick on the voyage Home. I don't want to be sick, Aunt Mary."

"I shouldn't think about it if I were you, dear," said Mrs. Ralston sensibly.

"But I want to think about it," said Tessa earnestly. "I want to think about every minute of it. I shall enjoy it so. Dear Uncle St. Bernard said in his letter the other day that we should be like the little pigs setting out to seek their fortunes. He says he is going to send me to school—only a day school though. Aunt Mary, shall I like going to school?"

"Of course you will, dear. What sensible little girl doesn't?"

"I'm sorry I'm going away from you," said Tessa suddenly. "But you'll have Uncle Jerry, won't you? Just the same as Aunt Stella will have darling Uncle Everard. I think I'm sorriest of all for poor Tommy."

"I daresay he will get over it," said Mrs. Ralston. "We will hope so anyway."

"He has promised to write to me," said Tessa rather wistfully. "Do you think he will forget to, Aunt Mary?"

"I'll see he doesn't," said Mrs. Ralston.

"Oh, thank you." Tessa embraced her tenderly. "And I'll write to you very, very often. P'raps I'll write in French some day. Would you like that?"

"Oh, very much," said Mrs. Ralston.

"Then I will," promised Tessa. "And oh, here they are at last! Take care of Whisky for me while I go and meet them!"

She was gone with the words—a little, flying figure with arms outspread, rushing to meet her friends.

"That child gets wilder and more harum-scarum every day," observed Lady Harriet, who was passing The Grand Stand in her carriage at the moment. "She will certainly go the same way as her mother if that very easy-going parson has the managing of her."

The easy-going parson, however, had no such misgivings. He caught the child up in his arms with a whoop of welcome.

"Well run, my Princess Bluebell! Hullo, Tommy! Who are you saluting so deferentially?"

"Only that vicious old white cat, Lady Harriet," said Tommy. "Hullo, Tessa! Your legs get six inches longer every time I look at 'em. Put her down, St. Bernard! She's going to race me to The Grand Stand."

"But I want to go and see Uncle Everard and Aunt Stella at The Nest," protested Tessa, hanging back from the contest. "Besides Aunt Mary says I'm not to get hot."

"You can't go there anyway," said Tommy inexorably. "The Nest is closed to the public for to-night. They are going to have a very sacred and particular evening all to themselves. That's why they wouldn't come in here with us."

"Are they love-making?" asked Tessa, with serious eyes. "Do you know, I heard a blue jay laughing up there this morning. Was that what he meant?"

"Something of that silly nature," said Tommy. "And he's going to be a public character is Uncle Everard, so he is wise to make the most of his privacy now. Ah, Bhulwana," he stretched his arms to the pine-trees, "how I have yearned for thee!"

"And me too," said Tessa jealously.

He looked at her. "You, you scaramouch? Of course not! Whoever yearned for a thing like you? A long-legged, snub-nosed creature without any front teeth worth mentioning!"

"I have! You're horrid!" cried Tessa, stamping an indignant foot. "Isn't he horrid, Uncle St. Bernard? If it weren't for that darling mongoose, I should hate him!"

"Oh, but it's wrong to hate people, you know." Bernard passed a pacifying arm about her quivering form. "You just treat him to the contempt he deserves, and give all your attention to your doting old uncle who has honestly been longing for you from the moment you left him!"

"Oh, darling!" She turned to him swiftly. "I'll never go away from you again. I can say that now, can't I?"

Her red lips were lifted. He stooped and kissed them. "It's the one thing I love to hear you say, my princess," he said.

The sun set in a glory of red and purple that night, spreading the royal colours far across the calm sky.

It faded very quickly. The night swooped down, swift and soundless, and in the verandah of the bungalow known as The Nest a red lamp glowed with a steady beam across the darkness.

Two figures stood for a space under the acacia by the gate, lingering in the evening quiet. Now and then there was the flutter of wings above them, and the white flowers fell and scattered like bridal blossoms all around.

"We must go in," said Stella. "Peter will be disappointed if we keep the dinner waiting."

"Ah! We mustn't hurt his august feelings," conceded Everard. "We owe him a mighty lot, my Stella. I wish we could make some return."

"His greatest reward is to let him serve us," she answered. "His love is the kind that needs to serve."

"Which is the highest kind of love," said Everard holding her to him. "Do you know—Hanani discovered that for me."

She pressed close to his side. "Everard darling, why did you keep that secret so long?"

"My dear!" he said, and was silent.

"Well, won't you tell me?" she urged. "I think you might."

He hesitated a moment longer; then, "Don't let it hurt you, dear!" he said. "But—actually—I wasn't sure that you cared—until I was with you in the temple and saw you—weeping for me."

"Oh, Everard!" she said.

He folded her in his arms. "My darling, I thought I had killed your love; and even though I found then that I was wrong, I wasn't sure that you would ever forgive me for playing that last trick upon you."

"Ah!" she whispered. "And if I—hadn't—forgiven—you?"

"I should have gone away," he said.

"You would have left me?" She pressed closer.

"I should have come back to you sometimes, sweetheart, in some other guise. I couldn't have kept away for ever. But I would never have intruded upon you," he said.

"Everard! Everard!" She hid her face against him. "You make me feel so ashamed—so utterly—unworthy."

"Don't darling! Don't," he whispered. "Let us be happy—to-night!"

"And I wanted you so! I missed you so!" she said brokenly.

He turned her face up to his own. "I missed myself a bit, too," he said. "I couldn't have played the Hanani game if Peter hadn't put me up to it. Darling, are those actually tears? Because I won't have them. You are going to look forward, not back."

She clung to him closely, passionately. "Yes—yes. I will look forward. But, oh, Everard, promise me—promise me—you will never deceive me again!"

"I don't believe I could, any more," he said.

"But promise!" she urged.

"Very well, my dear one. I promise. There! Is that enough?" He kissed her quivering face, holding her clasped to his heart. "I will never trick you again as long as I live. But I had to be near you, and it was the only way. Now—am I quite forgiven?"

"Of course you are," she told him tremulously. "It wasn't a matter for forgiveness. Besides—anyhow—you were justified. And,—Everard,—" her breathing quickened a little; she just caught back a sob—"I love to think—now—that your arms held our baby—when he died."

"My darling! My own girl!" he said, and stopped abruptly, for his voice was trembling too.

The next moment very tenderly he kissed her again.

"Please God he won't be the only one!" he said softly.

"Amen!" she whispered back.

In the acacia boughs above them the blue jay suddenly uttered a rippling laugh of sheer joy and flew away.

The Keeper of the Door

PART I

CHAPTER I

THE LESSON

"Then he's such a prig!" said Olga.

"You should never use a word you can't define," observed Nick, from the depths of the hammock in which his meagre person reposed at length.

She made a face at him, and gave the hammock a vicious twitch which caused him to rock with some violence for several seconds. As he was wont pathetically to remark, everyone bullied him because he was small and possessed only one arm, having shed the other by inadvertence somewhere on the borders of the Indian Empire.

Certainly Olga—his half-brother's eldest child—treated him with scant respect, though she never allowed anyone else to be other than polite to him in her hearing. But then she and Nick had been pals from the beginning of things, and this surely entitled her to a certain licence in her dealings with him. Nick, too, was such a darling; he never minded anything.

Having duly punished him for snubbing her, she returned with serenity to the work upon her lap.

"You see," she remarked thoughtfully, "the worst of it is he really is a bit of a genius. And one can't sit on genius—with comfort. It sort of flames out where you least expect it."

"Highly unpleasant, I should think," agreed Nick.

"Yes; and he has such a disgusting fashion of behaving as if—as if one were miles beneath his notice," proceeded Olga. "And I'm not a chicken, you know, Nick, I'm twenty."

"A vast age!" said Nick.

For which remark she gave him another jerk which set him swinging like a pendulum.

"Well, I've got a little sense anyhow," she remarked.

"But not much," said Nick. "Or you would know that that sort of treatment after muffins for tea is calculated to produce indigestion in a very acute form, peculiarly distressing to the beholder."

"Oh, I'm sorry! I forgot the muffins." Olga laid a restraining hand upon the hammock. "But do you like him, Nick? Honestly now!"

"My dear child, I never like anyone till I've seen him at his worst. Drawing-room manners never attract me."

"But this man hasn't got any manners at all," objected Olga. "And he's so horribly satirical. It's like having a stinging-nettle in the house. I believe—just because he's clever in his own line—that he's been spoilt. As if everybody couldn't do something!"

"Ah! That's the point," said Nick sententiously. "Everybody can, but it isn't everybody who does. Now this young man apparently knows how to make the most of his opportunities. He plays a rattling hand at bridge, by the way."

"I wonder if he cheats," said Olga. "I'm sure he's quite unscrupulous."

Nick turned his head, and surveyed her from under his restless eyelids. "I begin to think you must be falling in love with the young man," he observed.

"Don't be absurd, Nick!" Olga did not even trouble to look up. She was stitching with neat rapidity.

"I'm not. That's just how my wife fell in love with me. I assure you it often begins that way." Nick shook his head wisely. "I should take steps to be nice to him if I were you, before the mischief spreads."

Olga tossed her head. She was slightly flushed. "I shall never make a fool of myself over any man, Nick," she said. "I'm quite determined on that point."

"Dear, dear!" said Nick. "How old did you say you were?"

"I am woman enough to know my own mind," said Olga.

"Heaven forbid!" said Nick. "You wouldn't be a woman at all if you did that."

"I don't think you are a good judge on that subject, Nick," remarked his niece judiciously. "In fact, even Dr. Wyndham knows better than that. I assure you the antipathy is quite mutual. He regards everyone who isn't desperately ill as superfluous and uninteresting. He was absolutely disappointed the other day because, when I slipped on the stairs, I didn't break any bones."

"What a fiend!" said Nick.

"And yet Dad likes him," said Olga. "I can't understand it. The poor people like him too in a way. Isn't it odd? They seem to have such faith in him."

"I believe Jim has faith in him," remarked Nick. "He wouldn't turn him loose on his patients if he hadn't."

"Of course, Sir Kersley Whitton recommended him," conceded Olga. "And he is an absolutely wonderful man, Dad says. He calls him the greatest medicine-man in England. He took up Max Wyndham years ago, when he was only a medical student. And he has been like a father to him ever since. In fact, I don't believe Dr. Wyndham would ever have come here if Sir Kersley hadn't made him. He was overworked and wouldn't take a rest, so Sir Kersley literally forced him to come and be Dad's assistant for a while. He told Dad that he was too brilliant a man to stay long in the country, and Dad gathered that he contemplated making him his own partner in the course of time. The sooner the better, I should say. He obviously thinks himself quite thrown away on the likes of us."

"Altogether he seems to be a very interesting young man," said Nick. "I must really cultivate his acquaintance. Is he going to be present to-night?"

"Oh, I suppose so. It's a great drawback having him living in the house. You see, being his hostess, I have to be more or less civil to him. It's very horrid," said Olga, upon whom, in consequence of her mother's death three years before, the duties of housekeeper had devolved. "And Dad is so fearfully strict too. He won't let me be the least little bit rude, though he is often quite rude himself. You know Dad."

"I know him," said Nick. "He's licked me many a time, bless his heart, and richly I deserved it. Help me to get out of this like a good kid! I see James the Second and the twins awaiting me on the tennis-court. I promised them a sett after tea."

He rolled on to his feet with careless agility, his one arm encircling his young niece's shoulders.

"I shouldn't worry if I were you," protested Olga. "It's much too hot. Don't waste your energies amusing the children! They can quite well play about by themselves."

"And get up to mischief," said Nick. "No, I'm on the job, overlooking the whole crowd of you, and I'll do it thoroughly. When old Jim comes home he'll find a model household awaiting him. By the way, I had a letter from him this afternoon. The kiddie is stronger already, and Muriel as happy as a queen. I shall hear from her to-morrow."

"Don't you wish you were with them?" questioned Olga. "It would be much more fun than staying here to chaperone me."

Nick looked quizzical. "Oh, there's plenty of fun to be had out of that too," he assured her. "I take a lively interest in you, my child; always have."

"You're a darling," said Olga, raising her face impulsively. "I shall write and tell Dad what care you are taking of us all."

She kissed him warmly and let him go, smiling at the tuneless humming that accompanied his departure. Who at a casual glance would have taken Nick Ratcliffe for one of the keenest politicians of his party, a man whom friend and foe alike regarded as too brilliant to be ignored? He had even been jestingly described as "that doughty champion of the British Empire"—an epithet that Olga cherished jealously because it had not been bestowed wholly in jest.

His general appearance was certainly the reverse of imposing, and in this particular, to her intense gratification, Olga resembled him. She had the same quick, pale eyes, with the shrewdness of observation that never needed to look twice, the same colourless brows and lashes and insignificant features; but she possessed one redeeming point which Nick lacked. What with him was an impish grin of sheer exuberance, with her was a smile of rare enchantment, very fleeting, with a fascination quite indescribable but none the less capable of imparting to her pale young face a charm that only the greatest artists have ever been able to depict. People were apt to say of Olga Ratcliffe that she had a face that lighted up well. Her ready intelligence was ardent enough to illuminate her. No one was ever dull in her society. Certainly in her temperament at least there was nothing colorless. Where she loved she loved intensely, and she hated in the same way, quite thoroughly and without dissimulation.

Maxwell Wyndham, for instance, the subject of her recent conversation with Nick, she had disliked wholeheartedly from the commencement of their acquaintance, and he was perfectly aware of the fact. He could not well have been otherwise, but he was by no means disconcerted thereby. It even seemed as if he took a malicious pleasure in developing her dislike upon every opportunity that presented itself, and since he was living in the house as her father's assistant, opportunities were by no means infrequent.

But there was no open hostility between them. Under Dr. Ratcliffe's eye, his daughter was always frigidly polite to the unwelcome outsider, and the outsider accepted her courtesy with a sarcastic smile, knowing exactly how much it was worth.

Perhaps he was a little curious to know how she meant to treat him during her father's absence, or it may have been sheer chance that actuated him on that sultry evening in August, but Nick and his three playfellows had only just settled down to a serious sett when the doctor's assistant emerged from the house with his hands deep in his pockets and a peculiarly evil-smelling cigarette between his firm lips, and strolled across to the shady corner under the walnut-trees where the doctor's daughter was sitting.

She was stitching so busily that she did not observe his approach until escape was out of the question; but she would not have retreated in any case. It was characteristic of her to display a bold front to the people she disliked.

She threw him one of her quick glances as he reached her, and noted with distaste the extreme fieriness of his red hair in the light of the sinking sun. His hair had always been an offence to her. It was so obtrusive. But she could have borne with that alone. It was the green eyes that mocked at everything from under shaggy red brows that had originally given rise to her very decided antipathy, and these Olga found it impossible to condone. People had no right to mock, whatever the colour of their eyes.

He joined her as though wholly unaware of her glance of disparagement.

"I fear I am spoiling a charming picture," he observed as he did so. "But since there was none but myself to admire it, I felt at liberty to do so."

Again momentarily Olga's eyes flashed upwards, comprehending the whole of his thick-set figure in a single sweep of the eyelids. He was exceedingly British in build, possessing in breadth what he lacked in height. There was a bull-dog strength about his neck and shoulders that imparted something of a fighting look to his general demeanour. He bore himself with astounding self-assurance.

"Have you had any tea?" Olga inquired somewhat curtly. She was inwardly wondering what he had come for. He usually had a very definite reason for all he did.

"Many thanks," he replied, balancing himself on the edge of the hammock. "I am deeply touched by your solicitude for my welfare. I partook of tea at the Campions' half an hour ago."

"At the Campions'!" There was quick surprise in Olga's voice.

It elicited no explanation however. He sat and swayed in the hammock as though he had not noticed it.

After a moment she turned and looked at him fully. The green eyes were instantly upon her, alert and critical, holding that gleam of satirical humour that she invariably found so exasperating.

"Well?" said Olga at last.

"Well, fair lady?" he responded, with bland serenity.

She frowned. He was the only person in her world who ever made her take the trouble to explain herself, and he did it upon every possible occasion, with unvarying regularity. She hated him for it very thoroughly, but she always had to yield.

"Why did you go to the Campions'?" she asked, barely restraining her irritation.

"That, fair lady," he coolly responded, "is a question which with regret I must decline to answer."

Olga flushed. "How absurd!" she said quickly. "Dad would tell me like a shot."

"I am not Dad," said the doctor's assistant, with unruffled urbanity. "Moreover, fair lady—"

"I prefer to be called by my name if you have no objection, Dr. Wyndham," cut in Olga, with rising wrath.

He smiled at something over her head. "Thank you, Olga. It saves trouble certainly. Would you like to call me by mine? Max is what I generally answer to."

Olga turned a vivid scarlet. "I am Miss Ratcliffe to you," she said.

He accepted the rebuff with unimpaired equanimity. "I thought it must be too good to be true. Pardon my presumption! When you are as old as I am you will realize how little it really matters. You are genuinely angry, I suppose? Not pretending?"

Olga bit her lip in silence and returned to her work, conscious of unsteady fingers, conscious also of a scrutiny that marked and derided the fact.

"Yes," he said, after a moment, "I should think your pulse must be about a hundred. Leave off working for a minute and let it steady down!"

Olga stitched on in spite of growing discomfiture. The shakiness was increasing very perceptibly. She could feel herself becoming hotter every moment. It was maddening to feel those ironical eyes noting and ridiculing her agitation. From exasperation she had passed to something very nearly resembling fury.

"Leave off!" he said again; and then, because she would not, he laid a detaining hand upon her work.

Instantly and fiercely her needle stabbed downwards. It was done in a moment, almost before she realized the nature of the impulse that possessed her. Straight into the back of his hand the weapon drove, and there from the sheer force of the impact broke off short.

Olga exclaimed in horror, but Max Wyndham made no sound of any sort. The cigarette remained between his lips, and not a muscle of his face moved. His hand with the broken needle in it was not withdrawn. It clenched slowly, that was all.

The blood welled up under Olga's dismayed eyes, and began to trickle over the brown fist. She threw a frightened glance into his grim face. Her anger had wholly evaporated and she was keenly remorseful. But it was no matter for an apology. The thing was beyond words.

"And now," said Max Wyndham, coolly removing the ash from his cigarette, "perhaps you will come to the surgery with me and get it out."

"I?" stammered Olga, turning very white.

"Even so, fair lady. It will be a little lesson for you—in surgery. I hope the sight of blood doesn't make you feel green," said Max, with a one-sided twitch of the lips that was scarcely a smile.

He removed his hand to her relief, and stood up. Olga stood up too, but she was trembling all over.

"Oh, I can't! Indeed, I can't! Dr. Wyndham, please!" She glanced round desperately. "There's Nick! Couldn't you ask him?"

"Unfortunately this is a job that requires two hands," said Max. "Besides, you did the mischief, remember."

Olga gasped and said no more. Meekly she laid her work on the chair by the hammock and accompanied him to the house. It was the most painful predicament she had ever been in. She knew that there was no escape for her, knew, moreover, that she richly deserved her punishment; yet, as he held open the surgery-door for her, she made one more appeal.

"I'm sure I can't do it. I shall do more harm than good, and hurt you horribly."

"Oh, but you'll enjoy that," he said.

"Indeed, I shan't!" Olga was almost in tears by this time. "Couldn't you do it yourself with—with a forceps?"

"Afraid not," said Max.

He went to a cupboard and took out a bottle containing something which he measured into a glass and filled up with water.

"Fortify yourself with this," he said, handing it to her, "while I select the instruments of torture."

Olga shuddered visibly. "I don't want it. I only want to go."

"Well, you can't go," he returned, "until you have extracted that bit of needle of yours. So drink that, and be sensible!"

He pulled out a drawer with the words, and she watched him, fascinated, as he made his selection. He glanced up after a moment.

"Olga, if you don't swallow that stuff soon, I shall be—annoyed with you."

She raised it at once to her lips, feeling as if she had no choice, and drank with shuddering distaste.

"I always have hated *sal volatile*," she said, as she finished the draught.

"You can't have everything you like in this world," returned Max sententiously. "Come over here by the window! Now you are to do exactly what I tell you. Understand? Put your own judgment in abeyance. Yes, I know it's bleeding; but you needn't shudder like that. Give me your hand!" She gave it, trembling. He held it firmly, looking straight into her quivering face. "We won't proceed," he said, "until you have quite recovered your self-control, or you may go and slit a large vein, which would be awkward for us both. Just stand still and pull yourself together."

She found herself obliged to obey. The shrewd green eyes watched her mercilessly, and under their unswerving regard her agitation gradually died down.

"That's better," he said at length, and released her hand. "Now see what you can do."

It seemed to Olga later that he took so keen an interest in the operation as to be quite insensible of the pain it involved. She obeyed his instructions herself with a set face and a quaking heart, suppressing a sick shudder from time to time, finally achieving the desired end with a face so ghastly that the victim of her efforts laughed outright.

"Whom are you most sorry for, yourself or me?" he wanted to know. "I say, please don't faint till you have bandaged me up! I can't attend to you properly if you do, and I shall probably spill blood over you and make a beastly mess."

Again his insistence carried the day. Olga bandaged the torn hand without a murmur.

"And now," said Dr. Max Wyndham, "tell me what you did it for!"

She looked at him then with quick defiance. She had endured much in silence, mainly because she had known that she had deserved it; but there was a limit. She was not going to be brought to book as though she had been a naughty child.

"You had yourself alone to thank for it," she declared with indignation. "If—if you hadn't interfered and behaved intolerably, it wouldn't have happened."

"What a naïve way of expressing it!" said Max. "Shall I tell you how I regard the 'happening'?"

"You can do as you like," she flung back. She was longing to go, but stood her ground lest departure should look like flight.

Max took out and lighted another cigarette before he spoke again. Then: "I regard it," he said very deliberately, "as a piece of spiteful mischief for which you deserve a sound whipping—which it would give me immense pleasure to administer."

Olga's pale face flamed scarlet. Her eyes flashed up to his in fiery disdain.

"You!" she said, with withering scorn. "You!"

"Well, what about me?"

Carelessly, his hands in his pockets, Max put the question. Quite obviously he did not care in the smallest degree what answer she made. And so Olga, being stung to rage by his unbearable superiority, cast scruples to the wind.

"I'd do the same to you again—and worse," she declared vindictively, "if I got the chance!"

Max smiled at that superciliously, one corner of his mouth slightly higher than the other. "Oh, no, you wouldn't," he said. "For one thing, you wouldn't care to run the risk of having to sew me up again. And for another, you wouldn't dare!"

"Not dare! Do you think I am afraid of you?"

Olga stood in a streak of sunlight that slanted through the wire blind of the doctor's surgery and fell in chequers upon her white dress. Her pale eyes fairly blazed. No one who had ever seen her thus would have described her as colourless. She was as vivid in that moment as the flare of the sunset; and into the eyes of the man who leaned against the table coolly appraising her there came an odd little gleam of satisfaction—the gleam that comes into the eyes of the treasure-hunter at the first glint of gold.

Olga came a step towards him. She saw the gleam and took it for ridicule. The situation was intolerable. She would be mocked no longer.

"Dr. Wyndham," she said, her voice pitched rather low, "do you call yourself a gentleman?"

"I really don't know," he answered. "It's a question I've never asked myself."

"Because," she said, speaking rather quickly, "I think you a cad."

"Not really!" said Max, smiling openly. "Now I wonder why! Sit down, won't you, and tell me?"

The colour was fading from her face again. She had made a mistake in thus assailing him, and already she knew it. He only laughed at her puny efforts to hurt him, laughed and goaded her afresh.

"Why am I not a gentleman?" he asked, and drew in a mouthful of smoke which he puffed at the ceiling. "Because I said I should like to give you a whipping? But you would like to tar and feather me, I gather. Isn't that even more barbarous?" He watched the smoke ascend, with eyes screwed up, then, as she did not speak, looked down at her again.

She no longer stood in the sunlight, and the passing of the splendour seemed to have left her cold. She looked rather small and pinched—there was even a hint of forlornness about her. But she had learned her lesson.

As he looked at her, she clenched her hands, drew a deep breath, and spoke. "Dr. Wyndham, I beg your pardon for hurting you, and for being rude to you. I can't help my thoughts, of course, but I was wrong to put them into words. Please forget—all I've said!"

"Oh, I say!" said Max, opening his eyes, "that's the cruellest thing you've done yet. You've taken all the wind out of my sails, and left me stranded. What is one expected to say to an apology of that sort? It's outside my experience entirely."

Olga had turned to the door, but at his words she paused, looking back. A glimmer of resentment still shone in her eyes.

"If I were in your place," she said, "I should apologize too."

"Oh, no, you wouldn't," said Max. "Not if you wished to achieve the desired effect. You see, I've nothing to apologize for."

"How like a man!" exclaimed Olga.

"Yes, isn't it? Thanks for the compliment! Strange to say, I am much more like a man than anything else under the sun. I say, are you really going? Well, I forgive you for being naughty, if that's what you want. And I'm sorry I can't grovel to you, but I don't feel justified in so doing, and it would be very bad for you in any case. By the way—er—Miss Ratcliffe, I think you will be interested to learn that my visit to the Campions was of a social and not of a professional character. That was all you wanted to know, I think?"

Olga, holding the door open, looked across at him with surprise that turned almost instantly to half-scornful enlightenment.

"Oh, that's it, is it?" she said.

"That's it," said Max. "Quite sure you don't want to know anything else?"

Again he puffed the smoke upwards and watched it ascend.

"Why on earth couldn't you have said so before?" said Olga.

He turned at that and surveyed her quite seriously. "Oh, that was entirely for your sake," he said.

"For my sake!" said Olga. Sheer curiosity impelled her to remain and probe this mystery.

"Yes," said Max, with a sudden twinkle in his green eyes. "You know, it isn't good for little girls to know too much."

As the door banged upon her retreat, he leaned back, holding to the edge of the table, and laughed with his chin in the air.

Life in the country, notwithstanding its many drawbacks, was turning out to be more diverting than he had anticipated.

CHAPTER II
THE ALLY

"Ah, my dear, there you are! I was just wondering if I would come over and see you."

Violet Campion reined in her horse with a suddenness that made him chafe indignantly, and leaned from the saddle to greet Olga, who had just turned in at the Priory gates.

Olga was bicycling. She sprang from her machine, and reached up an impetuous hand, as regardless of the trampling animal as its rider.

"Pluto is in a tiresome mood to-day," remarked his mistress. "I know he won't be satisfied till he has had a good beating. Perhaps you will go on up to the house while I give him a lesson."

"Oh, don't beat him!" Olga pleaded. "He's only fresh."

"No, he isn't. He's vicious. He snapped at me before I mounted. It's no good postponing it. He'll have to have it." Violet spoke as if she were discussing the mechanism of a machine. "You go on up the drive, my dear, while I take him across the turf."

But Olga lingered. "Violet, really—I know he will throw you or bolt with you. I wish you wouldn't."

Violet's laugh had a ring of scorn. "My dear child, if I were afraid of that, I had better give up riding him altogether."

"I wish you would," said Olga. "He is much too strong for a woman to manage."

Violet laughed again, this time with sheer amusement, and then, with dark eyes that flashed in the sunlight, she slashed the animal's flank with her riding-whip. He uttered a snort that was like an exclamation of rage, and leaped clean off the ground. Striking it again, he reared, but received a stinging cut over the ears that brought him down. Then furiously he kicked and plunged, catching the whip all over his glossy body, till with a furious squeal he flung himself forward and galloped headlong away.

Olga stood on the drive and watched with lips slightly compressed. She knew that as an exhibition of skilled horsemanship the spectacle she had just witnessed was faultless; but it gave her no pleasure, and there was no admiration in the eyes that followed the distant galloping figure with the merciless whip that continued active as long as she could see it.

As horse and rider passed from sight beyond a clump of trees, she remounted her bicycle, and rode slowly towards the house.

Old and grey and weather-stained, the walls of Brethaven Priory shone in the hot sunlight. It had been built in Norman days a full mile and a half inland; but more than the mile had disappeared in the course of the crumbling centuries, and only a stretch of gleaming hillside now intervened between it and the sea. The wash and roar of the Channel and the crying of gulls swept over the grass-clad space as though already claim had been laid to the old grey building that had weathered so many gales. Undoubtedly the place was doomed. There was something eerily tragic about it even on that shining August afternoon, a shadow indefinable of which Olga had been conscious even in her childish days.

She looked over her shoulder several times as she rode in the direction in which her friend had disappeared, but she saw no sign of her. Finally, reaching the house, she went round to a shed at the back, in which she was accustomed to lodge her bicycle.

Here she was joined by an immense Irish wolf-hound, who came from the region of the stables to greet her.

She stopped to fondle him. She and Cork were old friends. As she finally returned to the carriage-drive in front of the house, he accompanied her.

The front door stood open, and she went in through its Gothic archway, glad to escape from the glare outside. The great hall she thus entered had been the chapel in the days of the monks, and it had the clammy atmosphere of a vault. Passing in from the brilliant sunshine, Olga felt actually cold.

179

It was dark also, the only light, besides that from the open door, proceeding from a stained-glass window at the farther end—a gruesome window representing in vivid colours the death of St. John the Baptist.

A carved oak chest, long and low, stood just within, and upon this the girl seated herself, with the great dog close beside her. Her ten-mile bicycle ride in the heat had tired her.

There was no sound in the house save the ticking of an invisible clock. It might have been a place bewitched, so intense and so uncanny was the silence, broken only by that grim ticking that sounded somehow as if it had gone on exactly the same for untold ages.

"What a ghostly old place it is, Cork!" Olga remarked to her companion. "And you actually spend the night here! I can't think how you dare."

In response to which Cork smiled with a touch of superiority and gave her to understand that he was too sensible to be afraid of shadows.

They were still sitting there conversing, with their faces to the sunlit garden, when there came the sound of a careless footfall and Violet Campion, her riding-whip dangling from her wrist, strolled round the corner of the house, and in at the open door.

She was laughing as she came, evidently at some joke that clung to her memory.

"Look at me!" she said. "I'm all foam. But I've conquered his majesty King Devil for once. He's come back positively abject. My dear, do get up! You're sitting on my coffin!"

Olga got up quickly. "Violet, what extraordinary things you think of!"

The other girl laughed again, and stooping raised the oaken lid. "It's not in the least extraordinary. Look inside, and picture to yourself how comfy I shall be! You can come and see me if you like, and spread flowers—red ones, mind. I like plenty of colour."

She dropped the lid again carelessly, and took a gold cigarette-case from her pocket. The sunlight shone generously upon her at that moment, and Olga Ratcliffe told herself for the hundredth time that this friend of hers was the loveliest girl she had ever seen. Certainly her beauty was superb, of the Spanish-Irish type that is world-famous,—black hair that clustered in soft ringlets about the forehead, black brows very straight and delicate, skin of olive and rose, features so exquisite as to make one marvel, long-lashed eyes that were neither black nor grey, but truest, deepest violet.

"Don't look at me like that!" she said, with gay imperiousness. "You pale-eyed folk have a horrible knack of making one feel as if one is under a microscope. Your worthy uncle is just the same. If I weren't so deeply in love with him, I might resent it. But Nick is a privileged person, isn't he, wherever he goes? Didn't someone once say of him that he rushes in where angels fear to tread? It's rather an apt description. How is he, by the way? And why didn't you bring him too?"

She stood on the step, with the sunlight pouring over her, and daintily smoked her cigarette. Olga came and stood beside her. They formed a wonderful contrast—a contrast that might have seemed cruel but for the keen intelligence that gave such vitality to the face of the doctor's daughter.

"Oh, Nick is playing cricket with the boys," she said. "He is wonderfully good, you know, and takes immense care of us all."

"A positive paragon, my dear! Don't I know it? A pity he saw fit to throw himself away upon that very lethargic young woman! I should have made him a much more suitable wife—if he had only had the sense to wait a few years instead of snatching the first dark-eyed damsel who came his way!"

"Oh, really, Violet! And fancy calling Muriel lethargic! She is one of the deepest people I know, and absolutely devoted to Nick—and he to her."

"Doubtless! doubtless!" Violet flicked the ash delicately from her cigarette. "I am sure he is the soul of virtue. But how comes it that the devoted Muriel can tear herself from his side to go a-larking on the Continent with the grim and masterful Dr. Jim?"

"Oh, I thought you knew that. It is for the child's benefit. Poor little Reggie has a delicate chest, and Redlands doesn't altogether suit him. Dad positively ordered him abroad, and when Muriel demurred about taking him out of Dad's reach (she has such faith in him, you know), he arranged to go too if Nick would leave Redlands and come and help me keep house. You see, Dad couldn't very well leave me to look after Dr. Wyndham singlehanded."

"My dear, of course not!" Up went the violet eyes in horror at the bare suggestion. "You scandalize me. An innocent child like you! Not to be thought of for a moment! Rather than that, I would have come and shared the burden with you myself!"

"That's exactly what I have come to ask you to do," said Olga eagerly. "Do say you can! You can't think how welcome you will be!"

"My dear, you're so impetuous!" Violet was just a year her junior, but this fact was never recognized. "Pray give me time to deliberate. You forget that I also have a family to consider. What will Bruce say if I desert him at a moment's notice?"

"I'm sure Bruce won't mind. Can't we go and ask him?"

"Presently, my child. He is not at home just at present. Neither is Mrs. Bruce." The daintiest grimace in the world testified to the opinion entertained by the speaker for the latter. "Moreover, Bruce and I had a difference of opinion this morning and are not upon speaking terms. So unfortunate that he is so *difficile*. By the way, he is hand and glove with the new assistant. Were you aware of that?"

"I knew that he came to tea here yesterday," said Olga.

"Oh! And how did you find that out?"

"He told me."

"You mean you asked him!"

"Indeed, I didn't!" Olga refuted the charge with indignation. "I don't take the smallest interest in his doings."

"Not really?" Her friend looked at her with a comprehending smile. "Don't you like the young man?" she enquired.

"I detest him!" Olga declared with vehemence.

Again the slender little finger flicked the ash from the cigarette. "But what a mistake, dear!" murmured the owner thereof. "Young men don't grow on every gooseberry bush. Besides, one can never tell! The object of one's detestation might turn out to be the one and only, and it's so humiliating to have to change one's mind."

"I shall never change mine with regard to Dr. Wyndham," Olga said with great determination. "I should hate him quite as badly even if he were the only man in the world."

But at that the cigarette was suddenly whisked from the soft lips and pointed full at her. "Allegro,"—it was Violet Campion's special name for her, and she uttered it weightily,— "mark my words and ponder them well! You have met your fate!"

"Violet! How dare you say such a thing?" Olga turned crimson with indignant protest. "I haven't! I wouldn't! It's horrid of you to talk like that!"

"Quite indecent, dear, I admit. But have you never noticed how indecent the truth can be? What a pity to waste such a lovely blush on me! I presume he hasn't begun to make love to you yet?"

"Of course he hasn't! No man would be such a fool with you within reach!" thrust back Olga, goaded to self-defence.

"But I am not within reach," said Violet, with a twirl of the cigarette.

"Far more so than I," returned Olga with spirit. "Anyhow, he never went out of his way to have tea with me."

A peal of laughter from her companion put a swift end to her indignation. Violet was absolutely irresistible when she laughed. It was utterly impossible to be indignant with her.

"Then you think if I am there perhaps he will be persuaded to stay at home to tea?" she chuckled mischievously. "Well, my dear, I'll come, and we will play at battledore and shuttlecock to your heart's content. But if the young man turns and rends us for our pains— and I have a shrewd notion that's the sort of young man he is—you mustn't blame me."

She tossed away her cigarette with the words, and turned inwards, sweeping Olga with her with characteristic energy. She was never still for long in this mood.

They passed through the great hall to a Gothic archway in the south wall, close to the wonderful stained window. Olga glanced up at it with a slight shiver as she passed below.

"Isn't it horribly realistic?" she said.

The girl beside her laughed lightly. "I rather like it myself; but then I have an appetite for the horrors. And they've made the poor man so revoltingly sanctimonious that one really can't feel sorry for him. I'd cut off the head of anybody with a face like that. It's a species that still exists, but ought to have been exterminated long ago."

With her hand upon Olga's arm, she led her through the Gothic archway to a second smaller hall, and on up a wide oak staircase with a carved balustrade that was lighted halfway up by another great window of monastic design but clear glass.

Olga always liked to pause by this window, for the view from it was magnificent. Straight out to the open sea it looked, and the width of the outlook was superb.

"Oh, it's better than Redlands," she said.

"I don't think so," returned Violet. "Redlands is civilized. This isn't. Picture to yourself the cruelty of bottling up a herd of monks here in full view of their renounced liberty. Imagine being condemned to pass this window a dozen times in the day, on the way to that dreary chapel of theirs. A refinement of torture with which the window downstairs simply can't compete. How they must have hated the smell of the sea, poor dears! But I daresay they didn't open their windows very often. It wasn't the fashion in those days."

She drew Olga on to the corridor above, and so to her own room, a cheerful apartment that faced the Priory grounds.

"If I am really coming to stay with you, I suppose I must pack some clothes. Does the young man dress for dinner, by the way?"

"Oh, yes. It's very ridiculous. We all do it now. It's such a waste of time," said the practical Olga. "And I never have anything to wear."

"Poor child! That is a drawback certainly. I wonder if you could wear any of my things. I shouldn't like to eclipse you."

"I'm sure I couldn't, thank you all the same." Olga's reply was very prompt. "As to eclipsing me, you'll do that in any case, whatever you wear."

Violet looked at her with dancing eyes. "I believe you actually want to be eclipsed! What on earth has the young man been doing? He seems to have scared you very effectually."

"Oh, I'm not afraid of him!" Olga spoke with her chin in the air. "But I detest him with all my heart, and he detests me."

"In fact, you are at daggers drawn," commented Violet. "And you want me to come and divert the enemy's attention while you strengthen your defences. Well, my dear, as I said before, I'll come. But—from what I have seen of Dr. Maxwell Wyndham—I don't think I shall make much impression. If he means to gobble you up, he certainly will do so, whether I interfere or not. I've a notion you might do worse, green eyes and red hair notwithstanding. He will probably whip you soundly now and then and put you in the corner till you are good. But you will get to like that in time. And I daresay he will be kind enough to let you lace up his boots for a treat in between whiles."

Olga's pale eyes flashed. "You are positively mad this afternoon, Violet!"

"Oh, no, I'm not. I haven't had a mad spell for a long time. I am only extraordinarily shrewd and far-seeing. Well, dear, what shall I bring to wear? Do you think I shall be appreciated in my red silk? Or will that offend the eye of the virtuous Nick?"

"No, you are not to wear that red thing. Wear white. I like you best in white."

"And black?"

"Yes, black too. But not colours. You are too beautiful for colours."

"Ridiculous child! That red thing, as you call it, suits me to perfection."

"I know it does. But I don't like it. You make me think of Lady Macbeth in that. Besides, it's much too splendid for ordinary occasions. Yes, that pale mauve is exquisite. You will look lovely in that. And this maize suits you too. But you look positively dangerous in red."

"I must leave the business of selection to you, it seems," laughed Violet. "Well, I am to be your guest, so you shall make your own choice. By the way, how shall I get to Weir?

Mrs. Bruce has the car, and will probably not return till late. And Bruce is using the dog-cart. That only leaves the luggage-cart for me."

"I'll fly round to Redlands for the motor. Nick won't mind. You get your things packed while I'm gone."

Olga deposited an armful of her friend's belongings upon the bed, and turned to go.

Nick's property of Redlands was less than a mile away, and all that Nick possessed was at her disposal. In fact, she had almost come to look upon Redlands as a second home. It would not take her long to run across to the garage and fetch the little motor which Nick himself had taught her years ago to drive. Lightly she ran down the oak stairs and through the echoing hall once more. The vault-like chill of the place struck her afresh as she passed to the open door. And again involuntarily she shivered, quickening her steps, eager to leave the clammy atmosphere behind.

Passing into the hot sunshine beyond the great nail-studded door was like entering another world. She turned her face up to the brightness and rejoiced.

CHAPTER III
THE OBSTACLE

Redlands had always been a bower of delight to Olga's vivid fancy. The house, long, low, and rambling, stood well back from the cliffs in the midst of a garden which to her childhood's mind had always been the earthly presentment of Paradise. Not the owner of it himself loved it as did Olga. Many were the hours she had spent there, and not one of them but held a treasured place in her memory.

As she turned in at the iron gate, the music of the stream that ran through the glen rose refreshingly through the August stillness. She wished Nick were with her to enjoy it too.

The temptation to run down to the edge of the water was irresistible. It babbled with such delicious coolness between its ferns. The mossy pathway gleamed emerald green. Surely there was no need for haste! She could afford to give herself five minutes in her paradise. Violet certainly would not be ready yet.

She sat down therefore on the edge of the stream, and gave herself up to the full enjoyment of her surroundings. An immense green dragon-fly whirred past her and shot away into the shadows. She watched its flight with fascinated eyes, so sudden was it, so swift, and so unerringly direct. It reminded her of something, she could not remember what. She wrestled with her memory vainly, and finally dismissed the matter with slight annoyance, turning her attention to a wonderful coloured moth that here flitted across her line of vision. It was an exquisite thing, small, but red as coral. Only in this fairyland of Nick's had she ever seen its like. Lightly it fluttered through the chequered light and shade above the water, shining like a jewel above the shallows, the loveliest thing in sight. And then, even under her watching eyes came tragedy. Swift as an arrow, the green dragon-fly darted back again, and in an instant flashed away. In that instant the coral butterfly vanished also.

Olga exclaimed in incredulous horror. The happening had been too quick for her eyes to follow, but her comprehension leaped to the truth. And in that moment she realized what it was of which the dragon-fly reminded her. It was of Max Wyndham sitting on the surgery-table watching her with that mocking gleam in his green eyes, as though he knew her to be at her mercy whether she stayed or fled.

It was unreasonable of course, but that fairy tragedy in the glen increased her dislike of the man a hundredfold. She felt as if he had darted into her life, armed in some fashion with the power to destroy. And she longed almost passionately to turn him out; for no disturbing force had ever entered there before. But she knew that she could not.

She went on up to the house in sober mood. It had been left to the care of the servants since Nick's departure. She found a French window standing open, and entered. It was the drawing-room, all swathed in brown holland. Its dim coolness was very different from the stony chill of the Priory. She looked around her with a restful feeling of being at home, despite the brown coverings. Many were the happy hours she had spent here both before and after Nick's marriage. It had always been her palace of delight.

As she paused in the room, she remembered that there was a book Nick had said he wanted out of the library. This room was a somewhat recent addition to the house and shut away from the rest of the building by a long passage. She passed from the drawing-room, and made her way thither.

It surprised her a little to find the door standing open, but it was only a passing wonder. The light that came in through green sun-blinds made her liken it in her own mind to a chamber under the sea. She went to a book-shelf in a dark corner, and commenced her hunt.

"If you are looking for Farrow's *Treatise on Party Government*," remarked a casual voice behind her, "I've got it here."

Olga started violently. Any voice would have given her a surprise at that moment, but the voice of Max Wyndham was an absolute shock that set every nerve on edge.

He laughed at her from the sofa, on which he sprawled at length. "My good child, your nerves are like fiddle-strings after a frost. Remind me to make you up a tonic when we get back! Did you bicycle over?"

Olga ignored the question. She was for the moment too angry to speak.

"Sit down," he said. "You ought to know better than to scorch on a day like this. You deserve a sunstroke."

"I didn't scorch," declared Olga, stung by this injustice. "I'm not such an idiot. You seem to think I haven't any sense at all!"

"My thoughts are my own," said Max. "Why didn't you say you were coming? You could have motored over with me."

"I didn't so much as know you would be in this direction. How could I?" said Olga. "And even if I had known—" she, paused.

"You would have preferred sunstroke?" he suggested.

"That I can quite believe. Well, here is the book!" He swung his legs off the sofa. "I dropped in to fetch it myself, as your good uncle seemed to want it, and then became so absorbed in its pages that I couldn't put it down. We seem to have a rotten Constitution altogether. Wonder whose fault it is."

Olga took the book with a slight, contemptuous glance. That he had been interested in the subject for a single moment she did not believe. She wondered that he deemed it worth his while to feign interest.

"Are you taking a holiday to-day?" she enquired bluntly.

He smiled at that. "I cut off an old man's toe at the cottage hospital this morning, vaccinated four babies, pulled out a tooth, and dressed a scald. What more would you have? I suppose you don't want to be vaccinated by any chance?"

Olga passed the flippant question over. "It's a half-holiday then, is it?" she said.

"Well, as it happens, fair lady, it is, all thanks to Dame Stubbs of 'The Ship Inn' who summoned me hither with great urgency and then was ungrateful enough to die before I reached her."

"Oh!" exclaimed Olga. "Is old Mrs. Stubbs dead?"

"She is," said Max.

She turned upon him. "And you've just come—from her death-bed?"

He arose and stretched himself. "Even so, fair lady."

Olga stared at him incredulously. "You actually—don't care?" she asked slowly.

"Not much good caring," said Max.

"What did she die of?" questioned Olga.

He hesitated for a second. Then, "cancer," he said briefly.

"Did she suffer much?" She asked the question nervously as if she feared the answer.

"It doesn't matter, does it?" said Max, thrusting his hands into his pockets.

"I don't see why you shouldn't tell me that." Olga spoke with a flash of indignation. "It does matter in my opinion."

"Nothing that's past matters," said Max.

"I don't agree with you!" Hotly she made answer, inexplicably hurt by his callous tone. "It matters a lot to me. She was a friend of mine. If I had known she was seriously ill, I'd have gone to see her. You—I think you might have told me."

She turned with the words as if to go, but Max coolly stepped to the door before her. He stretched a hand as if to open it, but paused, holding it closed.

"I was not aware that the old woman was a friend of yours," he said. "But it wouldn't have done much good to anyone if you had seen her. She probably wouldn't have known you."

"I might have taken her things at least," said Olga.

"Which she wouldn't have touched," he rejoined.

She clenched her hands unconsciously. Why was he so maddeningly cold-blooded?

"Do you mind opening the door?" she said.

But he remained motionless, his hand upon it. "Do you mind telling me where you are going?" he said.

Her eyes blazed. "Really, Dr. Wyndham, what is that to you?"

He stood up squarely and faced her, his back against the door. "I will answer your question when you have answered mine."

She restrained herself with an effort. How she hated the man! Conflict with him made her feel physically sick; and yet she had no choice.

"I am going down to 'The Ship' at once," she said, "to see her daughter."

"Pardon me!" said Max. "I thought that was your intention. I am sorry to have to frustrate it, but I must. I assure you Mrs. Briggs will have plenty of other visitors to keep her amused."

"I am going nevertheless," said Olga.

She saw his jaw coming into sudden prominence, and her heart gave a hard quick throb of misgiving. They stood face to face in the dimness, neither uttering a word.

Several seconds passed. The green eyes were staring at the bookshelves beyond Olga, but it was a stony, pitiless stare. Had he any idea as to how formidable he looked, she wondered? Surely—surely he did not mean to keep her against her will! He could not!

She collected herself and spoke. "Dr. Wyndham, will you let me go?"

Instantly his eyes met hers. "Certainly," he said, "if you will promise me first not to go to 'The Ship' till after the funeral."

She felt her face gradually whitening. "But I mean to go. Why shouldn't I?"

"Simply because it wouldn't be good for you," he made calm reply.

"How ridiculous!" They were the only words that occurred to her. She spoke them with vehemence.

He received them in silence, and she saw that a greater effort would be necessary if she hoped to assert her independence with any success.

It was essential that she should do so, and she braced herself for a more determined attempt. "Dr. Wyndham," she said, throwing as much command into her voice as she could muster, "open that door—at once!"

She saw again that glint in his eyes that seemed to mock her weakness. He stood his ground. "Fair lady," he said, "with regret I refuse."

She made a sharp movement forward, nerved for the fray by sheer all-possessing anger. She gripped the handle of the door above his hand and gave it a sharp wrench. He would not—surely he would not—struggle with her! Surely she must discomfit him—rout him utterly—by this means!

Yes, she had won! The sheer unexpectedness of her action had gained the day! Her heart gave a great leap of triumph as he took his hand away. But the next instant it stood still. For in the twinkling of an eye he had taken her by the shoulders holding her fast.

"That is the most foolish thing you ever did in your life," he said, and his words came curt and clipped as though he spoke them through his teeth.

Something about him restrained her from offering any resistance. She stood in silence, her heart jerking on again with wild palpitations. The grip of his hands was horribly close;

she almost thought he was going to shake her. But his eyes under their bristling brows held her even more securely. Under their look she was suddenly hotly ashamed.

"You are going to make me that promise," he said.

But she stood silent, trying to muster strength to defy him.

"What do you want to go for?" he demanded.

"I want to know—I want to know—" She stammered over her answer; it was uttered against her will.

"Well? What?" Still holding her, he put the question. "I can tell you anything you want to know."

"But you won't!" Olga plucked up her spirit at this. "It's no good asking you anything. You never answer."

"I will answer you," he said.

"And besides—" said Olga.

"Yes?" said Max.

"You're so horrid," she burst out, "so cold-blooded, so—so—so unsympathetic!"

To her own amazement and dismay, she found herself in tears. In the same instant she was free and the door left unguarded; but she did not use her freedom to escape. Somehow she did not think of that. She only leaned against the wall with her hands over her face and wept.

Max, with his hands deep in his pockets, strolled about the room, whistling below his breath. The gleam had died out of his eyes, but the brows met fiercely above them. His face was the face of a man working out a difficult problem.

Suddenly he walked up to her, and stood still.

"Look here," he said; "can't you manage to be sensible for a minute? If you go on in this way you will soon get hysterical, and I don't think my treatment for hysterics would appeal to you. Olga, are you listening?"

Yes, she was listening—listening tensely, because she could not help herself.

"I'm sorry you think me a brute," he proceeded. "I don't think anyone else does, but that's a detail. I am also sorry that you're upset about old Mrs. Stubbs, though I don't see much sense in crying for her now her troubles are over. I think myself that it was just as well I didn't reach her in time. I should only have prolonged her misery. That's one of the grand obstacles in the medical career. I've kicked against it a good many times." He paused.

"She did suffer then?" whispered Olga, commanding herself with an effort.

"When she wasn't under the influence of morphia—yes. That was the only peace she knew. But of course it affected her brain. It always does, if you keep on with it."

Olga's hands fell. She straightened herself. "Then—you think she is better dead?" she said.

He squared his great shoulders, and she felt infinitely small. "If I could have followed my own inclination with that old woman," he said, "I should have given her a free pass long ago. But—I am not authorized to distribute free passes. On the contrary, it's my business to hang on to people to the bitter end, and not to let them through till they've paid for their liberty to the uttermost farthing."

She glanced at him quickly. Cynical as were his words, she was aware of a touch of genuine feeling somewhere. She made swift response to it, almost before she realized what she was doing.

"Oh, but surely the help you give far outweighs that!" she said. "I often think I will be a nurse when I am old enough, if Dad can spare me."

"Good heavens, child!" he said. "Do you want to be a gaoler too?"

"No," she answered quickly. "I'll be a deliverer."

He smiled his one-sided smile. "And I wonder how long you will call yourself that," he said.

She had no answer ready, for he seemed to utter his speculation out of knowledge and not ignorance. It made her feel a little cold, and after a moment she turned from the subject.

"I am going back to the Priory," she said. "Shall I take that book, or will you?"

It was capitulation, but he gave no sign that he so much as remembered that there had been a battle. Obviously then her defeat had been a foregone conclusion from the outset.

"You needn't bicycle back," he said. "I've got the car here. And I'm going to the Priory myself."

Olga's eyes opened wide at the announcement. "In—deed!" she said, with somewhat daring significance.

"In—deed!" he responded imperturbably. "Is it a joke?"

She felt herself colouring, and considered it safer to leave the question unanswered. "I can't go back in our car," she said. "Violet Campion will be with me, so I have come to fetch Nick's."

"Oh—ho!" said Max keenly. "Coming to stay?"

Very curiously she resented his keenness. "I suppose you have no objection," she said coldly.

"I am enchanted," he declared. "But why not come with me in the car? If you take the one from here, you will only have to bring it back, for you can't house it at Weir."

"But I should have to come back in any case to fetch my bicycle," Olga pointed out.

"No, you needn't! Mitchel can ride that home, and you can drive the motor. You can drive, I'm told?"

"Of course, I can. I often drive Dad." Olga spoke with pride.

"Do you really? Why did you never tell me that before? Afraid I should want you instead of Mitchel?" He looked at her quizzically.

"It wouldn't make much difference if you did," said Olga. It was really quite useless to attempt to be polite to him if he would come so persistently within snubbing distance. Besides, she really did not owe him any courtesy, after the way he had dared to treat her.

But he only laughed at her, and turned to the door. "I shouldn't be so cocksure of that if I were you," he said, opening it with a flourish. "I have a wonderful knack of getting what I want."

She flung him the gauntlet of her contemptuous defiance as she passed him. "Really?" she said.

He took it up instantly, with disconcerting assurance. "Yes, really," he said.

And to Olga all unbidden there came a sudden little tremor of shuddering remembrance as there flashed across her inner vision the spectacle of a green dragon-fly swooping upon a poor little fluttering scarlet moth.

CHAPTER IV
THE SETTING OF THE WATCH

To return to the Priory with her *bête-noir* seated in triumph beside her was a trick of fortune that Olga had been very far from anticipating. There was no help for it, however, for he was determined to go thither, notwithstanding her assurance that the master of the house was from home. He leaned back at his ease and watched her drive with frank criticism.

"I had no idea you were so accomplished," he remarked, as they skimmed up the long Priory drive. "I should have thought you were much too nervous to drive a car."

Olga was never nervous except in his presence, but she would have rather died than have had him know it.

"Nick taught me," she said, "years ago, when he first lost his arm. It's about the only thing he can't do himself."

"I've noticed that he's fairly agile," commented Max. "What did he have his arm cut off for? Couldn't he make himself conspicuous enough in any other way?"

Olga's cheeks flamed. "He was wounded in action," she said shortly.

Max cocked one corner of his mouth. "And so entered Parliament in a blaze of glory," he said. "Vote for the Brave! Vote for the Veteran! Vote for the One-Armed Hero! Never mind his politics! That empty sleeve must have been absolutely invaluable to him in his electioneering days."

187

But joking on this subject was more than Olga could bear. The sight of the empty sleeve was enough to bring tears to her eyes at times even now. To hear it thus lightly spoken of was intolerable.

"How dare you say such a thing!" she exclaimed. "As if Nick—Nick!—would ever stoop to take advantage of a thing like that. Nick, who might have won the V.C., only—" She broke off with vehement self-repression. "I'm an idiot to argue with you!" she said.

"Don't be too hard on yourself!" said Max kindly. "Your imbecility takes quite an attractive form, I assure you. So our gallant hero occupies the shrine of your young affections, does he? It must be rather cramping for him. Is he never allowed to come out and stretch himself?"

Olga said no word in answer. Her lips were firmly closed.

"Poor chap!" said Max. "He must find it a tight squeeze, notwithstanding his size. If you don't slow up pretty soon, fair lady, you will knock the Priory into a heap of ruins."

"I know what I'm about," breathed Olga.

He caught the remark and threw it back with his customary readiness. "Do you really? I humbly beg to question that statement. If you did know, you would proceed with caution."

Olga applied her brake and brought the car adroitly to a standstill in front of the house before replying. Then she flung him a challenging glance.

"Yes," he said with deliberation. "I don't question your cleverness, fair lady;—only your wisdom. You are too prone to let your feelings run away with you, and that is the most infectious disorder that I know."

She laughed, avoiding his eyes, and hotly aware of a certain embarrassment that made reply impossible. "Perhaps, when you have quite finished your lecture, you will get out," she said, "and let me do the same. It's hot sitting here."

"Evidently," said Max.

He turned and descended, held up a hand to her, then, as she ignored it, stooped to guard her dress from the wheel. She whisked it swiftly from his touch, and ran in through the open door, encountering the master of the house just coming out with a suddenness that involved a collision.

He held her up with a sharp, "Hullo, hullo! Why don't you look where you are going?"

And Olga, crimson and breathless, extricated herself with more of speed than dignity. "I'm so sorry, Colonel Campion. The sun is so blazing, I didn't see you. I've come to fetch Violet. She has promised to spend a few days with me while Dad is away."

Colonel Campion's thin, bronzed face was grim, but he raised no objection to the projected visit. He turned at once to Max.

"Hullo, Wyndham! You, is it? Come in and have a drink."

And Olga, feeling herself dismissed, hastened away to find her friend. She stood somewhat in awe of Colonel Campion, despite the fact that his young half-sister defied him continually with impunity. There was something fateful and forbidding about him. He made her think of a man labouring perpetually under a burden which he resented, but was compelled to bear. She wondered what he and Max Wyndham could have in common as she paused at the sea-window on the stairs to cool her cheeks. He had certainly been pleased in his gloomy fashion to see Max, though he had not troubled to give her a welcome.

She found that Violet had not proceeded much further with her packing than when she had left her more than an hour before. She was in fact lying at careless ease half-dressed upon the bed, deeply immersed in a book with a lurid paper cover. She scarcely raised her eyes at Olga's entrance.

"Back already. My dear, you are like quicksilver. Well have I named you Allegro! It suits you to perfection. Sit down—anywhere! I really can't attend to you for a few minutes. This is the beastliest thing I've ever read. You shall have it when I've finished. It's all about the Turkish massacres in Armenia—revolting—absolutely revolting—" Her voice trailed off into a semi-conscious murmur and ceased. The beautiful eyes, dilated with horror, devoured the open page.

188

Olga contemplated her for a moment, then went to the bedside. "Violet, do put down that hateful book! How can you read such disgusting things? Violet!" as her remonstrance elicited no response, "do get up and let us pack your things! Dr. Wyndham is downstairs."

"What?" Violet looked at her this time, but with a mazed expression as of one half-asleep. "Who? The great Objectionable himself? How did you inveigle him here? By nothing short of witchcraft, I will swear. Those pale eyes of yours are rather witch-like, do you know? Did you fly over on a broomstick to fetch him? And why?"

Olga possessed herself of the book, and shut it with decision. "I came upon him at Redlands, and as he has got the car with him, we may as well go back in it. He said he was coming here in any case."

"Really, dear? I wonder why." Violet made a futile effort to recapture her book. "You might let me have it. I must know what became of those unlucky girls when the convent was taken. They mutilated most of the nuns with their scimitars. But the pupils—Allegro, let me have it, dear! I shan't sleep a wink to-night till I know the worst."

"You won't sleep if you do," said Olga magisterially.

"You shan't read any more. It's a disgusting, filthy book and you shan't have it. Get up and dress, and don't be horrid!"

"Horrid!" Violet broke into a gay laugh and the strained look passed in a moment from her eyes. "I was all that was beautiful a little while ago. You're quite right though. It is a foul book, and the man who wrote it is a downright beast. Take it away, and never let me see it again!"

She sprang from the bed, and began to do up her hair rapidly before the glass. Olga laid down the book, and busied herself with folding the various articles of raiment that littered the room.

"I think we ought to be quick," she said.

"To be sure! We mustn't keep his Objectionable Majesty waiting. Why didn't you bring him up with you? It would have kept him amused."

"Violet! As if I could!"

"Oh, couldn't you? I thought doctors were allowed anywhere. And I am sure this young man of yours is not lightly shocked. What was he doing at Redlands?"

Olga hesitated momentarily. "He had been sent for to 'The Ship,' to attend old Mrs. Stubbs," she said then. "But he didn't get there in time."

"Oh! Is she dead? I should think he is pretty savage with her, isn't he?"

"Why should you think so?" Olga glanced round in surprise.

"He's the sort of person to resent anyone dying without his express permission, I should imagine. I know I should never dare to die with him looking on;" Lightly the gay voice made answer. The speaker turned from the glass, her vivid face aglow with merriment. "Really, Olga, if you're quite determined to do my packing, I think I will run down and entertain him."

"You needn't trouble to do that. He is with your brother." Olga proceeded deftly with her task as she spoke. "We found him in the hall as we came in."

"Bruce back already! How tiresome of him! I meant to have just left a message, and now we shall have a wordy argument instead."

"Is Colonel Campion ever wordy?" asked Olga, trying to imagine this phenomenon.

"No, I supply the words and he the argument generally. You might just hook me down the back, dear; do you mind? What do you think his latest craze is? Mrs. Bruce is run down, so nothing will serve but we must all go for a yachting cruise in the Atlantic. I have told him flatly that I will not be one of the party. I detest being on the sea, and as to being boxed up in a yacht with those two—my dear, it would be unspeakable! I should simply leap overboard, I know I should, and I told him so. He has sulked ever since."

"Ah well, you are coming to us," said Olga consolingly. "So he can go without you now with a clear conscience."

"So he can. Mrs. Bruce will be enchanted. She hates me, though she pretends not to and thinks I don't know. Isn't it funny of her? Allegro, you're a darling!" Impulsively she whizzed round and kissed her friend. "You are the one person in the world who loves me, and the only one I love!"

"Violet dearest, how can you say so?"

"The truth, dear, I assure you. I fell in love last winter when we were at Nice with a boy with the most romantic, heavenly eyes you ever saw—an Italian. And then he went and spoilt everything by falling in love with me. I hated him then. He became cheap and very nasty. He only liked my outer covering too, and was not in the least interested in the creature that lived inside."

"You apparently only cared for his eyes," observed Olga.

"Yes, exactly, dear. How clever you are! I should like to have brought them away with me as trophies. But he didn't love me enough for that, and nothing else would have satisfied me. Have you put that hateful, revolting book quite out of reach? I think you had better. If I get it again, you won't take it away so easily a second time."

"I can't think what makes you like such beastly things," said Olga, sitting down upon it firmly.

"Nor I, dear. It's just the way I'm made. I don't like them either. I hate them. That's where the fascination comes in. There! Let me put on my hat, and I am ready. I suppose I must veil myself? We mustn't dazzle the impressionable Max, must we? He must accustom his sight to me gradually. Never mind the rest of those things, Allegro! Françoise can finish, and send them on by the luggage-cart in the evening. Come along, let us face the dragon and get it over."

She linked her arm in Olga's once more, and drew her to the door. Olga carried the book with her for safety, determined that her friend should feast no more on horrors.

"What a little tyrant you are!" laughed Violet. "I am coming to protect you from the dragon, but I shall probably end by protecting the dragon from you. Do you keep a censorious eye upon the literature he reads also?"

"I leave him quite alone," said Olga, "unless he interferes with me."

"Ah! And then, I suppose, you scratch him heartily Poor young man! But I should imagine he is quite capable of clipping your claws if they get in his way. My dear, your fate will be no easy one. I should begin to treat him kindly if I were you."

"I shall never do that," said Olga with conviction.

She was somewhat dismayed as they passed through the archway into the hall to find Max and his host still there; but as they were at the further end and apparently deeply engrossed in conversation, she decided that Violet's gay remarks were scarcely likely to have made any impression, even if they had penetrated so far.

Both men looked up at their entrance, and Max at once moved to meet them.

"I've turned up again at risk of boring you, Miss Campion," he observed. "I chanced to find myself in this direction, so had to yield to the temptation of coming here."

"Oh, don't apologize!" laughed Violet, giving him two fingers. "Of course, I know that it's Bruce you come to see. I wish you would prescribe him a temper tonic. He needs one badly, don't you, Bruce? So Granny Stubbs has given you the slip, has she? How impertinent of her! Aren't you very angry?"

Max shrugged his shoulders with a glance at Olga's tight lips. "I never expend my emotions in vain," he said. "It's a waste of time as well as energy, and I have other purposes for both."

"Then you are never angry?" enquired Violet.

"Never, unless I can punish the offender," smiled Max.

"How frightfully practical! Dear me! I shall have to be exceedingly careful not to offend you. I wonder what form your punishments usually take. Are they made to fit the crime?"

"Usually," said Max, and again he glanced at Olga.

Her eyelids flickered as though she were aware of his look, but she did not raise them.

"You make me quite nervous," declared Violet. "Do you know I have actually promised to come and help keep house for you and the redoubtable Captain Ratcliffe? I'm beginning to think I've been rather rash."

"On the contrary," said Max. "It was quite a wise move on your part, and it shall be mine to see that you do not regret it."

Her gay laugh rang through the old hall. "Bruce is looking quite scandalized, and I don't wonder. Will you and Adelaide be able to support life without me, Bruce? It's a purely formal question, so you needn't answer it if you don't wish. Oh, do let us have some tea! I'm so thirsty. Please ring the bell, Dr. Wyndham! It's close to you. Look at Olga cuddling that naughty book of mine! Don't you think you ought to take it away from her? It's not fit for an innocent maiden to handle even with gloves on."

"What book is it?" It was Colonel Campion who spoke in the harsh tone of one issuing a command.

Olga coloured fierily. "I was taking it away with me to burn on the garden bonfire," she said.

"Give it to me!" he said.

"No, don't, Allegro! It isn't yours to give. You may give it to Dr. Wyndham if you like, but not to Bruce."

"I am not going to give it to anyone," Olga said rather shortly.

"Pardon!" said Max, holding out his hand. "I should like to sample Miss Campion's taste in literature."

She drew back, but his hand remained outstretched. After a moment, reluctantly, she surrendered the book. He took it, and began to turn the pages.

"Nothing ever shocks a medical man," observed Violet. "He is inured to the worst. Come along, dear! This place is like a vault. Let us get into the sunshine and leave him to wallow till tea appears."

They went out together to Olga's immense relief, and spent the next ten minutes in playing with the motor, in the driving of which Violet had lately developed a keen interest.

When they returned, the book had disappeared and the incident was apparently forgotten. They had tea to the accompaniment of much light-hearted chatter on the parts of Violet and Max Wyndham. Colonel Campion sat in heavy silence, and Olga instinctively held aloof. There was something in Max's attitude that puzzled her, but it was something so intangible that she could not even vaguely define it to herself. All his careless banter notwithstanding, she was fully convinced in her own mind that he was not in the smallest degree dazzled or so much as attracted by the brilliant beauty that so dominated her own imagination. Though he laughed and joked in his customary cynical strain, she had a feeling that his mental energies were actually employed elsewhere. He was like a man watching behind a mask. Watching—for what?

Suddenly she remembered again the tragedy she had witnessed in the glen that afternoon, and her heart recoiled.

Was it the atmosphere of the place that made her morbid? Or was there indeed some evil influence at work in her friend's life which she by her headlong action had somehow rendered active?

Before they left the Priory, she had begun to repent almost passionately the impulse that had taken her thither. But wherefore she thus repented she could not have explained.

CHAPTER V
THE CHAPERON

"It's very kind of Olga to provide us with distractions," said Nick, as he dropped into an arm-chair, with a cigar, "but I almost think we are better off without them. If I see much of that girl, it will upset my internal economy. Is she real by any chance?"

"Haven't you ever seen her before?" asked Max.

"Several times, but never for long together. Jove! What a face she has!" He turned his head sharply, and looked up at Max who stood on the hearth-rug. "You're not wildly enthusiastic over her anyhow," he observed. "Are you really indifferent or only pretending?"

"I?" The corners of Max's mouth went down. He stuffed his pipe into one of them and said no more.

Nick continued to regard him with interest for some seconds. Suddenly he laughed. "Do you know, Wyndham," he said, "I should awfully like to give you a word of advice?"

"What on?" Max did not sound particularly encouraging. He proceeded to light his pipe with exceeding deliberation. He despised cigars.

Nick closed his eyes. "In my capacity of chaperon," he said. "It's a beastly difficult position by the way. I'm weighed down by responsibility."

"So I've noticed," remarked Max drily.

"Well, you haven't done much to lighten the burden," said Nick. "I suppose you haven't realized yet that I am one of the gods that control your destiny."

"Well, no; I hadn't." Max leaned against the mantelpiece and smoked, with his face to the ceiling. "I knew you were a species of deity of course. I've been told that several times. And I humbly beg to offer you my sympathy."

"Thanks!" Nick's eyes flashed open as if at the pulling of a string. "If it isn't an empty phrase, I value it."

"I don't deal in empty phrases as a rule," said Max.

"Quite so. Only with a definite end in view? I hold that no one should ever do or say anything without a purpose."

"So do I," said Max.

Nick's eyes flickered over him and closed again. "Then, my dear chap," he said, "why in Heaven's name make yourself so damned unpleasant?"

"So what?" said Max.

"What I said." Coolly Nick made answer. "It's not an empty phrase," he added. "You will find a meaning attached if you deign to give it the benefit of your august consideration."

Max uttered a grim, unwilling laugh. "I suppose you are privileged to say what you like," he said.

"I observe certain limits," said Nick.

"And you never make mistakes?"

"Oh, yes, occasionally. Not often. You see, I'm too well-meaning to go far astray," said Nick, with becoming modesty. "You must remember that I'm well-meaning, Wyndham. It accounts for a good many little eccentricities. I think you were quite right to make her extract that needle. I should have done it myself. But you are not so wise in resenting her refusal to kiss the place and make it well. I speak from the point of view of the chaperon, remember."

"Who told you anything about a needle?" demanded Max, suddenly turning brick-red..

"That's my affair," said Nick.

"And mine!"

"No, pardon me, not yours!" Again his eyes took a leaping glance at his companion.

Doggedly Max faced it. "Did she tell you?"

"Who?" said Nick.

"Olga." He flung the name with half-suppressed resentment. His attitude in that moment was aggressively British. He looked as he had looked to Olga that afternoon, undeniably formidable.

But Nick remained unimpressed. "I shan't answer that question," he said.

"You needn't," said Max grimly.

"That's why," said Nick.

"Oh! I see." Max's eyes searched him narrowly for a moment, then returned to the ceiling. "Does she think I'm in love with her?" he asked rather curtly.

"Well, scarcely. I shouldn't let her think that at present if I were you. In my opinion any extremes are inadvisable at this stage."

"I suppose you know I am going to marry her?" said Max.

"Yes, I've divined that."

"And you approve?"

"I submit to the inevitable," said Nick with a sigh.

Max smiled, the smile of a man who faces considerable odds with complete confidence. "She doesn't—at present."

Nick's grin of appreciation flashed across his yellow face and was gone. "No, my friend. And you'll find her very elusive to deal with. You will never make her like you. I suppose you know that."

"I don't want her to," said Max.

"You make that very obvious," laughed Nick. "It's a mistake. If you keep bringing her to bay, you'll never catch her. She's always on her guard with you now. She never breathes freely with you in the room, poor kid."

"What is she afraid of?" growled Max.

"You know best." Nick glanced up again with sudden keenness. "Don't harry the child, Wyndham!" he said, a half-whimsical note of pleading in his voice. "If you know you're going to win through, you can afford to let her have the honours of war. There's nothing softens a woman more."

"I don't mean to harry her." Max turned squarely round upon him. "But neither have I the smallest intention of fetching and carrying for her till she either kicks me or pats me on the head. I shouldn't appreciate either, and it's a method I don't believe in."

"There I am with you," said Nick. "But for Heaven's sake, man, be patient! It's no joke, I assure you, if the one woman takes it into her head that you are nothing short of a devouring monster. She will fly to the ends of the earth to escape you sooner than stay to hear reason."

Max smiled in his one-sided fashion. "Has that been your experience?"

Nick nodded. There was a reminiscent glitter in his eyes. "My courtship represented two years' hard labour. It nearly killed me. However, we've made up for it since."

"I don't propose to spend two years over mine," said Max.

Nick's eyes flashed upwards, meeting those of the younger man with something of the effect of a collision. His body however remained quite passive, and his voice even sounded as if it had a laugh in it as he made response.

"I think you're a decent chap," he said, "and I think you might make her happy; but I'm damned if she shall marry any man—good, bad, or indifferent—before she's ready."

"You also think you could prevent such a catastrophe?" suggested Max cynically.

Nick grinned with baffling amiability. "No, I don't think. I know. Quite a small spoke is enough to stop a wheel—even a mighty big wheel—if it's going too fast."

And again, more than half against his will, Max laughed. "You make a very efficient chaperon," he said.

"It's my speciality just now," said Nick.

He closed his eyes again peaceably, and gave himself up to his cigar.

Max, his rough red brows drawn together, leaned back against the mantelpiece and smoked his pipe, staring at the opposite wall. There was no strain in the silence between them. Both were preoccupied.

Suddenly through the open window there rippled in the fairy notes of a mandolin, and almost at once a voice of most alluring sweetness began to sing:

"O, wert thou in the cauld blast,
On yonder lea, on yonder lea,
My plaidie to the angry airt,
I'd shelter thee, I'd shelter thee.
Or did misfortune's bitter storms
Around thee blaw, around thee blaw,
Thy bield should be my bosom,
To share it a', to share it a'."
"Or were I in the wildest waste,
Sae black and bare, sae black and bare,
The desert were a paradise,
If thou wert there, if thou wert there.
Or were I monarch o' the globe,

> Wi' thee to reign, wi' thee to reign,
> The brightest jewel in my crown
> Wad be my queen, wad be my queen."

As the song died out into the August night, Nick rose. "That girl's a siren," he said. "Come along! We're wasting our time in here."

Max stooped laconically to knock the ashes from his pipe. His face as he stood up again was quite expressionless. "You lead the way," he said. "Are you going to leave your cigar behind? I suppose cigarettes are allowed?"

"I should think so, as the lady smokes them herself." Nick opened the door with the words, but paused a moment looking back at his companion quizzically. "Good luck to you, old chap!" he said.

Max's hand came out of his pocket with a jerk. He still had it bandaged, but he managed to grip hard with it nevertheless. But he did not utter a word.

They passed into the drawing-room with the lazy, tolerant air of men expecting to be amused; and Olga, with all her keenness, was very far from suspecting aught of what had just passed between them.

She and Violet were both near the open window, the latter with her instrument lying on her knee, its crimson ribbons streaming to the floor. She herself was very simply attired in white. The vivid beauty of her outlined against the darkness of the open French window was such as to be almost startling. She smiled a sparkling welcome.

"Dr. Wyndham, I've decided to call you Max; not because I like it,—I think it's hideous,—but because it's less trouble. I thought it as well to explain at the outset, so that there should be no misunderstanding."

"That is very gracious of you," said Max.

"You may regard it exactly as you please," she said majestically, "so long as you come when you're called. Allegretto, why do you move? I like you sitting there."

"I promised to go and say good-night to the boys," said Olga, who had sprung up somewhat precipitately at Max's approach. "Sit on the sofa, Nick, and keep a corner for me! I'm coming back."

She was gone with the words, a vanishing grey vision, the quick closing of the door shutting her from sight.

Violet leaned back in her chair, and dared the full scrutiny of Max's eyes.

"What a disturber of the peace you are!" she said. "What did you want to come here for before you had finished your smoke?"

"That was your doing," said Nick. "You literally dragged us hither. I'm inclined to think it was you who disturbed the peace."

"I?" She turned upon him. "Captain Ratcliffe—"

"Pray call me Nick!" he interposed. "It will save such a vast amount of trouble as well as keep you in the fashion."

She laughed. "You're much funnier than Max because you don't try to be. What do you mean by saying that I dragged you here? Was it that silly old song?"

"In part," said Nick cautiously.

"And the other part?"

"I won't put that into words. It would sound fulsome."

"Oh, please don't!" she said lightly. "And you, Max, what did you come for?"

He seated himself in the chair which Olga had vacated. "I thought it was time someone came to look after you," he said.

"How inane! You don't pretend to be musical, I hope?"

He leaned back, directly facing her. "No," he said. "I don't pretend."

"Never?" she said.

He smiled in his own enigmatical fashion. "That is the sort of question I never answer."

She nodded gaily. "I knew you wouldn't. Why do you look at me like that? I feel as if I were being dissected. I don't wonder that Olga runs away when she sees you coming. I shall myself in a minute."

He laughed. "Surely you are accustomed to being looked at!"

"With reverence," she supplemented, "not criticism! You have the eye of a calculating apothecary. I believe you regard everybody you meet in the light of a possible patient."

"Naturally," said Max. "I suppose even you are mortal."

"Oh, yes, I shall die some day like the rest of you," she answered flippantly. "But I shan't have you by my death-bed. I shouldn't think you had ever seen anybody die, have you?"

"Why not?" said Max.

"Nobody could with you standing by. You're too vital, too electric. I picture you with your back against the door and your arms spread out, hounding the poor wretch back into the prison-house."

Max got up abruptly and moved to the window. "You have a vivid imagination," he said.

She laughed, drawing her fingers idly across the strings of her mandolin.

"Quite nightmarishly so sometimes. It's rather a drawback for some things. How are you enjoying that book of mine? Do you appreciate the Arabian Nights' flavour in modern literature?"

"It's a bit rank, isn't it?" said Max.

She laughed up at him. "I should have thought you would have been virile enough to like rank things. To judge by the tobacco you smoke, you do."

"Poisonous, isn't it?" said Nick. "I suppose it soothes his nerves, but it sets everyone else's on edge."

Violet stretched out her hand to a box of cigarettes that stood on a table within reach. "You would probably feel insulted if I offered you one of these," she said, "but I practically live on them."

"Very bad for you," said Max.

She snapped her fingers at him. "Then I shall certainly continue the pernicious habit. Do you know Major Hunt-Goring? It was he who gave them to me. He thinks he is going to marry me,—but he isn't!"

"Great Lucifer!" said Nick.

She turned towards him. "What an appropriate name! I wish I'd thought of it. Do you know him?"

"Know him!" Nick's grimace was expressive. "Yes, I know him."

"Well?"

"Rather better than he thinks."

She laughed again, lightly, inconsequently, irresistibly. "He's a fascinating creature. It is his proud boast that he has kissed every girl in the neighbourhood except me."

"What an infernal liar!" said Nick.

"How do you know?" Gaily she challenged him. "It's quite probably true. He is exceedingly popular with the feminine portion of the community. I notice that friend Max maintains a shocked silence."

"Not at all," said Max. "I was only wondering why he had made an exception of you."

She tossed her head. "Can't you guess?"

"No, I can't," he returned daringly. "I should have thought you would have been the first on the list."

"How charming of you to say so!" said Violet. "Perhaps you are not aware of the fact that the sweetest fruit is generally out of reach."

"You might have let me say that," said Nick. "But the man is a liar in any case, and I hope he will give me the opportunity to tell him so."

Violet regarded him with interest. "I had no idea you were so pugnacious. Do you always tell people exactly what you think of them? Is it safe?"

"Quite safe for him," said Max.

"Why?" Violet turned back to him, her fingers carelessly plucking at the instrument on her knee.

Max made prompt and unflattering reply. "Because he's so obviously gimcrack that no one dares do anything to him for fear he should tumble to pieces."

"Many thanks!" said Nick.

Violet's peal of laughter mingled with the weird notes of her mandolin, and Olga, returning, desired to be told the joke.

Nick pulled her down beside him on the sofa. "Come and take care of me, Olga *mia*! I'm being disgracefully maligned. Can't you persuade Miss Campion to sing to us, by way of changing the subject?"

"Who has been maligning you?" demanded Olga, looking at Max with very bright eyes.

He looked straight back at her with that gleam in his eyes which with any other man would have denoted admiration but which with him she well knew to be only mockery.

"I admit it, fair lady," he said. "I threw a clod of mud at your hero. I thought it would be good for him. However, you will be relieved to hear that it went wide of the mark. He still sits secure in his tight little shrine and smiles magnanimously at my futility."

Olga's hand slipped into Nick's. "He's the biggest man you've ever seen!" she declared, with warmth.

"Please don't fight over my body!" remonstrated Nick. "I never professed to be more than a minnow among Tritons, and quite a lean minnow at that."

"You're not, Nick!" declared his champion impetuously. "You're a giant!"

"In miniature," suggested Max. "He is actually proposing to go and kick Major Hunt-Goring because—" He broke off short.

Into Olga's face of flushed remonstrance there had flashed a very strange look, almost a petrified look, as if she had suddenly come upon a snake in her path.

"Why?" she said quickly.

"Oh, never mind why," said Max, passing rapidly on. "That wasn't the point. We were trying to picture Hunt-Goring's amusement. He stands about seven feet high, doesn't he? And your redoubtable uncle—What exactly is your height, Ratcliffe?"

"Nick, why do you want to kick Major Hunt-Goring?" Very distinctly Olga put the question. She was evidently too proud to accept help from this quarter.

"It's a chronic craving with me," said Nick. "But Miss Campion has kindly undertaken the job for me. I am sure she is infinitely better equipped for the task than I am, and she will probably do it much more effectually."

"But not yet!" laughed Violet. "I like his cigarettes too well. Why do you look like that, Allegro? Doesn't he send you any?"

"If he did," said Olga, with concentrated passion, "I'd pick them up with the tongs and put them in the fire!"

Max laughed in a fashion that made her wince, but Nick's fingers squeezed hers protectingly.

"You don't like him any better than I do apparently," he said lightly. "But I suppose we must tolerate the man for Jim's sake. He wouldn't thank us for eliminating all his unpleasant patients during his absence. Now, Miss Campion, a song, please! The most sentimental in your *repertoire*!"

She flashed him her gay smile and flung the streaming ribbons over her arm. There was a gleam of mischief in her eyes as, without preliminary, she began to sing. Her voice was rich and low and wonderfully pure.

> In vain all the knights of the Underworld woo'd her,
> Though brightest of maidens, the proudest was she;
> Brave chieftains they sought, and young minstrels they sued her,
> But worthy were none of the high-born Ladye.
> "Whomsoever I wed," said this maid, "so excelling,
> That Knight must the conqu'ror of conquerors be;
> He must place me in halls fit for monarchs to dwell in;—
> None else shall be Lord of the high-born Ladye!"
> Thus spoke the proud damsel, with scorn looking round her
> On Knights and on Nobles of highest degree;

> Who humbly and hopelessly left as they found her,
> And worshipp'd at distance the high-born Ladye.
> At length came a Knight from a far land to woo her,
> With plumes on his helm like the foam of the sea;
> His vizor was down—but, with voice that thrill'd through her,
> He whisper'd his vows to the high-born Ladye.
> "Proud maiden, I come with high spousals to grace thee,
> In me the great conqu'ror of conquerors see;
> Enthron'd in a hall fit for monarchs I'll place thee,
> And mine thou'rt for ever, thou high-born Ladye!"
> The maiden she smil'd and in jewels array'd her,
> Of thrones and tiaras already dreamt she;
> And proud was the step, as her bridegroom convey'd
> her In pomp to his home, of that high-born Ladye.
> "But whither," she, starting, exclaims, "have you led me?
> Here's nought but a tomb and a dark cypress tree;
> Is *this* the bright palace in which thou wouldst wed me?"
> With scorn in her glance, said the high-born Ladye.
> "Tis the home," he replied, "of earth's loftiest creatures."
> Then he lifted his helm for the fair one to see;
> But she sunk on the ground—'twas a skeleton's features,
> And Death was the Lord of the high-born Ladye!

The beautiful voice throbbed away into silence, and the mandolin jarred and thrummed upon the floor. Violet Campion sat staring straight before her with eyes that were wide and fixed.

Olga jumped up impulsively. "Violet, why did you sing that gruesome thing? Do you want to give us all the horrors?"

She picked up the mandolin with a swish of its red ribbons, and laid it upon the piano, where it quivered and thrummed again like a living thing, awaking weird echoes from the instrument on which it rested.

Then she turned back to her friend. "Violet, wake up! What are you looking at?"

But Violet remained immovable as one in a trance.

Olga bent over her, touched her. "Violet!"

With a quick start, as though suspended animation had suddenly been restored, Violet relaxed in her chair, leaning back with careless grace, her white arms outstretched.

"What's the matter, Allegretto? You look as if you had had a glimpse of the conqueror of conquerors yourself. I shall have to come and sleep with you to frighten away the spooks."

"I don't think I shall ever dare to go to bed at all after that," said Nick.

She laughed at him lazily. "Get Max to sit up with you and hold your hand! The very sight of him would scare away all bogies."

"The sign of a wholesome mind," said Max.

She turned towards him. "Not at all! Scepticism only indicates gross materialism and lack of imagination. There is nothing at all to be proud of in the possession of a low grade of intelligence."

Max's mouth went down, and Violet's face flashed into her most bewitching smile.

"I don't often get the opportunity to jeer at a genius," she said. "You know that I am one of your most ardent admirers, don't you?"

"Is that the preliminary to asking a favour?" said Max.

She broke into a light laugh. "No, I never ask favours. I always take what I want. It's much the quickest way."

"Saves trouble, too," he suggested.

"It does," she agreed. "I am sure you follow the same plan yourself."

"Invariably," said Max.

"It's a plan that doesn't always answer," observed Nick, in a grandfatherly tone. "I shouldn't recommend it to everybody."

"And it's horribly selfish," put in Olga.

"My dear child, don't be so frightfully moral!" protested Violet. "I can't rise to it. Nick, why doesn't it always answer to take what one wants?"

"Because one doesn't always succeed in keeping it," said Nick.

"He means," said Max, a spark of humour in his eyes, "that a champion,—no, a chaperon—sometimes comes along to the rescue of the stolen article. But—from what I've seen of life—I scarcely think the odds would be on the side of the chaperon. What is your opinion, Miss Campion?"

"If the chaperon were Nick, I should certainly put my money on him," she answered lightly.

"And lose it!" said Max.

"And win it!" said Olga.

"Order! Order!" commanded Nick. "Once more I refuse to be the bone of contention between you. You will tear me to shreds among you, and even the great Dr. Wyndham might find some difficulty in putting me together again. Olga, give us some music!"

"I can't, dear," said Olga.

He frowned at her. "Why not?"

She hesitated. "I'm not in the mood for it. At least—"

"Am I the obstacle?" asked Max.

She could not control her colour, though she strove resolutely to appear as if she had not heard.

He turned to Violet, faintly smiling. "Shall we take a stroll in the garden?"

She rose, flinging a gay glance at Olga. "Just two turns!" she said.

He held aside the curtain for her, and followed her out, with a careless jest. The two who were left heard them laughing as they sauntered away. Olga rose with a shiver.

"What's the matter?" said Nick.

To which she answered, "Nothing," knowing that he would not believe her, knowing also that he would understand enough to ask no more.

She went to the piano, put aside the mandolin, and began to play. Not even to Nick, her hero and her close confidant, would she explain the absolute repugnance that the association of Max Wyndham with her friend had inspired in her.

But though she played with apparent absorption, her ears were strained to catch the sound of their voices in the garden behind her, the girl's light chatter, her companion's brief, cynical laugh. For she knew by the sure intuition which is a woman's inner and unerring vision, that jest or trifle as he might his keen brain was actively employed in some subtle investigation too obscure for her to fathom, and that behind his badinage and behind his cynicism there sat a man who watched.

CHAPTER VI
THE PAIN-KILLER

"I am going over to Brethaven to see Mrs. Briggs to-day," Olga announced nearly a week later, waylaying Max after breakfast on his way to the surgery with the air of one prepared to resist opposition. "Are you wanting the car this morning, Dr. Wyndham?"

She knew that he would be engaged at the cottage-hospital that morning, but it was one of Dr. Ratcliffe's strict rules that the car should never be used unprofessionally without express permission from himself or his assistant. Naturally Olga resented having to observe this rule in her father's absence and her manner betrayed as much, but she was too conscientious to neglect its observance.

"You don't propose to go alone, I suppose?" said Max, pausing.

This was another of her father's rules and one which Olga had often vainly attempted to persuade him to rescind. Under these circumstances, Max's question seemed little short of an insult.

"I don't see what that has to do with it," she said.

Max looked at his watch, then turned squarely and faced her. "With me, you mean. Very likely not. But there is a remote connection or I shouldn't ask. Are you going to take Nick with you?"

"He is going part of the way," said Olga, striving for dignity.

"Only part?"

"As far as the station," she returned, almost in spite of herself.

"Going up to town, is he?" said Max. "Well, that doesn't help much. Take one of the boys!"

"I don't want one of the boys," Olga spoke with sudden irritation. "Violet is going with me," she said.

His face changed very slightly, almost imperceptibly. "In that case you must take Mitchel," he said.

"How absurd!" exclaimed Olga.

"No, it isn't absurd. It's quite reasonable from my point of view. If you can't take Mitchel with you, I can't spare the car."

He smiled a little as he pronounced this decision, but quite plainly his mind was made up.

Olga bit her lip in exasperation. "Do you think I am not to be trusted to take care of her?" she asked him scornfully. "I shall ask Nick if I need do anything so ridiculous!"

"Here he is," said Nick, coming lightly up behind her with the words. "What's the trouble now? If you are requiring my valuable advice, it is quite at your service."

Olga turned to him at once. "Nick, it's really too silly for words. Dr. Wyndham makes mountains out of molehills."

"That's very ingenious of him," commented Nick. "I shouldn't harass the man if I were you, Olga. He's been out all night."

Olga pounced upon this fact. "I expect Mitchel has too, then, so he just won't be able to go."

"No," said Max. "I didn't take the car or Mitchel. It chanced to be a case in the village, and I bicycled."

"Who was it?" asked Olga eagerly; and then restrained herself with annoyance. "But of course you won't tell me. You're much too professional."

"Keep to the point!" ordered Nick.

Olga slipped a coaxing arm round his neck. "Nick, don't you think it absurd that Violet and I shouldn't motor over to Brethaven without a man to take care of us? I am quite certain Dad wouldn't object."

"There you are wrong," said Max. "If your father were here, he would forbid it—as I do."

He spoke with emphasis, and glanced again at his watch as he did so.

"He doesn't object to my going alone with one of the boys," said Olga. "It's only Violet who is too precious to go motoring without a full-grown escort. As if I weren't quite capable of taking care of her!"

"It's not that at all," said Max curtly. "I can't stop to argue, so please make up your mind what you are going to do. I'm sorry you've been dragged into the discussion, Ratcliffe. I daresay it seems a senseless one to you, but I have my reasons."

Nick looked at him for a moment, a quick gleam of comprehension behind his flickering eyelids. "It won't hurt you to take Mitchel, Olga *mia*," he said.

"Oh, Nick!" There was deep reproach in Olga's voice, and at sound of it Max smiled with dry humour.

Nick laughed outright, openly heartless. "My beloved chicken, who is making mountains out of molehills now? I would escort you myself if I hadn't got to attend this committee meeting in town,—a million plagues upon it! Come along and open my letters for me! We are wasting time."

"I do think you needn't take his part," said Olga, as Max disappeared into the surgery. "He's quite bullying and tyrannical enough without that."

"I'm inclined to sympathize with the young man myself," said Nick. "He wouldn't bully you if you weren't so nasty."

"Nick, I'm not nasty!"

"I should detest you if I were Max," said Nick, squeezing her affectionately with his one wiry arm.

"It isn't my fault we are antipathetic," protested Olga. "For goodness' sake, Nick, don't start liking him! But I'm sure you don't in your heart of hearts. You simply couldn't."

"Why not?" said Nick.

"Oh, Nick, you don't! You know you don't! He's so cold-blooded and cynical."

"Do you want to know what he was up to last night?" said Nick.

"Yes, tell me!" said Olga.

"He was sent for last thing by some people who live in that filthy alley—near the green pond. A child was choking. They thought it had swallowed a pin. When he got there, he found it was diphtheria at its most advanced stage. The child was at death's door. He had to perform an operation at a moment's notice, hadn't got the proper paraphernalia with him, and sucked the poison out himself."

"Good heavens, Nick!" said Olga, turning very white. "And the child?"

"The child is better. It is to be taken to the hospital to-day."

"Will it—won't it—have an effect on him?" gasped Olga.

"Heavens knows," said Nick.

"And that's why he didn't come down to breakfast," she said. "How did you find out about it? He didn't tell you?"

"He couldn't help it," said Nick. "He stole my bath this morning, and when I arrived he was lying in it face downwards boiling himself in some filthy disinfectant that made the bathroom temporarily uninhabitable. Naturally I lodged a complaint, and finally got at the whole story. By the way, he said I wasn' to tell you; but I told him I probably should. That's only a detail, but I mention it in case you should be tempted to broach the subject to him. I shouldn't advise you to do so, as I think you will probably find him rather touchy about it."

"But, Nick!" Olga's eyes had begun to shine. "It was very—fine of him," she said. "I wish I'd known before I was so cross to him. I—I should have made allowances if I had known."

"Quite so," said Nick. "Well, you can begin now if you feel so inclined, though I suppose the young man did no more than his duty after all."

"Oh, Nick, a man isn't obliged to go so far as that!" she exclaimed reproachfully. "There are plenty who wouldn't."

"Doubtless," agreed Nick, looking faintly quizzical. "It was the action of a fool—but a brave fool. We'll grant him that much, shall we?"

She laughed a little, her cheek against his shoulder. "Don't poke fun at me! It isn't fair. You know he isn't a fool perfectly well."

"By Jove! You are getting magnanimous!" laughed Nick.

"No, I'm not. I'm only trying to be fair. One must be that," said Olga, whose honest soul abhorred injustice of any description.

"Oh, of course," said Nick. "You'll have to spoil him now to make up for having been so—'horrid,' I think, is the proper term, isn't it? It's the most comprehensive word in the woman's vocabulary, comprising everything from slightly disagreeable to damned offensive."

"Really, Nick!"

Nick grinned. "Pardon my unparliamentary language!"

"But Nick, I've never been—that!" protested Olga.

"A matter of opinion!" laughed Nick.

But Olga did not laugh, she only flushed a little and changed the subject.

About an hour later, Max, taking his hat from a peg in the hall, preparatory to departing for the cottage-hospital, discovered the lining thereof to be pulled away in order to accommodate a twisted scrap of paper which had been pinned to it in evident haste.

He carried the hat to the consulting-room and there detached and examined its contents. He smoothed out the crumpled morsel with his customary deliberation, drawing his shaggy red brows together over a few lines of minute writing which became visible as he did so.

"Dear Max," he read, "I'm sorry I've been a beast to you lately. Please don't take any notice of this but let us just be friends for the future. Yours,

"Olga."

There was no mockery in the green eyes as they deciphered the impulsive note, nor did the somewhat hard lips smile. Max stood for some seconds after reading it, staring fixedly at the paper, and when at length he looked up his face wore a guarded expression with which many of his patients were familiar. He took a pocket-book from an inner pocket and laid the crumpled scrap within it. Then, without more ado, he put on his hat and departed.

Olga was by that time spinning merrily along the road to Brethaven, having parted with Nick at the railway-station. Violet was seated beside her, and the old servant Mitchel sat sourly behind them. He had a rooted objection to the back-seat, and held the opinion that a woman at the wheel was out of place.

Olga, however, was not prepared to yield on this point at least. She had brought him against her will, and she meant to forget him if possible. But it was not long before Violet had extracted from her an account of the discussion that had resulted in Mitchel's unwilling presence. She was not very anxious to supply the information, but Violet was insistent and soon possessed herself of the full details of the argument which she seemed to find highly amusing.

"Oh, my dear, he's in love with me of course!" she said "I discovered that the first night I was with you. Hence his solicitude."

"I'm not so sure of that," said Olga.

"What! You haven't noticed it? My dear child, where are your eyes? Haven't you seen the way he watches me?"

Yes, Olga had seen it; but somehow she did not think it meant that. She said so rather hesitatingly.

"What else could it mean?" laughed Violet. "But you needn't be afraid, dear. I'm not going to have him. He's much too anatomical for me, too business-like and professional altogether. I'd sooner die than have him attend me."

"Would you?" said Olga. "But why? He's very clever."

"That's just it. He's too clever to have any imagination. He would be quite unscrupulous, quite merciless, and utterly without sympathy. Can't you picture him making you endure any amount of torture just to enable him to say he had cured you? Oh yes, he's diabolically clever, but he is cruel too. He would take the shortest cut, whatever it meant. He wouldn't care what agony he inflicted so long as he gained his end and made you live."

"I don't think he is quite so callous as that," Olga said, but even as she said it she wondered.

"You will if he ever has to doctor you," rejoined Violet. "I wonder what Mrs. Briggs thought of him. We'll find out to-day."

Mrs. Briggs was the daughter of the old woman who had died the preceding week at "The Ship Inn," whither they were bound that morning. She had nursed Violet in her infancy, and was a privileged acquaintance of both girls.

They found her busy pastry-making, for the business of the establishment had not been suspended during her recent troubles. She greeted them both hospitably, though not without a hint of reproach, which found expression in words when she had come to the end of a detailed account of the funeral.

"I thought you'd 'a' been round long ago," she said. "Your flowers was lovely, Miss Olga. You ought to 'a' seen 'em a-layin' on pore mother. I made sure as you'd want to. And you too, Miss Violet. I kept the coffin open till the very last minute, thinkin' as you'd come."

"That was very sweet of you, Mrs. Briggs," said Violet. "It was all Dr. Wyndham's fault that we didn't. I'm staying there, you know, and whatever he says is law. I'm sure I don't know why, but there it is."

"Well, there!" said Mrs. Briggs. "I might 'a' known. Pore mother was frit to death o' he. 'There's black magic in 'im' she says to me. It was the day as she was took, too. 'Black magic,' she says. 'I've a-begged 'im to let me die easy, but Lor' bless yer, 'e don't take no more notice than if 'e were the Spink,'" Mrs. Briggs glanced over her shoulder. "But there's one thing as you'll both be glad to know," she said, lowering her voice confidentially, "she died easy, pore soul, in spite of 'im. 'E don't know 'ow that was."

"What?" gasped both girls in a breath.

Mrs. Briggs went to the door, peered out, softly closed it. Her eyes shone craftily as she returned. She took up her rolling-pin, holding it impressively between her floury hands.

"Two days afore pore mother went," she began, with an air of gruesome mystery, "Dr. Wyndham, 'e came and examined 'er, and 'urt 'er cruel, 'e did. I thought 'e'd 'ave killed 'er afore 'e'd finished. Well, just afore 'e left, 'e come to me with a dark blue bottle, and 'e says: 'Look 'ere, Mrs. Briggs, she won't last out the week. She's quiet now,' 'e says, 'for I've given 'er a dose as'll last for some hours. But when that's exhausted,' 'e says, 'the pain'll come back. And so I'm goin' to give you this.' 'E 'olds it up to the light, and looks at it. 'It's good stuff,' 'e says. 'It's warranted to kill pain. But it ain't a thing to play with. You give 'er a teaspoon of it,' 'e says, 'but only if she's took with bad pain. But she mustn't 'ave more than one in twenty-four hours,' 'e says. 'You mind that. And if you 'ave to give it to 'er, you send at once for me. If you don't send,' 'e says, 'I won't be 'eld responsible for the consequences.' With that 'e goes, and pore mother she seemed to take a turn, and all that day and the next she seemed to drowse like and not take much notice o' things. The neighbours come in and look at 'er, but she didn't seem to know. We 'ad two quiet nights with 'er, and then all of a sudden in the middle of the afternoon she started screamin' and writhin'. Oh, lor, Miss Olga, you never see the like. It was just as if she were bein' tortured over a slow fire. Well, Briggs, 'e was fair unmanned by it. 'For 'eaven's sake,' 'e says, 'give 'er the medicine as the doctor left, and I'll go and tell 'im as you've done it.' And off 'e goes, though it was gettin' latish and no one to attend to the bar. Well, I fetched the medicine, and I took it to 'er, and I says, "Ere you are, mother,' I says, 'you 'ave a dose o' this. It'll kill the pain.' I gave it 'er in a teaspoon like 'e said, and she took it. But there, it didn't make no more difference to 'er than if it 'ad been water.'" Mrs. Briggs heaved a sob, and picked up a corner of her apron to wipe her eyes. "I told 'er as I dursn't give 'er any more because of what the doctor 'ad said, and I said as 'ow Briggs 'ad gone for him, and 'e'd know 'ow to quiet 'er when 'e came. But the very thought of 'im seemed to drive 'er crazy. And then she said that about the black magic, and 'ow 'e'd never be persuaded to let 'er die easy. And then she says to me. 'But you didn't shake the bottle,' she says. 'I expect the stuff that kills the pain is all at the bottom.' And I thought there might be somethin' in it, so I fetched the bottle again and shook it up. And I thought I'd give 'er just 'alf a dose more in case she 'adn't 'ad enough. But just as I was a-goin' to pour it out there was such a rappin' down in the bar, that I 'ad to just give it 'er and run. I was back in under a minute, and there was pore mother a-sittin' up in bed and a-smilin' at me as if all 'er troubles was past, and says she, 'Annie,' she says, 'I've 'ad enough and I don't want no more,' she says; 'it's killed the pain.' And then she laid down in bed still smilin', and says she, 'You tell the doctor when 'e comes as I'm sorry to 'a' fetched 'im for nothin', but I couldn't wait—.' And—if you'll believe me, Miss Olga,—those was the last words she spoke." Again vigorously Mrs. Briggs dried her eyes. "She just dropped off to sleep as easy as easy, and I left 'er and went back to the bar. There was a stick by the bedside, and I knew I should 'ear 'er knock if she wanted me. But she didn't knock, and she didn't knock, and I kept thinkin' to myself what a nice sleep she was 'avin', and I wouldn't disturb 'er till the doctor came. And then all of a sudden, it came into my mind to wonder about that there medicine. And I just run up to see. And there I found 'er a-laying' dead, and *the stuff in the bottle were 'alf-gone!*"

Mrs. Briggs's information was imparted in a whisper and punctuated by sniffs. Her two listeners exchanged awe-stricken glances.

"How did you know she was dead?" asked Violet. "What did she look like?"

"My dear," said Mrs. Briggs, with solemn pride, "anyone as 'as seen death as often as I 'ave don't need to look twice."

Mrs. Briggs occupied the exalted position of layer-out in chief in Brethaven village, and right proud was she of her calling. It had been handed down from mother to daughter in her family for the past four generations. She literally swelled with importance as she resumed her narrative and her pastry-rolling at the same moment.

"Well, there she lay, pore dear, and I saw as the Lord 'ad took 'er right enough, and 'er troubles was well over. But there was this 'ere medicine-bottle, and I 'ad to think pretty quick about that; for just as I picked it up I 'eard the doctor's motor come round the corner. It came to me all in a minute, it did, and I upped with the water-jug and filled it to all but a spoonful of the top. For I knew what 'is first thought would be," said Mrs. Briggs grimly. "And I wasn't minded to let myself in for any questions. Yer see, my dear, 'e'd told me 'isself as the pore creature couldn't last the week. Well, I stuck the bottle on the shelf, and went to meet 'im. 'She's gone, sir,' I says. He come right past me without a word and stoops over the bed. And then, sure enough, quite sharp and sudden says 'e, 'You give 'er the pain-killer?' 'Just as you told me, sir,' I says, and with that I showed 'im the bottle. 'E took it into 'is 'and, and 'e give me a very straight look, and says 'e, frowning, 'Well, she'll never want any more of that.' And 'e just took it straight downstairs and emptied the bottle into the sink."

"He knew!" exclaimed Olga involuntarily.

"Lor' bless yer, no!" Mrs. Briggs's tone held unquestioning conviction. "'E was frownin' to 'isself all the time, and I could see as 'e was pretty mad that 'e'd come too late. I weren't sorry myself," she asserted boldly. "For I'd 'oped against 'ope after 'is last visit that 'e'd never see pore mother again alive. I couldn't 'a' stood it! There, I just couldn't."

Quite unexpectedly Mrs. Briggs suddenly broke down and dropped into a chair. Violet sprang to comfort, while Olga took possession of the rolling-pin and continued the pastry-making with deft hands.

After an interval poor Mrs. Briggs managed to recover somewhat of the hard demeanour that usually characterized her. "I've no call to fret," she said. "And don't you go rubbin' my dirty face with your clean 'andkerchief, Miss Violet. I ain't fit for you to touch, my dear."

"I'm only trying to get off the flour," explained Violet. "But I'm afraid you'll have to wash it after all. It's all gone into paste."

"And there's Miss Olga a-makin' my tarts for me like a ministerin' angel," said Mrs. Briggs, with a watery smile. "It's a pity you couldn't 'a' seen 'er in 'er coffin; for it was a beautiful coffin. Briggs said it was as fine a one as 'e'd seen. Well, well! She's gone, pore soul. And now you young ladies must try some of my rhubarb wine."

She rose briskly, and went to a cupboard. "We drank some of it at the funeral," she said. "And everyone liked it—even Briggs. But I thought I'd save the rest for when you came. Miss Olga always likes my rhubarb wine."

The rhubarb wine proved at least a welcome distraction, and under its genial influence Mrs. Briggs's spirits rose. She was quite cheery by the time her two visitors took their leave. They left her waving farewell from her doorstep, the patches of paste still upon her ruddy countenance, but with no other traces of her recent distress visible.

"Rum old thing!" said Violet. "I want to go round to the Priory and see Cork and Pluto next. I like to drop in unexpectedly when Bruce is away, and make sure that they are treated properly."

"We haven't much time," observed Olga.

"Oh, nonsense! Make time! We're not slaves," said Violet imperiously.

And Olga turned in the direction of the Priory without further words. It always took less time to yield to her friend's behests than to argue against them.

CHAPTER VII
THE PUZZLE

The visit to the Priory occupied some time, as Olga had foreseen. There were some things that Violet wanted to fetch from her own room and this entailed a search, for her possessions were always in the wildest disorder. Olga waited for her in the hall, chafing at the delay, since she knew that the car would be required by Max early in the afternoon to take him on his rounds.

Mitchel remained outside in the hot sunshine, severe disapproval in every line of him. Olga felt decidedly out of patience with him. As if it were her fault!

She sat on the old oak chest that Violet gaily called her coffin, and stared at the gruesome east window, while her thoughts dwelt upon the story she had just heard from Mrs. Briggs's lips. Had Max really intended to place freedom within the old woman's reach? For some reason wholly inexplicable she longed to know. She recalled the words he had uttered that day in the library of Redlands, his half-cynical talk of "a free pass," his reference to himself as "gaoler." Was it possible that she had formed a wrong impression of him? And if in this matter, perhaps in others also. Perhaps after all she had mistaken his attitude towards Violet. Perhaps after all he was human enough to feel the strong attraction of the girl's beauty. Perhaps after all he was beginning to care. And if so, what then? She felt her face burn in the coolness. Somehow she did not want him to be hurt, to suffer as she knew that other men had been made to suffer by the gay inconsequence of her friend. Only a week ago she had desired his ignominious downfall. To-day she wanted to save him from it. She had a desperate longing to warn him that Violet's favour was a thing of nought, that her treatment of him had all been planned between them beforehand, that it was all a game.

She could not picture him at any woman's feet. Yet undoubtedly Violet was hard to resist; their intimacy had grown apace during the past few days. And Violet knew so well how to wield her power, when to scorn and when subtly to flatter. She had never yet received a check in her triumphant career, and she boasted openly of her conquests.

No, Olga was fain to admit it. All her own private aversion notwithstanding, she did not want this man added to the list of victims. Cynical and even overbearing though he might be, she no longer desired to see him humiliated. And her face glowed more and more hotly as she remembered that it was she who had set the trap.

She fully realized, however, that an appeal to Violet at this stage would be worse than futile. Violet was too set on her mischievous course to do other than laugh and pursue it with renewed zest for her capture. Of course there remained Nick, chosen adviser and confidant; but for some reason Olga shrank from discussing Max with him. She had an uneasy dread lest Nick's intelligence should leap ahead of her and disclose to her with disconcerting suddenness facts and possibilities with which she was quite unprepared to reckon. She visualized his grin of amused comprehension over the means she had devised for her own deliverance and the unpleasant quandary in which it had placed her. Nick's sense of humour was at times almost too keen. She smiled faintly to herself over this reflection. She could not deny that there were points in the situation which appealed even to her own.

Yet she was more ashamed than amused. The discovery that Max was human had somehow altered everything, and made her own conduct appear dastardly. She had acted maliciously albeit, in self-defence; but now that it seemed that her point might pierce his armour, she wanted to withdraw it. She shrank unspeakably from seeing him vanquished. It would have hurt her to find him at her own feet, but the bare thought of him at Violet's— Violet who had no mercy upon old or young, who would trample him underfoot without a pang and pass gaily on—that thought was unbearable.

Of course she might be wrong. It was still possible that her original conception of him might be the correct one. He had a passion for his profession, she knew. It was quite possible that this had inspired his taking that awful risk the night before, quite possible also that a hopeless case did not appeal to him and that he had not therefore greatly cared how soon or in what manner Mrs. Stubbs had passed out through the prison-door which it was his work to guard. She realized vaguely that this form of callousness was not so hideous as she had at first deemed it. She also began to realize that for a man who had seen suffering and death in many forms and who found himself finally powerless to alleviate the one or avert the other, the inevitable end could not possess the tragic significance which it possessed for others.

Either point of view of his character was possible. She did not know him well enough to decide to her own satisfaction which was actually the true one. But the fact remained that she had delivered him to Violet to be tormented, and that before he had given any sign of suffering she had repented the rash act. He might be capable of suffering or he might not; but she had a passionate desire to know him safe before the fire had begun to kindle.

Violet's return at length broke up her reflections. She awoke from her reverie with a start to exclaim upon the lateness of the hour. It was already close upon luncheon-time.

"We shall have to scorch," laughed Violet.

And scorch they did at a rate that made the sober Mitchel swear inarticulately almost throughout the journey. They met with no mishap, however, and finally reached Weir flushed, dishevelled, but exultant.

Max came from the direction of the surgery as they entered.

"Can I speak to you a moment?" he said to Olga and drew her into her father's little smoking-room at the side of the hall almost before the words were uttered.

Olga faced him with a racing heart, burningly reminiscent of the note she had left in his hat, the note she had asked him to ignore.

He must have seen her embarrassment, for his green eyes studied her without mercy; but when he spoke it was not upon the subject of her overture.

"Look here!" he said. "Hunt-Goring is here. Do you mind if I ask him to luncheon?"

The news was unexpected. Olga gave a sharp, involuntary start. "Major Hunt-Goring!" she stammered. "Why—what is he doing here?"

"He walked over with a broken thumb for me to mend," said Max, still grimly watching her. "It's some way back to The Warren, and he's a bit used up. I fancy your father would make him lunch here under the circumstances, but you must do as you think best. It's not my house."

The colour sank rapidly from Olga's face under his look. "Oh, Dr. Wyndham," she said breathlessly, "do you think we need?"

He frowned at her agitation. "Of course, we needn't," he said. "If you don't want him, he can go to 'The Swan.' He is in the surgery at the present moment. I must go back and see how he is getting on."

"Wait a moment!" Olga broke in rapidly. "I—I'm afraid you're right. Dad would certainly keep him. Oh, why isn't Nick here? He needn't have chosen to-day to break this thumb."

"Kismet!" said Max, with a cynical lift of the shoulders. "I gather you don't like the man?"

She shrank at the question: it was almost a shudder. "No!"

He turned to the door. "Well, pull yourself together. I daresay he won't eat you. And you'll have Miss Campion to protect you. She would be proof against a dozen monsters."

He cast her a glance with the words that made her aware of a certain not very abstruse meaning behind them. Olga's cheeks burned again. Did he know, then? Had he guessed why Violet was in the house? Was that the reason of his curious vigilance, his guarded acceptance of her favours? She was possessed by an almost overwhelming desire to know, and yet no words could she find in which to ask.

"Well?" said Max, pausing in the act of opening the door. "You were going to say—"

She raised her eyes with a conscious effort, and nerved herself to speak.

"Max," she said desperately, "please don't mind my asking! It isn't from idle curiosity. Do you like her?" She saw the rough red brows go up, and swiftly repented her temerity. "I only asked," she faltered, "because—"

"Well?" Max said again. "It would be interesting to know why you asked."

She compelled herself to answer him, or perhaps it was he who compelled. In any case, with her head bent, her answer came.

"I had been thinking that perhaps you were getting fond of her, and—and—I should be sorry if that happened, because I know she isn't in earnest. I know she is only playing with you."

The words ran out in a whisper. She dared not look at him. She could only watch with fascinated eyes the brown fingers that gripped the door-knob.

"She has told you that?" asked Max.

She quivered at the question. It was horribly difficult to answer. "I know it is so," she murmured.

She was thankful that he did not press her to be more explicit. He stood for a moment in silence; then: "Isn't it possible," he said in a very level tone, "for a woman to set out to catch a man and to end by being caught herself?"

"Not for Violet," said Olga.

"I wonder," said Max.

She looked up at him quickly, caught by something in his tone. His eyes, alert and green, looked straight into hers.

"Did you really think I was falling in love with her?" he said.

Olga hesitated.

"She thinks so?" he questioned.

"Yes." Against her will she answered. It was as if he wrung the word from her.

He smiled a grim smile. "Many thanks for your warning!" he said. "I take a deep interest in Miss Campion, as you seem to have divined. But the danger of my falling a victim to her charms is very remote. You need harbour no further anxieties on my account."

He opened the door as he spoke, and Olga passed out, uncertain whether to be glad or sorry that she had brought herself to speak.

She went upstairs to Violet and acquainted her with the fact of Major Hunt-Goring's presence and its cause.

"I do wish Nick had been here," she said in conclusion.

"He may elect to stay for ever so long. I don't know what we shall do with him."

Violet, however, was by no means dismayed by the prospect. "Oh, I enjoy Major Hunt-Goring," she said. "You leave him to me. I'll entertain him."

"Hateful man!" said Olga.

Whereat Violet laughed and pinched her cheek. "You know you like him!"

"I detest him!" said Olga quickly.

It was certainly with no excess of cordiality that a few minutes later she greeted her guest. He was standing in the hall with one arm in a sling when she and Violet descended the stairs, an immense man of about five-and-forty with a very decided military bearing and dark eyes of covert insolence.

Max was with him, and Olga experienced a very novel feeling of relief to see him there. She advanced and shook hands with extreme frigidity.

"I am sorry you have had an accident," she said.

"Very good of you," said Major Hunt-Goring, his eyes boldly passing her to rest upon Violet. "Managed to crack my thumb tinkering at my old motor. Dr. Wyndham tells me that you have been kind enough to ask me to lunch. How do you do, Miss Campion? Charmed to meet you! Someone told me you were yachting in the Atlantic."

"Heaven forbid!" said Violet. "Yachting is simply another word for imprisonment to me. I told Bruce I should certainly drown myself if I went with them."

"I should like to introduce you to a form of yachting that is not imprisonment," said Hunt-Goring.

Violet laughed. "Oh, I should have to be mistress of the yacht for that."

"Even so," he rejoined significantly.

"And I shouldn't have any men on board with the exception of the sailors," she went on.

"And the captain," said Hunt-Goring.

"Oh, dear me, no! I would be my own captain."

"You'd be horribly bored before the first week was out," observed the major, as he followed her into the dining-room.

She laughed gaily. "There isn't a single man of my acquaintance in whose company I shouldn't be bored to extinction long before that."

"Oh, come!" he protested. "You don't speak from experience. You condemn us untried."

"I know you all too well," laughed Violet.

"You know me not at all," declared Hunt-Goring. "I appeal to Miss Ratcliffe. Am I the sort of man to bore a woman?"

"I am no judge," said Olga somewhat hastily. "I never have time to be bored with anyone. Will you sit here, please? I am sorry to say my uncle is in town to-day."

"Where are the three boys?" asked Max.

Olga turned to him with relief. "They have gone for an all-day paper-chase with the Rectory crowd and taken lunch with them."

"Why didn't you go too?" he asked. "Too lazy?"

"Too busy," she returned briefly.

"That's only an excuse," said Max.

She glanced at him. "It's a sound one anyhow."

"What are you going to do this afternoon?" he asked.

"Mend."

"Mend what?"

"Stockings," said Olga.

"Great Scot!" said Max. "Do you mend the stockings of the entire family?"

"Including yours," said Olga.

"Oh, I say!" he protested. "That wasn't in the contract, was it? Pitch 'em into my room. I'll mend them myself or do without."

"One pair more or less doesn't make much difference," said Olga. "As to doing without,—well, of course, you're a man or you wouldn't make such a suggestion."

"You've thrown that in my teeth before," he observed. "I think you might remember that I am hardly responsible for my sex. It's my misfortune, not my fault."

She smiled, her sudden brief smile, but made no rejoinder.

Major Hunt-Goring and Violet, who had undertaken to cut up his meal for him, were engrossed in a frothy conversation which it was obvious that neither desired to have interrupted.

Max glanced towards them before he abruptly started another subject with Olga.

"How is Mrs. Briggs?"

Olga coloured hotly. "Oh, she seemed all right."

Max surveyed her rather pointedly. "Well? What had she got to say about me?"

"About you?" said Olga.

He laughed and looked away. "Even so, fair lady. I conclude it was something you would rather not repeat. I had already fathomed the fact that I was not beloved by Mrs. Briggs."

"It's your own fault," said Olga, speaking on the impulse to escape from a difficult subject. "You have such a knack of making all your patients afraid of you."

"Really?" said Max.

"Oh, don't be supercilious!" she said quickly. "You know it's true."

"It must be if you say so," he rejoined, "though there again it is more my misfortune than my fault. If my patients elect to make me the butt of their neurotic imagination, surely I am more to be pitied than blamed."

"No, I don't pity you at all," Olga said. "It's want of sympathy, you know. You go and do a splendid thing like—like—" She stopped suddenly.

"Please go on!" said Max. "Let's hear my good points, by all means!"

But Olga was in obvious confusion. "I didn't mean to mention it," she said. "It just slipped out. I was really thinking of—what happened last night."

He frowned instantly. "Who told you anything about it?"

"Nick."

"I should like to wring his skinny little neck," said Max.

"How dare you?" said Olga indignantly.

"You don't think I'm afraid of you, do you?" he said, with a smile.

"No," she admitted rather grudgingly. "I don't think you are afraid of anyone or anything. But it is a pity you spoil things by being so—unfriendly."

"Are you speaking on Mrs. Briggs's behalf or your own?" asked Max.

She met his eyes with a feeling of reluctance. "Well, I do hate quarrelling," she said.

"I never quarrel," said Max placidly.

"Oh, but you do!" she exclaimed. "How can you say such a thing?"

"No, I don't!" said Max. "I go my own way, that's all. If anyone tries to stop me, well, they get knocked down and trampled on. I don't call that quarrelling. It simply happens in the natural course of things."

"No wonder people don't like you!" said Olga.

"Don't you like me?" said Max.

He put the question with obvious indifference, yet his green eyes still studied her critically. Olga poured out some water with a hand so shaky that it splashed over. He reached forward and dabbed it up with his table-napkin.

"Well?" he said.

"I don't know," she murmured somewhat incoherently.

"Don't know! But you knew this morning!" The green eyes suddenly laughed at her. "I say, don't try to drink that yet!" he said. "You'll choke if you do. Go on! Tell me some more about Mrs. Briggs! Did she give you any of that filthy concoction she calls rhubarb wine?"

"It isn't filthy! It's delicious," declared Olga. "You can't have tasted it."

"Oh, yes, I had some the day the old woman died. In fact, I was trying to sleep off the effects that afternoon, when you caught me in Uncle Nick's library. It's horribly strong stuff. I suppose that is what made you so late for luncheon?"

"Indeed, it wasn't! We went to the Priory before coming home."

"Oh! What for?"

"Some things Violet wanted."

"What things?" said Max.

She looked at him in surprise. "I'm sure I don't know. I'm not so inquisitive as you are. You had better ask Violet."

"Ask me what?" said Violet, detaching her attention from Major Hunt-Goring for a moment.

"Nothing," said Max. "I was only wondering how many glasses of rhubarb wine you had at 'The Ship.'"

Carelessly he rallied her on the subject, carelessly let it pass. And Olga was left with a newly-awakened doubt at her heart. What was the reason for the keen interest he took in her friend? Had he really told her the truth when repudiating the possibility of his falling in love with her? She fancied he had; and if so, why was he so anxious to inform himself of her most trivial doings? It was a puzzle to Olga—a puzzle that for some reason gave her considerable uneasiness. Against her will and very deep down within her, she was aware of a lurking distrust that made her afraid of Max Wyndham. She felt as if he were watching to catch her off her guard, ready at a moment's notice to turn to his own purposes any rash confidence into which she might be betrayed. And she told herself with passionate self-reproach that she had already been guilty of disloyalty to her friend.

During the rest of luncheon she exerted herself to keep the conversation general, Max seconding her efforts as though unconscious of her desire to avoid him. In fact, he seemed wholly unaware of any change in her demeanour, and Olga noted the fact with relief, the while she determined to exclude him rigidly for the future from anything even remotely approaching to intimacy. Watch as they might, the shrewd green eyes should never again catch her off her guard.

CHAPTER VIII
THE ELASTIC BOND

Major Hunt-Goring was quite obviously in his element. To Olga's dismay he showed no disposition to depart when they rose from the luncheon-table. Violet suggested a move to the garden, and he fell in with the proposal with a readiness that plainly showed that he had every intention of inflicting his company upon them for some time longer.

"It's confoundedly lonely up at The Warren," he remarked pathetically, as he lounged after her into the sunshine.

Violet laughed over her shoulder, an unlighted cigarette between her teeth. "You're hardly ever there."

"No. Well, it's a fact. I can't stand it. I'm a sociable sort of chap, you know. I like society."

"Why don't you marry?" laughed Violet.

"That's a question to which I can find no answer," he declared. "Why—why, indeed!"

"Hateful man!" murmured Olga, looking after them. "How I wish he would go!"

"Leave them alone for a spell," advised Max. "Go and mend your stockings in peace! Miss Campion is quite equal to entertaining him unassisted."

But Olga hesitated to pursue this course, and finally collected her work and followed her two guests into the garden.

Max departed upon his rounds, and a very unpleasant sense of responsibility descended upon her.

She took up a central position under the lime-trees that bordered the tennis-court, but Major Hunt-Goring and Violet did not join her. They sauntered about the garden-paths just out of earshot, and several times it seemed to Olga that they were talking confidentially together. She wondered impatiently how Violet could endure the man at such close quarters. But then there were many things that Violet liked that she found quite unbearable.

Slowly the afternoon wore away. The young hostess still sat under the limes, severely darning, but Violet and her companion had disappeared unobtrusively into a more secluded part of the garden. For nearly half an hour she had heard no sound of voices. She wondered if she ought to go in search of them, but her pile of work was still somewhat formidable and she was both to leave it. She continued to darn therefore with unflagging energy, till suddenly a hand touched her shoulder and a man's voice spoke softly in her ear.

"Hullo, little one! All alone? What has become of the fiery-headed assistant?"

She flung his hand away with a violent gesture. So engrossed had she been with getting through her work that she had not heard his step upon the grass.

"Are you just off?" she asked him frigidly. "Will you have anything before you go?"

Hunt-Goring laughed—a soft, unpleasant laugh. "Many thanks!" he said. "I was just asking myself that question. Generous of you to suggest it though. Perhaps you—like myself—are feeling bored."

He lowered himself on to the grassy bank beside her chair, smiling up at her with easy insolence. Olga did not look at him. Handsome though he undoubtedly was, he was the one man of her acquaintance whose eyes she shrank from meeting. His very proximity sent a shiver of disgust through her. She made a covert movement to edge her chair away.

"Where is Miss Campion?" she said.

He laughed again, that hateful confidential laugh of his. "She has gone indoors to rest. The heat made her sleepy. I suggested the hammock, but she wouldn't run the risk of being caught napping. I see that there is small danger of that with you."

Olga stiffened. She was putting together her work with evident determination. "I will see you off," she said.

"You seem in a mighty hurry to get rid of me," he said, without moving.

She laid her mending upon the grass and rose. "I am busy—as you see," she returned.

He looked at her for a moment, then very deliberately followed her example. He stood looking down at her from his great height, a speculative smile on his face.

"You've soon had enough of me, what?" he suggested.

Olga's pale eyes gleamed for an instant like steel suddenly bared to the sun. She said nothing whatever, merely stood before him very stiff and straight, plainly waiting for him to go.

"It's a pity to outstay one's welcome," he said. "I wouldn't do that for the world. But what about that kiss you offered me just now?"

"I?" said Olga, quivering disdain in the word.

"You, my little spitfire!" he said genially. "And it won't be the first time, what? Come now! You're always running away, but you should reflect that you're bound to be caught sooner or later. You didn't think I was going to let you off, did you?"

She stood before him speechless, with clenched hands.

He drew a little nearer. "You pay your debts, don't you? And what more suitable opportunity than the present? You are so elusive nowadays. Why, I haven't seen you except from afar since last Christmas. You were always such a nice, sociable little girl till then."

"Sociable!" whispered Olga.

"Well, you were!" He laughed again in his easy fashion. "Don't you remember what fun we had at the Rectory on Christmas Eve, and how you came to tea with me on the sly a few days after, and how we kissed under the mistletoe, and how you promised—"

"I promised nothing!" burst out Olga, with flashing eyes.

"Oh, pardon me! You promised to kiss me again some day. Have you forgotten? I hardly think your memory is as short as that."

He drew nearer still, and slipped a cajoling arm about her. "Why are we in such a towering rage, I wonder? Surely you don't want to repudiate your liabilities! You promised, you know."

She flung up a desperate face to his. "Very well, Major Hunt-Goring," she said breathlessly. "Take it—and go!"

He bent to her. "But you must give," he said.

"Very well," she said again. "It—it will be the last!"

"Will it?" he questioned, pausing. "In that case, I feel almost inclined to postpone the pleasure, particularly as—"

"Don't torture me!" she said in a whisper half—choked.

Her eyes were tightly shut; but Hunt-Goring's were looking over her head, and a sudden gleam of malicious humour shone in them. He turned them upon the white, shrinking face of the girl who stood rigid but unresisting within the circle of his arm. And then very suddenly he bent and kissed her on the lips.

She shivered through and through and broke from him with her hands over her face.

"But you didn't pay your debt, you know," said Hunt-Goring amiably. "I won't trouble you now, however, as we are no longer alone. Another day—in a more secluded spot—"

No longer alone! Olga looked up with a gasp. Her face was no longer pale, but flaming red. She seemed to be burning from head to foot.

And there, not a dozen paces from her, was Maxwell Wyndham, carelessly approaching, his hands in his pockets, his hat thrust to the back of his head, a faint, supercilious smile cocking one corner of his mouth, his whole bearing one of elaborate unconsciousness.

This much Olga saw; but she did not wait for more. The situation was beyond her. An involuntary exclamation of dismay escaped her, an inarticulate sound that seemed physically wrung from her; and then, without a second glance, ignominiously she turned and fled.

The sound of Hunt-Goring's oily laugh followed her as she went, and added speed to her flying feet.

It was several minutes later that Max entered the surgery, carrying an armful of stockings, and found her scrubbing her face vigorously over the basin that was kept there. She had turned on the hot water, and a cloud of steam arose above her head.

"Don't scald yourself!" said Max. "Try the pumice!"

"Oh, go away!" gasped Olga, with a furious stamp.

"Not going," said Max.

He fetched out a clean towel, and placed it within her reach. Then he sat down on the table and waited, whistling below his breath.

Olga grabbed the towel at last and buried her face in it. "Do you want to make me—hate you?" She flung at him through its folds.

"Don't be silly!" said Max.

"I'm not!" she cried stormily. "I'm not! It's you who—who make bad worse—always!"

He stood up abruptly. "No, I don't. I help—when I can. Sit down, and stop crying!"

"I'm not crying!" she sobbed.

"Then take that towel off your face, and behave sensibly. I'll make you drink some *sal volatile* if you don't."

"I'm sure you won't. I—I—I'm not a bit afraid of you!" came in muffled tones of distress from the crumpled towel.

"All right. Who said you were?" said Max. "Sit down now! Here's a chair. Now—let me have the towel! Yes, really, Olga!" He loosened her hold upon it, and drew it away from her with steady insistence. "There, that's better. You look as if you'd got scarlet fever. What did you want to boil yourself like that for? Now, don't cry! It's futile and quite unnecessary. Just sit quiet till you feel better! There's no one about but me, and I don't count."

He turned to the pile of stockings he had brought in with him, and began to sort them into pairs.

"By Jove! You're in the middle of one of mine," he said. "I'll finish this."

He thrust his hand into it and prepared to darn.

"Oh, don't!" said Olga. "You—you will only make a mess of it."

He waved his hand with airy assurance.

"I never make a mess of anything, and I'm a lot cleverer than you think. What train is Nick coming home by?"

"I don't know. The five-twenty probably."

He glanced at the clock. "Half an hour from now. And where is the fair Violet?"

"I don't know. He said she had gone in. I suppose I ought to go and see."

"Sit still!" said Max, frowning over his darning. "She is probably reading some obscene novel, and won't be wanting you."

"Max!"

"I apologize," said Max.

Olga smiled faintly. "It's horrid of you to talk like that."

"It's me," said Max.

She dried the last of her tears. "What—what did you do with him?"

"Packed him into the motor and told Mitchel to drive him home."

"I wish Mitchel would run into something and kill him!" said Olga, with sudden vehemence.

Max's brows went up. "Afraid I didn't give Mitchel instructions to that effect."

He spoke without raising his eyes, being quite obviously intent upon his darning. Olga watched him for a few seconds in silence. Finally she gave herself a slight shake and rose.

"You're doing that on the right side," she said.

"It's the best way to approach this kind of hole," said Max.

She came and stood by his side, still closely watching him.

"Dr. Wyndham!" she said at last, her voice very low.

"Please don't make me nervous!" said Max.

"Don't, please!" she said. "I want to speak to you seriously."

He drew out his needle with a reflective air. "Are you going to ask me to prescribe for you?"

"No."

"Then don't call me 'Dr. Wyndham'!" he said severely. "I don't answer to it, except in business hours."

She smiled faintly. "Max, then! Will you do me a favour?"

Max's eyes found hers with disconcerting suddenness. "On one condition," he said.

"What is it?"

The corner of his mouth went up. "I will name my condition when you have named your favour."

She hesitated momentarily. "Oh, it isn't very much," she said. "I only want you not to tell—Nick, or anyone—about—about what happened this afternoon."

"Why isn't Nick to know?" asked Max.

"He would be so angry," she said, "and he couldn't do any good. He would only go and get himself hurt."

"Would you care to know what Hunt-Goring said to me after you had effected a retreat?" asked Max.

The hot colour began to fade out of her cheeks. "Yes," she said, under her breath.

"He said—you know his breezy style: 'Don't be astonished! Miss Ratcliffe and I understand one another. In fact, we've been more or less engaged for a long time, though it isn't generally known.'"

"Max!" Olga started back as if from a blow. "He never said—that!"

"Yes, he did. I guessed it was a lie," said Max, "in spite of appearances."

She winced. "It is a lie!" she said with vehemence. "You—you told him so?"

"I was not in a position to do that," said Max. "But if you authorize me to do so—"

"Yes—yes?" she said feverishly.

"I can only do it if you accept my condition," he said.

"That means you want me to tell you everything," she said.

"No, it doesn't. I know quite as much as I need to know, and I shan't believe anything he may be pleased to say on the subject. It's up to you to tell me as much or as little as you like. No, the condition is this, and there is nothing in it that you need jib at. If you really want me to give him the lie, you must furnish me with full authority. You must put me in a position to do it effectually."

He was looking straight into her face of agitation. There was a certain remorselessness about him that made him in a fashion imposing. Olga quivered a little under the insistence of his eyes, but she flinched no more.

"Yes?" she said. "Well, I do authorize you. It's got to be stopped somehow. I never dreamed of his saying that."

"Quite so," said Max. "But that isn't enough. You will have to go a step further. Give me a free hand! It's the only way if you don't want Nick rushing in. Give me the right to protect you! I promise to use it with discretion."

He smiled very slightly with the words; but Olga only gazed at him uncomprehendingly.

"How? I don't know what you mean."

He held out his hand to her abruptly. "Don't faint!" he said. "Let me tell him—as a dead secret—that you are engaged to me!"

Olga gasped.

Max got up. "Only as a temporary expedient," he said. "I'll let you go again—when you wish it."

His hand remained outstretched, and after a very considerable pause she laid hers within it.

"But really," she said, with an effort, "I don't think we need do anything so desperate as that."

"A desperate case requires a desperate remedy sometimes," said Max, with a humorous twinkle in his eyes "It doesn't mean anything, but we must floor this rascal somehow. Is it a bargain?"

She hesitated. "You won't tell anyone else?"

"Not a soul," said Max.

She still hesitated. "But—he won't believe you."

"He will if I refer him to you," said Max.

Olga pondered the matter. "Are you sure it's the only way?"

"If you don't want Nick to know," he said.

"And what if he—spreads it abroad?" she hazarded.

"We can always treat it as idle gossip, you know," said Max. "Imminent but not actual—the sort of thing over which we blush demurely and say nothing."

She smiled in spite of herself. "It's very good of you," she said with feeling.

"Not a bit," said Max. "I shall enjoy it. I think it ought to put an effectual stop to all unwelcome amenities on his part. We'll try it anyhow."

He released her hand, and resumed his darning, still looking quizzical.

Olga lingered, dubiously reminding herself that only a few hours before she had distrusted this man whom circumstance now made her champion.

"Scissors, please!" said Max.

She gave them to him absently. He held out the unsevered wool, his eyes laughing at her over it.

"You can do the cutting," he said.

She complied, and in the same instant she met his look. "Max," she said rather breathlessly, "I—don't quite like it."

"All right," he said imperturbably. "Don't do it!"

She paused, looking at him almost imploringly. "You're sure it won't mean anything?"

"It can mean as much or as little as you like," said Max.

"I didn't mean—quite that," faltered Olga. "But—it won't be—it never could be—like a real engagement; could it?"

"Like, yet unlike," said Max. "It will be a sort of elastic and invisible bond, made to stretch to the utmost limit, never breaking of itself, though capable of being severed by either party at a moment's notice."

Olga drew a breath of relief. "If that is really all—"

"What more could the most exacting require?" said Max.

What indeed! Yet the phrase struck Olga somehow as being not wholly satisfactory. Perhaps even then, vaguely she began to realize that the species of bond he described might prove the most inviolable of all. But she raised no further argument, doubts notwithstanding; for, in face of his assurance, there seemed nothing left to say.

CHAPTER IX
THE PROJECT

The sound of Nick's cheery, untuneful humming seemed to invest all things with a more normal and wholesome aspect. Olga went to meet him with unfeigned delight.

He put his arm around her, flashing a swift look over her as he did it. "Well, Olga *mia*. I trust there has been no more bickering in my absence."

"No, I've made friends with Max," she said. "Come and have tea!"

He went through the house with her to the garden where tea awaited him. Max was seated alone beside the little table under the trees.

"You're not a very large party," commented Nick.

"Best we can do under the circumstances," said Max. "The kids are still paper-chasing, and Miss Campion, overcome by the heat, has retired to bed. I propose to follow her example if the company will excuse me. I only put in two hours last night, and may have to attend another case to-night. Here, Ratcliffe, you can have my chair."

"Are you coming down to dinner?" asked Olga.

"I am," he said.

"Because you needn't. I can send it up."

"Thanks! I'll come down," said Max.

He turned away towards the house, but stopped abruptly as Violet suddenly sauntered forth. She was yawning as she came.

"Good people, pray excuse me! I'm always sleepy after a motor-run. What has become of the dear major, Allegro? You haven't banished him already!"

"Did you think he was going to live here?" said Olga, with a very unwonted touch of asperity.

"I expect he will, dear, now he knows I'm here." Violet subsided into the vacant chair with a languid smile at Nick who offered it to her. Her eyes were wonderfully bright, but the lids were heavy. "I'm horribly sleepy still," she said. "Give me some tea, quick, to wake me up! Max, I haven't the energy to amuse you, so you may consider yourself excused."

"Many thanks!" said Max. "I am going to give myself the pleasure of waiting upon you."

"Nick can do that," said Olga. "Do go and get a rest!"

213

"My dear, if you show yourself so anxious to be rid of him, he'll stay," protested Violet. "Haven't you discovered that yet? You should display an elegant indifference, a pray-stay-if-you've-a-mind-to-but-don't- imagine-that-I-want-you kind of attitude. There are not many men who can face that for long." She broke off to yawn. "No, thanks. Nothing to eat. I'm too sleepy. Well, Nick, have you settled the affairs of the nation satisfactorily?"

"On the contrary. The nation is trying to settle mine," said Nick.

"Oh, really! What more could anyone want you to do?"

"I'm specially qualified for many things, it seems," said Nick modestly. "What has Hunt-Goring been here for?"

"Managed to break his thumb," said Max.

"Yes, and stayed philandering all the afternoon," chimed in Violet. "How did you manage to get rid of him, Allegro? He wouldn't go for me."

"Dr. Wyndham came back early and sent him home in the car," said Olga, with a slight effort.

"I was bored to death with him," declared Violet. "I simply deserted him at last because I couldn't keep my eyes open. Give me my *tea strong, please,* or I shall fall *asleep again* under your eyes."

"Do you mind if I smoke?" said Max.

"Not in the least; quite delighted."

He offered her his cigarette-case. "P'raps you'll join me."

"No, thanks. I've been smoking all the afternoon." She stretched up her arms behind her head; they were bare to the elbow, soft and white and rounded. Her eyelids began to droop a little more. She snuggled down into the chair, plainly on the verge of slumber.

And in that moment Olga looked at Max. He was intently watching the girl, so intently that he was oblivious of everything else; and into her mind, all-unbidden, there flashed again the memory of the green dragon-fly—the monster of the stream—darting upon the little scarlet moth. It sent a curious revulsion of feeling through her. For the moment she felt physically sick.

Then impetuously, desperately, she intervened, "Violet, dear, wake up and have your tea! It's this horrid thundery weather that is affecting you. I've felt it myself. Max, you won't get much of a rest if you don't go soon."

Instantly his eyes were turned upon her, and she was conscious of the sudden quickening of her heart; for she saw at a glance that he resented her interference.

"Go on, Max!" grinned Nick. "Why can't you take a graceful hint, man? There may be another luckless little brat wanting you to-night."

"One thing at a time," said Max curtly.

He took out a cigarette and lighted it, a frown between his shaggy brows. He looked neither at Violet nor Olga but his attitude was one of stubborn determination.

"Are you waiting to see me drink my tea?" asked Violet, rousing herself in response to Olga's hand on her arm.

"I am," he said.

"Oh, well, that's soon done," she said, and raised the cup to her lips.

Max smoked on, taciturn and frowning. Violet finished her tea, and asked for more. He finished his cigarette and turned to her.

"I wonder if you would let me try one of yours."

"Not now, I'm afraid," she made answer. "I left my case upstairs."

He lighted another of his own and rose.

"Good-night!" said Nick.

"I shall be down to dinner," Max responded gruffly, and sauntered away.

"Ill-tempered cuss!" said Nick. "What's the matter with him?"

"He's jealous," said Violet.

"Of whom?" Nick was frankly curious.

"Of Major Hunt-Goring. He's been dangling after me half the afternoon. How would you like me to marry him, Allegro?"

"Who?" said Olga, turning crimson.

214

"Oh, not Max, you may be sure!" Her friend laughed mischievously. "Max is only an interlude."

"And Hunt-Goring the main theme?" suggested Nick.

She laughed again indifferently. "Perhaps, I can't say I'm enamoured of him, though. He's rather a brute at heart, underneath the oil-silk. Well, I'm going to lie in the hammock and sleep."

She got up, stretched luxuriously, and strolled away over the grass.

Nick watched her go with flickering, observant eyes; but he made no comment upon her. Only as she passed from sight, he made an odd little grimace as if dismissing a slightly distasteful subject from his mind. Then he turned to his niece.

"Well, my chicken, you've had a busy afternoon."

"A beastly afternoon, Nick!" she responded warmly. "And I'm very glad it's over, and I don't want to talk about it. Tell me about your doings instead! What were you wanted for?"

"Prepare for a shock!" said Nick. "I haven't got over it myself yet. They want to pack me off to India again. I told 'em I couldn't go, but they seem to take it for granted that I shall. Don't know what Muriel will say to it, I'm sure. They say it would be only a six months' job, but I have my doubts of that."

"Nick! India!"

"India, my child—naked and unadulterated India! The Imperial Commissioners have quite decided that I'm the man for the job. I kept on saying 'Can't!' and 'Won't!' But that didn't make the least difference. Old Reggie Bassett's doing, I'll lay a wager. He will have it that my genius is thrown away in England. And they inform me rather brutally that my seat in Parliament would be far more easily filled than this Sharapura post. Also the young Rajah has done me the honour to ask for me. We went pig-sticking together once—years ago, and I chanced to head off Piggie at a critical moment for young Akbar. On the strength of that, he wants me to go and be his political adviser for a few months. It seems the State is in rather a muddle. His father was a shocking old shuffler, and there are plenty of *budmashes* about, if report says true. But this young Rajah is anxious to get things straightened out, and the Commissioner wants a report made and so on. Altogether," Nick paused with a smile on his yellow face, "they were very persuasive," he said.

"Nick! You're going!" Olga exclaimed.

He laughed. "If you want my impartial opinion as to that," he said, "I believe I am."

She drew a deep breath. Her eyes were shining. "Oh, how I wish I were a man! I'd come with you."

"Ladies are admitted," said Nick.

"Ah! I wonder what Muriel will say," she said. "Does she like India?"

"India is a large place," he pointed out. "She doesn't like Ghawalkhand, and she isn't keen on Simla—which is sheer prejudice on her part. Sharapura she has never seen. It's a small State in the very middle of the Empire. There are rivers and jungles and tigers and snakes—quite a lot of snakes; a decent little capital and a hill-station, healthy enough though not very high. The natives are exactly like monkeys. I learnt to speak their lingo one winter from a villainous bearer I had when some of us were stationed there. There is a small native garrison in cantonments at the capital. There is also a fort and a race-course. I won the Great Mogul's Cup there—a memorable occasion. My mount was a wall-eyed lanky brute of a Waler, with the action of a camel. But he had the spirit of an Olympian, and we won at a canter."

Nick stopped. His eyes also had begun to shine. Olga was listening enraptured.

"How I wish I was Muriel!" she said. "Of course she'll want to go, Nick. It sounds perfectly enchanting."

"Especially the tigers and snakes," laughed Nick. "Poor Muriel! It's rather a shame to ask her. She had an overdose of the East at the outset, and she has never got over it."

"Oh, but that's æons ago!" protested Olga.

"I know; but it went deep." Nick leaned back abruptly, with closed eyes. "I wonder if I can bring myself to refuse finally and conclusively—without telling her," he said ruminatively.

"Never, Nick!" Olga sprang from her chair. "You shan't think of such a thing! Nick! A heaven-sent chance like that! Oh, it wouldn't be fair. I'm sure she would say so. You must—you must tell her!"

Nick's hand clenched upon the arm of his chair. He kept his eyes shut. "You see, dear," he said, "there's the kiddie too. I'm an unnatural beast. I'd actually forgotten him for the moment. One-eyed of me, wasn't it?"

"Nick—darling!" Suddenly Olga was kneeling beside his chair; she put her arms about his neck. "You shan't call yourself anything so horrid!" she said. "Dad and I will take care of little Reggie. You know you can trust him to me, Nick. I'll watch over him day and night."

"Bless your heart!" said Nick. He lodged his head against her shoulder after the fashion she most loved. "You're a sweet little pal," he said. "But I doubt if Muriel would consent to go so far away from him, and I'm a selfish hound myself to contemplate such a thing. No; don't contradict me! It's rude. I'm that, and several other things besides. I'd no idea I was so much in the grip of the East. It's a curious thing. One feels it in the blood. It's six years—more—since I climbed on to the shelf, and I've been quite smug and self-satisfied most of the time. There's been a twinge of regret every now and then, but nothing I couldn't whistle away. But now—" his words quickened; he spoke them whimsically, yet passionately, in her ear—"between you and me, I'd give an eye, an ear, or a leg—anything I possess in duplicate—to come off the shelf, and have one more fling. I'm stiff! I'm stiff! And, ye gods, I'm only four-and-thirty! I always thought I'd go till sixty at least. I entered Parliament just to keep going; but that's only a steady progress downhill—a sort of frog's march in which you kick and are kicked, but don't do much besides. I'm a fighter, kiddie. I wasn't made to ornament the shelf. I'm not a hero; only an ordinary, restless, discontented mortal. They told me this afternoon that it was time I did something, that I was dropping out, that I should ossify if I sat still much longer. (A good term that; worthy of our friend Max!) And, by Heaven, they're right! But how can I help it? I know in my heart of hearts that it would be sheer brutality to spring this on Muriel now."

He ceased to speak, and there fell a silence. Olga's arms clasped him very tightly. Her cheek pressed his forehead. It was not often that Nick opened his heart to her thus. Only twice before had it ever happened, and on each occasion he had been in trouble—once when the woman he loved had sent back his engagement ring through her, and once again nearly two years later when that same woman—Muriel, his wife—had lain at death's door all through one dreadful night while they two, close pals, had waited huddled together in the passage outside her room. Those two occasions were sacred to Olga, never spoken of to any, shrined deep in the most inner, most secret recesses of her heart. Nick's confidence had ever been her most cherished possession. It thrilled her now with something more than pride; and through her silence her sympathy came out to him in a flood of understanding which needed no verbal expression.

She spoke at last very softly, almost in a whisper. "Nick, you know, don't you, that you are dearer to me than anyone else in the world?"

He put up his hand and patted her cheek. "What! Still?" he said.

"Still, Nick? What do you mean?"

"Nothing at all," said Nick promptly. "Go on!"

She took his hand and held it. "Nick darling, do you remember how I came and kept house for you—years ago, at Redlands, when I was a child?"

"Rather!" said Nick. "Bully, wasn't it?"

She hesitated a little. "Nick, I'm going to make a perfectly awful suggestion."

"Don't mind me!" said Nick.

She laughed faintly. "I don't, dear,—formidable as you can be. It only flashed into my mind that if Muriel feels she really can't leave Reggie, and if she can possibly bear to part with you and you with her, could you possibly put up with me as a substitute for those few months and take me instead, if Dad could spare me?"

"By Jove!" said Nick, sitting up.

"I know it's great cheek of me to suggest it," Olga hastened to say. "For of course I know I'd be a very poor substitute; but at least I could keep a motherly eye on you, and see that you were properly clothed and fed. And Muriel herself couldn't possibly love you more."

"By Jove!" Nick said again. Olga's face flushed and eager was close to his. He bent suddenly forward and kissed it. "And what about you, my chicken?" he said.

"I, Nick? I should love it!" she said, with candid eyes raised to his. "You can't imagine how much I should love it."

"You'd be homesick," said Nick.

"Nick! With you!"

He was looking at her with shrewd, flickering eyes. "Do you mean to say," he said, "that there is no one here that you would mind leaving for so long?"

"There's Dad of course," she said. "But—don't you think perhaps Muriel wouldn't mind taking care of him for me if I took care of you for her?"

Nick broke into a laugh. "Excellent, my child! Most ingenious! Jim and Muriel are fast allies. But—Jim is not the only person you would leave behind. You ought to consider that before you get too obsessed by this enchanting idea. It's pretty beastly, you know, to feel that half the world stretches between you and—someone you might at any moment develop a pressing desire to see."

Olga frowned at him. "What are you driving at, Nick?"

"I'm only indicating the obvious," said Nick.

"No, you're not, dear. You're hinting things."

"In that case," said Nick, "you are at liberty to treat me with the contempt I deserve. Look here! We won't talk about this any more to-day. The subject is too indigestible. We'll sleep on it, and see what we think of it to-morrow."

"You're not going to write to Muriel to-night?" asked Olga.

"Not to-night. They've given me a week to make up my mind."

"And when would you have to go?"

"Some time towards the end of next month, or possibly the beginning of October. But as we're not going," said Nick, "I move that the discussion be postponed."

He smiled into her eyes, a baffling, humorous smile, and rose.

"But it was a ripping idea of yours," he said. "I'm quite grateful to you for mentioning it. There are some chocolates in the hall for you. Don't give them all to Violet, charm she never so wisely."

"Oh, Nick, you darling! Fancy your remembering me! Do let's have some at once!"

They went indoors together with something of the air of conspirators, and in the close companionship of her hero Olga managed to forget that she had so recently been driven to another man for protection. In fact, the interview in the surgery, with the episode that had preceded it, was completely crowded out of her mind by this new and dazzling idea that had flashed so suddenly into her brain, and which seemed already to have altered the course of her life.

Many and startling were the visions that filled her sleeping hours that night but each one of them served but to impress upon her the same thing. When she arose in the morning she told herself with a little shiver of sheer excitement that the gates of the world were opening to her, and that soon she would actually behold those wonders of which till then she had only dreamed.

CHAPTER X
THE DOOR

When remembrance of the previous day's happenings came to Olga, she was already so deeply engrossed in household duties that she was able to dismiss the matter without much difficulty. It was one of the busiest mornings of the week, and no sooner had she finished indoors than she donned a sun-bonnet and big apron and betook herself to the raspberry-bed to gather fruit for jam.

The day was hot, and Violet had established herself in the hammock under the lime-trees with a book and a box of cigarettes. The three boys had gone with Nick on a fishing expedition, and all was supremely quiet.

The sun blazed mercilessly down upon Olga as she toiled, but she would not be discouraged. The raspberries were many and ready to drop with ripeness, and the jam-making could not be deferred. So intent was she that she really almost forgot the physical discomfort in her anxiety to accomplish her task. She had meant to do it in the cool of the previous evening, but her talk with Nick had driven the matter absolutely from her mind.

So she laboured in the full heat of a burning August day, till her head began to throb and her muscles to ache so unbearably that it was no longer possible to ignore them. It was at the commencement of the last row but one (they were very long rows) that she became aware that her energies were seriously flagging. The rest of the garden seemed to be swimming in a haze around her, but she stubbornly ignored that, and bent again to her work, fixing her attention once more with all her resolution upon the great rose-red berries that were waiting to be gathered. She must finish now. She had promised herself to clear the bed by luncheon-time. But it was certainly very hard labour, harder than she had ever found it before. She began to feel as if her limbs were weighted, and the fruit itself danced giddily before her aching eyes.

Suddenly she heard a step on the ash-path near her. She looked up, half-turning as she did so. The next instant it was as if a knife had suddenly pierced her temples. She cried out sharply with the pain of it, staggered, clutched wildly at emptiness, and fell. The contents of her basket scattered around her in spite of her desperate efforts to save them, and this disaster was to Olga the climax of all. She went into a brief darkness in bitterness of spirit.

Not wholly did she lose consciousness, however, for she knew whose arms lifted her, and even very feebly tried to push them away. In the end she found herself sitting on an old wooden bench in the shade of the garden-wall, with her head against Max's shoulder, and his hand, very vital and full of purpose, grasping her wrist.

"Oh, Max," she said, with a painful gasp, "my raspberries!"

"Damn the raspberries!" growled Max. His hand travelled up to her head and removed the sun-bonnet while he was speaking. "Don't move till you feel better!" he said. "There's nothing to bother about."

He pressed her temples with a sure, cool touch. She closed her eyes under it.

"But I must get on," she said uneasily. "I want to make the jam this afternoon."

"Do you?" said Max grimly.

She was silent for a little. He kept his hand upon her head, and she was glad of its support though she wished it had not been his.

"It must be nearly luncheon-time," she said at last, with an effort.

"It is," said Max. "We will go indoors."

"Oh, but I must pick up my raspberries first, and—there's a whole row—more—to gather yet."

"You will have to leave that job for someone else," he said. "You are not fit for it. Are you quite mad, I wonder?"

"It had to be done," said Olga. "I must finish now—really I must finish." She took his hand from her head and slowly raised it. Instantly that agonizing pain shot through her temples again. She barely suppressed a cry.

"What is it?" he said.

"My head!" she gasped. "And oh, Max, I do feel so sick."

He stood up. "Come along!" he said. "I'm going to carry you in."

She raised a feeble protest to which he paid no more attention than if it had been the buzzing of a fly. Very steadily and strongly he lifted her.

"Put your head on my shoulder!" he said, and she obeyed him like a child.

They encountered no one on the way back to the house. Straight in and straight upstairs went Max, finally depositing her upon her bed. He seemed to know exactly how she felt, for he propped her head high with a skill that she found infinitely comforting, and drew the window-curtains to shade her eyes. Then very quietly he proceeded to remove her shoes.

"Thank you very much," murmured Olga. "Don't bother!"

He came and stood beside her and again felt her pulse. "Look here," he said. "As soon as you feel a little better, you undress and slip into bed. I'll come up again in half an hour and give you something for your head. Understand?"

"Oh, no!" Olga said. "No! I can't go to bed, really. I'll lie here for a little while, but I shall be quite all right presently."

Max continued to feel her pulse. He was frowning a good deal. "You will do as I say," he said deliberately. "You are to go to bed at once, and you won't come down again for the rest of the day."

There was so much of finality in his speech that Olga became aware of the futility of argument. She felt moreover totally unfit for it. She only hazarded one more protest.

"But what about Violet?"

"She can take care of herself," he said. "I will tell her."

There was no help for it. Olga gave in without further protest. But she did venture to say as he released her hand, "Please don't bother about bringing me anything! I couldn't possibly take it."

"Leave that to me!" said Max brusquely.

He left her then, to her unutterable relief. There was no doubt about it; she was feeling very ill, so ill that the business of undressing was almost more than she could accomplish. But she did manage it at last, and crept thankfully into bed, laying her throbbing head upon the pillow with the vague wonder if she would ever have the strength to lift it again.

From that she drifted into a maze of pain that blurred all thought, and from which she only roused herself to find Max once more by her side. He was watching her closely.

"Is your head very bad?" he asked.

"Yes," she whispered.

"I've got some stuff here that will soothe it," he said.

"Just drink it down, and then see if you can get a sleep."

His tone was so gentle that had her pain been less severe Olga might have found room for amazement. As it was, she began very weakly to cry.

"Now don't be silly!" said Max. "You needn't move. I'll do it all."

He slipped his arm under the pillow, and lifted her. She commanded herself and drank from the medicine-glass he held to her lips.

"What queer stuff!" she said. "Is it—is it 'the pain-killer'?"

"What do you know about 'the pain-killer'?" he said.

She shrank a little at the question, and he did not pursue it. He laid her down again, settled the pillows, and left her.

Olga lay very still. She felt as if a strange glow were dawning in her brain, a kind of mental radiance, inexpressibly wonderful, absorbing her pain as mist is absorbed by the sun. Gradually it grew and spread till the pain was all gone, swamped, forgotten, in this curious flood of warmth and ecstasy. It was the most marvellous sensation she had ever experienced. Her whole being thrilled responsive to the glow. It was as though a door had been opened somewhere above her and she were being drawn upwards by some invisible means, upwards and upwards, light as gossamer and strangely transcendentally happy, towards the warmth and brightness and wonder that lay beyond.

Up and still up her spirit seemed to soar. Of her body she was supremely, most blissfully, unconscious. She felt as one at the entrance of a dream-world, a world of unknown unimagined splendours, a world of golden atmosphere, of ineffable rapture, and she was floating up through the ether, eager-spirited, wrapt in delight.

And then quite suddenly she knew that Max had returned to her side. His hand was laid upon her arm, his fingers sensitive and ruthless closed upon her pulse.

In that instant Olga also knew that her dream-world was fading from her, her paradise was lost. Softly, inexorably, the door that had begun to open to her closed. The hand that grasped her drew her firmly back to earth and held her there.

In her disappointment she could have wept, so vital, so entrancing, had been the vision. Piteously she tried to plead with him, but it was as though an obscuring veil had been dropped upon her. She could only utter unintelligible murmurings. She sought for words and found them not.

And then she heard his voice quite close to her, very tender and reassuring.

"Don't vex yourself, sweetheart! It's all right—all right."

His hand smoothed her brow; she almost fancied that he kissed her hair, but she was not certain and it did not seem to matter. Surely nothing could ever matter again since the closing of that door!

A brief confusion was hers, a brief wandering in dark places, and then a slow deepening of the dark, the spreading of a great silence....

The last thing she heard was the steady ticking of a watch that someone held close to her. The last thing her brain registered was the close, unvarying grip of a hand upon her wrist....

It was many hours—it might have been years to Olga—before she awoke. Very slowly her clogged spirit climbed out of the deep, deep waters of oblivion in which it had been steeped. For a long time she lay with closed eyes, semi-conscious, not troubling to summon her faculties. At last very wearily she opened them, and found Nick seated beside her, alertly watching.

"Hullo!" she murmured languidly.

"Hullo, darling!" he made soft response. "Had a nice sleep?"

She stared at him vaguely. "What are you sitting there for?"

"Taking care of you," said Nick.

She frowned, collecting her wits with difficulty. "It's night, isn't it?"

"Half-past one," said Nick.

"My dear!" She opened her eyes a little wider. "But what are you waiting for? Why don't you go to bed?"

"I like sitting up sometimes," said Nick. "Keeps me in form."

She turned her head on the pillow. "Is Max here?"

"No," said Nick.

"But—he has been?" she persisted.

"Yes. He's been in now and then."

"Ah!" Olga frowned still more. "Am I ill, Nick?" she asked, with a touch of nervousness.

His lean hand sought and held hers. "You've had a touch of sun, dear," he said, "but you've slept it off. Max is quite satisfied about you. You'll feel a bit rotten for a day or two, but that's all."

"How horrid!" said Olga.

"Don't worry!" said Nick. "I'm here. I shall stick like a leech for the future. You will never be out of my sight again in your waking hours."

She squeezed his hand. "Poor old Nick! I'm dreadfully sorry. But I had to get those raspberries. Oh, what's that?"

She started violently at the soft opening of the door. Nick got up, but she clung to him so fast that he could not leave her side. He bent down over her.

"It's all right, darling. It's only Max with some refreshments. We'll leave you in peace as soon as you have broken your fast."

"I don't want Max," she whispered. "Please send him away!"

"I'll go like a bird," Max said, "if you will let me take your pulse first. It isn't much to ask, is it?"

He set down a tray he was carrying, and came and stood beside Nick. Outlined against the dim light shed by a shaded night-lamp, he looked gigantically square and strong.

"I won't hurt you, Olga," he said. "Won't you trust me?"

Again his voice was softened to a great gentleness; yet it compelled. In another second Nick had withdrawn himself, and Max stood alone beside her bed. He stooped low over her, put back the hair from her forehead, looked intently into her eyes.

"Are you in pain?" he asked.

"No," she whispered back.

"You are sure? It doesn't hurt you to move your eyes?"

"No," she said again.

He passed his hand again over her forehead, felt her face, her temples, finally turned his attention to her pulse. As he took out his watch, she remembered again the two things that had outlasted all other impressions before she had sunk into her long sleep. And with this memory came another. She raised her eyes to his grave face.

"Max!"

"In a moment!" said Max.

But it was many moments before he laid her hand down.

"You will be all right when you have eaten something," he said then, "and had another sleep. Is there something you want to say to me?"

His tone was kind, but his manner repressive. She wished the light had not been so dim upon his face.

"Max," she said, with an effort, "why—why did you close the door?"

She fancied he smiled, grimly humorous, at the question. She was sure his eyes gleamed mockery. He was silent for a space, and then: "Ask me some other time!" he said.

She breathed a sigh of disappointment. She knew she would never have the courage.

He waited a few seconds more, then as she remained silent he laid his hand again on hers and pressed it lightly.

"Good-night!" he said.

She scarcely responded, nor did he wait for her to respond. In another moment he had turned from her, and was talking in a low voice to Nick.

A minute later he went softly out, and she saw no more of him that night.

Nick remained for some little time longer, waiting on her with the tenderness of a woman. It was wonderful to note how little his infirmity hampered him. There were very few things that Nick could not accomplish with one hand as quickly as the rest of the world with two.

But Olga, having recovered the full possession of her faculties, would not permit him to sacrifice any more of his night's rest to her.

"I shall be perfectly all right," she declared. "If I'm not, you are only in the next room, and I can rap on the wall."

"Yes, but will you?" said Nick.

"Of course I will."

"Is it a promise?"

She caught his hand and kissed it. "Yes, dear Nick, a promise."

"All right," said Nick. "I'll go."

But he was obviously loth to leave her, and she detained him to assure him how greatly she loved to be in his care.

"Max tells me I am not in the least fitted to look after you," he said rather ruefully, "and I believe he's right."

The humility of this speech was so extraordinary that it nearly took Olga's breath away.

"My dear Nick," she said, "what nonsense! Surely you don't—seriously—care what Max says?"

"Don't you?" said Nick.

She began to answer in the negative, but tripped up unexpectedly. "I—I can't quite say. I haven't really thought about it. But—anyhow—it's no business of his, is it?"

"He thinks it is," said Nick.

"Why?" She suddenly put out her hand to him with a little shiver. "Nick, you haven't told him about—that scheme of ours?"

"Yes, I have," said Nick.

"Oh, why?" There was unmistakable distress in the question.

Nick knelt down beside her. "Olga, I had to. He's a clever chap, cleverer than Jim even. I wanted to know if I'd better go on with it, if he thought—in view of to-day's misfortune—it might upset your health, supposing you were allowed to go. I couldn't run the risk of that."

"What did he say?" said Olga.

Nick chuckled a little. "He said that your normal health appeared to be up to the average young woman's, but he hadn't sounded you in any way, and—"

"And he shan't!" interjected Olga, with vehemence.

"And so couldn't say for certain," ended Nick. "But—I'll tell you this—he doesn't like our precious scheme—at all."

"Why not?" said Olga. "What has it got to do with him?"

"I don't know," said Nick.

"Why didn't you ask him?"

"My dear, you can do that in the morning—before I write to Muriel."

"I will," said Olga firmly. "It's my belief that you're afraid of him," she added, a moment later.

"No, I'm not," said Nick simply.

"Then why are you so careful of his feelings?"

"I shouldn't like to see him writhing in hell," said Nick. "I've done it myself, and I know exactly what it feels like."

"Really, Nick!"

"Yes, really, little sweetheart. You know or p'raps you don't know—what fools men can be."

"I know they can be quite unreasonable and very horrid sometimes," said Olga. "Nick dear, you'll promise me, won't you, that if Muriel agrees and Dad agrees you won't let an outsider like Max stand in our way?"

"Is he an outsider?" asked Nick humorously.

"He is so far as I am concerned," said Olga. "I can't imagine why you take any notice of him."

"Are you sure you don't yourself?" asked Nick.

"Oh, in some things perhaps. But not in a matter of this sort. I think he is very interfering," said Olga resentfully.

Nick smiled and rose. "I shouldn't be too hard on him, kiddie. Doubtless he has his reasons."

"I should like to know what they are," said Olga.

He stooped for a final kiss. "I daresay—if you were to ask him prettily—he would tell you."

"Oh, no, he wouldn't," she said. "He never tells me anything, even if I beg him." She slipped her arms round his neck and held him closely for a moment. "Nick darling, you will work that lovely scheme of ours if you possibly can—promise me!—in spite of anything Max may say or do!"

"You don't mind hurting his feelings?" asked Nick.

"Oh, well,"—she hesitated—"he couldn't care all that. It's only his love of interference."

"Or his love of you? I wonder which!" whispered Nick.

"Nick! Nick!" Wonder, dismay, incredulity, mingled in the cry.

But Nick had already slipped free from the clinging of her arms, and he did not pause in answer.

"Good-night, Olga *mia*!" he called back to her softly from the door. "Don't forget to knock on the wall if you feel squeamish!"

And with that he was gone. The latch clicked behind him, and she was alone.

CHAPTER XI
THE IMPOSSIBLE

Could it be true? Sleeping and waking, sleeping and waking, all through the night Olga asked herself the question; and when morning came she was still unconvinced. Nothing in Max's manner had ever given her cause to imagine for an instant that he cared for her. Never for an instant had she seriously imagined that he could care. Till quite recently she had believed that a very decided antipathy had existed between them. True, it had not thriven greatly since the writing of her note; but that had been an event of only two days before. She was sure he had not cared for her before that. He could not have begun to care since! And if he had, how in wonder could Nick have come to know?

Certainly he knew most things. His uncanny shrewdness had moved her many a time before to amazement and admiration. This quickness of intellect was hers also, but in a far smaller degree. She could leap to conclusions herself and often find them correct. But Nick—Nick literally swooped upon the truth with unerring precision. She had never known him to miss his mark. But this time—could he be right this time? It was such a monstrous notion. Its very contemplation bewildered her, carried her off her feet, made her giddy. She began to be a little frightened, to cast back her thoughts over all her intercourse with Max to ascertain if she had ever given him the smallest reason for loving her. Most emphatically she had never felt drawn towards him. In fact, she had often been repelled. In all their skirmishes she had invariably had the worst of it. He had simply despised her resistance, treating it as a thing of nought. And yet—there was no denying it—their intimacy had grown. Who but an intimate friend could have made that suggestion for encompassing her deliverance from the persecutions of that hateful man? Her face burned afresh over the memory of this. It had certainly been a desperate remedy—one to which she would never have given her consent could she for a single instant have suspected that it had been dictated by anything more than a friendly desire for her welfare.

Surely, argued her practical mind, he could never have been so foolish as to let himself care deeply for one who so obviously had only the most casual regard for him! She knew women did these silly things, but surely not men—and hard-headed men like Max!

Besides, what could he possibly see in her? Was it not Violet upon whom his attention was constantly focussed? And small wonder, his own repudiation of sentiment notwithstanding! Did not all men look at her with dazzled eyes? Even Nick paid her that much homage, though Olga was privately a little doubtful as to whether he altogether liked her brilliant friend.

No, she had never for an instant seriously contemplated this possibility which Nick had whispered into her ear. She wondered what had made him do it? Had he meant to put her on her guard. Or—staggering thought!—had he thought to wake her heart to some response? Was he taking Max's part? Did he want her to be kind to him?

She pictured Max's wrath, sardonically expressed, should he ever become acquainted with that move of Nick's. She fancied he did not much like Nick and that suspicion of itself was quite sufficient to present him in an unfavourable light to her half-involuntary criticism. How could she ever possibly begin to care for a man who did not admire her hero? Oh, why had she ever placed herself under an obligation to him, ever consented to the forging of that bond between them, elastic though it might be?

Of course it could be severed. He had said so. And severed it should be at once. But why had she ever suffered it? It weighed upon her intolerably now that she realized in what foundry its links had been cast. Even her enemy's impertinences would be easier to bear—now that she knew.

Again, as morning broke, she told herself that this thing was an impossibility after all, that Nick had been misled, or had spoken in jest. It seemed the only sane conclusion by the practical light of day, and, reassured, at last she slipped into untroubled slumber. Yes, she was sure Max was much too shrewd to let himself be caught by a girl who did not even want him. He would never waste his valuable time over such as she.

Yet while she slept, a curious memory came to her—a memory that was half a dream—of a hand that had stroked her head with a sure and soothing touch, of lips very near her hair that had whispered words of tenderness. It was not a disturbing dream by any means. She slept through it into a deeper peace with a smile upon her face.

She was finally aroused without ceremony by Violet, who skipped airily into the room, clad in a daring sea-green wrapper that revealed more of her charms than it concealed.

"Oh, my dear soul, are you awake?" was her greeting, as she perched herself on the foot of the bed. "I've just had the very sweetest note from Hunt-Goring accompanied by a box of the most exquisite Eastern cigarettes—'Companions of the Harem,' he says they are called. And how are you feeling now, you poor wan thing? What interesting shadows you have developed! I wish I could make my eyes look like that. The revered Max suffered agonies about you last night, and nearly slew me with a glance because I dared to touch my mandolin after dinner. Poor little Nick was rather blue too though he did at least try to be courteous. What made you go and get sunstroke, Allegretto? Rather unnecessary, wasn't it? He was quite obviously at your feet without that. Of course you realize how completely my wiles have been thrown away on him. I declare I was never so humiliated in my life. However, I daresay I shall get over it. If I don't, I shall take refuge in Hunt-Goring's harem. Good gracious! What now?"

A smart rap at the door had interrupted her plans for her future. She sprang off the end of Olga's bed, and stood poised on one foot, listening.

"Can I come in?" asked Max on the other side of the door.

Olga's face flushed scarlet. Violet shot her a glance of mock dismay.

"My dear, I wonder which would be the least improper," she said. "To go or to remain?"

"For pity's sake, put something on!" urged Olga. "There's my dressing-gown. Take that!"

But Violet had already snatched up a bath-towel which she draped about her with scarf-like effect.

"This will do quite well and is infinitely more artistic. Pray come in, Dr. Wyndham! The patient is quite ready for you."

Max came in. He scarcely looked at either girl, but halted just inside the room, holding the door wide open.

"One at a time, Miss Campion, please!" he said curtly.

"Dear, dear!" laughed Violet, with audacious mirth. "Then you had better call again later when I have concluded my visit."

He turned his eyes straight upon her; they were piercingly green in the morning light. "Your visit," he said, "is a direct violation of my orders. I must trouble you to conclude it at once."

He had never used that tone to her before. She opened her eyes very wide, meeting his look with the utmost nonchalance.

"Dear me!" she said. "How fierce we are this morning! And what if Olga prefers my company to yours?"

"That has nothing to do with it," he returned. "I am here professionally.".

"And if Olga is not requiring your professional services?" she suggested daringly.

"Oh, Violet dear, I think you had better go," interposed Olga nervously. "You can come back again when you are dressed."

Violet's beautiful eyes suddenly gleamed. She moved to the door, stepping daintily with her bare feet.

"Dr. Wyndham," she said, "I congratulate you on your conquest. It has been a ridiculously easy capture, but I warned her she had met her fate long ago. No doubt she has wisely decided that to run away any longer would be a waste of energy. *En tout cas,*—" she made an airy gesture of the hands,—"my blessing be upon you both!"

And with that, lightly she crossed the threshold, and was gone, flitting like a sunbeam from the room.

Quietly Max closed the door. He did not look at Olga, but walked straight to the window and stood there with his back turned and his hands in his pockets, staring outwards.

"I hope you don't object to an early visit," he said, after a moment. "I want to get my rounds done in good time to-day, and I didn't like to leave without seeing you first."

"I don't mind at all," stammered Olga in reply. "But—really, there's no reason for you to—to bother about me. I've had a good night, and—and I'm going to get up."

"Really?" he said. "You're not going raspberry picking, I hope?"

She laughed somewhat tremulously. Violet's vindictive thrust had embarrassed rather than hurt her. She looked at the great square shoulders that intervened between her eyes and the morning sunshine, and wondered why he did not turn. Was it possible that he could be feeling embarrassed too? She could scarcely imagine it; but yet the position was sufficiently intolerable for him also.

"I'm afraid the raspberries will have to go," she said regretfully, "unless the boys—"

"They would probably eat 'em as fast as they picked 'em," observed Max grimly. "I know boys."

Again, rather feebly, she laughed. "It seems a pity," she said.

"I shouldn't worry," said Max. "Besides, it's Sunday. You couldn't make jam on Sunday in any case."

"I could, though," said Olga, "if the fruit wouldn't keep till Monday."

He laughed. "What an admirably practical spirit!"

"Thank you!" said Olga. "That's the first nice thing you have ever said to me."

"Oh, no, it isn't!" said Max. "May I come and take a survey now?"

"I can't imagine what you are waiting for," she returned with renewed spirit.

She could meet him on the old fencing-ground without a tremor; at least so she fancied. But the next instant he disconcerted her in the most unexpected fashion.

"I have been waiting for your pulse to steady down," he said coolly.

"Oh!" said Olga.

He left the window and came to her side. She gave him her hand with an abrupt, childish movement.

"It's great nonsense!" she said, with burning cheeks. "You can't possibly make me out ill."

She saw one side of his mouth go up. He took out his watch, but he looked at her.

"You don't imagine that I want to keep you as a patient, do you?" he said.

"You know you always like people best when they are ill," she retorted.

"Do I?" he said.

"Well, don't you?"

"I wonder what makes you think so," he said.

She looked straight up at him with something of defiance. "You never bother to be nice to people unless they are ill."

He frowned a little. "I've been as nice as you would let me," he said.

"Yes, yes," said Olga rather hurriedly. "Of course we are friends. But, Max, there's something I want to say to you. It's very particular. Be quick with my pulse!"

He let her hand slip from his. "It's about a hundred and fifty," he observed, "but that seems to be the normal rate with you. I don't think you had better talk to me now unless it's to be a professional consultation. You can get up if you want to, and I will give Nick a list of the things you are not to do."

He would have gone with the words, but imperiously she detained him.

"You must wait a minute now. I want to speak about—about that compact we made the other day. You—you knew I was only joking, didn't you? You didn't—really—? tell Major Hunt-Goring—that?"

"Yes, I did," said Max. "And do you generally go and cry into the surgery towel when you are enjoying a joke?"

"Oh, Max! You told him?" Her face was tragic. "And what did he say?"

"He congratulated me," said Max.

"Max!"

"My dear girl, I'm telling you the truth; but really, since you have discharged yourself as cured, this has become a highly improper situation. Don't you think we had better postpone this discussion to a more suitable moment?"

Max was openly laughing into her face of distress. She suddenly felt abundantly reassured. He could not—surely—look and speak like this if he dreamed of wooing her in earnest!

"I don't want any discussion," she hastened to tell him. "Only—please, do go and tell Major Hunt-Goring that—that—there's been a mistake, and—in short—"

"In short that you've thrown me over?" said Max. "Oh, thanks, no! You can tell him that—if you wish!"

"He must be told," she said.

"I don't see why." Max smiled upon her with good-natured indulgence. "Have you suddenly taken fright at something?" he asked.

She smiled also, but a little anxiously. "I'm afraid it wasn't a very wise move after all. I want to put an end to it."

"You can't put an end to an engagement that doesn't exist," he said. "You will have to wait till I propose, and then you can go and tell everyone—including Hunt-Goring—that you have said No."

It was impossible to treat the matter seriously. She had a feeling that he was deliberately restraining her from so doing, deliberately offering her an easy means of escape from her own indiscretion. She seized upon it, eager to convince him that she had never deemed him in earnest.

"Do propose soon then!" she said. "And let us get it over!"

He turned to the door. "Given a suitable opportunity," he said, "if shall be done to-night."

"To-night!" she echoed sharply.

She caught the mocking gleam of his eyes for an instant, and her heart misgave her.

"Really, Max!" she said, in a tone of protest.

"Yes, really," said Max. "Good-bye!"

He was gone. She heard him stride away down the passage, and go downstairs. A little later she heard the banging of the surgery-door and the sound of his feet on the gravel. They passed under her window. They paused.

"Olga," he called up to her, "do you mind if a pal of mine comes to lunch?"

Her heart gave a great jolt at the sound of his voice. She swallowed twice before she found her own.

"Who is it?" she called then.

"Someone very nice," he assured her, and she caught a laugh in the words. "Someone you'll like."

"Anyone I know?" she asked.

"No."

She heard him strike a match to light a cigarette. He would not be looking upwards then. Impulse moved her. She left her bed and went to the window.

He was standing immediately below her, a thick-set, British figure of immense strength. A brisk breeze was blowing. She watched him nursing the flame between his hands, firm, powerful hands, full of confidence. The flame flickered and went out. Instantly he threw up his head and saw her. His cigarette was alight.

She drew back sharply as he waved her an airy salute.

"Adieu, fair lady!" called the mocking voice. "I conclude the aforementioned pal may come, then?"

He did not wait for her answer. She heard him whistling cheerily as he went in the direction of the coach-house, and the ting of his bicycle-bell a moment after as he rode away. When that reached her ears, Olga sat down very suddenly on the edge of her bed with the limpness of relaxed tension, and realized that she was feeling very weak.

CHAPTER XII
THE PAL

Nick's letter to his wife was written that morning while Olga lay on the study-sofa, comfortably lazy for once, and listened to the scratching of his pen.

The boys had been sent to church, Violet was again devouring a book and smoking Major Hunt-Goring's cigarettes in the hammock, and all was very quiet.

"I suppose I had better write to Jim too," Nick said, as he looked up at length from his completed epistle.

"I was just thinking I would," said Olga.

"No. Writing is strictly prohibited by your medical adviser." Nick grinned over his shoulder. "I'll send him a line myself."

"Don't let him be worried about me," said Olga. "I really don't know why I'm being so lazy. I feel quite well."

"And look—charming," supplemented Nick.

"Don't be silly, dear! You know I'm as hideous as—"

"As I am? Oh, no, not quite, believe me. I always pride myself I am unique in that respect. Now you mustn't talk," said Nick judiciously, "or you will spoil my inspiration. Who's that going across the lawn?"

He was writing rapidly as he spoke. Olga raised herself on her elbow to look.

"How on earth did you know? I never heard anyone. Oh!"

"What's the matter?" said Nick.

"It's Major Hunt-Goring!"

Nick ceased to write and peered into the garden. "It's all right. He's only violeting. An interesting pastime!" He turned unexpectedly and gave her one of his shrewd glances. "You don't seem pleased," he observed.

"Oh, Nick, he's so hateful! And—and Violet actually likes him."

"Every woman to her taste," said Nick. "Why shouldn't she?"

Olga was silent.

Nick returned to his writing. "I'll go and kick him for you if you like," he said. "Let me just finish my letter to Jim first, though, or it may never get written."

His pen resumed its energetic progress, and Olga fell into a brown study.

Half an hour later Nick turned swiftly and looked at her. Her eyes met his instantly.

"Not asleep?" he said.

"No, Nick. Only thinking."

"What about?"

"India," said Olga.

He got up and came and sat on the edge of the sofa. "Look here, kiddie," he said, "if you've thought better of it, just mention the same before I post these letters. I shall understand."

She smiled at him, her quick, sweet smile. "Nick, you're a darling! But I haven't."

"Quite sure?" said Nick.

"Quite sure," she replied with emphasis.

He looked a little quizzical. "By the way, did you ask Max—what you wanted to know?"

She knew that she coloured, but she faced him notwithstanding. "No, I didn't. I decided it wasn't important enough."

"Oh, all right," said Nick. He got up. "Now can I trust you to lie quietly here while I go and post these letters?"

"Of course you can," she said.

"I shan't be more than five minutes," he said, turning to the door.

She watched him go, and then closed her eyes, slightly frowning. She wished with all her heart that Major Hunt-Goring had not seen fit to come again, even though it was obviously her friend and not herself that he had come to see.

She was still pondering the unpleasant subject when the housemaid suddenly presented herself at the open door.

"Cook wants to know what she's to do about the raspberries, miss."

"Raspberries!" said Olga, with a start. "Oh, I'm afraid they're done for. It's no good thinking about them. I will go round to-morrow, and see if there are any left worth having. But I expect they will all be spoilt by this hot sun."

The girl looked at her, slightly mystified. "But they've been gathered, miss. Didn't you know? Cook thought you had done them yourself before you took ill."

Olga put her hand to her head. "No, I didn't. I hadn't finished. I dropped them all too."

"Well, they're in the pantry now, miss, and cook was wondering if she hadn't better start the jam first thing in the morning."

"Who brought them in?" asked Olga quickly.

The housemaid didn't know. She departed to ask.

Olga leaned back again on her cushions. She was growing a little tired of inactivity, notwithstanding the undeniable languor that had succeeded the previous day's headache.

The sound of voices in the hall outside, however, dispelled her boredom almost before she had time to recognize it. She suddenly remembered Max's pal, and started up in haste to smooth her rumpled hair. Surely Max would not be so inconsiderate as to bring him straight in to her without a moment's preparation!

This was evidently his intention, however, for she heard their footsteps drawing nearer, and she was possessed by a momentary shyness so acute that she nearly fled through the window. It really was too bad of Max!

"Come in here!" she heard him say, and with an effort she braced herself to encounter the stranger.

He entered, paused a second, and came forward. And in that second very strangely and quite completely her embarrassment vanished. She found herself shaking hands with a large, kindly man, who looked at her with deep-set, friendly eyes and asked her in a voice of marvellous softness how she was.

Her heart warmed to him on the instant, and she forgave Max forthwith.

"I am quite well," she said. "Have you walked from the station? Please sit down!"

He was years older than Max, she saw, this man whom the latter had so airily described as his pal. There was a bald patch on the back of his head, and his brows were turning grey. His face was clean-shaven, and she thought his mouth the kindest and the saddest she had ever seen.

"Yes, I walked," he said. "Max brought me across the fields. It was very pleasant. There is a good breeze to-day."'

"I am sure you must be thirsty," Olga said, mindful of the honours of the house. "Max, please go and find something to drink and bring it here!"

"No, no, my dear fellow! I can wait," protested the newcomer. But Max had already departed upon his errand. He turned back smiling to the girl. "I know you were lying on the sofa when I came in. Please lie down again!"

"I've had more than enough of it," she assured him. "I don't think lying still suits me. I only did it to please Nick. He will be in directly."

"Nick is your brother?" he asked.

Olga's smile flashed out. "Not quite. He is three parts brother to one part uncle. That is to say, he is Dad's half-brother, but nearer my age than Dad's."

He nodded in humorous comprehension. "And your father is away, Max tells me. I hope you don't mind being taken by storm like this? I am sorry to miss him, for we are old friends. We don't often meet, as I haven't a great deal of time at my disposal. I reserved to-day, however, as I rather particularly wanted to see Max."

"You will manage to come again perhaps, when Dad is at home," said Olga.

He smiled courteously. "I shall certainly try. And you are his eldest daughter?"

"His only daughter," she said. "There are three boys as well."

"Ah! And you have been left in charge?"

"Nick and I," she said; and then moved to sudden confidence, "I expect you have heard of Nick, haven't you? Nick Ratcliffe of Wara! He is an M.P. too."

"Oh, is he that Ratcliffe?" Her listener displayed immediate interest. "Yes, of course I have heard of him, Miss Ratcliffe. He is a man of renown, isn't he? It will give me much pleasure to meet him."

"You'll like him awfully!" said Olga, with shining eyes.

It was at this point that Nick himself pushed open the door with a peremptory, "Now then, Olga, what about your promise? Hullo!" He stopped short, and stood blinking rapidly at the visitor. "I thought it was Hunt-Goring you had got here," he observed. "Introduce me, please!"

Olga hesitated in momentary confusion. "Max didn't tell me your name, you know," she said to the stranger. "This is Captain Ratcliffe of Wara."

"Monkey!" said Nick briefly. "Plain Ratcliffe of no-where in particular is my description."

The big man rose with outstretched hand. "I know you well by repute, and I am very pleased to meet you. My name is Whitton—Kersley Whitton."

"Goodness!" ejaculated Olga. "Max might have told me!"

He laughed at her quietly. "Told you what? Didn't he say I was a friend of his?"

"So you've been entertaining a celebrity unawares!" laughed Nick. "I hope you have been on your best behaviour, my child."

"But Miss Ratcliffe must be accustomed to celebrities," said Sir Kersley Whitton, "since she has to entertain you and Max Wyndham every day."

"Is Max a celebrity too, then?" asked Olga quickly.

"He is going to be one," the great doctor answered, with conviction.

"You mean he will—someday—be like you?" she said.

He smiled at that. "He will be a greater man than I am," he said.

"An interesting collection!" commented Nick. "Heroes past, present, and to come! You will pardon me for putting myself first. My little halo went out long ago."

"Nick! How absurd you are!"

"My dear, it's my *rôle* to be absurd. I am the clown in every tragedy I come across—the comic relief man—the buffoon in every side-show. Hence my Frontier laurels, because I kept on dancing when everyone else was dead. The world likes dancers—virtuous or otherwise." Nick broke off with his elastic grimace. "If I go on, you'll think I'm trying to be clever. Sir Kersley, come and have a drink!"

"I'm bringing drinks," said Max's voice from the hall. "I say, Ratcliffe,"—he entered with the words—"do go and dislodge that leech Goring. He's in the garden with Miss Campion. Tell him I don't want to see either him or his beastly thumb for a week. I'll call in next Sunday, if I've nothing better to do. Say I'm engaged if he asks for me now."

"I'll say you're dead if you like," said Nick cheerily. "Shall I say you're dead too, Olga?"

"Say she's engaged also," said Max.

Olga glanced up sharply, but he was not looking at her. He was occupied in pouring out a drink for his friend, which he brought to him almost immediately.

"That's how you like it measured to a drop. Sorry there's no ice to be had. It doesn't grow in these parts."

"I'd have got out the best glass if I'd known," murmured Olga regretfully.

Max threw up his head and laughed. "What a good thing I didn't tell her, eh, Kersley?" He leaned a careless hand on Sir Kersley's shoulder. "She doesn't know what a taste you have for the simple life."

Olga's eyes opened wide at the familiarity of speech and action. Sir Kersley faintly smiled.

"Since Miss Ratcliffe received me so kindly as a friend of yours," he said, "I hope she will continue to regard me in that light, and dispense with all unnecessary ceremony. Miss Ratcliffe, I drink to our better acquaintance!"

"How nice of you!" said Olga.

"I return thanks on Miss Ratcliffe's behalf," said Max. "How long has the Hunt-Goring monstrosity been here?"

Olga's face clouded. "Oh, ages! Do you think Nick will persuade him to go?"

"He can't stop to lunch if he isn't asked," said Max.

"An unwelcome visitor?" asked Sir Kersley.

"Yes, a neighbour of ours," explained Olga. "He lives about two miles away at a place called The Warren. He is retired from the Army. He shoots and hunts in the winter and loafs all the summer."

"A very horrid man," said Max with a twinkle. "He broke his thumb the other day and we haven't been quit of him since. You see, Miss Ratcliffe has a most beautiful friend staying with her with whom we all fall in love at first sight. Some of us fall out again and some of us don't. Hunt-Goring—presumably—belongs to the latter category."

"And you?" asked Sir Kersley.

"Oh, I am too busy for frivolities of that sort," said Max. "My mind is entirely occupied with drugs. Ask Miss Ratcliffe if it isn't!"

Olga looked a little scornful. It suddenly seemed to her that Max Wyndham required a snub. She was spared the trouble of administering one, however, by the reappearance of the housemaid.

She rose. "Do you want me, Ellen?"

"Oh, no, miss. It's all right," was Ellen's breezy reply. "I only just come to say as it was Dr. Wyndham as brought in them raspberries—early this morning."

Ellen disappeared as Max popped the cork of a soda-water bottle with unexpected violence. He clapped his hand over the top and carried it bubbling to the window.

"Awfully sorry," he said. "The beastly stuff is so up this weather."

Olga followed him with his glass. "Thank you for rescuing my raspberries," she said.

Max rubbed himself down with a handkerchief and took the glass from her. He was somewhat red in the face. He looked at her with a queer smile.

"Confound that girl!" he said.

"Have you discovered any specially beneficial properties In raspberries?" asked Sir Kersley in the tone of one seeking information.

"Not yet. I'm experimenting," said Max.

And Olga laughed, though she could scarcely have said why.

"There goes Nick, escorting the undesirable," observed Max, a moment later. "I begin to think there really must be a spark of genius in that little uncle of yours. Hunt-Goring looks as if he had been kicked, while the swagger of Five Foot Nothing defies description. Ah! And here comes Miss Campion! She looks as if—" He broke off short.

Olga bent forward sharply to catch a glimpse of her friend, and then as swiftly checked herself and remembered her guest. She moved sedately back into the room, only to discover that he also had risen, to look out of the window over Max's shoulder.

Instinctively she glanced at him. His deep-set eyes were fixed intently as if held by a vision. But his face was drawn in painful lines. She had a curious feeling of foreboding as she watched him. There was something fateful in his look. It passed in a moment. Almost before she knew it, he had turned back to her and was courteously conversing.

She gave him her attention with difficulty. Her ears were strained to catch the sound of Violet's approach. She was possessed by a ridiculous longing to rush out to her, to keep her from entering this man's presence, to warn her—to warn her—Of what? She had not the faintest idea.

By a great effort of will, she controlled herself, but the impulse yet remained—a striving, clamouring force, impotent but insistent.

There came the low, sweet notes of Violet's voice. She was singing a Spanish love-song.

Sir Kersley Whitton fell silent. He looked at the door. Max wheeled from the window. Olga waited tensely for the coming of her friend.

The door swung back and she entered. With her careless Southern grace she sauntered in upon them.

"Good Heavens!" she said, breaking off in the middle of her song. "Is it a party of mutes?"

Olga hastily and with evident constraint introduced the visitor, at sound of whose name Violet opened her beautiful eyes to their widest extent.

"How do you do? I had no idea a lion was expected. Why wasn't I told?"

"He is not one of the roaring kind," said Max.

Violet was looking with frank curiosity into Sir Kersley's face. "I'm sure I've met you somewhere," she said. "I wonder where."

He smiled slightly—a smile which to Olga's watching eyes was infinitely sad.

"I don't think you have," he said. "You may have seen my portrait."

"Ah, that's it!" She regarded him with a new interest. "I have! I believe I've got it somewhere."

"Do you collect the portraits of celebrities?" asked Max.

She shook her head. "Oh, no! It's among my mother's things. It must have been taken years ago. You were very handsome—in those days, weren't you?"

"Was I?" said Sir Kersley.

"Yes. That's why I kept you. There was a bit of your hair with it, but I burnt that." Violet's brows knitted suddenly. "My mother was handsome too," she said. "I wonder why you jilted her!"

Sir Kersley made a slight movement, so slight that it seemed almost involuntary. "That, my child," he said quietly, "is a very old story."

She laughed her gay, winning laugh. "Oh, of course! I expect you have jilted dozens since then. It's the way of the world, isn't it?"

He looked into the exquisite face, still faintly smiling. "It's not my way," he said.

There fell a sudden silence, and Olga sent an appealing glance towards Max. He came forward instantly and clapped a practical hand upon his friend's shoulder.

"Come and have a wash, Kersley!" he said, and with characteristic decision marched him away.

As they went, Violet broke once more into the low, sweet refrain of her Spanish love-song.

CHAPTER XIII
HER FATE

"How extraordinary men are!" Violet stretched her arms high above her head and let them fall. Her eyes were turned contemplatively towards the sinking sun. "This man for instance who might have been—who should have been—my father. He loved her, you know; he must have loved her, or he wouldn't have remained single all these years. And she worshipped him. Yet on the very eve of marriage—he jilted her. Extraordinary!"

"How do you know she worshipped him?" Olga spoke with slight constraint; it seemed to her that the matter was too sacred for casual discussion.

"How do I know? My dear, it is written in black and white on the back of his photograph. 'The only being I have it in me to love—sovereign lord of my heart!' Fancy writing that of any man! I couldn't, could you?"

"I don't know," said Olga soberly.

Violet laughed. "You're such a queer child! One day you come flying to me for protection, and almost the day after, you—"

"Please, Violet!" Olga broke in sharply. "You know I don't like it!"

"Oh, very well, my dear, very well! The subject is closed. We will return to the renowned Sir Kersley. He was watching me all luncheon-time. Did you notice?"

Olga had noticed. "Are you very like your mother?" she asked.

"I am better-looking than she ever was," said Violet, without vanity. "You see, my father, Judge Campion (he was nearly sixty when he married her, by the way), was considered the handsomest man in India at the time. She was a Californian, and very Southern in temperament, I believe. I often rather wish I could have seen her, though she would probably have hated me for not being the child of the man she loved. She died almost before I was born however. I daresay it's as well. I'm sure we shouldn't have got on."

"Violet! How can you say those things?"

"I always say whatever occurs to me," said Violet. "It's so much simpler. Mrs. Briggs was all the mother I ever knew or wanted. Of course as soon as Bruce settled down, I was taken to live with them. But I never liked either of them. They always resented the Judge's second marriage."

"Why didn't he take care of you himself?" asked Olga.

"My dear, he was dead. He died before she did. He was assassinated by a native before they had been married three months. I've always thought it was rather poor-spirited of her to die too; for of course she never cared for him. She must have married him only to pique Kersley. By the way, Major Hunt-Goring met them in his subaltern days. He said everyone fell in love with her. I supposed that included himself, and he smiled and said, 'Calf-love, señorita!' Allegro, I wonder if I really like that man."

"I'm sure you don't," said Olga quickly. "You couldn't."

231

"But I must amuse myself with someone," reasoned Violet pathetically. "Besides, he gives me such lovely cigarettes. Have one, Allegretto. Do!"

"No!" said Olga almost fiercely.

"I will, Miss Campion." Coolly Max came forward from the open window behind them. "You promised me one, you know."

"Did I?" She tossed him her cigarette-case carelessly. "They are not made for masculine palates. However, as you are so anxious—"

"Thank you," he said.

He opened the case. Violet was lying back with eyes half-closed. Olga's eyes were keenly watching. He glanced up and met them.

Abruptly he held up a warning finger. For one instant his eyes commanded her, compelled her. Then deliberately he extracted two cigarettes, slipped one into his pocket, stuck the other between his lips. She watched him in silence.

He returned the case to its owner with the slight, cynical smile she knew so well, and began to smoke.

"What time is Sir Kersley Whitton going?" asked Violet.

"Soon. His train starts at seven."

Olga rose suddenly. "Well, I am going to the evening service," she announced, with a touch of aggressiveness. "Are you coming, Violet?"

"No, dear," said Violet.

"Nor you either," said Max, blowing a cloud of smoke upwards.

She looked at him. "Why not?"

"Doctor's orders," he said imperturbably.

Violet laughed a little. Olga's face flamed.

"That is absurd! I am going!"

"Where's Nick?" said Max unexpectedly.

"Somewhere in the garden with Sir Kersley. I believe they went to see the vine."

"Then go to him," said Max; "tell him I have forbidden you to go to church to-night, and see what he says."

"I won't," said Olga.

She passed him without a second glance, and went indoors.

Violet laughed again. Max turned towards her. "Excuse me a moment!" he said, and therewith followed Olga into the house.

He overtook her at the foot of the stairs and stopped her without ceremony.

"Olga, what do you want to go to church for?"

She turned upon him in sudden, quivering anger. "Max, leave me alone! How dare you?"

His hand was on her arm. He kept it there. He looked steadily into her eyes.

"I dare because I must," he said. "You have had a tiring day, and you will end it with a racking headache if you are not careful."

"What does it matter?" she flashed back.

He did not answer her. "What are you so angry about?" he said. "Tell me!"

She was silent.

"Olga," he said, "it isn't quite fair of you to treat me like this."

"I shall treat you how I like," she said.

"No, no, you won't!" he said.

His voice was quiet, yet somehow it controlled her. Her wild rebellion began to die down. For a few seconds she stood in palpitating silence. Then, almost under her breath: "Max," she said, "why did you take that other cigarette?"

She saw him frown. "Why do you want to know?"

Her hands clenched unconsciously. "You are always watching Violet—always spying upon her. Why?"

"I can't tell you," he said briefly and sternly.

"You can," she said slowly, "if you will."

"I won't, then," said Max.

She flinched a little, but persisted. "Don't you think I have a right to know? It was I who brought her here. She is—in a sense—under my protection."

"What are you afraid of?" Max demanded curtly.

She shivered. "I don't know. I believe you are trying to get some power over her."

"You don't trust me?" he said, in the same curt tone.

"I don't know," she said again.

"You do know," he said.

She was silent. There seemed nothing left to say.

He released her arm slowly. "I am sorry I can't be quite open with you," he said. "But I will pledge you my word of honour that whatever I do is in your friend's interest. Will that make things any easier?"

Her eyes fell before his. "I—was a fool to ask you," she said.

He did not contradict the statement. "You are going to have a rest now," he said, "before the headache begins."

It had begun already, but she did not tell him so. "I would rather go to church," she said.

Max looked stubborn.

"I always do go," she protested into his silence. "It will do me good to go."

"All right," he said, with his one-sided smile. "Then I must go too, that's all."

"What for?" she asked quickly.

"To bring you home again when you begin to be ill."

"I'm not going to be ill!" she declared indignantly.

"No," he said. "And you're not going to church either. I'm sorry to thwart your pious intentions, but in your father's absence—"

"Oh, don't begin that!" she broke in irritably.

"Well, don't you be silly!" said Max good-humouredly. "You know you don't really want to go. It's only because you are cross with me."

"It isn't!" she said.

"All right. It isn't. Now go and lie down like a good child! I shall come and prescribe for you if you don't."

Was it mockery that glinted in his eyes as he thus smilingly quelled her resistance? She asked herself the question as she slowly mounted the stairs. It was a look she had come to know singularly well of late, a look that she resented instinctively because it made her feel so small and puny. It was a look that told her more decidedly than any words that he would have his way with her, resist him as she might.

She heard the church-bells ringing as she went to her room, but the impulse to obey their summons had wholly left her. She lay down wearily upon her bed. She wished there were not so many problems in life. She had an uneasy sensation as of being caught in the endless meshes of an invisible net that compassed her whichever way she turned.

She did not sleep, but the rest did her good. Undeniably it had been a tiring day. It was growing dark when a tentative scratch at the door told her of Nick's presence there.

She called him eagerly in. "Has Sir Kersley gone? I hope he didn't think me rude. Max made such a fuss about my resting. So I thought—"

"Quite right, my chicken!" Nick came softly to her side. "Max explained your absence. How's the head?"

"Oh, it's all right now. Nick, how soon will Dad and Muriel get your letters?"

"The day after to-morrow," said Nick.

She took his hand and squeezed it. "And we shall hear—when?"

"On Thursday night—with luck," said Nick.

She carried the hand impulsively to her lips. "Nick, you are a darling!"

He laughed. "Same to you! But we won't count on it too much or we may find ourselves crying for the moon, which is the silliest amusement I know. How do you like Sir Kersley Whitton?"

"Oh, very much. You heard about—about Violet's mother having been engaged to him, I suppose?"

"He told me himself," said Nick.

233

"What did he tell you, Nick?"

Nick hesitated momentarily. "He spoke in confidence," he said then.

"You won't tell me?" she asked quickly.

"Sorry; I can't," said Nick.

Olga sat up. A sudden idea had begun to illumine her brain. "Nick tell me this—anyhow! Did Violet's mother do—something dreadful?"

"Look here, Olga *mia!*" said Nick severely. "I know you can't help being a woman, but you're not to look at your neighbour's cards. It's against the rules."

She laughed a little. "Forgive me, Nick! I suppose supper is ready. I'll come down."

They went down together, to find Violet thrumming her mandolin in the twilight for the benefit of Max who was stretched at full length on the drawing-room sofa. The three boys were scudding about the garden like puppies.

As Olga and Nick entered, Violet looked up from her instrument. "I'm wondering if Sir Kersley would like to adopt me as well as Max. Do you think he would?"

"Exceedingly doubtful," said Max, rising.

"Why?"

"You would take up too much of his valuable time," he rejoined. "A man has to think of that, you know."

"Only horrid sordid men like you!" she retorted.

He uttered his dry laugh. "A professional man must think of his career."

She tossed her head. "Is that your creed—that there is no time for a woman in a professional man's life?"

Max laughed again. "She mustn't be too beautiful, anyhow."

She sprang suddenly to her feet. The mandolin jarred and jangled upon the ground. "Are you listening, Allegro?" she said, and through her deep voice there ran a sinister note that seemed to mingle, oddly vibrant, with the echoing strings of the instrument. "A professional man can admit only a plain woman into his life. The other kind is too distracting, since he must think of his career."

Nick cut in upon the words with the suddenness of a sabre-thrust. "Oh, we all say that till we meet the right woman, and then, be she lovely or hideous, the career bobs under like a float and ceases to count."

Max grunted. "Does it? Well, you ought to know."

"Let's go and have supper," said Olga, and turned from the room.

Violet stooped to pick up her mandolin. Nick lingered to summon the boys. Max entered the dining-room in Olga's wake.

"Give me five minutes in the surgery presently," he said as he did so.

She glanced round at him sharply. "Why?"

He raised his brows. "Because I ask you to." He halted at the sideboard to cut some bread. "Going to refuse?" he asked.

"No," said Olga.

"Thanks!"

He went on with his cutting with the utmost serenity, and almost immediately they were joined by the rest of the party.

It was a somewhat rowdy meal. Violet appeared to be in one of her wildest moods. Her eyes shone like stars, and her merriment rippled forth continuously like a running stream. The boys were uproarious, and Nick was as one of them. In the midst of the fun and laughter, Olga sat rather silent. Max, drily humorous, took his customary somewhat supercilious share in the general conversation, but he made no attempt to draw her into it. She almost wished he would do so, for she felt as if he purposely held aloof from her.

Rising from the table at length, she was aware of an urgent impulse to shirk the interview for which he had made request. Valiantly she held it in check, but it did not have a very soothing effect upon her nerves.

The whole party rose together, and she slipped away to the kitchen to discuss domestic matters with the cook. She knew that Max saw her go, knew with sure intuition that he would seize the opportunity of her return to secure those few minutes alone with her that he had desired.

She was not mistaken. He was waiting for her by the baize door that led to the surgery when she emerged. With a brief, imperious gesture he invited her to pass through. The door closed behind them, and they were alone together.

"Come along into the consulting-room," said Max.

She turned thither without question. The room was in darkness. Max went forward and lighted the gas. Then, without pause, he wheeled and faced her.

"Are you angry with me still?"

Olga stood still by the table. "You haven't brought me in here to—quarrel, have you?" she said, a hint of desperation in her voice.

He smiled very slightly. "I have not. Sit down, won't you? You're looking very fagged."

He pulled forward an arm-chair, and she sat down with a nervous feeling that she was about to face a difficult situation. He relaxed into his favourite position, lounging against the table, his hands deep in his pockets.

"I want a word with you about Hunt-Goring," he said.

She looked up startled. "What about him?"

"He was here to-day, wasn't he?" proceeded Max.

"Yes. He came to see Violet."

Max grunted. "I suppose you know his little game?"

Olga's eyes widened. "No, I don't. What is it?"

He looked at her for a moment or two in silence. "Do you really imagine that you succeed in effacing yourself when you hide behind the beautiful Miss Campion?" he asked then.

The quick colour rose in her face. "What an absurd question!" she said.

"Why absurd?"

"As if anyone could possibly prefer me to Violet!"

"I know at least two who do," said Max.

"Who?" She flung the question almost angrily, as though she uttered it against her will.

Very deliberately he answered her. "Hunt-Goring and myself."

She started. Her face was burning now. Desperately she strove to cover her confusion, or at least to divert his attention from it. "I am quite sure Major Hunt-Goring doesn't! He—he wouldn't be so silly!"

"We are neither of us that," remarked Max with a twist of the lips that was hardly a smile. "I suppose you don't feel inclined to tell me exactly what the fellow's hold over you is."

"You said you didn't want to know!" she flashed back.

Max's green eyes were regarding her very intently. She resented their scrutiny hotly, but she could not bring herself to challenge it.

"Quite so, fair lady, I did," he responded imperturbably. "But as this affair has developed into something of the nature of a duel between the gallant major and myself it might be as well, for your sake as much as mine, that I should know what sort of ground I am standing on."

"A duel!" echoed Olga.

He smiled a little. "Hunt-Goring has no intention of letting you stay engaged to me if he can by any means prevent it."

"Oh, Max!" She met his look for an instant. "But—but—what can it really matter to him—one way or the other?"

"I conclude he wants you for himself," said Max.

She turned suddenly white. "He doesn't! He couldn't! Max!" She turned to him almost imploringly. "He doesn't really want me! It's not possible!"

"I should say he wants you very much indeed," said Max. "But you needn't be scared on that account. He isn't going to have you."

That reassured her somewhat. She essayed a shaky laugh. "You'll think me a shocking coward," she said. "But—do you know, I'm horribly frightened at him."

"Are you frightened at me too?" Max enquired unexpectedly.

She shook her head without looking at him.

"Quite sure?" he persisted.

She raised her eyes with a feeling that he must be convinced of this at all costs. "Of course I'm not," she said.

He leaned down towards her on one elbow, his hands still deep in his pockets. "Will you be engaged to me in earnest then?" he said. "Will you marry me?"

She stared at him. "Max!"

The humorous corner of his mouth went up. "Don't let me take your breath away! I say, what's the matter? You're as white as a ghost. Do you want some *sal volatile*?"

She forced a rather piteous smile. "No—no! I'm quite all right. But, Max—"

He pulled one hand free and laid it upon her clasped ones. "You can't stand me at any price, eh?"

She shook her head again. "Are you suggesting that I should—marry you, just to get away from Major Hunt-Goring?"

"I suppose you would rather marry me than him," said Max.

She laughed faintly. Her eyes were upon his hand—that hand which she had so ruthlessly stabbed not so very long before. The red scar yet remained. For the first time she felt genuinely sorry for having inflicted it.

"But there is no question of my marrying him, is there?" she said at last. "He has never even hinted at such a thing."

"That's true," said Max grimly. "You see, he has begun to realize by this time that you are not precisely fond of him."

She shivered involuntarily. "I hate him, Max!"

"He thrives on that," observed Max drily.

"Oh, not really!" she protested. "He couldn't want to marry me against my will."

"My good child," said Max, "if you had had the bad taste to flirt with him, he would have tired of you long ago. As it is—" he paused.

She looked up. "As it is?"

He uttered a curt laugh, and sat up, thrusting his hand back into his pocket. "Well—he won't be happy till he gets you."

Olga sprang to her feet. "But, Max, he couldn't marry me against my will! That sort of thing isn't done nowadays."

Max looked at her, his shrewd eyes very cynical. "Quite true!" he said.

"Then—then—" She stood hesitating, looking at him doubtfully—"what is there to be afraid of?" she asked at length.

"Oh, don't ask me!" said Max.

She felt the blood rush back to her face, and turned sharply from him.

"You—you don't help me much," she said.

He got to his feet abruptly. "You won't accept my help," he returned. "You've got yourself into a nasty hole, and you can't climb out alone, and you won't let me pull you out."

Olga was silent.

He stood a moment, then turned to the doctor's writing-table and sat down. "It's no good talking round and round," he said. "You'll have to tell Nick or your father. I can't do anything further. It's not in my power."

He opened a blotter with an air of finality, found a sheet of paper, and began to write.

Olga turned at the sound of his pen, and watched him dumbly. He had apparently dismissed her and her small affairs from his mind. His hand travelled with swift decision over the paper. He was evidently immersed in his own private concerns. He wrote rapidly and without a pause.

Very suddenly, without turning, he spoke again. "How did you like Kersley?"

The question astonished her. She had almost forgotten their visitor of a few hours before. But she managed to answer with enthusiasm.

"I liked him immensely."

"He is the greatest friend I possess," Max said, still writing. "He made me."

"I thought you seemed very intimate," observed Olga.

He laughed. "We are. I pulled him through a pretty stiff illness once. The mischief was that he wanted to die. I made him live." A note of grim triumph sounded in his voice, but he still continued to write.

"Was he grateful?" Olga asked.

"No. He fought like a mule. But I had my own way. It was tough work. I crocked up myself afterwards. And then it was his turn." Max jerked up his head. "After that," he said, "we became pals. He was only my patron before; since, we have been—something more than brothers."

He paused. Olga said nothing. She was wondering a little why he had chosen to make this confidence.

Suddenly he turned in his chair and enlightened her. "If you want to know what sort of animal I am," he said, his eyes going direct to hers, "if you want to know if I am worthy of a woman's confidence—in short, if I'm a white man or—the other thing, ask Kersley Whitton. For he is the only person in the world who knows."

The words were blunt, perhaps all the more so for the unwonted touch of fiery feeling which Olga was quick to detect in their utterance. They moved her strangely. It was almost as if he had flung open his soul to her, challenging her to enter and satisfy herself. And something very deep within her awoke and made swift response almost before she knew.

"But I don't need to ask him, Max," she said. "I know that for myself."

"Really?" said Max.

He stretched out his hand to her, without rising. His manner had changed completely. It was no longer passionate, but intensely quiet.

She came to him slowly, feeling compelled. She laid her hand in his.

His eyes were still upon hers. "I can't marry you against your will, can I?" he said. "It's not done nowadays."

She smiled a little. "I'm not afraid of that."

"Shall we go on being engaged, then," he said, "and see how we like it? We won't tell anyone yet—if you'd rather not."

She hesitated. "But—if I go to India with Nick?"

He frowned momentarily. "Well. I shouldn't ask you to marry me first."

Olga's face cleared somewhat. This was reassuring. It might very well lead to nothing after all.

"But," said Max impressively, "you wouldn't get engaged to any other fellow without letting me know."

She laughed at that. "I certainly shan't marry anyone out there."

Max looked grim. "You will give me the first refusal in any case?"

"But I needn't promise anything?" she said quickly.

"No, you needn't make any promise. Just bear me in mind, that's all; though I don't suppose for a moment that you could forget me if you tried," said Max with the utmost calmness.

"Why do you say that?" said Olga rather breathlessly.

It suddenly seemed to her that she had gone a little further than she had intended. She made an instinctive effort to get back while the way remained open.

But she was too late. She felt his hand tighten. For a moment she caught that gleam in his eyes which always disconcerted her.

And then it was gone, even as his hand released hers. He turned back to the writing-table with his supercilious smile.

"Because, fair lady," he said, "you have met your fate. If Hunt-Goring pesters you any further, of course you will let me know. Hadn't you better go now? The little god in the shrine will be jealous. And I have work to do."

And Olga went, somewhat precipitately, her heart throbbing in such a clamour of confused emotions that she hardly knew what had happened or even if she had any real cause for distress.

CHAPTER XIV
THE DARK HOUR

He had not made love to her! That was the thought uppermost in Olga's mind when the wild tumult of her spirit gradually subsided. He had not so much as touched upon his own feelings at all. Not the smallest reason had he given her for imagining that he cared for her, and very curiously this fact inclined her towards him more than anything else. Had he proposed to her in any more ardent fashion, she would have been scared away. Possibly he had fathomed this, and again possibly he had not wanted to be ardent. He was hard-headed, practical, in all he did. She was sure that his profession came first with him. He probably thought that a wife would be a useful accessory, and he was kind-hearted enough to be willing to do her a good turn at the same time that he provided for his own wants.

Violet's malicious declaration regarding a professional man's preference for a plain woman recurred to her at this point and made her feel a little cold. She did not know very much about men, and she had to admit to herself that it might quite easily be the truth. And then she thought of Hunt-Goring, reflecting with a shudder that that explanation would not account for his preference, if indeed what Max said were true and he actually did prefer her to Violet at whose feet he was so obviously worshipping.

She wondered if she ought to tell Max all about the man, and shuddered again at the bare thought. Not that there was much to tell, but even so, it was enough to set the blood racing in her veins and to make her hotly ashamed. She remembered with gratitude that he had not pressed her to be open on this point. He had left the matter almost at the first sigh of her reluctance to discuss it. She liked him for that. It furnished proof of a kindly consideration with which she had not otherwise credited him. It also furnished proof that he did not think very seriously of the matter. And for that also, lying awake in the moonlight, Olga secretly blessed her champion. Hard of head and cool of heart he might be, but he was undoubtedly a white man through and through.

From that she began to wonder if she really had met her fate, and if so, what life with him would be like, whether she would find it difficult, whether they would quarrel much, whether—whether they would ever fall in love. Of course there were plenty of people in the world who didn't, excellent people to whom romance in that form came not. Olga had always been quite sure that she was not romantic. She had always loved cricket and hockey and all outdoor sports. She had even—quite privately—been a little scornful over such shreds of romance as had come beneath her notice, dismissing them as paltry and ridiculous. Possibly also Violet's scoffing attitude towards her adorers had fostered her indifference.

No, on the whole she decided that it was verging upon foolish sentimentality to contemplate the possibility of falling in love. She was convinced Max would think so, even pictured to herself the one-sided smile that such nonsense would provoke. Doubtless he deemed her too sensible to waste time and thought over anything so absurd. He would even quite possibly be extremely annoyed if she ever ventured beyond the limits of rational friendship which he had marked out. Olga's sense of humour vibrated a little over this thought. He was always so scathing about her worship of Nick. He would certainly find no use for such feminine trash himself.

And yet—and yet—through her mind, vague as a dream, intangible yet not wholly elusive, there floated once more the memory of a voice that had reassured, a hand that had lulled her to rest. Had he really spoken that word of tenderness? Had his lips really touched her hair? Or had it all been a trick of her fancy already strung to fantastic imaginings by that magic draught?

She told herself that she would have given all she had to know if the dream were true and then found herself trembling from head to foot lest haply she might one day find that it had been so. Yes, on the whole she was relieved, thankful beyond measure, that he had not made love to her. Things were better as they were.

The church clock struck one as she arrived at this comfortable conclusion, and she turned her back to the moonlight and composed herself for slumber. Her thoughts wandered off down another track;—India as Nick had described it to her, a land of rivers and jungles, tigers and snakes, natives that were like monkeys, horses that moved like camels, pigs with tusks that had to be hunted and slain. Elephants too! He had left out the elephants, but they crowded in royal array into Olga's quick imagination. She and Nick would often go elephant-riding in the jungle. Mysterious word! It held her like a spell. Tall trees and winding undergrowth, a gloom well-nigh impenetrable, creatures that hid and spied upon them as they passed! Perhaps they would go tiger-hunting together. She thrilled at the thought, picturing herself creeping down one of those dim glades, rifle in hand, in search of the enemy. Nick would certainly have to teach her to shoot. He was a splendid shot, she knew. She believed that she could be a good shot too. It would not be easy to mark the striped body sliding through the undergrowth, but it would be a serious thing to miss. Olga's eyes closed. She began to wander down that jungle path, in search of the monster that lurked there. The lust of the hunt was upon her. She was about to secure the largest tiger that had ever been seen.

Her breath came quickly. Her blood ran hot. She forgot all lesser things in the ardour of the chase. The elephants had disappeared. She was running on foot through the jungle, eager and undismayed. Ah! What was that? Something that moved and was still. Two points that shone out suddenly ahead of her! Green eyes that gleamed triumphant mockery! Her heart stopped beating. Those eyes! Those eyes! They struck terror to her soul.

Headlong she turned and fled. Back through the jungle with the anguished speed of fear. The ground was sodden. It seemed to hold her flying feet. She tore them free, only to plunge deeper at every step, while behind her, swift and remorseless, followed her fate.

Wildly she struggled, powerless but persistent, till at last her strength was gone. She sank in utter impotence.

And then he came to her, he lifted her, he held her in his arms, pressed sickening kisses upon her lips; and suddenly she knew that she had fled from a myth to hurl herself into the power of her enemy. She had eluded her fate but to find herself at the mercy of a devil.

Gasping and half-suffocated she awoke, starting upright in a cold sweat of fear. Her heart was pumping as if it would burst. Her starting eyes searched and searched for the face of her captor. Her ears were strained for the sound of his soft, hateful laugh.

Ah! He was at the door! She heard a hand feeling along the panels, heard the handle turn! As one paralyzed she sat and waited.

Softly the door opened.

"Allegro!" whispered a hushed voice.

Olga turned swiftly with outflung arms. "Oh, come in, dear! Come in! I've had such a ghastly dream! You've come just in the nick of time."

Softly the door closed. Violet came to her, wonderful in the moonlight, a white mystery with shining eyes. She stood beside the bed, suffering herself to be clasped in her friend's arms.

"What have you been dreaming about?" she said.

"Oh, sheer nonsense of course," said Olga, hugging her in sheer relief. "All about that hateful Hunt-Goring man. Get into bed beside me and help me to forget him!"

But Violet remained where she was.

"Allegro," she said, "I've had—a bad dream—too."

"Have you, dear? How horrid!" said the sympathetic Olga. "What can we both have had for supper, I wonder?"

Violet uttered a hard little laugh. "Oh, it wasn't that! I haven't been asleep at all. I generally do sleep after Hunt-Goring's cigarettes. But to-night I couldn't. They only seemed to make things worse." She sat down abruptly on the edge of the bed. "Don't cuddle me, Allegro! I'm so hot."

Olga leaned back on her pillows, with a curious sense of something gone wrong. "Shall I light a candle?" she said.

"No. It's light enough. I hate an artificial glare, Allegro!"

"Well, dear?" said Olga gently.

Violet was sitting with her back to the moonlight, her face in deep shadow. Her black hair was loosely tied back and hung below her waist. Olga stretched out a hand and touched the silken ripples caressingly.

Violet threw back her head restlessly. "I'm going to give up Hunt-Goring," she said.

"My dear, I am glad!" said Olga fervently.

Violet laughed again. "I only encouraged him for the sake of his cigarettes. But I'm going to give up them too. The opium habit grows on one so."

"Opium!" echoed Olga sharply.

"Opium, dear child! It's a cunning mixture and most seductive. The astute Max little knew what he was inhaling this afternoon." Violet's words had a curious tremor in them as of semi-tragic mirth.

Olga listened in horrified silence. So this was the secret of Max's peculiar behaviour! If he did not know by this time, then she did not know Max Wyndham.

"Yes," Violet went on. "Hunt-Goring is counting on those cigarettes of his to get me under his influence. I know. But I'm tired to death of the man. I'm going to pass him on to you."

"I hate him!" said Olga quickly.

"Oh, yes, dear! But he has his points. You'll find he can be quite amusing. Anyhow, take him off my hands for a spell. It isn't fair to make me do all your entertaining."

"Why don't you snub him?" said Olga, with some impatience. "It certainly isn't my fault that he comes here."

"Allegro, don't be horrid! I didn't refuse to help you when you wanted help." There was actually a pleading note in Violet's voice.

Olga responded to it instantly, with that ready warmth of hers that was the secret of her charm. "My dear, you know I would do anything in my power for you. But I can't—possibly—be nice to Major Hunt-Goring. I do detest him so."

"You detest Max Wyndham," said Violet quickly. "But you manage to be nice to him."

The words rang almost like an accusation. For the moment Olga felt quite incapable of replying. She lay in silence.

"Allegro!" Again she heard that note of pleading, vibrant this time, eager, almost passionate.

With an effort Olga brought herself to answer. "I've changed my mind about him. We are friends."

"Friends!" Violet sprang from the bed, and stood tense, quivering, with an arrow-like straightness that made her superb. Her eyes glittered as she faced the moonlight that poured through the unshaded window. "Does that mean you—care for him?" she demanded.

Olga hesitated. Violet in this mood was utterly unfamiliar to her, a strange and tragic personality before which she felt curiously small and ill at ease, even in some unaccountable fashion guilty.

"Dear, please don't ask me such startling questions!" she said. "I can't possibly answer you."

"Why not?" said Violet. Her hands were clenched. Her whole body seemed to be held in rigid control thereby.

"Because—" again Olga hesitated, considered, finally broke off lamely "I don't know."

"You do know!" There was actual ferocity in the open contradiction. Violet was directly facing her now. Her eyes shone so fiercely, so unnaturally, bright that a queer little sensation of doubt pricked Olga for the first time, setting every nerve and every muscle on the alert for she knew not what. "You do know, Allegro! And so do I!" The full voice took a deeper note, it throbbed the words. "Do you think I haven't watched you, seen what was going on? Do you think it has all been nothing to me—nothing to see you spoiling my chances day by day—nothing to feel you drawing him away from me—nothing to know—to know—" she suddenly flung her clenched hands wide open to the empty moonlight—"to know that you have set your heart on the only man I ever loved—you who wanted me to help you to get away from him—and have shouldered me aside?"

Her voice broke. She turned to the girl in the bed with eyes grown terrible in their wild anguish of pain. "Allegro!" she cried. "Allegro! Give him up! Give him up—if not for my sake—for your own! You couldn't—be happy—with him!"

With the words she seemed to crumple as though all power had suddenly left her, and sank downwards upon the floor, huddling against the bed with agonized sobbing, her black head bowed almost to the floor.

Olga was beside her in an instant, stooping over her, wrapping warm arms about her. "My darling, don't, don't!" she pleaded. "You know I would never do anything to hurt you. I never dreamed of this indeed—indeed!"

Violet made a passionate movement to thrust her away, but she would not suffer it. She held her close.

"Violet dearest, don't cry like this! There is no need for it. Really, you needn't be so distressed. There, darling, come into bed with me. You'll be ill if you cry so. Violet! Violet!"

But Violet was utterly beyond control, and her paroxysm of weeping only grew more and more violent, till after some minutes Olga became seriously frightened. She stood up, and began to ask herself what she must do.

It was then that to her intense relief the door slid open and Nick's head was poked enquiringly in.

"Hullo!" he said softly. "Anything wrong?"

She motioned him to enter, being on the verge of tears herself.

"Nick, she's hysterical! What am I to do?"

"Better fetch Max," he said.

But the words were hardly out of his mouth before Max himself pushed the door wide open and entered!

He bore a small lamp in his hand which threw his somewhat grim features into strong relief. He made a weird figure in his night-attire, and his red hair looked as if it had been brushed straight on end.

He looked at neither Olga nor Nick, merely for a single instant at the shivering, sobbing girl on the floor, ere he set down his lamp with decision and turned to the washing-stand.

Olga stood and watched him as one fascinated. He was quite deliberate in all he did. With the utmost calmness he took up a tumbler and poured out some cold water.

Then very quietly he went to Violet, bent over her, gathered the dark hair back upon her shoulders.

She started at his touch, started and cried out in wild alarm, raising her head. And Max, with a set intention which seemed to Olga scarcely short of brutal, dashed a spray of water full into her deathly face.

She flinched away from him with another cry, gasping for breath and staring up at him as one in nightmare terror.

"You!" she uttered voicelessly. "You!"

He held what was left of the water to her lips. "Drink!" he said with insistence.

She tried feebly to resist. Her teeth chattered against the glass.

"Drink!" Max said again relentlessly.

Olga stooped swiftly forward and slipped a supporting arm around her. Violet drank a little, and turned to her, weakly sobbing.

"Allegro, send him away! Send him away!"

"Yes, dear, yes; he's going now," murmured Olga soothingly.

Max gave the glass to Nick with the absolute detachment of the professional man, and proceeded to take Violet's pulse. He watched her closely as he did so, with shaggy brows drawn down.

Violet gazed at him wide-eyed. She was no longer sobbing, but she shivered from head to foot.

"Yes," said Max at last, in the tone of one continuing an interrupted conversation. "Well, now you are going back to bed."

Violet shrank against Olga. "Let me stay with you, Allegro!" she murmured piteously.

"Of course you shall, dear," Olga made quick reply.

But in the same instant she saw Max elevate one eyebrow and knew that this suggestion did not meet with his approval.

"You will sleep better in your own room," he said. "Come along! Let me help you."

He put his arm about her and lifted her to her feet; but she clung fast to Olga still.

"I won't go without you, Allegro," she cried hysterically.

"My dear, of course not!" Olga answered. She caught up her dressing-gown and wrapped it round her friend. "You're as cold as ice," she said.

They helped her back to her own room between them, almost carrying her, for she seemed to have no strength left.

Max said nothing further of any sort till she was safely in bed, then somewhat brusquely he turned to Olga.

"Put on your dressing-gown and go down to the surgery! I want a bottle out of the cupboard there. It's a poison bottle, labelled P.K.R.; you can't mistake it. Third shelf, left-hand corner. The keys are in your father's desk. You know where. Put on your slippers too, and take a candle! Mind you don't tumble downstairs!" His eyes travelled to the doorway where Nick hovered. "Go with her, will you?" he said. "Bring back a medicine-glass too! There's one on the surgery mantelpiece."

He turned back to Violet again, stooping low over her, his hand upon her wrist.

Olga fled upon her errand with the speed of a hare, leaving Nick to follow with a candle. Even as she went she heard a cry behind her, but she sped on with a feeling that Max was compelling her.

When Nick joined her a few seconds later she had already found the keys and was fumbling in the dark for the cupboard-lock.

They found the medicine-bottle exactly where Max had said, and Olga snatched it out, seized the glass, and was gone. She was back again in Violet's bedroom barely two minutes after she had left it, but the instant she entered she was conscious of a change. Violet was lying quite straight and stiff with glassy eyes upturned. Max was bending over her, tight-lipped, motionless, intent. He spoke without turning his head.

"Just a teaspoonful—not a drop more. The rest water."

Olga poured out the dose, controlling her hands with difficulty.

"Not a drop more," he reiterated. "There's sudden death in that. Finished? Then give it to me!"

He raised Violet up in bed and took the glass from Olga. A curious perfume filled the room—a scent familiar but elusive. Olga stood breathing it, wondering what it brought to mind.

Max held the glass against the pale lips, and suddenly she remembered. It was the magic draught he had given to her two days before.

Violet seemed to be unconscious, but she drank nevertheless very slowly, with long pauses in between. Gradually the glassy look passed from her eyes, the long lashes drooped.

Max held out the empty glass to Olga. "You go back to bed now," he said. "She will sleep for some time."

"I can't leave her," Olga whispered.

He was lowering the senseless girl upon the pillow and made no reply. Having done so, he stooped and set his ear to her heart for a space of several seconds. Then he stood up and turned quietly round.

"You can't do anything more. Thanks for fetching that stuff! Why didn't you put on your slippers as I told you?"

His manner was perfectly normal. He left the bedside and took up the medicine-bottle, holding it against the lamp.

"Are you sure she will be all right?" whispered Olga.

"Quite sure," he said.

She turned her attention to the bottle also. "What is that stuff?" she asked.

He looked at her, and for an instant she saw his sardonic smile. "It's sudden death if you take enough of it," he said.

"Yes, I know," said Olga. "It's what you call 'the pain-killer,' isn't it?"

"Exactly," said Max, "Hence the legend on the label. But what do you know about the pain-killer? Who told you about it? I know I didn't."

"It was Mrs. Briggs," said Olga, and then turned hotly crimson under his eyes.

There fell a sudden silence; then, "You go back to bed," said Max. "And you are to settle down and sleep, mind. Don't lie awake and listen."

"You are sure she will sleep till morning?" said Olga, lingering by the bed.

"Yes." He put his hand on her shoulder, and wheeled her towards the door. "There's Nick waiting to tuck you up. Run along! I am going myself immediately."

She went, more to escape from his presence than for any other reason. There was undoubtedly something formidable about Max Wyndham at that moment notwithstanding his light speech, something that underlay his silence, making her curiously afraid thereof.

She did not lie and listen when she returned to bed, but a very long time passed before she slept.

CHAPTER XV
THE AWAKENING

Olga slept late on the following morning, awaking at length with a wild sense of dismay at having done so. She leaped up as the vivid memory of the night's happenings rushed upon her, and, seizing her dressing-gown, ran out into the passage and so to Violet's room.

Very softly she turned the door-handle, and peeped in. The curtains were drawn, but the morning-breeze blew them inwards, admitting the full daylight. Violet was lying awake with her face to the door.

"That you, Allegro? Come in!" she called. "I've had the oddest night."

Olga slipped in and went to her. The beautiful eyes were very wide open. They gazed up at her wonderingly. The forehead above them was slightly drawn.

"I've been dead," said Violet slowly. "I've just come to life."

"My darling!" Olga said.

"Yes. Isn't it queer? It was so strange, Allegro. I went right up to the very door of Paradise. But I suffered a lot first. I suffered—horribly. And when I got there—the door was shut in my face." Violet uttered a curious little laugh that had in it a note of pain. "That was when I died," she said.

Olga stooped to kiss her. "It was a dream," she said.

"Oh, but it wasn't," said Violet. She threw her arms unexpectedly around Olga's neck, and held her very tightly, as if she were afraid. "Allegro," she said under her breath, "I believe I left my soul behind. It's up there, waiting for the door to open. I hope it won't get lost."

The words sent a sharp chill through Olga. She held her friend closely, protectingly. "Darling, I don't think you are quite awake yet," she said very tenderly. "Stay in bed for a little while, and I'll dress and get your breakfast."

"Oh, no! Oh, no! I'm going to get up!" Quickly Violet made reply, almost feverishly. "I couldn't possibly lie still and do nothing. I've got to find the way out. It's very dark, but I daresay I shall manage. Blind people learn to, don't they? And that's what has happened to me, really. I've gone blind, Allegro, blind inside."

She put Olga from her, and prepared to rise. Her eyes were very bright, but there was a curiously furtive look about them. They seemed afraid to look.

"Wait anyhow till you have had some tea," urged Olga. "I'll run down and order it."

"No, don't go, Allegro! Don't leave me! I don't want to be alone." Impetuously Violet stretched out her hands to her. "Don't go!" she pleaded. "I'm so afraid—he—will come. And I don't want him to know anything about it. You won't tell him? Promise, Allegro!"

"Who, dear?" Olga asked the question though she knew the inevitable answer. She was becoming seriously uneasy, though she sought to reassure herself with the thought that

243

Violet's nerves were of the high-strung order and could scarcely have failed to suffer from the strain they had undergone.

Violet answered her with obvious impatience. "Why, Max, of course! Who else? Promise you won't tell him, Allegro!"

"Tell him what, dear?" questioned Olga.

Violet started up from her bed and sprang to the open door. She closed it and stood facing Olga with arms outstretched across it. Her breath came pantingly through dilated nostrils.

"You're not to tell him—not to tell him—what I have just told you. If he knows I'm trying to get out, he'll stop me. Don't you understand? Oh, don't you understand?" A fury of impatience sounded in her voice; she quivered from head to foot. "He keeps the door," she said. "And he never sleeps. Why, even last night he was there. Didn't you see him? Those dreadful green eyes—like—like a tiger in the dark? Olga—" suddenly and passionately she began to plead "—you won't tell him, dearest! You couldn't be so cruel! Can't you see what it means to me? Don't you realize that it's my better self that's gone? And I've got to follow—I must follow. If he doesn't know, perhaps I shall manage to slip through when he isn't looking. Dear, you wouldn't have me kept a prisoner—against my will? He's so hard, Allegro—so hard and merciless. And he keeps the door so close. I should have got away last night if it hadn't been for him. So you won't tell him, will you? You'll promise me you won't!"

Olga listened to the appeal with a heart that seemed turned to stone. She knew not what to say or do.

"It's my only chance!" urged Violet, in a voice that was beginning to break. "Oh, how can you hesitate? Are you all in league against me? Allegro! Allegro!"

"There, dear, there! It's all right. Don't worry!" Swiftly Olga collected herself and spoke. "There's nothing to be afraid of. No one shall keep you against your will."

"You promise, Allegro?" Violet looked at her doubtfully, yet as if she wished to be reassured.

"Yes, of course, dear. Now really you must let me go and dress. It's eight o'clock, and I shan't be ready for breakfast."

Violet came slowly away from the door. She did not look wholly satisfied, but she said no more; and Olga hastened back to her room with deadly misgiving at her heart. She felt as if there were tragedy in the very air. It seemed to be closing in upon her, a dread mist of unfathomable possibilities.

She dressed with nervous haste, and hurried downstairs, wondering a little that Max had not bestirred himself to ascertain the effect of his treatment.

She wondered still more when she found him calmly established behind the morning paper in an arm-chair in the dining-room. He laid it aside at her entrance, and rose to greet her.

"Well?" he said, with her hand in his.

She looked up to find his eyes piercingly upon her. They shone intensely green in the morning light.

She removed her hand somewhat abruptly. There was something in his manner that she resented, without knowing why. "Well?" she said.

"How do you find yourself this morning?" asked Max.

"I'm perfectly well, thank you," said Olga briefly.

"Ready to start jam-making?" he suggested.

Olga went to the coffee-urn. "I really don't know," she said. "I've had other things to think about."

He smiled a little, the superior, one-sided smile she most detested. "You mustn't let the fruit go bad," he observed, "after all my trouble."

Olga peered into the coffee-urn, without replying. Max in an exasperating mood could be very exasperating indeed. He pulled out the chair next to her, and sat down.

"And how is the beautiful Miss Campion?" he said.

Olga looked at him. She could not help it.

"Well?" said Max.

She coloured hotly. "I wonder you haven't been to see for yourself," she said.

"Perhaps I have," said Max.

She turned from his open scrutiny, and began to pour out the coffee with a hand not wholly steady.

"I presume—if you had—you wouldn't ask me," she said.

He lodged his chin on his hand, the better to study her. "In making that presumption, fair lady," he said, "you are not wholly justified. Has it never occurred to you that I might entertain a certain veneration for your opinion on a limited number of subjects?"

Olga set down the coffee-urn and squarely turned upon him. "Have you seen her this morning?" she asked him point-blank.

"Yes, I have seen her," he said.

"Then you know as much as I do," said Olga.

"Not quite," he returned. "I soon shall however. Did she seem pleased to see you this morning?"

"Of course," said Olga.

"And why 'of course'? Do you never disagree?" He asked the question banteringly, yet his eyes were still upon her, unflaggingly intent.

"We never quarrel," said Olga.

"I see. You have differences of opinion; is that it? And what happens then? Is there never a tug of war?" Max's smile became speculative.

"No, never," said Olga.

"Never?" He raised his red brows incredulously. "Do you mean to say you give in to her at every turn? She can be fairly exacting, I should imagine."

"I would give her anything she really wanted if it lay in my power," said Olga very steadily.

"Would you?" said Max. He suddenly ceased to smile. "Even if it chanced to be something you wanted rather badly yourself?"

She nodded. "Wouldn't you do as much for someone you loved?"

"That depends," said Max cautiously.

"Oh, of course!" said Olga quickly. "You're a man!"

He laughed. "You've made that remark before. I assure you I can't help it. No, I certainly wouldn't place all my possessions at the disposal of even my best friend. There would always be—reservations."

He looked at her with a smile in his eyes, but Olga did not respond to it. An inner voice had suddenly warned her to step warily. She took up the coffee-urn again.

"I wouldn't give much for that kind of friendship," she said.

"But is it always in one's power to pass on one's possessions?" questioned Max. "I maintain that the possessions are entitled to a voice in the matter."

"I don't understand you," said Olga, in a tone that implied that she had no desire to do so.

"No?" said Max indifferently. "Well, I think unselfishness should never be carried to extremes. Some women have such a passion for self-sacrifice that they will stick at nothing to satisfy it. The result is that unwilling victims get offered up, and you will admit that that is scarcely fair."

Olga handed him his coffee. "Will you cut the ham, please?" she said.

"Do you catch my meaning yet?" asked Max, not to be thwarted.

She shook her head. "But really it doesn't matter, and it's getting late."

"Sorry to keep you," he replied imperturbably, "but when I take the trouble to expound my views, I like to guard against any misunderstanding. Just tell me this, and I shall be satisfied. If you were at a ball, and you had a partner you liked and who liked you, and you came upon your friend crying because she wanted that particular partner—would you give him up to her?"

"Of course I should," said Olga. "I don't call that a very serious self-sacrifice."

"No?" said Max. He gave her a very peculiar look, and pursed his lips for an instant as if about to whistle. "And if the unfortunate partner objected?"

Olga began vigorously to cut some bread. "He would have to put up with it," she said.

Max rose without comment and went to the ham. There followed a somewhat marked silence as he commenced to carve it. Then: "Pardon my persistence, fair lady," he said. "But just one more question—if you've no objection. Suppose you were my partner and Hunt-Goring the forlorn friend, do you think I should be justified in passing you on to him? It would be a considerable self-sacrifice on my part."

"Oh, really!" exclaimed Olga, in hot exasperation. "What absurd question will you ask next?"

He looked across at her with a complacent smile. "You see, I'm only a man," he said coolly. "But that illustrates my point. It's not always possible to pass on all one's possessions, is it? It may answer in theory but not in practice. I think you catch my meaning now?"

"Hadn't you better have your breakfast?" said Olga, with a glance at the clock.

Max's eyes followed hers. "Where's Nick? Has he overslept himself?"

"He has not," said Nick, entering at the moment. "It is not a habit of his. Well, Olga, my child, how goes the world this morning?"

She turned with relief to greet him. His genial personality was wonderfully reassuring. He kissed her lightly, and took up his correspondence.

"Let me open them!" she said.

He stood by and watched her while she did it. She was very deft in all her ways, but to-day for some reason her hands were not quite so steady as usual.

Nick threw a sudden glance across at Max while he waited. "Miss Campion all right this morning?" he asked.

"Apparently," said Max, staring deliberately at a point some inches above Nick's head.

Nick pivoted round abruptly, and found Violet standing in the doorway directly behind him. He went instantly to meet her.

"Hullo, Miss Campion! You're just in time for breakfast. Come and have some!"

His tone was brisk and kindly. He took her hand and drew her forward. She submitted listlessly. Her face was white and her eyes deeply shadowed. She scarcely raised them as she advanced.

"Hullo, Nick!" she said indifferently. "Hullo, Allegro! No, I don't want any breakfast. I'm not hungry to-day." She reached the table, and for the first time seemed to become aware of Max, seated on the opposite side of it.

Her eyes suddenly opened wide. She stood still and faced him. "I want my cigarettes," she said, with slow emphasis.

Olga glanced at him sharply, in apprehension of she knew not what. Max's face, however, expressed no anxiety. He even faintly smiled.

"What! Haven't you got any? I shall be happy to supply you with some," he said, feeling in his pocket for his own case.

She leaned her hands upon the table in a peculiar, crouching attitude that struck Olga as curiously suggestive of an angry animal.

"I don't want yours," she said, in a deep voice that sounded almost like a menace. "I want my own!"

Max looked straight at her for a few seconds without speaking. Then, "I am sorry," he said very deliberately. "But you mustn't smoke that sort any more. They are not good for you."

"And you have dared to take them away?" she said.

He shrugged his shoulders. "I had no choice."

"No choice!" She echoed the words in a voice that vibrated very strangely. "You speak as if—as if—you had a right to confiscate my property."

"I have a right to confiscate that sort," said Max.

"What right?" She flung the question like a challenge, and as she flung it she straightened herself in sudden splendid defiance. All the pallor had gone from her face. She glowed with fierce, pulsing life.

Max remained looking at her. There was a glint of mercilessness in his eyes. "What right?" he repeated slowly. "If you saw a blind man walking over a precipice, would you say you hadn't the right to stop him?"

"I am not blind!" she flung back at him. "And I refuse to be stopped by you—or anyone!"

Max raised his red brows. "You amaze me," he said. "Then you are aware of the precipice?"

She clenched her hands. "I know what I am doing—yes! And I can guide myself. I refuse to be guided by you!"

"Violet!" Nervously Olga interposed. "Never mind now, dear! Do sit down and have some breakfast! The eggs are getting cold."

"Quite so," said Nick, putting down his letters abruptly. "The coffee also. Olga, you may tear up all my correspondence. It's nothing but bills. Miss Campion, wouldn't you like to butter some toast for me? You do it better than anyone I know. And I'm deuced hungry."

She turned away half-mechanically, met his smile of cheery effrontery, and suddenly flashed him a smile in return.

"What a gross flatterer you are!" she said "Allegro, aren't you jealous? Which piece of toast do you fancy, Nick? Can I cut up some ham for you as well?"

The tension was over and Olga breathed again. Max continued his breakfast with an inscrutable countenance, finished it, and departed to the surgery.

Violet did not so much as glance up at his departure. She was wrangling with Nick over the best means of attacking a boiled egg with one hand.

There was no longer the faintest hint of tragedy in her demeanour. Yet Olga went about her own duties with a heart like lead. She was beginning to understand Max's attitude at last; and it filled her with misgiving.

CHAPTER XVI
SECRETS

The rest of that day was passed in so ordinary a fashion that Olga found herself wondering now and then if she could by any chance have dreamed the events of the night.

During the whole of the morning she was occupied with her jam-making, while Violet lazed in the garden. Nick had planned a motor-ride in the afternoon, and they went for miles, returning barely in time for dinner. Violet was in excellent spirits throughout, and seemed unconscious of fatigue, though Olga was so weary that she nearly fell asleep in the drawing-room after the meal. Max was in one of his preoccupied moods, and scarcely addressed a word to anyone. Only when he bade her good-night she had a curious feeling that his hand-grip was intended to convey something more than mere convention demanded. She withdrew her own hand very quickly. For some reason she was feeling a little afraid of Max.

Yet on the following morning, so casual was his greeting that she felt oddly vexed with him as well as with herself, and was even glad when Violet sauntered down late as usual and claimed his attention. Violet, it seemed, had decided to ignore his decidedly arbitrary treatment of her. She had also apparently given up smoking, for she made no further reference to her vanished cigarettes, a piece of docility over which Olga, who had known her intimately for some years, marvelled much.

She was obliged to leave her that afternoon to go to tea with an old patient of her father's who lived at the other end of the parish, Violet firmly refusing at the last moment to accompany her thither. Nick had promised to coach the boys at cricket practice that day, and Olga departed with a slight feeling of uneasiness and a determination to return as early as possible.

It was not, however, easy to curtail her visit. The patient was a garrulous old woman, and Olga was kept standing on the point of departure for a full half-hour. In the end she almost wrenched herself free and hurried home at a pace that brought her finally to her own door so hot and breathless that she was obliged to sit down and gasp in the hall before she could summon the strength to investigate any further.

Recovering at length, she went in search of Violet, and found her lounging under the limes in luxurious coolness with a book.

She glanced up from this at Olga's approach and smiled. There was a sparkle in her eyes that made her very alluring.

"Poor child! How hot you are! People with your complexion never ought to get hot. What have you been doing?"

She stretched a lazy hand of welcome, as Olga subsided upon the grass beside her.

"I've been hurrying back," Olga explained. "I thought you would be lonely."

"Oh dear, no! Not in the least." Violet glanced down at her book, a little ruminative smile curving the corners of her red mouth.

Olga peered at the volume. "What is it? Something respectable for once?"

"Not in the least. It is French and very highly flavoured. I daresay you wouldn't understand it, dear," said Violet. "You're such an *ingénue*."

Olga made a grimace. "I'd rather not understand some things," she said bluntly.

Violet uttered a low laugh. "Dear child, you are so unsophisticated! When are you going to grow up?"

"I am grown up," said Olga. "But I don't see the use of studying the horrid side of life. I think it's a waste of time."

"There we differ," smiled Violet. "Perhaps, however, it doesn't matter so much in your case. It is only women who travel and see the world who really need to be upon their guard."

Olga smiled also at that. "Shall I tell you a secret?" she said.

"Do, dear!" Violet instantly stiffened to attention. The smile went out of her face; Olga almost fancied that she looked apprehensive.

"It's quite a selfish one," she said, seeking instinctively to reassure her. "It's only that—perhaps—when the autumn comes—I may go to India with Nick."

"Oh! Really! My dear, how thrilling!" The words came with a rush that sounded as if the speaker were wholeheartedly relieved. The smile flashed back into Violet's face. She lay back in her chair with the indolent grace that usually characterized her movements. "Really!" she said again. "Tell me all about it."

Olga told her forthwith, painting the prospect in the brilliant colours with which her vivid imagination had clothed it, while Violet listened, interested and amused.

"You'll remember it's a secret," she wound up. "We haven't heard from Dad or Muriel yet, and of course nothing can be settled till we do. If either should object, of course it won't come off."

"Oh, I won't tell a soul," Violet promised. "How exciting if you go, Allegro! I wonder if you will get married."

Olga laughed light-heartedly. "As if I should waste my precious time like that! No, no! If I go, I shall fill up every minute of the time with adventures. I shall go tiger-hunting with Nick, and pig-sticking, and riding, and—oh, scores of things. Besides, they're nearly all Indians at Sharapura, and one couldn't marry an Indian!"

"Couldn't one?" said Violet. "Wouldn't you like to be a ranee, Allegro? I would!" She looked at Olga with kindling eyes. "Just think of it, dear! The power, the magnificence, the jewels! Oh, I believe I'd do anything for riches."

"Violet! I wouldn't!"

Olga spoke with strong emphasis and Violet laughed—a short, hard laugh. "Oh, no, you wouldn't, I know! You were born to be a slave. But I wasn't. I was born to be a queen, and a queen I'll be—or die!" She suddenly glanced about her with the peculiar, furtive look that Olga had noticed the day before. "That's why I wouldn't marry Max Wyndham," she said, "for all the riches in the world! He is the One Impossible."

Olga felt her colour rising. She made response with an effort. "Don't you like him, then?"

"Like him!" Violet's eyes came down to her. They expressed a fiery chafing at restraint that made her think of a wild creature caged. "My dear, what has that to do with it? I wouldn't marry a man who didn't worship me, whatever my own feelings might be; and it isn't in him to worship any woman. No, he would only grind me under his heel, and I should probably kill him in the end and myself too." A passionate note crept into the deep voice. It seemed to quiver on the verge of tragedy; and then again quite suddenly she laughed. "But I don't feel in the least murderous," she said. "In fact, I'm at peace with all the world just now. Listen, Allegro! You've told me your secret. I'll tell you one of mine. But you must swear on your sacred honour that you will never repeat it to a soul."

Olga was in a fashion used to this form of affidavit. She had been the recipient of Violet's secrets before. She gave the required pledge with the utmost simplicity, little dreaming how soon she was to repent of it.

Violet leaned towards her and spoke in low, confidential tones. "So amusing, dear! I know you won't mind for once. It's Hunt-Goring again. He really is too ridiculous for words. He has hired a yacht, you must know—a nice little steam-yacht, Allegro. He walked over this afternoon to tell me about it. Don't look so horrified! There's much worse to come." She laughed again under her breath. "He has asked me—in fact, persuaded me—to go for a little trip in it one day next week. Of course I said No at first; and then he said you could come too to make it proper; so I consented. I'm sure you won't mind for once, and a breath of sea air will do me good."

She laid a hand of careless coaxing upon Olga's shoulder. But Olga's demeanour was very far from acquiescent.

"But, Violet!" she exclaimed, "how could you possibly accept for me? I'm not going! No; indeed, I'm not! Neither must you. It's the maddest project I ever heard of! Whatever made you imagine for one moment that I would agree to go?"

"Don't be ridiculous, Allegro!" Violet sounded quite unmoved. "Of course you'll go, unless—" she smiled a trifle maliciously—"you mean me to go alone, as I certainly shall if you are going to be tiresome about it. You wouldn't like me to do that, I suppose?"

Olga gazed at her helplessly. "Violet, what am I to say to you? How could you and I go off for a whole day with that detestable man? Why, it—it would start everyone talking!"

"My dear, no one will know," said Violet with composure. "Haven't you sworn to keep it a dead secret? He won't talk and neither shall I. So, you see, it's all perfectly safe. Not that there would be anything improper about it in any case. He is as old as you and me put together,—older I should say."

"Oh, but he's such a fiend!" burst forth Olga. "You said you were going to give him up only the other night."

"When?" said Violet sharply.

Olga hesitated. It was the first time she had made direct reference to that midnight episode.

"When did I say that?" insisted Violet.

Half-reluctantly Olga made reply, while Violet leaned forward and listened intently. "The night before last. You came to my room late, don't you remember?"

Violet's eyes had a startled look. "Yes?" she breathed. "Yes? What else?"

Olga looked straight up at her. "Dear, I don't think we need talk about it, need we? You were not yourself. I think you were half-asleep. You had been smoking those hateful cigarettes."

"Ah, but tell me!" insisted Violet. "Why did I come to you? What did I say? Was—was Max there?"

"He came in," faltered Olga. "He—guessed you weren't well. He helped you back to your own room. Don't you remember?"

"Yes—yes—I remember!" Violet's brows were drawn with the effort; there was a look of dawning horror in her eyes. "I remember, Allegro!" she said, speaking rapidly. "He—he was very brutal to me, wasn't he? He made me tell him where to find the cigarettes, and then—and then—yes, he took them away. I've hated him ever since." Again that vindictive note sounded in her voice. "I won't bear brutality from any man," she said. "Do you know, if I didn't hate him, I believe I should be afraid of him? I know you are, Allegro."

"Perhaps; a little," Olga admitted.

"Ah! I knew it. He can do anything he likes with you. But I am different." She lifted her head proudly. "I am no man's slave," she said. "He thinks that he has only to speak, and I shall obey. He was never more mistaken in his life."

"But, Violet, he was only treating you as a patient," Olga protested. "And he only took the cigarettes because—"

"I know why he took them." Quickly Violet interrupted. "And remember this, Allegro! Whatever happens to me in the future you must never, never let him attend me again. I suffered more from his treatment than I have ever suffered before, and I can never go through it again. You understand?" She looked at Olga with eyes that had in them the memory of a great pain. "It was torture," she said. "He forced his will upon mine. He crushed me down, so that I was at his mercy. It was like an overpowering weight. I thought my heart would stop. I don't know—even now—how it was I didn't die."

"He gave you the pain-killer, dear," said Olga soothingly. "That was what made you well again."

"The pain-killer!" Violet gazed at her bewildered. "What is—the pain-killer?" she said.

Olga shook her head. "I don't know what it is. He wouldn't tell me. He calls it—sudden death."

Violet gave a great start. "Good heavens, Allegro! And he gave me that?"

"Only enough to make you sleep," explained Olga. "He gave me some the other day, when the heat upset me. I liked it."

Violet's eyes were glittering very strangely. "And you—came back again after it?" she said. "Allegro, are you—sure?"

"Of course," said Olga. "I don't know what you mean, dear. Of course I came back, or I shouldn't be here now."

"No—no, of course not!" Violet lay back in her chair, gazing straight up through the limes at the flawless August sky. "So that is why I didn't die," she said. "He only let me go—half-way. If I'd only had a little more—a little more—" She broke off suddenly and threw a quick side glance at Olga. "What queer creatures doctors are!" she said. "They spend their whole lives fighting, with the certainty that they are bound to be conquered in the end."

"They are splendid!" said Olga, with shining eyes.

"Oh, do you think so? I never can. If they fought suffering only, it would be a different thing. That I could admire. But to fight death—" Violet made a curious little gesture of the hands—"it seems to me like tilting at a windmill," she said. "Everyone must die sooner or later."

"But no one wants to go before his time," observed a cool voice behind them. "Or if he does, he's a shirker and deserves to be kicked."

Both girls started as Max strolled carelessly up, hands in pockets, and propped himself against a tree close by.

His eyes travelled over Olga's face as he did so. "You've been overheated," he remarked.

She pulled her hat forward with a nervous jerk. "Who can help it this weather?"

He grunted disapproval. "You never see me in that condition. Pray continue your oration, Miss Campion! It was not my intention to interrupt."

But Violet had suddenly reopened her book and buried herself therein.

Max twisted his neck and peered over. After a brief space he grunted again and relaxed against the tree.

"Do you read French?" Olga asked, feeling the silence to be slightly oppressive.

He laughed drily. "Not that sort. I have no taste for it."

"But you know the language?" Olga persisted, still striving against silence.

"I've studied it," said Max. He paused a moment; then, "The best fellow I ever knew was a Frenchman," he said.

She looked up at him, caught by something in his tone. "A friend of yours?"

He took off his hat with a reverence which she would have deemed utterly foreign to his nature. "Yes, a friend," he said. "Bertrand de Montville."

"Oh, did you know him?" exclaimed Olga. "Why did you never tell me before? I shall never forget how miserable I was because he didn't live to be reinstated in the French Army. But it's years ago now, isn't it?"

"Six years," said Max.

"Yes, I remember. How I should like to have known him! But I was at school then. And you knew him well?"

"I was with him when he died," he said.

"Oh!" said Olga, and then with a touch of shyness, "I'm sorry, Max."

"No," he said. "You needn't be sorry. He was no shirker. His time was up."

"But wasn't it a pity?" she said.

He smiled a little. "I don't think he thought so. He was happy enough—at the last."

"But if he had only been vindicated first!" she said.

"Do you think that matters?" Max's smile became cynical.

"Surely it would have made a difference to him?" she protested. "Surely he cared!"

He snapped his fingers in the air. "He cared just that."

Violet looked up suddenly from her book. "And you—did you care—just that too?"

He seemed to Olga to contract at the question. "I?" he said. "I had other things to think about. Life is too short for grizzling in any case. And I chanced to have my sister to attend to at the same time."

"You have a sister?" said Olga, swift to intervene once more.

He nodded. "Did I never tell you? She is married to Trevor Mordaunt the writer. Ever heard of him?"

"Why, yes! Nick knows him, I believe."

"Very likely. He has an immense circle of friends. He's quite a good sort," said Max.

"And where do they live?" asked Olga, with interest.

"In Suffolk chiefly. Mordaunt bought our old home and gave it to Chris—my sister—when they married. My elder brother manages the estate for him."

"How nice!" said Olga. "And what is your sister like?"

Max smiled. "She is my twin," he said.

"Oh! Like you then?" Olga looked slightly disappointed.

Max laughed. "Not in the least. Can you imagine a woman like me? I can't. She has red hair or something very near it. And there the resemblance stops. I'll take you to see her some day—if you'll come."

"Thank you," said Olga guardedly.

"Don't mention it!" said Max. "There are two kiddies also—a boy and a girl. It's quite a domestic establishment. I often go there when I want a rest. My brother-in-law is good enough to keep special rooms for the three of us."

"Is there another of you then?" asked Olga.

"Yes, another brother—Noel. By the way, he won't be going there again at present, for he sailed for Bombay to join his regiment a year ago. That's the sum complete of us." Max straightened himself with a faintly ironical smile. "We are a fairly respectable family nowadays," he observed, "thanks to Mordaunt who has a reputation to think of. But we are boring Miss Campion to extinction. Can't we talk of something more amusing?"

Violet threw back her head with a restless movement, but she did not meet his eyes. "I am accustomed to amusing myself," she said.

He stooped to pick up a marker that had fallen from her book. "It is a useful accomplishment," he observed, as he handed it to her, "for those who have time to cultivate it."

She raised her arms with the careless, unstudied grace of a wild creature. Her eyes were veiled.

"I assure you it is far more satisfying than tilting at windmills," she said.

Max straightened himself. There seemed to Olga something pitiless about him, a deadliness of purpose that made him cruel. And in that moment she became aware of a strong antagonism between these two that almost amounted to open hostility.

"A matter of opinion," said Max. "I suppose we each of us have our patent method of killing time."

Violet uttered an indolent laugh. "Yours is a very strenuous one," she observed. "I believe you imagine yourself invincible in your own particular line, don't you?"

"Not at present," said Max, with his twisted smile.

She laughed again, mockingly. "Irresistible then, shall we say?"

He had turned to go, but he paused at the question and looked back at her, grimly ironical. Olga had a feeling that the green eyes comprehended her also.

"No," he said, with extreme deliberation. "Not even that. But—since you ask me—the odds are certainly very greatly in my favour."

And with that he turned on his heel, still smiling, and sauntered away.

As he went, Violet stooped towards Olga with a face gone suddenly white, and grasped her arm.

"Remember, Allegro!" she said. "Not a word about Hunt-Goring—to anyone! Not one single tiny suspicion of a hint!"

And Olga, looking into her eyes, read terror in her soul.

CHAPTER XVII
THE VERDICT

"It's a difficult position," said Nick.

"It's a damnable position," said Max. He stared across the white table-cloth with eyes that brooded under down-drawn brows. "I don't anticipate any sudden development if I can keep her off that cursed opium. But—I'd give fifty pounds to have her people within reach."

"Do you know where they are?" said Nick.

Max shrugged his shoulders. "They are cruising about the Atlantic to give Mrs. Bruce, who is neurotic, a rest-cure. Of course, when I undertook to keep an eye on the girl, I never anticipated this. Her brother was anxious about her, I thought somewhat unnecessarily. It was that blackguard Hunt-Goring who precipitated matters. I've given him a pretty straight warning, though Heaven alone knows what effect it will have."

"What did you say to him?" questioned Nick.

"I said that I had just discovered that he had been giving her cigarettes that contained opium. I warned him that it was criminally unsafe, that her brain was peculiarly susceptible to drugs, and that he would probably cause her death if he persisted; also, that if he did I would see that he was held responsible. What more could I say?"

"That was fairly direct certainly," said Nick. "And he?"

"He asked me to dine," said Max.

Nick laughed. "And you didn't accept?"

"Would you have accepted?" Max turned on him almost savagely.

"I think I should," said Nick. "There's nothing like studying the enemy from close quarters. But go ahead! Tell me more! When do you expect her people back?"

"Possibly in a fortnight. They have been gone that time already—rather more. And they expected to make a month of it."

Nick nodded. "We ought to be able to hold the fort for that time. What did your friend Sir Kersley think?"

Max lifted one eyebrow. "What did he say to you about it?"

Nick struck a match for his cigarette with considerable dexterity. "About Violet—practically nothing. About her mother—a good deal."

"I wonder why." Max spoke somewhat curtly.

Nick lighted his cigarette with a whimsical expression. "You don't seem to have noticed what an excellent confidant I make," he said.

"Ah, I know you are safe." There was conviction in Max's tone. "But Kersley is such a reserved chap. And—that ancient affair ruined his life."

"I gathered that," said Nick. "As a matter of fact, I knew a little of the affair before we met. He had been a doctor in my old regiment. It was five years after he retired that I joined; but most of the fellows knew the story. It reached me one way or another. I was deuced sorry for him when I heard the truth. Most people out there were of the opinion that he had treated her badly—was, in fact, to a very great measure responsible for the tragedy."

"That of course was not so," said Max deliberately. "She was responsible from first to last. She knew of the taint in her veins. He did not—till he detected it."

"Rather hard on her!" remarked Nick.

"Would you have married her?" The green eyes fixed him with sudden stern intentness.

Nick blinked rapidly for a few seconds. "I daren't answer that question," he said at length. "You see, I'm not a doctor."

Max rose abruptly. "Are doctors the only beings whoever think of the next generation?" he asked bitterly.

"There is a saying," said Nick, "that 'Love conquers all things.'"

"Pshaw!" said Max. "It never conquered heredity."

"I withdraw the proposition," said Nick. "But, I say, Wyndham!" He paused.

"Well?" Max swung round aggressively with hands in his pockets.

"Suppose the woman you loved developed that disease—would you throw her over?" Nick spoke tentatively.

Max flung back his head and stared at the ceiling. "Why do you ask?"

"Because I want to know what you are made of," replied Nick with simplicity.

Max turned and slowly walked to the window. "Yes," he said, with his back turned, "I should."

Nick was silent.

After a moment Max glanced round at him. "You wouldn't, I suppose?"

"No," said Nick.

"You would marry her regardless of the consequences?"

"If I were an ordinary man—perhaps," said Nick. "If I were a doctor—" he paused—"if I were a doctor, Max," he said again with a sudden smile, "I think I should tackle the situation from another standpoint. Either way, if she loved me and I loved her, I would marry her. As to the consequences—there wouldn't be any."

Max grunted. "Of course you are the exception to every rule."

"Who told you that?" thrust in Nick.

"It's been dinned into me ever since I met you." Half-churlishly Max made reply, and turning fell to pacing the room with the measured tread of one trained to step warily.

"And you believe it?" Nick leaned back in his chair peering forth through eyes half-closed.

"I do—more or less."

"Thanks!" said Nick. "And how goes the courtship?"

Max frowned heavily, without speaking.

"Pardon my asking," said Nick, "and consider the question answered!"

Max stopped squarely in front of him. "It doesn't go," he said briefly.

Nick's glance darted over him for an instant. "What method have you been employing? Coercion? Persuasion? Indifference? Or strategy?"

Max's hands showed clenched inside his pockets. "I'm leaving her alone," he growled.

"Then change your tactics at once!" said Nick. "Try an advance!"

"That's just the mischief. In the present damnable state of affairs, I am powerless. Violet Campion is hating me pretty badly, and—she—is thinking it clever to follow suit. She is avoiding me like the plague."

"That's sometimes a good sign," said Nick thoughtfully.

"Not in this case. It only means she is afraid of me."

Nick's glance flashed up at him again. "For any special reason?"

"I have given her none."

"Violet again?" queried Nick.

"Probably."

253

Nick ruminated. "You don't think it advisable to tell her how things are?"

"I?" The brief word sounded almost hostile. Max resumed his pacing on the instant. "I'm not an utter brute, Ratcliffe," he said, "whatever I may appear."

Nick sent a cloud of smoke upwards. "Would you call me a brute if I told her?" he asked.

"Yes, I should." Curt and prompt came the answer. "What is more, I won't have it done."

"She is a sensible little soul," contended Nick.

"She may be. But it would increase the difficulties a hundredfold. The girl herself would probably suspect something, and that would almost inevitably precipitate matters. No, the only possible course is to leave things alone for the present. The symptoms are slight, and though it is impossible to say from moment to moment what will happen, the chances are that if we can keep Hunt-Goring from doing any further mischief, the disease may remain in a stationary condition for some time. In that case you may manage to get Olga away on this tom-fool expedition of yours to India before any serious development takes place."

"I see," said Nick. "And you are convinced that a serious development is inevitable?"

"Absolutely." Max came strolling back from the window with eyes fixed and far-seeing. "It is as plain as a pike-staff to any professional man. Kersley detected it at once—as I knew he would; and that was before the midnight episode in Olga's room. Yes, it's bound to come. It may be gradual. It may even take the form of paralysis. But with her temperament I don't think that very likely. It will probably come suddenly as a sequel to some shock or violent agitation. But come—sooner or later—it must."

He spoke slowly, with the deliberation of absolute certainty. Reaching the mantelpiece he lodged himself against it and smoked with his eyes on the ceiling.

Nick watched him with a veiled scrutiny from the depths of his chair. "So that is the verdict," he said at last.

Max nodded without speaking.

"And how long have you known?"

"About a month."

"But you knew them before then?"

Max looked down at him with a slight gesture that passed unexplained. "As long as I have known the Ratcliffes," he said.

"It must have been something of a shock to you," suggested Nick.

Max's jaw hardened. "I was infinitely more interested in her when I knew," he said.

"Really?" said Nick.

"Yes, really." Max spoke with finality. "I assure you I am not impressionable," he added a moment later with the cynical twist of the lips that Olga knew so well. "And I never play with fire. That form of amusement doesn't attract me."

A sudden humorous glitter shone between Nick's half-closed eyelids. "But even serious people burn their fingers sometimes," he observed. "I presume you haven't proposed yet?"

"Yes, I have." Max spoke with dogged assertiveness.

Nick jerked upright. "The deuce you have!"

"You needn't excite yourself," Max assured him grimly. "We are not officially engaged yet—or likely to be. You needn't stick your spoke in. She knows I shan't marry her against her will."

"Oh, that's settled, is it?" Nick's eyes flashed over him with lightning rapidity.

"It is." Max began to smile. "And the marriage will take place some time before the end of next year."

The door opened abruptly while he was speaking, but he finished his sentence with extreme deliberation in spite of the fact that it was Olga who entered,—Olga, flushed and eager, vivid, throbbing with excitement. If she heard his words she paid no heed to them, but broke at once into breathless speech.

"Oh, Nick, it's the post! It's the post! A letter from Dad and another from Muriel; both for you!"

Nick stretched out his hand to her. "Come over here, kiddie! We'll read them together."

She sprang to him, knelt beside him, and warmly hugged him. Max remained propped against the mantelpiece, looking on, ignored by both.

"Muriel's first!" commanded Nick; and, with hands that shook, Olga slit open the envelope.

He put his arm about her shoulders as she withdrew the sheet and opened it out. "Yes, you can read it too. I know what's in it, bless her heart!"

So together they read the closely-written pages. There was silence in the room as they did so, broken only by the crackling of the paper, while Max Wyndham kept a motionless watch, his shaggy brows drawn close.

Suddenly Olga lifted her face. "Oh, Nick, isn't she a darling? I—I—it makes me feel such a beast!"

Nick's hand pinched her cheek in answer. His lips twitched a little, but he did not speak or raise his eyes.

She leaned her cheek against his shoulder. "I won't read any more, Nick. It's too private. May I open Dad's?"

He took his wife's letter between his fingers and dexterously folded it. "All right, Olga *mia!* Let us hear the verdict of the great Dr. Jim!"

He glanced up at Max with the words and instantly looked away.

Olga had apparently forgotten his very existence. She opened her father's letter still in quivering haste, and again there was a silence of several seconds while they read.

It was broken in a fashion which not one of the three anticipated. Quite suddenly Olga's lips began to quiver. She raised her head with the agitated gesture of one straining for self-control; and then in a moment the tears were running down her cheeks, and she covered her face and sobbed.

"Kiddie! Kiddie!" remonstrated Nick.

But it was Max who stooped and swiftly lifted her, holding her against his heart, stroking the fair hair with his steady capable hand. And surely there was magic in his touch, for almost immediately her weeping ceased. She looked up with slightly startled eyes, and drew herself gently but quite definitely from him.

"Thank you," she said, with a quaint touch of dignity. "You're very kind. Nick dear, I'm sorry. I—I'm all right now. Dad's very sweet to put it like that, pretending he doesn't mind a bit. I don't know how ever I shall say good-bye to him."

"You are really going then?" said Max.

She looked at him with a fleeting smile. "Yes, really!" she said.

"I congratulate you," he said.

Nick chuckled. "He is pretending he doesn't mind, too, Olga."

Olga flushed a little. "Oh, Max never pretends," she said. "Do you, Max?"

He smiled in his grim fashion. "It is not for me to contradict you," he said. "Permit me to congratulate you instead, and to hope that the East will not take as great liberties with your complexion as it has with Nick's."

"I'd rather be like Nick than anyone else in the world," she declared, with one arm wound about her hero's neck.

"Curious, isn't it?" grinned Nick.

"Almost incredible!" said Max.

"But quite true!" asserted Olga with vehemence.

Max swung around with his hands in his pockets, and sauntered to the door. Reaching it, he glanced back for a moment at the eager, girlish face, unperturbed, inscrutable.

"Strange as it may seem," he said, "I personally would rather that you remained like yourself."

"What cheek!" said Olga, as the door shut.

"Oh, isn't he allowed to say that?" enquired Nick.

She nestled to him, albeit half in protest. "Do let's talk about important things!" she said.

And Nick at once took the hint.

CHAPTER XVIII

SOMETHING LOST

Had Olga been a little less engrossed with the all-absorbing prospect that had just opened before her, she might have regarded as somewhat unusual the fact that Violet made no further mention of the proposed trip with Major Hunt-Goring during the week that followed. But, such was her preoccupation, she had even ceased to remember his existence. Little more than six weeks lay between her and the great adventure to which she was pledged, and she had already commenced her preparations. A visit to town would of course be inevitable, but this could not take place till Muriel's return at the end of the month. Nevertheless Olga, being woman to the core, found many things to do at home, and immersed herself in sewing with a zest that provoked Nick to much mirth.

Violet watched her lazily, with occasional offers to help which were seldom meant or taken seriously.

"I believe I shall come after you, Allegro," she said once. "It will be very dull without you."

"You know you are never dull in the shooting season," was Olga's sensible reply. "You never have time to think of me then."

"Quite true, dear," Violet admitted. "I wonder what sort of crowd Bruce will collect this year, and if any of them will want to marry me. He is always furiously angry when that happens. I can't imagine why. It amuses me," said Violet, with a yawn.

"Perhaps he doesn't want you to get married," suggested Olga.

"Apparently not. And yet I am sure he would be thankful to be rid of me. We never agree." The beautiful eyes gleamed mischievously. "I suppose he will expect me to marry a husband of his selection by-and-bye. He is very mediæval in some things."

"I don't believe you ever mean to marry at all," said Olga.

"Oh, yes, indeed I do!" Violet uttered her soft, low laugh. "But I am mediæval too, Allegro. Have you never noticed? I am waiting for the first man who is brave enough to run away with me."

It was on the day following this conversation that she prevailed upon Olga to leave her numerous occupations for an hour or so and motor her over to Brethaven to pay another visit to her old nurse, Mrs. Briggs. Nick wished to go over to Redlands to sort some papers, and offered his company as far as his own gates.

"You can walk to 'The Ship' from there," he said to Olga. "It's only half a mile, and after that you can run about the shore and amuse yourselves till I am ready to go back."

"Don't get up to mischief!" said Max briefly.

Violet gave him a quick look from under her lashes, but said no word.

It was a hot morning with a hint of thunder in the atmosphere. With Olga at the wheel, they set off soon after breakfast, leaving Max pumping his bicycle at the surgery-door with grim energy. He was going to the cottage-hospital that morning, a fact which left the motor at liberty till the afternoon.

Mile after mile of dusty road slid by, and Olga, with her heart in the future, sang softly to herself for sheer lightness of heart. She had ceased to trouble about Max, since he, quite obviously, had no intention of obtruding himself upon her. The problem—if problem there were—was evidently one that would keep until her return from India, and Olga was child enough to feel that that event was far too remote to trouble her now.

So, with a gay spirit, she piloted her two friends on that summer morning. No presentiment of evil touched her, no cloud was in her sky. Gaily she sped along the sunny road, little dreaming that that same sun that so gladdened her was to set upon the last of her youth.

The car was in a good mood also, and they hummed merrily past the little stone church of Brethaven and up to the great iron gate of Redlands just as the clock in the tower struck ten.

"Good business!" commented Nick, as he descended to open the gate. "That gives me two hours and a half. Don't be later than twelve-thirty, Olga *mia*, for starting back."

Olga promised, as she dexterously turned the car and ran in up the drive. He sprang upon the step, and so she brought him to his own door.

"Good-bye, Nick!" she said then, lifting her bright face.

He bent and lightly kissed her. "Good-bye! Don't go and get drowned, either of you, for my sake! Yes, you can leave the car here. It won't rain at present."

He stood on his own step and watched them go, with a motherly smile on his wrinkled face.

"Bless their hearts!" he murmured, as he finally turned away. "I'll swear it's all a mistake. She looks like a queen this morning; and as for Olga, if she has really given her heart to that ugly doctor chap I have never yet seen a woman in love."

He entered the house with the words, and straightway dismissed them from his mind.

"We will go to the shore first," Violet decreed. "Mrs. Briggs won't be expecting us so early. I hear that some more of the Priory land has been slipping into the sea. We must go and see it."

So to the shore they went. The slip was not a serious one. They made their way to the spot over loose sand and rocks, and dropped down in a sandy hollow to rest.

"Poor old Priory!" said Violet. "It's sure to be swallowed up like the rest some day. I wonder if I shall live to see it."

"Oh, surely not!" said Olga.

Violet laughed. "Do you think I am destined to die young then?"

"I can't imagine you dying or growing old," said Olga, with simplicity.

"My dear, what gross flattery!" Violet laughed again, her eyes upon the glittering sea. "Immortal youth! How divine it sounds! Allegro, I should hate to be old." She stretched out her arms to the sky-line. "I want to keep young for ever," she said. "Do you really think I shall? I sometimes think—" she paused.

"What?" said Olga.

She turned round to her with a little gesture of confidence. "I sometimes have a feeling, Allegro, that I must be getting old or dull or plain already. Men don't make love to me so much as they did."

"My dear, what nonsense!" exclaimed Olga, with burning cheeks.

"No, listen! It's true." There was almost a sound of tears in the deep voice. "It's quite true, Allegro. I am not so attractive as I was. I feel it. I know it. Something is lost. I don't know what it is. It went from me that night—you remember!—and it hasn't returned. I thought it was my soul at first. I still sometimes wonder." She laid a hand that quivered and clung upon Olga's arm. "And the dreadful part of it is, Allegro, that Max knows. He looks at me with the most deadly knowledge in his eyes—such wicked eyes they are, all green and piercing, and so cruel—so cruel."

A great shiver went through her, and then all in a moment—before Olga could utter a word—her mood had changed. She leaped suddenly to her feet, all sparkling animation and excitement.

"See! There is a yacht just come round the headland! How close it is! Oh, Allegro, wouldn't you love to go on the water this stifling day?"

"An easy wish to gratify!" observed a voice close to them.

Olga turned with a violent start. Violet merely glanced over her shoulder and smiled. Hunt-Goring, stepping lightly in canvas shoes, came airily forward over the sand, and bowed low.

"I am the *deus ex machina*," he said. "The yacht is mine—and entirely at your service."

Olga's face was crimson. She got quickly to her feet and stood stiffly silent.

Hunt-Goring was looking remarkably elegant, attired in white drill with a yachting cap which he carried in his hand.

"I seem to have come at an opportune moment," he said. "Really, the fates are more than kind. The yacht is making for Brethaven jetty to take me on board. If you ladies will come with me for a couple of hours' cruise, I need scarcely say how charmed I shall be."

He was looking at Violet as he spoke, and she made instant and impulsive reply. "Of course we will! It will be too delicious—the very thing I was longing for. What lucky chance sent you our way, I wonder?"

She gave him her hand, which he took with a gallantry that sent a quiver of disgust through Olga. With a sharp effort she spoke, hurriedly, nervously, but very much to the point.

"It's very good of you, but we can't possibly come. We must be getting back. You are going to see Mrs. Briggs, you know, Violet. And we promised Nick we wouldn't be late starting home from Redlands."

Violet's quick frown appeared like a sudden cloud. "My dear child, what nonsense! As if Mrs. Briggs mattered! And as for Nick, he won't be ready for more than two hours. You heard him say so."

But Olga stood her ground. "I don't see how we can possibly go—anyhow without telling Nick first. In fact, I would rather not."

Hunt-Goring was smiling—the smile of the man who has heard it all before. "Miss Olga is evidently afflicted with a tender conscience," he observed. "But if you really have two hours to spare and really care to go on the water, I do not see how Nick can reasonably object. Of course I have no desire to persuade you. I only beg that you will follow your inclinations."

"Of course!" said Violet quickly. "And we are coming—at least I am. Allegro, you can please yourself, but it will be very horrid of you if you won't come too."

Olga's pale eyes sparkled. "That depends on one's point of view," she said, with a touch of warmth. "You know what I think about it. I told you the other day."

"My dear, that is too ridiculous," declared Violet. "I never heard such rubbish in my life. Besides, it's only for a couple of hours. Major Hunt-Goring," appealing suddenly, "do tell her how absurd she is! What possible objection could there be to our going out with you for a morning's cruise?"

"None, I should say," smiled Hunt-Goring. "But doubtless Miss Olga has made up her mind and discussion would be only a waste of time. Shall we start?"

"Yes, we will!" agreed Violet impetuously. "I am simply dying for a breath of sea air. Ah, do give me a cigarette! I finished my last this morning."

And then Olga's eyes were opened, and she knew the reason of this man's ascendancy over her friend. The certainty went through her like the stab of a sword, and hard upon it came the realization that to desert Violet at that moment would be an act of treachery. So strong was the conviction that she did not dare to question it. It was as if a voice had spoken in her soul, and blindly she obeyed.

"I will come too," she said.

Violet beamed upon her instantly. "Well done, Allegro! I thought you couldn't be so unkind as to stay behind when I wanted you."

"A woman's second thoughts are always best," observed Hunt-Goring.

She looked him straight in the eyes. "I am going for Miss Campion's sake alone," she said.

He smiled at her with covert insolence. "You are a true woman," he said.

"Is that intended for a compliment or otherwise?" asked Violet.

"Otherwise, I think," said Olga, in a very low voice.

"Acquit me at least of idle flattery!" said Hunt-Goring, with a laugh.

CHAPTER XIX
THE REVELATION

It was certainly a perfect day for a cruise. The sea lay blue and still as a lake, so clear that the rocks made purple shadows in its crystal depths. Under any other circumstances, Olga would have revelled in the beauty of it, but there was no enjoyment for her that day. She stood on the deck of the yacht as she steamed away from the jetty, and watched the uneven shore recede with a feeling of impotence that was not without an element of fear. For it seemed to her that she was a prisoner, looking her last upon the liberty of her youth.

The vessel was of no inconsiderable size and moved swiftly through the still water, cleaving her way like a bird through space. It was not long before they passed the jutting headland that hid the little fishing-village from view; but Olga still stood motionless at the rail, fighting down the cold dread at her heart.

She could hear Violet's voice on the other side of the deck, gaily chattering to Hunt-Goring. The scent of their cigarettes reached her, and she clenched her hands. She was sure now that he had been supplying Violet with them secretly. She had been too deeply engrossed with her own affairs to think of this before, and bitterly did she blame herself for this absorption.

Poor Olga! It was the prelude to a life-long self-reproach.

They were heading out to sea now, running smoothly into the glaring sunshine. It poured upon her mercilessly where she stood, but she was scarcely aware of it. She gazed backward at the shore with eyes that saw not.

Suddenly a soft voice spoke at her shoulder. "What! Still sulking? Do you know you are remarkably like a boy?"

She turned with a great start, meeting the eyes she feared. "I don't know what you mean," she said, drawing sharply back.

He laughed his smooth, easy laugh. "I mean that you are behaving like a cub in need of chastisement. Do you seriously think I am going to put up with it—from a chit like you?"

She looked him up and down with a single flashing glance of clear scorn. "How much do you think I am going to put up with?" she said.

He leaned his arms upon the rail in an attitude of supreme complacence. "I may be the villain of the piece," he observed, "but I have no desire to be melodramatic. I have come over here to talk to you quietly and sensibly about the future. Of course if you—"

"What have you to do with my future?" she thrust in fiercely. She would have given all she had to be calm at that moment, but calmness was beyond her. Though her fear had utterly departed, she was quivering with indignation from head to foot.

Hunt-Goring kept his face turned downwards towards the swirl of water that leaped by them. He was quite plainly prepared for the question.

"Since you ask me," he responded coolly, "I should say—a good deal."

"In what way?" she demanded.

She could see that he was still smiling—that maddening, perpetual smile, and she thought that her sheer abhorrence of the man would choke her. But with all her throbbing strength she held herself in check.

He did not answer her at once. She waited, compelling herself to silence.

At length quite calmly he turned and faced her. "Well now, Olga, listen to me," he said. "I am a good deal older than you are, but I am still capable of a certain amount of foolishness. What I am now going to say to you, I have wanted to say for some time, but you have been so absurdly shy with me that—as you perceive—I have been obliged to resort to strategy to obtain a hearing."

He paused, for Olga had suddenly gripped the rail as if she needed support. Her face was deathly, but out of it the pale eyes blazed in fierce questioning.

"What do you mean?" she said. "What strategy?"

He laid his hand upon hers and gripped it hard. "Don't be hysterical!" he said. "I am paying you the compliment of treating you like a woman of sense."

She shrank away from him, but he continued to grip her hand with brutal force till the pain of it reached her consciousness and sent the blood upwards to her face. Then he let her go.

"Yes," he said coolly, "I have been laying my mine for some time now. It has not been particularly easy or particularly pleasant, but since I considered you worth a little trouble I did not grudge it. The long and the short of it is this: I fell in love with you last winter. You may remember that I caught your brothers poaching on my ground, and you came to me to beg them off. Well, I granted your request—for a consideration. You may remember the consideration also. You had been at great pains to snub me until that episode. I made you pay for the snubbing. I imposed a fine—do you remember?"

"I have loathed you ever since," she broke in.

"Oh, yes," he said. "I know that. That was what started the mischief. I am so constituted that resistance is but fuel to the flame. In that respect I believe I am not unique. It is a by no means remarkable trait of the masculine character, you will find. Well, I made you pay. It was to be two kisses, was it not? You gave me one, and then for some reason you fled. That left you in my debt."

"It is a debt I will never pay!" she declared passionately. "I will die first!"

He laughed. There was something in his eyes—something intolerable—that made her avert her own in spite of herself. In desperation she glanced around for Violet.

"She is asleep," said Hunt-Goring.

She turned on him then like a fury. "You mean you have drugged her!" she cried.

He shrugged his shoulders. "Not to that extent. You can wake her if you wish, but I think you had better hear me out first—for her sake also. It is better for all parties that we should come to a clear understanding."

With immense effort she controlled herself. "Very well. What do you wish me to understand?"

"Simply this," said Hunt-Goring. "I know very well that your engagement to Wyndham was simply a move in the game, and that you have not the faintest intention of marrying him. That is so, I think?"

She was silent, taken by surprise.

"I thought so," he continued. "You see, I am not so easy to hoodwink. And now I am going to act up to my villain's *rôle* and break that engagement of yours—which is no engagement. To put it quite shortly and comprehensibly—I am going to marry you myself."

She stared at him in gasping astonishment. "You!" she said. "You!"

He laughed into her eyes of horror. "You will soon get used to the idea," he said. "You see, Wyndham doesn't really want you, and I do. That is the one extenuating circumstance of my villainy. I want you so badly that I don't much care what steps I take to get you. And so long as you continue to hate me as heartily as you do now, just by so much shall I continue to want you. Is that quite plain?"

She was still staring at him in open repulsion. "And you think I would marry you?" she said breathlessly. "You think I would marry you?"

"I think you will have to," said Hunt-Goring, with his silky laugh. "I love you, you see." He added, after a moment, "I shan't be unkind to you if you behave reasonably. I am well off. I can give you practically anything you want. Of course you will have to give also; but that goes without saying. The point is, how soon can we be married?"

"Never!" she cried vehemently. "Never! Never!"

He looked at her, and again her eyes fell; but she continued, nevertheless, with less of violence but more of force.

"I don't know what you mean by suggesting such a thing. I think you must be quite mad—as I should be if I took you seriously. I am not going to marry you, Major Hunt-Goring. I have never liked you, and I never shall. You force me to speak plainly, and so I am telling you the simple truth."

"Thank you," said Hunt-Goring. "Well, now, let us see if I can persuade you to change your mind."

"You will never do that," she said quickly.

He smiled. "I wonder! Anyhow, let me try! It makes no difference to you that I love you?"

"No," she told him flatly. "None whatever. In fact, I don't believe it."

"I will prove it to you one day," he said. "But let that pass now, since it has no weight with you. I quite realize that I shall not persuade you to marry me for your own sake or for mine. But—I think you may be induced to consider the matter for the sake of—your friend."

"In what way?" Breathlessly she asked the Question. for again it was as if a warning voice spoke within her, bidding her to go warily.

He paused a moment. Then: "Has it never struck you that there is something rather—peculiar—about her?" he asked suavely.

She brought her eyes back to his in sharp apprehension. "Peculiar? No, never! What do you mean?"

"Are you quite sure of that?" he insisted.

She began to falter in spite of herself. "Never, until—until quite lately. Never till you gave her those—abominable—cigarettes."

"Believe me, there is no harm whatever in those cigarettes," he said. "I smoke them myself constantly. Try them for yourself if you don't believe me. They contain a minute quantity of opium, it is true, but only sufficient to soothe the nerves. No, those cigarettes are not responsible. That peculiarity which you have recently begun to notice is due to quite another cause. Surely you must have always known that she was different from other girls. Have you never thought her excitable, even unaccountable in some of her actions? Has she never told you of strange fancies, strange dreams? And her restlessness, her odd whims, her insatiable craving for morbid horrors, have you never taken note of these?"

He spoke with deliberate emphasis, narrowly watching the effect of his words.

Olga's hands were gripped fast together; her wide eyes searched his face.

"Oh, tell me what you mean!" she entreated, a piteous quiver in her voice. "Tell me plainly what you mean!"

"I will," he said. "Violet Campion's mother was a homicidal maniac. She killed her husband—this girl's father—in a fit of madness one night three months after their marriage. It happened in India, and was put down to native treachery in order to hush it up, but it was well known that no native was responsible for it. During the six months that followed, she was kept under restraint, hopelessly insane. It was in her blood—the worst form of insanity known. At the birth of the child she died. That will explain to you my exact meaning, and if you need corroboration you can go to Max Wyndham for it. She has begun to develop symptoms of her mother's complaint. All her peculiarities arise from incipient madness!"

"Oh, no!" Olga whispered, with fingers straining against each other. "It's not possible! It's not true!"

"It is absolutely true," he said. "And you know it is true. At the same time it is just possible that the disease may be arrested. Wyndham himself will tell you this. We discussed the matter quite recently. It may be arrested even for years if nothing happens to precipitate it. Of course her people will never let her marry, but she is not, I fancy, the sort of young woman to whom wedded bliss is essential. Naturally, all this has been kept from her. There are not many people who know of it. I am one, because I knew her mother both before and after her marriage, being a young subaltern at the time and stationed at the very place where the tragedy occurred. Wyndham is another, being the *protégé* of Kersley Whitton to whom the girl's mother was engaged and who was the first to discover the fatal tendency. She married Campion mainly out of pique because Whitton threw her over. He was a man of sixty, and his son was grown up at the time. I have often thought that he behaved with remarkable magnanimity when he adopted the child of the woman who had murdered his father."

Olga shivered suddenly and violently. The horror of the tale had turned her cold from head to foot. She no longer questioned the truth of it. She knew beyond all doubting that it was true.

The sun still shone gloriously, and the yacht slipped on through the shining water, throwing up the sparkling foam as she went. But to Olga the whole world had become a place of darkness and of the shadow of death. Whichever way she turned, she was afraid.

"Oh, why have you told me?" she said at last. "Why—why have you told me?"

"Can't you guess?" said Hunt-Goring.

"No!" Yet her breath came sharply with the word. If she did not guess, she feared.

He looked down at her for the first time unsmiling. "I have told you," he said, "that I mean to marry you, and—in keeping with the part of villain which you have assigned to me—I don't much care what I do to get you."

She met his look with all her quivering courage. "But what has this to do with that?" she said.

She saw his face harden, become cruel. "Miss Campion is nothing to me," he said brutally. "Either you give me your most sacred promise to marry me before the end of the year, or—I shall tell her the truth here and now, as I have just told it to you."

She shrank as though he had struck her. "Oh, you couldn't!" she cried out wildly. "You couldn't! No man could be such a fiend!"

He came a step nearer to her, and suddenly his eyes glowed with a fire that scorched her to the soul. "You had better not tempt me!" he said. "Or I may do that—and more also!"

She put her hands up to shield her face from his look, but he caught them suddenly and savagely into his own, overbearing her resistance with indomitable mastery.

"Promise me!" he said. "Promise me!"

His lips were horribly near her own. She strained away from him tensely, with all her strength. "I will not!" she panted. "I will not!"

"You shall!" he declared furiously. "Do you think I will be beaten by a child like you? I tell you, you shall!"

But still desperately she struggled against him, repeating voicelessly, "I will not! I will not!"

He gripped her fast, holding her face up mercilessly to his own. "You think I won't do it?" he said.

"I know you won't!" she gasped back. "You couldn't! No man—no man could!"

"I swear to you that I will!" he said.

"No!" she breathed. "No! No! No!"

She saw the fury on his face suddenly harden and turn cold. Abruptly he set her free.

"Very well," he said. "Marry you I will. But first I will show you that I am a man of my word."

He swung round upon his heel to leave her. But in that instant the warning voice cried out again in Olga's soul, compelling her to swift action. She sprang after him, caught his arm, clinging to it with all her failing strength.

"You will not!" she gasped out in an agony of entreaty. "You could not! You shall not!"

He stopped, looking down without pity into her face of supplication. "Then give me that promise!" he said.

She shook her head. "No, not that—not that!"

"Why not?" he insisted. "Are you hoping to catch your red-haired doctor? You are not likely to secure anyone else, and he will probably prove elusive."

She flinched at the gibing words, but still she held him back. "No, no! I don't want to marry anyone. I have always said so."

"Have you said so to him?" asked Hunt-Goring.

She was silent, but the quick blood ran to her temples betraying her.

"I thought not," he said. "So that is the explanation, is it? That is why you will have none of me, eh?"

"Oh, how can you be so hateful?" she cried vehemently.

He laughed. "You won't let me be anything else, I assure you I would be amiability itself if you would permit. Well now, which is it to be? You say you don't want to marry anyone. That, we have seen, is only a figure of speech. But since the red-haired doctor is not wanting you and I am—"

"You are wrong!" she broke in, with sudden heat.

Some hidden fire within her had kindled into flame at his words; it burned with a fierce strength. For the first time she challenged him without any sense of fear.

He looked at her in unfeigned astonishment. "I beg your pardon?"

"You are wrong!" she said again, and it was as if some inner force inspired the words. She spoke without conscious volition of her own. "Max Wyndham has asked me to marry him—and marry him I will!"

She never knew with what triumphant finality she spoke, but the effect of her words was instant and terrible. Even as they left her lips, she saw the dark blood rise in a wave to his forehead, swelling the veins there to purple cords. His eyes became suddenly bloodshot and glittered devilishly. His hands clenched, and she almost thought he was going to strike her.

With a desperate effort she faced him without a tremor, instinctively aware that courage alone could save her.

For fully thirty seconds he said no word, and as they slipped away she saw the dreadful wave of passion gradually recede. But even then he continued to glare at her till with a quiet movement she took her hand from his arm and turned away.

Then, as she stood at the deck-rail, at last he spoke. "So that is your last word upon the subject?"

She answered him briefly, "Yes."

She kept her face turned seawards. She was suddenly and overwhelmingly conscious of bodily weakness. All her strength seemed to have gone into that one great effort, that at the moment had seemed no effort at all. She felt as if she were going to faint, and gripped herself with all her quivering resolution, praying wildly that he might not notice.

He did not notice. For a few seconds more he stood behind her, while she waited, palpitating, for his next move. Then, very suddenly he turned and left her.

And Olga, instantly relaxing from a tension too terrible to be born, covered her face with her hands and shuddered over and over again in sick disgust.

It was many minutes before she recovered, minutes during which her mind seemed to be almost too stunned for thought. Very gradually at length she began to remember the words she had last uttered, the weapon she had used; and numbly she wondered at herself.

No, she had scarcely acted on her own initiative. Her action had been prompted by some force of which till that moment she had had no knowledge, a force great enough to lift her above her own natural impulses, great enough to help her in her sore strait, and to make all other things seem of small importance.

What would Max have said to that emphatic declaration of hers? But surely it was Max, and none other, who had inspired it. Surely—surely—ah, what was this that was happening to her? What magic was at work? She suddenly lifted her face to the dazzling summer sky. A brief giddiness possessed her—and passed. She was as one over whom a mighty wave had dashed. She came up from it, breathless, trembling, yet with a throbbing ecstasy at her heart such as she had never known before. For the impossible had happened to her. She realized it now. She—Olga Ratcliffe, the ordinary, the colourless, the prosaic—was caught in the grip of the Unknown Power, that Immortal Wonder which for lack of a better name men call Romance. And she knew it, she exulted in it, she stretched out her woman's hands to grasp it, as a babe will seek to grasp the sunshine, possessing and possessed.

In that moment she acknowledged that the bitter struggle through which she had just come had been indeed worth while. It had exhausted her, terrified her; but it had shown her her heart in such a fashion as to leave no room for doubt or misunderstanding. Even yet she quivered with the rapture of the revelation. It thrilled her through and through. For she knew that Max Wyndham reigned there in complete and undisputed possession. No other man had entered before him, or would ever enter after....

Slowly, reluctantly, she came back from her Elysium. She descended to earth and faced again the difficulties of the way.

She opened her eyes upon the yacht still running seawards, and decided that they must turn. She wondered if Hunt-Goring had regained his self-control, if he were ashamed of himself, if possibly he might bring himself to apologize, and what she should say to him if he did. Her heart felt very full. She knew she could not be very severe with him if he were really repentant.

Then she remembered Violet,—her friend....

CHAPTER XX
THE SEARCH

For the third time Nick looked at his watch. It was nearly one. He jumped to his feet with a grimace.

"What on earth are those girls up to?"

Rapidly he locked drawer after drawer of his writing-table, gathered up a sheaf of papers, and turned to go.

The library at Redlands overlooked a wide lawn that led through shrubberies to the edge of the cliff, up the face of which had been cut a winding path. He paused a moment considering this. Would they return from the shore by that way? If so, he would miss them if he went in search of them by the drive.

Impatiently he turned back towards the window, and in that moment he caught sight of a flying figure crossing the lawn,—Olga, with a white, strained face, hatless, dishevelled, gasping.

Nick's one arm fought with the heavy window and flung it up. In another second he had leaped out to meet her. She ran to him, stumbled ere she reached him, fell against him, helpless, sobbing, exhausted.

He held her up. "What is it? Violet? Is she drowned?" he questioned rapidly.

"No—no!" She gasped the words as she lay against his shoulder.

"All right then! Take your time! Come and sit down!" said Nick.

He supported her to the low window-sill, and she sank down upon it, still clinging to him with agonized gasping, voiceless and utterly spent.

He stood beside her, strongly grasping her hand. "Keep quite quiet!" he said. "It's the quickest in the end."

She obeyed him, as was her custom, leaning her head against him till gradually her breath came back to her and speech became possible.

"Oh, Nick!" she whispered then. "That any man—could be—so vile!"

"What man?" said Nick sharply.

"Major Hunt-Goring."

He stooped swiftly and looked into her face. "What has he been doing?"

"I'll tell you!" she said. "I'll tell you!"

And then, arrested possibly by something in that flashing regard, she raised herself and looked straight up at him.

"I can only tell you everything," she said, "if you will promise me not to go and quarrel with him—in fact, not to go near him. Will you promise, Nick?"

"I will not," said Nick.

"You must!" she said. "You must!"

"I will not," he said again.

She held his hand imploringly. "Not if I ask you—not if I beg you—"

"Not in any case," he said. "Now tell me the truth as quickly as you can."

She shook her head. "Nick, I can't. He is quite unscrupulous. He might kill you!"

"So he might," said Nick grimly. "He's crazy enough for anything. What has he been doing?"

"Is he crazy?" she said, catching at the word.

"He's drug-ridden," said Nick, "and devil-ridden too upon occasion. Now tell me!"

She began to cry with her head against his arm. "Nick,—I'm frightened! I can't!"

"Oh, damn!" said Nick to the world at large. And then he gently released himself and knelt beside her. "Look here, Olga darling! There's nothing to frighten you. I'm not a headlong fool. There! Dry your eyes, and be sensible! What's the beast been up to? Made love to you, has he?"

His bony hand grasped hers again very vitally, very reassuringly. Almost insensibly she yielded herself to his control. Quiveringly she began to tell him of the morning's happenings.

Perhaps it was as well that she did not see Nick's face as she did so, or she might have found it difficult to continue. As it was she spoke haltingly, with many pauses, describing to him Hunt-Goring's arrival and invitation, her own dilemma, her final surrender.

"I couldn't help it, Nick," she said, still fast clinging to his hand. "I couldn't let her go alone."

"Go on," said Nick.

And then she told him of Hunt-Goring's overture, her own sick repulsion for the man, his persistence, his brutality.

At that abruptly Nick broke in. "Before you go any farther—has he ever made love to you before?"

She answered him because she had no choice. "Yes, Nick. But I always hated him."

"And you didn't tell me," he said.

There was no note of reproach in his tone, yet in some fashion it hurt her.

"Nick—darling, you—you've only got one arm," she said. "And he's such a great, strong bully."

Nick uttered a sudden fierce laugh. His hand was clenched. "You women!" he said, and for some reason Olga felt overwhelmingly foolish.

"Well, finish!" he commanded. "No half-measures, mind! Just the whole truth!"

And Olga stumbled on. She repeated with quivering lips Hunt-Goring's story of the taint in Violet's blood, of the tragedy that had preceded her birth.

"Nick," she said, turning piteous eyes upon his face, "I know it must be partly true, but do you think it is really quite as bad as that? I believed it at the time. But—but—perhaps—"

He shook his head. "It's true," he said briefly.

"True that she is going—mad? Oh, Nick—Nick!"

He slipped his arm around her. "And the devil told her, did he?"

She leaned her forehead on his shoulder in an agony of quivering recollection. "Because I wouldn't listen to him—because—because—"

"Pass on," said Nick. "He told her. What happened?"

But she could not tell him. "It was too dreadful—too dreadful!" she moaned.

"Where is she now?" he pursued. "You can tell me that anyhow."

"She has gone to Mrs. Briggs," Olga whispered. "She said she would know everything. She had been her nurse from the beginning. She—she is in a terrible state, Nick. I only came away to tell you. I thought you would be getting anxious, or I wouldn't have left her. I ran up the cliff path. It was quickest."

"We will go back to her in the motor," Nick said.

He got to his feet, his arm still about her, raising her also.

"Come now!" he said. "Pull yourself together, kiddie! You will need all the strength you can muster. Come inside and have a drain of brandy before we start!"

He led her within. She was shivering as one with an ague, but she made desperate efforts to control herself.

Nick was exceedingly matter-of-fact. There was never anything tragic about him. He made her drink some brandy and water, and while she did so he scribbled a brief note.

"I will send off my own man in the motor with this to Max," he said. "He had better come."

Olga looked up sharply. "It's no manner of use sending for him, Nick. She vows she will never see him again."

"We will have him all the same," said Nick. "He is the man for the job."

He went off and despatched his message, and then, returning, went out with her to the motor in which they had arrived so gaily but a few hours before.

"Now go steady, my chicken!" he said, as he got in beside her. "It wouldn't serve anyone's turn to have a spill at this juncture."

His yellow face smiled cheery encouragement into hers, and Olga felt subtly comforted.

"Oh, I am glad I've got you, Nick," she said. "You're such a brick in any trouble."

"Don't tell anyone!" said Nick. "But that's my speciality."

The midday sun was veiled in a thick haze, and the heat was intense. The dust lay white upon the hedges, and eddied about their wheels as they passed. The sea stretched away indefinitely into the sky, leaden, motionless, with no sound of waves.

"I am sure there will be a storm," said Olga.

"A good thing if there is," said Nick.

"Yes, but Violet is terrified at thunder. She always has been."

"It won't break yet," he said.

Almost noiselessly the motor sped along the dusty road. All Olga's faculties became concentrated upon her task, and she spoke no more.

They reached the village. It seemed to be deserted in the slumbrous stillness. There was not so much as a dog to be seen.

Suddenly Nick spoke. "What became of Hunt-Goring?"

The colour leaped into her pale, tense face. "He landed us at the jetty, and went away again in his yacht."

"Let us hope he will go to the bottom!" said Nick.

She shook her head, a gleam of spirit answering his. "Men like that never do."

They ran unhindered through the village and came to "The Ship." The inn-door gaped upon the street. There was not a soul in sight.

Olga brought the car to a stand. "We had better go straight in, Nick."

"Certainly," said Nick.

She peeped into the bar and found it empty. Together they entered the narrow passage. The unmistakable odour of beer and stale tobacco was all-prevalent. The air was heavy with it. They reached the foot of the steep winding stairs, and Olga paused irresolutely.

"There doesn't seem to be anyone downstairs. Will you wait while I run up?"

"No," said Nick. "I'm coming too."

They ascended therefore, and commenced to search the upper regions. But the same absolute quiet reigned above as below. Only the loud ticking of a cuckoo-clock at the head of the stairs aggravated the stillness.

Olga opened one or two doors along the passage and looked into empty rooms, and finally turned round to Nick with scared eyes.

"What can have happened? Where can she be gone?"

As she uttered the words, there fell a heavy footstep in the sanded passage below, and the sound of a man's cough came up to them.

Nick wheeled. "Hi, Briggs! Is that you?"

"Briggs it is," said a thick voice.

Nick descended the stairs with Olga behind him, and encountered the owner thereof at the bottom. He was a large-limbed man with a permanent slouch and a red and sullen countenance that very faithfully bore witness to his habits. He stood and regarded Nick with a fixed and somewhat aggressive stare.

"Where's the missis?" he said.

"That's just what I want to know," said Nick.

Briggs uttered an uneasy guffaw as if he suspected the existence of a joke that had somewhat eluded him. His eyes rolled upward to Olga, and back to Nick.

"Well, she ain't 'ere seemin'ly," he remarked.

"Don't you know where she is?" demanded Nick.

Briggs grinned foolishly. "That's tellin'!" he observed facetiously.

Nick turned from him. "Come along, Olga! They are not here evidently. It's no use trying to get any sense out of this drunken beast."

"But, Nick—" said Olga in distress.

"We will go down to the shore," he said. "Here, you Briggs! Stand back, will you?"

Briggs was blocking the narrow passage with his great bull-frame, and showed no disposition to let them pass. He seemed to think he had a grievance, and he commenced to state it in a rambling, disjointed fashion, holding them prisoners on the stairs while he did so.

Nick bore with him for exactly ten seconds, and then, clean and straight, with lightning swiftness, his one hand shot forward. It was a single hard blow, delivered full on the jaw with a force that nearly carried Nick with it, and it sent the offender staggering backwards on his heels in bellowing astonishment. The opposite wall saved him from falling headlong, but the impact was considerable, and tendered him quite incapable of recovering his He subsided slowly onto the floor with a flood of language that at least testified to the fact that his injuries were not severe.

Nick's arm went round Olga in a flash. He almost lifted her over the legs of the prostrate Briggs and hurried her down the passage. As they emerged into the smoky sunlight, she heard him laugh, and marvelled that he could.

"On second thoughts," he said, with the air of one resuming an interrupted discussion, "I think we will go to the Priory. If she is not there, she is probably on the way."

"She would go by the cliffs," Olga said.

"Yes, I know. But Mrs. Briggs is with her. We had better motor," said Nick.

So they set off again along the glaring road.

It began to seem like a nightmare to Olga. She drove as one pursued by horrors unspeakable. Once or twice Nick spoke to her, and she knew that she obeyed his instructions, though what they were she could never afterwards remember. On and on they went, flying like cloud-shadows on a windy day, yet—so it seemed to Olga—drawing no nearer to their goal, until quite suddenly she found herself staring at the great Priory gate-posts with their huge stone balls while Nick wrestled with the fastenings of the gates.

They opened before her, and she drove slowly through with a curious sensation as of entering an unknown country, though she had known the Priory grounds from childhood. Nick clambered in beside her as she went, and then they were off again running swiftly up the long drive with its double line of yews to the house.

Memory awoke within her then, and she called to mind that day that seemed so long ago when she had encountered Violet, superbly confident, conquering the rebellious Pluto. The cry of a gull came to her now as then, and it sounded like a cry of pain.

They came within sight of the old grey walls. Silent and tragic, they stood up against the mist-veiled sky. The sunlight had turned to an ominous copper glow. And in that moment Olga was afraid, with that sick apprehension of evil that comes upon occasion even to the brave. She gave no sign of it, but it was coiled like a serpent about her heart from then onwards.

The front-door stood open, its Gothic archway gaping wide and mysterious. Still with that nightmare dread upon her, she descended and passed into the old chapel of the monks.

The stained window at the end cast a lurid stream of light along half its length. She caught her breath in an irrepressible shudder. She thought she had never before realized how gruesomely horrible that window was.

Nick's hand closed upon her elbow, and she breathed again. "Shall we go and investigate upstairs?" he said.

Mutely she yielded to the suggestion. They went down the long vault-like hall, and turned through the archway in the south wall close to the window. As they did so, a sudden sound rent the ghostly stillness, a sound that echoed and echoed from wall to wall, dying at last into a shrill thread of sound that seemed to merge into the cry of a sea-gull over the leaden waters. As it died, there came a noise of running feet in the corridor above, and a white-faced maid-servant rushed gasping down the wide oak stairs.

Olga sprang to intercept her. "Jane, what is the matter? Where is Miss Violet? Have you seen her?"

She caught the terrified girl by the shoulders, holding her fast while she questioned her.

Jane stopped perforce in her headlong flight. "Oh, lor, Miss Olga, do let me go! Miss Violet's upstairs—with Mrs. Briggs. She's in a dreadful taking, and don't seem to know what she's doing. Did you hear her scream? Mrs. Briggs says it's hysterics, but it don't sound like that to me. It's made my blood run cold."

Olga released as swiftly as she had captured her, and started for the stairs. Nick was close behind her. They ascended almost together, past the great window that looked upon the sea, and so on to the oak-panelled corridor that led to Violet's room.

The great wolf-hound Cork came to meet them here, wagging a wistful tail and lifting questioning eyes. He made no attempt to hinder their advance, obviously regarding them as friends in need.

Olga's hand caressed him as she passed, and he came and pressed against her as she stopped outside the closed door. Softly she turned the handle, only to discover that the door was locked. She bent her head to listen, and heard a broken sobbing that was like the crying of a child.

Her face quivered in sympathy. She stooped and put her lips to the key-hole. "Violet—Violet darling—let me in! Let me be with you!"

Instantly the sobbing ceased, but it was Mrs. Briggs's voice that made answer. "You can't come in, Miss Olga, only unless you're by yourself. Miss Violet's still very upset-like, and she ain't wanting anyone but me."

There was authority in the announcement. Mrs. Briggs was not without considerable strength of character, and she knew how to keep her head in an emergency.

Olga looked at Nick.

"I should wait if I were you," he counselled. "She is sure to want you later on."

She nodded silently, and bent over Cork. The strain of the past few hours was beginning to tell upon her. Her tears fell unrestrained upon the great dog's head.

Nick strolled away to the head of the stairs, and stood there like a sentinel, searching the blurred expanse of sea through the open window with alert, restless eyes.

Several minutes passed; then there came the sound of the key turning in the lock. Olga stood up hastily, dashing away her tears. Mrs. Briggs's head appeared in the aperture.

"Miss Olga," she said in a strenuous whisper, "Miss Violet would like to speak to you if so be as you're alone. But she won't have anyone else."

"There is only Captain Ratcliffe here," said Olga.

"Then p'raps he'll be good enough to wait outside," said Mrs. Briggs, with the air of a general issuing his orders. "You can come in, Miss Olga, and for pity's sake soothe the pore dear as much as you can. She's well-nigh wore herself out."

Olga glanced round for Nick, and found him at her side.

"Look here, Olga," he said, speaking in a rapid whisper, "you are not to lock that door. Understand? I say it!"

She hesitated. "But if———"

"I won't have it done," he said. "You must pretend to lock it. Mind, if I find that door locked, I shall have it forced, and take you away."

"But she may ask me, Nick," Olga objected.

"If she does, you must lie to her," he said inexorably.

Olga abandoned the discussion somewhat reluctantly, anticipating difficulties.

He laid his hand for an instant on her arm as she prepared to enter. "You understand I am in earnest, don't you?" he said.

She looked into his queer, yellow face with a feeling that was almost awe as she answered meekly. "Yes, Nick."

"And don't forget it," he said, as he let her go.

CHAPTER XXI
ON THE BRINK

"Is that you, Allegro? There is no one with you?"

Violet raised herself from her pillows, turning a haggard face to meet her friend. She looked as if years had passed over her. Her great eyes shone out of dark circles. They looked beyond Olga in evident apprehension.

"It's only me, darling," said Olga, going swiftly to her.

Feverish hands caught and held her. "Goodness, child! How cold you are!" exclaimed Violet. "Mrs. Briggs, I can do without you now. You had better go and look after Briggs." She broke into a brief laugh. "He always gets up to mischief as soon as your back is turned."

"He can very well look after 'imself," said Mrs. Briggs austerely. "And I'm not a-goin' to leave you like this, my dearie. But I'll tell you what I will do. I'll go down to the kitchen and make them lazy hussies stir themselves and get you a meal of some sort."

In the days when Mrs. Briggs had been Violet's nurse she had reigned supreme in the Priory kitchen, and she still regarded it as an outlying portion of her dominions.

Violet leaned back upon her pillows with exhaustion written plainly on her pale face. "Oh, do as you like, Nanny! But I don't want anything. I've got my cigarettes."

Mrs. Briggs grunted, and turned to go. The patient Cork here seized the opportunity to assert himself, and gently but firmly pressed into the room.

"Drat the dog!" said Mrs. Briggs.

"Leave him alone!" Violet commanded. "He knows how to take care of me."

As Cork was fully determined to enter, no effort on Mrs. Briggs's part would have availed to stop him, and Mrs. Briggs, realizing this, sniffed and departed.

The huge animal lay down by the foot of the bed and heaved a sigh of satisfaction as he dropped his nose upon his paws.

And then Violet turned her face to Olga, sitting on the bed, and whispered, "Does he know?"

"Who?" whispered back Olga.

"Max, of course! Who else?"

Olga hesitated. Violet's hands were gripping her very tightly. "Know what, dear?" she said at last.

A quick frown drew Violet's forehead. "Oh, you know what I mean. Does he know about my going mad? Have you told him?"

"My dearest,"—keen distress rang in Olga's voice—"don't—don't talk like that! You're not mad! You're not mad!"

Violet's frown changed into a very strange smile. "Oh yes, but I am," she said. "I've been mad for some time now. It's been gradually coming on, but to-day—to-day it is moving faster—much faster." Her low voice quickened. "I haven't much sanity left, Allegro. I can feel it slipping from me inch by inch like a paid-out rope. Only enough left now to know that I am mad. When I don't know that any longer, I shall have lost it all."

"Dearest! Dearest!" moaned Olga. "Won't you try to forget it—try to think of other things for a little?"

Violet continued as if she had not heard her. "You know, it's curious that it never occurred to me before. I've had such queer sensations—all sorts of funny things going on inside me. It began like a curious thirst—a very horrible sort of craving, Allegro. That was what made me take to those cigarettes. I never felt it when I was smoking them. They made me so deliriously sleepy. It was terrible when—he—took them away. I felt as if he had pushed me over a deep abyss. I really can't do without them. They make me float when I'm going to sink."

She paused, and passed a weary hand across her brow. "Why have I been crying so, Allegro? I hardly ever cry. Was I sorry for someone? Was it my mother? Fancy her doing—that!" The heavy eyes grew suddenly wide and bright. "I wonder if she would have killed me too if she had lived. I know exactly what made her do it. I should have done it myself—yes, and revelled in it. Can't you imagine it? The night and the darkness, and oneself lying there pretending to be asleep and waiting—waiting—for the man one hated." Suddenly the wide eyes glowed red. "Think of it—think of it, Allegro!—how one would feel for the point of the knife when one heard his step, and hide it away under the pillow when at last he came in. How one's flesh would creep when he lay down! How one's ears would shout and clamour while one waited for him to sleep! And then—and then—when he began to breathe slowly and one knew that he was unconscious—how inch by inch one would draw out one's hand with the knife and raise the bedclothes, and plunge it hard and deep into his breast! Would he struggle, Allegro? Would he open his eyes to see his own life-blood spout out? Would he be frightened, or angry, or just surprised? I think he would be surprised, don't you? He wouldn't give his wife credit for hating him so much. Men don't, you know. They never realize how far hatred will drive a woman until it pushes her over the edge. I think he would hardly believe his own eyes even then, unless he saw her laughing!" A burst of wild laughter broke from Violet's lips, but she smothered it with her handkerchief.

"I mustn't laugh," she said, "though I'm sure she did. And I want to talk to you seriously, Allegro."

"Dear, do lie down and rest!" Olga urged her gently. "That hateful story has given you a shock. Do try and remember that there's nothing new about it. It all happened years ago. And you are no different now than you were this morning before you heard it."

Violet leaned her head back again upon the pillows, but her eyes roved unceasingly. "But then I was mad this morning," she said, "only I didn't know it. Do you know, I think madness is a sort of state in which people lose their souls and yet go on living. Or else the soul goes blind. I've thought of that too. But I think my soul has gone on. I shall go and find it presently. You must help me."

"Of course I will help you, darling," Olga promised soothingly.

"Yes. But it won't be easy," said Violet, frowning upwards. "I've got to go into a great space of lost souls, and I shan't find it very easily. It was his fault. He never ought to have brought me back that night. That's the worst of doctors. They are so keen about the body, but they don't study the soul at all. They behave exactly as if the soul weren't there."

"Look here, dear," said Olga, with sudden inspiration, "wouldn't you like to talk to Nick about it? He's so clever. I always ask him about puzzling things."

"Nick?" Violet's eyes came round to her. "He's a soldier, isn't he? He has killed people."

"I don't know. I suppose so," said Olga. "He is just outside. May I fetch him?"

"Oh, yes, I don't mind Nick. He's got some sense. But I won't have Max, Allegro. He is not to come near me. I've found him out, and I hate him!" The deep voice suddenly grew deeper. A flame of fierce resentment leaped up in the roving eyes. "I know now exactly why he has been so attentive all this time. I thought—I used to think—he was in love with me—like other men. But I know now that he was only making a study of me, because he knew that I was going mad. Bruce must have told him that. I've often wondered why he and Bruce were so friendly. I know now that they were in league against me. Bruce never liked me—naturally. No one ever liked me but you, Allegro."

"Shall I call Nick?" said Olga, gently bringing her back to the point.

"Oh, if you like. But no! Cork would never let any man come in here. I will come downstairs. We'll have some lunch, and then smoke." Violet sprang from the bed with sudden decision. "Heavens!" she exclaimed, as she caught a glimpse of herself in her glass. "What a hag I look! I can't go down in this. It looks like a bedgown. Find me something, Allegro! That red silk will do. I believe everything else is at Weir. You will have to send my things back, for I am going to stay here now. I've had enough of Max Wyndham's tyranny. I must have my own way or I shall rave."

With impulsive hands she tore off her tumbled muslin dress, and arrayed herself in the flaming evening robe which Olga had once condemned. Olga raised no protest now. She gave her silent assistance. The horrors of that day had so closed in upon her that she felt fantastically convinced that nothing she did or left undone could make any difference, or hinder for the fraction of an instant the fate that so remorselessly pursued them and was surely every moment drawing nearer. The fear at her heart had so wound itself into her very being that she was no longer conscious of it. It possessed her like an evil spell.

So she stood by, sometimes helping, always watching, while her friend's tragedy leaped from point to point like a spreading forest-fire breeding destruction.

"You are not afraid of me, Allegro?" Violet asked her suddenly, as she arranged her black hair with swift, feverish movements.

And Olga answered with truth. "No, dear. I should never be that."

"Not whatever happened? That's right. I'm not really dangerous—so long as you keep Max out of my way. But, mind—I must never see him again, never—never—while I live!" She turned from the glass, facing Olga with eyes in which an awful fire had begun to burn. "I know him!" she said. "I know him! He will want to shut me up—to keep me as a specimen for him—and men like him—to study. He and Bruce will do it between them if they get the chance. But they won't—they won't! Allegro—darling, you must help me to get away. I can't—can't—be imprisoned for life. You will help me? Promise me! Promise!"

"I promise, dearest!" Olga made answer very earnestly.

Something of relief softened the agony in the dark eyes. Very suddenly Violet took her friend's face between her hands and passionately kissed her on the lips.

"I love you, Allegro!" she said. "And I trust you—and you only—till death."

It was then—at first but dimly—that Olga began to realize that the burden laid upon her might be heavier than she could bear, and yet that she alone must bear it even if it crushed her to the earth.

Passing out at length into the passage, she felt Violet's hand close with a convulsive pressure upon her arm, and she knew that here was fear such as she had never before encountered or imagined,—the deadly, unfathomable fear of a mind that hovered on the brink of the abyss.

She caught the hand warmly, protectingly, into her own. And she swore then and there a solemn, inward oath that, cost what it might, the trust reposed in her should not be in vain. When her friend turned to her for help in extremity, she should not find her lacking.

For of such stuff was Olga Ratcliffe fashioned, and her loyalty was that same loyalty which moves men even unto the sacrifice of their lives.

CHAPTER XXII
OVER THE EDGE

Marshalled by Mrs. Briggs, the Priory servants brought them luncheon, laying a table at one side of the great entrance-hall, for all the lower rooms were shuttered and closed.

Violet, with the great dog Cork vigilant and silent beside her, sat before it as one wrapt in reverie. Now and then she roused herself to answer at random some remark from Nick, but for the most part she sat mutely brooding.

The meal was but a dreadful farce to Olga. She was waiting, she was listening, she was watching. It seemed ludicrous to her stretched nerves to be seated there with food before her, when every instant she expected the devastating power that lurked behind the stillness to burst forth and engulf them. It was like sitting at the very mouth of hell, feeling the blistering heat, and yet pretending that they felt it not.

Darker and darker grew the day. They sat in a close, unearthly twilight. Though the huge entrance-door was flung wide, no breath of air reached them, no song of birds or sound of moving leaf. Once Olga turned her eyes to the far glimmer of the east window, but she turned them instantly away again, and looked no more. For it was as though a hand were holding up a dim lantern on the other side to show her the dreadful scene, casting a stain of crimson across the space where once had stood the altar.

Looking back later, she realized that it was only Nick's presence that gave her strength to endure that awful suspense. She had never admired him more than she did then, his shrewdness, his cheeriness, his strength. There was not the faintest suggestion of strain in his attitude. With absolute ease he talked or he was silent. Only in the deepening gloom she caught now and then the quick glitter of his eyes, and knew that like herself he was watching.

Slowly the minutes wore away, the darkness grew darker. From far away there came a low, surging sound. The storm-wind was rising over the sea.

Nick turned his head to listen. "Now for one of our patent storms!" he said. "Brethaven always catches it pretty strong. Remember that night you developed scarlet fever, at Redlands, Olga *mia*, and your devoted servant went down to a certain cottage on the shore to fetch a certain lady to nurse you?"

Olga did remember. It was one of the cherished memories of her childhood. "I told Muriel a secret about you that night, Nick," she said, responding with an effort.

He nodded. "For which act of treachery you possess my undying gratitude. Did you ever hear that story, Miss Campion?"

He offered her his cigarette-case with the words, and she turned her brooding eyes upon him. "Thanks!" she said. "I will have one of my own. Yes, I know that story. Your wife must be a very brave woman."

"She had me to take care of her," pointed out Nick.

Violet laughed with a touch of scorn.

"Oh, quite so," he said. "But I bear a charmed life, you should remember. No one ever drowns in my boat."

She leaned her chin upon her hand, and surveyed him through the weird twilight. "You are a strong man," she said slowly, "and you don't think much of Death."

"Not much," said Nick, striking a match on the heel of his boot.

The flame flared yellow on his face, emphasizing its many lines. His eyelids flickered rapidly, never wholly revealing the eyes behind.

"You wouldn't be afraid to die?" she pursued, still watching him.

His cigarette glowed and he removed the match; but the flame remained, burning with absolute steadiness between his fingers.

"I certainly shan't be afraid when my turn comes," he said, with confidence.

"Tell me," she said suddenly, "your idea of Death!"

His look flashed over her and back to the match he still held. The flame had nearly reached his fingers.

"Death," he said, "is the opening—and the closing—of a Door."

She leaned eagerly forward. "You think that?"

"Just that," said Nick. He smiled and blew out the match, just in time. "But—as you perceive—I am afraid of pain—that is, when I think about it."

She scarcely seemed to hear. "And have you ever seen anyone die?"

"Plenty," said Nick.

"Ah, I forgot! You've killed men, haven't you?" There was suppressed excitement in her voice.

Nick threw up his head and smoked towards the oak-beamed roof. "When I had to," he said, with brevity.

"Ah!" The word leaped from her like a cry of triumph. "Did you ever kill anyone with a knife? What did it feel like?"

"I shan't tell you," said Nick rudely. "It isn't good for anyone to know too much."

An abrupt silence followed his refusal. The surging of the sea had risen to a continuous low roar; and from the garden came the sound of trembling leaves. The storm was at hand.

"Do you think I don't know?" said Violet, and laughed.

Quickly Olga rose, as if her nerves were on edge, and went towards the open door. As she did so, a violet glare lit the hall from end to end, quivered, and was gone. She stopped dead, and in the awful silence that succeeded she heard the wild beat of her heart rising, rising, rising, in a tumult of sudden fear.

Violet remained at the table, staring, as one transfixed. She was gazing at the open door. Nick leaned swiftly forward and took her hand. So much Olga saw in the dimness before the thunder with a fierce crash burst forth overhead.

Ere it died away there came a shriek, wild, horrible, unearthly. It pierced Olga through and through, turning her cold from head to foot. Another shriek followed it, and yet another; and then came a dreadful, sobbing utterance in which words and moans were terribly mingled.

Olga caught at her self-control, as it were, with both hands, and went swiftly back to the table. Violet was on her feet. She had wrenched herself free, and was wildly pointing.

"No! No! No!" she cried. "Take him away!" Mortal terror was in her starting eyes. Suddenly perceiving Olga, she turned and clung to her. "Allegro! You promised! You promised!"

Then it was that Olga realized that someone had entered during that awful peal of thunder, and was even then advancing quietly down the hall. It needed not a second flickering flash to reveal him. Her heart told her who it was.

With Violet pressed close in her arms, she spoke. "Max, stop!"

She never knew whether it was the note of authority or of desperation in her voice that induced him to comply; but he stopped on the instant a full twenty feet from where they stood.

"What's the matter?" he said.

Brief, matter-of-fact, almost contemptuous, came his query. Yet Olga thrilled at the sound of it, feeling strengthened, reassured, strangely unembarrassed.

"It's this horrid storm," she said. "Violet's upset. Ah, here is Mrs. Briggs! Darling, wouldn't you like to go upstairs and lie down again till it's over? Do, dearie! I'll look after Nick and Max."

But Violet's straining arms clung faster. "He'll follow me!" she whispered.

"No, indeed he won't, dear. I won't allow it," said Olga, and she spoke with absolute confidence born of this new, strange feeling of power. "You needn't be afraid of that," she said, with motherly, shielding arms about her. "Won't you go with Mrs. Briggs? I will come up presently. Really there's nothing to be afraid of. The storm won't hurt you."

"And you won't let Max come?" Violet was suffering herself to be led towards the further door. She was shivering violently and moved spasmodically, as though the impulse to escape strongly urged her.

"I promise," Olga said.

She passed under the archway with her, paused there while another furious burst of thunder rolled above them: then gently surrendered her to Mrs. Briggs, and turned back herself into the hall.

She found Max and Nick standing together in the gloom.

"I came up here on the chance," the former was saying, "and got here just in time. Hullo! Is that a wolf?"

It was Cork, who crouched bristling against the table, with bared fangs, watching him. Olga went to him and took him by the collar.

"He's all right," she said. "I think he doesn't like strangers."

She led him also across the hall, took him to the foot of the stairs, and returned.

She felt Max's eyes upon her as she came up. He seemed to be regarding her in a new light.

"Well?" he said. "Why this hysteria? Is it due to the storm or—some other cause?"

She hesitated, finding it somehow difficult to give an answer to his cool questioning.

"I'll tell him, shall I?" said Nick.

She came and slipped her hand into his. "Yes, Nick."

He squeezed her fingers hard. "Our friend Hunt-Goring has been sticking his oar in," he said. "This—hysteria has been caused by him."

"You mean he has told her the whole story?" said Max.

"Yes," said Olga.

He considered the matter for a few seconds in silence. "And how long has this sort of thing been going on?" he asked then.

Again she hesitated.

He looked at her. "It's no good trying to keep anything from me," he observed. "I've seen it coming for a long while."

"Oh, Max!" she burst forth involuntarily. "Then it really is—"

A vivid flash of lightning and instant crashing thunder drowned her words. Instinctively she drew nearer to Nick. On many a previous occasion they had watched a storm together with delight. But to-day her nerves were all a-quiver, and its violence appalled her.

As the noise died away, Max looked about the shadowy place. "Is there any means of lighting this tomb?" he asked.

Apparently there was not. Olga believed there were some electric switches somewhere but she had forgotten where.

Max began to stroll about in search of them.

"Here comes the rain!" said Nick. "It will be lighter directly."

The rain came quite suddenly in an immense volume, that beat with deafening force upon the roof, drowning all but the loudest crashes of thunder. For a few seconds the darkness was like night. Then, swift and awful, there came a flash that was brighter than the noonday sun. It streaked through the stained-glass window, showing the dreadful picture like a vision to those below it, throwing a stream of vivid crimson upon the floor; then glanced away into the dark.

There came a sound like the bursting of shell that shook the very walls to their foundation. And through it and above it, high and horrible as the laughter of storm-fiends there came a woman's laugh....

In that instant Nick's hand suddenly left Olga's. He leaped from her side with the agility of a panther, and hurled himself into the darkness of the archway that led to the inner hall.

Something dreadful was happening there, she knew not what; and her heart stood still in terror while peal after peal of that awful laughter rang through the pealing thunder.

Then came another flash of lighting, keen as the blade of a sword, and she saw. There, outlined against the darkness of the archway, red-robed and terrible, stood Violet. Her right hand was flung up above her head, and in her grasp was a knife that she must have taken from the table. She was laughing still with white teeth gleaming, but in her eyes shone the glare of madness and the red, red lust of blood.

The picture flashed away and the thunder broke forth again, but the fiendish laughter continued for seconds till suddenly it turned to a piercing scream and ceased. Only the echoes of the thunder remained and a dreadful sound of struggling on the further side of the archway, together with a choking sound near at hand as of some animal striving against restraint.

Olga stumbled blindly forward. "Nick! Nick! Where are you? What has happened?" she cried, in an agony.

Instantly his voice came to her. "Here, child! Don't be scared! I'm holding the dog."

She groped her way to him, nearly falling over Cork, who was dragging against his hand.

The great dog turned to her, whining, and, reassured by her presence, ceased to resist.

"That's better," said Nick, with relief. "Can you hold him?"

She slipped her hand inside his collar! "Nick! What has happened?" she whispered, for her voice was gone.

Dimly she discerned figures in the inner hall, but there was no longer any sound of struggling. And then quite suddenly Max came back through the archway.

"Lend me a hand, Ratcliffe!" he said. "I'm bleeding like a pig."

CHAPTER XXIII
AS GOOD AS DEAD

So cool was his utterance, so perfectly free from agitation his demeanour, that Olga wondered if she could have heard aright. Then she saw him go to the table and prepare to remove his coat, and she knew that there could be no mistake.

The frozen horror of the past few seconds fell from her, and strength came in its place—the strength born of emergency. "I shall help you better than Nick," she said.

"If you don't faint," said Max.

She spoke a reassuring word to Cork and let him go. He moved away at once in uneasy search for his mistress, and she turned round to Max. Nick was already helping him out of his coat.

The storm had lulled somewhat, and the gloom had begun to lighten. As she drew near him she saw his right arm emerge from the coat. The shirt-sleeve was soaked with blood from shoulder to cuff.

"It's the top of the shoulder," said Max. "Only a flesh wound. Make a wet pad of one of those table-napkins and bind it up tight. I'll go back to the cottage-hospital presently and get it dressed."

With the utmost calmness he issued his directions, and Olga found herself obeying almost mechanically. Nick helped her to cut away the shirt and expose the wound. It was a deep one, and had been inflicted from the back.

"Quite a near shave," said Max, with composure. "That flash of lightning came just in time. I saw the reflection in one of those oak panels."

"Will this stop the bleeding?" asked Olga doubtfully.

"Yes, if you get the pressure on the right place. Pull it hard! That's the way! Don't mind me!" He was speaking through clenched teeth. "I daresay Nick knows all about first aid."

Nick did; and under his supervision the injury was bandaged at length with success.

"First-rate!" said Max approvingly. "I congratulate the pair of you. Now I will have a brandy and soda, if you have no objection. Olga must have one too. I'm never anxious about Nick. He always comes out on top."

He watched Olga pour him out a drink according to instructions. The storm was passing, and every instant the gloomy place grew lighter. Glancing at him, as she placed the tumbler before him, she saw his face fully for the first time, and noted how drawn and grey it was.

He smiled at her abruptly. "All right, Olga! You must drink the first quarter."

"Oh, no!" said Olga quickly.

"Oh, yes!" he rejoined imperturbably. "Tell her to, Nick! I know your word is law."

Nick had strolled across the hall to pick up something that lay upon the floor. As he returned, Olga was hastily gulping the prescribed dose.

Max turned towards him. "Yes. Take care of that!" he said. "It's done enough damage." He took the glass that Olga held out to him, and deliberately drained it. Then he rose, and took up his coat. "I must get into this if possible," he said.

Silently, with infinite care, Olga helped him.

Nick stood with the knife in his hand. "What are you going to do now?" he said.

Max's brows went up. "My dear fellow, what do you suppose? I am going to attend to my patient."

"Where is she?" said Nick.

"Upstairs. Mrs. Briggs went to look after her. I'm going to give her a composing draught," said Max, plunging his hand into a side-pocket.

"Oh, Max!" exclaimed Olga.

He turned to her. "There will be no repetition of this," he said grimly. "Miss Campion is exhausted and probably more or less in her right mind by now."

"But she won't be if you go to her," Olga said, and in her eagerness she drew near to him and laid a light hand on his sleeve. "Max, you mustn't go to her—indeed—indeed. I have promised her that you shall not. As you have seen for yourself, the very sight of you is enough to send her demented."

"Oh, it's for her sake, is it?" said Max; but he stood still, suffering her hand on his arm.

Her eyes were raised to his, very earnestly beseeching him. "Yes, for her sake," she said. "You would do her much more harm than good. Let me take the composing draught to her! Oh, Max, really it is the only way. Please be reasonable!"

Her voice trembled a little. She knew well that where his patients were concerned he would endure no interference. Again and again he had made this clear to her. But this was an exceptional case, and she prayed that as such he might view it.

She wondered a little that Nick did not come to her aid, but he stood aloof as if unwilling to be drawn into the discussion. Max seemed to have completely forgotten his existence.

"Look here," he said finally. "The matter isn't so desperate as you seem to think, but if I give in, so must you. There are several questions I shall have to ask, and I must have a clear answer."

"I will tell you anything in my power," she said.

"Very well," he said. "Tell me first—if you can—why Miss Campion hates me so violently."

His manner was curtly professional. He looked straight into her eyes with cool determination in his own.

She answered him, but her answer did not come very easily. "I think she feels that you have had her under supervision all along, and she resents it."

"Quite true," he said. "I have. Is that why she wants to kill me?"

"Not entirely." Olga was plainly speaking against her will.

But Max was merciless. "And the other reason?"

She locked her fingers very tightly together. "It—it would be a breach of confidence to tell you that," she said.

"I see," said Max. "She was annoyed because I didn't fulfil expectations by falling in love with her. She misunderstood my attitude; was that it? You did so yourself at one time, if I remember aright."

"Yes," admitted Olga reluctantly.

"I don't know quite how you managed it," he commented. "However, we are none of us infallible. Now tell me—without reservation—exactly what passed this morning between you two girls and Hunt-Goring."

With quivering lips she began to tell him. There were certain items of that conversation with Hunt-Goring, of which, though they were branded deep upon her mind, she could not bring herself to speak. It was a difficult recital in any case, and the grim silence with which he listened did not make it any easier.

"Have you told me everything?" he asked at last.

She answered steadily. "Everything that concerns Violet!"

He looked at her very closely for a few moments, and she saw his mouth take a cynical, downward curve.

"Hunt-Goring has my sympathy," he observed enigmatically. "Well, I think you are right. I had better keep out of the way for the present. I shall know better what course to take in the morning. Her state of mind just now is quite abnormal, but she may very well have settled down a little by that time. She will probably go through a stage of lethargy and depression after this. Her brother should be back again in a week's time. We may manage to ward off another outbreak till then. But, mind, you are not to be left alone with her during any part of that week. There must always be someone within call."

"I shall be within call," said Nick.

Max glanced at him. "Yes, you will be quite useful no doubt. But I must have a nurse as well."

"A nurse!" exclaimed Olga.

He looked back at her. "You don't seriously suppose I am going to leave you and Mrs. Briggs—and Nick—in sole charge?"

"But, Max," she protested, almost incoherent in her dismay, "she will be herself again to-morrow or the next day! This isn't going to last!"

"What do you mean?" he said.

She controlled herself with a sharp effort, warned of the necessity to do so by his tone.

"I mean that—hysteria—isn't a thing that lasts long as a rule."

"It isn't hysteria," he said.

She flinched in spite of herself. "But you think she will get better?" she urged.

He was silent a moment, looking at her. "I will tell you exactly what I think, Olga," he said then, in a tone that was utterly different from any he had used to her before. "For you certainly ought to know now. The tale you heard this morning was true—every word of it. I heard it myself from Bruce Campion and also from Kersley Whitton. Kersley was engaged to marry her mother when he detected in her a tendency to madness which he afterwards discovered to be an hereditary taint in her family. It is a disease of the brain which is absolutely incurable. It is in fact a peculiarly rapid decay caused by a kind of leprous growth which nothing can arrest. In some cases it causes total paralysis of every faculty almost at the outset, in others there may be years of violent mania before the inevitable paralysis sets in. Either way it is quite incurable, and if it takes the form of madness it is only intermittent for the first few weeks. There are no lucid intervals after that."

He paused. Olga was listening with white face upturned. She spoke no word; only the agony in her eyes spoke for her.

He went on very quietly, with a gentleness to which she was wholly unaccustomed. "It has been coming on for some little time now. I hoped at first that it would be slow in developing, and so at first it appeared to be. Sometimes, at the very beginning, it is not possible to detect it with any certainty. It is only when the disease has begun to manifest itself unmistakably that it moves so rapidly. It was because I feared a sudden development that I asked Sir Kersley to come down. He was of the opinion that that was not imminent, that three months or even six might intervene. I feared he was mistaken, but I hoped for the best. Of course a sudden shock was more than sufficient to precipitate matters. But I knew that she was less likely to encounter any in your society than anywhere else. Nick wanted me to warn you, but—rightly or wrongly—I wouldn't! I thought you would know soon enough."

He paused again, as if to give her time to blame him; but still she spoke no word, still she waited with face upturned.

He went on gravely and steadily. "I knew that opium was a very dangerous drug for her to take in however minute a quantity, but I hoped I had put a stop to that. I could not foresee to-day's events. Hunt-Goring is no favourite of mine, but I never anticipated his taking such a step. I did not so much as know that he was in a position to do so. He suppressed that fact on the sole occasion on which Miss Campion's name was mentioned between us."

Olga spoke for the first time, her stiff lips scarcely moving. "I think he is a devil," she said slowly.

Max made a gesture expressive of indifference on that point. "People who form the drug habit are seldom over-squeamish in other respects," he said. "He has certainly hastened matters, but he is not responsible for the evil itself. That has been germinating during the whole of her life."

"And—that—was why Sir Kersley jilted her mother?" Olga spoke in a low, detached voice. She seemed to be trying to grasp a situation that eluded her.

"It was." Max answered with a return to his customary brevity; his tone was not without bitterness. "Kersley was merciful enough to think of the next generation. He was a doctor, and he knew that hereditary madness is the greatest evil—save one—in the world. Therefore he sacrificed his happiness."

"What is the greatest evil?" she asked, still with the air of bringing herself painfully back as it were from a long distance.

He was watching her shrewdly as he answered. "Hereditary vice—crime."

"Is crime hereditary?"

"In nine cases out of ten—yes."

"And that is worse than—madness?"

"I should say much worse."

"I see." She passed a hand across her eyes, and very suddenly she shivered and seemed to awake. "Oh, is it quite hopeless?" she asked him piteously. "Are you sure?"

"It is quite hopeless," he said.

"She can never be herself again—not even by a miracle?"

"Such miracles don't happen," said Max, with grim decision. "It is much the same as a person going blind. There are occasional gleams for a little while, but the end is total darkness. That is all that can be expected now." He added, a hint of compassion mingling with the repression of his voice: "It is better that you should know the whole truth. It's not fair to bolster you up with false hopes. You can help now—if you have the strength. You won't be able to help later."

"But I will never leave her!" Olga said.

"My dear child," he made answer, "in a very little while she won't even know you. She will be—as good as dead."

"Surely she would be better dead!" she cried passionately.

"God knows," said Max.

He spoke with more feeling than he usually permitted himself, and at once changed the subject. "What we are at present concerned in is to make her temporarily better. Now you know this stuff?" He took a bottle from his pocket. "I am going to put it in your charge. Give her a teaspoonful now in a wine-glass of water, as you did before. I hope it will make her sleep. If it doesn't, give her a second dose in half an hour. But if she goes off without that second dose, all the better. Remember, it is rank poison. She ought to sleep for some hours then, and when she wakes I think she will probably be herself for a little. That's quite clear, is it?"

He was looking at her closely as he handed her the bottle; but she met the look with absolute steadiness. She had plainly recovered her self-control, and was ready to shoulder her burden once more.

"I quite understand," she said.

He laid his hand for a moment on her arm, and smiled at her with abrupt kindliness.

"Stick to it, Olga!" he said. "I am counting on you."

She smiled back bravely, though her lips quivered. She did not say a word.

But Nick answered for her, his arm thrust suddenly about her waist. "And so you can, my son," he said. "She is the pluckiest kid I know."

CHAPTER XXIV
THE OPENING OF THE DOOR

"Allegro!"

The utterance was very faint, yet it reached Olga, sitting, as she had sat for hours, by her friend's side, watching the long, still slumber that had followed Max's draught.

She bent instantly over the girl upon the bed, and warmly clasped her hand. "I am here, darling."

The shadows were lengthening. Evening was drawing on. Very soon it would be dark.

"Allegro!" The low voice said again. It held a note of unutterable weariness, yet there was pleading in it too. The hand Olga had taken closed with a faint, answering pressure.

"Are you wanting anything?" whispered Olga, her face close to the face upon the pillow, the beautiful face she had watched, with what a passion of devotion, during the long, long afternoon.

"Have you been here all the time?" murmured Violet.

"Yes, dear."

"How sweet of you, Allegro!" The dark eyes opened wider; they seemed to be watching something very intently, something that Olga could not see. "I suppose you thought I was asleep," she said.

"Yes, dear."

"I wasn't," said Violet. "I was just—away."

Olga was silent. The clasp of her hand was very close.

"My dear," Violet said, "I've been there again."

"Where, dearest?"

"I've been right up to the Gate of Heaven," she said. "It's very lovely up there, Allegro. I wanted to stay."

"Did you, dear?"

"Yes. I didn't mean to come back again. I didn't want to come back." A sudden spasm contracted her brows. "What happened before I went, Allegro? I'm sure something happened."

Very tenderly Olga sought to reassure her. "You were ill, dear. You were upset. But you are better now. Don't let us think about it."

"Ah! I remember!" Violet raised herself abruptly. Her eyes shone wide with terror in the failing light. "Allegro!" she said. "I—killed him!"

"No, no, dear!" Olga's hand tenderly pressed her down again. "He is only—a little—hurt. You didn't know what you were doing."

But recollection was dawning in the seething brain. One memory after another pierced through the turmoil. "I had to do it!" she whispered. "He is so cruel. He keeps me back. He holds the door when I want to get away. Allegro, why won't he let me go? I'm nothing to him. He doesn't love me. He doesn't—even—hate me." A great shudder ran through her. She fell back upon the pillow as though her strength were gone. "Oh, why won't he open the door and let me go?" She moaned piteously. "Why does he keep bringing me back? I know I shall kill him. I shall be driven to it. And it's such a horrible thing to do—that dreadful soft feeling under the knife, and the blood—the blood—oh, Allegro!"

She tried to raise herself again, and was caught into Olga's arms. She turned her face into her neck and shuddered.

"I'm not mad now," she whispered. "Really I'm not mad now! But I soon shall be. I can feel it coming back. My brain is like—a fiery wheel. Oh, don't let it come again, Allegro! Help me—help me to get away—before it comes again!"

Olga strained her to her heart, saying no word.

"They'll shut me up," the broken whisper continued. "I shall never find my soul again. I shan't even have you, and there's no one else I love. All the rest are strangers. Only he will come and look at me with his cruel, cold green eyes, and I shall kill him—I know I shall kill him—unless they bind me hand and foot. Allegro! Allegro!" She was shivering violently now. "Perhaps they will do that. It's happened before, hasn't it? 'Bound hand and foot and cast into outer darkness.' That's hell, isn't it? Oh, Olga, shall I be sent to hell if I kill him?"

"My darling, hush, hush!" Olga's arms held her faster still. "There is no such place," she said—"at least not in the sense you mean. You are torturing yourself, dear one, and you mustn't. Don't dwell on these dreadful things! You are quite, quite safe, here in my arms, with the love of God round us. Think of that, and don't be afraid!"

"But I am afraid," moaned Violet. "It's the outer darkness, Allegro. And you won't be there. And the door will be shut—always shut. Oh, can't you do anything to save me? You're not like Max. You're not paid to keep people back. Can't you—can't you find a way out for me? Couldn't you open the prison-door before he comes again, and let me slip through? I've never been a prisoner before. I've always come and gone as I liked. And now—twice over—he has dragged me back from the Gate of Paradise. Oh, Allegro, I shall never get there unless you help me. Quick, dear, quick! Help me now!"

She had turned in Olga's arms. She raised an imploring face. She clung about her neck.

"Isn't there a way of escape?" she urged feverishly. "Can't you think of one?"

But Olga looked back in silence, white and still.

"Allegro, don't you love me? Don't you want me to be happy?" Incredulity, despair were in the pleading voice. "Don't you believe in paradise either, Allegro? Do you want me to be shut away in the dark—buried alive—buried alive?"

There was suddenly a note of anguish in the appeal. Violet drew herself slowly away, as though her friend's arms had ceased to be a haven to her.

But instantly, with a swiftness that was passionate, Olga caught her back.

"I would die for you, my darling! I would sell my soul for you!" she said, and fierce mother-love throbbed in her voice. "But what can I do? O God! what can I do?"

Her voice broke, and she stilled it sharply, as if taken off her guard.

"Can't you open the door for me?" Violet begged again. "Don't you know how?"

But still Olga had no answer for the cry. Only she held her fast.

There followed a long, long pause; then again Violet spoke, more collectedly than she had spoken at all.

"Do you know what that man said to me this morning? He told me I should be a homicidal maniac—like my mother. I didn't realize at the time what that meant. I was too horrified. I know now. And it was the truth. That's what I want you to save me from. Allegro, won't you save me?"

"My darling, how can I?" The words were spoken below Olga's breath. The gathering darkness was closing upon them both.

Violet freed a hand and softly stroked her cheek. "Don't be afraid, dear! No one—but I—will ever know. And I— Allegro, I shall bless you for ever and ever. Wait!" She suddenly started, with caught breath. "Are we alone?"

"Mrs. Briggs is outside, dear," Olga told her gently.

"Oh! Dear old Nanny! She would never hold me back. She would understand. Do you remember how she told us—that afternoon—about her mother?"

Yes, well Olga remembered. She had never forgotten. Back upon her mind flashed that vivid memory, and with it the memory of Max's eyes, green and intent, searching her face on the night that he had asked, "What do you know about the pain-killer?"

Violet's voice brought her back. "Where is he, Allegro? Is he still here?"

"No." Almost unconsciously Olga also spoke in a whisper. "He has gone back to Weir," she said. "He had to go; but—"

"But he will come back?" gasped Violet.

"Yes."

"Ah! And he may be here—at any time?" The words came quick and feverish; again that painful trembling seized her.

"He won't come in here," Olga said steadfastly.

"He will! He will!" breathed Violet. "I know him. There is nothing—he will not do—for the sake of his—profession." She broke off, gripping Olga with tense strength. "And I've nothing to defend myself with!" she panted. "They have taken—the knife—away!"

Tenderly Olga soothed her panic. "It will be all right, dear. I can take care of you. I can keep him away."

Violet relaxed against her again, exhausted rather than reassured. "And where is Nick?" she murmured presently.

"Downstairs, darling; in the hall."

"On guard," said Violet quickly. "What shall I do? Oh, what shall I do?"

"My dearest, no! Only he wouldn't leave me. You know what pals we are," urged Olga. "Besides, you like Nick."

"Oh, yes; he amuses me. He is clever, isn't he? What was that he said about—about the opening—and the shutting—of a Door?"

Spasmodically the words fell. The failing brain was making desperate efforts against the gathering dark.

"He was speaking of Death," said Olga, her voice very low.

"Yes, yes! He said he wouldn't be afraid. And I'm sure he knew. He must have seen Death very often."

"I don't know, darling."

"Of course, the opening of the Door is to let us escape," ran on the feverish whisper. "And then it shuts, and we can't get back. But no one ever wants to get back, Allegro. Who ever wanted to go back into the prison-house—and the dreadful, dreadful dark?"

But Olga made no answer. With set face and quiet eyes she was waiting. And already at the heart of her she knew that when the moment came she would not flinch.

"And how lovely to be free—to be free!" Soft and eager came the whisper from her breast. "Never to be dragged back any more. To leave the dark behind for ever and ever. For it isn't dark up there, you know. It's never dark up there. You can see the light shining even through the Gates. And God couldn't be angry, Allegro. Do you think He could?"

"Not with you, my darling! Not with you!"

"So you'll let me go," said Violet, with growing earnestness. "You'll help me to go, Allegro? You will? You will?"

"My darling, I will!" Quick and passionate came the answer. The time had come.

For a few moments the arms that held her tightened to an almost fierce embrace; then slowly relaxed.

"Dear heart, I knew you would," said Violet.

She leaned back upon her pillow as Olga gently let her go, and through the deepening dusk she watched her with eyes of perfect trust.

There followed a pause, the tinkle of glass, the sound of liquid being poured out. Then Olga was with her again, very still and quiet.

Softly the door opened. "Anything I can do, Miss Olga?" murmured Mrs. Briggs.

"Nothing, thank you," said Olga.

"That young Dr. Wyndham—'e's just come back," said Mrs. Briggs.

Olga turned for a moment from the bed. The glass was in her hand.

"Go down to him, Mrs. Briggs," she said. "Ask him to wait five minutes."

"Allegro!" There was agonized appeal in the cry.

She turned back instantly. "It's all right, dearest. It's all right. Mind how you take it! There! Let me! Your hand is trembling."

She leaned over her friend, supporting her, holding the glass to her lips.

"Drink it slowly!" she whispered to the quivering girl. "You are quite safe—quite safe."

And Violet drank,—at first feverishly, then more steadily, and at last she took the glass into her own hand and slowly drained it. Olga waited beside her, took it quietly from her; set it down.

"Quite comfy, sweetheart?"

"Quite," said Violet. And then, "Come quite close, Allegro dear!"

Olga sat down upon the bed, and took her into her arms, "You don't mind the dark?" she whispered.

And Violet answered. "No. I've passed it. I'm not afraid of anything now."

There fell a silence between them. A great, all-enveloping peace had succeeded the turmoil. Violet's breathing was short but not difficult. She lay nestled in the sheltering arms like a weary child. And slowly the seconds slipped away.

There came a faint sound outside the door as of muffled movements, and Cork, from his post at the foot of the bed, raised his head and deeply growled.

Sleepily the head on Olga's shoulder stirred. "It doesn't matter now," said Violet's voice, speaking softly. "He can never bring me back again." And then, still more softly, in a kind of breathless ecstasy, "The Door is opening, Allegro—darling! Let me—go!"

The words went into a deep sigh that somehow did not seem to end. Olga waited a moment or two, listening tensely, then rose and laid her very tenderly back upon the pillow. She knew that even as she did so, her friend passed through ...

Slowly she turned from the bed, as one in a dream, unconscious of tragedy, untouched by fear or agitation or any emotion whatsoever. All feeling seemed to be unaccountably suspended.

The figure of a big man met her on the threshold. She looked at him with wide, incurious eyes, recognizing him without surprise.

"You are too late," she said.

He started, and bent to look at her closely.

From the deep shadow behind her arose Cork's ominous growl. She turned back into the room.

"May I come in?" Sir Kersley asked in his gentle voice.

With her hand upon Cork's collar, she answered him. "Yes, come in. I am afraid it is rather dark. Will you wait while Mrs. Briggs brings a candle?"

Someone else had entered behind Sir Kersley. She heard a quick, decided tread; and again more ferociously Cork growled.

"Take that dog away!" ordered Max.

Mechanically she moved to obey, Cork accompanying her reluctantly. In the passage she found a strange woman in a nurse's uniform, and Nick. He came to her instantly, and she felt his arm about her with a vague sensation of relief.

"Still sleeping?" he asked.

She answered him quite calmly; at that moment it was no effort to be calm.

"No, Nick; she has gone away."

"What?" he said sharply.

"Won't you take her downstairs?" interposed the nurse, and Olga wondered a little at the compassion in her voice. "She would be the better for a cup of tea."

"So she would," said Nick. "Come along, Olga *mia!*"

His arm was about her still. They went down the wide dim stairs, he and she and the great wolf-hound who submitted to Olga's hand upon him though plainly against his own judgment.

There were candles in the hall, making the vast place seem more vast and ghostly. The east window was discernible only as a vague oblong patch of grey against the surrounding darkness.

"The electric light has gone wrong," said Nick, as she looked at him in momentary surprise.

"I see," she said. "It must have been the storm." She looked down at Cork pacing beside her. "Poor fellow!" she murmured. "He doesn't understand."

"Come and sit down!" said Nick.

Tea had been spread in the place of luncheon. He led her to the table and pulled forward a chair. She sank into it with a sudden shiver.

"Cold?" he said.

"Yes, horribly cold, Nick," she answered.

She tried to smile, but her lips were too stiff. A very curious feeling was creeping over her, a species of cramp that was mental as well as physical. She leaned back in her chair, staring straight before her, seeing nothing.

Nick went round to the tea-pot. She heard him pouring out, but she could not turn her head.

"I ought to do that," she said.

"All right, dear. I'm capable," he answered.

And then in his deft fashion he came to her with the cup, and sat on the arm of her chair, holding it for her.

"Don't try to talk," he said. "Just drink this and sit still."

She leaned her head against him, feeling his vitality as one feels the throb of an electric battery.

"Do you think God is angry with me, Nick?" she said. "She wanted to go—so dreadfully."

"God is never angry with any of us," he answered softly. "We are not big enough for that. There, drink it, sweetheart! It will do you good."

She raised her two hands slowly, feeling as if they were weighted with iron fetters. With flickering eyes he watched her, in a fashion compelling though physically he could not help. She lifted the cup and drank.

The candlelight reeled and danced in her eyes. Her dazed senses began to awake. "Nick!" she exclaimed suddenly and sharply.

"Here, darling!" came his prompt reply.

She set down the empty cup, and clasped her hands tightly together. "Nick!" she said again, in a voice of rising distress.

His hand slid down and held hers. "What is it, kiddie?"

She turned to him impulsively. "Oh, Nick, I've made a great mistake—a great mistake! I ought not to have let her go alone. She will be frightened. I should have gone with her."

"My child," Nick said, "for God's sake—don't say any more! This isn't the time."

And even as she wondered at the unwonted vehemence of his speech, she knew that they were no longer alone.

Max came swiftly through the shadowy archway and moved straight towards her. A white sling dangled from his neck, but it was empty. She thought his hands were clenched.

Scarcely knowing what she did, she rose to meet him, forcing her rigid limbs into action. He came to her; he took her by the shoulders.

"Olga," he said, "how did this happen?"

She faced him, but even as she did so she was conscious of an awful coldness overwhelming her, as though at his touch her whole body had turned to ice. His eyes looked straight into hers, searching her with intolerable minuteness, probing her through and through. And from those eyes she shrank in nameless terror; for they were the eyes of her dream, green, ruthless, terrible. He looked to her like a man whose will might compel the dead.

For a long, long space he held her so, silent but merciless. She did not attempt to resist him. She felt that he had already forced his way past her defences, that he was as it were dissecting and analyzing her very soul. She had not answered his question, but she knew that he would not repeat it. She knew that he did not need an answer.

And then the coldness that bound her became by slow degrees a numbness, paralyzing her faculties, extinguishing all her powers. There arose a great uproar in her brain, the swirl as of great waters engulfing her. She raised her head with a desperate gesture. She met the searching of his eyes, and goaded as it were to self-defence, with the last of her strength, she told him the simple truth.

"I have opened the Door!" she said. "I have set her free!"

She thought his face changed at her words, but she could not see very clearly. She had begun to slip down and down, faster and ever faster into a fathomless abyss of darkness from which there was no deliverance. And as she went she heard his voice above her, brief, distinct, merciless: "And you will pay the price." ... The darkness closed over her head....

CHAPTER XXV
THE PRICE

That darkness was to Olga but the beginning of a long, long night of suffering—such suffering as her short life had never before compassed—such suffering as she had never imagined the world could hold.

It went in a slow and dreadful circle, this suffering, like the turning of a monstrous wheel. Sometimes it was so acute that she screamed with the red-hot agony of it. At other times it would draw away from her for a space, so that she was vaguely conscious that the world held other things, possibly even other forms of torture. Such intervals were generally succeeded by intense cold, racking, penetrating cold that nothing could ever alleviate, cold that was as Death itself, freezing her limbs to stiffness, congealing the blood in her veins, till even her heart grew slower and slower, and at last stood still.

Then, when it seemed the end of all things had come, some unknown power would jerk it on again like a run-down watch in which the key had suddenly been inserted, and she would feel the key grinding round and round and round in a winding-up process that was even more dreadful than the running-down. Then would come agonies of heat and thirst, a sense of being strung to breaking-point, and her heart would race and race till, appalled, she clasped it with her fevered hands and held it back, feeling herself on the verge of destruction.

And through all this dreadful nightmare she never slept. She was hedged about by a fiery ring of sleeplessness that scorched her eyeballs whichever way she turned, giving her no rest. Sometimes indeed dreams came to her, but they were waking dreams of such vivid horror as almost to dwarf her reality of pain. She moved continually through a furnace that only abated when the exhausted faculties began to run down and the deathly chill took her into fresh torments.

Once, lying very near to death, she opened her sleepless eyes upon Max's face. He was stooping over her, holding her nerveless hand very tightly in his own while he pressed a needle-point into her arm. That, she knew, was the preliminary to the winding-up process. It had happened to her before—many times she fancied.

She made a feeble—a piteously feeble—effort to resist him. On the instant his eyes were upon her face. She saw the green glint of them and quivered at the sight. His face was as carved granite in the weird light that danced so fantastically to her reeling brain.

"Yes," he said grimly. "You are coming back."

Then she knew that his will, indomitable, inflexible, was holding her fast, heedless of all the longing of her heart to escape. Then she knew that he, and only he, was the unknown power that kept her back from peace, forcing her onward in that dread circle, compelling her to live in torment. And in that moment she feared him as the victim fears the torturer, not asking for mercy, partly because she lacked the strength and partly because she knew—how hopelessly!—that she would ask in vain.

He did not speak to her again. He was fully occupied, it seemed, with what he had to do. Only, when he had finished, he put his hand over her eyes, compelling them to close, and so remained for what seemed to her a long, long time. For a while she vibrated like a sensitive instrument under his touch, and then very strangely there stole upon her for the first time a sense of comfort. When he took his hand away, she was asleep....

Max turned at last from the bed, nodded briefly to the nurse, and went as silently as a shadow from the room.

Another shadow waited for him on the threshold, and in the light of the passage outside the room they stood face to face.

"She will live," said Max curtly.

"And—" said Nick. He was blinking very rapidly as one dazzled.

"Yes; her reason is coming back. She knew me just now."

"Knew you!"

Max nodded without speaking.

Nick turned his yellow face for a moment towards the open window on the stairs. His lips twitched a little. He said no word.

Max leaned against the wall, and passed his handkerchief over his forehead. Sharp as a ferret, Nick turned.

"Come downstairs, old chap! You've been working like a nigger for the past fortnight. You'll knock up if you are not careful."

Max went with him in silence.

At the foot of the stairs he spoke again. "I shall hand her over to Dr. Jim now. She will do better with him than with me as she gets more sensible."

And so a new presence came into Olga's room, and the figure of her dread appeared no more before her waking eyes. Not at first did she realize the change, for it was only fitfully that her brain could register any definite impression. But one day when strong hands lifted her, something of familiarity in the touch caught her wavering intelligence. She looked up and saw a rugged face she knew.

"Dad!" she said incredulously.

"Of course!" said Dr. Jim bluntly. "Only just found that out?"

She made a feeble attempt to cling to him, smiling a welcome through tears. "Oh, Dad, where have you been?"

"I?" said Dr. Jim. "Why, here to be sure, for the past week. Now we won't have any talking. You shut your eyes like a sensible young woman and go to sleep!"

He had always exacted obedience from her. She obeyed him now. "But you won't go away again?" she pleaded.

"Certainly not," he said, and took her hand into his own.

The last thing she knew was the steady pressure of his fingers on her pulse.

From that time her strength began very slowly to return. The suffering grew less and less intense, till at last it visited her only when she tried to think. And this she was sternly forbidden to do by Dr. Jim, whose word was law.

She was like a little child in those days, conscious only of the passing moment, although even then at the back of her mind she was aware of a monstrous shadow that was never wholly absent day or night. Her father and the nurse were the only people she saw during those early days, and she came to watch for the former's coming with a child's eager impatience.

"I dreamed about Nick last night," she told him one morning. "I wish he would come home, don't you?"

"What do you want Nick for?" he said, possessing himself of her wrist as usual.

"I don't know," she said, knitting her brows. "But it's such a long while since he went away."

He laid his hand on her forehead, and smoothed the lines away. "If you're a good girl," he said, "you shall go and stay with Nick at Redlands when you are well enough."

She looked up at him with puzzled eyes. "I thought Nick was in India, Daddy."

"He was," said Dr. Jim. "But he has come back."

"Then he is at Redlands?" she asked eagerly.

He met her look with his black brows drawn in a formidable frown. "Go slow!" he said. "Yes, he is staying at Redlands."

"Oh, may he come and see me?" she begged.

Dr. Jim considered the point. "If you will promise to keep very quiet," he said finally, "I will let you see him for five minutes only."

"Now?" she asked eagerly.

"Yes, now," said Dr. Jim.

He rose with the words and went out of the room, leaving her struggling to fulfil his condition.

She thought he would return to satisfy himself on this point, but he did not. When the door opened again it was to admit Nick alone.

She held out her arms to him, and in a second he was beside her, holding her fast.

"My poor little chicken!" he said, and though there seemed to be a laugh in his voice she fancied he was in some fashion more moved than she.

"They've cut off all my hair, Nick," she said. "That's the worst of scarlet fever, isn't it?"

"Hair will grow again, sweetheart," he said. "At least, yours will. Mine won't. I'm going as bald as a coot."

They laughed together over this calamity which was becoming undeniably obvious.

"You never did have much thatch, did you, Nick?" she said. "And I suppose India has spoilt what little you had."

"It's nice of you not to set it down to advancing years," said Nick. "Muriel does."

"Muriel? Have you seen her lately?"

"This morning," said Nick.

"Oh?" There was surprised interrogation in Olga's voice. "Where is she, then?"

"At Redlands," said Nick; then, seeing her puzzled look: "We're married, you know, sweetheart."

"Oh?" she said again. "I didn't know."

"It's some time ago now," said Nick. "We've got a little kiddie called Reggie. He's at Redlands too."

"I remember now," Olga smiled understanding. "How is Reggie?" she asked.

"Oh, going strong," said Nick. "He'll soon be as big as I am."

She stretched up a shaky hand to stroke his parchment face. "You're the biggest man I know, Nick," she said softly. "Dad says I may come and stay with you at Redlands. Will you have me?"

"Rather!" said Nick. "There's your own room waiting for you."

"Dear Nick!" she murmured. "You are good to me."

She lay still for a few seconds, holding his hand. Her eyes were wandering round the room. They reached him at last, alert and watchful by her side.

"Nick!" she said.

"What is it, kiddie?"

"There's something I can't remember," she said. "And it hurts me when I try. Nick, what is it?"

He answered her at once with great gentleness. "It's nothing you need worry your head about, dear. I know and so does Jim. You leave it to us till you are a bit stronger."

But she continued to look at him with trouble in her eyes. "I feel as if someone is calling me," she said.

"But that is not so," said Nick quickly and firmly. "Believe me, there is nothing for it but patience. Wait till you are stronger."

She submitted to the mandate, conscious of her own inability to do otherwise; but there was a touch of reproach in her voice as she said, "I thought you would help me, Nick."

"I will," he promised, "when the time comes."

That comforted her somewhat, for she trusted him implicitly; and when Dr. Jim came in he found her quite tranquil.

Thereafter Nick was permitted to see her for a little every day, and she welcomed his visits with enthusiasm.

She would have welcomed Muriel also, but Dr. Jim had decreed that one visitor in the day was enough. She would see Muriel as soon as she was well enough to go to Redlands.

"I really think I am well enough to go now," she confided to Nick one morning. "Do try and persuade Dad."

Nick undertook to do so, with the result that late that night Dr. Jim came in, wrapped her in blankets, head and all as though she had been an infant, and carried her away.

It was a masterly move and achieved with such precision on his part that she had scarcely time to be surprised or excited before she was lying, still in his arms, in a motor and travelling rapidly through the darkness. He uncovered her face then and gave her his blunt permission to come up and breathe.

She clung to him delightedly. "Oh, Dad, isn't it fun? But you're going to stay at Redlands too?"

"For the present," said Dr. Jim.

"Who is taking your patients?" she asked him unexpectedly.

"A fellow from London, a youngster," said Dr. Jim. "Now no more talking, my girl! I'll have you in bed in five minutes and you must be fast asleep in ten."

She laid her cropped head down upon his shoulder, and asked no more.

But she could not wholly repress her astonishment when she abruptly found herself at Redlands. The adventure had all the suddenness of a fairy-tale. "We must have been scorching!" she exclaimed. "Why, we seem to have flown here!"

"It's necessary sometimes," said Dr. Jim.

His words did not wholly explain matters, but they effectually closed her lips; and she asked no more as he bore her up to the room she always occupied when staying in Nick's house. And thereafter she slept more peacefully and naturally than she had slept for a very long time.

In the morning she found another wonder awaiting her; for it was not the nurse who came to her bedside, but Muriel, grave and gentle and motherly, and somehow the sight of her seemed to unveil much that till then had been a mystery to Olga.

She greeted her very lovingly. "You can't imagine what it feels like to see you again," she whispered, with her arms round Muriel's neck. "But I do hope you and Dad haven't hurried back from Switzerland because of me."

Muriel smiled at her with great tenderness. "My darling, don't you know how precious you are?"

"Then you did!" said Olga. "I feel a horrid pig. How is Reggie?"

"He is splendid," said Reggie's mother, in the deep voice that always indicated depth of feeling also. "Much too gay and giddy to come and see you yet. Even Jim is satisfied with him. I couldn't ask for more than that, could I?"

She brought her a cup of milk and sat by the bed while she drank it. There was never any perturbing element in Muriel's presence. She carried ever with her the gracious quietness of a mind at rest.

Olga drank her milk with a most unwonted feeling of serenity. "Reggie certainly mustn't come near me yet," she said. "It would be awful if he caught it."

"There is nothing to catch, dear," said Muriel, as she took back the cup.

"Not scarlet fever?" said Olga in surprise.

"You haven't had scarlet fever," Muriel told her gently. "It was brain fever, following upon sunstroke. That is why we have to keep you so quiet."

"Oh!" said Olga. "Nick never told me that!"

"I don't suppose Dr. Jim would let him. But I told him I should." Muriel's hand, cool and reassuring, held hers. "There is no object in keeping it from you," she said. "You are getting well again, and you always had plenty of sense, dear. I know you will be sensible now."

"I'll certainly try," said Olga.

She lay quiet then for some time, apparently engrossed in thought though not distressed thereby. She turned her head at last and asked a sudden question.

"Will Nick go to India without me, Muriel?"

"No, dear. He is going to wait till you can go too," Muriel answered.

"Oh, Muriel!" She carried the quiet hand impulsively to her lips.

Muriel smiled. "Are you so anxious to go?"

"I should just think I am! But I know I'm horridly selfish. How can you bear to let him go?"

"My dear," Muriel said, "I don't think I could bear to keep him when I know he wants to go. You will have to take care of him for me."

"Oh, I will!" said Olga earnestly.

Very little more passed between them on the subject then, but it filled Olga's mind throughout the day, even to the exclusion of that sinister shadow that still lurked at the back of her consciousness.

Nick did not visit her until the evening, and then she at once began to talk of the topic that so occupied her thoughts.

"Do you know, I had actually forgotten about going to Sharapura, Nick?" she said. "I'm so glad I've remembered. It's something to be quick and get well for."

"Hear, hear!" said Nick, with a whoop of delight.

She laughed at his enthusiasm, and he suddenly recollected himself and entreated her to keep calm.

"If Jim knew I had made you laugh, he'd kick me to a jelly, and give you a blue pill."

Whereat she laughed a little more. "That would be more like Max than Daddy Jim." And there suddenly she stopped short, the colour flooding her pale face. "Why," she said, frowning confusedly, "I had forgotten Max too. How is Max?"

"He's all right," said Nick lightly. "Shall I give him your love?"

"Oh, no!" she said quickly. "Don't give him anything of mine! He—wouldn't understand."

"All right, my chicken," said Nick, with cheery unconcern. "He's got a little brother in the East by the way. I wonder if we shall run across him."

She did not echo the wonder. Her forehead was drawn in the old, painful lines, and she scarcely responded to the rest of his airy conversation.

When Dr. Jim visited her later in the evening he grunted disapproval.

"What's the matter now?" he asked her, with keen eyes on her troubled face.

"I don't know," she murmured wistfully.

"Yes, you do. Come, tell me!" He sat down on the edge of the bed with the evident determination to get at the root of the matter.

She held back for a little, but finally, finding him obdurate, sat up and drew herself within the circle of his arm.

"There, my dear! What is it?" said Dr. Jim.

She hid her face on his shoulder. "Dad, it—it's something to do with Max," she whispered.

"Max? Who is Max?" demanded Dr. Jim inquisitorially, the while he cuddled her close.

"Oh, you know, dear,—Dr. Wyndham," she murmured.

"Oh! So you call him Max, do you?" said Jim drily. "That's an innovation, so far as I am concerned."

"I couldn't help it," she faltered, hiding her face a little lower. "He made me."

"Did he indeed?" said Dr. Jim. "Well? What's the trouble?"

"I—I can't remember," she whispered forlornly.

"Are you in love with him?" asked Dr. Jim abruptly.

She lifted her face with a great start. "No!" she gasped breathlessly.

He looked at her with a semi-humorous frown. "Well, that's something definite to go upon anyhow. Can't stand him at any price, eh?"

She smiled a little doubtfully. "I couldn't at one time. But now—now—"

"Yes? Now?" said Dr. Jim.

"I'm just—afraid of him," she said, a piteous quiver in her voice.

"What for?" Dr. Jim sounded stern, but his hold was very comforting.

"That's just it," said Olga. "I don't remember. I can't remember. But I know he is angry—for some reason. I think—I think I must have done—something he didn't like. Anyhow—I know he is angry."

Dr. Jim grunted again. "Does that matter?" he asked after a moment.

She clung to him very fast. "It will matter—when I see him again."

"And if you don't see him again?" said Dr. Jim.

"Oh, Dad!" she said, with a deep breath.

"Well?" he persisted. "Would that simplify matters? Would that set your mind at rest?"

"Oh, yes, it would!" she said, with immense relief.

He gave her an abrupt kiss, and laid her down. "Very well then. That's settled," he said. "You shan't see him again. Now go to sleep!"

But though she knew he would keep his promise, she was not wholly satisfied, nor did sleep come to her very readily. Her mind was vaguely disturbed. The thought of Max had set her brain in a turmoil which she literally dared not attempt to pursue to its source. She was beginning to be desperately afraid of the mystery she could not penetrate.

She was not so well in the morning, and Dr. Jim rigidly refused to allow either Nick or Muriel at her bedside.

He himself was there during the greater part of the day, watching her, waiting upon her, with a vigilance that never slackened. She suffered a good deal of pain, but his unremitting care did much to alleviate it, and in the evening she was better again, albeit considerably weakened.

After that, her progress was slow, and finding the effort of thought beyond her, she was forced wearily to give up the attempt to think. Even when at length her strength returned sufficiently for her to be carried downstairs and laid on a couch in the garden, the mystery still remained a mystery, and for some reason unintelligible even to herself she had grown content to leave it so. She avoided all thought of it with a morbid dread that was in part physical; for any attempt at concentration in those days always entailed a headache that rendered her practically blind and speechless for hours.

Meantime, they sought to keep her occupied with thoughts of her coming adventure in the East with Nick. There were many preparations to be made, and Muriel tackled them with a steady energy that could not fail to excite Olga's interest. She even roused herself to assist, though Dr. Jim would not permit her to do much, and would often rise and take the work out of her hands when her eyes began to droop.

She had her hours of great depression also, when life was nothing but a burden and she would weep without knowing why. On these occasions Nick was invaluable. He had a wonderful knack of banishing those tears, and in his cheery presence the burden was never insupportable.

It was on Nick's wiry strength that she leaned when she tottered forth for her first walk in the garden. She would probably have wept over her weakness if he had not made her laugh at it instead. It was a morning of soft misty sunshine in the early autumn, and a robin trilled his gay greeting to them as they slowly crept along.

"Jolly little beggar!" said Nick. "Robins always appeal tome. They know how to be cheerful in adversity. Care to go down to the glen, sweetheart? I'll haul you back again."

Yes, Olga would go to the glen. It was a favourite haunt with both of them. The sun glinted on the narrow pathway as they went. The twinkle of the stream was like fairy laughter, with every now and then a secret gurgle as of a laugh suppressed.

They halted on the mossy bank, Nick's arm affording active support. Olga looked down thoughtfully into the running water.

"The last time I was here," she said slowly, "was on the day I went to the Priory to—ask—Violet—to come and stay with me. That must be ages ago."

"Oh, ages!" said Nick.

She turned to him with a puzzled air. "I wonder Violet hasn't been to see me, Nick. Where is she?"

His flickering eyes were searching the stream. "She's gone away," he said.

"Oh! Where has she gone?"

"Haven't a notion," he said indifferently.

"I wonder I haven't heard," mused Olga. "I suppose she hasn't written?"

"Not to my knowledge," said Nick. His attention was obviously still fixed upon the babbling water.

"Oh, well, she hardly ever does write," commented Olga. "And you don't know where she is gone?"

"I do not," said Nick.

At this point his preoccupation seemed to strike her. "What are you looking at?" she asked.

He nodded towards a clump of ferns that fringed the bank. "I thought I saw my friend the scarlet butterfly. There is a beauty lives hereabouts. Yes; by Jove, there he is! See him, Olga?"

Even as he spoke the scarlet butterfly emerged from its hiding place and fluttered down the stream.

Olga uttered a sharp cry that brought Nick's eyes to her face. "What's the matter, kiddie? What is it?"

For a moment she was too overcome to tell him. Then: "Oh, Nick," she said, "I saw that butterfly the last time I was here. It was fluttering along just like that. And then—all of a sudden—a dreadful green dragon-fly flashed out on it, and—and—I didn't see it any more."

"Cheer up!" said Nick. "Evidently it escaped."

"Oh, I wonder!" she said, in a voice of puzzled distress. "I do wonder!"

His shrewd glance returned to the moth quivering like a flower petal in the breeze. "Well, there it is!" he said cheerily. "Let's give it the benefit of the doubt."

Her face did not wholly clear. "I wish I knew," she said. "Do you really think it can be the same, Nick?"

"I've never seen more than one," said Nick, "so it would appear to be a more artful dodger than you took it for. I don't see friend dragon-fly anywhere about."

She shuddered suddenly and convulsively. "No, and I hope he isn't here. Do you know what he made me think of? Max; so strong, so merciless, and so horribly clever."

"I'm clever too," said Nick modestly.

"Oh, but in a different way," protested Olga.

Again his quick eyes flashed over her. "I think you are rather hard on Max myself," he said unexpectedly.

"I?" said Olga.

"Yes, you, my dear. You've no right to regard him in that unwholesome light. He doesn't deserve it. He is quite a decent sort; a little too managing perhaps, but that's just his way. You might go further and fare much worse."

He paused, but Olga said no word. She only palpitated against his arm.

He continued after a moment with the quick decision characteristic of him. "I'm not going to pursue the subject, but just this once—in justice to the man—I must have my say. You asked me once if I liked him, and I was not in a position to tell you. I will tell you now. I like him thoroughly. He's a man after my own heart, straight and clean and staunch. If you ever want someone to trust—trust him! He'd stand by you to perdition."

"Oh, do you think that of him, Nick?" she said, as one incredulous.

"Yes, dear, I do," said Nick. "Well, that's all I have to say. Suppose we begin to crawl back!"

But Olga waited a moment, watching with fascinated eyes the speck of scarlet that still trembled in the sunshine. It fluttered from sight at last, and with a sigh she turned.

"I wonder if it got away!" she murmured again, as if to herself. "I do wonder!"

But to Max, in spite of Nick's spirited eulogy, she made no further reference.

Nick dined at his brother's house at Weir that evening, alone with Max Wyndham. The boys had gone back to school, and the house was almost painfully quiet. Even Nick seemed to feel a certain depression in the atmosphere, for his cheerful chatter was decidedly fitful, and when he and Max were seated opposite to one another smoking it ceased altogether.

Out of a long silence came Max's voice. "When did you say you were starting for the East?"

"Three weeks next Friday," said Nick.

Max grunted, and the silence was renewed.

It was Nick's voice, cracked and careless, that next broke the spell. He seemed to speak on the edge of a laugh. "It's just six years ago since the woman I wanted went to India. Curious, isn't it?"

"What's curious?" said Max.

Nick explained, still with a suspicion of humour in his words: "Well, the funny part of it was that she hoped and believed she was going to get away from me. However, I viewed the matter otherwise, and—I followed her."

"Did you though?" said Max. "And how did the lady take it? Was she pleased?"

"My dear chap, she didn't know." The laugh was more apparent now. Nick removed his cigar to indulge it. "I was most careful not to get in her way, you understand. I was simply there—if wanted."

"And events proved you justified, I suppose?" Max sounded interested after a cynical and quite impersonal fashion.

"They did," said Nick. His own elastic grin appeared for an instant and was gone. "Events can generally be trimmed to suit your purpose," he said, "if you are sufficiently in earnest."

"That has not been my experience," observed Max briefly.

"Perhaps you haven't tried," said Nick.

Silence descended once more, and Nick was rude enough to fall asleep.

An hour later he awoke with extreme alertness in response to a remark from Max as to the lateness of the hour.

"Yes, by Jove," he said. "I must be getting back. By the way, Wyndham, did I mention to you that Sharapura is the name of the place we are going to? It's quite an interesting corner of the Empire, and declared by medical experts to be a top-hole neighbourhood for studying malaria."

"Is that a recommendation?" asked Max grimly.

Nick's smile was geniality itself. "It is," he answered; "a very strong recommendation." He thrust out a friendly hand. "Good-night, my son, and good luck to you!"

Max's grip was hard and sustained. He looked into the grinning, humorous face, and almost in spite of himself his own mouth took a humorous twist.

"So that's what you came to say, is it?" he said. "Well, good-night, you old rotter, and—thanks!"

Nick mounted his horse and rode back in the moonlight, singing a tuneless but very sentimental love lyric to the stars.

Part II
CHAPTER I
COURTSHIP

"It must be great fun gettin' married," said the chief bridesmaid pensively to the best man. "Why don't you go and get married, Noel?"

"I'm going to," said Noel.

"Oh, are you?" with suddenly-awakened interest. "Soon?"

Noel screwed up his Irish eyes and laughed. "In twelve years or thereabouts."

"Oh!" A pair of wide blue eyes regarded him attentively. "Twelve years is a very long time," observed the chief bridesmaid gravely.

"It is, isn't it?" said Noel, with a large sigh.

"P'raps you'll be dead then," suggested the chief bridesmaid.

"What a jolly idea! P'raps I shall. In that case, the marriage will not take place."

She sat down on his knee, and slipped a kindly arm round his neck. "I hope you won't be dead, Noel," she said, in the careful tone of one not wishing to be taken too seriously.

The best man smiled all over his merry face. "I shall do my best to survive for your sake," he said.

She nodded thoughtfully. "But why aren't you goin' to get married sooner?"

He surveyed her with his head on one side. "My little sweetheart is only pocket size at present," he said. "I'm waiting for her to grow up."

"Oh! Is she little like me?" asked the chief bridesmaid, looking slightly disappointed.

"She's just like you, sweetheart," said Noel, with cheery assurance. "She has eyes of wedgewood blue, and hair of golden down, a mouth like a rose, and the jolliest little turn-up nose in the world. And she's going to be six next birthday."

This classic description was an instant revelation to the chief bridesmaid. She blushed very sweetly, with pleasure unfeigned in which shyness had no part. "Oh, Noel!" she breathed, in rapturous anticipation. "But why must we wait till we're growed up?"

"We!" said Noel, who was twenty-two and a crack shot in the Regiment.

She kissed him propitiatingly. "I mean—dear Noel—. why can't we go and get married now? I'm sure Mummy wouldn't mind."

"H'm! I wonder!" said Noel.

"I do love you so very much," said the chief bridesmaid, with eyes of shining sincerity. "And you are just the beautifullest soldier *I* ever saw!"

He threw back his head in a laugh that showed his white teeth, to his small adorer's huge delight. He was certainly a very gallant figure in his red and gold uniform with his sword dangling at his side; and his winning Irish ways gained him popularity wherever he went.

It was true that the chief bridesmaid's mother shook her head at him, and called him fickle, but then his fickleness was of so open and boyish an order that it could hardly be regarded as a fault, especially since no one—with the exception of the chief bridesmaid—ever took him seriously. And to her at least young Noel Wyndham was always tenderly faithful in his allegiance.

On the present occasion, though nominally he had been acting as best man to a brother officer, he had spent most of his time in the service of the muslin-frocked, bare-legged atom who now sprawled upon his knee with all the privilege of old acquaintance, assuring him of her whole-hearted devotion and admiration.

He had just been giving her tea and wedding-cake, of which latter she had eaten the sugar and he the cake, a wise division which had pleased them both.

"Will we have a cake just like this when we're married, Noel?" she asked seductively, casting an affectionate glance towards the empty plate.

"Oh, rather!" said Noel. "Several storeys high, big enough to last a whole year."

"Oh, Noel!" she murmured ecstatically.

And, "Oh, Noel!" said her mother, suddenly coming up behind them.

The chief bridesmaid laughed roguishly over Noel's shoulder. "I like weddin's," she said.

Noel set her down and rose. "My dear Mrs. Musgrave, I've been hunting for you everywhere. Have you had any tea?"

She smiled at him with amused reproof. A very sweet smile had Mrs. Musgrave, but it was never very mirthful. She had lost all her mirth with her youth. Though she could not have been much over thirty, her hair was silver white.

"I was only in the next room," she said. "Yes, thank you; the padre gave me tea. We must be going. Peggy and I. Will left some time ago, directly after the bride and bridegroom."

"Ah, Will is a paragon of industry. I believe he thinks more of that beastly old reservoir of his than of the whole population of Sharapura put together. But surely you needn't go yet? Don't!" pleaded Noel, with his most persuasive smile.

"No, don't let's, Mummy!" begged the child, clinging to her hero's hand. "Noel and me, we're goin' to be married, we are."

"So we are," said Noel. "And we're going to church on the Rajah's state elephant, and we're going to make him trumpet all the way there and all the way back. I hope we are not springing it on you too suddenly," he added, with a laugh. "It's the usual thing, isn't it, for the best man to marry the chief bridesmaid?"

"I should say it depended a little on their respective ages," smiled Mrs. Musgrave. "Are you going to find my 'rickshaw? It is later than I thought, and I am expecting visitors."

"Ah, I know," said Noel. "Captain and Mrs. Nick of Wara, isn't it?"

"Not Mrs. Nick," she corrected him. "I wish it had been. She is my greatest friend. But she can't leave England because of their child."

"There's a lady of some description coming in his train," asserted Noel. "I have it on unimpeachable authority."

"Yes, she is his niece. I knew her as a child, a giddy little thing—rather like Nick himself."

"Mrs. Musgrave! Is that how you describe one of our most celebrated heroes? Nick Ratcliffe—the one and only—the most romantic specimen of our modern British chivalry—beloved of women like yourself, respected by men like me! Did I hear aright?"

She laughed. "Oh, don't be absurd! He is the least imposing person in the world, I assure you."

"And the lady, his niece?" questioned Noel. "Is she married by the way?"

"Oh, no. She is quite a girl."

"A real live girl in this wilderness!" ejaculated Noel. "I say, may I drop in a little later and see her? Dear Mrs. Musgrave, say Yes!" He stooped and gallantly kissed her hand. "As your daughter's *fiancé*, I think you might ask me to dine. I'll be so awfully good if you will. I say, Peggy, ask Mummy to invite me to dinner to-night, and I'll come and say good-night to you in bed."

"Oh, yes!" cried Peggy, jumping with eagerness. "He may come, mayn't he, Mummy? And I'll save up my prayers," she added to Noel, "and say them to you!"

"Hear, hear!" said Noel. "Come, Mrs. Musgrave, you haven't the heart to refuse me such an innocent pleasure as that. I'm sure you haven't, so thank you kindly, I'll come. Shall I?"

"Of course you are quite irresistible," said Mrs. Musgrave. "But I don't—really—think it would be very kind of me to have guests on their first night. The poor child is sure to be too tired for chatter."

"But I shan't chatter," protested Noel. "I'll be as quiet as a mouse. Come, Mrs. Musgrave, don't be cruel! Remember you're dealing with your future son-in-law, who is absolutely devoted to you; and don't refuse me the only favour I've ever asked!"

He gained his end. Noel Wyndham was an adept at that, having made a study of it all his life.

Mrs. Musgrave, reflecting that the most fascinating young officer in the cantonment could scarcely be unwelcome in the eyes of a young English girl, however tired she might be, finally allowed herself to be persuaded by cajolery on his part and earnest pleading on Peggy's to include him at her dinner-table.

"If you don't mind taking the risk of being de trop," she said, "you may come."

"I'll take any risk," he declared ardently; and, having gained his point, kissed her hand again and departed to summon her 'rickshaw, with Peggy mounted on his shoulder.

CHAPTER II
THE SELF-INVITED GUEST

When Noel Wyndham entered Mrs. Musgrave's drawing-room that night, he was wearing his most alluring smile. He was evidently prepared to charm and be charmed; and his host, who privately regarded this addition to the party as a decided nuisance, could not but extend to him a cordial welcome. Will Musgrave, though grave and even by some deemed austere, was never churlish. He was a civil engineer of some repute, and had earned for himself a reputation for hard work which was certainly well deserved.

Nick Ratcliffe had been his close friend from boyhood, and the chance that had stationed him within a short distance of the native city of Sharapura in which Nick was for the next few months to take up his abode was regarded by both as a singularly happy one. It was not surprising therefore that he could not bring himself to look upon Noel's advent on that, their first evening together, with much enthusiasm.

His wife had broken the news with semi-humorous apologies. "I couldn't resist him, Will. You know what that boy is. Really I didn't ask him. He asked himself."

"Oh, all right," Will had replied, with resignation. "You'll have to look after him, and see he doesn't try to flirt too outrageously at first sight."

"I'll try," she had assented somewhat dubiously.

For Noel always flirted with every woman he met, herself included, and it was really quite impossible to stop him, or even to discourage him. He only laughed at snubs, and pursued his airy flights with keener zest.

She was not in the drawing-room when the self-invited guest arrived, and it fell to her husband to receive and entertain him. Noel, however, was extremely easy to entertain at all times. He was never bored.

"It was so awfully good of Mrs. Musgrave to let me come," he observed to his host, on shaking hands. "I had to beg jolly hard, I can tell you. She thought your other visitors might consider me one too many. But I'm sure they won't, and I'm immensely keen on meeting them. Have they arrived?"

"Two hours ago," said Will Musgrave.

"That's all right. My brother-in-law knows Ratcliffe, but I've never had the good luck to meet him. Something of a fire-eater, isn't he?"

Will laughed. "Oh, quite a giant in his own line."

Noel nodded. "Just as well. They are wanting a giant pretty badly up at the city if report says true. That young Akbar needs a firm hand. He passed us on parade yesterday, went by like the devil, kicking up a dust fit to choke the lot of us. Beastly young cad!"

"Ah! He isn't over fond of the Indian Army," said Will.

"The Indian Army would give him a damn good hiding if it got the chance," returned Noel, in righteous indignation. "I hope Ratcliffe will rub that into him well. The place is simply swarming with malcontents, and he encourages them. I believe they even flatter themselves we are afraid of 'em."

"I shouldn't say anything of that kind before Miss Ratcliffe," said Will. "She has just got over a severe illness, and may be nervous."

"Great Scotland! This isn't the place for anyone with nerves!" ejaculated Noel. "I heard this morning that there's a most ferocious man-eater in the Khantali district. I'm longing to have a shot at him, but they say he's as cunning as Beelzebub, and never shows unless he has some game on. And the jungle's so beastly thick all round there. It doesn't give anyone a chance. Why can't His Objectionable Excellency turn his hand to something useful, and clear some of it away? By the way, I tried to catch a *karait* this morning. I am going to start a menagerie for Peggy's edification. But our *khit*, who is a very officious person when he isn't wrapt in contemplation of nothing in particular, interfered and killed the little beast before I had time to explain. I told him he was a silly ass, but he seemed to think he had done something praiseworthy. What's the best remedy for a *karait's* bite?"

"The only known remedy is to sit down and die with as good a grace as possible," said Nick, entering at the moment. "But it's just as well to be sure it is a *karait* before you take those measures, as there are more hopeful remedies for other species." He held out his hand to Noel with a cheery smile. "Pleased to meet you. I have already made the acquaintance of one member of your illustrious family."

"Have you though?" said Noel. "That's rather a handicap for me, isn't it?"

Nick's glance travelled swiftly over him and passed. "If you're as good a chap as your brother, you'll do," he said.

"Oh, I'm not," said Noel hastily. "If you're talking about Max, he's the only respectable Wyndham there is, and that's only because he hasn't time to be anything else. He wrote and told me you were coming here. I was at Budhpore then, but I set to work double quick and got myself transferred."

"What for?" said Nick.

Noel winked confidentially. "I wanted to see the fun," he said.

Again for the passage of a second Nick's eyes regarded him, and then over the shrewd, yellow face there flashed a sudden smile. "Are you a cricketer?" said Nick.

"You bet I am!" said Noel boyishly.

Nick nodded. "I was myself once."

"Only once, Nick?" protested Musgrave, with a smile that was scarcely humorous.

Nick turned to him with a semi-rueful grimace. "Oh, my cricketing days are over. All I'm good for now is to teach other fellows the rules of the game."

At this point a high voice made itself heard in the distance, imperiously demanding Noel's presence.

"Oh, Jupiter!" exclaimed Noel. "That's Peggy! Excuse me, you chaps! She has been saving up her prayers for my benefit, and I came early on purpose!"

He was gone with the words, with all an ardent lover's alacrity, and Will Musgrave smiled.

"He's a heady youngster, but there's real stuff in him."

"Sound, is he?" said Nick.

"I should say so; but fancy he's a bit fiery," said Will.

There was nothing to denote fieriness in Noel's attitude as he composed himself a few seconds later for the ceremony of Peggy's devotions. It was a very simple ceremony, but conducted with extreme decorum, Peggy's *ayah* being sternly dismissed as a preliminary.

Noel sat on the edge of the bed while its small owner knelt upon it, head bowed in hands and lodged upon his shoulder. He had made a tentative movement to encircle her with his arm, but this had been gently but quite firmly forbidden.

"You mustn't cuddle while I'm sayin' my prayers," said Peggy. "You must put your hands together and shut your eyes. That's what Mummy does."

Noel complied with these instructions, but when Peggy was fairly launched he ventured to violate the last and steal a look at the fair head that rested against his shoulder.

Peggy was saying the Lord's Prayer with evident enjoyment. Noel listened with respect. There was the swish of a woman's dress in the passage outside. He listened to that also, his dark eyes watching the half-open door. His attention began to wander.

"Noel!" said a small, hurt voice at his side.

Noel's eyes shut as if at the pulling of a string. "Sorry, Peg-top! Go ahead!"

"You mustn't call me Peg-top when I'm sayin' my prayers!" protested Peggy. "I wanted you to say Amen."

"Amen," said Noel humbly.

"It's no good now." There was a sound of tears in Peggy's voice. "You've just spoilt it all."

"Oh, I say!" pleaded Noel. "Well, try again! I'll say it next time."

"Can't," said Peggy. "It's wrong to keep on sayin' the same thing."

"I never heard that before," said Noel.

"It's in the Bible," asserted Peggy.

"Is it?" Noel sounded faintly incredulous.

"Yes, it is." There was a touch of indignation in Peggy's rejoinder. "It's what the heathen do," she said.

Noel ventured to open his eyes, and found hers fixed severely upon him. "Well, I'm awfully sorry," he said. "What had we better do?"

"You're not sorry," said Peggy accusingly. "Your eyes are all laughy."

"I'll swear they're not," declared Noel. "But I say, hadn't you better finish? Then we can have a cuddle."

"But I can't finish," said Peggy.

"Why not?"

"'Cos you interrupted, and I can't begin again." There was more than the sound of tears this time; the blue eyes were suddenly swimming in them. "And I haven't said my hymn, and you don't care a bit," she said in a voice that quivered ominously. Matters were evidently getting desperate.

"Yes, but you can say the rest," argued Noel, with the feeling that he was losing ground every instant. "What do you generally say next?"

"No, I can't. It wouldn't be sayin' them properly, and God doesn't listen if you don't say them properly."

Here was a formidable difficulty; but Noel's brain was fertile. He had a sudden inspiration. "Look here!" he said. "I'll say the first part again for you, and you can say Amen. I haven't said mine yet, you know, so it doesn't matter for me. Then you can go on and finish. Will that do?"

Peggy gave the matter her grave consideration, and decided that it would. "But you must kneel down," she said.

There was no sound in the passage now. Noel peered in that direction, but detected nothing. Patiently he slipped on to his knees, and began to recite the Lord's Prayer.

Considering the difficulties under which he laboured, he acquitted himself with considerable credit. Peggy at least was fully satisfied, a fact to which her fervent "Amen"! abundantly testified. She took up her own petitions at once quite impressively, albeit with slightly accelerated speed to make up for lost time. At the end of her hymn she paused.

"Would you like me to ask God to make me grow up quick so that we can be married soon, Noel?" she asked.

"I shouldn't." said Noel.

"Not?" The wedgewood-blue eyes opened wide.

"No. Very likely you won't want to marry me when you're grown up," Noel explained.

Peggy was amazed at the bare suggestion of such a possibility. "Why, of course I'll want to marry you," she declared, hugging him. "You're the wery nicest man that ever was."

"No, I'm not. I'm a rotter," Noel made brief and unvarnished reply. "No one knows what I am—except myself. And no one ever will," he added almost fiercely. And then, with lightning change of front, he laughed. "Never mind! We'll go on being sweethearts. That's better than nothing, isn't it?"

Peggy was looking at him very seriously. "I'd go on lovin' you even if—if—you was to kill someone," she said.

"Thanks, Peg-top! Well, I've never done that yet, though there's no knowing how soon I may begin," said Noel carelessly.

"Oh, but it's very wicked to kill people." There was shocked reproof in Peggy's tone.

"Depends," said Noel judicially. "Sometimes it's the only thing to do."

"Oh, Noel!" Peggy's disapproval was evidently struggling with her loyalty.

Something white gleamed in the doorway, and Noel's eyes suddenly sparkled. He abandoned the argument without a second thought.

"Pray come in!" he said. "Peggy is holding a reception. She always receives at this hour. Now, Peggy, stand up and tell this lady my name!"

"May I really come in for a moment?" said Olga. She stood hesitating on the threshold, a slim, girlish figure. "Don't let me disturb you! Mrs. Musgrave thinks she must have left her rings here. How do you do?"

She gave her hand to Noel who had moved to meet her He laughed audaciously into her face.

"Awfully pleased to meet you, Miss—er—Ratcliffe! Why didn't you come in before? I was in a beastly tight fix, and should have been glad of your assistance. I knew you were there."

"Did you?" she said. The smile that had grown so rare flashed over her face in response to his. "I wasn't eavesdropping really," she assured him. "I was only waiting for a suitable moment to present myself."

"Could any moment be anything else?" he asked her, bowing deeply.

She laughed at that without the faintest coquetry. "Very easily, I should say. Isn't little Peggy going to bed?"

"Of course she is," said Noel. "Hop in, infant! We've been officiating at a wedding to-day, she and I, and the excitement has turned our heads a little. That's the way, mavourneen!" as Peggy, a little shy in the presence of the newcomer, slipped into her bed. "You didn't introduce me though, did you?"

Peggy held his hand in embarrassed silence.

"Peggy scarcely knows me herself yet," said Olga. "Don't you think we might manage without?"

"I dared not have suggested it myself," said Noel, with an ease that belied him. "If we do that, we may as well pretend we're old acquaintances at once."

"Perhaps," said Olga. She was searching for her hostess's rings and spoke with a somewhat absent air.

"Especially as my name is Wyndham," he said.

She stopped short in her search and seemed to stiffen. Then slowly she turned towards him. "You are Max's—Dr. Wyndham's—brother!"

"I have that honour," said Noel drily.

She stood quite still for a moment; then: "I knew he had a brother in India," she said. "But I didn't know we were likely to meet."

"That," said Noel, "was partly his doing and partly mine. He wrote and told me that Captain Ratcliffe was coming to Sharapura, and I at once took steps to get myself transferred to the battalion here."

"Oh! Then you know Nick?"

"By repute," smiled Noel. "A good many people in India can say the same, though he may be without honour in his own country."

"Indeed he isn't!" said Olga proudly. "He is a hero wherever he goes."

"And you have come to take care of him?" asked Noel.

She faced him. "Did you know I was coming?"

"No. I thought it was Mrs. Ratcliffe. Max writes an abominable fist."

She seemed relieved. "Yes, I have come to take care of him. He never takes care of himself."

"And you know how to make him do as he is told?" asked Noel.

She smiled. "Oh, yes, I am quite capable. It isn't the first time I have taken care of him. We are very old pals."

"I envy you both," said Noel. "Is this what you are looking for?"

He had spied a ring under the edge of Peggy's biscuit-plate. He held it out to her with a graceful flourish.

But at this point Peggy, who had begun to feel neglected, overcame her shyness and shrilly intervened.

"Noel, that's not the way! You should say, 'With this ring—'"

"Peggy!" Noel interrupted, "you're going too fast. I'm much too old to travel at that pace. I will say good-night to you before you get me into trouble."

He stooped to kiss her, but Peggy was clinging like a marmoset round his neck when he stood up again. His brown face laughed through her curls.

"We're a horribly spoony couple," he said to Olga. "We've known each other just six weeks, and we got engaged to-day."

"Do you often get engaged like that?" asked Olga.

"Oh, rather!" said Noel. "It's much more fun than getting married. Cheaper too, and not so monotonous!" Again he laughed. "I assure you it's the easiest thing in the world to get engaged. Never tried it?"

It was unpardonably audacious; but that was Noel Wyndham's way, and somehow no one ever took offence.

Olga did not take offence, but she winced ever so slightly; a fact which Noel obviously failed to observe, being occupied with the difficult task of releasing himself from Peggy's ardent embraces.

When he finally obtained his freedom and stood up, Olga had passed out again into the passage. He threw a last kiss to his small sweetheart, and hurried after her.

CHAPTER III
THE NEW LIFE

"It isn't in the least what I thought it would be," said Olga.

"Nothing ever is," said Nick.

He was sprawling on a *charpoy* on the verandah of their new abode, smoking a cigarette with lazy enjoyment.

Though within sound of the native city, their bungalow stood well outside. It was surrounded by a compound of many tangled shrubs that gave it the appearance of being more isolated than it actually was. Not so very far away from it, down in the direction of Will Musgrave's growing reservoir, there stood a *dâk*-bungalow; and immediately beyond this were corn-fields and the native village that clustered along the edge of the river. The cantonments were well out of sight, more than a mile away along the dusty road, further than the polo-ground and race-course.

Behind the bungalow, approached only through a dense mass of tall jungle grass, stretched the jungle, mile upon mile of untamed wilderness, home of wild pig and jackals, monkeys and flying foxes. Very quiet by day was that long dark tract of jungle, but at night strange voices awoke there that seemed to Olga like the crying of unquiet spirits. Neither by day nor night did she feel the smallest desire to explore it.

The native city of Sharapura held infinitely greater fascinations for her. Some of its buildings were beautiful, and she was keenly interested in its inhabitants. She never entered it, however, save under Nick's escort. He was very insistent upon this point, and he would never suffer her to linger in the long, narrow bazaar, with its dim booths and crafty, peering faces.

Down by the river there was a mosque about which pigeons circled and cooed perpetually, but beggars were so plentiful all round it that it was next to impossible to pause near the spot without being beset on all sides, a matter of real regret to the English girl, who longed to wander or stand and admire at will.

In His Excellency the Rajah she was frankly disappointed. He had been educated in England, and had acquired a patronizing condescension of demeanour which she found singularly unattractive. He never treated her with familiarity, but she did not like the look of his dusky eyes. They always smiled, but to her there was something unpleasant behind the smile. In her private soul she deemed him treacherous.

He invariably wore European costume, with the exception of his green turban with its flowing puggaree. He was an excellent and graceful horseman, and spoke English with extreme fluency.

Nick spent a good many hours of every day at the Palace, and they were always on the best terms; yet Olga never saw him go without a pang of anxiety or return without a thrill of relief.

Probably her recent severe illness had had a lasting effect upon her nerves, for she was never easy in his absence, though Daisy Musgrave did much to reassure her. She had taken Olga under her wing as naturally as though they had been related, and they were much together.

The old life had begun to seem very far away to Olga, her childhood as remote as a half-forgotten dream. The blank space in her memory remained as a patch of darkness through which her thread of life had run indeed but of which no record remained. She had ceased to attempt to read the riddle, half in dread and half in sheer helplessness. It did not seem to matter. Surely, as Max had once said to her, nothing mattered that was past.

She did not spare much thought for Max either just then, instinctively avoiding all mention of him. She had a vague consciousness that was more in the nature of a nightmare memory than an actual happening, that they had parted in anger. Sometimes there would rush over her soul the recollection of piercing green eyes that searched and searched and would not spare, and her heart would beat in a wild dismay and she would shrink in horror from the vision. But it was not often that this came to her now. She had learned to ward it off, to put away the past, to live in the present.

For nearly a month she had been established with Nick in the bungalow on the outskirts of the city, and the novelty of things had begun to wear off. She was not strong enough to go out very much, and beyond a few calls with Nick and a dinner or two at the cantonments she had not seen much of the social life of Sharapura.

That night, however, they were to attend a State dinner at the Palace, to which all the officers of the battalion and their wives had been bidden. Olga was relieved to know that the Musgraves were also going, for at present she was intimate with no one else, with the possible exception of Noel, who visited them in a fashion which he described as "entirely unofficial" almost every day. He seemed to entertain a vast admiration for Nick, and as Olga was wholly in sympathy with him on this great point, they did not find it difficult to agree upon smaller matters. She even bore with his bare-faced Irish compliments, mainly

297

because she knew he did not mean them and she found it easier to be amused than offended.

The new life was undeniably one of considerable interest, and now and then, more particularly when she went for her morning ride with Nick—a function which Noel almost invariably attended when off duty, appearing with a brazen smile and not the faintest suggestion of an excuse—the old zest would awake within her, almost deluding her into the belief that her lost youth had returned.

She still had her hours of depression and strange heart-heaviness so alien to her nature, and even in her lighter moments she was far more restrained than of yore—shrewd still, quick of understanding still, but infinitely graver, more womanly, more reserved.

Nick, who watched her as tenderly as a mother, sometimes asked himself if after all he and Jim had done the right thing. Her remoteness worried him. She seemed to live in a world of her own, asking no questions, making no confidences. Not that she ever barred him out. He was well aware that she had not the vaguest desire to keep him at a distance. But her old spontaneity, her child-like demonstrativeness, seemed to have gone, and a nameless shadow haunted the eyes that once had been so clear.

They often sat together on the verandah as now, when the day's work was done, sometimes talking, sometimes silent, always in complete accord.

Olga's remark that the India to which Nick had introduced her was wholly unlike her expectations had been called forth by some comment of his upon the Rajah's exceedingly British tastes.

"I thought things would be much more primitive," she said.

And Nick laughed, and after a long draught of whisky and soda observed that possibly they were more primitive than she imagined. After which he stretched himself luxuriously, and asked her if she were aware that they were within a week of Christmas Day.

"Of course," she said. "Did you imagine I had forgotten? It seems so strange to have nothing to do."

He sat up very abruptly with his knees drawn up to his chin and blinked at her with extreme rapidity. "Olga," he said, "I believe you're homesick."

The colour that of old had been so quick to rise faintly tinged her face as she shook her head. "Oh, no, Nick! Don't be absurd! How could I be, with you?"

"I'm not absurd—on this occasion," returned Nick.

"It's the fashion for absentees to be homesick all the world over at Christmas-time. However, we are not bound to follow the fashion. How are we going to celebrate the occasion? Have you any ideas to put forward?"

"None, Nick."

He nodded. "That makes it all the easier for me. Shall we give a picnic at Khantali—you and I? It won't be much fag for you if you drive over with Daisy Musgrave. Noel can take most of the provisions in his dog-cart. He's a useful youngster. How does that strike you? There is a ruined temple or a mosque at Khantali, I believe, and you like that sort of thing."

He paused. She was listening with far-away eyes. "Yes, I shall like that," she said. "It is very nice of you to think of it."

Nick straightened his knees and got up. "Do you know what I would do if I had two hands, Olga *mia*?" he said.

She looked up questioningly. His face was for the moment grim.

"I would take you by the shoulders and give you a jolly good shaking," he said.

She opened her eyes in astonishment. "Really, Nick!"

"Yes, really," he said. "You didn't hear a word of what I said just now."

"Oh, but I did!" she protested, flushing in earnest this time. "I heard you and I answered you."

"Oh, yes, you answered me," he said, "as kindly and indulgently as if I had been prattling like Peggy Musgrave. I won't put up with it any longer, my chicken. Understand?"

He put his hand under her chin and turned her face upwards.

She quivered a little and the tears sprang to her eyes. "I'm sorry, Nick," she said.

He shook his head at her. "I won't have you sorry. That's just the grievance. Be hurt, be indignant, be angry! Sulk even! I know how to treat sulks. But don't cry, and don't be sorry! I shall be furious if you cry."

She smiled up at him wistfully, saying nothing.

"Fact of the matter is," proceeded Nick, "you're spoilt. It's high time I put my foot down. If you don't wake up, I'll make you take a cold bath every morning and swing dumb-bells for half an hour after it."

She began to laugh. "I love to see you playing tyrant, Nick."

He let her go. "I'm not playing, my child. I'm in sober, deadly earnest. Have you made up your mind yet what you're going to say to young Noel when he asks you to marry him?"

She started. "Oh, really, Nick!" she said again, this time with a touch of annoyance in her tone.

He smiled as he heard it. "It's coming, I assure you. You see, the station is short of girls, and our young friend is impressionable. He is the sort of amorous swain who gets engaged to a dozen before he settles down to marriage with one. The question for you to decide is, are you going to be one of the dozen?"

"No, that I certainly am not." Olga spoke with undoubted emphasis, and having spoken rose and laid her hands upon Nick's shoulders. "I don't think he would be so silly as to ask me," she said. "And if he did, I certainly should not be silly enough to say Yes."

"I'm glad to hear that anyway," said Nick briskly. "I was afraid you might accept him out of sheer boredom."

"Nick! I'm not bored!"

He looked at her quizzically, as if he did not quite believe her.

"I am not bored," she reiterated, with something like vehemence. "I am happier with you than with anyone else in the world."

"Really?" said Nick, still smiling.

"Don't you believe me?" she said.

He laughed. "Not quite, dear; but that's not your fault. What are you going to wear to-night?"

Nick could switch himself from one subject to another as easily as a monkey leaps from tree to tree, and when once he had made the leap no persuasion could ever induce him to return. Olga knew this, and abandoned the discussion, albeit slightly dissatisfied.

They separated soon after to dress for the Rajah's dinner. Olga had chosen a dress of palest mauve, and very fair and delicate she looked in it. In a crowd of girls she would doubtless have been passed over by all but the most observant, but she was not one of a crowd at Sharapura. There were not many girls in that region, or Noel Wyndham's volatile fancy had scarcely strayed in her direction.

She told herself this with a faint smile, as she took a final glance at herself when her *ayah* had finished. There never had been any personal vanity about Olga, and that night she told herself she looked positively ugly. What in the world did Noel see in her, she wondered? It seemed incredible that any man could find anything to admire in the colourless image that confronted her.

And yet as she went up the Palace steps with Nick into the blaze of light that awaited them, he was the first to greet her, and she saw his eyes kindle at the sight of her after a fashion that made her heart contract with a sudden pain for which at the moment she was wholly at a loss to account.

"I say, you look topping!" he said, smiling down at her with pleasing effrontery. "Do you know you are very nearly late? I've been watching out for you for the past ten minutes."

"What a waste of time!" said Olga; but she returned his smile, for she could not do otherwise.

"No! Why? I had nothing better to do," he assured her. "And my patience is well rewarded. Hope you're keen on music. I've brought my banjo for the Rajah's edification. It's better than a tomtom anyway. I wonder if the fates have put us next to each other. I'll lay you five rupees to a sixpence that they haven't."

Olga refused to take this generous offer, saying she had no sixpences to spare him, a remark which he declared to be both premature and uncalled for.

"You shouldn't kick a man before he's down," he said. "It's bad policy. If you have to sit next to me after that, it will serve you right."

But when she found that he actually was to be her neighbour she was far from quarrelling with the destiny that made him so. He was so blithe and gay of heart, so blandly impudent, the very wine seemed to shine the redder for his presence. It was not in her nature to flirt with any man, but it was utterly impossibly not to enjoy his society. Less and less did she believe that his butterfly pursuit of her had in it the smallest element of serious intention. He was altogether too young and giddy for such things. She dismissed the matter without further misgiving.

CHAPTER IV
THE PHANTOM

Without Noel she would have found that State dinner as dreary as it was pompous. The Rajah was occupied with discussing the laws of British sport with Colonel Bradlaw who regarded himself as an authority on such matters, and expressed his opinions ponderously and at extreme length.

Nick was far away down the long table, seated beside Daisy Musgrave, obviously to their mutual satisfaction. A bubbling oasis of gaiety surrounded them. Evidently the general atmosphere of state and ceremony was less oppressive in that quarter.

"Where would you be without me to take care of you?" said Noel, boldly intercepting her glance in their direction.

"I am not at all bad at taking care of myself," she told him.

"I say—forgive me—I don't believe that," said Noel, with calm effrontery. "You would simply fall a prey to the first ogre who came along."

Olga elevated her chin slightly. "That shows how much you know about me."

"I know a great deal," said Noel, with an ardent glance. "And that's what makes me want to know much more. You know, you're horribly tantalizing, if you will allow me to say so."

"In what way?" She spoke coolly; there was a hint of challenge in the grey eyes she turned upon him.

He laughed without embarrassment. "I can't quite explain. There's something so elusively attractive—or do I mean attractively elusive?—about you. I call you 'the will-o'-the-wisp girl' to my own private soul."

"I hope your own private soul is too sensible to encourage such nonsense," said Olga severely.

He looked at her, sheer mischief dancing in his Irish eyes. "Come and see it some day and judge for yourself!" he said. "I can fix up a *séance* any time. It would always be at home to you. I'm sure you would get on together."

It was hard to restrain a smile; Olga permitted herself one of strictly limited proportions.

"I will show you a glimpse presently if you would care to see it," proceeded Noel.

"Oh, please don't trouble!" said Olga.

"Afraid of being bored?" he asked.

She laughed. "Perhaps."

He leaned towards her. Her laugh was reflected in his eyes, but she did not hear it in his voice as he said, "Do you mean that? Do I really bore you?"

She met his look for a moment, and her heart quickened a little. Quite suddenly she realized that this man, young though he was, possessed a wonderful power of attraction. She wondered if he himself were aware of it, and rapidly decided that he had made the discovery in his cradle. Of one thing she was certain. She did not want to fall in love with him. He drew her indeed, but it was against her will.

"Well?" he said. "Have you made up your mind yet?"

She smiled. "Oh, no, you don't bore me," she said.

"Thanks awfully! It's not generally considered a family failing of the Wyndhams. Every other rascality under the sun, but not that."

"What a fascinating family you seem to be!" said Olga.

He made a wry face. "In a sense. Did you find Max fascinating?"

He put the question carelessly; yet she suspected he had a reason for asking it. She felt the tell-tale blood rising in her face.

"You don't like him?" said Noel.

She hesitated.

"I don't mind your saying so in the least," he assured her. "He's a queer chap—a bit of a genius in his own line; but geniuses are trying folk to live with. How did he get on with your father?"

"Oh, Dad likes him," she said.

"He's not much of a ladies' man," remarked Noel. "I suppose he has chucked that job by this time, and gone back to Sir Kersley Whitton. Lucky beggar! He seems to be able to do anything he likes."

"I didn't know he was going to leave," said Olga quickly.

"No? I believe he said something about it in his letter to me. He is always rather sudden," said Noel. "Too much beastly electricity in his composition for my taste."

"Do you often hear from him?" Olga asked abruptly.

"Once in a blue moon. Why?" His dark eyes interrogated her, but she would not meet them.

"I just wondered," she said.

"No. I scarcely ever hear," said Noel. "He wrote, I suppose, to tell me of your good uncle's advent. He had probably heard from my sister that some of us were stationed here. Anyhow I lost no time in getting myself transferred for the pleasure of making his acquaintance. I was inclined to regret the move just at first. It's rather a hole, isn't it? But the moment I saw you—" Olga stiffened slightly, and he at once passed on with the agility of a practised skater on thin ice: "I say, what a ripping little sportsman your uncle is! He is actually talking of taking up polo again. Did you know?"

"Polo!" Olga stared at him. "Nick! How could he?"

"Heaven knows! I suppose he would hang on with his knees, and swipe when he got the chance. He'd need some deuced intelligent ponies though."

"He couldn't possibly do it!" Olga declared. "He mustn't try."

"Think you can prevent him?" asked Noel curiously.

"He won't if I beg him not to," she said.

"Oh, that's how you manage him, is it? Does he always come to heel that way?"

Olga's eyes flashed a loving glance down the table towards her hero. "There is no one in the world like Nick," she said softly.

"It's good to be Nick," remarked Noel, with his impudent smile. "It's quite evident that he can do no wrong."

She laughed and turned the subject. Nick was too near and dear to discuss with an outsider.

They began to talk of polo. A match had been arranged for Boxing Day. Noel was a keen player, and had plenty to say about it.

The Rajah was also a keen player, and after a little he disengaged himself from Colonel Bradlaw's endless reminiscences and joined in the conversation, which speedily became general.

A display of fireworks had been provided for the entertainment of the guests, and when the long State dinner was over they repaired to a marble balcony that overlooked some of the Palace gardens.

Will Musgrave came and joined Olga as she stepped out between the carved pillars. She greeted him with a smile of welcome. They were old friends. As a child she had known him before his marriage, though she had seen nothing of him since. There was something in the quiet strength of the man that appealed to her. He gave her confidence.

"Well, Olga," he said, "how do you like India?"

They stood together by the fretted marble balustrade, looking down upon the illuminated gardens that stretched away dim and mysterious into the night.

Olga did not directly answer the question. "I am not really acquainted with her yet," she said.

He uttered a short sigh. "She is a hard mistress. I don't advise you to get too intimate. She has a way of turning and rending her slaves, which is ungrateful, to say the least of it."

"But you are not sworn to her service for ever," said Olga.

He laughed with a touch of sadness. "Until she kicks me out. Like Kipling's Galley Slave, I'm chained to the oar. It's all very well so long as one remains in single blessedness, but it's mighty hard on the married ones. Take my advice, Olga; never marry an Indian man!"

"I'm never going to marry anyone," said Olga, with quiet decision.

"Really!" said Will Musgrave.

She turned her head towards him. "You sound surprised."

He smiled a little. "I beg your pardon. I was only surprised at the way in which you said it—as if you had been married for years, and knew the best and the worst."

There was a slight frown on Olga's face. She looked as if she were trying to remember something. "Oh, no, it wasn't like that," she said. "But somehow I don't feel as if I could ever like a man well enough to marry him. I don't want to fall in love."

"Too much trouble?" suggested Will.

She nodded, the frown still between her eyes. "It doesn't seem worth while," she said rather vaguely. "It's such a waste."

Will looked at her with very kindly eyes. "I see," he said gently.

She met the look and read his thought. Almost involuntarily she answered it. "I've never been in love myself," she told him simply. "But somehow I know just what it feels like. It's a wonderful feeling, isn't it? Like being caught up to the Gates of Paradise." She paused, and the puzzled frown deepened. "But one comes back again—nearly always," she said. "That's why I don't think it seems worth while."

"I see," Will said again. He was silent for a moment while a great green rocket rushed upwards with a hiss and burst in a shower of many-coloured stars. Then as they watched them fall he spoke very kindly and earnestly. "But it is worth while all the same—even though one may be turned back from Paradise. Remember—always remember—that it's something to have been there! Not everyone gets so far, and those who do are everlastingly the richer for it." He paused a moment, then added slowly, "Moreover, those who have been there once may find their way there again some day."

Another rocket soared high into the night and broke in a golden rain. From a few yards away came Nick's cracked laugh and careless speech.

"Here comes the *chota-bursat*, Daisy! It's high time you went to the Hills."

Daisy Musgrave's answer was instant and very heartfelt. "Oh, not yet, thank Heaven! We have three months more together, Will and I."

"You must make him leave his beastly old reservoir to the sub when the hot weather comes," said Nick, "and go for a honeymoon with you."

"If he only could!" said Daisy.

A sombre smile crossed Will's face as he turned it towards his wife. "I'm listening, Daisy," he said.

She came quickly to his side, and in the semi-darkness Olga saw her hand slip within his arm. "I'm feeling sentimental to-night," she said, in a voice that tried hard to be gay. "It's Nick's fault. Will, I want another honeymoon."

"My dear," he made answer in his deep, quiet voice, "you shall have one."

The rattle of squibs drowned all further speech, and under cover of it Olga made her way to Nick.

"They're awfully fond of each other, those two," she confided to him.

"Bless their hearts! Why shouldn't they?" said Nick tolerantly. "Are you getting tired, my chicken? Do you want to go home to roost?"

She was a little tired, but he was not to hurry on her account. "It's quite restful out here," she said.

He put his arm about her. "What did the infant Don Juan talk about all dinner-time?"

She laughed with a touch of diffidence. "He is quite a nice boy, Nick."

"What ho!" said Nick. "I thought he was making the most of his time."

She pinched his fingers admonishingly. "Don't be a pig, Nick! We—we talked of Max—part of the time."

"Oh, did we?" said Nick.

"Yes. Did you know he was thinking of leaving Dad?"

"I did," said Nick.

There was a moment's silence; then: "Dear, why didn't you tell me?" she asked, her voice very low.

"Dear, why should I?" said Nick.

She did not answer, though his flippant tone set her more or less at her ease.

"Any more questions to ask?" enquired Nick, after a pause.

With an effort she overcame her reticence. "He has actually gone then?"

"Bag and baggage," said Nick.

"Nick, why?"

"I understand he never was a fixture," said Nick.

"No. I know. But—but—I didn't think of his going so soon," she murmured.

"You don't seem pleased," said Nick.

"You see, I had got so used to him," she explained. "He was like a bit of home."

"I'm sure he would be vastly flattered to hear you say so," said Nick.

She laughed rather dubiously. "Has Dad got another assistant then?"

"I don't know. Very likely. You had better ask him when you write."

"And he has gone back to Sir Kersley Whitton?" she ventured.

"My information does not extend so far as that," said Nick.

She turned her attention to the blaze of coloured fire below them, and was silent for a space.

Suddenly and quite involuntarily she sighed. "Nick!"

"Yours to command!" said Nick.

She turned towards him resolutely. "Be serious just a moment! I want to know something. He didn't leave Dad for any special reason, did he?"

"I've no doubt he did," said Nick. "He has a reason for most of his actions. But he didn't confide it to me."

She gave another sharp sigh, and said no more.

Colonel Bradlaw came up and joined them, and after a little the Rajah also. He stationed himself beside Olga, and began to talk in his smooth way of all the wonders in the district she had yet to see.

She wished he would not take the trouble to be gracious to her, but he was always gracious to European ladies and there was no escape. The British polish over the Oriental suavity seemed to her a decidedly incongruous mixture. She infinitely preferred the purely Oriental.

"My *shikari* has told me of a man-eater at Khantali," he said presently. "You have not seen a tiger-hunt yet? I must arrange an expedition, and you and Captain Ratcliffe will join?"

Olga explained that she had never done any shooting.

"But you will like to look on," he said.

She hesitated. "I am afraid," she said, after a moment, "I don't like seeing things killed."

"No?" said the Rajah politely.

She wondered if the dusky eyes veiled contempt, and felt a little uncomfortable in consequence of the wonder.

"You have never killed—anything?" he asked, in a tone of courteous interest.

"Nothing bigger than a beetle," said Olga.

"Really!" said the Rajah.

This time she was sure he was feeling bored, and she began to wish that Noel would reappear and lighten the atmosphere.

As if in answer to the wish, there came the sudden tinkle of a stringed instrument in one of the marble recesses behind them, and almost immediately a man's voice, very soft and musical, began to sing:

> "O, wert thou in the cauld blast,
> On yonder lea, on yonder lea,
> My plaidie to the angry airt,
> I'd shelter thee, I'd shelter thee.
> Or did misfortune's bitter storms
> Around thee blaw, around thee blaw,
> Thy bield should be my bosom,
> To share it a', to share it a'."

The voice ceased; the banjo thrummed on. Olga's hands were fast gripped upon the marble lattice-work. She stood tense, with white face upraised.

The Rajah was wholly forgotten by her, and he stepped silently away to join another of his guests. The new English girl presented an enigma to him, but it was one in which he did not take much interest. All her fairness notwithstanding, she was not even pretty, according to his standard, and he had seen a good many pretty women.

Again through the dimness the clear voice came. It held a hint—a very carefully restrained hint—of passion.

> "Or were I in the wildest waste,
> Sae black and bare, sae black and bare,
> The desert were a paradise
> If thou wert there, if thou wert there.
> Or were I monarch o' the globe,
> Wi' thee to reign, wi' thee to reign,
> The brightest jewel in my crown
> Wad be my queen, wad be my queen."

The song was ended; the banjo throbbed itself into silence. Olga's hands went up to her face. She wanted to keep the silence, to hold it fast, while she chased down that elusive phantom that dodged her memory.

Ah! A voice beside her, Nick's arm through hers! She raised her face. The phantom had fled.

"After that serenade, I move that we take our departure," said Nick. "The youngster has a decent voice, so far as my poor judgment goes. Are you ready?"

Yes, she was ready. She longed to be gone, to get away from the careless, chattering crowd, to work out her problem in solitude and silence.

With scarcely a word she went with him, and they made their farewells together.

At the last moment Noel, his eyes very bright and coaxingly friendly, caught her hand and boldly held it.

"Did you catch it?" he asked.

She looked at him uncomprehendingly. "Catch what?"

He laughed. The pressure of his fingers was intimately close. "That glimpse I promised you," he said.

"Ah!" Understanding dawned in Olga's eyes, and in the same instant she removed her hand. "No, I'm afraid I didn't. I was thinking of something else. Good-bye!"

"Oh, I say!" protested Noel, actually crest-fallen for once.

Nick swallowed a chuckle, and clapped him on the shoulder. "Good-night, minstrel boy! Mind you bring the harp along to my Christmas picnic! We are not all so unappreciative as Olga."

Noel looked for a second as if he were on the verge of losing his temper, but the next he changed his mind and laughed.

"You bet I will, old chap!" he said, and wrung Nick's hand with cordiality.

Nick's chuckle became audible as they drove away. "He can't accuse you of encouraging him anyhow, Olga *mia*," he remarked. "If you keep it up at this pace, you'll soon choke him off."

Olga's answer was to draw very close to him, and to utter a great sigh.

"Wherefore?" whispered Nick.

She was silent for a moment, then: "I sometimes wish you were the only man in the world, Nick," she said, with quivering emphasis.

"Gracious heaven!" said Nick. "Don't make me giddy!"

She laughed a little, but there was a sound of tears behind. "Men are so silly," she said.

"Abject fools!" said Nick. "There's never more than one worth crying about."

"What do you mean, Nick?"

"Nothing—nothing!" said Nick. "I was just demonstrating my foolishness, that's all."

Whereat she laughed again in a somewhat doubtful key, and asked no more.

CHAPTER V
THE EVERLASTING CHAIN

It was a very thoughtful face that met Nick at the breakfast table on the following morning. But Nick's greeting was as airy as usual. He made no comments and asked no questions.

The day was Sunday, a perfect day of Indian winter, cloudless and serene. The tamarisks in the compound waved their pink spikes to the sun, and in the palm-trees behind them bright-eyed squirrels dodged and flirted. A line of cypresses bounded the garden, and the sky against which they stood was an ardent blue.

"What is the programme for to-day?" said Nick, when the meal was nearly over.

Olga leaned her chin on her hand, and looked across at him. "Shall you go to church, Nick?"

The cantonments boasted a small church and a visiting chaplain who held one service in it every Sunday.

Nick considered the matter in all its bearings while he stirred his coffee.

"No," he said finally; "I think I shall stay at home with you this morning."

"How do you know I am not going?" said Olga.

Nick grinned. "I'm awfully good at guessing, Olga *mia*."

She smiled rather wanly. "Well, I'm not going, as a matter of fact. I had a stupid sort of night."

Nick nodded. "I shan't take you out to dinner again for a long time."

"It wasn't that," she said. "At least, I don't think so. It was that song. Why did Noel sing it?"

"For reasons best known to himself," said Nick, taking out his cigarette-case.

She rose and went round to his side to strike a match for him, but reaching him she suddenly knelt and clasped her arms about his neck.

"Nick," she whispered, "I'm frightened."

His arm went round her instantly. "What is it, my chicken?"

She held him closely for a while in silence; then, her face hidden, she told him of the trouble at her heart.

"That song has been haunting me all night long. I feel as if—as if—someone—were calling me, and I can't quite hear or understand. Nick, where—where is Violet?"

It had come at last. Once before she had confronted him with that question, and he had turned it aside. But to-day, he knew that he must face and answer it.

He laid his cheek against her hair. "Olga darling, I think you know, but I'll tell you all the same. She has—gone on."

Very gently he spoke the words, and after them there fell a silence broken only by the scolding of a couple of parroquets in a mimosa-tree near the verandah.

Nick did not stir. His lips twitched a little above the fair head, and his yellow face showed many lines; but there was no tension in his attitude. His pose was alert rather than anxious.

305

Olga lifted her face at last. She was very white, but fully as composed as he.

"That," she said slowly, "was the thing I couldn't remember."

He nodded. "It was."

Her hands clasped the front of his coat with nervous force. She looked him straight in the face.

As of old, the flickering eyes evaded her. They met and passed her over a dozen times, but imparted nothing.

"Nick," she said, "will you please tell me how it happened? I am strong enough to bear it now, and indeed—indeed, I must know."

"I have been waiting to tell you," Nick said. "Put on a hat, and we will go in the garden."

She rose at once. Somehow his brief words reassured her. She felt no agitation, was scarcely aware of shock. In his presence even the shadow of Death became devoid of all superstitious fears. In some fashion he made fear seem absurd.

Nick waited for her on the verandah with his face turned up to the sky. He scarcely looked like a man bracing himself for a stiff ordeal, but it was not his way to stoop under his burdens. He had learned to tread jauntily while he carried a heart like lead.

When Olga joined him, he put his hand through her arm and led her forth. The path wound along between the tangle of shrubs and lower growth till it reached the cypresses, and here was a shady stretch where they could pace to and fro in complete privacy.

Arrived here, Nick spoke. "It wasn't altogether news to you, was it?"

She passed her hand across her eyes in the old, puzzled way. "I didn't remember," she said, "and yet I wasn't altogether surprised. I think somehow at the back of my mind—I suspected."

"You remember now," said Nick.

She looked at him with troubled eyes. "No, I don't, dear. That's just it. I—I can't remember. It—frightens me." She clasped his hand with fingers that trembled.

"No need to be frightened," said Nick. "You were ill, you know; first the heat and then the shock. After brainfever, people very often do forget."

"Ah, yes," she said, with a piteous kind of eagerness. "But it is coming back now. I only want you to help a little." She stood suddenly still. "Nick, you are not afraid of Death, I know. Wasn't it you who called it the opening of a Door?"

"It is—just that," said Nick.

"But the body," she said, "the body dies."

"The body," he said, "is like a suit of clothes that you lay aside till the time comes for it to be renovated and made wearable again."

"Ah! She couldn't die, could she, Nick?" Olga's eyes implored him. "Not she herself!" she urged. "She was so full of life. I can't realize it. I can't—I can't! Tell me how it happened! Surely I never saw her dead! Whatever came after, I never could have forgotten that!"

"Tell me how much you do remember, kiddie," Nick said gently. "And I will fill in the gaps."

Her forehead contracted in a painful frown. "It's so difficult," she said, "so disjointed—like a dreadful dream. I know she was horribly afraid of Max. And then there was Major Hunt-Goring. I can't believe she ever liked him. It was only because he—flattered her, and gave her those dreadful cigarettes."

"Probably," said Nick.

"That morning when he invited us to go on his yacht is the last thing I can remember clearly," she said. "I didn't want to go, but—she—insisted. After that, my mind is just a jumble of impressions that don't fit into each other. I seem to remember being on the yacht, and Major Hunt-Goring and Violet laughing together. And then he came and told me an awful thing about her mother. He wanted me to say I would marry him, and I wouldn't because I hated him so. And after that he was so furious, he went and told her too."

Olga stopped with horror in her eyes. The effort to remember was plainly torturing her, yet Nick made no effort to help her.

"And after that?" he said.

"Oh, after that, there seems to come a blank. I remember her face, and how I held her in my arms and tried to comfort her. And then—oh, it's just like a dreadful dream!—I was running in the sun, running, running, running, never seeming to get anywhere. The next thing I really remember is being at the Priory and having lunch in that awful storm, and Max coming—do you remember?—do you remember? And how I kept him away from her? Poor child, he terrified her so." Olga was shuddering now from head to foot. Her eyes were wide and staring, as though fixed upon some fearful vision.

Nick did not attempt to interrupt her. He waited, alert and silent, for the vision to come to an end.

The end was not far off. She went on speaking rapidly, as if more to herself than to him. She seemed indeed to have forgotten him for the moment.

"What a frightful storm it was! That flash of lightning—how it shone through the east window—and the floor was all red as if—as if—" She broke off; her hand clenched unconsciously upon Nick's. "Did you see her?" she whispered. "Or was it only a nightmare? She—was trying—to—to—kill Max—in the dark!"

"She was not herself," said Nick. His voice was low and soothing; he spoke as if he feared to awake her.

"No—no! She was mad—like her mother. Oh, Nick, how beautiful she was!"

Suddenly the tension passed. Olga covered her face and began to cry.

His arm tightened about her; he drew her on up the shady walk. "And that is all you remember, kiddie?" he said.

She slipped her arm round his neck as they walked. "No, I remember two things more." She forced back her tears to tell him. "I remember Max's arm all soaked with blood. It stained my dress too. And I remember his saying that—that it was a hopeless case, and that she—Violet—was as good as dead. After that—after that——"

Nick waited. "After that?" he said.

She turned to him, her face anguished, piteous, appealing. "I can't get any further than that, Nick. It's just a dreadful darkness that makes me afraid. I think I begged him not to go to her. But I know he went, because—when he came down again"—her voice faltered; bewilderment showed through her distress—"when he came down again—" she repeated the words like a child conning a lesson, then stopped, staring widely. "Ah, I don't remember," she cried hopelessly. "I don't remember—except that I think—when he came down again—it was all over. And he seemed to be angry with me. Why was he angry with me, Nick? Why? Why?"

She began to tremble violently; but Nick's arm, strong and steadfast, drew her on.

"He wasn't angry," said Nick. "Up to that point you are all right, but there your imagination runs away with you. It's not surprising. He looks grim enough when he's on the job. But that's his way. We know too much of him, you and I, to take him over seriously."

"Then he really wasn't angry?" Olga said, relief struggling with doubt in her voice.

Nick began to smile. "He really wasn't," he said.

She gave a sharp sigh. "I've been so afraid sometimes. But why—why did he look so strange?"

"Doctors don't like being beaten," said Nick.

"But then, he knew it was hopeless—he said so. Was he angry because of his arm? Was he angry with her, do you think? Oh, Nick, my brain—my brain! It does whirl so! It won't let me think quietly."

"There is no need to make it think any more," said Nick, with quick decision. "Give it a rest! You've got hold of the main points, and that's enough for anyone. You mustn't fret either, dear. Remember, we are all going the same way. God knows why we take these things so hard. I suppose it's our silly little minds that won't let us look ahead."

"If we only could look ahead!" murmured Olga. "If we could only know!"

Nick's eyes sent a single flashing glance over the cypresses. His arm clasped her closely and very tenderly. "That's just where the trick of believing comes in," he said. "I don't see how those who honestly believe in the love of God can help believing that all is well with those who have gone on. To my mind it follows as the inevitable sequence. Those who doubt it are putting a limit to the Illimitable and placing a lower estimate on the love of God than they place upon their own. But we are all such wretched little pigmies—even the biggest of us. We are apt to forget that, don't you think? Horribly apt to try and measure the Infinite with a foot-rule. And see what comes of it! Only a deeper darkness and a narrowing of our own miserable limitations. We never get any further that way, Olga *mia*. Speculating and dogmatizing don't help us. We are up against the Unknown like a wall. But the love of God shines on both sides of it; and till the Door opens to us also, that's as much as we shall know."

He paused. Olga was listening with rapt attention. Her tears were gone, but the clasp of her hand was feverishly tense. Her breath came quickly.

"Go on, Nick!" she whispered. "Tell me more of the things you believe!"

He smiled whimsically. "My dear, I'm afraid I'm not over-orthodox. You see, I've knocked about a bit and seen something of other men's beliefs. The love of God is the backbone of my religion, and all that doesn't go with that, I discarded long ago. If Christianity doesn't mean that, it doesn't mean anything. I've no use for the people who think that none but their own select little circle will go to heaven. Such Gargantuan smugness takes one's breath away. It is almost too colossal to be funny. One wonders where on earth they get it from. I suppose it's a survival of the Dark Ages, but even then surely people had brains of some description."

"But death, Nick!" she said. "Death is such a baffling kind of thing."

"Yes, I know. You can't grasp it or fathom it. You can only project your love into it and be quite sure that it finds a hold on the other side. Why, my dear girl, that's what love is for. It's the connecting link that God Himself is bound to recognize because it is of His own forging. Don't you see—don't you know it is Divine? That is why our love can hold so strongly—even through Death. Just because it is part of His plan—a link in the everlasting Chain that draws the whole world up to Paradise at last. It's so divinely simple. One wonders how anyone can miss the meaning of it."

Olga's rapt face relaxed. She smiled at him—a very loving, comprehending smile. "Yes, I see it when you put it like that, Nick, of course. It is only just at first Death seems so staggering—such a plunge into the dark."

"But there is nothing in the dark to frighten us," Nick said. "If some of us died and some didn't, it would be terrible, I grant. But we are all going sooner or later. No one is left behind for long. To my mind there's a vast deal of comfort in that. It doesn't leave much time for grousing when we simply can't help moving on."

She squeezed his hand. "I wonder where I'd be without you, Nick."

Nick's grin flashed magically across his face. "I'm only a man, kiddie," he observed, "and I seem to have been gassing somewhat immoderately. However, them's my sentiments, and you can take 'em or leave 'em according to fancy."

Thereafter for a space they talked of Violet, touching no tragic note, recalling her as an absent friend. Olga dwelt fondly upon the thought of her, scarcely realizing her loss. The new life she had entered had done much to soften the blow when it should fall. Here in a strange land she did not feel her friend's death as she would inevitably have felt it at Weir. Circumstances combined with Nick's sheltering presence to lift the weight which otherwise must have pressed heavily upon her. Moreover, the longer she contemplated the matter, the more completely did she realize that it had not come to her with the force of a sudden calamity. Deep within her she had carried a nameless dread that had hung upon her like an iron fetter. She had longed—yet trembled—to know the truth. Now that burden seemed lifted from her, and she was conscious of relief. Before, she had feared she knew not what; but now she feared no longer. She was weary beyond measure, too weary for grief or wonder, though she did ask Nick, faintly smiling, why they had kept the truth from her for so long.

"I should have found it easier if I had known," she said.

But Nick shook his head with the wisdom of an old man. "You weren't strong enough to know," he said.

She did not contest the point, reflecting that Nick, with all his shrewdness, was but a man, as he himself admitted.

She asked him presently, somewhat haltingly, if he would give her the details of her friend's death. "Max was there, I know. But he never tells one anything. It was one of the reasons why I never got on with him."

A hint of the old resentment was in her tone, and Nick smiled at it. "Poor old Max! You always were down on him, weren't you? But there is really nothing to tell, dear. She just went to sleep, and her heart stopped. They said it was not altogether surprising, considering her state of health."

"Who said?" questioned Olga.

"Sir Kersley Whitton and Max. Max sent for him, you know."

"Oh, did he? Yes, I remember now. I saw him just for a moment." Again her brow contracted. "Oh, I wish I could remember everything clearly, Nick!" she said.

"Never mind, my chicken! Don't try too hard!" Cheery and reassuring came Nick's response. "Don't you think you have thought enough for one day? Shall we tell Kasur to order the horses, and go for a canter?"

She turned beside him. "Yes, I shall like that. But—why did you say I was always hard on Max?"

"The result of observations made," he answered lightly.

She smiled with a hint of wistfulness, and said no more. The child Olga would have argued the point. The woman Olga held her peace.

Undoubtedly Nick had stepped off his pedestal that day. She loved him none the less for it, but she wondered a little.

And Nick, philosopher and wily tactician, grinned at his fallen laurels and let them lie. He had that day accomplished the most delicate task to which he had ever set his hand. Behind the mask of masculine clumsiness he had subtly worked his levers and achieved his end. And he was well satisfied with the result.

Let her pity his limitations after a woman's immemorial fashion! How should she recognize the wisdom of the serpent which they veiled?

CHAPTER VI
CHRISTMAS MORNING

It was the strangest Christmas Day Olga had ever known, but she certainly had no time to be homesick.

She was roused by Nick scratching seductively at her window from the verandah, and, admitting him, she found him waiting to present a jeweller's box which contained a string of moonstones exquisitely set in silver. It was one of the most beautiful things she had ever seen, and she was delighted with it.

Through the medium of her *ayah* she had purchased a carved sandal-wood box from the bazaar for Nick, which she now presented, modestly hoping he didn't hate the smell.

"I adore it," declared Nick, sniffing it loudly. "It's just the East to me. I shall steep my ties in it. Many thanks, Olga *mia!* Thine ancient uncle values the gift for the sake of the giver." He kissed her, and sat down on the edge of the bed, dangling his feet in a pair of violently coloured Oriental slippers. "I see His Excellency has sent us a thing like a clothes-basket full of fruit. Very kind of him, but a trifle overwhelming. There is no mail in yet, but some local parcels have arrived which the *khit* is sorting with the face of a judge. Ah, here comes your little lot!" as the *ayah* softly opened the door. "Shall I remove myself?"

"Of course not, Nick! Smoke a cigarette while I open them. They can't be anything very much."

The *ayah,* smiling broadly, laid two parcels on the table by Olga's bedside. A third one, which was very small, she dropped with a mysterious gesture into her hand.

"What can this be?" questioned Olga. "Sambaji, what is it?"

But Sambaji shook her head. "Miss *sahib,* how should I know?"

Olga suddenly turned crimson. She held out the tiny packet to Nick.

"You open it!" she said. "I'm sure it's something I don't want."

Nick made no movement to take it! "Sorry, dear. Two hands are better than one," he said.

Sambaji withdrew, still smiling.

Olga looked at the thing in the palm of her hand. She was trembling a little. "I don't want it, Nick," she said almost piteously.

Nick was heartless enough to laugh.

"Don't!" she pleaded, real distress in her tone. "Can't I send it back unopened?"

"Whom do you propose to send it to?" asked Nick, still chuckling.

She smiled faintly in spite of herself. "It's pretty certain where it comes from, isn't it?"

"Is it?" said Nick.

"Well, isn't it?" she persisted, still dubiously eyeing the unwelcome gift.

"I really can't say. But I don't see why you should be afraid of it in any case. To judge by the size of it, I shouldn't say it could be a very dangerous explosive."

She smiled again with obvious reluctance, and began to study the address on the packet. It was written in a very minute hand.

There followed a pause; then with abrupt resolution Olga's fingers began to work at the outer covering.

Nick watched her, amusement on his yellow face. "I'm not quite sure that two hands are better than one when they shake like that," he observed. "Ah, here comes the dedication!" as a tiny strip of paper fluttered from Olga's fingers. "It reminds me—vividly—of my own courtship. Quite sure you don't want me to go?"

"Nick!" she protested, with burning cheeks. "It's very horrid of you to laugh. Do you know what it is?"

"I can almost guess," he said, as a small leather case emerged from the paper. "I've seen 'em before."

Olga opened the case. It was lined with white velvet, and in the centre of it there flashed and glittered a diamond and emerald ring.

"Hullo!" said Nick.

Olga looked up at him with gleaming eyes. "Nick! How—how dare he!"

"It is pretty daring certainly," agreed Nick. "It's a valuable trifle—that."

Olga closed the case with a resolute snap. "I shall send it back at once."

"Hadn't you better read the dedication?" suggested Nick.

She took up the strip of paper, stretched it out, frowned at it. The writing on this also was minute. After a moment she read it out. "'*Dum spiro spero. N.W.*' Just as I thought!"

"Do you know what it means?" asked Nick.

She shook her head vigorously. "And I don't want to know."

"Oh, that's a pity," he said. "Pray let me enlighten your ignorance. It means, '*While I breathe I hope*'—a very proper sentiment which does the young man infinite credit."

"I can't imagine how you can laugh," said Olga fierily, tearing the strip to fragments. "Can't you see I'm really angry?"

"My dear child, that's why!" chuckled Nick. "It's the best thing I've seen for a long time. The young man has all my gratitude. He has done more for my little pal than I with the best intentions could ever do myself."

She stretched out her hand to him then with a little smile. "Nick, you silly old boy! Well, tell me what to do!"

"Quite sure you don't like him?" questioned Nick.

"No. I do like him." Olga's smile deepened. "But I think it was outrageous of him to send me this thing. And I shall have to tell him so."

"I should," said Nick. "You will have ample opportunities when we get to Khantali. Take the thing with you and give it back to him there. Afterwards, if it seems necessary, I'll tell him to moderate the pace if you like. But the boy's a gentleman. I don't think it will be necessary." He smiled at her quizzically. "I knew it was coming, Olga *mia*. I can smell a love affair fifty miles away. But I shouldn't be persuaded to have him if I were you. He's altogether too young for matrimony by about ten years. Let him wait for Peggy Musgrave to grow up. He will be of a marriageable age by that time."

Olga laughed, and turned to her other parcels. Nick's worldly wisdom struck her as being a little funny when she knew herself to be so infinitely wiser than he.

She found the two remaining packets to contain presents from the Musgraves, some beautiful Indian embroidery from Daisy and a pair of little Hindu gods in carved ivory from Will. Nick stopped to admire these, and then betook himself to his own room to dress.

Left alone, Olga took up the ring-case once more, and slowly opened it. The stones glinted in the morning light, the diamonds white and intense, the emeralds piercingly green. She wondered why he had chosen emeralds; they seemed to her to belong to something in which he had no part. At the back of her mind there hovered a vague, elusive something like an insect on the wing. Suddenly it flashed into her full consciousness, and her eyes widened and grew dazed. She saw not the shimmering iridescence of the stones, but a darting green dragon-fly which for one fleeting instant poised before her vision and the next was gone. A sharp shudder assailed her. She closed the case....

When she met Nick again there was no trace of agitation about her. She seated herself behind the coffee-pot, and told him she had decided to go to church.

"I congratulate you," said Nick. "So have I."

They were half-way through breakfast when there came the ring of spurred heels on the verandah.

"Hullo!" said Nick. "Enter amorous swain!"

The colour leaped to Olga's face. She said nothing, and she certainly did not smile a welcome when Noel's brown face peered merrily in upon them.

"Happy Christmas to you, good people! May I come and break my fast, with you? I've been all round the town and this is the last port of call."

"Come in by all means!" said Nick. "Have you brought your harp?"

Noel clapped a free and easy hand upon his shoulder. "No, I haven't. I can't harp on a full heart alone. I've tied the Tempest to your garden palings. I hope he won't carry 'em away, for I can't pay any damages, being broke in every sense of the word! Good-morning, Olga! I'm calling everyone by their Christian names this morning in honour of the day. It's my birthday, by the way; hence my romantic appellation."

He dropped into a bamboo-chair and stretched out his arms with a smile of great benignity.

"I've even been to see Badgers," he said. "He was in his bath and didn't want to admit me. However, I gained my end, I generally do," said Noel complacently, with one eye cocked at Olga's rigidly unresponsive face.

"Who is Badgers?" asked Nick.

"Why, the C.O. of course. I didn't find him in at all a Christmas spirit; but it was beginning to sprout before I left. I say, I hope you are providing lots of beef for our consumption, Nick. It's the first Christmas I've spent out of England, and I don't want to be homesick. Any form of indigestion rather than that!" He turned suddenly upon Olga. "Why does the lady of the ceremonies preserve so uncompromising an attitude? I feel chilled to the marrow."

She controlled her blush before it could overwhelm her, and very sedately she made answer. "I am not feeling very pleased with you; that's why."

"Great heaven!" said Noel. "What on earth have I done?"

"You might have the decency to let me finish my breakfast in peace," protested Nick. "My appetite can't thrive in a stormy atmosphere."

Noel turned to him, smiling persuasively. "Can't you take your breakfast into the garden, old chap? I want to thresh this matter out at once. I'm sure you have your niece's permission to retire."

But at that, Olga rose from the table. "Suppose we go into the garden, Mr. Wyndham," she said.

Noel sprang up with a jingle of spurs. "By all means!"

"Get a hat, Olga!" said Nick.

She threw him a fleeting smile and departed.

Noel propped himself against the window-frame and waited. He did not appear greatly disconcerted by the turn of events. Without an effort he conversed with Nick on the chances of the forthcoming polo-match.

When Olga came along the verandah a minute later he stepped out and joined her with a smile.

They passed side by side down the winding path that led to the cypress walk. Olga's face was pale. She looked very full of resolution.

"I am quite sure you know what I am going to say," she said very quietly at length.

"You haven't wished me a happy Christmas yet," remarked Noel, still smiling his audacious smile. "Can it be that?"

Olga's face remained grave. "No," she said. "I don't feel friendly enough for that."

"I say, what have I done?" said Noel.

She stopped and faced him, and he suddenly saw that she was very nervous. She held out to him a little packet wrapped in tissue-paper.

"Mr. Wyndham," she said, speaking rapidly to cover her agitation, "you couldn't seriously expect me to accept this, whatever your motive for sending it. Please take it back, and let me forget all about it as quickly as possible!"

Noel's hand clasped hers instantly, packet and all. "My dear girl," he said softly, "don't be upset,—but you're making a mistake."

She looked up, meeting the Irish eyes with a tremor of reluctance. In spite of herself, she spoke almost with entreaty. For there was something about him that stirred her very deeply. "Please don't make things hard!" she said. "You know you have no right. I never gave you the smallest reason to imagine I would take such a gift from you."

Noel was still smiling; but there was nothing impudent about his smile. Rather he looked as if he wished to reassure her. "How did you know where it came from?" he said.

The colour she had been so studiously restraining rushed in a wave over her face. "Of course—of course I knew! Besides, there was a line with it."

"May I see the line?" said Noel.

She stared at him, her agitation increasing. What right had he to be so cool and unabashed?

"I tore it up," she said.

"What for?" said Noel.

Her eyes gleamed momentarily. "I was angry."

"Angry with me?" he questioned.

"Yes."

"Does it make you angry to know that a man cares for you?" he said.

Her eyes fell before the sudden fire that kindled in his with the words. "Don't!" she said rather breathlessly. "Please don't!"

"You ought to be sorry for me," he whispered, "not angry."

She turned her face aside. "Of course—that—would not make me angry. Only—only—you had no right to—to send me—a present—a valuable present."

"And if I didn't?" said Noel.

She looked at him in sheer astonishment. He still held her hand with the packet clasped in it.

"What if I am not the delinquent after all?" he said.

"What do you mean?" Her eyes met his again, wide and incredulous.

"What if I tell you that this packet—whatever it contains—did not come from me?"

He asked the question with a faint smile that set some chord of memory vibrating strangely in her soul. But she could not stop to wrestle with memory then. His words demanded her instant attention.

"Not come from you!" she repeated, as one dazed. "But it did! Surely it did!"

"Most surely it didn't!" said Noel.

She freed her hand and opened it, gazing at the subject of their discussion almost with fear. "Mr. Wyndham!"

"Call me Noel!" he said. "There's nothing in that. Everybody does it. And don't be upset on my account! It was a perfectly natural mistake. I'm deeply in love with you. But—all the same—this present did not come from me."

"It had your initials," she said, still only half believing.

"Then it was probably a hoax," said Noel.

"Oh, no! That's not possible. It—it—you see, it's valuable." Olga's voice was almost piteous.

"I say, don't mind!" he said. "It's just some other fellow's impudence. I'll kick him for you if I get the chance. You're quite sure about my initials?"

"Quite," she said.

"And what else was there?"

She frowned, "Only a Latin motto."

"Tell me!" he said persuasively.

She continued to frown. "It was '*Dum spiro spero*.'"

"Great Scott!" he said. "Do you think I should have been as presumptuous as that? I should have just said, '*With Noel's love*,' and you wouldn't have had the heart to fling it back again."

She smiled, not very willingly. "I can't understand it at all."

"I can," he said boldly. "I've known there was another fellow, ever since the first night I met you. But I've been hoping against hope that he didn't count. Does he count then?"

Olga turned sharply from him. She was suddenly trembling. "No!" she whispered.

He drew a step nearer to her. "Olga—forgive me—is that the truth?"

She controlled herself and turned back to him. "There is no one in India who would have sent me this," she said. "I can't account for it—in any way. Please forgive me for accusing you of what you haven't done. And—and—"

She stopped short, for he had caught her hands in an eager, boyish clasp. "Olga, don't—there's a dear!" he begged with headlong ardour. "I don't love you any the less because I didn't do it. I believe myself it's a beastly hoax, and I'm just as furious as you are. But, I say, can't we found a partnership on it? Is it asking too much? Pull me up if it is! I don't want to be premature. Only I won't have you sick or sorry about it, anyhow so far as I am concerned. You were quite right in thinking that I loved you. I do, dear, I do!"

"But you mustn't!" she said. She left her hands in his, but the face she raised was tired and sad and unresponsive. "I feel a dreadful pig, Noel," she said, speaking as if it were an effort. "I almost made you say it, didn't I? And it's just the one thing I mustn't let you say. You're so nice, so kind, such a jolly friend. But you're not—not—not—"

"Not eligible as a husband," suggested Noel.

"Don't use that horrid adjective!" she protested. "You make me feel worse and worse."

He laughed, his sudden, boyish laugh. "No, but there's nothing to feel bad about, really. And you didn't make me say it. I said it because I wanted to. Also, you're not bound to take me seriously. I'm not always in earnest—as you may have discovered. Look here, you've warned me off. Can't we talk about something else now?"

"If you're sure you don't mind," she said, smiling rather wistfully.

He cocked his eyebrows humorously. "Of course I mind. I mind enormously. But that's of no consequence. By the way, I suppose your funny little uncle isn't given to playing practical jokes?"

"Nick? Why no!" Olga surveyed him in astonishment. "Nick is the soul of wisdom," she said.

"Is he though?" Noel looked amused. "I must get him to give me a few hints," he observed. "I wonder if he has left any breakfast. You know, I haven't had any yet."

"Oh, let us go back!" said Olga turning. "And please do forget all about this tiresome misunderstanding! Promise you will!"

He waved his hand. "The subject is closed and will never be reopened by me without your permission. At the same time, let me confess that I have presumed so far as to procure a small Christmas offering for your acceptance. You won't refuse it, will you?"

Olga looked up dubiously; but the handsome young face that looked back would only laugh.

"What is it?" she said at length.

Gaily he made answer. "It's a parrot—quite a youngster. I picked him up in the bazaar. He isn't properly fledged yet, but he promises well. I'm keeping him for a bit to educate him. But if you won't have him, I shall wring his neck."

"I'm sure you wouldn't!" she exclaimed.

He continued to laugh, though her face expressed horror. "And you will be morally responsible; think of that! It's tantamount to being guilty of murder. Horrible idea, isn't it? You—who never in your life killed so much as a moth! Hullo! What's up?"

For Olga had made a sudden, very curious gesture, almost as if she winced from a threatened blow. Her face was white and strained; she pressed her hands very tightly over her heart.

"What's up?" he repeated, in surprise.

She gazed at him with the eyes of one coming out of a stupor. "I don't know," she said. "I had a queer feeling as if—as if—" She paused, seeming to wrestle with some inner, elusive vision. "There! It's gone!" she said, after a moment, disappointment and relief curiously mingled in her voice. "What were we talking about? Oh, yes, the parrot! It's very kind of you. I shall like to have it."

"I've christened it Noel," he remarked, with some complacence. "It's a Christmas present, you see."

"I see," said Olga, beginning to smile. "And you are teaching it to talk?"

"I'm only going to teach it one sentence," he said.

"Oh, what is it?"

He gave her a sidelong glance. "I don't think I'd better tell you."

"But why not?"

"It'll make you cross."

Olga laughed. Somehow she could not help feeling indulgent. Moreover, the interview was nearly at an end, for they were nearing the bungalow, and Nick's white figure was visible on the verandah.

"In that case," she said, "you had better not educate it any further."

"Oh, it won't make you cross on the bird's lips," Noel assured her.

"Has it got lips?" she asked. "What a curious specimen it must be!"

"I say, don't laugh!" he besought her, with dancing eyes. "It's not a joke, I assure you. I'll tell you what I'm teaching it to say if you like. But I shall have to whisper it. Do you mind?"

Again she found him hard to resist, albeit she did not want to yield. "Well?" she said.

They were close to the bungalow now. Noel came very near. "Of course you can wring the little brute's neck if it displeases you," he said, "but it's a corky youngster and I don't much think you will. He's learning to say, 'I love you, Olga.'"

Olga looked up on the verge of protest, but before she could utter it Nick's gay, cracked voice hailed them from above; and Noel, briskly answering, deprived her of the opportunity.

CHAPTER VII
THE WILDERNESS OF NASTY POSSIBILITIES

When Nick heard of the mistake that had been made, he raised his eyebrows till he could raise them no further and then laughed, laughed immoderately till Olga was secretly a little exasperated.

They did not have much time for discussing the matter, and for some reason Nick did not seem anxious to do so. If he had his own private opinion, he did not impart it to Olga, and, since he seemed inclined to treat the whole affair with levity, she did not press him for it. For she herself was regarding matters very seriously.

Noel's candid adoration was beginning to assume somewhat alarming proportions, and she had a feeling that it was undermining her resolution. She was not exactly afraid, but she did not feel secure. He appealed, in some fashion wholly inexplicable, to her inner soul. His very daring attracted her. By sheer audacity he weakened her powers of resistance. And yet she knew that he would not press her too hard. With all his impetuosity, he was so quick to understand her wishes, so swift to respond to the curb. No, he would not capture her against her will. But therein she found no comfort. For he was drawing her by a subtler method than that. His boyish homage, his winning ardour, these were weapons that were infinitely harder to resist. There was scarcely a woman in Noel Wyndham's acquaintance who had not at one time or another felt the force of his fascination. He exerted it instinctively, often almost unconsciously, and now that he had deliberately set himself to attract he wielded his power with marvellous effect. His warmth, his gaiety, his persistence, all combined to make of him a very gallant knight; and Olga was beginning to find that it hurt her to resist the magnetism by which he held her. And yet—and yet—deep in the soul of her she knew how little she had to give. That haunting memory which yet invariably eluded her made her vaguely conscious that far down in the most secret corner of her heart was a locked door which would never open to him. She herself scarcely knew what lay behind it, but none the less was it sacred. Not even to Nick—trusted counsellor and confidant—would that door ever open; perhaps to none....

The Christmas service roused her somewhat from the contemplation of her perplexities, and after it there were friends to greet—Colonel Bradlaw and his merry little wife, Will Musgrave, Daisy, and the radiant Peggy.

They made a cheery crowd as they assembled in the hot sunshine before Nick's bungalow a little later and discussed their final arrangements for the picnic at Khantali.

The Bradlaws had a waggonette, and Daisy and Peggy were to drive with them. Noel had a dog-cart in which he boldly announced that Olga must accompany him.

Olga wanted to ride, but Nick declared that this would overtire her, adding with a grin that he would occupy the back seat in the dog-cart if Noel had no objection.

Noel grinned also, and expressed his delight; but at the last moment a couple of his brother-subalterns came up and took forcible possession of Nick, protesting that such a celebrity could not be permitted to take a back seat and insisting that he should travel in the place of honour in their dog-cart. Nick, finding himself outnumbered, submitted with no visible discomfiture, and the procession, being completed by about a dozen equestrians, finally started with much laughter and *badinage* upon the long, rough journey through the jungle to Khantali.

The *khitmutgar* watched the start with grave, inscrutable eyes and finally turned back into the bungalow with the aloofness of a dweller in another sphere. The all-pervading Christmas cheer seemed to have gone to the *sahibs'* heads already. Perhaps he wondered in what condition they would return.

"I say, you don't mind?" said Noel coaxingly, as they drew ahead along the dusty road.

And Olga answered lightly, "I'm not going to mind anything or think of anything serious all day long."

He laughed. "I'm with you there. It's a jolly world, isn't it? And it's a shame to spoil it. As a matter of fact, I tried to get Peggy for a companion, but her mother wouldn't hear of it. I am too headlong and Peggy is too precious."

Olga laughed. "The Rajah was talking about a man-eating tiger at Khantali only the other day."

"Oh, yes, there is one too. But I'm afraid we are not very likely to come across him."

"Afraid! Do you want to then?"

Noel's eyes shone with enthusiasm. "I'm just aching to get a shot at one of these creatures. I've never so much as seen one in the wild yet. If the Rajah gets up an expedition I hope he'll take me along."

"He asked me if I would go," said Olga.

"Did he though? Very affable of him! I hope you said No!"

She laughed at his tone. "Well, yes, I did. But it was only because I didn't think I should like it."

"Not like a tiger-hunt!" ejaculated Noel.

She coloured a little. "Do you really like seeing things die?"

"Oh, that!" said Noel. "You're squeamish, are you? No, I'm never taken that way myself. That is in great part why I came here. I hoped—everyone thought—there was going to be some sort of shindy. But—I suppose it's the result of your clever little uncle's tactics—it seems to have fizzled out. Very satisfactory for him no doubt, but rather rough luck on us."

"Was there really any danger?" Olga asked.

"Oh, rather! The city was simply swarming with *budmashes*, and it was said that the priests had begun to preach a *jehad* against the British *raj*. Then there was a bomb found on the parade-ground one night, close under the fort. It would have blown a good many of us sky-high if it had exploded, and damaged the fort as well. Badgers was quite indignant. You see the fort has just been painted and generally smartened up in anticipation of General Bassett coming this way. He is expected on a tour of inspection in a few weeks, and we naturally want to look our best when the officer commanding the district is around. Hence the righteous wrath of Badgers!"

"I never heard of all this," said Olga, from whose ears the seething unrest of the State had been studiously kept by Nick.

"No?" said Noel. "Well, there's no chance now of any fun here. I'm pinning all my hopes on the possibility of a shine on the Frontier."

Olga looked at his brown, alert face with its restless Irish eyes, and understood. "You never think of the horrid part, do you?" she said.

He laughed, and flicked his whip at a wizened monkey-face that peered at them round the bole of a tree. "What do you mean by the horrid part?"

She hesitated.

He turned his gay face to her. "Do you mean the hardships or the actual fighting?"

She gave a little shudder. Even in that brilliant warmth of sunshine she was conscious of a sense of chill. "I mean—the killing," she said. "It seems to me one could never forget that. It—it's such a frightful responsibility."

"It's all part of the game," said Noel. "I couldn't kill a man on the sly. But when the chances of being killed oneself are equal—well, I don't see anything in it."

"I see." Olga was silent a moment; then, with a curious eagerness: "And was that what you were thinking of that night when you told Peggy that sometimes it was the only thing to do?" she asked. "Forgive my asking! But I've wondered often what you meant by that."

"Great Scott!" said Noel, with a frown of bewilderment. "What night? What were we talking about?"

She explained with a touch of embarrassment. "It was the night I arrived. Don't you remember I came upon you hearing her say her prayers?—in fact you were saying them with her. I liked you for doing that," she said simply.

"Thank you," said Noel with equal simplicity. "I remember now. The kiddie said something about it being wicked to kill people, didn't she?"

"Yes. And you said—it was just before I interrupted you—you said that sometimes it was the only thing to do."

Noel nodded. "I remember. Well, can't you imagine that? Don't you agree that when a man is fighting for his country, or in defence of someone, he is justified in slaying his enemies?"

Olga was frowning also, the old, troubled frown of perplexity. "Oh, of course, when you put it like that," she said; then put her hand to her head with a puzzled air. "But that wasn't quite what I meant."

"What did you mean?" said Noel.

She shook her head. "I don't quite know. It's difficult to express things. Whenever I try to discuss anything I always seem to lose the thread."

Noel grinned boyishly. "Good for me! You'd jolly soon floor me if you didn't. Look at that parroquet, I say! He flashes like an emerald, and see that imp of a monkey! He's actually daring to rebuke us for trespassing. I call this road a disgrace to the State, don't you? If I were the Rajah—by the way, the Rajah isn't coming, is he?"

Olga thought it possible. She knew he had been asked, but he had not returned any definite reply. She hoped he would be prevented.

"Oh, don't you like him?" said Noel. "I detest him myself. That's partly why I'm so keen on smashing his team to-morrow. He's a slippery customer, he and that wily old dog Kobad Shikan. They'd erupt, the two of them, if they dared and overwhelm us all. But—they daren't!" And Noel turned his face upwards, and laughed an exceeding British laugh.

"I wonder how you know these things," said Olga, watching him.

"What? I don't know 'em of course. I'm only assuming," said Noel. "I only play about on the surface, as it were, and draw my own conclusions as to the depths. It's quite a fascinating game, and nobody's any the worse or the wiser."

"And you think Kobad Shikan untrustworthy?" questioned Olga.

"My dear girl, could anyone with any sense whatever think him anything else? Could he have run the show for so many years if he had been anything less than a crafty old schemer? Oh, you bet he hasn't been Prime Minister and Lord High Treasurer all this time for nothing. What does Nick think of him?"

"Nick never discusses any of them." Olga was considerably astonished by these revelations. "I thought it was fairly plain sailing," she said.

"Did you though? Well, Nick is a genius, as everyone knows. He is probably in the thick of everything, and knows all that goes on. He'll be a C.S.I. before he's done."

"Oh, do you think so?" said Olga, with shining eyes.

"Rather! It's pretty evident. You wait till old Reggie comes along, and ask him. He is a great backer of Nick's. So am I," said Noel modestly. "I'd back him against all the Kobad Shikans in the Empire."

This, as Noel had doubtless foreseen, proved a fruitful topic of conversation and lasted them during a considerable part of their drive. Nearly the whole of the way lay through the jungle, here and there narrowing to little more than a track over which great forest-trees stretched their boughs. It was all new country to Olga, and the quiet, sunless depths as they advanced, held her awe-struck, spellbound. She gazed into the thick undergrowth with half-fearful curiosity. Once, at a sudden loud flapping of wings, she started and changed colour.

"There must be so many wild things there," she said.

"Teeming with 'em," said Noel. "We've come along at a rattling pace. Shall we pull up and wait for the rest to turn up?"

But Olga did not want to linger on the jungle-road. "Besides we've got most of the provisions," she pointed out. "And I want to get things arranged a little before anyone comes."

They pressed on, therefore, past glades, obscure and gloomy, where the flying-foxes hung in branches from the trees, and the little striped squirrels leaped and scuttled from bough to bough, where the blue jays laughed with abandoned mirth and the parroquets squabbled unceasingly, and cunning monkey-faces peered forth, grimaced, and vanished.

"This place is full of critics," declared Noel. "Can't you feel the nasty remarks they're making?"

Olga laughed and slightly shivered. "It isn't a very genial atmosphere, is it? But I think we must be nearly there. Doesn't that look like a break in the trees ahead?"

She was right. They were coming to a clearing in the jungle. Gradually it opened before them. The trees gave place to shrubs, and the shrubs to tall *kutcha*-grass which Olga viewed with deep suspicion.

"How easily a tiger could hide there!" she said.

Noel laughed aloud. "I daresay the brute's a myth, but in any case they never come out in the day-time. Are you really nervous, or only pretending?"

She was not pretending, but she did not tell him so. The *kutcha*-grass was very thick, quite impenetrable. It stretched like a solid wall on each side of them for a considerable distance—a choked wilderness of coarse weed that grew higher than their heads.

"I say, what a charming spot!" said Noel. "Did Nick choose it for the scenery, do you think, or the excellence of the road?"

They were bumping in and out of dusty holes with a violence that threatened repeatedly to overturn them altogether.

Olga laughed rather hysterically. "I'm sure the champagne will be quite unmanageable after all this shaking up. And just look what a lather your horse is in!"

"It's a case of the wicked uncle and the lost babes over again," declared Noel. "It also smacks of *The Pilgrim's Progress*. Old Bunyan would have made some good copy out of this. He'd have dubbed you Mistress Timorous and me Master Overbold."

Olga laughed again more naturally. Noel could be very wholesome and reassuring when he liked.

"And this beastly jungle-grass," he proceeded, "is the Wilderness of Nasty Possibilities. Hold up, Tinker, my lad, and get out of it as fast as you can!"

Tinker was obviously most anxious to comply. He bent all his sweating energies to the task. The road—if such it could be called—bent in a wide curve through the high grass. As they gradually rounded this, it became evident that that stage of the journey was nearly over. The thick walls opened out. They had a glimpse of wider country ahead dotted with mango-trees.

"Hooray!" sang out Noel. "We return to civilization!"

But it was not a very populous civilization which they were approaching. They came within view of a domed temple indeed, but it was a temple set among ruins. There was no sign of any inhabitant, near or far.

"There's a well somewhere," said Olga. "Nick said we were to camp there."

"So be it!" said Noel. "It's Nick's funeral. Let us find his precious well!"

They emerged from the jungle-road with relief, and approached a group of mango-trees. These led in a somewhat broken grove to the temple which stood amidst stunted palms and cypresses. The mid-day sun was fierce, and the shade of the mangoes was welcome. For about a hundred yards they travelled over a road that was nearly choked by stones and grass, and then somewhat unexpectedly they discovered the well.

It was plainly very ancient, its round stone mouth crumbling with age. All about it and over its edges grew the coarse grass. It must have been many years since native women had foregathered there to discuss the affairs of forgotten Khantali. Above it, on rising ground, stood the temple, domed, mysterious, deserted.

"A place for satyrs to dance in, what?" suggested Noel. "We ought to have come here by moonlight. Let's get down and investigate. The others can't be far behind."

"Yes, let us fix on a place before they come!" said Olga. "It will save such a lot of discussion."

"Excellent notion! I'll tie up Tinker to one of these trees. I don't call this a very promising site for a bean-feast," said Noel, wrinkling his nose. "It's so beastly stuffy."

"Yes, we will try the temple first," said Olga. "It stands higher. There will be much more air there."

They descended. There was still no sign of the rest of the party. "I expect they gave us a start to keep out of the beastly dust," said Noel. "They'll be here directly. Nick has pitched on a secluded corner anyhow. I shouldn't think the foot of man had trodden it for a thousand years."

Olga laughed. "I wonder. It's better than the jungle, isn't it? I don't feel nearly so creepy here."

"What price tigers?" grinned Noel.

"Oh, I've got over that," she declared. "But I didn't like your Wilderness of Nasty Possibilities."

He flashed her a merry look. "You ought not to be afraid with Master Overbold by your side. As for the tiger, we may meet him yet."

"Oh, no, we shan't!" she asserted with confidence. "It would be too ludicrously like a fairy-tale."

"Horribly ludicrous!" said Noel. "Well, come along and look for him!"

So side by side they started.

CHAPTER VIII
THE SOUL OF A HERO

The way was exceedingly rough and here and there almost overgrown with coarse weeds. Near the temple, the ground ascended fairly steeply, and the path narrowed so that it was impossible to walk abreast.

"Wonder if there are any of those jolly little *karaits* about," speculated Noel. "If you don't mind, I'll go first."

"I believe I saw a scorpion!" said Olga, as he took the lead.

He laughed at her over his shoulder. "Or a lizard! Stick to it, Mistress Timorous! You'll develop a taste for adventure soon."

"Oh, I'm not a coward really," she protested. "At least I never used to be!"

"You are the sweetest girl in the world," said Noel, in a tone that reduced Olga to instant and uncompromising silence.

She could not refuse his hand, however, when he paused to help her over the rough places. It was an utter impossibility to be ungracious to Noel for long. He was far too seductive.

They reached the top of the ascent and found themselves close to the temple. The place was a ruin. Blocks of stone, that once had been part of its structure, were scattered in all directions; and, advancing, they presently stumbled upon the monstrous head of a broken idol.

"This is the temple of Dagon," said Noel dramatically. "I don't think it's a very suitable place for a picnic. One might find bits of human sacrifices about and that would spoil the appetite."

"Oh, don't be gruesome!" Olga besought him. "Let's go in, as we are here."

They crossed the stone-strewn space through the shadowy cypresses, and entered under the dome. The place was dark and very eerie. Their footsteps echoed weirdly, and instantly there ensued a wild commotion overhead of owls and flying-foxes.

Olga started violently, and Noel looked upwards with a laugh that echoed and echoed in sinister repetition.

"What a ghastly place!" whispered Olga, as it died away at last.

The whisper was taken up and repeated from wall to wall till the further darkness swallowed it. Olga's hand went out instinctively and closed upon Noel's arm. Her nerves were not strung to this.

Almost before she knew it, he had drawn her to him, and slipped the arm about her. She looked up swiftly to protest, but the words were never spoken. They died upon her lips. For even as she opened them to speak there came an awful sound from the darkness.

It began deep and low, swelling in volume till it filled the building, reverberating from stone to stone, vibrating along the broken floor—a growl rising to a furious snarl—the unmistakable voice of an angry beast.

Olga stood as one petrified, feeling the arm around her tighten to a grip, but too lost in horror to take any note thereof. Staring widely into the darkness before them, she saw two points of light, red, ominous, advancing as it were by swift stealth out of the deep shadow.

At the same moment, Noel by a sudden, wholly unexpected movement thrust her behind him.

"Go!" he said. "Go for your life! Get back to Tinker and warn the rest! I'll keep the brute from following you."

His voice was short and authoritative; it held compulsion. In that moment of emergency he was a boy no longer, but a man, cool and strong and undismayed—a man to command obedience.

"Go quickly!" he said. "Remember it's up to you to warn them. This other is my job. Good-bye!"

He spoke without turning his head; yet the very brevity of his speech seemed to give her strength. Mechanically, she moved to obey.

Later she never remembered passing out of that place of horror. She went, hardly knowing what she did. The sudden smiting of the sunshine between the cypress boughs was the first she knew of having left the temple behind her. As one stricken blind, she moved, too stunned for panic.

And then—how it happened she was utterly unable to realize—as if he had dropped from the sky a man stood suddenly in her path.

He wore a pith helmet dragged forward over his eyes, and she was too dazzled by the sun to see his face. But there was something—something in his gait, his figure, his attitude—that sent a wild thrill through her, waking her to vivid, pulsing life. With an incoherent cry she clutched him by the arm.

"The tiger!" she gasped. "The tiger!"

"Where?" he said.

She pointed back over her shoulder, her eyes dilated, anguished. "In the temple,—and Noel is there! He will be killed!"

In a single movement he had freed his arm and was gone. She heard his feet racing over the stones, and she turned up her face to the blinding sunshine and frantically prayed....

Minutes—or could it have been only seconds?—passed. From below her came Tinker's frightened neigh. She could hear him stamping in the undergrowth. But she had no further thought of going to him. That spot with all its terrors held her chained.

Suddenly from behind her there came a loud report—a nerve-shattering sound. She whizzed round. He had a gun, then. She had not seen that he had a gun.

But what had happened? What? What? She was trembling so that she could barely stand, yet she forced her quaking limbs to move. Back she stumbled, back through the glaring sunlight. Once she fell, and saw a lizard—or was it a scorpion?—flick from her path. And then she was up again, panting, sobbing, utterly unnerved, but struggling with all her failing strength to reach the ruined temple, to see for herself what lay there.

An awful silence brooded across the stony space. It was as though a curse had fallen upon it. She tried to lift her voice, to call to Noel, to make some sound in the stillness. But her throat was powerless.

She thought he must be dead. She thought that her brain had tricked her, that she had only dreamed of the coming of the second man, had dreamed of the gun-shot, had dreamed all but those dreadful gleaming eyes coming stealthily nearer and nearer out of the dark.

Again she tried to call, and again piteously she failed. She reached the temple staggering, her hands stretched gropingly before her. And even as she did so, the silence was rent by a sound that convinced her wholly that she was indeed dreaming—a sound that echoed and echoed through the gloom, making her pulses leap again in spite of her—the sound of a ringing British laugh.

She fell against the broken marble of the doorway, her hands pressed fast over her face. She was struggling with herself, consciously striving to nerve herself to go in and find his dead body. Of any personal danger she was past thinking. Had the tawny body of their enemy sprung out upon her then she would scarcely have known fear.

And so when Noel came suddenly to her, caught her hands into his own, making her look up, his brown face bent close to hers, she simply gazed at him uncomprehendingly, not believing that she saw him.

Swift concern flashed into his eyes. He drew her to him and held her in his arms. "Olga,—Olga dear, don't you know me?" he said. "You've had a beastly fright, haven't you? But the brute's dead, and no one else is any the worse. There, there! It's all right. Did you think I was killed and eaten?"

He was holding her closely now. His voice came softly, on a winning note of tenderness, into her ear. "And would you have cared—would you have cared—darling—if I had been?"

But she leaned against him quivering and speechless, unresisting, unresponding.

He held her for a space in silence, patting her shoulder reassuringly. But it was not in him to be silent for long. After a few seconds he was speaking again with cheery confidence.

"Let's get out of this ghastly place! The rest of the party must be coming along now. It was a nasty experience, wasn't it? But you're getting better, eh? That chap with the gun came up just in time to save my bacon. You saw him, didn't you?"

"Yes," she whispered feebly.

His arms relaxed a little. He looked down into her face. "Better now?"

With an effort she answered him. "Yes,—getting better."

"Can you walk?" he said. "Or shall I carry you?"

That roused her somewhat. "Oh, let me walk!" she said; and, after a moment: "Forgive me for being foolish! It—it was the shock. I shall be all right now. Just let me hold your arm."

He gave it, still looking at her in a fashion which she was at no loss to understand. Instinctively she sought to divert his attention. "Tell me what happened! Who—who was the man with the gun?"

His expression changed a little. A momentary shadow crossed his face. He answered her with a touch of restraint. "Oh, he's a fellow I've met before. You'll see him again, I daresay. He has been chasing around after this infernal tiger since early morning. Had a shot at the brute once and wounded him. Been hunting for him ever since."

"All alone?" asked Olga in amazement.

Noel nodded. "Cracked thing to do, but as he's bagged his game I suppose he'll do it again."

"And what is he doing now?" asked Olga, as they descended the narrow path.

"Oh, he was going to clear out. He was awfully disgusted that the skin wasn't worth having. And there wasn't much of the head left." Noel made a face. "I shouldn't advise any of our picnic party to go near that beastly temple. It's a deal too sacrificial just now. Hullo! Here come some of 'em at last! You'll be glad to get back under Nick's wing."

He smiled at her quizzically, and Olga smiled back reassured. But reaching the lower ground, she detained him for an instant.

"Noel," she said rather haltingly, "there are some things beyond words, and—and I think this is one of them. But I shall never forget what you did. It—it was—magnificent."

"Great Scotland!" said Noel. He spoke banteringly, but she could not meet his eyes. "And you think I could have done anything else?"

She smiled rather wistfully. "Not you—perhaps," she said. "But it was fine of you all the same."

"And you're—not sorry—I wasn't eaten?" he suggested.

She gave him her hand with a gesture half-appealing. "We won't talk about it," she said. "It just won't bear talking about."

Her voice trembled a little but she was plainly anxious that he should not notice it. He stood a moment silent, holding her hand. From the direction of the jungle-road there came the sounds of the approaching party—the rattle of hoofs and jingle of bells mingling with laughing voices and gay shouts. It seemed incredible that a bare ten minutes had elapsed since their own arrival upon the scene.

Noel's hand tightened a little upon hers. He bent with a certain serious gallantry that became him well, and carried it to his lips.

"My lady's wishes shall be obeyed always," he said gravely.

She knew that he meant her to ascribe a full meaning to his words. And she let herself be reassured, for that she knew him now to possess the soul of a hero.

CHAPTER IX
THE MAN WITH THE GUN

In after-days when Olga looked back upon the rest of that Christmas picnic, she could remember very little in detail of what took place. Her mind was so fully occupied with the adventure in the ruined temple that the events immediately following it made but a slight impression upon her.

That they lunched at length by the ancient well, that Nick and the Musgraves petted and made much of her, that Noel considerately amused himself with the care and entertainment of Peggy, all these things she was able afterwards vaguely to recall, but none of them remained vividly in her memory.

During the afternoon she rested, with Daisy sitting by her side and Nick smoking a few yards away, until presently the Rajah rode up unescorted and occupied Nick's attention for the remainder of the time. He came and shook hands with Olga later and congratulated her on her escape, but his manner seemed to her perfunctory and somewhat absent. Remembering Noel's words, she wondered what schemes were developing behind those dusky eyes.

Her thoughts, however, did not dwell on him; they were curiously active in another direction. Over and over again she saw herself stumbling over the stones under the cypresses and finding herself all-suddenly face to face with a man in a pith helmet. She was haunted by the thought of him, though she had not in the glare discerned him fully. She had seen him as one sees a shadow on a sheet, a momentary impression, suggestive but wholly elusive, capable of stirring her to the depths but yet too vague to grasp.

Even to her own secret heart she could not account for the wild suspicion to which that lightning glimpse had given birth. The man was probably a very ordinary Briton under ordinary circumstances. That he had a breadth of shoulder that imparted the impression of power and somewhat discounted his height, that his first appearance had been so leisurely that he might have been strolling in an English garden—the sauntering vision flashed across her as she had often seen it, hands deep in pockets, and stubby brier-pipe between his teeth—that his brevity of speech had impelled her to clearness of brain and prompt reply—all these were but incidents that might have characterized the coming of any stranger. And yet whenever she recalled any one of these details, she found her heart beating up against her throat as though it would choke her.

And why had he disappeared so suddenly, this stranger with the gun? How she wished she had had the presence of mind to turn back into the temple to find him! Why had Noel spoken of him with such evident restraint? Had he been under orders so to speak? She almost resolved to ask him, but realized immediately that for some reason she could not. Besides, had he not said she would see him again? And when she saw him—when she saw him—again she had to still the tumult of her heart—doubtless she would tell herself how utterly unreasonable her agitation concerning him had been. She would make the acquaintance of a total stranger and wonder how he had ever reminded her of the one man in her world who alone had had the power to move her thus.

So, over and over again she reassured herself, considering the matter and dismissing it, only to admit it over and over again for further consideration.

Nick made unflattering comment upon her jaded appearance when the time came to return, and bundled her unceremoniously into the Musgraves' dog-cart before Noel could put in a claim. Olga was in some sense relieved, for she did not want to talk, and Daisy fully understood and left her in peace during the drive back to Sharapura.

The brief twilight came upon them just before they reached their destination, and when they stopped before the bungalow it was nearly dark. The stately *khitmutgar* was waiting for them, and helped Olga to descend. He stood by with massive patience while the Musgraves bade her farewell and drove away; then with extreme dignity he addressed her.

"There is a strange *sahib* in the drawing-room, who waits to see the Miss *sahib*," he said.

Olga's heart gave a wild bound. "To see me? What name, Kasur?"

"Miss *sahib*, he gave no name. 'She knows me,' he said. 'I will announce myself.'"

Olga turned to the verandah steps, as if drawn thereto by some unseen magnetic force. Sedately Kasur followed.

"Will the Miss *sahib* await the return of Ratcliffe *sahib*?" he suggested decorously.

She turned at the head of the steps. Her eyes were alight, feverish. She was strung to so high a pitch of excitement that she scarcely knew what she did.

"No, I can't wait," she threw back to him. "But Ratcliffe *sahib* will be in directly. Tell him when he comes." And with that she was gone, running swiftly, as one who obeys an urgent call.

The lamps were alight in the drawing-room and the glare streamed out across the verandah. It dazzled her as she entered, but yet she did not pause. Not till that moment did she realize how great a void the absence of one man had made in her life. Not till that moment did she understand the reason of the crushing sense of loss which for so long had been with her. Perhaps she did not fully understand it then, but there was no hiding the sudden rapture of gladness at her heart. It pierced her almost with a sense of pain, and with it came a stabbing certainty that this was no new thing—that sometime, somewhere, she had felt it all before.

He was on his feet lounging against the mantelpiece as she entered, but he straightened himself to meet her, and dazzled though she was, she saw his outstretched hand.

As it closed upon her own, she found her voice, though panting between tears and laughter. "Max! You—you!"

"A happy Christmas to you!" said Max.

He grasped her hand very firmly. How well she remembered that strong restraining grip! How often had she felt the controlling magic of it! Once she had even hotly resented it; but to-day—to-day—

She saw his mouth go up at one corner in the old, quizzing way. "'If my heart by signs can tell—'" he began, and ended, openly smiling, "I should almost dare to fancy you were—well, shall we say not annoyed?—to see me."

"Annoyed!" she laughed, still struggling with an outrageous desire to cry.

He looked at her critically. "You haven't grown any plumper since I saw you last, fair lady. Do you live on air in these parts? You will be flattered to hear that your resemblance to the great Nick is more pronounced than ever. Where is he, by the way? I hope he hasn't been eaten by a tiger, though I scarcely think any tiger, would be such a fool as to expect to find any nourishment in him."

"Oh, don't be horrid!" she said, laughing more naturally. "That's too gruesome a joke after what happened this afternoon."

"I wasn't joking," said Max. "I'm a serious-minded person. And what did happen this afternoon—if it isn't indiscreet to ask?"

She raised her eyes to his in astonishment. "But you were there!" she said.

"Who told you so?" demanded Max.

"I saw you myself, I spoke to you. I told you about—about Noel being in the temple—with the tiger." She halted a little over the explanation.

Max smiled at her—a curious smile that seemed to express relief. "I didn't think you recognized me in a helmet," he said. "Yes, I was there. I'd been on the brute's track since daybreak. I'm told that it's the proper thing to let natives do all the stalking in this country. But to my mind that's half the fun. Gives the tiger a sporting chance, too."

"You were actually hunting it all by yourself!" said Olga, with a quick shudder.

Her hand still lay in his; he gave it a sudden sharp squeeze. "Don't shiver like that! It's a sign of too vivid an imagination. Yes, I was all on my own, and enjoyed it. It was my first tiger too. I've learned quite a lot about the Indian jungle to-day. What made Nick choose the haunts of a man-eater for his Christmas party? Was it one of his little jokes?"

"We didn't believe in the man-eater," said Olga, beginning to make subtle efforts to recover possession of her hand. "There hadn't been one so near for years, and Nick said he thought it was bunkum."

"There," said Max, "he did not display his usual shrewdness of intelligence. Where is the little god by the way?"

"He's following on with Noel. They stopped behind to finish packing."

Max's fingers closed more firmly upon hers, so that without open resistance she could not free herself. "Noel seems to have developed into quite a picturesque cavalier," he observed impersonally.

He was watching her, she knew; and over her face there ran a great wave of colour. She was furiously aware of it even before she saw his faint smile. Desperately she sought to turn the subject.

"Why didn't you come back to us when the tiger was dead?" she said. "Why didn't you let Noel tell me you were there?"

She caught the old glint of mockery in his eyes as he made reply. "As you have foreseen, fair lady," he observed, "one answer will suffice for both questions. It was not my turn just then. Moreover, you knew I was there."

"I wasn't absolutely sure," she protested quickly. "I thought it probable that I had made a mistake."

"Didn't you expect to see me?" he asked her coolly.

She stared at him. "How could I? I never dreamed of your being in India."

He passed the question by. "And yet you were the only person in India whom I took the trouble to inform of my arrival."

Her eyes widened. "What can you mean?"

"Didn't you get a message from me this morning?" he asked.

"From you?" she said incredulously.

"I sent you a message," said Max.

Her hand leaped suddenly in his. So that was the explanation! She began to tremble. "I—didn't understand," she said piteously.

She wished he would turn his eyes from her face, but he kept them fixed upon her. "I wonder who got the credit for it," he said.

She turned from his scrutiny in quivering silence. But her hand remained in his.

He took her gently by the shoulder. "Olga, tell me!" he said.

"I didn't know it came from you," she whispered.

"Why not? I wrote a line with it."

"Yes, but—but—"

"But—" said Max, with quiet insistence.

She tried to laugh. "It was very absurd of me. The initials weren't very clear. I thought they were—someone else's."

"Noel's?" he said.

She nodded.

There was a brief silence, during which she dared not look round. Then he spoke, his voice drily humorous. "I suppose you thanked him for it then?"

"No, I didn't," she said. "At least—at least—I was vexed, but I didn't want to hurt his feelings."

"No?" said Max, in the same cynical tone.

Her hand slipped free at last. She spoke more firmly. "I told him I couldn't accept it."

"Poor Noel!" observed Max. He took his hand from her shoulder also, and she knew that he thrust it into his pocket. "And what did he say to that?"

She hesitated. "Well, of course he—he explained—that he hadn't sent it."

"And you believed him?"

"Of course I did. He—we thought perhaps it was a hoax."

Max grunted; she wondered if he were seriously displeased. And then abruptly he turned her thoughts in another direction. "Well, now that you know the truth,—what are you going to do about it?"

The question came with the utmost coolness, but yet in some fashion it sounded like a challenge. She felt compelled to turn and face him.

Thick-set and British, he confronted her. "Before you decide," he said, "there's just one little thing I should like you to remember. You may not have been in love with me—I don't think you were; but you engaged yourself to me quite a long time ago."

Olga's hands were locked together. But she met the challenge unflinching, unafraid. Quite suddenly she knew how to answer it. Yet she waited, not answering, her pale eyes shining, her whole being strung to throbbing expectation.

He came a step nearer to her, looking at her very intently. "Well?" he said.

She made a little fluttering movement with her clasped hands. Her face was raised unfalteringly to his. "I haven't forgotten," she said.

"But you thought I had," said Max.

Her lips quivered. "So many things have happened since then," she said, in a low voice.

"What of that?" he said, and suddenly there was a deep note in his voice that she had never heard before. "Do you think that so long as the world holds us both I would be content without you?"

The words were few, but they thrilled her as never had she been thrilled before. There came again to her that breathless feeling as though an immense wave had suddenly burst over her. She raised her face gasping, half-frightened. She even had a wild impulse to turn and flee.

But it was gone on the instant, for very suddenly Max Wyndham's arms closed about her, holding her fast, and she had no choice but to surrender. With a sob she yielded herself to him, clinging very tightly, her face hidden with a desperate shyness against his shoulder.

He spoke no word of love, simply holding her in silence during those first great moments. But at length his hand came up and lay quietly, reassuringly, upon her head. She quivered under it for a little. He waited till she was still.

"Olga," he said then, speaking very softly, "will you tell me something?"

"Perhaps," she whispered back.

"Why are you afraid of me? You never used to be."

She clung a little closer to him and was silent.

"Don't you know?" he said.

"Not altogether." Tremulously she made answer.

"I've had a feeling—all this time—that you were angry with me for some reason."

"For what reason?" he said.

"That's what I never could remember."

The hand upon her head moved and lightly stroked her cheek; then very gently but with evident determination turned her face upwards. His eyes, green and piercing, looked straight into her soul.

"You think that still?" he asked.

"No." Panting, she answered him; for deep within her, memory stirred afresh. The phantom of her dread lurked once more darkly in the background. The last time those eyes had searched her thus, her soul had been in agony. Wherefore? Wherefore? She struggled to remember.

And then in a flash all was gone. The past went from her. She was back again in the present, with the throbbing consciousness of Max's arms enfolding her, and the overwhelming knowledge that Max loved her filling all her world.

"You're not afraid now," he said.

"No," she answered softly.

"Then—" he set her free, bending to her, his face close to hers—"I may go on 'breathing and hoping,' may I, without running any risk of scaring you away?"

She laughed—a faint, sweet laugh more eloquent than words, realizing fully that, albeit her defences were down, he would not enter her citadel until she gave him leave.

His chivalrous regard for her went straight to her heart. In Noel it would not have surprised her, but in Max it was so unexpected that for a moment she hardly knew how to meet it.

He waited with the utmost patience, his smile, subtly softened but still unmistakably humorous, hovering at the corner of his mouth.

And so after a moment, half-laughing, with a face on fire, she reached out, took the red head between her hands, and bestowed a very small, shy kiss upon his cheek.

The next instant he held her crushed against his heart while his lips pressed hers with all the fiery passion of a man's worship....

It must have been several minutes later that a cracked voice was suddenly uplifted in the verandah singing a plantation love-song with more of pathos than tunefulness.

Olga started at the sound, started violently and guiltily, and slipped out of reach with a scarlet countenance.

"Nick!" she whispered.

Max glanced at the open window, raised his brows, shrugged his shoulders, and strolled across to it. Nick it was, stationed at a discreet distance, but dimly discernible in the darkness.

"Let me go to him first!" murmured Olga.

She passed Max with a touch of the hand and a fleeting smile, and was gone.

Nick's plaintive lament came to an abrupt conclusion two seconds later, and Max turned back into the room with his hands thrust deep in his pockets, and one side of his mouth cocked at an angle expressive of extreme satisfaction. He had dared a good deal that day, far more than Olga vaguely dreamed, and events had proved him more than justified.

CHAPTER X
A TALK IN THE OPEN

Noel dined with the Musgraves that night. His mood was hilarious throughout, but he seemed for some reason unwilling to discuss the adventure he had shared with Olga in the temple, and of their rescuer he scarcely spoke at all. He seemed in fact to have practically dismissed the whole matter from his mind, and when he bade them farewell at the end of the evening Daisy acknowledged to her husband that she was disappointed.

"I felt so sure he had begun to care for Olga," she said. "He doesn't often miss his opportunities, that boy."

"Perhaps Olga doesn't chance to care for him," suggested Will, with his arm round his wife's waist. "That does happen sometimes, you know."

She smiled, her cheek against his shoulder. "I can't imagine any girl resisting Noel's charms if he were the first comer—as I fancy he must be," she said.

"I wonder if he is," said Will. "She told me the other night she had never been in love, but she seemed to know so much about the disease that I rather doubted her veracity."

"Fancy your living to call it a disease!" said Daisy, with a faint sigh.

He stooped and kissed her. "Oh, I'm not a cynic, my dear," he said. "Shall we call it an incurable affection of the heart instead?"

"That's almost as bad," she protested.

"I said incurable," pleaded Will. "I ought to know, for I fell a victim to it long ago."

She laughed softly against his shoulder. "Well, if you will have it so, it's very infectious, you know. And I am a victim too."

His arm tightened. "Mine was always a hopeless case, Daisy," he murmured half wistfully.

She turned her lips up to his. "When it attacks old folks—like you and me, dear—it always is," she said.

He kissed her again, lingeringly and in silence. There had been a time of which neither ever spoke when Will's love for his wife had been to her a thing of little value. He had not been the first comer. That time had passed long since, and with it the last of their youth. But though for them romance was no more, they had become lovers in a sense more true. Their lives were bound up together and woven into one by the Loom of God.

Whatever opportunities Noel might have missed that day, he certainly did not permit the thought of them to depress him. With his customary jauntiness, he took his departure; but he did not return straight to his quarters at the cantonments. He turned his steps in the direction of the *dâk*-bungalow, whistling in the starlight as he went.

A chilly wind was blowing, and the dust swirled about his feet. The road gleamed white and deserted before him. He swung along it, erect and British, caring nothing for dust or cold. From far away, in the direction of the jungle, there came the desolate cry of a jackal; but near at hand there was no sound but the rush of the wind past his ears and the swish of the dust along the way.

He came at length within sight of the *dâk*-bungalow and saw beyond it the lights of the native city. Nick's bungalow, tucked away amongst its trees, was not visible.

"They're horribly near that treacherous hound," he murmured to himself, as he strode along. "I wonder if Nick realizes the risk. They might be murdered in their beds any night, and none of us down at the cantonments any the wiser. The Rajah and old Kobad Shikan would be horrified of course. It's so easy to be horrified—afterwards."

Unconsciously he quickened his steps. Somehow the danger had always seemed remote until that night. Had the day's adventure unsettled his nerves, or had he hitherto always underrated it? How ghastly it would be if—His thoughts broke off short. A figure had detached itself from the vagueness in front of him, and a whiff of rank tobacco smoke came suddenly to his nostrils.

Noel straightened himself and quickened his stride. He had the soldier's instinct for making the most of his height. The square, lounging figure that sauntered towards him looked almost short by comparison.

They met about fifty yards from the *dâk*-bungalow. "Hullo!" said Max.

His tone was coolly fraternal, but his hand came out at the same time and Noel remembered the grip of it for some minutes after.

"What on earth have you come out here for?" he said.

Max smoked a pipe in one corner of his mouth and smiled with the other. "Like the girls," he said, "I've come out to get married."

"You're not going to marry Olga!" said Noel quickly and fiercely.

"That's just what I want to talk to you about," said Max. "Shall we walk?" He took his brother by the arm and led him forward. "I thought a talk in the open would be preferable. My hutch in this beastly little inn is not precisely inviting. I go to Nick's bungalow tomorrow."

"The devil you do!" said Noel.

The hand on his arm was not removed. It closed very slowly and surely. "Look here, old chap," Max said, "say what you like to me and welcome, if it does you any good. But there is no actual necessity for you to express your feelings. For I know what they are; and—I'm infernally sorry."

The words were quietly uttered, but they sent a shock of amazement through Noel. He stood still and stared. He had never heard anything of the kind from Max before.

Steadily Max drew him on. "When I wrote you that letter in the autumn, I meant you to do exactly what you have done. I didn't of course anticipate playing such a heathen trick on you as cutting you out. I regarded myself at that time as out of the running. Circumstances which there is no need to discuss had set dead against me, and I had reason to believe that she might need an able-bodied man's protection. Nick is all very well as a moral force, but physically he is a negligible quantity. I didn't fancy the idea of her coming out here with the chance of the aforementioned danger cropping up."

"What danger?" said Noel, abruptly.

Max hesitated a moment. "It's rather a long story. There was another fellow—a great hulking bounder. I was half afraid he might follow her out here and make himself objectionable. I thought you would probably get friendly with her, and she might turn to you for help if she needed it. You're the sort of chap a woman would turn to. And anyhow, I know you're sound fundamentally."

"Do you?" murmured Noel.

Max went on. "At that time I never thought of coming out here myself. It was Nick who first suggested it at a time when I believed my chances to be *nil*. And gradually the idea took hold of me. We had been almost engaged before. And though I didn't believe in my luck any longer, I thought I would have one last shot. Kersley backed me as usual. I am to go into partnership with him when I get back. He urged me to come, even said I owed it to her. I wasn't so sure of that myself, but events have proved him justified. I thought in any case I should only hurt myself and that wouldn't matter much. Afraid I behaved like a selfish ass. But I didn't know how far matters had gone, or even if they were likely to move at all. She isn't the sort of girl that attracts at first sight. It never occurred to me to be attracted till I found out how badly she disliked me. Then I used to bait her, and I liked her spirit. After that—" an odd, tender note had crept into his voice; he stopped abruptly.

Noel set his teeth and tramped along in dogged silence.

For a few seconds Max followed his example; then took up his discourse at the final point. "So I chanced a final throw and came out here; I thought at the worst she could only send me away again, and I should be no more badly off than I was before. Well, I got here, and the first thing. I heard was that Nick was giving a picnic at Khantali, and that there was a man-eater there. My informant was a native groom at the inn. He seemed to believe in the man-eater, and as I had equipped myself with a Winchester with the idea of solacing myself with big game when I had been given my *congé*, I armed myself and went to have a look for him. You know the rest. I must admit I was nearly as staggered as she was when I saw her come out of the temple. As soon as I had a moment for thought, it occurred to me that I should be probably one too many if I presented myself then. It was your chance, not mine; so I decided with your connivance to lie low. This evening I called to see the result. I fully expected to be told that you and she were engaged, and I went prepared to congratulate. But directly I saw her, I knew that it was otherwise. And I realized that my luck had turned."

"She accepted you?" Curt and straight came the words.

"She did." Calmly and deliberately Max made answer. "I had sent her a ring earlier in the day, which little attention, it seems, she had attributed to you."

"Yes; she tried to return it this morning." Noel spoke with his eyes fixed straight ahead.

"She is wearing it to-night," said Max.

Noel tramped on again in silence.

Suddenly he stopped, facing round upon his brother with a gesture that was openly passionate. "Damn it, Max! You're deuced cool, I must say! Aren't there girls enough in England without your posting out here to take the one I want? She's half in love with me already. I'd have won her over in another week—in less! Very likely to-morrow!"

Max stood still. They had nearly reached the gate that led into Nick's compound. The rustle of the cypresses in the night-wind came to them as they faced each other. Noel's hands were clenched, Max's well out of sight in the depths of his pockets.

He did not speak at once, but there was no hint of irresolution in his attitude.

"Yes," he said, after a moment. "You jolly nearly died for her, and if anyone has a right to her, you have. But, my dear chap, you can't get away from the fact that she was mine before you ever met her. I know that now. I didn't before to-night, though so far as I am concerned, she has been the only girl in the world for a very long time. Not knowing it, I'd have been quite ready—I'd be ready now—for you to have her; glad even. But knowing it—well, it rather alters the case, doesn't it? You see," his mouth twisted a little in the old cynical curve, "we can't hand her about and barter for her like a bale of goods. She's a woman; and—whether we like it or not—in these things the woman must have the casting vote."

"It's so beastly unfair!" Noel broke in hotly, boyishly. "Why the devil couldn't you stay away a little longer?"

"And suppose I had!" For the first time Max spoke sternly. "Suppose I had!" he repeated, with eyes that suddenly shot green in the starlight. "Suppose you had won her before I came—suppose you'd been engaged, and I had come along afterwards! What then?"

"You'd have been too late," said Noel, the dogged note in his voice.

"You wouldn't have set her free?" Max flung the question with brief contempt.

"No!" Noel flung back the answer fiercely.

"Not if you had known she cared for me first?" Max's voice was suddenly quiet and chill. It expressed a cold curiosity, no more.

Noel writhed before it. "Confound you, no!" he cried violently.

There fell a sudden deep silence. Max stood quite motionless during the passage of seconds, watching, waiting, while Noel stood before him, fiercely threatening.

Then, very abruptly, as if he had suddenly discovered that there was nothing to wait for, he turned on his heel.

"Good-night!" he said, and walked away.

He went with his customary, sauntering gait, but there was absolute decision in his movements. It was quite obvious that he had no intention of returning.

And Noel made no attempt to call him back. He stood with his black brows drawn, and dumbly watched him go.

At the end of thirty seconds, he wheeled slowly round, and turned his sullen face towards Nick's bungalow. As he did so, there was a slight movement near the gate as of someone stealthily retreating.

Instantly suspicion leaped, keen-edged with anxiety, into his brain. In a flash his former fears rushed back upon him. They were so horribly near the native city, so horribly undefended. He remembered the bomb on the parade-ground, and felt momentarily physically sick.

In another instant he was speeding to the open gate. He turned sharply in between the cypresses, and was met by a white-clad, cringing figure that bowed to the earth at his approach.

Noel stopped dead in sheer astonishment. So sudden had been the apparition that he scarcely restrained himself from running into it. Then, being in no pacific mood, his astonishment passed into a blaze of anger.

"What the devil are you sneaking about here for?" he demanded. "What are you doing?"

The muffled figure before him made another deep salaam. "Heaven-born, I am but a humble seller of moonstones. Will his gracious excellency be pleased to behold his servant's wares?"

It was ingratiatingly spoken—the soft answer that should have turned away wrath; but Noel's tolerance was a minus quantity that night. Moreover, he had had a severe fright, and his Irish blood was up.

"You may have moonstones," he said, "but you didn't come here to sell them. The city's full of you infernal *budmashes*. It's a pity you can't be exterminated like the vermin you are. Be off with you, and if I ever catch you skulking round here again, I'll give you a leathering that you'll never forget for the rest of your rascally life!"

The moonstone-seller bowed again profoundly. "Yet even a rat has its bite," he murmured in a deferential undertone into his beard.

He turned aside, still darkly muttering, and shuffled past Noel towards the road.

Noel swung round on his heel as he did so, and administered a flying kick by way of assisting his departure. Possibly it was somewhat more forcible than he intended; at least it was totally unexpected. The moonstone-seller stumbled forward with a grunt, barely saving himself from falling headlong.

A momentary compunction pricked Noel, for the man was obviously old, and, by the peculiar fashion in which he recovered his balance, he seemed to be crippled also. But the next moment he was laughing, though his mood was far from hilarious. For, with an agility as comical as it was surprising, the moonstone-seller gathered up his impeding garment and fled.

He was gone like a shadow; the garden lay deserted; Noel's bitterness of soul returned. He glanced towards the darkness of the cypresses where they had walked only that morning, and a great misery rose and engulfed his spirit. A second or two he stood hesitating, irresolute. Should he go in and see her? Vividly her pale face came before him, but glorified with a radiance that was not for him. No, he could not endure it. By to-morrow he would have schooled himself. To-morrow he would wish her joy. But to-night—to-night—he drained the cup of disappointment for the first time in his gay young life and found it bitter as gall.

With a fierce gesture he flung round and tramped away.

CHAPTER XI
THE FAITHFUL WOUND OF A FRIEND

All the social circle of Sharapura and most of the native population usually assembled on the polo-ground to witness the great annual match between the Rajah's team and the officers stationed at the cantonments. It was to be followed by a dance at the mess-house in the evening, to which all English residents far and near had been bidden, and which the Rajah himself and his chief Minister, Kobad Shikan, had promised to attend.

The day was a brilliant one, and Olga looked forward to its festivities with a light heart. The thought of Noel was the only bitter drop in her cup of happiness, but instinct told her that his wound would be but a superficial one. She was sorry on his behalf, but not overwhelmingly so. As Nick had wisely observed, it would be far more fitting for him to wait and marry Peggy Musgrave. They were eminently well suited to each other, and would be playfellows all their lives.

She expected Max to present himself in the course of the morning, and he did not disappoint her. He made his casual appearance soon after Nick had departed for the Palace, and found her in the garden. Not alone, however, for Daisy had arrived before him to see how Olga fared after the previous day's adventure.

Max, strolling out to them, was met by Olga in a glowing embarrassment which he was far from sharing, and introduced forthwith to Daisy as "Noel's brother."

Daisy, who had just been listening to a somewhat halting account of his unexpected arrival the day before, marked her very evident confusion and leaped to instant comprehension. So this was the cause of Noel's reticence! She shook hands with Max with a very decided sense of disappointment, resenting his intrusion on Noel's behalf, and with womanly criticism marvelling that this thick-set unromantic Englishman could ever have held the girl's fancy when Noel, the handsomest officer in the district, had been so obviously at her feet.

She heaved a little sigh for Noel even while she said, smiling, "I have just been hearing of your dramatic arrival yesterday, Dr. Wyndham. You could scarcely have chosen a more thrilling moment."

He smiled also, with slight cynicism. "Yes, there were plenty of thrills for all of us," he said. "Have you heard the latest?"

Daisy's eyes travelled from him to Olga, who stretched out her left hand, bearing Max's ring upon it, and said, very sweetly and impulsively: "Oh, Mrs. Musgrave, I was just going to tell you about it. Please don't think me deceitful! It—it—it only happened last night."

"My darling child!" Daisy said. She took the outstretched, trembling hand and folded it in a soft, warm clasp. Her eyes went back to Max, whose expression became more ironical than ever under her scrutiny. It was as if he observed and grimly ridiculed her jealousy on his brother's behalf. And Daisy's resentment turned to a decided sense of hostility. She discovered quite suddenly but also quite unmistakably that she was not going to like this young man.

She was sure the green eyes under their shaggy red brows saw and mocked her antipathy. There was even a touch of insolence about him as he said: "I'm afraid it's taken your breath away, but it is not such a sudden arrangement as it appears. Strange to say all women don't fall in love with me at first sight. Olga, for instance, did quite the reverse, didn't you, Olga?"

His eyes mocked Olga now openly and complacently. Daisy told herself indignantly that she had never in her life witnessed anything so disgustingly cold-blooded. He positively revolted her. She saw him as a husband, selfish, supercilious, accepting with condescension his young wife's eager devotion, and her congratulations died on her lips. For Daisy was a woman with whom a man's homage counted for much. She had been accustomed to it all her life and its absence was an offence unpardonable. And then suddenly Olga overcame her shyness, and boldly came to the rescue.

"Max, don't make Mrs. Musgrave think you a beast! It isn't fair to me. He isn't a bit like this really," she added to Daisy. "It's all affectation. Nick knows that."

Daisy laughed. The girlish speech helped her, if it did not remove her doubts.

She gave her free hand to Max, saying, "I suppose we are none of us ourselves to strangers, but, since you are engaged to Olga, I hope you will not place me in that category. You are very, very lucky to have won her, and I wish you both every happiness."

Max bowed, still with a hint of irony. "It's nice of you not to condole with Olga," he said. "I feel inclined to myself. Perhaps, if I am not wanted, I may be allowed to go and have a smoke on the verandah. I am expecting my traps to turn up directly," he added to Olga.

"Oh, we must come and see about them," she said. "The *khit* will show you your room. Max is going to put up with us now," she told Daisy, with a smile that pleaded with her friend to be lenient.

Daisy's hand still held hers. "That is nice, dear," she said. "I must be getting back to Peggy. Is your *fiancé* coming to the regimental dance to-night?"

"Oh, Max,"—Olga's eyes shone upon him,—"you will, won't you? But of course you will. Noel will have settled that."

The corner of Max's mouth went down. "Noel is not in the habit of settling my affairs great or small," he observed. "If I go at all, it will be in the little god's train and under his auspices alone. But I warn you I'm not much of a dancer."

"What nonsense!" said Olga. "All doctors dance. It's part of their hospital training."

"Is it?" said Max. "Then my medical education is incomplete. My partners generally prefer to sit out after the first round."

"I shan't sit out with anyone," declared Olga. "It's such a waste of time. One can do that any day."

"So one can," said Max. "I hope you are not hurrying away on my account, Mrs. Musgrave. My business here is not urgent. It will very well wait."

He was evidently in an incurably cynical mood, and Olga gave him up in despair. She went with Daisy to the gate, and, with her arms round her neck, besought her, half-laughing, not to be misled by appearances.

"I was myself," she confessed. "I actually hated him once. But now—but now—"

"But now it's all right," smiled Daisy. "Run back to him, dear child! I should imagine he is the sort of young man who doesn't like to be kept waiting."

That was all the criticism she permitted herself, but Olga, returning slowly to Max on the verandah, was regretfully aware that the impression he had made upon this friend of hers was far from favourable.

"It isn't nice of you, Max," she began, as she reached him. "It really isn't nice of you."

But she got no further than that for the moment, for Max literally lifted her off her feet, holding her fast in his arms while he kissed the colour into her white face, finally lowering her into Nick's favourite hammock and dexterously settling her therein.

"You shouldn't!" she protested feebly. "You shouldn't! And indeed I'm not going to lie here."

"You are going to do as you are told, fair lady," he responded grimly. "What have you been lying awake half the night for?"

"I didn't," she began. "At least—" seeing his look of open incredulity—"it couldn't have been so long as that. And I—I had a lot of things to think about. No, Max, you're not to feel my pulse! Max, I won't have it!"

She pulled desperately, and freed herself. Max thrust his hands into his pockets, faintly smiling, and stood over her, contemplating her.

"Well, tell me all the things you had to think about!" he said.

She shook her head, flushed still and slightly distressed. "No, Max."

He stooped over her, searching her face. "Do you like being engaged, Olga?" he asked.

She sat up quickly and leaned against him, her hands clasped upon his arm.

"I'm happy enough to—to want to cry," she said, a slight catch in her voice.

He held her closely again, her head against his heart. "No, that's not the reason," he said softly into her ear. "Something is bothering you, isn't it?"

She swallowed once or twice and nodded. "I'm—foolish," she managed to utter after a moment.

"Never mind if you can't help it!" he said. "Tell me what it's about!"

But she was silent.

"Afraid I shan't understand?" he questioned.

Her hand nestled into his, but she kept her face down. "I wrote a long, long letter to Dad last night," she remarked irrelevantly, after a pause. "He—I'm afraid he'll be rather surprised."

"I wonder," said Max.

She glanced up for an instant. "Did he know you were coming out here to me?" she asked.

"He did." There was a queer note of dry exultation in Max's reply.

"Oh, Max!" Her head went back to its resting-place. "He thought I didn't like you, you know. What—what did he say?"

"He told me I was a fool," said Max.

Olga laughed. "Dear Dad! I suppose he thought you were wasting your time over a wild goose chase."

"Yes; he didn't anticipate my catching my wild goose, I admit. Kersley on the other hand was so confident that he practically hoofed me out of England. He wants a married partner, you know, so perhaps he was not altogether disinterested."

Again the complacent note sounded in Max's voice.

Olga's fingers closed tightly on his hand. "Is that why you are so anxious to get married?" she asked, in a muffled voice.

Max's fingers responded so swiftly and so mercilessly that she cried out with the pain. "Max! How brutal!"

"You deserved it," said Max without compunction.

"But I didn't! I only asked a simple question," she protested.

"No, you didn't; it was a compound one." He opened his hand and sternly regarded the crushed fingers. "If you develop claws, Olga," he said, "you must expect trouble."

She laughed again. "It isn't a question of developing: they're there—full-grown. Do you remember that day I stabbed you with my darning-needle?"

"I do," said Max. He turned his hand over and showed her a small white scar on the back. "I suppose you never realized that that was the beginning of everything?"

"It wasn't with me!" declared Olga. "I could have slain you that night!"

"Because I told you you ought to be whipped," said Max. "It was quite true, you know. Dr. Jim would have said the same. He would probably have done it too."

"I'm sure he wouldn't!" Olga lay back in the hammock with the scarred hand between her own. "Dad is very just. He would have realized that you were quite insufferable."

"That wouldn't have justified you, my child," maintained Max.

She snapped her fingers at him. "I'd do it again to-day if you were as horrid as you were then."

"Not you!" said Max.

She opened her eyes. "You think I wouldn't dare?"

He looked back at her with composure. "It is more a matter of caring than daring, my dear," he said. "Your heart wouldn't be in it. But you are afraid of me all the same."

She coloured and turned the subject. "When is Sir Kersley going to make you his partner?"

"Directly I return," said Max.

"And when will that be?"

He considered a moment. "I expect to reach England in a month from now."

"Max!" She sat up again quickly. "Oh, you're not going so soon!" she said.

He put his arm round her shoulders. "But you will be coming back yourself in April. Nick told me so."

"In April! But that's æons away!" protested Olga.

His eyes looked down into hers, and the old gleam which once she had taken for mockery hovered there. Her own eyes flickered and sank before it. There was something quick and fiery in it that she could not meet.

"I'll take you back with me," he said, "if you will come."

She started a little. "Oh, no!" she said.

"Why 'Oh, no'?" he enquired.

She was silent for a moment, her face downcast. "I couldn't leave Nick—possibly—out here," she said then.

"Why not? Can't the little god take care of himself?"

"No. And I wouldn't let him if he could. I shouldn't feel easy about him. He—he—I feel as if he is trying to walk a tight rope every day."

"It's a sort of thing he ought to do very well, I should say," observed Max. "But what is he doing it for?"

She looked up. "He thinks he is getting on splendidly," she said. "He and the Rajah are such friends! But the Rajah isn't everybody, and I'm not sure even of him. Someone tried to blow up the fort with a bomb not so very long ago."

"Oh, that's the game, is it?" said Max. "You think a similar little joke might be played on Nick, and if so you want to be there to see."

She smiled faintly, in a sense relieved that he did not treat the matter too seriously. "It makes one a little nervous for him," she said, "though of course there may be no reason for it."

"I see," said Max. "It's just a nightmare, is it?"

He was watching her intently, and under his look her heart quickened a little.

"It may be all nonsense, yes," she admitted. "But in any case I won't leave Nick out here. He is in my special charge."

He laughed. "Well, there's no appealing against that. You will be home in April then. Will you marry me on Midsummer Day?"

Olga's eyelids flickered and fell. "I must think about it," she said.

He pinched her cheek. "Say Yes," he said.

She turned her face impulsively; her lips just touched his hand. "I wonder if I shall, Max," she said.

"Say Yes," he repeated, still softly but with insistence.

She leaned her head against him. "I'd like to say Yes," she said. "But somehow—somehow—I have a feeling that—that—"

"My dear," said Max very practically, "don't be silly!"

She turned and clung to him very tightly. "Max, I—I've got something—on my mind."

His arm, very steady and strong, grew close about her. "Tell me!" he said.

Haltingly she complied. "You will think me morbid. I can't help it. Max, all last night—all last night—I felt as if—as if a spirit were with me—calling—calling—calling, trying to make me understand something, trying to—to warn me—of some danger—I couldn't see."

She broke off in tears. It seemed impossible to put the thing into words. It was so intangible yet in her eyes so portentous. Max's hand was on her head, stilling her agitation. She wondered if he thought her very absurd, but he did not leave her long in doubt.

"There's nothing to cry about, my dear," he said. "Your nerves were a bit strung up after the tiger episode, that's all. They will quiet down in a day or two. All the same"—his hand pressed a little—"I'm glad you told me. A trouble shared is only half a trouble, is it? And I have a right to all your troubles now."

He took her handkerchief, and dried her eyes with the utmost kindness; then turned her face gently upwards.

"Is that quite all?" he asked.

She tried to smile, with quivering lips.

"Not quite?" he questioned. "Come, I may as well know, mayn't I?"

"I don't know that there is anything gained by telling you," she said. "You never liked talking about your cases to me."

He frowned a little. "My dear girl, what particular case is it you have on your mind?"

She hesitated. "You won't be vexed?"

"Vexed? No!" he said; but he continued to frown slightly notwithstanding.

"I hope you won't be," Olga said, "because I simply can't argue about it. Max, I sometimes think to myself that if—you hadn't known—and Violet hadn't come to know—about—about her mother—things might have been—very different."

"Meaning I should have fallen in love with her?" said Max.

She nodded. "It may be a breach of confidence, but—I think I'll tell you now. Max, she cared for you."

She spoke the words with an effort, her eyes turned from him. Perhaps she was afraid that she might encounter cynicism in the vigilant green eyes, and she could not have endured it at that moment.

But at least there was none in his voice when he said: "Yes, I know she did. That was what made her hate me so badly afterwards. I am very sorry, Olga; but, for your comfort let me tell you this. I should never—under any circumstances—have come to care for her. You won't like me for saying it, but she was never more to me than a very interesting case, and, apart from medical investigation, she would simply not have existed so far as I was concerned. She didn't appeal to me."

Olga winced a little. "Oh, Max, but she was so beautiful!" she urged wistfully.

He made a slight gesture of impatience. "I don't dispute it. But what of it? My brain is not the sort to be turned by beauty. There was too much of it for my taste. She was exotic. That type of beauty gives me indigestion."

Olga looked at him reproachfully. "You didn't like her, Max?"

"Not much," said Max.

She made a movement as if she would withdraw herself from him, but he quietly and very resolutely held her still. "Although you knew she cared for you!" she said.

"Yes, in spite of that;" said Max. "In fact, I felt a bit vexed with her for complicating matters in that fashion. Goodness knows I never gave her the smallest reason for it!"

Olga laughed faintly, with an unwonted touch of bitterness. "It's a pity women are such doting fools," she said.

He looked at her attentively. "Did you say that?" he asked.

She met his look, not without defiance. "Yes, and I meant it too. It's such a wicked waste. And I think— I think—in her case it was something far worse. I believe it was that which in a very great measure helped to unhinge her mind."

"How could I help it?" demanded Max almost fiercely. "I never wanted her to care."

"That was just the cruel part of it," said Olga. "It was just your utter indifference that broke her heart."

"Good heavens!" said Max.

He let her go very abruptly and leaned against one of the verandah posts as if he needed support.

Olga tilted herself over the side of the hammock and stood up. "You couldn't help not caring," she said. "But—you might have been a little kinder. You needn't have made her hate and fear you."

Max surveyed her grimly from under drawn brows. "My dear," he said, "you simply don't know what you are talking about."

That fired her. A quiver of passion went suddenly through her. She faced him as she had faced him in the old days with a courage that sustained itself.

"Indeed, I know!" she said. "Better than it is in your power to understand. Oh, I know now what made her—hate you so."

The last words came with a rush, almost under her breath; but they were fully audible to the man lounging before her.

He did not speak at once, and yet he did not give the impression of being at a loss. He continued to lounge while he contemplated her with eyes of steady inscrutability.

He spoke at length with extreme deliberation. "And so you want to take me to task for breaking her heart, do you?"

"She was my friend," said Olga quickly.

He stood up slowly. "And would you have liked it better if I had made love to her?"

She flinched as if that stung. "No—no! But you might have been kind—you might have been kind—since you knew she cared. If you hadn't made such a study of her, she would never have looked your way. That was the cruel part of it—the dreadful, cold-blooded part."

"What do you mean by kind?" said Max. "You don't seem to realize that the poor girl was mad. If I had been soft with her she would have been beyond my control at once."

"Oh, but she wasn't mad then," Olga's hands clasped each other tightly. "Max," she said, and there was no longer indignation in her voice—it held only pain, "I'm afraid you and I have a good deal to answer for."

"Perhaps," said Max. He was frowning still; but he did not appear angry. She did not wholly understand either his look or tone. "I suppose she thought I treated her badly," he said.

Olga nodded silently.

"She told you so?" His voice sounded stern; yet, still he did not seem to be angry.

"No, never." Almost involuntarily she answered him. "But she did say—once—that you cared only for your profession, that it was not in you to—to worship any woman."

"And you think that too?" he said.

His voice was softer now; it moved her subtly. She turned her face away from him and stifled a sob in her throat.

"No; but, Max—to build our life-happiness on—on the ruin of hers; that—that—is what troubles me."

"But my dear girl!" he said. He took her two hands clasped into his. "I can't reason with you, Olga," he said. "You are quite unreasonable, and you know it. If you were any other woman, I should say that you felt in the mood for a good cry and so were raking up any old grievance for a pretext. As you are you, I won't say that. But I absolutely prohibit crying in my presence. If you want to indulge in tears, you must wait till I am out of the way."

She smiled at him faintly. "Max, I—I loved her-so; and I wasn't even with her—when she died."

Max was silent, suddenly and conspicuously silent, so that she knew on the instant that he had no sympathy to bestow on this point.

Yet an inner longing that was passionate urged her to brave his silence. Pleadingly she raised her face to his.

"Max, you were there, I know. Tell me—tell me about it!"

But he looked straight back at her with eyes that told her nothing, and she saw that his face was hard. For a little she tried to withstand him, mutely beseeching him; but at length her eyes fell before his.

And then Max spoke, briefly yet not unkindly. "My dear Olga, believe me, in nine cases out of ten it is better to forget those things that are behind; and this is one of the nine. I can't tell you anything on that subject, so we had better regard it as closed."

It was a bitter disappointment to her; but she saw that there was no appealing against his decision. She made as though she would turn away.

But he stopped her with quiet mastery. "No, I won't have that," he said. "I am not so cold-blooded as you think. I haven't hurt you—really, Olga!"

A note of tenderness sounded in his voice. She yielded to him, albeit under protest.

"But you have!" she said.

He held her in his arms again. He kissed her drooping lips. "Well, if I have," he said, "it's the faithful wound of a friend. Can't you forgive it?"

That Max should ever ask forgiveness was amazing. Her bitterness went out like the flare of a match. She laid her head against his neck.

"Max—dear, I didn't mean to be horrid!"

"You couldn't be if you tried," he said.

She clung faster to him. "How can you say so? I've hardly ever been anything else to you."

"When are you going to reform?" said Max, with his lips against her forehead.

"Now," said Olga into his neck.

"Really?" Max's voice came down to her very softly. "Then—won't you say Yes to the Midsummer Day project?"

She was silent for a little, as if considering the matter or summoning her resolution. Then with sudden impulse she lifted her face fully to his.

"Yes, Max," she said.

CHAPTER XII
A LETTER FROM AN OLD ACQUAINTANCE

It was universally acknowledged that the Rajah's Prime Minister, Kobad Shikan, was the most magnificent figure on the polo-ground that afternoon. The splendour of his attire was almost dazzling. He literally glittered with jewels. And his snow-white beard added very greatly to the general brilliance of his appearance. It was not his custom to attend social gatherings at all. Unlike the Rajah, he was by no means British in his tastes; and he never wore European costume. At the same time no one had ever detected any anti-British sentiments in him. He walked with such extreme wariness that no one actually knew what his sentiments were.

Why he had decided to grace the occasion with his presence was a matter for conjecture. Owing possibly to his habitual reticence, he was no favourite with the English portion of the community. Daisy Musgrave had nicknamed him Bluebeard long since, and Peggy firmly believed that somewhere in the depths of the Rajah's Palace this old man kept his chamber of horrors.

"What on earth has he come for, Nick?" murmured Olga, as they found places in the pavilion.

Nick laughed, a baffling laugh. "I asked him to come," he said.

"You, Nick! Why?"

He frowned at her. "Don't ask questions, little girl! Ah, that's a fine pony down there! Ye gods! What wouldn't I give to have another fling at the game!"

"Oh, but you never must!" said Olga quickly. "I couldn't bear you to take that risk indeed."

"You'd like to wrap me up in cotton-wool and seal me in a safe," laughed Nick.

"No; but, Nick, you are so reckless," she said, with loving eyes upon him. "It would be madness, wouldn't it, Max?"

Max's shrewd look rested for a moment on his host. "Little gods sometimes accomplish what mere mortals would never dream of attempting," he said. "How soon do you expect to be Viceroy, Nick?"

"Oh, not for a year or two," said Nick. "I haven't talked it over with my wife yet. There's no knowing. She may object. Wives are sometimes hard to please, you know." He flung a humorous glance at Max, and turned to leave them. "You will excuse me, I am sure, with the utmost pleasure. I am going to play spelicans with Kobad Shikan."

He was gone, and Olga turned to Max, smiling somewhat uneasily. "I wish he wouldn't," she said.

"What? Play spelicans? I should think he might prove as great an adept at that as walking the tight rope," said Max. "Ah, here comes your friend Mrs. Musgrave! She went home and told her husband this morning that I was the most objectionable young man she had ever met."

Olga's eyes widened with indignation. "Max, I'm sure she didn't, and if she did it was entirely your own fault. I believe you wanted her to think so."

"Some people have an antipathy to red hair," observed Max. "You had yourself at one time, I believe. Hullo! Is that our gallant Noel in polo-kit? What a magnificent spectacle!"

It was Noel following Daisy, whose rickshaw he had just spied, and bearing the proud Peggy on his shoulder.

He came straight to Olga, smiling with supreme ease, lowered Peggy from her perch, and dropped into the vacant seat beside her. Daisy passed on with a smile to join the Bradlaws. Peggy remained, glued to her hero's side.

"I say," said Noel, "I hope you haven't been thinking me beastly rude, Olga. I've been wishing you happiness with all my heart all the morning, but I simply couldn't get round to tell you so."

It was charmingly spoken. Her hand lay in his while he said it. He did not seem to observe his brother on her other side. But Peggy observed him and clung to Noel's shoulder with wide, fascinated eyes fixed upon the stranger.

"Noel," cut in the high, baby voice, "isn't that an ugly man? Who's that ugly man, Noel?"

Noel squeezed Olga's hand and set it free to lift the small questioner to his knee.

"That handsome gentleman, Peggy, is my brother, and he is going to marry this pretty lady—whom you know. Any more questions?"

Peggy stared at Olga very seriously. "Do you want to marry him, Miss Ratcliffe?" she asked.

"Of course she does," said Max. "Everyone wants to marry me. It's a sort of disease that spreads like the plague."

Peggy's eyes returned to him and fixed him with grave attention.

"I don't want to marry you," she announced with absolute decision.

"You'd rather have the plague, eh?" suggested Noel.

"No," said Peggy, and turned to him with her sweet, adoring smile. "But I'm goin' to marry you; aren't I, Noel?"

"Hear, hear!" said Noel with enthusiasm.

"Highly suitable," said Max.

"I hope you will both be very happy," said Olga, with a touch of earnestness that she emphasized with a secret pressure of Noel's arm.

"We shall be as happy as the day is long," said Noel, smiling straight into her eyes. "Now, little sweetheart," turning to Peggy, "I must be off. We've got some tough work in front of us."

"I hope you'll win," said Olga.

He stood up, looking very straight and handsome. His dark eyes, laughing downwards, seemed to challenge her to detect any shadow of disappointment in them.

"Win! Why, of course we shall. We're going to lick Akbar & Co. into the middle of next week—for the honour of the Regiment and Badgers."

He cast an impudent glance over his shoulder towards his commanding officer, with whom, however, he was a supreme favourite; smiled again at Olga while wholly overlooking Max, then swung around on his heel and departed.

Peggy stood for a moment watching him go, then with sudden resolution put aside the arm Olga had passed around her and ran after him.

"Highly suitable," Max said again.

Olga turned to him. "That's what Nick says. But it's such a long while for him to wait, poor boy."

"That wouldn't hurt him," said Max. "Do him all the good in the world, in fact. He's too much of a spoilt darling at present."

"Oh, Max, how can you say so? He is so splendid."

Max's mouth curved downwards. He said nothing.

"Max!" Olga's voice was anxious; it held a hint of pleading also, "you haven't—quarrelled, have you?"

Max turned deliberately and looked at her. "I never quarrel," he said.

"But you don't seem to be on very good terms," she said.

"The boy is such a puppy," Max said.

"Oh, he isn't!" she protested, flushing swiftly and very hotly. "He—he is the very nicest boy I know."

He laughed a little. "I believe you would have married him if I hadn't come along just in time."

Olga turned her burning face to the field. She was silent for a space, studying the mixed crowd assembled there, till, feeling his eyes persistently upon her, she was at length impelled to speak.

"It is quite possible," she said in a low voice.

"Really? You like him well enough for that?" Max's voice was quite calm, even impersonal. He spoke as one seeking information on a point that concerned him not at all.

Again for a time Olga was silent while the deep flush slowly died out of her face. At last with a little gesture of confidence only observable by him, she slipped her hand under his arm. "I wasn't in love with him, Max," she whispered. "But—I think—perhaps I could have been."

He pressed her hand to him with no visible movement. "And now?" he said.

"Ah, no, not now," she murmured, half-laughing. "You have quite put an end to that."

They were interrupted. Colonel Bradlaw had just heard of their engagement from Daisy, and came up to make Max's acquaintance and to offer his pompous felicitations.

Before these were over the game began, greatly to Olga's relief. She took a keen interest in it, and marked the adroit celerity with which the Rajah's team took the field with anxiety. The Rajah himself was an excellent player, and he was obviously on his mettle. Moreover, his ponies were superior to those of the British team; and the odds were plainly in his favour.

"Oh, he mustn't win; he mustn't!" said Olga feverishly.

"Don't get excited!" Max advised. "Follow the example of Nick's Oriental friend in front of us. He doesn't look as if red-hot pincers would make him lose his dignity."

"Horrid old man!" breathed Olga.

And yet Kobad Shikan was conversing with Nick with exemplary courtesy, giving no adequate occasion for such criticism.

"Is he another *bête-noir* of yours then?" asked Max.

She laughed a little. "Yes, I think he is detestable, and I believe he hates us all."

"Poor old man!" said Max.

All through that afternoon of splendid Indian winter, they watched the polo, talking, laughing, or intimately silent. All through the afternoon Nick remained with Kobad Shikan, airily marking time. And all through the afternoon Noel distinguished himself, whirling hither and thither, hotly, keenly, untiringly pressing for the victory. If the Rajah were on his mettle, so undoubtedly was he. He had never played so brilliantly before, and the wild applause he gained for himself should have been nectar to his soul. Yet to many it almost seemed that he did not hear it. He laughed throughout the game, but it was with set teeth, and once in a close encounter with the Rajah his eyes flamed open fury into the face of the Oriental as the latter swept the ball out of his reach.

It was a splendid fight, but the British team were outmatched. In the end, after a fierce struggle, they were beaten by a single goal.

Victors and vanquished came to the pavilion later and had tea with their supporters. But Noel did not return to Olga's side. He kept at a distance, surrounded by an enthusiastic group of fellow-subalterns.

Peggy, restrained by her mother from joining him, watched him with longing eyes; but she watched in vain. Noel did not so much as glance in their direction, and very soon he departed altogether with a brother-officer.

"Wyndham seems down on his luck," observed Major Forsyth, Noel's Major, to Daisy, to whom he had just brought tea. "He's no need to be. He played like a dozen devils."

She smiled with that touch of tenderness that all women had for Noel. "I expect he doesn't like being beaten, poor boy."

"He hasn't learned the art of taking it gracefully," said the Major. "But he shouldn't show temper. It's a sign of coltishness that I don't care for."

"Ah, well, he's young," said Daisy, with a sigh. "He'll get over that."

Her thoughts dwelt regretfully upon the young officer as she returned with Peggy. She believed that she understood Noel better than anyone else did just then.

Peggy did not understand him at all, and was deeply hurt by her cavalier's defection. She did think he might have said good-bye to her before he went.

Will, meeting them at the gate of their own compound, laughed down his small daughter's grievance. "Do you really suppose he could remember a midget like you?" he asked, as he tossed her on to his shoulder. "You expect too much of us, my baby."

"You wouldn't have goed away like that, Daddy," she protested, locking her small fingers lovingly under his chin.

"Ah, well, I'm old, you see," said Will. "I've learned how to please—or should I say how not to displease?—you sensitive ladies."

"Did Mummy teach you?" asked Peggy with interest.

Will laughed with his eyes on his wife's face. "On that subject," he said, "she taught me absolutely all I know."

Daisy smiled in return. "I set you some hard lessons, didn't I, Will?" she said. "Why, how late we are! I had no idea the evening mail was in. Peggy, run to *ayah*, darling! Only one letter for me! Who on earth is it from?"

She took it up and inspected the handwriting on the envelope.

"It's a bold enough scrawl," said Will. "Some male acquaintance apparently."

"No one interesting, I am sure," said Daisy.

She opened the envelope as she stood, withdrew the letter, and glanced at the signature.

The next instant she flushed suddenly and hotly. "That man!" she ejaculated.

"What man?" said Will.

She turned to the beginning of the letter. "Oh, it's no one you know, dear. A man I met long ago at Mahalaleshwar—that time you were at Bombay, soon after we married. He was a shocking flirt. So was I—in those days. But he got too serious at last, and I had to cut and run. I daresay there wasn't any real harm in him. It was probably all my own fault. It always is the woman's fault, isn't it?"

She twined her arm in his, looking up into his face with a little smile, half-mocking, half-wistful.

He stooped to kiss her. "Well, what does the bounder want?"

"Oh, nothing much," she said. "Simply, he finds himself in this direction after big game, and, having heard of our being here, he wants to know if we will put him up for a night or two—for the sake of old times, he has the effrontery to add."

"Do you want him?" asked Will, the echo of a fighting note in his voice.

She smiled again as she heard it. "No, not particularly. I am really indifferent. But I think it would look rather silly to refuse, don't you? Besides, it would be good for him to see how old and staid I have become."

Will looked slightly grim. Nevertheless, he did not argue the point. "All right, Daisy. Do as you think best!" he said.

She returned to her letter, still holding his arm. "That's very wise of you, Will," she said softly. "Then I suppose I shall write and tell him to come."

"What's the fellow's name?" asked Will.

Daisy turned again to the signature. "Merton Hunt-Goring. He was a major in the Sappers, but he has retired now, he says. He can't be very young. He was no chicken in those days. I didn't really like him, you know; but he amused me."

Will smiled. "Poor darling! Your bore of a husband never did that."

She rubbed her cheek against his shoulder. "Dear old duffer! When are we going for that honeymoon of ours? And what shall we do with Peggy? Don't say we've got to wait till she is safely married to Noel!"

Will's eyes opened. Never since Peggy's birth had Peggy's mother tolerated the possibility of leaving her. He had always believed that her whole soul centred in the child, and he had been content to believe it; such was the greatness of his love.

"You would never bear to leave Peggy behind," he said.

She laughed at him, her soft, mocking laugh of mischievous, elusive charm. "Do you suppose I shall want a child to look after when I am on my honeymoon? Of course I should leave her behind—not alone with *ayah*, of course. But that could be arranged. Anyhow, it is high time she learned to toddle alone on her own wee legs for a little. She is very independent already. She wouldn't really miss me, you know."

"Wouldn't she?" said Will. "But what of you? Your heart would ache for her from the moment you left her to the moment of your return."

She laughed again, lightly, merrily, her cheek against his sleeve.

"Not with my own man to keep me happy. There were no Peggies in the Garden of Eden, were there?" Then, as he still looked doubtful, "Oh, Will,—my own dearest one—how blind—how blind thou art!"

That moved him, touching him very nearly. He suddenly flushed a deep red. His arm went swiftly round her. "Daisy, Daisy—" he whispered haltingly, "I am not—not more to you than our child?"

She turned her face up to his; her eyes were full of tears though she was smiling still. "More to me than all the world, dear," she whispered back; "dearer to me than my hope of heaven."

She had never spoken such words to him before; he had never dreamed to hear them on her lips. It was not Daisy's way to express herself thus. In the far-off days of their courtship she had ever, daintily yet firmly, kept him at a distance. Since those days she had suffered shipwreck—a shipwreck from which his love alone had delivered her; but though the bond between them had drawn them very close, he had never pictured himself as ruling supreme in his wife's heart.

He was strongly moved by the revelation; but it was utterly impossible to put his feeling into words. He could only stoop and kiss her with a murmured, "God bless you, Daisy!"

They parted then, she to follow Peggy and superintend the evening tub, he to return to his desk and his work.

But his work did not flourish that evening; and presently, waxing impatient, he rose and went to seek her, drawn as a needle to a magnet.

He found her dressed for the regimental ball, and such was the witchery of her in her gown of shimmering black that he stood a moment in the doorway of her room as though hesitating to enter.

She turned from her table smiling her gay, sweet smile. Her silvery hair shone soft and wonderful in the lamplight.

"Ah, my dear Will," she said, "are you coming to for once? I wish you would. Do leave that stuffy old work—just to please me!" She went to meet him, with hands coaxingly outstretched. "It's getting late," she said, "I'll help you to dress."

He took the hands, gazing at her as if he could not turn his eyes away. "There's not much point in my trying to work to-night," he said, his voice very deep and a trifle husky. "I see and think of nothing but you. Great heavens, Daisy, how lovely you are!"

She laughed at him with tender raillery. "Dearly beloved gander, there is no one in the world thinks so but you."

"You've turned my head to-night," he said, still gazing at her. "By Heaven, I believe I'm falling in love with you all over again."

"Ah, well, it's to some purpose this time," she laughed, "for I'm very badly smitten too."

He did not laugh; he could not. "Daisy," he said, "we will have that honeymoon."

She pressed towards him with eagerness none the less because she pretended it to be half-feigned. "Will, you darling! When? When?"

His arms clasped her. His chest was heaving. "Very soon," he said, speaking softly down into her upraised face. "I've been thinking, dear—thinking very hard, ever since you asked me. I can get long leave in about three months—if I work for it. We'll go Home for the summer, you and I and the kiddie. If you are sure you can bear it, we will take her to Muriel Ratcliffe—and leave her in her charge."

He paused.

"Go on!" breathed Daisy. "And then?"

"Then we will go away together—you and I—you and I—right away into the country, and be—alone."

Daisy drew a deep breath. Her eyes were shining. She spoke no word. Only, after a moment, her hands stole upwards and clasped his neck.

"Will it do?" said Will.

She nodded mutely.

He held her closely. "Daisy, forgive me for asking—it won't hurt you to go back to England?"

Her eyes met his with absolute candour. "No, dear," she said.

"I was thinking," he said, stumbling a little, "sometimes old scenes, you know—they bring back—old heartaches."

"My heart will never ache—in that way," she answered gently, "while I have you." She paused a moment; then: "I'd like you to understand, Will," she said. "It isn't that I have forgotten. I have simply passed on. One does, you know. And I think that is—sometimes—how the last come to be first. It doesn't hurt me any longer to remember my old love. And it mustn't hurt you either. For it isn't a thing that could ever again come between us. Nothing ever could, Will. We are too closely united for that. And it is your love, your faith, your patience, that have made it so."

She ended with her head back, her lips raised to his, and in the kiss that passed between them there was something sacred, something in the nature of a bond.

Yet in a moment she was smiling again, the while she slipped from his close embrace. "And now you are going to dress for the ball. Come, you won't refuse me just for to-night—just for to-night!"

She pleaded with him like a girl and she proved irresistible. Half dazzled by her, he surrendered to her wiles.

"I will come if you like, Daisy; but I'm afraid I shall only be in the way. My dancing has grown very rusty from long disuse."

"What nonsense!" she protested. "Why, I only married you for the sake of your dancing. If you don't come, I shall spend the whole evening dancing with Nick."

"Oh, I'm not afraid of Nick!" said Will. "He is as safe as the Bank of England."

"Is he?" said Daisy. "You wait till you catch us alone some day. I tell you frankly, Will, I've kissed Nick more than once!"

"My dear," he said, "your frankness is your salvation. You have my full permission to do so as often as you meet."

She made a face at him, and finally freed herself. "Many thanks! But you wouldn't like me to create a scandal by dancing with him all the evening, I am sure. So," giving him a small, emphatic push, "go at once and dress your lazy self, and do your duty as a husband for once!"

"Shall I be adequately rewarded for it?" questioned Will, looking back as he turned to go.

She blew him an airy kiss. "Yes, you shall have half my waltzes."

He still lingered. "And the other half?"

"The other half," said Daisy, "will be divided equally between Nick and my prospective son-in-law."

And at that Will laughed like a merry boy and moved away. "I know I can cut out Noel," he said as he went. "As for Nick, he is welcome to as many as he can get."

CHAPTER XIII
A woman's prejudice

The evening was marked for ever in Olga's calendar as the merriest of her life. She was positively giddy with happiness, and she danced as she had never danced before. No one deemed her colourless or insignificant that night. She was radiant, and all who saw her felt the glow.

The only flaw in her joy was a slight dread of Noel; but this he very quickly dispelled, singling her out at once to plead for dances.

"You've saved a few for me, I know," he said, in his wheedling Irish way, and she saw at once that, whatever his inner feelings, he had no intention of wearing his heart on his sleeve.

She showed him her programme. "Yes, I've kept quite a lot for you to choose from," she said.

He flashed her a glance from his dark eyes that made her drop her own. "All right then," he said coolly. "I'll take 'em all."

She raised no protest though she had not quite expected that of him. She felt she owed it to him—as if in short she ought to give him anything he asked for to make up for what she had been compelled to withhold.

Max, sauntering up a little later, took her programme and looked at it with brows slightly raised. He gave it back to her, however, without comment.

Noel was the best dancer in the room, and Olga fully appreciated the fact. She loved Nick's dancing also, but it always brought to notice his crippled state, a fact which he never seemed to mind, but which she had never wholly ceased to mourn.

It was a great surprise to her to see Will Musgrave on the scene. When he came to her side her programme was full.

"Oh, knock off one of Nick's!" he said. "I owe him one."

But she would not do this till Nick's permission had been obtained and Nick had airily secured Daisy as a substitute.

Her dances with Max were spent chiefly in a very dark corner of the verandah, as he maintained that she was in a highly feverish condition and rest and quiet were essential. There was certainly some truth in the assertion though she indignantly denied it, and the intervals passed thus undoubtedly calmed her and kept her from reaching too high a pitch of excitement.

Max was exceedingly composed and steady. He danced with Daisy Musgrave, and provoked her to exasperation by his *sang-froid*.

"He is quite detestable," she told her husband later. "What on earth Olga can see to like in him is a puzzle I can never hope to solve. Noel is worth a hundred of him."

At which criticism Will laughed aloud. "There is no accounting for woman's fancies, my dear Daisy. And I must say I think young Noel would prove something of a handful."

"Anyhow he is human," retorted Daisy. "But this young man of Olga's is as self-contained and unapproachable as a camel. I'd rather deal with a sinner than a saint any day."

"Is Dr. Wyndham a saint?" questioned Will.

She laughed with just a touch of hardness. "A very scientific one, I should say. He has the most merciless eyes I ever saw."

She expressed this opinion a little later to Nick who took her in to supper, and for once found him in disagreement with her.

"Dearest Daisy," he said, "you can't expect a genius to look and behave like an ordinary mortal. That young man is already one of the most brilliant members of his profession. He has practically the world at his feet, and he'd be a fool if he didn't know it. I quite admit he may be merciless, but he is magnetic too. He can work with his mind as well as his hands, and he is never at a loss. Now that is the sort of man I admire. I think Olga has shown excellent taste."

"I don't!" declared Daisy emphatically. "I simply can't understand it, Nick. He may be an excellent match for her from a worldly point of view, but from a romantic standpoint—" She broke off with an expressive gesture—"I suppose it is a love-match?"

Nick laughed, blinking very rapidly as her eyes sought his. "Look at the kiddie's face if you want to know! She is as happy as a lark. Also, I seem to remember someone once saying to me that there wasn't a man in the universe that some woman couldn't be fool enough to love."

Daisy smiled in spite of herself. "I know I did. But some attachments are quite unaccountable all the same. I suppose if you are satisfied, I ought to be; but, you know, there is something about that young man that puts me in mind of a destroying angel. There's a tremendous power for shattering things hidden away in him somewhere. He may be a genius. I daresay he is. But one feels he wouldn't stick at anything that came in his way. If he failed he would simply trample his failure underfoot without scruple and go on. He is ruthless, Nick, or he couldn't have cut out poor Noel so overwhelmingly. I always thought till yesterday that Noel's chances were very good."

"I never favoured Noel's addresses," said Nick lightly. "He wants more ballast, to my mind. Whatever Max may be, at least he's solid. He wouldn't capsize in a gale."

Daisy laughed. "I see you are not to be influenced by a woman's prejudice. I daresay you are right, but there is also something in what I say or my instinct is very seriously at fault."

"On that point," said Nick politely, "chivalry does not permit me to express an opinion. Also, you are far too lovely to thwart, if I may use an old friend's privilege to tell you so."

She laughed carelessly enough though her cheeks flushed a little. "You are a gross flatterer, Nick."

"On the contrary," he said, "I worship at the shrine of Truth. You are more beautiful to-night than I have ever before seen you."

She laughed again with a hint of something that was not careless. "I'm glad you think so." She paused a moment; then: "Nick," she said softly, "dear old friend, Will and I are going for our second honeymoon this year!"

Carefully subdued though it was Nick heard the note of exultation in her voice. His own magic smile flashed across his face. Under the table his hand gripped hers.

"Thanks for telling me, dear!" he said, in a rapid whisper. "Long life and happiness to you both!"

For the rest of his time with her, he was gay and inconsequent. Very thorough was the understanding between them. They had been pals for many years.

When he left her, it was to go in search of Olga whose name was the only one left on his programme.

He found her with Noel on the verandah whither they had just betaken themselves for some air after the heat of the supper-room. He broke in upon them without ceremony.

"Look here, Olga *mia*! I've got to go. I'm afraid I shall have to cut our dance. You can give it to Max with my love. Daisy will take care of you here, and he can bring you home."

"Got to go, Nick! Why?" She turned to him in surprise. "You're not going to the Palace at this time of night surely! Why, the Rajah is still here, isn't he?"

"Great Lucifer, no!" said Nick. "But I've got some business to see to that won't keep. You'll be all right with Max to take care of you. Good-night!" He kissed her lightly. "See you in the morning! Don't overtire yourself, and don't get up early! Good-night, Noel!"

He would have departed with the words, but Noel detained him. "I say, Nick! I've been wanting a word with you all day, but couldn't get it in. If I lived where you do, I should keep a pretty sharp look-out. I caught an old brute of a moonstone-seller (at least that's what he called himself) prowling about your place only last night, and kicked him off the premises."

Nick stood still. His eyes flickered very rapidly as he faced Noel in the dimness. "Awfully obliged to you, my son," he said, and in his cracked voice there sounded a desire to laugh. "But that poor old seller of moonstones happens to be a very particular friend of mine. You needn't kick him again."

"What?" said Noel. "That mangy old cur a friend of yours?"

"He isn't mangy," said Nick. "And he's been very useful to me in one way and another; will be again, I daresay."

"My dear chap," Noel protested, "you don't mean to say you trust those people? You shouldn't really. It's madness. They are treachery incarnate, one and all."

Nick laughed flippantly. "Even treachery is a useful quality sometimes," he declared, as he turned to go. "Don't you worry yourself, my boy. I can walk on cat's ice as well as anyone I know."

He was gone, humming his favourite waltz as he departed; and Noel turned back to his partner with a grunt of discontent.

"He'll play that game once too often if he isn't careful," he said.

"Is there really any danger?" Olga asked.

"I should say so," he answered, "but it seems I am of no account."

"Oh, he didn't mean that," she said quickly.

He looked at her. "He is not the only person who thinks so, Olga."

She slipped a friendly hand on to his arm. "Noel," she said, "you don't think I think so, do you?"

He laid his hand on hers and pressed it silently. They stood together in the semi-darkness, isolated for the moment, very intimately alone.

"Noel," Olga whispered at length, a tremor of distress in the words, "you mustn't think that; please—please, you must never think that!"

He moved a little, stooped to her. "Olga," he said, speaking quickly, "I'm not blaming you. You couldn't help it. It's just my damned luck. But—if I'd met you—first—I'd have won you!"

The words came hot and passionate. His hand gripped hers with unconscious force. She made no attempt to free herself. Neither did she contradict him, for she knew that he spoke the truth.

Only, after a moment, she said, looking up at him, "I'm so dreadfully sorry."

"You couldn't help it," he reiterated almost savagely. "Anyhow you're happy; so I ought to be satisfied. I should be too, if I didn't have a sort of feeling that you'd have been happier with me. P'raps I'm a cad to tell you, but it's hit me rather hard."

He broke off, breathing heavily. She drew nearer to him, stroking his shoulder softly with her free hand. "Dear Noel, I love you for telling me," she said. "I feel dreadfully unworthy of your love. But I'm very, very grateful for it. You know that, don't you? And I—I'd marry you if my heart would let me, but,—dear, it won't."

He forced a laugh. "I know you would. That's just the damnable part of it. Life is an infernal swindle, isn't it? It's brimful of this sort of thing." He stood up with a jerk, and pulled himself together. "Forgive me, Olga! I didn't mean to let off steam in this way. I'm a selfish hound. Forget it! Only promise me that if you ever want a friend to turn to, you'll turn to me."

"Indeed I will!" she said very earnestly.

He held her hands very tightly for a moment and let them go; but they clung to his. She looked up at him appealingly.

"Noel," she said, with slight hesitation, "please—for my sake—be friendly with Max!"

He drew back instantly with a boyish gesture of distaste. "Oh, all right," he said.

She saw that he would not endure pressure on this point, and refrained from pursuing it; but his reception of her request was a disappointment to her. Somehow she had come to expect greater things from Noel.

The rest of the evening slipped away magically. She danced a great many dances without any sense of fatigue; but when it was all over at last a great weariness descended upon her. She drove back with Max, so utterly spent that she could hardly speak.

Yet, as they entered Nick's bungalow, she roused herself and turned to him with her own quick smile. "It's been the happiest evening of my life," she said.

"Really!" said Max.

She slipped the cloak from her shoulders and went close to him. The love in her eyes gave them a glory that was surely not of earth. She took him by the shoulders, those clear, shining eyes raised to his.

"I'm afraid you've had a dull time," she said. "I hope you haven't hated it."

"Not at all," said Max.

Yet a hint of cynicism still lingered about him as he said it. He stood passive within her hold.

She pressed a little nearer to him. "Max, you didn't mind my giving all those dances to Noel? You—understood?"

He began to smile. "My dear girl, yes!"

"You are sure?" she insisted.

He took her upraised face between his hands. "I have always understood you," he said.

"I can't help being sorry for him, can I?" she said wistfully.

He bent and kissed her. "It's a wasted sentiment, my child; but if it pleases you to be sorry, I have no objection."

"He is much nicer than you think," she pleaded.

He laughed at that. "I've known him from his cradle. He's a typical Wyndham, you know. They are all charming in one sense, and all rotten in another."

"Oh, Max!" she protested.

"I'm an exception," he said; "neither charming nor rotten. Now, my dear, since your estimable little chaperon has deserted you it's up to me to send you to bed. Do you want a drink before you go?"

She leaned her head against his shoulder. "No, I don't want anything. I feel as if I had had too much already. I don't want to go to bed, Max. I don't want to end this perfect day."

"There is always to-morrow," he said.

"No; but to-morrow won't be the same. And the time goes so fast. Very soon you will be going too."

"It will soon be Midsummer Day," smiled Max.

She gave a sudden, sharp shiver. "Lots of things may happen before then."

He held her closely to him for a moment, and in the thrilling pressure of his arms she felt his love for her vibrate; but he made no verbal answer to her words.

Slowly at length she released herself. "Well, I suppose I must say good-night. I hope you will be comfortable. You are sure you have all you want?"

"Quite sure," he said.

"Then good-night!" She went back for a moment into his arms. "I wonder Nick isn't here. Do you think he can have gone to bed?"

"Haven't an idea," said Max. "Anyhow I don't want him. And it's high time you went. Good-night, dear!"

Again closely he held her; again his lips pressed hers. Then, his arm about her, he led her to the door.

They parted outside, she glancing backward as she went, he standing motionless to watch her go. At the last she kissed her hand to him and was gone.

He turned back into the room with an odd, unsteady smile twitching the corner of his mouth.

The hand with which he helped himself to a drink shook slightly, and he looked at it with contemptuous attention. His favourite briar was lying in an ash-tray, where he had left it earlier in the day. He took it up, filled and lighted it. Then he sauntered out on to the verandah, drink in hand.

The night was dark and chill. He could barely discern the cypresses against the sky. He sat down in a hammock-chair in deep shadow and proceeded to smoke his pipe.

From far away, in the direction of the jungle, there came the haunting cry of a jackal, and a little nearer he heard the weird call of an owl. But close at hand there was no sound. He lay in absolute stillness, gazing along the verandah with eyes that looked into the future.

Minutes passed. His pipe went out, and his drink remained by his side forgotten. He wandered in the depths of reverie….

Suddenly from the compound immediately below him there came a faint rustle as of some living creature moving stealthily, and in a second Max was back in the present. He sat up noiselessly and peered downwards.

The faint rustle continued. His thoughts flashed to the tiger he had slain the day before at Khantali. Could this be another prowling in search of food? He scarcely thought so, yet the possibility gave him a sensation of bristling down the spine. He remained motionless in his chair, however, alert, listening.

Softly the intruder drew near. He heard the tamarisk bushes part and close again. But he heard no sound of feet. It was a cat-like advance, slow and wary.

He wondered if the creature could see him there in the dark, wondered if he were a fool to remain but decided to do so and take his chances. Max Wyndham's belief in his own particular lucky star was profound.

Nearer and nearer drew the unseen one, came close to him, seemed to pause,—and passed. Max was holding his breath. His hands were clenched. He was strung for vigorous resistance.

But as he realized that the danger—if danger there had been—was over, his muscles relaxed. A moment later with absolute noiselessness he rose and leaned over the verandah-rail, intently watching.

Seconds passed thus and nothing happened. The rustling sound grew fainter, faded imperceptibly at length into the stillness of the night. Could it have been a jackal, Max asked himself?

He stood up and looked once more along the verandah. Nick's room was just round the corner of the bungalow. The nocturnal visitor had gone in that direction. With noiseless tread he followed.

He reached the corner. The soft glow of a night-lamp lay across the verandah. The window was open. He paused a second, then strode softly up and looked in.

A bamboo-screen was pulled across the room, hiding the bed. The lamp was burning behind it. As Max stood at the window, a turbaned figure came silently round the screen. It was the figure of an old man, grey-bearded, slightly bent, clad in a long native garment. For a moment he stood, then stepped to the window and closed it swiftly in Max's face. So sudden and so noiseless was the action that Max was taken wholly by surprise. He did not so much as know whether his presence had been observed.

Then the blind came down with the same noiseless rapidity, and he was left in darkness.

Mindful of the mysterious visitor in the compound, he turned about and felt his way back to the corner of the bungalow, deciding that the lighted drawing-room was preferable to the dark verandah.

Reaching the corner and within sight of the lamplight, he stopped again and listened. But the compound was still and to all appearance deserted. He waited for a full minute, but heard no sound beyond a faint stirring of the night-wind in the cypresses. Slowly at length he turned and retraced his steps, contemptuously wondering if the mysterious East had tampered with his nerves.

It was evident that his host had retired for the night with the assistance of his bearer, and he decided to follow his example. He closed and bolted the windows and went to his own room.

CHAPTER XIV
SMOKE FROM THE FIRE

"It always used to be regarded as anything but a model State," smiled Major Hunt-Goring, as he lay in a long chair and watched Daisy's busy fingers at work on a frock for Peggy. "I suppose our friend Nicholas Ratcliffe has changed all that, however. A queer little genius—Nick."

"He is my husband's and my greatest friend," said Daisy.

"Really!" Hunt-Goring laughed silkily. "Do you know, Mrs. Musgrave, that's the fifth time you have mentioned your husband in as many minutes? If I remember aright, he used not to be so often on your lips."

Daisy glanced up momentarily. "And now," she said, "he is never out of my thoughts."

"Really!" Hunt-Goring said again. He looked at her very attentively for a few seconds before he relaxed again with eyes half-closed. "That is *très convenant* for you both," he observed. "I enjoy the unusual spectacle of a wife who is happy as well as virtuous."

Daisy stitched on in silence. Privately she wondered how she had ever come to be on intimate terms with the man, and condemned afresh the follies of her youth.

"Have you been Home since I had the pleasure of your society at Mahalaleshwar I will not say how many years ago?" asked Hunt-Goring, after a pause.

"I went Home the following year," said Daisy. "We thought—we hoped—it would make our baby boy more robust to have a summer in England."

"Oh, have you a boy?" said Hunt-Goring, without much interest.

"He died," said Daisy briefly.

Hunt-Goring looked bored, and the conversation languished.

Into the silence came Peggy, fairy-footed, gay of mien. She flung impulsive arms around her mother's neck and pressed a soft cheek coaxingly to hers.

"Mummy, Noel is comin' to teach me to ride this morning. I may go, mayn't I?"

"My darling!" said Daisy, in consternation. "He never said anything to me about it."

Peggy laughed, nodding her fair head with saucy assurance. "He promised, Mummy."

"But, dearie," protested Daisy, "you can't ride Noel's horse. You'd be frightened, and so would Mummy."

Peggy laughed again, the triumphant laugh of one who possesses private information. "Noel wouldn't let me be frightened," she said, with confidence.

"Who is Noel?" asked Hunt-Goring.

Peggy looked at him. She was not quite sure that she liked this friend of her mother's, and her look said as much. "Noel is an officer," she said proudly. "He's the pwettiest officer in the Regiment, and I love him."

"Ha!" Hunt-Goring laughed. "You inherit your mother's tastes, my child." He looked across at Daisy. "She always preferred the pretty ones."

"I know better now," said Daisy, without returning his look.

He laughed again and stretched himself. "What became of that handsome cousin of yours who paid you a visit in the old M'war days?"

"Do you mean Blake Grange?" Daisy's voice suddenly sounded so remote and cold that Peggy turned and regarded her in round-eyed astonishment.

"Yes, that was the fellow. He got trapped at Wara along with General Roscoe and Nick Ratcliffe. What happened to him? Was he killed?"

"No, not then." Slowly Daisy lifted her eyes; slowly she spoke. "He gave his life in England the following year to save some shipwrecked sailors."

"Did he, though? Quite a hero!" Hunt-Goring's eyes met hers and insolently held them. "Were you present at the sacrifice?"

"Yes," she answered him briefly, but there was tragedy in her eyes.

"Ah!" said Hunt-Goring softly. "That made a difference to you."

She did not answer; she leaned her cheek against Peggy's fair head in silence.

"My dear lady," said Hunt-Goring, "you always took things too seriously."

She gave a brief sigh, and took up her work again. "Life is rather a serious matter, I find," she said, with a smile that was scarcely gay.

"Nonsense!" said Hunt-Goring.

"Don't you find it so?" Daisy did not look up again; she stitched on rapidly with the child leaning against her knee.

"I?" he said. "Oh, sometimes it seems so, when things don't fit. But I don't care, you know. I have a volatile mind, I am glad to say."

"Are you never afraid of growing old?" asked Daisy.

He laughed his soft, self-satisfied laugh. "Oh, really, you know, I don't think they will let me do that at present."

"You never think of getting married?" asked Daisy.

Hunt-Goring's smile changed a little, grew subtly harder. "Most people think of it at one time or another." he observed. "But personally I do not regard myself as a marrying man."

"And you are never lonely?" she said.

"I am seldom alone, my dear Mrs. Musgrave," he said.

She turned the conversation. "Where have you been living since your retirement?"

"I took a place in England in the hunting-country—quite a decent place."

"Ah? Where?"

"About two miles from a little town called Weir." Hunt-Goring spoke deliberately, still watching his hostess's slim fingers at work.

"Why!" Swiftly Daisy looked up. "That is where the Ratcliffes live—Jim Ratcliffe and Olga. Olga is out here now with Nick. Did you know?"

Hunt-Goring nodded to each sentence. "I know it all. I know Jim Ratcliffe, and a burly old monster he is. I know Nick of Redlands—also the sedate Mrs. Nick. And, last but not least, I know—Olga."

He spoke mockingly; his look was derisive.

"I had no idea you had been living there," said Daisy.

"I was the hornet in the hive," said Hunt-Goring with his lazy laugh. "It's rather a hole of a place, though I liked The Warren well enough. I'm not going back there. You can tell Olga so with my love."

"She and Nick are dining here to-night," observed Daisy, "so you will be able to tell her yourself."

"What! To meet me!" It was Hunt-Goring's turn to look surprised. He did so with an accompanying sneer. "How did you describe me, I wonder? You couldn't have mentioned my name."

Daisy regarded him steadily for a moment. "Is there any reason why she should not meet you?" she asked.

"None whatever," said Hunt-Goring, with a shrug. "Needless to say, I shall be quite charmed to meet her."

At this point the conversation was interrupted by the sudden appearance of Noel. He came out through the French window of the drawing-room with his habitual air of cheery assurance, and was instantly pounced upon by Peggy who hailed him with delight.

He caught her up in his arms. "Well, little sweetheart, are we going for our ride? What does Mummy say?" He laughed down at Daisy, the child mounted high on his shoulder.

Daisy laughed back because she could not help it. "Oh, Noel, you are incorrigible! I don't think I dare trust her to you. Why do you suggest these headlong things?"

"But, my dear Mrs. Musgrave," he protested, "does any harm ever come to her when she is with me? You know I would guard her with my life!"

"Yes, I know," smiled Daisy. "But I am not sure that that would be a very great safeguard. You are so reckless yourself. By the way, let me introduce Major Hunt-Goring—an old friend. Major Hunt-Goring—Mr. Wyndham!"

Noel nodded careless acknowledgment. Hunt-Goring merely lifted his brows momentarily. He did not greatly care for the boy's familiarity with his hostess. It was a privilege which he did not wish to share.

"Well, shall we start?" said Noel. "I've brought one of my polo mounts for Peggy," he added to Daisy. "You know the Chimpanzee. He's as quiet as a lamb. Come and give us a send-off! Really you needn't be anxious."

He patted her arm coaxingly, reassuringly, and Hunt-Goring took out his cigarette-case. He was plainly bored to extinction.

Daisy left him with a smiling apology. She did not suggest that he should accompany them, and he did not offer to do so.

"I don't like that man," declared Peggy as Noel bore her away. "He looks so ugly when he smiles."

"Only the Daisies and Peggies of this world manage to look pretty always," observed Noel gallantly.

For which dainty compliment Daisy frowned upon him. "My vanity days are over," she said, "but do remember that hers are yet to come!"

They went round to the front of the bungalow where Noel had left the mounts; and after a good deal of discussion and many injunctions Peggy was, to her huge delight, perched astride the Chimpanzee, a creature of almost human intelligence who plainly took a serious view of his responsibilities, to Daisy's immense relief.

She watched them ride away together at length at a walking pace, Noel on his tall Waler leading the polo-pony, from whose back Peggy waved her an ardent farewell; and finally went back to her guest feeling reassured. Noel evidently had no intention of taking any risks with Peggy in his charge.

"It's very good of him," she remarked, as she sat down again on the verandah.

Hunt-Goring opened his eyes a quarter of an inch. "I beg your pardon?"

"Oh, nothing," said Daisy, feeling slightly annoyed. "He's a nice boy, that's all; and I am grateful to him for being so kind to my little Peggy."

"It probably answers his purpose," said Hunt-Goring, smothering a yawn.

Daisy took up her work again in silence.

Hunt-Goring finished his cigarette in dreamy ease before he spoke again.

She thought he was half-asleep when unexpectedly he accosted her, referring to the subject in which he had seemed to take but slight interest.

"Did you say that puppy's name was Wyndham?"

"He isn't a puppy," said Daisy, quick to defend her friend.

He smiled his tolerant amusement. "My dear little woman, that wasn't the point of my enquiry."

Daisy stiffened. She suddenly began to sew very fast indeed, without speaking. Her pretty lips were compressed, but Hunt-Goring seemed sublimely unconscious of the fact. He smiled to himself as at some inward thought.

"You did say his name was Wyndham, I think?" he said, after a moment.

"I did," said Daisy.

"There was a fellow of the same name who lived at Weir," observed Hunt-Goring. "He was the doctor's assistant; had to leave in something of a hurry, I believe. There was the beginning of a scandal, but it was hushed up—strangled at birth, so to speak."

"What?" said Daisy. She looked across at him swiftly, her dignity and work alike forgotten.

Hunt-Goring still smiled placidly. "I daresay it might be described as a regrettable incident. It concerned the sudden death of a young girl at which event the said Dr. Wyndham presided. I really shouldn't have mentioned it if it hadn't been for the familiarity of the name."

"They are brothers," said Daisy.

"Really! That is strange." Again Hunt-Goring barely concealed a yawn. "Olga Ratcliffe used to be somewhat smitten with the young man in what I might call her calf days. Doubtless she has got over that by now, especially as the girl who died was a friend of hers."

"But she can't know of that!" said Daisy quickly. "She has been very ill, you know—an illness brought on by the shock of it all."

"Indeed!" said Hunt-Goring, and became significantly silent.

Daisy continued to look at him. "She has not got over it," she said slowly at length, speaking as though uttering her thoughts aloud. "He is out here now, arrived only last week. And—they are engaged to be married."

"*Chacun à son goût!*" observed Hunt-Goring.

She made a sharp movement of impatience. "Oh, don't be so cold-blooded! Tell me—do tell me—the whole story!"

"My dear Daisy," said Hunt-Goring daringly, "there is practically nothing more to tell."

"But there must be," Daisy argued, ignoring side-issues. "How did the gossip arise? There is never smoke without some fire."

"True," said Hunt-Goring. "But for the truth of the gossip I will not vouch. It ran in this wise. The girl was beautiful—and gay. The man—well, you have had some experience of the species; you know what they are. Trouble arose; there was madness in the girl's family. She became demented; and a certain magic draught did the rest. It was risky of course; but it was a choice of evils. He chose the surest means of protecting his reputation—which, I believe, is considered valuable in his profession."

"Oh, it isn't possible!" protested Daisy. "It simply can't be. How did you hear all this?"

Hunt-Goring laughed. "How does one ever hear anything? I told you I didn't vouch for the truth of it."

"I wonder what I ought to do," said Daisy.

"Do?" He looked at her. "What do you contemplate doing? Is it up to you to do anything?"

Daisy scarcely saw or heard him. "I am thinking of little Olga. She is engaged to him. She—can't know of this evil tale."

"She probably does," said Hunt-Goring. "They were very intimate—she and Violet Campion."

"It isn't possible," Daisy said again. "Why, I believe she was actually with the poor girl when she died. Nick told me a little. He said it had been very sudden and a severe shock to her."

"I should say it was," said Hunt-Goring.

She looked at him. "You were there at the time?"

"I was at The Warren—yes." He spoke with an easy air of unconcern.

Daisy leaned towards him. "And Nick—do you think Nick knew?"

Hunt-Goring looked straight back at her. "I think," he said deliberately, "that I should scarcely trouble to tackle Nick on the subject. He knows exactly what it suits him to know."

"What do you mean?" Daisy spoke sharply, nervously.

"Merely that he and the young man are—and always have been—hand and glove," explained Hunt-Goring smoothly. "Nick is a very charming person no doubt, but—"

"Be careful!" warned Daisy.

He made her a smiling bow. "But," he repeated with emphasis, "he is not sentimentally particular in a matter of ethics. He looks to the end rather than the means. Also you must remember he is a man and not a woman. A man's outlook is different."

"Do you mean that Nick would overlook a thing of this kind?" asked Daisy.

Hunt-Goring nodded thoughtfully. "I think he would condone many things that you would regard as inexcusable, even monstrous. Otherwise, he would scarcely have been selected for his present job."

Daisy was silent.

"And you must remember," Hunt-Goring proceeded, "that this young Wyndham is a rising man—a desirable *parti* for any girl. He will probably never make another blunder of that description. It is too risky, especially for a man who means to climb to the top of the tree."

"You really think it possible then that Nick knows?" Daisy still looked doubtful.

"I think it more than possible." Hunt-Goring spoke with confidence. "I am sorry if it shocks you, but, you know, he is really too shrewd a person not to know current gossip and its origin."

This was a straight shot, and it told. Daisy acknowledged it without argument.

"But Olga!" she said. "Olga can't know."

"Perhaps not," admitted Hunt-Goring. "And—in that case—it would be advisable to leave her in ignorance; would it not?"

He took out another cigarette with the words, flinging her a sidelong glance as he did it.

But Daisy was silent, looking straight before her.

"Surely," said Hunt-Goring, through a cloud of aromatic smoke, "whether there is anything in the tale or not, the fewer that know of it—the better."

"Oh, I don't know." Daisy spoke as if compelled. "No woman ought to be married blindfold. It is too great a risk."

Hunt-Goring leaned back again in his chair. "If I were in your place, I should maintain a discreet silence," he said.

"I don't think you would," said Daisy.

He inhaled a long breath of smoke. "If I didn't, I should approach the girl herself—find out what she knows—and, with great discretion, put her on her guard. I don't think you would gain much by opening up the matter in any other quarter."

"You mean it would be no good to discuss it with Nick?" said Daisy.

Hunt-Goring looked at the end of his cigarette. "Perhaps I do mean that," he said. "He would probably prevent it coming to Olga's knowledge if he had set his heart on the match."

"He couldn't prevent my telling her," said Daisy quickly.

"No?" Hunt-Goring gave utterance to his silky laugh. "Well," he said, "my experience of Nick Ratcliffe is not a very extensive one; but I should certainly say that he knows how to get his own way in most things. Perhaps you have never come into collision with him?"

Daisy coloured suddenly, and was silent.

Hunt-Goring laughed again. "You see my point, I perceive," he remarked. "Well, I leave the matter in your hands, but—if you really wish to warn the girl, I should not warn Nick Ratcliffe first."

He spoke impressively, notwithstanding his laugh. And Daisy accepted his advice in silence.

Much as she loved Nick, she knew but too well how a struggle with him would end, and she shrank from risking a conflict. Besides, there was Olga to be thought of. She resumed her sewing with a puckered brow. Certainly Olga must be warned.

There might be no truth in the story, but then rumours of that description never started themselves. And Max Wyndham—well she had been prejudiced against him from the beginning in spite of the fact that Nick was all in his favour. He was ruthless and unscrupulous; she was sure of it. How he had ever managed to win Olga was a perpetual puzzle to her. Perhaps he really was magnetic, as Nick had said. But she believed it to be an evil magnetism. As a lover, he was the coolest she had ever seen.

"Altogether objectionable," had been her verdict from the outset.

And now came this monstrous tale to confirm her previous opinion. Impulsively Daisy decided that Olga must not be left in ignorance. Marriage was too great a speculation for any risk of that kind to be justifiable. She felt she owed it to the girl to warn her—to save her from a possible life-long misery. These things had such a ghastly knack of turning up afterwards. And Olga was so young, so trusting—

"Are you going to take my advice?" asked Hunt-Goring.

She looked up with a start. "What advice?"

"As to maintaining a discreet silence," he said.

His eyes were half-closed; she could not detect the narrowness of his scrutiny.

"No," she answered. "I shall certainly speak to Olga. It wouldn't be right—it wouldn't be fair—not to do so." Her look was suddenly appealing. "There is a free-masonry among women as well as men," she said. "We must keep faith with one another at least."

Hunt-Goring closed his eyes completely, and smiled a placid smile. "Dear Mrs. Musgrave," he said, "you are a true woman."

And she did not hear the note of exultation below the lazy appreciation of his words.

CHAPTER XV
THE SPREADING OF THE FLAME

Certainly Major Hunt-Goring was the last person Olga expected to meet at the Musgraves' dinner-party that night, and so astounded was she for the moment at the sight of him that she came to a sudden halt on the threshold of the drawing-room.

"Hullo!" murmured Max's voice behind her. "Here's a dear old friend!"

Max's hand gently pushed her forward, and in an instant she had mastered her astonishment. She met the dear old friend with heightened colour indeed, but with no other sign of agitation. He smiled upon her, upon Max, upon Nick, with equal geniality.

"Quite a gathering of old friends!" he remarked.

"Quite," said Nick. "Have you only just come out?"

"No, I've been out some weeks. I came after tiger," said Hunt-Goring, with his eyes on Olga, who had passed on to her host.

"You won't find any in this direction," said Nick. "Wyndham bagged the last survivor on Christmas Day, and a mangy old brute it was."

"I daresay I shall come across other game," said Hunt-Goring, bringing his eyes slowly back to Nick.

Nick laughed. "It's not particularly plentiful here. You'll find it a waste of time hunting in these parts."

"Oh, I have plenty of time at my disposal," smiled Hunt-Goring.

Nick's eyes flickered over him. He also was smiling. "Perseverance deserves to be rewarded," he said.

"And usually is," said Hunt-Goring. He held out his hand to Max. "Ah, Dr. Wyndham, I'm delighted to meet you again. You will be gratified to hear that, thanks to your skilful treatment, my thumb has mended quite satisfactorily."

Max looked at the hand critically; he did not offer to take it. "I am—greatly gratified," he said.

Hunt-Goring withdrew it, still smiling. "May I congratulate you on your engagement," he said.

Max's mouth went down ironically. "Certainly if you feel so disposed," he said.

Hunt-Goring laughed easily. "You young fellows have all the luck," he said. "When do you expect to be married?"

"On Midsummer Day," said Max.

"Really!" Hunt-Goring's laugh was silken in its softness. "Your plans are all cut and dried then. Yet, you know, 'there's many a slip,' etc."

"Not under my management," said Max.

He looked hard and straight into the other man's eyes, and turned aside.

Nick had already joined his hostess, and was making gay conversation about nothing in particular.

Noel came in late, acknowledged everyone with a deep salaam, and attached himself instantly to Olga.

With relief she found that he was to take her in to dinner. He was in a mood of charming inconsequence, and under his easy guidance she gradually recovered from the shock of her enemy's appearance on the scene.

"I hear on the best authority that General Bassett is expected in a fortnight," he told her. "We are going to treat him royally. You ladies will have to work hard."

"Max will be on his way Home by then," said Olga, with a sigh.

He laughed. "Well, I shall be left, and I shan't let you grizzle. We must organize a *fête* week. You and I will be the head of the committee. I'll come round to-morrow, and we'll draw up a plan to submit to old Badgers; merely a matter of form, you know. He'll consent to anything. We will have a fancy-dress ball for one thing, and a picnic or two, and some races and gymkhanas. Perhaps we might manage some private theatricals."

"Oh, we couldn't possibly!" protested Olga. "We could never get anything up in time."

But Noel was not to be discouraged. He proceeded to sketch out a lavish programme of entertainments with such energy and ingenuity that at length he managed to infuse her with some of his enthusiasm, and the end of dinner came upon her as a surprise.

Will, Hunt-Goring, Max, and Nick sat down to play bridge when it was finally over—at the suggestion of Hunt-Goring, who displayed not the smallest desire to seek her out. It seemed as though all memory of their former relations had passed completely from his mind. Neither by word nor look did he attempt to recall old times.

And gradually Olga became reassured. His fancy for her had quite obviously evaporated. He scarcely so much as glanced her way.

Could it have been mere coincidence that had brought him there? she began to ask herself. Stranger things had happened; and he was plainly on intimate terms with his hostess, rather more intimate than Daisy's manner seemed to justify. But then familiarity with women was one of his main characteristics, as she knew but too well. He had not been able to exercise this much at Weir. She suspected that boredom alone had induced him to pursue her so persistently.

In any case, it was over. He cared for her no more and was at no pains to conceal the fact, which she on her part recognized with profound relief.

She went with Daisy to the drawing-room, leaving the card-players established in Will's especial den. Noel airily accompanied them, and sang a few songs at the piano, as much for his own pleasure as theirs. He was in a particularly charming mood, and was evidently determined to enjoy himself to the utmost.

But he was not minded to give them too much of his society, and presently he slipped away to take a peep at Peggy.

"I shan't wake her," he said; but apparently he found his small adorer awake, for he did not return.

"He's a dear boy," said Daisy.

Olga assented warmly. "I shall love him for a brother."

Daisy smiled faintly. "Poor Noel! I'm afraid that is scarcely the sort of appreciation he wants."

Olga flushed. She was standing near the window, her girlish face outlined against the dark. Very young and slender she looked standing there, scarcely more than a child; and Daisy's heart went out to her in a sudden rush of almost passionate tenderness. She rose impulsively and joined her. She slipped a warm arm round her waist.

Olga glanced at her in momentary surprise, then swiftly responded to the caress. She leaned her cheek against Daisy's shoulder.

"You see," she said, "I met Max first."

"I see, dear," said Daisy. She hesitated a moment. "And Max is your ideal of all that a man should be?" she asked then.

"Oh, no!" said Olga. She gave a little laugh. "No; Nick is that, and always has been. I don't think anyone could idealize Max, do you?"

"But you love him?" said Daisy.

Olga looked at her with clear, direct eyes. "Oh, yes, I love him. But I don't try to think he is nicer than he really is. Nice or horrid, I love him just the same."

"Do you know any horrid things about him, then?" Daisy asked.

Olga laughed again. "I knew the horrid part of him first," she said. "Why, I—I almost hated him once."

"And then you changed your mind," said Daisy.

The love-light glowed softly in Olga's eyes as she answered, "Yes, dear Mrs. Musgrave; he made me."

Daisy uttered a sharp, involuntary sigh. "I hope he is all you believe him to be," she said.

"But why do you say that?" questioned Olga. "I'm afraid you don't like him."

Daisy hesitated. "I am afraid I know too much about him," she said at length.

Olga looked at her in surprise. "Has Noel been telling you things?"

Daisy shook her head.

"Oh, then it's that detestable Major Hunt-Goring!" said Olga, adding quickly: "Please forgive me for running down your guest; but he really is a hateful man."

"I don't care for him myself, dear," said Daisy.

"He has only come here to make mischief," said Olga, with conviction. "I guessed it the moment I saw him. He hates me because—because—" she faltered a little—"because I wouldn't marry him. As if I possibly could!" she ended fierily. "And as if he would have really liked it if I had!"

"Oh, is that it?" said Daisy, in a tone of enlightenment.

Olga nodded. "He's a beast, Mrs. Musgrave. And what has he been telling you about Max?"

Daisy hesitated. She was assailed by sudden misgiving. Was it all a ruse? She did not trust Major Hunt-Goring. She believed him fully capable of vindictiveness, and yet, so subtle had been his strategy, he had not seemed vindictive. He had repeated the story idly in the first place, and, finding she took it seriously, he had advised her to hold her peace. No, she would do him justice at least. She was convinced that he had not been deliberately malicious in this case. It had not been his intention to work evil.

"Tell me what he said!" said Olga.

Her tone was imperative; yet Daisy still hesitated. "Do you know, dear, I don't think I will," she said.

"Please—you must!" said Olga, with decision. "It concerns me as much as it does him."

"I am not sure that it really concerns either of you," Daisy said. "It was just a piece of gossip which may—or may not—have had any foundation."

"Still, tell me!" Olga insisted. "Forewarned is fore-armed, isn't it? And things do get so distorted sometimes, don't they?"

"Well, dear—" Daisy was beginning to wish herself well out of the matter—"it is not a pretty story. You and Nick may possibly have heard of it. Quite possibly you know it to be untrue. Major Hunt-Goring told me it was sheer gossip, and he would not vouch for the truth of it. It concerned the death of your friend Violet Campion."

"Ah!" said Olga. She breathed the word rather than uttered it. All the colour went out of her face. "Go on!" she whispered. "Go on!"

"You know the tale?" said Daisy.

"Tell me!" said Olga.

Reluctantly Daisy complied. "It was whispered that there had been an understanding between them, that the poor girl went mad with trouble, and that—to protect himself from scandal—he gave her a draught that ended her life."

Briefly, baldly, fell the words, spoken in an undertone, with evident unwillingness. They went out into silence, a silence that had in it something dreadful, something that no words could express.

It was many seconds before Daisy ventured a look at the girl's face, though her arm was still about her. When she did, she was shocked. For Olga was gazing straight before her with eyes wide and glassy—the eyes of the sleep-walker who stares upon visions of horror which no others see.

As Daisy moved, she moved also, went to the window, stepped straight out into the night. Dumbly Daisy watched her. She had obeyed her instinct in speaking, but now she knew not what to say or do.

Slowly at length Olga turned. She came back into the room. The glassy look had gone out of her eyes. She appeared quite normal. She went to Daisy, and laid gentle hands upon her shoulders.

"You did quite right to tell me," she said. "It is something that I certainly ought to know."

Her face was deathly, but she smiled bravely into Daisy's troubled eyes.

"My dear, my dear," Daisy said in distress, "I do pray that I haven't done wrong."

"You haven't," Olga said. "It was dear of you to tell me, and I'm very grateful."

She kissed Daisy very lovingly and let her go. There was nothing tragic in her manner, only an unwonted aloofness that kept the elder woman from attempting to pursue the subject.

The return of Noel a few minutes later was a relief to them both. He came in full of animation and merriment, precipitating himself upon them with a gaiety that overlooked all silences. As Daisy was wont to say, Noel was the most useful person she knew for filling in tiresome gaps. He did it instinctively, without so much as seeing them.

In his cheery company the rest of the evening slid lightly by. Olga encouraged him to be frivolous. She seemed to enjoy his society more than she had ever done before; and Noel was nothing loth to be encouraged.

When the card-players joined them, they were busily engaged in drawing up a programme for what Noel termed "the Bassett week," and so absorbed were they that they did not so much as glance up till Nick came between them and demanded to know what it was all about.

Max, cynically tolerant, looked on from afar; and Daisy, who had been feeling somewhat conscience-stricken at his entrance, rapidly found herself detesting him more heartily than ever. She was glad when Major Hunt-Goring drifted to her side and engaged her in conversation, and she more nearly resumed her old intimacy with him in consequence than she had done before.

The party broke up late, as Olga, Noel, and Nick continued their discussion until their elaborate schemes were complete. By that time Max and his host had retired for a final smoke, and had to be unearthed by Nick, who declared himself scandalized to find anyone still up at such an immoral hour.

Olga was standing with Noel, dressed for departure, waiting to go, when Hunt-Goring sauntered up to her.

"Well, Miss Ratcliffe," he said conversationally, "and how do you like India?"

It was the first time he had deliberately accosted her. She glanced up at him sharply, and made a slight, instinctive movement away from him. At once, albeit almost imperceptibly, Noel moved a little nearer to her. She was conscious of his intention to protect, and threw him a brief smile as she made reply.

"I am enjoying it very much."

"Really!" said Hunt-Goring. "And you are engaged to be married, I hear?"

Olga did not instantly reply. It was Noel who answered shortly: "Yes, to my brother. No objection, I suppose?"

It was aggressively spoken. Noel had quite obviously taken a dislike to the newcomer, a sentiment which Olga knew to be instantly reciprocated by the calm fashion in which Hunt-Goring ignored his intervention.

She found him waiting markedly for her reply, and braced herself to enter the arena. "Is it news to you?" she asked coldly.

He laughed his soft, hateful laugh. "Well, scarcely, since you, yourself, informed me of the approaching event some months before it took place."

Noel made a slight gesture of surprise, and the colour rose in a hot wave to Olga's face; but she looked steadily at Hunt-Goring and said nothing.

He went on, smoothly satirical. "I used to think the odds were in favour of Miss Campion, you know. You will pardon me for saying that I don't think there are many girls who could have cut her out."

Olga's face froze to a marble immobility. "There was no question of that," she said.

"No?" Hunt-Goring's urbanity scarcely covered his incredulity. "I fancied she took the opposite view. Well, well, the poor girl is dead and out of the running. I consider Max Wyndham is a very lucky man."

He spoke with significance and Noel's eyes, jealously watching Olga's face, saw her flinch ever so slightly. A hot wave of anger rose within him; his hands clenched. He turned upon Hunt-Goring.

"If you have anything offensive to say," he said, in a furious undertone, "say it to me, you damned coward!"

Hunt-Goring looked at him at last. "I beg your pardon?" he said.

Noel was on the verge of repeating his remark when, quick as a flash, Olga turned and caught his arm.

"Noel, please, please!" she gasped breathlessly. "Not here! Not now!"

He attempted to resist her, but she would not be resisted. With all her strength she pulled him away, her hands tightly clasped upon his arm. And it was thus that they came face to face with Max, sauntering in ahead of his host.

He glanced at them both, but showed no surprise, though both Olga's agitation and Noel's anger were very apparent.

"Look here, you two," he said, "Nick and I can't be kept waiting any longer. We value our beauty-sleep if you don't. And Mr. Musgrave is longing to see the last of us."

"Not at all," said Will courteously. "But Nick has suddenly developed a violent hurry to be gone. My wife is trying to pacify him, but she won't hold him in for long."

"Let us go!" said Olga. She took her hand from Noel's arm, but looked at him appealingly.

"All right," he said gruffly. "I suppose I had better go too."

"High time, I should say," observed his brother. "Good-night!"

Noel did not look at him or respond. He turned aside without a word, and left the room.

Max made no further comment of any sort, but Olga was aware of his green eyes studying her closely. Like Noel she avoided them. She shook hands hurriedly with Will, and went out to Nick and Daisy.

As Max turned to follow her, she heard Hunt-Goring's smiling voice behind him. "Good-bye, Dr. Wyndham! Delighted to have met you again—you and your *fiancée*. I have just been congratulating Miss Olga on her conquest."

Max went out as though the sneering words had not reached him, but his face was so grim when he said good-bye to Daisy that she felt almost too guilty to look at him. She held Olga to her very closely at the last, and saw her go with a passionate regret. Whether she had acted rightly or wrongly she did not know; but she felt that she had wrecked the girl's happiness, and the spontaneity of Olga's answering embrace did not reassure her.

CHAPTER XVI
THE GAP

"Now, my chicken, to roost!" said Nick.

He turned to give her his paternal embrace, but paused as Olga very slightly drew back from it.

They stood in the dining-room which they had entered on arrival. Max had lounged across to the mantelpiece, and propped himself against it in his favourite attitude. He looked on as it were from afar.

"Please," Olga said rather breathlessly, and she addressed Nick as though he were the only person in the room, "I want to ask you something before we say good-night."

"Something private?" asked Nick.

She put her hand to her throat; her face was ghastly. Her voice came with visible effort. "It concerns—Max," she said.

Max neither moved nor spoke. He was looking very fixedly at Olga. There was something merciless in his attitude.

Nick flashed a swift glance at him, and slipped his arm round the girl. She was quivering with agitation, yet she made as if she would free herself.

"Please, Nick!" she said imploringly. "I want to be strong. Help me to be strong!"

"All right, dear," he said gently. "You can count on me. What's the trouble? Hunt-Goring again?"

She shivered at the name. "No—no! At least—not alone. He hasn't worried me."

She became silent, painfully, desperately silent, while she fought for self-control.

Again Nick glanced across at Max. "Pour out a glass of wine!" he said briefly.

Max stood up. He went to the table, and very deliberately mixed a little brandy and water. His face, as he did it, was absolutely composed. He might have been thinking of something totally removed from the matter in hand.

Yet, as he turned round, the air of grimness was perceptible again. He held out the glass to Nick. "I think I'll go," he said.

"No!" It was Olga who spoke. She stretched out a detaining hand. "I want you—please—to stay. I—I—"

She faltered and stopped as Max's hand closed quietly and strongly upon hers.

"Very well," he said. "I'll stay. But drink this like a sensible girl! You're cold."

She obeyed him, leaning upon Nick's shoulder, and gradually the deadly pallor of her face passed. She drew her hand out of Max's grasp, and relinquished Nick's support.

"I'm dreadfully sorry," she said, and her voice came dull and oddly indifferent. "You are both so good to me. But I think one generally has to face the worst things in life by oneself. Nick, I asked you a little while ago to fill in a gap in my memory—to tell me something I had forgotten. Do you remember?"

"I do," said Nick. Like Max, he was watching her closely, but his eyes moved unceasingly; they glimmered behind his colourless lashes with a weird fitfulness.

Olga was looking straight at him. She had never stood in awe of Nick.

"You didn't do it," she said in the same level, tired voice. "You put me off. You refused to fill in the gap."

"Well?" said Nick. His tone was abrupt; for the first time in all her knowledge of him it sounded stern.

But Olga remained unmoved. "Would you refuse if I asked you to do it now?" she said.

"Perhaps," he answered.

She turned from him to Max. "You would refuse too?" she said, and this time there was a tremor of bitterness in her voice. "You always have refused."

"It happens to be my rule never to discuss my cases with anyone outside my profession," he said.

"And that was your only reason?" A sudden pale gleam shot up in Olga's eyes; she stiffened a little as though an electric current ran through her as she faced him.

"It is the only one I have to offer you," Max said.

He also sounded stern; and in a flash she grasped her position. They were ranged against her—the two she loved best in the world—leagued together to keep from her the truth. A quiver of indignation went through her. She turned abruptly from them both.

"You needn't take this trouble any longer," she said. "I—know!"

"What do you know?" It was Max's voice, curt and imperative.

He took a step forward; his hand was on her shoulder. But she wheeled and flung it from her with an exclamation that was almost a cry of horror.

"Don't touch me!" she said.

He stood confronting her, hard, pitiless, insistent. Of her gesture he took no notice whatever. "What do you know?" he repeated.

She answered him with breathless rapidity, as if compelled. "I know that you made her love you—that when you knew the truth about her you gave her up. I know that you ruined her first—and deserted her afterwards for me. I know that you terrified her into secrecy, and then, when—when her brain gave way and there was no way of escape for you—I know that you—that you—that you—"

Her lips stiffened. She could not say the word. For several seconds she strove with it inarticulately; then suddenly, wildly, she flung out her hands, urging him from her.

"Oh, go! Go! Go!" she cried. "Let me never see you again!"

He did not go. He stood absolutely still, watching her.

But she was scarcely aware of him any longer. For her strength had suddenly deserted her. She was sunk against the wall with her hands over her face, sobbing terrible, tearless sobs that shook her from head to foot.

Nick started towards her, but Max stretched out a powerful arm, and kept him back. "No, Nick," he said firmly. "This is my concern. You go, like a good chap. I'll come to you presently."

"I will not!" said Nick flatly.

He gripped the opposing arm at the elbow so that it doubled abruptly. But Max wheeled upon him on the instant and held him fast.

"Look here," he said, "I'm in earnest."

"So am I," said Nick.

They faced one another for a moment in open conflict; then half-contemptuously Max made an appeal.

"Don't let us be fools!" he said. "It's for her sake I want you to go. I'll tell you why later. If you butt in now, you will make the biggest mistake of your life."

"Take your hands off me!" said Nick.

He complied. Nick went straight to Olga. "Olga," he said, "for Heaven's sake, be reasonable! Give him a chance to set things straight!"

It was urgently spoken. His hand, vital and very insistent, closed upon one of hers, drawing it down from her face.

She looked at him with hunted eyes. "Nick," she said, "tell him—to go!"

"I can't, dear," he made answer. "You've made an accusation that no man could take lying down. You'll have to face it out now."

"But it's the truth!" she said.

"It's a damnable lie!" said Nick.

"Nick," it was Max's voice measured and deliberate, "will you leave me to deal with this?"

Olga's hand turned in Nick's and clung to it. "You needn't go, Nick," she said hurriedly.

"Yes, I'm going," said Nick. "You can come to me afterwards if you like. I shall be in my room."

He squeezed her hand and relinquished it. His yellow face was full of kindness, but she saw that he would not be persuaded to remain. In silence she watched him go.

Then slowly, reluctantly, she turned to Max. He was standing watching her with fixed, implacable eyes.

"Well?" he said, as she looked at him. "Do you really want me to deny this preposterous story?"

She leaned against the wall, facing him. She felt unutterably tired—as if she were too weary to take any further interest in anything. Neither his denial nor Nick's could make the tale untrue.

"It doesn't make much difference," she said drearily.

"Thanks!" said Max shortly.

And then, as if suddenly making up his mind, he came to her and took her almost roughly by the shoulders.

"Olga," he said, "how dare you believe this thing of me?"

She looked at him and her face quivered. "You have never told me the truth," she said.

"And so you are ready to believe any calumny," said Max. His hands pressed upon her; his red brows were drawn together.

At any other moment she would have deemed him formidable, but she was beyond fear just then.

"If you would only tell me what to believe—" she said.

"And if I won't?" He broke in upon her almost fiercely. "If I demand your trust on this point—as I have a right to demand it on every point—what then? Are you going to give me everything except that?"

She shook her head. "No, Max."

"What do you mean?" he demanded.

She answered him steadily enough. "I mean that unless you can tell me the truth—the truth, Max," there was a piteous touch in her repetition of the words—"I can never give you—anything."

"Meaning you won't marry me?" he said.

Steadily she answered him. "Yes, I mean just that."

He continued to hold her before him. His face grew harder, grimmer than before. "And you think I will suffer myself to be thrown over?" he said.

That pierced her lethargy, quickened her to resistance. "I think you have no choice," she said.

Max's jaw set itself like an iron clamp. "There you show your absolute ignorance," he said, "of me—and of yourself."

"You couldn't hold me against my will," she said quickly.

"Could I not?" said Max.

Something of fear crept about her heart, hastening its beat. But she faced him unflinching. "No," she said.

He was silent; but she had an inexplicable feeling that the green eyes were drawing her gradually, mercilessly, against her will. Yet she resisted them, summoning all her strength.

And then she became aware that his hold had tightened and grown close. She awoke to the fact very suddenly, as one coming out of a trance, and swiftly, nervously, she sought to free herself.

Instantly his arms were about her. He gathered her to him with a force that compelled. He crushed her lips with his own in kisses so fierce and so passionate that she winced from them in actual pain, not sparing her till she sank in his arms, spent, unresisting, crying against his shoulder.

He made no attempt to comfort her; his hold was sustaining, but grimly devoid of all tenderness. Later she knew that he had fought a desperate battle for her happiness and his own, and it was no moment for relaxation.

He spoke to her at last, curtly, over her bowed head, "And you think—you dare to think—that I have ever loved another woman."

"I don't know what to think," she whispered, hiding her face lower on his breast.

"Then think this," he said, and there was a ring of iron in his voice, "that for no slander whatever will I hold myself answerable, either to you or to anyone else. I shall not defend myself from it. I shall not deny it. And because of it I will not suffer myself to be jilted. Is that enough?"

He spoke with indomitable resolution, but there must have been some yielding quality in the last words, for she suddenly found strength to lift her head again and turn her face up to his.

"Max," she said imploringly, "I believe I have wronged you, and I do beg you to forgive me.—But, Max, there is one thing that—for my peace of mind—you must tell me. Please, Max, please!"

She set her clasped hands against him, beseeching him with her whole soul. He looked down into her eyes, and his own were no longer stern but quite impenetrable. He spoke no word.

"I have always known," she said, faltering a little under his look, "always felt that there was something—something strange about—Violet's sudden death. Max, tell me—tell me—she didn't—make away with herself?"

She uttered the question with a shrinking dread that seemed to run shuddering through her whole body. And because he did not instantly reply, her face whitened with a sick suspense.

"Oh, she didn't!" she gasped imploringly. "Say she didn't! I—I think it would break my heart if—if—if—that—had happened."

"You must remember that she was not responsible for her actions," Max said.

Olga was trembling all over. "Then she did?"

He avoided the question. "Her life was over," he said, "in any case."

"Then she did?" Again sharply she put the question, as though goaded thereto by an intolerable pain. "Max," she said, "oh, Max, I could bear anything better than that! I don't believe it of her! I can't believe it!"

"But why torture yourself in this way?" he said. "What do you gain by it?"

"Because I must, I must!" she answered feverishly. "I dream about her night after night—night after night. My mind is never at rest about her. She seems to be calling to me, trying to tell me something. And I never can get to her or hear what it is. It's all because I can't remember. And sometimes I feel as if I shall go mad myself with trying."

"Olga!" Briefly and sternly he checked her. "You are getting hysterical. Don't you think there has been enough of this? If you go any further, you will regret it."

"But I must know!" she said. "Max, was it so? Did she take her own life?"

"She did not!"

Quietly he answered her, so quietly that for a moment she could hardly believe that he had given a definite reply. She stared at him incredulously.

"You are telling me the truth?" she said piteously at length. "You won't try to deceive me any more?"

"I have told you the truth," he said.

"Then—then—" She still gazed at him with wide eyes, eyes in which a certain horror gradually dawned and spread. "I am sure she did not die a natural death," she said with conviction.

Max was silent, grimly, inexorably silent.

She disengaged herself slowly from him. Her forehead drew itself into the old painful lines. She passed an uncertain hand across it.

As if in answer to the gesture he spoke, bluntly, almost brutally. "If you will have it, you shall; but remember, it is final. Miss Campion was suffering from a hideous and absolutely incurable disease of the brain which had developed into homicidal madness. She might have lived for years—a blinded soul fettered to a brain of raving insanity. What her life would have been, only those who have seen can picture. But, mercifully for her—rightly or wrongly is not for me to say—her torment was brought to an early end. In fact, almost before it had begun, a friend gave her deliverance. She died—as you know—suddenly."

"Ah!" With a cry she broke in upon him. "It was—the pain-killer!"

"It was." He scarcely opened his lips to reply, and instantly closed them in a single unyielding line. His eyes never left her face.

As for Olga, she stood a moment, as one stunned past all feeling; then turned from him and moved away. "So it was—your doing," she said, in a curious, stifled voice as if she were scarcely conscious of speaking at all.

He did not answer her. The words scarcely demanded an answer.

She reached the table unsteadily, and sat down, leaning her elbow upon it, her chin on her hand. Her eyes gazed right away down far vistas unbounded by time or space.

"It isn't the first time, is it?" she said. "You did it once before. I suppose—" her voice dropped still lower; she seemed to be speaking to herself—"as a Keeper of the Door, you think you have the right."

"Will you tell me what you mean?" he said.

She did not turn her head. She still gazed upon invisible things. "Do you remember poor old Mrs. Stubbs? You helped her, didn't you, in the same way?"

"I?" said Max.

The utter astonishment of his voice reached her. She turned and looked at him. "She died in the same way," she said.

"But—great heavens above—not with my connivance!" he exclaimed.

She continued to look at him, but with that same far look, as though she saw many things besides. "Yet—you knew!" she said.

He made a curt gesture of repudiation. "I suspected—perhaps. I actually knew—nothing."

"I see," she said, with a faint smile. "She just slipped through—and you looked the other way."

"Nothing of the sort!" he said sternly. "I did my utmost—as I have always done my utmost—to prolong life. It is my duty—the first principle of my profession; and I hold it—I always have held it—as sacred."

"And yet—you let Violet's go," she said.

He swung round almost violently and turned his back. "I will not discuss that point any further," he said.

She looked at him with an odd dispassionateness. She still seemed to be searching the distant past. "You never liked her," she said at last slowly. "And she was horribly afraid of you—afraid of you!" A sudden tremor of awakening life ran through the words. The stunned look began to pass. Again the horror looked out of her eyes. "She was so afraid of you that—when she went mad—she tried to kill you. Ah, I see now!" She caught her breath sharply—"You—you were afraid too!"

He remained with his back turned upon her, motionless as a statue.

"And so—and so—" Her eyes came swiftly back to the present and saw him only. The horror in them had become vivid, anguished. She rose and stretched an accusing finger towards him. "That was why you ended her life!" she said. "It was—to save—your own!"

He wheeled round at that and faced her with that in his eyes which she had never before seen there—a look that sent the blood to her heart. "By Heaven, Olga," he said, "you go—rather far!"

He came towards her slowly. There was something terrible about him at that moment, something that held her fettered and dumb before him, though—so great was her horror—she would have given all she had to turn and flee.

He halted before her, looking down into her face with a curious intentness. "You really believe that?" he said. "You can't conceive such a thing as this—utterly and inexcusably wrong as I admit it to be—you can't conceive it to have been done from a motive of mercy?"

She shrank away from him as from a thing unclean. The impulse to escape was still strong upon her, urging her to a wild resistance. She met the pitiless eyes that watched her like a creature at bay. "You never did anything in mercy yet!" she said. "There is no mercy in you!"

"Indeed!" he said, and uttered a brief, grating laugh that made her shudder. "In that case, I'm afraid I can't help you any further. I'm at the end of my resources."

Olga drew herself together with a supreme effort, mustering all her strength. "It is the end of everything," she said. "I can never marry you now. I never want to see you again."

He met her look implacably, with eyes that seemed to beat down her own. "I have told you that I won't submit to that," he said.

She caught her breath with a convulsive movement of protest. Perhaps never before had she so clearly realized the ruthlessness of the man and his strength.

"I can't help it," she said. "I can never marry you. Even if—if we had been married, I could not have stayed with you—after this."

She saw his mouth harden to cruelty at her words, and instinctively she drew back from him; but in the same instant his hands closed upon her wrists and she was a captive.

"Doesn't it occur to you," he said, "that you are bound to me in honour—unless I set you free?"

He spoke with the utmost calmness, but her heart misgave her. She saw herself at his mercy, an impotent prisoner striving against him, vainly beating out her will against the iron of his. In that moment she realized fully that not by strength could she prevail, and desperately she began to plead.

"But you will set me free, Max! You wouldn't—you couldn't—hold me against my will!"

"Couldn't I?" said Max, and grimly smiled. "There is nothing whatever that I couldn't do with you, Olga,—with—or without—your will."

She shivered sharply and uncontrollably, not attempting to contradict him.

"And that being so," he said, "it is not my intention to set you free. There is no earthly reason why you should not marry me, and therefore I hold you to your engagement. That is quite understood, is it?"

His hold tightened upon her. She saw that he meant every word, and her heart died within her. Her strength was running out swiftly, swiftly. Very soon it would be utterly gone. She cast a desperate glance upwards, and made one last supreme effort. "But, Max," she pleaded, "I thought you loved me."

His face was set in iron lines, but she thought it softened ever so slightly at her words. Had she pierced the one vulnerable point in his armour at last? She wondered, scarcely daring to hope.

"Well?" he said.

Only the one word; but somehow, inexplicably, her heart cried shame upon her, as though she had put a good weapon to an unworthy use. She stood before him, trying vainly to drive it home. But she could not. Further words failed her.

"I see," he said at last. "You think out of my love for you I ought to be willing to give you up. Is that it?"

She nodded mutely, not daring to look at him, still overwhelmed with that shamed sense of doing him a wrong.

"I see," he said again. "And—if it would be for your happiness to let you go—I might perhaps be equal to the sacrifice." His voice was suddenly cynical, and she never guessed that he cloaked an unwanted emotion therewith. "But take the other view of the case. You know you would never be happy away from me."

"I couldn't be happy with you—now," she murmured.

He bent slightly towards her as if not sure that he had heard aright. "Do you really mean that?" he asked.

She was silent.

"Olga!" he said insistently.

Against her will she raised her eyes, and met his close scrutiny. Against her will she answered him, breathlessly, out of a fevered sense of expediency. "Yes—yes, I do mean it! Oh, Max, you must—you must let me go!"

But he held her still. "You have appealed to my love," he said. "I appeal to yours."

But that was more than she could bear; the sudden tension snapped the last shreds of her quivering strength. She broke down utterly, standing there between his hands.

He made no attempt to draw her to him. Perhaps he did not wholly trust himself. Neither did he let her go; but there was no element of cruelty about him any longer. In silence, with absolute patience, he waited for her.

She made a slight effort at last to free herself, and instantly he set her free. She sat down again at the table, striving desperately for self-control. But she could not even begin to speak to him, so choked and blinded was she by her tears.

A while longer he waited beside her; then at length he spoke. "If you really honestly feel that you can't marry me, that to do so would make for misery and not happiness; if in short your love for me is dead—I will let you go."

The words fell curt and stern, but if she had seen his face at the moment she would have realized something of what the utterance of them cost.

But her own face was hidden, her paroxysm of weeping yet shook her uncontrollably.

"Is it dead?" he said, and stooped over her, holding the back of her chair but not touching her.

She made a convulsive movement, whether of flinching from his close proximity or protest at his words it was impossible to say.

He waited a moment or two. Then: "If it isn't," he said, "just put your hand in mine!"

He laid his own upon the table before her, upturned, ready to clasp hers. His face was bent so low over her that his lips were almost on her hair. She could have yielded herself to his arms without effort.

But she only stiffened at his action, and became intensely still. In the seconds that followed she did not so much as breathe. She was as one turned to stone.

For the space of a full minute he waited; and through it the wild beating of her heart rose up in the stillness, throbbing audibly. But still she sat before him mutely, making no sign.

Then, after what seemed to her an eternity of waiting, very quietly he straightened himself and took his hand away.

She shrank away involuntarily with a nervous contraction of her whole body. For that moment she was unspeakably afraid.

But he gave her no cause for fear. He bore himself with absolute self-possession.

"Very well," he said. "That ends it. You are free."

With the words he turned deliberately from her, walked to the door, passed quietly out. And she was left alone.

CHAPTER XVII
THE EASIEST COURSE

"I won't be a party to it," said Nick.

"You can't help yourself."

Bluntly Max made reply. He lounged against the window while his host dressed. The presence of the stately *khitmutgar* who was assisting Nick was ignored by them both.

"I can generally manage to help myself," observed Nick.

Max's mouth took its most cynical downward curve. "You see, old chap, this chances to be one of the occasions on which you can't. It's my funeral, not yours."

Nick sent a brief glance across. "You're a fool, Max," he said.

"Thanks!" said Max. He took his pipe from his pocket and commenced to fill it with extreme care. There was something grimly ironical about his whole bearing. He did not speak again till his task was completed and the pipe alight. Then very deliberately through a cloud of rank smoke, he took up his tale. "It is one of the most interesting cases that have ever come under my notice. I am only sorry that I shall not be able to continue to keep it under my own personal supervision."

Nick laughed, a crude, cracked laugh. "It seems a pity certainly, since you came to India for that express purpose. I suppose you think it's up to me to continue the treatment?"

"Exactly," said Max.

"Well, I'm not going to." Again Nick's eyes flashed a keen look at Max's imperturbable countenance. "I held my peace last night," he said, "because matters were too ticklish to be tampered with. But as to keeping it up——"

Max thrust his hands deep into his pockets. "As to keeping it up," he said, "you've no choice; neither have I. It may be a matter for regret from some points of view, but a matter of the most urgent expediency it undoubtedly is. I tell you plainly, Nick, this is not a thing to be played with. There are some risks that no one has any right to take. This is one."

He looked at Nick, square-jawed and determined; but Nick vigorously shook his head.

"I am not with you. I don't agree. I never shall agree."

Max's cynical smile became more pronounced. "Then you will have to act against your judgment for once. There is no alternative. And I shall go Home by the first boat I can catch."

"And leave her to fret her heart out," said Nick.

Max removed his pipe, and attentively regarded the bowl. After nearly a minute he put it back again and stared impenetrably at Nick. "She won't do that," he said.

"I'll tell you what she will do," said Nick. "She will go and marry that wild Irish brother of yours."

Max continued to look at him. His mouth was no longer cynical, but cocked at a humorous angle. "I say, what a clever little chap you are!" he said. "Whatever made you think of that?"

Nick grinned in spite of himself. Disagree as he might with Max Wyndham, yet was he always in some subtle fashion in sympathy with him.

"I suppose she might do worse," he admitted after a moment. "He's a well-behaved youngster as a general rule."

"Given his own way, quite irreproachable," said Max "He's not very rich, but he's no slacker. If he doesn't break his neck at polo, he'll get on."

"Oh, he's brilliant enough," said Nick. "I suppose he can be trusted to look after her. He's full young."

"He'll grow," said Max.

A brief silence fell between them. Max continued to smoke imperturbably. There was not the faintest sign of disappointment in his bearing. He looked merely ruminative.

Nick was thoughtful also. He sat and watched his man fasten his gaiters with those flickering eyes of his that never seemed to concentrate upon one point and yet missed nothing.

"What are you going to do about Hunt-Goring?" he asked suddenly.

"Do about him?" Max sounded supremely contemptuous. He raised one eyebrow in supercilious interrogation.

"Well, he dealt this hand," said Nick.

"With Mrs. Musgrave's kind assistance," supplemented Max.

Nick made a grimace. "Who told you that?"

"No one." Max blew a cloud of smoke upwards. "You're not the only person with brains, Nick," he observed, with sardonic humour. "But look here! Your friend Mrs. Musgrave is not to be meddled with in this matter. You leave her alone and Hunt-Goring too! He's killing himself by inches with opium, so he won't interfere with anyone for long. And she will prove a useful friend to Noel if allowed to take her own way."

"You really mean to take this lying down?" said Nick.

"It's the easiest course," said Max.

"So far as you are concerned?" Nick abruptly turned in his chair; but his scrutiny was of the briefest. He did not seem to look at Max at all; nor did he apparently expect an answer to his query, for he went on almost immediately. "It's damnable luck for both of you. Old man, are you sure it's all right?"

There was no subtlety in the question. Nick had long since abandoned subtlety in his dealings with Max Wyndham, a fact which indicated that he held him in very high esteem.

Max's response expressed appreciation of the fact. He took his hand from his pocket and carelessly stretched it out. "I am absolutely sure," he said. "Make your mind easy on that point!"

Their hand-grip was silent and brief. It ended the discussion by mutual consent.

At once Max changed the subject. "Is that chap your *khit* or your valet or what?"

"He is all three combined," said Nick. "Why? Think I work him too hard?"

The Indian showed his teeth in a splendid smile, but said nothing.

"No, but where's the other fellow?" said Max.

"What other fellow?" Nick thrust his one arm with vigour into his riding-coat.

"The chap I saw here the other night—an old chap. I came along the verandah to tell you there was someone sneaking in the compound, and he shut the window in my face. I presumed he was head-nurse or bearer, or whatever you are pleased to call them in these parts."

"Oh, that fellow!" said Nick. "Quite a venerable old chap, you mean? Rather scraggy—not over-clean?"

"That's the man," said Max.

Nick laughed. "Great Scott! You didn't seriously, think he was my bearer, did you? No, he's an old moonstone-seller who comes to see me occasionally. He's not so disreputable as he looks. I find him handy in the matter of bazaar politics, with which I consider it useful to keep in touch."

Max received the information with a nod. His green eyes were watching Nick's lithe movements with thoughtful intentness.

"How long is this job going to last?" he asked abruptly.

"Heaven knows," was Nick's airy response.

Max was silent a moment; then: "You will send her away if it gets too hot?" he said.

Nick took up his riding-switch. "It's a tricky climate," he observed, "but I am keeping an eye on the weather. I don't anticipate anything of the nature of a heat-wave at present."

Max grunted. "Are you sure your barometer is a trustworthy one?"

Nick smiled. "I have every reason to believe so." He turned and clapped a kindly hand on Max's shoulder. "All right, old chap. Don't be anxious! I'll take care of her," he said.

Max looked at him. "You had better take care of yourself too," he said.

"Trust me!" laughed Nick.

There came a knock at the door, to which Kasur responded. It was Olga's *ayah*. A few whispered words passed between them, then the *khitmutgar* softly closed it and approached Nick.

"Miss *sahib* is tired this morning, and cannot ride with the *sahibs*. She asks that you will go to her, *sahib*, before you leave."

Nick glanced at Max. "You had better come too."

But Max shook his head. "No. I'll be on the verandah if she wants me, but I don't think she will."

Nick went to the door in silence; but ere he reached it Max spoke again.

"Nick!"

"Well?" Nick paused as if reluctant.

Very deliberately Max followed him. They stood face to face. "You will remember what I have said," Max said, with slow emphasis.

"I'm not very likely to forget it," said Nick.

"And you will abstain from interference in this matter?" Max's voice was emotionless, but it had a certain quality of compulsion notwithstanding.

Nick's eyes darted over him. His whole frame stiffened slightly. "If you think I am going to bind myself hand and foot by a promise, you're mistaken," he said.

"I am only asking you to let matters take their course," said Max, unmoved.

"Circumstances may make that impossible," said Nick.

"They may. In that case, you are free to act as you think fit. But I don't think they will—and—damn it, Nick, it isn't much to ask. It's for her sake."

A tinge of feeling suddenly underran his speech. He flushed slowly and deeply; but he stood his ground.

As for Nick, he turned again to the door with his switch tucked under his arm. "All right," he said. "I accept the amendment."

He was gone with the words, almost as though he feared he had already yielded too far. Probably to no other man would he have yielded a single inch.

The interview had ended in a fashion extremely distasteful to him, yet he entered Olga's presence cheerily, with no sign of discontent.

"Hullo, my chicken! Not riding this morning? Haven't you slept?"

He sat down on the bed with Olga's arms very tightly round his neck, and prepared himself to make the best of a very bad business.

The night before he had soothed her in the midst of her distress with all a mother's tenderness, but by daylight he discarded the maternal *rôle* and resumed his masculine limitations.

"Come!" he said coaxingly to the fair head pillowed against his shoulder. "You're going to be a sensible kiddie now? You're going to forget all yesterday's nonsense? Max won't say any more if you don't. You've just got to kiss and be friends."

Olga little dreamed that thus cheerily he made his last stand for a hope which he knew to be forlorn.

She raised her head and looked at him with eyes that shone with the brilliance which follows the shedding of many tears. "It's no good ever thinking of that, Nick," she said, speaking quickly and nervously. "I've been awake all night, thinking—thinking. But there's no way out. I can't marry him. I can't even see him again. And, Nick,—I want you, please, to give him back his ring."

"My dear, you're not in earnest!" said Nick.

"Yes, yes, I am, dear. And I can't argue about it. My head whirls so. Oh, Nick, why didn't you tell me when I asked you to fill in the gap? It's such a mistaken kindness—if you only knew it—to keep back the truth—whatever it may be."

Nick groaned melancholy acquiescence. "But can't you forgive him, sweetheart? Most women can forgive anything. And you never used to be vindictive."

"I'm not vindictive," she made swift reply. "It isn't that I want to punish him. Oh, don't you understand? He may have acted up to his lights. And even if—if he had been anything but a doctor, I think it would have been a little different. But he—he knew so exactly what he was doing. And oh, Nick, I couldn't possibly marry a man who had done—that. I should never forget it. It would prey on me so, just as if—as if—I had been a party to it!" A violent shiver went through her. She clung closer to him. The horror had frozen in her eyes to a wide and glassy terror.

"Easy, easy!" said Nick gently. "We won't get hysterical. But isn't it a pity to do anything in a hurry? You won't feel so badly in a week or a fortnight. Don't do anything final yet! Put him off for a bit. He'll understand."

But Olga would not listen to this suggestion. "I must be free, Nick!" she said feverishly. "I can't be bound to him any longer. Oh, Nick, do help me to get free!"

"My dear child, you are free," Nick assured her. "But take my advice; don't shake him off completely. Give him just a chance, poor chap! Wait six months before you quite make up your mind to have done with him. You'll be sure to want him back if you don't."

But still Olga would not listen. "Oh, Nick, please stop!" she implored him. "I've been through it all a hundred times already, and indeed I know my own mind. If it were to drag on over six months, I don't think I could possibly bear it. No, no! It must be final now. Nick—dear, don't you understand?"

He nodded. "Yes, I do understand, Olga *mia*; but I think you are making a big mistake. The horror of the thing has blinded you temporarily. You are incapable of forming a clear judgment at present. By and by you will begin to see better. That's why I want you to wait."

"But I can't wait," she said. "It—it is like a dreadful wound, Nick. I want to bind it up quick—quick, before it gets any worse,—to hide it,—to try and forget it's there. I can't—I daren't—keep it open. I think it would kill me."

There was actual agony in her voice, and Nick saw that he had made his last stand in vain. Yet not instantly did he abandon it. Once more he thrust past her defences, though she sought so desperately to keep him out.

"It's not for us to judge each other, is it?" he said. "Be merciful, Olga! Don't you think there may have been—extenuating circumstances?"

She looked at him with quivering lips, and dumbly shook her head.

"Listen!" he said. "When Muriel and I were flying from Wara, I killed a man with my hands under her eyes. It was a ghastly business. I did it to save her life and my own. But—like you—she didn't look at the motive—only at the deed. And in consequence I became a thing abhorrent in her sight. She didn't get over it for a long time. But she forgave me at last. Can't you be equally generous? Or don't you love him well enough?"

Olga's hands clasped one another very tightly. She answered him under her breath. "I expect that's it, Nick, I don't love him any more at all. It has killed my love."

"Then you never loved him," said Nick with conviction.

She made no attempt to contradict him. Only her strained white face seemed to implore him to torture her no further. He saw it, and his heart smote him.

"I hate to hurt you, my chicken," he said. "But, dear, you're making such a hideous muddle of your life. I hate that even worse."

She flung her arms about his neck; she pressed her lips to his yellow face. "Darling Nick, never mind about me, never mind!" she whispered. "I am doing simply what I must do. I can scarcely think or feel yet. Only I know that I must get free. It isn't that I'm hard. It's just that I have no choice. Your case was different. You had to do it. But this—" her words sank, became scarcely audible—"Nick, could anything extenuate—this?"

"God knows," said Nick. He paused a moment, then added: "I sometimes think, if the whole truth were known, there would be an extenuating circumstance for every mortal offence under the sun."

She did not argue the point. She seemed beyond argument. "Very likely," she said. "But really I have no choice. You see, we were such friends—such friends. And then she loved him, while he—he had nothing but a professional interest for her, till he found her case to be hopeless, and then he lost even that. That's what made it so horrible—so impossible. If he had loved her—even a little—I could have understood. But as it was—Oh, Nick, don't you see?"

Yes, he did see. It was useless to reason with her. She was like a captive bird beating wild wings for freedom and wholly unable to gauge its awful desolation when won.

For the second time he had to own himself beaten. For the second time he withdrew his forces from the field.

"Well, dear, I'm sorry," was all he said, but it conveyed much.

When he quitted her presence a little later he carried with him the ring that Max had given her and a brief and piteous message to her lover that he would not try to see her again.

Max received both in grim silence, and within half an hour of so doing he had gone.

CHAPTER XVIII
ONE MAN'S LOSS

"Oh, damn!" said Noel.

He had made the remark several times before that morning, but he made it with special emphasis on this occasion in response to the news that his brother was waiting to see him.

Hot and cross from the parade-ground, he rolled off his horse and turned towards his quarters. The animal looked after him with a faint whinny of hurt surprise, and sharply Noel flung round again.

The *saice* grinned, but was instantly quelled to sobriety by his master's scowl. The horse whinnied again, and tucked a confiding nose under the young officer's arm.

"All right, old man! Here you are!" said Noel.

He fished out a lump of sugar and stuffed it between the sensitive lips that nibbled at his sleeve, kissed the white star between the soft brown eyes, whispered an endearing word into the cocked ear, slapped the glossy neck, and finally departed.

His face resumed its scowl as he entered the room where Max sprawled in a bamboo chair with his feet on another and the petted terrier of the establishment seated alertly on his chest. Max smiled at sight of it and stretched forth a lazy hand.

"Excuse my rising! I daren't incur this creature's displeasure."

Noel took the creature by the neck and removed it. Max's hand remained outstretched, but that he ignored.

"What have you come for?" he demanded gruffly.

"I should have said, 'What can I do for you?'" observed Max to the ceiling. "If you are thinking of having a drink, perhaps you will allow me to join you."

Noel went to the door and grumpily yelled an order. After which he jingled back, unbuckled his sword, and flung it noisily on the table.

Max turned his head very deliberately and regarded him.

His scrutiny was a prolonged one, and Noel finally waxed impatient under it. "Well, what are you staring at me for?" he enquired aggressively.

With a sudden movement Max removed his feet from the second chair and sat up. "Sit down there!" he said.

The words fell curt and sharp, a distinct order which Noel obeyed almost before he knew what he was doing. He dropped into the chair and sat directly facing his brother, a kind of surly respect struggling with the evident hostility of his expression.

His dog, feeling neglected, sprang on to his knees and licked his sullen face.

Max uttered a short laugh that was not unfriendly. "Oh, stop being a silly ass, Noel!" he said. "What on earth do you want to quarrel with me for? It's the most unprofitable game under the sun."

Noel sat stiffly upright, holding the dog at arm's length. "It's no fault of mine," he said.

His eyes were obstinately lowered in a mule-like refusal to meet his brother's straight regard. He looked absurdly like a schoolboy brought up for punishment.

Max considerately stifled a second laugh. "All right, it's mine," he said. "And I've come to apologize. Understand? I've come to make unconditional restitution of my ill-gotten gains. I'm just off to Bombay, to shake the dust of this accursed country off my feet, and to leave you in undisputed possession of the spoil. How's that appeal to you, you sulky young hound?"

Noel's eyes shot upwards at the epithet, though the supercilious good-humour of its utterance made it somehow impossible to raise any furious protest.

The entrance of his servant with drinks helped very materially to save his dignity. He pulled the table to him without rising and began to pour them out.

"Lemon?" he asked briefly.

"No, thanks. I'll have a plain soda. And if you've no objection we will thresh this matter out at once as I have to be off in ten minutes. I suppose you took in what I said just now?"

Noel held out a glass to him, his brown hand not quite steady. "May as well be explicit," he said gruffly.

"Quite so. Then my engagement to Olga Ratcliffe is at an end. Is that plain enough for you?"

Again the boy's eyes glanced upwards, meeting the imperturbable green eyes opposite for the fraction of a second. "Really?" he said.

"Yes, really." Max took a slow gulp from his glass and set it down. "Pleased?" he enquired.

Noel did not answer. His own drink remained untouched at his elbow. "Whose doing is it?" he enquired.

"Hers."

"What! Doesn't she care for you after all?" There was a sudden quiver in the question that belied the studied calm of the speaker.

Max took up his glass and drank again. "She can't stand me at any price," he said.

"Then what have you been doing?" There was no attempt to disguise the fierceness of the query. Noel started forward in his chair with hands clenched, and his dog slid to the ground.

"Take it easy!" said Max. "I'm not going to let you into that secret. It wouldn't be good for your morals. Besides, there's no time to go into that now. All I want to say to you is that there's a clear road in front of you and the odds are all in your favour. Go straight and I believe you'll win!"

Noel leaned nearer. His face was a curious blend of eagerness and resentment. "Do you mean—you've found out—that she'd sooner have me after all?" he blurted out.

Max looked at him, and a queer, half-pitying smile curved his grim mouth. "Yes, I suppose it amounts to that," he said, after a moment.

"Oh, I say!" said Noel.

He got up abruptly, and walked to the end of the room. Coming back, he gave a sharp gasp as of one rising from deep water, and the next moment very suddenly he laughed.

"I say," he said again, speaking jerkily, "is it the sun—or what? I feel as if—you'd hit me between the eyes."

Max nodded towards the table. "Have your drink, boy, and pull yourself together! You haven't won her yet, remember. You've got some uphill work before you still."

Noel stopped at the table, and raised his glass. His hand shook palpably, and the smile on Max's face became almost one of tenderness. He watched him in silence as he drank, then lifted his own glass.

"Here's to your success!" he said.

Noel's eyes came down to him. They had the rapt look of a man who sees a vision. "Oh, man," he suddenly exclaimed, "you don't know how I worship her!"

And then abruptly he realized what he had said and to whom, and flushed darkly, averting his look.

Max got to his feet, and faced him across the table. "You've got to worship her always," he said, and in his voice there throbbed some remote echo as of an imprisoned passion deep in his hidden soul. "She'll need the utmost you can offer."

Noel looked back at him again, and the shamed flush died away. He leaned impulsively forward, suddenly, boyishly remorseful for his churlishness.

"Max! Max, old boy! I'm an infernal brute!" he declared. "I was actually forgetting that you—that you——"

"You're quite welcome to forget that," interposed Max grimly. He moved round the table, and clapped a friendly hand on the boy's shoulder. "I shall make it my business to forget it myself," he said. "But look here, don't be headlong! She isn't quite ready for you yet. I speak as a friend; go slow!"

Noel looked at him, and again the hot blood rose to his forehead. He gripped the hand on his shoulder, and held it fast. "I say, Max," he said, an odd sort of deference in his tone, "she doesn't know—does she—what a much better chap you are than I?"

The corner of Max's mouth went up. "Don't talk bosh!" he said.

"I'm not," persisted Noel. "You're doing what I hadn't the spunk to do. I think she ought to know that."

Max's smile passed from amusement to cynicism. "Do you seriously think a woman loves a man for his good points?" he said.

"No; but you've no right to put her off with an inferior article," persisted Noel.

"My good chap, I! I tell you it was her own choice." Max almost laughed.

"But you care for her?" Noel's dark eyes became suddenly intent and shrewd, and the boyishness passed from his face. "See here, Max, I won't take any sacrifices," he said. "I may be a selfish brute, but I'm not quite such a swine as that. You care for her."

"Which fact is beside the point," said Max. His fingers suddenly answered Noel's grip with the strength of a restraining force. "If there is any sacrifice anywhere," he said, "it's not offered to you, so make your mind easy on that head. As I said before, she won't have me at any price. If she would, I shouldn't be here now. You see," again his mouth twisted, "I'm not so ultra-generous myself. But I don't see why we should both be losers, especially as you had half won her before I came along. So go ahead and good luck to you!"

He disengaged his hand and lightly slapped Noel's shoulder as a preliminary to taking his departure. But Noel, with a swift return to boyhood, caught him by the arms. "I don't know what to say to you, old chap," he said, quick feeling in the words. "You've made me feel like a murderer."

"My dear chap, what rot!"

"No, it's not rot! I've hated you like the devil. I'm beastly ashamed—beastly sorry. I'll do anything to atone—anything under the sun. Give me something to do for you, Max, old boy! I can't stand myself if you go like this."

He spoke impulsively enough, but there was more than mere impulse in his speech. Hot-headed repentance it might be, but it was the real thing.

Max stood still, faintly smiling. "My dear lad, there's nothing you can do for me that you won't do twice as well for yourself," he said. "I'm glad you care for her, and I'm not sorry you hated me for getting in your way. You might let me know when it's time to congratulate. That's all I can think of at the present moment—except, yes, one thing!"

"What?" said Noel.

Max's face hardened somewhat. "That fellow Hunt-Goring," he said. "He's the chap I told you of. Keep clear of him!"

Noel stiffened. "I should like to kill him," he said.

"Yes, but you can't. He's more than a match for you. He once had some hold over Olga—something very slight. I never bothered to find out what. But she has broken away and he is an enemy in consequence. Watch out for him, but don't fall foul of him! He won't worry you for long. He is taking opium enough to kill an ox every day of his life."

"Is he though? Well, no one will weep for him."

"Unless it's Mrs. Musgrave," observed Max drily.

"She doesn't like the bounder," declared Noel with conviction. "Look here; sit down again! I've seen nothing of you yet."

"No, I can't stop, thanks. I've said good-bye to everyone else, and time is up. Don't go and get smashed up at polo! If she doesn't want you now, she will very soon. Bear that in mind!"

Noel's dark eyes shone. "The only risks I'm likely to take would be for her safety. I wish to Heaven Ratcliffe could be made to see the danger they are in."

Max smiled a little. "I've been talking to him. We touched on that point. He knows—rather more on the subject than we do."

"But he makes light of it," Noel protested. "The place is infested with *budmashes* and he rather encourages them than otherwise. I myself kicked an old blackguard of a moonstone-seller—or so he described himself—off his premises only the other night."

Max broke into a laugh. "Did you though?"

"Yes. What is there to laugh at? Wouldn't you have done the same? And when I told Nick the day after, he described the old beggar as a friend of his."

Max was still laughing. "What a devil of a fellow you are! I've seen the old gentleman myself. I rather think he is a friend. How did he take the kicking?"

"Oh, I don't know. He cursed a bit and went. What's the joke, I say?"

Noel's voice was imperious. He was always somewhat impatient of matters beyond his comprehension. But Max turned the subject off.

"You're such a peppery chap—always wanting to fight someone. Well, I must be gone. You'll remember not to fight Hunt-Goring?"

"No. I shan't fight the brute unless he interferes." Noel followed him to the door and stood a moment. "I say, Max," he suddenly said, "was this affair Hunt-Goring's doing?"

"What affair?" Max spoke as one bored with the subject.

But Noel persisted. "Was it thanks to Hunt-Goring that this split with Olga came about?"

Max faced about. There was a very peculiar smile in his green eyes. "Well," he said very deliberately, "I don't say Hunt-Goring's influence has been exactly a genial one. But that fact in itself would not have much difference. The main reason is the one I have given you. If you are not satisfied with that—then you will never be satisfied with anything—and you won't deserve to be." He held out his hand. "Good-bye, lad! And again—good luck!"

Noel wrung the hand. They looked each other in the eyes, and Noel spoke impulsively as his habit was, but with genuine feeling. "Good-bye, old chap! I hope you'll get to the tip-top of the tree and stay there." He added, seeing Max's mouth go down, "But I know very well there's a bigger thing than success in the world, and if I can ever help you to it—by God, old boy, I will!"

He said it hurriedly, expecting it to be received with irony. But there was no trace of cynicism left in Max's face as he gave him a final grip, and turned away with the one word: "Thanks!"

When he had gone, Noel returned to the room with sober gait, and paused in the middle of it to pick up his sword.

"I wonder if he cares much," he murmured half aloud.

He stood by the table with eyes absently fixed, going over in his mind the conversation that had just passed, recalling the leisurely, supercilious tones, the semi-ironical kindness with which his brother had revealed the situation. Why had he troubled himself to do so? For a space Noel wondered.

And then very suddenly the words, "You've got to worship her always," flashed through his mind. Those words were the key to everything. He realized that fully. And again he was conscious of shame. Yes, Max did care. That was beyond all questioning. He cared enough to do what he—Noel—had wholly failed to do. His love was great enough to efface itself, a form of love—the rarest and the highest—of which he himself was as yet incapable. He could stand between the girl and death without a second's hesitation; but he could not live and sacrifice his happiness to hers.

Again the hot blood mounted to his forehead and slowly sank again. And in those few moments Noel Wyndham stepped into manhood and faced his soul anew. If she loved him, he would marry her and give her all he had; withholding nothing. She should not be a loser because she had loved him better than Max.

He would give her a love as strong and as worthy. He would make her happiness his aim and his goal, his watch-word and his prize. No sacrifice should ever be too great for her. He would offer all he had.

No; never should she come to repent her preference—to regret the love she had refused. She had chosen him—the lesser before the greater; and she should not find him wanting. She should not be disappointed in him. Never, never now should his love fail her!

Impulsive as always, he lifted his sword and kissed the hilt with reverence. "So help me, God!" he swore.

CHAPTER XIX
A FIGHT WITHOUT A FINISH

It was not the same Olga who went back into the busy little Anglo-Indian community at Sharapura after the breaking of her engagement, though it was only those intimate with her who marked the change. To the rest of the world she was as she had ever been, quiet and gentle, perhaps a little colourless, possibly in the eyes of some even insignificant, —"too reserved to be interesting," according to Colonel Bradlaw who liked a woman to have plenty of vivacity and mirth in her composition.

To those who knew her best—to Nick, to Daisy, and to Noel—she was changed, though it was a change of which she herself was scarcely aware. Her re-awakened spontaneity had gone again. She asked sympathy of none. Even to Nick she made no confidences. She had become wholly woman, and she had learned as it were to stand alone. She preferred her solitude.

Of Noel she seemed a little shy at first, until by frank good-fellowship he overcame this. Noel's courtship was apparently at a standstill. He made no open attempt to further his cause with her, though every day he sought her out with cheery friendliness, never overstepping the mark, never giving her the smallest occasion for embarrassment. And thus every day her confidence in him grew. She came to rely upon him in a fashion that she scarcely realized, depending upon his consideration and unfailing chivalry more than she knew. She had never liked him better than she liked him then, in the first desperate bitterness of her trouble. He asked so little of her, was so readily pleased with her mere friendship, and though at the back of her mind she knew that this was only his pleasant method of marking time she was none the less grateful to him for his patience. He helped her through her dark hours without seeming in the least aware that she needed help. He demanded rather than offered sympathy, and in giving it she found herself oddly soothed. She was glad that Noel wanted her, glad that he regarded her co-operation as quite indispensable to his schemes. He occupied her thoughts at a time when private reflection was torture. The misery was there perpetually at her heart, but he gave her no time to dwell upon it. He carried her along with him with an impetus which she had no desire to resist.

Nick watched his tactics from afar with unwilling admiration, wryly admitting to himself that they were precisely the tactics he would have pursued. He saw that the fulfilment of his prediction was merely a matter of time, and prepared himself to yield to the inevitable with as good a grace as he could muster. He was in fact more in sympathy with Noel than with Olga just then. The boy was undoubtedly developing under this new influence. The spoilt side of his nature was giving place to a new manliness that was infinitely more attractive, and Nick found it impossible not to accept him with approval.

Sir Reginald Bassett's visit was to take place early in February, and great were the preparations in progress for his entertainment. Daisy Musgrave found herself swept into the vortex of Noel's energies, and she on her part did her best to interest her guest therein. It was a futile effort on her part. Hunt-Goring only laughed at her and paid her lazy compliments. Why he stayed on was a problem that she was wholly at a loss to solve. Quite privately she had begun to wish very much that he would go. She was heartily tired of being for ever on her guard, and she never dared to be otherwise with him. Not that she found it really difficult to keep him at a distance. He was too indolent for that. When she withdrew herself, he never troubled to pursue. His attentions were never ardent. But he never failed to take advantage of the smallest lapse on her part. She could never be at her ease with him.

Will Musgrave was inclined to smile at his wife's difficulties. Perhaps he was not wholly sorry that the follies of her youth should thus come home to her. He did not like Hunt-Goring much, but the man never gave offence.

"I suppose he'll go when he's tired of us," said Will philosophically.

"And meantime neither Olga nor Noel will come near the place with him in it," sighed Daisy. "I don't believe he will ever go."

He laughed at that and pinched her cheek. "We shall though, little wife. That honeymoon of ours comes nearer every day."

She smiled an eager, girlish smile. "Dear old Will!" she murmured softly.

It was on that same evening that Noel broke his rule and raced in to give Daisy some important information with regard to his schemes for what he termed "the Bassett week."

He was full of excitement and declared himself unable to remain for a single moment more than his business demanded.

"I'm going to dine with Nick," he told her. "In fact, I'm due there now."

"I never see anything of Nick nowadays," said Daisy.

"No; nor do I. He's at the Palace, morning, noon, and night. Can't see the attraction myself. But no doubt he thinks he's doing something great. By the way, you're coming round to old Badgers' to-morrow, I suppose? We are going to hold a meeting of the committee. Olga will be there of course."

"How is Olga?" asked Daisy.

"Oh, all right. Why don't you go round and see her?" Noel asked the question with some curiosity. He had begun to wonder lately if there could have been a disagreement between them.

Daisy smiled with a touch of wistfulness. She had scarcely seen Olga since the breaking of her engagement. "I seem to have so little time nowadays. The last time I went, she was busy too."

"Oh, she's sure to be busy till Bassett week," laughed Noel. "I'm seeing to that. It's good for her, you know."

"Yes, I know," said Daisy. She added in a lower tone, for Hunt-Goring was smoking on the verandah outside the window, "I am glad you are taking care of her, Noel. She needs that."

Noel coloured a little. "I do what I can. So does Nick. But I wish you would go and see her. She wants a pal of her own sex."

"I am not so sure of that," said Daisy. "Ah, here's Peggy! I thought you wouldn't escape without seeing her."

Peggy's entrance was of the nature of a whirlwind. It completely diverted the thoughts of both. She was scantily clad in a bath-towel which she held tightly gripped with both hands about her small person. Her feet left little wet dabs on the floor as she pattered in.

"Oh, Noel!" she cried. "You horrid, horrid Noel! I've been callin' you for ever so long. And I was in my bath. I thought you'd like to see me in my bath."

"Peggy!" exclaimed her mother, scandalized.

Peggy's *ayah*, also scandalized, hovered in the doorway.

Peggy, herself, from the safe shelter of Noel's arms, smiled securely upon both.

"You mustn't tickle me," she said to her protector, "or I shall come undone. Why hasn't you been to take me for another ride, Noel?"

"Sweetheart—" he began with compunction.

But Peggy interrupted very decidedly. "No, you needn't make excuses. And I'm not goin' to be your sweetheart any more—ever—not till you take me for another ride."

"Oh, don't be cruel!" besought Noel. "I've been so shockingly busy lately. It wasn't that I forgot you, Peggy. I couldn't do that if I tried. So give me a kiss, little sweetheart, and let's be friends! I vow I'll tickle you if you won't."

Peggy, however, was nothing daunted by this threat. She kept her face rigidly turned over his shoulder. "When will you take me for another ride?" she demanded imperiously.

"Peggy," her mother broke in again, "I can't have you behaving like this, dear. It isn't decent. Go back to *ayah* at once!"

Peggy peeped mischievously over Noel's shoulder. "If I get down again, I shall come all undone," she said.

"By Jove, what a calamity!" said Noel. "Haven't you got a pin or something to hold the thing together?"

She tightened her arms about his neck. "You carry me back!" she whispered ingratiatingly. "An' I'll give you three booful kisses!"

Noel succumbed at once. "Can't resist that!" he remarked to Daisy. "I'll take her back and slap her for you, shall I?"

"I wish you would," said Daisy.

"He daren't!" declared Peggy.

"Ho! Daren't he?" laughed Noel. "That's the rashest thing you ever said in your life. Come along, you scaramouch, and we'll see about that!"

He bore her away, with her draperies slipping from her, followed by the *ayah* whose open horror was surveyed by Peggy with eyes of shining amusement. A little later her shrill squeals announced the fact that Noel was carrying out his threat after a fashion which she found highly enjoyable, and Noel subsequently emerged in a somewhat heated and tumbled condition and bade Daisy a hasty farewell.

"I've chastised the imp, but she's quite unregenerate. Glad I'm not her mother. I've sworn a solemn oath to take her out on the Chimpanzee to-morrow. I haven't time, but that's a detail. I'll work it somehow, if you don't mind having her ready by ten. I'll race round after parade."

"I ought not to let her go," Daisy protested.

He laughed at that. "Yes, yes, you must. I've promised. Good-bye! Ten o'clock then!"

He shook her hand and departed, singing as he went.

Hunt-Goring from the verandah watched him all-unperceived.

"The whelp seems pleased with himself," he observed to Daisy, with a sneering smile. "I presume that Fortune—in the form of Miss Olga Ratcliffe—favours the brave."

"He's very handsome, isn't he?" said Daisy, smiling back not without a touch of malice. "Who could help favouring such an Adonis?"

"Not you, I'm sure," said Hunt-Goring, "or the charming Peggy either. But I'm a little sorry for the red-haired doctor, you know. I feel in a measure responsible for that tragedy."

"The responsibility was mine," said Daisy gravely.

He turned his lazy eyes upon her. "Ah, to be sure! You wanted an excuse to procure that young man his *congé*, I believe. I hope you realize that you are in my debt for just so much as the excuse was worth."

Daisy made a quick movement of exasperation. "Do you never give women credit for being sincere?" she said.

"Only when they are angry," said Hunt-Goring, taking out his cigarette-case. "Now join me, won't you? Sincerity is such a heating quality. I shouldn't cultivate it if I were you."

But Daisy declined somewhat curtly. It was quite evident that her patience was wearing very thin.

Hunt-Goring did not press her. He smiled and subsided with obvious indifference. Perhaps he deemed it wiser not to try her too far, or perhaps he lacked the energy to pursue the matter.

He had taken to spending most of his time on the verandah, smoking his endless cigarettes and dreamily watching the world go by. He seemed almost to have forgotten that he was a guest, and, her exasperation notwithstanding, Daisy could not bring herself to remind him of the fact. For the man was changed. Day after day she realized it more and more clearly. Day after day it seemed to her that he dropped a little deeper into his sea of lethargy. His interest flagged so quickly where once it had been keen. He grew daily older while she watched. And a curious pity for him kept her from actively disliking him, although his power to attract her was wholly gone. She found herself bearing with him simply because he cared so little.

It was quite otherwise with Noel, who was frankly disgusted to find himself confronted with him on the following morning when, true to his promise, he made his appearance with Peggy's mount. Hunt-Goring was just preparing to establish himself on the verandah when Noel came striding along it in search of his small playmate. They so nearly collided in fact that it was impossible for either to overlook the other's presence.

Noel drew back sharply with his quick scowl. They had not met since the evening on which he had so furiously challenged him to battle on Olga's behalf. For Olga's sake, and perhaps a little in deference to Max's warning, he had refrained from following up the challenge, but he was more than ready to do so even yet; and his attitude said as much as he stood aside in glowering silence for the other man to pass.

Hunt-Goring however was plainly in a genial mood. He paused to bestow his smiling scrutiny upon the young officer. "Let me see! Surely we have met before?"

"We have," said Noel bluntly.

"I fear the occasion has slipped my memory," said Hunt-Goring.

A wiser man would have passed on. But Noel had not yet attained to years of discretion. He stood his ground and explained.

"We met at dinner here. Captain and Miss Ratcliffe were here too—and my brother."

"Oh, ah! I remember now. Quite an amusing evening, was it not?" Hunt-Goring laughed gently. "You were rather vexed with me for chaffing her about her engagement. I have always thought a little chaff was legitimate on such occasions."

"When it isn't objectionable," said Noel gruffly.

Hunt-Goring laughed again. "Do you know why the engagement was broken off?"

Noel drew himself up sharply. "That, sir, is neither your affair nor mine."

Hunt-Goring took out his cigarette-case. "Well, it was mine in a way," he observed complacently. "I pulled the strings, you know."

"Ah!" It was an exclamation of anger rather than of surprise. The blood mounted in a great wave to Noel's forehead. He looked suddenly dangerous. "I guessed it was your doing," he said, in a furious undertone.

Hunt-Goring continued to smile. "He wasn't a very suitable *parti* for her, my dear fellow. There was a certain episode in his past that wouldn't bear too close an investigation. Very possibly you have not been let into that secret. Your brother was not over-anxious to have it noised abroad."

Noel's hands were clenched. He seemed to be restraining himself from a violent outburst with immense difficulty.

"My brother," he said with emphasis, "is the gentleman of our family. He has never yet done anything that couldn't have been proclaimed from the house-tops."

Hunt-Goring uttered his sneering laugh. "What touching loyalty! My dear fellow, your brother is the biggest blackguard of you all, if you only knew it."

"You lie!" Violently came the words; they were as the sudden bursting of the storm. Something electric seemed suddenly to have entered into Noel. He became as it were galvanized by fury.

But still Hunt-Goring laughed. "Oh, not on this occasion, I assure you. I have too little at stake. I wonder why you imagined the engagement was broken off. I suppose your brother gave you a reason of sorts."

Noel's eyes shone red. "He gave me to understand that you had had a hand in it. I guessed it in fact. I knew what an infernal blackguard you were."

"Order! Order!" smiled Hunt-Goring. "After all, my share in the matter was a very small one. Most men have a past, you know. When you have lived a little longer, you will recognize that. So he didn't tell you why he had been thrown over? Left you to make your own inferences, I suppose? Or perhaps she made the flattering suggestion that she had bestowed her affections upon—someone more captivating? I fancy she is wisely determined to secure as good a bargain as possible—for which one can scarcely blame her. And a man with so lively a past as your brother's would scarcely be a safe partner for one who values peace and prosperity."

"How dare you make these vile insinuations in my hearing?" burst forth Noel. "Do you think I'm made of sawdust? Tell me what you mean, or else retract every single word you've said!"

Hunt-Goring held up a cigarette between his fingers and looked at it. The fury of Noel's attitude scarcely seemed to reach his notice. He leaned against the balustrade of the verandah, still faintly smiling.

"I would tell you the whole story with pleasure," he said, "only I am not quite sure that it would be good for you to know."

"Oh, damn all that!" broke in Noel, goaded to exasperation by his obvious indifference. "If you want to save your skin, you'd better speak out at once!"

"To save my skin!" Hunt-Goring's eyes left their contemplation of the cigarette and travelled to his face. They held a sneer that was well-nigh intolerable, and yet which somehow restrained Noel for the moment. "What a very headlong young man you are!" pursued Hunt-Goring, in his soft voice. "I've done nothing to you. I haven't the smallest desire to quarrel with you. Nor have I given you any occasion for offence. It was Mrs. Musgrave—not I—who imparted the regrettable tale of your brother's shortcomings to his *fiancée*. In some fashion she conceived it to be her duty to do so."

"You meant her to do it!" flashed back Noel.

"Ah! that is another story," smiled Hunt-Goring. "We are not discussing motives or intentions. I think. But she will tell you—if you care to ask her—that I advised her strongly against the course she elected to pursue."

"You would!" said Noel bitterly. "Well, get on! Let's hear this precious story. I've no doubt it's a damned lie from beginning to end, but if it's going the round I'd better know it."

"It may be a lie," said Hunt-Goring diplomatically. "But it was not concocted by me. I should conclude, however, from subsequent events that some portion of it bears at least some sort of resemblance to the truth." He stopped to light his cigarette while Noel looked on fuming. "The story is a very ordinary one, but might well prove somewhat damning to a doctor's career. It concerned a young lady with whom your brother was—somewhat intimate."

"Did you know her?" thrust in Noel.

Hunt-Goring looked at the end of his cigarette with a thoughtful smile. "Yes, I knew her rather well. I was not, however, prepared to lend my name to cloak a scandal—even to oblige your brother who had transferred his attentions to Miss Olga, so he had to take his own measures." He looked up with a glitter of malice in his eyes. "The girl died," he said, "rather suddenly. That's all the story."

It was received in a dead silence that lasted for the breathless passage of a dozen seconds. Then: "You—skunk!" said Noel.

He did not raise his voice to say it, but there was that in his tone that was more emphatic than violence. It warned Hunt-Goring of danger as surely as the growl of a tiger. His lazy complacence suddenly gave place to alertness. He straightened himself up. But even then he had not the sense to refrain from his abominable laugh.

"I've noticed," he said, "that present-day puppies are greater at snarling than fighting. I told you this story because you asked for it. Now I'll tell you one you didn't ask for. Max Wyndham transferred his attentions to Olga Ratcliffe, not because he cared for her, but because he wanted to put a spoke in my wheel. Little Olga and I were very thick at one time. You didn't know that, I daresay?"

"I don't believe it!" said Noel, breathing heavily.

Hunt-Goring inhaled a deep breath of smoke and blew it forth again in gentle puffs. "Ah! She never told you that? She was always a secretive young woman. Yes, we had some very jolly times together on the sly, till one day the doctor-fellow caught us kissing under the apple-trees. Then of course she was afraid he'd split, so it was all up." He smiled insolently into Noel's blazing eyes. "I flatter myself that she missed those stolen kisses," he said. "I must go round one of these days—when the dragon is out of ear-shot—and make up for it."

That loosed the devil in Noel at last. He took a swift step forward. His right hand gripped his riding-whip.

"If you ever go near her again," he said, "I'll break every bone in your body! You liar—you damned blackguard—you cur!"

Full into Hunt-Goring's face he hurled his furious words. He was more angry in that moment than he had ever been in his life. The force of his anger carried him along as a twig borne on a racing current. Till that instant he had forgotten that he carried his riding-whip. The sudden remembrance of it flashed like a streak of lightning through his brain.

Before he knew what he was doing, almost as if a will swifter than his own were at work, he had sprung upon Hunt-Goring and struck him a swinging blow across the shoulders.

Only that one blow, however! For Hunt-Goring was not an easy man to thrash. Ten years before, he had been the strongest man in his regiment, and he was powerful still. Before Noel could strike again, he was locked in an embrace that threatened to crush him to a pulp.

In awful silence they strained and fought together, and in a second or two it came to Noel through the silence that he had met his match. The Irish blood in him leaped exultant to the fray. He laughed a breathless laugh, and braced his muscles to a fierce resistance. He had been spoiling for a fight with this man for a long time.

But it was impossible to do anything scientific in that constrictor-like hold, and as they swayed and strove he began to realize that unless he could break it, it would very speedily break him. Hunt-Goring's face, purple and devilish, with lips drawn back and teeth clenched upon his cigarette, glared into his own. There was something unspeakably horrible about the eyes. They turned upwards, showing the whites all shot with blood.

"The man's a maniac!" was the thought that ran through Noel's brain.

His heart had begun to pump with painful hammering strokes. Not much of a fight this! Rather a grim struggle for life against a power he could not break. He braced himself again to burst that deadly grip. In his ears there arose a great surging. He felt his own eyes begin to start. By Heaven! Was he going to be squeezed to death ignominiously on the strength of that single blow? He gathered himself together for one mighty effort—the utmost of which he was capable—to force those iron arms asunder.

For about six seconds they stood the strain, holding him like a vice; then very suddenly they parted—so suddenly that Noel almost staggered as he drew his first great gasp of relief. Hunt-Goring reeled—almost fell—back against the wall of the bungalow. The sweat was streaming down his forehead. His face was livid. His eyes, sinister and awful, were turned up like the eyes of a dead man. He was chewing at his cigarette with a ceaseless working of the jaws indescribably horrible to watch.

Noel realized on the instant that the struggle was over, with small satisfaction to either side. He stood breathing deeply, all the mad blood in him racing at fever speed through his veins, burning to follow up the attack but conscious that he could not do so. For the man who leaned there facing him was old—a bitter fact which neither had realized until that moment—too old to fight, too old to thrash.

Noel swung round and turned his back upon him, utterly disgusted with the situation. He picked up his riding-whip with a savage gesture and stared at it with fierce regret. It was a serviceable weapon. He could have done good work with it—on a younger man.

Hunt-Goring made a sudden movement, and he wheeled back. The livid look had gone from the man's face. He stood upright, and spat the cigarette from his lips. His eyes had drooped again, showing only a malicious glint between the lids. Yet there was something about him even then that made Noel aware that he was very near the end of his strength.

He was on the verge of speaking when there came the sudden rush of Peggy's eager feet, and she darted out upon the verandah, and raced to Noel with a squeal of delight.

Noel caught her in his arms. He had never been more pleased to see her. He did not look at Hunt-Goring again, and the words on Hunt-Goring's lips remained unspoken.

"Let's go! Let's go!" cried Peggy.

And Noel turned as if the atmosphere had suddenly become poisonous, and bore her swiftly away.

A few seconds later, Daisy, running out to see the start, came upon Hunt-Goring upright and motionless upon the verandah, and was somewhat surprised by the rigidity of his attitude. He relaxed almost at once, however, and sat down in his usual corner.

"I had no idea Noel was here," she said. "Has he been waiting long?"

"Not long," said Hunt-Goring. "I have been entertaining him."

"Isn't he a nice boy?" said Daisy impetuously. "Look at him in the saddle—so splendidly young and free!"

Hunt-Goring was silent a moment. Then, as he took out his cigarette-case, he remarked: "He is so altogether charming, Mrs. Musgrave, that I can't help thinking that he must be one of those fortunate people 'whom the gods love.'"

"But what a horrid thing to say!" protested Daisy. "I'm sure Noel won't die young. He is so full of vitality. He couldn't!"

Hunt-Goring smiled upon his cigarettes. "I wonder," he said slowly, and chose one with the words. "I—wonder!"

CHAPTER XX
THE POWER OF THE ENEMY

It so chanced that Noel did not find himself in any intimate conversation with Olga again until the great week arrived, and General Sir Reginald Bassett came upon the scene with much military pomp and ceremony.

Olga avoided all talk of a confidential nature with him with so obvious a reluctance that he could not force it upon her in the brief spaces of time which he had at his disposal when they met. They had become close friends, but the feeling that this friendship depended mainly upon his forbearance never left Noel, and he could not fail to see that she shrank from the bare mention of Max's name.

He bided his time, therefore, since there was no urgent need to broach the subject forthwith and he was still by no means sure of his ground. He would have discussed the matter with Nick, but Nick was never to be found. He came and went with astonishing rapidity, bewildering even Olga by the suddenness of his moves. Vaguely she heard of unrest in the city, but definite information she had none. Nick eluded all enquiries; but it seemed to her that the yellow face grew more wrinkled every day, and the shrewd eyes took on a vigilant, sleepless look that troubled her much in secret. The thought of him kept her from brooding overmuch upon her own trouble. She did not want to brood. If her own nights were sleepless, she took a book and resolutely read. She would not yield an inch to the ceaseless, weary ache of her heart, and very sternly she denied herself the relief of tears. Too much of her life had been wasted already, in the pursuit of what was not. She would not waste still more of it in bitter, fruitless mourning over that which was.

Perhaps it was the bravest stand she had ever made, and what it cost her not even Nick might guess. Certainly he had less time to bestow upon her than ever before. They met at meals, and very often that was all. But Olga, with her curious, new reserve, was not needing his companionship just then. Her attitude towards her beloved hero had subtly changed. Beloved he was still and would ever be, but he no longer dwelt apart from all other men on the special little pedestal on which her worship had placed him. He was no longer the demi-god of her childish adoration. Olga had grown up, and was shedding her illusions one by one. Nick was a man and she was a woman. Therefore it followed as a natural sequence that though she was fully capable of understanding him, she herself was—and must ever remain—a being beyond his comprehension. Not superior to him; Olga never aspired to be that. But with her woman's knowledge she realized that even Nick had his limitations. There were certain corners of her soul which he could never penetrate. He would have understood the wild crying of her heart, but her steady stifling of that crying would have been beyond him. Simply he stood on another plane, and he would not understand that her heart must break before she could listen to its passionate entreaty. Nor could she explain herself to him. She belonged to the inexplicable and unreasonable race called woman. Her motives and emotions were hidden, and she could never hope to make them understood even by the shrewdest of men.

So she veiled her sorrow from him, little guessing how the vigilant eyes took in that also when they did not apparently so much as glance her way.

On the morning of the day on which Sir Reginald was to arrive, he kept her waiting for breakfast, a most unusual occurrence. Olga was occupied with a letter from her father, one of his brief, kindly epistles that she valued for their very rarity; and it was not till this was finished that she realized the lateness of the hour.

Then in some surprise she went along the verandah in search of him.

His window stood open as usual. She paused outside it. "Nick, aren't you coming?"

There was no reply to her call, and she was about to repeat it when Kasur the *khitmutgar* came along the verandah behind her.

"Miss *sahib*, Ratcliffe *sahib* has not yet come back from the city," he said.

Olga turned in astonishment. "The city, Kasur! How long has he been there? When did he go?"

The man looked at her with the deferential vagueness which only the Oriental can express. "Miss *sahib*, how should I know? My lord goes in the night while his servant is asleep."

"In the night!" Again incredulously she repeated his words. "And to the city! Kasur, are you sure?"

Kasur became more vague. "Perhaps he goes to the cantonments, Miss *sahib*. How should I know whither he goes?"

It was an unsatisfactory conversation, obviously leading in every direction but the one desired. Olga turned from him, impatient and perplexed. She went slowly back round the corner of the bungalow to the breakfast-table, set in the shade of the cluster-roses that climbed over the verandah, and sat down before it with a sinking heart. What did this mean? Was it true that Nick went nightly and by stealth to the city? What did he do there?

And how came he to be there at this hour? Moment by moment her uneasiness grew. The conviction that Nick was in danger came down upon her like a bird of evil omen, and inaction became intolerable. She turned in her chair with the intention of calling to Kasur to order her horse that she might go in search of him. But in that instant a voice spoke to her from the compound immediately below her, arresting the words on her lips,—a whining, ingratiating voice.

"*Mem-sahib!*" it said. "*Mem-sahib!*"

She looked down and saw an old, old man, more like a monkey than a human being, standing huddled in a ragged *chuddah* on the edge of the path. He seemed to be looking at her, obviously he must have seen her sitting there, and yet to Olga his eyes looked blind. They stared straight up at the sky while he spoke, and there was a dreadful paleness about them, a lifeless hue that contrasted very strangely with the deep copper of his bearded face.

"Do not be alarmed, most gracious!" he begged in a thin reedy voice. "I come with a message from the captain *sahib*. He has been detained in the city; but all is well with him. He bids me to say that he desires the *mem* to eat alone this morning, but to have no fear. He will be with her again ere the sun has reached its height."

Olga leaned upon the balustrade of the verandah and looked down at her strange visitor. She was not sorry that she was thus raised above him, for he was very dirty. The voluminous *chuddah* in which he was swathed looked as if it had wrapped him in those selfsame folds for many years.

"But what is the *sahib* doing?" she asked. "Why doesn't he come?"

The old man wagged a deferential beard. "Excellency, how should a poor old seller of moonstones know?"

"Oh!" Olga suddenly became interested in the messenger. "You are the moonstone-seller, are you?" she said. "Have you ever been here before?"

He bent himself before her in a low salaam. "I am my lord's most humble servant," he told her meekly. "A very poor man, most gracious,—a very poor man. I come here at my lord's bidding—when he needs me."

Olga's brow puckered. "How queer!" she said. "I wonder I have never seen you before. Perhaps you only come at night."

"Only at night, most gracious," he said.

He made as if he would hobble away, but she called to him to wait, while she ran to her room to fetch a few *annas* for him. It took her but a second or two to find what she wanted, but when she emerged again upon the verandah her visitor had disappeared.

She stood and searched the compound with astonished eyes, but no sign of him was visible. He must have removed himself with considerable rapidity for so old a man, and remembering his extreme poverty, Olga was puzzled. She had never known a native run away from *backsheesh* before.

She sat down to her solitary breakfast, no longer actively anxious concerning Nick, but still by no means easy. She was firmly convinced that he was running risks in the city, and she longed to have him back.

The morning dragged away. She would not leave the bungalow lest he should return in her absence. She busied herself with the making of a fancy-dress which she and her *ayah* had concocted for the coming ball at the mess-house. It was to be quite an important affair, and every European within reach was to attend—according to Noel's decree. He had persuaded his colonel to have a purely European function for once, pleading that it would be so much more like Home; and Colonel Bradlaw, albeit with hesitation, had yielded the point. So to that one night's entertainment no native guests had been invited.

Noel was looking forward to the event with an enthusiasm that simply swept Olga along with it. She could not help being interested and in a measure excited. It was an absolute impossibility to be lukewarm about anything over which Noel was enthusiastic. He kindled enthusiasm wherever he went. Native fancy-dresses were tabooed by the regulations. Noel was supremely contemptuous of all things native. He meant to go as Dick Turpin himself, and she had promised to support him in a dress of the same period. It had taken considerable thought and skill to manufacture, but it was now well on the road to completion, and she sat and stitched at it throughout the morning, trying to stifle her uneasiness in the attention which it demanded.

It was not an easy matter. She found herself starting at every sound, and pausing to listen with nerves on edge. Still she persisted, determined not to give way to them; and she was in fact gradually schooling herself to a calmer frame of mind, when suddenly a thing happened that bereft her in a moment of all the composure she had striven so hard to attain. A man's hand shot—swiftly and stealthily—from behind her and covered her eyes in a flash, while a man's voice, soft and exultant, said mockingly above her head, "Guess!"

Olga uttered a cry that would have been a shriek had not the hand very swiftly shifted its position from her eyes to her mouth. She looked up into a face she knew—a face whose eyes of evil triumph made her heart stand still, and all her strength went suddenly from her. She turned as white as death and sank back into the chair from which she had half-risen. The total unexpectedness of the thing deprived her of all powers of resistance. She sat as one stunned.

He took his hand from her lips and brutally kissed them, laughing as she shrank away from him in sick horror. The gleaming mockery of his eyes was a thing she dared not meet.

"You will never guess what I have come for," he said, hanging over her, his hand gripping both of hers, his face still horribly near.

Her lips moved voicelessly in answer. She could not utter a word.

"You're awfully pleased to see me, aren't you?" he said. "That's nice of you. I wonder when you mean to pay that debt of yours—that old, sweet debt."

He spoke softly, smilingly, his eyes devouring her the while. She closed her own to avoid them. Her heart did not seem to be beating at all. She felt as if she were going to die of sheer horror there in his arms.

Softly again his voice came to her. "Come, you mustn't faint. That wouldn't be at all good for you. Open your eyes! Don't be afraid! Open them!"

They opened quiveringly, almost against her will. He was holding her closely, as if he anticipated some sudden resistance. But his eyes were on her still, burningly, possessively, menacingly. She met them shrinking, and felt as if thereby she gave herself to him body and soul.

He began to laugh again—that soft, silky laugh. "You're such a silly child," he said; "you always expect the worst. It's not wise of you. Aren't you old enough to know that yet?"

She found her voice at last, and with it came the consciousness of the slow, slow beating of her heart. "Let me go!" she said, in a breathless whisper.

"Presently; on one condition," he said.

"No, now!" The beating had begun to quicken a little, to harden into a distinct throbbing. But she felt deadly cold. Her hands, powerless in that unrelenting grasp, were as ice.

"Now don't be foolish!" said Hunt-Goring. "You're absolutely at my mercy, and it's very poor policy on your part not to recognize that fact. Just listen! You want me to let you go, you say. Well, I will let you go—for one small consideration on your part. You've never paid that debt of yours. You will pay it now—in full, freely, both arms round my neck. Come, I've a right to ask that much. It's just a whim that you can't refuse to gratify."

"I can refuse!" The words leaped from Olga. Her strength was returning, her heart quickening with every instant. "At least you can't make me do that!" she said.

"You would rather do it than marry me, I presume?" he said.

"I will never do either!" She stirred at last in his hold. She did not shrink from his eyes any longer; rather she challenged them as she stiffened herself to rise.

Hunt-Goring laughed in her face. "Oh, won't you?" he said. "I fancy you said that once before—and lived to regret it. It really is not wise of you to defy me. I warn you! I warn you!" His hold tightened upon her with sudden brutality, quelling her effort at freedom. "There are worse things than marriage," he said. "Are you utterly ignorant, I wonder, or deliberately foolhardy? Why do you always force upon me the *rôle* of villain? I tell you again, you are not wise!"

"I don't know what you mean," Olga said. She sat quite still in his hold now, for she knew that resistance was useless. Like Noel, she suddenly wondered if he were indeed sane. His eyes were unlike any she had ever seen in a human being. They glared upon her so devilishly, so murderously. She faced them with all her courage. "I don't know what you mean," she repeated. "I think you must be mad to persecute me in this way. I have always said that I would never marry you."

"But you will change your mind," he said.

She kept her eyes on his. "I shall never change my mind," she said very distinctly.

He laughed again, his lower lip between his teeth. "Even if I were mad," he said, "wouldn't you be wiser to humour me? Have you forgotten what happened when you flouted me before?"

"No, I have not forgotten." A quiver of anger went through Olga, and she suffered it, for it helped her courage. "I shall never forgive you for that," she said—"never, as long as I live!"

Hunt-Goring continued to laugh, and his laugh was an insult. "I shall get over that," he told her. "I don't want your forgiveness—especially as you had yourself alone to thank for that episode. But come now! About marrying me. You'd better give in at once; you'll have to in the end. And there are plenty of advantages to outweigh your present disinclination. For instance, my life is not considered a good one. As my widow, you would be quite a wealthy woman. Doesn't that appeal to you? And I'll give you plenty of rope even while I'm alive. I shan't interfere with your pleasures. Come, I shouldn't make such a bad husband. I'm quite respectable nowadays. I should want a little attention of course, but you wouldn't find me exacting. You'll get quite fond of me in time."

Olga barely repressed a shudder. "Never!" she said. "No, never!"

"Never?" said Hunt-Goring. He stooped a little lower over her, his arm about her shoulders despite her sick disgust. "Why never? You've sent that doctor chap about his business, haven't you?"

"He has gone, yes." She answered him briefly to hide the intolerable pain at her heart the words called up.

"But you're still hankering after him; is that it?" sneered Hunt-Goring. "Well, then, listen to me! I hold that man's future in my hands. I can ruin him utterly or—I can forbear. I'm not over-fond of him, as you know. I should rather like to see him ruined, though it would give me some little trouble to do it. What say you? I am the gladiator in the arena. I shall slay or spare—at your word alone."

Again his eyes overwhelmed her, so that she could not meet them. A great shiver went through her. She began to pant a little. "I—don't understand," she said. "You know nothing—but gossip. You—you can prove nothing."

"Can I not?" said Hunt-Goring. "You haven't a very high opinion of my intelligence, have you? Colonel Campion—I believe you know him—is scarcely the man to sit still when such gossip as that reaches his ears. As for the proofs, I know how to find them. The worthy Mrs. Briggs was on the spot, you may remember. Her evidence would be valuable. And there are other well-known means which I needn't go into now. But I assure you the circumstances themselves, properly handled, are sufficiently suspicious. You would not care to see your friend Max on his trial for murder, I presume?"

She shivered again, shivered from head to foot. She did not utter a word.

"No, I thought not," said Hunt-Goring, after a moment. "It would be especially painful for you, as your evidence also would be required. You see the position quite clearly, don't you? Come, hadn't you better give in now—and save further trouble?"

She was silent still. Only her breath came fast—as the breath of one who nears exhaustion.

Hunt-Goring waited a little, watching her white face. "Come!" he said, "I don't want to play the villain any longer. Can't you give me something better to do? I always dance to your piping."

She spoke at last, forcing her trembling lips to utterance; after repeated effort. "Go—please!" she said.

"Go?" said Hunt-Goring.

"Yes! go!" She raised her eyes for an instant, piteously entreating, to his. "I—can't talk to you now,—can't—think even. I—will see you again—later."

"When?" he said.

Her breast was rising and falling. She could not for several seconds answer him. Then: "At the ball—on Thursday," she whispered.

"You will give me my answer then?" he said.

"Yes."

He smiled—a cruel smile. "After due consultation with Nick, I suppose? No, my dear. I think not. We'll keep this thing a secret for the present—and I'll have my answer now."

"I can't answer you now!" She flung the words wildly, and rose up between his hands with desperate strength. "I can't—I can't!" she cried. "You must give me—a little time. I shan't consult—Nick or anyone. I only want—to think—by myself."

"Really?" said Hunt-Goring.

"Yes, really." She set her hands against his breast, holding him from her, yet beseeching him. "Oh, you can't refuse me this!" she urged. "It's—too small a thing. I've got to find out if—if—if I can possibly do it."

"You won't run away?" he said.

"No—no! I've nowhere to go."

"And you mention the matter to no one—on your oath—till we meet again?" His eyes were cruel still, but they were not cold. They shone upon her with a fierce heat.

She could not avoid them, though they seemed to burn her through and through. "I promise," she said through white lips.

"Very well. Till Thursday then." He let her go; and then, as if repenting, caught her suddenly back to him, savagely, passionately. "I'll have that kiss anyway," he said, "whether you take me or not. It's the price of my good behaviour till Thursday. Come, a kiss never hurt anyone, so it isn't likely to kill you."

She did not resist him. She even gave him her lips; but she was shaking as one in an ague, and her whole weight was upon him as he crushed her in his arms. So deathly was her face that after a moment even he was slightly alarmed.

He put her down again in the chair with a laugh that was not wholly self-complacent. "That's all right, then. I'll leave you to get used to the idea. You will give me my answer on Thursday, then, and we will decide on the next step. I don't mean to be kept waiting, you know. I've had enough of that."

She did not answer him or move. She was staring straight before her, with hands fast gripped together in her lap.

He bent a little. "What's the matter? I haven't hurt you. Aren't you well?"

"Quite," she said, without stirring.

He laughed again—the soft laugh she so abhorred. "Jove! What a dance you've led me!" he said. "You'll have a good deal to make up for when the time comes. I shan't let you off that."

"Will you—please—go?" said Olga, in that still voice of hers, not looking at him yet, nor moving.

He laughed again caressingly. "Yes, I'll go. You want to have a good quiet think, I suppose. But there's only one way out, you know. You'll have to give in now. And the sooner the better."

"I shall see you on Thursday," she said.

"Yes, I shall be there. Keep the supper-dances for me! We'll find a quiet corner somewhere and enjoy ourselves. Till Thursday then! Good-bye!"

"Good-bye!" she said.

He was gone. Before her wide eyes he went away along the verandah, and passed from her sight, and there fell an intense silence.

Olga sat motionless as a statue, gazing straight before her. A squirrel skipped airily on to the further end of the verandah and sat there, washing its face. Below, on the path, a large lizard flicked out from behind a stone, looked hither and thither, spied the still figure, and darted away again. And then, somewhere away among the cypresses the silence was broken; a paroquet began to screech.

Olga stirred, and a great breath burst suddenly from her—the first she had drawn in many seconds. She stretched out her hands into emptiness.

"Oh, Max!" she said. "Max! Max!"

With that bitter cry, all her strength seemed to go from her. She bowed her head upon her knees and wept bitterly, despairingly….

It must have been a full quarter of an hour later that Nick came lightly along the verandah, paused an instant behind the bowed figure, then slipped round and knelt beside it.

"Kiddie! Kiddie! What's the matter?" he said.

His one arm gathered her to him, so that she lay against his shoulder in the old childish attitude, his cheek pressed against her forehead.

She was too exhausted, too spent by that bitter paroxysm of weeping, to be startled by his sudden coming. She only clung to him weakly, whispering, "Oh, Nick, have you come back at last?"

"But of course I have," he said. "Have you been worrying about me? I sent you a message."

"I know. But I—I couldn't help being anxious." She murmured the words into his neck, her arms tightening about him.

"What a silly little sweetheart!" he said. "Is that what you've been crying for?"

She was silent.

He passed rapidly on. "You mustn't cry any more, darling. Old Reggie will be here soon, you know. He'll think I've been bullying you. Have you been sitting here by yourself all the morning? Why didn't you go down to Daisy Musgrave?"

"I didn't want to, Nick. I—I don't in the least mind being by myself," she told him, mastering herself with difficulty. "Tell me what you've been doing—all this time!"

"I?" said Nick. "Watching and listening chiefly. Not much else. Is the post in? Come and help me read my letters!"

"They're here." Olga turned and began to feel about with one hand under her work.

"All right. I'll find 'em." He let her go, and fished out his correspondence himself. She was glad that he did not look at her very critically or press further for the cause of her woe.

He sat down on the mat at her feet, and proceeded to read his letters as she handed them to him.

After a little, she took up her work again. She had quite regained her composure, only she was utterly weary—too weary to feel anything but a numb aching. All violent emotion had passed.

Suddenly Nick dropped his correspondence, and turned. "Kiddie," he said. "I'm going to chuck this job."

She looked down at him with a surprise that would have been greater but for her great weariness. "Really, Nick?"

"Yes, really. I've done my poor best, but to make a success would be a life job. Moreover," Nick's eyes suddenly gleamed, "the Party want me—or say they do. There's going to be a big tug of war in the summer, and they want me to help pull. I'm rather good at pulling," here spoke Nick's innate modesty, "and so I've got to be there.'"

"We are going Home then?" Olga's voice was low. She spoke as one whom the decision scarcely touched.

Nick leaned back luxuriously against her knees. "Yes, sweetheart, Home—Home to Muriel and the kiddie—Home to good old Jim. You won't be sorry to see your old Dad again?"

"No," she said; then, as his brows went up, she stooped forward and kissed the top of his head. "But you've been very good to me, Nick," she said. "I—I've been happier with you, dear, than I could have been with anyone."

"Save one," said Nick, flashing a swift look upwards. "And you've struck him off the list, poor beggar."

She checked him quickly, her hand on his shoulder. "Please, Nick!" she whispered.

He nodded wisely. "Yes, that hurts, doesn't it? But you're not the only one to suffer. Ever think of that?"

She did not answer him. With a quiver in her voice she changed the subject. "When do you think we shall go Home then, Nick?"

"Soon," said Nick. "Very soon. They say I can't be spared much longer. Awfully sweet of 'em, isn't it? As for this immoral little State, it ought to be put under martial law for a spell. It won't be, of course; but old Reggie will understand. He'll take measures, and relieve me of my stewardship as soon as may be. I'm sorry in a way, but I only bargained for six months. And I want to get back to Muriel." He turned to her again, with his elastic smile. "But you've been a dear little pal. You've kept me from pining," he said. "Wish your affairs might have ended more cheerily; but we won't discuss that. Let's see; you don't know Sir Reginald Bassett, do you?"

"No, dear."

"Nor Lady Bassett his wife. Good for you. Pray that you never may, and the odds are in favour of the prayer being granted. She has decided not to come after all."

"Not to come, Nick! Why, I thought it was all settled!"

Nick grinned. "Her heart has failed her at the last moment. She doesn't like immoral States." He waved a letter jubilantly in the air. "No matter, my dear. We shall get on excellently without her. She isn't your sort at all." He broke into a laugh. "She's the only woman of my acquaintance I don't love, and the only one—literally—who doesn't love me."

"How horrid of her, Nick! I'm sure I should hate her."

"I'm sure you would, dear. So it's just as well—all things considered—that you are not going to meet. Well, I must go and get respectable." He rose with a quick, lithe movement, but paused, looking down at her quizzically to ask: "What did you think of my friend the moonstone-seller? Pretty, isn't he?"

She smiled for the first time. "I'm sure he's quite disreputable. He disappeared in the most mysterious fashion. I wonder if he's lurking about anywhere still, waiting to murder us in our beds."

"I wonder," said Nick.

But he did not trouble himself to look round for the mysterious one, nor did the possibility of being murdered seem to disturb him greatly. He went away to his room, humming a love-song below his breath. And Olga knew that his thoughts were far away in England, where Muriel was waiting to welcome him Home.

CHAPTER XXI
THE GATHERING STORM

Looking back in after days, the time that elapsed between the coming of Sir Reginald Bassett and the night of the Fancy-Dress Ball at the mess-house was to Olga as a whirling nightmare. She took part in all the gaieties that she and Noel had so busily planned, but she went through them as one in the grip of some ghastly dream, beholding through all the festivities the shadow of inexorable Fate drawing near. For she was caught in the net at last, hopelessly, irrevocably enmeshed. From the very outset she had realized that. There could no longer be any way of escape for her, for she could not accept deliverance at the price that must be paid for it. She did not so much as seek to escape, knowing her utter helplessness. Rebellion was a thing of the past. Her spirit was broken. Had she been still engaged to Max, the struggle, though hopeless, would have been more fierce. But since that was over, there was little left to fight for on her own account. Hate and loathe the man as she might, she was forced to own his mastery. To pass from the desert to an inferno was not so racking a contrast as if he had dragged her direct from her paradise.

Later, when the first paralysis of despair had passed, when her captor came to take full possession, she would rebel again wildly, madly. There would be a frightful struggle between them, the last fierce effort of her instinct to be free from a bondage that revolted her. Vaguely, from afar, she viewed that inevitable battle, and in her mind the conviction grew that she would not survive it. The thing was too monstrous. It would kill her.

But for the present her power of resistance was dead. Max must be protected, and this was the only way. She did not dare to think of him in those days, save as it were in the abstract. He filled a certain chamber in her heart which she never entered. He had gone out of her life more completely than if he had died, for she cherished no tender memory of him. She turned away from the bare thought of him, and in the naked horrors of the night, when she lay cold and staring while the hours crawled by, she deliberately banished him from her mind. She was going to do this thing for his sake—this thing that she firmly believed would kill her—but she barred him away from her agony. Not even in thought could she endure his presence at the sacrifice.

So, without struggle, those awful days passed, and she mingled with the gay crowd, instinctively hiding the plague-spot in her soul. Each day she encountered Hunt-Goring at one function or another, meeting the gleam in his dark eyes with no outward tremor but with a heart gone cold. He made no attempt to be alone with her; he was content to bide his time, knowing that the game was his. And each night the memory of his hateful kisses wound like a thread of evil through her brain, banishing all rest.

It was on the afternoon preceding the Ball that Nick called her out to the verandah where he and Sir Reginald were sitting. She liked Sir Reginald, he was genial and kindly and exceedingly easy to entertain.

He drew forward a chair beside him as she approached. "Come and join us, Miss Ratcliffe! Nick and I have been having a very lengthy confab. I am afraid you will accuse me of monopolizing him."

Olga came to the chair and sat beside him. "I hope you have been telling him to stop his visits to the native quarter at night," she said. "They are very bad for him. Look how thin he is getting!"

Nick laughed, but Sir Reginald shook his head. "If I may be allowed to say so, I don't think you are either of you looking very robust," he said. "India plays tricks with us, doesn't she? It doesn't do to let her get too strong a hold. I think Nick will be in a position to take you Home before the end of next month, Miss Ratcliffe. His work here is practically done, and a very brilliant service he has rendered the Government. It has been a very delicate task, and he has accomplished it with marked ability."

"Oh, is it finished?" said Olga.

"Not finished—no!" said Nick. "And never will be with Kobad Shikan in power. But I rather fancy the days of that old gentleman's supremacy are drawing to an end. I've been teaching friend Akbar a thing or two lately. He is beginning to see which way the cat jumps, and to realize that the only way to hold his own is to hold by his masters. I've been the antidote to a big dose of sedition administered by the hoary Kobad, and I fancy I've brought him round. Kobad's influence is undermined in all directions, and I fancy the old sinner is beginning to know it."

"I knew he was a horrid old man!" said Olga.

Nick laughed again. "He entertains a very lively hatred for all of us that nothing will ever eradicate. But he belongs to the old *régime*, so what could one expect? I have even heard it whispered that he served with the rebel sepoys in the Mutiny. However, his day is done. Akbar is no longer under his influence. He will strike out a line for himself now. I've won him round to the British raj, and if he isn't assassinated by Kobad's people, he'll do. It's a pity they can't have martial law for a bit," he added to Sir Reginald. "They would settle in half the time. Hang a few, shoot a few, and—"

"Nick!" said Olga, in astonishment.

He stretched out his one hand and laid it on her knee. "And flog a few," he finished, smiling at her. "There would be some chance for the State then. Yes, I'm a blood-thirsty creature. Didn't you know? One can't wear gloves for this game."

Olga held his hand in silence. She had learned more of Nick in the past five months than she had ever known before. Undoubtedly he had become more of the man to her and less of the hero. She did not love him any the less for it, but her attitude towards him was different.

She knew he had divined the change, and suspected him of being amused thereby—a suspicion which he strengthened by saying with a laugh, "You didn't know I could be such a brute, did you?"

She smiled back a little wistfully. "I begin to think you could be almost anything, Nick," she said.

He shot her a swift glance, and it seemed to her for a moment that he was looking for a double meaning to her words. But apparently he found none, for he smiled again with the comfortable remark, "Ah, well, it's a useful faculty if exercised with discretion. What are you going to wear to-night? Let's hear all about it!"

That was the new Nick all over, displaying the male denseness with which she had never been wont to credit him. She gave him details of her costume without much ardour, he listening with careless comments.

"You don't sound very keen," he said suddenly. "I believe you're getting *blasé*."

"These things get a little monotonous, don't they?" said Sir Reginald.

His smile was sympathetic. She felt inexplicably that he understood her better than did Nick. He had fathomed the deadly weariness that Nick had overlooked.

"Go on!" commanded Nick. "Who are you going to dance with?"

She hesitated a little, and he turned his hand and pinched her fingers somewhat mercilessly. "Noel of course—he's too handsome to refuse, isn't he? And the rest of the boys will expect their share, doubtless. But remember—the supper-dances are mine."

She started a little. "Oh, Nick dear, I'm afraid I've promised those already."

"To whom?" said Nick swiftly.

"Major Hunt-Goring." Her voice was low; she did not look at him as she uttered the name.

Nick's eyebrows shot upwards with lightning rapidity; then drew into a frown. He was silent for a moment before he said very decidedly, "I'm not going to let you dance with Hunt-Goring, so you may as well pass his dances on to me. If he wants to know the reason, he can ask me—and I shall be delighted to tell him."

He spoke in a fighting tone; there was fight in the grip of his hand. Olga noted it, and foresaw trouble.

"I'm afraid it's too late now, Nick," she said rather wearily. "I must keep my engagements."

Nick turned and sent one of his keen glances over her. "You won't keep this one," he told her. "I am simply not going to allow it. Those supper-dances are mine, so make up your mind to that!"

He spoke with a finality that made protest seem futile. It seemed to Olga that the yellow face had never looked so grim. She made no further effort to withstand him, aware that to do so would entail a battle of wills which could only end in her defeat. Perhaps deep in the heart of her she was even thankful for this brief reprieve.

She said nothing therefore, and Sir Reginald considerately turned the subject by asking Nick what disguise he intended to assume.

"I?" said Nick. "I haven't absolutely decided, sir. I've got a fool's dress somewhere that might serve."

He turned, releasing Olga's hand, to take a screw of paper from a salver with which Kasur at that moment approached him.

He glanced at Sir Reginald as he did so, muttered a word of excuse, and deftly opened it. The next instant he crumpled it again in his hand, and spoke over his shoulder to the waiting native.

"Say I will see the moonstone before it is sent away!"

The man departed, and Nick rose. "Afraid I shall have to go to the Palace, sir. Olga, you must take care of Sir Reginald in my absence."

"What! Now, Nick?" Olga looked up in swift surprise.

"Yes, now, my child. Good-bye!" He stooped and lightly kissed her. "I daresay I shan't be late back. If I am, you must go to the Ball without me, and get Sir Reginald to take care of you. I shall turn up some time, you may be sure."

"Important, is it?" asked Sir Reginald.

Nick nodded. "I ought to go, sir. Don't wait for me. I shall follow on if I'm late. In any case," he turned to Olga, "I shall be in time for those supper-dances."

His look flashed over her with a species of quizzical tenderness. "And you are not to give any dances to Hunt-Goring, mind, whatever the bounder says."

He was gone. Free, careless, upright, he strode humming along the verandah and swung round the corner out of sight.

A brief silence descended upon the two who were left. Olga glanced once or twice at Sir Reginald, whose brows were drawn in deep thought.

At length, with slight hesitation she spoke, voicing the anxiety that had been growing within her for many days. "Sir Reginald, do you think he is in any danger when he goes to the city?"

The old soldier came out of his reverie, and met her eyes. He smiled at her, albeit his own were grave. "He is extremely shrewd and capable," he said. "I do not think there is much likelihood of his being taken unawares."

"But it is dangerous?" Olga insisted.

"There is a certain amount of risk certainly." Gravely he admitted the fact. "But I think you need not be over-anxious," he added, with a kindly smile. "Nick is one of those clever people who always manage to win through somehow. They always used to say of him on the Frontier that he bore a charmed life. He has a positive genius for wriggling out of tight corners."

He wished to reassure her, she saw; but somehow she did not feel reassured. The conviction was growing upon her that Nick was exposing himself to a danger that would have appalled her had she realized it to its fullest extent.

She said no more to Sir Reginald, but her heart sank. The clouds were gathering thicker and ever thicker on her horizon. She did not dare to look forward any more.

CHAPTER XXII
THE REPRIEVE

"I say, you're magnificent!" said Noel. His hand closed tightly upon Olga's with the words. He looked her up and down with a free admiration too boyish to be offensive. "You're an absolute darling in that get-up!" he told her with enthusiasm.

It was impossible to be indignant. Olga tried and failed. She had not been aware till that moment that she was making a particularly brave show in her eighteenth-century costume, with her pink satin finery and powdered hair. But there was no mistaking the adulation in the boy's eyes, and even in the midst of her misery she felt a little glow of gratification. He was looking alluringly disreputable in his highwayman's dress, and the dark eyes shone upon her with fascinating audacity as he lifted her hand to his lips.

"So you haven't brought Nick with you?" he said, speaking with laughing haste to cut short her half-hearted rebuke.

"No, Nick was called away," she said. "He'll come later if he can."

"Called away, was he?" Noel paused, with her programme in his hand. "Is that what you are looking so worried about?"

She tried to laugh. "Yes, I am rather worried about him. I am afraid he is taking—big risks."

"Little idiot!" said Noel. "When he's got you to look after. But what do you mean by risks? Where has he gone?"

"I don't know," she said, with a shake of the head. "I don't know anything, Noel. He said something about going to see a moonstone, but I think that was only a blind. He can be rather subtle, you know, when he likes."

"Confound him!" said Noel. "Why doesn't he turn his attention to taking care of you? I've been wanting to have a talk to you for days, but I couldn't work it somehow."

Olga held out her hand for her programme; it shook ever so slightly. "I don't think we have anything very important to talk about," she said.

"But we have!" he said impetuously. "At least I have. Oh, damn!—a million apologies! I couldn't help it!—here's that brute Hunt-Goring. You're not going to dance with him? Say you're full up!"

Hunt-Goring, attired as a Turk, was crossing the room towards them. Olga cast a single glance over her shoulder, and turned to Noel with panic in her eyes.

"I've forgotten something," she said in a palpitating whisper. "I must run back to the cloak-room. Wait for me!"

She was gone with the words, fleeing like a hunted creature, till the gathering crowd hid her from sight.

Hunt-Goring smiled, and turned aside. He had no pressing desire for a public meeting. His turn was coming,—the very fact of her flight proclaimed it,—and he could very well afford to wait. He would make her pay full measure for that same waiting.

He passed Noel's scowl with a lazy sneer. The young man would pay also, and that reflection was nectar to his soul. Carelessly he betook himself to the verandah. The dancing did not attract him—so he had told Daisy Musgrave earlier in the day, a remark of which she had been swift to take advantage. For her weariness of her guest was very nearly apparent by that time, and it was a relief to be able to relax her duties as hostess for that evening at least.

The dancing began to the strains of the regimental band, and soon the motley throng were all gathered in the ball-room. It did not look like an all-British assembly, but the nationality of the laughing voices was quite unmistakable. All talked and laughed as they danced, and the hubbub was considerable.

Into it Olga came stealing back, and paused nervously in the doorway to look on. Daisy, dressed as a water-nymph, waved her a gay greeting over her husband's shoulder. Olga smiled and waved back, striving to smother away out of sight the sick fear at her heart.

Someone touched her shoulder, and she started round almost with a cry.

Noel bent to her. "Sorry I made you jump. Look here! There's no one in the ante-room. Come and sit out with me!"

He offered his arm, and she took it thankfully without a word. They went away together.

The ante-room was dimly lighted, and comparatively quiet, though the music and laughter and swish of dancing feet were fully audible there. Noel found her a comfortable chair, and seated himself upon the arm thereof.

He did not speak at once, but after a little, as Olga sat in silence, he turned and looked down at her.

She raised her eyes at once and smiled. "You must think me very foolish," she said.

"No, I don't," he rejoined bluntly. "That brute is enough to scare any woman. You hate him, don't you?"

There was insistence in his tone, insistence mingled with a touch of anxiety. But Olga did not answer him.

"Don't let us talk about him!" she said, with a shiver she could not repress.

Noel's mouth hardened a little. "I'm very sorry," he said. "But we must. He's been circulating a lot of lies about—Max." He paused an instant, looking straight down at her. "Max is a good chap, you know," he said. "It's up to me to defend him."

Olga's face quivered, but she kept her eyes lifted. "You can't," she said, her voice very low.

"Can't I, though?" Hotly he threw back the words. "You don't mean to say you believe it?"

"I know it is true," she said.

"My dear Olga,—" he began.

But she checked him, her hand upon his arm. "Noel," she said, "truly I can't talk about this. But that story is—true, in part at least. Max admitted it—himself—to me."

"Impossible!" ejaculated Noel.

Her fingers closed over his sleeve; her hold was beseeching. "I can't argue with you, Noel," she said. "But I know it is true. You see, I was there."

He stared at her in stupefaction. "Olga, I can't believe it!"

"It is true," she said again.

"But—" Noel began to waver in spite of himself—"if you were there, you must have known all along!"

Her brows drew into the old lines of perplexity. "You see, I was ill," she said. "I—I didn't remember. I don't remember all the details even now. I only know that—it happened. Max told me so—when I asked him."

"Good heavens above!" ejaculated Noel.

She went on drearily, as if he had not spoken. "That was the end of everything between us; and it's just as well now. For I shouldn't have been able to marry him even if it hadn't been."

"Why not?" said Noel.

She looked away from him, and was silent.

He leaned down towards her, and spoke quickly, urgently.

"Olga dear, forgive me for asking, but I must know. Don't you really love him?"

She made a little unconscious gesture of the hands as of pushing something from her. "No," she said.

"But you did?" he insisted.

She leaned her elbow on her knee, lodging her chin upon her hand. "I thought I did—once," she said slowly. "But—it was a mistake."

"It couldn't have been," he said.

She nodded slowly two or three times, not turning her head. "Yes," she said, with the air of one clinching an argument. "It was a mistake."

Noel was silent for a few moments. There was something in her set profile that hurt him. He longed to see her full face. But she did not move. She seemed almost to have forgotten that he was there.

He moved at last, bending nearer. "Olga!" he whispered.

"Yes?" Still she did not turn.

He slipped down to his knees beside her. "Olga!" he said again very pleadingly.

She stirred then, stirred and looked him full in the eyes. And all his life Noel remembered the awful despair that looked out at him from her soul "I—can't!" she said.

He clasped her two hands between his own. "Can't you even think of it?" he urged, under his breath. "You know—you said—you'd have married me if—if—poor old Max hadn't come first. I wouldn't cut him out for worlds; but that's happened already, hasn't it? Surely there's no one else?"

But Olga made no answer. Only the despair in her eyes deepened to a dumb agony.

"Darling," he whispered, gathering her hands up and holding them against his face, "I'd be awfully good to you. And I want you—I do want you. Won't you even consider it?"

A great shiver went through Olga.

"Won't you have my love?" he said.

But still for a little she was silent. It seemed that no words would come.

Then, as he pressed his lips to the hands he had taken, something seemed suddenly to break loose within her. With a great sob she leaned her head upon his shoulder. "Noel! Noel! I—can't!"

His arms clasped her in a moment; he held her close. "Dearest, what is it? Why can't you?"

She answered him with her face hidden and in a voice so low that he barely caught the words. "I am—not free!"

"Not free!" Sharply he repeated the phrase. Suspicion, keen-edged as a rapier, ran swiftly through him. His arms tightened. "Olga, tell me what you mean! Who is it? Not—not that devil Hunt-Goring!"

She did not answer him, save by her silence and the convulsive shudder that went through her at his words. But that in itself was answer enough, and over her head Noel swore a deep and terrible oath.

Only a few yards away the lilting waltz-music was quickening to a finish. In a few moments more their privacy would be invaded by the giddy dancers.

"Listen!" said Noel, and his voice fell short and stern. "He shan't have you! That I swear! It's monstrous—it's unthinkable! Why, he's old enough to be your father. And he's got the opium-habit. Max told me so. Olga, I say, haven't you the strength of mind to refuse him? If the brute pesters you, why don't you tell Nick?"

Slowly Olga raised herself, quitting his support. "I've promised not to tell anyone," she said dully. "You mustn't know either."

"But, my dear girl, something must be done," he objected. "You can't let him ride over you roughshod. You don't mean—you can't mean—to let him marry you?"

"I can't help it," she said.

"Can't help it!" He stared at her. "He really has some hold over you then? What is it?"

She was silent. The last crashing chords of the first waltz were being played. Noel got to his feet. His boyish face was set in grim lines.

"Do you want me to go and kill him?" he said.

"No!" She sprang up also, quickened to sudden fear by his words. "You're not to go near him," she said, "Noel, promise me you won't! Oh, if you only knew—how much harder—your interference makes things! Don't you see—I've given him my word to consult no one!" She was panting uncontrollably; her hands were fast closed upon his arm. "I refused him once before," she told him feverishly, "and he—he punished me—cruelly. I can't—I daren't—refuse him again!"

"You'd sooner marry him?" Noel stared at her incredulously.

She flung out her hands with a wide, despairing gesture. "Yes—yes—I would sooner marry him!"

The music had stopped. There came the sound of approaching voices. Their privacy was at an end.

Yet for full ten seconds Noel stood widely gazing at the girl before him with eyes in which surprise, hurt pride, and smouldering passion mingled; then very abruptly, as the first chattering couple reached the half-open door, he swung away from her.

"All right!" he said. "Good-bye!"

He went straight out without a glance behind, nearly running into the gay invaders.

Olga, with the instinct to escape notice, turned as swiftly to the window. She went out upon the verandah, blindly groping her way, scarcely aware of her surroundings. And a figure waiting there in the dimness laughed a cruel laugh and roughly caught her.

"'You'd sooner marry him,' eh?" gibed a voice close to her ear. "My dear, that's the wisest resolution you ever made in your life!"

She did not cry out or attempt to resist him. She had known that her fate was sealed. Only, as his lips sought hers, she shrank away with every fibre of her being in sick revolt, and for the first time in her life she begged for mercy.

"Please—please—give me to-night!" she pleaded. "Only to-night! Yes, I will marry you. But don't—don't ask—any more of me—to-night!"

He paused, still holding her in his arms, feeling the wild beat of her heart against his own, softened in spite of himself by that quivering, agonized appeal.

"And if I let you go to-night, what will you give me to-morrow?" he said.

"I shall be—your *fiancée*—to-morrow," she whispered, gasping.

"And you will marry me—when?"

"You shall decide," she murmured faintly.

He laughed rather brutally. "A somewhat empty favour, my dear, since I should have decided in any case. But if you give me your promise to come to me like a sensible girl, without any more nonsense of any kind—"

"I will!" she said. "I will!"

"Then—" he released her with the words—"I give you your freedom—till to-morrow. Go—and make the most of it!"

He had not kissed her. She slipped from his arms, thankful for his forbearance, and sped away down the veranda like a shadow.

As for Hunt-Goring, he cursed himself for a soft fool and took out his cigarettes to wile away what promised to be an evening of infernal dullness.

CHAPTER XXIII
THE GIFT OF THE RAJAH

Olga danced that night with the feeling that she danced upon her grave, reminding herself continually, as the hours slipped by, that it was her last night of freedom.

The failure of Nick to appear for the supper-dances diverted her thoughts from this but to send them with ever-growing anxiety into a new channel. Where was Nick? What was happening to him? What could be delaying him?

She had no partner to take her in to supper, refusing each one that offered with the repeated declaration that she must wait for Nick. But Nick came not, and momentarily her uneasiness increased.

Sir Reginald came to her at last, his kindly face full of sympathy. "There is probably no occasion for alarm, my dear," he said. "Come, give me the pleasure of your company at supper!"

She had to yield, for he would take no refusal; but she could eat nothing notwithstanding his utmost solicitude. She was in a state of mind to start at every sudden sound, and the food he put before her remained untasted on her plate.

Sir Reginald watched over her with fatherly concern, but he could do nothing to alleviate her anxiety. In his own private soul he shared it to a considerable degree.

As they left the supper-room together, she turned to him piteously. "Oh, do you think I might go back and see if he has returned? Really, I can't—I can't dance any more!"

"Wait a little longer!" he counselled. "You needn't dance of course. Stay quietly with me! He may walk in at any moment."

She longed to go, but could not refuse a suggestion so kindly proffered. She stayed with him therefore, glad of his protecting presence, refusing to dance any more on the plea of fatigue.

The whirling scene wearied her unspeakably. She found herself watching Noel, who was frankly flirting with every woman in the room. It was doubtless a safe pastime, but behind her gnawing anxiety a little spark of resentment kindled and burned. How hopelessly fickle he was!

Hunt-Goring had apparently removed himself from the gay company altogether, for she saw him not at all. His absence was the only palliating circumstance in that hour of sick suspense.

It was growing late and the remaining dances were few, when a native orderly entered the room and stepped up to Colonel Bradlaw, who was standing with Sir Reginald. He murmured a few low words to which the Colonel listened with a frown. It was his habit to frown always at the unexpected.

He turned after a moment to Sir Reginald. "There's a messenger arrived from the Palace with a box of sweets or something. What?" breaking off ferociously as the orderly's lips moved soundlessly.

"Moonstones, *sahib*," murmured the orderly with deference.

"Moonstones," repeated the Colonel, in a tone of vast contempt, "to be presented to the lady wearing the best make-up in the room. What on earth am I to do, sir?"

"Accept with thanks, I should say," said Sir Reginald, with a smile.

"Oh, I don't mean that," said the Colonel, frowning still more. "But who the dickens is going to decide as to the merits of the ladies' costumes? Not I—and not my wife! It's too big a responsibility—that."

Sir Reginald laughed. "That is a serious consideration, certainly. I should make them decide themselves. Vote by ballot. That ought to satisfy everyone."

The Colonel turned to the waiting orderly. "Very well. Tell the messenger to come in!" He made a sign to Noel, who had just ceased to dance, that brought the young man to his side.

"Look here, Wyndham! You organized this show, so you may as well take on this job. The Rajah has sent a prize for the lady wearing the best costume."

Noel frowned also at the news. "Confound him! What for, sir?"

"Oh, I suppose he wants to make himself popular," said the Colonel, still mightily contemptuous. "We can't refuse it anyway. Arrange for the ladies to vote by ballot, will you? They will probably all vote for themselves," he added to Sir Reginald. "But that's a detail. And I say, Noel, get a table from somewhere, will you? It's your show, not mine."

Noel smiled upon his commanding-officer, an impudent, affectionate smile. He and Badgers were close allies. "Very good, sir, I'll see to it," he said, and departed.

Under his directions a table was brought in and placed at the end of the room. The dancing was stopped temporarily, and the dancers lined up against the walls. Noel, armed with a sheaf of note-paper went the round, tearing off slips and distributing them as he went.

While this was in progress, the Rajah's messenger was admitted and conducted to the table behind which stood Sir Reginald with Olga and Colonel Bradlaw. He was a very magnificent person, turbaned and glittering; he bore himself like the servant of an emperor. In his hands he carried with extreme care an ivory casket, exquisitely carved, with a lock of wrought Indian gold. The key, also of gold, lay on the top of the casket.

The gift was plainly a costly one, and every eye in the room followed it.

The messenger reached the table and bowed low. "With the compliments of His Highness the Rajah of Sharapura!" he said, and deposited the casket upon the table.

The Colonel glanced at Sir Reginald who at once responded. "Convey our thanks to the Rajah," he said, "and say that the gracious gift will be much appreciated! I shall give myself the pleasure of calling upon him to assure him of this in person to-morrow."

The messenger salaamed again deeply, and withdrew.

"I wish he'd keep his precious moonstones!" grumbled the Colonel. "They are more bother than they're worth. Hurry up, there, Noel! It's getting late."

"Just finished, sir," came Noel's cheery answer. "I must just get a hat to hold the ballot-papers."

He did not offer a paper to Olga, who still kept her place by Sir Reginald, her young face white and tired under the pile of fair, powdered hair.

"I think I shall go when this is over," she whispered to Sir Reginald.

"So you shall," he said kindly. "I will escort you myself. I expect we shall find Nick waiting for us," he added, with a smile. "Some business has delayed him, I have no doubt."

She tried to smile in answer, but her lips quivered in spite of her. She turned her face aside, ashamed of her weakness.

Noel came up with the ballot-papers, and emptied them out upon the table without a glance at her.

"I must get you to help," said Sir Reginald, drawing her gently forward.

"I can manage, sir," said Noel shortly.

But the Colonel broke in, "Nonsense, Wyndham! One scrutineer isn't enough."

And Noel pushed across a handful of papers to Olga without lifting his eyes.

With fingers that trembled slightly, she began to sort, assisted by Sir Reginald. Several of the papers bore her own name, a fact which at first she scarcely noticed, but which very soon became too conspicuous to be ignored.

"I believe it's yours," murmured Sir Reginald at her elbow.

"Oh, impossible!" she said, flushing.

But in a very few minutes the suspicion was verified. Noel looked up from his sorting with a brief, "You've won!"

Olga raised her eyes swiftly, but he instantly averted his, and turned to communicate the result to the Colonel.

The latter shook hands with her, and shouted the news in his loudest parade voice to the assembled company. There ensued applause and congratulations that Olga would gladly have foregone. Then, as her friends began to press round, Sir Reginald stepped forward.

"It is my proud privilege," he said, "to present to Miss Ratcliffe in the Rajah's name his very handsome gift."

He took the golden key from the top of the casket and handed it with a bow to Olga.

She took it with a murmur of thanks, and stood hesitating, possessed by a very curious feeling of dread.

"Open it!" said Noel impatiently.

"Open it for her!" said Sir Reginald, divining a certain amount of nervousness as the cause of her hesitation.

Noel held out a hand for the key, and she gave it to him. There was a sudden hush and a little thrill of expectation in the motley crowd gathered round as he turned to fit it into the lock.

The key did not fit in very easily; it seemed to meet with some obstruction. With a frown Noel pulled it out again. "What's the matter with the thing?" he said irritably.

"Try it the other way up!" suggested Sir Reginald.

"I believe it's a hoax," said a man in the crowd.

Noel turned the key upside down amid an interested silence, and began to insert it again in the lock.

As he did so, there came a sudden cry from the background, a man's voice shrill and warning.

"Leave the thing alone! It's a bomb! I tell you, it's a bomb!"

"What?" The crowd scattered backwards as though a thunderbolt had fallen in its midst, and a woman shrieked in panic.

A man—wild, unkempt, ragged—tore like a maniac over the polished floor, making for the group at the table, waving one skinny arm.

"Noel! You damn' fool! Leave the thing alone!"

Noel whizzed round with the key in his hand. "Hullo,—Nick!" he said.

"Leave it alone! Leave it alone!" The voice dropped to a hoarse croak. The man was close to the table now, and in amazement Olga recognized the face of the old moonstone-seller. But it was convulsed with a terror such as she had never seen on the face of any man.

The bony hand darted out towards the casket, and her heart stood still. She knew that hand—wiry, energetic, capable.

"Nick!" she whispered. "Nick!"

He brushed her aside, and, again in that dry, breathless croak, "There isn't—a moment—to lose!" he said.

In another instant he would have had the shining thing in his grasp, but in that instant Noel's wits leaped to full understanding. He wheeled, caught the newcomer by his tattered garment, and flung him violently away.

"All right, you old joker!" he said. "My job!"

Dazed with horror, though still scarcely realizing, Olga saw him turn and lift the ivory casket, holding it clasped firmly between his hands. Then, with a set face, stepping warily, he moved to the window close behind.

In the other part of the room women were crying and men deeply cursing; but there near the table no one uttered a sound, till the ragged creature on the floor sprang up crying hoarsely for a pail of water.

Noel's figure passed through the open window as he did so, smoothly, unfalteringly, and so out upon the dark verandah.

Deftly, warily, he made his way. The thing between his hands weighed heavily. It would have been no job for a one-armed man.

He passed down the verandah with every nerve strung to the moment's emergency. Unquestionably he was not afraid, but he could have wished that the place had been better illuminated. His progress would have been considerably quicker.

He neared the flight of six steps that led down to the compound, and suddenly became aware of a dark figure lounging in a wicker-chair ahead of him. He saw the glow of a cigarette.

He raised his voice. "Hi, you! Clear out! Git—if you value your life! There's going to be an explosion!"

He did not slacken his pace as he uttered his warning. He dared not pause. His whole heart was set on reaching the compound in time.

The figure in the chair turned towards him. He heard the creak of the bamboo. But it made no movement to rise.

"Confound you! Take your chance then!" said Noel between his teeth.

He came closer. He saw in a momentary glance the face behind the cigarette. Heavy, drugged eyes looked up to his. Then in the dimness he heard a sudden movement, a snarling, devilish laugh.

The next instant he kicked against an obstruction, staggered, fought madly to recover himself, tripped a second time, and with a yell of rage fell headlong.

There came a flash of blinding, intolerable brightness—a roar as of the roar of a cannon, stunning, deafening, devastating,—the smaller sound of wood splintering and falling,—and then a dumb and awful silence more fearful than Death.

* * * * *

The first to arrive on that scene of darkness and destruction was the old moonstone-seller. He seemed to be gifted with eyes of extraordinary keenness, for he made his way unerringly, with the agility of a monkey among the splintered *débris*. One corner of the mess-house had completely gone, leaving a gaping hole into the ante-room. Dimly the lamps within shone upon the wreckage. The crowd from the ball-room, horror-stricken, fearful, were gathered about the doorway. The atmosphere was thick with dust and smoke.

Light as an acrobat the moonstone-seller stepped among the ruins, then paused to listen.

"Is there anyone here?" he asked aloud. "Noel, are you here?"

There was no answer. The awful, tragic silence closed in upon his words.

But it did not daunt him. Cautiously he crept a little further forward. And now there came a voice from the room behind him, Colonel Bradlaw's voice, harsh with suspense.

"Is the boy dead?"

"Don't know yet, sir," came back the answer. "Will you send a lantern? Ah! Hullo!"

Something had moved against his foot. Something writhed and groaned.

The searcher stooped. "Hullo!" he said again. "Noel, is it you, lad? I'm here. I'll help you."

A voice answered him—a smothered inarticulate voice. A groping hand came up, clutching for deliverance. There came the slip and crackle of broken wood beneath which some living object struggled and fought for freedom.

The one wiry arm of the moonstone-seller went down to the rescue. It did good service that night—such service as astonished even its owner when he had time to think.

The man under the *débris* was making titanic efforts, thrusting his way upwards with desperate, frantic strength. Once as he strove he uttered a sharp, agonized cry, and the man above him swore in fierce, instinctive sympathy.

"Where are you hurt, old chap? Keep your head, for Heaven's sake! Where is it worst?"

The gasping voice made answer with spasmodic effort: "My head—my face—my eyes! Oh, God,—my eyes!"

There followed a cough as if something choked all utterance, and then again that mute, gigantic struggle for freedom.

It was over at last. Out of the wreckage there staggered the dreadful likeness of a man. The lantern had been brought and shone full upon the ghastly sight. He was torn, battered, half-naked, and the whole of his face was blackened and streaming with blood.

"Noel! Is it Noel?" asked Colonel Bradlaw.

And the man himself made answer, spitting forth the blood that impeded his utterance.

"Yes, it's me! But I'm done, sir! I'm done! Bring a light someone! I can't see—where I'm going!"

The moonstone-seller's arm was round him, holding him up. "All right, lad! I've got you!" he said.

"But bring a light! Bring a light!" A note of panic ran through the reiterated words "Confound it! I must see—I will see—I—"

"My dear lad, you can't see for a minute." It was Nick's voice, quick and soothing. "This infernal blood has got into your eyes. Come and have them attended to! You'll be better directly."

"No! It's not the blood! It's not the blood!" The words tumbled over each other, well-nigh incoherent in their fevered utterance. And suddenly Noel flung up his arms above his head with a wild and anguished cry. "My God! I'm blind! I'm blind!"

With the cry his strength—that fiery strength born of emergency—collapsed quite suddenly. His knees doubled under him. He fell forward in utter, overwhelming impotence, and lay prone and senseless at the Colonel's feet....

CHAPTER XXIV
THE BIG, BIG GAME OF LIFE

It was many hours later that understanding returned to Noel.

He came to himself abruptly, in utter darkness, with the horror of it still strong within his soul. His head was swathed in bandages. He turned it to and fro with restless jerks.

"And will ye please to lie quiet?" said the voice of the Irish regimental surgeon peremptorily by his side.

Noel, also Irish, collected his forces and made reply. "No. Why the devil should I? Where am I? What's going to happen to me? Am I—am I blind for life?"

The falter in the words spoke to the tenseness of his suspense. The doctor answered instantly, with more of kindliness than judgment. "Faith, no! It's not so bad as that. But ye'll have to pretend ye are for the present, or, egad, ye will be before ye've done. We brought ye to the Musgraves' shanty. Mrs. Musgrave wanted the care of ye. Damn' quare taste on her part, I'm thinking. And now ye're not to talk any more; but drink this stuff like a good boy and go to sleep."

Noel drank with disgust; the taste of blood was still in his mouth. He had never been ill in his life before, and he had not the smallest intention of obeying the doctor's orders.

"Let's hear what happened!" he said impatiently. "Oh, leave me alone, do! When can I have this beastly bandage off my eyes?"

"Not for a very long while, my son." The doctor's voice was jaunty, but the eyes that looked at the blind, swathed face were full of pity. "And don't ye go loosening it when my back's turned, or it isn't meself that'll be answerable for the consequences."

"Oh, damn the consequences!" said Noel. "I want to get up."

"And that ye can't!" was the doctor's prompt rejoinder. "Ye'll just lie quiet till further orders. Ye'll find yourself as weak as a rat moreover, when ye start to move about. It's only the fever in your veins that makes ye want to try."

Noel straightened himself in the bed. He was becoming aware of a fiery, throbbing torture beneath the bandages. With clenched teeth and hands hard gripped he set himself to endure.

But in a few minutes he turned his head again. "Are you still there, Maloney?"

"Still here, my son," said Maloney.

"Well, go and find someone—anyone who knows—to tell me exactly what happened last night."

"I can tell ye meself," began Maloney.

But Noel interrupted. "No; not you! You're such a liar. No offence meant! You can't help it. Find—find Nick, will you?"

"It isn't visitors ye ought to be having with your pulse in this state," objected Maloney.

"Do as I say!" commanded Noel stubbornly.

His will prevailed. The Irish doctor saw the futility of argument, and departed, having extracted a promise from his patient not to move during his absence.

And then came silence as well as darkness, an awful sense of being entombed, an isolation that appalled him added to the torture that racked. With an acuteness of consciousness more harrowing than delirium, he faced this thing that had come upon him, grabbing all his courage to endure the ordeal.

He felt as if his brain were on fire, each nerve-centre agonizing separately in the intolerable, all-enveloping flames. And through the dreadful stillness he heard the beat, beat, beat, of his heart, like the feet of a runaway along a desert road.

He turned his head again restlessly from side to side. The agony was beginning to master him. His powers of endurance were dwindling.

Suddenly he found himself speaking, scarcely knowing what he said, feeling that he must cry out or die.

"Lighten our darkness, we beseech Thee, O God!" Just the one sentence over and over to save him from raving insanity. "Lighten our darkness! Lighten our darkness! Lighten our darkness, we beseech Thee!"

He broke off abruptly. What was the good? Prayers were for white-souled children like Peggy. Was it likely that any cry of his would pierce the veil?

Yet the words came back to him, so urgent was his distress, so unbearable the silence of his desert. He said them again with a desperate earnestness, and almost instinctively began to listen for an answer. He felt almost a child again himself in his utter need, as he wrestled to drive the awful darkness from his soul. But no answer came to his cry and the brave heart of him slowly sank. He was deserted then, hurled down into hell to die a living death. In a single flashing second he had been torn from the world he loved—that bright, gay world in which he had revelled all his life—and flung into this inferno of endless darkness. The iron began to bite into his soul.

The glory of his youth was quenched. From thenceforth he would hear the music from afar, he would be barred out from the splendour of life, he would wander along the outside edge of things, forlorn and lonely. His popularity, his brilliance, his joy of living, had all been crushed to atoms with that single, sledge-hammer blow of Fate. Better—ten thousand times better—to have killed him outright! For this thing was infinitely worse than death.

The iron drove in a little deeper. His spirit, his pride, awoke and rebelled, raging impotently. He would not bear the burden. He would die somehow. He would find a means, do what they would to stop him. He would escape—somehow—from this particular hell. He would not be chained between life and death. He would burst the bonds. He would be free!

His pulses rose to fever pitch. He started up upon the bed. Now was the time—now—now! He might not have another chance. And there must be some means to his hand—some way out of this awful darkness!

The madness of fever urged him. In another moment he would have been on his feet, at grips with the fate that bound him; but even as he gathered himself together for the effort, something happened.

The door opened and a woman entered. He heard the swish of her draperies, and his heart gave a great throb and paused.

"Who is it?" he said, and his voice was harsh and dry even to his own hearing. "Who is it? Speak to me!"

She spoke, and his heart, released from the sudden check, leaped on at a pace that nearly suffocated him. "It's I, Noel,—Olga! They said I might come and see you. You don't mind?"

"Mind!" he said, and suddenly a great sob burst from him. He felt out towards her with hands that wildly groped. "Let me feel you!" he entreated. "I—I'll let you go again!"

And then very suddenly her arms were all around him, closing him in, lifting him out of his hell. "Noel! My own Noel!" she whispered. "My own, splendid boy!"

He held her fast, his battered head pillowed against her while he fought for self-control. For many seconds he could not utter a word. And in the silence the world he knew opened its gates to him again and took him back. The darkness remained indeed, but it had been lightened. The horror of it no longer tore his soul. The iron had been withdrawn.

He moved at last, drawing her hand to his lips. "Olga, you don't know what you've saved me from. I was—in hell."

"Lie down, dear!" she murmured softly. "I'm going to take care of you now." She added, as she shook up the pillow, "It's my business, isn't it?"

He sank back with a sense of great comfort, holding her hand fast in his. It made the darkness less dark to hold her so.

"I want to know what happened," he said. "Sit down and tell me!"

"And you will try to keep quiet," she urged gently.

"Yes—yes! But don't keep anything back! Tell me everything!"

"I will, dear," she said, "though really there isn't much to tell. Is that quite comfy? You're not in bad pain?"

"I can bear it," he said. "Go on! Let's hear!"

So, sitting by his side, her hand in his, Olga told him.

The plot had been of Kobad Shikan's devising. Nick had been on the watch for it for some time, had penetrated the city nightly in the garb of a moonstone-seller, collecting evidence, and—most masterly stroke of all—he had drawn the Rajah into partnership with him. It was due to Nick's influence alone that the Rajah had not been caught in Kobad Shikan's toils. Thanks to Nick's steady call upon his loyalty, he had remained staunch. But Kobad Shikan had been too powerful a tactician to overthrow openly. They had been forced to work against him in secret.

"The Rajah calls Nick his brother," said Olga.

"Like his cheek!" said Noel. "Not that I can talk myself. I took the liberty of kicking him off his own premises once." He chuckled involuntarily at the recollection and commanded her to continue.

So Olga went on to tell of old Kobad's final coup and of how the Rajah, receiving news of some mischief afoot, had sent an urgent message of warning that had taken Nick straight to the Palace. Thence he had gone in disguise to the haunts of Kobad Shikan's conspirators, but here he had received a check. Kobad Shikan, fearing treachery among his followers, had taken elaborate precautions to conceal his proceedings, and for hours Nick had been kept searching vainly for a clue. Then at last he had succeeded in running the truth to earth, had discovered the whole ghastly plot barely half an hour before the time fixed for its consummation, and had raced to the mess-house with his warning.

"And that's all, is it?" said Noel.

"Yes, that's all; except that old Kobad has disappeared. Nick seems sorry, but everyone else is glad."

"And what about—Hunt-Goring?" said Noel at last.

Olga's fingers tightened in his hold. "Oh, did you know he was there?" she said.

Briefly he made answer. "Yes, he tripped me. I believe he was half-drunk with opium or something. What happened? Was he killed?"

Noel's voice was imperious. She answered him instantly, seeing he demanded it.

"Yes."

Noel drew a deep breath. "Thank God for that!" he said. "Then you are free!"

Olga was silent.

"You are free?" he repeated, with quick interrogation.

Yet an instant longer she hesitated. Then she leaned her head against his pillow with a little sob. "No,—I'm not free, Noel. I—have given myself—to you!"

"Because I'm blind!" he said.

"No, dear, no! Once free—I should have come to you—in any case."

"Would you?" he said. "Would you? You're quite sure? You're not saying it out of pity? I won't have you marry me out of pity, Olga. I couldn't stand it."

"Oh, you needn't be afraid of that!" she said. Then a moment later, "When I marry you," she murmured softly, "it will be—for love."

There was no mistaking the sincerity of the words, though even then as it were in spite of himself he knew that the passionate adoration he had poured out to her had awakened no answering rapture in her heart. The very fashion of her surrender told him this. He might come first with her indeed, but the full gift was no longer hers to offer.

"I wonder if you will be happy with me," he said, after a moment.

"It is my only chance of happiness," she made answer.

"How do you know?" There was curiosity in his voice: he made a movement of impatient impotence, putting a hand that trembled up to his bandaged head.

She took the hand, and drew it softly down. "I will tell you how I know," she said. "I know because when I thought you were killed I felt—I felt as if the world had stopped. And since then—since I knew that you would live—I have been able to think of only you—only you." Her voice broke upon a sound of tears. "That awful fear for you opened my eyes," she whispered. "I haven't been able to think of Major Hunt-Goring's death or anything else at all. I've even deserted Nick." Valiantly, through her tears, she smiled. "I never did such a thing as that before for anyone."

He clasped her hands tightly as he lay. "Don't cry, sweetheart!" he whispered. "You're not crying—for me?"

"I can't help it," she whispered back. "I can't bear to think of you suffering,—you, Noel, you!"

"Don't cry!" he said again, and this time there was a hint of grimness in his voice. "I shall win through—somehow—for your sweet sake. Maloney told me I wasn't blind just now. That, I know, was a lie. Or at least he didn't believe it himself. Personally I feel as if my eyes have been blown clean out of my head. But—blind or otherwise—I'll stick to it, I'll stick to it, Olga. I'll make you happy, so help me, God!"

"My dearest!" she murmured. "My dearest!"

"And you're not to cry over me," he said despotically. "You're not to fret—ever. If you do, I—I shall be furious." He uttered a quivering laugh. "We'll play the game, dear, shall we, the big, big game of life? It won't be easy, God knows; but He lightened my darkness—very first time of asking too. So perhaps He'll give us a tip now and then as to the moves."

He fell silent for a space, and she wondered if he were growing drowsy. Then as she sat motionless by his side, closely watching him, she saw the boyish lips part in their own sunny smile.

"Go and tell Mrs. Musgrave to hoist a flag!" he said. "Say it's the luckiest day of my life!"

The lips quivered a little over the words, but they continued bravely to smile.

And Olga understood. The boy had shouldered his burden with all his soldier's spirit, and nothing would daunt him now. He had begun to play the game.

She herself rose to the occasion with instant resolution, forcing back the tears he would not suffer, brave because he was brave.

"I shall tell her to hoist one for us both," she said, "and to keep it flying as long as we are under her roof."

CHAPTER XXV
MEMORIES THAT HURT

"Well, Max! You're just off then?" Sir Kersley Whitton looked up with a smile to greet his partner as he entered.

"Just off," said Max.

He came to Sir Kersley, seated at his writing-table, and paused beside him. It was a day in April, showery, shot with fleeting gleams of sunshine that sent long golden shafts across the doctor's room.

"You will bring the boy here then?" said Sir Kersley.

"Yes, straight here. It's very good of you, Kersley." Max's hand lay for a moment on the great man's shoulder.

"Nonsense, my dear fellow! I'm as keen as you are." Sir Kersley leaned back in his chair. "I only hope we may be successful," he said. "Is he likely to be a good patient?"

"Quite the reverse, I should say." Max sounded grim. "But I expect I can manage him."

Sir Kersley smiled again. "Just as you managed me a couple of years ago, eh? Yes, I should say you will be fully competent in that respect. You have a way with you, eh, Max? What was it this Indian doctor said?"

"He believed a cure possible, but only under the most favourable conditions. The boy was in no state then to undergo an operation, and he funked the job." Max's tone was contemptuous.

"Ah, well! It's as well he didn't attempt it in that case," said Sir Kersley. "He will stand a better chance with us. And what about Captain Ratcliffe and Olga? Will they go straight home?"

"No," said, Max. He paused a moment, then said rather shortly, "I had a line from Dr. Jim. He says she won't leave Noel. He and Mrs. Ratcliffe are coming up to meet them, but he expects to go back alone."

"Captain and Mrs. Ratcliffe will stay in town with Olga, then?" asked Sir Kersley.

"I believe so."

Sir Kersley's grey eyes regarded him thoughtfully. "And she is still in the dark with regard to Miss Campion's death?" he asked, after a moment.

Max's eyes came swiftly downwards, meeting his look with something of the effect of a challenge. "Yes, absolutely," he said.

"It's an extraordinary case," observed Sir Kersley.

Max said nothing whatever. He took his pipe from his pocket, and began to fill it with a face of sardonic composure.

"I wonder if she ever asks herself how it came about," said Sir Kersley.

"Why should she?" said Max gruffly.

"My dear fellow, she must have wondered how it happened—why all details were kept from her—and so on."

"Why should she?" said Max again aggressively. "The subject is a painful one. She is willing enough to avoid it. Of course," he paused momentarily, "Noel doesn't know about that affair either. No one knows besides ourselves, but Dr. Jim and Nick."

"In my opinion Noel ought to know," said Sir Kersley, with quiet decision. "It would be a terrible thing for Olga if some day—after they were married—she remembered, and he were in ignorance of it."

Again Max's hand pressed his friend's shoulder, but this time the pressure was one of warning. "Kersley," he said, "I've been into all that. I've weighed every possible contingency that might arise. And I have decided against telling Noel. As you say, it would be a terrible thing if she ever remembered; but if Noel is left in ignorance, the chances are she never will remember. To tell him would be to put a shadow between them which he would never forget and she would in time come to be aware of. It would wreck their happiness sooner or later. No; in Heaven's name, leave them in peace!"

"I think you are wrong," Sir Kersley said. He was looking straight up into Max's face with eyes of shrewd kindliness. "I think it is extremely improbable that she never will remember. And I think, moreover, that it is hardly to be desired that she should not."

"I disagree with you!" said Max harshly.

"Yes, my dear fellow, I know you do. You are no impartial judge. You want—very naturally—to save her from any suffering. And I don't think you will succeed. If you could have persuaded her to marry you, you might have done it. Forewarned is forearmed; you would have known how to safeguard her. But utter ignorance is no safeguard at all. I don't think she would thank you for it—if she knew."

Max's mouth twisted in its most cynical smile. "I wonder," he said.

Sir Kersley said no more. Beyond the bare fact of his brief engagement and its rupture, Max had confided in him not at all. He had left him to infer that she had been caught by a nearer attraction in his absence—an inference which her present engagement to his brother had seemed to confirm. And Sir Kersley had been far too considerate to probe for further enlightenment. But he was not privately by any means satisfied with regard to the matter of Max's long and fruitless journey. He was not accustomed to seeing Max beaten, and the spectacle hurt him.

He urged his opinion no further, for it was evident that Max was firmly determined to withstand it; but when Max had gone he sat and contemplated the matter with a troubled frown. There seemed to be something he had not fathomed behind Max's silence.

As for Max he departed for the docks with that air of grimness that had somewhat grown on him of late. Though bound upon a welcoming errand, he knew that it was not going to be a particularly easy one.

He was somewhat late in arriving, and the great steamer had already come to her moorings. Among the waiting crowd he discerned Dr. Jim and Muriel, but he did not make his way to them. He knew they would meet later, and he was not feeling sociable that afternoon.

So he stood aloof and waited, searching the many faces that lined the deck-rails for the one face that alone he longed to see. He spied her at last, and was conscious of a momentary pang that he fiercely stifled. She was standing there at the rail above him, waving her handkerchief to Dr. Jim. Nick was on one side of her, also madly waving and yelling with futile energy. On the other side stood Noel. And at sight of him Max's grim face softened to tenderness.

"There's grit in the boy," he murmured.

For Noel, with a black shade covering his bandaged eyes, was obviously as merry as any there. He was holding Peggy Musgrave perched on his shoulder, and his thin, brown face was upturned and laughing. There seemed to be some joke going on between them, for Peggy was also chuckling vigorously, and as Max watched she slipped a caressing hand round Noel's chin and tenderly kissed him.

Daisy and Will Musgrave were standing next to them, but they were plainly not thinking of Peggy or her cavalier. They were very close together and hand in hand.

It was nearly an hour later that Max joined the party as they came ashore. Noel's pleasure at meeting him was very obvious. He gripped him by both hands.

"Old chap, you're a brick to come and meet me!" he said. "I was thinking of asking Trevor, but I'd ten times sooner have you."

"Trevor's away," Max said. "I've come to take possession of you altogether. I suppose you've no objection?"

"Objection!" laughed Noel. He pushed his hand through his brother's arm. "You'll have to pilot me," he said. "I'm getting used to things, but I can't find my way in a crowd yet."

And then came the meeting with Olga. It was very brief. For barely the fraction of a second her hand lay in Max's. Her greeting was quite inaudible.

Noel turned to her. "Olga, Max wants me to clear out at once with him. You're going to Marriot's with Nick of course. I shall come round and see you to-night."

"Perhaps Olga will come and see you instead," said Max. "Is Dr. Jim spending the night in town? Bring him to dine! I will speak to him, shall I?"

He passed on and made the arrangement with Dr. Jim, not waiting for her reply.

Then came a general rallying of the party, introductions and good-byes, fervent embraces from Peggy, good wishes and invitations on all sides, and at last the final departure of the two Wyndhams in Sir Kersley Whitton's motor.

Noel removed his hat and leaned back with a sigh. "It's been a ripping voyage," he said. "But I'm deuced glad it's over." He added with a laugh, as Max made no comment. "I shall miss Peggy though. She's been blind man's dog to me all through."

"Let us hope you won't need a dog to lead you about much longer!" said Max.

Whereat Noel's hand came out gropingly, with a certain diffidence. "Oh, man," he said, "I haven't dared to think of that!"

Max grasped the hand. "I'll do my best for you, old chap," he said. "But you'll need a thundering lot of patience."

"I've been cultivating that," said Noel. "The only thing I can't stand is not to know the truth."

"I shan't keep you in the dark," said Max. "It's not my way."

He was as good as his word. A few hours later he made his first examination of the injury, and curtly gave it as his opinion that it was not beyond remedy.

"I don't profess to be infallible," he said. "But there certainly seems to be just a chance that the sight has not been absolutely destroyed. I'm afraid you'll have a good deal to go through if it is to be restored, though. It will be a tough job for all concerned."

"Oh, I'm not afraid of that," said Noel sturdily. "I've the very best of reasons for sticking to it."

"Ah!" said Max, with his twisted smile. "I haven't congratulated you yet."

Noel turned with a quick movement. "I say, Max," he said, with a touch of embarrassment, "you weren't quite straight with me over that, were you?"

"I don't know what you mean," said Max in a voice that was utterly devoid of expression.

Noel's face was red, but he stuck to his point. "You didn't tell me why she broke with you," he said.

"Who did?" demanded Max.

"Hunt-Goring."

Max swallowed a remark which sounded more savage suppressed than if it had been fully audible.

"You had a row with him then?"

"Yes, I did. I couldn't help it. I told him it was a damned lie," said Noel.

Max grunted.

Noel proceeded with a hint of that doggedness that characterized them both. "After that, I saw Olga; it was before we got engaged. And I told her it was a lie too."

Max grunted again, stubbornly refraining from question or comment.

Noel, equally stubborn, continued. "She said it was the truth—said you had admitted it to her. I didn't—quite—believe it even then. Thinking about it since, I am pretty sure you didn't do actually that. Or if you did, it was a lie."

Max maintained an uncompromising silence.

Noel waited a moment, then squarely tackled him. "Max, why did you lie to her?"

"And if I didn't?" said Max very deliberately.

Noel made instant and winning reply. "Oh, you needn't ask me to believe that tomfool tale, old chap! I know you too well for that."

"All right," said Max. "Then you know quite as much as is good for you. If you want to be ready in time to meet your fiancée, you had better let Kersley's man lend you a hand with your dressing. I will send him to you."

He was at the door with the words. Noel heard him open it and go out. He sat where Max had left him with a puzzled frown between his brows.

"I wish I knew the fellow's game," he murmured. "I wish—"

He broke off. What was the good of wishing? Moreover, to be quite honest, perhaps he was more or less satisfied with things as they were. Max had probably got over his disappointment to a certain extent by this time. It was quite obvious that he had no desire or intention to reopen the matter. No, on the whole perhaps it was indiscreet to probe too deeply. Every man had a right to his own secrets. And meantime, Olga was his—was his, and there remained this glorious possibility that his sight might be restored also.

He put up his hands suddenly, covering those useless, tortured eyes. A very curious tremor went through him. His heart began to throb thick and hard. It seemed too good to be true. Since that first awful day he had not fought against Fate, refraining himself even in his worst hours of darkness and suffering, and now it seemed that Fate was going to be kind after all. Like Job, he was to receive all—and more also—that he had lost.

He broke into a quivering laugh. "Good old Job!" he said. "We're not all such lucky beggars as that."

And then again that odd little tremor went through him. It was like a warning, almost a presentiment. His hands fell. He sat straight and still, as one waiting for a sign. No, such things didn't happen. Luck like Job's was apocryphal, abnormal, outside the bounds of human possibility. They might give him back his sight, but—He stopped here as if brought up by a sudden obstacle.

"I wonder if I'm a fool to have that operation," he said. "I wonder if—she—will like me as well if I get back my sight."

The doubt pressed cold at his heart. She had been so divinely kind to him ever since the catastrophe. She had literally given herself up to him, making his darkness light. And vaguely he knew that she had loved the doing of it, had loved to know that he needed her. How would it be, he asked himself, when he needed her thus no longer? Would she love him as well in strength as in weakness? Would she be as near to him when he no longer needed her to lead him by the hand?

He sprang to his feet with a gesture of fierce impatience. He flung the doubt away. Her love was not fashioned of so slender a fabric as this. What right had he to question it thus?

But yet, despite all self-reproach, the doubt remained, repudiate it as he might. It went with him even into her loved presence, refusing to be dislodged.

She came with her father to dine in accordance with Max's invitation. The evening passed with absolute smoothness. Sir Kersley and Dr. Jim were old friends, and had a good deal to say to one another. Max was present at the table, but withdrew early, alleging that he had a serious case to attend. Olga and Noel were left to themselves.

They retired to Sir Kersley's drawing-room and spent the rest of the evening there. Olga was evidently tired, and Noel provided most of the conversation. Noel was never silent for any length of time. He lay on the sofa talking with cheery inconsequence, scarcely pausing for any response, till presently he worked round to the subject of his blindness—a subject which by tacit consent they seldom discussed.

"Max has had a look at me," he said. "He thinks they may be able to switch the light on again. They will have to tighten up a few screws, or something of the kind. He didn't let me into the whole ghastly process, but gave me to understand it wouldn't be exactly a picnic. I don't know how long it's going to take; some time, I fancy. You'll pay me a visit now and then, won't you?"

It was then that Olga came very suddenly out of her silence, moved impulsively to him, and knelt by his side, her hands on his.

"Noel!" she said.

He turned to her swiftly, gathering her hands up to his lips. "What, darling?"

"Noel,—" she paused an instant, then with a rush came the words—"let us be married very soon! Let us be married—before the operation!"

"My darling girl!" said Noel in astonishment.

"Yes," she said rapidly. "I mean it! I wish it! Dad knows that I wish it. So does Nick. Nick is very good, you know. He—he is going to settle some money on me on my twenty-first birthday. So that needn't be a difficulty. We shall have enough to live upon."

"And you think I'm going to live on you?" said Noel, still with her hands pressed hard against his cheek.

"No," she said. "No. You've got something, I expect. That—with mine—would be enough."

"I've got what my good brother-in-law allows me—besides my pay," said Noel. "I daresay—if the worst happened—he would make a settlement too. But I can't count on that. Besides—the worst isn't going to happen. So cheer up, darling! I shall go back to Badgers yet. Poor old boy! It was decent of him to pay me the compliment of being so cut up, wasn't it? I mustn't forget to send him a cable when the deed is done."

He was switching the conversation into more normal channels with airy inconsequence, but Olga gently brought him back to the point.

"Won't you consider my suggestion?" she said.

He smiled then, his quick, boyish smile. "My darling, I have considered it. I'm afraid it isn't practicable. But thank you a million times over all the same!"

"Noel!" There was keen disappointment in her voice. "Why isn't it practicable?"

He let her hands go, and reached out, drawing her to him. "Don't tempt me, sweetheart!" he said softly. "I'm hound enough as it is to dream of letting you join your life to mine under present conditions. But this other is out of the question. I simply won't do it, dear, so don't ask me!"

"But why not?" she pleaded very earnestly. "I have told you I wish it."

He smiled—a smile that was very tender and yet whimsical also. "So like you, darling," he said. "But it can't be done. There are always chances to be taken in a serious operation;

but I don't mean to take more than I can help. I'm not going to chance making you a widow almost before you are a wife."

"Oh, but, Noel—" she protested.

"Yes, really, darling. It's my final word on the subject. We will be married just as soon after the operation as can be decently managed. But not before it, sweetheart. Any fellow who let you do that would be a cur of the lowest degree."

He was holding her in his arms with the words. Her head was against his shoulder. A man had entered the conservatory behind them from an adjoining room, lounging in with his feet in carpet slippers that made no sound.

"And suppose—" it was Olga's voice very low and quivering—"suppose the operation doesn't succeed,—shall you—shall you refuse to marry me then?"

"Not much," said Noel cheerily. "If I'm alive and kicking, I shall want you all the more. No!" He caught himself up sharply. "I don't mean that! I couldn't want you more. Ill or well, I should want you just the same. I only meant—" his voice grew subtly softer, he spoke with great tenderness, his lips moving against her forehead—"I only meant that 'the desert were a paradise, if thou wert there, if thou wert there.'"

She raised her head quickly. There were tears in her eyes. "Noel, how strange that you should say that!"

"Say what, dear?"

"That old song," she said rather incoherently. "It—it has memories for me—memories that hurt."

"What memories?" he asked.

But she could not tell him, and he passed the matter by.

The man in the conservatory drew back with his hands deep in his pockets, and went back by the way he had come.

CHAPTER XXVI
A FOOL'S ERRAND

Dr. Jim's expectations, so far as Olga was concerned, were fulfilled. When he went back to Weir, she remained in town with Nick and Muriel. But he did not go back alone. Will, Daisy, and Peggy went with him. Daisy's love for Dr. Jim was almost as great as her love for Nick, and Will had spent his boyhood under his care.

There was a cottage close to the doctor's house which Daisy had tenanted seven or eight years before when she had been obliged to come Home for her health and Will had been left behind in India. Dr. Jim had managed to secure this cottage a second time, and here they were soon installed with all the joy of exiles in an English spring.

"But we are not going to forego the honeymoon," Will said on their first evening, as he and Daisy stood together in the ivy-covered porch.

She laughed—that little laugh of hers half-gay, half-sad, that seemed like a reminiscence of more mirthful days. "Isn't this romantic enough for you?"

He slipped his arm about her waist. "I'm not altogether sure that I did right to let you come here," he said.

"Oh, nonsense!" She leaned her head against him with a very loving gesture. "I am not so morbid as that. I love to be here, and close to dear old Jim. He hasn't altered a bit. He is just as rugged—and as sweet—as ever."

Will laughed. "How you women, do love a masterful man!"

"Oh, not always," said Daisy. "There are certain forms of mastery in a man which to my mind are quite intolerable. Max Wyndham for instance!"

"What! You've still got your knife into him? I'm sorry for the man myself," said Will. "It must be—well, difficult, to say the least of it, to see his brother come home in possession of his girl and to keep smiling."

"He doesn't care!" said Daisy scathingly. "Geniuses haven't time to be human."

"I wonder," said Will.

He knew, and had never ceased to regret, his wife's share in the accomplishment of Max's discomfiture; and he fancied that secretly, her antipathy notwithstanding, she had begun to regret it also.

He changed the subject, and they went on to talk of Noel.

"Olga tells me that they think of operating next Sunday," Daisy said. "How anxious she will be, poor girl! I am thankful she has Nick and Muriel to take care of her. It has been a terrible time for her all through."

"Poor child!" said Will compassionately.

He shrewdly suspected that the time that lay ahead of Olga would be harder to face than any she had yet experienced.

Olga herself had already begun to realize that. Noel's refusal to consider her suggestion had surprised and disappointed her. She had not anticipated his refusal, though she fully understood it and respected him for it. But it made matters infinitely more difficult for her. She longed for the time when Max's part should be done and he should have passed finally out of her life. Not that he intruded upon her in any way. He scarcely so much as glanced in her direction; but his very presence was a perpetual trial to her. She had a feeling that the green eyes were watching continually for some sign of weakness, even though they never looked her way.

Nick was a great comfort to her in those days, but she felt that even he did not wholly grasp the difficulties of the situation. He supported her indeed, but he did not realize precisely where lay the strain. And it was the same with Dr. Jim. He had accepted her engagement without demur after a gruff enquiry as to whether she loved the fellow. But he had not asked for any details, and had made no reference to her former engagement. She supposed that he found out all he wanted to know on this subject from Nick; and she was grateful for his forbearance, albeit, after a woman's fashion, slightly hurt by it.

She had not, however, much time for reflection of any sort during those first days in town. Noel occupied all her thoughts.

On the day before that fixed for the operation, he went into a private nursing-home. He was extremely cheery over all the preparations, and made himself exceedingly popular with his nurses before he had been more than a few hours in the place.

Even Max was somewhat surprised by the boy's fund of high spirits, and Sir Kersley openly expressed his admiration.

"You Wyndhams are a very remarkable family," he said to Max that night.

Max smiled sardonically in recognition of the compliment. "But the boy has more backbone than I thought," he admitted. "I don't think he will give us much trouble after all, thanks to Olga."

"Ah!" Sir Kersley said. "You think this is due to her?"

"In a great measure," said Max.

Sir Kersley's face was grave. "I am afraid the strain is telling upon her," he said.

"You think she looks ill?" Max shot the question with none of his customary composure.

"No, not actually ill," Sir Kersley said, without looking at him. "But she is too thin in my opinion, and she looks to me very highly strung."

"She always was," said Max.

"Yes; well, she mustn't have a nervous break-down if we can prevent it," said Sir Kersley gently.

"No," Max agreed curtly. "She has got to keep up for Noel's sake."

That seemed to be his main idea just then—his brother's welfare. Very resolutely he kept his mind fixed, with all the strength of which it was capable, upon that one object, and he was impatient of every distraction outside his profession.

Late that night he went round for a last look at Noel, and was told by a smiling nurse that he had "gone to sleep as chirpy as a cricket." He went in to see him, and found him slumbering like an infant. The pulse under Max's fingers was absolutely normal, and an odd smile that had in it an element of respect touched Max's grim lips. Certainly the boy had grit.

The first sound he heard when he arrived at the home on the following day was Noel's heartiest laugh. He was enjoying a joke with one of the nurses who was Irish herself and extremely gay of heart. But the moment Max entered, he sobered and asked for Olga.

Olga was in the building with Nick, but they had thought it advisable to keep visitors away from him on the morning of the operation. Noel, however, was absolutely immovable on the point, refusing flatly to proceed until he had seen her. So for five short minutes Olga was admitted and left alone with him.

More than once during those minutes his cheery laugh made itself heard again. He had a hundred and one things to say, not one of which could Olga ever remember afterwards save the last, when, holding her close to him, he whispered, "And if I don't come out of it, sweetheart, you're to marry another fellow; see? No damn' sentimental rot on my account, mind! I never was good enough for you, God knows! There! Run along! Good-bye!"

His kiss was the briefest he had ever given her, but there was something in the manner of its bestowal that pierced her to the heart. Her own farewell was inarticulate. She was only just able to restrain her tears.

But she mastered her weakness almost immediately, for Max was waiting in the passage outside. He was talking to a nurse, and she would have slipped past him without recognition; but he broke off abruptly and joined her, walking back with her to the room where Nick was waiting.

"Look here!" he said, "I don't think you need be so anxious, I give you my word I believe the operation will be a success."

It was so contrary to his custom to express an opinion in this way that Olga raised her eyes almost involuntarily to gaze at him.

His eyes met and held them instantly. He looked at her with a species of stern kindness that seemed to thrust away all painful memories.

"Even if it isn't a success," he said, "I won't let him die, I promise you. Now, will you follow my advice for once?"

"Yes," she murmured, wondering at her own docility.

He smiled upon her with instant approval, and her heart gave a wild leap that almost made her gasp. "That's wise of you," he said in that voice of cool encouragement that she remembered so well—so well! "Then get Nick to take you for a walk that'll last for an hour and a half. Go and look at the frogs in the Serpentine! Awfully interesting things—frogs! And have a glass of milk before you start! Good-bye!"

Strong and steady, his hand closed upon hers, gave it a slight admonitory shake and set it free.

The next moment he had turned and was striding back along the corridor. Olga stood and watched him out of sight, but he did not turn his head.

* * * * *

The search for frogs in the Serpentine was scarcely as engrossing a pastime as Nick could have desired for the amusement of his charge on that sunny April morning, but he did his valiant best to keep her thoughts on the move. He compelled her to talk when she yearned to be silent, and again in a vague, disjointed fashion Olga wondered at his lack of penetration. Yet, since he was actually obtuse enough to misunderstand her preoccupation and to be even mildly hurt thereby, she exerted herself for his sake to respond intelligently to his remarks. So, with cheery indifference on his part and aching suspense on hers, they passed that dreadful interval of waiting.

On the return journey Olga's knees shook so much that they would scarcely support her; and then it was that Nick seemed suddenly to awake to the situation. He gave her a swift glance, and abruptly offered his arm.

"There, kiddie, there!" he said softly. "Keep a stiff upper lip! It's nearly over."

She accepted his help in silence, and in silence they pursued their way. Nick looked at her no more, nor spoke. His lips were twitching a little, but he showed no other sign of feeling.

So they came at last to the tall building behind its iron railings that hid so many troubles from the world.

The door opened to them, and they went within.

Silence and a curious, clinging perfume met them as they entered.

Olga stood still. She was white to the lips. "Nick," she said, in a voiceless whisper, "Nick, that is—the pain-killer!"

And then, very quietly from a room close by, Max came to them. He glanced at Nick and nodded. There was an odd, exultant look in the green eyes. He took Olga's hands very firmly into his own.

"It's all right," he said.

She stared at him, trying to make her white lips form a question.

"It's all right," he said again. "Well over. As satisfactory as it could possibly be. Now don't be silly!" Surely it was the Max of old times speaking! "Pull up while you can! Come in here and sit down for a minute! I am going to take you to see him directly."

That last remark did more towards restoring Olga's self-control than any of the preceding ones. She went with him submissively, making strenuous efforts to preserve her composure. She even took without a murmur the wineglass of *sal volatile* with which he presented her.

Max stood beside her, still holding one of her hands, his fingers grasping her wrist, and talked over her head to Nick.

"Absolutely normal in every way. Came round without the least trouble. He'll be on his legs again in a fortnight. Of course we shan't turn him loose for a month, and he will have to live in the dark. But he ought to be absolutely sound in six weeks from now."

"And—he will see?" whispered Olga.

Max bent and laid her hand down. He looked at her closely for a moment. "Yes," he said. "There is no reason why he shouldn't make a complete recovery. Are you all right now? I promised to let him have a word with you."

She stood up. "Yes, I am quite all right. Let us go!"

Her knees still felt weak, but she steadied them resolutely. They went out side by side.

In silence Max piloted her. When they reached the darkened room he took her hand again and led her forward. The cheerful Irish nurse was at the bedside, but she drew away at their approach. And Olga found herself standing above a swathed, motionless figure in hushed expectancy of she knew not what.

The hand that held hers made as if to withdraw itself, but she clung to it suddenly and convulsively, and it closed again.

"All right," said Max's leisurely tones. "He's a bit sleepy still. Noel!" He bent, still holding her hand. "I've brought Olga, old chap, as I promised. Say good-night to her, won't you?"

The voice was the voice of Max Wyndham, but its tenderness seemed to rend her heart. She could have wept for the pain of it, but she knew she must not weep.

The figure in the bed stirred, murmured an incoherent apology, seemed to awake.

"Oh, is Olga there?" said Noel drowsily. "Take care of her, Max, old boy! Make her as happy as you can! She's awfully—fond—of you—though I'm not—supposed—to know."

The voice trailed off, sank into unconsciousness. Max's hand had tightened to a hard grip. He straightened himself and spoke, coldly, grimly.

"He isn't quite himself yet. I'm afraid I've brought you on a fool's errand. You can kiss him if you like. He probably won't know."

But Olga could not. She turned from the bed with the gesture of one who could bear no more, and without further words he led her from the room.

CHAPTER XXVII
LOVE MAKES ALL THE DIFFERENCE

"I've been prayin' for you, dear Noel," said Peggy importantly, with her arms round her hero's neck.

"Have you, though?" said Noel. "I say, little pal, how decent of you! How often?"

"Ever so many times," said Peggy. "Every mornin', every evenin', and after grace besides."

"By Jove!" said Noel. "What did you say?"

"I said," Peggy swelled with triumph, "'Lighten Noel's darkness, we beseech Thee, O Lord!'"

"Why, that's what I said!" ejaculated Noel.

"Did you?" cried Peggy excitedly. "Did you really? Oh, Noel, then that's how it was, isn't it?"

"Quite so," said Noel.

He sat on the sofa in Daisy's little drawing-room with his small playfellow on his knee. They had not seen each other for six weeks. And in those weeks Noel had been transformed from a blind man to a man who saw, albeit through thick blue spectacles that emphasized the pallor of illness to such an alarming degree that Daisy had almost wept over him at sight.

Peggy, more practical in her sympathy, had gathered him straightway to her small but ardent bosom, and refused to let him go.

So they sat in the drawing-room tightly locked and related to each other all the doings of their separation.

"I wonder you're not afraid of me in these hideous goggles," Noel said once.

To which Peggy replied with indignation. "I'm not a baby!"

"And Olga has gone to Brethaven, has she?" he asked presently.

"Yes," said Peggy wisely. "Dr. Jim said she must have some sea air to make her fat again. So Captain Nick came yesterday and took her away. And d'you know," said Peggy, "I'm goin' there too very soon?"

"What ho!" said Noel. "Are they going to let you stay there all by yourself?"

Peggy nodded. "Daddy and Mummy are goin' away all by theirselves, so I'm goin' away all by myself."

"And who's going to slap you and put you to bed when you're naughty?" Noel enquired rudely. "Nick?"

"No!" said Peggy, affronted, "Captain Nick's a gentleman!"

"Is he though? Nasty snub for Noel Wyndham Esquire!" observed Noel. "Sorry, Peggy! Then unless Mrs. Nick rises nobly to the occasion, I'm afraid you'll go unslapped. Dear, dear! What a misfortune! I shall have to come down now and then and see what I can do."

Peggy embraced him again ecstatically at this suggestion. "Yes, dear Noel, yes! Come often, won't you?"

"Rather!" said Noel cheerily. "I believe I'm going to be married some time soon by the way," he added as an afterthought.

Peggy's face fell. "Oh, Noel, not really!"

"Why not really?" said Noel.

Peggy explained with a little quiver in her voice. "You did always say that when I was growed up you'd marry me."

"Oh, is that all?" said Noel. "That's easily done. I'll get permission to have two. Whom does one ask? The Pope, isn't it? I'll go and cultivate his acquaintance on my honeymoon."

"What's a honeymoon?" said Peggy.

Noel burst into his merriest laugh and sprang to his feet. "It's the nicest thing in the world. I'll tell you all about it when we're married, Peg-top! Meantime, will you take me to see the great Dr. Jim? I want to inveigle him into lending me his motor."

"Oh, are you goin' to Brethaven?" asked Peggy eagerly. "Take me! Do, dear Noel!"

"What for?" said Noel.

"Reggie lives there," said Peggy. "And Reggie's got some rabbits—big, white ones."

"But suppose they don't want you?" objected Noel.

"S'pose they don't want *you*?" countered Peggy, clinging ingratiatingly to his hand. "Then—you can come and play with me and the rabbits—and Reggie."

Noel stooped very suddenly and kissed her. "What an excellent idea, Peg-top!" he said. "There's nothing more useful when the road is blocked than to secure a good line of retreat."

Peggy looked up at him with puzzled eyes, but she did not ask him what he meant.

* * * * *

It was on that same afternoon that Olga found herself wandering along the tiny glen in the Redlands grounds that had been her favourite resort in childhood. It was only two days since she had left town, urged thereto by Dr. Jim who insisted that she had been there too long already. Nick, moreover, who had patiently chaperoned her for the past five weeks, was wanting to rejoin his wife who had returned to Redlands soon after Noel's operation. And Noel himself, though still undergoing treatment at his brother's hands, had so far recovered as to be able to leave the home and take up his abode temporarily with Sir Kersley Whitton and Max. He had cheerily promised to follow her in a day or two; and Olga, persuaded on all sides, had yielded without much resistance though not very willingly. She had a curious reluctance to return to her home. Something—that hovering phantom that she had almost forgotten—had arisen once more to menace her peace. And she was afraid; she knew not wherefore.

She was happier in Noel's society than in any other. To see him daily growing stronger was her one unalloyed pleasure, and, curiously, when with him she was never so acutely conscious of that chill shadow. Of Max she saw practically nothing. He was always busy, almost too busy to notice her presence, it seemed—a fact that hurt her vaguely even while it gave her relief.

There was another fact that imparted the same kind of miserable comfort, and that was that Noel, though impetuous and loving as ever, never made any but the most casual allusions to their marriage. She could only conclude that he was waiting to make a complete recovery, and she would not herself broach the subject a second time. She did not actually want him to speak, but it grieved her a little that he did not do so. She did not for a moment doubt his love, but she felt that she did not possess the whole of his confidence, and the feeling made her vaguely uneasy. She had been so ready to give all that he had desired. How was it he was slow to take?

These thoughts were running persistently in her mind as she moved along the edge of the stream. It was a day in the end of May, fragrant with many perfumes, crystallized with spring sunshine—such a day as she would have revelled in only last year. Only last year! How many things had happened since then! She was almost afraid to think.

There came the sound of feet on the drive above, and a cracked voice hailed her. "Hullo, Olga *mia*! How are you amusing yourself?"

She looked up with a smile. Last year she would have sprung to meet him; but she seemed to have outgrown all her impulsiveness lately. She moved to meet him indeed, but he was at her side before she had moved a couple of yards.

He caught her hand in his, and drew her to the water's edge. His eyes flickered over her and went beyond.

"Hullo! There goes the green dragon-fly!" he said.

She looked round startled. "Oh, Nick, where?"

"Gone away!" said Nick unconcernedly. "He'll come back again, I'll wager. What's the programme for this morning, kiddie? Anything special?"

"Nothing," said Olga.

Again rapidly his eyes comprehended her. "I'm going up to the Priory myself," he announced unexpectedly. "Care to come?"

She started again, coloured, then went very white. "I—don't know, Nick," she faltered.

"Might as well, dear," said Nick persuasively. "There's no one there. Did I tell you about the landslip? There was a bad one last February, and the old place is beginning to crack in all directions. It's been condemned as unsafe, and Campion is going to clear out bag and baggage. He hasn't lived there, you know, since last summer. They've taken to travelling. Wouldn't you like to come and see it once more before it is dismantled?"

Olga was standing very still. She did not seem to be breathing; only the hand Nick had taken vibrated in his hold.

"Don't come if you don't like!" he said. "But it's your last chance. They are going to start clearing it to-morrow. I've got to go myself to fetch poor old Cork. You remember Cork? Campion has handed him over to me."

Yes, Olga remembered Cork. She drew in a deep breath and spoke. "Dear old dog! I'm glad you are going to have him. Yes, Nick, I'll come. But is the place really doomed? What will happen to it?"

"It will probably fall in first," said Nick, "and the next big landslide it will go over the cliff."

"How—dreadful!" said Olga, and added half to herself, "Violet was wondering only that morning if she would—would—live to see it."

"Ah!" said Nick. He was leading her through the glen that led down to the shore. "It was bound to happen some time," he said, "but they didn't think it would be so soon."

Olga went with him as one moving in a dream, submitting though not of her own conscious volition.

Nick said no more. He had chosen the shortest route, and his main object was to accomplish the distance without disturbing her thoughts.

They came out at length upon the shore, where the stream from the glen gurgled and fell in bubbling cascades into its channel on the beach. The sun poured full over a sea of blue and purple, threaded with silvery pathways here and there.

Olga paused for a moment, as it were instinctively, because from her earliest childhood she had always paused in just that spot to drink in the beauty of the scene.

Nick waited beside her, alert but patient. When she turned along the beach, he turned also, walking close to her over the stones, saying no word.

They came to the hollow in the rocks where she and Violet had rested on that summer morning, and again Olga paused with her face to the sea. A curious little spasm passed across it as she looked. Far away a white sail floated over the blue, and the cries of circling gulls came to them over the water. There was no other sound but the long, long roar of the sea.

Again, in utter silence, Olga turned, pursuing her way. They reached the cliff-path that still remained intact, and began to climb.

The way was steep, but she did not seem aware of it. Nick, lithe and agile, followed her step for step. His yellow face was full of anxious wrinkles. He looked neither to right nor left, watching her only.

Olga never paused in the ascent. She went unswervingly, as though drawn by some magnetic force above. Reaching the summit of the cliff, she turned at once from the Redlands ground, and struck across towards the boundary of the Priory. Nick fell into pace beside her again, vigilant as an eagle guarding its young in the first terrifying flight, not offering help, but ready to give it at the first sign of weakness.

But Olga gave no such sign. Only as they came in sight of the old grey building, standing stark and gaunt above them, she uttered a sudden sigh that seemed to break from her in spite of rigid restraint. And a moment later she quickened her pace.

They passed at length around a buttressed corner and so on to the yew-lined drive that led to the front of the house. The Gothic archway gaped wide to the spring sunshine. Olga came swiftly to it, and there stood suddenly still.

"Nick!" she said. "Nick!"

Her voice was vibrant, her eyes widely staring into the gloom within.

He slipped his arm about her, that wiry arm of great strength that had served her so often. "I am here, darling," he said soothingly.

Olga turned to him in piteous appeal. "Nick," she whispered, "where is she? Where? Where?"

He answered her steadfastly, with the absolute conviction of one who knew. "She is there beyond the Door, dear. You'll find her some day, waiting for you where it is given to all of us to wait for those we love."

But Olga only trembled at his words. "What door, Nick?" she asked. "Do you—do you mean Death?"

"We call it Death," he said.

She scarcely heard his answer. She was shaking from head to foot. "Oh, Nick," she gasped, "I'm frightened—I'm frightened! I daren't go on!"

His arm encircled her more strongly still. He almost lifted her forward over the threshold into the cold and gloomy hall. "Don't be frightened, darling! I'm with you," he said.

She would have hung back, but her strength was gone. She tottered weakly whither he led. In a moment she was sitting on the old oak chest with her face to the sunshine, just as she had sat on that golden afternoon when she had come to summon Violet to her aid.

She covered her face and shivered. Surely the place was haunted—haunted! In a grim procession memories began to crowd upon her. With shrinking vision she beheld, and all the while Nick stood beside her, holding her hand, sustaining even while he compelled.

"Do you remember?" he said, and again, as she shrank and quivered, "Do you remember?"

There was something ruthless about him during those moments, something she had never encountered before, something against which she knew she would oppose herself in vain. For the first time she saw the man as he was, felt the colossal strength of him, quivered beneath his mastery. He was forcing her towards an obstacle from which every racked nerve winced in horror. He was driving her, and he meant to drive her, into conflict with a force that threatened to overwhelm her utterly.

"Oh, let me go, Nick! Let me go!" she cried in agonized entreaty. "It's more than I can bear."

He knelt beside her; he held her close. "Darling," he said, "face it—face it just this once! It's for your own peace of mind I'm doing it."

And then she knew that no cry of hers would move him. He was ready to help her—if he could; but he would not suffer her to flee before that dread procession that had begun to wind like a fiery serpent through her brain. So, in a quivering anguish of spirit such as she had never before known, she sat and faced it, faced the advancing phantom from the shadowy presence of which she had so often shrunk appalled. And the beat of her heart rose up in the silence above the sound of the sea till she thought the mad race of it would kill her.

Slowly the seconds throbbed away, the torture swept towards her. She was as one who, fascinated, watches a forest-fire while he waits to be engulfed.

Presently, from the shadows behind, the great dog Cork came like a ghost and gave them stately welcome. He licked Olga's quivering hands, standing beside her in earnest solicitude.

Nick rose to his feet and moved a little away. His hand was hard clenched against his side. He could not help, it seemed. He could only look on in impotence, while she suffered.

Slowly at last Olga raised her head and looked at him with tragic eyes. Her face was white and strained, but she had in a measure regained her self-control.

"I am going upstairs," she said, "just for a little while. Don't come with me, Nick! Wait for me! Wait for me!"

She rose with the words, swayed a little, then recovered herself, and, with her hand on Cork's head, moved slowly away down the great hall.

Dumbly Nick stood and watched the slim young figure with the wolf-hound pacing gravely beside it. At the end, immediately below the east window, she paused, and he saw her drawn face upraised to the dreadful picture above her; then, still slowly, she turned, and, with the dog, passed out of sight under the southern archway.

For a long, long space he waited in the utter stillness. He had faced a good many difficulties in his life and endured a good many adversities, but this thing stood by itself, unique in his experience, with a pain that was all its own. He would have given much to have gone with her, to have held her up while the storm raged round her, to have borne with her that which, it seemed, she could only bear alone. But, since this was denied him, he could only wait with set teeth while his little pal went through that fiery trial of hers, wait and picture her agonizing in solitude, wait till she should come back to him with all the gladness gone for ever from her eyes,—a woman who could never be young again.

Slowly the minutes dragged on till half an hour had passed. He fell to pacing up and down in a fever of anxiety. Would she never come back? She had begged him to wait for her, but he began to feel he could not wait any longer. The suspense was becoming intolerable.

Desperately he marked another quarter of an hour crawl by leaden-footed, moment by moment. And still she did not come. He went for the last time to the open door and looked forth restlessly. The warmth of the spring sunshine spread everywhere like a benediction. It was only within those walls of crumbling stone that it found no place. A sudden shiver went through him. He turned abruptly inwards. She should not stay alone in the vault-like solitude any longer. Surely anything—anything—must be better for her than that!

With quick strides he went down the old dim hall that once had been the chapel of the monks, turned sharply through the second archway, and approached the staircase beyond. And then very suddenly he stopped. For there above him at the open staircase-window that looked upon the sea stood Olga.

The afternoon sunshine streamed in upon her, and she seemed to be stretching out her hands to it, basking in the generous glow. Her face was upturned to the splendour. Her eyes were closed.

For a moment or two Nick stood narrowly watching her, then as suddenly as he had come he withdrew. For Olga's lips were moving, and it seemed to him that she was no longer alone....

He went back to the porch and stood in the sunshine waiting with renewed patience.

Ten minutes later a moist nose nozzled its way into his hand. He looked down into Cork's eyes of faithful friendliness. Then, hearing a light footfall, he turned. Olga had come back to him at last.

Straight to him she came, moving swiftly. Her face was still pale and very wan, but the strained look had utterly passed away. Her eyes sought his with fearless confidence, and Nick's heart gave a jerk of sheer relief. He had expected tragedy, and he beheld—peace.

She reached him. She laid her hands upon his shoulders. A tremulous smile hovered about her lips. "Nick—Nick darling," she said, "why—why—why didn't you tell me all this long ago?"

He stood before her dumb with astonishment. For once he was utterly and completely at a loss.

She slipped her hand through his arm, and drew him out. "Let us go into the sun!" she said. And then, as the glow fell around them, "Oh, Nick, I'm so thankful that I know the truth at last!"

"Are you, dear?" he said. "Well, I certainly think it is time you knew it now."

"I ought to have known it sooner," she said. "Why did you—you and Max—let me believe—a lie?"

He hesitated momentarily. "We thought it would be easier for you than the truth," he said then.

"You mean Max thought so," she said quickly. "You didn't, Nick!"

"Perhaps not," he admitted.

"I'm sure you didn't," she said. "You know me better than that." Again she stood still in the sunshine, lifting her face to the glory. "Love conquers so many things," she said.

"All things," put in Nick quickly.

She looked at him again. "I don't know about all things, Nick," she said.

"I have proved it," he said.

She shook her head slowly. "But I haven't." She passed from the subject as if it were one she could not bear to discuss openly. "What made you think the truth would hurt me so, I wonder? It was only the first great shock I couldn't bear. That nearly killed me. But now that it is over—and I can see clearly again—Nick, tell me,—as her friend—her only friend—could I have done anything else?"

Nick was silent. He had asked himself the same question many times, and had not found an answer.

"Nick," she said pleadingly, "none but a friend could have done it. It was—an act of love."

"I know it was," he said.

"And yet you blame me?" Her voice was low, full of the most earnest entreaty.

"You blamed Max," he pointed out.

"Oh, but Max didn't love her!" He heard a note of quick pain in her voice. "Oh, don't you see," she said, "how love makes all the difference? Surely that was what St. Paul meant when he said that love was the fulfilling of the law. Nick, you must agree with me in this. It was utterly hopeless. Think of it! Think of it! If she had been living now!" A sudden hard shiver went through her. "Nick, if I had been in her place—wouldn't you have done the same for me?"

"I don't know," he said.

But she clung to him more closely. "You do know, dear! You do know!"

And then Nick did a strange, impulsive thing. He suddenly flung down his reserve and bared to her his inmost soul.

"Yes, Olga *mia*, I do know," he said. "I would have done the same for you. I nearly did the same for Muriel when we were in a tight corner long ago at Wara. But whether it's right or whether it's wrong, God alone can judge. It may be we take too much upon us, or it may be He means us to do it. That is what I have never yet decided. But I solemnly believe with you that love makes all the difference. Love is the one extenuating circumstance which He will recognize and pass. It isn't the outward appearance that counts. It's just the heart of things."

He stopped. Olga was listening with earnest attention, her pale face rapt. For a moment, as he ceased to speak, their eyes met, and between them there ran the old electric current of sympathy, re-connected and entire.

"Oh, Nick," she said, "you never fail me! You always understand!"

But Nick shook his head in whimsical denial. "No, not always, believe me,—being but a man. But I've learnt to hide my ignorance by taking the difficult bits for granted. For instance, I didn't expect you to take this thing so sensibly. If I had, I should have acted very differently long ago."

"Do you call me sensible, Nick?" she said, with a wistful smile.

"Not in all respects, dear," said Nick. "But you have shown more sense than I expected on this occasion."

"Did you expect me to be very badly upset?" she asked. "Nick, shall I tell you something? You'll think me fanciful perhaps. Yet I don't know. Very likely you will understand. I've had a feeling for such a long, long time that she—that Violet—was calling to me, and I could never hear what she wanted to say. To-day—at last—I have been in touch with her, and I know that all is well." She turned her face up to the sun again, speaking with closed eyes. "I know that she is safe. I know that she is happy. And—Nick—Nick—" her voice thrilled on the words—"I know that she loves me still."

Nick bared his head with reverence. His face was strangely moved, but the restless eyes were steadfast as he made reply: "That, dear, is just the Omnipotence of Love. You can't explain it. It's too great a thing to grasp. You can only feel the pull of the everlasting Chain that binds us to those beyond."

"It is wonderful," she whispered, "wonderful!"

"It is Divine," said Nick.

CHAPTER XXVIII
A SOLDIER AND A GENTLEMAN

When Nick returned to Redlands, he was alone. Olga had gone down again to the shore. She wanted to be by herself a little longer, she said. He didn't mind? No, Nick minded nothing, so long as all went well with her; and, on her promise that all should be well, he left her with Cork for guardian.

He went back to Redlands over the cliffs, entering his own grounds by a low wire fence, and thence turning inwards towards the garden. The sounds of gay voices reached him as he approached, and he speedily found himself caught in a lively ambush that consisted of Peggy, Reggie, and Noel. He naturally fled for his life, but was overtaken by the latter and held down while the two accomplices rifled his pockets. By the rules of the game all coppers found therein were confiscated, and this regulation having been duly observed, the prisoner was allowed to sit up and converse with his principal captor while the rest of the gang divided the spoils.

"Have a cigarette?" said Noel.

"Thanks! Mighty generous of you!" Nick righted his tumbled attire and accepted the proffered weed. "If it isn't a rude question, what are you doing here?"

Noel's eyes laughed across at him gaily through the blue spectacles. "I should have thought you might have guessed that I'm spending a night or two with the Musgraves, but I am under a solemn oath to return to Max by noon on Friday in order to have another dose of some infernal stuff with which he is peppering my eyes. He didn't much want me to come away, as it meant postponing the torture for a few hours. But I managed to get on the soft side of him for once, though he is holding himself in preparation for an immediate summons in case my vision should take advantage of my absence from him to play any nasty tricks."

"I see," said Nick. "And how is the vision?"

"Oh, all right, so far as it goes. Gives me beans upon occasion, for which Max always swears at me as if it were my fault. I'm not allowed to see by artificial light at all, so after sunset I join the bats. Lucky for me the sun sits up late just now. By the way, I had a positively gushing epistle from old Badgers this morning. He seems almost hysterical at the thought of getting me back again; says that married or single, I've got to go." Noel stopped to take in a long breath of smoke; then, very abruptly, "Where's Olga?" he demanded.

Nick nodded in the direction whence he had come. "Down on the shore."

Noel was on his feet in a second. "All right. You can be nurse for a bit now. See you later!"

He would have swung away with the words, but Nick had also risen, and with a swift word he detained him. "I say, Noel!"

Noel stopped. "Hullo!"

"Look here!" said Nick rapidly. "She isn't wanting anyone just yet. We have just been to the Priory, she and I—in accordance with Sir Kersley's advice, of which I told you. She is having a quiet think. Don't disturb her!"

Noel stood still. He had stiffened somewhat at the words, but there was no dismay discernible about him. He faced that which had to be faced without flinching.

"You mean she knows?" he asked slowly.

"Yes," said Nick. "But I didn't tell her."

"Did she remember, then?"

"Yes. It all came back to her."

"What effect did it have? Was she—is she very badly upset?" The sharp falter in the words betrayed more than the speaker knew.

Nick turned away from him, grinding his heel into the turf. "No. She took it remarkably quietly on the whole—seemed relieved to know the truth."

"And Max—did she mention him?"

"Yes. She seemed glad to know that he was not responsible, but rather hurt that he had thought it necessary to concoct a lie for her benefit."

"Exactly what I should have felt myself," said Noel. He paused a moment; then: "It was decent of you to let me into that secret," he observed.

"Oh, that was Sir Kersley's doing." Nick still spoke with his back half-turned. "He tackled me on the subject, said you ought to know, but that Max was averse to it. Then I told him why. It seems that he hadn't the vaguest notion till then as to why the engagement was broken off."

Noel nodded. "Just like Max! He's a bit too clever sometimes. Well, what did he say when he knew?"

"He said that if Max wouldn't take the responsibility of setting matters right, he would. And he advised me to tell you everything straight away; which I did," said Nick, "at peril of my life. I don't know how Max will take it, but it will doubtless be on my devoted head that his wrath will descend."

"You'll survive that," said Noel. "But look here! Tell me more about Olga! Wasn't she horribly shocked—just at first?"

"It was touch and go," said Nick. "I followed Sir Kersley's advice throughout. He didn't want me to tell her outright, and I didn't. The whole thing came to her gradually. Yes, it was a bit of a strain to begin with. But she has come through it all right. Give her time to settle, and I don't think she will be any the worse."

"I see," said Noel. He relaxed very suddenly, and passed a boyishly familiar arm around Nick's shoulders. "Well, that cooks my goose, quite effectually, doesn't it? Lucky it's come to me gradually too. I shouldn't have relished it all in a lump. The only person who is going to have a shock over this little business is Max. And you'll admit he deserves one."

"What are you going to do?" asked Nick.

"Do? Send him a wire of course."

"Who? Max?"

"Yes, Max. And I shall say, 'Come at once. Urgent. Noel.' That'll fetch him," said Noel with a twinkle. "He's making a speciality of me just now. He ought to be here before eight."

"And what about Olga?"

"Leave Olga to me!" said Noel.

Nick glanced up at him, and abruptly did so. "You're a sportsman, my son," he observed affectionately. "But to return to Max, doesn't it occur to you that it may not be precisely convenient for him to come posting down here at a moment's notice? He's an important man, remember."

But Noel here displayed a touch of his old imperious spirit. "Who the devil cares for Max?" he demanded. "He's just got to come; and if he doesn't like it, he can go hang. Surely a fellow may be permitted to settle who is to be asked to his own funeral!"

"Oh, if you put it like that—" said Nick.

"Well, it is like that; see?" There was a comic touch to Noel's tragedy notwithstanding, and Nick divined with a satisfaction that he was careful to conceal that the *rôle* he had taken upon himself was not altogether distasteful to him. The funeral arrangements obviously had their attractive side.

"Well, my boy, fix it up as you think best!" he said, giving him as ample a squeeze as his one arm could compass. "You're a soldier and a gentleman, and whatever you do will have my full approval."

"What ho!" said Noel, highly gratified.

They parted then, going their several ways. Noel to send his message, Nick in pursuit of the two children. And so the rest of the afternoon wore away.

Muriel had tea laid in the old oak-panelled dining-room, and thither Nick presently marshalled his charges, to find his wife serenely waiting for them in solitude.

"Hasn't Olga come in yet?" he asked.

"Yes, dear, some time ago. But she looked so tired, poor child!" said Muriel. "I persuaded her to go up to her room and lie down. She has had some tea."

"She will be all right?" asked Nick quickly.

"I think so. She looks quite worn out. She seems to need a sleep more than anything," said Muriel.

He gave her a quick look. "You saw Noel?"

"Yes. He came in and talked for a few minutes after he left you. He seems a very nice boy." A faint smile touched Muriel's lips.

Nick laughed, pulling her hand round his neck as she brought him his tea. "Lost your heart to him, eh? It's quite the usual thing to do. Where has he gone?"

"He came over in Jim's motor, and has gone away in it again. He didn't say where he was going."

"Gone away without me!" ejaculated Peggy in consternation.

"He'll come back again, my chicken. Don't you worry!" said Nick. "Here! Have a jam sandwich!"

"I want Noel," said Peggy. "Where is Noel?"

413

"He has gone out on business," said Nick. "Which reminds me," he added to Muriel. "His brother Max will probably be here this evening to spend the night."

"Max!"

"Yes. Don't mention it upstairs! Noel is pulling the wires, so be prepared for anything."

"What wires is Noel pullin'?" Peggy wanted to know.

"Telegraph wires," said Reggie brightly.

"Yes, telegraph wires," chuckled Nick. "I think I'll just go up for a second, Muriel. I shan't wake her up if she's asleep."

He was gone with the words, swift and noiseless as a bird on the wing, and five seconds later was scratching very softly at Olga's door.

Her voice bade him enter immediately, and he went in.

She was lying on her bed, but the blind was up and the windows wide. She held out her arms to him.

"Nick—darling!"

"Ever yours to command!" said Nick. He went to her, stooping while the arms wound round his neck.

She held him tightly. "Nick," she whispered, "is Noel still here?"

"No, darling. Do you want him?"

She drew a sharp breath. "I—I'm afraid I—dodged him a little while ago. I simply couldn't meet him just then. Has he been looking for me? Did he wonder where I was?"

"Don't think so," said Nick. "He was playing with the kids. He is spending a couple of nights with the Musgraves, and he brought Peggy over."

"And he has gone again?" Faint wonder sounded in her voice.

"Only temporarily. He wanted to send a message to someone from the post-office; but he is coming back—presumably—for Peggy."

"I see." She was silent for a few moments, and Nick sat down on the edge of the bed. "Nick," she said at length, speaking with obvious effort, "will he—will he be very hurt, do you think, if—if I don't see him to-day?"

"Shouldn't say so, darling," said Nick.

She slipped her hand into his. "I've got to do a lot of thinking, Nick," she said rather piteously.

"Can I help?" said Nick.

She shook her head with a quivering smile. "No, dear. It's a—it's a one-man job. But, if you don't mind, tell Noel I'm rather tired, but I'll come over to Weir in the morning. I'm going to tell him everything," she ended, squeezing his hand very tightly.

"Quite right, dear," said Nick.

"Yes, but—before I tell him—I want to—to write to Max." Olga's voice was very low. "I must put things right with him first. I must ask him to forgive me."

"Forgive you, sweetheart!"

"Yes, for—for being very unkind to him." Olga's lips quivered again, and suddenly her eyes were full of tears. "I feel as if—as if I've been running into things in the dark, and doing a lot of harm," she said. "Of course everything is quite over—quite over—between us. He will understand that. But I want—I want to be friends with him—if—he—will let me. Nick dear, that's all. Hadn't you better go and have your tea?"

"And leave you to weep?" said Nick, with his face screwed up. "No, I don't think so."

"I'm not going to," she assured him. "I'm going to be—awfully sensible. Really I am. Kiss me, Nick darling, and go!"

He bent over her. "You mustn't cry," he urged pathetically.

She clasped him close. "No, I won't! I won't! Nick—dearest, you're the very sweetest man in the world. I always have thought so, and I always shall. There!"

"Ah, well, it's a comparatively harmless illusion," said Nick, with his quizzical grimace. "I'll endeavour to live up to it. Sure you want me to go?"

"Yes. You must go, dear. I'm sure Muriel is wanting you. I've monopolized you long enough. You—you'll tell Noel, won't you? Is he all right?"

"At the very top of his form," said Nick.

She smiled. "I'm so very glad. Give him my love, Nick, my—my best love."

"I will," said Nick. He stood up. "He's a fine chap—Noel," he said. "He deserves the best, and I hope—some day—he'll get it."

With which enigmatical remark, he wheeled and left her.

CHAPTER XXIX
THE MAN'S POINT OF VIEW

That letter to Max was perhaps the hardest task that Olga had ever undertaken. She spent the greater part of three hours over it, oblivious of everything else; and then, close upon the dinner-hour, tore up all previous efforts in despair and scribbled a brief, informal note that was curiously reminiscent of one she had written once in a moment of impulsive penitence and pinned inside his hat.

"Dear Max," it ran, "I want to tell you that everything has come back to me, and I am very, very sorry. Will you forgive me and let us be friends for the future? Yours, Olga."

This letter she addressed and stamped and took downstairs with her, laying it upon the hall-table to be posted. Thence she passed on to the library to find a book she wanted.

The glow of sunset met her on the threshold, staying the hand she raised to the electric switch. She moved slowly through the dying light to the window and stood before it motionless, gazing forth into the glory. It poured around her in a rosy splendour, lighting her pale, tired face. For several minutes she stood drinking in the beauty of it, with a feeling at her heart as of unshed tears.

Then at last with a long sigh she slowly turned, and moved across to a row of bookshelves. Perhaps there was light enough for her purpose after all. She began to search along the backs of the books with her face close to them.

"Are you looking for Farrow's *Treatise on Party Government* by any chance?" asked a leisurely voice behind her.

She sprang round as if a gun had been discharged in the room. She stared widely, feeling back against the bookshelves for support.

He was lounging on the edge of the table immediately facing her—a square strong figure, with hands in his pockets, the red light of the sunset turning his hair to fire.

"Because if you are," he continued, a note of grim humour in his voice, "I'm afraid you won't find it—to-night. What's the matter with you, fair lady? You don't seem quite pleased to see me."

"I am pleased," she whispered. "I am pleased."

But her voice was utterly gone. Her throat worked spasmodically. She put up both hands to it as if she were choking.

He stood up abruptly and came to her. He took her hands and drew them gently away. "I shall begin to think I'm bad for you if you do that," he said. "What's the matter, child? Did I frighten you?"

"No!" she whispered back. "No! It was only—only—"

"Only—" he said. "Look here! You mustn't cry. It's one better than fainting, I admit; but I'm not going to let you do either if I can help it. Come over here to the window!"

He led her unresisting, one steady arm upholding her.

"Do you know," he said, "a curious thing happened just now? I'd only been in the house twenty minutes or so when, coming downstairs to look for you, I discovered a letter in the hall addressed to me. I took the liberty of opening and reading it, in spite of the fact that it was plainly intended for the post." He paused. "I thought that would make you angry," he observed, looking down at her critically.

She uttered a desperate little laugh and tried to disengage herself from his arm. "No, I'm glad you've got it," she said rather breathlessly.

"It was a very silly letter," remarked Max, calmly frustrating the attempt. "It didn't say half it might have said, and what it did say wasn't to the point."

"Yes, it was," she maintained quickly. "It—it—I meant to say just that."

"Then all I can say is that you have quite missed the crux of the situation," said Max. "Why are you very, very sorry? Why do you want me to forgive you? And why in the name of wonder do you suggest that we should become friends when you know that we are so constituted as to be incapable of being anything but the dearest of enemies?"

He looked down again suddenly into her quivering, averted face. "Still I shall value that letter," he said, "if only as a sample of the sweet unreasonableness of women. Are you still very sorry, Olga?"

She moved at the utterance of her name, moved and made a more decided effort to free herself.

"Not a bit of good," said Max. "Don't you know I'm waiting for the kiss of peace?"

"I can't!" she protested swiftly. "I can't!"

"Can't what?" said Max.

Her lips were trembling, but she shed no tears. He seemed in some magic fashion to keep her from that.

"I can't kiss you, Max, really—really!" she said.

"Why not?" said Max.

She was silent, but he persisted, still holding her pressed to him.

"Tell me why not! Is it because you don't want to Or you think you ought not to? Or because you are just—shy?"

She caught the smile in his voice and pictured the cocked-up corner of his mouth. "I think I ought not to," she murmured, with her head still turned from him.

"Conscientious objections?" suggested Max.

"Don't laugh!" she whispered.

"My dear child, I'm as serious as a judge. What are the objections?"

"There is—Noel," she said.

"You will have to chuck Noel," said Max coolly.

That vitalized her very effectually; she turned on him with burning cheeks. "Max, how dare you—how dare you suggest such a thing!"

His eyes met hers, green and dominant. She saw again that old mocking gleam of conscious mastery with which he had been wont to exasperate her. He answered her with a directness almost brutal.

"Because you don't love him."

"I do love him!" she declared fiercely. "I do love him!"

"Better than me?" said Max.

She shrank visibly from the question. "I love him too well to throw him over," she said.

His lips twisted cynically. "That is curious," he said.

She winced again from that which he left unsaid. "Oh, Max, don't hurt me!" she pleaded. "Try—try to understand!"

It was an appeal for mercy. But Max would not hear. He took her by the shoulders, compelling her to face him. "So you really mean to marry Noel," he said. "Do you think you will be happy with him?"

"I could never be happy if I didn't," she answered rather incoherently.

Max frowned. "Look here!" he said. "It's no good expecting me to understand if you won't even answer my questions."

She quivered in his hold. "You ask such—impossible things," she said.

"They are only impossible," Max said relentlessly, "because you are afraid to tell me the truth. You are afraid to tell me that you are sacrificing yourself. You are afraid to be honest—even with yourself."

"I am not!" she protested fierily. "Max, you have no right——"

"I have a right." He broke in upon her sternly. "I have the first and foremost right. Remember, you were mine before you were his. You gave yourself to me because you loved me. You only threw me over because of a fancied unworthiness. Now I am cleared of that, do you think you owe me nothing more than an apology?"

"Oh, but, Max," she pleaded, "think of Noel! Think of Noel!"

"Well?" said Max, "then think of him! Don't you think he can make a better bargain for himself than marriage with a woman who doesn't love him best? Why, nearly every woman he meets falls in love with him, and could offer him more than you do. You women who are so keen on sacrificing yourselves never look at the man's point of view, and so the only thing he really wants, you make it impossible for him to get."

"Max! Max!" she cried in distress.

"Well, isn't it so?" said Max. "Just admit that, and p'raps I won't bully you any more. You know he doesn't come first with you—and never would."

"But I could make him happy," she said.

"Oh, could you? And suppose his happiness depended upon yours? Suppose he were man enough to want you to be happy too? Could you do that for him?"

She hesitated.

He pressed on without mercy. "Could you drive me utterly out of your thoughts, your dreams? Could you stifle every regret, every secret longing? Could you empty your heart of me and put him in my place? Tell me! Could you?"

But she could not tell him. She only turned her face from him and wept.

He set her free then, just as he had set her free on that day long ago when her will had first bruised itself against the iron of his. He went away from her, went to the door as if he would leave her; then stood still, and after a space came back.

She trembled at his coming. She had a feeling that he had armed himself with another, stronger weapon to overcome her resistance.

He stopped in front of her. "Olga," he said, "have you thought about me at all?"

She made a sharp gesture—the involuntary wincing of the victim from the knife.

He went on, very quietly, as if he had not seen. "Do you think I'm going to be happy without you? I've got my career, haven't I, and all my brilliant successes? How much do you think they are worth to me? How far do you think they are going to satisfy me—make up for that which you have taken away?"

He paused, but she could not answer him, could not so much as lift her eyes to his.

He went on. "A little while ago you appealed to my love, and—I don't claim to be more than human—it stood the strain. I appealed to yours, and you sent me about my business. You had some excuse. I had deceived you. But this time—this time—are you going to do the same this time, Olga?"

"I can't help it!" she whispered through her tears.

He came nearer to her, but he did not touch her. "Is that the truth?" he said. "Don't you love me well enough? Is that it? Is my love so little to you that you can afford to throw it away? You know I love you, don't you? You believe in my love?" His voice suddenly vibrated; his hands clenched. "It's stood a good deal," he said. "But, by Heaven! I don't think it will stand this!"

She lifted her face suddenly. "Max, stop! I can't bear it!"

"Neither can I!" He flung back fiercely. "It's too much to ask—too much to give! Olga, you shall come to me! You shall! You shall!"

He caught her to him with the words, holding her mercilessly in a grip that was savage. She felt the hard, passionate beat of his heart against her own. And she gasped and gasped again, as one suddenly immersed in deep waters.

She did not resist him, for she could not. He had her a helpless captive before she could even begin. Perhaps she might not have done so in any case. It was a point she never was able to decide. But from the moment his lips met hers the battle was over. With or without her will her lips clung to his; the flame of his passion kindled an answering flame in her; and the love which she had striven so desperately to restrain leaped forth to him in wild, exultant freedom, so that she forgot all the world beside.

* * * * *

"So that's settled!" said Max a little later into the flushed face that lay against his shoulder. "It's taken a mighty long time to make you see reason."

"It isn't reason," said Olga faintly. "And oh, Max, what—what am I to say to Noel?"

Max's one-sided smile appeared. "I should just say, 'Thank you kindly, sir,' if it were me. There's nothing else left to say."

"Oh, but there is!" she protested.

"There isn't," said Max. "He is coming over to congratulate us to-morrow."

"Max!" She opened her eyes wide and lifted her head. "Max, you don't mean——"

"Yes, I do," said Max imperturbably. "Why do you suppose I came tearing down here to-night, leaving Kersley to kill all my patients as well as his own?"

"Not—surely—to see me?" said Olga, wonderingly.

He laughed grimly. "No. It was to see Noel. Odd how we both put him first, isn't it? The young cub sent me a message that brought me down post-haste, expecting to find him in a state of collapse. Instead of which I found him gaily awaiting me at the station to tell me he had run himself out—or some bosh of the kind—and it was now my innings, and I was to go in and win. On my soul, Olga, he was enjoying himself up to the hilt."

"But why didn't you tell me this before?" said Olga quickly.

Max's mouth went up a little higher. "Various reasons, fair lady."

"Don't be horrid!" she protested, giving him a shake. "And how did it happen? How did he come to know anything? I haven't seen him to-day. It must have been Nick!"

"Yes. I'm going to throttle Nick presently. I've often wanted to. After which I shall turn him into a mummy and send him to India to be worshipped as the little god of intrigue. I daresay he'll get on all right in that capacity. It ought to suit him down to the ground. He's a born meddler."

"How absurd you are!" Olga laughed in spite of herself. "Where is Nick? Don't you think we had better go and find him?"

It was at this point that the handle of the door was turned ostentatiously the wrong way, struggled with, sworn at, and finally put right.

"May I come in?" said Nick, briskly opening the door. "Muriel and I have finished dinner. We knew you wouldn't be wanting any."

"Nick!" Olga exclaimed. "I'm sure you haven't!"

"All right, we haven't," said Nick. "That is to say, we have saved you a little in case you were prosaic enough to want it. Max, my son, your presence here is an honour for which I have scarcely made fit preparation, but I am none the less proud to entertain you, and as your uncle-in-law elect I bid you welcome."

He held out his hand which Max took with a dry, "Thanks! One can't scrag a man under his own roof, I suppose, though it's a sore temptation."

"You will have ample opportunity in the future," Nick assured him genially, "though, as I think I told you long ago, I'm the most well-meaning little cuss that ever walked the earth. I threatened once to put a spoke in your wheel, didn't I? Well, I never did it. I've been pushing and straining to get it out of the bog ever since. And now I've done it, you want to scrag me. Olga, the man's a blood-thirsty scoundrel. If you have the smallest regard for my feelings, you will kick him out of the house at once."

But Olga was holding the two clasped hands in hers, and she would not let them part. "Nick, you're a darling—a darling! And Max knows it, don't you, Max? It was dear of you to make the wheels go round. They would never have done it without you, and we shall never, never forget it as long as we two shall live."

"Amen!" said Max.

"Bless your hearts!" said Nick benevolently. "Well, come and have something to eat!"

He turned towards the door, but Olga hung back. "Is—is Noel here?" she asked.

"Heavens, no!" said Nick. "He eloped with Peggy long ago."

"Oh!" A note of relief sounded in her voice. "I shall see him to-morrow," she said.

"Yes, he'll be over to-morrow." Nick shot her a swift look in the twilight. "Meantime, I have a message to give you from him," he said.

"So have I," cut in Max.

"I know what it is!" said Olga quickly.

"His love," said Max.

"His best love," said Nick.

There was an instant's silence in the room; then Olga bent her head and murmured softly, "God bless him!"

CHAPTER XXX

THE LINE OF RETREAT

"No," said Daisy, with decision. "I shall never like Dr. Wyndham, though I am quite willing to admit that he may be admirable in many ways. He is not my ideal of a nice husband, but then of course—" she dimpled prettily—"I'm only just back from my honeymoon, and I've been thoroughly spoilt."

Will smiled upon her indulgently. "It's just as well we don't all like the same people. He looked happy enough anyhow."

"In his lordly, cynical fashion," objected Daisy. "He was quite the most self-possessed bridegroom I ever saw."

"Just as well perhaps," commented Will. "Olga was positively shaking with nervousness. Dr. Jim went grimly armed with a brandy-flask and smelling-salts."

"Will, did he really? How like him!"

"Yes. Sir Kersley told me. But he added that it is a well-known fact that brides never faint, so Jim's precautions were quite unnecessary. He also said—But perhaps it's hardly fair to tell you that!"

"What?" said Daisy eagerly. "Of course tell me! Tell me at once, Will!"

Will smiled again. "Well, if I must! He told me that Max himself was anything but as serene as he looked and had been dosing with bromide to steady his nerves."

Daisy broke into a laugh. "No, you certainly shouldn't have told me that! How mean of Sir Kersley! Still, it's nice to know that Max is a little human now and then. I shall like him better now. And so I don't mind telling you something in return. I've been making the most discreet enquiries, and I haven't unearthed the vaguest rumour of that tale Major Hunt-Goring told me. I believe it was all his own invention after all."

"Very likely," said Will. "Opium-smokers often get delusions."

Daisy caught and kissed her husband's hand. "How very charitable of you, Will! You're a perpetual antidote to my poison. Did you observe Nick during the ceremony? He was grinning like a Hindu idol—just as if he'd done it all."

"He has his finger in most pies," observed Will. "I daresay it wasn't altogether absent from this one. Muriel looked supremely proud of her C.S.I."

"And she has reason to be," declared Daisy warmly. "He is quite a king in his own line. I'm so glad he got the Star."

"It's time he got something of the sort certainly," said Will. "I suppose he'll be good now for another six years. Then he'll send the boy to school and inveigle her back to the East."

But Daisy shook her head. "No. I think she'll keep him now. This country is wanting men very badly—and there's plenty to be done."

"Oh, he's a bulwark of the Empire," smiled Will. "He'll do the work of ten. Where's the kiddie gone?"

"She's somewhere with Noel. Did you see those two come out of church together? It was the sweetest sight," said Daisy with enthusiasm.

"She ought to have been walking with Reggie," observed Will.

"Yes, I'm afraid she deserted him. But he ran after Dr. Jim. They are great pals. But Peggy and Noel—" Daisy suddenly laughed—"oh, Will, I do love that boy!" she said. "It is good to see him his gay, handsome self again. See, there they are together now, sitting on the grass! I wonder what they are talking about."

"Probably discussing to-day's event," said Will.

"And wishing it had been their turn," laughed Daisy. A guess which, as it chanced, was not altogether wide of the mark! Peggy, the while she leaned against her cavalier, was remarking at that very moment that she thought Midsummer Day the nicest day in all the year for a "weddin'."

"Why?" said Noel.

"All the fairies gets married then," said Peggy.

"Silly little duffers!" said Noel unsympathetically.

She looked at him round-eyed, then slipped a soft hand into his. "DearNoel, don't you like weddin's?"

Noel cut short an involuntary sigh. "Not always, Peggy," he said.

"Not when you're best man and I'm chief bridesmaid?" persisted Peggy, with her cheek against his shoulder.

He laughed, without much gaiety. "Oh, well, of course that makes a difference," he said.

There was a pause during which Peggy rubbed her cheek up and down his coat in tender silence. At last coaxingly, "Why didn't you like this weddin', dear Noel?" she asked.

But at that he broke into a half-shamed laugh and springing up snatched her high into his arms. "I'll tell you when we're married, Peg-top," he promised her. "Till then—let's have some fun!"

"Yes, yes!" cried Peggy, laughing down at him alluringly. "Let's have some fun!"

And that ended the conversation.

The Way of an Eagle

PART I

CHAPTER I

THE TRUST

The long clatter of an irregular volley of musketry rattled warningly from the naked mountain ridges; over a great grey shoulder of rock the sun sank in a splendid opal glow; from very near at hand came the clatter of tin cups and the sound of a subdued British laugh. And in the room of the Brigadier-General a man lifted his head from his hands and stared upwards with unseeing, fixed eyes.

There was an impotent, crushed look about him as of one nearing the end of his strength. The lips under the heavy grey moustache moved a little as though they formed soundless words. He drew his breath once or twice sharply through his teeth. Finally, with a curious groping movement he reached out and struck a small hand-gong on the table in front of him.

The door slid open instantly and an Indian soldier stood in the opening. The Brigadier stared full at him for several seconds as if he saw nothing, his lips still moving secretly, silently. Then suddenly, with a stiff gesture, he spoke.

"Ask the major sahib and the two captain sahibs to come to me here."

The Indian saluted and vanished like a swift-moving shadow.

The Brigadier sank back into his chair, his head drooped forward, his hands clenched. There was tragedy, hopeless and absolute, in every line of him.

There came the careless clatter of spurred heels and loosely-slung swords in the passage outside of the half-closed door, the sound of a stumble, a short ejaculation, and again a smothered laugh.

"Confound you Grange! Why can't you keep your feet to yourself, you ungainly Triton, and give us poor minnows a chance?"

The Brigadier sat upright with a jerk. It was growing rapidly dark.

"Come in, all of you," he said. "I have something to say. As well to shut the door, Ratcliffe, though it is not a council of war."

"There being nothing left to discuss, sir," returned the voice that had laughed. "It is just a simple case of sitting tight now till Bassett comes round the corner."

The Brigadier glanced up at the speaker and caught the last glow of the fading sunset reflected on his face. It was a clean-shaven face that should have possessed a fair skin, but by reason of unfavourable circumstances it was burnt to a deep yellow-brown. The features were pinched and wrinkled—they might have belonged to a very old man; but the eyes that smiled down into the Brigadier's were shrewd, bright, monkey-like. They expressed a cheeriness almost grotesque. The two men whom he had followed into the room stood silent among the shadows. The gloom was such as could be felt.

Suddenly, in short, painful tones the Brigadier began to speak.

"Sit down," he said. "I have sent for you to ask one among you to undertake for me a certain service which must be accomplished, but which I—" he paused and again audibly caught his breath between his teeth—"which I—am unable to execute for myself."

An instant's silence followed the halting speech. Then the young officer who stood against the door stepped briskly forward.

"What's the job, sir? I'll wager my evening skilly I carry it through."

One of the men in the shadows moved, and spoke in a repressive tone. "Shut up, Nick! This is no mess-room joke."

Nick made a sharp, half-contemptuous gesture. "A joke only ceases to be a joke when there is no one left to laugh, sir," he said. "We haven't come to that at present."

421

He stood in front of the Brigadier for a moment—an insignificant figure but for the perpetual suggestion of simmering activity that pervaded him; then stepped behind the commanding officer's chair, and there took up his stand without further words.

The Brigadier paid no attention to him. His mind was fixed upon one subject only. Moreover, no one ever took Nick Ratcliffe seriously. It seemed a moral impossibility.

"It is quite plain to me," he said heavily at length, "that the time has come to face the situation. I do not speak for the discouragement of you brave fellows. I know that I can rely upon each one of you to do your duty to the utmost. But we are bound to look at things as they are, and so prepare for the inevitable. I for one am firmly convinced that General Bassett cannot possibly reach us in time."

He paused, but no one spoke. The man behind him was leaning forward, listening intently.

He went on with an effort. "We are a mere handful. We have dwindled to four white men among a host of dark. Relief is not even within a remote distance of us, and we are already bordering upon starvation. We may hold out for three days more. And then"—his breath came suddenly short, but he forced himself to continue—"I have to think of my child. She will be in your hands. I know you will all defend her to the last ounce of your strength; but which of you"—a terrible gasping checked his utterance for many labouring seconds; he put his hand over his eyes—"which of you," he whispered at last, his words barely audible, "will have the strength to—shoot her before your own last moment comes?"

The question quivered through the quiet room as if wrung from the twitching lips by sheer torture. It went out in silence—a dreadful, lasting silence in which the souls of men, stripped naked of human convention, stood confronting the first primaeval instinct of human chivalry.

It continued through many terrible seconds—that silence, and through it no one moved, no one seemed to breathe. It was as if a spell had been cast upon the handful of Englishmen gathered there in the deepening darkness.

The Brigadier sat bowed and motionless at the table, his head sunk in his hands.

Suddenly there was a quiet movement behind him, and the spell was broken. Ratcliffe stepped deliberately forward and spoke.

"General," he said quietly, "if you will put your daughter in my care, I swear to you, so help me God, that no harm of any sort shall touch her."

There was no hint of emotion in his voice, albeit the words were strong; but it had a curious effect upon those who heard it. The Brigadier raised his head sharply, and peered at him; and the other two officers started as men suddenly stumbling at an unexpected obstacle in a familiar road.

One of them, Major Marshall, spoke, briefly and irritably, with a touch of contempt. His nerves were on edge in that atmosphere of despair.

"You, Nick!" he said. "You are about the least reliable man in the garrison. You can't be trusted to take even reasonable care of yourself. Heaven only knows how it is you weren't killed long ago. It was thanks to no discretion on your part. You don't know the meaning of the word."

Nick did not answer, did not so much as seem to hear. He was standing before the Brigadier. His eyes gleamed in his alert face—two weird pin-points of light.

"She will be safe with me," he said, in a tone that held not the smallest shade of uncertainty.

But the Brigadier did not speak. He still searched young Ratcliffe's face as a man who views through field-glasses a region distant and unexplored.

After a moment the officer who had remained silent throughout came forward a step and spoke. He was a magnificent man with the physique of a Hercules. He had remained on his feet, impassive but observant, from the moment of his entrance. His voice had that soft quality peculiar to some big men.

"I am ready to sell my life for Miss Roscoe's safety, sir," he said.

Nick Ratcliffe jerked his shoulders expressively, but said nothing. He was waiting for the General to speak. As the latter rose slowly, with evident effort, from his chair, he thrust out a hand, as if almost instinctively offering help to one in sore need.

General Roscoe grasped it and spoke at last. He had regained his self-command. "Let me understand you, Ratcliffe," he said. "You suggest that I should place my daughter in your charge. But I must know first how far you are prepared to go to ensure her safety."

He was answered instantly, with an unflinching promptitude he had scarcely expected.

"I am prepared to go to the uttermost limit, sir," said Nicholas Ratcliffe, his fingers closing like springs upon the hand that gripped his, "if there is a limit. That is to say, I am ready to go through hell for her. I am a straight shot, a cool shot, a dead shot. Will you trust me?"

His voice throbbed with sudden feeling. General Roscoe was watching him closely. "Can I trust you, Nick?" he said.

There was an instant's silence, and the two men in the background were aware that something passed between them—a look or a rapid sign—which they did not witness. Then reckless and debonair came Nick's voice.

"I don't know, sir. But if I am untrustworthy, may I die to-night!"

General Roscoe laid his free hand upon the young man's shoulder.

"Is it so, Nick?" he said, and uttered a heavy sigh. "Well—so be it then. I trust you."

"That settles it, sir," said Nick cheerily. "The job is mine."

He turned round with a certain arrogance of bearing, and walked to the door. But there he stopped, looking back through the darkness at the dim figures he had left.

"Perhaps you will tell Miss Roscoe that you have appointed me deputy-governor," he said. "And tell her not to be frightened, sir. Say I'm not such a bogey as I look, and that she will be perfectly safe with me." His tone was half-serious, half-jocular. He wrenched open the door not waiting for a reply.

"I must go back to the guns," he said, and the next moment was gone, striding carelessly down the passage, and whistling a music-hall ballad as he went.

CHAPTER II
A SOLDIER'S DAUGHTER

In the centre of the little frontier fort there was a room which one and all of its defenders regarded as sacred. It was an insignificant chamber, narrow as a prison cell and almost as bare; but it was the safest place in the fort. In it General Roscoe's daughter—the only white woman in the garrison—had dwelt safely since the beginning of that dreadful siege.

Strictly forbidden by her father to stir from her refuge without his express permission, she had dragged out the long days in close captivity, living in the midst of nerve-shattering tumult but taking no part therein. She was little more than a child, and accustomed to render implicit obedience to the father she idolised, or she had scarcely been persuaded to submit to this rigorous seclusion. It would perhaps have been better for her physically and even mentally to have gone out and seen the horrors which were being daily enacted all around her. She had at first pleaded for at least a limited freedom, urging that she might take her part in caring for the wounded. But her father had refused this request with such decision that she had never repeated it. And so she had seen nothing while hearing much, lying through many sleepless nights with nerves strung to a pitch of torture far more terrible than any bodily exhaustion, and vivid imagination ever at work upon pictures more ghastly than even the ghastly reality which she was not allowed to see.

The strain was such as no human frame could have endured for long. Her strength was beginning to break down under it. The long sleepless nights were more than she could bear. And there came a time when Muriel Roscoe, driven to extremity, sought relief in a remedy from which in her normal senses she would have turned in disgust.

It helped her, but it left its mark upon her—a mark which her father must have noted, had he not been almost wholly occupied with the burden that weighed him down. Morning and evening he visited her, yet failed to read that in her haunted eyes which could not have escaped a clearer vision.

423

Entering her room two hours after his interview with his officers regarding her, he looked at her searchingly indeed, but without understanding. She lay among cushions on a *charpoy* of bamboo in the light of a shaded lamp. Young and slight and angular, with a pale little face of utter weariness, with great dark eyes that gazed heavily out of the black shadows that ringed them round, such was Muriel Roscoe. Her black hair was simply plaited and gathered up at the neck. It lay in cloudy masses about her temples—wonderful hair, quite lustreless, so abundant that it seemed almost too much for the little head that bore it. She did not rise at her father's entrance. She scarcely raised her eyes.

"So glad you've come, Daddy," she said, in a soft, low voice. "I've been wanting you. It's nearly bedtime, isn't it?"

He went to her, treading lightly. His thoughts had been all of her for the past few hours and in consequence he looked at her more critically than usual. For the first time he was struck by her pallor, her look of deathly weariness. On the table near her lay a plate of boiled rice piled high in a snowy pyramid. He saw that it had not been touched.

"Why, child," he said, a sudden new anxiety at his heart "you have had nothing to eat. You're not ill?"

She roused herself a little, and a very faint colour crept into her white cheeks. "No, dear, only tired—too tired to be hungry," she told him. "That rice is for you."

He sat down beside her with a sound that was almost a groan. "You must eat something, child," he said. "Being penned up here takes away your appetite. But all the same you must eat."

She sat up slowly, and pushed back the heavy hair from her forehead with a sigh.

"Very well, Daddy," she said submissively. "But you must have some too, dear. I couldn't possible eat it all."

Something in his attitude or expression seemed to strike her at this point, and she made a determined effort to shake off her lethargy. A spoon and fork lay by the plate. She handed him the former and kept the latter for herself.

"We'll have a picnic, Daddy." she said, with a wistful little smile. "I told *ayah* always to bring two plates, but she has forgotten. We don't mind, though, do we?"

It was childishly spoken, but the pathos of it went straight to the man's heart. He tasted the rice under her watching eyes and pronounced it very good; then waited for her to follow his example which she did with a slight shudder.

"Delicious, Daddy, isn't it?" she said. And even he did not guess what courage underlay the words.

They kept up the farce till the pyramid was somewhat reduced; then by mutual consent they suffered their ardour to flag. There was a faint colour in the girl's thin face as she leaned back again. Her eyes were brighter, the lids drooped less.

"I had a dream last night, Daddy," she said, "such a curious dream, and so vivid. I thought I was out on the mountains with some one. I don't know who it was, but it was some one very nice. It seemed to be very near the sunrise, for it was quite bright up above, though it was almost dark where we stood. And, do you know—don't laugh, Daddy, I know it was only a silly dream—when I looked up, I saw that everywhere the mountains were full of horses and chariots of fire. I felt so safe, Daddy, and so happy. I could have cried when I woke up."

She paused. It was rather difficult for her to make conversation for the silent man who sat beside her so gloomy and preoccupied. Save that she loved her father as she loved no one else on earth, she might have felt awed in his presence.

As it was, receiving no response, she turned to look, and the next instant was on her knees beside him, her thin young arms clinging to his neck.

"Daddy, darling, darling!" she whispered, and hid her face against him in sudden, nameless terror.

He clasped her to him, holding her close, that she might not again see his face and the look it wore. She began to tremble, and he tried to soothe her with his hand, but for many seconds he could find no words.

"What is it, Daddy?" she whispered at last, unable to endure the silence longer. "Won't you tell me? I can be very brave. You said so yourself."

"Yes," he said. "You will be a brave girl, I know." His voice quivered and he paused to steady it. "Muriel," he said then, "I don't know if you have ever thought of the end of all this. There will be an end, you know. I have had to face it to-night."

She looked up at him quickly, but he was ready for her. He had banished from his face the awful despair that he carried in his soul.

"When Sir Reginald Bassett comes—" she began uncertainly.

He put his hand on her shoulder. "You will try not to be afraid," he said. "I am going to treat you, as I have treated my officers, with absolute candour. We shall not hold out more than three days more. Sir Reginald Bassett will not be here in time."

He stopped. Muriel uttered not a word. Her face was still upturned, and her eyes had suddenly grown intensely bright, but he read no shrinking in them.

With an effort he forced himself to go on. "I may not be able to protect you when the end comes. I may not even be with you. But—there is one man upon whom you can safely rely whatever happens, who will give himself up to securing your safety alone. He has sworn to me that you shall not be taken, and I know that he will keep his word. You will be safe with him, Muriel. You may trust him as long as you live. He will not fail you. Perhaps you can guess his name?"

He asked the question with a touch of curiosity in the midst of his tragedy. That upturned, listening face had in it so little of a woman's understanding, so much of the deep wonder of a child.

Her answer was prompt and confident, and albeit her very lips were white, there was a faint hint of satisfaction in her voice as she made it.

"Captain Grange, of course, Daddy."

He started and looked at her narrowly. "No, no!" he said. "Not Grange! What should make you think of him?"

He saw a look of swift disappointment, almost of consternation, darken her eyes. For the first time her lips quivered uncertainly.

"Who then, Daddy? Not—not Mr. Ratcliffe?"

He bent his head. "Yes, Nick Ratcliffe. I have placed you in his charge. He will take care of you."

"Young Nick Ratcliffe!" she said slowly. "Why, Daddy, he can't even take care of himself yet. Every one says so. Besides,"—a curiously womanly touch crept into her speech—"I don't like him. Only the other day I heard him laugh at something that was terrible—something it makes me sick to think of. Indeed, Daddy, I would far rather have Captain Grange to take care of me. Don't you think he would if you asked him? He is so much bigger and stronger, and—and kinder."

"Ah! I know," her father said. "He seems so to you. But it is nerve that your protector will need, child; and Ratcliffe possesses more nerve than all the rest of the garrison put together. No, it must be Ratcliffe, Muriel. And remember to give him all your trust, all your confidence. For whatever he does will be with my authority—with my—full—approval."

His voice failed suddenly and he rose, turning sharply away from the light. She clung to his arm silently, in a passion of tenderness, though she was far from understanding the suffering those last words revealed. She had never seen him thus moved before.

After a few seconds he turned back to her, and bending kissed her piteous face. She clung closely to him with an agonised longing to keep him with her; but he put her gently from him at last.

"Lie down again, dear," he said, "and get what rest you can. Try not to be frightened at the noise. There is sure to be an assault, but the fort will hold to-night."

He stood a moment, looking down at her. Then again he stooped and kissed her. "Good-bye, my darling," he said huskily, "till we meet again!"

And so hurriedly, as if not trusting himself to remain longer, he left her.

CHAPTER III

THE VICTIM OF TREACHERY

There came again the running rattle of rifle-firing from the valley below the fort, and Muriel Roscoe, lying on her couch, pressed both hands to her eyes and shivered. It seemed impossible that the end could be so near. She felt as if she had existed for years in this living nightmare of many horrors, had lain down and had slept with that dreadful sound in her ears from the very beginning of things. The life she had led before these ghastly happenings had become so vague a memory that it almost seemed to belong to a previous existence, to an earlier and a happier era. As in a dream she now recalled the vision of her English school-life. It lay not a year behind her, but she felt herself to have changed so fundamentally since those sunny, peaceful days that she seemed to be a different person altogether. The Muriel Roscoe of those days had been a merry, light-hearted personality. She had revelled in games and all outdoor amusements. Moreover, she had been quick to learn, and her lessons had never caused her any trouble. A daring sprite she had been, with a most fertile imagination and a longing for adventure that had never been fully satisfied, possessing withal so tender and loving a heart that the very bees in the garden had been among her cherished friends. She remembered all the sunny ideals of that golden time and marvelled at herself, forgetting utterly the eager, even passionate, craving that had then been hers for the wider life, the broader knowledge, that lay beyond her reach, forgetting the feverish impatience with which she had longed for the day of her emancipation when she might join her father in the wonderful glowing East which she so often pictured in her dreams. Of her mother she had no memory. She had died at her birth. Her father was all the world to her; and when at last he had travelled home on a brief leave and taken her from her quiet English life to the strange, swift existence of the land of his exile, her soul had overflowed with happiness.

Nevertheless, she had not been carried away by the gaieties of this new world. The fascinations of dance and gymkhana had not caught her. The joy of being with her father was too sacred and too precious to be foregone for these lesser pleasures, and she very speedily decided to sacrifice all social entertainments to which he could not accompany her. She rode with him, camped with him, and became his inseparable companion. Undeveloped in many ways, shy in the presence of strangers, she soon forgot her earlier ambition to see the world and all that it contained. Her father's society was to her all-sufficing, and it was no sacrifice to her to withdraw herself from the gay crowd and dwell apart with him.

He had no wish to monopolise her, but it was a relief to him that the constant whirl of pleasure about her attracted her so little. He liked to have her with him, and it soon became a matter of course that she should accompany him on all his expeditions. She revelled in his tours of inspection. They were so many picnics to her, and she enjoyed them with the zest of a child.

And so it came to pass that she was with him among the hills of the frontier when, like a pent flood suddenly escaping, the storm of rebellion broke and seethed about them, threatening them with total annihilation.

No serious trouble had been anticipated. A certain tract of country had been reported unquiet, and General Roscoe had been ordered to proceed thither on a tour of inspection and also, to a very mild degree, of intimidation. Marching through the district from fort to fort, he had encountered no shadow of opposition. All had gone well. And then, his work over, and all he set out to do satisfactorily accomplished, his face towards India and his back to the mountains, the unexpected had come upon him like a thunderbolt.

Hordes of tribesmen, gathered Heaven knew how or whence, had suddenly burst upon him from the south, had cut off his advance by sheer immensity of numbers, and, hemming him in, had forced him gradually back into the mountain fastnesses through which he had just passed unmolested.

It was a stroke so wholly new, so subtly executed, that it had won success almost before the General had realised the weight of the disaster that had come upon him. He had believed himself at first to be involved in a mere fray with border thieves. But before he reached the fort upon which he found himself obliged to fall back, he knew that he had to cope with a general rising of the tribes, and that the means at his disposal were as inadequate to stem the rising flood of rebellion as a pebble thrown into a mountain stream to check its flow.

The men under his command, with the exception of a few officers, were all native soldiers, and he soon began to have a strong suspicion that among these he numbered traitors. Nevertheless, he established himself at the fort, determined there to make his stand till relief should arrive.

The telegraph wires were cut, and for a time it seemed that all communication with the outside world was an impossibility. Several runners were sent out, but failed to break through the besieging forces. But at last after many desperate days there came a message from without—a scrap of paper attached to a stone and flung over the wall of the fort at night. News of the disaster had reached Peshawur, and Sir Reginald Bassett, with a hastily collected force, was moving to their assistance.

The news put heart into the garrison, and for a time it seemed that the worst would be averted. But it became gradually evident to General Roscoe that the relieving force could not reach them in time. The water supply had run very low, and the men were already subsisting upon rations that were scarcely sufficient for the maintenance of life. There was sickness among them, and there were also many wounded. The white men were reduced to four, including himself, the native soldiers had begun to desert, and he had been forced at last to face the fact that the end was very near.

All this had Muriel Roscoe come through, physically scathless, mentally torn and battered, and she could not bring herself to realise that the long-drawn-out misery of the siege could ever be over.

Lying there, tense and motionless, she listened to the shots and yells in the distance with a shuddering sense that it was all a part of her life, of her very being, even. The torture and the misery had so eaten into her soul. Now and then she heard the quick thunder of one of the small guns that armed the fort, and at the sound her pulses leaped and quivered. She knew that the ammunition was running very low. These guns did not often speak now.

Then, during a lull, there came to her the careless humming of a British voice, the free, confident tread of British feet, approaching her door.

She caught her breath as a hand rapped smartly upon the panel. She knew who the visitor was, but she could not bring herself to bid him enter. A sudden awful fear was upon her. She could neither speak nor move. She lay, listening intently, hoping against hope that he would believe her to be sleeping and go away.

The knock was not repeated. Dead silence reigned. And then quickly and decidedly the door opened, and Nick Ratcliffe stood upon the threshold. The light struck full upon his face as he halted—a clever, whimsical face that might mask almost any quality good or bad.

"May I come in, Miss Roscoe?" he asked.

For she had not moved at his appearance. She lay as one dead. But as he spoke she uncovered her face, and terror incarnate stared wildly at him from her starting eyes. He entered without further ceremony, and closed the door behind him. In the shaded lamplight his features seemed to twitch as if he wanted to smile. So at least it seemed to her wrought-up fancy.

He gazed greedily at the plate of rice on the table as he came forward. "Great Jupiter!" he said. "What a sumptuous repast!"

The total freedom from all anxiety or restraint with which he made this simple observation served to restore to some degree the girl's tottering self-control. She sat up, sufficiently recovered to remember that she did not like this man.

"Pray have some if you want it," she said coldly.

He turned his back on it abruptly. "No, don't tempt me," he said. "It's a fast day for me. I'm acquiring virtue, being conspicuously destitute of all other forms of comfort. Why don't you eat it yourself? Are you acquiring virtue too?"

He stood looking down at her quizzically, under rapidly flickering eyelids. She sat silent, wishing with all her heart that he would go away.

Nothing, however, was apparently further from his thoughts. After a moment he sat down in the chair that her father had occupied an hour before. It was very close to her, and she drew herself slightly away with a small, instinctive movement of repugnance. But Nick was sublimely impervious to hints.

"I say, you know," he said abruptly, "you shouldn't take opium. Your donkey of an *ayah* ought to know better than to let you have it."

Muriel gave a great start. "I don't"—she faltered. "I—I—"

He shook his head at her, as though reproving a child. "Pussy's out," he observed. "It is no good giving chase. But really, you know, you mustn't do it. You used to be a brave girl once, and now your nerves are all to pieces."

There was a species of paternal reproach in his tone. Looking at him, she marvelled that she had ever thought him young and headlong. Almost in spite of herself she began to murmur excuses.

"I can't help it. I must have something. I don't sleep. I lie for hours, listening to the fighting. It—it's more than I can bear." Her voice quivered, and she turned her face aside, unable to hide her emotion, but furious with herself for displaying it.

Nick said nothing at all to comfort her, and she bitterly resented his silence. After a pause he spoke again, as if he had banished the matter entirely from his mind.

"Look here," he said. "I want you to tell me something. I don't know what sort of a fellow you think I am, though I fancy you don't like me much. But you're not afraid of me, are you? You know I'm to be trusted?"

It was her single chance of revenge, and she took it. "I have my father's word for it," she said.

He nodded thoughtfully as if unaware of the thrust. "Yes, your father knows me. And so"—he smiled at her suddenly—"you are ready to trust me on his recommendation? You are ready to follow me blindfold through danger if I give you my hand to hold?"

She felt a sharp chill strike her heart. What was it he was asking of her? What did those words of his portend?

"I don't know," she said. "I don't see that it makes much difference how I feel."

"Well, it does," he assured her. "And that is exactly what I have come to talk about. Miss Roscoe, will you leave the fort with me, and escape in disguise? I have thought it all out, and it can be done without much difficulty. I do not need to tell you that the idea has your father's full approval."

They were her father's own words, but at sound of them she shrank and shivered, in sheer horror at the coolness with which they were uttered. He might have been asking her to stroll with him in the leafy quiet of some English lane.

Could it be, she asked herself incredulously, could it be that her father had ever sanctioned and approved so ghastly a risk for her? She put her hand to her temples. Her brain was reeling. How could she do this thing? How could she have permitted it to be even suggested to her? And then, swift through her tortured mind flashed his words: "There will be an end. I have had to face it to-night." Was it this that he had meant? Was it for this that he had been preparing her?

With a muffled exclamation she rose, trembling in every limb. "I can't!" she cried piteously, "oh, I can't! Please go away!"

It might have been the frightened prayer of a child, so beseeching was it, so full of weakness. But Nick Ratcliffe heard it unmoved. He waited a few seconds till she came to a stand by the table, her back towards him. Then with a sudden quiet movement he rose and followed her.

"I beg your pardon," he said. "But you can't afford to shirk things at this stage. I am offering you deliverance, though you don't realise it."

He spoke with force, and if his aim had been to rouse her to a more practical activity, he gained his end. She turned upon him in swift and desperate indignation. Her voice rang almost harsh.

"How can you call it deliverance? It is at best a choice of two horrible evils. You know perfectly well that we could never get through. You must be mad to suggest such a thing. We should be made prisoners and massacred under the very guns of the fort."

"I beg your pardon," he said again, and his eyelids quivered a little as if under the pressure of some controlled emotion. "We shall not be made prisoners. I know what I am saying. It is deliverance that I am offering you. Of course you can refuse, and I shall still do my utmost to save you. But the chances are not equal. I hope you will not refuse."

The moderation of this speech calmed her somewhat. In her first wild panic she had almost imagined that he could take her against her will. She saw that she had been unreasonable, but she was too shaken to tell him so. Moreover, there was still that about him, notwithstanding his words, that made her afraid to yield a single inch of ground lest by some hidden means he should sweep her altogether from her precarious foothold. Even in the silence, she felt that he was doing battle with her, and she did not dare to face him.

With a childish gesture of abandonment, she dropped into a chair and laid her head upon her arms.

"Oh, please go away!" she besought him weakly. "I am so tired—so tired."

But Ratcliffe did not move. He stood looking down at her, at the black hair that clustered about her neck, at the bowed, despairing figure, the piteous, clenched hands.

A little clock in the room began to strike in silvery tones, and he glanced up. The next instant he bent and laid a bony hand upon her two clasped ones.

"Can't you decide?" he said. "Will you let me decide for you? Don't let yourself get scared. You have kept so strong till now." Firmly as he spoke, there was somehow a note of soothing in his voice, and almost insensibly the girl was moved by it. She remained silent and motionless, but the strong grip of his fingers comforted her subtly notwithstanding.

"Come," he said, "listen a moment and let me tell you my plan of campaign. It is very simple, and for that reason it is going to succeed. You are listening now?"

His tone was vigorous and insistent. Muriel sat slowly up in response to it. She looked down at the thin hand that grasped hers, and wondered at its strength; but she lacked the spirit at that moment to resent its touch.

He leaned down upon the table, his face close to hers, and began to unfold his plan.

"We shall leave the fort directly the moon is down. I have a disguise for you that will conceal your face and hair. And I shall fake as a tribesman, so that my dearest friend would never recognise me. They will be collecting the wounded in the dark, and I will carry you through on my shoulder as if I had got a dead relation. You won't object to playing a dead relation of mine?"

He broke into a sudden laugh, but sobered instantly when he saw her shrink at the sound.

"That's about all the plan," he resumed. "There is nothing very alarming about it, for they will never spot us in the dark. I'm as yellow as a Chinaman already. We shall be miles away by morning. And I know how to find my way afterwards."

He paused, but Muriel made no comment. She was staring straight before her.

"Can you suggest any amendments?" he asked.

She turned her head and looked at him with newly-roused aversion in her eyes. She had summoned all her strength to the combat, realising that now was the moment for resistance if she meant to resist.

"No, Mr. Ratcliffe," she said, with a species of desperate firmness very different from his own. "I have nothing to suggest. If you wish to escape, you must go alone. It is quite useless to try to persuade me any further. Nothing—nothing will induce me to leave my father."

Whether or not he had expected this opposition was not apparent on Nick's face. It betrayed neither impatience nor disappointment.

"There would be some reason in that," he gravely rejoined, "if you could do any good to your father by remaining. Of course I see your point, but it seems to me that it would be harder for him to see you starve with the rest of the garrison than to know that you had escaped with me. A woman in your position is bound to be a continual burden and anxiety to those who protect her. The dearer she is to them, so much the heavier is the burden. Miss Roscoe, you must see this. You are not an utter child. You must realise that to leave your father is about the greatest sacrifice you can make for him at the present moment. He is worn out with anxiety on your behalf, literally bowed down by it. For his sake, you are going to do this thing, it being the only thing left that you can do for him."

There was more than persuasion in his voice. It held authority. But Muriel heard it without awe. She had passed that stage. The matter was too momentous to allow of weakness. She had strung herself to the highest pitch of resistance as a hunted creature at bay. She threw back her head, a look of obstinacy about her lips, her slight figure straightened to the rigidity of defiance.

"I will not be forced," she said, in sharp, uneven tones. "Mr. Ratcliffe, you may go on persuading and arguing till doomsday. I will not leave my father."

Ratcliffe stood up abruptly. A curious glitter shone in his eyes, and the light eyebrows twitched a little. She felt that he had suddenly ceased to do battle with her, yet that the victory was not hers. And for a second she was horribly frightened, as though an iron trap had closed upon her and held her at his mercy.

He walked to the door without speaking and opened it. She expected him to go, sat waiting breathlessly for his departure, but instead he stood motionless, looking into the dark passage.

She wondered with nerves on edge what he was waiting for. Suddenly she heard a step without, a few murmured words, and Nick stood on one side. Her father's Sikh orderly passed him, carrying a tray on which was a glass full of some dark liquid. He set it down on the table before her with a deep salaam.

"The General Sahib wishes Missy Sahib to have a good night," he said. "He cannot come to her himself, but he sends her this by his servant, and he bids her drink it and sleep."

Muriel looked up at the man in surprise. Her father had never done such a thing before, and the message astonished her not a little. Then, remembering that he had shown some anxiety regarding her appearance that evening, she fancied she began to understand. Yet it was strange, it was utterly unlike him, to desire her to take an opiate. She looked at the glass with hesitation.

"Give him my love, Purdu," she said finally to the waiting orderly. "Tell him I will take it if I cannot sleep without."

The man bowed himself again and withdrew. To her disgust, however, Nick remained. He was looking at her oddly.

"Miss Roscoe," he said abruptly, "I beg you, don't drink that stuff. Your father must be mad to offer it to you. Let me take the beastliness away."

She faced him indignantly. "My father knows what is good for me better than you do," she said.

He shrugged his shoulders. "I don't profess to be a sage. But any one will tell you that it is madness to take opium in this reckless fashion. For Heaven's sake, be reasonable. Don't take it."

He came back to the table, but at his approach she laid her hand upon the glass. She was quivering with angry excitement.

"I will not endure your interference any longer," she declared, goaded to headlong, nervous fury by his persistence. "My father's wishes are enough for me. He desires me to take it, and so I will."

She took up the glass in a sudden frenzy of defiance. He had frightened her—yes, he had frightened her—but he should see how little he had gained by that. She took a taste of the liquid, then paused, again assailed by a curious hesitancy. Had her father really meant her to take it all?

Nick had stopped short at her first movement, but as she began to lower the glass in response to that disquieting doubt, he swooped suddenly forward like a man possessed.

For a fleeting instant she thought he was going to wrest it from her, but in the next she understood—understood the man's deep treachery, and with what devilish ingenuity he had worked upon her. Holding her with an arm that felt like iron, he forced the glass back between her teeth, and tilted the contents down her throat. She strove to resist him, strove wildly, frantically, not to swallow the draught. But he held her pitilessly. He compelled her, gripping her right hand with the glass, and pinning the other to her side.

When it was over, when he had worked his will and the hateful draught was swallowed, he set her free and turned himself sharply from her.

She sprang up trembling and hysterical. She could have slain him in that instant had she possessed the means to her hand. But her strength was more nearly exhausted than she knew. Her limbs doubled up under her weight, and as she tottered, seeking for support, she realised that she was vanquished utterly at last.

She saw him wheel quickly and start to support her, sought to evade him, failed—and as she felt his arms lift her, she cried aloud in anguished helplessness.

What followed dwelt ever after in her memory as a hideous dream, vivid yet not wholly tangible. He laid her down upon the couch and bent over her, his hands upon her, holding her still; for every muscle, every nerve twitched spasmodically, convulsively, in the instinctive effort of the powerless body to be free. She had a confused impression also that he spoke to her, but what he said she was never able to recall. In the end, her horror faded, and she saw him as through a mist bending above her, grim and tense and silent, controlling her as it were from an immense distance. And even while she yet dimly wondered, he passed like a shadow from her sight, and wonder itself ceased.

Half an hour later Nicholas Ratcliffe, the wit and clown of his regiment, regarded by many as harebrained or wantonly reckless, carried away from the beleaguered fort among the hostile mountains the slight, impassive figure of an English girl.

The night was dark, populated by terrors alive and ghastly. But he went through it as one unaware of its many dangers. Light-footed and fearless, he passed through the midst of his enemies, marching with the sublime audacity of the dominant race, despising caution— yea, grinning triumphant in the very face of Death.

CHAPTER IV
DESOLATION

Out of a deep abyss of darkness in which she seemed to have wandered ceaselessly and comfortlessly for many days, Muriel Roscoe came haltingly back to the surface of things. She was very weak, so weak that to open her eyes was an exertion requiring all her resolution, and to keep them open during those first hours of returning life a physical impossibility. She knew that she was not alone, for gentle hands ministered to her, and she was constantly aware of some one who watched her tirelessly, with never-failing attention. But she felt not the smallest interest regarding this faithful companion, being too weary to care whether she lived or fell away for ever down those unending steeps up which some unseen influence seemed magnetically to draw her.

It was a stage of returning consciousness that seemed to last even longer than the period of her wandering, but this also began to pass at length. The light grew stronger all about her, the mists rolled slowly away from her clogged brain, leaving only a drowsing languor that was infinitely restful to her tired senses.

And then while she lay half-dreaming and wholly content, a remorseless hand began to bathe her face and head with ice-cold water. She awoke reluctantly, even resentfully.

"Don't!" she entreated like a child. "I am so tired. Let me sleep."

"My poor dear, I know all about it," a motherly voice made answer. "But it's time for you to wake."

She did not grasp the words—only, very vaguely, their meaning; and this she made a determined, but quite fruitless, effort to defy. In the end, being roused in spite of herself, she opened her eyes and gazed upwards.

And all his life long Nick Ratcliffe remembered the reproach that those eyes held for him. It was as if he had laid violent hands upon a spirit that yearned towards freedom, and had dragged it back into the sordid captivity from which it had so nearly escaped.

But it was only for a moment that she looked at him so. The reproach faded swiftly from the dark eyes and he saw a startled horror dawn behind it.

Suddenly she raised herself with a faint cry. "Where am I?" she gasped. "What—what have you done with me?"

She stared around her wildly, with unreasoning, nightmare terror. She was lying on a bed of fern in a narrow, dark ravine. The place was full of shadow, though far overhead she saw the light of day. At one end, only a few yards from her, a stream rushed and gurgled among great boulders, and its insistent murmur filled the air. Behind her rose a great wall of grey rock, clothed here and there with some dark growth. Its rugged face was dented with hollows that looked like the homes of wild animals. There was a constant trickle of water on all sides, an eerie whispering, remote but incessant. As she sat there in growing panic, a great bat-like creature, immense and shadowy, swooped soundlessly by her.

She shrank back with another cry, and found Nick Ratcliffe's arm thrust protectingly about her.

"It's all right," he said, in a matter-of-fact tone. "You're not frightened at flying-foxes, are you?"

Recalled to the fact of his presence, she turned sharply, and flung his arm away as though it had been a snake. "Don't touch me!" she gasped, passionate loathing in voice and gesture.

"Sorry," said Nick imperturbably. "I meant well."

He began to busy himself with a small bundle that lay upon the ground, whistling softly between his teeth, and for a few seconds Muriel sat and watched him. He was dressed in a flowing native garment, that covered him from head to foot. Out of the heavy enveloping folds his smooth, yellow face looked forth, sinister and terrible to her fevered vision. He looked like some evil bird, she thought to herself.

Glancing down, she saw that she was likewise attired, save that her head was bare. The hair hung wet on her forehead, and the water dripped down her face. She put up her hand half-mechanically to wipe the drops away. Her fear was mounting rapidly higher.

She knew now what had happened. He had drugged her forcibly—she shivered at the remembrance—and had borne her away to this dreadful place during her unconsciousness. Her father was left behind in the fort. He had sanctioned her removal. He had given her, a helpless captive, into this man's keeping.

But no! Her whole soul rose up in sudden fierce denial of this. He had never done this thing. He had never given his consent to an act so cowardly and so brutal. He was incapable of parting with her thus. He could never have permitted so base a trick, so cruel, so outrageous, a deed of treachery.

Strength came suddenly to her—the strength of frenzy. She leaped to her feet. She would escape. She would go back to him through all the hordes of the enemy. She would face anything—anything in the world—rather than remain at the mercy of this man.

But—he had not been looking at her, and he did not look at her,—his arm shot out as she moved, and his hand fastened claw-like upon her dress.

"Sorry," he said again, in the same practical tone. "But you'll have something to eat before you go."

She stooped and strove wildly, frantically, to shake off the detaining hand. But it held her like a vice, with awful skeleton fingers that she could not, dared not, touch.

"Let me go!" she cried impotently. "How dare you? How dare you?"

Still he did not raise his head. He was on his knees, and he would not even trouble himself to rise.

"I can't help myself," he told her coolly. "It's not my fault. It's yours."

She made a final, violent effort to wrest herself free. And then—it was as if all power were suddenly taken from her—her strained nerves gave way completely, and she dropped down upon the ground again in a quivering agony of helplessness.

Nick's hand fell away from her. "You shouldn't," he said gently. "It's no good, you know."

He returned to his former occupation while she sat with her face hidden, in a stupor of fear, afraid to move lest he should touch her again.

"Now," said Nick, after a brief pause, "let me have the pleasure of seeing you break your fast. There is some of that excellent boiled rice of yours here. You will feel better when you have had some."

She trembled at the sound of his voice. Could he make her eat also against her will, she wondered?

"Come!" said Nick again, in a tone of soft wheedling that he might have employed to a fractious child. "It'll do you good, you know, Muriel. Won't you try? Just a mouthful—to please me!"

Reluctantly she uncovered her face, and looked at him. He was kneeling in front of her, the *chuddah* pushed back from his face, humbly offering her an oatmeal biscuit with a small heap of rice piled upon it.

She drew back shuddering. "I couldn't eat anything—possibly," she said, and even her voice seemed to shrink. "You can. You take it. I would rather die."

Nick did not withdraw his hand. "Take it, Muriel," he said quietly. "It is going to do you good."

She flashed him a desperate glance in which anger, fear, abhorrence, were strongly mingled. He advanced the biscuit a little nearer. There was a queer look on his yellow face, almost a bullying look.

"Take it," he said again.

And against her will, almost without conscious movement, she obeyed him. The untempting morsel passed from his hand to hers, and under the compulsion of his insistence she began to eat.

She felt as if every mouthful would choke her, but she persevered, urged by the dread certainty that he would somehow have his way.

Not until the last fragment was gone did she feel his vigilance relax, but he ate nothing himself though there remained several biscuits and a very little of the rice.

"You are feeling better?" he asked her then.

A curious suspicion that he was waiting to tell her something made her answer almost feverishly in the affirmative. It amounted to a premonition of evil tidings, and instinctively her thoughts flew to her father.

"What is it?" she questioned nervously. "You have something to say."

Nick's face was turned from her. He seemed to be gazing across the ravine.

"Yes," he said, after a moment.

"Oh, what?" she broke in. "Tell me quickly—quickly! It is my father, I know, I know. He has been hurt—wounded—"

She stopped. Nick had lifted one hand as if to silence her. "My dear," he said, his voice very low, "your father died last night—before we left the fort."

At her cry of agony he started up, and in a second he was on his knees by her side and had gathered her to him as though she had been a little child in need of comfort. She did not shrink from him in her extremity. The blow had been too sudden, too overwhelming. It blotted out all lesser sensibilities. In those first terrible moments she did not think of Nick at all, was scarcely conscious of his presence, though she vaguely felt the comfort of his arms.

And he, holding her fast against his breast, found no consolation, no word of any sort wherewith to soothe her. He only rocked her gently, pressing her head to his shoulder, while his face, bent above her, quivered all over as the face of a man in torture.

Muriel spoke at last, breaking her stricken silence with a strangely effortless composure. "Tell me more," she said.

She stirred in his arms as if to free herself from some oppression, and finally drew herself away from him, though not as if she wished to escape his touch. She still seemed to be hardly aware of him. He was the medium of her information, that was all. Nick dropped back into his former attitude, his hands clasped firmly round his knees, his eyes, keen as a bird's and extremely bright, gazing across the ravine. His lips still quivered a little, but his voice was perfectly even and quiet.

"It happened very soon after the firing began. It must have been directly after he left you. He was hit in the breast, just over the heart. We couldn't do anything for him. He knew himself that it was mortal. In fact, I think he had almost expected it. We took him into the guardroom and made him as easy as possible. He lost consciousness before he died. He was lying unconscious when I came to you."

Muriel made a sharp movement. "And you never told me," she said, in a dry whisper.

"I thought it best," he answered with great gentleness. "You could not have gone to him. He didn't wish it."

"Why not?" she demanded, and suddenly her voice rang harsh again. "Why could I not have gone to him? Why didn't he wish it?"

Nick hesitated for a single instant. Then, "It was for your own sake," he said, not looking at her.

"You mean he suffered?"

"While he remained conscious—yes." Nick spoke reluctantly. "It didn't last long," he said.

She scarcely seemed to hear him. "And so you tricked me," she said; "you tricked me while my father was lying dying. I was not to see him—either then or after—for my own sake! And do you think"—her voice rising—"do you think that you were in any way justified in treating me so? Do you think it was merciful to blind me and to take from me all I should ever have of comfort to look back upon? Do you think I couldn't have borne it all ten thousand times easier if I could have seen and known the very worst? It was my right— it was my right! How dared you take it from me? I will never forgive you—never!"

She was on her feet as the passionate protest burst from her, but she swayed as she stood and flung out her arms with a groping gesture.

"I could have borne it," she cried again wildly, piteously. "I could have borne anything—anything—if I had only known!"

She broke into a sudden, terrible sobbing, and threw herself down headlong upon the earth, clutching at the moss with shaking, convulsive fingers, and crying between her sobs for "Daddy! Daddy!" as though her agony could pierce the dividing barrier and bring him back to her. Nick made no further attempt to help her. He sat gazing stonily out before him in a sphinx-like stillness that never varied while the storm of her anguish spent itself at his side.

Even after her sobs had ceased from sheer exhaustion he made no movement, no sign that he was so much as thinking of her.

Only when at last she raised herself with difficulty, and put the heavy hair back from her disfigured face, did he turn slightly and hold out to her a small tin cup.

"It's only water," he said gently. "Have some."

She took it almost mechanically and drank, then lay back with closed eyes and burning head, sick and blinded by her paroxysm of weeping.

A little later she felt his hands moving about her again, but she was too spent to open her eyes. He bathed her face with a care equal to any woman's, smoothed back her hair, and improvised a pillow for her head.

And afterwards she knew that he sat down by her, out of sight but close at hand, a silent presence watching over her, till at last, worn out with grief and the bitter strain of the past weeks, she sank into natural, dreamless slumber, and slept for hours.

CHAPTER V
THE DEVIL IN THE WILDERNESS

It was dark when Muriel awoke—so dark that she lay for a while dreamily fancying herself in bed. But this illusion passed very quickly as her brain, refreshed and active, resumed its work. The cry of a jackal at no great distance roused her to full consciousness, and she started up in the chill darkness, trembling and afraid.

Instantly a warm hand grasped hers, and a low voice spoke. "It's all right," said Nick. "I'm here."

"Oh, isn't it dark?" she said. "Isn't it dark?"

"Don't be frightened," he answered gently. "Come close to me. You are cold."

She crept to him shivering, thankful for the shielding arm he threw around her.

"The sunrise can't be far off," he said. "I expect you are hungry, aren't you?"

She was very hungry, and he put a biscuit into her hand. The very fact of eating there in the darkness in some measure reassured her. She ate several biscuits, and began to feel much better.

"Getting warmer?" questioned Nick. "Let me feel your hands." They were still cold, and he took them and thrust them down against his breast. She shrank a little at the touch of his warm flesh.

"It will make you so cold," she murmured.

But he only laughed at her softly, and pressed them closer. "I am not easily chilled," he said. "Besides, it's sleeping that makes you cold. And I haven't slept."

Muriel heard the news with astonishment. She was no longer angry with Nick, and her fears of him were dormant. Though she would never forget and might never forgive his treachery, he was her sole protector in that wilderness of many terrors, and she lacked the resolution to keep him at arm's length. There was, moreover, something comforting in his presence, something that vastly reassured her, making her lean upon him almost in spite of herself.

"Haven't you slept at all?" she asked him in wonder. "How in the world did you keep awake?"

He did not answer her, only laughed again as though at some secret joke. He seemed to be in rather good spirits, she noticed, and she marvelled at him with a heavy pain at her heart that was utterly beyond expression or relief.

She sat silent for a little, then at length withdrew her hands, assuring him that they were quite warm.

"And I want to talk to you," she added, in a more practical tone than she had previously managed to assume. "Mr. Ratcliffe, you may be in command of this expedition, but I think you ought to tell me your plans."

"Call me Nick, won't you?" he said. "It'll make things easier. You are quite welcome to know my plans, such as they are. I haven't managed to develop anything very ingenious during all these hours. You see we are, to a certain extent, at the mercy of circumstances. This place isn't more than a dozen miles from the fort, and the hills all round are infested with tribesmen. I hoped at first that we should get clear in the night, but you were asleep, and on the whole it seemed best to lie up for another day. We might make a bolt for it tomorrow night if all goes well. I have a sort of instinct for these mountains. There is always plenty of cover for those who know how to find it. It will be slow progress, of course, but we will keep moving south, and, given luck, we may fall in with Bassett's relief column before many days."

So with much serenity he disclosed his plans, and Muriel marvelled afresh at the confidence that buoyed him up. Was he really as sublimely free from anxiety as he wished her to believe, she wondered? It was difficult to think otherwise, even though he had admitted that they were governed by circumstance. She began to think that there was magic in him, some hidden reserve force upon which he could always draw when all other resources failed.

Another matter had also caught her attention, and this she presently decided to investigate. She had never thought of Nick Ratcliffe as in any sense a remarkable person before.

"Did you actually carry me ten miles?" she asked.

"Something very near it," said Nick.

"How in the world did you do it?" Her interest was quickened. Undoubtedly there was something uncanny in this man's strength.

"You're not very heavy, you know," he said.

His arm was still around her, and she suffered it; for the darkness still frightened her when she allowed herself to think.

"Have you had anything to eat?" she asked him next.

"Not quite lately," said Nick. "I've been smoking. I wonder you didn't notice it."

His tone was somehow repressive, but she ignored it with a growing temerity. After all, he did not seem such an alarming person on a nearer acquaintance.

"Does smoking do as well as eating?" she asked.

"Much better," said Nick promptly. "Care to try?"

She shook her head in the darkness. "I don't think you are telling the truth," she said.

"What?" said Nick.

He spoke carelessly, but she did not repeat her assertion. A sudden shyness descended upon her, and she became silent. Nick was quiet too, and she wondered what was passing in his mind. But for the tenseness of the arm that encircled her, she could have believed him to be dozing. The silence was becoming oppressive when abruptly he broke it.

"See!" he said. "Here comes the dawn!"

She started and stared in front of her, seeing nothing.

"Over to your left," said Nick. And turning she beheld a lightening of the darkness high above them.

She breathed a sigh of thankfulness, and watched it grow. It spread rapidly. The walls of the ravine showed ghostly grey, then faintly pink. Through the dimness the boulders scattered about the stream stood up like mediaeval monsters, and for a few panic-stricken seconds Muriel took the twining roots of a rhododendron close at hand for the coils of a gigantic snake. Then as the ordinary light of day filtered down into the gloomy place she sighed again with relief, and looked at her companion.

He was sitting with his chin on his hand, gazing across the ravine. He did not stir or glance in her direction. His yellow face was seamed in a thousand wrinkles.

A vague misgiving assailed her as she looked at him. There was something unnatural in his stillness.

"Nick!" she said at length with hesitation.

He turned sharply, and in an instant the ready grin leaped out upon his face. "Good morning," he said lightly. "I was just thinking how nice it would be to go down there and have a wash. We've got to pass the time somehow, you know. Will you go first?"

His gaiety baffled her, but she did not feel wholly reassured. She got up slowly, and as she did so, her attention was caught by something that sent a thrill of dismay through her.

"Don't look at my feet, please," said Nick. "They won't bear inspection at present."

She turned horrified eyes to his face, as he thrust them down into a bunch of fern. "How dreadful!" she exclaimed. "They are all cut and gashed. I didn't know you were barefooted."

"I wasn't," said Nick. "I've got some sandals here. Don't look like that! You make me want to cry. I assure you it doesn't hurt in the least."

He grinned again as he uttered this cheerful lie, but Muriel was not deceived.

"You must let me bind them up," she said.

"Not for the world," laughed Nick. "I couldn't walk with my feet in poultice-bags, and we shall have some more rough marching to do to-night. Now don't you worry. Run along like a good girl. I'm going to say my prayers."

It was flippantly spoken, but Muriel realised that it would be better to obey. She turned about slowly, and began to make her way down to the stream.

The sunlight was beginning to slant through the ravine, and here and there the racing water gleamed silvery. It was intensely refreshing to kneel and bathe face and hands in its icy coldness. She lingered long over it. Its sparkling purity seemed to reach and still the throbbing misery at her heart. In some fashion it brought her peace.

She would have prayed, but she felt she had no prayer to offer. She had no favour to ask for herself, and her world was quite empty now. She had no one in her heart for whom to pray.

Yet for awhile she knelt dumb among the lifeless stones, her face hidden, her thoughts with the father whose loss she had scarcely begun to realise. It might be that God would understand and pity her silence, she thought drearily to herself.

The rush of the water drowned all sound but its own, and the memory of Nick, waiting above, faded from her consciousness like a dream. Her brain felt numb and heavy still. She did not want to think. She leaned her head against a rock, closing her eyes. The continuous babble of the stream was like a lullaby.

Under its soothing influence she might have slept, a blessed drowsiness was stealing over her, when suddenly there flashed through her being a swift warning of approaching danger. Whence it came she knew not, but its urgency was such that instinctively she started up and looked about her.

The next instant, with a sound half-gasp, half-cry, she was on her feet, and shrinking back against her sheltering boulder in the paralysis of a great horror. There, within a few yards of her and drawing nearer, ever nearer, with a beast-like stealth, was a tall, black-bearded tribesman. Transfixed by terror, she stood and gazed at him, waiting dumbly, cold from head to foot, feeling as though her very heart had turned to stone.

Nearer he came, and yet nearer, soundlessly over the stones. His eyes, gleaming, devilish, were to her as the eyes of a devouring monster. In her agony she tried to shriek aloud, but her voice was gone, her throat seemed locked. She was powerless.

Close to her, for a single instant he paused; then, as in a lightning flash, she saw the narrow, sinewy hand and snake-like arm dart forward to seize her, felt every muscle in her body stiffen to rigidity in anticipation of its touch, and shrank—shrank in every nerve though she made no outward sign of shrinking.

But on the instant, with a panther-like spring, sure, noiseless, deadly, another figure leapt suddenly across her vision. There followed a violent struggle in front of her, a confused swaying to and fro, a cry choked instantly and terribly, the tinkling sound of steel falling upon stone. And then both figures were on the ground almost at her feet, locked together in mortal combat, fighting, fighting like demons in a silence that throbbed with the tumult of unrestrained savagery.

Later she never could remember how long it took her to realise that the second apparition was Nick, or if she had known it from the first. She felt herself hovering upon the brink of a great emptiness, a void immense, and yet all her senses were alive and tingling with horror. With agonised perception of what was passing, she yet felt numbed: as though her body were dead, but still contained a vital, tortured soul.

And it was thus that she presently saw Nick's face bent above the black-bearded face of his enemy; and remembered suddenly and horribly a picture she had once seen of the devil in the wilderness.

With his knees he was gripping the writhing body of his fallen foe. With his hands—it came upon her as she watched with a shock of anguished comprehension—he was deliberately and with deadly intention choking out the man's life.

"Curse you! Die!" she heard him say and his voice sounded like the snarl of a wild beast. His upper lip was drawn back, the lower one was between his teeth, and from it the blood dripped continuously upon his hands and upon the dark throat he gripped.

"Give me that knife!" he suddenly said, with an upward jerk of the head.

A dagger was lying almost within his reach, close to her foot. She could have kicked it towards him had not her body been fast bound in that deathly inertia. But her whole soul rose up in wild revolt at the order. She tried to cry out, to implore him to have mercy, but she could not make a sound. She could only stand in frozen horror, and witness this awful thing.

She saw Nick shift his grip to one hand and reach out with the other for the weapon. He grasped it and recovered himself. A great darkness was descending upon her, but it did not come at once. It hovered before her eyes, and seemed to pass, and again she saw the horror at her feet; saw Nick, bent to destroy like an eagle above his prey, merciless, full of strength, terrible; saw the man beneath him, writhing, convulsed, tortured; saw his upturned face, and starting eyes; saw the sudden downward swoop of Nick's right hand, the flash of the descending steel.

In her agony she burst the spell that bound her, and shrieking turned to flee from that awful sight.

But even as she moved, the darkness came suddenly back upon her, enveloping her, overwhelming her—a darkness that could be felt. For a little she fought against it

437

frantically, impotently. Then her feet seemed to totter over the edge of a dreadful, formless silence. She knew that she fell.

CHAPTER VI
WHEN STRONG MEN FAIL

"Wake up!" said Nick softly. "Wake up! Don't be afraid."

But Muriel turned her face from the light with a moan. Memory winged with horror was sweeping back upon her, and she wanted never to wake again.

"Wake up!" Nick said again, and this time there was insistence in his voice. "Open your eyes, Muriel. There is nothing to frighten you."

Shuddering, she obeyed him. She was lying once more upon her couch of ferns, and he was stooping over her, looking closely into her face. His eyes were extraordinarily bright, like the eyes of an eagle, but the lids flickered so rapidly that he seemed to be looking through her rather than at her. There was a wound upon his lower lip, and at the sight she shuddered again, closing her eyes. She remembered that the last time she had looked upon that face, it had been the face of a devil.

"Oh, go away! Go away!" she wailed. "Let me die!"

"I will go away," he answered swiftly, "if you will promise to drink what is in this cup."

He pressed it against her hand, and she took it almost mechanically. "It is only brandy and water," he said. "You will drink it?"

"If I must," she answered weakly.

"You must," he rejoined, and she heard him rise and move away. She strained her ears to listen, but she very soon ceased to hear him; and then raising herself cautiously, she drank. A warm thrill of life ran through her veins with the draught, steadying her, refreshing her. But it was long before she could bring herself to look round.

The miniature roar of the stream was the only sound to be heard, and when at length she glanced downwards there was no sign anywhere of the ghastly spectacle she had just witnessed. She saw the rock behind which she had knelt, and again a violent fit of shuddering assailed her. What did that rock conceal?

Nevertheless she presently took courage to rise, looking about her furtively, half afraid that Nick might pop up at any moment to detain her. For she felt that she could not stay longer in that place, whatever he might say or do. The one idea that possessed her was to get away from him, to escape from his horrible presence, whither she neither knew nor cared. If he appeared to stop her then, she thought that she would go raving mad.

But she saw nothing of him as she stood there, and with deep relief she began to creep away. Half a dozen yards she covered, and then stood suddenly still with her heart in her throat. There, immediately in front of her, flung prone upon the ground with his face on his arms, was Nick. He did not move at her coming, did not seem to hear. And the thought came to her to avoid him by a circuit, and yet escape. But something—a queer, indefinable something—made her pause. Why was he lying there? Had he been hurt in that awful struggle? Was he—was he unconscious? Was he—dead?

She fought back the impulse to fly, not for its unworthiness, but because she felt that she must know.

Trembling, she moved a little nearer to the prostrate, motionless figure.

"Nick!" she whispered under her breath.

He made no sign.

Her doubt turned to sudden, overmastering fear that pricked her forward in spite of herself.

"Nick!" she said again, and finding herself close to him she bent and very slightly touched his shoulder.

He moved then, and she almost gasped with relief. He turned his head sharply without raising himself, and she saw the grim lines of his lean cheek and jaw.

"That you, Muriel?" he said, speaking haltingly, spasmodically. "I'm awfully sorry. Fact is—I'm not well. I shall be—better—directly. Go back, won't you?"

He broke off, and lay silent, his hands clenched as if he were in pain.

Muriel stood looking down at him in consternation. It was her chance to escape—a chance that might never occur again—but she had no further thought of taking it.

"What is it?" she asked him timidly, "Can I—do anything?"

And then she suddenly saw what was the matter. It burst upon her—a startling revelation. Possibly the sight of those skeleton fists helped her to enlightenment. She turned swiftly and sped back to their camping ground.

In thirty seconds or less, she was back again and stooping over him with a piece of brown bread in her hand.

"Eat this," she ordered, in a tone of authority.

Nick's face was hidden again. He seemed to be fighting with himself. His voice came at length, muffled and indistinct.

"No, no! Take it away! I'll have a drain of brandy. And I've got some tobacco left."

Muriel stooped lower. She caught the words though they were scarcely audible. She laid her hand upon his arm, stronger in the moment's emergency than she had been since leaving the fort.

"You are to eat it," she said very decidedly. "You shall eat it. Do you hear, Nick? I know what is the matter with you. You are starving. I ought to have seen it before."

Nick uttered a shaky laugh, and dragged himself up on to his elbows. "I'm not starving," he declared. "Take it away, Muriel. Do you think I'm going to eat your luncheon, tea, and dinner, and to-morrow's breakfast as well?"

"You are going to eat this," she answered.

He flashed her a glance of keen curiosity. "Am I?" he said.

"You must," she said, speaking with an odd vehemence which later surprised herself. "Why should you go out of your way to tell me a lie? Do you think I can't see?"

Nick raised himself slowly. Something in the situation seemed to have deprived him of his usual readiness. But he would not take the bread, would not even look at it.

"I'm better now," he said. "We'll go back."

Muriel stood for a second irresolute, then sharply turned her back. Nick sat and watched her in silence. Suddenly she wheeled. "There!" she said. "I've divided it. You will eat this at least. It's absurd of you to starve yourself. You might as well have stayed in the fort to do that."

This was unanswerable. Nick took the bread without further protest. He began to eat, marvelling at his own docility; and suddenly he knew that he was ravenous.

There was very little left when at length he looked up.

"Show me what you have saved for yourself," he said.

But Muriel backed away with a short, hysterical laugh.

He started to his feet and took her rudely by the shoulder. "Do you mean to say—" he began, almost with violence; and then checked himself, peering at her with fierce, uncertain eyes.

She drew away from him, all her fears returning upon her in a flood; but at her movement he set her free and turned his back.

"Heaven knows what you did it for," he said, seeming to control his voice with some difficulty. "It wasn't for your own sake, and I won't presume to think it was for mine. But when the time comes for handing round rewards, may it be remembered that your offering was something more substantial than a cup of cold water."

He broke off with a queer sound in the throat, and began to move away.

But Muriel followed him, an unaccountable sense of responsibility overcoming her reluctance.

"Nick!" she said.

He stood still without turning. She had a feeling that he was putting strong restraint upon himself. With an effort she forced herself to continue.

"You want sleep, I know. Will you—will you lie down while I watch?"

He shook his head without looking at her.

"But I wish it," she persisted. "I can wake you if—anything happens."

"You wouldn't dare," said Nick.

"I suppose that means you are afraid to trust me," she said.

He turned at that. "It means nothing of the sort. But you've had one scare, and you may have another. I think myself that that fellow was a scout on the look-out for Bassett's advance guard. But Heaven only knows what brought him to this place, and there may be others. That's why I didn't dare to shoot."

He paused, his light eyebrows raised, surveying her questioningly; for Muriel had suddenly covered her face with both hands. But in another moment she looked up again, and spoke with an effort.

"Your being awake couldn't lessen the danger. Won't you—please—be reasonable about it? I am doing my best."

There was a deep note of appeal in her voice, and abruptly Nick gave in.

He moved back to their resting-place without another word, and flung himself face downwards beside the nest of fern that he had made for her, lying stretched at full length like a log.

She had not expected so sudden and complete a surrender. It took her unawares, and she stood looking down at him, uncertain how to proceed.

But after a few seconds he turned his head towards her and spoke.

"You'll stay by me, Muriel?"

"Of course," she answered, that unwonted sense of responsibility still strongly urging her.

He murmured something unintelligible, and stirred uneasily. She knew in a flash what he wanted, but a sick sense of dread held her back. She felt during the silence that followed as though he were pleading with her, urging her, even entreating her. Yet still she resisted, standing near him indeed, but with a desperate reluctance at her heart, a shrinking unutterable from the bare thought of any closer proximity to him that was as the instinctive recoil of purity from a thing unclean.

The horror of his deed had returned upon her over-whelmingly with his brief reference to it. His lack of emotion seemed to her as hideous callousness, more horrible than the deed itself. His physical exhaustion had called her out of herself, but the reaction was doubly terrible.

Nick said no more. He lay quite motionless, hardly seeming to breathe, and she realised that there was no repose in his attitude. He was not even trying to rest.

She wrung her hands together. It could not go on, this tension. Either she must yield to his unspoken desire, or he would sit up and cry off the bargain. And she knew that sleep was a necessity to him. Common-sense told her that he was totally unfit for further hardship without it.

She closed her eyes a moment, summoning all her strength for the greatest sacrifice she had ever made. And then in silence she sat down beside him, within reach of his hand.

He uttered a great sigh and suffered his whole body to relax. And she knew by the action, though he did not speak a word, that she had set his mind at rest.

Scarcely a minute later, his quiet breathing told her that he slept, but she sat on by his side without moving during the long empty hours of her vigil. He had trusted her without a question, and, as her father's daughter, she would at whatever cost prove herself worthy of his trust.

CHAPTER VII
THE COMING OF AN ARMY

Through a great part of the night that followed they tramped steadily southward. The stars were Nick's guide, though as time passed he began to make his way with the confidence of one well-acquainted with his surroundings. The instinct of locality was a sixth sense with him. Hand in hand, over rocky ground, through deep ravines, by steep and difficult tracks, they made their desperate way. Sometimes in the distance dim figures moved mysteriously, revealed by starlight, but none questioned or molested them. They passed from rock to rock through the heart of the enemy's country, unrecognised, unobserved. There were times when Nick grasped his revolver under his disguise, ready,

ready at a moment's notice, to keep his word to the girl's father, should detection be their portion; but each time as the danger passed them by he tightened his hold upon her, drawing her forward with greater assurance.

They scarcely spoke throughout the long, long march. Muriel had moved at first with a certain elasticity, thankful to escape at last from the horrors of their resting-place. But very soon a great weariness came upon her. She was physically unfit for any prolonged exertion. The long strain of the siege had weakened her more than she knew.

Nevertheless, she kept on bravely, uttering no complaint, urged to utmost effort by the instinctive desire to escape. It was this one idea that occupied all her thoughts during that night. She shrank with a vivid horror from looking back. And she could not see into the dim blank future. It was mercifully screened from her sight.

At her third heavy stumble, Nick stopped and made her swallow some raw brandy from his flask. This buoyed her up for a while, but it was evident to them both that her strength was fast failing. And presently he stopped again, and without a word lifted her in his arms. She gasped a protest to which he made no response. His arms compassed her like steel, making her feel helpless as an infant. He was limping himself, she noticed; yet he bore her strongly, without faltering, sure-footed as a mountain goat over the broken ground, till he found at length what he deemed a safe halting-place in a clump of stunted trees.

The sunrise revealed a native village standing among rice and cotton fields in the valley below them.

"I shall have to go foraging," Nick said.

But Muriel's nerves that had been tottering on the verge of collapse for some time here broke down completely. She clung to him hysterically and entreated him not to leave her.

"I can't bear it! I can't bear it!" she kept reiterating. "If you go, I must go too. I can't—I can't stay here alone."

He gave way instantly, seeing that she was in a state of mind that bordered upon distraction, and that he could not safely leave her. He sat down beside her, therefore, making her as comfortable as he could; and she presently slept with her head upon his shoulder. It was but a broken slumber, however, and she awoke from it crying wildly that a man was being murdered—murdered—murdered—and imploring him with agonised tears to intervene.

He quieted her with a steady insistence that gained its end, though she crouched against him sobbing for some time after. As the sun rose higher her fever increased, but she remained conscious and suffering intensely, all through the heat of the day. Then, as the evening drew on, she slipped into a heavy stupor.

It was the opportunity Nick had awaited for hours, and he seized it. Laying her back in the deep shadow of a boulder, he went swiftly down into the valley. The last light was passing as he strode through the village, a gaunt, silent figure in a hillman's dress, a native dagger in his girdle. Save that he had pulled the *chuddah* well over his face, he attempted no concealment.

He glided by a ring of old men seated about a fire, moving like a shadow through the glare. They turned to view him, but he had already passed with the tread of a wolf, and the mud wall of one of the cottages hid him from sight.

Into this hut he dived as though some instinct guided him. He paid no heed to a woman on a string-bedstead with a baby at her breast, who chattered shrilly at his entrance. Preparations for a meal were in progress, and he scarcely paused before he lighted upon what he sought. A small earthen pitcher stood on the mud floor. He swooped upon it, caught it up, splashing milk in all directions, clapped his hand yellow and claw-like upon the mouth, and was gone.

There arose a certain hue and cry behind him, but he was swiftly beyond detection, a fleeing shadow up the hillside. And the baffled villagers, returning, found comfort in the reflection that he was doubtless a holy man and that his brief visit would surely entail a blessing.

By the time they arrived at this conclusion, Nick was kneeling by the girl's side, supporting her while she drank. The nourishment revived her. She came to herself, and thanked him.

"You will have some too," said she anxiously.

And Nick drank also with a laugh and a joke to cloak his eagerness. That draught of milk was more to him at that moment than the choicest wine of the gods.

He sat down beside her again when he had thus refreshed himself. He thought that she was drowsy, and was surprised when presently she laid a trembling hand upon his arm.

He bent over her quickly. "What is it? Anything I can do?"

She did not shrink from him any longer. He could but dimly see her face in the strong shadow cast by the moonlight behind the trees.

"I want just to tell you, Nick," she said faintly, "that you will have to go on without me when the moon sets. You needn't mind about leaving me any more. I shall be dead before the morning comes. I'm not afraid. I think I'm rather glad. I am so very, very tired."

Her weak voice failed.

Nick was stooping low over her. He did not speak at once. He only took the nerveless hand that lay upon his arm and carried it to his lips, breathing for many seconds upon the cold fingers.

When at length he spoke, his tone was infinitely gentle, but it possessed, notwithstanding, a certain quality of arresting force.

"My dear," he said, "you belong to me now, you know. You have been given into my charge, and I am not going to part with you."

She did not resist him or attempt to withdraw her hand, but her silence was scarcely the silence of acquiescence. When she spoke again after a long pause, there was a piteous break in her voice.

"Why don't you let me die? I want to die. Why do you hold me back?"

"Why?" said Nick swiftly. "Do you really want me to tell you why?"

But there he checked himself with a sharp, indrawn breath. The next instant he laid her hand gently down.

"You will know some day, Muriel," he said. "But for the present you will have to take my reason on trust. I assure you it is a very good one."

The restraint of his words was marked by a curious vehemence, but this she was too ill at the time to heed. She turned her face away almost fretfully.

"Why should I live?" she moaned. "There is no one wants me now."

"That will never be true while I live," Nick answered steadily, and his tone was the tone of a man who registers a vow.

But again she did not heed him. She had suffered too acutely and too recently to be comforted by promises. Moreover, she did not want consolation. She wanted only to shut her eyes and die. In her weakness she had not fancied that he could deny her this.

And so when presently he roused her by lifting her to resume the journey, she shed piteous tears upon his shoulder, imploring him to leave her where she was. He would not listen to her. He knew that it was highly dangerous to rest so close to habitation, and he would not risk another day in such precarious shelter.

So for hours he carried her with a strength almost superhuman, forcing his physical powers into subjection to his will. Though limping badly, he covered several miles of wild and broken country, deserted for the most part, almost incredibly lonely, till towards sunrise he found a resting-place in a hollow high up the side of a mountain, overlooking a winding, desolate pass.

Muriel was either sleeping or sunk in the stupor of exhaustion. There was some brandy left in his flask, and he made her take a little. But it scarcely roused her, and she was too weak to notice that he did not touch any himself.

All through the scorching day that followed, she dozed and woke in feverish unrest, sometimes rambling incoherently till he brought her gravely back, sometimes crying weakly, sometimes making feeble efforts to pray.

All through the long, burning hours he never stirred away from her. He sat close to her, often holding her in his arms, for she seemed less restless so; and perpetually he gazed out with terrible, bloodshot eyes over the savage mountains, through the long, irregular line of pass, watching eagle-like, tireless and intent, for the deliverance which, if it came at all, must come that way. His face was yellow and sunken, lined in a thousand wrinkles like the face of a monkey; but his eyes remained marvellously bright. They looked as if they had not slept for years, as if they would never sleep again. He was at the end of his resources and he knew it, but he would watch to the very end. He would die watching.

As the sun sank in a splendour that transfigured the eternally white mountain-crest to a mighty shimmer of rose and gold, he turned at last and looked down at the white face pillowed upon his arm. The eyes were closed. The ineffable peace of Death seemed to dwell upon the quiet features. She had lain so for a long time, and he had fancied her sleeping.

He caught his breath, feeling for his flask, and for the first time his hands shook uncontrollably. But as the raw spirit touched her lips, he saw her eyelids quiver, and a great gasp of relief went through him. As she opened her eyes he stayed his hand. It seemed cruel to bring her back. But the suffering and the half instinctive look of horror passed from her eyes like a shadow, as they rested upon him. There was even the very faint flicker of a smile about them.

She turned her face slightly towards him with the gesture of a child nestling against his breast. Yet though she lay thus in his arms, he felt keenly, bitterly, that she was very far away from him.

He hung over her, still holding himself in with desperate strength, not daring to speak lest he should disturb the holy peace that seemed to be drawing all about her.

The sunset glory deepened. For a few seconds the crags above them glittered golden as the peaks of Paradise. And in the wonderful silence Muriel spoke.

"Do you see them?" she said.

He saw that her eyes were turned upon the shining mountains. There was a strange light on her face.

"See what, darling?" he asked her softly.

Her eyes came back to him for a moment. They had a thoughtful, wondering look.

"How strange!" she said slowly. "I thought it was—an eagle."

The detachment of her tone cut him to the heart. And suddenly the pain of it was more than he could bear.

"It is I—Nick," he told her, with urgent emphasis. "Surely you know me!"

But her eyes had passed beyond him again. "Nick?" she questioned to herself. "Nick? But this—this was an eagle."

She was drawing away from him, and he could not hold her, could not even hope to follow her whither she went. A great sob broke from him, and in a moment, like the rush of an overwhelming flood from behind gates long closed, the anguish of the man burst its bonds.

"Muriel!" he cried passionately. "Muriel! Stay with me, look at me, love me! There is nothing in the mountains to draw you. It is here—here beside you, touching you, holding you. O God," he prayed brokenly, "she doesn't understand me. Let her understand,—open her eyes,—make her see!"

His agony reached her, touched her, for a moment held her. She turned her eyes back to his tortured face.

"But, Nick," she said softly, "I can see."

He bent lower. "Yes?" he said, in a choked voice. "Yes?"

She regarded him with a faint wonder. Her eyes were growing heavy, as the eyes of a tired child. She raised one hand and pointed vaguely.

"Over there," she said wearily. "Can't you see them? Then perhaps it was a dream, or even—perhaps—a vision. Don't you remember how it went? 'And behold—the mountain—was full—of horses—and chariots—of—fire!' God sent them, you know."

443

The tired voice ceased. Her head sank lower upon Nick's breast. She gave a little quivering sigh, and seemed to sleep.

And Nick turned his tortured eyes upon the pass below him, and stared downwards spellbound.

Was he dreaming also? Or was it perchance a vision—the trick of his fevered fancy? There, at his feet, not fifty yards from where he sat, he beheld men, horses, guns, winding along in a narrow, unbroken line as far as he could see.

A great surging filled his ears, and through it he heard himself shout once, twice, and yet a third time to the phantom army below.

The surging swelled in his brain to a terrific tumult—a confusion indescribable. And then something seemed to crack inside his head. The dark peaks swayed giddily against the darkening sky, and toppled inwards without sound.

The last thing he knew was the call of a bugle, tense and shrill as the buzz of a mosquito close to his ear. And he laughed aloud to think how so small a thing had managed to deceive him.

PART II
CHAPTER VIII
COMRADES

The jingling notes of a piano playing an air from a comic opera floated cheerily forth into the magic silence of the Simla pines, and abruptly, almost spasmodically, a cracked voice began to sing. It was a sentimental ditty treated jocosely, and its frivolity rippled out into the mid-day silence with something of the effect of a monkey's chatter. The *khitmutgar* on the verandah would have looked scandalised or at best contemptuous had it not been his rôle to express nothing but the dignified humility of the native servant. He was waiting for his mistress to come out of the nursery where her voice could be heard talking imperiously to her baby's *ayah*. He had already waited some minutes, and he would probably have waited much longer, for his patience was inexhaustible, had it not been for that sudden irresponsible and wholly tuneless burst of song. But the second line was scarcely ended before she came hurriedly forth, nearly running into his stately person in her haste.

"Oh, dear, Sammy!" she exclaimed with some annoyance. "Why didn't you tell me Captain Ratcliffe was here?"

She hastened past him along the verandah with the words, not troubling about his explanation, and entered the room whence the music proceeded at a run.

"My dear Nick," she cried impulsively, "I had no idea!"

The music ceased in a jangle of wrong notes, and Nick sprang to his feet, his yellow face wearing a grin of irrepressible gaiety.

"So I gathered, O elect lady," he rejoined, seizing her outstretched hands and kissing first one and then the other. "And I took the first method that presented itself of making myself known. So they beguiled you to Simla, after all?"

"Yes, I had to come for my baby's sake. They thought at first it would have to be home and no compromise. I'm longing to show him to you, Nick. Only six months, and such a pet already! But tell me about yourself. I am sure you have come off the sick list too soon. You look as if you had come straight from a lengthy stay with the *bandar-log*."

"*Tu quoque!*" laughed Nick. "And with far less excuse. Only you manage to look charming notwithstanding, which is beyond me. Do you know, Mrs. Musgrave, you don't do justice to the compromise? I should be furious with you if I were Will."

Mrs. Musgrave frowned at him. She was a very pretty woman, possessing a dainty and not wholly unconscious charm. "Tell me about yourself, Nick," she commanded. "And don't be ridiculous. You can't possibly judge impartially on that head, as you haven't the smallest idea as to how ill I have been. I am having a rest cure now, you must know, and I don't go anywhere; or I should have come to see you in hospital."

"Good thing you didn't take the trouble," said Nick. "I've been sleeping for the last three weeks, and I am only just awake."

Mrs. Musgrave looked at him with a very friendly smile. "Poor Nick!" she said. "And Wara was relieved after all."

He jerked up his shoulders. "After a fashion. Grange was the only white man left, and he hadn't touched food for three days. If Muriel Roscoe had stayed, she would have been dead before Bassett got anywhere near them. There are times when the very fact of suffering actively keeps people alive. It was that with her."

He spoke briefly, almost harshly, and immediately turned from the subject. "I suppose you were very anxious about your cousin?"

"Poor Blake Grange? Of course I was. But I was anxious—horribly anxious—about you all." There was a quiver of deep feeling in Mrs. Musgrave's voice.

"Thank you," said Nick. He reached out a skeleton finger and laid it on her arm. "I thought you would be feeling soft-hearted, so I have come to ask you a favour. Not that I shouldn't have come in any case, but it seemed a suitable moment to choose."

Mrs. Musgrave laughed a little. "Have you ever found me anything but kind?" she questioned.

"Never," said Nick. "You're the best pal I ever had, which is the exact reason for my coming here to-day. Mrs. Musgrave, I want you to be awfully good to Muriel Roscoe. She needs some one to help her along just now."

Mrs. Musgrave opened her eyes wide, but she said nothing at once, for Nick had sprung to his feet and was restlessly pacing the room.

"Come back, Nick," she said at last. "Tell me a little about her. We have never met, you know. And why do you ask this of me when she is in Lady Bassett's care?"

"Lady Bassett!" said Nick. He made a hideous grimace, and said no more.

Mrs. Musgrave laughed. "How eloquent! Do you hate her, too, then? I thought all men worshipped at that shrine."

Nick came back and sat down. "I nearly killed her once," he said.

"What a pity you didn't quite!" ejaculated Mrs. Musgrave.

Nick grinned. "Sits the wind in that quarter? I wonder why."

"Oh, I hate her by instinct," declared Mrs. Musgrave recklessly, "though her scented notes to me always begin, 'Dearest Daisy'! She always disapproved of me openly till baby came. But she has found another niche for me now. I am not supposed to be so fascinating as I was. She prefers unattractive women."

"Gracious heaven!" interjected Nick.

"Yes, you may laugh. I do myself." Daisy Musgrave spoke almost fiercely notwithstanding. "She's years older than I am anyhow, and I shall score some day if I don't now. Have you ever watched her dance? There's a sort of snaky, coiling movement runs up her whole body. Goodness!" breaking off abruptly. "I'm getting venomous myself. I had better stop before I frighten you away."

"Oh, don't mind me!" laughed Nick. "No one knows better than I that she is made to twist all ways. She hates me as a cobra hates a mongoose."

"Really?" Daisy Musgrave was keenly interested. "But why?"

He shook his head. "You had better ask Lady Bassett. It may be because I had the misfortune to set fire to her once. It is true I extinguished her afterwards, but I don't think she enjoyed it. It was a humiliating process. Besides, it spoilt her dress."

"But she is always so gracious to you," protested Daisy.

"Honey-sweet. That's exactly how I know her cobra feelings. And that brings me round to Muriel Roscoe again, and the favour I have to ask."

Daisy shot him a sudden shrewd glance. "Do you want to marry her?" she asked him point blank.

Nick's colourless eyebrows went up till they nearly met his colourless hair. "Dearest Daisy," he said, "you are a genius. I mean to do that very thing."

Daisy got up and softly closed the window. "Surely she is very young," she said. "Is she in love with you?"

She did not turn at the sound of his laugh. She had almost expected it. For she knew Nick Ratcliffe as very few knew him. The bond of sympathy between them was very strong.

"Can you imagine any girl falling in love with me?" he asked.

"Of course I can. You are not so unique as that. There isn't a man in the universe that some woman couldn't be fool enough to love."

"Many thanks!" said Nick. "Then—I may count upon your support, may I? I know Lady Bassett will put a spoke in my wheel if she can. But I have Sir Reginald's consent. He is Muriel's guardian, you know. Also, I had her father's approval in the first place. It has got to be soon, you see, Daisy. The present state of affairs is unbearable. She will be miserable with Lady Bassett."

Daisy still stood with her back to him. She was fidgeting with the blind-cord, her pretty face very serious.

"I am not sure," she said slowly, "that it lies in my power to help you. Of course I am willing to do my best, because, as you say, we are pals. But, Nick, she is very young. And if—if she really doesn't love you, you mustn't ask me to persuade her."

Nick sprang up impulsively. "Oh, but you don't understand," he said quickly. "She would be happy enough with me. I would see to that. I—I would be awfully good to her, Daisy."

She turned swiftly at the unwonted quiver in his voice. "My dear Nick," she said earnestly, "I am sure of it. You could make any woman who loved you happy. But no one—no one—knows the misery that may result from a marriage without love on both sides—except those who have made one."

There was something almost passionate in her utterance. But she turned if off quickly with a smile and a friendly hand upon his arm.

"Come," she said lightly. "I want to show you my boy. I left him almost in tears. But he always smiles when he sees his mother."

"Who doesn't?" said Nick gallantly, following her lead.

CHAPTER IX
THE SCHOOL OF SORROW

The aromatic scent of the Simla pines literally encircled and pervaded the Bassetts' bungalow, penetrating to every corner. Lady Bassett was wont to pronounce it "distractingly sweet," when her visitors drew her attention to the fact. Hers was among the daintiest as well as the best situated bungalows in Simla, and she was pleasantly aware of a certain envy on the part of her many acquaintances, which added a decided relish to the flavour of her own appreciation. But notwithstanding this, she was hardly ever to be found at home except by appointment. Her social engagements were so numerous that, as she often pathetically remarked, she scarcely ever enjoyed the luxury of solitude. As a hostess she was indefatigable, and being an excellent bridge-player as well as a superb dancer, it was not surprising that she occupied a fairly prominent position in her own select circle. In appearance she was a woman of about five-and-thirty—though the malicious added a full dozen years more to her credit—with fair hair, a peculiarly soft voice, and a smile that was slightly twisted. She was always exquisitely dressed, always cool, always gentle, never hasty in word or deed. If she ever had reason to rebuke or snub, it was invariably done with the utmost composure, but with deadly effect upon the offender. Lady Bassett was generally acknowledged to be unanswerable at such times by all but the very few who did not fear her.

There were not many who really felt at ease with her, and Muriel Roscoe was emphatically not one of the number. Her father had nominated Sir Reginald her guardian, and Sir Reginald, aware of this fact, had sent her at once to his wife at Simla. The girl had been too ill at the time to take any interest in her destination or ultimate disposal. It was true that she had never liked Lady Bassett, that she had ever felt shy and constrained in her presence, and that, had she been consulted, she would probably have asked to be sent to England. But Sir Reginald had been too absorbed in the task before him to spend much thought on his dead comrade's child at that juncture, and he had followed the simplest course that presented itself, allowing Nick Ratcliffe to retain the privilege which General Roscoe himself had bestowed. Thus Muriel had come at last into Lady Bassett's care, and she was only just awaking to the fact that it was by no means the guardianship she would have chosen for herself had she been in a position to choose. As the elasticity of her youth gradually asserted itself, and the life began to flow again in her veins, the power to suffer returned to her, and in the anguish of her awakening faculties she knew how utterly she was alone. It was in one sense a relief that Lady Bassett, being caught in the full swing of the Simla season, was unable to spare much of her society for the suddenly bereaved girl who had been thrust upon her. But there were times during that period of dragging convalescence when any presence would have been welcome.

She was no longer acutely ill, but a low fever hung about her, a species of physical inertia against which she had no strength to struggle. And often she wondered to herself with a dreary amazement, why she still lived, why she had survived the horrors of that flight through the mountains, why she had been thus, as it were, cast up upon a desert rock when all that had made life good in her eyes had been ruthlessly swept away. At such times there would come upon her a loneliness almost unthinkable, a shrinking more terrible than the fear of death, and the future would loom before her black as night, a blank and awful desert which she felt she could never dare to travel.

Sometimes in her dreams there would come to her other visions—visions of the gay world that throbbed so close to her, the world she had entered with her father so short a time before. She would hear again the hubbub of laughing voices, the music, the tramp of dancing feet. And she would start from her sleep to find only a great emptiness, a listening silence, an unspeakable desolation.

If she ever thought of Nick in those days, it was as a phantom that belonged to the nightmare that lay behind her. He had no part in her present, and the future she could not bring herself to contemplate. No one even mentioned his name to her till one day Lady Bassett entered her room before starting for a garden-party at Vice-Regal Lodge, a faint flush on her cheeks, and her blue eyes brighter than usual.

"I have just received a note from Captain Ratcliffe, dear Muriel," she said. "I have already mentioned to him that you are too unwell to think of receiving any one at present, but he announces his intention of paying you a visit notwithstanding. Perhaps you would like to write him a note yourself, and corroborate what I have said."

"Captain Ratcliffe!" Muriel echoed blankly, as though the name conveyed nothing to her; and then with a great start as the blood rushed to her white cheeks, "Oh, you mean Nick. I—I had almost forgotten his other name. Does he want to see me? Is he in Simla still?"

She turned her hot face away with a touch of petulance from the peculiar look with which Lady Bassett was regarding her. What did she mean by looking at her so, she wondered irritably?

There followed a pause, and Lady Bassett began to fasten her many-buttoned gloves.

"Of course, dear," she said gently, at length, "there is not the smallest necessity for you to see him. Indeed, if my advice were asked, I should recommend you not to do so; for after such a terrible experience as yours, one cannot be too circumspect. It is so perilously easy for rumours to get about. I will readily transmit a message for you if you desire it, though I think on the whole it would be more satisfactory if you were to write him a line yourself to say that you cannot receive him."

"Why?" demanded Muriel, with sudden unexpected energy. She turned back again, and looked at Lady Bassett with a quick gleam that was almost a challenge in her eyes. "Why should I not see him? After all, I suppose I ought to thank him. Besides—besides—why should I not?"

She could not have said what moved her to this unwonted self-assertion. Had Lady Bassett required her to see Nick she would probably have refused to do so, and listlessly dismissed the matter from her mind. But there was that in Lady Bassett's manner which roused her antagonism almost instinctively. But vaguely understanding, she yet resented the soft-spoken words. Moreover, a certain perversity, born of her weakness, urged her. What right had Lady Bassett to deny her to any one?

"When is he coming?" she asked. "I will see him when he comes."

Lady Bassett yielded the point at once with the faintest possible shrug. "As you wish, dear child, of course; but I do beg of you to be prudent. He speaks of coming this afternoon. But would you not like him to postpone his visit till I can be with you?"

"No, I don't think so," Muriel said, with absolute simplicity.

"Ah, well!" Lady Bassett spoke in the tone of one repudiating all responsibility. She bent over the girl with a slightly wry smile, and kissed her forehead. "Good-bye, dearest! I shouldn't encourage him to stay long, if I were you. And I think you would be wise to call him Captain Ratcliffe now that you are living a civilised life once more."

Muriel turned her face aside with a species of bored patience that could scarcely be termed tolerance. She did not understand these veiled warnings, and she cared too little for Lady Bassett and her opinions to trouble herself about them. She had never liked her, though she knew that her father had conscientiously tried to do so for the sake of his friend, Sir Reginald.

As Lady Bassett went away she rubbed the place on her forehead which her cold lips had touched. "If she only knew how I hate being kissed!" she murmured to herself.

And then with an effort she rose and moved wearily across the room to ring the bell. Since by some unaccountable impulse she had decided to see Nick, it might be advisable, she reflected, to give her own orders regarding his visit.

Having done so, she lay down again. But she did not sleep. Sleep was an elusive spirit in those days. It sometimes seemed to her that she was too worn out mentally and physically ever to rest naturally again.

Nearly an hour passed away while she lay almost unconsciously listening. And then suddenly, with a sense of having experienced it all long before, there came to her the sound of careless footsteps and of a voice that hummed.

It went through her heart like a sword-thrust as she called to mind that last night at Fort Wara when she had clung to her father for the last time, and had heard him bid her good-bye—till they should meet again.

With a choked sensation she rose, and stood steadying herself by the back of the sofa. Could she go through this interview? Could she bear it? Her heart was beating in heavy, sickening throbs. For an instant she almost thought of escaping and sending word that she was not equal to seeing any one, as Lady Bassett had already intimated. But even as the impulse flashed through her brain, she realised that it was too late. The shadow of the native servant had already darkened the window, and she knew that Nick was just behind him on the verandah. With a great, sobbing gasp, she turned herself to meet him.

CHAPTER X
THE EAGLE SWOOPS

He came in as lightly and unceremoniously as though they had parted but the day before, a smile of greeting upon his humorous, yellow face, words of careless good-fellowship upon his lips.

He took her hand for an instant, and she felt rather than saw that he gave her a single, scrutinising glance from under eyelids that flickered incessantly.

"I see you are better," he said, "so I won't put you to the trouble of saying so. I suppose dear Lady Bassett has gone to the Vice-Regal garden-party. But it's all right. I told her I was coming. Did you have to persuade her very hard to let you see me?"

Muriel stiffened a little at this inquiry. Her agitation was rapidly subsiding. It left her vaguely chilled, even disappointed. She had forgotten how cheerily inconsequent Nick could be.

"I didn't persuade her at all," she said coldly. "I simply told her that I should see you in order—"

"Yes?" queried Nick, looking delighted. "In order—"

To her annoyance she felt herself flushing. With a gesture of weariness she dismissed the sentence and sat down. She had meant to make him a brief and gracious speech of gratitude for his past care of her, but somehow it stuck in her throat. Besides, it was quite obvious that he did not expect it.

He came and sat down beside her on the sofa. "Let's talk things over," he said. "You are out of the doctor's hands, I'm told."

Muriel was leaning back against the cushions. She did not raise her heavy eyes to answer. "Oh, yes, ever so long ago. I'm quite well, only rather tired still."

She frowned slightly as she gave this explanation. Though his face was not turned in her direction, she had a feeling that he was still closely observant of her.

He nodded to himself twice while he listened and then suddenly he reached out and laid his hand upon both of hers as they rested in her lap. "I'm awfully pleased to hear you are quite well," he said, in a voice that seemed to crack on a note of laughter. "It makes my business all the easier. I've come to ask you, dear, how soon you can possibly make it convenient to marry me. To-day? To-morrow? Next week? I don't of course want to hurry you unduly, but there doesn't seem to be anything to wait for. And—personally—I abhor waiting. Don't you?"

He turned towards her with the last words. He had spoken very gently, but there seemed to be an element of humour in all that he said.

Muriel's eyes were wide open by the time he ended. She was staring at him in blank astonishment. The flush on her face had deepened to crimson.

"Marry you?" she gasped at length, stammering in her confusion. "I? Why—why—whatever made you dream of such a thing?"

"I'll tell you," said Nick instantly, and quite undismayed. "I dreamed that a certain friend of mine was lonely and heart-sick and sad. And she wanted—horribly—some one to come and take care of her, to cheer her up, to lift her over the bad places, to give her things which, if they couldn't compensate for all she had lost, would be anyhow a bit of a comfort to her. And then I remembered how she belonged to me, how she had been given to me by her own father to cherish and care for. And so I plucked up courage to intrude upon her while she was still wallowing in her Slough of Despair. And I didn't pester her with preliminaries. We're past that stage, you and I, Muriel. I simply came to her because it seemed absurd to wait any longer. And I just asked her humble-like to fix a day when we would get up very early, and bribe the padre and sweet Lady Bassett to do likewise, and have a short—very short—service all to ourselves at church, and when it was over we would just say good-bye to all kind friends and depart. Won't you give the matter your serious consideration? Believe me, it is worth it."

He still held her hand closely in his while he poured out his rapid explanation, and his eyebrows worked up and down so swiftly that Muriel was fascinated by them. His eyes baffled her completely. They were like a glancing flame. She listened to his proposal with more of bewilderment than consternation. It took her breath away without exactly frightening her. The steady grasp of his hand and the exceedingly practical tones of his voice kept her from unreasoning panic; but she was too greatly astounded to respond very promptly.

"Tell me what you think about it," he said gently.

But she was utterly at a loss to describe her feelings. She shook her head and was silent.

After a little he went on, still quickly, but with less impetuosity. "It isn't just a sudden fancy of mine—this. Don't think it. There's nothing capricious about me. Your father knew about it. And because he knew, he put you in my care. It was his sole reason for trusting you to me. I had his full approval."

He paused, for her fingers had closed suddenly within his own. She was looking at him no longer. Her memory had flashed back to that last terrible night of her father's life. Again she heard him telling her of the one man to whom he had entrusted her, who would make it his sole business to save her, who would protect her life with his own, heard his speculative question as to whether she knew whom he meant, recalled her own quick reply, and his answer—and his answer.

With a sudden sense of suffocation, she freed her hand and rose. Once more her old aversion to this man swept over her in a nauseating wave. Once more there rose before her eyes the dread vision which for many, many nights had haunted her persistently, depriving her of all rest, all peace of mind—the vision of a man in his death-struggle, fighting, agonising, under those merciless fingers.

It was more than she could bear. She covered her eyes, striving to shut out the sight that tortured her weary brain. "Oh, I don't know if I can!" she almost wailed. "I don't know if I can!"

Nick did not move. And yet it seemed to her in those moments of reawakened horror as if by some magnetic force he still held her fast. She strove against it with all her frenzied strength, but it eluded her, baffled her—conquered her.

When he spoke at length, she turned and listened, lacking the motive-power to resist.

"There is nothing to frighten you anyhow," he said, and the tone in which he said it was infinitely comforting, infinitely reassuring. "I only want to take care of you; for you're a lonely little soul, not old enough, or wise enough to look after yourself. And I'll be awfully good to you, Muriel, if you'll have me."

Something in those last words—a hint of pleading, of coaxing even—found its way to her heart, as it were, against her will. Moreover, what he said was true. She was lonely: miserably, unspeakably lonely. All her world was in ashes around her, and there were times when its desolation positively appalled her.

But still she stood irresolute. Could she, dared she, take this step? What if that phantom of horror pursued her relentlessly to the day of her death? Would she not come in time to shrink with positive loathing from this man whose offer of help she now felt so strangely tempted in her utter friendlessness to accept?

It was impossible to answer these tormenting questions satisfactorily. But there was nothing—so she told herself—to be gained by waiting. She had no one to advise her, no one really to mind what happened to her, with the single exception of this friend of hers, who only wanted to take care of her. And after all, since misery was to be her portion, what did it matter? Why should she refuse to listen to him? Had he not shown her already that he could be kind?

A sudden warmth of gratitude towards him stirred in her heart—a tiny flame springing up among the ashes of her youth. Her horror sank away like an evil dream.

She turned round with a certain deliberation that had grown upon her of late, and went back to Nick still seated on the sofa.

"I don't care much what I do now," she said wearily. "I will marry you, if you wish it, if—if you are quite sure you will never wish you hadn't."

"Well done!" said Nick, with instant approval. "That's settled then, for I was quite sure of that ages ago."

He smiled at her quizzically, his face a mask of banter. Of what his actual feelings were at that moment she had not the faintest idea.

With a piteous little smile in answer she laid her hand upon his knee. "You will have to be very patient with me," she said tremulously. "For remember—I have come to the end of everything, and you are the only friend I have left."

He took her hand into his own again, with a grasp that was warm and comforting. "My dear," he said very kindly, "I shall always remember that you once told me so."

CHAPTER XI
THE FIRST FLIGHT

Muriel lay awake for hours that night, going over and over that interview with Nick till her tired brain reeled. She was not exactly frightened by this new element that had come into her life. The very fact of having something definite to look forward to was a relief after dwelling for so long in the sunless void of non-expectancy. But she was by no means sure that she welcomed so violent a disturbance at the actual heart of her darkened existence. She could not, moreover, wholly forget her fear of the man who had saved her by main force from the fate she would fain have shared with her father. His patience—his almost womanly gentleness—notwithstanding, she could not forget the demon of violence and bloodshed that she knew to be hidden away somewhere behind that smiling, yellow mask.

She marvelled at herself for her tame surrender, but she felt it to be irrevocable nevertheless. So broken was she by adversity, that she lacked the energy to resist him or even to desire to do so. She tried to comfort herself with the thought that she was carrying out her father's wishes for her; but this did not take her very far. She could not help the doubt arising as to whether he had ever really gauged Nick's exceedingly elusive character.

Tired out, at last she slept, and dreamed that an eagle had caught her and was bearing her swiftly, swiftly, through wide spaces to his eyrie in the mountains.

It was a long, breathless flight fraught with excitement and a nameless exultation that pierced her like pain. She awoke from it with a cry that was more of disappointment than relief, and started up gasping to hear horses' hoofs dancing in the compound below her window to the sound of a cracked, hilarious voice.

She almost laughed as she realised what it was, and in a moment all her misgivings of the night vanished like wraiths of the darkness. He had extracted a promise from her to ride with him at dawn, and he meant to keep her to it. She got up and pulled aside the blind.

A wild view-halloa greeted her, and she dropped it again sharply; but not before she had seen Nick prancing about the drive on a giddy, long-limbed Waler, and making frantic signs to her to join him. Another horse with a side-saddle was waiting, held by a grinning little *saice*. The sun was already rising rapidly behind the mountains. She began to race through her toilet at a speed that showed her to have caught some of the fever of her cavalier's impatience.

She wondered what Lady Bassett thought of the disturbance (Lady Bassett never rose early), and nearly laughed aloud.

Hastening out at length she found Nick dismounted and waiting for her by the verandah-steps. He sprang up to meet her with an eager whoop of greeting.

"Hope you enjoyed my serenade. Come along! There's no time to waste. Jakko turned red some minutes ago. Were you asleep?"

Muriel admitted the fact.

"And dreaming of me," he rattled on, "as was sweet and proper?"

She did not answer, and he laughed like a boy, rudely but not insolently.

"Didn't I know it? Jump up! We're going to have a glorious gallop. I've brought some slabs of chocolate to keep you from starvation. Ready? Heave ho! My dear girl, you're disgracefully light still. Why don't you eat more?"

"You're as thin as a herring yourself," Muriel retorted, with a most unwonted flash of spirit.

He lifted his grinning face to her as she settled herself in the saddle, and then uncovering swiftly he bent and kissed the black cloth of her habit, humbly, reverently, as became a slave.

It sent a queer thrill through her, that kiss of his. She felt that it was in some fashion a revelation; but she was still too blinded by groping in dark places to understand its message. As they trotted side by side out of the compound, she knew her face was burning, and turned it aside that he might not see.

It was a wonderful morning. There was intoxication in the scent of the pines. The whole atmosphere seemed bewitched. They gave their horses the rein and raced with the wind through an enchanted world. It was the wildest, most alluring ride that she had ever known, and when Nick called a halt at last she protested with a flushed face and sparkling eyes.

Nevertheless, it was good to sit and watch the rapid transformation that the sun-god was weaving all about them. She saw the spurs of Jakko fade from pink to purest amber, and then in the passage of a few seconds gleam silver in the flood of glory that topped the highest crests. And her heart fluttered oddly at the sight, while again she thought of the eagle of her dream, cleaving the wide spaces, and bearing her also.

She glanced round for Nick, but he had wheeled his horse and was staring out towards the plains. She wondered what was passing in his mind, for he sat like a statue, his face turned from her. And suddenly the dread loneliness of the mountains gripped her as with a chilly hand. It seemed as if they two were alone together in all the world.

She walked over to him. "I'm cold, Nick," she said, breaking in upon his silence almost apologetically. "Shall we go?"

He stretched out a hand to her without turning his head, without speaking. But she would not put her own within it, for she was afraid.

After a long pause he gave a sudden sharp sigh, and pulled his horse round. "Eh? Cold? We'll fly down to Annandale. There's plenty of time before us. By the way, I want to introduce you to a friend of mine—Daisy Musgrave. Ever heard of her? She and Blake Grange are first cousins. You'll like Daisy. We are great chums, she and I."

Muriel had heard of her from Captain Grange. She had also once upon a time met Daisy's husband.

"I liked him, rather," she said. "But I thought he must be very young."

"So he is," said Nick. "A mere infant. He's in the Civil Service, and works like an ox. Mrs. Musgrave is very delicate. She and the baby were packed off up here in a hurry. I believe she has a weak heart. She may have to go home to recruit even now. She doesn't go out at all herself, but she hopes I will take you to see her. Will you come?"

Muriel hesitated for a moment. "Nick," she said, "are you telling—everybody—of our—engagement?"

"Of course," said Nick, instantly. "Why not?"

She could not tell him, only she was vaguely dismayed.

"I told Lady Bassett yesterday evening," he went on. "Didn't she say anything to you?"

"Oh, yes. She kissed me and said she was very pleased." Muriel's cheeks burned at the recollection.

"How nice of her!" commented Nick. He shot her a sidelong glance. "Dear Lady Bassett always says and does the right thing at the right moment. It's her speciality. That's why we are all so fond of her."

Muriel made no response, though keenly aware of the subtlety of this speech. So Nick disliked her hostess also. She wondered why.

"You see," he proceeded presently, "it is as well to be quite open about it as we are going to be married so soon. Of course every one realises that it is to be a strictly private affair. You needn't be afraid of any demonstration."

It was not that that had induced her feeling of dismay, but she could not tell him so.

"And Mrs. Musgrave knows?" she questioned.

"I told her first," said Nick. "But you mustn't mind her. She won't commit the fashionable blunder of congratulating you."

Muriel laughed nervously. She longed to say something careless and change the subject, but she was feeling stiff and unnatural, and words failed her.

Nick brought his horse up close to hers.

"There's one thing I want to say to you, Muriel, before we go down," he said.

"Oh, what?" She turned a scared face towards him.

"Nothing to alarm you," said Nick, frowning at her quizzically. "I wanted to say it some minutes ago only I was shy. Look here, dear." He held out to her a twist of tissue-paper on the palm of his hand. "It's a ring I want you to wear for me. There's a message inside it. Read it when you are alone."

Muriel looked at the tiny packet without taking it. She had turned very white. "Oh, Nick," she faltered at last, "are you—are you—quite sure?"

"Quite sure of what?" questioned Nick. "Your mind? Or my own?"

"Don't!" she begged tremulously. "I can't laugh over this."

"Laugh!" said Nick sharply. And then swiftly his whole manner changed. "Yes, it's all right, dear," he said, smiling at her. "Take it, won't you? I am—quite—sure."

She took it obediently, but her reluctance was still very manifest. Nick, however, did not appear to notice this.

"Don't look at it now," he said. "Wait till I'm not there. Put it away somewhere for the present, and let's have another gallop."

She glanced at him as she slipped his gift into her pocket. "Won't you let me thank you, Nick?" she asked shyly.

"Wait till you've seen it," he returned. "You may not think it worth it. Ready? One! Two! Three!"

In the scamper that followed, the blood surged back to her face, and her spirits rose again; but in her secret heart there yet remained a nameless dread that she was as powerless to define as to expel.

CHAPTER XII
THE MESSAGE

Lady Bassett was still invisible when Muriel returned to the bungalow though breakfast was waiting for them on the verandah. She passed quickly through to her room and commenced hasty preparations for a bath. It had been a good ride, and she realised that, though tired, she was also very hungry.

She slipped Nick's gift out of the pocket of her riding-habit, but she would not stop to open it then. That should come presently, when she had the whole garden to herself, and all the leisure of the long summer morning before her. She felt that in a sense she owed him that.

But a note that caught her eye lying on the table she paused to open and hastily peruse. The writing was unfamiliar to her—a dashing, impetuous scrawl that excited her curiosity.

"Dear Miss Roscoe," it ran,—"Don't think me an unmitigated bore if you can help it. I am wondering if you would have the real kindness to waive ceremony and pay me a visit this afternoon. I shall be quite alone, unless my baby can be considered in the light of a social inducement. I know that Nick contemplates bringing you to see me, and so he shall, if you prefer it. But personally I consider that he would be decidedly *de trop*. I feel that we shall soon know each other so well that a formal introduction seems superfluous. Let me know your opinion by word of mouth, or if not, I shall understand. Nick, being of the inferior species, could hardly be expected to do so, though I admit that he is more generously equipped in the matter of intellect than most.—Your friend to be,

"Daisy Musgrave."

Muriel laid down the letter with a little smile. Its spontaneous friendliness was like a warm hand clasping hers. Yes, she would go, she decided, as she splashed refreshingly in her bath, and that not for Nick's sake. She knew instinctively that she was going to discover a close sympathy with this woman who, though an utter stranger to her, yet knew how to draw her as a sister. And Muriel's longing for such human fellowship had already driven her to extremes.

She had the note in her hand when she finally joined Lady Bassett upon the verandah.

Lady Bassett, though ever-gracious, was seldom at her best in the morning. She greeted the girl with a faint, wry smile, and proffered her nearest cheek to be kissed.

"Quite an early bird, dear child!" was her comment. "I should imagine Captain Ratcliffe's visitation awakened the whole neighbourhood. I think you must not go out again with him before sunrise. I should not have advised it this morning if you had consulted me."

Muriel flushed at the softly-conveyed reproof. "It is not the first time," she said, in her deep voice that was always deepest when indignation moved her. "We have seen the sun rise together and the moon rise too, before to-day."

Lady Bassett sighed gently. "I am sure, dearest," she said, "that you do not mean to be uncouth or unmannerly, far less—that most odious of all propensities in a young girl—forward. But though my authority over you were to be regarded as so slight as to be quite negligible, I should still feel it my duty to remonstrate when I saw you committing a breach of the conventions which might be grievously misconstrued. I trust, dear Muriel, that you will bear my protest in mind and regulate your actions by it in the future. Will you take coffee?"

Muriel had seated herself at the other side of the table, and was regarding her with wide, dark eyes that were neither angry nor ashamed, only quite involuntarily disdainful.

After a distinct pause she decided to let the matter drop, reflecting that Lady Bassett's subtleties were never worth pursuing.

"I am going to see a friend of Nick's this afternoon," she said presently. "I expect you know her—Mrs. Musgrave."

Lady Bassett's forehead puckered a little. It could hardly be called a frown. "Have you ever met Mrs. Musgrave?" she asked.

"No, never. But she is Nick's friend, and of course I know her cousin, Captain Grange, quite well."

Lady Bassett made no comment upon this. "Of course, dear," she said, "you are old enough to please yourself, but it is not usual, you know, to plunge into social pleasures after so recent a bereavement as yours."

The sudden silence that followed this gentle reminder had in it something that was passionate. Muriel's face turned vividly crimson, and then gradually whitened to a startling pallor.

"It is the last thing I should wish to do," she said, in a stifled voice.

Lady Bassett continued, softly suggestive. "I say nothing of your marriage, dear child. For that, I am aware, is practically a matter of necessity. But I do think that under the circumstances you can scarcely be too careful in what you do. Society is not charitably inclined towards those who even involuntarily transgress its rules. And you most emphatically are not in a position to do so wilfully."

She paused, for Muriel had risen unexpectedly to her feet. Her eyes were blazing in her white face.

"Why should you call my marriage a matter of necessity?" she demanded. "Sir Reginald told me that my father had provided for me."

"Of course, of course, dear." Lady Bassett uttered a faint, artificial laugh. "It is not a question of means at all. But, there, since you are so childishly unsophisticated, I need not open your eyes. It is enough for you to know that there is a sufficiently urgent reason for your marriage, and the sooner it can take place, the better. But in the meantime, let me counsel you to be as prudent as possible in all that you do. I assure you, dear, it is very necessary."

Muriel received this little homily in silence. She did not in the least understand to what these veiled allusions referred, and she decided impatiently that they were unworthy of her serious consideration. It was ridiculous to let herself be angry with Lady Bassett. As if it mattered in the least what she said or thought! She determined to pay her projected visit notwithstanding, and quietly said so, as she turned at length from the table.

Lady Bassett raised no further remonstrance beyond a faint, eloquent lift of the shoulders. And Muriel went away into the shady compound, her step firmer and her dark head decidedly higher than usual. She felt for Nick's gift as she went, with a little secret sensation of pleasure. After all, why had she been afraid? All girls wore rings when they became engaged to be married.

Reaching her favourite corner, she drew it forth from its hiding-place, a quiver of excitement running through her.

She was sitting in the hammock under the pines as she unwrapped it. The hot sunshine, glinting through the dark boughs overhead, flashed upon precious stones and dazzled her as the wisp of tissue-paper fell from her hand.

And in a moment she was looking at an old marquise ring of rubies in a setting of finely-wrought gold. Her heart gave a throb of sheer delight at the beauty of the thing. She slipped it impetuously on to her finger, and held it up to the sunlight.

The rubies shone with a deep lustre—red, red as heart's blood, ardent as flame. She gazed and gazed with sparkling, fascinated eyes.

Suddenly his words flashed into her mind. A message inside it! She had been so caught by the splendour of the stones that she had not looked inside. She drew the ring from her finger, and examined it closely, with burning cheeks.

Yes, there was the message—three words engraved in minute, old-fashioned characters inside the gold band. They were so tiny that it took her a long time to puzzle them out. With difficulty at length she deciphered the quaint letters, but even then it was some time before she grasped the meaning that they spelt.

It flashed upon her finally, as though a voice had spoken into her ear. The words were: OMNIA VINCIT AMOR. And the ring in her hand was no longer the outward visible sign of her compact. It was a love-token, given to her by a man who had spoken no word of love.

CHAPTER XIII
THE VOICE OF A FRIEND

"So you didn't bring Nick after all. That was nice of you," said Daisy Musgrave, with a little, whimsical smile. "I wanted to have you all to myself. The nicest of men can be horribly in the way sometimes."

She smiled upon her visitor whom she had placed in the easiest chair and in the pleasantest corner of her drawing-room. Her pretty face was aglow with friendliness. No words of welcome were needed.

Muriel was already feeling happier than she had felt for many, many weary weeks. It had been an effort to come, but she was glad that she had made it.

"It was kind of you to ask me," she said, "though of course I know that you did it for Nick's sake."

"You are quite wrong," Daisy answered instantly. "He told me about you, I admit. But after that, I wanted you for your own. And now I have got you, Muriel, I am not going to stand on ceremony the least bit in the world. And you mustn't either; but I can see you won't. Your eyes are telling me things already. I don't get on with stiff people somehow. Lady Bassett calls me effusive. And I think myself there must have been something meteoric about my birth star. Doubtless that is why I agree so well with Nick. He's meteoric, too." She slipped cosily down upon a stool by Muriel's side. "He's a nice boy, isn't he?" she said sympathetically. "And is that his ring? Ah, let me look at it! I think I have seen it before. No, don't take it off! That's unlucky."

But Muriel had already drawn it from her finger. "It's beautiful," she said warmly. "Do you know anything about it? It looks as if it had a history."

"It has," said Daisy. "I remember now. He showed it to me once when I was staying at his brother's house in England. I know the Ratcliffes well. My husband used to live with them as a boy. It came from the old maiden aunt who left him all his money. She gave it to him before she died, I believe, and told him to keep it for the woman he was sure to love some day. Nick was an immense favourite of hers."

"But the ring?" urged Muriel.

Daisy was frowning over the inscription within it, but she was fully aware of the soft colour that had flooded the girl's face at her words.

"OMNIA VINCIT AMOR," she read slowly. "That is it, isn't it? Ah, yes, and the history of it. It's rather sad. Do you mind?"

"I am used to sad things," Muriel reminded her, with her face turned away toward the mountains.

Daisy pressed her hand gently. "It is a French ring," she said. "It belonged to an aristocrat who was murdered in the Reign of Terror. He sent it by his servant to the girl he loved from the steps of the guillotine. I don't know their names. Nick didn't tell me that. But she was English."

Muriel had turned quickly back. Her interest was aroused. "Yes," she said eagerly, as Daisy paused. "And she?"

"She!" Daisy's voice had a sudden hard ring in it. "She remained faithful to him for just six months. And then she married an Englishman. It was said that she did it against her will. Still she did it. Luckily for her, perhaps, she died within the year—when her child was born."

Daisy rose abruptly and moved across the room. "That was more than a hundred years ago," she said, "and women are as great fools still. If they can't marry the man they love—they'll marry—anything."

Muriel was silent. She felt as if she had caught sight of something that she had not been intended to see.

But in a moment Daisy came back, and, kneeling beside her, slipped the ring on to her finger again. "Yet love conquers all the same, dear," she said, passing her arm about the girl. "And yours is going to be a happy love story. The ring came finally into the possession of the lady's grandson, and it was he who gave it to Nick's aunt—the maiden aunt. It was her engagement ring. She never wore any other, and she only gave it to Nick when her fingers were too rheumatic to wear it any longer. Her lover, poor boy, was killed in the Crimea. There! Forgive me if I have made you sad. Death is not really sad, you know, where there is love. People talk of it as if it conquered love, whereas it is in fact all the other way round. Love conquers death."

Muriel hid her face suddenly on Daisy's shoulder. "Oh, are you quite sure?" she whispered.

"I am quite sure, darling." The reply was instant and full of conviction. "It doesn't need a good woman to be quite sure of that. Over and over again it has been the only solid thing I have had to hold by. I've clung to it blindly in outer darkness, God only knows how often."

Her arms tightened about Muriel, and she fell silent. For minutes the room was absolutely quiet. Then Muriel raised her head.

"Thank you," she whispered. "Thank you so much."

Her eyes were full of tears as her lips met Daisy's, but she brushed them swiftly away before they fell.

Daisy was smiling at her. "Come," she said, "I want to show you my baby. He is just the wee-est bit fractious, as he is cutting a tooth. The doctor says he will be all right, but he still threatens to send us both to England."

"And you don't want to go?" questioned Muriel.

Daisy shook her head. "I want to see my cousin Blake," she said lightly, "when he comes marching home again. Did you hear the rumour that he is to have the V.C.? They ought to give it to Nick, too, if he does."

"Oh, I shouldn't think so. Nick didn't do anything. At least," Muriel stumbled a little, "nothing to be proud of."

Daisy laughed and caught her face between her hands. "Except save his girl from destruction," she said. "Doesn't that count? Oh, Muriel, I know exactly what made him want you. No, you needn't be afraid. I'm not going to tell you. Wild horses sha'n't drag it from me. But he's the luckiest man in India, and I think he knows it. What lovely hair you have! I'll come round early on your wedding-day and do it for you. And what will you wear? It mustn't be a black wedding whatever etiquette may decree. You look too pathetic in black, and it's a barbarous custom anyway. I have warned my husband fairly that if he goes into mourning for me, I'll never speak to him hereafter again. He is coming up to see us next week, and to discuss our fate with the doctor. Have you ever met Will?"

"Once," said Muriel. "It was at a dance at Poonah early last summer."

"Ah! When I was at Mahableshwar. He is a good dancer, isn't he? He does most things well, I think."

Daisy smiled tolerantly as she indicated the photograph of a boy upon the mantelpiece. "He isn't sixteen," she said; "he is nearly twenty-eight. Now come and see his son and the light of my eyes." She linked her arm in Muriel's, and, still smiling, led her from the room.

CHAPTER XIV
THE POISON OF ADDERS

The week that followed that first visit of hers was a gradual renewal of life to Muriel. She had come through the darkest part of her trouble, and, thick though the shadows might still lie about her, she had at last begun to see light ahead. She went again and yet again to see Daisy, and each visit added to her tranquillity of mind. Daisy was wonderfully brisk for an invalid, and her baby was an endless source of interest. Even Lady Bassett could not cavil when her charge spoke of going to nursery tea at Mrs. Musgrave's. She made no attempt to check the ripening friendship, though Muriel was subtly aware that she did not approve of it.

She also went every morning for a headlong gallop with Nick who, in fact, would take no refusal in the matter. He came not at all to the house except for these early visits, and she had a good many hours to herself. But her health was steadily improving, and her loneliness oppressed her less than formerly. She spent long mornings lying in the hammock under the pines with only an occasional monkey far above her to keep her company. It was her favourite haunt, and she grew to look upon it as exclusively her own. There was a tiny rustic summer-house near it, which no one ever occupied, so far as she knew. Moreover, the hammock had been decorously slung behind it, so that even though a visitor might conceivably penetrate as far as the arbour, it was extremely unlikely that the hammock would come into the range of discovery.

Even Lady Bassett had never sought her here, her time being generally quite fully occupied with her countless social engagements. Muriel often wondered that that garden on the mountainside in which she revelled seemed to hold so slight an attraction for its owner. But then of course Lady Bassett was so much in demand that she had little leisure to admire the beauties that surrounded her.

Growing daily stronger, Muriel's half-childish panic regarding her approaching marriage as steadily diminished. She enjoyed her rides with Nick, becoming daily more and more at her ease with him. They seldom touched upon intimate matters. She wore his ring, and once she shyly thanked him for it. But he made no further reference to the words engraved within it, and she was relieved by his forbearance.

Nick, on his part, was visiting Daisy Musgrave every day, and sedulously imbibing her woman's wisdom. He had immense faith in her insight and her intuition, and when she entreated him to move slowly and without impatience he took a sterner grip of himself and resolutely set himself to cultivate the virtue she urged upon him.

"You mustn't do anything in a hurry," Daisy assured him, "either before your marriage or after. She has had a very bad shock, and she is only just getting over it. You will throw everything back if you try to precipitate matters. She is asleep, you know, Nick, and it is for you to waken her, but gradually—oh, very gradually—or she will start up in the old nightmare terror again. If she doesn't love you yet, she is very near it. But you will only win her by waiting for her. Never do anything sudden. Always remember what a child she is, though she has outgrown her years. And children, you know, though they will trust those they love to the uttermost, are easily frightened."

Nick knew that she was right. He knew also that he was steadily gaining ground, and that knowledge helped him more than all Daisy's counsels. He was within sight, so he felt, of the great consummation of all his desires, and he was drawing daily nearer.

Their wedding-day was little more than a week away. He had already made full preparation for it. It was to be as quiet a ceremony as it was possible to arrange. Daisy Musgrave had promised to be there, and he expected her husband also. Lady Bassett, whose presence he realised with a grimace to be indispensable, would complete the wedding-party.

He had arranged to leave Simla directly the service was over, and to go into Nepal. It would not be his first visit to that most wonderful country, and it held many things that he desired to show her. He expected much from that wedding journey, from the close companionship, the intimacy that must result. He would teach her first beyond all doubting that she had nothing to fear, and then—then at last, as the reward of infinite patience, he would win her love. His blood quickened whenever he thought of it. Alone with her once more among the mountains, in perfect security, surrounded by the glory of the eternal snows, so he would win her. They would come back closely united, equipped to face the whole world hand-in-hand, so joined together that no shadow of evil could ever come between them any more. For they would be irrevocably made one. Thus ran the current of his splendid dream, and for this he curbed himself, mastered his eagerness, controlled his passion.

On the day that Daisy's husband arrived, he considerately absented himself from their bungalow, knowing how the boy loved to have his wife to himself. He had in consequence the whole afternoon at his disposal, and he contemplated paying a surprise visit to his betrothed. He had ridden with her that morning, and he did not doubt that she was to be found somewhere in Lady Bassett's compound. So in fact she was, and had he carried out his first intention, he would have explored behind the summer-house and found her in her retreat. But he did not after all pay his projected visit. A very small matter frustrated his plans—a matter of no earthly importance, but which he always looked upon afterwards as a piece of the devil's own handiwork. He remembered some neglected correspondence, and decided to clear it off. She would not be expecting him, possibly she might not welcome his intrusion. And so, in consequence of that rigid self-restraint that he was practising, he suffered this latter reflection to sway him in the direction of his unanswered letters, and sat down to his writing-table with a strong sense of virtue, utterly unsuspicious of the evil which even at that moment was drawing near imperceptibly but surely to the girl he loved.

She was lying in her hammock with an unread book on her knees. It was a slumberous afternoon, making for drowsiness. The mountains were wrapped in a vague haze, and the whole world was very still. Very far overhead, the pines occasionally whispered to one another, but below there was no movement, save when a lizard scuttled swiftly over the pine-needles, and once when an enquiring monkey-face peered at her round the red bole of a pine.

It was all very restful, and Muriel was undeniably sleepy. She had ridden farther than usual with Nick that morning, and it did not take much to tire her. Lady Bassett had gone to a polo-match, she knew, and she luxuriated in undisturbed solitude. It lay all about her like a spell of enchantment. With her cheek pillowed on her hand she presently floated into serene slumber. It was like drifting down a tidal river into a summer sea....

Her awakening was abrupt, almost startling. She felt as if some one had touched her, though she realised In a moment that this was impossible; for she was still alone. No one was in sight. Only from the arbour a few feet away there came the sound of voices, and the tinkle of tea-cups.

Visitors evidently! Lady Bassett had returned and brought back a couple of guests with her. She frowned impatiently over the discovery, realising that she was a prisoner unless she elected to show herself. For her corner behind the summer-house was bounded by the wall of the compound, and there was no retreat save by the path that led to the bungalow, and this wound in front of the arbour itself.

It was very annoying, but there was no help for it. She knew very few people in Simla, and neither of the voices that mingled with Lady Bassett's was familiar to her. It did not take her long to decide that she had no desire for a closer acquaintance with their owners. One was a man's voice, sonorous and weighty, that sounded as if it were accustomed to propound mighty problems from the pulpit. The other was a woman's, high-pitched as the wail of a cat on a windy night, that caused the listening girl to nestle back on her pillow with the instant resolution to remain where she was until the intruders saw fit to depart, even if by so doing she had to forego her tea.

She opened her book with an unwarrantable feeling of resentment. Of course Lady Bassett could not know she was there, and of course she was at liberty to go whither she would in her own garden. But no one likes to have their cherished privacy invaded even in ignorance. And Lady Bassett might surely have concluded that she would be out somewhere under the pines.

Well, they probably would not stay for long, and she was in no hurry. With a faint sigh of lingering annoyance she began to read.

But the piercing, feline voice soon pounded flail-like into her consciousness, scattering her thoughts with ruthless insistence.

"Of course," it asserted, "it was the only thing he could possibly do. No man with any decent feeling could have done otherwise. But it was a little hard on him. Surely you agree with me there?"

Lady Bassett's voice, soft and precise, made answer. "Indeed I think he has behaved most generously in the matter. As you say, it would have been but a gentleman's duty to make an offer of marriage, considering all the circumstances. But he went further than that. He actually insisted upon the arrangement. I suppose he felt bound to do so as the poor child's father had placed her in his charge. She is quite unformed still, and is very far from realising her grave position. Indeed, I scarcely expected her to accept him without the urgent reason for the match being explained to her; for it is quite obvious that she does not care for him in that way. Poor child, she is scarcely old enough to know the true meaning of love. It is very sad for them both."

A gentle sigh closed the sentence. Muriel's book had slid down upon a cushion of pine-needles. She had raised herself in the hammock, and was staring at the rustic woodwork of the summer-house as though she saw a serpent twining there.

There followed a brief silence. Then came the man's voice, deliberate and resounding.

"I am sure it must have caused you much anxiety, dear Lady Bassett. With my knowledge of Nicholas Ratcliffe I confess that I should have felt very grave misgivings as to whether he were endowed with the chivalry to fulfil the obligation he had incurred. My esteem for him has increased fourfold since I heard of his intention to shoulder his responsibilities thus courageously. I had not deemed him capable of such a sacrifice. I sincerely trust that he will be given strength to carry it through worthily."

"I shall not feel really easy till they are married," confessed Lady Bassett.

"Ah!" The sonorous voice broke in again with friendly reproof. "But—pardon me—does not that indicate a certain lack of faith, Lady Bassett? Since the young man has been led to see that the poor girl has been so sadly compromised, surely we may trust that he will be enabled to carry out his engagement. I consider it doubly praiseworthy that he has taken this action on his own initiative. I may tell you in confidence that I was seriously debating with myself as to whether it were not my duty to approach him on the subject. But the news of his engagement relieved me of all responsibility. It is no doubt something of a sacrifice to a man of his stamp. We can only trust that he will be duly rewarded."

Here the shrill, feline voice suddenly made itself heard, tripping in upon the deeper tones without ceremony.

"Oh, but poor Nick! I can't picture him married and done for. He has always been so gay. Why, look at him with Daisy Musgrave! I know for a fact that he goes there every day at least, and she refusing to receive any one else. I call it quite scandalous."

"My dear! My dear!" It was Lady Bassett's turn to reprove. "Not quite every day surely!"

"I do assure you that isn't the smallest exaggeration," protested her informant. "I had it from Mrs. Gybbon-Smythe who never misstates anything. It was she who first told me of this engagement, and she considered that Nick was positively throwing himself away. A mere chivalrous fad she called it, and declared that it would simply ruin his prospects. For it is well known that married officers are almost invariably passed over by the powers that be. And he is regarded as so promising too. Really I am almost inclined to agree with her. Just a little more tea, dear, if I may. Your tea is always so delicious, and doubly so out here under the pines."

The soft jingling of tea-cups ensued, and through it presently came Lady Bassett's gentle tones. They sounded as if she were smiling.

"Well, all I can say is, I was unspeakably relieved when I heard that Captain Ratcliffe had decided to treat the matter as a point of honour and marry dear Muriel. She is a sweet girl and I am devoted to her, which made it doubly hard for me. For I should scarcely have dared to venture, after what has happened, to ask any of my friends to receive her. Naturally, she shrinks from speaking of that terrible time, but I understand that she spent no less than three nights alone in the mountains with him. And that fact in itself would be more than sufficient to blight any girl's career from a social standpoint. I often think that the rules of our modern etiquette are very rigid, though I know well that we cannot afford to disregard them." Again came that soft, regretful sigh; and then in an apologetic tone, "*You* will say, I know, that for the good of the community this must be so, but you are great enough to make allowances for a woman's weakness. And I must confess that I cannot but feel the pity of it in such a case as this."

"Indeed, Lady Bassett, I think your feminine weakness does you credit," was the kind response this elicited. "We must all of us sympathise most deeply with the poor little wanderer, who, I am well assured, could not be in better hands than she is at the present moment. Your protecting care must, I am convinced, atone to her in a very great measure for all that she has been called upon to undergo."

"So sweet of you to say so!" murmured Lady Bassett. "Words cannot express my reluctance to explain to her the actual state of affairs, or my relief that I have been able to avoid doing so with a clear conscience. Ah! Your cup is empty! Will you let me refill it? No? But you are not thinking of leaving me yet, surely?"

"Ah, but indeed we must. We are dining with the Boltons to-night, and going afterwards to the Parkers' dance. You will be there of course? How delightful! Then we shall soon meet again."

The penetrating voice was accompanied by the sounds of a general move, and there ensued the usual interchange of compliments at departure, Lady Bassett protesting that it had been so sweet of her friends to visit her, and the friends assuring her of the immense pleasure it had given them to do so. All the things that are never said by people who are truly intimate with each other were said several times over as the little party moved away. Their voices receded into the distance, though they continued for a while to prick through the silence that fell like a velvet curtain behind them.

Finally they ceased altogether. The summer-house was empty, and an enterprising monkey slipped down the trunk of a tree and peered in. But he was a nervous beast, and he had a feeling that the place was not so wholly devoid of human presence as it seemed. He approached cautiously, gibbering a little to himself. It looked safe enough, and there was some dainty confectionery within. But, uneasy instinct still urging him, he deemed it advisable to peer round the corner of the summer-house before he yielded to the promptings of a rapacious appetite.

The next instant his worst fears were realised, and he was scudding up the nearest tree in a panic.

There, on the ground, face downwards on the pine-needles, lay a human form. True, it was only a woman lying there. But her silence and her stillness were eloquent of tragedy even to his monkey-intelligence. From a safe height he sat and reviled her till he was tired for having spoilt his sport. Finally, as she made no movement, he forgot his grievance, and tripped airily away in quest of more thrilling adventures.

But the woman remained prone upon the ground for a long, long time.

CHAPTER XV
THE SUMMONS

Nick's fit of virtue evaporated with his third letter, and he got up, feeling that he had spent an unprofitable afternoon. He also discovered that he was thirsty, and while quenching his thirst he debated with himself whether he would after all stroll round to the Musgraves. He and Will were old school-fellows, and the friendship between them was of the sort that wears forever. He was moreover dissatisfied with regard to Daisy's appearance, and he wanted to know the doctor's verdict.

He had just decided to chance his welcome and go, when a note was brought to him which proved to be from Will himself.

"DEAR OLD NICK," it ran,—"I have been wanting to shake your hand ever since I heard of your gallant return from the jaws of death. Well done, old chap, if it isn't a stale sentiment!

"Will you come and dine with us? Do thy diligence, for though we are neither of us the best of company, we both want you. The doctor has ordered Daisy and the youngster home. They are to leave before the *chota-bursat*. Damn the *chota-bursat*, and the whole beastly show!—Yours ever,

"WILL"

Nick considered this outburst with a sympathetic frown, and at once despatched an answer in the affirmative. He had almost expected the news. It had been quite plain to him that Daisy was not making any progress towards the recovery of her strength. Her quick temperament would not allow her to be listless, but he had not been deceived. And he was glad that Will had come up at length to see for himself.

It was horribly unlucky for them both, he reflected, for he knew that Will could not accompany his wife to England. And the thought presently flashed across him,—How would it go with him if he ever had to part with Muriel in that way? Having once possessed her, could he ever bear to let her go again? Would he not rather relinquish his profession for her sake, dear though it was to him? He had made her his own by sheer dogged effort. He had planned for her, fought for her, suffered for her,—almost he had died for her. Now that she was his at last, he knew that he could never let her go.

He turned impetuously to a calendar on his writing-table, and ticked off another day. There were only six left before his wedding-day. He counted them with almost savage exultation. Finally he tossed down the pencil with a sudden, quivering laugh, and stood up with wide-flung arms. She was his—his—his! No power or force of circumstance could ever come between them now. He would trample every obstacle underfoot.

But there were no obstacles left. He had overcome them all. He had won her fairly; and the reward of patience was very near.

For the first time he slackened the bonds of his self-restraint; and instantly the fire of his passion leapt up, free and fierce, overflowing its confines in a wide-spread, molten stream that carried all before it.

When later he departed to keep his engagement, he was as a man treading upon air. Not a dozen yards from the gate one of Lady Bassett's servants met him and presented a note. He guessed it was from Muriel, and the blood rose in a hot wave to his head and pounded at his temples as he opened it. It was the first she had ever written to him.

"I must see you at once,—M."

That was all. He dismissed the waiting native, and returned to his room. There he wrote a note to Will Musgrave warning him that he had been delayed.

Then he suddenly straightened himself and stood tense. Something had happened. He was sure of it. That urgent summons rang in his brain like a cry for help. Some demand was about to be made upon him, a demand which he might find himself ill-equipped to meet. He was not lacking in courage. He could meet adversity without a quiver. But for once he was not sure of himself. He was not prepared to resist any sudden strain that night.

Several minutes passed before he moved. Then, glancing down, he saw her message fast gripped in his hand. With a swift, passionate movement he carried the paper to his lips. And he remembered suddenly how he had once held her hand there and breathed upon the little cold fingers to give them life. He had commanded himself then. Was he any the less his own master now? And was he fool enough to destroy all in a moment that trust of hers which he had built up so laboriously? He felt as if a fiend had ensnared him, and with a fierce effort he broke free. Surely he was torturing himself in vain. She had only sent for him to explain that she could not ride with him in the morning, or some other matter equally trifling. He would go to her at once since she had desired it, and set her mind at rest on whatever subject happened to be troubling it.

And so with steady tread he left the house once more. She had called him for the first time. He would not keep her waiting.

CHAPTER XVI
THE ORDEAL

The drawing-room was empty when he entered it, the windows standing flung wide to the night. Strains of dance music were wafted in from somewhere lower down the hill, and he guessed that Lady Bassett would be from home. The pine-trees of the compound stood black and silent. There seemed to be a hush of expectancy in the air.

He stood with his back to the room and his face to the mountains. The moon was still below the horizon, but stars blazed everywhere with a marvellous brightness. It was a night for dreams, and he thought with a quickening heart of the nights that were coming when they two would be alone once more among the hills, no longer starved and fleeing for their lives, but wandering happily together in an enchanted world where the past was all forgotten, and the future gleamed like the peaks of Paradise.

At sound of a quiet footfall, he turned back into the room. Muriel had entered and was closing the door behind her. At first sight he fancied that she was ill, so terribly did her deep mourning and heavy hair emphasise her pallor. But as she moved forward he reassured himself. It was growing late. Doubtless she was tired.

He went impetuously to meet her, and in a moment he had her hands in his; but they lay in his grasp cold and limp, with no responding pressure. Her great eyes, as they looked at him, were emotionless and distant, remote as the lights of a village seen at night across a far-reaching plain. She gave him no word or smile of welcome.

A sudden dark suspicion flashed through his brain, and he drew her swiftly to the light, looking at her closely, searchingly.

"What have you been doing?" he said.

She fathomed his suspicion, and faintly smiled. "Nothing—nothing whatever. I have never touched opium since the night you—"

He cut in sharply, as if the reminiscence hurt him. "I beg your pardon. Well, what is it then? There's something wrong."

She did not contradict him. Merely with a slight gesture of weariness, she freed herself and sat down.

Nick remained on his feet, looking down at her, waiting grimly for enlightenment.

It did not come very readily. Seconds had passed into minutes before she spoke, and then her words did not bear directly upon the matter in hand.

"I hope it was quite convenient to you to come to-night. I was a little afraid you would have an engagement."

He remembered the urgency of her summons and decided that she spoke thus conventionally to gain time. On another occasion he might have humoured such a whim, but to-night it goaded him almost beyond endurance. Surely they had passed that stage, he and she.

With an effort he controlled himself, but it sounded in his voice as he made reply.

"My engagement to you stands before any other. What is it you want to say to me?"

Her expression changed slightly at his words, and a shade of apprehension flitted across her face. She threw him a swift upward glance, half-scared, half-questioning. Unconsciously her hands locked themselves together.

"I want you not to be vexed, Nick," she said, in a low voice.

He made an abrupt movement. "My dear girl, don't be silly. What's the trouble? Let me hear it and have done."

His tone was reassuring. She looked up at him with more confidence.

"Yes, I am silly," she acknowledged. "I'm perfectly idiotic to fancy for a moment that it can make any difference to you. Nick, I have been thinking things over seriously, and—and—I find that I can't marry you after all. I hope you won't mind, though of course—" she uttered a little laugh that was piteously insincere—"I know you will feel bound to say you do. But—anyhow—you needn't say it to me, because I understand. I thought it was only fair to let you know at once."

"Thank you," said Nick, and there was that in his voice which was like the sudden snapping of a tense spring.

She saw his hands clench with the words, and an overwhelming sense of danger swept over her. Instinctively she started to her feet. If a tiger had leapt in upon her through the window she could not have been more terrified.

Nick took a single stride towards her, and she stopped as if struck powerless. His face was the face she had once seen bent over a man in his death-agony, convulsed with passion, savage, merciless,—the face of a devil.

She shrank away from him in nameless terror, gasping and panic-stricken. "Nick," she whispered, "are you—mad?"

He answered her jerkily in a strangled voice that was like the snarl of a beast. "Yes—I am mad. If you try to run away from me now—I won't answer for myself."

She gazed at him with widening eyes. "But, but—" she faltered—"I—I don't understand. Oh, Nick, you frighten me!"

It was the cry of a child, lost, bewildered, piteous. Had she withstood him, had she sought to escape, the demon in him would have burst the last restraining bond, and have shattered in one moment of unshackled violence all the chivalrous patience which during the last few weeks he had spent his whole strength to achieve.

But that cry of desolation pierced straight through his madness, cutting deeper than reproach or protest, wounding him to the heart.

With a sound that was half-sob, half-groan, he turned his back upon her and covered his face.

For a space of seconds he stood so, not moving, seeming not even to breathe. And Muriel, steadying herself by the mantelpiece, watched him with a panting heart.

Then abruptly, moving with a quick, light tread that made no sound, he crossed the room to one of the wide-flung windows and stopped there.

From across the quiet garden there came the strains of "The Blue Danube," fitful, alluring, plaintive—that waltz to which countless lovers have danced and wooed and whispered through the years. Muriel longed intensely to shut it out, to stop her ears, to make some noise to drown it. Her nerves were all on edge, and she felt as if its persistent sweetness would drive her mad.

Surely Nick felt the same; but if he did, he made no sign. He stood without movement with his face to the night, gripping the woodwork of the window with both hands, every bone of them standing out in sharp, skeleton lines.

She watched him, fascinated, for a long time, but he did not stir from his tense position. He seemed to have utterly forgotten her presence in the room behind him. And still that maddening waltz kept on and on and on till she felt sick and dazed with listening to it. It seemed as if for the rest of her life she would never again be free from those haunting strains.

The soft shutting of the window made her start and quiver. Nick had moved at last, and her heart began to throb thick and fast as he turned. She tried to read his face, but she could not even see it. There was a swimming mist before her eyes, and her limbs felt powerless, heavy as lead.

In every nerve, she felt him drawing near, and in an agony of helplessness she awaited him, all the surging horror of that night when he had drugged her rushing back upon her with tenfold force. Again she saw him as she had seen him then, monstrous, silent, terrible, a man of superhuman strength, whose mastery appalled her. Again in desperate fear she shrank from him, seeking wildly, fruitlessly, for a way of escape.

And then came the consciousness of his arm about her, supporting her; and the voice that had quieted her wildest delirium was speaking in her ear.

"The goblins are all gone, dear," she heard him say. "Don't be frightened."

He led her gently to a sofa and made her sit down, bending over her and softly rubbing her cold cheek.

"Tell me when you're better," he said, "and we'll talk this thing out. But don't be frightened anyway. It's all right."

The tenderness of voice and touch, the sudden cessation of all tension, the swift putting to flight of her fear, all combined to produce in her a sense of relief so immense that the last shred of her self-control went from her utterly. She laid her head down upon the cushions and burst into a storm of tears.

Nick's hand continued to stroke and soothe, but he said no more while her paroxysm of weeping lasted. He who was usually so ready of speech, so quick to console, found for once no words wherewith to comfort her.

Only when her distress had somewhat spent itself, he bent a little lower and dried her tears with his own handkerchief, his lips twitching as he did it, his eyes flickering so rapidly that it was impossible to read their expression.

"There!" he said at last. "There's nothing to cry about. Finish what you were saying when I interrupted you. I think you were in the middle of throwing me over, weren't you? At least, you had got through that part of it, and were just going to tell me why."

His tone was reassuringly flippant.

Looking up at him, she saw the old kindly, quizzical look on his face. He met her eyes, nodding shrewdly.

"Let's have it," he said, "straight from the shoulder. You're tired of me, eh?"

She drew back from him, but with no gesture of shrinking. "I'm tired of everything—everything," she said, a little passionate quiver in her voice. "I wish—I wish with all my heart, you had left me to die."

"Is that the grievance?" said Nick. He sat down on the head of the sofa, and drove his fist into the cushion. "If I could explain things to you, I would. But you're such a chicken, aren't you, dear, and about as easily scared? Since when have you harboured this grudge against me?"

The gentle banter of his tone did not deceive her into imagining that she could trifle with him, nor was she addicted to trifling. She made answer with a certain warmth of indignation that seemed to have kindled on its own initiative and wholly without her volition.

"I haven't, I don't. I'm not so absurd. It isn't that at all."

"You're not tired of me?" queried Nick.

"No."

"If I were to die to-morrow for instance—and there's no telling, you know, Muriel,—you'd be a little sorry?"

Again, though scarcely aware of it, she resented the question. "Why do you ask me that? Of course I should be sorry."

"Of course," acquiesced Nick. "But all the king's horses and all the king's men wouldn't bring me back again. That's the worst of being mortal. You can't dance at your own funeral."

"What do you mean?" There was a note of exasperation in Muriel's voice. She saw that he had an object in view, but his method of attaining it was too tortuous for her straightforward understanding.

He explained himself with much patience. His mood had so completely changed that she could barely recall to mind the vision that had so appalled her but a few minutes before.

"What I mean is that it's infernal to think that some one may be shedding precious tears on your grave and you not there to see. I've often wondered if one could get a ticket of leave for such an occasion." He smiled down at her with baffling directness. "I should value those tears unspeakably," he said.

Muriel made a slight movement of impatience. The discussion seemed to her inconsequent and unprofitable.

Nick began to enumerate his points. "You're not tired of me—though I see I'm boring you hideously; put up with it a little longer, I've nearly finished—and you'd shed quite a respectable number of tears if I were to die young. Yes, I am young though as ugly as Satan. I believe you think I'm some sort of connection, don't you? Is that why you don't want to marry me?"

He put the question with startling suddenness, and Muriel glanced up quickly, but was instantly reassured. He was no more formidable at that moment than a grinning schoolboy. Still she did not feel wholly at her ease with him. She had a curious suspicion that he was in some fashion testing her.

"No," she answered, after a moment. "It is nothing of that sort."

"Quite sure there is a reason?" he asked quizzically.

Her white cheeks flushed. "Yes, of course. But—I would rather not tell you what it is."

"Quite so," said Nick. "I suppose that also is 'only fair'?"

Her colour deepened. He made her feel unaccountably ashamed. "I will tell you if you wish to know," she said reluctantly. "But I would rather not."

Nick made an airy gesture. "Not for the world! My intelligence department is specially fitted for this sort of thing. Besides, I know exactly what happened. It was something like this." He passed his hand over his face, then turned to her with a faint, wry smile so irresistibly reminiscent of Lady Bassett that Muriel gasped with a sudden hysterical desire to laugh.

He silenced her by beginning to speak in soft, purring accents. "You know, darling Muriel, I have never looked upon Nicholas Ratcliffe as a marrying man. He is such a gay butterfly." (This with an indulgent shake of the head.) "Indeed, I have heard dear Mrs. Gybbon-Smythe describe him as a shocking little flirt. And they say he is fond of his glass too, but let us hope this is an exaggeration. I know for a fact that he has a very violent temper, and this may have given rise to the rumour. I assure you, dearest, he is quite formidable, notwithstanding his size. But there, if I tell you any more you will think I am prejudiced against him, whereas we are really the greatest friends—the greatest possible friends. I only thought it kind to warn you not to expect too much. It is a mistake so many young girls make, and I want you to be as happy as you can, poor child."

Muriel was laughing helplessly when he stopped. The mimicry of voice and action was so perfect, so free from exaggeration, so sublimely spontaneous.

Nick did not laugh with her. Behind his mask of banter he was watching, watching closely. He had clad himself in jester's garb to feel for the truth. Perhaps she realised something of this as she recovered herself, for again that glance, half-questioning, half-frightened, flashed up at him as she made reply.

"No, Nick. She never said that, indeed. I wouldn't have cared if she had. It was only—only—"

"I know," he broke in abruptly. "If it wasn't that, there is only one thing left that it could have been. I don't want you to tell me. It's as plain as daylight. Let me tell you instead. It's all for the sake of your poor little personal pride. I know—yes, I know. They've been throwing mud at you, and it's stuck. You'd sooner die than marry me, wouldn't you? But what will you do if I refuse to set you free?"

She turned suddenly crimson. "You—you wouldn't, Nick! You couldn't! You haven't—the right."

"Haven't I?" said Nick, with an odd smile. "I thought I had."

He looked down at her, and a queer little flame leaped up like an evil spirit in his eyes, flickered an instant, and was gone. "I thought I had," he said again, in a different tone. "But we won't quarrel about that. Tell me what you want to do."

Her answer came with a vehemence that perhaps he had hardly expected. "Oh, I want to get away—right away. I want to go home. I—I hate this place."

"And every one in it?" suggested Nick.

"Almost." Muriel spoke recklessly, even defiantly. She was fighting for her freedom, and the battle was infinitely harder than she had anticipated.

He nodded. "The sole exception being Mrs. Musgrave. Do you know Mrs. Musgrave is going home? You would like to go with her."

Muriel looked at him with sudden hope. "Alone with her?" she said.

"Oh, I'm not going," declared Nick. "I'm going to Khatmandu for my honeymoon."

The hope died out of Muriel's eyes. "Don't—jeer at me, Nick," she said, in a choked voice. "I can't bear it."

"Jeer!" said Nick. "I!" He reached down suddenly and took her hand. The light sparkled on the ring he had given her, and he moved it slowly to and fro watching it.

"I am going to ask you to take it back," she said.

He did not raise his eyes. "And I am going to refuse," he answered promptly. "I don't say you must wear it, but you are to keep it—not as a bond, merely in remembrance of a promise which you will make to me."

"A promise—" she faltered.

Still he did not look up. He was watching the stones with eyes half-shut.

"Yes," he said, after a moment. "I will let you go on the sole condition that you give me this promise."

She began to tremble a little. "What is it?" she whispered.

He glanced at her momentarily, but his expression was enigmatical. She felt as if his look lighted and dwelt upon something beyond her.

"Simply this," he said. "You'll laugh, I daresay; but if you are able to laugh it won't hurt you to promise. I want your word of honour that if you ever change your mind about marrying me, you will come to me like a brave woman and tell me so."

Thus, quite calmly, he made known to her his condition, and in the amazed silence with which she received it he continued to flash hither and thither the wonderful rays that shone from the gems upon her hand. He did not appear to be greatly concerned as to what her answer would be. Simply with an inscrutable countenance he waited for it.

"Is it a bargain?" he asked at last.

She started with an involuntary gesture of shrinking. "Oh, no, Nick! How could I promise you that? You know I shall never change my mind."

He raised his eyebrows ever so slightly. "That isn't the point under discussion. If it's an impossible contingency, it costs you the less to promise."

He kept her hand in his as he said it, though she fidgeted to be free. "Please, Nick," she said earnestly, "I would so much rather not."

"You prefer to marry me at once?" he asked, and suddenly it seemed to her that this was the alternative to which he meant to drive her.

She rose in a panic, and he rose also, still keeping her hand. His face looked like a block of yellow granite.

"Must it—must it—be one or the other?" she panted.

He looked at her under flickering eyelids. "I have said it," he remarked.

Her resistance flagged, sank, rose again, and finally died away. After all, why should she hesitate? What was there in such an undertaking as this to send the blood so wildly to her heart?

"Very well," she said faintly at last. "I promise. But—but—I never shall change my mind, Nick—never—never."

He was still looking at her with veiled, impenetrable eyes. He paid no attention to her protest. It was as if he had not so much as heard it.

"You've done your part," he said. "Now hear me do mine. I swear to you—before God—that I will never marry you unless you ask me to."

He bent with the words, and solemnly, reverently, he pressed his lips upon the hand he held.

Muriel waited, half-frightened still, and wholly awestruck. She did not know Nick in this mood.

But when he straightened himself again, the old whimsical smile was on his face, and she breathed a sigh of relief. With a quick, caressing movement he took her by the shoulders.

"That's over then," he said lightly. "Turn over and start another page. Go back to England, go back to school; and let them teach you to be young again."

They were his last words to her. Yet an instant longer he waited, and very deep down in her heart something that was hidden there stirred and quivered as a blind creature moves at the touch of the sun. It awoke a vague pain within her, that was all.

The next moment Nick had turned upon his heel and was departing.

She heard him humming a waltz tune under his breath as he went away with his free British swagger. And she knew with no sense of elation that she had gained her point.

For good or ill he had left her, and he would not return.

PART III
CHAPTER XVII
AN OLD FRIEND

"There!" said Daisy, standing back from the table to review her handiwork with her head on one side. "I may be outrageously childish, but if Blake fails to appreciate this masterpiece of mine, I shall feel inclined to turn him out-of-doors, and leave him to spend the night on the step."

Muriel, curled up in the old-fashioned window-seat, looked round with her low laugh. "It's snowing hard," she remarked.

Daisy did not heed her. "Come and look at it," she said.

The masterpiece in question consisted of an enormous red scroll bearing in white letters the words: "Welcome to the Brave."

"It never before occurred to me that Blake was brave," observed Daisy. "He is so shy and soft and retiring. I can't somehow feel as if I am going to entertain a lion. He ought to be here by this time. Let's go and hang my work of art in the hall."

She slipped her hand through Muriel's arm, and glanced at her sharply when she felt it tremble.

"It will be good to see him again, won't it?" she said.

"Yes," Muriel agreed, but there was a little tremor in her voice as well.

Very vividly were the circumstances under which she had last seen this man in her mind that night. Eight months that were like as many years stretched between that tragic time and the present, but the old wild horror had still the power to make her blood turn cold, the old wound had not lost its ache. These things had made a woman of her before her time, but yet she was not as other women. It seemed that she was destined all her life to live apart, and only to look on at the joys of others. They did not attract her, and she had no heart for gaiety. Yet she was not cold, or Daisy had not found in her so congenial a companion. But even Daisy seldom penetrated behind the deep reserve that had grown over the girl's sad young heart. They were close friends, but their friendship lay mainly in what they left unsaid. For all her quick warmth, Daisy too had her inner shrine—a place so secret that she herself never entered it save as it were by stealth.

But something of Muriel's mood she understood on that bitter night in January on which they awaited the coming of Blake Grange, and her close hand-pressure conveyed as much as they passed out together into the little hall that glowed so snugly in the firelight.

"He is sure to be frozen, poor boy," she said. "I hope Jim Ratcliffe won't forget to send the motor to the station as he promised."

"I am quite sure he never forgets anything," Muriel declared, with reassuring confidence.

Daisy laughed lightly. "Yes, he's very dependable, deliciously solid, isn't he? A trifle domineering perhaps, but all doctors are. They rule us weak women with a rod of iron. I am a little afraid of Dr. Jim myself, and most unfortunately he knows it."

Muriel's silence expressed a certain scepticism that provoked another laugh from Daisy. She was almost frivolously light-hearted that night.

"It's a fact, I assure you. Have you never noticed how docile I am in his presence? I always feel as if I want to confess all my sins to him. I should like intensely to have his opinion upon some of them. I think it would do me good."

"Then why not ask for it?" suggested Muriel.

"For the reason aforementioned—a slavish timidity." Daisy broke off to carol a few bars of a song. "I've known the Ratcliffe family ever since I became engaged to Will," she said presently. "Jim Ratcliffe, you know, was left his guardian, and he was always very good to him. Will made his home with them and he and Nick are great pals, just like brothers. I should think Dr. Jim had his hands full with the two of them." Again Daisy stopped to sing. Muriel was stooping over the fire. It was seldom that Nick's name was mentioned between them, though the fact that Daisy had placed herself and her baby in the hands of his half-brother formed a connecting link which could not always be ignored. She always dropped into silence when a reference was made to him. Not in the most casual conversation had Daisy ever heard her utter his name.

Having successfully fixed her message of welcome in a prominent position, she joined the girl in front of the fire. Her face was flushed and her eyes were sparkling. Muriel thought that she had never seen her look so well or so happy.

"You're quite excited," she said.

Daisy put up a hand to her hot cheek. "Yes, isn't it absurd? I hope Dr. Jim won't come with him, or he will be cross. But I can't help it. Blake and I have been chums all our lives, and of course I am glad to see him after all this while. So nice, too, not to have Lady Bassett looking on."

There was a spice of venom in this, over which Muriel smiled in her sad way.

"Does she disapprove?" she asked.

Daisy nodded impatiently. "She chose altogether to overlook the fact that we are first cousins. It was intolerable. But—" again came her light laugh—"everything is intolerable till you learn to shrug your shoulders and laugh. Hark! Surely I heard something!"

Both listened intently. Footsteps were approaching the door. Daisy sprang to open it.

But it was only the evening post, and she came back holding a letter with a very unwonted expression of disappointment.

"From Will," she said. "I forgot it was mail night. I don't suppose there is anything very exciting in it."

She pushed the flimsy envelope into the front of her dress and fell again to listening.

"Can he have missed the train? Surely it's getting very late. A fog on the line perhaps. No! What's that? Ah! It really is this time. That's the horn, and, yes, Jim Ratcliffe's voice."

In a moment she had the door open again, and was out upon the step crying welcome to her guest.

Muriel crouched a little lower over the fire. Her hands were fast gripped together. It was more of an ordeal than she had thought it possibly could be.

An icy blast blew in through the open door, and she heard Dr. Ratcliffe's voice, sharp and curt, ordering Daisy back into the house. Then came another voice, slow and soft as a woman's, and for an instant Muriel covered her face, overwhelmed by bitter memory.

When she looked up they were entering the hall together, Daisy, radiant, eager, full of breathless questioning; Blake, upright, soldierly, magnificent, wearing the shy, pleased smile that she so well remembered.

He did not at once see her, and she stood hesitating, till Daisy, who was clinging to her cousin's arm, turned swiftly round and called her.

"Muriel, dear, where are you? Why are you hiding yourself? See, Blake! Here is Muriel Roscoe! You knew we were living together?"

He saw her then, and came across to her, with both hands outstretched.

"Forgive me, Miss Roscoe," he said, with his pleasant smile. "You know how glad I am to meet you again."

He looked down at her with eyes full of frank and friendly sympathy, and the grasp of his hands was such that she felt it for long after. It warmed her through and through, but she could not speak just then, and with ready understanding he turned back to Daisy.

"Dr. Ratcliffe told me you had sent him to fetch me from the station," he said. "I am immensely grateful to you and to him."

Daisy was greeting the doctor with much animation and a hint of mischief.

"I knew you would come," she laughed. "You never trust me to take care of myself, do you?"

He brushed some flakes of snow from her dress. "Events prove me to be justified," he remarked dryly. "Since Will has put you in my care, I labour under a twofold responsibility. What possessed you to go out in that murderous north-easter?"

He frowned at her heavily, his black brows meeting, but notwithstanding her avowal of a few minutes before, Daisy only grimaced in return. He was generally regarded as somewhat formidable, this gruff, square-shouldered doctor, with his iron-grey hair and black moustache, and keenly critical eyes. There was no varnish in his curt speech, no dissimulation in any of his dealings. It was said of him that he never sugared his pills. But his popularity was wide-spread nevertheless. His help was sought in a thousand ways outside his profession. To see his strong face melt into a smile was like sunshine on a gloomy day, the village mothers declared.

But Daisy's gay effrontery did not manage to provoke it at that moment.

"You have no business to take risks," he said. "How's the boy?"

Daisy sobered instantly. "His teeth have been worrying him rather to-day. *Ayah* is with him. I left her crooning him to sleep. Will you go up?"

Jim Ratcliffe nodded and turned aside to the stairs. But he had not reached the top when Muriel overtook him, moving more quickly than was her wont.

"Let me come with you, doctor," she said.

He put his hand on her arm unceremoniously. "Miss Roscoe," he said, "I have a message for you—from my scapegrace Olga. She wants to know if you will play hockey in her team next Saturday. I have promised to exert my influence—if I have any—on her behalf."

Muriel looked at him in semi-tragic dismay. "Oh, I can't indeed. Why, I haven't played for ages,—not since I was at school. Besides—"

"How old are you?" he cut in.

"Nearly twenty," she told him. "But—"

He brought his hand down sharply on her shoulder. "I shall never call you Miss Roscoe again. You obtained my veneration on false pretences, and you have lost it for ever. Now look here, Muriel!" Arrived at the top of the stairs, he stood still and confronted her with that smile of his that so marvellously softened his rugged face. "I am thirty years older than you are, and I haven't lived for any part of them with my eyes shut. I've been wanting to give you some advice—medical advice—for a long time. But you wouldn't have it. And now I'm not going to offer it to you. You shall take the advice of a friend instead. You join Olga's hockey team, and go paper-chasing with her too. The monkey is a rare sportswoman. She'll give you a good run for your money. Besides, she has set her heart on having you, and she is a young woman that likes her own way, though, to be sure, she doesn't always get it. Come, you can't refuse when a friend asks you."

It was difficult, certainly, but Muriel plainly desired to do so. She had escaped from the whirling vortex of life with strenuous effort, and dragged herself bruised and aching to the bank. She did not want to step down again into even the minutest eddy of that ruthless flood. Moreover, in addition to this morbid reluctance she lacked the physical energy that such a step demanded of her.

"It's very kind of your little daughter to think of asking me," she said. "But really, I shouldn't be any good. I get tired so quickly. No, there's nothing the matter with me," seeing his intent look. "I'm not ill. I never have been actually ill. Only—" her voice quivered a little—"I think I always shall be tired for the rest of my life."

"Skittles!" he returned bluntly. "That isn't what's the matter with you. Go out into the open air. Go out into the north-east wind and sweep the snow away. Shall I tell you what is wrong with you? You're stiff from inaction. It's a species of cramp, my dear, and there's only one remedy for it. Are you going to take it of your own accord, or must I come round with a physic spoon and make you?"

She laughed a little, though the deep pathos of her shadowed eyes never varied. Daisy's merry voice rose from the lower regions gaily chaffing her cousin.

"Goodness, Blake! I shouldn't have known you. You're as gaunt as a camel. Haven't you got over your picnic at Fort Wara yet? You're almost as scanty a bag of bones as Nick was six months ago."

Blake's answer was inaudible. Dr. Ratcliffe did not listen for it. He had seen the swift look of horror that the brief allusion had sent into the girl's sad face, and he understood it though he made no sign.

"Very well," he said, turning towards the nursery. "Then I take you in hand from this day forward. And if I don't find you in the hockey-field on Saturday, I shall come myself and fetch you."

There was nothing even vaguely suggestive of Nick about him, but Muriel knew as surely as if Nick had said it that he would keep his word.

CHAPTER XVIII
THE EXPLANATION

"Now," said Daisy briskly, "you two will just have to entertain each other for a little while, for I am going up to sit with my son while *ayah* is off duty."

"Mayn't we come too?" suggested her cousin, as he rose to open the door.

She stood a moment and contemplated him with shining eyes. "You are too magnificent altogether for this doll's house of ours," she declared. "I am sure this humble roof has never before sheltered such a lion as Captain Blake Grange, V.C."

"Only an ass in a lion's skin, my dear Daisy," said Grange modestly.

She laughed. "An excellent simile, my worthy cousin. I wish I had thought of it myself."

She went lightly away with this thrust, and Grange, after a brief pause, turned slowly back into the room.

Muriel was seated in a low chair before the fire. She was working at some tiny woollen socks, knitting swiftly in dead silence.

He moved to the hearthrug, and stood there, obviously ill at ease. A certain shyness was in his nature, and Muriel's nervousness reacted upon him. He did not know how to break the silence.

At length, with an effort, he spoke. "You heard about Nick Ratcliffe's wound, I expect, Miss Roscoe?"

Muriel's hands leapt suddenly and fell into her lap. "Nick Ratcliffe! When was he wounded? No, I have heard nothing."

He looked down at her with an uneasy suspicion that he had lighted upon an unfortunate subject.

"I thought you would have heard," he said. "Didn't Daisy know? He came back to us from Simla—got himself attached to the punitive expedition. I was on the sick list myself, so did not see him, but they say he fought like a dancing dervish, and did a lot of damage too. Every one thought he would have the V.C., but there was a rumour that he refused it."

"And—he was wounded, you say?" Muriel's voice sounded curiously strained. Her knitting lay jumbled together in her lap. Her dark face was lifted, and it seemed to Grange, unskilled observer though he was, that he had never seen deeper tragedy in any woman's eyes.

Somewhat reluctantly he made reply. "He had his arm injured by a sword-thrust at the very end of the campaign. He made light of it for ever so long till things began to look serious. Then he had to give in, and had a pretty sharp time of it, I believe. He's better again now, though, so his brother told me this evening. I never heard any details. I daresay he's all right again." He stooped to pick up a completed sock that had fallen. "He's the sort of chap who always comes out on top," he ended consolingly.

Muriel stiffened a little as she sat. She had a curious longing to hear more, and an equally curious reluctance to ask for it.

"I never heard anything about it—naturally," she remarked.

Grange, having fitted the sock on to two fingers, was examining it with a contemplative air. It struck her abruptly that he was trying to say something. She waited silently, not without apprehension. She had no idea as to how much he knew of what had passed between herself and Nick.

"I say, Miss Roscoe," he blurted out suddenly, "do you hate talking about these things—very badly, I mean?"

She looked up at him, and was surprised to see emotion on his face. It had an odd effect upon her, placing her unaccountably at her ease with him, banishing all her stiffness in a moment. She remembered with a quick warmth at her heart how she had always liked this man in those far-off days of her father's protection, how she had always found something reassuring in his gentle courtesy.

"No," she said, after a moment, speaking with absolute sincerity. "I can't bear to with—most people; but I don't think I mind with you."

She saw his pleasant smile for an instant. He laid the sock down upon her knee, and in doing so touched and lightly pressed her hand.

"Thank you," he said simply. "I know I'm not good at expressing myself, but please believe that I wouldn't hurt you for the world. Miss Roscoe, I have brought some things with me I think you will like to have—things that belonged to your father. Sir Reginald Bassett entrusted them to me—left them, in fact, in my charge, as he found them. I was coming home, and I asked leave to bring them to you. Perhaps you would like me to fetch them?"

She was on her feet as he asked the question, on her face such a look of eagerness as it had not worn for many weary months.

"Oh, please—if you would!" she said, her words falling fast and breathless. "It has been—such a grief to me—that I had nothing of his to—to treasure."

He turned at once to the door. The desolation that those words of hers revealed to him went straight to his man's heart. Poor little girl! Had the parting been so infernally hard as even now to bring that look to her eyes? Was her father's memory the only interest she had left in her sad young life? And all the evening, save for that first brief moment of their meeting, he had been thinking her cold, impassive, even cynical.

With a deep pity in his soul he departed on his errand.

Returning with the soft tread which was his peculiarity, he surprised her with her face in her hands in an attitude of such abandonment that he drew back hesitating. But, suddenly aware of him, she sprang up swiftly, with no sign of tears upon her face.

"Oh, come in, come in!" she said impatiently. "Why do you stand there?"

She ran forward to meet him with hands hungrily outstretched, and he put into them those trifles which were to her so infinitely precious—a cigarette-case, a silver match-box, a pen-knife, a little old prayer-book very worn at the edges, with all the gilt faded from its leaves. She gathered them to her breast closely, passionately. All but the prayer-book had been her gifts to the father she had worshipped. With a wrung heart she called to mind the occasion upon which each had been offered, his smile of kindly appreciation, the old-world courtliness of his thanks. With loving hands she laid them down one by one, lingering over each, seeing them through a blur of tears. She was no longer conscious of Grange, as reverently, even diffidently, she opened last of all the little shabby prayer-book that her father had been wont to take with him on all his marches. She knew that he had cherished it as her mother's gift.

It opened upon a scrap of white heather which marked the Service for the Burial of the Dead. Her tears fell upon the faded sprig, and she brushed her hand swiftly across her eyes, looking more closely as certain words underlined caught her attention. Other words had been written by her father's hand very minutely in the margin.

The passage underlined was ... "not to be sorry as men without hope, for them that sleep ..." and in a moment she guessed that her father had made that mark on the day of her mother's death. It was like a message to her, the echo of a cry.

The words in the margin were so small that she had to carry them to the light to read them. And then they flashed out at her as if sprung suddenly to light on the white paper. There, in the beloved handwriting, sure and indelible, she read it, and across the desert of her heart, voiceless but insistent, there swept the hunger-cry of a man's soul: OMNIA VINCIT AMOR.

It pulsed through her like an electric current, seeming to overwhelm every other sensation, shutting her off as it were from the home-world to which she had fled, how fruitlessly, for healing. Once more skeleton fingers held hers, shifting to and fro, to and fro, slowly, ceaselessly, flashing the deep rays that shone from ruby hearts hither and thither. Once more—But she would not bear it! She was free! She was free! She flung out the hand that once had worn those rubies, and, resisting wildly, broke away from the spell that the words her father had written had woven afresh for her.

It might be true that Love conquered all things—he had believed it—but ah, what had this uncanny force to do with Love? Love was a pure, a holy thing, the bond imperishable—the Eternal Flame at which all the little torches of the world are lighted.

Moreover, there was no fear in Love, and she—she was sick with fear whenever she encountered that haunting phantom of memory.

With a start she awoke to the fact that she was not alone. Blake Grange had taken her out-flung hand, and was speaking to her softly, soothingly.

"Don't grieve so awfully, Miss Roscoe," he urged, a slight break in his own voice. "You're not left friendless. I know how it is. I've felt like it myself. But it gets better afterwards."

Muriel suffered him with a dawning sense of comfort. It surprised her to see tears in his eyes. She wondered vaguely if they were for her.

"Yes," she said, after a pause. "It does get better, I know, in a way. Or at least one gets used to an empty heart. One gets to leave off listening for what one will never, never hear any more."

"Never is a dreary word," said Grange.

She bent her head silently, and again his heart overflowed with pity for her. He looked down at the hand that lay so passively in his.

"I hope you will always think of me as a friend," he said.

She looked up at him a quick gleam of gratitude in her eyes. "Thank you," she said. "Yes, always."

He still held her hand. "You know," he said, blundering awkwardly, "I always blamed myself that—that I wasn't the one to be with you when you escaped from Wara. I might have been. But I—I wasn't prepared to pay the possible price."

She was still looking at him with those aloof, tragic eyes of hers. "I don't quite understand," she said, "I never did understand—exactly—why Nick was chosen to protect me. I always wished it had been you."

"It ought to have been," Grange said, with feeling. "It should have been. I blame myself. But Nick is a better fighter than I. He keeps his head. Moreover, he's a savage in some respects. I wasn't savage enough."

He smiled with a hint of apology.

Muriel repressed a shudder at his words. "I don't understand," she said again.

He hesitated. "It's a difficult thing to explain to you," he said reluctantly. "You see, the fellow who took charge of you had to be prepared for—well—anything. You know what devils those tribesmen are. There was to be no chance of your falling into their hands. It didn't mean just fighting for you, you understand. We would all have done that to the last drop of our blood. But—your father—was forced to ask of us—something more. And only Ratcliffe would undertake it. He's a queer chap. I used to think him a rotter till I saw him fight, and then I had to change my mind. That was, I believe, the main reason why General Roscoe selected him as your protector. He knew he could trust the fellow's nerve. The rest of us were like women compared to Nick."

He paused. Muriel's eyes had not flinched from his. She heard his explanation as one not vitally concerned.

"Have I made myself intelligible?" he asked, as she did not speak.

"Do you mean I was to be shot if things went wrong?" she returned, in her deep, quiet voice.

He nodded. "It must have been that. Your father saw it in that light, and so did we. Of course you are bound to see it too. But we stuck at it—Marshall and I. There was only Nick left, and he volunteered."

"Only Nick left!" she repeated slowly. "Nick would stick at nothing, Captain Grange."

"I honestly don't think he would," said Grange. "Still, you know, he's awfully plucky. He would have gone any length to save you first."

She drew back with a sudden shrinking of her whole body. "Oh, I know, I know!" she said. "I sometimes think there is a devil in Nick."

She turned aside, bending once more over her father's things, putting them together with unsteady fingers. So this was the answer to the riddle—the secret of his choice for her! She understood it all now.

472

After a short pause, she spoke again more calmly. "Did Nick ever speak to you about me?"

"Never," said Grange.

"Then please, Captain Grange"—she stood up again and faced him—"never speak to me again about him. I—want to forget him."

Very young and slight she looked standing there, and again he felt his heart stir within him with an urgent pity. Vague rumours he had heard of those few weeks at Simla during which her name and Nick Ratcliffe's had been coupled together, but he had never definitely known what had taken place. Had Nick been good to her, he wondered for the first time? How was it that the bare mention of him was unendurable to her? What had he done that she should shudder with horror when she remembered him, and should seek thus with loathing to thrust him out of her life?

Involuntarily the man's hands clenched and his blood quickened. Had the General's trust been misplaced? Was Nick a blackguard?

Finding her eyes still upon him, he made her a slight bow that was wholly free from gallantry.

"I will remember your wish, Miss Roscoe," he said. "I am sorry I mentioned a painful subject to you, though I am glad for you to know the truth. You are not vexed with me, I hope?"

Her eyes shone with sincere friendliness. "I am not vexed," she answered. "Only—let me forget—that's all."

And in those few words she voiced the desire of her soul. It was her one longing, her one prayer—to forget. And it was the one thing of all others denied to her.

In the silence that followed, she was conscious of his warm and kindly sympathy, and she was grateful for it, though something restrained her from telling him so.

Daisy, coming lightly in upon them, put an end to their tête-à-tête. She entered softly, her face alight and tender, and laid her two hands upon Grange's great shoulders as he sat before the fire.

"Come upstairs, Blake," she whispered, "and see my baby boy. He's sleeping so sweetly. I want you to see him first while he's good."

He raised his face to her smiling, his hands on hers. "I am sure to admire anything that belongs to you, Daisy," he said.

"You're a dear old pal," responded Daisy lightly. "Come along."

When they were gone Muriel spied Will Musgrave's letter lying on the ground by Grange's chair as it had evidently fallen from Daisy's dress. She went over and picked it up. It was still unopened.

With an odd little frown she set it up prominently upon the mantelpiece.

"Does Love conquer after all?" she murmured to herself, and there was a faint twist of cynicism about her lips as she asked the question. There seemed to be so many forms of Love.

CHAPTER XIX
A HERO WORSHIPPER

"Well played! Oh, well played! Miss Roscoe, you're a brick."

The merry voice of the doctor's little daughter Olga, aged fourteen, shrilled across the hockey-ground, keen with enthusiasm. She was speeding across the field like a hare to congratulate her latest recruit.

"I'm so pleased!" she cried, bursting through the miscellaneous crowd of boys and girls that surrounded Muriel. "I wanted you to shoot that goal."

She herself had been acting as goal-keeper at her own end of the field, a position of limited opportunities which she had firmly refused to assign to the new-comer. A child of unusual character was Olga Ratcliffe, impulsive but shrewd, with quick, pale eyes which never seemed to take more than a brief glance at anything, yet which very little ever escaped. At first sight Muriel had experienced a certain feeling of aversion to her, so marked was the likeness this child bore to the man whom she desired so passionately to shut out of her very memory. But a nearer intimacy had weakened her antipathy till very soon it had altogether disappeared. Olga had a swift and fascinating fashion of endearing herself to all who caught her fancy and, somewhat curiously, Muriel was one of the favoured number. What there was to attract a child of her quick temperament in the grave, silent girl in mourning who held aloof so coldly from the rest of the world was never apparent. But that a strong attraction existed for her was speedily evident, and Muriel, who was quite destitute of any near relations of her own, soon found that a free admittance to the doctor's home circle was accorded her on all sides, whenever she chose to avail herself of it.

But though Daisy was an immense favourite and often ran into the Ratcliffes' house, which was not more than a few hundred yards away from her own little abode, Muriel went but seldom. The doctor's wife, though always kind, was too busy to seek her out. And so it had been left to the doctor himself to drag her at length from her seclusion, and he had done it with a determination that would take no refusal. She did not know him very intimately, had never asked his advice, or held any confidential talk with him. At the outset she had been horribly afraid lest he should have heard of her engagement to Nick, but, since he never referred to her life in India or to Nick as in any fashion connected with herself, this fear had gradually subsided. She was able to tell herself thankfully that Nick was dropping away from her into the past, and to hope with some conviction that the great gulf that separated them would never be bridged.

Yet, notwithstanding this, she had a fugitive wish to know how her late comrade in adversity was faring. Captain Grange's news regarding him had aroused in her a vague uneasiness, which would not be quieted.

She wondered if by any means she could extract any information from Olga, and this she presently essayed to do, when play was over for the day and Olga had taken her upstairs to prepare for tea.

Olga was the easiest person in the world to deal with upon such a subject. She expanded at the very mention of Nick's name.

"Oh, do you know him? Isn't he a darling? I have a photograph of him somewhere. I must try and find it. He is in fancy dress and standing on his head—such a beauty. Weren't you awfully fond of him? He has been ill, you know. Dad was very waxy because he wouldn't come home. He might have had sick leave, but he wouldn't take it. However, he may have to come yet, Dad says, if something happens. He didn't say what. It was something to do with his wound. Dad wants him to leave the Army and settle down on his estate. He owns a big place about twelve miles away that an old great-aunt of his left him. Dad thinks a landowner ought to live at home if he can afford to. And of course Nick might go into Parliament too. He's so clever, and rich as well. But he won't do it. So it's no good talking."

Olga jumped off the dressing-table, and wound her arm impulsively through Muriel's. "Miss Roscoe," she said coaxingly, "I do like you most awfully. May I call you by your Christian name?"

"Why, do!" Muriel said. "I should like it best."

"Oh, that's all right," said Olga, well pleased. "I knew you weren't stuck-up really. I hate stuck-up people, don't you? I'm awfully pleased that you like Nick. I simply love him—better almost than any one else. He writes to me sometimes, pages and pages. I never show them to any one, and he doesn't show mine either. You see, we're pals. But I can show you his photograph—the one I told you about. It's just like him—his grin and all. Come up after tea, and I'll find it."

And with her arm entwined in Muriel's she drew her, still talking eagerly, from the room.

CHAPTER XX
NEWS FROM THE EAST

"I have been wondering," Grange said in his shy, rather diffident way, "if you would care to do any riding while I am here."

"I?" Muriel looked up in some surprise.

474

They were walking back from church together by a muddy field-path, and since neither had much to say at any time, they had accomplished more than half the distance in silence.

"I know you do ride," Grange explained, "and it's just the sort of country for a good gallop now and then. Daisy isn't allowed to, but I thought perhaps you—"

"Oh, I should like to, of course," Muriel said. "I haven't done any riding since I left Simla. I didn't care to alone."

"Ah! Lady Bassett rides, doesn't she? She is an accomplished horsewoman, I believe?"

"I don't know," Muriel's reply was noticeably curt. "I never rode with her."

Grange at once dropped the subject, and they became silent again. Muriel walked with her eyes fixed straight before her. But she did not see the brown earth underfoot or the bare trees that swayed overhead in the racing winter wind. She was back again in the heart of the Simla pines, hearing horses' feet that stamped below her window in the dawning, and a gay, cracked voice that sang.

Her companion's voice recalled her. "I suppose Daisy will stay here for the summer."

"I suppose so," she answered.

Grange went on with some hesitation. "The little chap doesn't look as if he would ever stand the Indian climate. What will happen? Will she ever consent to leave him with the Ratcliffes?"

"I am quite certain she won't," Muriel answered, with unfaltering conviction. "She simply lives for him."

"I thought so," Grange said rather sadly. "It would go hard with her if—if—"

Muriel's dark eyes flashed swift entreaty. "Oh, don't say it! Don't think it! I believe it would kill her."

"She is stronger, though?" he questioned almost sharply.

"Yes, yes, much stronger. Only—not strong enough for that. Captain Grange, it simply couldn't happen."

They had reached a gate at the end of the field. Grange stopped before it, and spoke with sudden, deep feeling.

"If it does happen, Muriel," he said, using her Christian name quite unconsciously, "we shall have to stand by her, you and I. You won't leave her, will you? You would be of more use to her than I. Oh, it's—it's damnable to see a woman in trouble and not be able to comfort her."

He brought his ungloved hand down upon the gate-post with a violence that drew blood; then, seeing her face of amazement, thrust it hastily behind him.

"I'm a fool," he said, with his shy, semi-apologetic smile. "Don't mind me, Miss Roscoe. You know, I—I'm awfully fond of Daisy, always was. My people were her people, and when they died we were the only two left, as it were. Of course she was married by that time, and there are some other relations somewhere. But we've always hung together, she and I. You can understand it, can't you?"

Muriel fancied she could, but his vehemence startled her none the less. She had not deemed him capable of such intensity.

"I suppose you feel almost as if she were your sister," she remarked, groping half-unconsciously for an explanation.

Grange was holding the gate open for her. He did not instantly reply.

Then, "I don't exactly know what that feels like," he said, with an odd shame-facedness. "But in so far as that we have been playfellows and chums all our lives, I suppose you might describe it in that way."

And Muriel, though she wondered a little at the laborious honesty of his reply, was satisfied that she understood.

She was drifting into a very pleasant friendship with Blake Grange. He seemed to rely upon her in an indefinable fashion that made their intercourse of necessity one of intimacy. Moreover, Daisy's habits were still more or less those of an invalid, and this fact helped very materially to throw them together.

To Muriel, emerging slowly from the long winter of her sorrow, the growing friendship with this man whom she both liked and admired was as a shaft of sunshine breaking across a grey landscape. Insensibly it was doing her good. The deep shadow of a horror that once had overwhelmed her was lifting gradually away from her life. In her happier moments it almost seemed that she was beginning to forget.

Grange's suggestion that they should ride together awoke in her a keener sense of pleasure than she had known since the tragedy of Wara had darkened her young life, and for the rest of the day she looked forward eagerly to the resumption of this her favourite exercise.

Daisy was delighted with the idea, and when on the following morning Grange ransacked the town for suitable mounts and returned triumphant, she declared gaily that she should take no further trouble for her guest's entertainment. The responsibility from that day forth rested with Muriel.

Muriel was by no means loth to assume it. They got on excellently together, and their almost daily rides became a source of keen pleasure to her. Winter was fast merging into spring, and the magic of the coming season was working in her blood. There were times when a sense of spontaneous happiness would come over her, she knew not wherefore. Jim Ratcliffe no longer looked at her with stern-browed disapproval.

She and Grange both became regular members of Olga's hockey team. They shared most of their pursuits. Among other things she was learning the accompaniments of his songs. Grange had a well-cultivated tenor voice, to which Daisy the restless would listen for any length of time.

Altogether they were a very peaceful trio, and as the weeks slipped on it almost seemed as if the quiet home life they lived were destined to endure indefinitely. Grange spoke occasionally of leaving, but Daisy would never entertain the idea for an instant, and he certainly did not press it very strongly. He was not returning to India before September, and the long summer months that intervened made the date of his departure so remote as to be outside discussion. No one ever thought of it.

But the long, quiet interval in the sleepy little country town, interminable as it might feel, was not destined to last for ever. On a certain afternoon in March, Grange and Muriel, riding home together after a windy gallop across open country, were waylaid outside the doctor's gate by one of the Ratcliffe boys.

The urchin was cheering at the top of his voice and dancing ecstatically in the mud. Olga, equally dishevelled but somewhat more coherent, was seated on the gate-post, her long legs dangling.

"Have you seen Dad? Have you heard?" was her cry. "Jimmy, come out of the road. You'll be kicked."

Both riders pulled up to hear the news, Jimmy squirming away from the horses' legs after a fashion that provoked even the mild-tempered Grange to a sharp reproof.

"You haven't heard?" pursued Olga, ignoring her small brother's escapade as too trifling to notice at such a supreme moment. "But you haven't, of course, if you haven't seen Dad. The letter only came an hour ago. It's Nick, dear old Nick! He's coming home at last!" In her delight over imparting the information Olga nearly toppled over backwards, only saving herself by a violent effort. "Aren't you glad, Muriel? Aren't you glad?" she cried. "I was never so pleased in my life!"

But Muriel had no reply ready. For some reason her animal had become suddenly restive, and occupied the whole of her attention.

It was Grange who after a seconds hesitation asked for further particulars. "What is he coming for? Is it sick leave?"

Olga nodded. "He isn't to stay out there for the hot weather. It's something to do with his wound. He doesn't want to come a bit. But he is to start almost at once. He may be starting now."

"Not likely," put in Jimmy. "The end of March was what he said. Dad said he couldn't be here before the third week in April."

"Oh, well, that isn't long, is it?" said Olga eagerly. "Not when you come to remember that it's three years since he went away. I do think they might have given him the V.C., don't you? Captain Grange, why hasn't he got the V.C.?"

Grange couldn't say, really. He advised her to ask the man himself. He was observing Muriel with some uneasiness, and when she at length abruptly waved her whip and rode sharply on as though her horse were beyond her control, he struck spurs into his own and started in pursuit.

Muriel passed her own gate at a canter, but hearing Grange behind her she soon reined in, and they trotted some distance side by side in silence.

But Grange was still uneasy. The girl's rigid profile had that stony, aloof look that he had noted upon his arrival weeks before, and that he had come to associate with her escape from Wara.

Nevertheless, when she presently addressed him it was in her ordinary tone and upon a subject indifferent to them both. She had received a shock, he knew, but she plainly did not wish him to remark it.

They rode quite soberly back again, and separated at the door.

CHAPTER XXI
A HARBOUR OF REFUGE

To Daisy the news that Grange imparted was more pleasing than startling. "I knew he would come before long if he were a wise man," she said.

But when her cousin wanted to know what she meant, she would not tell him.

"No, I can't, Blake," was her answer. "I once promised Muriel never to speak of it. She is very sensitive on the subject."

Grange did not press for an explanation. It was not his way. He left her moodily, a frown of deep dissatisfaction upon his handsome face. Daisy did not spend much thought upon him. Her interests at that time were almost wholly centred upon her boy who was so backward and delicate that she was continually anxious about him. She was, in fact, so preoccupied that she hardly noticed at dinner that Muriel scarcely spoke and ate next to nothing.

Grange remarked both facts, and his moodiness increased. When Daisy went up to the nursery, he at once followed Muriel into the drawing-room. She was standing by the window when he entered, a slim, straight figure in unrelieved black; but though she must have heard him, she neither spoke nor turned her head.

Grange closed the door and came softly forward. There was an unwonted air of resolution about him that made him look almost grim. He reached her side and stood there silently. The wind had fallen, and the sky was starry.

After a brief silence Muriel dropped the blind and looked at him. There was something of interrogation in her glance.

"Shall we go into the garden?" she suggested. "It is so warm."

He fell in at once with the proposal. "You will want a cloak," he said. "Can I fetch you one?"

"Oh, thanks! Anything will do. I believe there's one of Daisy's in the hall."

She moved across the room quickly, as one impatient to escape from a confined space. Grange followed her. He was not smoking as usual. They went out together into the warm darkness, and passed side by side down the narrow path that wound between the bare flower-beds. It was a wonderful night. Once as they walked there drifted across them a sudden fragrance of violets.

They reached at length a rustic gate that led into the doctor's meadow, and here with one consent they stopped. Very far away a faint wind was stirring, but close at hand there was no sound. Again, from the wet earth by the gate, there rose the magic scent of violets.

Muriel rested her clasped hands upon the gate, and spoke in a voice unconsciously hushed.

"I never realised how much I liked this place before," she said. "Isn't it odd? I have been actually happy here—and I didn't know it."

"You are not happy to-night," said Grange.

She did not attempt to contradict him. "I think I am rather tired," she said.

"I don't think that is quite all," he returned, with quiet conviction.

She moved, turning slightly towards him; but she said nothing, though he obviously waited for some response.

For awhile he was discouraged, and silence fell again upon them. Then at length he braced himself for an effort. For all his shyness he was not without a certain strength.

"Miss Roscoe," he said, "do you remember how you once promised that you would always regard me as a friend?"

She turned fully towards him then, and he saw her face dimly in the starlight. He thought she looked very pale.

"I do," she said simply.

In a second his diffidence fell away from him. He realised that the ground on which he stood was firm. He bent towards her.

"I want you to keep that promise of yours in its fullest sense to-night, Muriel," he said, and his soft voice had in it almost a caressing note. "I want you—if you will—to tell me what is the matter."

Muriel stood before him with her face upturned. He could not read her expression, but he knew by her attitude that she had no thought of repelling him.

"What is it?" he urged gently. "Won't you tell me?"

"Don't you know?" she asked him slowly.

"I only know that what we heard this afternoon upset you," he answered. "And I don't understand it. I am asking you to explain."

"You will only think me very foolish and absurd."

There was a deep quiver in the words, and he knew that she was trembling. Very kindly he laid his hand upon her shoulder.

"Can't you trust me better than that?" he asked.

She did not answer him. Her breathing became suddenly sharp and irregular, and he realised that she was battling for self-control.

"I don't know if I can make you understand," she said at last. "But I will try."

"Yes, try!" he said gently. "You won't find it so very difficult."

She turned back to the gate, and leaned wearily upon it.

"You are very kind. You always have been. I couldn't tell any one else—not even Daisy. You see, she is—his friend. But you are different. I don't think you like him, do you?"

Grange hesitated a little. "I won't go so far as to say that," he said finally. "We get on all right. I was never very intimate with the fellow. I think he is a bit callous."

"Callous!" Muriel gave a sudden hard shudder. "He is much worse than callous. He is hideously, almost devilishly cruel. But—but—he isn't only that. Blake, do you think he is quite human? He is so horribly, so unnaturally strong."

Grange heard the scared note in her voice, and drew very close to her. "I think," he said quietly, "that—without knowing it—you exaggerate both his cruelty and his strength. I know he is a queer chap. I once heard it said of him that he has the eyes of a snake-charmer, and I believe it more or less. But I assure you he is human—quite human. And"—he spoke with unwonted emphasis—"he has no more power over you—not an inch—than you choose to give him."

Muriel uttered a faint sigh. "I knew I should never make you understand."

Grange was silent. He might have retorted that she had given him very little information to go upon, but he forebore. There was an almost colossal patience about this man. His silence had in it nothing of resentment.

After a few seconds Muriel went on, her voice very low. "I would give anything—all I have—not to meet him when he comes back. But I don't know how to get away from him. He is sure to seek me out. And I—I am only a girl. I can't prevent it."

Again there sounded that piteous quiver in her words. It was like the cry of a lost child. Grange heard it, and clenched his hands, but he did not speak. He was gazing straight ahead, stern-eyed and still.

Muriel scarcely noticed his attitude. Having at length broken through her barrier of reserve, she found a certain relief in speech.

"I might go away, of course," she said. "I expect I shall do that, for I don't think I could endure it here. But I haven't many friends. My year in India seemed to cut me off from every one. It's a little difficult to know where to go. And then, too, there is Daisy."

She paused, and suddenly Grange spoke, with more abruptness than was his wont.

"Why do you think he is sure to seek you out? Did he ever say so?"

She shivered. "No, he never said so. But—but—in a way I feel it. He is so merciless. He always makes me think of an eagle swooping down on its prey. No doubt you think me very fanciful and ridiculous. Perhaps I am. But once—in the mountains—he told me that I belonged to him—that he would not let me go, and—and—I have never been able to forget it."

Her voice sank, and it seemed to Grange that she was crying in the darkness. Her utter forlornness pierced him to the heart. He leaned towards her, trying ineffectually to see her face.

"My dear little girl," he said gently, "don't be so distressed. He deserves to be kicked for frightening you like this."

"It's my own fault," she whispered back. "If I were stronger, or if Daddy were with me—it would be different. But I am all alone. There is no one to help me. I used to think it didn't matter what happened to me, but I am beginning to feel it does."

"Of course it does," Grange said. His hand felt along the rail for hers, and, finding them, held them closely. Her weakness gave him confidence. "Poor child!" he murmured softly. "Poor little girl! You do want some one to take care of you."

Muriel mastered herself with an effort. It was not often now that she gave way so completely.

"It's only now and then," she said. "It's better than it used to be. Only somehow I got frightened when I heard that Nick was coming. I daresay—when I begin to get used to the idea—I shan't mind it quite so much. Never mind about my silly worries any more. No doubt I shall get wiser as I grow older."

She tried to laugh with the words, but somehow no laugh came. Grange's great hand closed very tightly upon hers, and she looked up in surprise.

Almost instantly he began to speak, very humbly, but also very resolutely. "Muriel," he said, "I'm an unutterable fool at expressing things. I can only say them straight out and hope for the best. You want a protector, don't you? And I—should like to be the one to protect you if—if it were ever possible for you to think of me in that light."

He spoke with immense effort. He was afraid of scaring her, afraid of hurting her desolate young heart, afraid almost of the very impulse that moved him to speak.

Absolute silence reigned when he ended.

Muriel had become suddenly rigid, and so still that she did not seem to breathe. For several seconds he waited, but still she made no sign. He had not the remotest clue to guide him. He began to feel as if a door had unexpectedly closed against him, not violently, but steadily, soundlessly, barring him out.

It was but a fleeting impression. In a few moments more it was gone. She drew a long quivering breath, and turned slightly towards him.

"I would rather trust myself to you," she said, "than to any one else in the world."

She spoke in her deep, sincere voice which gave him no doubt that she meant what she said, and at once his own trepidation departed. He put his arm around her, and pressed her close to him.

"Come to me then," he said very tenderly. "And I will take such care of you, Muriel, that no one shall ever frighten you again."

She yielded to his touch as simply as a child, leaning her head against him with a little, weary gesture of complete confidence. She was desperately tired of standing alone.

"I know I shall be safe with you," she whispered.

"Quite safe, dear," he answered gravely. He paused a moment as though irresolute; then, still holding her closely, he bent and kissed her forehead.

He did it very quietly and reverently, but at the action she started, almost shrank. One of those swift flashes of memory came suddenly upon her, and as in a vision she beheld another face bending over her—a yellow, wrinkled face of terrible emaciation, with eyes of flickering fire—eyes that never slept—and heard a voice, curiously broken and incoherent that seemed to pray. She could not catch the words it uttered.

The old wild panic rushed over her, the old frenzied longing to escape. With a sobbing gasp she turned in Grange's arms, and clung to him.

"Oh, Captain Grange," she panted piteously, "promise—promise you will never let me go!"

Her agitation surprised him, but it awaked in him a responsive tenderness that compassed her with a strength bred rather of emergency than habit.

"My little girl, I swear I will never let you go," he said, with grave assurance. "You are quite safe now. No one shall ever take you from me."

And it was to Muriel as if, after long and futile battling in the open sea, she had drifted at last into the calm heaven which surely had always been the goal of her desires.

CHAPTER XXII
AN OLD STORY

Jim Ratcliffe was in the drawing-room with Daisy when they returned. He scrutinised them both somewhat sharply as they came in, but he made no comment upon their preference for the garden. Very soon he rose to take his leave.

Grange accompanied him to the door, and Muriel, suddenly possessed by an overwhelming sense of shyness, bent over Daisy and murmured a hasty goodnight.

Daisy looked at her for a moment. "Tired, dear?"

"A little," Muriel admitted.

"I hope you haven't been catching cold—you and Blake," Daisy said, as she kissed her.

Muriel assured her to the contrary, and hastened to make her escape. In the hall she came face to face with Blake. He met her with a smile.

"What! Going up already?"

She nodded. Her face was burning. For an instant her hand lay in his.

"You tell Daisy," she whispered, and fled upstairs like a scared bird.

Grange stood till she was out of sight; then turned aside to the drawing-room, the smile wholly gone from his face.

Daisy, from her seat before the fire, looked up with her gay laugh. "I'm sure there is a secret brewing between you two," she declared. "I can feel it in my bones."

Grange closed the door carefully. There was a queer look on his face, almost an apprehensive look. He took up his stand on the hearthrug before he spoke.

"You are not far wrong, Daisy," he said then.

She answered him lightly as ever. "I never am, my dear Blake. Surely you must have noticed it. Well, am I to be let into the plot, or not?"

He looked at her for a moment uneasily. "Of course we shall tell you," he said. "It—it's not a thing we could very well keep to ourselves for any length of time."

A sudden gleam of understanding flashed into Daisy's upturned face, and instantly her expression changed. With a swift, vehement movement she sprang up and stood before him.

"Blake!" she exclaimed, and in her voice astonishment, dismay, and even reproach were mingled.

He averted his eyes from hers. "Won't you congratulate me, Daisy?" he said, speaking almost under his breath.

Daisy had turned very white. She put out both hands, and leaned upon the mantelpiece.

"But, my dear Blake," she said, after a moment, "she is not for you."

"What do you mean?" Grange's jaw suddenly set itself. He squared his great shoulders as if instinctively bracing himself to meet opposition.

"I mean"—Daisy spoke very quietly and emphatically—"I mean, Blake, that she is Nick's property. She belonged to Nick before ever you thought of wanting her. I never dreamed that you would do anything so shabby as to step in at the last moment, just when

Nick is coming home, and cut him out. How could you do such a thing, Blake? But surely it isn't irrevocable? You can't have said anything definite?"

Grange's face had become very stern. He no longer avoided her eyes. For once he was really angry, and showed it.

"You make a mistake," he told her curtly. "I have done nothing whatever of which I am ashamed, or of which any man could be ashamed. Certainly I have taken a definite step. I have proposed to her, and she has accepted me. With regard to Nick Ratcliffe, I believe myself that the fellow is something of a blackguard, but in any case she both fears and hates him. He can have no shadow of a right over her."

"You forget that he saved her life," said Daisy.

"Is she to hold herself at his disposal on that account? I must say I fail to see the obligation."

There was even a hint of scorn in Grange's tone. At sound of it, Daisy turned round and laid her hand winningly upon his arm.

"Dear old boy," she said gently, "don't be angry. I'm not against you."

He softened instantly. It was not in him to harbour resentment against a woman. He took her hand, and heaved a deep sigh.

"No, Daisy," he said half sadly, "you mustn't be against me. I always count on you."

Daisy laughed a little wistfully. "Always did, dear, didn't you? Well, tell me some more. What made you propose all of a sudden like this? Are you—very much in love?"

He looked at her. "Perhaps not quite as we used to understand the term," he said, seeming to speak half-reluctantly.

"Oh, we were very extravagant and foolish," rejoined Daisy lightly. "I didn't mean quite in that way, Blake. You at least are past the age for such feathery nonsense, or should be. I was—aeons and aeons ago."

"Were you?" he said, and still he looked at her half in wonder, it seemed, and half in regret.

Daisy nodded at him briskly. The colour had come back to her face. "Yes, I have arrived at years of discretion," she assured him. "And I quite agree with Solomon that childhood and youth are vanity. But now let us talk about this. Is she in love with you, I wonder? I must be remarkably blind not to have seen it. How in the world I shall ever face Nick again, I can't imagine."

Grange frowned. "I'm getting a bit tired of Nick," he said moodily. "He crops up everywhere."

Daisy's face flushed. "Don't you ever again say a word against him in my hearing," she said. "For I won't bear it. He may not be handsome like you; but for all that, he's about the finest man I know."

"Good heavens!" said Blake. "As much as that!"

She nodded vehemently. "Yes, quite as much. And he loves her, too, loves her with his whole soul. Perhaps you never knew that they would have been married long ago in Simla if Muriel hadn't overheard some malicious gossip and thrown him over. How in the world she made him let her go I never knew, but she did it, though I believe it nearly broke his heart. He came to me afterwards and begged me to keep her with me as long as I could, and take care of her."

"All this," broke in Grange, "is what you promised never to speak of?"

"Yes," she admitted recklessly. "But it is what you ought to know—what you must know—before you go any further."

"It will make no difference to me," he observed. "It is quite obvious that she never cared for him in the smallest degree. Why, my dear girl, she hates the man!"

Daisy gave vent to a sigh of exasperation. "When you come to talk about women's feelings, Blake, you make me tired. You will never be anything but a great big booby in that respect as long as you live."

Grange became silent. He never argued with Daisy. She had always had the upper hand. He watched her as she sat down again, her pretty face in the glow of the fire; but though fully aware of the fact, she would not look at him.

"She is a dear girl, and you are not half good enough for her," she said, stooping a little to the blaze.

"I know that," he answered bluntly. "I wasn't good enough for you, either, but you would have had me—once."

She made a dainty gesture with one shoulder. "That also was aeons ago. Why disturb that poor old skeleton?"

He did not answer, but he continued to watch her steadily with eyes that held an expression of dumb faithfulness—like the eyes of a dog.

Daisy was softly and meditatively poking the fire. "If you marry her, Blake," she said, "you will have to be enormously good to her. She isn't the sort of girl to be satisfied with anything but the best."

"I should do my utmost to make her happy," he answered.

She glanced up momentarily. "I wonder if you would succeed," she murmured.

For a single instant their eyes met. Daisy's fell away at once, and the firelight showed a swift deepening of colour on her face.

As for Blake, he stood quite stiff for a few seconds, then with an abruptness of movement unusual with him, he knelt suddenly down beside her.

"Daisy," he said, and his voice sounded strained, almost hoarse, "you're not vexed about it? You don't mind my marrying? It isn't—you know—it isn't—as if—"

He broke off, for Daisy had jerked upright as if at the piercing of a nerve. She looked at him fully, with blazing eyes. "How can you be so ridiculous, Blake?" she exclaimed, with sharp impatience. "That was all over and done with long, long ago, and you know it. Besides, even if it hadn't been, I'm not a dog in the manger. Surely you know that too. Oh, go away, and don't be absurd!"

She put her hand against his shoulder, and gave him a small but vehement push.

He stood up again immediately, but he did not look hurt, and the expression of loyalty in his eyes never wavered.

There was a short pause before Daisy spoke again.

"Well," she said, with a brief sigh, "I suppose it's no good crying over spilt milk, but I wish you had chosen any girl in the world but Muriel, Blake; I do indeed. You will have to write to Sir Reginald Bassett. He is her guardian, subject to his wife's management. Perhaps she will approve of you. She hated Nick for some reason."

"I don't see how they can object," Grange said, in the moody tone he always used when perplexed.

"No," said Daisy. "Nor did Nick. But Lady Bassett managed to put a spoke in his wheel notwithstanding. Still, if Muriel wants to marry you—or thinks she does—she will probably take her own way. And possibly regret it afterwards."

"You think I shall not make her happy?" said Grange.

Daisy hesitated a little. "I think," she said slowly, "that you are not the man for her. However,"—she rose with another shrug—"I may be wrong. In any case you have gone too far for me to meddle. I can't help either of you now. You must just do what you think best." She held out her hand. "I must go up now. Baby is restless to-night, and may want me. Good-night."

Blake stooped, and carried her hand softly and suddenly to his lips. He seemed for an instant on the verge of saying something, but no words came. There was a faint, half-mocking smile on Daisy's face as she turned away. But she was silent also. It seemed that they understood each other.

CHAPTER XXIII
THE SLEEP CALLED DEATH

It was an unspeakable relief to Muriel that, in congratulating her upon her engagement, Daisy made no reference to Nick. She did not know that this forbearance had been dictated long before by Nick himself.

The days that followed her engagement had in them a sort of rapture that she had never known before. She felt as a young wild creature suddenly escaped from the iron jaws of a trap in which it had long languished, and she rioted in the sense of liberty that was hers. Her youth was coming back to her in leaps and bounds with the advancing spring.

She missed nothing in Blake's courtship. His gentleness had always attracted her, and the intimacy that had been growing up between them made their intercourse always easy and pleasant. They never spoke of Nick. But ever in Muriel's heart there lay the soothing knowledge that she had nothing more to fear. Her terrible, single-handed contests against overwhelming odds were over, and she was safe. She was convinced that, whatever happened, Blake would take care of her. Was he not the protector she would have chosen from the beginning, could she but have had her way?

So, placidly and happily, the days drifted by, till March was nearly gone; and then, sudden and staggering as a shell from a masked battery, there fell the blow that was destined to end that peaceful time.

Very late one night there came a nervous knocking at Muriel's door, and springing up from her bed she came face to face with Daisy's *ayah*. The woman was grey with fright, and babbling incoherently. Something about "baba" and the "mem-sahib" Muriel caught and instantly guessed that the baby had been taken ill. She flung a wrap round her, and hastened to the nursery.

It was a small room opening out of Daisy's bedroom. The light was turned on full, and here Daisy herself was walking up and down with the baby in her arms.

Before Muriel was well in the room, she stopped and spoke. Her face was ghastly pale, and she could not raise her voice above a whisper, though she made repeated efforts. "Go to Blake!" she panted. "Go quickly! Tell him to fetch Jim Ratcliffe. Quick! Quick!"

Muriel flew to do her bidding. In her anxiety she scarcely waited to knock at Blake's door, but burst in upon him headlong. The room was in total darkness, but he awoke instantly.

"Hullo! What is it? That you, Muriel?"

"Oh, Blake!" she gasped. "The child's ill. We want the doctor."

He was up in a moment. She heard him groping for matches, but he only succeeded in knocking something over.

"Can't you find them?" she asked. "Wait! I'll get you a light."

She ran back to her own room and fetched a candle. Her hands were shaking so that she could scarcely light it. Returning, she found Grange putting on his clothes in the darkness. He was fully as flurried as she.

As she set down the candle there arose a sudden awful sound in Daisy's room.

Muriel stood still. "Oh, what is that?"

Grange paused in the act of dragging on his coat. "It's that damned *ayah*," he said savagely.

And in a second Muriel understood. Daisy's *ayah* was wailing for the dead.

She put her hands over her ears. The dreadful cry seemed to pierce right through to her very soul. Then she remembered Daisy, and turned to go to her.

Out in the passage she met the white-faced English servants huddling together and whispering. One of them was sobbing hysterically. She passed them swiftly by.

Back in Daisy's room she found the *ayah* crouched on the floor, and rocking herself to and fro while she beat her breast and wailed. The door that led into the nursery was closed.

Muriel advanced fiercely upon the woman. She almost felt as if she could have choked her. She seized her by the shoulders without ceremony. The *ayah* ceased her wailing for a moment, then recommenced in a lower key. Muriel pulled her to her feet, half-dragged, half-led her to her own room, thrust her within, and locked the door upon her. Then she returned to Daisy.

She found her sunk in a rocking-chair before the waning fire, softly swaying to and fro with the baby on her breast. She looked at Muriel entering, with a set, still face.

"Has Blake gone?" she asked, still in that dry, powerless whisper.

Muriel moved to her side, and knelt down. "He is just going," she began to say, but the words froze on her lips.

She remained motionless for a long second, gazing at the tiny, waxen face on Daisy's breast. And for that second her heart stood still; for she knew that the baby was dead.

From the closed room across the passage came the muffled sound of the *ayah's* wailing. Daisy made a slight impatient movement.

"Stir the fire," she whispered. "He feels so cold."

But Muriel did not move to obey. Instead she held out her arms.

"Let me take him, dear," she begged tremulously. Daisy shook her head with a jealous tightening of her clasp. "He has been so ill, poor wee darling," she whispered. "It came on so suddenly. There was no time to do anything. But he is easier now. I think he is asleep. We won't disturb him."

Muriel said no more. She rose and blindly poked the fire. Then—for the sight of Daisy rocking her dead child with that set, ashen face was more than she could bear—she turned and stole away, softly closing the door behind her.

Again meeting the English servants hovering outside, she sent them downstairs to light the kitchen fire, going herself to the dining-room window to watch for the doctor. Her feet were bare and freezing, but she would not return to her room for slippers. She felt she could not endure that awful wailing at close quarters again. Even as it was, she heard it fitfully; but from the nursery there came no sound.

She wondered if Blake had gone across the meadow to the doctor's house—it was undoubtedly the shortest cut—and tried to calculate how long it would take him.

The waiting was intolerable. She bore it with a desperate endurance. She could not rid herself of the feeling that somehow Nick was near her. She almost expected to see him come lightly in and stand beside her. Once or twice she turned shivering to assure herself that she was really alone.

There came at last the click of the garden-gate. They had come across the drenched meadows. In a transient gleam of moonlight she saw the two figures striding towards her. Grange stopped a moment to fasten the gate. The doctor came straight on.

She ran to the front door and threw it open. The wind blew swirling all about her, but she never felt it, though her very lips were numb and cold.

"It's too late!" she gasped, as he entered. "It's too late!"

Jim Ratcliffe took her by the shoulders and forced her away from the open door.

"Go and put something on," he ordered, "instantly!"

There was no resisting the mastery of his tone. She responded to it instinctively, hardly knowing what she did.

The *ayah's* paroxysm of grief had sunk to a low moaning when she re-entered her room. It sounded like a dumb creature in pain. Hastily she dressed, and twisted up her hair with fingers that she strove in vain to steady.

Then noiselessly she crept back to the nursery.

Daisy was still rocking softly to and fro before the ore, her piteous burden yet clasped against her heart. The doctor was stooping over her, and Muriel saw the half-eager, half-suspicious look in Daisy's eyes as she watched him. She was telling him in rapid whispers what had happened.

He listened to her very quietly, his keen eyes fixed unblinking upon the baby's face. When she ended, he stooped a little lower, his hand upon her arm.

"Let me take him," he said.

Muriel trembled for the answer, remembering the instant refusal with which her own offer had been met. But Daisy made no sort of protest. She seemed to yield mechanically.

Only, as he lifted the tiny body from her breast, a startled, almost a bereft look crossed her face, and she whispered quickly, "You won't let him cry?"

Jim Ratcliffe was silent a moment while he gazed intently at the little lifeless form he held. Then very gently, very pitifully, but withal very steadily, his verdict fell through the silent room.

"He will never cry any more."

Daisy was on her feet in a moment, the agony in her eyes terrible to see. "Jim! Jim!" she gasped, in a strangled voice. "He isn't dead! My little darling,—my baby,—the light of my eyes; tell me—he isn't—dead!"

She bent hungrily over the burden he held, and then gazed wildly into his face. She was shaking as one in an ague.

Quietly he drew the head-covering over the baby's face. "My dear," he said, "there is no death."

The words were few, spoken almost in an undertone; but they sent a curious, tingling thrill through Muriel—a thrill that seemed to reach her heart. For the first time, unaccountably, wholly intangibly, she was aware of a strong resemblance between this man whom she honoured and the man she feared. She almost felt as if Nick himself had uttered the words.

Standing dumbly by the door, she saw the doctor stoop to lay the poor little body down in the cot, saw Daisy's face of anguish, and the sudden, wide-flung spread of her empty arms.

The next moment, her woman's instinct prompting her, she sprang forward; and it was she who caught the stricken mother as she fell.

CHAPTER XXIV
THE CREED OF A FIGHTER

It was growing very hot in the plains. A faint breeze born at sunset had died away long ago, leaving a wonderful, breathless stillness behind. The man who sat at work on his verandah with his shirt-sleeves turned up above his elbows sighed heavily from time to time as if he felt some oppression in the atmosphere. He was quite a young man, fair-skinned and clean-shaven, with an almost pathetically boyish look about him, a wistful expression as of one whose youth still endured though the zest thereof was denied to him. His eyes were weary and bloodshot, but he worked on steadily, indefatigably, never raising them from the paper under his hand.

Even when a step sounded in the room behind him, he scarcely looked up. "One moment, old chap!" He was still working rapidly as he spoke. "I've a toughish bit to get through. I'll talk to you in a minute."

There was no immediate reply. A man's figure, dressed in white linen, with one arm quite invisible under the coat, stood halting for a moment in the doorway, then moved out and slowly approached the table at which the other sat.

The lamplight, gleaming upwards, revealed a yellow face of many wrinkles, and curious, glancing eyes that shone like fireflies in the gloom.

He stopped beside the man who worked. "All right," he said. "Finish what you are doing."

In the silence that followed he seemed to watch the hand that moved over the paper with an absorbing interest. The instant it rested he spoke.

"Done?"

The man in the chair stretched out his arms with a long gesture of weariness; then abruptly leapt to his feet.

"What am I thinking of, keeping you standing here? Sit down, Nick! Yes, I've done for the present. What a restless beggar you are! Why couldn't you lie still for a spell?"

Nick grimaced. "It's an accomplishment I have never been able to acquire. Besides, there's no occasion for it now. If I were going to die, it would be a different thing, and even then I think I'd rather die standing. How are you getting on, my son? What mean these hieroglyphics?"

He dropped into the empty chair and pored over the paper.

"Oh, you wouldn't understand if I told you," the other answered. "You're not an engineer."

"Not even a greaser of wheels." admitted Nick modestly. "But you needn't throw it in my teeth. I suppose you are going to make your fortune soon and retire—you and Daisy and the imp—to a respectable suburb. You're a very lucky chap, Will."

"Think so?" said Will.

He was bending a little over his work. His tone sounded either absent or dubious.

Nick glanced at him, and suddenly swept his free right hand across the table. "Put it away!" he said. "You're overdoing it. Get the wretched stuff out of your head for a bit, and let's have a smoke before dinner. I'll bring her out to you next winter. See if I don't!"

Will turned towards him impulsively. "Oh, man, if you only could!"

"Only could!" echoed Nick. "I tell you I will. Ten quid on it if you like. Is it done?"

But Will shook his head with a queer, unsteady smile. "No, it isn't. But come along and smoke, or you will be having that infernal neuralgia again. It was confoundedly good of you to look me up like this when you weren't fit for it."

Nick laughed aloud. "Man alive! You don't suppose I did it for your sake, do you? Don't you know I wanted to break the journey to the coast?"

"Odd place to choose!" commented Will.

Nick arose in his own peculiarly abrupt fashion, and thrust his hand through his friend's arm.

"Perhaps I thought a couple of days of your society would cheer me up," he observed lightly. "I daresay that seems odd too."

Will laughed in spite of himself. "Well, you've seen me with my nose to the grindstone anyhow. You can tell Daisy I'm working like a troop-horse for her and the boy! Jove! What a knowing little beggar that youngster used to be! He isn't very strong though, Daisy writes."

"How often do you hear?" asked Nick.

"Oh, the last letter came three weeks ago. They were all well then, but she didn't stop to say much because Grange was there. He is staying with them, you know."

"You haven't heard since then?" There was just a hint of indignation in Nick's query.

Will shook his head. "No. She's a bad correspondent, always was. I write by every mail, and of course, if there were anything I ought to know, she would write too. But they are leading a fairly humdrum existence just now. She can't have much to tell me."

Nick changed the subject. "How long has Grange been there?"

"I don't know. Some time, I think. But I really don't know. They are very old pals, you know, he and Daisy. There was a bit of a romance between them, I believe, years ago, when she was in her teens. Their people wouldn't hear of it because they were first cousins, so it fizzled out. But they are still great friends. A good sort of fellow, I always thought."

"Too soft for me," said Nick. "He's like a well-built ship adrift without a rudder. He's all manners and no grit—the sort of chap who wants to be pushed before he can do anything. I often ached to kick him when we were boxed up at Wara."

Will smiled. "The only drawback to indulging in that kind of game is that you may get kicked back, and a kick from a giant like Grange would be no joke."

Nick looked supremely contemptuous. "Fellows like Grange don't kick. They don't know how. That's why I had to leave him alone."

He turned into Will's sitting-room and stretched himself out upon an ancient *charpoy* furnished with many ancient cushions that stood by the window.

Will gave him a cigarette, and lighted it. "I wonder how many nights I have spent on that old shake-down," he remarked, as he did it.

Nick glanced upwards. "Last year?"

Will nodded. "It was like hell," he said, with terrible simplicity. "I came straight back here, you know, after Daisy left Simla. I suppose the contrast made it worse. Then, too, the sub was ill, and it meant double work. Well," with another sigh, "we pulled through somehow, and I suppose we shall again. But, Nick, Daisy couldn't possibly stand this place more than four months out of the twelve. And as for the kiddie—"

Nick removed his cigarette to yawn.

"You won't be here all your life, my son," he said. "You're a rising man, remember. There's no sense in grizzling, anyhow, and you're getting round-shouldered. Why don't you do some gymnastics? You've got a swimming bath. Go and do a quarter of a mile breaststroke every day. Jupiter! What wouldn't I give to"—He broke off abruptly. "Well, I'm not going to cry for the moon either. There's the *khit* on the verandah. What does he want?"

Will went out to see. Nick, idly watching, saw the native hand him something on a salver which Will took to the lamp by which he had been working. Dead silence ensued. From far away there came the haunting cry of a jackal, but near at hand there was no sound. A great stillness hung upon all things.

To Nick, lying at full length upon the cushions, there presently came the faint sound of paper crackling, and a moment later his friend's voice, pitched very low, spoke to the waiting servant. He heard the man softly retire, and again an intense stillness reigned.

He could not see Will from where he lay, and he smoked on placidly for nearly five minutes in the belief that he was either answering some communication or looking over his work. Then at last, growing impatient of the prolonged silence, he lifted his voice without moving.

"What in the world are you doing, you unsociable beggar? Can't you tear yourself away from that beastly work for one night even? Come in here and entertain me. You won't have the chance to-morrow."

There was no reply. Only from far away there came again the weird yell of a jackal. For a few seconds more Nick lay frowning. Then swiftly and quietly he arose, and stepped to the window.

There he stopped dead as if in sudden irresolution; for Will was sunk upon his knees by the table with his head upon his work and his arms flung out with clenched hands in an attitude of the most utter, the most anguished despair. He made no sound of any sort; only, as Nick watched, his bowed shoulders heaved once convulsively.

It was only for a moment that Nick stood hesitating. The next, obeying an impulse that he never stopped to question, he moved straight forward to Will's side; and then saw—what he had not at first seen—a piece of paper crumpled and gripped in one of his hands.

He bent over him and spoke rapidly, but without agitation. "Hullo, old boy! What is it! Bad news, eh?"

Will started and groaned, then sharply turned his face upwards. It was haggard and drawn and ghastly, but even then its boyishness remained.

He spoke at once, replying to Nick in short, staccato tones. "I've had a message—just come through. It's the kiddie—our little chap—he died—last night."

Nick heard the news in silence. After a moment he stooped forward and took the paper out of Will's hand, thrusting it away without a glance into his own pocket. Then he took him by the arm and hoisted him up. "Come inside!" he said briefly.

Will went with him blindly, too stricken to direct his own movements.

And so he presently found himself crouching forward in a chair staring at Nick's steady hand mixing whiskey and water in a glass at his elbow. As Nick held it towards him he burst into sudden, wild speech.

"I've lost her!" he exclaimed harshly. "I've lost her! It was only the kiddie that bound us together. She never cared a half-penny about me. I always knew I should never hold her unless we had a child. And now—and now—"

"Easy!" said Nick. "Easy! Just drink this like a good chap. There's no sense in letting yourself go."

Will drank submissively, and covered his face. "Oh, man," he whispered brokenly, "you don't know what it is to be despised by the one being in the world you worship."

Nick said nothing. His lips twitched a little, that was all.

But when several miserable seconds had dragged away and Will had not moved, he bent suddenly down and put his arm round the huddled shoulders. "Keep a stiff upper lip, old chap," he urged gently. "Don't knock under. She'll be coming to you for comfort presently."

"Not she!" groaned Will. "I shall never get near her again. She'll never come back to me. I know. I know."

"Don't be a fool!" said Nick still gently. "You don't know. Of course she will come back to you. If you stick to her, she'll stick to you."

Will made a choked sound of dissent. Nevertheless, after a moment he raised his quivering face, and gripped hard the hand that pressed his shoulder. "Thanks, dear fellow! You're awfully good. Forgive me for making an ass of myself. I—I was awfully fond of the little nipper too. Poor Daisy! She'll be frightfully cut up." He broke off, biting his lips.

"Do you know," he said presently in a strained whisper, "I've wanted her sometimes—so horribly, that—that I've even been fool enough to pray about it."

He glanced up as he made this confidence, half expecting to read ridicule on the alert face above him, but the expression it wore surprised him. It was almost a fighting look, and wholly free from contempt.

Nick seated himself on the edge of the table, and smote him on the shoulder. "My dear chap," he said, with a sudden burst of energy, "you're only at the beginning of things. It isn't just praying now and then that does it. You've got to keep up the steam, never slack for an instant, whatever happens. The harder going it is, the more likely you are to win through if you stick to it. But directly you slack, you lose ground. If you've only got the grit to go on praying, praying hard, even against your own convictions, you'll get it sooner or later. You are bound to get it. They say God doesn't always grant prayer because the thing you want may not do you any good. That's gammon—futile gammon. If you want it hard enough, and keep on clamouring for it, it becomes the very thing of all others you need—the great essential. And you'll get it for that very reason. It's sheer pluck that counts, nothing else—the pluck to go on fighting when you know perfectly well you're beaten, the pluck to hang on and worry, worry, worry, till you get your heart's desire."

He sprang up with a wide-flung gesture. "I'm doing it myself," he said, and his voice rang with a certain grim elation. "I'm doing it myself. And God knows I sha'n't give Him any peace till I'm satisfied. I may be small, but if I were no bigger than a mosquito, I'd keep on buzzing."

He walked to the end of the room, stood for a second, and came slowly back.

Will was looking at him oddly, almost as if he had never seen him before.

"Do you know," he said, smiling faintly, "I always thought you were a rotter."

"Most people do," said Nick. "I believe it's my physiognomy that's at fault. What can any one expect from a fellow with a face like an Egyptian mummy? Why, I've been mistaken for the devil himself before now." He spoke with a semi-whimsical ruefulness, and, having spoken, he went to the window and stood there with his face to the darkness.

"Hear that jackal, Will?" he suddenly said. "The brute is hungry. You bet, he won't go empty away."

"Jackals never do," said Will, with his weary sigh.

Nick turned round. "It shows what faithless fools we are," he said.

In the silence that followed, there came again to them, clear through the stillness, and haunting in its persistence, the crying of the beast that sought its meat from God.

CHAPTER XXV
A SCENTED LETTER

There is no exhaustion more complete or more compelling than the exhaustion of grief, and it is the most restless temperaments that usually suffer from it the most keenly. It is those who have watched constantly, tirelessly, selflessly, for weeks or even months, for whom the final breakdown is the most utter and the most heartrending.

To Daisy, lying silent in her darkened room, the sudden ending of the prolonged strain, the cessation of the anxiety that had become a part of her very being, was more intolerable than the sense of desolation itself. It lay upon her like a physical, crushing weight, this absence of care, numbing all her faculties. She felt that the worst had happened to her, the ultimate blow had fallen, and she cared for nought besides.

In those first days of her grief she saw none but Muriel and the doctor. Jim Ratcliffe was more uneasy about her than he would admit. He knew as no one else knew what the strain had been upon the over-sensitive nerves, and how terribly the shock had wrenched them. He also knew that her heart was still in a very unsatisfactory state, and for many hours he dreaded collapse.

He was inclined to be uneasy upon Muriel's account as well, at first, but she took him completely by surprise. Without a question, without a word, simply as a matter of course, she assumed the position of nurse and constant companion to her friend. Her resolution and steady self-control astonished him, but he soon saw that these were qualities upon which he could firmly rely. She had put her own weakness behind her, and in face of Daisy's utter need she had found strength.

He suffered her to have her way, seeing how close was the bond of sympathy between them, and realising that the very fact of supporting Daisy would be her own support.

"You are as steady-going as a professional," he told her once.

To which she answered with her sad smile, "I served my probation in the school of sorrow last year. I am only able to help her because I know what it is to sit in ashes."

He patted her shoulder and called her a good girl. He was growing very fond of her, and in his blunt, unflattering way he let her know it.

Certain it was that in those terrible days following her bereavement, Daisy clung to her as she had never before clung to any one, scarcely speaking to her, but mutely leaning upon her steadfast strength.

Muriel saw but little of Blake though he was never far away. He wandered miserably about the house and garden, smoking endless cigarettes, and invariably asking her with a piteous, dog-like wistfulness whenever they met if there were nothing that he could do. There never was anything, but she had not the heart to tell him so, and she used to invent errands for him to make him happier. She herself did not go beyond the garden for many days.

One evening, about three weeks after her baby's death, Daisy heard his step on the gravel below her window and roused herself a little.

"Who is taking care of Blake?" she asked.

Muriel glanced down from where she sat at the great listless figure nearing the house. "I think he is taking care of himself," she said.

"All alone?" said Daisy.

"Yes, dear."

Daisy uttered a sudden hard sigh. "You mustn't spend all your time with me any longer," she said. "I have been very selfish. I forgot. Go down to him, Muriel."

Muriel looked up, struck by something incomprehensible in her tone. "You know I like to be with you," she said. "And of course he understands."

But Daisy would not be satisfied. "That may be. But—but—I want you to go to him. He is lonely, poor boy. I can hear it in his step. I always know."

Wondering at her persistence, and somewhat reluctant, Muriel rose to comply. As she was about to pass her, with a swift movement Daisy caught her hand and drew her down.

"I want you—so—to be happy, dearest," she whispered, a quick note of passion in her voice. "It's better for you—it's better for you—to be together. I'm not going to monopolise you any longer. I will try to come down to-morrow, if Jim will let me. It's hockey day, isn't it? You must go and play as usual, you and he."

She was quivering with agitation as she pressed her lips to the girl's cheek. Muriel would have embraced her, but she pushed her softly away. "Go—go, dear," she insisted. "I wish it."

And Muriel went, seeing that she would not otherwise be pacified.

She found Blake depressed indeed, but genuinely pleased to see her, and she walked in the garden with him in the soft spring twilight till the dinner hour.

Just as they were about to go in, the postman appeared with foreign letters for them both, which proved to be from Sir Reginald and Lady Bassett.

The former had written briefly but very kindly to Grange, signifying his consent to his engagement to his ward, and congratulating him upon having won her. To Muriel he sent a fatherly message, telling her of his pleasure at hearing of her happiness, and adding that he hoped she would return to them in the following autumn to enable him to give her away.

Grange put his arm round his young *fiancée* as he read this passage aloud, but she only stood motionless within it, not yielding to his touch. It even seemed to him that she stiffened slightly. He looked at her questioningly and saw that she was very pale.

"What is it?" he asked gently. "Will that be too soon for you?"

She met his eyes frankly, but with unmistakable distress. "I—I didn't think it would be quite so soon, Blake," she faltered. "I don't want to be married at present. Can't we go on as we are for a little? Shall you mind?"

Blake's face wore a puzzled look, but it was wholly free from resentment. He answered her immediately and reassuringly.

"Of course not, dear. It shall be just when you like. Why should you be hurried?"

She gave him a smile of relief and gratitude, and he stooped and kissed her forehead with a soothing tenderness that he might have bestowed upon a child.

It was with some reluctance that she opened Lady Bassett's letter in his presence, but she felt that she owed him this small mark of confidence.

There was a strong aroma of attar of roses as she drew it from the envelope, and she glanced at Grange with an expression of disgust.

"What is the matter?" he asked. "Nothing wrong, I hope?"

"It's only the scent," she explained, concealing a faint sense of irritation.

He smiled. "Don't you like it? I thought all women did."

"My dear Blake!" she said, and shuddered.

The next minute she threw a sharp look over her shoulder, suddenly assailed by an uncanny feeling that Nick was standing grimacing at her elbow. She saw his features so clearly for the moment with his own peculiarly hideous grimace upon them that she scarcely persuaded herself that her fancy had tricked her. But there was nothing but the twilight of the garden all around her, and Blake's huge bulk by her side, and she promptly dismissed the illusion, not without a sense of shame.

With a gesture of impatience she unfolded Lady Bassett's letter. It commenced "Dearest Muriel," and proceeded at once in terms of flowing elegance to felicitate her upon her engagement to Blake Grange.

"In according our consent," wrote Lady Bassett, "Sir Reginald and I have not the smallest scruple or hesitation. Only, dearest, for Blake Grange's sake as well as for your own, make quite sure *this time* that your mind is fully made up, and your choice final."

When Muriel read this passage a deep note of resentment crept into her voice, and she lifted a flushed face.

"It may be very wicked," she said deliberately, "but I hate Lady Bassett."

Grange looked astonished, even mildly shocked. But Muriel returned to the letter before he could reply.

It went on to express regret that the writer could not herself return to England for the summer to assist her in the purchase of her trousseau and to chaperon her back to India in the autumn; but her sister, Mrs. Langdale, who lived in London, would she was sure, be delighted to undertake the part of adviser in the first case, and in the second she would doubtless be able to find among her many friends who would be travelling East for the winter, one who would take charge of her. No reference was made to Daisy till the end of the letter, when the formal hope was expressed that Mrs. Musgrave's health had benefited by the change.

"She dares to disapprove of Daisy for some reason," Muriel said, closing the letter with the rapidity of exasperation.

Grange did not ask why. He was engrossed in brushing a speck of mud from his sleeve, and she was not sure that he even heard her remark.

"You—I suppose you are not going to bother about a trousseau yet then?" he asked rather awkwardly.

She shook her head with vehemence. "No, no, of course not. Why should I hurry? Besides, I am in mourning."

"Exactly as you like," said Grange gently. "My leave will be up in September, as you know, but I am not bound to stay in the Army. I will send in my papers if you wish it."

Muriel looked at him in amazement. "Send in your papers! Why no, Blake! I wouldn't have you do it for the world. I never dreamed of such a thing."

He smiled good-humouredly. "Well, of course, I should be sorry to give up polo, but there are plenty of other things I could take to. Personally, I like a quiet existence."

Was there just a shade of scorn in Muriel's glance as it fell away from him? It would have been impossible for any bystander to say with certainty, but there was without doubt a touch of constraint in her voice as she made reply.

"Yes. You are quite the most placid person I know. But please don't think of leaving the Army for my sake. I am a soldier's daughter remember. And—I like soldiers."

Her lip quivered as she turned to enter the house. Her heart at that moment was mourning over a soldier's unknown grave. But Grange did not know it, did not even see that she was moved.

His eyes were raised to an upper window at which a dim figure stood looking out into the shadows. And he was thinking of other things.

CHAPTER XXVI
THE ETERNAL FLAME

Daisy maintained her resolution on the following day, and though she did not speak again of going downstairs, she insisted that Muriel should return to the hockey-field and resume her place in Olga's team. It was the last match of the season, and she would not hear of her missing it.

"You and Blake are both to go," she said. "I won't have either of you staying at home for me."

But Blake, when Muriel conveyed this message to him, moodily shook his head. "I'm not going. I don't want to. You must, of course. It will do you good. But I couldn't play if I went. I've strained my wrist."

"Oh, have you?" Muriel said, with concern. "What a nuisance! How did you manage it?"

He reddened, and looked slightly ashamed. "I vaulted the gate into the meadow this morning. Idiotic thing to do. But I shall be all right. Never mind about me. I shall smoke in the garden. I may go for a walk."

Thus pressed on all sides, though decidedly against her own inclination, Muriel went. The day was showery with brilliant intervals. Grange saw her off at the field-gate.

"Plenty of mud," he remarked.

"Yes, I shall be a spectacle when I come back. Good-bye! Take care of yourself." Muriel's hand rested for an instant on his arm, and then she was gone—a slim, short-skirted figure walking swiftly over the grass.

He stood leaning on the gate watching her till a clump of trees intervened between them, then lazily he straightened himself and began to stroll back up the garden. He was not smoking. His face wore a heavy, almost a sullen, look. He scarcely raised his eyes from the ground as he walked.

Nearing the house the sudden sound of a window being raised made him look up, and in an instant, swift as a passing cloud-shadow, his moodiness was gone. Daisy was leaning on her window-sill, looking down upon him.

Though she had not spoken to him for weeks, she gave him no greeting. Her voice even sounded a trifle sharp.

"What are you loafing there for?" she demanded. "Why didn't you go with Muriel to the hockey?"

He hesitated for a single instant. Then—for he never lied to Daisy—quite honestly he made reply. "I didn't want to."

Her pale face frowned down at him, though the eyes had a soft light that was like a mother's indulgence for her wayward child.

"How absurd you are! How can you be so lazy? I won't have it, Blake. Do you hear?"

He moved forward a few steps till he was immediately below her, and there stood with uplifted face. "What do you want me to do?"

"Do!" echoed Daisy. "Why, anything—anything rather than nothing. There's the garden-roller over there by the tool-shed. Go and get it, and roll the lawn."

He went off obediently without another word, and presently the clatter of the roller testified to his submissive fulfilment of her command. He did not look up again. Simply, with his coat off and shirt-sleeves turned above his elbows, he tackled his arduous task, labouring up and down in the soft spring rain, patient and tireless as an ox.

He had accomplished about half his job when again Daisy's voice broke imperiously in upon him.

"Blake! Blake! Come in! You'll get wet to the skin."

He stopped at once, straightening his great frame with a sigh of relief. Daisy was standing at the drawing-room window.

He pulled on his coat and went to join her.

She came to meet him with sharp reproach. "Why are you so foolish? I believe you would have gone on rolling if there had been an earthquake. You must be wet through and through." She ran her little thin hand over him. "Yes, I knew you were. You must go and change."

But Grange's fingers closed with quiet intention upon her wrist. He was looking down at her with the faithful adoration of a dumb animal.

"Not yet," he said gently. "Let me see you while I can."

She made a quick movement as if his grasp hurt her, and in an instant she was free.

"Yes, but let us be sensible," she said. "Don't let us talk about hard things. I'm very tired, you know, Blake. You must make it easy for me."

There was a piteous note of appeal in her voice. She sat down with her back to the light. He could see that her hands were trembling, but because of her appeal he would not seem to see it.

"Don't you think a change would be good for you?" he suggested.

"I don't know," she answered. "Jim says so. He wants me to go to Brethaven. It's only ten miles away, and he would motor over and look after me. But I don't think it much matters. I'm not particularly fond of the sea. And Muriel assures me she doesn't mind."

"Isn't it at Brethaven that Nick Ratcliffe owns a place?" asked Grange.

"Yes. Redlands is the name. I went there once with Will. It's a beautiful place on the cliff—quite thrown away on Nick, though, unless he marries, which he never will now."

Grange looked uncomfortable. "It's not my fault," he remarked bluntly.

"No, I know," said Daisy, with a faint echo of her old light laugh. "Nothing ever was, or could be, your fault, dear old Blake. You're just unlucky sometimes, aren't you? That's all."

Blake frowned a little. "I play a straight game—generally," he said.

"Yes, dear, but you almost always drive into a bunker," Daisy insisted. "It's not your fault, as we said before. It's just your misfortune."

She never flattered Blake. It was perhaps the secret of her charm for him. To other women he was something of a paladin; to Daisy he was no more than a man—a man moreover of many weaknesses, each one of which she knew, each one of which was in a fashion dear to her.

"We will have some tea, shall we?" she said, as he sat silently digesting her criticism. "I must try and write to Will presently. I haven't written to him since—since—" She broke off short and began again. "I got Muriel to write for me once. But he keeps writing by every mail. I wish he wouldn't."

Grange got up and walked softly to the window. "When do you think of going back?" he asked.

"I don't know." There was a keen note of irritation in the reply. Daisy leaned suddenly forward, her fingers locked together. "You might as well ask me when I think of dying," she said, with abrupt and startling bitterness.

Grange remained stationary, not looking at her. "Is it as indefinite as that?" he asked presently.

"Yes, quite." She spoke recklessly, even defiantly. "Where would be the use of my going to a place I couldn't possibly live in for more than four months in the year?

Besides—besides—" But again, as if checked by some potent inner influence, she broke off short. Her white face quivered suddenly, and she turned it aside. Her hands were convulsively clenched upon each other.

Her cousin did not move. He seemed to be unaware of her agitation. Simply with much patience he waited for her end of the sentence.

It came at last in a voice half-strangled. She was making almost frantic efforts to control herself. "Besides, I couldn't stand it—yet. I am not strong enough. And he—he wouldn't understand, poor boy. I think—I honestly think—I am better away from him for the present"

Blake made no further inquiries. From Daisy's point of view, he seemed to be standing motionless, but in reality he was quite unconsciously, though very deliberately, pulling the tassel of the blind-cord to shreds.

The clouds had passed, and the sun blazed down full upon him, throwing his splendid outline into high relief. Every detail of his massive frame was strongly revealed. There was about him a species of careless magnificence, wholly apart from arrogance, unfettered, superb.

To Daisy, familiar as she was with every line of him, the sudden revelation of the sunlight acted like a charm. She had been hiding her eyes for many days from all light, veiling them in the darkness of her grief, and the splendour of the man fairly dazzled her. It rushed upon her, swift, overmastering as a tidal wave, and before it even the memory of her sorrow grew dim.

Blake, turning at last, met her eyes fixed full upon him with that in their expression which no man could ignore. She had not expected him to turn. The movement disconcerted her. With a sharp jerk She averted her face, seeking to cover that momentary slip, to persuade him even then, if it were possible, into the belief that he had not seen aright.

But it was too late. That unguarded look of hers had betrayed her, rending asunder in an instant the veil with which for years she had successfully baffled him.

In a second he was on his knees beside her, his arms about her, holding her with a close and passionate insistence.

"Daisy!" he whispered huskily. And again, "Daisy!"

And Daisy turned with a sudden deep sob and hid her face upon his breast.

CHAPTER XXVII
THE EAGLE CAGED

In spite of Olga's ecstatic welcome, Muriel took her place on the hockey-field that afternoon with a heavy heart. Her long attendance upon Daisy had depressed her. But gradually, as the play proceeded, she began to forget herself and her troubles. The spring air exhilarated her, and when they returned to the field after a sharp shower her spirits had risen. She became even childishly gay in the course of a hotly-contested battle, and the sadness gradually died out of her eyes. She had grown less shy, less restrained, than of old. Youth and health, and a dawning, unconscious beauty had sprung to life upon her face. She was no longer the frightened, bereft child of Simla days. She no longer hid a monstrous fear in her heart. She had put it all away from her wisely, resolutely, as a tale that is told.

The wild wind had blown the hair all loose about her face by the time the last goal was won. Hatless, flushed, and laughing, she drew back from the fray, Olga, elated by victory, clinging to her arm. It was a moment of keen triumph, for the fight had been hard, and she enjoyed it to the full as she stood there with her face to the sudden, scudding rain. The glow of exercise had braced every muscle. Every pulse was beating with warm, vigorous life.

She laughed aloud in sheer exultation, a low, merry laugh, and turned with Olga to march in triumphant procession from the field.

In that instant from a gate a few yards away that led into the road there sounded the short, imperious note of a motor-horn, repeated many times in a succession of sharp blasts. Every one stood to view the intruder with startled curiosity for perhaps five seconds. Then there came a sudden squeal of rapture from Olga, and in a moment she had torn her arm free and was gone, darting like a swallow over the turf.

Muriel stood looking after her, but she was as one turned to stone. She was no longer aware of the children grouped around her. She no longer saw the fleeting sunshine, or felt the drift of rain in her face. Something immense and suffocating had closed about her heart. Her racing pulses had ceased to beat.

A figure familiar to her—a man's figure, unimposing in height, unremarkable in build, but straight, straight as his own sword-blade—had bounded from the car and scaled the intervening gate with monkey-like agility.

He met the child's wild rush with one arm extended; the other—Muriel frowned sharply, peering with eyes half closed, then uttered a queer choked sound that had the semblance of a laugh—in place of the other arm there was an empty sleeve.

Through the rush of the wind she heard his voice.

"Hullo, kiddie, hullo! Hope I don't intrude. I've come over on purpose to pay my respects."

Olga's answer did not reach her. She was hanging round her hero's neck, and her head was down upon Nick's shoulder. It seemed to Muriel that she was crying, but if so, she received scant sympathy from the object of her solicitude. His cracked, gay laugh rang out across the field.

"What? Why, yesterday, to be sure. Spent the night in town. No, I know I didn't. Never meant to. Wanted to steal a march on you all. Why not? I say, is that—Muriel?"

For the first time he seemed to perceive her, and instantly with a dexterous movement he had disengaged himself from Olga's clinging arms and was briskly approaching her. Two of the doctor's boys sprang to greet him, but he waved them airily aside.

"All right, you chaps, in a minute! Where's Dr. Jim? Go and tell him I'm here."

And then in a couple of seconds more they were face to face.

Muriel stared at him speechlessly. She felt cold from head to foot. She had known that he was coming. She had been steeling herself for weeks to meet him in an armour of conventional reserve. But all her efforts had come to this. Swift, swift as the wind over wheat, his coming swept across her new-born confidence. It wavered and bent its head.

"Does your Excellency deign to remember the least and humblest of her servants?" queried Nick, with a deep salaam.

The laugh in his tone brought her sharply back to the demand of circumstance. Before the watching crowd of children, she forced her white lips to smile in answer, and in a moment she had recovered her self-possession. She remembered with a quick sense of relief that this man's power over her belonged to the past alone—to the tale that was told.

The hand she held out to him was almost steady. "Yes, I remember you, Nick," she said, with chilly courtesy. "I am sorry you have been ill. Are you better?"

He made a queer grimace at her words, and for the second that her hand lay in his, she knew that he looked at her closely, piercingly.

"Thanks—awfully," he said. "As you may have noticed, there is a little less of me than there used to be. I hope you think it's an improvement."

She felt as if he had flung back her conventional sympathy in her face, and she stiffened instinctively. "I am sorry to see it," she returned icily.

Nick laughed enigmatically. "I thought you would be. Well, Olga, my child, what do you mean by growing up like this in my absence? You used to be just the right size for a kid, and now you are taller than I am."

"I'm not, Nick," the child declared with warmth. "And I never will be, there!"

She slid her arm again round his neck. Her eyes were full of tears.

Nick turned swiftly and bestowed a kiss upon the face which, though the face of a child, was so remarkably like his own.

"Aren't you going to introduce me to your friends?" he said.

"There's no need," said Olga, hugging him closer. "They all know Captain Ratcliffe of Wara. Why haven't you got the V.C., Nick, like Captain Grange?"

"Didn't qualify for it," returned Nick. "You see, I only distinguished myself by running away. Hullo! It's raining. Just run and tell the chauffeur to drive round to the house. You can go with him. And take your friends too. It'll carry you all. I'm going the garden way with Muriel."

Muriel realised the impossibility of frustrating this plan, though the last thing in the world that she desired was to be alone with him. But the distance to the house was not great. As the children scampered away to the waiting motor-car she moved briskly to leave the field.

Nick walked beside her with his free, elastic swagger. In a few moments he reached out and took her hockey-stick from her.

"Jove!" he said. "It did me good to see you shoot that goal."

"I had no idea you were watching," she returned stiffly.

He grinned. "No, I saw that. Fun, wasn't it? Like to know what I said to myself?"

She made no answer, and his grin became a laugh. "I'm sure you would, so I'll tell you. I said, 'Prayer Number One is granted,' and I ticked it off the list, and duly acknowledged the same."

Muriel was plainly mystified. He was in the mood that most baffled her. "I don't know what you mean," she said at last.

Nick swung the hockey-stick idly. His yellow face, for all its wrinkles, looked peculiarly complacent.

"Let me explain," he said coolly; "I wanted to see you young again, and—my want has been satisfied, that's all."

Muriel looked sharply away from him, the vivid colour rushing all over her face. She remembered—and the memory seemed to stab her—a day long, long ago when she had lain in this man's arms in the extremity of helpless suffering, and had heard him praying above her head, brokenly, passionately, for something far different—something from which she had come to shrink with a nameless, overmastering dread.

She quickened her pace in the silence that followed. The rain was coming down sharply. Reaching the door that led into the doctor's walled garden, she stretched out her hand with impetuous haste to push it open.

Instantly, with disconcerting suddenness, Nick dropped the hockey-stick and swooped upon it like a bird of prey.

"Who gave you that?" he demanded.

He had spied a hoop of diamonds upon her third finger. She could not see his eyes under the flickering lids, but he held her wrist forcibly, and it seemed to her that there was a note of savagery in his voice.

Her heart beat fast for a few seconds, so fast that she could not find her voice. Then, almost under her breath, "Blake gave it to me," she said. "Blake Grange."

"Yes?" said Nick. "Yes?"

Suddenly he looked straight at her, and his eyes were alight, fierce, glowing. But she felt a curious sense of scared relief, as if he were behind bars,—an eagle caged, of which she need have no fear.

"We are engaged to be married," she said quietly.

There fell a momentary silence, and a voice cried out in her soul that she had stabbed him through the bars.

Then in a second Nick dropped her hands and stooped to pick up the hockey-stick. His face as he stood up again flashed back to its old, baffling gaiety.

"What ho!" he said lightly. "Then I'm in time to dance at the wedding. Pray accept my heartiest congratulations!"

Muriel murmured her thanks with her face averted. She was no longer afraid merely, but strangely, inexplicably ashamed.

CHAPTER XXVIII
THE LION'S SKIN

The news of Nick's return spread like wildfire through the doctor's house, and the whole establishment assembled to greet him. Jim himself came striding out into the rain to shake his hand and escort him in.

His "Hullo, you scapegrace!" had in it little of sentiment, but there was nothing wanting in his welcome in the opinion of the recipient thereof.

Nick's rejoinder of "Hullo, you old buffer!" was equally free from any gloss of eloquence, but he hooked his hand in the doctor's arm as he made it, and kept it there.

Jim gave him one straight, keen look that took in every detail, but he made no verbal comment of any sort. His heavy brows drew together for an instant, that was all.

It was an exceedingly clamorous home-coming. The children, having arrived in the motor, swarmed all about the returned hero, who was more than equal to the occasion, and obviously enjoyed his boisterous reception to the uttermost. There never had been any shyness about Nick.

Muriel, standing watching in the background with a queer, unaccountable pain at her heart, assured herself that the news of her engagement had meant nothing to him whatever. He had managed to deceive her as usual. She realised it with burning cheeks, and ardently wished that she had borne herself more proudly. Well, she was not wanted here. Even Olga, her faithful and loving admirer, had eyes only for Nick just then. As for Dr. Jim, he had not even noticed her.

Quietly she stole away from the merry, chattering group. The hall-door stood open, and she saw that it was raining heavily; but she did not hesitate. With a haste that was urged from within by something that was passionate, she ran out hatless into the storm.

The cracked, careless laugh she knew so well pursued her as she went, and once she fancied that some one called her by name. But she did not slacken speed to listen. She only dashed on a little faster than before.

Drenched and breathless, she reached home at length, to be met upon the threshold by Blake. In her exhaustion she almost fell into his arms.

"Hullo!" he said, steadying her. "You shouldn't run like that. I never dreamed you would come back in this, or I would have come across with an umbrella to fetch you."

She sank into a chair in the hall, speechless and gasping, her hair hanging about her neck in wildest disorder.

Blake stood beside her. He was wearing his worried, moody look.

"You shouldn't," he said again. "It's horribly bad for you."

"Ah, I'm better," she gasped back. "I had to run—all the way—because of the rain."

"But why didn't you wait?" said Blake. "What were they thinking of to let you come in this down-pour?"

"They couldn't help it." Muriel raised herself with a great sobbing sigh. "It was nobody's fault but my own. I wanted to get away. Oh, Blake, do you know—Nick is here?"

Blake started. "What? Already? Do you mean he is actually in the place?"

She nodded. "He came up in a motor while we were playing. I suppose he is staying at Redlands, but I don't know. And—and—Blake, he has lost his left arm. It makes him look so queer." She gave a sudden, uncontrollable shudder. The old dumb horror looked out of her eyes. "I thought I shouldn't mind," she said, under her breath. "Perhaps—if you had been there—it would have been different. As it was—as it was—" She broke off, rising impetuously to her feet, and laying trembling hands upon his arms. "Oh, Blake," she whispered, like a scared child. "I feel so helpless. But you promised—you promised—you would never let me go."

Yes, he had promised her that. He had sworn it, and, sick at heart, he remembered that in her eyes at least he was a man of honour. It had been in his mind to tell her the simple truth, just so far as he himself was concerned, and thereafter to place himself at her disposal to act exactly as she should desire. But suddenly this was an impossibility to him. He realised it with desperate self-loathing. She trusted him. She looked to him for protection. She leaned upon his strength. She needed him. He could not—it almost seemed as if in common chivalry he could not—reveal to her the contemptible weakness which lay like a withering blight upon his whole nature. To own himself the slave of a married woman, and that woman her closest friend, would be to throw her utterly upon her own resources at a time when she most needed the support and guidance of a helping hand. Moreover, the episode was over; so at least both he and Daisy resolutely persuaded themselves. There had been a lapse—a vain and futile lapse—into the long-cherished idyll of their romance. It must never recur. It never should recur. It must be covered over and forgotten as speedily as might be. They had come to their senses again. They were ready, not only to thrust away the evil that had dominated them, but to ignore it utterly as though it had never been.

So, rapidly, the man reasoned with himself with the girl's hands clasping his arm in earnest entreaty, and her eyes of innocence raised to his.

His answer when it came was slow and soft and womanly, but, in her ears at least, there was nothing wanting in it. She never dreamed that he was reviling himself for a blackguard even as he uttered it.

"My dear little girl, there is nothing whatever for you to be afraid of. You're a bit overstrung, aren't you? The man isn't living who could take you from me."

He patted her shoulder very kindly, soothing her with a patient, almost fatherly tenderness, and gradually her panic of fear passed. She leaned against him with a comforting sense of security.

"I can't think how it is I'm so foolish," she told him. "You are good to me, Blake. I feel so safe when I am with you."

His heart smote him, yet he bent and kissed her. "You're not quite strong yet, dear," he said. "It takes a long time to get over all that you had to bear last year."

"Yes," she agreed with a sigh. "And do you know I thought I was so much stronger than I am? I actually thought that I shouldn't mind—much—when he came. And yet I did mind—horribly. I—I—told him about our engagement, Blake."

"Yes, dear," said Blake.

"Yes, I told him. And he laughed and offered his congratulations. I don't think he cared," said Muriel, again with that curious, inexplicable sensation of pain at her heart.

"Why should he?" said Blake.

She looked at him with momentary irresolution. "You know, Blake, I never told you. But I was—I was—engaged to him for about a fortnight that dreadful time at Simla."

To her relief she marked no change in Blake's courteously attentive face.

"You need not have told me that, dear," he said quietly.

"No, I know," she answered, pressing his arm. "It wouldn't make any difference to you. You are too great. And it was always a little bit against my will. But the breaking with him was terrible—terrible. He was so angry. I almost thought he would have killed me."

"My dear," Blake said, "you shouldn't dwell on these things. They are better forgotten."

"I know, I know," she answered. "But they are just the very hardest of all things to forget. You must help me, Blake. Will you?"

"I will help you," he answered steadily.

And the resolution with which he spoke was an unspeakable comfort to her. Once more there darted across her mind the wonder at her father's choice for her. How was it—how was it—that he had passed over this man and chosen Nick?

Blake's own explanation of the mystery seemed to her suddenly weak and inadequate. She simply could not bring herself to believe that in a supreme moment he could be found wanting. It was unthinkable that the giant frame and mighty sinews could belong to a personality that was lacking in a corresponding greatness.

So she clung to her illusion, finding comfort therein, wholly blind to those failings in her protector which to the woman who had loved him from her earliest girlhood were as obvious and well-nigh as precious as his virtues.

CHAPTER XXIX
OLD FRIENDS MEET

"I must be getting back," said Nick.

He was sprawling at ease on the sofa in Jim's study, blinking comfortably at the ceiling, as he made this remark.

Jim himself had just entered the room. He drew up a chair to Nick's side.

"You will be doing nothing of the sort to-night," he returned, with a certain grimness. "The motor has gone back to Redlands for your things. I saw to that an hour ago."

"The deuce you did!" said Nick. He turned slightly to send a shifting glance over his brother. "That was very officious of you, Jimmy," he remarked.

"Very likely," conceded the doctor. "I have to be officious occasionally. And if you think that I mean to let you out of my sight in your present state of health, you make a big mistake. No, lie still, I tell you! You're like a monkey on wires. Lie still! Do you hear me, Nick?"

Nick's feet were already on the ground, but he did not rise. He sat motionless, as if weighing some matter in his mind.

"I can't stay with you, Jimmy," he said at last. "I'll spend to-night of course with all the pleasure in the world. But I'm going back to Redlands to-morrow. I have a fancy for sleeping in my own crib just now. Come over and see me as often as you feel inclined, the oftener the better. And if you care to bring your science to bear upon all that is left of this infernally troublesome member of mine, I shall be charmed to let you. You may vivisect me to your heart's content. But don't ask me to be an in-patient, for it can't be done. There are reasons."

Jim frowned at him. "Do you know what will happen if you don't take care of yourself?" he said brusquely. "You'll die."

Nick burst into a laugh, and lay back on the cushions. "I was driven out of India by that threat," he said. "It's getting a bit stale. You needn't be afraid. I'm not going to die at present. I'll take reasonable precautions to prevent it. But I won't stay here, that's flat. I tell you, man, I can't."

He glanced again at Jim, and, finding the latter closely watching him, abruptly shut his eyes.

"I'm going to open Redlands," he said, "and I will have Olga to come and keep house for me. It'll be good practice for her. I'll take her back with me to-morrow, if you have no objection."

"Fine mischief you'll get up to, the pair of you," grumbled Jim.

"Very likely," said Nick cheerily. "But we shan't come to any harm, either of us. To begin with, I shall make her wait on me, hand and foot. She'll like that, and so shall I."

"Yes, you'll spoil her thoroughly." said Jim. "And I shall have the pleasure of breaking her in afterwards."

Nick laughed again. "What an old tyrant you are! But you needn't be afraid of that. I'll make her do as she's told. I'm particularly good at that. Ask Muriel Roscoe."

Jim's frown deepened. "You know of that girl's engagement to Grange, I suppose?"

Nick did not trouble to open his eyes. "Oh, rather! She took care that I should. I gave her my blessing."

"Well, I don't like it," said Jim plainly.

"What's the matter with him?" questioned Nick.

"Nothing that I know of. But she isn't in love with him."

Nick's eyelids parted a little, showing a glint between. "You funny old ass!" he murmured affectionately.

Jim leaned forward and looked at him hard.

"Quite so," said Nick in answer, closing his eyes again. "But you don't by any chance imagine she's in love with me, do you? You know how a woman looks at a worm she has chopped in half by mistake? That's how Muriel Roscoe looked at me to-day when she expressed her regret for my mishap."

"She wouldn't do that for nothing," observed Jim, with a hint of sternness.

"She wouldn't," Nick conceded placidly.

"Then why the devil did you ever give her reason?" Jim spoke with unusual warmth. Muriel was a favourite of his.

But he obtained scant satisfaction notwithstanding.

"Ask the devil," said Nick flippantly. "I never was good at definitions."

It was a tacit refusal to discuss the matter, and as such Jim accepted it.

He turned from the subject with a grunt of discontent. "Well, if I am to undertake your case, you had better let me look at you. But we'll have a clean understanding first, mind, that you obey my orders. I won't be responsible otherwise."

Nick opened his eyes with a chuckle. "I'll do anything under the sun to please you, Jimmy," he said generously. "When did you ever find me hard to manage?"

"You've given me plenty of trouble at one time and another," Jim said bluntly.

"And shall again before I die," laughed Nick, as he submitted to his brother's professional handling. "There's plenty of kick left in me. By the way, tell me what you think about Daisy. I must call on her to-morrow before I leave."

This intention, however, was not fulfilled, for Daisy herself came early to the doctor's house to visit him. Far from well though she was, she made the effort as a matter of course. Nick was too near a friend to neglect. Blake did not accompany her. He was riding with Muriel.

She found Nick stretched out in luxurious idleness on a couch in the sunshine. He made a movement to spring to meet her, but checked himself with a laugh.

"This is awfully good of you, Daisy. I was coming to see you later, but I'm nailed to this confounded sofa for the next two hours, having solemnly sworn to Jim that nothing short of battle, murder or sudden death should induce me to move. I'm afraid I can't reasonably describe your coming as any of these, so I must remain a fixture. It's Jimmy's rest cure."

He reached out his hand to Daisy, who took it in both her own. "My poor dear Nick!" she said, and stooping impulsively kissed him on the forehead.

"Bless you!" said Nick. "I'm ten times better for that. Sit down here, won't you? Pull up close. I've got a lot to say."

Of sympathy for her recent bereavement, however, he said no word whatever. He only held her hand.

"There's poor old Will," he said: "I spent the night with him on my way down. He's beastly homesick—sent all sorts of messages to you. You'll be going out in the winter?"

"It depends," said Daisy.

"He's breaking his heart for you, like a silly ass," said Nick. "How long has Muriel been engaged to Grange?"

Daisy started at the sudden question.

"It's all right," Nick assured her. "I'm not a bit savage. It'll be a little experience for her. When did it begin?"

Daisy hesitated. "Some weeks ago now."

Nick nodded. "Exactly. As soon as she heard I was coming. Funny of her. And what of Grange? Is he smitten?"

Daisy flushed painfully, and tried to laugh. "Don't be so cold-blooded, Nick. Of course he—he's fond of her."

"Oh, he—he's fond of her, is he?" said Nick. He looked at her suddenly, and laughed with clenched teeth. "I'm infernally rude, I know. But why put it in that way? Should you say I was 'fond' of her?"

Daisy met his darting, elusive glance with a distinct effort. "I shouldn't say you were fond of any one, Nick. The term doesn't apply where you are concerned. There never were two men more totally different than you and Blake. But he isn't despicable for all that. He's a child compared to you, but he's a good child. He would never do wrong unless some one tempted him."

"That's so with a good many of us," remarked Nick, sneering faintly. "Let us hope that when the account comes to be totted up, allowance will be made."

Daisy's hand upon his banished the sneer. "Be fair, Nick," she urged. "We are not all made with wills of iron. I know you are bitter because you think he isn't good enough for her. But would you think any man good enough? Don't think I wanted this. I was on your side. But I—I was busy at the time with—other things. And I didn't see it coming."

Nick's face softened. He said nothing.

She bent towards him. "I would have given anything to have stopped it when I knew. But it was too late. Will you forgive me, Nick?"

He patted her hand lightly. "Of course, of course. Don't fret on my account."

"But I do," she whispered vehemently. "I do. I know—how horribly—it hurts."

Nick's fingers closed suddenly upon hers. His eyes went beyond her.

"Mrs. Musgrave," he said, "I am gifted with a superhuman intelligence, remember. I know some cards by their backs."

Daisy withdrew her hand swiftly. His tone had been one of warning. She threw him a look of sharp uneasiness. She did not ask him what he meant.

"Tell me some more about Will," she said. "I was thinking of writing to him to-day."

And Nick forthwith plunged into a graphic account of the man who was slaving night and day in the burning Plains of the East for the woman of his heart.

CHAPTER XXX
AN OFFER OF FRIENDSHIP

It was with unspeakable relief that Muriel learned of Nick's departure. That he had elected to take Olga with him surprised her considerably and caused her some regret. Grange had discovered some urgent business that demanded his presence in town, and she missed the child in consequence more than she would otherwise have done.

Daisy was growing stronger, and was beginning to contemplate a change, moved at last by Jim Ratcliffe's persistent urging. There was a cottage at Brethaven which, he declared, would suit her exactly. Muriel raised no objection to the plan. She knew it would be for Daisy's benefit, but her heart sank whenever she thought of it. She was glad when early in June Blake came back to them for a few days before starting on a round of visits.

He approved of the Brethaven plan warmly, and he and Muriel rode over one morning to the little seaside village to make arrangements. Muriel said no more to him upon the subject of Nick. On this one point she had come to know that it was vain to look for sympathy. He had promised to help her indeed, but he simply did not understand her nervous shrinking from the man. Moreover, Nick had made it so abundantly evident that he had no intention of thrusting himself upon her that there could be no ground for fear on that score. Besides, was not her engagement her safeguard?

As for Blake, her silence upon the matter made him hope that she was getting over her almost childish panic. With all the goodwill in the world, he could not see that his presence as watch-dog was required.

Yet, as they turned from the cottage on the shore with their errand accomplished, he did say after some hesitation, "Of course, if for any reason you should want me when I am away, you must let me know. I would come at once."

She thanked him with a heightened colour, and he had a feeling that his allusion had been unwelcome. They rode up from the beach in silence.

Turning a sharp corner towards the village where they proposed to lunch, they came suddenly upon a motor stationary by the roadside. A whoop of cheery recognition greeted them before either of them realised that it was occupied, and they discovered Nick seated on the step, working with his one hand at the foot-brake. Olga was with him, endeavouring to assist.

Nick's face grinned welcome impartially to the newcomers. "Hullo! This is luck. Delighted to see you. Grange, my boy, here's a little job exactly suited to your Herculean strength. Climb down like a good fellow, and lend a hand."

Grange glanced at Muriel, and with a slight shrug handed her his bridle. "I'm not much good at this sort of thing," he remarked, as he dismounted.

"Never thought you were for a moment," responded Nick. "But I suppose you can do as you're told at a pinch. This filthy thing has got jammed. It's too tough a job for a single-handed pigmy like me." He glanced quizzically up at Muriel with the last remark, but she quickly averted her eyes, bending to speak to Olga at the same instant.

Olga was living in the seventh heaven just then, and her radiant face proclaimed it. "I'm learning to drive," she told Muriel. "It's the greatest fun. You would just love it. I know you would." She stood fondling the horses and chattering while the two men wrestled with the motor's internal arrangements, and Muriel longed desperately to give her animal the rein and flee away from the mocking sprite that gibed at her from Nick's eyes. Whence came it, this feeling of insecurity, this perpetual sense of fighting against the inevitable? She had fancied that Blake's presence would be her safeguard, but now she bitterly realised that it made no difference to her. He stood as it were outside the ropes, and was powerless to intervene.

Suddenly she saw them stand up. The business was done. They stood for a second side by side—Blake gigantic, well-proportioned, splendidly strong; Nick, meagre, maimed, almost shrunken, it seemed. But in that second she knew with unerring conviction that the greater fighter of the two was the man against whom she had pitted her quivering woman's strength. She knew at a single glance that for all his bodily weakness Nick possessed the power to dominate even so mighty a giant as Blake. What she had said to herself many a time before, she said again. He was abnormal, superhuman even; more—where he chose to exert himself, he was irresistible.

The realisation went through her, sharp and piercing, horribly distinct. She had sought shelter like a frightened rabbit in the densest cover she could find, but, crouching low, she heard the rush of the remorseless wings above her. She knew that at any moment he could rend her refuge to pieces and hold her at his mercy.

Abruptly he left Blake and came to her side. "I want you and Grange to come to Redlands for luncheon," he said. "Olga is hostess there. Don't refuse."

"Oh, do come!" urged Olga, dancing eagerly upon one leg. "You've never been to Redlands, have you? It's such a lovely place. Say you'll come, Muriel."

Muriel scarcely heard her. She was looking down into Nick's face, seeking, seeking for the hundredth time, to read that baffling mask.

"Don't refuse," he said again. "You'll get nothing but underdone chops at the inn here, and I can't imagine that to be a weakness of yours."

She gave up her fruitless search. "I will come," she said.

"It's exactly as you like, you know, Muriel," Grange put in awkwardly.

She understood the precise meaning of Nick's laugh. She even for a moment wanted to laugh herself. "Thank you. I should like to," she said.

Nick nodded and turned aside. "Olga, stop capering," he ordered, "and drive me home."

Olga obeyed him promptly, with the gaiety of a squirrel. As Nick seated himself by her side, Muriel saw her turn impulsively and rub her cheek against his shoulder. It gave her a queer little tingling shock to see the child's perfect confidence in him. But then—but then—Olga had never looked on horror, had never seen the devil leap out in naked fury upon her hero's face.

They waited to let the car go first, Olga proudly grasping the wheel; then, trotting briskly, followed in its wake.

Muriel had an uneasy feeling that Blake wanted to apologise, and she determined that he should not have the opportunity. Each time that he gave any sign of wishing to draw nearer to her, she touched her horse's flank. Something in the nature of a revelation had come to her during that brief halt by the roadside. For the first time she had caught a glimpse, plain and unvarnished, of the actual man that inhabited the giant's frame, and it had given her an odd, disturbing suspicion that the strength upon which she leaned was in simple fact scarcely equal to her own.

The way to Redlands lay through leafy woodlands through which here and there the summer sea gleamed blue. Turning in at the open gates, Muriel uttered an exclamation of delight. She seemed to have suddenly entered fairyland. The house, long, low, rambling, roofed with thatch, stood at the end of a winding drive that was bordered on both sides by a blaze of rhododendron flowers. Down below her on the left was a miniature glen from which arose the tinkle of running water. On her right the trees grew thickly, completely shutting out the road.

"Oh, Blake!" she exclaimed. "What a perfect paradise!"

"Like it?" said Nick; and with a start she saw him coolly step out from a shadowy path behind them and close the great iron gate.

Impulsively she pulled up and slipped to the ground. "Take my horse, Blake," she said. "I must run down to that stream."

He obeyed her, not very willingly, and Nick with a chuckle turned and plunged after her down the narrow path. "Go straight ahead!" he called back. "Olga is waiting for you at the house."

He came up with Muriel on the edge of the fairy stream. Her face was flushed and her eyes nervous, but she met him bravely. She had known in her heart that he would follow. As he stopped beside her, she turned with a little desperate laugh and held out her hand.

"Is it peace?" she said rather breathlessly.

She felt his fingers, tense as wire, close about her own. "Seems like it," he said. "What are you afraid of? Me?"

She could not meet his look. But the necessity for some species of understanding pressed upon her. She wanted unspeakably to conciliate him.

"I want to be friends with you, Nick," she said, "if you will let me."

"What for?" said Nick sharply.

She was silent. She could not tell him that her sure defence had crumbled at a touch. Somehow she was convinced that he knew it already.

"You never wanted such a thing before," he said. "You certainly weren't hankering after it the last time we met."

Her cheeks burned at the memory. Again she felt ashamed. With a great effort she forced herself to speak with a certain frankness.

"I am afraid," she said—"I have thought since—that I was rather heartless that day. The fact was, I was taken by surprise. But I am sorry now, Nick. I am very sorry."

Her tone was unconsciously piteous. Surely he must see that if they were to meet often, as inevitably they must, some sort of agreement between them was imperative. She must feel stable ground beneath her feet. Their intercourse could not be one perpetual passage of arms. Flesh and blood could never endure it.

But Nick did not apparently view the matter in the same light. "Pray don't be sorry," he airily begged her. "I quite understood. I never take offence where none is intended, and not always where it is. So dismiss the matter from your mind with all speed. There is not the smallest occasion for regret."

He meant to elude her, she saw, and she turned from him without another word. There was to be no understanding then, no friendly feeling, no peace of mind. She had trusted to his generosity, and it was quite clear that he had no intention of being generous.

As they walked by a mossy pathway towards the house, they talked upon indifferent things. But the girl's heart was very bitter within her. She would have given almost anything to have flung back his hospitality in his grinning, triumphant face, and have departed with her outraged pride to the farthest corner of the earth.

CHAPTER XXXI
THE EAGLE HOVERS

Luncheon in the low, old-fashioned dining-room at Redlands with its windows facing the open sea, with Olga beaming at the head of the table, would have been a peaceful and pleasant meal, had Muriel's state of mind allowed her to enjoy it. But Nick's treatment of her overture had completely banished all enjoyment for her. She forced herself to eat and to appear unconcerned, but she was quivering inwardly with a burning sense of resentment. She was firmly determined that she would never be alone with him again. He had managed by those few scoffing words of his to arouse in her all the bitterness of which she was capable. If she had feared him before, she hated him now with the whole force of her nature.

He seemed to be blissfully unconscious of her hostility and played the part of host with complete ease of manner. Long before the meal was over, Grange had put aside his sullenness, and they were conversing together as comrades.

Nick had plenty to say. He spoke quite openly of his illness, and declared himself to have completely recovered from it. "Even Jim has ceased his gruesome threats," he said cheerily. "There will be no more lopping of branches this season. Just as well, for I chance to have developed an affection for what is left."

"You're going back to the Regiment, I suppose?" Blake questioned.

"No, he isn't," thrust in Olga, and was instantly frowned upon by Nick.

"Speak when you're spoken to, little girl! That's a question you are not qualified to answer. I'm on half-pay at present, and I haven't made up my mind."

"I should quit in your place," Grange remarked, with his eyes on the dazzling sea.

"No doubt you would," Nick responded dryly. "And what should you advise, Muriel?"

The question was unexpected, but she had herself in hand, and answered it instantly. "I certainly shouldn't advise you to quit."

He raised his eyebrows. "Might one ask why?"

She was quite ready for him, inspired by an overmastering longing to hurt him if that were possible. "Because if you gave up your profession, you would be nothing but a vacuum. If the chance to destroy life were put out of your reach, you would simply cease to exist."

She spoke rapidly, her voice pitched very low. She was trembling all over, and her hands were clenched under the table to hide it.

The laugh with which Nick received her words jarred intolerably upon her. She heard nothing in it but deliberate cruelty.

"Great Lucifer!" he said. "You have got me under the microscope with a vengeance. But you can't see through me, you know. I have a reverse side. Hadn't you better turn me over and look at that? There may be sorcery and witchcraft there as well."

There might be. She could well have imagined it. But these were lesser things in which she had no concern. She turned his thrust aside with disdain.

"I am not sufficiently interested," she said. "The little I know is enough."

"Well hit!" chuckled Nick. "I retire from the fray, discomfited. Olga *mia*, I wish you would find the cigars. You know where they are."

Olga sprang to do his bidding. Having handed the box to Grange she came to Nick and stood beside him while she cut and lighted a cigar for him.

He put his arm round her for a moment, and she stooped a flushed face and kissed the top of his head.

"Run along," said Nick. "Take Muriel into the garden. She hasn't seen it all."

Muriel rose. "We mustn't be late in starting back," she remarked to Blake.

But Olga lingered to whisper vehemently in Nick's ear.

He laughed and shook his head. "Go, child, go! You don't know anything about it. And Muriel is waiting. You should never keep a guest waiting."

Olga went reluctantly. They passed out into the clear June sunshine together and down towards the shady shrubberies beyond the lawns.

"Can Nick play tennis?" Muriel asked, as they crossed a marked-out court.

"Yes, he can do anything," the child said proudly. "He was on horseback this morning, and he managed splendidly. We generally play tennis in the evening. He almost always wins. His services are terrific. I can't think how he does it. He calls it juggling. I try to manage with only one hand sometimes—just to keep him company—but I always make a mess of things. There's no one in the world as clever as Nick."

Muriel felt inclined to agree with her, though in her opinion this distinguishing quality was not an altogether admirable one. She infinitely preferred people with fewer brains. She would not, however, say this to Olga, and they paced on together under the trees in silence. Suddenly a warm hand slid within her arm, and Olga's grey eyes, very loving and wistful, looked up into hers.

"Muriel darling," she whispered softly, "don't you—don't you—like Nick after all?"

The colour rushed over Muriel's face in a vivid flood.

"Like him! Like him!" she stammered. "Why do you ask?"

"Because, dear—don't be vexed, I love you frightfully—you did hurt him so at lunch," explained Olga, pressing very close to her.

"Hurt him! Hurt him!" Again Muriel repeated her words, then, recovering sharply, broke into a sudden laugh. "My dear child, I couldn't possibly do such a thing if I tried."

"But you did, you did!" persisted Olga, a faint note of indignation in her voice. "You don't know Nick. He feels—tremendously. Of course you might not see it, for it doesn't often show. But I know—I always know—when he is hurt, by the way he laughs. And he was hurt to-day."

She stuck firmly to her point, notwithstanding Muriel's equally persistent attitude of incredulity, till even Muriel was conscious at last in her inner soul of a faint wonder, a dim and wholly negligible sense of regret. Not that she would under any circumstances have recalled that thrust of hers. She felt it had been dealt in fair fight; but even in fair fight there come sometimes moments of regret, when one feels that the enemy's hand has been intentionally slack. She knew well that, had he chosen, Nick might have thrust back, instantly and disconcertingly, as his manner was. But he had refrained, merely covering up his wound—if wound there had been—with the laugh that had so wrung Olga's loving heart. His ways were strange. She would never understand him. But she would like to have known how deep that thrust had gone.

Could she have overheard the conversation between Nick and his remaining guest that followed her departure, she might have received enlightenment on this point, but Nick took very good care to ensure that that conversation should be overheard by none.

As soon as Grange had finished his coffee, he proposed a move to the library, and led the way thither, leaving his own drink untouched behind him.

The library was a large and comfortable apartment completely shut away from the rest of the house, and singularly ill-adapted for eavesdroppers. The windows looked upon a wide stretch of lawn upon which even a bird could scarcely have lingered unnoticed. The light that filtered in through green sun-blinds was cool and restful. An untidy writing-table and a sofa strewn with cushions in disorderly attitudes testified to the fact that Nick had appropriated this room for his own particular den. There was also a sun-bonnet tossed upon a chair which seemed to indicate that Olga at least did not regard his privacy as inviolable. The ancient brown volumes stacked upon shelves that ranged almost from floor to ceiling were comfortably undisturbed. It was plainly a sanctum in which ease and not learning ruled supreme.

Nick established his visitor in an easy-chair and hunted for an ash-tray. Grange watched him uncomfortably.

"I'm awfully sorry about your arm, Ratcliffe," he said at length. "A filthy bit of bad luck that."

"Damnable," said Nick.

"I've been meaning to look you up for a long time," Grange proceeded, "but somehow it hasn't come off."

Nick laughed rather dryly. He was perfectly well aware that Grange had been steadily avoiding him ever since his return. "Very good of you," he said, subsiding upon the sofa and pulling the cushions about him. "I've been saving up my congratulations for you all these weeks. I might have written, of course, but I had a notion that the spoken word would be more forcible."

Grange stirred uneasily, neither understanding nor greatly relishing Nick's tone. He wished vehemently that he would leave the subject alone.

Nick, however, had no such intention. A faint fiendish smile was twitching the corners of his lips. He did not even glance in Blake's direction. There was no need.

"Well, I wish you joy," he said lightly.

"Thank you," returned Grange, without elation and with very little gratitude. In some occult fashion, Nick was making it horribly awkward for him. He longed to change the subject, but could find nothing to say—possibly because Nick quite obviously had not yet done with it.

"Going to get married before you sail?" he asked abruptly.

"I don't think so." Very reluctantly Grange made reply.

"Why not?" said Nick.

"Muriel doesn't want to be married till she is out of mourning," Grange explained.

"Why doesn't she go out of mourning then?"

Grange didn't know, hadn't even thought of it.

"Perhaps she will elect to wear mourning all her life," suggested Nick. "Have you thought of that?"

There was a distinct gibe in this, and Grange at once retreated to a less exposed position. "I am quite willing to wait for her," he said. "And she knows it."

"You're deuced easily pleased then," rejoined Nick. "And let me tell you—for I'm sure you don't know—there's not a single woman under the sun who appreciates that sort of patience."

Grange ignored the information with a decidedly sullen air. He did not regard Nick as particularly well qualified to give him advice upon such a subject.

After a moment Nick saw his attitude, and laughed aloud. "Yes, say it, man! It's quite true in a sense, and I shouldn't contradict you if it weren't. But has it never occurred to you that I was under a terrific disadvantage from the very beginning? Do you remember that I undertook the job that you shirked? Or do you possibly present the matter to yourself—and others—in some more attractive form?"

He turned upon his elbow with the question and regarded Grange with an odd expectancy. But Grange smoked in silence, not raising his eyes.

Suddenly Nick spoke in a different tone, a tone that was tense without vibrating. "It doesn't matter how you put it. The truth remains. You didn't love her then. If you had loved her, you must have been ready—as I was ready—to make the final sacrifice. But you were not ready. You hung back. You let me take the place which only a man who cared enough to protect her to the uttermost could have taken. You let me do this thing, and I did it. I brought her through untouched. I kept her—night and day I kept her—from harm of any sort. And she has been my first care ever since. You won't believe this, I daresay, but it's true. And—mark this well—I will only let her go to the man who will make her happy. Once I meant to be that man. You don't suppose, do you, that I brought her safe through hell just for the pleasure of seeing her marry another fellow? But it's all the same now what I did it for. I've been knocked out of the running." His eyelids suddenly quivered as if at a blow. "It doesn't matter to you how. It wasn't because she fancied any one else. She hadn't begun to think of you in those days. I let her go, never mind why. I let her go, but she is still in my keeping, and will be till she is the actual property of another man—yes, and after that too. I saved her, remember. I won the right of guardianship over her. So be careful what you do. Marry her if you love her. But if you don't, leave her alone. She shall be no man's second best. That I swear."

He ceased abruptly. His yellow face was full of passion. His hand was clenched upon the sofa-cushion. The whole body of the man seemed to thrill and quiver with electric force.

And then in a moment it all passed. As at the touching of a spring his muscles relaxed. The naked passion was veiled again—the old mask of banter replaced.

He stretched out his hand to the man who had sat in silence and listened to that one fierce outburst of a force which till then had contained itself.

"I speak as a fool," he said lightly. "Nothing new for me, you'll say. But just for my satisfaction—because she hates me so—put your hand in mine and swear you will seek her happiness before everything else in the world. I shall never trouble you again after this fashion. I have spoken."

Blake sat for several seconds without speaking. Then, as if impelled thereto, he leaned slowly forward and laid his hand in Nick's. He seemed to have something to say, but it did not come.

Nick waited.

"I swear," Blake said at length.

His voice was low, and he did not attempt to look Nick in the face, but he obviously meant what he said.

And Nick seemed to be satisfied. In less than five seconds, he had tossed the matter carelessly aside as one having no further concern in it. But the memory of that interview was as a searing flame to Blake's soul for long after.

For he knew that the man from whom Muriel had sought his protection was more worthy of her than he, and his heart cried bitter shame upon him for that knowledge.

It was with considerable difficulty that he responded to Nick's airy nothings during the half-hour that followed, and the unusual alacrity with which he seized upon his host's suggestion that he might care to see the garden, testified to his relief at being released from the obligation of doing so.

They went out together on to the wide lawn and sauntered down to a summer-house on the edge of the cliff, overlooking the whole mighty expanse of sea. It lay dreaming in the sunlight, with hardly a ripple upon the long white beach below. And here they came upon Muriel and Olga, sitting side by side on the grass.

Olga had just finished pulling a daisy to pieces. She tossed it away at Nick's approach, and sprang to meet him.

"It's very disappointing," she declared. "It's the fourth time I've done it, and it always comes the same. I've been making the daisies tell Muriel's fortune, and it always comes to 'He would if he could, but he can't.' You try this time, Nick."

"All right. You hold the daisy," said Nick.

Muriel looked up with a slightly heightened colour. "I think we ought to be going," she remarked.

"We have just ordered the horses for four o'clock," Grange said apologetically.

She glanced at the watch on her wrist—half-past three. Nick, seated cross-legged on the grass in front of her, had already, with Olga's able assistance, begun his game.

Swiftly the tiny petals fell from his fingers. He was very intent, and in spite of herself Muriel became intent too, held by a most unaccountable fascination. So handicapped was he that he could not even pull a flower to pieces without assistance. And yet—

Suddenly he looked across at her. "He loves her!" he announced.

"Oh, Nick!" exclaimed Olga reproachfully. "You cheated! You pulled off two!"

"He usually does cheat," Muriel observed, plucking a flower of grass and regarding it with absorption.

"So do you," retorted Nick unexpectedly.

"I!" She looked at him in amazement. "What do you mean?"

"I sha'n't tell you," he returned, "because you know, or you would know if you took the trouble to find out. Grange, I wish you would give me a light. Hullo, Olga, there's a hawk! See him? Straight above that cedar!"

All turned to look at the dark shape of the bird hovering in mid-air. Seconds passed. Suddenly there was a flashing, downward swoop, and the sky was empty.

Olga exclaimed, and Nick sent up a wild whoop of applause. Muriel gave a great start and glanced at him. For a single instant his look met hers; then with a sick shudder, she turned aside.

"You are cold," said Grange.

Yes, she was cold. It was as if an icy hand had closed upon her heart. As from an immense distance, she heard Olga's voice of protest.

"Oh, Nick, how can you cheer?"

And his careless reply. "My good child, don't grudge the poor creature his dinner. Even a bird of prey must live. Come along! We'll go in to tea. Muriel is cold."

They went in, and again his easy hospitality overcame all difficulties.

When at length the visitors rode away, they left him grinning a cheery farewell from his doorstep. He seemed to be in the highest spirits.

They were more than half-way home when Muriel turned impetuously to her companion, breaking a long silence.

"Blake," she said, "I am ready to marry you as soon as you like."

PART IV

CHAPTER XXXII
THE FACE IN THE STORM

Muriel saw very little of her *fiancé* during the weeks that followed their visit to Redlands. There was not indeed room for him at the cottage at Brethaven which she and Daisy had taken for the summer months. He had, moreover, several visits to pay, and his leave would be up in September.

Muriel herself, having once made her decision, had plenty to occupy her. They had agreed to adhere to Sir Reginald Bassett's plan for them, and to be married in India some time before Christmas. But she did not want to go to Lady Bassett's sister before she left England, and she was glad when Daisy declared that she herself would go to town with her in the autumn.

A change had come over Daisy of late, a change which Muriel keenly felt, but which she was powerless to define. It seemed to date from the arrival of Nick though she did not definitely connect it with him. There was nothing palpable in it, nothing even remotely suggestive of a breach between them; only, subconsciously as it were, Muriel had become aware that their silence, which till then had been the silence of sympathy, had subtly changed till it had become the silence of a deep though unacknowledged reserve. It was wholly intangible, this change. No outsider would have guessed of its existence. But to the younger girl it was always vaguely present. She knew that somewhere between herself and her friend there was a locked door. Her own reserve never permitted her to attempt to open it. With a species of pride that was largely composed of shyness, she held aloof. But she was never quite unconscious of the opposing barrier. She felt that the old sweet intimacy, that had so lightened the burden of her solitude, was gone.

Meanwhile, Daisy was growing stronger, and day by day more active. She never referred to her baby, and very seldom to her husband. When his letters arrived she invariably put them away with scarcely a glance. Muriel sometimes wondered if she even read them. It was pitifully plain to her that Will Musgrave's place in his wife's heart was very, very narrow. It had dwindled perceptibly since the baby's death.

On the subject of Will's letters, Nick could have enlightened her, for he always appeared at the cottage on mail-day for news. But Muriel, having discovered this habit, as regularly absented herself, with the result that they seldom met. He never made any effort to see her. On one occasion when she came unexpectedly upon him and Olga, shrimping along the shore, she was surprised that he did not second the child's eager proposal that she should join them. He actually seemed too keen upon the job in hand to pay her much attention.

And gradually she began to perceive that this was the attitude towards her that he had decided to assume. What it veiled she knew not, nor did she inquire. It was enough for her that hostilities had ceased. Nick apparently was bestowing his energies elsewhere.

Midsummer passed, and a July of unusual heat drew on. Dr. Jim and his wife and boys had departed to Switzerland. Nick and Olga had elected to remain at Redlands. They were out all day long in the motor or dogcart, on horseback or on foot. Life was one perpetual picnic to Olga just then, and she was not looking forward to the close of the summer holidays when, so her father had decreed, she was to return to her home and the ordinary routine. Nick's plans were still unsettled though he spoke now and then of a prospective return to India. He must in any case return thither, so he once told her, whether he decided to remain or not. It was not a pleasant topic to Olga, and she always sought to avoid any allusion to it. After the fashion of children, she lived in the present, and enjoyed it to the full: bathing with Muriel every morning, and spending the remainder of the day in Nick's society. The friendship between these two was based upon complete understanding. They had been comrades as long as Olga could remember. Given Nick, it was very seldom that she desired any one besides.

Muriel had ceased to marvel over this strange fact. She had come to realise that Nick was, and always must be, an enigma to her. In the middle of July, when the heat was so intense as to be almost intolerable, Daisy received a pressing invitation to visit an old friend, and to go yachting on the Broads. She refused it at first point-blank; but Muriel, hearing of the matter before the letter was sent, interfered, and practically insisted upon a change of decision.

"It is the very thing for you," she declared. "Brethaven has done its best for you. But you want a dose of more bracing air to make you quite strong again. It's absurd of you to dream of throwing away such an opportunity. I simply won't let you do it."

"But how can I possibly leave you all alone?" Daisy protested. "If the Ratcliffes were at home, I might think of it, but—"

"That settles it," Muriel announced with determination. "I never heard such nonsense in my life. What do you think could possibly happen to me here? You know perfectly well that a couple of weeks of my own society would do me no harm whatever."

So insistent was she, that finally she gained her point, and Daisy, albeit somewhat reluctantly, departed for Norfolk, leaving her to her own devices.

The heat was so great in those first days of solitude that Muriel was not particularly energetic. Apart from her early swim with Olga, and an undeniably languid stroll in the evening, she scarcely left the precincts of the cottage: No visitors came to her. There were none but fisher-folk in the little village. And so her sole company consisted of Daisy's *ayah* and the elderly English cook.

But she did not suffer from loneliness. She had books and work in plenty, and it was even something of a relief, though she never owned it, to be apart from Daisy for a little. They never disagreed, but always at the back of her mind there lay the consciousness of a gulf between them.

She was at first somewhat anxious lest Nick should feel called upon to entertain her, and should invite her to accompany him and Olga upon some of their expeditions. But he did not apparently think of it, and she was always very emphatic in assuring Olga that she was enjoying her quiet time.

She and Nick had not met for some weeks, and she began to think it more than probable that they would not do so during Daisy's absence. Under ordinary circumstances this expectation of hers would doubtless have been realised, for Nick had plainly every intention of keeping out of her way; but the day of emergency usually dawns upon a world of sleepers.

The brooding heat culminated at last in an evening of furious storm, and Muriel speedily left the dinner-table to watch the magnificent spectacle of vivid and almost continuous lightning over the sea. It was a wonder that always drew her. She did not feel the nervous oppression that torments so many women, or if she felt it she rose above it. The splendour of the rising storm lifted her out of herself. She had no thought for anything else.

For more than half an hour she stood by the little sitting-room window, gazing out upon the storm-tossed water. It had not begun to rain, but the sound of it was in the air, and the earth was waiting expectantly. There seemed to be a feeling of expectation everywhere. She was vaguely restless under it, curiously impatient for the climax.

It came at last, so suddenly, so blindingly, that she reeled back against the curtain in sheer, physical recoil. The whole sky seemed to burst into flame, and the crash of thunder was so instantaneous that she felt as if a shell had exploded at her feet. Trembling, she hid her face. The world seemed to rock all around her. For the first time she was conscious of fear.

Then as the thunder died into a distant roar, the heavens opened as if at a word of command, and in one marvellous, glittering sheet the rain burst forth.

She lifted her head to gaze upon this new wonder that the incessant lightning revealed. The noise was like the sharp rattle of musketry, and it almost drowned the heavier artillery overhead. The window was blurred and streaming, but the brilliance outside was such that every detail in the little garden was clear to her notwithstanding. And though she still trembled, she nerved herself to look forth.

An instant later she sprang backwards with a wild cry of terror. A face—a wrinkled face that she knew—was there close against the window-pane, and had looked into her own.

CHAPTER XXXIII

THE LIFTING OF THE MASK

Out of a curious numbness that had almost been a swoon there came to her the consciousness of a hand that rapped and rapped and rapped upon the pane. She had fled away to the farther end of the room in her panic. She had turned the lamp low at the beginning of the storm, and now it burned so dimly that it scarcely gave out any light at all. Beyond the window, the lightning flashed with an awful luridness upon the rushing hail. Beyond the window, looking in upon her, and knocking, knocking, knocking, stood the figure of her dread.

She came to herself slowly, with a quaking heart. It was more horrible to her than anything she had known since the days of her flight from the beleaguered fort; but she knew that she must fight down her horror, she knew as certainly as if a physical force compelled her that she would have to go to the window, would have to open to the man who waited there.

Slowly she brought her quivering body into subjection, while every nerve twitched and clamoured to escape. Slowly she dragged herself back to the vision that had struck her with that paralysis of terror. Resisting feebly, invisibly compelled, she went.

He ceased to knock, and, his face against the pane, he spoke imperatively. What he said, she could not hear in that tumult of mighty sound. Only she felt his insistence, answered to it, was mastered by it.

White-faced, with horror clutching at her heart, she undid the catch. His one hand, strong, instinct with energy, helped her to raise the sash. In a moment he was in the room, bare-headed, drenched from head to foot.

She fell back before him, but he scarcely looked at her. He shut the window sharply, then strode to the lamp, and turned it up. Then, abruptly he wheeled and spoke in a voice half-kindly, half-contemptuous. "Muriel, you're a little idiot!"

There was little in the words to comfort her, yet she was instantly and vastly reassured. She was also for the moment overwhelmingly ashamed, but he did not give her time to think of that.

"I couldn't get in any other way," he said. "I tried the doors first, hammered at them, but no one came. Look here! Olga is ill, very ill, and she wants you badly. Are you brave enough to come?"

"Oh!" Muriel said, with a gasp. "Now, do you mean? With—with you?"

He threw her an odd look under his flickering eyelids, and she noted with a scared minuteness of attention the gleam of the lamplight on their pale lashes. She had always hated pale eyelashes. They seemed to her untrustworthy.

"Yes," he told her grimly. "All alone—with me—in the storm. Shall you be afraid—if I give you my hand to hold? You've done it before."

Was he mocking her weakness? She could not say. She only knew that he watched her with the intensity of an eagle that marks its quarry. He did not mean her to refuse.

"What is the matter with Olga?" she asked.

"I don't know. I believe it is sunstroke. We were motoring in the mid-day heat. She didn't seem to feel it at the time, but her head ached when we got in. She is in a high fever now. I've sent my man on in the motor to fetch Jim's locum from Weir. I should have brought the dogcart myself, to fetch you, but I couldn't trust the horse in this."

"You left her alone to come here?" Muriel questioned.

He nodded. "I had no choice. She wished it. Besides, there were none but women-folk left. She's got one of them with her, the least imbecile of the lot, which isn't saying much. They're all terrified of course at the storm—all except Olga. She is never afraid of anything."

A frightful crash of thunder carried away his words. Before it had rolled away, Muriel was at the door. She made a rapid sign to him, and was gone.

Nick chafed up and down the room, waiting for her. The storm continued with unabated violence, but he did not give it a thought. He was counting the moments with feverish impatience.

Muriel's absence scarcely lasted for five minutes, but when she came back all trace of fear had left her. Her face showed quiet and matter-of-fact above the long waterproof in which she had wrapped herself. Over her arm she carried a waterproof cloak.

She held it out to him. "It's one of Daisy's, but you are to wear it. I think you must be mad to have come out without anything."

She put it round his shoulders; and he thanked her with a smothered laugh.

A terrific blast of wind and rain met them as they emerged from the cottage, nearly whirling Muriel off her feet. She made an instinctive clutch at her companion and instantly her hand was caught fast in his. He drew her arm close under his own, and she did not resist him. There was something reassuring in his touch.

Later she wondered if they spoke at all during that terrible walk. She could never recall a word on either side. And yet, though in a measure frightened, she was not panic-stricken.

The storm was beginning to subside a little before they reached Redlands, though the rain still fell heavily. In the intervals between the lightning it was pitch dark. They had no lantern, but Nick was undismayed. He walked as lightly and surely as a cat, and Muriel had no choice but to trust herself unreservedly to his guidance. She marvelled afterwards at the complete trust with which that night he had managed to inspire her, but at the time she never questioned it.

Yet when the lights of Redlands shone at last through the gloom, she breathed a sigh of relief. Instantly Nick spoke.

"Well done!", he said briefly. "You are your father's daughter still."

She knew that she flushed in the darkness, and was glad that he could not see her face.

"You must go and get dry, first of all," he went on. "I told them to light a fire somewhere. And you are to have some coffee too. Mind, I say it."

To this she responded with some spirit. "I will if you will."

"I must go straight to Olga," he said. "I promised I would."

"Not in your wet things!" Muriel exclaimed. "No, Nick! Listen! I am not wet, not as you are. Let me go to Olga first. You can send me some coffee in her room if you like. But you must go at once and change. Promise you will, Nick!"

She spoke urgently. For some reason the occasion seemed to demand it.

Nick was silent for a little, as if considering. Then as they finally reached the porch he spoke in a tone she did not altogether fathom.

"I say, you are not going to shut me out, you know."

She looked up in astonishment. "Of course not. I never dreamt of such a thing."

"All right," he said, and this time she knew he spoke with relief. "I will do as you like then."

A moment more, and he opened the door, standing aside for her to pass. She entered quickly, glad to be in shelter, and paused to slip off her streaming waterproof. He took it from her, passing his hand over her sleeve.

"You are sure you are not wet through?"

"Quite sure," she told him. "Take me straight up, won't you?"

"Yes. Come this way."

He preceded her up the wide stairs where he might have walked beside her, not pausing for an instant till he stood at Olga's door.

"Go straight in," he said then. "She is expecting you. Tell her, if she wants to know, that I am coming directly."

He passed on swiftly with the words, and disappeared into a room close by.

Very softly Muriel turned the door-handle and entered. Olga's voice greeted her before she was well in the room. It sounded husky and strained.

"Muriel! Dear Muriel! I'm so glad you've come. I've wanted you so you can't think. Where's Nick?"

"He is coming, dearest." Muriel went forward to the bed, and took in hers the two hands eagerly extended.

The child was lying in an uneasy position, her hair streaming in a disordered tangle about her flushed face. She was shivering violently though the hands Muriel held were burning. "You came all through this awful storm," she whispered. "It was lovely of you, dear. I hope you weren't frightened."

Muriel sat down beside her. "And you have been left all alone," she said.

"I didn't mind," gasped Olga. "Mrs. Ellis—that's the cook—was here at first. But she was such an ass about the thunder that I sent her away. I expect she's in the coal cellar."

A gleam of fun shone for an instant in her eyes, and was gone. The fevered hands closed tightly in Muriel's hold. "I feel so ill," she murmured, "so ill."

"Where is it, darling?" Muriel asked her tenderly.

"It's, it's all over me," moaned Olga. "My head worst, and my throat. My throat is dreadful. It makes me want to cry."

There was little that Muriel could do to ease her. She tied back the tossing hair, and rearranged the bedclothes; then sat down by her side, hoping she might get some sleep.

Not long after, Nick crept in on slippered feet, but Olga heard him instantly, and started up with out-flung arms. "Nick, darling, I want you! I want you! Come quite close! I think I'm going to die. Don't let me, Nick!"

Muriel rose to make room for him, but he motioned her back sharply; then knelt down himself by the child's pillow and took her head upon his arm.

"Stick to it, sweetheart!" he murmured softly. "There's a medicine man coming, and you'll be better presently." Olga cuddled against him with a sigh, and comforted by the close holding of his arm dropped presently into an uneasy doze.

Nick never stirred from his position, and mutely Muriel sat and watched him. There was a wonderful tenderness about him just then, a softness with which she was strangely familiar, but which almost she had forgotten. If she had never seen him before that moment, she knew that she would have liked him.

He seemed to have wholly forgotten her presence. His entire attention was concentrated upon the child. His lips twitched from time to time, and she knew that he was very anxious, intensely impatient under his stillness for the doctor's coming. She remembered that old trick of his. She had never before associated it with any emotion.

Suddenly he turned his head as if he had felt her scrutiny, and looked straight into her eyes. It was only for a moment. His glance flickered beyond her with scarcely a pause. Yet it was to her as if by that swift look he had spoken, had for the first time made deep and passionate protest against her bitter judgment of him, had as it were shown her in a single flash the human heart beneath the jester's garb.

And again very deep down in her soul there stirred that blind, unconscious entity, of the existence of which she herself had so vague a knowledge, feeling upwards, groping outwards, to the light.

There came upon her a sudden curious sense of consternation—a feeling as of a mental earthquake when the very foundations of the soul are shaken. Had she conceivably been mistaken in him? With all her knowledge of him, had she by some strange mischance—some maddening, some inexplicable misapprehension—failed utterly and miserably to see this man as he really was?

For the first time the question sprang up within her. And she found no answer to it—only that breathless, blank dismay.

Softly Nick's voice broke in upon her seething doubt. He had laid Olga back upon the pillow.

"The doctor is here. Do you mind staying with her while I go?"

"You'll come back, Nick?" the child urged, in her painful whisper.

"Yes, I'll come back," he promised. "Honest Injun!"

He touched her cheek lightly at parting, and Olga caught the caressing hand and pressed it against her burning lips. Muriel saw his face as he turned from the bed. It was all softened and quivering with emotion.

CHAPTER XXXIV
AT THE GATE OF DEATH

In the morning they knew the worst. Olga had scarlet fever.

The doctor imparted the news to Nick and Muriel standing outside the door of the sick-room. Nick's reception of it was by no means characteristic. For the first time in her life Muriel saw consternation undisguised upon the yellow face.

"Great Jupiter!" he said. "What a criminal ass I am!"

At another moment she could have laughed at the tragic force of his self-arraignment. Even as it was, she barely repressed a smile as she set his mind at rest. She needed no explanation. It was easy enough to follow the trend of his thoughts just then.

"If you are thinking of me," she said, "I have had it."

She saw his instant relief, though he merely acknowledged the statement by a nod.

"We must have a nurse," he said briefly. "We shall manage all right then. I'll do my turn. Oh, stuff!" at a look from the doctor. "I sha'n't hurt. I'm much too tough a morsel for microbes to feed on."

Possibly the doctor shared this opinion, for he made no verbal protest. It fell to Muriel to do this later in the day when the nurse was installed, and she was at liberty to leave Olga's room. Nick had just returned from the post-office whence he had been sending a message to the child's father. She came upon him stealing up to take a look at her. Seeing Muriel he stopped. "How is she?"

Muriel moved away to an open window at the end of the passage before she made reply. He followed her, and they stood together, looking out upon the sunset.

"The fever is very high," she said. "And she is suffering a good deal of pain. She is not quite herself at times."

"You mean she is worse?" He looked at her keenly.

It was exactly what she did mean. Olga had been growing steadily worse all day. Yet when abruptly he turned to leave her, Muriel laid a hasty hand upon his arm.

"Nick," she said, and her voice was almost imploring, "don't go in! Please don't go in!"

He stopped short. "Why not?"

She removed her hand quickly. "It's so dangerous—besides being unnecessary. Won't you be sensible about it?"

He gave his head a queer upward jerk, and stood as one listening, not looking at her. "What for?"

She could not think of any very convincing reason for the moment. Yet it was imperative that he should see the matter as she saw it.

"Suppose I had not had it," she ventured, "what would you have done?"

"Packed you off to the cottage again double quick," said Nick promptly.

It was the answer she had angled for. She seized upon it. "Well, tell me why."

He spun round on his heels and faced her. He was blinking very rapidly. "You asked me that question once before," he said. "And out of a sentimental consideration for your feelings—I didn't answer it. Do you really want an answer this time, or shall I go on being sentimentally considerate?"

She heard the old subtle jeering note in his voice, but its effect upon her was oddly different from what it had ever been before. It did not anger her, nor did it wholly frighten her. It dawned upon her suddenly that, though possibly it lay in his power to hurt her, he would not do so.

She answered him with composure. "I don't want you to be anything but sensible, Nick. And it isn't sensible to expose yourself to unnecessary risk. It's wrong."

"That's my lookout," said Nick.

It was indubitably; but she wanted very much to gain her point.

"Won't you at least keep away unless she asks for you?" she urged.

"You seem mighty anxious to get rid of me," said Nick.

"I am not," she returned quickly. "I am not. You know it isn't that."

"Do I?" he said quizzically. "It's one of the few things I shouldn't have known without being told. Well, I'm sorry I can't consent to be sensible as you call it. I am quite sure personally that there isn't the slightest danger. It isn't so infectious at this stage, you know. Perhaps by-and-by, when she is through the worst, I will think about it."

He spoke lightly, but she was aware of the anxiety that underlay the words. She said no more, reminding herself that argument with Nick was always futile, sometimes worse. Nevertheless she found some comfort in the smile with which he left her. He had refused to treat with her, but his enmity—if enmity it could be called—was no longer active. He had proclaimed a truce which she knew he would not break.

Olga was delirious that night, and privately Muriel was glad that she had not been able to exclude him; for his control over the child was wonderful. As once with a tenderness maternal he had soothed her, so now he soothed Olga, patiently, steadfastly, even with a certain cheeriness. It all came back to her as she watched him, the strength of the man, his selfless devotion.

She could see that both doctor and nurse thought very seriously of the child. The former paid a late visit, but said very little beyond advising her to rest if she could in an adjacent room. Both Nick and the nurse seconded this, and, seeing there was nothing that she could do, she gave way in the matter, lying down as she was with but small expectation of sleep. But she was wearier than she knew, and the slumber into which she fell was deep, and would have lasted for some hours undisturbed.

It was Nick who roused her, and starting up at his touch, she knew instantly that what they had all mutely feared had drawn very near. His face told her at a glance, for he made no effort to dissemble.

"The nurse thinks you had better come," was all he said.

She pushed the hair from her forehead, and turned without a word to obey the summons. But at the door something checked her, something cried aloud within her, bidding her pause. She stopped. Nick was close behind her. Swiftly, obedient to the voice that cried, she stretched out her hand to him. He gripped it fast, and she was conscious for an instant of a curious gladness, a willingness to leave it in his hold, that she had never experienced before. But at the door of Olga's room he softly relinquished it, and drew back.

Olga was lying propped on pillows, and breathing quickly. The nurse was bending over her with a glass, but Olga's face was turned away. She was watching the door.

As Muriel came to her, the light eyes brightened to quick intelligence, and the parted lips tried to speak. But no sound came forth, and a frown of pain succeeded the effort.

Muriel stooped swiftly and grasped the slender hand that lay clenched upon the sheet.

"There, darling! Don't try to talk. It hurts you so. We are both here, Nick and I, and we understand all about it."

It was the first time she had ever voluntarily coupled herself with him. It came to her instinctively to do it in that moment.

But Olga had something to say, something apparently that must be said. With infinite difficulty she forced a husky whisper. Muriel stooped lower to catch it, so low that her face was almost touching the face upon the pillow.

"Muriel," came haltingly from the parched lips, "there's something—I want—to say to you—about Nick."

Muriel felt the blood surging at her temples as the faint words reached her. She would have given anything to know that he was out of earshot.

"Won't you say it in the morning, darling?" she said, almost with pleading in her voice. "It's so late now."

It was not late. It was very, very early—the solemn hour when countless weary ones fall into their long sleep. And the moment she had spoken, her heart smote her. Was she for her own peace of mind trying to silence the child's last words on earth?

"No, never mind, dear," she amended tenderly. "I am listening to you. Tell me now."

"Yes," panted Olga. "I must. I must. You remember—that day—with the daisies—the day we saw—the hawk?"

Yes, well Muriel remembered it. The thought of it went through her like a stab.

"Yes, dear. What of it?" she heard herself say.

"Well, you know—I've thought since—that the daisies meant Nick, not—not—I can't remember his name, Muriel."

513

"Do you mean Captain Grange, dear?"

"Yes, yes, of course. He was there too, wasn't he? I'm sure now—quite sure—they didn't mean him."

"Very likely not, dear."

"And Muriel—do you know—Nick was just miserable—after you went. I sort of felt he was. And late—late that night I woke up, and I crept down to him—in the library. And he had his head down on the table—as if—as if—he was crying. Oh, Muriel!"

A sharp sob interrupted the piteous whisper. Muriel folded her arms about the child, pillowing the tired head on her breast. All the fair hair had been cut off earlier in the day. Its absence gave Olga a very babyish appearance.

Brokenly, with many gasping pauses, the pathetic little story came to an end. "I went to him—and I asked him what it was. And he—he looked up with that funny face he makes—you know—and he just said, 'Oh, it's all right. I've been feeding on dust and ashes all day long, that's all. And it's dry fare for a thirsty man!' He thought—I wouldn't know what he meant. But I did, Muriel. And I always wanted to tell you. But—somehow—you wouldn't let me. He meant you. He was hurt—so hurt—because you weren't kind to him. Oh, Muriel, won't you—won't you—try to be kind to him now? Please, dear, please!"

Muriel's eyes sought Nick, and instantly a thrill of surprise and relief shot through her. He had not heard that request of Olga's. She doubted if he had heard anything. He was sunk in a chair well in the background with his head on his hand, and looking at him she saw his shoulders shake with a soundless sob.

She looked away again with a sense of trespass. This—this was the man who had fought and cursed and slain under her eyes—the man from whose violence she had shrunk appalled, whose strength had made her shudder many a time. She had never imagined that he could grieve thus—even for his little pal Olga.

Tenderly she turned back to the child. That single glimpse of the man in pain had made it suddenly easy to grant her earnest prayer.

"I won't be unkind to him again, darling," she promised softly.

"Never any more?" insisted Olga.

"Never any more, my darling."

Olga made a little nestling movement against her. It was all she wanted, and now that the effort of asking was over she was very tired.

The nurse drew softly back into the shadow, and a deep silence fell in the room. Through it in a long, monotonous roar there came the sound of the sea breaking, eternally breaking, along the beach.

No one moved. Olga's breathing was growing slower, so much slower that there were times when Muriel, listening intently, fancied that it had wholly ceased. She held the little slim body close in her arms, jealously close, as though she were defying Death itself. And ever through the stillness she could hear her own heart beating like the hoofs of a galloping horse.

Slowly the night began to pass. The outline of the window-frame became visible against a faint grey glimmer. The window was open, and a breath of the coming dawn wandered in with the fragrance of drenched roses. A soft rain was falling. The patter of it could be heard upon the leaves.

Again Muriel listened for the failing breath, listened closely, tensely, her face bent low to the fair head that lay so still upon her breast.

But she heard nothing—nothing but her own heart quickening, quickening, from fear to suspense, from suspense to the anguish of conviction.

She lifted her face at last, and in the same instant there arose a sudden flood of song from the sleeping garden, as the first lark soared to meet the dawn.

Half-dazed, she listened to that marvellous outpouring of gladness, so wildly rapturous, so weirdly holy. On, ever on, pealed the bird-voice; on to the very Gates of Heaven, and it seemed to the girl who listened as though she heard a child's spirit singing up the steeps of Paradise. With her heart she followed it till suddenly she heard no more. The voice ceased as it had begun, ceased as a burst of music when an open door is closed—and there fell in its stead a silence that could be felt.

CHAPTER XXXV
THE ARMISTICE

She could not have said for how long she sat motionless, the slight, inert body clasped against her breast. Vaguely she knew that the night passed, and with it the wondrous silence that had lain like a benediction upon the dawn. A thousand living things awoke to rejoice in the crystal splendour of the morning; but within the quiet room the spell remained unlifted, the silence lay untouched. It was as though the presence of Death had turned it into a peaceful sanctuary that no mere earthly tumult could disturb.

She sat in a species of waking stupor for a long, long time, not daring to move lest the peace that enfolded her should be shattered. Higher and higher the sun climbed up the sky till at last it topped the cedar-trees and shone in upon her, throwing a single ray of purest gold across the foot of the bed. Fascinated, she watched it travel slowly upwards, till a silent, one-armed figure arose and softly drew the curtain.

The room grew dim again. The world was shut out. She was not conscious of physical fatigue, only of a certain weariness of waiting, waiting for she knew not what. It seemed interminable, but she would not seek to end it. She was as a soldier waiting for the order to quit his post.

There came a slight movement at last. Someone touched her, whispered to her. She looked up blankly, and saw the nurse. But understanding seemed to have gone from her during those long hours. She could not take in a word. There arose a great surging in her brain, and the woman's face faded into an indistinct blur. She sat rigid, afraid to move lest she should fall.

She heard vague whisperings over her head, and an arm that was like a steel spring encircled her. Someone lifted her burden gently from her, and a faint murmur reached her, such as a child makes in its sleep.

Then the arm that supported her gradually raised her up till she was on her feet. Mechanically she tried to walk, but was instantly overcome by a sick sense of powerlessness.

"I can't!" she gasped. "I can't!"

Nick's voice answered her in a quick, confident whisper. "Yes, you can, dear. It's all right. Hang on to me. I won't let you go."

She obeyed him blindly. There was nothing else to do. And so, half-led, half-carried, she tottered from the room.

A glare of sunlight smote upon her from a passage-window with a brilliance that almost hurt her. She stood still, clinging to Nick's shoulder.

"Oh, Nick," she faltered weakly, "why don't they—pull down the blinds?"

Nick turned aside, still closely holding her, into the room in which she had rested for the earlier part of the night.

"Because, thank God," he said, "there is no need. Olga is going to live."

He helped her down into an easy-chair, and would have left her; but she clung to him still, weakly but persistently.

"Oh, Nick, don't laugh! Tell me the truth for once! Please, Nick, please!"

He yielded to her so abruptly that she was half-startled, dropping suddenly down upon his knees beside her, the morning light full upon his face.

"I am telling you the truth," he said. "I believe you have saved her life. She has been sleeping ever since sunrise."

Muriel gazed at him speechlessly; but she no longer suspected him of trying to deceive her. If he had never told her the truth before that moment he was telling it to her then.

She gave a little gasping cry of relief unspeakable, and hid her face. The next moment Nick was on his feet. She heard his quick, light step as he crossed the threshold, and realised thankfully that he had left her alone.

A little later, a servant brought her a breakfast-tray with a message from the master of the house to the effect that he hoped she would go to bed and take a long rest.

It was excellent advice, and she acted upon it; for since the worst strain was over, sleep had become an urgent necessity to her. She wondered as she lay down if Nick were following the same course. She hoped he was, for she had a curiously vivid memory of the lines that sleeplessness had drawn about his eyes.

It was late afternoon when she awoke, and sat swiftly up with a confused sense of being watched.

"Don't jump like that!" a gruff voice said. "Lie down again at once. You are not to get up till to-morrow morning."

She turned with a shaky laugh of welcome to find Dr. Jim seated frowning by her side. He laid a compelling hand upon her shoulder.

"Lie down again, do you hear? There's nothing for you to do. Olga is much better, and doesn't want you."

"And Nick?" said Muriel.

They were the first words that occurred to her. She said them hurriedly, with heightened colour.

Jim Ratcliffe frowned more than ever. He was feeling her pulse. "A nice couple of idiots you are!" he grimly remarked. "You needn't worry about Nick. He has gone for a ride. As soon as he comes back, he will dine and go to bed."

"Can't I get up to dinner?" Muriel suggested.

She could scarcely have said why she made the proposal, and she was certainly surprised when Jim Ratcliffe fell in with it. He looked at his watch. "Well, you may if you like. You will probably sleep the better for it. But I'll have no nonsense, mind, Muriel. You're to do as you're told."

Muriel smiled acquiescence. She felt that everything was right now that Dr. Jim had returned to take the direction of affairs into his own hands. He had come back alone, and he intended to finish his holiday under Nick's roof. So much he told her before, with an abrupt smile, he thanked her for her care of his little girl and took himself off.

She almost regretted her decision when she came to get up, for the strain was telling upon her more than she had realised. Not since Simla days had she felt so utterly worn out. She was glad of the cup of tea which Dr. Jim sent in to her before she left her room.

Sitting on the cushioned window-seat to drink it, she heard the tread of a horse's feet along the drive, and with a start she saw Nick come into view round a bend.

Her first impulse was to draw back out of sight, but the next moment she changed her mind and remained motionless. Her heart was suddenly beating very fast.

He was riding very carelessly, the bridle lying on the horse's neck. The evening sun was shining full in his face, but he did not seem to mind. His head was thrown back. He rode like a returning conqueror, wearied it might be, but triumphant.

Passing into the shadow of the house, he saw her instantly, and the smile that flashed into his face was one of sheer exultation. He dropped the bridle altogether to wave to her.

"Up already? Have you seen old Jim?"

She nodded. It was impossible at the moment not to reflect his smile. "I am coming down soon," she told him.

"Come now," said Nick persuasively.

She hesitated. He was slipping from his horse. A groom came up and took the animal from him.

Nick paused below her window, and once more lifted his grinning, confident face.

"I say, Muriel!"

She leaned down a little. "Well?"

"Don't come if you don't want to, you know."

She laughed half-reluctantly, conscious of a queer desire to please him. Olga's words were running in her brain. He had fed on dust and ashes.

Yet still she hesitated. "Will you wait for me?"

"Till doomsday," said Nick obligingly.

And drawn by a power that would not be withstood, she went down, still smiling, and joined him in the garden.

CHAPTER XXXVI
THE EAGLE STRIKES

Olga's recovery, when the crisis of the disease was past, was more rapid than even her father had anticipated; and this fact, combined with a spell of glorious summer weather, made the period of her quarantine very tedious, particularly as Nick was rigidly excluded from the sick-room.

At Olga's earnest request Muriel consented to remain at Redlands. Daisy had written to postpone her own return to the cottage, having received two or three invitations which she wished to accept if Muriel could still spare her.

Blake was in Scotland. His letters were not very frequent, and though his leave was nearly up, he did not speak of returning.

Muriel was thus thrown upon Jim Ratcliffe's care—a state of affairs which seemed to please him mightily. It was in fact his presence that made life easy for her just then. She saw considerably more of him than of Nick, the latter having completely relegated the duties of host to his brother. Though they met every day, they were seldom alone together, and she began to have a feeling that Nick's attitude towards her had undergone a change. His manner was now always friendly, but never intimate. He did not seek her society, but neither did he avoid her. And never by word or gesture did he refer to anything that had been between them in the past. She even wondered sometimes if there might not possibly have been another interpretation to Olga's story. That unwonted depression of his that the child had witnessed had surely never been inspired by her.

She found the time pass quickly enough during those six weeks. The care of Olga occupied her very fully. She was always busy devising some new scheme for her amusement.

Mrs. Ratcliffe returned to Weir, and Dr. Jim determined to transfer Olga to her home as soon as she was out of quarantine. With paternal kindliness, he insisted that Muriel must accompany her. Daisy's return was still uncertain, though it could not be long delayed; and Muriel had no urgent desire to return to the lonely life on the shore.

So, to Olga's outspoken delight, she yielded to the doctor's persuasion, and on the afternoon preceding the child's emancipation from her long imprisonment she walked down to the cottage to pack her things.

It was a golden day in the middle of September and she lingered awhile on the shore when her work was done. There was not a wave in all the vast, shimmering sea. The tide was going out, and the shallow ripples were clear as glass as they ran out along the white beach. Muriel paused often in her walk. She was sorry to leave the little fishing-village, realising that she had been very happy there. Life had passed as smoothly as a dream of late, so smoothly that she had been content to live in the present with scarcely a thought for the future.

This afternoon she had begun to realise that her peaceful time was drawing to an end. In a few weeks more, she would be in town in all the bustle of preparation. And further still ahead of her—possibly two months—there loomed the prospect of her return to India, of Lady Bassett's soft patronage, of her marriage.

She shivered a little as one after another these coming events presented themselves. There was not one of them that she would not have postponed with relief. She stood still with her face to the sunlit sea, and told herself that her summer in England had been all too short. She had an almost passionate longing for just one more year of home.

A pebble skimming past her and leaping from ripple to ripple like, a living thing caught her attention. She turned sharply, and the next moment smiled a welcome.

Nick had come up behind her unperceived. She greeted him with pleasure unfeigned. She was tired of her own morbid thoughts just then. Whatever he might be, he was at least never depressing.

"I'm saying good-bye," she told him. "I don't suppose I shall ever come here again."

He came and stood beside her while he grubbed in the sand with a stick.

"Not even to see me?" he suggested.

"Are you going to live here?" she asked in surprise.

"Oh, I suppose so," said Nick, "when I marry."

"Are you going to be married?" Almost in spite of her the question leapt out.

He looked up, grinning shrewdly. "I put it to you," he said. "Am I the sort of man to live alone?"

She experienced a curious sense of relief. "But you are not alone in the world," she pointed out. "You have relations."

"You regard marriage as a last resource?" questioned Nick.

She coloured and turned her face to the shore. "I don't think any man ought to marry unless—unless—he cares," she said, striving hard to keep the personal note out of her voice.

"Exactly," said Nick, moving beside her. "But doesn't that remark apply to women as well?"

She did not answer him. A discussion on this topic was the last thing she desired.

He did not press the point, and she wondered a little at his forbearance. She glanced at him once or twice as they walked, but his humorous, yellow face told her nothing.

Reaching some rocks, he suddenly stopped. "I've got to get some seaweed for Olga. Do you mind waiting?"

"I will help you," she answered.

He shook his head. "No, you are tired. Just sit down in the sun. I won't be long."

She seated herself without protest, and he turned to leave her. A few paces from her he paused, and she saw that he was trying to light a cigarette. He failed twice, and impulsively she sprang up.

"Nick, why don't you ask me to help you?"

He whizzed round. "Perhaps I don't want you to," he said quizzically.

She took the match-box from him. "Don't be absurd! Why shouldn't I?" She struck a match and held it out to him. But he did not take it from her. He took her wrist instead, and stooping forward lighted his cigarette deliberately.

She did not look at him. Some instinct warned her that his eyes were intently searching her face. She seemed to feel them darting over her in piercing, impenetrable scrutiny.

He released her slowly at length and stood up. "Am I to have the pleasure of dancing at your wedding?" he asked her suddenly.

She looked up then very sharply, and against her will a burning blush rose up to her temples. He waited for her answer, and at last it came.

"If you think it worth your while."

"I would come from the other side of the world to see you made happy," said Nick.

She turned her face aside. "You are very kind."

"Think so?" There was a note of banter in his voice. "It's the first time you ever accused me of that."

She made no rejoinder. She had a feeling at the throat that prevented speech, even had she had any words to utter. Certainly, as he had discovered, she was very tired. It was physical weariness, no doubt, but she had an almost overmastering desire to shed childish tears.

"You trot back now," said Nick cheerily. "I can grub along quite well by myself."

She turned back silently. Why was it that the world seemed so grey and cold on that golden summer afternoon? She sat down again in the sunshine, and began to trace an aimless design in the sand with the stick Nick had left behind. Away in the distance she heard his cracked voice humming. Was he really as cheerful as he seemed, she wondered? Or was he merely making the best of things?

Again her thoughts went back to Olga's pathetic little revelation. Strange that she who knew him so intimately should never have seen him in such a mood! But did she know him after all? It was a question she had asked herself many times of late. She remembered how he had lightly told her that he had a reverse side. But had she ever really seen it, save for those brief glimpses by Olga's bedside, and as it was reflected in the child's whole-souled devotion to him? She wished with all her heart that he would lift the veil just once for her and show her his inner soul.

Again her thoughts passed to her approaching marriage. She had received a letter from Blake that day, telling her at length of his plans. He and Daisy had been staying in the same house, but he was just returning to town. He was to sail in less than a fortnight, and would come and say good-bye to her immediately before his departure. The letter had been courteously kind throughout, but she had not felt tempted to read it again. It contained no reference to their wedding, save such as she chose to attribute to the concluding sentence: "We can talk everything over when we meet." A sense of chill struck her when she recalled the words. He was very kind, of course, and invariably meant well; but she had begun to realise of late that there were times when she found him a little heavy and unresponsive. Not that she had ever desired any demonstration of tenderness from him, heaven knew. But the very consciousness that she had not desired this added to the chill. She was not quite sure that she wanted to see him again before he sailed. Certainly he had never bored her; but it was not inconceivable that he might do so. She shivered ever so slightly. It was not an exciting prospect—life with Blake. He was quite sure to be kind to her. He would consider her in every way. But was that after all quite all she wanted? A great sigh welled suddenly up from the bottom of her heart. Life was ineffably dreary—when it was not revoltingly horrible.

"Shall I tell you what is the matter?" said Nick.

She started violently, and found him leaning across the flat rock on which she was seated. His eyes were remarkably bright. She had a feeling that he suppressed a laugh as his look flickered over her.

"Sorry I made you jump," he said. "You ought to be used to me by this time. Anyhow you needn't be frightened. My venom was extracted long ago."

She turned to him with sudden, unconsidered impulse. "Oh, Nick," she said, "I sometimes think to myself I've been a great fool."

He nodded. Her vehemence did not seem to surprise him. "I thought it would strike you sooner or later," he said.

She laughed in spite of herself with her eyes full of tears. "There's not much comfort in that."

"I haven't any comfort to give you," said Nick, "not at this stage. I'll give you advice if you like—which I know you won't take."

"No, please don't! That would be even worse." There was a tremor in her voice. She knew that she had stepped off the beaten track; but she had an intense, an almost passionate longing to go a little further, to penetrate, if only for a moment, that perpetual mask.

"Don't let us talk of my affairs," she said. "Tell me of your own. What are you going to do?"

Nick's eyebrows went up. "I thought I was coming to your wedding," he remarked. "That's as far as I've got at present."

She made a gesture of impatience. "Do you never think of the future?"

"Not in your presence," laughed Nick. "I think of you—you—and only you. Didn't you know?"

She turned away in silence. Was he tormenting her deliberately? Or did he fail to see that she was in earnest?

There followed a pause, and then, urged by that unknown impulse that would not be repressed, she did a curious thing. She got up, and, facing him, she made a very earnest appeal.

"Nick, why do you always treat me like this? Why will you never be honest with me?"

There was more of pain than reproach in the words. Her voice was deep and very sad.

But Nick scarcely looked at her. He was pulling tufts of dried seaweed off the rock on which he leaned.

"My dear girl," he said, "how can you expect it?"

"Expect it!" she echoed. "I don't understand. What do you mean?"

He drew himself slowly to a sitting posture. "How can I be honest with you," he said, "when you are not honest with yourself?"

"What do you mean?" she said again.

He gave her an odd look. "You really want me to tell you?"

"Of course I do." She spoke sharply. The old scared feeling was awake within her, but she would not yield to it. Now or never would she read the enigma. She would know the truth, cost what it might.

"What I mean is this," said Nick. "You won't own it, of course, but you are cheating, and you are afraid to stop. There isn't one woman in ten thousand who has the pluck to throw down the cards when once she has begun to cheat. She goes on—as you will go on—to the end of her life, simply because she daren't do otherwise. You are out of the straight, Muriel. That's why everything is such a hideous failure. You are going to marry the wrong man, and you know it."

He looked up at her again for an instant as he said it. He had spoken with his usual shrewd decision, but there was no hint of excitement about him. He might have been discussing some matter of a purely impersonal nature.

Muriel stood mutely poking holes in the sand. She could find nothing to say to this matter-of-fact indictment.

"And now," Nick proceeded, "I will tell you why you are doing it."

She started at that, and looked up with flaming cheeks. "I don't think I want to hear any more, Nick. It—it's rather late in the day, isn't it?"

He shrugged his shoulders. "I knew you would be afraid to face it. It's easier, isn't it, to go on cheating?"

Her eyes gleamed for a moment. He had flicked a tender place. "Very well," she said proudly. "Say what you like. It will make no difference. But please understand that I admit none of this."

Nick's grin leapt goblin-like across his face and was gone. "I never expected it of you," he told her coolly. "You would sooner die than admit it, simply because it would be infinitely easier for you to die. You will be false to yourself, false to Grange, false to me, rather than lower that miserable little rag of pride that made you jilt me at Simla. I didn't blame you so much then. You were only a child. You didn't understand. But that excuse won't serve you now. You are a woman, and you know what Love is. You don't call it by its name, but none the less you know it."

He paused for an instant, for Muriel had made a swift gesture of protest.

"I don't think you know what you are saying," she said, her voice very low.

He sprang abruptly to his feet. "Yes," he said, speaking very rapidly. "That's how you will trick yourself to your dying day. It's a way women have. But it doesn't help them. It won't help you. For that thing in your heart—the thing that is fighting for air—the thing you won't own—the thing that drove you to Grange for protection—will never die. That is why you are miserable. You may do what you will to it, hide it, smother it, trample it. But it will survive for all that. All your life it will be there. You will never forget it though you will try to persuade yourself that it belongs to a dead past. All your life,"—his voice vibrated suddenly, and the ever-shifting eyes blazed into leaping flame—"all your life, you will remember that I was once yours to take or to throw away. And—you wanted me, yet—you chose to throw me away."

Fiercely he flung the words at her. There was nothing impersonal about him now. He was vitally, overwhelmingly, in earnest. A deep glow covered the parchment face. The man was as it were electrified by passion.

And Muriel gazed at him as one gazing upon sudden disaster. What was this, what was this, that he had said to her? He had rent the veil aside for her indeed. But to what dread vision had he opened her eyes?

The old paralysing fear was knocking at her heart. She dreaded each instant to see the devil leap out upon his face. But as the seconds passed she realised that he was still his own master. He had flung down the gauntlet, but he would go no further, unless she took it up. And this she could not do. She knew that she was no match for him.

He was watching her narrowly, she knew, and after a few palpitating moments she nerved herself to meet his look. She felt as if it scorched her, but she would not shrink. Not for a moment must he fancy that those monstrous words of his had pierced her quivering heart. Whatever happened later, when this stunned sense of shock had left her, she must not seem to take them seriously now, with his watching eyes upon her.

And so at last she lifted her head and faced him with a little quivering laugh, brave enough in itself, but how piteous she never guessed.

"I don't think you are quite so clever as you used to be, Nick," she told him, "though I admit,"—her lips trembled—"that you are very amusing sometimes. Blake once told me that you had the eyes of a snake-charmer. Is it true, I wonder? Anyhow, they don't charm me."

She stopped rather breathlessly, half-frightened by his stillness. Would he understand that it was not her intention to defy him—that she was only refusing the conflict?

For a few moments her heart beat tumultuously, and then came a great throb of relief. Yes, he understood. She had nought to fear.

He put his hand sharply over his eyes, turning from her. "I have never tried to charm you," he said, in a voice that sounded curiously choked and unfamiliar. "I have only—loved you."

In the silence that followed, he began to walk away from her, moving noiselessly over the sand.

Mutely she watched him, but she dared not call him back. And very soon she was quite alone.

CHAPTER XXXVII
THE PENALTY FOR SENTIMENT

It did not take Dr. Jim long to discover that some trouble or at the least some perplexity was weighing upon his young guest's mind. He also shrewdly remarked that it dated from the commencement of her visit at his house. No one else noticed it, but this was not surprising. There was always plenty to occupy the attention in the Ratcliffe household, and only Dr. Jim managed to keep a sharp eye upon every member thereof. Moreover, by a casual observer, there was little or nothing that was unusual to be detected in Muriel's manner. Quiet she certainly was, but she was by no means listless. Her laugh did not always ring quite true, that was all. And her eyes drooped a little wearily from time to time. There were other symptoms, very slight, wholly imperceptible to any but a trained eye, yet not one of which escaped Dr. Jim.

He made no comment, but throughout that first week of her stay he watched her unperceived, biding his time. During several motor rides on which she accompanied him he maintained this attitude while she sat all unsuspecting by his side. She had never detected any subtlety in this staunch friend of hers, and, unlike Daisy, she felt no fear of him. His blunt sincerity had never managed to wound her.

And so it was almost inevitable that she should give him his opportunity at last.

Late one evening she entered his consulting-room where he was busy writing.

"I want to talk to you," she said. "Is it very inconvenient?"

The doctor leaned back in his chair. "Sit down there," he said, pointing to one immediately facing him.

She laughed and obeyed, faintly blushing. "I'm not a patient, you know."

He drew his black brows together. "It's very late. Why don't you go to bed?"

"Because I want to talk to you."

"You can do that to-morrow," bluntly rejoined Dr. Jim. "You can't afford to sacrifice your sleep to chatter."

"I am not sacrificing any sleep," Muriel told him rather wearily. "I never sleep before morning."

He laid down his pen and gave her one of his hard looks. "Then you are a very silly girl," he said curtly at length.

"It isn't my fault," she protested.

He shrugged his shoulders. "You all say that. It's the most ordinary lie I know."

Muriel smiled. "I know you are longing to give me something nasty. You may if you like. I'll take it, whatever it is."

Dr. Jim was silent for a space. He continued to regard her steadily, with a scrutiny that spared her nothing. She sat quite still under it. He had never disconcerted her yet. But when he leaned suddenly forward and took her wrist between his fingers, she made a slight, instinctive effort to frustrate him.

"Be still," he ordered. "What makes you so absurdly nervous? Want of sleep, eh?"

Her lips trembled a little. "Don't probe too deep, doctor," she pleaded. "I am not very happy just now."

"Why don't you tell me what is the matter?" he asked gruffly.

She did not answer, and he continued frowning over her pulse.

"What do you want to talk to me about?" he asked at last.

She looked up with an effort. "Oh, nothing much. Only a letter from a Mrs. Langdale who lives in town. She is going to India in November, and says she will take charge of me if I care to go with her. She has invited me to go and stay with her beforehand."

"Well?" said Jim, as she paused.

"I don't want to go," she said. "Do you think I ought? She is Lady Bassett's sister."

"I think it would probably do you good, if that's what you mean," he returned. "But I don't suppose that consideration has much weight with you. Why don't you want to go?"

"I don't like strangers, and I hate Lady Bassett," Muriel answered, with absolute simplicity. "Then there is Daisy. I don't know what her plans are. I always thought we should go East together."

"There's no sense in waiting for Daisy's plans to develop," declared Jim. "She is as changeable as the wind. Possibly Nick will be able to make up her mind for her. I fancy he means to try."

"Nick! You don't mean he will travel with Daisy?" There was almost a tragic note in Muriel's voice. She looked up quickly into the shrewd eyes that watched her.

"Why shouldn't he?" said Jim.

"I don't know. I never thought of it." Muriel leaned back again, a faint frown of perplexity between her eyes. "Perhaps," she said slowly at length, "I had better go to Mrs. Langdale."

"I should in your place," said Jim. "That handsome soldier of yours won't want to be kept waiting, eh?"

"Oh, he wouldn't mind." The weariness was apparent again in her voice, and with it a tinge of bitterness. "He never minds anything," she said.

Jim grunted disapproval. "And you? Are you equally indifferent?"

Her pale face flushed vividly. She was silent a moment; then suddenly she sat up and met his look fully.

"You'll think me contemptible, I know," she said, a great quiver in her voice. "I can't help it; you must. Dr. Jim, I'll tell you the truth. I—I don't want to go to India. I don't want to be married—at all."

She ended with a swift rush of irrepressible tears. It was out at last, this trouble of hers that had been gradually growing behind the barrier of her reserve, and it seemed to burst over her in the telling in a great wave of adversity.

"I've done nothing but make mistakes," she sobbed "ever since Daddy died."

Dr. Jim got up quietly to lock the door. The grimness had passed from his face.

"My dear," he said gruffly, "we all of us make mistakes directly we begin to run alone."

He returned and sat down again close to her, waiting for her to recover herself. She slipped out a trembling hand to him, and he took it very kindly; but he said no more until she spoke.

"It's very difficult to know what to do."

"Is it? I should have said you were past that stage." His tone was uncompromising, but the warm grip of his hand made up for it. His directness did not dismay her. "If you are quite sure you don't care for the fellow, your duty is quite plain."

Muriel raised her head slowly. "Yes, but it isn't quite so simple as that, doctor. You see, it's not as if—as if—we either of us ever imagined we were—in love with each other."

Jim's eyebrows went up. "As bad as that?"

She leaned her chin on her hand. "I am sure there must be crowds of people who marry without ever being in love."

"Yes," said Jim curtly. "And kindle their own hell in doing it."

She started a little. "You think that?"

"I know it. I have seen it over and over again. Full half of the world's misery is due to it. But you won't do that, Muriel. I know you too well."

Muriel glanced up at him. "Do you know me? I don't think you would have expected me to accept him in the first place."

"Depends what you did it for," said Jim.

She fell suddenly silent, slowly twisting the ring on her finger. "He knew why," she said at last in a very low voice. "In fact—in fact he asked me for that reason."

"And the reason still exists?"

She bent her head. "Yes."

"A reason you are ashamed of?" pursued the doctor.

She did not answer, and he drew his great brows together in deep thought.

"You don't propose to take me any further into your confidence?" he asked at last.

She made a quick, impulsive movement. "You—you—I think you know."

"Will you let me tell you what I know?" he said.

She shrank perceptibly. "If—if you won't make it too hard for me."

"I can't answer for that," he returned. "It depends entirely upon yourself. My knowledge does not amount to anything very staggering in itself. It is only this—that I know a certain person who would cheerfully sacrifice all he has to make you happy, and that you have no more cause to fear persecution from that person than from the man in the moon."

He paused; but Muriel did not speak. She was still absently turning her engagement ring round and round.

"To verify this," he said, "I will tell you something which I am sure you don't know—which in fact puzzled me, too, considerably, for some time. He has already sacrificed more than most men would care to venture in a doubtful cause. It was no part of his plan to follow you to England. He set his face against it so strongly that he very nearly ended his mortal career for good and all in so doing. As it was, he suffered for his lunacy pretty heavily. You know what happened. He was forced to come in the end, and he paid the forfeit for his delay."

Again he paused, for Muriel had sprung upright with such tragedy in her eyes that he knew he had said enough. The next moment she was on her feet, quivering all over as one grievously wounded.

"Oh, do you know what you are saying?" she said, and in her voice there throbbed the cry of a woman's wrung heart. "Surely—surely he never did that—for me!"

He did not seem to notice her agitation. "It was a fairly big price to pay for a piece of foolish sentiment, eh?" he said. "Let us hope he will know better next time."

He looked up at her with a faintly cynical smile, but she was standing with her face averted. He saw only that her chin was quivering like a hurt child's.

"Come," he said at length. "I didn't tell you this to distress you, you know. Only to set your mind at rest, so that you might sleep easy."

She mastered herself with an effort, and turned towards him. "I know; yes, I know. You—you have been very kind. Good-night, doctor."

He rose and went with her to the door. "You are not going to lie awake over this?"

She shook her head. "Good-night," she said again.

He watched her down the passage, and then returned to his writing. He smiled to himself as he sat down, but this time wholly without cynicism.

"No, Nick, my boy," he said, as he drove his pen into the ink. "She won't lie awake for you. But she'll cry herself to sleep for your sake, you gibbering, one-armed ape. And the new love will be the old love before the week is out, or I am no weather prophet."

CHAPTER XXXVIII
THE WATCHER OF THE CLIFF

The gale that raged along the British coasts that autumn was the wildest that had been known for years. It swelled quite suddenly out of the last breezes of a superb summer, and by the middle of September it had become a monster of destruction, devastating the shore. The crumbling cliffs of Brethaven testified to its violence. Beating rain and colossal, shattering waves united to accomplish ruin and destruction. And the little fishing-village looked on aghast.

It was on the third day of the storm that news was brought to Nick of a landslip on his own estate. He had been in town ever since his guests' departure, and had only returned on the previous evening. He did not contemplate a long stay. The place was lonely without Olga, and he was not yet sufficiently proficient in shooting with one arm to enjoy the sport, especially in solitude. He was in fact simply waiting for an opportunity which he was convinced must occur before long, of keeping a certain promise made to a friend of his on a night of early summer in the Indian Plains.

It was a wild day of drifting squalls and transient gleams of sunshine. He grimaced to himself as he sauntered forth after luncheon to view the damage that had been wrought upon his property. The ground he trod was sodden with long rain, and the cedars beyond the lawn plunged heavily to and fro in melancholy unrest, flinging great drops upon him as he passed. The force of the gale was terrific, and he had to bend himself nearly double to meet it.

With difficulty he forced his way to the little summer-house that overlooked the shore. He marvelled somewhat to find it still standing, but it was sturdily built and would probably endure as long as the ground beneath it remained unshaken.

But beyond it a great gap yawned. The daisy-covered space on which they had sat that afternoon, now many weeks ago, had disappeared. Nothing of it remained but a crumbling desolation to which the daisies still clung here and there.

Nick stood in such shelter as the summer-house afforded, and looked forth upon the heaving waste of waters. The tide was rising. He could see the great waves swirling white around the rocks. Several land-slips were visible from this post of observation. The village was out of sight, tucked away behind a great shoulder of cliff; but an old ruined cottage that had been uninhabited for some time had entirely disappeared. Stacks of seaweed had been thrown up upon the deserted shore, and lay in great masses above the breakers. The roar of the incoming tide was like the continuous roll of thunder.

It was a splendid spectacle and for some time he stood, with his face to the driving wind, gazing out upon the empty sea. There was not a single vessel in all that wide expanse.

Slowly at last his vision narrowed. His eyes came down to the great gash at his feet where red earth and tufts of grass mingled, where the daisies had grown on that June day, where she had sat, proud and aloof, and watched him fooling with the white petals. Very vividly he recalled that summer afternoon, her scorn of him, her bitter hostility—and the horror he had surprised in her dark eyes when the hawk had struck. He laughed oddly to himself, his teeth clenched upon his lower lip. How furiously she had hated him that day!

He turned to go; but paused, arrested by some instinct that bade him cast one more look downwards along the howling shore. In another moment he was lying full length upon the rotten ground, staring intently down upon the group of rocks more than two hundred feet below him.

Two figures—a man and a woman—had detached themselves from the shelter of these rocks, and were moving slowly, very slowly, towards the path that led inwards from the shore. They were closely linked together, so much his first glance told him. But there was something in the man's gait that caught the eye and upon which Nick's whole attention was instantly focussed. He could not see the face, but the loose-slung, gigantic limbs were familiar to him. With all his knowledge of the world of men, he had not seen many such.

Slowly the two approached till they stood almost immediately beneath him, and there, as upon mutual impulse, they stopped. It was a corner protected from the driving blast by the crumbling mass of cliff that had slipped in the night. The rain was falling heavily again, but neither the two on the shore nor the solitary watcher stretched on the perilous edge of the cliff seemed aware of it. All were intent upon other things.

Suddenly the woman raised her face, and with a movement that was passionate reached up her arms and clasped them about the man's bent neck. She was speaking, but no sound or echo of words was audible in that tumult. Only her face lifted to the beating rain, with its passion of love, its anguish of pain, told the motionless spectator something of their significance.

It was hidden from him almost at once by the man's massive head; but he had seen enough, more than enough, to verify a certain suspicion which had long been quartered at the back of his brain.

Stealthily he drew himself back from the cliff edge, and sat up on the damp grass. Again his eyes swept the horizon; there was something of a glare in them. He was drenched through and through by the rain, but he did not know it. Had Muriel seen him at that moment she might have likened him with a shudder to an eagle that viewed its quarry from afar.

He returned to the house without further lingering, and spent the two hours that followed in prowling ceaselessly up and down his library.

At the end of that time he sat down suddenly at the writing-table, and scrawled a hasty note. His face, as he did so, was like the face of an old man, but without the tolerance of age.

Finishing, he rang for his servant. "Take this note," he said, "and ask at the Brethaven Arms if a gentleman named Captain Grange is putting up there. If he is, send in the note, and wait for an answer. If he is not, bring it back."

The man departed, and Nick resumed his prowling. It seemed that he could not rest. Once he went to the window and opened it to listen to the long roar of the sea, but the fury of the blast was such that he could scarcely stand against it. He shut it out, and resumed his tramp.

The return of his messenger brought him to a standstill.

"Captain Grange was there, sir. Here is his answer."

Nick grabbed the note with a gesture that might have indicated either impatience or relief. He held the envelope between his teeth to slit it open, and they left a deep mark upon it.

"Dear Ratcliffe," he read. "If I can get to you through this murderous storm, I will. Expect me at eight o'clock.—Yours,

B. Grange."

"All right," said Nick over his shoulder. "Captain Grange will dine with me."

With the words he dropped the note into the fire, and then went away to dress.

CHAPTER XXXIX
BY SINGLE COMBAT

By eight o'clock Nick was lounging in the hall, awaiting his guest, but it was more than a quarter of an hour later that the latter presented himself.

Nick himself admitted him with a cheery grin. "Come in," he said. "You've had a pretty filthy walk."

"Infernal," said Grange gloomily.

He entered with a heavy, rather bullied air, as if he had come against his will. Shaking hands with his host, he glanced at him somewhat suspiciously.

"Glad you managed to come," said Nick hospitably.

"What did you want to see me for?" asked Grange.

"The pleasure of your society, of course." Nick's benignity was unassailable, but there was a sharp edge to it somewhere of which Grange was uneasily aware. "Come along and dine. We can talk afterwards."

Grange accompanied him moodily to the dining-room. "I thought you were away," he remarked, as they sat down.

"I was," said Nick. "Came back last night. When do you sail?"

"On Friday. I came down to say good-bye."

"Muriel is at Weir," observed Nick.

"Yes. I shall go on there to-morrow. Daisy is only here for a night or two to pack up her things."

"And then?" said Nick.

Grange stiffened perceptibly. "I don't know what her plans are. She never makes up her mind till the last minute."

Nick laughed. "She evidently hasn't taken you into her confidence. She is going East this winter."

Grange looked up sharply. "I don't believe it."

"It's true all the same," said Nick indifferently, and forthwith forsook the subject.

He started other topics, racing, polo, politics, airily ignoring his guest's undeniable surliness, till at last Grange's uneasiness began to wear away. He gradually overcame his depression, and had even managed to capture some of his customary courtesy before the end of dinner. His attitude was quite friendly when they finally adjourned to the library to smoke.

Nick followed him into the room and stopped to shut the door.

Grange had gone straight to the fire, and he did not see him slip something into his pocket as he came forward.

But he did after several minutes of abstraction discover something not quite normal in Nick's silence, and glanced down at him to ascertain what it was.

Nick had flung himself into a deep easy-chair, and was lying quite motionless with his head back upon the cushion. His eyes were closed. He had been smoking when he entered, but he had dropped his cigar half consumed into an ash-tray.

Grange looked at him with renewed uneasiness, and looked away again. He could not help feeling that there was some moral tension somewhere; but he had never possessed a keen perception, he could not have said wherein it lay.

He retired into his shell once more and sat down facing his host in silence that had become dogged.

Suddenly, without moving, Nick spoke.

His words were slightly more deliberate than usual, very even, very distinct. "To come to the point," he said. "I saw you on the shore this afternoon—you and Mrs. Musgrave."

"What?" Grange gave a great start and stared across at him, gripping the arms of his chair.

Nick's face, however, remained quite expressionless. "I saw you," he repeated.

With an effort Grange recovered himself. "Did you though? I wondered how you knew I was down here. Where were you?"

There was an abrupt tremor behind Nick's eyelids, but they remained closed. "I was on the top of the cliff, on my own ground, watching you."

Dead silence followed his answer—a silence through which the sound of the sea half a mile away swelled terribly, like the roar of a monster in torment.

Then at last Nick's eyes opened. He looked Grange straight in the face. "What are you going to do?" he said.

Grange's hands dropped heavily from the chair-arms, and his whole great frame drooped slowly forward. He made no further attempt at evasion, realising the utter futility of such a course.

"Do!" he said wearily. "Nothing."

"Nothing?" said Nick swiftly.

"No, nothing," he repeated, staring with a dull intentness at the ground between his feet. "It's an old story, and the less said about it the better. I can't discuss it with you or any one. I think it was a pity you took the trouble to watch me this afternoon."

526

He spoke with a certain dignity, albeit he refused to meet Nick's eyes. He looked unutterably tired.

Nick lay quite motionless in his chair, inscrutably still, save for the restless glitter behind his colourless eyelashes. At length, "Do you remember a conversation we had in this room a few months ago?" he asked.

Grange shook his head slightly, too engrossed with his miserable thoughts to pay much attention.

"Well, think!" Nick said insistently. "It had to do with your engagement to Muriel Roscoe. Perhaps you have forgotten that too?"

Grange looked up then, shaking off his lethargy with a visible effort. He got slowly to his feet, and drew himself up to his full giant height.

"No," he said, "I have not forgotten it."

"Then," said Nick, "once more—what are you going to do?"

Grange's face darkened. He seemed to hesitate upon the verge of vehement speech. But he restrained himself though the hot blood mounted to his temples.

"I have never yet broken my word to a woman," he said. "I am not going to begin now."

"Why not?" said Nick, with a grin that was somehow fiendish.

Grange ignored the gibe. "There is no reason why I should not marry her," he said.

"No reason!" Nick's eyes flashed upwards for an instant, and a curious sense of insecurity stabbed Grange.

Nevertheless he made unfaltering reply. "No reason whatever."

Nick sat up slowly and regarded him with minute attention. "Are you serious?" he asked finally.

"I am absolutely serious," Grange told him sternly. "And I warn you, Ratcliffe, this is not a subject upon which I will bear interference."

"Man alive!" jeered Nick. "You must think I'm damned easily scared."

He got up with the words, jerking his meagre body upright with a slight, fierce movement, and stood in front of Grange, arrogantly daring.

"Now just listen to this," he said. "I don't care a damn how you take it, so you may as well take it quietly. It's no concern of mine to know how you have whitewashed this thing over and made it look clean and decent—and honourable—to your fastidious eye. What I am concerned in is to prevent Muriel Roscoe making an unworthy marriage. And that I mean to do. I told you in the summer that she should be no man's second best, and, by Heaven, she never shall. I had my doubts of you then. I know you now. And—I swear by all things sacred that I will see you dead sooner than married to her."

He broke off for a moment as though to get a firmer grip upon himself. His face was terrible, his body tense as though controlled by tight-strung wires.

Before Grange could speak, he went on rapidly, with a resolution more deadly if less passionate than before.

"If either of you had ever cared, it might have been a different matter. But you never did. I knew that you never did. I never troubled to find out your reason for proposing to her. No doubt it was strictly honourable. But I always knew why she accepted you. Did you know that, I wonder?"

"Yes, I did." Grange's voice was deep and savage. He glowered down upon him in rising fury. "It was to escape you."

Nick's eyes flamed back like the eyes of a crouching beast. He uttered a sudden, dreadful laugh. "Yes—to escape me," he said, "to escape me! And it has fallen to me to deliver her from her chivalrous protector. If you look all round that, you may see something funny in it."

"Funny!" burst forth Grange, letting himself go at last. "It's what you have been playing for all along, you infernal mountebank! But you have overreached yourself this time. For that very reason I will never give her up."

He swung past Nick with the words, goaded past endurance, desperately aware that he could not trust himself within arm's length of that gibing, devilish countenance.

He reached the door and seized the handle, wrenched furiously for a few seconds, then flung violently round.

"Ratcliffe," he exclaimed, "for your own sake I advise you not to keep me here!"

But Nick had remained with his face to the fire. He did not so much as glance over his shoulder. He had suddenly grown intensely quiet. "I haven't quite done with you," he said. "There is just one thing more I have to say."

Grange was already striding back like an enraged bull, but something in the voice or attitude of the man who leaned against the mantelpiece without troubling to face him, brought him up short.

Against his will he halted. "Well?" he demanded.

"It's only this," said Nick. "You know as well as I do that I possess the means to prevent your marriage to Muriel Roscoe, and I shall certainly use that means unless you give her up of your own accord. You see what it would involve, don't you? The sacrifice of your precious honour—and not yours only."

He paused as if to allow full vent to Grange's anger, but still he did not change his position.

"You damned cur!" said Grange, his voice hoarse with concentrated passion.

Nick took up his tale as if he had not heard. "But, on the other hand, if you will write and set her free now, at once—I don't care how you do it; you can tell any likely lie that occurs to you—I on my part will swear to you that I will give her up entirely, that I will never plague her again, will never write to her or attempt in any way to influence her life, unless she on her own initiative makes it quite clear that she desires me to do so."

He ceased, and there fell a dead silence, broken only by the lashing rain upon the windows and the long, deep roar of the sea. He seemed to be listening to them with bent head, but in reality he heard nothing at all. He had made the final sacrifice for the sake of the woman he loved. To secure her happiness, her peace of mind, he had turned his face to the desert, at last, and into it he would go, empty, beaten, crippled, to return no more for ever.

Across the lengthening silence Grange's voice came to him. There was a certain hesitation in it as though he were not altogether sure of his ground.

"I am to take your word for all that?"

Nick turned swiftly round. "You can do as you choose. I have nothing else to offer you."

Grange abandoned the point abruptly, feeling as a man who has lost his footing in a steep place and is powerless to climb back. Perhaps even he was vaguely conscious of something colossal hidden away behind that baffling, wrinkled mask.

"Very well," he said, with that dogged dignity in which Englishmen clothe themselves in the face of defeat. "Then you will take my word to set her free."

"To-night?" said Nick.

"To-night."

There was another pause. Then Nick crossed to the door and unlocked it.

"I will take your word," he said.

A few seconds later, when Grange had gone, he softly shut and locked the door once more, and returned to his chair before the fire. Great gusts of rain were being flung against the window-panes. The wind howled near and far with a fury that seemed to set the walls vibrating. Now and then dense puffs of smoke blew out across the hearth into the room, and the atmosphere grew thick and stifling.

But Nick did not seem aware of these things. He sat on unheeding in the midst of his dust and ashes while the storm raged relentlessly above his head.

CHAPTER XL
THE WOMAN'S CHOICE

With the morning there came a lull in the tempest though the great waves that spent themselves upon the shore seemed scarcely less mountainous than when they rode before the full force of the storm.

In Daisy Musgrave's cottage above the beach, a woman with a white, jaded face sat by the window writing. A foreign envelope with an Indian stamp lay on the table beside her. It had not been opened; and once, glancing up, she pushed it slightly from her with a nervous, impatient movement. Now and then she sat with her head upon her hand thinking, and each time she emerged from her reverie it was to throw a startled look towards the sea as though its ceaseless roar unnerved her.

Nevertheless, at sight of a big, loosely-slung figure walking slowly up the flagged path, a quick smile flashed into her face, making it instantly beautiful. She half rose from her chair, and then dropped back again, still faintly smiling, while the light which only one man's coming can kindle upon any woman's face shone upon hers, erasing all weariness and bitterness while it lingered.

At the opening of the door she turned without rising. "So you have come after all! But I knew you would. Sit down a minute and wait while I finish this tiresome letter. I have just done."

She was already scribbling last words as fast as her pen would move, and her visitor waited for her without a word.

In a few minutes she turned to him again. "I have been writing a note to Muriel, explaining things a little. She doesn't yet know that I am here; but it would be no good for her to join me, for I am only packing. I shall leave as soon as I can get away. And she too is going almost at once to Mrs. Langdale, I believe. So we shall probably not meet again at present. You will be seeing her this afternoon. Will you give it to her?"

She held the letter out to him, but he made no move to take it. His face was very pale, more sternly miserable than she had ever seen it. "I think you had better post it," he said.

She rose and looked at him attentively. "Why, what's the matter, Blake?" she said.

He did not answer, and she went on immediately, still with her eyes steadily uplifted.

"Do you know, Blake, I have been thinking all night, and I have made up my mind to have done with all this foolish sentimentality finally and for ever. From to-day forward I enter upon the prosaic, middle-aged stage. I was upset yesterday at the thought of losing you so soon. It's been a lovely summer, hasn't it?" She stifled a sigh half uttered. "Well, it's over. You have to go back to India, and we must just make the best of it."

He made a sharp movement, but said nothing. The next moment he dropped down heavily into a chair and sat bowed, his head in his hands.

Daisy stood looking down at him, and slowly her expression changed. A very tender look came into her eyes, a look that made her seem older and at the same time more womanly. Very quietly she sat down on the arm of his chair and laid her hand upon him, gently rubbing it to and fro.

"My own boy, don't fret, don't fret!" she said. "You will be happier by-and-by. I am sure of it."

He took the little hand from his shoulder, and held it against his eyes. At last after several seconds of silence he spoke.

"Daisy, I have broken my engagement."

Daisy gave a great start. A deep glow overspread her face, but it faded very swiftly, leaving her white to the lips. "My dear Blake, why?" she whispered.

He answered her with his head down. "It was Nick Ratcliffe's doing. He made me."

"Made you, Blake! What can you mean?"

Sullenly Grange made answer. "He had got the whip-hand, and I couldn't help myself. He saw us on the shore together yesterday afternoon, made up his mind then and there that I was no suitable partner for Muriel, got me to go and dine with him, and told me so."

"But Blake, how absurd!" Daisy spoke with a palpable effort. "How—how utterly unreasonable! What made you give in to him?"

Grange would not tell her. "I shouldn't have done so," he said moodily, "if he hadn't given his word that he would never pester Muriel again. She's well rid of me anyhow. He was right there. She will probably see it in the same light."

"What did you say to her?" questioned Daisy.

"Oh, it doesn't matter, does it? I didn't see her. I wrote. I didn't tell her anything that it was unnecessary for her to know. In fact I didn't give her any particular reason at all. She'll think me an infernal cad. And so I am."

"You are not, Blake!" she declared vehemently. "You are not!"

He was silent, still tightly clasping her hand.

After a pause, she made a gentle movement to withdraw it; but at that he turned with a sudden mastery and thrust his arms about her. "Daisy," he broke out passionately, "I can't do without you! I can't! I can't! I've tried,—Heaven knows how I've tried! But it can't be done. It was madness ever to attempt to separate us. We were bound to come together again. I have been drifting towards you always, always, even when I wasn't thinking of you."

Fiercely the hot words rushed out. He was holding her fast, though had she made the smallest effort to free herself he would have let her go.

But Daisy sat quite still, neither yielding nor resisting. Only at his last words her lips quivered in a smile of tenderest ridicule. "I know, my poor old Blake," she said, "like a good ship without a rudder—caught in a strong current."

"And it has been the same with you," he insisted. "You have always wanted me more than—"

He did not finish, for her hand was on his lips, restraining him. "You mustn't say it, dear. You mustn't say it. It hurts us both too much. There! Let me go! It does no good, you know. It's all so vain and futile—now." Her voice trembled suddenly, and she ceased to speak.

He caught her hand away, looking straight up at her with that new-born mastery of his that made him so infinitely hard to resist.

"If it is quite vain," he said, "then tell me to go,—and I will."

She tried to meet his eyes, but found she could not. "I—shall have to, Blake," she said in a whisper.

"I am waiting," he told her doggedly.

But she could not say the word. She turned her face away and sat silent.

He waited with absolute patience for minutes. Then at last very gently he took his arms away from her and stood up.

"I am going back to the inn," he said. "And I shall wait there till to-morrow morning for your answer. If you send me away, I shall go without seeing you again. But if—if you decide otherwise,"—he lowered his voice as if he could not wholly trust it—"then I shall apply at once for leave to resign. And—Daisy—we will go to the New World together, and make up there for all the happiness we have missed in the Old."

He ended almost under his breath, and she seemed to hear his heart beat through the words. It was almost too much for her even then. But she held herself back, for there was that in her woman's soul that clamoured to be heard—the patter of tiny feet that had never ceased to echo there, the high chirrup of a baby's voice, the vision of a toddling child with eager arms outstretched.

And so she held her peace and let him go, though the struggle within her left her physically weak and cold, and she did not dare to raise her eyes lest he should surprise the love-light in them once again.

It had come to this at last then—the final dividing of the ways, the definite choice between good and evil. And she knew in her heart what that choice would be, knew it even as the sound of the closing door reached her consciousness, knew it as she strained her ears to catch the fall of his feet upon the flagged path, knew it in every nerve and fibre of her being as she sprang to the window for a last glimpse of the man who had loved her all her life long, and now at last had won her for himself.

Slowly she turned round once more to the writing-table. The unopened letter caught her eye. She picked it up with a set face, looked at it closely for a few moments, and then deliberately tore it into tiny fragments.

A little later she went to her own room. From a lavender-scented drawer she took an envelope, and shook its contents into her hand. Only a tiny unmounted photograph of a laughing baby, and a ringlet of baby hair!

Her face quivered as she looked at them. They had been her dearest treasures. Passionately she pressed them to her trembling lips, but she shed no tears. And when she returned to the sitting-room there was no faltering in her step.

She poked the fire into a blaze, and, kneeling, dropped her treasures into its midst. A moment's torture showed in her eyes, and passed.

She had chosen.

CHAPTER XLI
THE EAGLE'S PREY

During the whole of that day Muriel awaited in restless expectancy the coming of her *fiancé*. She had not heard from him for nearly a week, and she had not written in the interval for the simple reason that she lacked his address. But every day she had expected him to pay his promised visit of farewell.

It was hard work waiting for him. If she could have written, she would have done so days before in such a fashion as to cause him almost certainly to abandon his intention of seeing her. For her mind was made up at last after her long torture of indecision. Dr. Jim's vigorous speaking had done its work, and she knew that her only possible course lay in putting an end to her engagement.

She had always liked Blake Grange. She knew that she always would like him. But emphatically she did not love him, and she knew now with the sure intuition which all women develop sooner or later that he had never loved her. He had proposed to her upon a mere chivalrous impulse, and she was convinced that he would not wish to quarrel with her for releasing him.

Yet she dreaded the interview, even though she was quite sure that he would not lose his self-control and wax violent, as had Nick on that terrible night at Simla. She was almost morbidly afraid of hurting his feelings.

Of Nick she rigidly refused to think at all, though it was no easy matter to exclude him from her thoughts, for he always seemed to be clamouring for admittance. But she could not help wondering if, when Blake had gone at last and she was free, she would be very greatly afraid.

She was sitting alone in her room that afternoon, watching the scudding rain-clouds, when Olga brought her two letters.

"Both from Brethaven," she said, "but neither from Nick. I wonder if he is at Redlands. I hope he will come over here if he is."

Muriel did not echo the hope. She knew the handwriting upon both the envelopes, and she opened Daisy's first. It did not take long to read. It simply contained a brief explanation of her presence at Brethaven, which was due to an engagement having fallen through, mentioned Blake as being on the point of departure, and wound up with the hope that Muriel would not in any way alter her plans for her benefit as she was only at the cottage for a few days to pack her possessions and she did not suppose that she would care to be with her while this was going on.

There was no reference to any future meeting, and Muriel gravely put the letter away in thoughtful silence. She had no clue whatever to the slackening of their friendship, but she could not fail to note with pain how far asunder they had drifted.

She turned to Grange's letter with a faint wonder as to why he should have troubled himself to write when he was so short a distance from her.

It contained but a few sentences; she read them with widening eyes.

"Fate or the devil has been too strong for me, and I am compelled to break my word to you. I have no excuse to offer, except that my hand has been forced. Perhaps in the end it will be better for you, but I would have stood by had it been possible. And even now I would not desert you if I did not positively know that you were safe—that the thing you feared has ceased to exist.

"Muriel, I have broken my oath, and I can hardly ask your forgiveness. I only beg you to believe that it was not by my own choice. I was fiendishly driven to it against my will. I came to this place to say good-bye, but I shall leave to-morrow without seeing you unless you should wish otherwise.

"B. Grange."

She reached the end of the letter and sat quite still, staring at the open page.

She was free, that was her first thought, free by no effort of her own. The explanation she had dreaded had become unnecessary. She would not even have to face the ordeal of a meeting. She drew a long breath of relief.

And then swift as a poisoned arrow came another thought,—a stabbing, intolerable suspicion. Why had he thus set her free? How had his hand been forced? By what means had he been fiendishly driven?

She read the letter through again, and suddenly her heart began to throb thick and hard, so that she gasped for breath. This was Nick's doing. She was as sure of it as if those brief, bitter sentences had definitely told her so. Nick was the motive power that had compelled Grange to this action. How he had done it, she could not even vaguely surmise. But that he had in some malevolent fashion come between them she did not for an instant doubt.

And wherefore? She put her hand to her throat, feeling suffocated, as the memory of that last interview with him on the shore raced with every fiery detail through her brain. He had marked her down for himself, long, long ago, and whatever Dr. Jim might say, he had never abandoned the pursuit. He meant to capture her at last. She might flee, but he was following, tireless, fleet, determined. Presently he would swoop like an eagle upon his prey, and she would be utterly at his mercy. He had beaten Grange, and there was no one left to help her.

"Oh, Muriel,"—it was Olga's voice from the window—"come here, quick, quick! I can see a hawk."

She started as one starts from a horrible dream, and looked round with dazed eyes.

"It's hovering!" cried Olga excitedly. "It's hovering! There! Now it has struck!"

"And something is dead," said Muriel, in a voiceless whisper.

The child turned round, saw something unusual in her friend's face, and went impetuously to her.

"Muriel, darling, you look so strange. Is anything the matter?"

Muriel put an arm around her. "No, nothing," she said. "Olga, will it surprise you very much to hear that I am not going to marry Captain Grange after all?"

"No, dear," said Olga. "I never somehow thought you would, and I didn't want you to either."

"Why not?" Muriel looked up in some surprise. "I thought you liked him."

"Oh, yes, of course I do," said Olga. "But he isn't half the man Nick is, even though he is a V.C. Oh, Muriel, I wish,—I do wish—you would marry Nick. Perhaps you will now."

But at that Muriel cried out sharply and sprang to her feet, almost thrusting Olga from her.

"No, never!" she exclaimed, "Never,—never,—never!" Then, seeing Olga's hurt face, "Oh, forgive me, dear! I didn't mean to be unkind. But please don't ever dream of such a thing again. It—it's impossible—quite. Ah, there is the gong for tea. Let us go down."

They went down hand in hand. But Olga was very quiet for the rest of the evening; and she did not cling to Muriel as usual when she said good-night.

CHAPTER XLII
THE HARDEST FIGHT OF ALL

It was growing late on that same evening when to Daisy, packing in her room with feverish haste, a message was brought that Captain Ratcliffe was waiting, and desired to see her.

Her first impulse was to excuse herself from the interview, for she and Nick had never stood upon ceremony; but a very brief consideration decided her to see him. Since he had come at an unusual hour, it seemed probable that he had some special object in view, and if that were so, she would find it hard to turn him from his purpose. But she resolved to make the interview as brief as possible. She had no place for Nick in her life just then.

She entered the little parlour with a certain impetuosity, that was not wholly spontaneous. "My dear Nick," she said, as she did so, "I can give you exactly five minutes, not one second more, for I am frightfully busy packing up my things to leave to-morrow."

He came swiftly to meet her, so swiftly that she was for the moment deceived, and fancied that he was about to greet her with his customary bantering gallantry. But he did not lift her fingers to his lips after his usual gay fashion. He only held her proffered hand very tightly for several seconds without verbal greeting of any sort.

Suddenly he began to speak, and as he did so she seemed to see a hundred wrinkles spring into being on his yellow face. "I have something to say to you, Mrs. Musgrave," he said. "And it's something so particularly beastly that I funk saying it. We have always been such pals, you and I, and that makes it all the harder."

He broke off, his shrewd glance flashing over her, keen and elusive as a rapier. Daisy faced him quite fully and fearlessly. The possibility of a conflict in this quarter had occurred to her before. She would not shirk it, but she was determined that it should be as brief as possible.

"Being pals doesn't entitle you to go trespassing, Nick," she said.

"I know that," said Nick, speaking very rapidly. "None better. But I am not thinking of you only, though I hate to make you angry. Mrs. Musgrave—Daisy—I want to ask you, and you can't refuse to answer. What are you doing? What are you going to do?"

"I don't know what you mean," she said, speaking coldly. "And anyhow I can't stop to listen to you. I haven't time. I think you had better go."

"You must listen," Nick said. She caught the grim note of determination in his voice, and was aware of the whole force of his personality flung suddenly against her. "Daisy," he said, "you are to look upon me as Will's representative. I am the nearest friend he has. Have you thought of him at all lately, stewing in those hellish Plains for your sake? He's such a faithful chap, you know. Can't you go back to him soon? Isn't it—forgive me—isn't it a bit shabby to play this sort of game when there's a fellow like that waiting for you and fretting his very heart out because you don't go?"

He stopped—his lips twitching with the vigour of his appeal. And Daisy realised that he would have to be told the simple truth. He would not be satisfied with less.

Very pale but quite calm, she braced herself to tell him. "I am afraid you are pleading a lost cause," she said, her words quiet and very distinct. "I am never going back to him."

"Never!" Nick moved sharply drawing close to her. "Never?" he said again; then with abrupt vehemence, "Daisy, you don't mean that! You didn't say it!"

She drew back slightly from him, but her answer was perfectly steady, rigidly determined. "I have said it, Nick. And I meant it. You had better go. You will do no good by staying to argue. I know all that you can possibly say, and it makes no difference to me. I have chosen."

"What have you chosen?" he demanded.

For an instant she hesitated. There was something almost fierce in his manner, something she had never encountered before, something that in spite of her utmost effort made her feel curiously uneasy, even apprehensive. She had always known that there was a certain uncanny strength about Nick, but to feel the whole weight of it directed against her was a new experience.

"What have you chosen?" he repeated relentlessly.

And reluctantly, more than half against her will, she told him. "I am going to the man I love."

She was prepared for some violent outburst upon her words, but none came. Nick heard her in silence, standing straight before her, watching her, she felt, with an almost brutal intentness, though his eyes never for an instant met her own.

"Then," he said suddenly at length, and quick though they were, it seemed to her that the words fell with something of the awful precision of a death-sentence, "God help you both; for you are going to destroy him and yourself too."

Daisy made a sharp gesture; it was almost one of shrinking. And at once he turned from her and fell to pacing the little room, up and down, up and down incessantly, like an animal in a cage. It was useless to attempt to dismiss him, for she saw that he would not go. She moved quietly to a chair and sat down to wait.

Abruptly at last he stopped, halting in front of her. "Daisy,"—he began, and broke off short, seeming to battle with himself.

She looked up in surprise. It was so utterly unlike Nick to relinquish his self-command at a critical juncture. The next moment he amazed her still further. He dropped suddenly down on his knees and gripped her clasped hands fast.

"Daisy," he said again, and this time words came, jerky and passionate, "this is my doing. I've driven you to it. If I hadn't interfered with Grange, you would never have thought of it."

She sat without moving, but the hasty utterance had its effect upon her. Some of the rigidity went out of her attitude. "My dear Nick," she said, "what is the good of saying that?"

"Isn't it true?" he persisted.

She hesitated, unwilling to wound him.

"You know it is true," he declared with vehemence. "If I had let him alone, he would have married Muriel, and this thing would never have happened. God knows I did what was right, but if it doesn't turn out right, I'm done for. I never believed in eternal damnation before, but if this thing comes to pass it will be hell-fire for me for as long as I live. For I shall never believe in God again."

He swung away from her as though in bodily torture, came in contact with the table and bowed his head upon it. For many seconds his breathing, thick and short, almost convulsed, was the only sound in the room.

As for Daisy, she sat still, staring at him dumbly, witnessing his agony till the sight of it became more than she could bear. Then she moved, reached stiffly forward, and touched him.

"You are not to blame yourself, Nick," she said.

He did not stir. "I don't," he answered, and again fell silent.

At last he moved, seemed to pull himself together, finally got to his feet.

"Do you think you will be happy?" he said. "Do you think you will ever manage to forget what you have sacrificed to this fetish you call Love,—how you broke the heart of one of the best fellows in the world, and trampled upon the memory of your dead child—the little chap you used to call the light of your eyes, who used to hold out his arms directly he saw you and cry when you went away?"

His voice was not very steady, and he paused but he did not look at her or seem to expect any reply.

Daisy gave a great shiver. She felt cold from head to foot. But she was not afraid of Nick. If she yielded, it would not be through fear.

A full minute crawled away before he spoke again. "And this fellow Grange," he said then. "He is a man who values his honour. He has lived a clean life. He holds an unblemished record. He is in your hands. You can do what you like with him—whatever your love inspires you to do. You can pull him back into a straight course, or you can wreck him for good and all. Which is it going to be, I wonder? It's a sacrifice either way,—a sacrifice to Love or a sacrifice to devils. You can make it which you will. But if it is to be the last, never talk of Love again. For Love—real Love—is the safeguard from all evil. And if you can do this thing, it has never been above your horizon, and never will be."

Again he stopped, and again there was silence while Daisy sat white-faced and slightly bowed, wondering when it would be over, wondering how much longer she could possibly endure.

And then suddenly he bent down over her. His hand was on her shoulder. "Daisy," he said, and voice and touch alike implored her, "give him up, dear! Give him up! You can do it if you will, if your love is great enough. I know how infernally hard it is to do. I've done it myself. It means tearing your very heart out. But it will be worth it—it must be worth it—afterwards. You are bound—some time—to reap what you have sown."

She lifted a haggard face. There was something in the utterance that compelled her. And so looking, she saw that which none other of this man's friend's had ever seen. She saw his naked soul, stripped bare of all deception, of all reserve,—a vital, burning flame shining in the desert. The sight moved her as had nought else.

"Oh, Nick," she cried out desperately, "I can't—I can't!"

He bent lower over her. He was looking straight down into her eyes. "Daisy," he said very urgently, "Daisy, for God's sake—try!"

Her white lips quivered, striving again to refuse. But the words would not come. Her powers of resistance had begun to totter.

"You can do it," he declared, his voice quick and passionate as though he pleaded with her for life itself. "You can do it—if you will. I will help you. You shan't stand alone. Don't stop to think. Just come with me now—at once—and put an end to it before you sleep. For you can't do this thing, Daisy. It isn't in you. It is all a monstrous mistake, and you can't go on with it. I know you better than you know yourself. We haven't been pals all these years for nothing. And there is that in your heart that won't let you go on. I thought it was dead a few minutes ago. But, thank God, it isn't. I can see it in your eyes."

She uttered an inarticulate sound that was more bitter than any weeping, and covered her face.

Instantly Nick straightened himself and turned away. He went to the window and leaned his head against the sash. He had the spent look of a man who has fought to the end of his strength. The thunder of the waves upon the shore filled in the long, long silence.

Minutes crawled away, and still he stood there with his face to the darkness. At last a voice spoke behind him, and he turned. Daisy had risen.

She stood in the lamplight, quite calm and collected. There was even a smile upon her face, but it was a smile that was sadder than tears.

"It's been a desperate big fight, hasn't it, Nick?" she said. "But—my dear—you've won. For the sake of my little baby, and for the sake of the man I love—yes, and partly for your sake too,"—she held out her hand to him with the words—"I am going back to the prison-house. No, don't speak to me. You have said enough. And, Nick, I must go alone. So I want you, please, to go away, and not to come to me again until I send for you. I shall send sooner or later. Will you do this?"

Her voice never faltered, but the misery in her eyes cut him to the heart. In that moment he realised how terribly near he had been to losing the hardest battle he had ever fought.

He gave her no second glance. Simply, without a word, he stooped and kissed the hand she had given him; then turned and went noiselessly away.

He had won indeed, but the only triumph he knew was the pain of a very human compassion.

Scarcely five minutes after his departure, Daisy let herself out into the night that lay like a pall above the moaning shore. She went with lagging feet that often stumbled in the darkness. It was only the memory of a baby's head against her breast that gave her strength.

CHAPTER XLIII
REQUIESCAT

"I believe I heard a gun in the night," remarked Mrs. Ratcliffe at the breakfast-table on the following morning.

"Shouldn't be surprised," said Dr. Jim. "I know there was a ship in distress off Calister yesterday. They damaged the lifeboat trying to reach her. But the wind seems to have gone down a little this morning. Do you care for a ride, Muriel?"

Muriel accepted the invitation gladly. She liked accompanying Dr. Jim upon his rounds. She had arranged to leave two days later, a decision which the news of Daisy's presence at Brethaven had not affected. Daisy seemed to have dropped her for good and all, and her pride would not suffer her to inquire the reason. She had, in fact, begun to think that Daisy had merely tired of her, and that being so she was the more willing to go to Mrs. Langdale, whose letters of fussy kindliness seemed at least to ensure her a cordial welcome.

She had discussed her troubles no further with Dr. Jim. Grange's letter had in some fashion placed matters beyond discussion. And so she had only briefly told him that her engagement was at an end, and he had gruffly expressed his satisfaction thereat. Her one idea now was to escape from Nick's neighbourhood as speedily as possible. It possessed her even in her dreams.

She went with Dr. Jim to the surgery when breakfast was over, and sat down alone in the consulting-room to wait for him. He usually started on his rounds at ten o'clock, but it wanted a few minutes to the hour and the motor was not yet at the door. She sat listening for it, hoping that no one would appear to detain him.

The morning was bright, and the wind had fallen considerably. Through the window she watched the falling leaves as they eddied in sudden draughts along the road. She looked through a wire screen that gave rather a depressing effect to the sunshine.

Suddenly from some distance away there came to her the sound of a horse's hoof-beats, short and hard, galloping over the stones. It was a sound that arrested the attention, awaking in her a vague, apprehensive excitement. Almost involuntarily she drew nearer to the window, peering above the blind.

Some seconds elapsed before she caught sight of the headlong horseman, and then abruptly he dashed into sight round a curve in the road. At the same instant the gallop became a fast trot, and she saw that the rider was gripping the animal with his knees. He had no saddle.

Amazed and startled, she stood motionless, gazing at the sudden apparition, saw as the pair drew nearer what something within her had already told her loudly before her vision served her, and finally drew back with a sharp, instinctive contraction of her whole body as the horseman reined in before the surgery-door and dismounted with a monkey-like dexterity, his one arm twined in the bridle. A moment later the surgery-bell pealed loudly, and her heart stood still. She felt suddenly sick with a nameless foreboding.

Standing with bated breath, she heard Dr. Jim himself go to answer the summons, and an instant later Nick's voice came to her, gasping and uneven, but every word distinct.

"Ah, there you are! Thought I should catch you. Man, you're wanted—quick! In heaven's name—lose no time. Grange was drowned early this morning, and—I believe it's killed Daisy. For mercy's sake, come at once!"

There was a momentary pause. Muriel's heart was beating in great sickening throbs. She felt stiff and powerless.

Dr. Jim's voice, brief and decided, struck through the silence. "Come inside and have something. I shall be ready to start in three minutes. Leave your animal here. He's dead beat."

There followed the sound of advancing feet, a hand upon the door, and the next moment they entered together. Nick was reeling a little and holding Jim's arm. He saw Muriel with a sharp start, standing as she had turned from the window. The doctor's brows met for an instant as he put his brother into a chair. He had forgotten Muriel.

With an effort she overcame the paralysis that bound her, and moved forward with shaking limbs.

"Did you say Blake was—dead?" she asked, her voice pitched very low.

She looked at Nick as she asked this question, and it was Nick who answered her in his quick, keen way, as though he realised the mercy of brevity.

"Yes. He and some fisher chaps went out early this morning in an ordinary boat to rescue some fellows on a wreck that had drifted on to the rocks outside the harbour. The lifeboat had been damaged, and couldn't be used. They reached the wreck all right, but there were more to save than they had reckoned on—more than the boat would carry—and the wreck was being battered to pieces. It was only a matter of seconds for the tide was rising. So they took the lot, and Grange went over the side to make it possible. He hung on to a rope for a time, but the seas were tremendous, and after a bit it parted. He was washed up two hours ago. He had been in the water since three, among the rocks. There wasn't the smallest chance of bringing him back. He was long past any help we could give."

He ended abruptly, and helped himself with a jerk to something in a glass that Jim had placed by his side.

Muriel stood dumbly watching. She noticed with an odd, detached sense of curiosity that he was shivering violently as one with an ague. Dr. Jim was already making swift preparations for departure.

Suddenly Nick looked up at her. His eyes were glittering strangely. "I know now," he said, "what you women feel like when you can only stand and look on. We have been looking on—Daisy and I—just looking on, for six mortal hours." He banged his fist with a sort of condensed fury upon the table, and leapt to his feet. "Jim, are you ready? I can't sit still any longer."

"Finish that stuff, and don't be a fool!" ordered Jim curtly.

Muriel turned swiftly towards him. "You'll take me with you!" she said very earnestly.

Nick broke in sharply upon the request. "No, no, Muriel! You're not to go. Jim, you can't—you shan't—take her! I won't allow it!"

But Muriel was clinging to Dr. Jim's arm with quivering face upraised. "You will take me," she entreated. "I was able to help Daisy before. I can help her now."

But even before she spoke there flashed a swift glance between the two brothers that foiled her appeal almost before it was uttered. With a far greater gentleness than was customary with him, but with unmistakable decision, Dr. Jim refused her petition.

"I can't take you now, child. But if Daisy should ask for you, or if there is anything under the sun that you can do for her, I will promise to let you know."

It was final, but she would not have it so. A sudden gust of anger caught her, anger against the man for whose sake she had one night shed so many bitter tears, whom now she so fiercely hated. She still clung to Jim. She was shaking all over.

"What does it matter what Nick says?" she urged pantingly. "Why give in to him at every turn? I won't be left behind—just because he wishes it!"

She would have said more. Her self-control was tottering; but Dr. Jim restrained her. "My dear, it is not for Nick's sake," he said. "Come, you are going to be sensible. Sit down and get your breath. There's no time for hysterics. I must go across and speak to my wife before I go."

He looked at Nick who instantly responded. "Yes, you be off! I'll look after her. Be quick, man, be quick!"

But when Dr. Jim was gone, his impatience fell away from him. He moved round the table and stood before her. He was steady enough now, steadier far than she.

"Don't take it too hard," he said. "At least he died like a man."

She did not draw away from him. There was no room for fear in her heart just then. It held only hatred—a fierce, consuming flame—that enabled her to face him as she had never faced him before.

"Why did you let him go?" she demanded of him, her voice deep and passionate, her eyes unwaveringly upon him. "There must have been others. You were there. Why didn't you stop him?"

"I stop him!" said Nick, and a flash of something that was almost humour crossed his face. "You seem to think I am omnipotent."

Her eyes continued to challenge him. "You always manage to get your own way somehow," she said very bitterly, "by fair means or foul. Are you going to deny that it was you who made him write that letter?"

He did not ask her what she meant. "No," he said with a promptitude that took her by surprise. "I plead guilty to that. As you are aware, I never approved of your engagement."

His effrontery stung her into what was almost a state of frenzy. Her eyes blazed their utmost scorn. She had never been less afraid of him than at that moment. She had never hated him more intensely.

"You could make him do a thing like that," she said. "And yet you couldn't hold him back from certain death!"

He answered her without heat, in a tone she deemed most hideously callous. "It was not my business to hold him back. He was wanted. There would have been no rescue but for him. They needed a man to lead them, or they wouldn't have gone at all."

His composure goaded her beyond all endurance. She scarcely waited for him to finish, nor was she wholly responsible for what she said.

"Was there only one man among you, then?" she asked, with headlong contempt.

He made her a curious, jerky bow. "One man—yes," he said. "The rest were mere sheep, with the exception of one—who was a cripple."

Her heart contracted suddenly with a pain that was physical. She felt as if he had struck her, and it goaded her to a fiercer cruelty.

"You knew he would never come back!" she declared her voice quivering uncontrollably with the passion that shook her. "You—you never meant him to come back!"

He opened his eyes wide for a single instant, and she fancied that she had touched him. It was the first time in her memory that she had ever seen them fully. Instinctively she avoided them, as she would have avoided a flash of lightning.

And then he spoke, and she knew at once that her wild accusation had in no way hurt him. "You think that, do you?" he said, and his tone sounded to her as though he barely repressed a laugh. "Awfully nice of you! I wonder what exactly you take me for."

She did not keep him in suspense on that point. If she had never had the strength to tell him before, she could tell him now.

"I take you for a fiend!" she cried hysterically. "I take you for a fiend!"

He turned sharply from her, so sharply that she was conscious of a moment's fear overmastering her madness. But instantly, with his back to her, he spoke, and her brief misgiving was gone.

"It doesn't matter much now what you take me for," he said, and again in the cracked notes of his voice she seemed to hear the echo of a laugh. "You won't need to seek any more protectors so far as I am concerned. You will never see me again unless the gods ordain that you should come and find me. It isn't the way of an eagle to swoop twice—particularly an eagle with only one wing."

The laugh was quite audible now, and she never saw how that one hand of his was clenched and pressed against his side. He had reached the door while he was speaking. Turning swiftly, he cast one flickering, inscrutable glance towards her, and then with no gesture of farewell was gone. She heard his receding footsteps die away while she struggled dumbly to quell the tumult of her heart.

CHAPTER XLIV
LOVE'S PRISONER

Late that evening a scribbled note reached Muriel from Dr. Jim.

"You can do nothing whatever," he wrote. "Daisy is suffering from a sharp attack of brain fever, caused by the shock of her cousin's death, and I think it advisable that no one whom she knows should be near her. You may rest assured that all that can be done for her will be done. And, Muriel, I think you will be wise to go to Mrs. Langdale as you originally intended. It will be better for you, as I think you will probably realise. You shall be kept informed of Daisy's condition, but I do not anticipate any immediate change."

She was glad of those few words of advice. Her anxiety regarding Daisy notwithstanding, she knew it would be a relief to her to go. The strain of many days was telling upon her. She felt herself to be on the verge of a break-down, and she longed unspeakably to escape.

She went to her room early on her last night at Weir, but not in order to rest the longer. She had something to do, something from which she shrank with a strange reluctance, yet which for her peace of mind she dared not leave neglected.

It was thus she expressed it to herself as with trembling fingers she opened the box that contained all her sacred personal treasures.

It lay beneath them all, wrapped in tissue-paper, as it had passed from his hand to hers, and for long she strove to bring herself to slip the tiny packet unopened into an envelope and seal it down—yet could not.

At last—it was towards midnight—she yielded to the force that compelled. Against her will she unfolded the shielding paper and held that which it contained upon the palm of her hand. Burning rubies, red as heart's blood, ardent as flame, flashed and glinted in the lamp-light. "OMNIA VINCIT AMOR"—how the words scorched her memory! And she had wondered once if they were true!

She knew now! She knew now! He had forced her to realise it. He had captured her, had kindled within her—by what magic she knew not—the undying Against her will, in spite of her utmost resistance, he had done this thing. Above and beyond and through her fiercest hatred, he had conquered her quivering heart. He had let her go again, but not till he had blasted her happiness for ever. None other could ever dominate her as this man dominated. None other could ever kindle in her—or ever quench—the torch that this man's hand had lighted.

And this was Love—this hunger that could never be satisfied, this craving which would not be stifled or ignored—Love triumphant, invincible, immortal—the thing she had striven to slay at its birth, but which had lived on in spite of her, growing, spreading, enveloping, till she was lost, till she was suffocated, in its immensity. There could never be any escape for her again. She was fettered hand and foot. It was useless any longer to strive. She stood and faced the truth.

She did not ask herself how it was she had ever come to care. She only numbly realised that she had always cared. And she knew now that to no woman is it given so to hate as she had hated without the spur of Love goading her thereto. Ah, but Love was cruel!

Love was merciless! For she had never known—nor ever could know now—the ecstasy of Love. Truly, it conquered; but it left its prisoners to perish of starvation in the wilderness.

A slight sound in the midnight silence! A timid hand softly trying the door-handle! She sprang up, dropping the ring upon her table, and turned to see Olga in her nightdress, standing in the doorway.

"I was awake," the child explained tremulously. "And I heard you moving. And I wondered, dear Muriel, if perhaps I could do anything to help you. You—you don't mind?"

Muriel opened her arms impulsively. She felt as if Olga had been sent to lighten her darkest hour.

For a while she held her close, not speaking at all; and it was Olga who at last broke the silence.

"Darling, are you crying for Captain Grange?"

She raised her head then to meet the child's gaze of tearful sympathy.

"I am not crying, dear," she said. "And—it wouldn't be for him if I were. I don't want to cry for him. I just envy him, that's all."

She leaned her head against Olga's shoulder, rocking a little to and fro with closed eyes. "Yes," she said at last, "you can help me, Olga, if you will. That ring on the table, dear,—a ring with rubies—do you see it?"

"Yes," breathed Olga, holding her very close.

"Then just take it, dear." Muriel's voice was unutterably weary; she seemed to speak with a great effort. "It belongs to Nick. He gave it to me once, long ago, in remembrance of something. I want you to give it back to him, and tell him simply that I prefer to forget."

Olga took up the ring. Her lips were trembling. "Aren't you—aren't you being nice to Nick any more, Muriel?" she asked in a whisper.

Muriel did not answer.

"Not when you promised?" the child urged piteously.

There was silence. Muriel's face was hidden. Her black hair hung about her like a cloud, veiling her from her friend's eyes. For a long time she said nothing whatever. Then at last without moving she made reply.

"It's no use, Olga. I can't! I can't! It's not my doing. It's his. Oh, I think my heart is broken!" Through the anguish of weeping that followed, Olga clasped her passionately close, frightened, by an intensity of suffering such as she had never seen before and was powerless to alleviate.

She slept with Muriel that night, but, waking in the dawning, just when Muriel had sunk to sleep, she crept out of bed and, with Nick's ring grasped tightly in her hand, softly stole away.

PART V
CHAPTER XLV
THE VISION

A gorgeous sunset lay in dusky, fading crimson upon the Plains, trailing to darkness in the east. The day had been hot and cloudless, but a faint, chill wind had sprung up with the passing of the sun, and it flitted hither and thither like a wandering spirit over the darkening earth.

Down in the native quarter a *tom-tom* throbbed, persistent, exasperating as the voice of conscience. Somewhere in the distance a dog barked restlessly, at irregular intervals. And at a point between *tom-tom* and dog a couple of parrots screeched vociferously.

Over all, the vast Indian night was rushing down on silent, mysterious wings. Crimson merged to grey in the telling, and through the falling dark there shone, detached and wonderful, a single star.

In the little wooden bungalow over against, the water-works a light had been kindled and gleamed out in a red streak across the Plain. Other lights were beginning to flicker also from all points of the compass, save only where a long strip of jungle lay like a blot upon the face of the earth. But the red light burned the steadiest of them all.

It came from the shaded lamp of an Englishman, and beneath it with stubborn, square-jawed determination the Englishman sat at work.

Very steadily his hand moved over the white paper, and the face that was bent above it never varied—a face that still possessed something of the freshness of youth though the set of the lips was firm even to sternness and the line of the chin was hard. He never raised his eyes as he worked except to refer to the notebook at his elbow. The passage of time seemed of no moment to him.

Yet at the soft opening of the door, he did look up for an instant, a gleam of expectancy upon his face that died immediately.

"All right, Sammy, directly," he said, returning without pause to his work.

Sammy, butler, bearer, and general factotum, irreproachable from his snowy turban to his white-slippered feet, did not take the hint to retire, but stood motionless just inside the room, waiting with statuesque patience till his master should deign to bestow upon him the favour of his full attention.

After a little Will Musgrave realised this, and with an abrupt sigh sat back in his chair and rubbed his hand across his forehead.

"Well?" he said then. "You needn't trouble to tell me that the mail has passed, for I heard the fellow half an hour ago. Of course there were no letters?"

The man shook his head despondingly. "No letters, sahib."

"Then what do you want?" asked Will, beginning to eye his work again.

Sammy—so dubbed by Daisy long ago because his own name was too sore a tax upon her memory—sent a look of gleaming entreaty across the lamp-lit space that separated him from his master.

"The dinner grows cold, sahib," he observed pathetically.

Will smiled a little. "All right, my good Sammy. What does it matter? I'm sure if I don't mind, you needn't. And I'm busy just now."

But the Indian stood his ground. "What will my mem-sahib say to me," he said, "when she comes and finds that my lord has been starved?"

Will's face changed. It was a very open face, boyishly sincere. He did not laugh at the earnest question. He only gravely shook his head.

540

"The mem-sahib will come," the man declared, with conviction. "And what will her servant say when she asks him why his master is so thin? She will say, 'Sammy, I left him in your care. What have you done to him?' And, sahib, what answer can her servant give?"

Will clasped his hands at the back of his head in a careless attitude, but his face was grim. "I don't think you need worry yourself, Sammy," he said. "I am not expecting the mem-sahib—at present."

Nevertheless, moved by the man's solicitude, he rose after a moment and laid his work together. He might as well dine, he reflected, as sit and argue about it. With a heavy step he passed into the room where dinner awaited him, and sat down at the table.

No, he was certainly not expecting her at present. He had even of late begun to ask himself if he expected her at all. It was five months now since the news of her severe illness had almost induced him to throw everything aside and go to her. He had only been deterred from this by a very serious letter from Dr. Jim, strongly advising him to remain where he was, since it was highly improbable that he would be allowed to see Daisy for weeks or even months were he at hand, and she would most certainly be in no fit state to return with him to India. That letter had been to Will as the passing knell of all he had ever hoped or desired. Definitely it had told him very little, but he was not lacking in perception, and he had read a distinct and wholly unmistakable meaning behind the guarded, kindly sentences. And he knew when he laid the letter down that in Dr. Jim's opinion his presence might do incalculable harm. From that day forward he had entertained no further idea of return, settling down again to his work with a dogged patience that was very nearly allied to despair.

He was undoubtedly a rising man. There were prospects of a speedy improvement in his position. It was unlikely that he would be called upon to spend another hot season in the scorching Plains. Steady perseverance and indubitable talent had made their mark. But success was dust and ashes to him now. He did not greatly care if he went or stayed.

That Daisy was well again, or on the high-road to recovery, he knew; but he had not received a single letter from her since her illness.

Jim's epistles were very few and far between, but Nick had maintained a fairly regular correspondence with him till a few weeks back when it had unaccountably lapsed. But then Nick had done unaccountable things before, and he did not set down his silence to inconstancy. He was probably making prodigious efforts on his behalf, and Will awaited every mail with an eagerness he could not quite suppress, which turned invariably, however, into a sick sense of disappointment.

That Daisy would ever return to him now he did not for an instant believe, but there remained the chance—the slender, infinitesimal chance—that she might ask him to go to her. More than a flying visit she would know he could not manage. His work was his living, and hers. But so much Nick's powers of persuasion might one day accomplish though he would not allow himself to contemplate the possibility, while week by week the chance dwindled.

So he sat alone and unexpectant at his dinner-table that night and made heroic efforts to pacify the vigilant Sammy whose protest had warmed his heart a little if it had not greatly assisted his appetite.

He was glad when the meal was over, and he could saunter out on to the verandah with his cigar. The night was splendid with stars; but it held no moon. The wind had died away, but it had left a certain chill behind; and somehow he was reminded of a certain evening of early summer in England long ago, when he and Daisy had strolled together in an English garden, and she had yielded impulsively to his earnest wooing and had promised to be his wife. He remembered still the little laugh half sweet, half bitter, with which she had surrendered, the soft raillery of her blue eyes that yet had not wholly mocked him, the dainty charm of her submission. She had not loved him. He had known it even then. She had almost told him so. But with a boy's impetuosity he had taken the little she had to give, trusting to the future to make her all his own.

Ah, well! He caught himself sighing, and found that his cigar was out. With something less than his customary self-suppression he pitched it forth into the darkness. He could not even smoke with any enjoyment. He would go indoors and work.

He swung round on his heel, and started back along the verandah towards his room from which the red light streamed. Three strides he took with his eyes upon the ground. Then for no reason that he knew he glanced up towards that bar of light. The next instant he stood still as one transfixed, and all the blood rushed in tumult to his heart.

There, motionless in the full glare—watching him, waiting for him—stood his wife!

CHAPTER XLVIT
THE HEART OF A MAN

She did not utter a single word or move to greet him. Even in that ruddy light she was white to the lips. Her hands were fast gripped together. She did not seem to breathe.

So for full thirty seconds they faced one another, speechless, spell-bound, while through the awful silence the cry of a jackal sounded from afar, seeking its meat from God.

Will was the first to move, feeling for his handkerchief mechanically and wiping his forehead. Also he tried to speak aloud, but his voice was gone. "Pull yourself together, you fool!" he whispered savagely. "She'll be gone again directly."

She caught the words apparently, for her attitude changed. She parted her straining hands as though by great effort, and moved towards him.

Out of the glare of the lamplight she looked more normal. She wore a grey travelling-dress, but her hat was off. He fancied he saw the sparkle of the starlight in her hair.

She came towards him a few steps, and then she stopped. "Will," she said, and her voice had a piteous tremble in it, "won't you speak to me? Don't you—don't you know me?"

Her voice awoke him, brought him down from the soaring heights of imagination as it were with a thud. He strode forward and caught her hands in his.

"Good heavens, Daisy!" he said. "I thought I was dreaming! How on earth—"

And there he stopped dead, checked in mid career, for she was leaning back from him, leaning back with all her strength that he might not kiss her.

He stood, still holding her hands, and looked at her. There was a curious, choked sensation at his throat, as if he had swallowed ashes. She had come back to him—she had come back to him indeed, but he had a feeling that she was somehow beyond his reach, further away from him in that moment of incredible reunion than she had ever been during all the weary months of their separation. This woman with the pale face and tragic eyes was a total stranger to him. Small wonder that he had thought himself to be dreaming!

With a furious effort he collected himself. He let her hands slip from his. "Come in here," he said, forcing his dry throat to speech by sheer strength of will. "You should have let me know."

She went in without a word, and came to a stand before the table that was littered with his work. She was agitated, he saw. Her hand was pressed against her heart, and she seemed to breathe with difficulty.

Instinctively he came to her aid with commonplace phrases—the first that occurred to him. "How did you come? But no matter! Tell me presently. You must have something to eat. You look dead beat. Sit down, won't—"

And there he stopped again, breaking off short to stare at her. In the lighted room she had turned to face him, and he saw that her hair was no longer golden but silvery white.

Seeing his look, she began to speak in hurried, uneven sentences. "I have been ill, you know. It—it was brain fever, Jim said. Hair—fair hair particularly—does go like that sometimes."

"You are well again?" he questioned.

"Oh, quite—quite." There was something almost feverish in the assertion; she was facing him with desperate resolution. "I have been well for a long time. Please don't send for anything. I dined at the dâk-bungalow an hour ago. I—I thought it best."

Her agitation was increasing. She panted between each sentence. Will turned aside, shut and bolted the window, and drew the blind. Then he went close to her; he laid a steady hand upon her.

"Sit down," he said, "and tell me what is the matter."

She sank down mutely. Her mouth was quivering; she sought to hide it from him with her hand.

"Tell me," he said again, and quietly though he spoke there was in his tone a certain mastery that had never asserted itself in the old days; "What is it? Why have you come to me like this?"

"I—haven't come to stay, Will," she said, her voice so low that it was barely audible.

His face changed. He looked suddenly dogged. "After twenty months!" he said.

She bent her head. "I know. It's half a lifetime—more. You have learnt to do without me by this. At least—I hope you have—for your own sake."

He made no comment on the words; perhaps he did not hear them. After a brief silence she heard his voice above her bowed head. "Something is wrong. You'll tell me presently, won't you? But—really you needn't be afraid."

Something in the words—was it a hint of tenderness?—renewed her failing strength. She commanded herself and raised her head. She scarcely recognised in the steady, square-chinned man before her the impulsive, round-faced boy she had left. There was something unfathomable about him, a hint of greatness that affected her strangely.

"Yes," she said. "Something is wrong. It is what I am here for—what I have come to tell you. And when it is over, I'm going away—I'm going away—out of your life—for ever, this time."

His jaw hardened, but he said nothing whatever. He stood waiting for her to continue.

She rose slowly to her feet though she was scarcely capable of standing. She had come to the last ounce of her strength, but she spent it bravely.

"Will," she said, and though her voice shook uncontrollably every word was clear, "I hardly know how to say it. You have always trusted me, always been true to me. I think—once—you almost worshipped me. But you'll never worship me any more, because—because—I am unworthy of you. Do you understand? I was held back from the final wickedness, or—or I shouldn't be here now. But the sin was there in my heart. Heaven help me, it is there still. There! I have told you. It—was your right. I don't ask for mercy or forgiveness. Only punish me—punish me—and then—let me—go!"

Voice and strength failed together. Her limbs doubled under her, and she sank suddenly down at his feet, sobbing—terrible, painful, tearless sobs that seemed to rend her very being.

Without a word he stooped and lifted her. He was white to the lips, but there was no hesitancy about him. He acted instantly and decidedly as a man quite sure of himself.

He carried her to the old *charpoy* by the window and laid her down.

Many minutes later, when her anguish had a little spent itself, she realised that he was kneeling beside her, holding her pressed against his heart. Through all the bitter chaos of her misery and her shame there came to her the touch of his hand upon her head.

It amazed her—it thrilled her, that touch of his; in a fashion it awed her. She kept her face hidden from him; she could not look up. But he did not seek to see her face. He only kept his hand upon her throbbing temple till she grew still against his breast.

Then at length, his voice slow and deep and very steady, he spoke. "Daisy, we will never speak of this again."

She gave a great start. Pity, even a certain measure of kindness, she had almost begun to expect; but not this—not this! She made a movement to draw herself away from him, but he would not suffer it. He only held her closer.

"Oh, don't, Will, don't!" she implored him brokenly. "For your own sake—let me go!"

"For my own sake, Daisy," he answered quietly,—"and for yours, since you have come to me, I will never let you go again."

"But you can't want me," she insisted piteously. "Don't be generous, Will. I can't bear it. Anything but that! I would rather you cursed me—indeed—indeed!"

His hand restrained her, silenced her. "Hush!" he said. "You are my wife. I love you, and I want you."

Tears came to her then with a rush, blinding, burning, overwhelming, and yet their very agony was relief to her. She made no further effort to loosen his hold. She even feebly clung to him as one needing support.

"Ah, but I must tell you—I must tell you," she whispered at last. "If—if you mean to forgive me, you must know—everything."

"Tell me, if it helps you," he answered, and he spoke with the splendid patience that twenty weary months had wrought in him. "Only believe—before you begin—that I have forgiven you. For—before God—it is the truth."

And so presently, lying in his arms, her face hidden low on his breast, she told him all, suppressing nothing, extenuating nothing, simply pouring out the whole bitter story, sometimes halting, sometimes incoherent, but never wavering in her purpose, till, like an evil growth that yet clung about her palpitating heart, her sin lay bare before him—the sin of a woman who had almost forgotten that Love is a holy thing.

He heard her to the end with scarcely a word, and when she had finished he made one comment only.

"And so you gave him up."

She shivered with the pain of that memory. "Yes, I gave him up—I gave him up. Nick had made me see the hopelessness of it all—the wickedness. And he—he let me go. He saw it too—at least he understood. And on that very night—oh, Will, that awful night—he went to his death."

His arms grew closer about her. "My poor girl!" he said.

"Ah, but you shouldn't!" she sobbed. "You shouldn't! You ought to hate me—to despise me."

"Hush!" he said again. And she knew that with that one word he resolutely turned his back upon the gulf that had opened between them during those twenty months—that gulf that his love had been great enough to bridge—and that he took her with him, bruised and broken and storm-tossed as she was, into a very sheltered place.

When presently he turned her face up to his own and gravely kissed her she clung to his neck like a tired child, no longer fearing to meet his look, only thankful for the comfort of his arms.

For a while longer he held her silently, then very quietly he began to question her about her journey. Had she told him that she had been putting up at the dâk-bungalow?

"Oh, only for a few hours," she answered. "We arrived this evening, Nick and I."

"Nick!" he said. "And you left him behind?"

"He is waiting to take me back," she murmured, her face hidden against his shoulder.

Again, very tenderly, his hand pressed her forehead. "He must come to us, eh, dear? I will sent the *khit* down with a note presently. But you are tired out, and must rest. Lie here while I go and tell Sammy to make ready."

It was when he came back to her that she began to see wherein lay the change in him that had so struck her.

From her cushions she looked up at him, piteously smiling. "How thin you are, Will! And you are getting quite a scholarly stoop."

"Ah, that's India," he said.

But she knew that it was not India at all, and her face told him so, though he affected not to see it.

He bent over her. "Now, Daisy, I am going to carry you to bed as I used—do you remember?—at Simla, after the baby came. Dear little chap! Do you remember how he used to smile in his sleep?"

His voice was hushed, as though he stood once more beside the tiny cot.

She sat up, yielding herself to his arms. "Oh, Will," she said, with a great sob, "if only he had lived!"

He held her closely, and lying against his breast she felt the sigh he stifled. His lips were upon the silvered hair.

"Perhaps—some day—Daisy," he said, under his breath.

And she, clinging to him, whispered back through her tears, "Oh, Will,—I do hope so."

CHAPTER XLVII
IN THE NAME OF FRIENDSHIP

It was very hot down on the buzzing race-course, almost intolerably so in the opinion of the girl who sat in Lady Bassett's elegantly-appointed carriage, and looked out with the indifference of boredom upon the sweltering crowds.

"Dear child, don't look so freezingly aloof!" she had been entreated more than once; and each time the soft injunction had reached her the wide dark eyes had taken to themselves a more utter disdain.

If she looked freezing, she was far from feeling it, for the hot weather was at its height, and Ghawalkhand, though healthy, was not the coolest spot in the Indian Empire. Sir Reginald Bassett had been appointed British Resident, to act as adviser to the young rajah thereof, and there had been no question of a flitting to Simla that year. Lady Bassett had deplored this, but Muriel rejoiced. She never wanted to see Simla again.

Life was a horrible emptiness to her in those days. She was weary beyond expression, and had no heart for the gaieties in which she was plunged. Idle compliments had never attracted her, and flirtations were an abomination to her. She looked through and beyond them with the eyes of a sphinx. But there were very few who suspected the intolerable ache that throbbed unceasingly behind her impassivity—the loneliness of spirit that oppressed her like a crushing, physical weight.

Even Bobby Fraser, who saw most things, could scarcely have been aware of this; yet certainly it was not the vivacity of her conversation that induced him to seek her out as he generally did when he saw her sitting apart. A very cheery bachelor was Bobby Fraser, and a tremendous favourite wherever he went. He was a wonderful organizer, and he invariably had a hand in anything of an entertaining nature that was going forward.

He had just brought her tea, and was waiting beside her while she drank it. Lady Bassett had left the carriage for the paddock, and Muriel sat alone.

Had she had anything on the last race, he wanted to know? Muriel had not. He had, and was practically ruined in consequence—a calamity which in no way seemed to affect his spirits.

"Who would have expected a rank outsider like that to walk over the course? Ought to have been disqualified for sheer cheek. Reminds me of a chap I once knew—forget his name—Nick something or other—who entered at the last minute for the Great Mogul's Cup at Sharapura. Did it for a bet, they said. It's years ago now. The horse was a perfect brute—all bone and no flesh—with a temper like the foul fiend and no points whatever—looked a regular crock at starting. But he romped home on three legs, notwithstanding, with his jockey clinging to him like an inspired monkey. It was the only race he ever won. Every one put it down to black magic or personal magnetism on the part of his rider. Same thing, I believe. He was the sort of chap who always comes out on top. Rum thing I can't remember his name. I had travelled out with him on the same boat once too. Have some more tea."

This was a specimen of most of Bobby Fraser's conversation. He was brimful of anecdotes. They flowed as easily as water from a fountain. Their source seemed inexhaustible. He never repeated himself to the same person.

Muriel declined his offer of more tea. For some reason she wanted to hear more of the man who had won the Great Mogul's Cup at Sharapura.

Bobby was more than willing to oblige. "Oh, it was sheer cheek that carried him through, of course. I always said he was the cheekiest beggar under the sun—quite a little chap he was, hideously ugly, with a face like a baked apple, and eyes that made you think of a cinematograph. You know the sort of thing. I used to think he had a future before him, but he seems to have dropped out. He was only about twenty when I had him for a stable-companion. I remember one outrageous thing he did on the voyage out. There was card-playing going on in the saloon one night, and he was looking on. One of the lady-players—well, I suppose I may as well call it by its name—one of them cheated. He detected it. Beastly position, of course. Don't know what I should have done under the circumstances, but anyhow he wasn't at a loss. He simply lighted a cigarette and set fire to the lady's dress."

Muriel's exclamation of horror was ample testimony to the fact that her keenest interest was aroused.

"Yes, awfully risky, wasn't it?" said Bobby. "We only thought at the time he had been abominably careless. I did not hear the rights of the case till afterwards, and then not from him. There was a fine flareup, of course—card-table overturned—ladies in hysterics—in the middle of the fray our gallant hero extinguishing the flames with his bare hands. He was profusely apologetic and rather badly scorched. The lady took very little harm, except to her nerves and her temper. She cut him dead for the rest of the voyage, but I don't think it depressed him much. He was the sort of fellow that never gets depressed. Hullo! There's Mrs. Philpot making violent signs. I suppose I had better go and see what she wants, or be dropped for evermore. Good-bye!"

He smiled upon her and departed, leaving her thoughtful, with a certain wistful wonder in her eyes.

Lady Bassett's return interrupted her reverie. "You have had some tea, I hope, dear? Ah, I thought Mr. Bobby Fraser was making his way in this direction. So sweet of him not to forget you when he has so many other calls upon his attention. And how are you faring for to-night? Is your programme full yet? I have literally not one dance left."

Lady Bassett had deemed it advisable to ignore the fact of Muriel's brief engagement to Captain Grange since the girl's return to India. She knew, as did her husband, that it had come to an end before Grange's death, but she withheld all comment upon it. Her one desire was to get the dear child married without delay, and she was not backward in letting her know it. Life at Ghawalkhand was one continuous round of gaiety, and she had every opportunity for forwarding her scheme. Though she deplored Muriel's unresponsiveness, she yet did not despair. It was sheer affectation on the girl's part, she would tell herself, and would soon pass. And after all, that queenly, aloof air had a charm that was all its own. It might not attract the many, but she had begun to fancy of late that Bobby Fraser had felt its influence. He was not in the least the sort of man she would have expected to do so, but there was no accounting for taste—masculine taste especially. And it would be an excellent thing for Muriel.

She was therefore being particularly gracious to her young charge just then—a state of affairs which Muriel endured rather than appreciated. She would never feel at her ease with Lady Bassett as long as she lived.

She was glad when they drove away at length, for she wanted to be alone. Those anecdotes of Bobby's had affected her strangely. She had felt so completely cut off of late from all things connected with the past. No one ever mentioned Nick to her now—not even her faithful correspondent Olga. Meteor-like, he had flashed through her sky and disappeared; leaving a burning, ineradicable trail behind him, it is true, but none the less was he gone. She had not the faintest idea where he was. She would have given all she had to know, yet could not bring herself to ask. It seemed highly improbable that he would ever cross her path again, and she knew she ought to be glad of this; yet no gladness ever warmed her heart. And now here was a man who had known him, who had told her of exploits new to her knowledge yet how strangely familiar to her understanding, who had at a touch brought before her the weird personality that her imagination sometimes strove in vain to summon. She could have sat and listened to Bobby's reminiscences for hours. The bare mention of Nick's name had made her blood run faster.

Lady Bassett did not trouble her to converse during the drive back, ascribing to her evident desire for silence a reason which Muriel was too absent to suspect. But when the girl roused herself to throw a couple of annas to an old beggar who was crouched against the entrance to the Residency grounds she could not resist giving utterance to a gentle expostulation.

"I wish you would not encourage these people, dearest. They are so extremely undesirable, and there is so much unrest in the State just now that I cannot but regard them with anxiety."

Muriel murmured an apology, with the inward reservation to bestow her alms next time when Lady Bassett was not looking on.

She found a letter lying on her table when she entered her room, and took it up listlessly, without much interest. Her mind was still running on those two anecdotes with which Bobby Fraser had so successfully enlivened her boredom. The writing on the envelope was vaguely familiar to her, but she did not associate it with anything of importance. Absently she opened it, half reluctant to recall her wandering thoughts. It came from a Hill station in Bengal, but that told her nothing. She turned to the signature.

The next instant she had turned back again to the beginning, and was reading eagerly. Her correspondent was Will Musgrave.

"Dear Miss Roscoe,"—ran the letter. "After long consideration I have decided to write and beg of you a favour which I fancy you will grant more readily than I venture to ask. My wife, as you probably know, joined me some months ago. She is in very indifferent health, and has expressed a most earnest wish to see you. I believe there is something which she wishes to tell you—something that weighs upon her heavily; and though I trust that all will go well with her, I cannot help feeling that she would stand a much better chance of this if only her mind could be set at rest. I know I am asking a big thing of you, for the journey is a ghastly one at this time of the year, but if of your goodness you can bring yourself to face it, I will myself meet you and escort you across the Plains. Will you think the matter carefully over? And perhaps you would wire a reply.

"I have written without Daisy's knowledge, as she seems to feel that she has forfeited the right to your friendship.—Sincerely yours,

"W. MUSGRAVE."

Muriel's reply was despatched that evening, almost before she had fully read the appeal. "Starting to-morrow," was all she said.

CHAPTER XLVIII
THE HEALING OF THE BREACH

Lady Bassett considered the decision deplorably headlong, and said so; but her remonstrances were of no avail. Muriel tossed aside her listlessness as resolutely as the ball-dress that had been laid out for the evening's festivity, and plunged at once into preparations for her journey. She knew full well that it was of no actual importance to Lady Bassett whether she went or stayed, and she did not pretend to think otherwise. Moreover, no power on earth would have kept her away from Daisy now that she knew herself to be wanted.

Though more than half of the three days' journey lay across the sweltering Plains, she contemplated it without anxiety, even with rejoicing. At last, the breach, over which she had secretly mourned so deeply, was to be healed.

The next morning at an early hour she was upon her way. She looked out as she drove through the gates for the old native beggar who had crouched at the entrance on the previous afternoon. He was not there, but a little way further she met him hobbling along to take up his post for the day. From the folds of his chuddah his unkempt beard wagged entreaty at the carriage as it passed. Impulsively, because of the gladness that was so new to her lonely heart, she leaned from the window and threw him a rupee.

Looking back upon the journey later, she never remembered its tedium. She was as one borne on the wings of love, and she scarcely noticed the hardships of the way.

Will Musgrave met her according to his promise at the great junction in the Plains. She found him exceedingly solicitous for her welfare, but so grave and silent that she hardly liked to question him. He thanked her very earnestly for coming, said that Daisy was about the same, and then left her almost exclusively to the society of her ayah.

The heat in the Plains was terrific, but Muriel's courage never wavered. She endured it with unfaltering resolution, hour after hour reckoning the dwindling miles that lay before them, passing over all personal discomfort as of no account, content only to be going forward.

But they left the Plains behind at last, and then came to the welcome ascent to the Hill station through a country where pine-trees grew ever more and more abundant.

At length at the close of a splendid day they reached it, and as they were nearing their destination Will broke through his silence.

"She doesn't know even yet that you are coming," he said. "I thought the suspense of waiting for you might be bad for her. Miss Roscoe—in heaven's name—make her happy if you can!"

There was such a passion of entreaty in his voice that Muriel was deeply touched. She gave him her hand impulsively.

"Mr. Musgrave," she said, "to this day I do not know what it was that came between us, but I promise—I promise—that if any effort of mine can remove it, it shall be removed to-night."

Will Musgrave squeezed her fingers hard. "God bless you!" he said earnestly.

And with that he left her, and went on ahead to prepare Daisy for her coming.

All her life Muriel remembered Daisy's welcome of that evening with a thrill of pain. They met at the gate of the little compound that surrounded the bungalow Will had taken for his wife, and though the light of the sinking sun smote with a certain ruddiness upon Daisy, Muriel was unspeakably shocked by her appearance.

Her white hair, her deathly pallor, the haunting misery of her eyes—above all, her silence—went straight to the girl's heart. Without a single word she gathered Daisy close in her warm young arms and so held her in a long and speechless embrace.

After all, it was Daisy who spoke first, gently drawing herself away. "Come in, darling! You must be nearly dead after your awful journey. I can't think how Will could ask it of you at this time of the year. I couldn't myself."

"I would have come to you from the world's end—and gladly," Muriel answered, in her deep voice. "You know I would."

And that was all that passed between them, for Will was present, and Daisy had already begun to lead her guest into the house.

As the evening wore on, Muriel was more and more struck by the great change she saw in her. They had not met for ten months, but twice as many years seemed to have passed over Daisy, crushing her beneath their weight. All her old sprightliness had vanished utterly. She spoke but little, and there was in her manner to her husband a wistful humility, a submission so absolute, that Muriel, remembering her ancient spirit, could have wept.

Will looked at her as if he longed to say something when she bade him good-night, but Daisy was beside her, and he could only give her a tremendous handgrip.

They went away together, and Daisy accompanied her to her room. But the wall of reserve that had been built up between them was not to be shattered at a touch. Neither of them knew exactly how to approach it. There was no awkwardness between them, there was no lack of tenderness, but the door that had closed so long ago was hard to open. Daisy seemed to avoid it with a morbid dread, and it was not in Muriel's power to make the first move.

So for awhile they lingered together, talking commonplaces, and at length parted for the night, holding each other closely, without words.

It seemed evident that Daisy could not bring herself to speak at present, and Muriel went to bed with a heavy heart.

She was far too weary to lie awake, but her tired brain would not rest. For the first time in many dreary months she dreamed of Nick.

He was jeering at her in devilish jubilation because she had changed her mind about marrying him, but lacked the courage to tell him so.

CHAPTER XLIX

THE LOWERING OF THE FLAG

The night was very far advanced when Muriel was aroused from her dreams by a sound which she drowsily fancied must have been going on for some time. It did not disturb her very seriously at first; she even subconsciously made an effort to ignore it. But at length a sudden stab of understanding pierced her sleep-laden senses, and in a moment she started up broad awake. Some one was in the room with her. Through the dumb stillness before the dawn there came the sound of bitter weeping.

For a few seconds she sat motionless, startled, bewildered, half afraid. The room was in nearly total darkness. Only in dimmest outline could she discern the long French window that opened upon the verandah.

The weeping continued. It was half smothered, but it sounded agonised. A great wave of compassion swept suddenly over Muriel. All in a moment she understood.

Swiftly she leaned forward into the darkness, feeling outwards till her groping hands touched a figure that crouched beside the bed.

"Daisy! Daisy, my darling!" she said, and there was anguish in her own voice. "What is it?"

In a second the sobbing ceased as if some magic had silenced it. Two hands reached up out of the darkness and tightly clasped hers. A broken voice whispered her name.

"What is it?" Muriel repeated in growing distress.

"Hush, dear, hush!" the trembling voice implored. "Don't let Will hear! It worries him so."

"But, my darling,—" Muriel protested.

She began to feel for some matches, but again the nervous hands caught and imprisoned hers.

"Don't—please!" Daisy begged her earnestly. "I—I have something to tell you—something that will shock you unutterably. And I—I don't want you to see my face."

She resisted Muriel's attempt to put her arms about her. "No—no, dear! Hear me first. There! Let me kneel beside you. It will not take me long. It isn't just for my own sake I am going to speak, nor yet—entirely—for yours. You will see presently. Don't ask me anything—please—till I have done. And then if—if there is anything you want to know, I will try to tell you."

"Come and lie beside me," Muriel urged.

But Daisy would not. She had sunk very low beside the bed. For a while she crouched there in silence while she summoned her strength.

Then, "Oh, Muriel," she suddenly said, and the words seemed to burst from her with a great sigh, "I wonder if you ever really loved Blake."

"No, dear, I never did." Muriel's answer came quiet and sincere through the darkness. "Nor did he love me. Our engagement was a mistake. I was going to tell him so—if things had been different."

"I never thought you cared for him," Daisy said. "But oh, Muriel, I did. I loved him with my whole soul. No, don't start! It is over now—at least that part of it that was sinful. I only tell you of it because it is the key to everything that must have puzzled you so horribly all this time. We always loved each other from the very beginning, but our people wouldn't hear of it because we were cousins. And so we separated and I used to think that I had put it away from me. But—last summer—it all came back. You mustn't blame him, Muriel. Blame me—blame me!" The thin hands tightened convulsively. "It was when my baby died that I began to give way. We never meant it—either of us—but we didn't fight hard enough. And then at last—at Brethaven—Nick found it out; and it was because he knew that Blake's heart was not in his compact with you that he made him write to you and break it off. It was not for his own ends at all that he did it. It was for your sake alone. He even swore to Blake that if he would put an end to his engagement, he on his part would give up all idea of winning you and would never trouble you any more. And that was the finest thing he ever did, Muriel, for he never loved any one but you. Surely you know it. You must know it by this time. You have never understood him, but you must have begun to realise that he has loved you well enough to set your happiness and well-being always far, far before his own."

Daisy paused. Her weeping had wholly ceased, but she was shivering from head to foot.

Muriel sat in silence above her, watching wide-eyed, unseeing, the vague hint of light at the open window. She was beginning to understand many things—ah, many things—that had been as a sealed book to her till then.

After a time Daisy went on. "No one will ever know what Nick was to me at that time, how he showed me the wickedness of it all, how he held me back from taking the final step, making me realise—even against my will—that Love—true Love—is holy, conquering all evil. And afterwards—afterwards—when Blake was gone—he stood by me and helped me to live, and brought me back at last to my husband. I could never have done it alone. I hadn't the strength. You see"—the low voice faltered suddenly—"I never expected Will to forgive me. I never asked it of him—any more than I am asking it of you."

"Oh, my darling, there is no need!" Muriel turned suddenly to throw impetuous arms about the huddled figure at her side. "Daisy! Daisy! I love you. Let us forget there has ever been this thing between us. Let us be as we used to be, and never drift apart again."

Tenderly but insistently, she lifted Daisy to the bed beside her, holding her fast. The wall between them was broken down at last. They clung together as sisters long parted.

Daisy, spent by the violence of her emotion, lay for a long time in Muriel's arms without attempting anything further. But at length with a palpable effort she began to speak of other things.

"You know, I have a feeling—perhaps it is morbid—that I am not going to live. I am sure Will thinks so too. If I die, Muriel,—three months from now—you and Nick must help him all you can."

"You are not going to die," Muriel asserted vehemently. "You are not to talk of dying, or think of it. Oh, Daisy, can't you look forward to the better time that is coming—when you will have something to live for? And won't you try to think more of Will? It would break his heart to lose you."

"I do think of him," Daisy said wearily. "I would do anything to make him happier. But I can't look forward. I am so tired—so tired."

"You will feel differently by-and-by," Muriel whispered.

"Perhaps," she assented. "I don't know. I don't feel as if I shall ever hold another child in my arms. God knows I don't deserve it."

"Do you think He looks at it in that way?" murmured Muriel, her arms tightening. "There wouldn't be much in life for any of us if He did."

"I don't know," Daisy said again.

She lay quiet for a little as though pondering something. Then at length hesitatingly she spoke. "Muriel, there is one thing that whether I live or whether I die I want with my whole heart. May I tell you what it is?"

"Of course, dear. What is it?"

Daisy turned in her arms, holding her in a clasp that was passionate. "My darling," she whispered very earnestly, "I would give all I have in the world to know you happy with—with the man you love."

Silence followed the words. Muriel had become suddenly quite still; her head was bent.

"Don't—don't bar me out of your confidence," Daisy implored her tremulously. "There is so little left for me to do now. Muriel—dearest—you do love him?"

Muriel moved impulsively, hiding her face in her friend's neck. But she said no word in answer.

Daisy went on softly, as though she had spoken. "He is still waiting for you. I think he will wait all his life, though he will never come to you again unless you call him. Won't you—can't you—send him just one little word?"

"How can I?" The words broke suddenly from Muriel as though she could no longer restrain them. "How can I possibly?"

"It could be done," Daisy said. "I know he is still somewhere in India though he has left the Army. We could get a message to him at any time."

"Oh, but I couldn't—I couldn't!" Muriel had begun to tremble violently. There was a sound of tears in her deep voice. "Besides—he wouldn't come."

"My dear, he would," Daisy assured her. "He would come to you directly if he only knew that you wanted him. Muriel, surely you are not—not too proud to let him know!"

"Proud! Oh, no, no!" There was almost a moan in the words. Muriel's head sank a little lower. "Heaven knows I'm not proud," she said. "I am ashamed—miserably ashamed. I have trampled on his love so often—so often. How could I ask him for it—now?"

"Ah, but if he came to you," Daisy persisted, "if in spite of all he came to you, you wouldn't send him away?"

"Send him away!" A sudden note of passion thrilled in Muriel's voice. She lifted her head sharply. With the tears upon her cheeks she yet spoke with a certain exultation. "I—I would follow him barefoot across the world," she said, "if—if he would only lift one finger to call me. But oh, Daisy,"—her confidence vanished at a breath—"where's the use of talking? He never, never will."

"He will if you let him know," Daisy answered with conviction. "Don't you think you can, dear? Give me just one word for him—one tiny message that he will understand. Only trust him this once—just this once! Give him his opportunity—he has never had one before, poor boy—and I know, I know, he will not throw it away."

"You don't think he will—laugh?" Muriel whispered.

"My dear child, no! Nick doesn't laugh at sacred things."

Muriel's face was burning in the darkness. She covered it with her hands as though it could be seen.

For a few seconds she sat very still. Then slowly but steadily she spoke.

"Tell him then, Daisy, from me, that 'Love conquers all things—and we must yield to Love.'"

CHAPTER L
EREBUS

Not another word passed between Daisy and Muriel upon the subject of that night's confidences. There seemed nothing further to be said. Moreover, there was between them a closer understanding than words could compass.

The days that followed passed very peacefully, and Daisy began to improve so marvellously in health and spirits that both her husband and her guest caught at times fleeting glimpses of the old light-hearted personality that they had loved in earlier days.

"You have done wonders for my wife," Will said one day to Muriel. And though she disclaimed all credit, she could not fail to see a very marked improvement.

She herself was feeling unaccountably happy in those days, as though somewhere deep down in her heart a bird had begun to sing. Again and again she told herself that she had no cause for gladness; but again and yet again that sweet, elusive music filled her soul.

She would have gladly stayed on with Daisy, seeing how the latter clung to her, for an indefinite period; but this was not to be.

Daisy came out on to the verandah one morning with a letter in her hand.

"My dear," she said, "I regret to say that, I must part with you. I have had a most touching epistle from Lady Bassett, describing at length your many wasted opportunities, and urging me to return you to the fold with all speed. It seems there is to be a State Ball at the palace—an immense affair to which the Rajah is inviting all the big guns for miles around—and Lady Bassett thinks that her dear child ought not to miss such a gorgeous occasion. She seems to think that something of importance depends upon it, and hints that I should be almost criminally selfish to deprive you of such a treat as this will be."

Muriel lifted a flushed face from a letter of her own. "I have heard from Sir Reginald," she said. "Evidently she has made him write. I can't think why, for she never wants me when I am with her. I don't see why I should go, do you? After all, I am of age and independent."

A very tender smile touched Daisy's lips. "I think you had better go, darling," she said.

Muriel opened her eyes wide. "But why—"

Daisy checked the question half uttered. "I think it will be better for you. I never meant to let you stay till the rains, so it makes little more than a week's difference. It sounds as if I want to be rid of you, doesn't it? But you know it isn't that. I shall miss you horribly, but you have done what you came to do, and I shall get on all right now. So I am not going to keep you with me any longer. My reasons are not Lady Bassett's reasons, but all the same it would be selfish of me to let you stay. Later on perhaps—in the winter—you will come and make a long stay; spend Christmas with us, and we will have some real fun, shall we, Will?" turning to her husband who had just appeared.

He stared for an instant as if he thought he had not heard aright, and there was to Muriel something infinitely pathetic in the way his brown hand touched his wife's shoulder as he passed her and made reply.

"Oh, rather!" he said. "We'll have a regular jollification with as many old friends as we can collect. Don't forget, Miss Roscoe! You are booked first and foremost, and we shall keep you to it, Daisy and I."

Two days later Muriel was on her way back to Ghawalkhand. She found the heat of the journey almost insupportable. The Plains lay under a burning pall of cloud, and at night the rolling thunder was incessant. But no rain fell to ease the smothering oppression of the atmosphere.

She almost fainted one evening, but Will was with her and she never forgot his kindly ministrations.

A few hours' journey from Ghawalkhand Sir Reginald himself met her, and here she parted with Will with renewed promises of a future meeting towards the end of the year.

Sir Reginald fussed over her kind-heartedly, hoped she had enjoyed herself, thought she looked very thin, and declared that his wife was looking forward with much pleasure to her return. The State was still somewhat unsettled, there had been one or two outrages of late, nothing serious, of course, but the native element was restless, and he fancied Lady Bassett was nervous.

She was away at a polo-match when they arrived, and Muriel profited by her absence and went straight to bed.

She could have slept for hours had she been permitted to do so, but Lady Bassett, returning, awoke her to receive her welcome. She was charmed to have her back, she declared, though shocked to see her looking so wan, "so almost plain, dear child, if one may take the liberty of an old friend to tell you so."

Neither the crooked smile that accompanied this gentle criticism nor the decidedly grim laugh with which it was received, was of a particularly friendly nature; but these facts were not extraordinary. There had never been the smallest hint of sympathy between them.

"I trust you will be looking much better than this two nights hence," Lady Bassett proceeded in her soft accents. "The Rajah's ball is to be very magnificent, quite dazzlingly so from all accounts. Mr. Bobby Fraser is of course behind the scenes, and he tells me that the preparations in progress are simply gigantic. By the way, dear, it is to be hoped that your absence has not damaged your prospects in that quarter. I have been afraid lately that he was transferring his allegiance to the second Egerton girl. I hope earnestly that there is nothing in it, for you know how I have your happiness at heart, do you not? And it would be such an excellent thing for you, dear child, as I expect you realise. For you know, you look so much older than you actually are that you really ought not to throw away any more opportunities. Every girl thinks she must have her fling, but you, dear, should soberly think of getting settled soon. You would not like to get left, I feel sure."

At this point Muriel sat up suddenly, her dark eyes very bright, and in brief tones announced that so far as she was concerned the second Egerton girl was more than welcome to Mr. Fraser and she hoped, if she wanted him, she would manage to keep him.

It was crudely expressed, as Lady Bassett pointed out with a sigh for her waywardness; but Muriel always was crude when her deeper feelings were disturbed, and physical fatigue had made her irritable.

She wished ardently that Lady Bassett would leave her, but Lady Bassett had not quite done. She lingered to ask for news of poor little Daisy Musgrave. Had she yet fully recovered from the shock of her cousin's tragic death? Could she bear to speak of him? She, Lady Bassett, had always suspected the existence of an unfortunate attachment between them.

Muriel had no information to bestow upon the subject. She hoped and believed that Daisy was getting stronger, and had promised, all being well, to spend Christmas with her.

Lady Bassett shook her head over this declaration. The dear child was so headlong. Much might happen before Christmas. And what of Mr. Ratcliffe—this was on her way to the door—had she heard the extraordinary, the really astounding news concerning him that had just reached Lady Bassett's ears? She asked because he and Mrs. Musgrave used to be such friends, though to be sure Mr. Ratcliffe seemed to have thrown off all his old friends of late. Had Muriel actually not heard?

"Heard! Heard what?" Muriel forced out the question from between lips that were white and stiff. She was suddenly afraid—horribly, unspeakably afraid. But she kept her eyes unflinchingly upon Lady Bassett's face. She would sooner die than quail in her presence.

Lady Bassett, holding the door-handle, looked back at her, faintly smiling. "I wonder you have not heard, dear. I thought you were in correspondence with his people. But perhaps they also are in the dark. It is a most unheard-of thing—quite irrevocable I am told. But I always felt that he was a man to do unusual things. There was always to my mind something uncanny, abnormal, something almost superhuman, about him."

"But what has happened to him?" Muriel did not know how she uttered the words; they seemed to come without her own volition. She was conscious of a choking sensation within her as though iron bands were tightening about her heart. It beat in leaps and bounds like a tortured thing striving to escape. But through it all she sat quite motionless, her eyes fixed upon Lady Bassett's face, noting its faint, wry smile, as the eyes of a prisoner on the rack might note the grim lines on the face of the torturer.

"My dear," Lady Bassett said, "he has gone into a Buddhist monastery in Tibet."

Calmly the words fell through smiling lips. Only words! Only words! But with how deadly a thrust they pierced the heart of the woman who heard them none but herself would ever know. She gave no sign of suffering. She only stared wide-eyed before her as an image, devoid of expression, inanimate, sphinx-like, while that awful constriction grew straiter round her heart.

Lady Bassett was already turning to go when the deep voice arrested her.

"Who told you this?"

She looked back, holding the open door. "I scarcely know who first mentioned it. I have heard it from so many people,—in fact the news is general property—Captain Gresham of the Guides told me for one. He has just gone back to Peshawur. The news reached him, I believe, from there. Then there was Colonel Cathcart for another. He was talking of it only this afternoon at the Club, saying what a deplorable example it was for an Englishman to set. He and Mr. Bobby Fraser had quite a hot argument about it. Mr. Fraser has such advanced ideas, but I must admit that I rather admire the staunch way in which he defends them. There, dear child! You must not keep me gossiping any longer. You look positively haggard. I earnestly hope a good sleep will restore you, for I cannot possibly take that wan face to the Rajah's ball'."

Lady Bassett departed with the words, shaking her head tolerantly and still smiling.

But for long after she had gone, Muriel remained with fixed eyes and tense muscles, watching, watching, dumbly, immovably, despairingly, at the locked door of her paradise.

So this was the key to his silence—the reason that her message had gone unanswered. She had stretched out her hands to him too late—too late.

And ever through the barren desert of her vigil a man's voice, vital and passionate, rang and echoed in a maddening, perpetual refrain.

"All your life you will remember that I was once yours to take or to throw away. And—you wanted me, yet—you chose to throw me away."

It was a refrain she had heard often and often before; but it had never tortured her as it tortured her now,—now when her last hope was finally quenched—now when at last she fully realised what it was that had once been hers, and that in her tragic blindness she had wantonly cast away.

CHAPTER LI
THE BIRD OF PARADISE

Muriel did not leave the Residency again until the evening of the State Ball at the palace. Scarcely did she leave her room, pleading intense fatigue as her excuse for this seclusion. But she could not without exciting remark, absent herself from the great function for which ostensibly she had returned to Ghawalkhand.

She wore a dress of unrelieved white for the occasion, for she had but recently discarded her mourning for her father, and her face was almost as devoid of colour. Her dark hair lay in a shadowy mass above her forehead, accentuating her pallor. Her eyes looked out upon the world with tragic indifference, unexpectant, apathetic.

"My dear, you don't look well," said Sir Reginald, as, gorgeous in his glittering uniform, he stood to hand her after his wife into the carriage.

She smiled a little. "It is nothing. I am still rather tired, that's all."

Driving through the gates she looked forth absently and spied the old beggar crouching in his accustomed place. He almost prostrated himself at sight of her, but she had no money with her, nor could she have bestowed any under Lady Bassett's disapproving eye. The carriage rolled on, leaving his obsequiousness unrequited.

Entering the glittering ballroom all hung with glowing colours was like entering a garden of splendid flowers. European and Indian costumes were mingled in shining confusion. A hubbub of music and laughter seemed to engulf them like a rushing torrent.

"Ah, here you are at last!" It was Bobby Fraser's voice at Muriel's side. He looked at her with cheery approval. "I say, you know, you're the queen of this gathering. Pity there isn't a king anywhere about. Perhaps there is, eh? Well, can you give me a dance? Afraid I haven't a waltz left. No matter! We can sit out. I know a cosy corner exactly fitted to my tastes. In fact I've booked it for the evening. And I want a talk with you badly. Number five then. Good-bye!"

He was gone, leaving Muriel with the curious impression that there really was something of importance that he wished to say to her.

She wondered what it was. That he was paying her serious attention she had never for a moment believed, nor had she given him the faintest encouragement to do so. She knew that Lady Bassett thought otherwise, but she had never rated her opinion very highly; and she had never read anything but the most casual friendliness in Bobby's attitude.

Still it disturbed her somewhat, that hint of intimacy that his words portended, and she awaited the dance he had solicited in a state of mind very nearly allied to apprehension. Lady Bassett's suggestions had done for her what no self-consciousness would ever have accomplished unaided. They had implanted within her a deep-rooted misgiving before which all ease of manner fled.

When Bobby Fraser joined her, she was so plainly nervous that he could not fail to remark it. He led her to a quiet corner above the garden that was sheltered from the throng by flowering tamarisks.

"I say," he said, "I hope you are not letting yourself get scared by these infernal budmashes. The reports have all been immensely exaggerated as usual."

"I am not at all scared," she told him. "But wasn't there an Englishman murdered the other day?"

"Oh, yes," he admitted, "but miles and miles away, right the other side of the State. There was nothing in that to alarm any one here. It might have happened anywhere. People are such fools," he threw in vindictively. "Begin to look askance at the native population, and of course they are on the *qui vive* instantly. It is only to be expected. It was downright madness to send a Resident here. They resent it, you know. But the Rajah's influence is enormous. Nothing could happen here."

"I wonder," said Muriel.

She had scarcely given the matter a thought before, but it was a relief to find some impersonal topic for discussion.

Bobby, however, had no intention of pursuing it further. "Oh, it's self-evident," he said. "They are loyal to the Rajah, and the Rajah is well-known to be loyal to the Crown. It's only these duffers of administrators that make the mischief." He broke into an abrupt laugh, and changed the subject. "Let us talk of something less exasperating. How did you get on while you were away? You must have found the journey across the Plains pretty ghastly."

She told him a little about it, incidentally mentioning Will Musgrave.

"Oh, I know him," he broke in. "An engineer, isn't he? Awfully clever chap. I met him years ago at Sharapura the time Nick Ratcliffe won the Great Mogul's Cup. I told you that story, didn't I?"

Yes, he had done so. She informed him of the fact with an immovable face. It might have been a subject of total indifference to her.

"You know Nick Ratcliffe, don't you?" he pursued, evidently following his own train of thought.

She flushed at the direct question. She had not expected it. "It is a very long time since I last saw him," she said, with a deliberate effort to banish all interest from her voice.

He was not looking at her. He could not have been aware of the flush. Yet he elected to push the matter further.

"A queer fish," he said. "A very queer fish. He has lost his left arm, poor beggar. Did you know?"

Yes, she knew; but she could hardly summon the strength to tell him so. Her fan concealed her quivering lips, but the hand that held it shook uncontrollably.

But he, still casual, continued his desultory harangue. "Always reminds one of a jack-in-the-box—that fellow. Has a knack of popping up when you least expect him. You never know what he will do next. You can only judge him by the things he doesn't do. For instance, there's been a rumour floating about lately that he has just gone into a Tibetan monastery. Heaven knows who started it and why. But it is absolutely untrue. It is the sort of thing that couldn't be true of a man of his temperament. Don't you agree with me? Or perhaps you didn't know him very well, and don't feel qualified to judge."

At this point he pulled out his programme and studied it frowningly. He was plainly not paying much attention to her reply. He seemed to be contemplating something that worried him.

It made it all the easier for her to answer. "No," she said slowly. "I didn't know him very well. But—that rumour was told to me as absolute fact. I—of course—I believed it."

She knew that her face was burning as she ended. She could feel the blood surging through every vein.

"If you want to know what I think," said Bobby Fraser deliberately, "it is that that rumour was a malicious invention of some one's."

"Oh, do you?" she said. "But—but why?"

He turned and looked at her. His usually merry face was stern. "Because," he said, "it served some one's end to make some one else believe that Nick had dropped out for good."

Her eyes fell under his direct look. "I don't understand," she murmured desperately.

"Nor do I," he rejoined, "for certain. I can only surmise. It doesn't do to believe things too readily. One gets let in that way." He rose and offered her his arm. "Come outside for a little. This place is too warm for comfort."

She went with him willingly, thankful to turn her face to the night. A dozen questions hovered on her lips, but she could not ask him one of them. She could only walk beside him and profess to listen to the stream of anecdotes which he began to pour forth for her entertainment.

She did not actually hear one of them. They came to her all jumbled and confused through such a torrent of gladness as surely she had never known before. For the bird in her heart had lifted its head again, and was singing its rapture to the stars.

CHAPTER LII

A WOMAN'S OFFERING

Looking back upon the hours that followed that talk with Bobby behind the tamarisks, Muriel could never recall in detail how they passed. She moved in a whirl, all her pulses racing, all her senses on the alert. None of her partners had ever seen her gay before, but she was gay that night with a spontaneous and wonderful gaiety that came from the very heart of her. It was not a gaiety that manifested itself in words, but it was none the less apparent to those about her. For her eyes shone as though they looked into a radiant future, and she danced as one inspired. She was like a statue waked to splendid life.

Swiftly the hours flew by. She scarcely noted their passage, any more than she noted the careless talk and laughter that hummed around her. She moved in an atmosphere of her own to a melody that none other heard.

The ball was wearing to a close when at length Lady Bassett summoned her to return. Lady Bassett was wearing her most gracious smile.

"You have been much admired to-night, dear child," she murmured to the girl, as they passed into the cloakroom.

Muriel's eyes looked disdainful for an instant, but they could not remain so. As swiftly the happiness flashed back into them.

"I have enjoyed myself," she said simply.

She threw a gauzy scarf about her neck, and turned to go. She did not want her evening spoilt by criticisms however honeyed.

The great marble entrance was crowded with departing guests. She edged her way to one of the pillars at the head of the long flight of steps, watching party after party descend to the waiting carriages. The dancing had not yet ceased, and strains of waltz-music came to her where she stood, fitful, alluring, plaintive. They were playing "The Blue Danube."

She listened to it as one in a dream, and while she listened the tears gathered in her eyes. How was it she had been so slow to understand? Would she ever make it up to him? She wondered how long he meant to keep her in suspense. It was not like him to linger thus if he had indeed received her message. She hoped he would come soon. The waiting was hard to bear.

She called to mind once more the last words he had spoken to her. He had said that he would not swoop a second time, but she could not imagine him doing anything else. He would be sudden, he would be disconcerting, he would be overwhelming. He would come on winged feet in answer to her call, but he would give her no quarter. He would neither ask nor demand. He would simply take.

She caught her breath and hastened to divert her thought, realising that she was on the verge of the old torturing process of self-intimidation which had so often before unnerved her.

The throng about her had lessened considerably. Glancing downwards, she discerned at the foot of the steps the old beggar who so persistently haunted the Residency gates, incurring thereby Lady Bassett's alarmed displeasure. He was crouching well to one side in the familiar attitude of supplication. There were dozens like him in Ghawalkhand, but she knew him by the peculiar, gibbering movement of the wiry beard that protruded from his chuddah. He was repulsive, but in a fashion fascinating. He made her think of a wizened old monkey who had wandered from his kind.

She had come to regard him almost in the light of a protege, and, remembering suddenly that he had besought an alms of her in vain some hours before, she turned impulsively to a man she knew who had just come up.

"Colonel Cathcart, will you lend me a rupee?"

He dived in his pocket and brought out a handful of money. She found the coin she wanted, thanked him with a smile, and began to descend the steps.

The old native was not looking at her. Something else seemed to have caught his attention. For the moment he had ceased to cringe and implore.

She heard Sir Reginald's voice above her. He was standing in talk with the Rajah while he waited for his wife.

And then—she was half-way down the steps when it happened—a sudden loud cry rang fiercely up to her, arresting her where she stood—a man's voice inarticulate at first, bursting from mere sound into furious headlong denunciation.

"You infernal hound!" it cried. "You damned assassin!"

At the same instant the old beggar at the foot of the palace steps sprang panther-like from his crouching position to hurl himself bodily at something that skulked in the shadows beyond him.

The marvellous agility of the action, the unerring precision with which he pounced upon his prey, above all, the voice that had yelled in execration, sent such a stab of amazed recognition through Muriel that she stood for a second as one petrified.

But the next instant all her senses were pricked into alertness by a revolver-shot. Another came, and yet another. They were fighting below like tigers—two men in native dress, swaying, straining, struggling, not three yards from where she stood.

She never fully remembered afterwards how she came to realise that Nick—Nick himself—was there before her in the flesh, fighting like a demon, fighting as she had seen him fight once long ago when every nerve in her body had been strung to agonised repulsion.

She felt no repulsion now—no shrinking of any sort, only a wild anguish of fear for his sake that drove her like a mad creature down the intervening steps, that sent her flashing between him and his adversary, that inspired her to wrench away the smoking revolver from the murderous hand that gripped it.

She went through those awful moments as a woman possessed, blindly obeying the compelling force, goaded by sheer, primaeval instinct to protect her own. It was but a conflict of seconds, but while it lasted she was untrammelled by any doubts or hesitations. She was sublimely sure of herself. She was superbly unafraid.

When it was over, when men crowded round and dragged her enemy back, when the pressing need was past, her courage fell from her like a mantle. She sank down upon the steps, a trembling, hysterical woman, and began to cry.

Some one bent over her, some one whispered soothing words, some one drew the revolver out of her weak grasp. Looking up, she saw the old native beggar upon whom she had thought to bestow her charity.

"Oh, Nick!" she gasped. "Nick!" And there stopped in sudden misgiving. Was this grotesque figure indeed Nick? Could it be—this man who had sat at the Residency gates for weeks, this man to whom she had so often tossed an alms?

Her brain had begun to reel, but she clung to the central idea, as one in deep waters clinging to a spar.

"Speak to me!" she entreated. "Only speak to me!"

But before he could answer, Bobby Fraser pushed suddenly forward, bent over, lifted her. "You are not hurt, Miss Roscoe?" he questioned anxiously, deep concern on his kindly face. "The damned swine didn't touch you? There! Come back into the palace. You're the bravest girl I ever met."

He began to help her up the steps, but though she was spent and near to fainting she resisted him.

"That man—" she faltered. "Don't—don't let him go!"

"Certainly not," said Bobby promptly. "Here, you old scarecrow, come and lend a hand!"

But the old scarecrow apparently had other plans for himself, for he had already vanished from the scene as swiftly and noiselessly as a shadow from a sheet.

"He is gone!" wailed Muriel. "He is gone! Oh, why did you let him go?"

"He'll turn up again," said Bobby consolingly. "That sort of chap always does. I say, how ghastly you look! Take my arm! You are not going to faint, are you? Ah, here is Colonel Cathcart! Miss Roscoe isn't hurt, sir—only upset. Can't we get her back to the palace?"

They bore her back between them, and left her to be tended by the women. She was not unconscious, but the shock had utterly unstrung her. She lay with closed eyes, listening vaguely to the buzz of excited comment about her, and wondering, wondering with an aching heart, why he had gone.

No one seemed to know exactly what had taken place, and she was too exhausted to tell. Possibly she would hot have told in any case. It was known only that an attempt had been made upon the life of the British Resident, Sir Reginald Bassett, and it was surmised that Muriel had realised the murderous intention in time to frustrate it. Certainly a native had tried to help her, but since the native had disappeared, his share in the conflict was not regarded as very great. As a matter of fact, the light had been too uncertain and the struggle too confused for even the eye-witnesses to know with any certainty what had taken place. Theories and speculations were many and various, but not one of them went near to the truth.

"Dear Muriel will tell us presently just how it happened," Lady Bassett said in her soft voice.

But Muriel was as one who heard not. She would not even open her eyes till Sir Reginald came to her, pillowed her head against him, kissed her white face, and called her his brave little girl.

That moved her at last, awaking in her the old piteous hunger, never wholly stifled, for her father. She turned and clung to him convulsively with an inarticulate murmuring that ended in passionate tears.

CHAPTER LIII
THE LAST SKIRMISH

Why had he gone? That was the question that vexed Muriel's soul through the long hours that followed her return to the Residency. Lying sleepless on her bed, she racked her weary brain for an answer to the riddle, but found none. Her brief doubt regarding him had long since fled. She knew with absolute certainty that it was Nick and no other who had yelled those furious words, who had made that panther-spring, who had leaned over her and withdrawn the revolver from her hold, telling her softly not to cry. But why had he gone just then when she needed him most?

Surely by now her message had reached him! Surely he knew that she wanted him, that she had lowered what he had termed her miserable little rag of pride to tell him so! Then why was he tormenting her thus—playing with her as a cat might play with a mouse? Was he taking his revenge for all the bitter scorn she had flung at him in the past? Did he think to wring from her some more definite appeal? Ah, that was it! Like a searchlight flashing inwards, she remembered her promise to him uttered long ago against her will—his answering oath. And she knew that he meant to hold her to that promise—that he would exact the very uttermost sacrifice that it entailed; and then perchance—she shivered at the unendurable thought—he would laugh his baffling, enigmatical laugh, and go his way.

But this was unbearable, impossible. She would sooner die than suffer it. She would sooner—yes, she would almost sooner—break her promise.

And then, to save her from distraction, the other side of the picture presented itself, that reverse side which he had once tauntingly advised her to study. If he truly loved her, he would not treat her thus. It would not gratify him to see her in the dust. If he still cared, as Daisy had assured her he did, it would not be his pleasure to make her suffer. But then again—oh, torturing question!—had that been so, would he have gone at that critical moment, would he have left her, when a look, a touch, would have sufficed to establish complete understanding?

Drearily the hours dragged away. The heat was great, and just before daybreak a thunder-storm rolled up, but spent itself without a drop of rain. It put the finishing touches to Muriel's restlessness. She rose and dressed, to sit by her window with her torturing thoughts for company, and awaited the day.

With the passing of the storm a slight draught that was like a shudder moved the scorched leaves of the acacias in the compound, quivered a little, and ceased. Then came the dawn, revealing mass upon mass of piled cloud hanging low over the earth. The breaking of the monsoon was drawing very near. There could be no lifting of the atmosphere, no relief, until it came.

She leaned her aching head against the window-frame in a maze of weariness unutterable. Her heart was too heavy for prayer.

Minutes passed. The daylight grew and swiftly overspread all things. The leaden silence began to be pierced here and there by the barking of a dog, the crowing of a cock, the scolding of a parrot. Somewhere, either in the compound or close to it, some one began to whistle—a soft, tentative whistle, like a young blackbird trying its notes.

Muriel remained motionless, scarcely heeding while it wove itself into the background of her thoughts. She was in fact hardly aware of it, till suddenly, with a great thrill of astonishment that shook her from head to foot, a wild suspicion seized her, and she started up, listening intently. The fitful notes were resolving into a melody—a waltz she knew, alluring, enchanting, compelling—the waltz that had filled in the dreadful silences on that night long ago when she had fought so desperately hard for her freedom and had prevailed at last. But stay! Had she prevailed? Had she not rather been a captive in spite of it all ever since?

On and on went the haunting waltz-refrain, now near, now far, now summoning, now eluding. She stood gripping the curtain till she could bear it no longer, and then with a great sob she mustered her resolution; she stepped out upon the verandah, and passed down between shrivelled trailing roses to the garden below.

The tune ceased quite suddenly, and she found herself moving through a silence that could be felt. But she would not turn back then. She would not let herself be discouraged. She had been frightened so often when there had been no need for fear.

On she pressed to the end of the path till she stood by the high fence that bordered the road. She could see no one. The garden lay absolutely deserted. She paused, hesitating, bewildered.

At the same instant from the other side of the fence, almost as if rising from the ground at her feet, a careless voice began to hum—a cracked, tuneless, unmistakable voice, that sent the blood to her heart with a force that nearly suffocated her.

"Nick!" she said, almost in a whisper.

He did not hear her evidently. His humming continued with unabated liveliness.

"Nick!" she said again.

Still no result. There was nothing in the least dramatic in the situation. It might almost have been described as ludicrous, but the white-faced woman in the compound did not find it so.

She waited till he had come to a suitable stopping place, and then, before he could renew the melody, she rapped with nervous force upon the fence.

There fell a most unexpected silence.

She broke it with words imploring, almost agonised. "Nick! Nick! Come and speak to me—for Heaven's sake!"

His flippant voice greeted her at once in a tone of cheerful inquiry. "That you, Muriel?"

Her agitation began to subside of itself. Nothing could have been more casual than his question. "Yes," she said in reply. "Why are you out there? Why don't you come in?"

"My dear girl,—at this hour!" There was shocked reproof in the ejaculation. Nick was evidently scandalised at the suggestion.

Muriel lost her patience forthwith. Was it for this that she had spent all those miserable hours of fruitless heart-searching? His trifling was worse than ridiculous. It was insufferable.

"You are to come in at once," she said, in a tone of authority.

"What for?" said Nick.

"Because—because—" She hesitated, and stopped, her face burning.

"Because—" said Nick encouragingly.

"Oh, don't be absurd!" she exclaimed in desperation. "How can I possibly talk to you there?"

"It depends upon what you want to say," said Nick. "If it is something particularly private—" He paused.

"Well?" she said.

"You can always come to me, you know," he pointed out. "But I shouldn't do that, if I were you. It would be neither dignified nor proper. And a girl in your position, dearest Muriel, cannot be too discreet. It is the greatest mistake in the world to act upon impulse. Let me entreat you to do nothing headlong. Take another year or so to think things over. There are so many nice men to choose from, and this absurd infatuation of yours cannot possibly last."

"Don't, Nick!" Muriel's voice held a curious mixture of mirth and sadness. "It—it isn't a bit funny to talk like that. It isn't even particularly kind."

"Ye gods!" said Nick. "Who wants to be kind?"

"Not you, evidently," she told him with a hint of bitterness. "You only aim at being intelligent."

"Well, you'll admit I hit the mark sometimes," he rejoined. "I'm like a rat, eh? Clever but loathsome."

She uttered a quivering laugh. "No, you are much more like an eagle, waiting to strike. Why don't you, I wonder, and—and take what you want?"

Nick's answering laugh had a mocking note in it. "Oh, I can play Animal Grab as well as anybody—better than most," he said modestly. "But I don't chance to regard this as a suitable occasion for displaying my skill. Uninteresting for you, of course, but then you are fond of running away when there is no one after you. It's been your favourite pastime for almost as long as I have known you."

The sudden silence with which this airy remark was received had in it something tragic. Muriel had sunk down on a garden-bench close at hand, lacking the strength to go away. It was exactly what she had expected. He meant to take his revenge in his own peculiar fashion. She had laid herself open to this, and mercilessly, unerringly, he had availed himself of the opportunity to wound. She might have known! She might have known! Had he not done it again and again? Oh, she had been a fool—a fool—to call him back!

Through the wild hurry of her thoughts his voice pierced once more. It had an odd inflection that was curiously like a note of concern.

"I say, Muriel, are you crying?"

"Crying!" She pulled herself together hastily. "No! Why should I?"

"I can tell you why you shouldn't," he answered whimsically. "No one ever ought to cry before breakfast. It's shocking for the appetite and may ruin the complexion for the rest of the day. Besides,—you've nothing to cry for."

"Oh, don't be absurd!" she flung back again almost fiercely. "I'm not crying!"

"Quite sure?" said Nick.

"Absolutely certain," she declared.

"All right then," he rejoined. "That being so, you had better dry your eyes very carefully, for I am coming to see for myself."

CHAPTER LIV
SURRENDER

She awaited him still sitting on the bench and striving vainly to quiet her thumping heart. She heard him come lightly up behind her, but she did not turn her head though she had no tears to conceal. She was possessed by an insane desire to spring up and flee. It took all her resolution to remain where she was.

And so Nick drew near unwelcomed—a lithe, alert figure in European attire, bare-headed, eager-faced. He was smiling to himself as he came, but when he reached her the smile was gone.

He bent and looked into her white, downcast face; then laid his hand upon her shoulder.

"But Muriel—" he said.

And that was all. Yet Muriel suddenly hid her face and wept.

He did not attempt to restrain her. Perhaps he realised that tears such as those must have their way. But the touch of his hand was in some fashion soothing. It stilled the tempest within her, comforting her inexplicably.

She reached up at last, and drew it down between her own, holding it fast.

"I'm such a fool, Nick," she whispered shakily. "You—you must try to bear with me."

She felt his fingers close and gradually tighten upon her own until their grip was actual pain.

"Haven't I borne with you long enough?" he said. "Can't you come to the point?"

She shook her head slightly. Her trembling had not wholly ceased. She was not—even yet she was not—wholly sure of him.

"Afraid?" he questioned.

And she answered him meekly, with bowed head. "Yes, Nick; afraid."

"Don't you think you might look me in the face if you tried very hard?" he suggested.

"No, Nick." She almost shrank at the bare thought.

"Oh, but you haven't tried," he said.

His voice sounded very close. She knew he was bending down. She even fancied she could feel his breath upon her neck.

Her head sank a little lower. "Don't!" she whispered, with a sob.

"What are you afraid of?" he said. "You weren't afraid to send me a message. You weren't afraid to save my life last night. What is it frightens you?"

She could not tell him. Only her panic was very real. It shook her from head to foot. A fierce struggle was going on within her,—the last bitter conflict between her love and her fear. It tore her in all directions. She felt as if it would drive her mad. But through it all she still clung desperately to the bony hand that grasped her own. It seemed to sustain her, to hold her up, through all her chaos of doubt, of irresolution, of miserable, overmastering dread.

"What is it frightens you?" he said again. "Why won't you look at me? There is nothing whatever to make you afraid!"

He spoke softly, as though he were addressing a scared child. But still she was afraid, afraid of the very impulse that urged her, horribly afraid of meeting the darting scrutiny of his eyes.

He waited for a little in silence; then suddenly with a sharp sigh he straightened himself. "You don't know your own mind yet," he said. "And I can't help you to know it. I had better go."

He would have withdrawn his hand with the words, but she held it fast.

"No, Nick, no! It isn't that," she told him tremulously. "I know what I want—perfectly well. But—but—I can't put it into words. I can't! I can't!"

"Is that it?" said Nick. His manner changed completely. He bent down again. She heard the old note of banter in his voice, but mingled with it was a tenderness so utter that she scarcely recognised it. "Then, my dear girl, in Heaven's name, don't try! Words were not made for such an occasion as this. They are clumsy tools at the best of times. You can make me understand without words. I'm horribly intelligent, as you remarked just now."

Her heart leapt to the rapid assurance. Was it so difficult to tell him after all? Surely she could find a way!

The tumult of her emotions swelled to sudden uproar, thunderous, all-possessing, overwhelming, so that she gasped and gasped again for breath. And then all in a moment she knew that the conflict was over. She was as a diver, hurling with headlong velocity from dizzy height into deep waters, and she rejoiced—she exulted—in that mad rush into depth.

With a quivering laugh she moved. She loosened her convulsive clasp upon his hand, turned it upwards, and stooping low, she pressed her lips closely, passionately, lingeringly, upon his open palm. She had found a way.

He started sharply at her action; he almost winced. Then, "Muriel!" he exclaimed in a voice that broke, and threw himself on his knees beside her, holding her fast in a silence so sudden and so tense that she also was awed into a great stillness.

Yet, after a little, though his face was pressed against her so that she could not see it or even vaguely guess his mood, she found strength to speak.

"I can tell you what I want now, Nick," she whispered. "Shall I tell you?"

He did not answer, did not so much as breathe. But yet she knew no fear or hesitancy. Her eyes were opened, and her tongue loosed. Words came easily to her now, more easily than they had ever come before.

"I want to be married—soon, very soon," she told him softly. "And then I want you to take me away with you into Nepal, as you planned ever so long ago. And let us be alone together in the mountains—quite alone as we were before. Will you, Nick? Will you?"

But again he had no answer for her. He did not seem able to reply. His head still lay against her shoulder. His arm was still tense about her. She fell silent, waiting for him.

At last he drew a deep breath that seemed to burst upwards from the very heart of him, and lifted his face with a jerk.

"My God!" he said. "Is it true?"

His voice was oddly uneven; he seemed to produce it with difficulty. But having broken the spell that bound him, he managed after a moment to continue.

"Are you quite sure you want to marry me,—quite sure that to-morrow you won't be scared out of your wits at the bare idea? Have you left off being afraid of me? Do you mean me really to take you at your word?"

"If you will, Nick," she answered humbly.

"If I will!" he echoed, with sudden passion. "I warn you, Muriel, you are putting yourself irrevocably in my power, and you will never break away again. You may come to loathe me with your whole soul, but I shall never let you go. Have you realised that? If I take you now, I take you for all time."

He spoke almost with violence, and, having spoken, drew back from her abruptly, as though he could not wholly trust himself.

But nothing could dismay her now. She had fought her last battle, had made the final surrender. Her fear was dead. She stretched out her hands to him with unfaltering confidence.

"Take me then, Nick," she said.

He took the extended hands with quick decision, first one and then the other, and laid them on his shoulders.

"Now look at me," he said.

She hesitated, though not as one afraid.

"Look at me, Muriel!" he insisted.

Then, as she kept her eyes downcast, he put his hand under her chin and compelled her.

She yielded with a little quivering murmur of protest, and so for the first time in her life she deliberately met his look, encountering eyes so wide and so piercingly blue that she had a moment's bewildered feeling of uncertainty, as though she had looked into the eyes of a stranger. Then the colourless lashes descended again and veiled them as of old. He blinked with his usual disconcerting rapidity and set her free.

"Yes," he said. "You've left off cheating. And if you really care to marry me—what's left of me—it's a precious poor bargain, but—I am yours."

His voice cracked a little. She fancied he was going to laugh. And then, while she was still wondering, his arm went round her again and drew her closely to him. She was conscious of a sudden, leaping flame behind the pale lashes, felt his hold tighten while the wrinkled face drew near,—and with a sob she clasped her arms about his neck and turned her lips to his.

CHAPTER LV
OMNIA VINCIT AMOR

"Funny, wasn't it?" said Nick, jingling a small handful of coins in front of his fiancée. "Quite a harvest in its way! I had no idea you were so charitable."

She caught his wrist. "You have no right to a single one of them. You obtained them under false pretences. What in the world induced you to do such a thing?"

Nick's hand closed firmly upon the spoil. "It was a sheer, heaven-sent inspiration," he declared. "Care to know how it came to me? It happened one night in the Indian Ocean when I was on the way out with Daisy. I was lying on deck under the stars, thinking of you, and the whole idea came to me ready-made. I didn't attempt to shape it; it shaped itself. I was hungering for the sight of you, and I knew you would never find me out. You never would have, either, if I hadn't had Daisy's message. I was just going to quit my lonely vigil when it reached me. But that altered my plans, and I decided with Fraser's assistance to face it out. You knew he was in the secret, of course? He is in every secret, that chap. As soon as I heard of Lady Bassett's ingenious little fiction about the Buddhist monastery, I was ready to take the wan path. But you were invisible, you know. I had to wait till you emerged. Then came last night's episode, and I had to take to my heels. I couldn't face a public exposure, and it wouldn't have been particularly pleasant for you, either. So now you have the whole touching story, and I think you needn't grudge me a rupee and a few annas as a reward for my devotion."

Muriel laughed rather tremulously. "I would have given you something better worth having—if I had known."

"Never too late," said Nick philosophically. "You can begin at once if you like. Let me have your hand. Hold it steady, my dear girl. Remember my limitations. You won't refuse any longer to wear my ring?"

"I will wear it gladly," she told him, as he fitted it back upon her finger. "I shall never part with it again."

Her eyes were full of tears, but she would not let them fall, and Nick was too intent upon what he was doing to notice.

"That imp Olga nearly broke her poor little heart when she gave it back to me," he said. "I think I shall have to send her a cable. What shall I say? OMNIA VINCIT AMOR? She is old enough to know what that means. And if I add, 'From Muriel and Nick,' she will understand. A pity she can't come to our wedding! I'd sooner have seen her jolly little phiz than all Lady Bassett's wreathed smiles. She is sure to smile, you know. She always does when she sees me." He broke off with a hideous grimace.

"Don't, Nick!" Muriel's voice trembled a little. "Why does she hate you so?"

"Can't imagine," grinned Nick. "It's a way some people have. Perhaps she will end by falling in love with me. Who knows?"

"Don't be horrid, Nick! Why won't you tell me?" Muriel laid a pleading hand upon his.

He caught it to his lips. "I can't tell you, darling, seeing she is a woman. An unpleasant adventure befell her once for which I was partially responsible. And she has hated me with most unseemly vehemence ever since."

A light began to break upon Muriel. "Was it something that happened on board ship?" she hazarded.

He gave her a sharp look. "Who told you that?"

She flushed a little. "Bobby Fraser. He didn't mention her name, of course. We—we were talking about you once."

Nick laughed aloud. "Only once?"

Her colour deepened. "You are positively ridiculous. Still, I wish it hadn't been Lady Bassett, Nick. I don't like to feel she hates you like that."

"It doesn't hurt me in the least," Nick declared. "Her poison-fang is extracted so far as I am concerned. She could only poison me through you. I always knew I had her to thank for what happened at Simla."

"Oh, but not her alone," Muriel said quickly. "You mustn't blame her only for that. I was prejudiced against you by—other things."

"I know all about it," said Nick. He was holding her hand in his, moving it hither and thither to catch the gleam of the rubies upon it. "You were a poor little scared rabbit fleeing from a hideous monster of destruction. You began to run that last night at Wara when I made you drink that filthy draught, and you have hardly stopped yet. I don't suppose it ever occurred to you that I would rather have died in torment than have done it." He broke into a sudden laugh. "But you needn't be afraid that I shall ever do it again. I can't do much to any one with only one arm, can I? You witnessed my futility last night. There's a grain of comfort in that, eh, darling?"

"Nick, don't, don't!" She turned to him impulsively and laid her cheek against his shoulder. "You—you don't know how you hurt me!"

"My dear girl, what's the matter?" said Nick. "I was only trying to draw your attention to my good points—such as they are."

"Don't!" she said again, in a choked voice. "It's more than I can bear. You would never have lost your arm but for me."

"Oh, rats!" said Nick, holding her closely. "Whoever told you that—"

"It was Dr. Jim."

"Well, Jim's an ass, and I shall tell him so. There, don't fret, darling. It isn't worth it. I could wish it hadn't happened for your sake, but I don't care a rap for my own."

"You are not to care for mine," she whispered. "I shall only love you the better for it."

"Then it will be a blessing to me after all," said Nick cheerily. "Do you know what we are going to do as soon as we are married, sweetheart? We are going to climb the highest mountain in the world, to see the sun rise, and to thank God."

She turned her face upwards with a quivering smile. "Let us be married soon then, Nick."

"At once," said Nick promptly. "Come along and tell Sir Reginald. He must be out of bed by this time. If he isn't I think the occasion almost justifies us in knocking him up."

They found Sir Reginald already upon the verandah, drinking his early coffee, and to Muriel's dismay he was not alone. It was later than she had imagined, and Colonel Cathcart and Bobby Fraser had both dropped in for a gossip, and were seated with him at the table smoking.

As she and Nick approached, Lady Bassett herself emerged through an open window behind the three men.

Nick began to chuckle. This was the sort of situation that appealed to his sense of humour. He began to chant an old-world ditty under his breath with appropriate words.

"Oh, dear, what will the Bassett say?"

Muriel uttered a short, hysterical laugh, and instantly they were discovered.

"Now what are you going to do?" said Nick.

"I don't know," she responded hurriedly. "Run away, I think."

"Not you," said Nick, grasping her hand very firmly. "You are going to face the music with me."

She gave in, half laughing, half protesting, and he led her up the steps with considerable pomp.

She need not have been so painfully embarrassed, for every one, with the exception of Bobby Fraser, looked at Nick, and Nick only, in speechless amazement, as though he had just returned from the dead.

Nick was sublimely equal to the occasion. He came to a standstill by the table, executed an elaborate bow in Lady Bassett's direction, then turned briskly to Sir Reginald.

"After two years' deliberation," he announced, "we have decided to settle our differences by getting married, and we are hoping, sir, that you will bestow your blessing upon our union."

"My good fellow!" gasped Sir Reginald. "This is a very great surprise!"

"Yes, I know," said Nick. "It was to me, too. But—though fully sensible of my unworthiness—I shall do my best to deserve the very high honour that has been done me. And I hope we may count upon your approval and support."

Again his bow included Lady Bassett. There was a mocking glint in the glance he threw her.

She came forward as though in answer to a challenge, her face unwontedly flushed. "This is indeed unexpected!" she declared, extending her hand. "How do you do, Captain Ratcliffe? You will understand our surprise when I tell you that some one was saying only the other day that you had entered a Tibetan monastery."

"Some one must have been telling a lie, dear Lady Bassett," said Nick. "I am sorry if it caused you any uneasiness on my account. I should certainly never have taken such a serious step without letting you know. I trust that my projected marriage will have a less disturbing effect."

Lady Bassett smiled her crooked smile, and raised one eyebrow. "Oh, I shall not be anxious on your account," she assured him playfully.

"Quite right, Lady Bassett," broke in Colonel Cathcart. "He'll hold his own, wherever he is. I always said so when he was in the Service."

"And a little over probably," put in Bobby Fraser. "Miss Roscoe, if you ever find him hard to manage, you send for me."

Muriel, from the shelter of Sir Reginald's arm, looked across at the speaker with a smile of unwonted confidence.

"Thank you all the same," she responded, "but I don't expect any difficulties in that respect."

"She is far more likely to fight my battles for me," remarked Nick complacently, "seeing my own fighting days are over."

"And what have you been doing with yourself all this time?" demanded Sir Reginald suddenly. "You have been singularly unobtrusive. What have you been doing?"

Nick's answering grin was one of sheer exuberance of spirit. "I've just been marking time, sir, that's all," he replied enigmatically. "A monotonous business for every one concerned, but it seems to have served its purpose."

Sir Reginald grunted a little, and looked uncomfortably at his wife's twisted smile. "And now you want to get married, do you?" he said.

"At once," said Nick.

"Well, well," said Sir Reginald, beginning to smile himself. "All's well that ends well, and Muriel is old enough to please herself. Mind you are good to her, that's all. And I wish you both every happiness."

"So do I," said Bobby Fraser heartily. "And look here, you jack-in-the-box, if you're wanting a best man to push you through, I'll undertake the job. It's a capacity in which I have often made myself useful."

"Right O!" laughed Nick. "But you won't find I want much pushing, old chap. I'm on my way to the top crag of Everest already."

"Ah, Captain Ratcliffe, be careful!" murmured Lady Bassett. "Do not soar too high!"

He bowed to her a third time, still with his baffling smile. "Thanks, dear Lady Bassett!" he said lightly. "But you need have no misgivings. Forewarned is forearmed, they say. And on this occasion, at least, I am wise—in time."

"And dear Muriel too, I wonder?" smiled Lady Bassett.

"And dear Muriel too," smiled Nick.

CHAPTER LVI
THE EAGLE SOARS

Night and a running stream—a soft gurgle of sound that was like a lullaby. Within the tent the quiet breathing of a man asleep; standing in the entrance—a woman.

There was a faint quiver in the air as of something coming from afar, a hushed expectancy of something great. A chill breath came off the snows, hovering secretly above the ice-cold water. The stars glittered like loose-hung jewels upon a sable robe.

Ah, that flash as of a sword across the sky! A meteor had fallen among the mountains. It was almost like a signal in the heavens—herald of the coming wonder of the dawn.

Softly the watcher turned inwards, and at once a gay, cracked voice spoke out of the darkness.

"Hullo, darling! Up and watching already! Ye gods! What a sky! Why didn't you wake me sooner? Have I time for a plunge?"

"Perhaps—if you will let me help you dress after it. Certainly not otherwise." The deep voice had in it a tremulous note that was like a caress. The speaker was looking into the shadows. The glory without no longer held her.

"All right then, you shall—just for a treat. Perhaps you would like to shave me as well?"

"Shave you!" There was scorn this time in the answering voice. "You couldn't grow a single hair if you tried!"

"True, O Queen! I couldn't. And the few I was born with are invisible. Hence my failure to distinguish myself in the Army. It is to be hoped the deficiency will not blight my Parliamentary career also—always supposing I get there."

"Ah, but you did distinguish yourself. I heard—once"—the words came with slight hesitation—"that you ought to have had the V.C. after the Wara expedition,—only you refused it."

"I wonder what gas-bag let that out," commented Nick. "You shouldn't believe all you hear, you know. Now, darling, I'm ready for the plunge, and I must look sharp about it too. Do you mind rummaging out a towel?"

"But, Nick, was it true?"

"What? The V.C. episode? Oh, I suppose so, more or less. I didn't want to be decorated for running away, you see. It didn't seem exactly suitable. Besides, I didn't do it for that."

"Nick, do you know you make me feel more contemptible every day?" There was an unmistakable quiver of distress in the words.

"My own girl, don't be a goose!" came the light response. "You don't honestly suppose I could ever regret anything now, do you? Why, it's a lost faculty."

He stepped from the tent, clad loosely in a bath sheet, and bestowed a kiss upon his wife's downcast face in passing. "Look here, sweetheart, if you cry while I'm in the water, I'll beat you directly I come out. That's a promise, not a threat. And by the way, I've got something good to tell you presently; so keep your heart up."

He laughed at her and went his way, humming tunelessly after his own peculiarly volatile fashion. She listened to his singing, as he splashed in the stream below, as though it were the sweetest music on earth; and she knew that he had spoken the truth. Whatever sacrifices he had made in the past, regret was a thing impossible to him now.

By the time he joined her again, she had driven away her own. The sky was changing mysteriously. The purple depth was lightening, the stars receding.

"We must hurry," said Nick. "The gods won't wait for us."

But they were ready first after all, and the morning found them high up the mountainside with their faces to the east.

Sudden and splendid, the sun flashed up over the edge of the world, and the snow of the mountain crests shone in roselit glory for a few magic seconds, then shimmered to gold—glittering as the peaks of Paradise.

They did not speak at all, for the ground beneath their feet was holy, and all things that called for speech were left behind. Only as dawn became day—as the sun-god mounted triumphant above the waiting earth—the man's arm tightened about the woman, and his flickering eyes grew steadfast and reverent as the eyes of one who sees a vision....

"'Prophet and priestess we came—back from the dawning,'" quoted Nick, under his breath.

Muriel uttered a long, long sigh, and turned her face against her husband's shoulder.

His lips were on her forehead for a moment; the next he was peering into her face with his usual cheery grin.

"Care to hear my piece of news?" he questioned.

She looked at him eagerly. "Oh, Nick, not the mail!"

He nodded. "Runner came in late last night. You were asleep and dreaming of me. I hadn't the heart to wake you."

She laughed and blushed. "As if I should! Do you really imagine that I never think of anyone else? But go on. What news?"

He pulled out two letters. "One from Olga, full of adoration, bless her funny heart, and containing also a rude message from Jim to the effect that Redlands is going to rack and ruin for want of a tenant while we are philandering on the outside edge of civilisation doing no good to anybody. No good indeed! I'll punch his head for that some day. But I suppose we really ought to be thinking of Home before long, eh, sweetheart?"

She assented with a smile and a sigh. "I am sure we ought. Dr. Jim is quite right. We must come back to earth again, my eagle and I."

Nick kissed her hair. "It's been a gorgeous flight hasn't it? We'll do it again—heaps of times—before we die."

"If nothing happens to prevent," said Muriel.

He frowned. "What do you say that for? Are you trying to be like Lady Bassett? Because it's a vain aspiration, so you may as well give it up at the outset."

"Nick, how absurd you are!" There was a slight break in the words. "I—I had almost forgotten there was such a person. No, I said it because—because—well, anything might happen, you know."

"Such as?" said Nick.

"Anything," she repeated almost inaudibly.

Nick pondered this for a moment. "Is it a riddle?" he asked.

She did not answer him. Her face was hidden.

He waited a little. Then, "I shall begin to guess directly," he said.

She uttered a muffled laugh, and clung to him with a sudden, passionate closeness. "Nick, you—you humbug! You know!"

Nick tossed his letters on the ground and held her fast. "My precious girl, you gave the show away not ten seconds ago by that blush of yours. There! Don't be so absurdly shy! You can't be shy with me. Look at me, sweet. Look up and tell me it's true!"

She turned her face upwards, quivering all over, yet laughing tremulously. "Yes, Nick, really, really!" she told him. "Oh, my darling, are you glad?"

"Am I glad?" said Nick, and laughed at her softly. "I'm the happiest man on earth. I shall go Home now without a pang, and so will you. We have got to feather the nest, you know. That'll be fun, eh, sweetheart?"

Her eyes answered him more convincingly than any words. They seemed to have caught some of the sunshine that made the world around them so glorious.

Some time elapsed before she remembered the neglected correspondence. Time was of no account up there among the mountains.

"The other letter, Nick, you didn't tell me about it. I fancied you might have heard from Will Musgrave."

"So I have," said Nick. "You had better read it. There's a line for you inside. It's all right. Daisy has got a little girl, both doing splendidly; Daisy very happy, Will nearly off his head with joy."

Muriel was already deep in Will's ecstatic letter. She read it with smiling lips and tearful eyes. At the end in pencil she found the line that was for her.

"Tell Muriel that all's well with me, and I want you both for Christmas.—Daisy."

Muriel looked up. "I promised to spend Christmas with them, Nick."

Nick smiled upon her quizzically. "By a strange coincidence, darling, so did I. I should think under the circumstances we might go together, shouldn't you?"

She drew his hand to her cheek. "We will go to them for Christmas then. And after that straight Home. Tell Dr. Jim when you write. But—Nick—I think we should like to feather the nest all ourselves, don't you?"

"Why, rather!" said Nick. "We'll do it together—just you and I."

"Just you and I," she repeated softly.

Later, hand in hand, they looked across the valley to the shining crags that glistened spear-like in the sun.

A great silence lay around them—a peace unspeakable—that those silver crests lifted into the splendour of Infinity.

They stood alone together—above the world—with their faces to the mountains.

And thus standing with the woman he loved, Nick spoke, briefly—it seemed lightly—yet with a certain tremor in his voice.

"Horses," he said—"and chariots—of fire!" And Muriel looked at him with memory and understanding in her eyes.

THE END

Printed in Great Britain
by Amazon